MEDIEVAL FOLKLORE

MEDIEVAL FOLKLORE

A Guide to Myths, Legends, Tales, Beliefs, and Customs

Edited by

Carl Lindahl
John McNamara
John Lindow

OXFORD

UNIVERSITY PRESS

2002

OXFORD
UNIVERSITY PRESS

Oxford New York
Auckland Bangkok Buenos Aires Cape Town Chennai
Dar es Salaam Delhi Hong Kong Istanbul Karachi Kolkata
Kuala Lumpur Madrid Melbourne Mexico City Mumbai Nairobi
São Paulo Shanghai Singapore Taipei Tokyo Toronto

and an associated company in Berlin

First published by ABC-CLIO, Inc., 2000, as a 2-volume set entitled
Medieval Folklore: An Encyclopedia of Myths, Legends, Tales, Beliefs, and Customs

Published by Oxford University Press, Inc.
198 Madison Avenue, New York, NY 10016

Oxford is a registered trademark of Oxford University Press

Library of Congress Cataloging-in-Publication Data
Medieval folklore : a guide to myths, legends, tales, beliefs, and
customs / editors, Carl Lindahl, John McNamara, John Lindow.
p. cm.
Originally published: Santa Barbara, Calif.: ABC-CLIO, c2000
ISBN 0-19-514772-3 (pbk.) — ISBN 0-19-514771-5 (cloth)
1. Folklore—Encyclopedias. 2. Civilization, Medieval—Folklore—
Encyclopedias. I. Lindahl, Carl, 1947–. II. McNamara, John. III. Lindow, John.
GR35 .M43   2002
398'.094'0902—dc21
2001058814

9 8 7 6 5 4 3 2 1

Printed in the United States of America
on acid-free paper

To those friends and family members
for the extraordinary good will, tolerance, and love
they extended us throughout this often seemingly endless process:

Thea Austen, Heather Bohannan, Sorrel Bohannan, John Haba, Leo Hackl,
Shawn Heilbron, Joel Klass, Alison Lindahl, Constance Lindahl, Kristin Lindahl,
Kitty Lindow, Cynthia Marshall McNamara, Kathleen McNamara,
Kelly McNamara, Maureen McNamara, the late Paul McNamara,
Wendy McNamara, and Bevin Santos.

This book is dedicated to them, and to the memory of Paul.

CONTENTS

CONTRIBUTORS AND THEIR ENTRIES

Alexander Argüelles
Handong University
Pohang, Republic of Korea
Dreams and Dream Poetry

Samuel G. Armistead
University of California at Davis
Davis, California
Hispanic Tradition

Michele Bacci
Scuola Normale Superiore
Pisa, Italy
Votive Offerings

E. J. W. Barber
Occidental College
Los Angeles, California
Spinning and Weaving

Pamela Berger
Boston College
Chestnut Hill, Massachusetts
Grain Miracle

Karen Bezella-Bond
Columbia University
New York, New York
Games and Play

Bettina Bildhauer
Pembroke College, University of Cambridge
Cambridge, England
Blood

Zoe Borovsky
University of Oregon
Eugene, Oregon
Sagas of Icelanders

Nancy M. Bradbury
Smith College
Northampton, Massachusetts
Romance

Erika Brady
Western Kentucky University
Bowling Green, Kentucky
Augustine of Hippo, Saint

Dorothy Ann Bray
McGill University
Montreal, Canada
Patrick, Saint; Wells and Springs

Nicholas N. Burlakoff
Southwest Planning Assoc., Inc.
Yonkers, New York
Ships

†Pack Carnes
Lake Forest College
Lake Forest, Illinois
Fable; Marie de France

Nicola Chatten
University of Saint Andrews
Fife, Scotland
Fabliau

Geert H. M. Claassens
Katholieke Universiteit Leuven
Leuven, Belgium
Charlemagne

Albrecht Classen
University of Arizona
Tucson, Arizona
Crusades; Foreign Races; Nibelungenlied; Saracen Princess; Tannhäuser

Lawrence M. Clopper
Indiana University
Bloomington, Indiana
Midsummer

Joyce Coleman
University of North Dakota
Grand Forks, North Dakota
Orality and Literacy

Melinda Sue Collins
Indiana University
Bloomington, Indiana
Accused Queen

Lisa H. Cooper
Columbia University
New York, New York
Tournament

Stephen D. Corrsin
Wayne State University
Detroit, Michigan
Sword Dance

Fabrizio Crivello
Scuola Normale Superiore
Pisa, Italy
Books of Hours

Hilda Ellis Davidson
University of Cambridge
Cambridge, England
Giants; Otherworldly Journey; Supernatural Weapons; Sword; Valkyries; Woman Warrior

Linda Davidson
University of Rhode Island
Kingston, Rhode Island
   James the Elder, Saint; Pilgrimage

Giuseppe C. Di Scipio
Hunter College, City University of New York
New York, New York
   Dante Alighieri; Decameron; Italian Tradition;
   Novella

Peter Dinzelbacher
Universität Salzburg
Salzburg, Austria
   Harrowing of Hell; Hell; Purgatory

Graham N. Drake
State University of New York at Geneseo
Geneseo, New York
   Homosexuality (male); Knights Templar

Thomas A. DuBois
University of Wisconsin
Madison, Wisconsin
   Baltic Tradition; Cross; Finno-Ugric Tradition;
   Sauna; Skis and Skiing

Joseph J. Duggan
University of California at Berkeley
Berkeley, California
   Cantar de mio Cid; Chanson de Roland

Maryjane Dunn
Independent Scholar
Lufkin, Texas
   James the Elder, Saint; Pilgrimage

Bradford Lee Eden
University of Nevada, Las Vegas
Las Vegas, Nevada
   Advent; Boy Bishop, Feast of the; Candlemas;
   Christmas; Dance; Fools, Feast of; New Year's

Mary Agnes Edsall
Columbia University
New York, New York
   Wine

J. K. Elliott
University of Leeds
Leeds, England
   Jesus Christ; Joseph, Saint; Virgin Mary

Deanna Delmar Evans
Bemidji State University
Bemidji, Minnesota
   Nine Worthies

Jonathan Evans
University of Georgia at Athens
Athens, Georgia
   Dragon

Cathalin B. Folks
Pellissippi State Technical Community College
Knoxville, Tennessee
   Gawain; Loathly Lady; Morgan le Fay

Judith Gilbert
Language and Culture Center,
   University of Houston
Houston, Texas
   Mermaid

Stephen O. Glosecki
University of Alabama at Birmingham
Birmingham, Alabama
   Bear; Shamanism; Totem; Wolf and Werewolf

Peter Goodrich
Northern Michigan University
Marquette, Michigan
   Merlin

Cynthia Whiddon Green
University of Houston
Houston, Texas
   Bagpipe; Harp

Valdimar Tr. Hafstein
University of California at Berkeley
Berkeley, California
   Dwarfs

William Hansen
Indiana University
Bloomington, Indiana
   Hamlet

Susan Haskins
Independent Scholar
London, England
   Mary Magdalen, Saint

Thomas Head
Hunter College and The Graduate Center,
   City University of New York
New York, New York
   Relics

Elissa R. Henken
University of Georgia at Athens
Athens, Georgia
   David, Saint; Gerald of Wales; Gildas; Maelgwn
   Gwynedd; Map, Walter; Nennius; Owain (sixth
   century); Owain Glyndwr; Sleeping King; Welsh
   Tradition

Constance B. Hieatt
Essex, Connecticut
   Foodways

Elliott Horowitz
Ramat-Gan, Israel
   Jews, Stereotypes of; Purim

Nicholas Howe
Ohio State University
Columbus, Ohio
   Anglo-Saxon Chronicle

Bonnie D. Irwin
Eastern Illinois University
Charleston, Illinois
  Assassins Nizari Ismaᶜilis; Frame Tale; Harun
  al-Rashid; Seven Sages, The; Thousand and
  One Nights

Madeleine Jeay
McMaster University
Hamilton, Canada
  Joan of Arc, Saint; Marriage Traditions; Rites of
  Passage

Karen Louise Jolly
University of Hawaii at Manoa
Honolulu, Hawaii
  Magic

Leslie Ellen Jones
Independent Scholar
Los Angeles, California
  Druids; Fairies

Malcolm Jones
University of Sheffield
Sheffield, England
  Bestiary; Burial Mounds; Cockaigne, Land of;
  Cuckold; Dance of Death; Eulenspiegel; Fool;
  Fools, Feast of; Green Man; Iconography; Man-
  uscript Marginalia; Misericords; Names, Per-
  sonal; Phallic Imagery; Punishments; Scatology;
  Sheela-na-Gig; Ships; Trickster; Wild Man;
  World Turned Upside Down

Henryk Jurkowski
Theatre Academy
Warsaw, Poland
  Puppets and Puppet Plays

Merrill Kaplan
University of California at Berkeley
Berkeley, California
  Runes and Runic Inscriptions

Richard Kieckhefer
Northwestern University
Evanston, Illinois
  Magic Manuals; Witchcraft

Samuel Kinser
Northern Illinois University
DeKalb, Illinois
  Carnival; Masking

Norris J. Lacy
Pennsylvania State University at University Park
University Park, Pennsylvania
  Arthur; Chrétien de Troyes; Grail; Tristan and
  Iseut

Eve Levin
Ohio State University
Columbus, Ohio
  Slavic Tradition, East

Shimon Levy
Tel Aviv University
Tel Aviv, Israel
  Passover Haggadah

Carl Lindahl
University of Houston
Houston, Texas
  Accused Queen; Becket, Saint Thomas;
  Chaucer, Geoffrey; English Tradition: Middle
  English Period; Folklore; Folktale; Guinefort,
  Saint; Loathly Lady; Marie de France; Motif;
  Myth; Peasants; Trickster; Valentine's Day,
  Saint; Wandering Jew

John Lindow
University of California at Berkeley
Berkeley, California
  Berserks; Burgundian Cycle; Scandinavian
  Mythology; Snorri Sturluson's Edda; Thor; Wild
  Hunt

Timothy J. Lundgren
University of Michigan
Ann Arbor, Michigan
  Outlaw; Robin Hood

Emily Lyle
University of Edinburgh
Edinburgh, Scotland
  Thomas Rhymer

Patricia Lysaght
University College Dublin
Dublin, Ireland
  Beltane; Lugnasa; Samhain

Elizabeth MacDaniel
Clarion University of Pennsylvania
Clarion, Pennsylvania
  Mandeville's Travels; Travel Literature

Ulrich Marzolph
University of Göttingen and
  Enzyklopädie des Märchens
Göttingen, Germany
  Arabic-Islamic Tradition

Adrienne Mayor
Independent Scholar
Princeton, New Jersey
  Griffin; Seven Sleepers of Ephesus; Sibyl

Cynthia Marshall McNamara
Southwest College,
  Houston Community College System
Houston, Texas
  Nuns

John McNamara
University of Houston
Houston, Texas
  Angels; Bede the Venerable; Brigid, Saint; Cæd-
  mon; Dreams and Dream Poetry; English Tradi-
  tion: Anglo-Saxon Period; Exemplum; Fable;
  Monks; Outlaw; Scottish Tradition

Binita Mehta
Independent Scholar
London, England
Prester John

Daniel F. Melia
University of California at Berkeley
Berkeley, California
Ulster Cycle

Wolfgang Mieder
University of Vermont
Burlington, Vermont
Blasons Populaires; Proverbs

Michelle Miller
University of Houston
Houston, Texas
Plow and Plowing; Sir Gawain and the Green Knight

Robert Mills
Pembroke College, University of Cambridge
Cambridge, England
Funeral Customs and Burial Rites; Memento Mori

Stephen A. Mitchell
Harvard University
Cambridge, Massachusetts
Scandinavian Tradition

Joseph Falaky Nagy
University of California at Los Angeles
Los Angeles, California
Irish Tradition

Tara Neelakantappa
Columbia University
New York, New York
Inns and Taverns

Paul B. Nelson
Indiana University
Bloomington, Indiana
Swan Knight

W. F. H. Nicolaisen
University of Aberdeen
Aberdeen, Scotland
Names, Place

John D. Niles
University of California at Berkeley
Berkeley, California
Beowulf

Dáithí Ó hÓgáin
University College Dublin
Dublin, Ireland
Celtic Mythology; Fenian Cycle

Lea Olsan
University of Louisiana at Monroe
Monroe, Louisiana
Medicine

Alexandra H. Olsen
University of Denver
Denver, Colorado
Apollonius of Tyre; Robert of Sicily

Ward Parks
Avatar Meher Baba Trust
Amednagar, India
Flyting

Leander Petzoldt
Institut für Europäische Ethnologie und Volkskunde
Innsbruck, Austria
German Tradition; Satan; Spirits and Ghosts

Ruth Petzoldt
Universität Regensburg
Regensburg, Germany
Vampire

Chiara Piccinini
Scuola Normale Superiore
Pisa, Italy
Gargoyles

Éva Pócs
Hungarian Academy of Sciences
Budapest, Hungary
Hungarian Tradition

Gillian S. Polack
Australian National University
Canberra, Australia
Chanson de Geste; William of Orange

Catharina Raudvere
Lund University
Lund, Sweden
Nightmare

Velma Bourgeois Richmond
Holy Names College
Oakland, California
Amicus et Amelius; Guy of Warwick

Brynley F. Roberts
Former Librarian, National Library of Wales
Aberystwyth, Wales
Annwfn (Annwn); Arthurian Lore; Brutus; Camlan; Geoffrey of Monmouth; Gododdin, Y; Gwynn ap Nudd; Lear, King; Map, Walter; Maxen Wledig; Myrddin; Nennius; Taliesin; Triads of the Island of Britain; Welsh Tradition

Nicola Royan
University of Glasgow
Glasgow, Scotland
Andrew's Day, Saint

Miri Rubin
Pembroke College, Oxford
Oxford, England
Eucharist

Joyce E. Salisbury
University of Wisconsin
Green Bay, Wisconsin
Bestiality

Sandra M. Salla
Lehigh University
Bethlehem, Pennsylvania
Carol; Fairy Lover

Francesca Canadé Sautman
The Graduate Center,
    City University of New York
New York, New York
Anne, Saint; French Tradition; Lesbians

Michèle Simonsen
University of Copenhagen
Copenhagen, Denmark
Animal Tale; Unibos

Jacqueline Simpson
Past President, Folklore Society (England)
Worthing, England
Amulet and Talisman; Evil Eye; George, Saint;
Sutton Hoo

Leigh Smith
Stephen F. Austin State University
Nacogdoches, Texas
Catherine of Alexandria, Saint; Courtly Love;
Knight; Richard the Lion-Heart; Unicorn

John Southworth
Independent Scholar
Ipswich, England
Minstrel

Lorraine K. Stock
University of Houston
Houston, Texas
Bal des Ardents; Charivari; Godiva, Lady; Wild
Woman

Kathleen Stokker
Luther College
Decorah, Iowa
Olaf, Saint

Jeff Sypeck
University of Maryland
College Park, Maryland
Ordeal

Timothy R. Tangherlini
University of California at Los Angeles
Los Angeles, California
Black Death; Eddic Poetry; Legend

Sandra H. Tarlin
University of Houston
Houston, Texas
Judith

Elizabeth Tucker
Binghamton University
Binghamton, New York
Childbirth

Martin W. Walsh
University of Michigan
Ann Arbor, Michigan
Drama; Festivals and Celebrations; Harvest Fes-
tivals and Rituals; Martinmas

Andrew Welsh
Rutgers University
New Brunswick, New Jersey
Culhwch and Olwen; Mabinogi; Riddle

David Williams
McGill University
Montreal, Canada
Saints, Cults of the

Myra Corinne Williams
University of Houston
Houston, Texas
Punishments

Lee Winniford
University of Houston
Houston, Texas
Becket, Saint Thomas; Dance

Roger Wood
Central College,
    Houston Community College System
Houston, Texas
Peasants' Revolts

Eli Yassif
Tel Aviv University
Tel Aviv, Israel
Golem; Jewish Tradition; Judah the Pious; Lilith

ALPHABETICAL LIST OF ENTRIES

PREFACE

Fully five centuries after their passing, the Middle Ages have never been more popular than they are today. Their heroes—King Arthur, Joan of Arc, Robin Hood—are named by twenty-first-century Americans as often as any hero now alive. Their supernatural villains—dragons, giants, dwarfs, witches—are the stuff of contemporary fairy tales, fantasy novels, and live-action role-playing games. Their lovers—Tristan and Iseut, Guinevere and Lancelot—persist as major figures in romantic opera and contemporary film. The focal image of today's fantasy world—the multi-turreted castle standing at the center of a Walt Disney theme park—is based upon modern notions of a medieval castle. No past era is more clearly and pervasively a part of our own than the Middle Ages.

More than any other aspect of medieval life, we know about its folklore—its traditional festivals, such as Carnival and the Feast of Fools; its courtly and martial games, including tournaments and lovers' serenades; its customs and beliefs, exemplified by the healing rituals of French and English kings; its extraordinary gods and heroes, such as Thor and Cú Chulainn; and its enduring legends, as expressed in such epics as *Beowulf*, the *Cantar de mio Cid,* and the *Chanson de Roland.*

Yet for all the present-day excitement generated by the medieval world, most of our impressions of its folklore come from the imaginative reconstructions of the past 200 years—from Victor Hugo's *Notre Dame de Paris* to Disney's *Hunchback of Notre Dame,* from Richard Wagner's *Ring of the Nibelungs* to recent *Thor* comic books, from Alfred, Lord Tennyson's *Idylls of the King* to T. H. White's *Once and Future King.* Most twenty-first-century Americans, asked what strikes them about this period, would mention a postmedieval stereotype—for example, the gargoyles of Notre Dame Cathedral in Paris, as much the products of the nineteenth-century architect Eugène Viollet-le-Duc as of any medieval sculptor; or the tale of how Robin Hood saved England from the clutches of King John, though this scenario owes more to Sir Walter Scott than to twelfth-century English intrigue.

This book seeks to reach beyond such modern imaginings to capture a sense of medieval folklore in its own time. Our work is dedicated to the conviction that no matter how exciting our fantasies about the Middle Ages may be, the real thing was even more engaging. We assumed the daunting task of presenting the folk cultures of medieval Europe in their own light and on their own terms. To that end, we asked our authors to craft their contributions according to some basic premises of current folklore studies.

Some Guiding Premises for the Study of Medieval Folklore

As imperishable as the heroes of medieval folklore seem to be, there is nothing more protean, volatile, and elusive than folklore itself. A much fuller description of the qualities of folklore is available in the entry Folklore in this volume. Here, we set out some of the premises that most informed us in planning this work.

Because folklore changes over time, medieval folklore should not be confused with earlier or later folkloric expressions. In the nineteenth century, when the term *folklore* was coined, many people assumed that folklore, like a fossil, preserves a frozen image of the ancient past. If one accepts this premise, then the folklore of any given time will be essentially the same in form, function, and meaning as the folklore of any other. To the contrary, through close observation, folklorists have noted that folklore tends to be extraordinarily dynamic, extremely prone to change with changing times and environments.

In describing medieval folklore, contributors often mentioned related phenomena from earlier or later periods, sometimes to demonstrate significant continuity, sometimes to demonstrate crucial differences over time in the development of a given custom, tale, or belief. We asked them to provide clarity to our readership by being very specific in dating and characterizing both medieval and nonmedieval phenomena.

Because folklore serves as the foundation for most other forms of cultural expression, it is so powerful, relevant, and pervasive that it will leave its traces even in the most official culture. Most medieval folklore comprised ephemeral acts and perishable expressions: oral tales, customs recorded only incidentally in writing, sung and instrumental performances delivered without the aid of musical notation, dances so often known to us now only by a drawing or a woodcut capturing only one frozen motion of the whole. Thus, many of the fullest and most vital expressions of medieval folklore disappeared centuries ago.

Nevertheless, folklore is such a pervasive force that even such a formal, institutional cultural phenomenon as the canonization of saints will reflect unofficial folk custom. Therefore, our entry Saints discusses both the official and unofficial aspects of the canonization process, just as the entry Ordeal considers both the official legal nature and the folkloric expressions of this institution.

Also, because all human groups and complex cultural activities possess their unofficial sides, folklore is everywhere, not merely limited to a certain social layer—it is not, for example, restricted to poor, rural populations or to the Celts. Not only peasants, but also knights possessed and practiced folklore in the Middle Ages. Therefore, this book contains entries describing the traditional practices of both groups. Entries such as Courtly Love and Tournament, for example, treat aristocratic play traditions, while the entries Harvest Festivals and Rituals and Midsummer devote themselves more pointedly to lower-class entertainments. Many entries, such as Carol, Dance, and Foodways, treat both upper- and lower-class expressions of traditional culture.

Because folklore is so strongly influenced by its environment, the study of folklore must proceed hand in hand with the study of its cultural context. Folklore inevitably changes when transmitted from one distinctive cultural environment to another. Thus the Welsh King Arthur (treated in the entry Arthurian Lore) is a figure distinctly different from the Arthur described in the twelfth-century French works of Chrétien de Troyes (see the entries Arthur and Chrétien de Troyes). Each of these figures embodies images and attitudes concerning kingship that are based on the folkloric traditions of its respective time, author, and audience. To begin to understand the folkloric meaning of these different Arthurs, it is necessary to know something about their various cultural milieux.

The editors have devoted as much space as possible to treating the largest tradition areas of medieval Europe as defined by common history, language, and other culture traits. Readers of this book are urged to get a sense of the diversity and complexity of the period by browsing the entries Arabic-Islamic Tradition, Baltic Tradition, English Tradition (both the Anglo-Saxon Period and the Middle English Period), Finno-Ugric Tradition, French Tradition, German Tradition, Hispanic Tradition, Hungarian Tradition, Irish Tradition, Italian Tradition, Jewish Tradition, Scandinavian Tradition, Scottish Tradition, Slavic Tradition (East), and Welsh Tradition.

The Entries

Following the precepts outlined above, we asked our contributors to structure their entries in a format designed to peel away postmedieval preconceptions and to recover as much as possible of the medieval folkloric world. Authors were to begin their articles with "the most concrete and least contestable evidence" so that readers would soon gather how much (or more often, how little) information is available to us, as well as the nature of that evidence.

In order to conserve space and maintain a steady focus, the editors have devoted relatively little space to discussing ways in which medieval folklore reflects ancient culture or presages traditions practiced today. Our aim is, rather, for the reader to experience the medieval phenomenon, to the very limited extent that it is possible to do so from such a vast remove in time. To this end, we asked contributors—even those writing about phenomena well documented in ancient times—to begin by presenting the most relevant medieval information. Medieval folklore would thus appear as a vital entity in its own right rather than as it has so often been interpreted—as a final footnote to an ancient practice, more important for what it suggests concerning distant origins than for what it reveals about medieval life.

The contributors responded creatively and in highly varied fashion, and we have striven to preserve the integrity of their individual voices, methodologies, and approaches. Some entries, such as Norris J. Lacy's entry Arthur and Brynley F. Roberts's entry Arthurian Lore, are impeccable models of precision in which the authors scrupulously lay out all the known facts and resist generalization. Other entries, such Stephen O. Glosecki's entry Totem, address phenomena that we cannot even prove to have existed in the Middle Ages, yet they do so in ways that clearly distinguish evidence from speculation. Although authors vary enormously in their willingness to speculate, the editors have attempted to minimize those differences by asking contributors to supply their most speculative interpretations at the end of each entry.

Audience

This is the first one-volume work of its kind. More-general works, including the *Dictionary of the Middle Ages* (13 vols., edited by J. R. Strayer, 1982–1989) and *Funk and Wagnalls Standard Dictionary of Folklore, Mythology, and Legend* (2nd ed., edited by Maria Leach, 1960), include medieval folklore as part of their overall designs. More-specific reference tools, such as *The Arthurian Encyclopedia* (2nd ed., edited by Norris J. Lacy, 1996), discuss the medieval and folkloric dimensions of their particular topics. But no previous one-volume work has devoted itself both broadly and exclusively to the subject of medieval folklore. Aware of the unique nature of our project, we attempt to address three distinct audiences:

Those who are entirely new to the academic study of both folklore and the Middle Ages. We assumed that this population would make up our largest audience. Accordingly, we strove for precision in language and clarity in presentation, as well as to characterize and define those concepts and terms that are not generally known outside the fields of folklore and medieval studies.

Those who have studied medieval culture but who have little knowledge of folklore, and vice versa. This text treats two areas of great appeal for nonspecialists even in the academic world. The fact is that the great majority of specialists in both medieval studies and folklore studies know very little about the other discipline. Thus, this book relies on a core group of contributors who are adept in both fields and who are committed to and experienced in reaching out to those who are novices in either.

Those who are specialists in both medieval studies and folklore. Because there has never previously been a one-volume companion to medieval folklore, we designed this book to serve as a site for consolidating a body of information currently available only in widely scattered sources. Each major article is structured to give a general survey of its topic; in sum, this book presents a larger body of specific information on medieval folklore than can be found in any other one-volume work of which we are aware. (Those seeking a thorough bibliographical treatment of the topics included in this book are urged to consult the two-volume *Medieval Folklore: An Encyclopedia of Myths, Legends, Tales, Beliefs, and Customs,* edited by Carl Lindahl, John McNamara, and John Lindow [2000].)

Scope
Because this book was designed to present not only individual items of lore but also their social and cultural contexts, the editors could have created a work many times the length of this one and still not have come close to exhausting our subject. Necessarily, then, the encyclopedia has been limited in its scope. These are the work's most significant boundaries:

1. A limited geographic range: this book concentrates on European folklore. Furthermore, the editors, bearing in mind an English-reading audience, focus more intently on England, Ireland, Scotland, and Wales than on other medieval cultures. The cultures that most strongly influenced and interacted with medieval Britain and Ireland—French, West Germanic, and Scandinavian—received somewhat less detailed but still substantial treatments. Arabic-Islamic, Baltic, East Slavic, Finno-Ugric, Hispanic, Hungarian, Italian, and Jewish folk cultures also figure significantly, but the scope of our project did not allow us to extend far beyond the boundaries of Europe. Thus, medieval Africa, East Asia, and South Asia are little mentioned.

2. In terms of time, we have concentrated on the period 500–1500 C.E. The relatively few people who died or events that transpired before 500 that are treated here—St. Peter and St. Augustine of Hippo, for example, or and the Hunnish slaughter of the Burgundians (referred to in the entries Burgundian Cycle and *Nibelungenlied*)—are discussed for their enormous influence on medieval folk traditions rather than for the ways they influenced and were influenced by premedieval folklore. On the opposite end of the time line, we have included a significant amount of postmedieval information, almost all of it from the sixteenth century, for two reasons: such records are often substantially richer than medieval records, and they provide information of special value for certain cultural regions, such as the Baltic and Finno-Ugric, in which medieval traditions continued largely unchanged into and sometimes beyond the sixteenth century.

3. Even within our areas of greatest concentration, we make no claim of completeness. A book of this size could easily have been devoted exclusively to the folklore of medieval saints, yet here we offer fewer than 20 entries on individual saints. Again, the folklore of medieval royalty could have handily filled this volume, yet this work devotes separate entries to only four historical rulers, Charlemagne, Harun al-Rashid, Olaf (who was also a saint), and Richard the Lion-Heart, as well as one legendary king, Arthur. In similar fashion, the book treats most of its major categories by devoting individual entries to a few of the most representative examples and discussing others in more general fashion. For example, there are separate articles on some wild animals (see, for example, Bear and Wolf and Werewolf) as well as some legendary beasts (see Griffin and Unicorn), but clerical lore concerning other animals is discussed in the entry Bestiary, and the entries Animal Tale, Bestiality, and Gargoyles also bring together significant amounts of medieval animal lore.

Finding Information
Although no one work, including this one, could present an exhaustive treatment of medieval folklore, we do offer the reader access to some of the most important aspects of the folk traditions of medieval Europe, and they also introduce some of the major current methods and tools of folklorists.

The book contains three classification systems for guiding readers to the information that they seek: first, the entries themselves, listed in alphabetical order; second, the list of cross-references following the heading "See also" at the end of each entry; and, third, the general index at the end of the book. Although this volume contains only 261 entries, it makes significant reference to thousands of aspects of medieval folklore. For example, Melusine, an otherworldly being featured in late-medieval French romances, does not have an entry devoted exclusively to her, but she does figure substantially in the entries on Fairies, Fairy Lover, Mermaid, and Myth; all of these references can be found by consulting the general index.

Finally, readers interested in folk narrative have five means of finding information on a desired topic: in addition to the three tools just listed, there are separate type and motif indexes provided just before the general index. Thus, readers interested in the tale known to folklorists as "The Dragon-Slayer" can find references not only in the general index but also in the tale type index, where "The

Dragon-Slayer" is listed as type AT 300, and the motif index, where motif B11.11, "Fight with dragon," refers to an important element in this particular tale.

Tools for Folklore Study

This work focuses primarily on expressions of folk culture and consequently devotes a relatively small amount of space to the theories and methods of folklorists. Nevertheless, certain articles were designed wholly or largely to convey information about the principles, methods, and theories of folklorists. The entry Folklore defines the field and describes some of its major contemporary approaches and methods. The entries on certain folklore genres—Blasons Populaires, Folktale, Harvest Festivals and Rituals, Legend, Myth, and Proverbs in particular—discuss some of the major past perspectives in the history of folklore studies as well as some of the more recent scholarly approaches.

In addition, the entries on Folktale and Motif discuss traditional approaches to the classification and comparative study of folk narrative. Folktale discusses the concept of the tale type, and Motif assesses the uses and weaknesses of the concept of the motif. Because many authors who wrote about folk narratives use the tale type numbers developed by Antti Aarne and Stith Thompson in their *Types of the Folktale* (3rd ed., 1961) as well as the motifs classified in Thompson's *Motif-Index of Folk-Literature* (2nd ed., 1955–1958), we have provided a tale type index and a motif index at the back of the book. Readers new to the study of types and motifs should read the entry Folktale before consulting the type index, and the entry Motif before consulting the motif index.

Our most persistent attempt to infuse folklore studies into this book lies in structuring the entries in ways that encourage readers to "think folkloricly," to consider folklore as a living process that both reflects and influences its social and cultural environment. We encourage readers to browse, reading the entries on culture areas (Baltic Tradition and Welsh Tradition, for example) and social groups (Knight, Monks, Nuns, Peasants) to consider how folklore reflects both its broadest cultural contexts and the specific values of the group that creates it; and surveying the entries on folklore genres (Animal Tale, Blasons Populaires, Folktale, Harvest Festivals and Rituals, Legend, Myth, Proverbs, Riddle) as well as the medieval literary and performance genres in which so much folklore is embedded (Drama, Flyting, Puppets and Puppet Plays, Romance). If the folklore of the Middle Ages lies beyond the experience of us all, the combined efforts of more than 100 authors will bring readers closer to those vanished traditions than any other one-volume work currently available.

ACKNOWLEDGMENTS

The editors gratefully acknowledge their sources of funding and project support. In 1993, 1996, and 1999 the University of Houston supplied Limited Grants in Aid, allowing the coeditors to retain Katherine Oldmixon, Sandra Jordan, and Myra Williams to perform editorial work related to this project. University of Houston English Department chairs Harmon Boertien and Wyman Herendeen generously supported the work by providing materials, computers, and services that would have been extremely difficult for us to do without. University of Houston English Department office manager Lynn Dale, Barbie DeVet, and Andrea Short performed numerous acts of assistance and kindness. Dean Lois Zamora of the University of Houston's College of Humanities, Fine Arts, and Communication assisted the project with allotments to help retain Myra Williams. Eric Granquist and Dan Jackson of the college's Computing Support Office contributed time and expertise to help establish a server and database for the project. David Rossi of the English Department Computer Writing Lab volunteered assistance in a number of technical matters.

We further acknowledge Gary Kuris, who first conceived of the project; Samuel Armistead, Michael Chesnutt, W. F. H. Nicolaisen, and J. Michael Stitt, who contributed substantially to the early planning; William Gillies, who generously reviewed the Pictish and Gaelic sections in the article on Scottish Tradition; and the members of our advisory board: Elissa R. Henken, Malcolm Jones, Samuel Kinser, Ulrich Marzolph, Stephen A. Mitchell, Brynley F. Roberts, Eli Yassif, and the late W. Edson Richmond.

Once more, we thank our contributors, whose names are listed beginning on page viii, both for sharing their expertise and for extending their patience throughout the long process of preparing this encyclopedia.

Among the people who gave generously of their time, we would particularly like to thank Elissa R. Henken, Malcolm Jones, and Brynley F. Roberts, who, together, are responsible not only for writing nearly one-seventh of all the entries that appear in this encyclopedia but also for offering considerable aid and advice on other aspects of the encyclopedia, recommending and contacting potential contributors, locating illustrations, and offering much-needed criticism.

Sabrina Sirocco of the University of California at Berkeley, and Jack Hall, James Williams, and Malcolm Williams of the University of Houston generously provided translations of seven entries initially written in German. Gerida Brown of the University of Houston's M. D. Anderson Library volunteered extensive time and expertise to check bibliographical citations.

Graduate and undergraduate students at the University of Houston provided exemplary editorial services: Katherine Oldmixon, Sandra Jordan, and Myra Williams gave the project far more than their grant moneys ever compensated them.

Former students Erin McAfee, Dr. Leigh Smith, Andrea Tinnemeyer, and Dr. Lee Winniford performed extraordinary eleventh-hour research.

Copy editor Kathy Delfosse and Todd Hallman and Martha Whitt of ABC-CLIO furthered the enterprise with an extraordinary mixture of expertise and inexplicable good humor, and Linda Robbins of Oxford University Press was most gracious in helping prepare the abridged edition.

A NOTE ON ORTHOGRAPHY

In adapting foreign-language text, we have tried to follow a principle of using forms most familiar to a nonspecialist audience and have aimed for consistency only within a given language, not across languages. Thus, for example, we have eliminated acute accent marks from Old Norse and retained them in Old Irish (but kept ö in Old Norse because it is frequently found in the familiar title *Völsunga Saga*). We have also uniformly edited personal and geographic names to the forms found in *Webster's New Biographical Dictionary* and *Merriam Webster's Geographical Dictionary*, even when this principle caused us personal distress (e.g., Harold Hardraada, a form in which only two of the five syllables might reasonably be defended and that otherwise vanished with Victorian scholarship).

We fully recognize that this system is imperfect, that it could never pretend to be fully consistent, and that our application of it may not have been faultless, but we believe that it was nevertheless the best way to serve the various groups we perceive to be our audience.

MEDIEVAL
FOLKLORE

Accused Queen.

Most often, a woman who is first abused in her parents' home and later slandered and otherwise persecuted in the home of her husband; more rarely, a woman falsely charged with adultery; a common figure in late-medieval romances, chronicles, and saints' lives, also known as the Calumniated Woman.

"The Maiden without Hands"

Tales about a woman victimized first as a daughter and then as a wife began to appear in force in thirteenth-century chronicles (*The Life of Offa I*, a Latin text written in England) and legendary romances (such as the French *La belle Helene* and *La manekine*) and grew progressively more popular as the Middle Ages wore on. The general plot has remained a staple in oral tradition into the present century; the oral form of the accused queen tale is identified by folklorists as "The Maiden without Hands" (AT 706).

In the most common medieval versions, the protagonist undergoes two threats of death and two long exiles before she is finally reunited with both the family of her birth and the family of her marriage. One of the earliest versions of the full-blown plot, Philippe de Remi's *La manekine* (French, c. 1270), presents particularly striking correspondences with the modern folktale:

The king of Hungary promises his dying queen that he will remarry only when he finds a woman who looks just like her. No such woman can be found outside the household, so the king's councilors, clamoring for a male heir, tell the king to marry his daughter Joie, his only child. At first reluctant, the king develops a love for his daughter and sets a wedding date. Joie cuts off her own hand to avoid the marriage. The king has her condemned to death, but sympathetic courtiers save her from her fate and set her out to sea in a sail-less, rudderless boat.

Joie prays, and divine guidance brings the boat ashore in Scotland, where she attracts the attention of the Scottish king. She will not reveal her name or family origin to him, so he calls her *La manekine* (Mannequin). Her silence, however, does not prevent him from falling in love with her, and the two are married in a joyous celebration that only the king's mother refuses to attend.

Five months after Manekine becomes pregnant with the king's child, he travels to France to join in a tournament, leaving her in his mother's care. Manekine gives birth to a son and has a letter sent to her husband announcing the birth. The evil mother-in-law intercepts the letter and replaces it with an announcement that Manekine has given birth to a monster. When the king receives the news, he replies with a letter instructing that mother and child be kept safe until his return, but his mother again replaces the original letter, this time with one ordering mother and son to be burned alive. Sympathetic councilors intervene and have two mannequins burned, while Manekine and her son are sent off secretly in a rudderless boat.

The boat lands in Rome, where a senator takes care of the mother and son. Meanwhile, the Scottish king learns the truth about his wife, imprisons his cruel mother, and sets off on a seven-year quest to find Manekine. He stops at the Roman senator's house, recognizes Manekine through a ring that he had given her (now worn by her son), and the two are reunited.

Another reunion is in the making. After many years Manekine's father, the king of Hungary, repents his desire to marry his daughter, and he goes on pilgrimage to Rome to seek absolution from the pope. He finds his daughter in Rome, and when the two are reconciled, his daughter readopts her birth name, Joie. The pope announces that Joie's severed hand has been found in the baptismal water, and God's voice orders the pope to reattach it. All live whole and happy.

Among the dozens of medieval romances and chronicles following this basic plot are fourteenth- and fifteenth-century works in German (*Mai und Beaflor*, Jason Enikel's *Weltkronik*, *Königstochter von Frankreich*, *Herzog Herpin*), French (*La comtesse d'Anjou*, *Alixandre roy de Hongrie*, *Yde et Olive*), Catalan (*El rey de Hungria*), Italian (*Regina Oliva*, *Novella della figlia del re di Dacia*), English (*Emare*, Chaucer's "Man of Law's Tale," and Gower's "Tale of Constance"), and Latin (*Ystoria regis Frachorum*).

A comparison of *La manekine* with recent oral folktales reveals extraordinary similarities, but also significant differences. This is the general outline of "The Maiden without Hands":

1. *Mutilation:* A maiden's hands are cut off to punish her for refusing to marry her own father or brother (or the maiden lops off her own hands, eyes, or breasts and sends them to her incestuous suitor, who has admired them; or a father carelessly sells his daughter to the devil, who forces him to cut off her hands; or a malicious sister-in-law effects the mutilation by slandering the maiden to her brother). The maiden is cast out.
2. *Royal marriage:* A king (usually out hunting) finds her in the woods, takes her home, sometimes has silver hands fashioned for her, and marries her. While her husband is away she bears a child and sends a letter to the king announcing the birth.
3. *Calumniation:* However, she is cast forth again because her resentful mother-in-law (or jealous sister-in-law, depraved father,

or the devil) exchanges the letter, substituting one falsely accusing her of giving birth to a changeling (or of eating her infant). When her compassionate husband sends a message ordering that his wife be cared for, the villain exchanges that letter for one commanding that she be put to death. Because of her incomparable beauty and gentleness, the would-be executioners are unable to kill the queen and instead exile her.

4. *Restoration:* While she is in the wilderness for the second time, her hands are miraculously restored, and she is reunited with her family.

La manekine and the other medieval accused queen romances most closely resemble the modern oral folktales in the central episodes, involving the cruel mother-in-law and the substituted letters, which have remained the most stable parts of the story for more than seven centuries. In other respects the differences between medieval and modern versions are many and striking. One of the major atmospheric differences is that the medieval woman usually undergoes two exiles in an open boat, while the märchen victim wanders in a forest. Other changes in the plot over time concern significant differences in treating issues of gender, sexuality, and maturity.

In the modern folktale incest is one of many possible causes for the exile of the innocent daughter, but in medieval romance the father's attempt to marry his daughter is almost always the cause. Sometimes, as in *La manekine*, the father is pushed toward incest by councilors who desire an heir. Sometimes, as in *Mai und Beaflor*, his long grief over the death of his wife slowly transforms into desire for his daughter. Elsewhere the king seems to go mad with sudden passion, as in *La comtesse d'Anjou*, where he conceives a great desire for his daughter as they play chess together. In other cases, as in *La belle Helene* and *La figlia del re di Dacia*, the devil infects the king with lust. In only a few of the romances is the incest motive missing, but they are among the most famous: Chaucer's "Man of Law's Tale," Gower's *Confessio Amantis*, and the Italian *Il pecarone*.

Second, though mutilation is common enough in medieval versions, it is not as common as in modern oral versions of "The Maiden without Hands"; furthermore, the medieval heroine—like Manekine, who cuts off her hand, or the heroine of Enikel's *Weltkronik*, who claws at her face until she looks "like the devil"—most often mutilates herself, whereas in the majority of oral tales the father or the devil mutilates the child. Thus, the typical medieval father is a sexual predator; the most common folktale father, a physical abuser of his child. By and large the romance heroine is slightly stronger than the märchen heroine in taking her fate into her own hands, so to speak. She may attempt to gain control over her situation, desperately, through self-mutilation, but also sometimes, less self-destructively, through a clever escape (as in the Latin *Columpnarium*) occasionally (as in the French *Yde et Olive*) disguised as a man. The romance heroine could be fairly characterized as more "grown up" than the oral folktale maiden.

A third major difference further points to the adult nature of the medieval heroine. Although the most stable part of the medieval and modern tale is the wicked mother-in-law who substitutes the letters, Margaret Schlauch has pointed out that in the later Middle Ages a male villain tended to enter the plot to subject the queen to further slander. In such romances the female persecutor is aided, either purposely or incidentally, by a male: in *Valentine and Nameless* the malign mother-in-law's accomplice is a reprobate bishop; in Chaucer's "Man of Law's Tale" Constance is calumniated first by the lustful knight (for murder) and later by her mother-in-law (for monster birth). In such romances, nonincestuous, adult sexuality supplements or replaces the father-daughter relationship.

Chronicle, Ballad, and Late-Medieval Romance Accounts

The false charge of adultery occurs independently in chronicle accounts before the first surviving version of "The Maiden without Hands" appears. Queen Gunhilda (also Gunhild), daughter of the English King Canute (also Cnut) the Great and wife of the German Emperor Henry III, is an early example. Married in 1036, Gunhilda died of the plague in 1038, apparently never having been the object of calumny. But writing circa 1125, the English chronicler William of Malmesbury relates that after years of married life Gunhilda was accused of adultery by a massive antagonist. The queen's champion was a young boy who succeeded in defeating her accuser, after which Gunhilda left her husband and entered a convent. (The story of Gunhilda later appears in ballad form in the seventeenth-century English "Sir Aldingar" and the sixteenth-century Danish "Ravengård og Memering.") A thirteenth-century French chronicle of the life of Edward the Confessor recounts a very similar story but identifies the champion as a dwarf named Mimecan. The account of St. Cunigund (married to Emperor Henry II in the early years of the eleventh century) partakes of many of the same motifs: calumniated wife; woman slandered as adulteress; physically abusive husband; trial by ordeal (walking barefoot over hot plowshares, carrying hot iron in her bare hands). As they must in märchen and ballads, wives in chronicles and saints' lives must fend off degenerate acquaintances, spousal battery, and slander and must avoid being burned to death. But unlike folktale wives, those in chronicles and hagiography often refuse to stay with their cruel husbands. The near absence of children in these narratives stands in stark contrast to the maiden without hands tales and romances, in which the children of the accused queen play an important role, motivating the plot and heightening pathos in the narrative.

Yet many later medieval romances incorporate the charge of adultery. When the mother-in-law is replaced as the persecutor, often the nature of the persecution changes. In such romances as *Hirlanda of Brittany* and *Charles le chauve* the villainous brother-in-law and the false steward, respectively, level the familiar folktale charges (animal or monster birth and infanticide), but increasingly a new slander takes center stage. The supremely persecuted Hirlanda, accused of giving birth to a monster and of murdering her child, is further vilified as an adulteress. The new charge of infidelity occurs frequently in calumniated woman romances, including a number of fourteenth- and fifteenth-century works: *Syr Tryamore*, *The Erle of Toulous*, *Valentine and Orson* (part of the Charlemagne cycle), and *Theseus de Cologne* (a long romance with three calumniated women). An earlier work, Ulrich von Zatzikhoven's Middle High German *Lanzelet*, belongs to the Arthurian cycle and is unusual in its depiction of Guinevere as an accused queen charged with the treasonous act of poisoning a knight. In these and many others of roughly the same period, the villain has become a power-hungry courtier, and his slander of choice is the charge of infidelity, while the heroine remains virtuous and sorely tried, perhaps even the victim of physical abuse. *Valentine and Orson's* beautiful pregnant Queen Bellissant rebuffs the lustful archbishop of Constantinople, resulting in his denouncing her as an adulteress and a traitor; her credulous husband (the emperor) savagely beats her before the court, deaf to her pleas for mercy for herself and her unborn child. However, the accused queen's role as blameless sufferer did not mean that she always met abuse passively, or even with pragmatic resignation. For example, in *Valentine and Nameless*, Queen Phila's mother-in-law and her accomplice, the false bishop, accuse the queen of infanticide. When the bishop affirms that Phila told him in the confessional that she had committed the crime, the outraged young queen yanks his hair, vigorously refuting his testimony. *Charles le chauve's* pregnant Queen Dorame is subjected to a tiresome and protracted suit by the lustful steward Butor: first he falsely reports her husband's death, then he tries to win her with logic, and when that tactic fails he tries to rape her. Dorame is fiercely chaste, however, and in the struggle she knocks out several of his teeth. Spirited persecuted heroines like Phila and Dorame have proven hardy, retaining salience for hundreds of years and inspiring late-twentieth-century writers of poetry and prose as they formerly caught the imagination of storytellers, ballad singers, chroniclers, and romance writers.

See also: Folktale; Lear, King; Swan Knight

—Melinda Sue Collins and Carl Lindahl

Advent. A time of preparation for the celebration of Christ's birth on December 25, generally the four-week period prior to Christmas.

From very early times, just before the onset of Advent there were festivals and celebrations associated with the autumn harvesting of crops, the slaughtering of livestock, and the preservation of foodstuffs for the long winter ahead. Among the numerous such festivals held throughout Europe, the Celtic Samhain—which developed into Halloween—is a good example of the ways people during the Middle Ages and beyond celebrated the harvest time with feasting while at the same time observing a time when otherworldly beings could enter the natural world. With the coming of Christianity to the north, such celebrations were assimilated to the Church calendar: Samhain coincided with All Saints' and All Souls' Days (November 1 and 2) as a time of experiencing the presence of those gone to the afterlife, and Advent actually began on the Sunday closest to St. Andrew's Day, the last day in November.

In the fourth century, when the Church fixed the date of Christ's birth on December 25, the concept of a spiritual time of preparation for this feast began to be developed. In the Gallic Church this time period took on a penitential character and was called *Quadragesima Sancti Martini*, the Forty Days' Fast of St. Martin, in honor of the Feast of St. Martin on November 11, when this fasting period would begin. On the other hand, in the Roman Church, the mood was one of festive and joyful preparation for Christ's birth, and by the sixth century, the focus was on a series of sermons or homilies on this theme. By the eighth century, when the Frankish Church accepted the Roman liturgy, the penitential seven-to-nine-week Advent observance of Gaul clashed with the festive four-week Advent celebration of Rome. By the thirteenth century, a long period of compromise had eventually determined the current mode for celebrating Advent, combining the four-week time period of Rome and the penitential character of Gaul, though the fasting obligations were not as severe as those of the Lenten observance.

During the medieval period Advent also came to be designated as the beginning of the Church year. The annual cycle begins with Christ's birth; it continues through the year with his Passion, Resurrection, and Ascension, the coming of the Holy Spirit, and the celebration of the Church Triumphant; and it concludes with the ceremonies during All Saints' and All Souls' Days, invoking the remembrance of those who have already passed away.

This leads to the subject of the Second Coming of Christ. Medieval Christians viewed Advent not only as a time of waiting and expectation before Christ's birth but also as analogous to the present time of waiting and expectation before Christ's Second Coming. Partly due to the analogies among these cyclical religious moments of expectation and fulfillment, Advent came to be regarded as the beginning of the Christian church year—a period encompassing the life of Christ, the life of the Church, and the eventual return of Christ to his people on earth.

The most visible symbols of the Advent season in modern times are the Advent wreath and the Advent calendar. The Advent wreath, on which four candles are lit progressively, one more each week, during the four weeks of Advent, originated in the sixteenth century among German Lutherans. The Advent calendar has been developed to assist children in the preparation for Christ's birth through a combination of pictures, symbols, and treats hidden behind "doors" on a large cardboard house, to be opened once a day until Christmas.

See also: Christmas; Harvest Festivals and Rituals; Martinmas; Samhain

—Bradford Lee Eden

Amicus et Amelius. One of the most popular stories of the Middle Ages, from the early eleventh to the fifteenth centuries, with versions in Latin, French, English, Italian, Spanish, Dutch, German, Norse, and Welsh; also a designation for a widespread group of related postmedieval folktales (AT 516C).

There are two groups of such stories: those in which the characteristics of romances predominate, and those that more closely resemble saints' lives. Both treat the ideal of friendship between two knights, include the ultimate test of child sacrifice, and have a strong didactic argument, but the moral exposition and details of the action differ, and there is much disagreement about interpretation.

The major romance versions, which vary widely and are mostly unrelated by source, include *Amys et Amillyoun* (Anglo-Norman, thirteenth century) and *Amis and Amiloun* (Middle English, fourteenth century): Amis and Amiloun are conceived on the same night and born on the same day. Sons of barons of Lombardy, the boys are so much alike in virtue, strength, beauty, and courtesy that none can tell them apart. They are adopted by the duke of Lombardy at the age of 12, swear eternal friendship, become knights at the age of 15, and are much admired and honored at court. When Amiloun returns home after his father's death, he has two exact golden cups made as mementos (and potential tokens of recognition) and presents one to his sworn brother Amis. Inevitably such praised young knights incur the envy of the jealous steward, who betrays Amis, after he reluctantly became the lover of the duke's daughter Belisaunt, a forth-putting maiden.

The hero denies the charge and is allowed a chance for judicial combat. Belisaunt and her mother offer themselves as hostages. Amis, afraid to fight because he would have to perjure himself, seeks his friend Amiloun, and the two exchange places. Amis sleeps with a sword of chastity (motif T351) between himself and Amiloun's wife, pleading illness.

Amiloun goes to the duke's court and fights, even though a voice warns that he will be punished with leprosy. He kills the steward and tells Amis, who returns and marries Belisaunt and ultimately becomes duke. Amiloun explains his actions to his own angry wife, who later drives him away when he develops leprosy. Accompanied by his nephew Amoraunt, Amiloun travels about as a beggar. Amis sends wine to him in his token cup, and Amiloun takes it in his duplicate cup. Amis believes that the leper has injured his friend and attacks him, until he recognizes his sworn brother, whom he treats kindly.

After a year both friends dream that Amiloun can be cured of leprosy by being washed in the blood of Amis's children (S268). Belisaunt agrees; Amis cuts the children's throats, and Amiloun is healed. Friendship triumphs as the highest good; the children are found alive in the nursery. Later the friends return to Amiloun's country and punish his evil wife. Amis and Amiloun die on the same day and are buried in Mortara, or in some romances, Amiloun returns to live with Amis.

The hagiographic version is older; the Latin *Vita Amici et Amilii* dates from the twelfth century, the French *Ami et Amile*, from circa 1200. Both are set in the eighth century, at the time of Charlemagne. The French version is stylistically similar to chansons de geste, and its details are closely tied to religion. Two fathers, one Germanic and one from the Auvergne region of France, take their boys to Rome in response to a dream; Amicus (Ami) and Amelius (Amile) become fast friends on the journey. They are baptized by the pope, who gives them identical cups as mementos. The two separate to sort out inheritance but soon seek each other. Each meets a pilgrim, who believes there is only one because they are so alike; not recognizing each other, they almost fight, but they then swear friendship on the hilt of a sword that contains relics.

At court Charlemagne receives and honors both. It is Amelius who loves the forward princess, and the steward accuses him of robbing the treasury. Amicus offers to substitute for him in the judicial combat, and the two change places. Realizing that he will be guilty of murder, Amicus tries to resolve the conflict but has to kill the steward. His leprosy is explained as God's chastisement of those he loves. Amicus's wife tries to kill him, but he flees to Rome, where Amelius meets him and recognizes him through the cups. The angel Raphael explains that the blood of Amelius's children will cure the leprosy. Amelius, after sustained self-questioning, decides to make the sacrifice. As the friends go to church in thanksgiving, bells ring to announce the miracle of healing. They find the children restored by the Virgin Mary, and devils enter Amicus's wife and kill her. Later the friends join Charlemagne's army against Didier in Lombardy and are killed at Mortara. They are buried in separate churches; miraculously, the two are united in one place. After his victory Charlemagne leaves priests and clerics to care for the tomb of Amicus and Amelius.

Rodulfus Tortarius's Latin poem (before 1175) refers to the sword of the epic hero Roland, but otherwise it is largely classical and pagan in references and attitude. The Anglo-Norman and Middle English romances contain many details of Christian belief. Many postmedieval folktales share significant traits with the medieval versions of the story of Amicus and Amelius. The widespread folktale "The Twins or Blood Brothers" (AT 303) parallels the medieval narrative: it features males who look identical, were born on the same day, and are separated in their travels, and it incorporates the motifs of the life tokens (E761) and the separating sword. The concluding episode of the medieval tale, centering on sacrifice and revivification of the children, is echoed in the oral folktale "Faithful John" (AT 516, 516C).

See also: Folktale; Romance; Sword

—Velma Bourgeois Richmond

Amulet and Talisman. Words that first appeared in European languages late in the Middle Ages to denote material objects thought to have some mysterious power to protect their owners from misfortune, disease, or witchcraft or to bring them wealth, success, and good luck.

There is considerable overlap between the two terms, and those scholars who do differentiate between them do not agree on their definitions. Some use *amulet* for "a passive protector or preventive charm" and *talisman* for one that has an "active principle" and "positive power" to procure a fortunate result. Others say an amulet is necessarily small enough to be carried on the person or worn as jewelry, whereas a talisman can be any size; others, that *amulet* is the broader term and can be used of anything, however natural or homely, which is thought to bring healing, protection, or luck—for example, a holed stone, a piece of coral, a wolf's tooth—whereas *talisman* has the more restricted meaning of an elaborate device constructed according to the rituals of learned magic. One reason for the difficulty is that the same object or class of objects can fulfill both functions. Astrological figures were often protective as well as active, while other objects changed their roles over time—a horseshoe on a Tudor door was a defensive measure against witchcraft, but on a modern wedding cake it is expected to confer good luck.

Talisman, the more closely definable term, en-tered English in the 1630s as a rendering of the Byzantine Greek *telesm*, the name for a magic statue defending a city or some hidden magic object to protect a building from harm. However, the Greek *telesm* was itself borrowed from Arabic *tilsam*, a metal plaque, jewel, or parchment bearing astrological designs, words, or letters that harness the powers of the planets and stars and the spirits associated with them. This astrological meaning persists in most seventeenth-century uses of the word, though in the nineteenth century (perhaps under the influence of Sir Walter Scott's famous novel *The Talisman*) it came to be used far more loosely.

Astrological talismans were based upon elaborate systems of occult knowledge; these were most fully developed by Renaissance intellectuals, such as Cornelius Agrippa (1486–1535) and John Dee (1527–1608), but their individual components were already present in the Middle Ages. One was the ancient idea, systematized by Bishop Isidore of Seville (c. 560–636), that all precious and semiprecious stones had "virtues" beneficial to the wearer—either for healing or for conferring power. Thirteenth-century lapidaries claim, for example, that any man wearing a ruby will be received with honor wherever he goes and can never be defeated in games or in battle; that the sapphire "is good for kings, queens, and great lords," gives deep joy, wisdom, and chastity to whoever gazes at it, and breaks iron fetters; and that the emerald "multiplieth a man's goods."

Such powers were increased by sacred words and symbols engraved on the gem or its metal setting. Names of God and of angels were especially potent; some were Hebrew, including the tetragrammaton JHVH (the letters forming the name of God), others Greco-Egyptian, others Arabic. Some were the initials of words, such as AGLA, for *Atha Gebri Leilan Adonai* (Thou art mighty forever, O Lord); others depended on numerology, since all individual letters had been assigned numbers. Thus, many rings have been found bearing the word ABRAXAS, the name of God, according to the Gnostic Basilides of Alexandria (fl. c. 125); its Greek letters have the value 365, supposedly corresponding not only to the days of the year but also to the number of eons, of ranks of angels, and of bones in a human body. Abraxas was represented as a bird-headed figure with snakes for legs; old gems with this image were reused in medieval times—for example, the intaglio ring buried with Bishop Seffried of Chichester (Sussex), who died in 1151. The names ascribed to angels and demons, by which they could be invoked and their powers harnessed, became increasingly numerous and fantastic throughout the period. At the beginning of the thirteenth century Michael Scot had already listed some whereby demons could be imprisoned inside a ring or bottle.

Arithmetical magic spread with Islamic culture

into Europe. Each of the seven planets had its "magic square" of numbers so arranged that in whichever direction they were added the result was the same. There were also "letter squares," most famously the classical *ROTAS-OPERA-TENET-AREPO-SATOR*, which, when arranged in box form,

```
R O T A S
O P E R A
T E N E T
A R E P O
S A T O R
```

delivered the same five-word sentence, vertically as well as horizontally, backward from the bottom as well as forward from the top. (The sentence has many possible translations, one of which is "Sator the plowman performs the work of wheels.") And the pattern can also be manipulated to yield the Christian message *PATER NOSTER A O*. It was said to extinguish fires if written on a wooden tablet and thrown into the flames.

An important symbolic pattern was the six-pointed star, which was called the Shield of David in Hebrew and Solomon's Seal in Arabic and in Byzantine Greek. It was the sign of Solomon's legendary authority to make demons serve him. Another was the five-pointed figure variously known as the pentagram, pentacle, or pentalpha (that is, five A's). It is first found in ancient Greece and the eastern Mediterranean as a decorative pattern, and to Gnostics and Neoplatonists in the early centuries C.E. it symbolized the perfect universe (four elements plus spirit). It reached medieval Europe via Jewish and Arab culture and was reinterpreted as representing the five wounds of Jesus—a symbol guaranteed to put demons to flight. In the poem *Sir Gawain and the Green Knight* it is painted on the hero's shield, presumably with defensive intent, though the poet does call it Solomon's Sign, implying knowledge of its talismanic function.

Solomon was respected as a virtuous wizard in medieval times, and manuals of magic were falsely ascribed to him, such as the famous *Key of Solomon*. These contained many designs for talismans to be inscribed on metal plaques under astrological conditions, with much prayer and invocation of spirits. Typically they would include a pentacle inscribed within a circle and surrounded by sacred words. They were used for finding treasure, winning women's love or great men's favor, destroying enemies, and the like.

Terms for "amulet" entered European languages at the end of the Middle Ages. The word *amulet* itself is of unknown derivation; however, the class of objects it applies to is extremely ancient. In fact, there has probably never been a period of history or prehistory during which people did not regard certain things as worth keeping for religio-magical protection against sickness, poison, spells, the attacks of enemies or wild animals, or simple bad luck. At their simplest these are natural objects such as animal teeth, horns, claws and bones, pointed stones, holed stones, and fossils of striking appearance; or they may be older human-made items no longer recognized as such and therefore credited with magical powers: stone axes to ward off thunderstorms, flint arrows to detect poisons, Romano-British glass rings interpreted as "snake stones" with healing powers. Various substances were regarded as intrinsically effective, notably coral, jet, and amber, as described by Pliny and other ancient authors. Medieval amulets containing some of these substances include the jet pendants made at Santiago (including, alongside religious items, old magic symbols such as eyes and hands) and the coral beads popular in Italy to ward off the evil eye from children. Museums, understandably, tend to display the more artistic and expensive amulets—for example, those where the protective object is mounted in silver or gold. Simple items are in any case likely to have perished. It is only in specialist collections such as the Pitt-Rivers Museum (Oxford) and the Horniman Museum (London) that one can see such things as a mole's paw carried by a farm laborer in the 1920s to ward off cramp and wonder how many medieval peasants may have done the same.

Folklorists have given special attention to amulets with proven precedents in pre-Christian culture. Representations of eyes have been used since ancient Egypt, especially in Mediterranean countries, and are probably related to the blue bead with an eyelike pattern widely used in the same regions. In ancient Rome the phallus brought good luck and warded off the evil eye, as its successor, the red or silver "Neapolitan horn," did in medieval Italy and still does. The pagan origins of mermaid and sea-horse figures as charms are also clear. Certain gestures were thought to ward off evil, notably making "horns" by extending the index and little fingers, the rest being folded; making "the fig," a sexual gesture, by thrusting the thumb between clenched fingers; and (in some countries) extending the hand palm outward. Small metal or bone hands making these gestures were worn as pendants.

But it must not be forgotten that throughout medieval Europe there were innumerable Christian objects worn or kept in the home as safeguards against misfortune; to assist in sickness, childbirth, or danger; or as a guarantee that one would not die suddenly and unshriven: medals, crosses, pilgrim badges, saints' emblems, ribbons or strips of paper alleged to be the exact length of Christ's body, papers inscribed with religious texts and sewn up in a pouch, wax disks stamped with the Lamb of God, and many more.

Naturally, it is usually the finer specimens that survive. Among many examples, one could cite the fifteenth-century Scottish Glenlyon brooch, bearing the names of the Three Magi and Christ's dying words, *consummatum est* (it is finished), which (according to various medieval texts) protect the wearer from bleeding, fever, thieves, epilepsy, storms, danger while traveling, and sudden death. A gold pendant discovered in 1985 near Middleham Castle in Yorkshire is engraved with representations of the Trinity, the Nativity, and various saints, and also with *JHVH* and the word *ANANYZAPTA*, supposed to cure epilepsy and drunkenness and to prevent "an evil death"; it also bears a large sapphire, a gem with many medicinal and protective powers. It is hollow and contains fragments of rich embroidery, presumed to be relics. In medieval Catholic culture, artifacts such as these were devotional objects. Protestant critics called them "superstitious idols," and now scholars categorize them as amulets.

See also: Evil Eye; Magic; Relics

—Jacqueline Simpson

Andrew's Day, Saint. The feast day for St. Andrew the Apostle, November 30, which was notable in the Western Church calendar for its proximity to Advent.

St. Andrew was believed to have been martyred around 60 C.E. on a cross in Patras, Greece, whence his relics were taken to Constantinople. He remains the patron saint of Patras, and his feast day is still important in Greek Orthodox liturgy, although earlier practice of his cult in the East is unclear. Claimed as the first evangelist of Georgia, Russia, and Ukraine, Andrew is also revered in Russian Orthodoxy. The cult of the saint came to the West in the fourth century, partly through the efforts of St. Ambrose, who presented relics, now lost, to his church in Milan. The cathedral in Amalfi, Italy, gained relics around 1208, and there, since 1304, both the clergy and lay folk have claimed that on days associated with St. Andrew, a liquid forms in a vessel suspended over the area known as the Apostle's tomb.

St. Andrew is also the patron saint of Scotland. According to early legend St. Andrew appeared to King Hungus in a dream, promising him victory over his enemies. In the meantime, an angel appeared to St. Rule (or Regulus), directing him to take relics of St. Andrew somewhere in the northwest, though not telling him specifically where. During St. Rule's travels, the angel later directed him to stop in Fife, Scotland, where the saint built the church of St. Andrews for the relics. Moreover, since King Hungus had already had his vision of St. Andrew, St. Rule was particularly welcome when he turned up with the relics at Kinrymont.

Despite the saint's importance, popular customs connected particularly with his feast day are rare. In Scotland, to honor the saint's patronage on his feast day, men and boys would trap rabbits and squirrels for "Andermas" dinner. Andermas dinner appears to have originated as a medieval custom, although time lines are of course a bit blurred in rural Scotland. The practice is also found in England from early times, and in postmedieval times, in shires where the saint's day marked a lace makers' holiday, mumming was also found.

See also: Advent; Relics; Saints, Cults of the; Scottish Tradition

—Nicola Royan

Angels. God's heavenly helpers who bring messages to earth and in various ways provide aid and protection to humans, named from the Greek word for "messengers," which was based on the Hebrew word with the same meaning.

Biblical Angels
Angels have a long biblical history. A "messenger of Yahweh" appears in numerous places in the Hebrew Bible, appearing to Hagar in the desert, preventing Abraham from sacrificing Isaac, speaking to Jacob in a dream and to Moses at the burning bush, and leading the Israelites through the Red Sea. The messenger is usually alone, but exceptions include the two angels who rescue Lot from Sodom and those whom Jacob sees in a dream going up and down the ladder to heaven. Eventually, some angels are given names: Raphael, who helps Tobit and his sons; Gabriel, who flies to Daniel as part of his vision; and Michael, described by Daniel as a "prince," who strives with the prince of Persia on behalf of Israel. These angels are all friends to the Chosen People, of course, but some figures may be fearful instruments of divine justice. Such is the case with the great winged creatures and the fiery sword that God posts outside Eden after expelling Adam and Eve.

The Christian New Testament continues this rich tradition of angels. Gabriel announces the coming births of both John the Baptist and Jesus; angels sing in the heavens at the birth of Jesus, and one tells the shepherds of the event; an angel appears to Joseph in a dream, reassuring him that Mary will give birth while still being a virgin; the angel reappears to Joseph in another dream warning him to flee with Mary and the child to Egypt; angels minister to Jesus after his temptation; at the Mount of Olives an angel comes from heaven to give Jesus strength during his agony; and angels by his empty tomb proclaim that he has risen from the dead. In the traditions of the early Church recorded in the Acts of the Apostles, angels also figure prominently in such instances as releasing Peter and John from prison, assuring Paul in a dream that his ship to Rome will arrive safely despite a terrible storm, and striking the proud Herod Agrippa with a horrible disease in which worms eat him alive. Numerous angels appear in the Revelation, or Apocalypse, especially Michael as leader of the forces that defeat Satan. On Judgment Day angels will separate the saved from the damned, leading the blessed to their heavenly reward. Thus, angels become far more than messengers, serving as powerful agents of divine power in both Jewish and Christian biblical traditions.

Early Medieval Angels

The popularity of angels continued to promote a rich lore in early and medieval Christian culture. Thus, by the second and third centuries, even theologians such as Clement of Alexandria (fl. c. 200–215) and Origen (fl. c. 222–254) recognized the special function of guardian angels in protecting humans, and Origen claimed that each person had a good angel on one side and a bad angel on the other, perhaps reflecting the dualistic tendencies in pre-Christian popular religion from the East (e.g., that associated with the followers of Mani). In the fourth-century Apocalypse of St. Paul, a man living in the saint's former house in Tarsus is visited by an angel who tells him to dig under the house and publish what he finds there. Twice he refuses to believe the angel, and so the third time the angel appears and scourges him, forcing him to break up the foundation of the house and there find a marble box. Terrified, he takes the box to a judge, who in turn sends it to Emperor Theodosius. When the emperor opens it he discovers St. Paul's own Revelation. In it Paul describes being transported to the Third Heaven where, among other things, he learns that dwelling within "every man and woman" there resides a guardian angel who reports each night to God about the person's good or sinful deeds during the day. By God's order, these guardian angels protect the virtuous who have renounced the world and seek to convert or inspire repentance in sinners who are "caught in the snares of the world." Later in the narrative, after viewing the torments of the damned in hell, St. Paul and St. Michael, together with other angels, ask God to relieve the sufferings of these sinners for a day—a motif that became common in many later visions of hell. The Apocalypse of St. Paul became so popular that it was translated into virtually all European languages, and it did much to spread lore about angels as well as influence later visions of the afterlife.

Although there was some biblical mention of various orders of angels, it was the *Celestial Hierarchy* of the Pseudo-Dionysius (late fifth or early sixth century) that was most influential in schematizing these orders for medieval tradition. Whoever the author was, he claimed to be Dionysius the Areopagite who was converted by St. Paul himself, and thus his *Celestial Hierarchy* appeared to have authority extending back to the apostolic age, an authority that was not seriously questioned until the end of the Middle Ages. In this work, not only is God seen as a Trinity, but there are three trinities of angelic orders, each with three further orders, all arranged in a hierarchy. At the top are seraphim, cherubim, and thrones; next come dominations, virtues, and powers; and finally principalities, archangels, and angels. Originally written in Greek, this scheme entered the West through the Latin translation of Abbot Hilduin of Saint-Denis (827), which also contained a legendary biography of the author, and then through the even more widely influential translation made by John Scotus Erigena (860–862) at the request of Charles the Bald.

Popular Cults

In the meantime the Church had become increasingly anxious about popular cults of angels, which spread rapidly and took various local forms. Thus, after earlier warnings had done little to stop such devotions to the angels, the Lateran Synod of 745, followed by subsequent councils, officially condemned as idolatry the popular tendency to name angels, thereby personalizing them as local spirits. Nevertheless, the Church did allow the naming of and devotion to the biblical angels Gabriel, Raphael, and Michael, along with Uriel. Though Uriel was not named in the Bible, he was sanctioned by ancient Jewish tradition and figured prominently in the mid-second-century Apocalypse of St. Peter, which as part of the apocryphal New Testament enjoyed great popularity and influence in the Middle Ages. Another exception, according to Jacobus de Voragine's *Legenda aurea* (The Golden Legend, c. 1260), was John the Baptist, whom many called an angel since he performed the function of an angel in proclaiming the coming of the Son of God.

The earliest known angelic cult sanctioned by the Church focused on the Feast of St. Michael and the Angels (September 29), especially after the widely reported apparition of St. Michael at Mount Gargano in Italy (c. 490); both Mount Gargano and Mont-Saint-Michel in France, where a later apparition took place (708), became the sites of famous monasteries dedicated to his cult. According to the earliest version of the *South English Legendary* (thirteenth century), popular tradition related that shortly after his first miracle at Mount Gargano St. Michael killed with lightning bolts some 600 Saracens who were attacking Christians at his mount—an example of the saint's military function and his association with mountains and hills. (Numerous churches dedicated to St. Michael are situated on high places.)

But perhaps St. Michael's most unusual miracle is his saving a pregnant woman in the sea. In the *South English Legendary* we read that a church of St. Michael was built on a mount at Toumbe, which was located "in the great sea" and thus accessible to pilgrims only at low tide. On the feast day of the saint a group of worshippers was making the crossing to the shrine when the tide suddenly came rushing in. All escaped the swift current except for a pregnant woman who could not keep up with the others. Yet through the help of St. Michael in his role as guardian angel ("guod wardein"), she floated on the turbulent waters, gave birth to her baby amid the waves, and survived in the sea with the infant for a whole year on fish and water provided by the saint.

Angels likewise affect individuals on a very personal level, either as protectors or as enforcers. Thus, according to Gregory the Great's immensely popular *Dialogues* (c. 593), a certain Equitus, disturbed by sexual temptations, had a nocturnal vision in which he was made a eunuch with an angel mysteriously in attendance, and afterward Equitus was no longer troubled. In *The Golden Legend*, after St. Catherine (Katherine) of Alexandria has been severely tortured angels treat her wounds and feed her in prison, and one of the angels later destroys the torture wheel that had caused her such suffering. Even so, angels could also deal harshly with saints when necessary, as Adomnán relates in his *Life of St. Columba* (c. 697) that when the saint did not want to follow an angel's directions, the angel struck him with a whip, leaving a blue mark as a sign of his punishment.

There are numerous legends in which "reliable witnesses" are reported to have had visions of saints being carried to heaven, at the very moment of their deaths, by crowds of angels. In his *Dialogues*, Gregory relates that no less a person than St. Benedict himself saw the soul of Bishop Germanus of Capua borne by angels to heaven "in a ball of fire." Bede's *Ecclesiastical History of the English People* (731), one of the greatest achievements of medieval historical writing, is filled with such accounts, all reported by (or at least to) reliable persons. For example, Bede relates that Egbert, "a most reverend man," reported that he was told by an eyewitness that St. Chad's soul was carried to heaven by angels. Bede goes on to say that "whether [Egbert] was speaking of himself or of another is uncertain, but what cannot be uncertain is that whatever such a man said must be true" (Bk. 4, ch. 3). In a later chapter (Bk. 4, ch. 23) Bede tells of a nun named Begu who lived in a monastery 13 miles away from the monastery over which St. Hilda presided as abbess. Despite this distance Begu saw the saint carried upward at the moment of her death in a great light, guided by angels to her heavenly reward. Lest this account seem to be founded on the testimony of Begu alone, Bede goes on to cite other witnesses as well. In such narratives we see a feature that folklore scholars recognize as common in legends, whether medieval or modern: the claim that however much the story may exceed our normal experience, it is "really true"—a claim that is generally supported by the statement that it happened to the person recounting the experience or was witnessed by some reliable person who told the story to the narrator.

Such claims are especially important in yet another kind of popular legend involving angels, the account of an out-of-body experience in which a human is guided by angels to a vision of the after-life. Following the second-century Apocalypse of St. Peter and the fourth-century Apocalypse of St. Paul there are numerous visions of heaven and hell in the Middle Ages (and of purgatory after the twelfth century), long before Dante's *Divine Comedy* in the fourteenth century. Bede gives two of these in his history, the visions of Fursa and of Dryhthelm. In the first, Fursa is led safely by angels through fires tormenting the damned, though at one point an evil spirit throws one of the damned against Fursa, burning him on the chin and shoulder. An angel explains that the burn is punishment for Fursa's earlier having accepted property from someone he knew to be a sinner. When Fursa returns to this world he bears the scars for the rest of his life, clear evidence of the truth of his account of his experience. In the case of Dryhthelm, we have a man who appears to die and is guided and protected by an angel through terrifying images of hell, whose torments include extreme cold as well as heat, until he returns to life and relates his vision to the holy monk Hæmgisl, who in turn relates it to Bede.

In some of these visions the angelic guide comments at length on the specific sins that have landed sinners in hell. For example, in the *Vision of Wetti* (824) the angel mentions various sins but focuses on those of a sexual nature, especially sodomy: "Again and again the angel introduced a discussion of sodomy ... five times and more he said that it should be avoided." While he does not define the sin specifically, commenting only that it is "contrary to nature," the angel does make it clear that

> not only does the violent contagion of this creeping disease infect the polluted soul of males who lie together, but it is even found in the ruin of many couples. Stirred up in madness by the instigation of devils and changed by the vexation of lust ... married ones change an immaculate marriage bed into a stain of disgrace as they prostitute themselves with devils.

This stress on sexual sins parallels the growing attention to them in contemporary penitential manuals for priests hearing confessions, and despite the qualification about married couples, his particular preoccupation with sodomy may be connected to the monk Wetti's urging—also in his vision—that his fellow monks (and nuns) undergo serious reforms of their practices in his time. It is worth noting that Wetti's admonitions are given special force by being put in the mouth of the angel guiding him through the afterlife.

This mention of devils also shows the medieval depiction of devils as fallen angels, following the great narratives of the war in heaven, won by St. Michael and the good angels when they cast Satan and the evil angels down to hell. Although rooted in the biblical Revelation, this story was greatly elaborated in the Middle Ages—for example, in the ninth-century Anglo-Saxon poem *Genesis B*, whose narrative power bears comparison with John Milton's *Paradise Lost*. These evil angels, or devils, frequently appear in medieval saints' lives as enticing tempters or dreadful enemies testing the virtue of the holy men and women who resist them (e.g., in Athanasius's fourth-century *Life of St. Anthony*, which, through Evagrius's translation, became a model for such narratives throughout Europe). Although guardian angels usually defeat devils and drive them away from the virtuous, sometimes the angels concede victory to their enemies. Bede tells of a young man who remains adamant in his life of sin despite all efforts to reform him. Shortly before his death he sees himself surrounded by hideous devils, the chief of whom is holding a large dark book detailing all his sins. Two angels appear with a very small white book containing the man's good deeds, but when they see the size of the devil's book they withdraw, and the devils drive the sinner down to hell.

Despite official Church efforts to control the views of the faithful about angels, including the fallen angels, popular lore extended the presence and powers of these figures into areas far beyond ecclesiastically accepted measure. In the *South English Legendary* both good and evil angels are believed to cause dreams, with nightmares being inspired by evil angels. These same evil angels lie with women and get them pregnant, or, having taken the shapes of women, they lie with men. Evil angels are also known to have special power in the woods, where they are better known as elves. Moreover, evil angels could sometimes assume an ethnic or even political significance. According to Felix's eighth-century *Life of St. Guthlac*, the saint, apparently living in a border area in England, spends a terrible night tormented by evil angels whom he recognizes as devils because they are shrieking in Welsh.

The earliest pictorial images of angels present them in glorified human forms, as wingless young men, often surrounded by bright light. In antiquity these figures sometimes appeared wearing the togas of Roman senators, thus conferring on them a conventional sign of dignity. In the Middle Ages the toga was often replaced by such signs of authority as a diadem, scepter, or codex. In the late-medieval mystery plays angels could be dressed in garments suggesting a liturgical function associated with the time of the dramatic action in the Church calendar. Art historians have traced the iconography of winged angels to the classical sculptures of Nike, goddess of victory, as these figures emerged in the fourth century. Seraphim could be recognized by their six wings (perhaps covered with eyes) and the color red, while cherubim had four wings and their color was the blue of the heavens. Whereas biblical angels were always masculine, in the Middle Ages they became idealized forms of beauty, and

in Renaissance paintings angels began to take on feminine qualities.

See also: Bede the Venerable; Hell; Iconography; Saints, Cults of the; Satan; Spirits and Ghosts

—John McNamara

Anglo-Saxon Chronicle. Annals of English history spanning the years from around 60 B.C.E. to 1154 C.E. and found in four major manuscript versions, conventionally designated as Parker (A), Abingdon (B and C), Worcester (D), and Peterborough or Laud (E).

Although these versions differ in some respects, their similarities are sufficiently strong that they are known collectively as the *Anglo-Saxon Chronicle*. Written in Old English, they share a core of material, the so-called Common Stock, that dates to the beginning of their composition during the reign of King Alfred in the 890s. The Common Stock draws heavily on written and oral sources; it begins the record of English history with Julius Caesar's attempted conquest of the island and focuses on ecclesiastical, political, and military events through 891. Whereas accounts of early history necessarily derive largely from written sources, with some material from oral tradition, as continuations of the *Chronicle* become more contemporaneous with the events they record, from the early 900s through 1154, they rely heavily on orally circulating stories and thus become more valuable to those working in medieval folklore.

The *Chronicle* contains a great wealth of information about the cultural practices and beliefs of the Anglo-Saxons scattered throughout its versions because its compilers went far beyond the expected record of political and religious conditions. They included events that affected daily life in early medieval England, such as the activities of outlaws and others on the social margins; the effects of severe weather on crops and domestic animals; outbreaks of murrain and other pestilence; fires in major urban areas; unusually high or low tides along the coastline and rivers; atmospheric conditions such as the aurora borealis; and noteworthy celestial occurrences such as eclipses, comets, and astronomical portents. For example, the E version entry for 1117 records that on the night of December 16 the sky was as red as if it were on fire. The chronicler notes this disturbance of the natural order immediately after recording the oppressive taxation policies of King Henry I. The audience of the *Chronicle* is thus invited to see this natural portent as a sign of divine displeasure with Henry's rule. Thus, contemporary interpretations of such events often appear in entries and are of particular interest.

The *Chronicle* also contains information about the origins and ancestors of the Anglo-Saxons. It records the migration of the Germanic tribes to Britain in 449 C.E. as well as extended genealogies (at various entries) that trace English rulers back to Germanic chieftains and divinities of continental Europe. The appearance of genealogies in the *Chronicle* indicates the importance of popular beliefs about ancestry, particularly the lasting value of such names as Woden and Geat, who lent legitimacy to the political power of those claiming such ancestry during the period.

Only the Peterborough (E) version of the *Chronicle* continues to record events beyond 1080, 14 years after the Norman Conquest. Until it ends in 1154, this version vividly records the Norman occupation of England from a native perspective. These later entries are of special value for the study of Anglo-Saxon beliefs, customs, and practices as they were affected by the pressures of Norman rule.

See also: English Tradition: Anglo-Saxon Period; Wild Hunt

—Nicholas Howe

Animal Tale. A fictional oral narrative in which animals perform the principal plot actions.

As a folklore genre, animal tales are distinct from the closely related genres of mimologisms and etiological legends. Mimologisms are verbal expressions and dialogues, sometimes introduced by a very short narrative, that interpret the sounds of animals in humorous ways. Etiological legends relate events, supposed to have taken place once in the distant past, to explain particularities of the animal and natural world still observable nowadays—for example, to tell why the bat is blind and flies only at night (AT 222A, a version of which appears as the twenty-third tale in the *Fables* of Marie de France), or to explain why the bear has no tail (AT 2, "The Tail-Fisher").

In certain cases animal tales so closely resemble etiological legends that they share the same plot, although the two genres put that plot to different uses. Medieval versions of "The Tail-Fisher," for example, pit the fox against the wolf: the fox convinces the wolf to use his tail as a fishing line. As the wolf sits on a hole in a frozen pond, waiting for the fish to bite, ice forms around his tail and traps him. Farmers arrive and beat the wolf; in order to survive he has to cut off his own tail. The version just summarized comes from the medieval *Roman de Renart*, a twelfth-century collection of fictional tales. But in some modern oral traditions the tale is told about a bear, and after the bear loses his tail in the ice, the narrator ends by explaining that this is why, today, bears have no tails.

Like "The Tail-Fisher," most animal tales feature two major characters. And, also like "The Tail-Fisher," most are simply structured stories of deceit involving two basic plot actions. First, there is the deceit or deception (the fox tricks the wolf into using his tail as a fishing line); second, the outcome, a sudden ending (the wolf is beaten and loses his tail). In the actual practice of story-

telling, however, a narrator may string together many such short tales into long narratives. Because the episodes are all similar in structure, they may occur in any order, thus allowing gifted performers great freedom to compose their own chains of episodes. Nevertheless, some chains have proved remarkably stable in practice. For example, in both medieval literature and recent oral tradition "The Tail-Fisher" is often prefaced by "The Theft of Fish" (AT 1), in which a hungry fox plays dead; fishermen find him in the road and, eager to skin him, throw him into their fish basket (or in the *Roman de Renart*, a cart full of eels); as the fishermen make their way home, the fox throws the fish out of the basket and then escapes to eat them.

The animal tales of oral folk tradition are organized around a few clear semantic oppositions: physical weakness combined with cunning conflicts with physical strength combined with stupidity. Wild animals conflict with domestic animals. These two sets of oppositions generally coincide, as both stupidity and savagery are stigmatized while cunning and domesticity are valorized. In European tradition strength and stupidity are most often embodied in the figure of the wolf, though in the Nordic countries the bear frequently fills this role. The trickster par excellence is the fox, but his status is more ambiguous. When opposed to domestic animals, he represents physical strength and is sometimes the loser, but when opposed to the wolf or bear, he is the embodiment of cunning, thus acquiring some of the traits normally attached to the human/domestic sphere.

In medieval literature animal tales were told for moral and edifying purposes, in fables and exempla; for didactic purposes, in bestiaries; but above all, for comic and satiric purposes, in the vast cycle of Reynard the Fox: the immensely popular and influential *Roman de Renart* (1174–1250), its antecedents in clerical Latin poetry, and its many continuations into the fifteenth century.

Fable and Exemplum Traditions

The oldest literary versions of animal tales in Western tradition are the medieval collection of fables called *ysopets* or *Romulus*, which transmit and adapt the fables of classical antiquity (Aesop and Phaedrus) throughout the Middle Ages. Generally speaking, the fable, of learned origin and cultivated by clerics, is written to convey a moral message; the animal tales of oral folk tradition, on the contrary, tend to be told for entertainment. This difference affects their respective narrative structures. For example, fables tend to end with a pointed moral, whereas animal tales seldom do.

Although medieval fables ultimately derive from the antique fables of Aesop and Phaedrus, a number of them are retellings of animal tales from folk traditions. Compilers of fable collections used a variety of sources. A case in point is the *Fables* of Marie de France, possibly the first such collection to appear in a European vernacular. It includes 20 stories derived from classical fable tradition as well some 12 fabliaux, but the remainder are animal tales rooted in medieval oral folk traditions. Three of the folk-derived fables feature the fox: "The Cock and the Fox" (AT 6), "The Fox and the Dove" (AT 62), and "The Fox and the Bear" (AT 36). Significantly, all three tales also appear in the major beast epic collections *Ysengrimus* and *Renart*. Eight others commonly associated with folk tradition feature the wolf. In contrast to the fox tales, the wolf tales seem to have come more immediately from clerical sources. In these tales animals fast, officiate at mass, and serve as bishops! One of Marie's wolf fables (no. 90) follows the plot of the popular tale of "The Wolf and the Seven Kids" (AT 123).

After 1250 medieval fables featuring the fox and the wolf are likely to borrow from the widely popular *Roman de Renart* rather than directly from folk tradition. For example, the *Liber parabolarum* (Book of Parables) by Odo de Cheriton contains 116 fables, of which 15 can be traced back to classical tradition through the *Romulus* and others to bestiaries, while several are connected with the cycle of Reynard the Fox. For example, Odo's fable 74 is the tale of "The Tail-Fisher" (AT 2). Fable 23, "De fraudibus vulpis et catti" (On the Tricks of the Wolf and the Cat), is a folktale: the cat's only trick saves him. When in danger, the cat climbs up the tree, whereas the fox is captured in spite of his many tricks (AT 105, "The Cat's Only Trick"). The protagonists of this fable are given the names—Reynard the Fox and Tibert the Cat—earlier bestowed upon them in the *Roman de Renart*, although the story itself does not appear in the *Roman*. Fables by Jean de Sheppey (between 1354 and 1377) include such narratives as "Lupus et vulpes in lardio" (The Wolf and the Fox in the Larder), a version of the popular animal tale "The Wolf Overeats in the Cellar" (AT 41, also found in the fables of Odo of Cheriton).

Preachers often employed animal tales in their sermons, first exploiting the entertaining features of the folktale to gain the attention of the audience and then shaping the tale to underscore moral points. Such tales, known as exempla, became increasingly popular in the later Middle Ages. The French exemplum collection *Chastoiement d'un père à son fils* (A Father's Warning to His Son) includes the tale of the wolf and fox in the well (AT 32). The *Chastoiement* is a translation of the eleventh-century *Disciplina clericalis* by Petrus Alfonsi, a Spanish Christian converted from Judaism. Alfonsi, in turn, had borrowed the tale from the Talmudic commentator Rachi. Through such channels, many Jewish and Arabic tales entered the written traditions and influenced the oral traditions of medieval Europe, especially from the thirteenth century forward, as the Latin tales were translated into European vernaculars.

The Roman de Renart

The animal tales of medieval written tradition are most richly represented by the vast and complex literature centered on the figure of Reynard the Fox.

Questions concerning the relationship between oral folk tradition and the *Roman de Renart*, as well as the *Roman's* sources of inspiration in general, have given rise to violent scholarly disputes. It is now clear that the animal tales written in Latin in poetic form by clerics and monks had a decisive influence. The earliest of these, "Ecbasis captivi" (The Escape of a Captive, written in 937), depicts animals and scenes later found in the *Roman de Renart*. Two centuries later appears *Ysengrimus*, a long satirical poem by the monk Nivard of Ghent (1149) and a direct precursor of *Renart*. *Ysengrimus* portrays the exploits of the fox Reinardus and his sustained feud with the wolf Ysengrimus; this is the earliest work in which animals are given personal names. In content and structure *Ysengrimus* displays strong similarities with the later *Renart*. For example, *Ysengrimus* contains a sequence of four episodes that would later appear, in the exact same order, in the earliest branch of the Renart cycle (branch II): Renart and the cock, Renart and the titmouse (though the role of titmouse is filled by a cock in *Ysengrimus*), Renart's insult of Isengrin's cubs, and his rape of Isengrin's wife.

These early animal epics in the form of Latin poetry are themselves inspired by Aesopian fables, but they are amply developed and are given an ecclesiastic twist through such features as the wolf dressed as a priest, which was a widespread religious topos in the Middle Ages.

Although undeniably influenced by the *Ysengrimus*, the *Roman de Renart* displays some distinctive innovations. Written in the vernacular, it appeals to a much larger audience, more interested in laughter than in philosophical and moral speculations. Plot and characters are no longer confined to monastic life.

Roman de Renart is not a unified work. Rather, it is a cycle of independent poems in the French vernacular, centered on the trickster figure of Reynard the Fox. These poems, called "branches," were composed at different times by different authors, most of them anonymous. Sometimes they relate a single episode, and sometimes a string of episodes. Although they sometimes refer to each other, these poems were meant to be read independently and therefore often overlap or contradict each other. The numerical order of the branches established by Ernest Martin in the 1880s is still used by scholars for practical purposes, although it differs both from the chronology of the events in the narration and from the presumed chronology of their writing.

As early as the thirteenth century, copyists tried to assemble the branches into comprehensive collections. Three different collections survive from the Middle Ages, none of which contains all 28 of the branches identified by scholars today. The choice of branches and their order of appearance are also different in the three collections. Furthermore, even the total of 28 branches is misleading because some branches (e.g., V) have been subdivided into subbranches a and b, each of which may be counted as a separate branch.

The earliest 6 branches were written between 1174 and 1178, another 12 between 1178 and 1205, and yet another 12 between 1225 and 1250. These three groups total about 25,000 lines.

The earliest six branches (II–Va, III, V, XV, IV, XIV) constitute the sections of the *Roman de Renart* that most strongly parallel the tales of oral folk tradition. In branches II and Va, the oldest poem of the *Roman* (1174–1177), written by a cleric, Pierre de Saint-Cloud, Renart catches the cock Chantecler by inducing him to crow with his eyes closed; Renart leaps and seizes the cock in his jaws (AT 61). Chantecler escapes by persuading Renart to talk and taking advantage of the situation to fly out of the fox's mouth (AT 6). Defeated by the cock, the fox then tries to beguile the titmouse into closing his eyes and kissing him, claiming that King Noble, the lion, has ordered peace among all animals. Suspicious, the titmouse touches Renart with a twig, and the fox snaps at it. The titmouse escapes unharmed (AT 62, "Peace among Animals"). Renart, pretending to make friends with Tibert the cat, proposes that the two run a race; Renart's plan is to steer Tibert into a trap, a pit dug in the path by a peasant; Tibert sees the pit and swerves just in time, but eventually steers Renart into it (AT 30). Renart flatters Tiecelin the raven into singing. Tiecelin drops his cheese and Renart gets hold of it (AT 57). The poem then turns to the origin of the mortal feud that opposes Renart and Isengrin the wolf. One day Renart finds himself by accident in the wolf's den, and Hersent, Isengrin's wife, makes advances to him. Renart embraces her, but fearing the return of Isengrin, he soon leaves, after having stolen her food and insulted her cubs. The cubs reveal their mother's behavior to their father. Isengrin forces Hersent to help him catch Renart. Renart flees to his den. Isengrin and Hersent pursue him with such speed that Hersent gets trapped, with her head in the den and her hindquarters outside. Renart goes out through another entrance and rapes her, while insulting Isengrin, who is witness to the scene.

In branch III Renart plays dead on the road. A peasant takes him up and throws him in his wagon, which is full of eels, and Renart throws them one by one out of the wagon (AT 1, "The Theft of Fish"). Isengrin, pursued by dogs, takes refuge in a monastery and puts on monk's robes.

Renart induces him to catch fish with his tail through a hole in the ice. The wolf's tail freezes fast, and when he is attacked and tries to escape, he loses his tail (AT 2, "The Tail-Fisher").

In branch V Renart helps Isengrin steal a ham, but the wolf tricks him and eats it alone. Renart tries in vain to eat the cricket. In branch XV Renart and Tibert the cat find a sausage. Tibert tricks Renart into letting him carry it, climbs up a cross, and eats the sausage alone. In branch IV (written in 1178), Renart dives in the well of the monastery, mistaking his reflection for his wife Hermeline (AT 34). When Isengrin arrives, Renart pretends that he is in heaven, inducing Isengrin to descend into the well in one bucket, thus bringing Renart up in the other one (AT 32). Branch XIV (written in 1178) features Renart and Tibert in the cellar (AT 41); Renart plays tricks on Primaut, a wolf whose adventures are very similar to those of Isengrin.

After 1178 the poems of the cycle diverge substantially from oral traditional animal tales and take on themes related to professional life and upper-class society. Branch I (1179) is devoted to the trial of Renart; branch VI (1190) to his duel with Isengrin and his becoming a monk; branch XII (1190) to Renart and Tibert in the cloister; branch VIII (1190) to Renart's pilgrimage; and branch Ia (1190–1195) to the siege of Renart's den Maupertuis. In branch Ib (1195) Renart becomes a *jongleur*; in branch VII (1195–1200) Renart confesses; in branch XI (1196–1200) he becomes emperor. Branch IX (1200) presents Renart, the peasant, and the bear; branch XVI, Renart's will; and branch XVII (1205), Renart's death and burial.

Characters in the *Roman de Renart*, especially in the earlier branches, are described as both humans and animals. Renart is a seigneur who owns a fortified castle, Maupertuis, and a fief, and who fights a duel with Isengrin. The society around him is a close reflection of the feudal world of the twelfth century. Yet he has to crawl on four legs through the kitchen garden in order to catch a chicken. The other protagonists, too, have their traditional animal characteristics: Brun the bear is clumsy and greedy; Tibert the cat is agile, fastidious, and hypocritical; Chantecler the cock vain and protective; and Bernart the donkey immensely credulous and silly. This does not apply to the female protagonists, however. Queen Fiere, the lioness, is as noble and beautiful as a queen in an Arthurian romance, Renart's wife Hermeline appears largely in the role of devoted wife and mother, Isengrin's wife Hersent is as sensuous and unfaithful as the wives in fabliaux— but these traits do not reflect the characteristics of their animal species in folk tradition.

From its very beginning the *Roman de Renart* displays both a comical and a satirical aspect. The balance between these two aspects changes progressively, from the more comical to the more satirical. The earliest branches, closer to folklore, introduce a strong parodic element alongside the simple comedy of traditional animal tales. Writers of the *Roman de Renart* continually parody the scenes and rhetorics of courtly literature, chansons de geste, legal procedures, and other realms of refined aristocratic and ecclesiastical life.

The *Roman de Renart* has had many continuations, new poems that can be considered as new branches in a way, but whose style and purpose infuse the figure of Renart and his adventures with more and more satire and less overt comedy. The characters also become increasingly anthropomorphic. In *Renart le bestourné* (1261), Rutebeuf delivers a violent attack on friars, as does the anonymous poem *Le couronnement de Renart* (1263–1270). *Renart le nouvel* (1289), by Jacquemart Gielée, is a long allegoric and didactic poem, a prose adaptation often copied and published in the course of the following 300 years. New branches were composed in the fourteenth century. The anonymous *Roman de Renart le contrefait* (1319–1342) is an enormous work of encyclopedic knowledge.

The first six branches of the *Roman de Renart* inspired *Reinhart Fuchs*, written about 1190 in Alsatian, a German dialect, by Heinrich le Glichezâre. A new branch of *Renart* developed in Italy: *Rainardo e Lisengrino*, written in Franco-Italian dialect in the thirteenth century.

English-language versions of the Renart tales are relatively rare before the fifteenth century. The short thirteenth-century poem "The Fox and the Wolf" relates the story of Renart and Isengrin in the well. Renart next appears in the last years of the fourteenth century in Chaucer's "Nun's Priest's Tale," a free adaptation of the episode of Renart and Chantecler the cock.

The popularity and diffusion of the *Roman de Renart* has been especially strong in the countries north of France. The Flemish poem *Reinaert de Voes* (c. 1250), which combines and translates several French branches, inspired a prose adaptation in Dutch (published 1479). The Dutch version was in turn translated into English by Caxton under the title of *History of Raynard the Fox* (1481) and became the source of a number of German and Scandinavian translations and reworkings in subsequent centuries, even serving as the main source of inspiration of Goethe's *Reinecke Fuchs.*

Numerous allusions in chansons de geste, fabliaux, and other literary works testify that by the twelfth century all classes of society were already very familiar with the tales of Renart. A verse in Gautier de Coincy's *Miracles de Notre-Dame* implies that scenes from the Renart epic were painted even in priests' houses (Pocquet ed., col. 59, vers. 168–172). The extraordinary popularity of the animal epic created around the figure of the trickster fox is perhaps best attested by the fact that since the thirteenth century the personal name of the protagonist, *Renart* (adapted from the German name *Raginhard*, "He who wins

through cunning"), has replaced *goupil* to mean "fox" in the French language—and has become the basis of another French word, *renardie* (hypocrisy or craftiness).

Renart the trickster is cruel, unscrupulous, vicious by inclination as much as by necessity, and, above all, cunning. Originating partly in the animal tales of medieval folklore, but mostly in the learned Latin animal poems written by clerics influenced by the fables of Phaedrus, the *Roman de Renart* and its continuations have become the most powerful expression of the satiric spirit of the Middle Ages. Progressively, the trickster figure of Reynard the Fox becomes the symbol of cunning and of hypocrisy, two aspects of evil, one of the major preoccupations of medieval culture.

See also: Bestiary; Fable; Marie de France; Trickster

—Michèle Simonsen

Anne, Saint. According to ancient and medieval legend, the mother of the Virgin Mary, and therefore grandmother of Jesus.

Although she is not mentioned in the New Testament, St. Anne and her husband St. Joachim are named as the parents of the Virgin Mary in the second-century apocryphal Gospel of James, also known as the Protevangelium, or Earlier Gospel, since it treats of events before the Virgin Mary's conception and the birth of Jesus as related in the canonical gospels. According to the Gospel of James, Joachim and Anne were unable to have children, and he retreated to the wilderness until receiving a sign from God, while Anne remained at home singing songs of sorrow and praying. Both were subsequently visited by angels declaring God's favor, and when Joachim hurried home he was embraced by his wife Anne, who told him she was to become pregnant through a miracle. After Mary is born Anne takes her to her room, which she has made into a kind of sanctuary, where she nurses and cares for her until the child's presentation in the temple a year later; Mary spends another two years in Anne's sanctuary before her parents place her as a virgin in the temple at age three.

No doubt aided by the developing devotion to the Virgin Mary, Anne herself came to be venerated as a saint in the early Church. Justinian had a church built for her in Constantinople, and by the tenth century a feast honoring her miraculous conception was being celebrated in Naples. The practice soon spread to northern Europe. She continues to be venerated in parts of Europe and Canada.

In medieval Italy she was revered by embroiderers, who kept her feast day under penalty of seeing their labor destroyed, a practice also followed by washerwomen. She was the great intercessor for women in childbirth, but she has also been a patron to woodworkers, seamstresses, and seafarers; Hugh of Lincoln became her devotee while threatened by a storm at sea. According to the *trinubium* tradition, Anne was married subsequently to Cleophas and Salome after Joachim, a tradition criticized by some Church Fathers but accepted by Peter Lombard and Guillaume Durand. She thus gave birth to holy progeny, including the two other Marys, Mary Jacobus and Mary Salome; and from them, to James the Lesser and the Greater, John the Evangelist, Simon, and Jude, all offshoots of one sacred tree of which Anne was the root. This tradition also gained wide circulation because it was related in Jacobus de Voragine's immensely popular *The Golden Legend* (c. 1260).

Her position in folk religion derives from a variety of symbolic associations, including verbal plays and the Latin meanings of her name, linking her to the year (*annus*) and thus to the figure of Anna Perenna (who personified the year in Roman popular tradition) and, in a pun on the French word *âne*, to a humble beast, the ass.

Her legend was widely known through the Middle Ages in several traditions focusing on her belatedly fertile marriage to Joachim. A unique French text, the *Romanz de Saint Fanuel et de Sainte Anne et de Nostre Dame et de Nostre Seigneur et de ses Apostres* (Romance of St. Fanuel, St. Anne, and Our Lady and Our Lord and His Apostles), which is extant in eight different manuscripts and alluded to indirectly in Wace's poem *The Conception of Our Lady*, tells us that she was not "engendered by a man" and had no mother but, rather, was carried in the thigh of a holy man, Fanuel, and "impregnated" after he wiped the juice of apples endowed with curative power on it. Anne, the girl born of this wonder, was exposed in an empty eagle's nest, where she grew up and whence she instructed the king's seneschal, Joachim, to spare the deer he was about to strike, so impressing him that he married her.

St. Anne was invoked by woodworkers, especially joiners and turners, and one of the lead tokens used by guilds and societies represents her instructing the Virgin in reading on one side (a characteristic feature of the medieval iconography of St. Anne) and with the compass and other measuring instruments on the other. This association has been variously ascribed to the profession of her son-in-law Joseph or to the notion that she made the first true tabernacle.

She was also associated with the grapevine from the time of John Damascene, who wrote of her bringing forth a fertile vine, producing a delicious grape, and this power is also invoked in the litanies of the church of Apt, which claimed to have Anne's relics from the time of Charlemagne.

She was also credited with many healing and curative powers. They appear in a list compiled by the German monk Johannes Trithemius in the sixteenth century. Besides those mentioned, she cured melancholics, protected those among enemies or thieves, guarded against sudden death and assisted the dying, and was invoked against plagues. Water consecrated to St. Anne's worship held a wonderful healing value in France, Italy, England, and Germany: it lessened fevers and helped parturients and those who had lost their minds. Finally, in many parts of France she was associated with wells and springs and consequently with the regulation of drought.

See also: Saints, Cults of the; Virgin Mary

—Francesca Canadé Sautman

Annwfn [Annwn].

Annwfn [Annwn]. The otherworld in Welsh mythology and folklore, probably either *an-* (intensive prefix) and *dwfn* (deep), thus "very deep," or *an-* (negative) and *dwfn* (world), thus "not world."

Annwfn is sometimes located across the sea, and both real offshore islands and unspecified islands are portrayed as the otherworld. For example, in the Four Branches of the Mabinogi, Gwales (an island now called Grassholm off the Pembrokeshire coast), where time stands still, is the scene of an extended sojourn of feasting and pleasure, while in an early poem in the Book of Taliesin, "Preiddau Annwfn" (The Spoils of Annwfn), the otherworld is an unnamed island (unless Ynys Wair, now Lundy Island in the Bristol Channel, is intended). In this poem Arthur leads an expedition to the otherworld to win a treasure and to rescue a prisoner. "Three shiploads we went; save seven none returned" from this expedition to the island, which is given a number of descriptive titles: Fortress of Intoxication, Four-Cornered Fortress, Glass Fortress (a title that recalls an account in the *Historia Brittonum* [History of the Britons] of a raid upon a glass tower in the ocean from which only one shipload escaped). In other sources Annwfn is contiguous with this world, and the passage from one to the other is analogous to traveling from familiar to unfamiliar territory, becoming lost. Thus, in the First of the Four Branches of the Mabinogi, during the course of a hunt near his own court Pwyll becomes separated from his friends; he encounters the king of Annwfn and accompanies him to the otherworld. This appears to be a feature transmitted to Arthurian romance, in which hunts and journeys through forests are frequently the prologues to magical encounters. Mounds are often liminal areas where the boundaries between the two worlds become blurred. For example, the Mound of Arberth in the Four Branches of the Mabinogi is a place where mortals encounter otherworldly persons. Peredur meets an otherworldly lady who directs his journey and whom he "marries" at a mound. The magical properties of other hills are recorded in Welsh folklore: Crug Mawr (Cardiganshire), Cadair Idris (Meirionethshire), Glastonbury Tor. Though there is no suggestion that Annwfn may be entered through such hills or mounds, it is nevertheless frequently regarded as being underground and may be entered through caves, lakes, bogs, or other orifices.

All these locations—islands, unfamiliar territory, underground dwellings—have been considered the homes of the fairies throughout medieval and into modern Welsh folklore. In west Wales the "Children of Rhys Ddwfn" was a name for the fairies whose home consisted of islands lying a short distance off the coast of Pembrokeshire. Gerald of Wales recounts the sojourn of a man named Elidyr in fairyland, a delightful land of meadows and woods that he reached through a dark underground tunnel. Stories of fairy rings and fairy dances are common throughout Wales, and a number of late-medieval poems have as their theme tales of travelers becoming lost in the marshes and bogs of the Welsh hills and of being led astray by the fairies.

Annwfn is usually conceived of as a single kingdom, subject to the same tensions as this world. In the First of the Four Branches of the Mabinogi, although Arawn, head of Annwfn, is king of Annwfn, he is, nevertheless, challenged by Hafgan, "a king in Annwfn," presumably a *subregulus*, if, indeed, such strictly realistic approaches to this type of story are appropriate. There are other references in Welsh to the head of Annwfn *(Pen Annwfn)*; however, this title is not always applied to the same figure.

Annwfn is not the world of the dead. In a poem in the Book of Taliesin the otherworld is portrayed as a land of feasting and never-ending pleasure, a place whose inhabitants are harmed by neither plague nor age. The same concept underlies the story of Arthur's passing to the Isle of Avalon to be healed of his wounds after his last battle. The timeless feast at Gwales is typical of views of Annwfn and is reflected in the sixteenth-century *Life of St. Collen*, when the saint ascends Glastonbury Tor to meet Gwynn ap Nudd, "king of Annwfn and the fairies." He finds awaiting him the fairest castle he has ever seen, the finest retinues of courtiers and musicians to welcome him, and the most luxurious table imaginable. Annwfn became equated with hell, and its people with devils (as is made clear in references in the story *Culhwch and Olwen*), and Collen, recognizing the illusion that was intended to ensnare him, sprinkled holy water over all, causing the castle and its folk to disappear.

See also: Celtic Mythology; Gerald of Wales;
Gwynn ap Nudd; Mabinogi; Taliesin
—Brynley F. Roberts

Apollonius of Tyre. A classical romance that remained popular throughout the Middle Ages and Renaissance; also, the first romance in English.

Apollonius of Tyre probably derives from Hellenistic times, since the names of the characters and settings are from Greece and Anatolia. The first Latin reference to this work is in the *Carmina* of Venantius Fortunatus (written c. 566–568). Fortunatus compares his wanderings with those of Apollonius. The earliest surviving version is the Latin prose *Historia Apollonii Regis*

Tyri (Story of Apollonius, King of Tyre) in ninth-century manuscripts. There are numerous medieval Latin versions, including a brief poem in the *Carmina Burana* (1230–1250) and a version in the fourteenth-century *Gesta Romanorum* (Deeds of the Romans), and there are translations and adaptations in almost all the European vernaculars, including Hungarian. The most famous Renaissance retelling of *Apollonius* is Shakespeare's *Pericles* (1607), and T. S. Eliot's "Marina" is a modern version.

The earliest English version is a fragmentary eleventh-century Old English prose work. This version and a 1,737-line version in John Gower's *Confessio Amantis* (The Lover's Confession) are of the greatest interest to students of the English Middle Ages.

Apollonius is a story that deals with the trials and triumphs of virtuous love. The story begins in folktale fashion, "*Fuit quidam ...*" [There was once ...]. The cruel king Antiochus of Antioch is living incestuously with his beautiful daughter and putting all her suitors to death. Apollonius discovers the father-daughter incest, and Antiochus tries to assassinate him. Apollonius flees to sea and is shipwrecked in Cyrene, where he marries the daughter of King Archistrates. On their voyage home, the young wife gives birth to a daughter during a tempest and apparently dies. Her body is placed in a coffin and thrown overboard, but it washes ashore near Ephesus. She is revived by a physician and placed in the temple of Artemis. Apollonius entrusts his infant daughter to foster parents in Tarsus and returns to Tyre. His daughter, Tharsia, grows up beautiful and accomplished and incites the hatred of her foster parents, who decide to kill her. She is kidnapped instead by pirates, who sell her to a brothel keeper in Mytilene. She manages to preserve her virginity. When Apollonius returns to Tarsus 14 years after he left his daughter there, he is told that Tharsia is dead and falls into a deep despair. He puts out to sea, and a tempest drives the ship to Mytilene. Apollonius and Tharsia are reunited. Apollonius is instructed in a dream to go to Ephesus, and in the temple of Artemis he meets his wife. The family is reunited and lives long and happily thereafter.

The Apollonius story is little discussed by modern scholars. The Old English version is found in a manuscript of Wulfstan's *Homilies* and copied by the same scribe. This version of *Apollonius* is the first romance in English. This preeminence is especially noteworthy because Old English prose otherwise consists of chronicles, homilies, and documentary materials. The presence of this romance amid such disparate genres suggests that the taste for literature of entertainment including wonders and sensationalism existed before the conquest as well as after. There seem to be relatively few connections between the story of Apollonius and Old English poetry such as *Beowulf*. As a hero, Beowulf, always eager for confrontation, diverges sharply from Apollonius, who flees in disguise.

Apollonius contains interesting threads common to both the Old and Middle English periods (e.g., love between members of the upper classes of the kind popularized by the romances of Chrétien de Troyes). The Old English *Apollonius* has more in common with Gower's version in the *Confessio Amantis* than with most other works in Old English literature.

Gower's narrative "The Tale of Apollinus" is little discussed. The tale occupies most of the *Confessio's* Book 8, which is devoted to the laws of marriage and includes three stories of incest as prologue to the story of Antiochus: namely those of Caligula, Amon, and Lot. At the end of Book 8, Amans (the Lover) meets Venus for the second time and learns that his love cannot prosper because he is old. Although the tale of Apollonius is always structurally loose, Gower emphasizes parallels—especially those parallels concerning three father-daughter relationships, between: Antiochus and his daughter; Archistrates and his daughter; Apollonius and Tharsia. The tale is related to the end of Book 8 primarily through its exploration of the theme of natural and unnatural love. It is related to the *Confessio* as a whole through its theme of love that unites passion and reason.

Like all Greek romances, *Apollonius of Tyre* includes many stock motifs, situations, and characters that are common in folk tradition: long voyages that reveal the sea as a metaphor for the transience of life; tempests; shipwrecks; pirates; wicked foster parents; prophetic dreams; separations and reunions; love affairs; virginity miraculously preserved. In one episode set in Cyrene, the shipwrecked Apollonius is befriended by a compassionate fisherman; this is a motif found in many Greek romances. A study of these elements both in the Latin *Apollonius* and in vernacular works would demonstrate the folklore roots behind the written medieval versions.

See also: Romance

—Alexandra H. Olsen

Arabic-Islamic Tradition. The folkloric culture of the peoples of the Islam-dominated Mediterranean and Middle Eastern regions.

The defining basis of Arabic-Islamic tradition resides in the religious concepts of Islam, which originated against the backdrop of Judaism and Christianity in pagan Arabia. As Islamic culture spread into regions beyond Arabia, it absorbed and integrated traditions of various origins, ranging from Greek and Persian antiquity to the North African Berber cultures.

History

When the Arabs entered the theater of international history at the beginning of the seventh century, the culture of the Arabian Peninsula was dominated by tribal structures. Pagan religion focused on a central sanctuary in Mecca, including the sacred black stone incorporated in the Kaaba as well as the holy well Zamzam that, according to tradition, was dug by Abraham. While essentially polytheistic, pre-Islamic Arabic paganism had developed a certain hierarchy of deities, founding a nucleus for the subsequent development of the strict Islamic monotheism. Popular religious practices included such elements as charms and divination exercised by various means, such as interpreting lines in the ground (geomancy) or marks on the shoulder blade of a sheep (scapulimancy). Belief in supernatural beings was widespread, particularly in the demonic beings known as jinn (source of the English "genie") often associated with desert wells, as well as the cannibal *ʿifrît* or *ghûl* (source of the English "ghoul").

The mission of the prophet Muhammad (d. 632) resulted in the propagation of the religion of Islam (*islâm*, "absolute submission") and the constitution of a new era, initiated by Muhammad's exodus (*hijra*) from Mecca to Medina in the year 621. The obligation to spread the new religion (*jihâd*, "holy war") soon became a unifying force, supplying to the Arabs an overwhelming military verve. Arabic conquests in the first century of the new era included North Africa and Spain in the West and the Levantine, Mesopotamian, Caucasian, and Iranian territories in the East. In Western Europe the Islamic onslaught was only reversed by the battles at Tours and Poitiers in present-day France in the year 732. Even though the Christian rulers soon strove to regain the Andalusian territories (*reconquista*), the last remaining Islamic kingdom in Granada was not conquered until 1492, when Isabella of Castile and Ferdinand of Aragon prevailed. Their conquest and the ensuing political stability also resulted in the release of organizational and financial resources that enabled Christopher Columbus to explore the Americas. Meanwhile, other Mediterranean regions, such as Sicily and Malta, had also experienced periods of Islamic domination. Moreover, in the course of the fourteenth through the sixteenth centuries, the eastern Mediterranean regions of Anatolia and the Balkans had been conquered by the Islamic Ottoman dynasty, whose progress toward central Europe was halted in 1683 when the Ottoman army was kept from conquering Vienna. In Palestine and the Levant, the Crusades (beginning in 1096) not only resulted in the temporary conquest of Jerusalem and the occupations of territories of the Holy Land (until 1291, when the last Christian fortress fell to Islam) but also served as a unique opportunity for cultural contact between the medieval European and Arabic-Islamic cultures.

Cultural Contacts

In terms of cultural heritage, Arabic-Islamic tradition is a sibling of Christian European traditions. In addition to translating, researching, discussing, and preserving ancient Greek scientific heritage, it also incorporated constituents of other cultures, such as of the partly hellenized Iranian tradition that in turn also drew on elements of Indo-Iranian origin. Thus, beyond exposing the West to its own distinct characteristics, Arabic-Islamic culture also served as the predominant vehicle for the preservation of previous cultural heritage and as a channel for transmitting knowledge of the ancient world to the West. Areas of cultural contact include military confrontations as well as commercial relationships and peaceful coexistence in a multicultural environment.

Notably, the Islamic dominion of Spain constituted a period of productive cultural contact. In an atmosphere of religious tolerance, Arabic scientific works were translated into Latin, often with the active cooperation of Jews converted to Christianity. Medieval trade relations resulted in numerous contacts that show traces of Eastern influence far beyond the obvious, even as far north as Iceland. Even warfare, though dominated by the perception of the Islamic enemy as brutish and bloodthirsty (consider, for example, the "Saracen" as portrayed in the *Chanson de Roland*), also contributed to transmitting notions of an educated and chivalrous cultural counterpart as exemplified in the noble Saladin (Salah ad-Din, ruled 1169–1193), founder of the Ayyubîd dynasty and legendary opponent of the English king Richard the Lion-Heart during the Third Crusade.

The knowledge passed on from or via the Arabs to medieval Europe predominantly relates to philosophy, the natural sciences (notably algebra, astronomy, and alchemy), medicine, geography, and architecture. Islamic artistic influences on Europe included love poetry and the concept of courtly love. Arabic-Islamic tradition possessed wandering poets and singers; whether these served as models for the European troubadour is a subject of some debate. The phenomenon of the English morris dance obviously relates to a tradition of Islamic Spain, the Andalusian *morisco*, or morris ("Moorish") dance, recorded as early as 1149. Above all, cultural contacts between the Arabic-Islamic cultural sphere and Christian Europe can be traced in numerous instances of narrative literature.

Popular Literature

The most influential of all works of narrative literature transmitted to the medieval West through Arabic-Islamic culture is the collection known by the name of its two protagonist jackals, *Kalila and Dimna*. Originating from the Indian *Panchatantra* (Five [Books of] Wisdom), the book was first brought to Persia by Burzoy, physician to the Achaemenid ruler Anosharvan (531–579). From a middle-Persian translation, now lost, Abu Muhammad ibn al Muqaffaᶜ in the eighth century prepared an Arabic adaptation, which in turn was translated into Greek (eleventh century), Hebrew (early twelfth century), and Spanish (mid-thirteenth century). The Latin version, *Directorium vitae humanae* (Guide Book for Human Life), prepared about 1270 by the converted Jewish author John of Capua, became the source of a large number of translations into European vernacular languages.

Kalila and Dimna contains narratives that might best be termed instructive stories (exempla) or, since they often deal with animal characters, fables. The narratives are linked by a frame story that serves as an umbrella bringing together tales featuring various protagonists and dealing with various topics. In *Kalila and Dimna*, as in other similar works, the frame story consists of a conversation or dispute, in the course of which exemplary tales are employed by the opposing parties in order to illustrate their relevant points. Other influential Arabic-Islamic frame tales include the religious romance *Barlaam and Josaphat*, an adaptation of the Indian legend of Buddha, and the *Sindbâd-nâme/Syntipas*, an originally Persian collection of tales about the wiles of women, anonymously translated into Latin in the early twelfth century as *Historia septem sapientium* (History of the Seven Sages). In medieval Western literature the Eastern narrative device of the frame story appeared in a wide range of works, including Chaucer's *Canterbury Tales* and Boccaccio's *Decameron*. The *Disciplina clericalis* (Clerical Discipline), compiled in the early twelfth century by Petrus Alfonsi, a Spanish Jew converted to Christianity, draws heavily on material originating from Arabic-Islamic tradition. The *Disciplina clericalis* was the first European collection of short narratives and was highly influential in inaugurating a new genre in European literature.

While the above-mentioned collections exemplify scholarly, written tradition, there is evidence indicating that oral tradition also contributed much to the transmission of Arabic-Islamic popular narratives to the medieval West. The most famous of all Eastern frame tales is the *Thousand and One Nights*, commonly known as *The Arabian Nights*. It begins when King Shahzamân becomes aware of his wife's sexual infidelity, kills her, and travels to visit his brother Shahrayar. There, he remains depressed until by chance he notices that his brother's fate is by no means different. When both set out on a journey, they are forced to make love to a woman who is being kept by a demon in a chest; her ability to seduce men even when guarded by a supernatural being demonstrates to the brothers the ultimate success of the wiles of women. Shahrayar subsequently decides to distrust women altogether, kills each of his wives after her wedding night, and is reformed only after Shahrazad manages to stay alive and win his trust with 1,001 nights of storytelling. The Italian authors Giovanni Sercambi (1348–1424) and Ludovico Ariosto (1474–1533) present evidence that some version of this frame story was known to medieval Italy. In Sercambi's *Novella d'Astolfo*, a king, made melancholic by his wife's infidelity, recovers after undergoing an adventure similar to that experienced by the two royal brothers Shahrayar and Shahzamân when they made love to the woman kept in the chest. The story of King Jocondo and his brother Astolfo being deceived by their respective wives in Ariosto's *Orlando furioso* (canto 28) is also reminiscent of the frame story of the *Thousand and One Nights*.

In medieval epics, particularly Wolfram von Eschenbach's *Parzival* and the anonymous travel romance *Herzog Ernst*, a number of narrative motifs from Arabic-Islamic tradition appear, of which the most popular ones are the magnetic mountain and the city of brass. Besides exempla, fables, märchen, and elements of chivalrous romance, even comic narratives can be shown to have been transmitted from Arabic-Islamic tradition via Latin versions to the West. A case in point is the work of Jacques de Vitry, who served as bishop of the Palestinian town of Acre between 1216 and 1227. His collections of sermons, particularly the *Sermones feriales et communes* (Holiday and Saint's-Day Sermons) and the *Sermones communes vel quotidiani* (Saint's-Day and Everyday Sermons), preserved in their original Latin, contain a number of short narratives of Arabic origin, such as the one about the peasant who fell unconscious when smelling roses but was revived by smelling dung. A number of Jacques de Vitry's anecdotes are introduced by the remark "*Audivi …*" [I have heard …], strongly suggesting that he relied on oral sources. The above anecdote in later European tradition appears in the genre of fabliaux (French humorous verse narratives) as *Le vilain mire* (The Peasant Doctor) and serves as a reminder that the fabliaux as well as other short medieval narrative genres might well contain elements retaining Arabic-Islamic influence.

Trade and diplomatic relations exerted great impact on the transmission of popular narratives, even in clerical circles, as demonstrated by the papal secretary Poggio Bracciolini's *Liber facetiarum* (Book of Comic Tales), compiled around 1450 and containing numerous anecdotes of Arabic-Islamic origin. A convincing example of the lasting impression of medieval Arabic jocular tradition is the fact that the Sephardic Jewish community expelled from Spain after the Christian conquest in 1492 and ultimately settling in the Balkans even today remembers the popular Arabian trickster character Juha under his original name.

See also: Crusades; Frame Tale; Harun al-Rashid; Hispanic Tradition; Jewish Tradition; *Seven Sages, The*; *Thousand and One Nights*

—Ulrich Marzolph

Arthur. Legendary British hero and king, savior of Britain during a turbulent period.

Arthur's story is historically linked with events following the Roman withdrawal from Britain around 410 C.E., but evidence concerning his very existence is scattered and contested. There clearly was never a historical King Arthur with a Round Table and a castle known as Camelot, but there may well have been one or many historical figures whose exploits provided the germ of the legend that was to develop.

Early Traditions
Early documents that could shed light on the genesis of the legend are scarce. Gildas, the sixth-century author of *De excidio et conquestu Britanniae* (On the Ruin and Conquest of Britain) discusses the Saxon invasion of Britain after the Roman departure and notes that those wars culminated in the "siege of Mount Badon," a battle that would later be attributed to Arthur. Gildas does not, however, mention Arthur by name, a fact that some scholars have taken as evidence of Arthur's nonexistence.

The first reference to Arthur may have been made around 600 C.E. in a Welsh composition titled *The Gododdin*, which praises a certain warrior but adds that "he was no Arthur." This reference, which may have been added to the work later, nevertheless demonstrates that Arthur was already reputed to be an extraordinary, if not legendary, military figure. His fame would grow steadily. In the ninth century, the *Historia Brittonum* (History of the Britons), perhaps by a Welsh cleric named Nennius, names Arthur and enumerates his major battles, but he is described not as a king but as a *dux bellorum* (war leader). Only in the twelfth century would he become King Arthur. It was at that time, with Geoffrey of Monmouth's *Historia regum Britanniae* (History of the Kings of Britain, c. 1138), that Arthur received for the first time a full biography that includes his conception, birth, youth, conquests, marriage, and an extended period of peace. From Geoffrey the legend of Arthur spread throughout Europe, and the king would quickly become a figure of romance and overt fiction. That is the King Arthur we still know, but that status itself says nothing either for or against his historical existence.

Debates on Arthur's Life and Death
This last question—whether or not Arthur had actually lived—was often and hotly debated during the Middle Ages. Chroniclers disagreed with one another; Robert Mannyng of Brunne, John Hardyng, and other chroniclers accepted him, sometimes uncritically, as real, while others, like William of Newburgh, concluded that he was a creation of fiction or legend. Still others assumed that beneath an overlay of fanciful elaborations there was a kernel of truth. Among them was William of Malmesbury, who attested to his belief in Arthur's historicity by lamenting the fact that reality had been obscured or contaminated by so many fictional details.

Differences of opinion concerned not only Arthur's existence but also his character and the legitimacy of his rule. Geoffrey's *Historia* presented Arthur as an enemy of the Scots, and the Plantagenets in effect claimed Arthur as an English king. These developments presented a dilemma to Scottish chroniclers. Until the very late Middle Ages, most expressed admiration for Arthur, although John of Fordun, in his *Chronica gentis Scotorum* (Chronicle of the Scottish People, 1385), suggested that Scots (such as Gawain and Modred, or Mordred) and not Arthur should have occupied the throne. During the fifteenth century and beyond, many Scottish chroniclers (such as Hector Boece in 1527) dismissed or condemned Arthur as a corrupt and illegitimate ruler.

Debates concerning Arthur were influenced by historical events, most notably by the ostensible discovery at Glastonbury Abbey around 1191 of Arthur's body and that of his queen. Gerald of Wales (in his *De principes instructione*, 1193) tells us that Henry II, having learned from a Welsh bard the location of the bodies, informed the abbot, who before long ordered excavations in the abbey cemetery. Found were a large lead cross, whose inscription identified the spot as the grave of Arthur and his queen, and the remains of a man and a woman. It was concluded that the king had been discovered. The bodies were removed to a tomb before the altar in the abbey church, where they remained until the monasteries were dissolved during the sixteenth century. At that time they disappeared. The lead cross has also disappeared, although we have a 1607 drawing of it published in William Camden's *Britannia*.

Scholars have not agreed about the historical value of this discovery. Many, suspicious of motives—Glastonbury Abbey had burned in 1184 and needed money for rebuilding—have declared it a hoax intended to attract pilgrims and therefore income. Others have argued that the burial was clearly earlier than the twelfth century, though in the present state of our knowledge it is impossible to date it to the "Arthurian era" of post-Roman Britain.

In any event this discovery is important for several reasons. The English, Welsh, and Scottish rulers all had a stake in claiming the legendary Arthur as their own. The Plantagenets, as noted, were particularly intent on doing so, a fact that may account for Henry's privileged information about the grave. In the next century, after claiming Arthur's crown from the Welsh in 1278, Edward I held an elaborate ceremony at Glastonbury, during which the bodies were displayed as one might display the holiest of relics. The ceremony was an important effort by Edward to establish himself as Arthur's legitimate successor.

For legend and folklore, the importance of the 1191 discovery is that the grave, if authentic, would by definition shatter the belief in Arthur's return. From the early Middle Ages on, many believed that Arthur had not been killed but only gravely wounded and that he had been taken away (to a cave or to a place named Avalon, most frequently identified with Glastonbury). He would eventually return in the hour of Britain's greatest need. (Arthur is only one among a number of legendary figures around whom such beliefs coalesced; folklorists know the motif as culture hero's expected return, motif A580.) A narrative written by Hermann of Tournai in 1113 documents the belief, which must have existed much earlier. Hermann reported that during the course of a religious observance, violence broke out because someone dared to contend that Arthur was really dead. The growing legend of Arthur's survival is attested as well by others, including William of Malmesbury, who in 1125 wrote in his *Gesta regum Anglorum* (Deeds of the Kings of England) that "Arthur's grave is nowhere beheld, so that ancient songs say that he is still to come." A great many writers rejected this element of the Arthurian story, and Caxton's version of Sir Thomas Malory's *Le Morte Darthur* (printed 1485) leaves the question open, but the notion of the "once and future king" persisted in literature and thrived in the popular imagination.

The question of Arthur's existence or nonexistence did not diminish his appeal as a literary and legendary figure, either during the Middle Ages or since. Geoffrey's text was adapted into French by Wace in 1155 in his *Roman de Brut* (Romance of Brutus). Soon afterward the Arthurian court was transformed into the setting for courtly fiction. The greatest French author of romances, Chrétien de Troyes (fl. 1165–1191), set all five of his major works in an Arthurian context, but even as he made the Arthurian court into a powerful symbol of chivalric accomplishment he diminished the king himself. He remade Arthur into an often ineffectual and sometimes almost comical figure, though, paradoxically, a virtuous and respected one as well. (Some scholars have suggested that this transformation is the natural result of a French author writing of a British king.) In Chrétien Arthur is a secondary figure, and the romances center on particular knights of the Round Table—Lancelot, Yvain, Gauvain, Perceval, and others. Even in biographical (as opposed to episodic) romances, the same principle holds in part; in the French Lancelot-Grail cycle (c. 1215–1235) and in Sir Thomas Malory's *Le Morte Darthur* (c. 1470) the authors concentrate on Arthur until his kingdom is firmly established and then focus primarily on other knights and their adventures. Arthur thereafter remains an inspirational but often peripheral figure.

Arthur's Character and Popularity

Arthur's virtues, of which there were many, and his vices, which were generally considered few, vary from text to text. He is almost always presented as compassionate and generous. He is rarely wrathful, although the Middle English alliterative *Morte Arthure* (late fourteenth century) is a dramatic exception; nor is he a notably proud person, except when he is presented as a conqueror. He is generally faithful to his knights and to his queen, but there are glaring exceptions to the latter generalization. He lies with more than one woman besides his wife, and in some texts he cruelly rejects Guinevere in favor of the False Guinevere, an impostor. More commonly, though, even when he is required (by law, by his barons, or by his own judgment) to arrest or reject the queen, he does so with more sorrow than anger. The majority of authors after Chrétien follow him in presenting a spiritually imperfect king, and the French *Queste del saint Graal* (Quest for the Holy Grail, c. 1225) dramatizes the spiritual imperfection of Arthur and his court by emphasizing the superiority of the Grail ideal.

Yet it is apparent that the Arthur who maintained a strong hold on the popular imagination was the great, pious, generous, and compassionate king, not the weak, indecisive, and morally flawed figure. When Jacques de Longuyon (early fourteenth century) proposed a list of heroes to be respected and emulated, he included Arthur among them. He listed Nine Worthies: three pagans (Hector, Julius Caesar, and Alexander), three Christians (Charlemagne, Arthur, and Godfrey de Bouillon), and three Jews (Joshua, David, and Judas Maccabaeus). Here, despite his frequently ambiguous and occasionally negative depiction in literature, Arthur served as a symbol of glory, valor, and virtue, and the Nine Worthies (or often the Three Christian Worthies) were the frequent subjects of literary depictions as well as depictions in painting, tapestry, and other forms.

Whatever the fact of Arthur's existence, his appeal was so strong that reality began to imitate legend, and beginning in the thirteenth century Arthurian enthusiasts organized chivalric pageants called "Round Tables." Including jousts, feasting, and other activities, these pageants often featured participants who assumed Arthurian names and coats of arms. In 1446 René d'Anjou even built an "Arthurian" castle for the event.

Theories of Origin

Given the enduring popularity of the legend, it is unsurprising that the search has continued for a historical Arthur or for the historical models around whom his legend coalesced. There have been theories of a northern Arthur, a Welsh Arthur, even occasionally a Continental Arthur. Among the theories that attempt to explain the genesis of the legend, two have received a good deal of attention in recent years. These two, which are not mutually exclusive, are the Riothamus theory and the "Sarmatian Connection."

The former, suggested as early as 1799, by Sharon Turner, has been developed most systematically by Geoffrey Ashe. The notion concerns "Riothamus" (the word *riothamus* is an honorific meaning "high" or "supreme king" rather than a proper name). Indeed, a British high king called Riothamus is known to have existed. He crossed the channel in 468 C.E. to conduct military operations against the Britons' enemies in Gaul, as Geoffrey of Monmouth's *Historia* tells us Arthur did. This Riothamus (who may be identifiable with one Lucius Artorius Castus) is the only Briton of his time who figures in Continental records. He thus may be either "Arthur" or, at least, the historical figure around whom the Arthurian legend crystallized.

The so-called Sarmatian Connection concerns horse nomads sent to Britain from Eastern Europe as auxiliaries for the Roman army. It is thought that their customs and beliefs may well have been merged with stories of an emerging hero to shape the Arthurian legend as we would come to know it. Among the striking connections with the Arthurian story are the symbolism of an upright naked sword (reminiscent of the sword in the stone), battle ensigns carrying the image of a dragon, and sacred cauldrons (perhaps related to the Grail) used in rituals.

Despite the appeal of these and other theories, the majority of scholars remain skeptical, and there are those who assert that the truth behind the Arthurian legend is unknowable. Thus far, that is correct.

See also: Arthurian Lore; Chrétien de Troyes; Geoffrey of Monmouth; Grail; Nine Worthies; Sleeping King

—Norris J. Lacy

Arthurian Lore. Traditional narratives and motifs, attitudes, and beliefs associated with Arthur, his court, and his followers.

The legend of Arthur was one of the most productive themes of medieval literature in Western Europe. Grounded in popular beliefs in the Celtic-speaking regions of Great and Little Britain—primarily Wales, Cornwall, and Brittany—Arthurian tales were adapted first by Norman, Anglo-Norman, and French authors and then by others, especially German and English. Arthurian lore is preserved mainly in literary narrative genres—histories, *vitae sanctorum* (saints' lives), prose and verse romances, poems—and its stories and episodes are therefore found at some remove from their primary oral forms.

Nevertheless, though the legend takes many forms in various cultural contexts, it has some salient features. There is a core Arthurian entourage and a number of characteristic types of adventure (hunts; quests; journeys to unknown regions; combats with monsters, giants, or hags, or with other knights). There developed an Arthurian ethos of service and magnanimity centered upon Arthur's court. But the two themes that caught the imagination of writers and of their audiences (leaving aside the related but independent Merlin and Grail legends) were the abduction of Arthur's wife Guinevere and, especially, Arthur's final defeat, death, and prophesied return. These became the enduring features of the legend, which developed on the one hand into one of the great tragedies of world literature and on the other into a symbol of renewal and restoration.

Early Fragments of Legends

The earliest Arthurian texts derive from Wales and are written in Welsh or Latin. In these Arthur assumes a range of roles: he is variously termed hero, warrior, king, emperor, or simply leader. The ninth-century *Historia Brittonum* (History of the Britons), written in southeast Wales and often attributed to Nennius, has two stories of Arthur in a section describing some of the *mirabilia* (wonders) of Britain. Both seek to explain the names of features in the topography of south Wales, and it is possible that the Arthurian associations are secondary. One explains the name of a spring in present-day Herefordshire, Llygad Amr, "The Eye [i.e., fountain] of Amr [or Anir]," now Gamberhead, by identifying it as the spot where *Arthur miles* (Arthur the warrior) killed his own son Amr. Amr's grave, a tumulus, is nearby and cannot be accurately measured. Although this son is named again in a later Welsh romance, he does not appear to be a traditional character, and he seems to have been created from the place name. In this instance, a common motif may simply have been given an Arthurian context.

The other wonder is Carn Cabal (now Corn Gaffallt), a stone atop a cairn above the Wye valley in Builth, which bears the footprint of Arthur's dog Cabal (Cafall, in modern Welsh orthography), impressed upon it during the hunt for the boar Porcum Troit. This familiar explanation of a peculiarly marked stone is linked to another common motif, for though the stone may be removed it always returns to its original location. The Arthurian association provides a more specific context. *Cafall* is Old Welsh for "horse," and as the name of Arthur's hound it reflects the gigantic size of the dog and, by implication, of its owner. These two stories are the earliest examples of a widespread element in Arthurian folklore, the use of Arthur's name to identify topographic features. In 1113 Hermann of Tournai noted Arthur's Chair and Arthur's Oven in the West country, and there are scores of later examples throughout Britain. Nevertheless, it cannot be assumed that every Arthur's Seat, Quoit, Bed, or Stone had an onomastic tale attached to it, though they are certainly evidence of the popularity and magnetism of Arthurian associations.

The Earliest Surviving Welsh Tales

The hunting of the boar Porcum Troit (named Twrch Trwyd or Trwyth, in Welsh) by Arthur and his men was, however, a well-established tale. It forms a major part of the eleventh-century Welsh story "How Culhwch Won Olwen" (*Culh-* *wch and Olwen*). Twrch Trwyth is there said to have been a king transformed into a swine for his sins. Between his ears are the shears and comb that the hero Culhwch must obtain to shave his future father-in-law, the giant Ysbaddaden, before the wedding feast. The hunt takes Arthur, who is Culhwch's kinsman and helper, and his men from Ireland across south Wales to the Severn valley and thence along the Cornish peninsula until the boar is driven off the cliffs of Land's End and his magic implements snatched away. Hunts of magic animals, boars and stags especially, are frequent in Celtic legends, often as a means of leading the hero to an arranged tryst or enchantment, but the tale of Twrch Trwyth is of a boar hunted for its own enchantment and for the capture of magic talismans (though into this narrative have been interwoven a host of onomastic elements).

Culhwch and Olwen, the earliest extant Arthurian story, has other characteristic Arthurian episodes: journeys to free prisoners and to gain treasures; combats with monsters, giants, and witches—all in a magical, supernatural world. Although they have been brought together within a single narrative about winning the giant's daughter, no doubt many if not all of these adventures had an independent existence. In addition to the hunting of Twrch Trwyth (one of two boar hunts found in the tale), *Culhwch and Olwen* contains at least two other quests that belonged to earlier traditions: the first of these is the release of Mabon son of Modron, originally divine beings (the Maponos and Matrona whose names are found on Romano-British altars), from his prison in Caerloyw (which may mean "shining fortress"), in Gloucester. The second is the expedition to Ireland to win the cauldron of Diwrnach the Irishman. The two quests echo a ninth- or tenth-century Welsh poem "The Spoils of Annwfn," apparently spoken by the archetypal bard Taliesin. The poem recalls a disastrous expedition undertaken by Arthur, in his ship Prydwen, and two other shiploads of men to Annwfn, the Welsh otherworld—variously called here the Glass Fortress, the Fairy Fortress, and the Fortress of Intoxication—from which only seven men returned. The allusions to the features of the otherworld are similar to those found in early Irish literature, but the purpose of the voyage was to free a prisoner, Gweir, and to win the richly ornamented cauldron of the head of Annwfn; kindled by the breath of nine maidens, its peculiarity was that it would not "boil the meat of a coward." The same cauldron, now that of Dyrnwch the giant, is listed elsewhere as one of the 13 treasures of Britain, all of which appear to be, in origin, otherworld talismans. It seems likely that Diwrnach's cauldron in *Culhwch and Olwen* is another version of the same story, one that seems to have been a common type: of expeditions to win otherworld treasures—even if, in *Culhwch and Olwen*, Ireland has replaced Annwfn as the site of the cauldron.

Taliesin is not usually one of Arthur's followers, but a number of other characters named in the list in *Culhwch and Olwen* reappear in another early dialogue poem in which Arthur, seeking entrance at the gate of a fort, is made to declare the worth of his men. What follows is a catalog of heroes and warriors—pride of place being given to Cai (Kay) and Bedwyr (Bedivere)—and a series of allusions to their exploits against human enemies and supernatural monsters and hags. Another poem describes the heroism of Emperor Arthur in a human battle. Even more allusive are references to Arthur in the Welsh Triads of the Island of Britain. The general outlines of the persona of Arthur remain unchanged, but there are hints of an extensive lost Arthurian literature.

Arthur in the Saints' Lives
Supernatural combats are portrayed in a negative way in some saints' lives of the twelfth century. In these renditions of combat in saints' lives, written in Latin but using Welsh and Breton traditions, Arthur, often *quidam tirranus* (a certain king), now fights but fails to slay dragons. He challenges his rivals, no longer giants but monks or hermits. No longer victorious, he is discomforted and ridiculed. He is not heroic but avaricious and jealous. The nature of the Arthurian adventure has not changed, but the narrator has; rather than a writer of heroic poetry, the author is a cleric presenting his story to reflect the viewpoints of the saints, Arthur's rivals from ecclesiastical folklore. The saint challenges Arthur to win not his kingdom but, rather, the loyalty of Arthur's followers; this he accomplishes by overcoming Arthur and all he stands for. In making Arthur the villain of choice, the authors are acknowledging his importance; in this inverted sense, the *vitae sanctorum* are evidence of the same Arthurian lore as the early Welsh poems and *Culhwch and Olwen*.

Most of these episodes may be no more than conventional composed stories in which Arthur fills the slot of the stereotyped villain, but the *Life of Gildas* (c. 1130), by Caradog of Llancarfan, has two episodes that appear to be genuine fragments of Arthurian lore. One concerns the long-standing enmity of Arthur and Hueil, Gildas's brother; this rivalry also appears in the writings of Gerald of Wales and survives as a Welsh folktale at least as old as the sixteenth century. The second is the earliest account of the abduction of Arthur's wife (called Guennuvar by Caradog and generally known as Gwenhwyfar in Welsh): Melwas, king of *aestiva regio* (the summer country), carries the queen to Glastonbury, which the author calls *Urbs Vitrea* (Glass City). After a year's search, Arthur learns that she is a captive in Glastonbury and besieges the city to win her back. Gildas intervenes to have Gwenhwyfar returned to Arthur peaceably. The fact that the hero saint outshines Arthur by restoring Gwenhwyfar without a fight demonstrates that

this particular version of the story is steeped in clerical values. Yet the abduction theme recurs constantly in Arthurian literature: in an obscure Welsh dialogue poem, in the *Lancelot* of Chrétien de Troyes (where the abductor is Meleagant and the rescuer Lancelot, her lover), and in later romances.

Geoffrey and Other Twelfth-Century Treatments
In Geoffrey of Monmouth's *History of the Kings of Britain* (c. 1138), the queen's infidelity with Arthur's nephew Modred (in Welsh, Medrawd) and the latter's treachery are the cause of the final battle of Camlan, where Arthur is killed. Geoffrey created a potent mix of Welsh legend and tradition, classical and contemporary Latin writings, and creative imagination to present Arthur, the European emperor. Beneath this portrayal can be found some nuggets of genuine tradition: Arthur's sword Caliburnus (Excalibur), forged in the otherworld; Prydwen, his shield (not his ship, as in "The Spoils of Annwfn"); his wife and companions. Arthur fought the giant Ritho, who claimed his beard for his cloak of pelts (as Arthur had shaved the beard of Dillus in *Culhwch and Olwen*), and the obscene giant of Mont-Saint-Michel. Making Modred play the role of Melwas may be Geoffrey's error, and the battle of Camlan may not have been the result of any enmity between Arthur and Modred, but that the battle was the traumatic catastrophe of the Welsh Arthurian legend seems clear in the light of allusions found in the Triads, *Culhwch and Olwen*, and poetry. It became the focus for related incidents and developed its own group of traditions. Geoffrey claims that Arthur was taken to *Insula Avallonis* (the Isle of Avalon) to be healed of his wounds, a circumspect allusion to the belief in his eventual return. In his poem *The Life of Merlin*, Geoffrey developed the theme of Arthur's passing after Camlan, and his description of the "island of apples," ruled over by nine sisters who recall the nine maidens of the poem "The Spoils of Annwfn," and of the healing powers of Morgen, the chief of them, accurately reflects Irish and Welsh descriptions of the otherworld.

One of the Welsh "Stanzas of the Graves" (in the Black Book of Carmarthen) merely states that a grave for Arthur would be a wonder of the world, presumably because he had not died, but Geoffrey's contemporary William of Malmesbury, writing in 1125, is clearer, stating that "the grave of Arthur is nowhere to be seen, and that ancient songs prophesy his return," a belief that was given powerful expression when a near riot erupted in Bodmin, Cornwall, because some visiting monks were foolish enough to voice their doubts, according to the 1113 account given by Hermann of Tournai. Other twelfth-century writers, including Henry of Huntingdon, Gerald of Wales, and Étienne de Rouen, refer to this belief, which was to become the most abiding piece of Arthurian folklore. The earliest narratives of the king's survival, those of Geoffrey of Monmouth and Wace, tell of Arthur's passing to an otherworld island to be healed of his wounds and to await the hour and occasion of his messianic return. A more popular form of the theme is the cave legend of the sleeping lord. The earliest of these stories is related by Gervase of Tilbury in his *Otia imperialia* (Imperial Pastimes, c. 1211), which locates the cave in Mount Etna, Sicily, but a sixteenth-century Welsh chronicler provides the earliest evidence locating the legend in Wales, at south Cadbury.

Romance Traditions
Some familiar Arthurian themes are found for the first time in French romances. Arthurian stories, and perhaps an Arthurian legend as a frame of reference and context for them, were clearly well established in early and medieval Britain, as the narratives and allusions found in Welsh and in Latin attest. Arthurian heroes, stories, and ambiance apparently had a particular appeal for Normans in England, Wales, and Brittany, and these were transmitted to the French and Anglo-Norman cultural environments where Arthurian romance, verse, and, later, prose flourished, but it cannot be assumed that either the plots or all the episodes contained in the romances have a Welsh or other Celtic origin or that anything more has been borrowed in many cases than a traditional Welsh or Breton personal name. Wace, in *Roman de Brut* (Chronicle of Brutus, 1155), is the first to refer to the Round Table, established to prevent discord over claims of precedence at court and about which "Britons tell many wondrous tales," he claims. No such tales, however, have survived.

Stories of Arthur's begetting and boyhood may have been an element in his legend, but the celebrated incident of the Sword in the Stone, whereby Arthur's claim to royal leadership is confirmed when he alone is able to withdraw a sword from a block of stone, occurs first in Robert de Boron's *Merlin* (early thirteenth century). But French Arthurian romance has types of tales that can be more easily paralleled in Celtic stories. The most common of these are the hunt of the white stag, the transformed hag, journeys to enchanted castles and forests, magic fountains and mists, quests for wondrous objects, and the wasteland. These "Arthurian commonplaces" derive from Celtic mythological themes that may or may not have been associated with Arthur in their native, primary forms but that were part of the totality of Brythonic narrative themes and motifs that together with Arthurian elements gave medieval Arthurian romance its particular flavor.

That Arthur and some close companions— Cai (Kay), Bedwyr (Bedivere), Gwalchmai (Gauvain, Gawain)—were popular folklore figures is clear. Stories about them can be retrieved, complete or in allusions. What is more debatable is whether this Arthurian lore was so many individual pieces or whether they existed within a legendary frame. Most Arthurian stories center on widespread motifs—combats, monsters, witches, and the like—and they are, therefore, movable. But the fixed elements—including the abduction and loss of Guinevere, the battle of Camlan, the death and return of Arthur, and an ethos of service found even in *Culhwch and Olwen* and the *Life of Cadoc*—suggest that one can refer to an early Arthurian legend. Whether any of this has a historical basis is irrelevant. Much of what is said of Arthur, even in the Latin chronicle texts, is expressed in terms that are recognizable as popular themes and motifs of myth and folktale.

See also: Annwfn; Arthur; Camlan; *Culhwch and Olwen*; Geoffrey of Monmouth; Gerald of Wales; Merlin; Myrddin; Nennius; Taliesin

—Brynley F. Roberts

Assassins Nizari Isma'ilis [Nizari Isma'ilis].
A medieval Shi'i Muslim sect known for its use of political assassination.

The Isma'ilis take their name from Muhammad ibn Isma'il (d. 760 C.E.), who, although he predeceased his father Ja'far al-Sadiq, was accepted by many as having achieved the high spiritual state of imam. The Nizari branch is named for Abu Mansur Nizar (d. 1095), a caliph of the Fatimid dynasty. The Isma'ilis inhabited many regions of the Middle East in the medieval period, but their authority was centered in Syria and Persia, which came under their control when Hasan-i Sabbah seized the Fortress of Alamut in 1090. Outnumbered by Sunni Muslims and beset by schisms, the Isma'ilis turned to political assassination in the Fatimid (909–1171) and post-Fatimid periods as a means of self-preservation. Training for these missions took place in secret, apparently in several of the fortresses controlled by the Nizaris, but the assassinations were often public and spectacular, inspiring many legends about the Nizaris and their leaders.

Contrary to European legend and history, most Nizari assassinations were directed at other Muslims, and the term *Assassin* derives from *hashishiyya*, first used to describe the *fida'is* in the twelfth century. Although the term literally means "hashish user," it is now believed to have been used by other Muslims as a broad insult meaning "social outcast" or "irreligious." Persian Isma'ilis were rarely if ever referred to by this term; they were more commonly known as *mulhidun* (apostates). Nonetheless, *Assassin*, first used in a European chronicle by Burchard of Worms in 1175, became the common Western term for all Nizaris.

Legends concerning the Nizaris were not limited to Western traditions. Muslim legends also circulated, particularly in the twelfth and thirteenth centuries, when the Nizaris attained political prominence in Persia and Syria. Though the Nizaris were too few to undermine Sunni authority, their great influence led to exaggerated tales of their training and exploits. The Sunni legend tradition consisted of attributing all assassinations to Nizaris, thus magnifying the strength of the sect and its impact on the medieval Muslim political scene. As the Frankish crusaders came into contact with Muslims, stories of the efficient Assassins spread into European lore. Stories that they targeted Christians became more and more prevalent, and many deaths during the Crusades themselves were attributed to the Nizari Assassins.

Europeans, not able to understand the Shi῾i martyrology that would cause one to willingly sacrifice one's life in a murder attempt, created tales of young men trained as assassins in compounds where their minds were controlled by drugs. That addicts would be neither efficient nor effective as assassins was not considered as the legends were perpetuated both in oral tradition and in historical texts, such as that of Arnold of Lübeck (d. 1212). Western legend combined the Shi῾i belief that martyrs immediately entered Paradise and the Persian tradition of planting lavish gardens into images of hedonistic training centers where the drug-crazed young Assassins were deluded into believing that Paradise existed on earth and that if they completed their missions, they would be allowed to return to it.

Loyalty to the Nizari movement became in legend loyalty to a single leader, Rashid al-Din Sinan (d. 1192), also known as the Old Man of the Mountain. Henry of Champagne was purportedly treated to a demonstration in 1194, when the Old Man of the Mountain ordered his followers to commit suicide by leaping off the wall of his fortress. This story is believed to have been inspired by a late romance in which Alexander the Great intimidated an enemy by ordering troops to commit suicide. By the end of the thirteenth century the legend was widely accepted enough to be included in chronicles, and the loyalty of the Assassins was so renowned that Provençal troubadours adopted them as role models for lovers, who declared themselves to be as devoted as Assassins. Ibn Jubayr and other Arab historians apparently adapted the death-leap story from its European origins into Arabic chronicles as well, where it supported the notion that the Nizaris were fanatical.

Originally separate legend strands, the hashish addiction, Paradise fantasy, and suicide cult became facets of one story and were granted historical authority in the writings of Marco Polo (1254–1324) and his scribe Rustichello. Polo stopped at the Persian fortress Alamut on his travels; there he claimed to have heard several reports concerning the Old Man, inexplicably in Persia instead of Syria, who convinced his young adherents that his garden was indeed Paradise. The Assassins were administered an opium potion that enhanced their fantasies and enabled them to be manipulated into killing the Old

Man's enemies in order to regain access to Paradise. Most subsequent renderings of Assassin legends can be traced back to Marco Polo's composite version of the fourteenth century.

See also: Arabic-Islamic Tradition; Crusades; Travel Literature

—Bonnie D. Irwin

Augustine of Hippo, Saint (354–430).
Bishop and saint, designated one of the four principal Doctors of the Catholic Church.

Augustine was born in Tagaste, Numidia (North Africa), to a pagan municipal official and a Christian mother. His spiritual journey toward conversion, culminating in his baptism in 387, is recounted unforgettably in the *Confessions*. His written works were so extensive that his biographer and cataloger Possidius claimed that no single person could read them all. His influence on Christian theology has been incalculable, but perhaps equally pervasive has been his influence on what might be termed the "flavor" of medieval Christian culture.

The nature of Augustine's ethnic origin has been a matter of scholarly debate: fourth-century Numidians appear to have been closely related to modern Berbers. Although she was a devout Christian, Augustine's mother had been reprimanded for maintaining graveside rituals of pagan origin (*Confessions* 6, 2); her name, Monica, may derive from that of a Numidian mother goddess. Augustine's education was rigorously classical, but certain preoccupations and values evince African influence: ecstatic intensity of emotional attachment directed toward the divine as well as the human, and a portentous sense of the created world as a kind of text from which universal meaning may be inferred, whether by divinatory interpretation or the construction of elaborate allegorical schema.

Augustine was an acute observer of human behavior; his interest in traditional belief was intellectual, practical, and on occasion personal. The critical point in his conversion occurred when he was in the depths of a spiritual crisis and heard a nearby voice chanting, "Take up and read; take up and read." His first reaction was to consider whether this might not be part of some children's game. His decision to take the advice of the mysterious voice as a prompting to a bibliomantic ritual—opening the Bible and reading the first passage he saw—resulted in his emotional breakthrough to belief.

Official Christian teaching as *doctrina publica* had emerged toward the end of the second century and was thus relatively recent in Augustine's time, and the process of shaping a central core of belief distinct from "optional" beliefs and practices (comprising what Adolph Harnack has called "Christianity of the second rank") was still being negotiated. A conscientious pastor after his conversion, Augustine was especially concerned with the necessary process of riddling through pre-Christian traditions of belief to determine which would support the new faith, which might undermine it, and which might be "baptized" through allegorical reinterpretation. A skilled rhetorician as well as a scholar, he was preoccupied with the distinction between orality and the written word: he was fascinated by his mentor Ambrose's habit of reading without moving his lips (*Confessions* 6, 3).

Augustine's concern with folklore is expressed in the three primary roles of his life. As a theologian, his absorption in consensual symbols as a vehicle for both meaning and communion, human and divine, is most movingly set forth in the dialogue *De magistro* between himself and his son Adeodatus, whose mother was a woman with whom Augustine had a relationship before becoming a priest. In their conversation, in a manner both serious and playful, Augustine demonstrates both the necessity for symbolic communication and its limitations. Although he claims "I am afraid I shall appear ridiculous, because I set out on so long a journey with the consideration of signs and not of the realities they signify," he concludes "there is absolutely nothing that can be taught without signs."

As a preacher, he made daring rhetorical use of popular beliefs, especially in his oral commentaries on the Psalms. For example, glossing the line "the voice of the Lord perfecting the stags," Augustine alludes to the popular belief that a stag could draw serpents from their dens by means of the sweetness and power of its breath, illuminating an otherwise opaque verse (one that is, in fact, a mistranslation). The "perfected" stag becomes an image for the power of Christ over calumny, "for the voice of the Lord has above all led to perfection those who know how to control and discountenance enemy tongues" (*Enarrationes*, Psalm 28).

Third, as an ecclesiastical administrator, he attempted to define criteria by which orally transmitted accounts of miraculous "wonders," the "urban legends" of his time, could be evaluated with both intellectual rigor and reverence—an issue still unresolved in our own day. Although early in his conversion he averred that the time of miracles had passed, in later life he was sufficiently impressed by a series of cures resulting from contact with shrines to the holy in his domain to institute a formal procedure for documenting each event, requiring a written affidavit from the recovered patient to be proclaimed in church and later filed in the bishop's library, thus ensuring that any exaggerations or garbling of the account in oral circulation could be checked against this first-person testimony.

In his great work *The City of God,* he related miracles that could be verified from his own time and locale. For example, he related a story of a kind familiar to folklorists: a fellow townsman of Hippo, a tailor named Florentius, lost his coat, prayed to the Twenty Martyrs for a new one, was ridiculed by the young men of the town, found a fish on the shore, and took it to a cook, who cut it open to find inside the fish a gold ring. Thus, the tailor got his new coat through a miracle (22, 8). Similar material of interest to folklorists in that same work would include his discussion of Adam and Eve's realization of their nakedness after the Fall, which involuntarily "moved" their sexual organs with lust (14, 17); his speculations about the origin of giants through intercourse with ordinary women (15, 23); the abominations of rites of the Great Mother, as celebrated by castrati (7, 26); his description of pagan hydromancy as a form of divination in which the images of gods (actually demons) appeared in water (7, 35); and the helpful information that peacock's flesh has antiseptic power (21, 4).

Approached on his deathbed by a dream-prompted sufferer hoping for a miraculous cure, Augustine remarked wryly that if he had such powers he would apply them to his own affliction—but he laid gentle hands on the man nonetheless.

See also: Saints, Cults of the

—Erika Brady

$\mathcal{B}$agpipe. A musical instrument of unknown but ancient origin.

Suetonius attests to Nero's ability on the bagpipe, Procopius writes that the bagpipe was used
by the imperial Roman army, and historians suggest that the Roman soldiers introduced the bagpipe into England. Two distinct types of the bagpipe have been documented in medieval Europe:
the conical chanter, which produced a loud
piercing sound, and the cylindrical chanter,
which gave off a soft buzzing tone. Although
both single drone and droneless pipes were played
in the Middle Ages, the multidrone bagpipe common today seems to be a postmedieval invention.

The bagpipe is considered predominantly a
folk instrument in Western European traditions,
and its music accompanied weddings, dances,
and festivals. The instrument did maintain a
connection to royalty: in 1290, for example, Edward I of England memorialized his queen,
Eleanor, by having bagpipes play while crosses
dedicated to her memory were erected. It was
also common practice for pipers to accompany
religious pilgrims. In the early fifteenth century,
Thomas Arundel, archbishop of Canterbury, remarked that bagpipes could drive away a pilgrim's
hurt, and Chaucer's Miller seems to accurately
reflect this practice as he pipes the pilgrims forth
to Canterbury.

The bagpipe possessed traditional associations
with gluttony, animal lust, and the male genitals.
Carved images of pigs with bagpipes can be
found at Beverley Minster in England and at
Melrose Abbey in Scotland. According to a
chronicle of Bruges, Belgium, for the years from
1477 to 1491, when crimes and executions rose
at an alarming rate, one of the worst criminals
was a musician "called Anthuenis, and he was
known as a soothsayer, who used to play the bagpipes, and he was put to death for things that are
better not reported."

The manuscript evidence, however, such as
Très riches heures and the *Cloisters Apocalypse*, depicts both shepherds and angels playing bagpipes
at Christ's birth. Such a wide range of associations highlights the diverse attitudes displayed
toward the bagpipe by Western medieval culture.
—Cynthia Whiddon Green

Bal des Ardents. The "dance of the burning
men," one of the most infamous incidents in the
late-fourteenth-century reign of France's King
Charles VI, which was less a ball than a danse
macabre.

The Bal des Ardents occurred on January 28,
1393, at a festivity celebrating the wedding of
two members of the royal household, hosted by
the king at the Hotel de St. Pol, one of the favorite residences of Charles and Queen Isabeau.
The bride was one of the queen's favorite ladies-
in-waiting. Six members of court, one of whom
was Charles himself, dressed in costumes and performed a dance as an entertainment for guests at
the reception. Either by accident or by design the
flammable costumes ignited, and four of the
dancers died of the burns. Although the king fortuitously escaped death, the incident caused a
scandal because of the tragic but avoidable deaths
of four participants. While the general outlines of
the story remain similar from account to account,
there are significant inconsistencies in the details
about the event supplied in the respective versions written by contemporary chroniclers of affairs of court during Charles VI's late-fourteenth-
century reign.

One royal chronicler, the Monk of St. Denis,
interprets the event as a charivari. The Monk
emphasizes that the party celebrated the third
marriage, to a German lord, of one of Queen Isabeau's favorite ladies-in-waiting. Remarriages and
marriages to outsiders or foreigners were both violations of social taboos that could precipitate
the enactment of charivari, a ritual of humiliation aimed at transgressors against local socio-
sexual mores. After generally condemning the
practice of humiliating remarrying widows by
means of a charivari, the Monk of St. Denis reports that King Charles VI and five other
courtiers nevertheless planned a spectacle directed at the newlyweds being feted. The masked
dancers entered the hall in frightful disguises that
rendered them unrecognizable. In line with his
earlier censorious remarks, the Monk thus implies that the dance of Charles VI and his costumed cohorts was a charivari. This chronicler
profoundly criticizes the behavior of the king and
his courtiers, especially their disgraceful postures,
obscene gestures, and bestial cries, which he
compares to the howling of wolves. When somebody, either accidentally or purposefully, tossed a
spark toward one of the charivari participants,
the dancers' highly flammable costumes ignited.
Of the six charivari participants, only the king
and one other dancer survived; the other four
participants died painfully of their burns. As the
Monk reports the Bal des Ardents, the perpetrators of the purported charivari, not the newlyweds, became the inadvertent victims of their
own guising, a sign, in his opinion, of poetic justice and divine retribution. Regardless of the actual intent of Charles VI and the other dancers,
the Monk's implication that the dancing at this
wedding feast constituted a charivari permits him
to reaffirm a recent ecclesiastical critique of the
custom and to criticize the monarch's foolish lack
of decorum.

But the most famous account of this event, by
Jean Froissart in his late-fourteenth-century
Chroniques, does not mention the motif of charivari and instead emphasizes the specific costumes
worn by the dancers in what may have been
meant only as an entertaining masque. In Froissart's chronicle Charles VI and the other five

courtiers impersonated *hommes sauvages* by wearing highly flammable costumes that resembled the body fur of the legendary medieval Wild Man. Froissart adds specific details about the guests, emphasizes the preventive measures taken to ensure the dancers' safety (torches or other sources of fire were forbidden during the dance), and mentions that the dancers, with the exception of the king, were attached to each other. Froissart also adds material about the spectators' marveling reactions to the dance and explains that, separated from the other Wild Men and passing by his wife, the king walked over to a group of female guests at the party and engaged in a conversation with the duchess of Berry. (Though the duchess was the king's aunt—her husband the duke of Berry was Charles's uncle—she was the youngest woman at the reception.) Of all the chroniclers, Froissart provides the most detail about the occasioning of the fire and identifies the cause of the blaze: the king's brother, Duke Louis of Orléans, arrived late and carried a torch to the dancers for closer inspection and (either accidentally or deliberately) set off a conflagration. Igniting one costumed link in this human chain lit them all. Pandemonium broke out among the horrified guests. When the dancers caught fire, the duchess of Berry protected the king by covering him with her dress, thus saving his life. The only survivors of the debacle were the king and one other dancer, who threw himself into a tub of fresh water used for rinsing flasks and goblets and thus doused the flames.

Whereas the Monk focuses his critique on the practice of charivari in his account, Froissart's version is more concerned with the inadvisability of the king's having participated in the dance; the significance of the specific folk figure being impersonated in the furry costumes, the Wild Man of the woods; the way the king escapes being burned, by perhaps-unsuitable engagement with a young woman; the culpability of the king's brother; and the ensuing scandal when news of the tragedy spread throughout Paris. Froissart's version of the Bal des Ardents seems designed to excoriate the monarch responsible for the tragedy that occurred at a wedding party he hosted.

See also: Charivari; Dance; Wild Man

—Lorraine K. Stock

Baltic Tradition. The folkloric culture of medieval Livonia and Lithuania.

The southeast coast of the Baltic Sea was home to a number of peoples belonging to two cultural complexes: the Balts (speakers of languages in a conservative branch of the Indo-European language family, comprising Latvian, Lithuanian, and Prussian) and the Baltic Finns (speakers of a highly Indo-Europeanized branch of the Finno-Ugric language family, comprising Estonian, Finnish, Ingrian, Karelian, Livonian, Vepsian, and Votic). During the medieval period the majority of these peoples were forcibly consolidated into the realm of Livonia, ruled by the Teutonic Knights. Lithuanians, however, maintained their independence, rising to the status of empire during the thirteenth through the early fifteenth centuries, before finally succumbing to Polish domination. The medieval folk culture of the region was marked by the strong persistence of native traditions, overlaid by Christian, German, and Hanseatic influences.

The Livonian Rhymed Chronicle of the thirteenth century describes the peoples of the Baltic region thus: "All these pagans have most unusual customs. They dwell together of necessity, but they farm separately, scattered about through the forests. Their women are beautiful and wear exotic clothing. They ride in the ancient manner and their army is very strong whenever it is assembled." From such remarks, along with archaeological and later ethnographic evidence, it is possible to characterize early medieval Baltic life. Shifting slash-and-burn agriculture was the rule, supplemented by hunting and fishing. Loanwords for agricultural implements and many crops indicate that agriculture passed from the Balts to the Baltic Finns. Intermarriage among all the groups appears to have been prevalent. Women wore elaborate headdresses, breastplates, and jewelry, adopting styles developed elsewhere but modifying them to fit native tastes. Armies were assembled when needed, and hill forts were sometimes maintained for defense.

During the Viking Age, Baltic amber became a prime commodity throughout Europe and the Middle East. Viking traders from the island of Gotland in the West and from Novgorod in the East vied for control of the Baltic trade, but the various peoples of the region remained independent. Both Western and Eastern Christianity entered the region but failed to take root. Sporadic pirating of trading ships made the Baltic region uncertain ground for merchant interests.

In the twelfth century, however, German merchants from Lübeck entered the region, establishing a post among the Livonians (Livs) on the western Dvina River near the site of Riga. They profited from the regional cooperation of Saxon and Danish rulers and found the area lucrative. In the 1180s, soon after the creation of the settlement, the Augustinian priest Meinhard arrived to Christianize the populace. The subsequent Livonian crusade grew increasingly militaristic, spawning an order of German monastic knights, the Fratres Militae Christi, or Swordbrothers. These crusaders, recruited from Germany and Scandinavia, subdued one tribe after another, establishing fortresses at key defensive sites (e.g., Riga, Tallinn, Tartu, and Daugavpils), forcing native nobles into vassal status, pressing peasants into military service, and levying taxes to sustain their new institutions. The consolidated realm became known as Livonia. In the mid-thirteenth century the Swordbrothers merged with the larger Teutonic Knights, an order occupied in the conquest of Prussia.

In opposition to the Swordbrothers and Teutonic Knights, a coalition of Lithuanian tribes formed under the leadership of King Mindaugas. In 1260 Mindaugas abandoned the Christian faith—which he had accepted in the 1250s—and began to war actively against the German crusaders. The Lithuanians and closely related Samogitians damaged the German effort through frequent raiding. Lithuanian warriors pushed eastward as well, conquering Slavic cities abandoned by the Tartar retreat. The Lithuanian empire begun by Mindaugas was continued by a succession of worthy kings in the fourteenth century and eventually extended from the Baltic to the Black Sea. The empire fell in the early fifteenth century with the triumph of Poland and the nominal conversion of the Lithuanians to Christianity.

Following conversion, the entire Baltic region came to be dominated by German Hanseatic interests. The cities founded for defensive purposes became trading centers similar to those of northern Germany and Scandinavia. The peasant economy was greatly restructured to accord with the feudal system. The countryside continued to harbor a great many traditions, however, that predated contact and domination.

Pre-Christian Religions

The overtly mercantile nature of the Baltic crusades did little to endear common people to their new religion. Furthermore, although Pope Innocent II (1130–1143) had urged the use of the Baltic vernaculars in prayer and preaching as early as 1138, nearly all of the region's clergy and services were German throughout the medieval period. The strong resistance to Christianity among the Lithuanians further bolstered the region's pre-Christian beliefs, so that the entire medieval period can be viewed as a negotiation between pre-Christian and Christian traditions.

Little is known of the religions of the Baltic Finns, although the beliefs of the Finns and Karelians further north were fairly well preserved. German and Polish chronicles provide glimpses of pre-Christian Prussian and Lithuanian religions. From these references it appears that the Balts possessed a religious system similar to that of other Indo-European peoples. In particular, the sources indicate a triad of male deities worshipped in conjunction with sacred oak groves at sites such as Romowe. A fierce god of the dead—associated with hanging, skulls, night rides, and fury and depicted as old, sometimes one-eyed, and green-bearded—was known by the various names Patollus, Pecullus, and Velinas. A thunder god—associated with perpetual fires and oracle priests and depicted as middle-aged and black-bearded—was known as Perkūnas. Finally, a youthful, beardless Potrimpos or Natrimpe was associated with agrarian fertility, good fortune,

grain, milk, snakes, and a priestess class. Potrimpos merges with a wide range of "lower-order" deities associated with the earth, harvest, and fertility, including Zvempatis and Zvemyna, master and mistress of the earth. Many of these lower deities are male. References to a divine smith (Kalvelis), a woodland goddess, and deities associated with healing abound in late-medieval accounts of Lithuanian culture.

Although German conquest obliterated much of early Latvian (Lett) religion, we know of a supreme god, Dievs (or Debestêvs), and a thunder god, Perkuons. The sun and moon were viewed as husband and wife, and their daughters were said to play with the sons of the celestial dieties. A goddess of birth and fate, Laima, is mentioned in many folksongs and was known among the Lithuanians as well. A variety of female lower-order dieties presided over water, fire, sea, and wind. Household spirits and the spirits of deceased relatives were venerated and feared among all the Balts and Baltic Finns.

Folksongs

In the Baltic region, native meters and genres of folksong persisted throughout the medieval period. A trochaic or trochaic-dactylic meter characterized Baltic-Finnic, Latvian, and Lithuanian songs, although each culture possessed its own devices and aesthetics. The Baltic-Finnic song tradition was strongly alliterative, and line-pair parallelism was a regular feature. The Latvian *daina* was terse (usually only two lines long) with some alliteration and much parallelism. The longer and more rhythmically variable Lithuanian *dainas* rarely relied on alliteration, rhymed occasionally, and possessed both elaborate parallelism and a nuanced use of diminutives.

Peasant life finds poignant expression in the folk music of the region, including songs concerning the life of orphans, wives, and shepherds. Ritual songs associated with weddings, harvest, birth, death, and holidays are plentiful and varied from village to village throughout the region. Courtship, too, was accompanied by singing, sometimes subdued and lyrical, other times bawdy and erotic. Although epics exist throughout the region, lyrical songs predominate; they were performed primarily by women. Traditional Baltic instruments include a small zither (Lithuanian *kankles*, Latvian *kokle*, Estonian *kannel*), panpipes, and various forms of wooden trumpets. The bagpipes were popular in the later Middle Ages, but the violin arrived relatively late.

Calendar Customs

Scholars disagree about the origin and age of Baltic calendar customs: some regard traditions connected with the agricultural year as pre-Christian, while others posit their introduction with Christianity. At any rate, during the Middle Ages festivities connected with sowing, the harvest, and the solar year were celebrated on the feast days of Christian saints. Important festivals were associated with St. George (spring planting), St. John's Eve (Midsummer), St. Anthony, a feast of the dead, Christmas, Easter, and others. Particularly striking were customs involving the creation of an idol or effigy, such as the Latvian Jumis or Estonian Metsik, Peko, or Tunn. Communal work was undertaken as a festival of its own, known in Latvian as *talka*, in Estonian, *talgud*. Such work parties combined heavy harvest labor with feasting, drinking, and dance.

See also: Finno-Ugric Tradition; Slavic Tradition, East

—Thomas A. DuBois

Bear [*Ursus arctos arctos*]. The Eurasian brown bear, ranging from Spain to Siberia and as far south as India; eponym and heraldic charge, as at Bern, Switzerland, since at least 1224; trained to perform (motif K1728) and victimized in spectacles from Roman to modern times.

Bears were exported to the Roman Empire by the Germanic peoples, whose descendants preserved much ursine lore. In Norway and Denmark, Migration Age nobles were buried on bearskins, with bear claws or with clay models of bear claws. Claws have been recovered from Viking York, as has a bear's canine, partly pierced, from Norse Orkney (now a northern Scottish island). Ursiform ornament has a long history in Scandinavia, from Paleolithic petroglyphs through Neolithic clubs to brooches found on Gotland (an island east of Sweden) and on to the sword hilts and spear sockets of the Vendel period. Best known is a Torslunda die depicting a man flanked by two bearlike figures. These apparently whispering beasts parallel tales of the whispering bear (J1488).

The bear figures prominently in the folklore of Europe; in southern French tradition it is Ursus who seeks his shadow on Candlemas. Linking bear lore with St. Blaise, Emmanuel Le Roy Ladurie notes that "the bear's resounding fart of dehibernation celebrated the primordial rite of spring" (*Carnival in Romans* [1980], p. 99). *Roman de Renart* tells how Bruin lost his tail (AT 2). Icelandic sagas suggest totemic relationships between humans and bears: humans have bear fathers, mothers, and sons. This circumpolar theme may be reflected in Hallmund, who in *Grettir's Saga* lives in a cave under a glacier with his mysterious daughter. In Norway Grettir kills a bear, keeping its pelt and claws. He has been called a "bear hero," as have Beowulf, Bjarki, and Bodvar. Retold in *Hrolf's Saga*, the legend of Bjarki (Little Bear)—son of Björn (He-Bear) and Bera (She-Bear)—involves shapeshifting (G263.1.1), sorcery, bear marriage (B601.1), and breach of taboo (B635.1.1).

Germanic bear lore reflects lost ritual. The Eddic poem *Sigrdrífumál* prescribes carving runes *á bjarnar hrammi* (on a bear claw): fangs and claws

were talismans. Sympathetic magic inspired ursiform design that gave bear power to warriors—for example, the *berserkir* (bear shirts) were fanatical warriors dedicated to Odin, who worked themselves into battle rage. Saxo Grammaticus says men drank bear blood to attain ursine strength. According to Arent, initiation rites may even have pitted men against bears. Onomastic applications were common: like Björn, the name *Beowulf* (Wolf of the Bees) may be taken to mean "bear"; these terms presuppose names based on bruin's color or craving for honey. There are many such euphemisms—sweetfoot, wintersleeper, grandfather, forest king—coined for the one that wintered in the underworld, summered upon middle earth, and haunted heaven forever in the constellation called Great Bear by many besides the Romans (cf. Finnish *Otava*).

The Celts had a bear deity (A132.5) analogous to the Arcadian Kallisto. According to Rhys Carpenter, the Greeks also associated the bear with Zalmoxis, Odysseus's progenitor Arkeisios, and the oracle at Trophonios. Derivations from Celtic *airth* (including perhaps the name Arthur), Italic *ursus*, and Hellenic *arktos* reflect the Indo-European root word for bear, **rks*—a term long gone from Germanic (scholars have suggested that tribal hunting taboos on speaking the name of the bear led to the disappearance of the term). Place names like Björnhövda (Bear's Head) imply that the Swedes, like the Finns, had a bear cult. The Finno-Ugric bear hunt involved rich drama, with a "marriage" and feasting followed by the solemn burial of the reassembled skeleton—except for the skull, which was placed high in a tree. Totem and shamanic guardian, the bear was a natural fertility figure, too, reborn each spring along with the green shoots and summer birds. It was the most anthropomorphic animal of the North, hallowed by the rhythm of death and resurrection.

See also: Candlemas; Finno-Ugric Tradition

—Stephen O. Glosecki

Becket, Saint Thomas (c. 1120–1170). Chancellor of England (1155–1162), archbishop of Canterbury (1162–1170), and the most extensively venerated English saint—famous since the twelfth century for his martyrdom at the hands of four knights in Canterbury Cathedral but even more celebrated in medieval times, almost from the moment of his death, for his afterlife as a miracle worker.

Although postmedieval legendry, seeking to identify Thomas Becket with the cultural underdogs of post-Conquest England, has sometimes portrayed him as Anglo-Saxon in descent, he was in fact of Norman parentage. Born in London as the city was becoming a major cultural center, Becket became known as London's saint almost as much as he was Canterbury's. His friend William Fitzstephen, who wrote a *vita* (saint's life) of Thomas in the 1170s, prefaced his sacred biography with a description of London, for "St. Thomas has adorned both these cities, London by his rising and Canterbury by his setting."

Early Life

Biographers and scholars searching for the seeds of greatness in what is known of Thomas Becket's early life have been generally both puzzled and disappointed by the sketchiness of his education and his seeming lack of any clear aim or purpose. Although he was a bright, attractive youth, possessed of unusually keen senses and a wonderful memory (total recall, it is said), Thomas was an indifferent student who preferred field sports, such as hunting with hawks and hounds, to strict application to his studies. Nevertheless, it is known that he attended Merton, which served as a preparatory school, and after some years there entered one of the three principal schools of London, possibly St. Paul's. From the London grammar school, at age 16 or so, he went to Paris, where he would most likely have followed the arts curriculum, though there is evidence Thomas had not thoroughly mastered the subjects. The motivation for some of the changes in young Thomas's life is not clear, but certainly his father's financial misfortunes and then the deaths of both parents (it was his mother who had insisted on his studies and recognized his talents) affected his decisions. Forced to make his own living after his father fell on bad times, he was apprenticed as an accountant to a banker friend of his father's, Osbern Huitdeniers, and he also acted as clerk and auditor to the sheriffs of London. In these capacities he added a knowledge of the world of politics, diplomacy, and finance to what he already knew, through his father's contacts, of the interests and manners of the court circle.

As long as he was alive, Thomas's father, Gilbert Becket, was a prime agent in his son's advancement, so it is hard to know whether he arranged for the young man's introduction into the household of Theobald, archbishop of Canterbury, or whether this move was due to Thomas's desire for an ecclesiastical rather than an administrative career. Whatever the case, probably in the winter of 1143–1144 at age 25, Thomas joined the archbishop's household as a clerk. In this cathedral community, one of the most distinguished in the country, Thomas was doubtless groomed for an administrative post such as the archdeaconry, to which he was appointed in 1154 through Theobald's influence. But advancement followed hard upon advancement; only weeks later, also through Theobald's influence, Thomas was appointed chancellor to the new English king, Henry II. For both men, king and gifted, ambitious commoner, it was a fateful development. As was his nature (a trait that baffles some biographers), Thomas Becket gave to his new master his complete loyalty and his best efforts. The chancellorship gave Thomas

the opportunity to indulge a taste for opulence and ostentation—lavish entertainments with gold and silver plate and exquisite foods, fine horses, a convoy of ships when he crossed the English Channel. The extent to which his intimate friendship with Henry II involved Thomas in debauchery is somewhat debatable; certainly the two rode together, hunted, hawked, and gamed together. Some biographers insist that Thomas remained chaste in his private life and ate and drank in moderation. It is likewise suggested that during these years of achievement and success Thomas Becket was aware of trying to serve two masters, the king and the Church, the secular and the spiritual. That being the case, his proper allegiance was made manifest to him in 1162, when Henry II appointed him archbishop of Canterbury.

As Archbishop

No doubt the English king was convinced that he could control an archbishop as easily as he had controlled a chancellor. The king failed to understand—and the concept boggles the minds of some of Thomas's biographers—that Thomas Becket applied himself wholeheartedly and single-mindedly to whatever job he accepted without any residual sympathies or loyalties. From the time he was ordained a priest in order to serve as archbishop, Thomas was a churchman. Perhaps such had been his inclination from the early days of his mother's instruction, or perhaps his avid dedication to his duties was in part a matter of practical expedient. In any event, he brooked no intrusion on the Church's authority. For centuries in England, through a variety of political upheavals, the issue of the division between the functions and offices of the Church and royal power had been held somewhat in abeyance. Thomas's appointment came at a time when circumstances at last brought the issue to a head and when a group of men, all of them powerful and gifted but each of them seriously flawed, were brought together to engage in debate and combat: Thomas and Henry II, of course, as well as Pope Alexander III, Thomas's rival and archenemy Gilbert Foliot, and others. The confrontation came immediately. Thomas's rebuff of King Henry in the matter of clerical immunity led to Henry's presenting the Constitutions of Clarendon, a number of which were unacceptable not just to Thomas but to the Church hierarchy in Rome, and the ensuing bitter quarrel led to Thomas's escape from England and exile first in Rome and then in France. His exile lasted for six years, during which the quarrel continued through a complex web of emissaries and letters.

On January 19, 1170, the often indecisive Alexander III commanded that the English king and archbishop resolve their differences, with harsh penalties for both if they refused. Thomas returned to England amid scenes of rejoicing and omens of disaster. Rumors and a number of hostile incidents indicated that the archbishop was not safe on English soil. However, as his entourage made its way through the countryside, the streets and roadways were lined with cheering multitudes. It was a reception that neither Thomas nor Henry II could ignore. Henry had arranged to be out of the country, but there were those who were willing to act on his behalf. On Tuesday, December 29, 1170, four knights—Hugh of Moreville, William de Tracy, Reginald Fitz Urse, and Richard le Breton—murdered Thomas in the cathedral at Canterbury.

As Martyr and Saint

If the event had been staged to inspire public reaction and the immortality of the victim, it would not have been more effective. The church was full of people. The archbishop's courage in facing his assailants and his final words, "I accept death in the name of Jesus and his Church," were seen and heard by many. The murder was especially brutal and grisly; one knight sliced through the dying archbishop's skull while another scattered his brains across the stones. The night was stormy, with lightning and thunder. The monks who prepared the body for burial—in secret and without ceremony—discovered under Thomas's habit a hair shirt and drawers infested with vermin and concluded that his martyrdom by sword was more endurable than his self-inflicted, continuous martyrdom. Furthermore, more than any other moment of medieval history, the occasion was recorded by men of learning who could describe it in detail; four of the nine biographers who wrote about Thomas Becket were present at the martyrdom.

Thus, within hours of Thomas's death, his heroic afterlife began. Although for a short time the royal agents in Canterbury acted vigorously to prevent the murder having vexatious consequences, threatening monks and hampering pilgrims, they could not control the rapid spread of information or the burgeoning cult among the common people. In a matter of days reports and tales of signs and wonders began to pour in. Shortly after Whitsun, Robert de Broc's brother, William, was cured at Becket's tomb. Soon the cathedral, for a while left desolate and deserted, was changed into a kind of field-dressing station that was visited by a steady stream of the sick and indigent. The heart of the cult was the blood of the martyr, which at first the monks were hesitant to administer for both theological and practical reasons. Eventually they diluted the blood in wine or water or presented pilgrims with small patches of Thomas's blood-soaked garments. However, anything associated with the martyr—his cloak, scraps of the hair shirt, proximity to his tomb—was in time believed to have miraculous powers.

A monk named Benedict collected a series of oral testimonies concerning miracles experienced by those who prayed to St. Thomas; these are remarkable in the extent to which they record the experiences of the lower classes. In 1172 William of Canterbury, another monk, incorporated Benedict's together with his own collection, probably as part of a project to obtain the status of sainthood for Thomas, for the posthumous miracles known as *signa* (signs) were necessary evidence for canonization. These books may never have been presented in evidence, because Thomas was canonized speedily, within two years and two months of his death, on February 21, 1173. A year later, in July 1174, Henry crossed from Normandy to England in a tempest and did public penance at Canterbury, asking for pardon and being scourged by the whole community of monks. Louis VII, king of France, who had given Thomas sanctuary during his exile, paid a similar visit.

Fifty years after Becket's death his remains were removed from the crypt and reinterred in the newly completed Trinity Chapel on a raised portion of the ground floor of the cathedral. In subsequent centuries, so many pilgrims would visit this site that their feet wore down the stone steps leading up to the shrine. The new shrine was surrounded by the 12 tall "miracle windows," each depicting some of Thomas's miracles, and many closely following the tales earlier collected by Benedict and William. Much of the glass has been destroyed, but the surviving scenes are remarkable in depicting very few nobles but many common people. Quite clearly, the numerous lower-class pilgrims visiting the shrine could find echoes of their own status even within surroundings that were probably the most ornate and lavish they had ever experienced.

Some of the stories represented in the miracle windows present rather simple lessons in charity toward the lower classes. In the tale of Eilward of Westoning, a man who steals from his neighbors is blinded and mutilated by order of a magistrate. Thomas visits him in his bed and restores his sight. A group of pilgrims, moved by the miracle, give Eilward alms, which he promptly gives away to a beggar. The moral is clear: Thomas's mercy supersedes rough worldly justice; those who follow Thomas learn that generosity to the poor cancels crime and undoes punishment.

In other stories peasants are forgiven their faults and given redress for the inequities they suffer when they fail their lords. One of the glass stories traces the fortunes of Richard Sunieve, a herdsman who fell asleep while tending the horses of his lord. Awaking, he was stricken with leprosy, which can be read as punishment for failing to do the work of his master. Richard traveled to Thomas's shrine and was healed. St. Thomas thus serves as a mediator who can be invoked to lessen the pains of the peasants. God and their masters may punish peasants who do not attend to the good of their lords, but Thomas, if not an equalizer, intervenes to clear the slate and spare them from disproportionate punishment.

If Thomas sometimes helps peasants avoid punishment, he also calls upon the lower orders to help him punish godless nobles. Perhaps the most striking instance of this is found in the complex tale of the Fitzeisulf windows. The nine panels recount an episode of the plague that kills Sir Jordan Fitzeisulf's nurse and threatens to kill his son. Water from St. Thomas's shrine cures the son, and Sir Jordan vows to pay a visit of thanks to the cathedral. When Fitzeisulf forgets to make the journey, the saint appears to a leprous crippled beggar, Gimp, and tells him to warn the family. Gimp delivers the warning from his sickbed, but Sir Jordan does not heed him. So Becket appears, like the avenging archangel Michael, hovering over the family with a sword drawn to deal out death. Most of the family and its servants fall ill; the oldest Fitzeisulf son dies; and Sir Jordan finally makes his too-long-delayed pilgrimage to pay homage to St. Thomas. This is probably the most revolutionary text of all. To punish a negligent noble, Thomas enlists the help of a leprous beggar. Gimp becomes the human voice of the saint, warning that a failure of generosity will lead to terrible vengeance.

It may be said that at a crucial time and under mostly accidental circumstances, Archbishop Thomas Becket died for the freedom of the spiritual authority of the Church and died proclaiming that he knew what he was doing and was willing to die for this cause. The reverberations of his death affected the course of history in a limited way and for a limited time. St. Thomas's influence as an ongoing source of folkloric materials of great richness and variety has been, however, much longer lasting.

See also: Blood; Pilgrimage; Saints, Cults of the
—Lee Winniford and Carl Lindahl

Bede the Venerable (673–735).

Monastic theologian and historian of early England, whose works are rich sources of legends circulating in oral tradition.

Born in territory attached to the monastery of St. Peter and St. Paul—which had sites at both Wearmouth (now Monkwearmouth) and Jarrow in northern England—Bede was brought to the monastery at age seven and lived there for the rest of his life studying, teaching, and writing the many works that earned his reputation as the most distinguished scholar of his time.

Though much of his learning came from books, Bede also collected numerous legends from oral tradition, especially for his great *Ecclesiastical History of the English People* (731), which provides some memorable examples: that scrapings taken from an Irish manuscript and mixed with water was a cure for snakebite (1, 1); that St. Albans displayed power over a river before his martyrdom and that after his beheading the executioner's eyes popped out onto the ground (1, 7); that St. Germanus debated the Pelagian heretics before a crowd that finally judged him the victor when the saint defeated his opponents in a miracle contest (1, 17–18); that splinters from King (later St.) Oswald's cross, mixed in water, would cure sick humans and animals (3, 2); that so many people dug dirt from the spot where Oswald fell to mix with water for cures that they made a hole as deep as a man is tall (3, 9); that oil from the holy Aidan had power to calm the stormy sea (3, 15); that the same Aidan's prayers were responsible for averting the destruction by fire of the royal city of Bamburgh (3, 16); that the saintly Chad likewise had the power to calm storms (4, 3); that Imma's fetters kept falling off despite repeated efforts by his captors to chain him (4, 22); that Hilda's mother had a dream when the abbess was still an infant betokening, through a brightly shining necklace, the precious jewel that her daughter would later become for all Britain (4, 23); that St. Cuthbert's relics effected marvelous cures (4, 30–32); that the hermit Oethelwald had power to calm the stormy sea long enough for visitors to return from his island to the mainland (5, 1); that Bishop John chastised the abbess at Watton for bleeding a young nun on the fourth day of the moon (5, 3); that the hermit Dryhthelm related a terrifying, highly imaginative description of his traveling to the otherworld (5, 12); that when a dying man refused to confess his sins, demons inserted into different parts of his body sharp objects that, when they met, caused his death and damnation (5, 13); and that many people took soil from the spot where Hædde died, mixing it with water to cure illnesses in humans and cattle—and producing a large hole in the ground by their digging (5, 18).

From Bede's accounts of the transmission of these legends it appears that Anglo-Saxon monastic communities were not so insulated as is often claimed. Such legends did not observe institutional boundaries; rather, they passed generally from popular oral culture to the monasteries, circulated orally among and within various monastic communities, and often flowed from the monastery to popular culture. For example, in his *Vita Sancti Cuthberti* (Life of St. Cuthbert), Bede recounts an early miracle of Cuthbert's in which he saved monks from drowning (ch. 3). Toward the end of this account he describes how this legend was performed and circulated orally for generations among the local people before being related to Bede by a monk who heard the story in a live performance by a member of that folk tradition. While such legends did eventually get written down by a writer like Bede, they continued in oral tradition, sometimes reappearing in later written versions as well.

In Alfred the Great's reign (871–899), Latin literacy had so far declined even among the clergy—according to Alfred's famous preface to the translation of Pope Gregory the Great's *Pastoral Care*—that a translation of Bede's history into Old English became a major event in Alfred's translation program. This late-ninth-century Old English Bede substantially reduces the scholarly apparatus and simplifies the style of the original for reading aloud to nonliterate audiences. As such, it is plausible to conceive of this version as a "re-oralizing" of the largely oral traditional legends written into Bede's Latin text, thus providing a more complicated view of the relations between orality and literacy in early medieval contexts than has been recognized in much earlier scholarship.

See also: Cædmon; English Tradition: Anglo-Saxon Period; Monks; Nuns; Orality and Literacy
—John McNamara

Beltane [Bealtaine, May Day]. In Ireland, the festival heralding the summer season.

Basic to the Celtic conception of time was the twofold division of the year into a winter period followed by a summer period. The summer part of the year began at Beltane, identified as May 1 in the Julian calendar. This twofold division of the year in Ireland is well attested in early and medieval literary texts in the Irish language, as is the further subdivision of winter and summer, giving four smaller seasons of three months each as the standard division of the year in Ireland.

The celebration of Beltane—in line with the celebration of the other major seasonal festivals in Ireland—commenced on the eve of the festival at sunset (and in modern oral tradition the preternatural power associated with this festival in particular was considered to be most potent between sunset on May Eve and midday on May Day). Thus, *Oíche Bhealtaine* (the night of May, May Eve) referred to the last day of April. The change of the calendar from the Old Style to the New Style around the mid-eighteenth century meant that 11 days were dropped from the reckoning, giving rise to such popular conceptions as New May Eve (*Oíche Bhealtaine úr*) on April 30, and New May Day (*Lá Bhealtaine úr*) on May 1, while May 11 became known as Old May Eve (*Oíche Shean Bhealtaine*) and May 12 as Old May Day (*Lá Shean Bhealtaine*). Thus, the period "between the two Mays" (*idir an dá Bhealtaine*), that is, between New May Eve and Old May Eve, was perceived as a hiatus during which certain farm activities, such as transferring stock to the mountain pastures, should be carried out. Hiring fairs, at which farmers took on farm servants and workers for the seasonal summer and autumn work, were held on May 11 and 12 in many places in Ireland, especially in Ulster. This also applied to some livestock fairs. The most important beliefs and customs connected with Beltane, however, transferred over time to New May Day, and this day was perceived as the appropriate time to observe the festival in order to avail oneself of its beneficent import and to avoid its potential dangers.

May Day inaugurates the summer season, when there is renewed life in the natural world, with trees in leaf, wildflowers in bloom, and a plentiful supply of fresh grass for the milk cows. It has strong agricultural and pastoral connotations, for it marked a new phase in the annual round of farming life and involved a considerable amount of reorganization on the farm, especially in relation to cattle.

It is also the bright half of the year, when the sun is high in the sky and when nature is favorable. These attributes of the season may be reflected in the festival's name, Beltane—which is also in Ireland the name of the first month of the summer season. The word, whose first element, *bel*, probably means "shining," "brilliant," or "favorable" and whose second, *teine*, means "fire," may be connected with the ancient Celtic god Belenus, possibly a solar deity. In modern folklore certain acts considered to involve magic were forbidden at sunset and sunrise, and the connection with fire, manifested in the lighting of bonfires, is an enduring aspect of the celebration of the festival.

The mythological significance of the festival of Beltane is attested in medieval literature, where it is claimed that it was on this festival that the Sons of Mil, the ancestors of the Gaels, landed in Ireland for the first time in the southwest of the country. They succeeded in wresting the sovereignty of Ireland from their predecessors, the Tuatha Dé Danann. Despite their defeat, however, the Tuatha Dé Danann deprived the Gaels of the basic foodstuffs—grain and milk—by means of magic, forcing the Gaels to come to terms with them.

The perception that milk cows and the milk yield could be adversely affected by magical acts continued to find expression in literature in Ireland during the medieval and later periods and also in the oral tradition. Milk magic is especially connected with the festival of Beltane, presumably because this feast signaled the commencement of the dairying season. The performance of milk magic is attributed to women especially, probably because they have traditionally been largely responsible for the care of the milk cows and the production and sale of dairy products. A persistent motif in narratives referring to the performance of milk magic is that some women could shapeshift, transforming themselves into hares in order to suck the milk from the cows lying in the fields. This is mentioned by Gerald of Wales (Giraldus Cambrensis) in his late-twelfth-century *Topography of Ireland* and by the English historian William Camden in his *Britannia* in the mid-sixteenth century, and it has remained a persistent element of the oral tradition in relation to Beltane in Ireland and in other parts of Europe.

A variety of verdure customs, concerned with protecting and promoting the milk yield and dairy produce, especially butter, and with welcoming the summer, are associated with the celebration of Beltane. Camden in his *Britannia* mentions the setting up of a green bough before the house in order to have an abundance of milk during the dairying season, and Sir Henry Pier's statement in his *Description of the County West-Meath* (1682) that a green bush placed before the house was strewn with yellow flowers undoubtedly strengthens its association with the production of milk and butter and with their protection and promotion. The May growths are intended to promote what they symbolize—the green leaves are representative of pasture and the yellow flowers are particularly associated with dairy produce. The erection before the house of a "May bush," with bunches of yellow flowers tied to its branches, is an enduring aspect of the celebration of Beltane, the festival of May, in parts of the eastern region of Ireland to the present day.

See also: Irish Tradition; Lugnasa; Samhain

—Patricia Lysaght

Beowulf. Anglo-Saxon heroic poem telling of fabulous events set in ancient Scandinavia.

The unique copy, written out by two scribes working about 1000 C.E., is found on folios 129a–198b of British Library MS Cotton Vitellius A.xv. There are no other medieval records of either the poem or its hero, but many of the characters and events to which the poet alludes in passing (such as Weland the Smith and Sigemund the Dragon-Slayer) are known in variant forms from other such early Germanic sources as the *Poetic Edda* and *Völsunga Saga*.

No other work of the early-medieval imagination provides such a detailed representation of Germanic society; no other puts the art of heroic poetry on such sustained display; no other provides such a wealth of information concerning the Anglo-Saxons' view of their legendary past. In language charged with ornamental epithets, the poet gives either sustained or glancing attention to such bedrock Germanic institutions as the feud, gift giving, cremation funerals, wergild, fosterage, exile, female exogamy, ritualistic drinking, the use of the harp, boasting, and flyting, as well as to the physical appearance of armaments, ships, and halls.

Theories of Date and Composition

While the first modern scholars to edit and translate *Beowulf* attributed it to a period as early as the Age of Migrations of the Germanic tribes, recent scholarship has dated the poem progressively closer to the date of the manuscript itself. Opinion is now divided between those who accept an eighth-century date of composition and those who favor the late ninth or tenth century, when a united Anglo-Scandinavian kingdom ruled by members of the West Saxon royal line was forming. Theories of monkish interpolation have generally been discarded, as has the old theory that the epic was stitched together from separate lays. Instead, most current scholars view the poem as a unified composition, the result of a gifted Christian poet's meditation about the remote pagan past.

No one knows how the poem was composed. Some scholars attribute it to a learned author who happened to write in the vernacular. Others see it as the work of a singer steeped in a traditional oral-formulaic technique, like epic songs recorded in the Balkans and Greece in recent times. The current tendency is to see the poem as in some sense oral-derived rather than as either a completely literary composition or the verbatim record of a normal oral performance. If the text came into being through the collaboration of a singer, a patron, and one or more scribes, like the poems attributed to Cædmon by Bede (*Historia ecclesiastica* 4, 24), then surely it was edited in the process of being written down, and its length and elaborate ornamentation may partly reflect the special conditions of an unusual process of textualization.

Folktale Analogs

Some scholars see the poem as closely indebted to Celtic tradition, particularly to the Old Irish tale known as "The Hand and the Child." In stories of this type, the hero wrenches off a long, demonic arm that reaches into a hall in an attempt to abduct a prince's newborn child. He then traces the wounded monster to a body of water and kills him. In its two-part action, its switch between a hall and a watery setting, and its lurid focus on a severed arm, the tale has much in common with the Grendel episode in *Beowulf*, and yet in the Old English poem there is no child or attempted kidnapping, nor does the arm appear as a threat in its own right. Among other motifs that have been held to show Celtic influence are the hero's swimming prowess, his battle rage, his use of a giant-wrought sword, and the choice of a mighty female creature as adversary. If such elements do derive from Celtic sources, whether via the folklore of a subjugated British population or via Ireland, then they have been assimilated to the Anglo-Saxon worldview while being adapted to a setting in the Germanic past.

The poem consists of two main episodes into which other materials are freely introduced, including historical and legendary digressions, retrospective speeches, and gnomic and elegiac passages. First Beowulf, a young Geatish warrior, vanquishes Grendel, a cannibalistic creature who for many years has terrorized the hall of Hrothgar, king of the Danes; then, after Grendel's mother avenges her son, Beowulf seeks her out and kills her in her underwater home (lines 1–2,199). After many years, now having become the aged king of the Geats, Beowulf dies in victorious combat against a huge firedrake (lines 2,200–3,182). While the plot of the dragon fight is too simple for this episode to be traced to a single source, the Grendel episode has been linked to a widely distributed European folktale known as the "Bear's Son" tale, or, more properly, "The Three Stolen Princesses" (AT 301). Like *Beowulf*, this international tale type features the adventures of a strong hero (sometimes with ursine attributes or parentage) who first puts one ogre into flight, then follows its tracks into a nether region where he dispatches a second, sometimes female, ogre. Similar story elements are found in the thirteenth-century *Grettir's Saga* and other Old Icelandic tales, and *Hrolfs Saga Kraka* includes a somewhat comic analog in its account of the monster-slayer Bödvar Bjarki, who is literally the son of a bear. It cannot be shown, however, that AT 301 existed during the Middle Ages in the same form as in recent tradition. Very likely both *Beowulf* and its Icelandic analogs represent a specialized northwest European reflex, set in a pseudohistorical context, of a very ancient two-part mythic-hero tale of a monster slaying.

Christian Influences

Although the poem is set in the pagan Continental homeland of the English peoples, nothing in it is inconsistent with Christian teachings. On the one occasion when the Danes offer sacrifice at a pagan shrine, the narrator vehemently condemns their error. Other scenes that contribute to what has been called the "pagan coloring" of the poem, such as the ship funeral at its start and the cremation burial at its end, are presented with such stately decorum as to elicit admiration for great kings and ceremonies rather than anxiety about theological doctrines. No pagan gods are mentioned by name. No word is breathed about such repugnant rites as human sacrifice, although divination is mentioned in passing and the dragon's treasure bears a curse. Beowulf, Hrothgar, and other main characters talk and act like pious monotheists, as if by their innate power of reason they are endowed with a knowledge of such matters as the Creation, Providence, Hell, and Doomsday. In addition, the narrator, who knows more than the characters do, informs us that Grendel is descended from Cain, that God sent Beowulf to the Danes as a savior, that the huge sword the hero finds in Grendel's lair was made by giants before the Flood, and that Beowulf's soul departs from his body at death "to seek out the judgment of the righteous." By such means the audience is assured that the heroes and kings of the ancient north, rather like the patriarchs of Old Testament times, acted out their fates in a world subject to God's will.

The Hero and the Monsters

At the center of the poem, lending the story such unity as it has, is the character of Beowulf himself. We are left wondering whether he has supernatural powers or is merely exceptionally strong. His maternal uncle, Hygelac, was renowned for his gigantic size, as is reported in the medieval Latin compendium known as the *Liber monstrorum* (Book of Monsters). His tribe, the Geats, while identifiable with the Gautar of southern Sweden, seems also to be linked through medieval pseudogeography with both the Jutes,

whom Bede names as one of the founding tribes of England, and the Getae, an imaginary "proto-Germanic" tribe of the ancient north. True to both his tribal associations and his folktale affinities, Beowulf is described as not only the biggest of his band of warriors but also the strongest human being alive at that time, and he proves his might by wrenching the arm off a creature who is literally of gigantic stature. In addition, he can swim in the seas for days, fully armed in his mail coat, and he can survive underwater for longer than seems humanly possible. The poet makes it clear that God himself favors Beowulf, at least in his two first fights. On the other hand, nothing is said about Beowulf's having other than normal parentage, and the plot of the poem shows him to be mortal. Unlike heroes of the "Strong John" type, but much like the biblical patriarchs or the saints of the New Dispensation, Beowulf seems to win victory as much through his piety and fierce moral integrity as through his physical strength. He is larger than life; he is also, in his ultimate vulnerability, completely human. Like the hero, the monsters of *Beowulf* occupy an ambiguous realm between the natural and the supernatural. Grendel and his mother are not just cannibalistic ogres; they are literally devilish, and the eerie, icy pool in which they make their home is reminiscent of medieval theologians' descriptions of the mouth of hell. The dragon, while never described as demonic, is a figure for the devil in medieval typology outside *Beowulf*, and some scholars have argued that he carries at least some of that typological weight in this poem as well. On the other hand, the Anglo-Saxons believed in the flesh-and-blood existence of dragons and cannibalistic giants, to judge from the place names built on the elements *thyrs* (monster) and *drake* (dragon) that dot the English landscape. Books of pseudo-science known to the English—in particular the collection known as *Marvels of the East* (a copy of which directly precedes *Beowulf* in the hand of the first scribe)—confirmed that such creatures existed in at least the exotic regions of the world, and a Wiltshire charter of 931 refers to a "Grendel's mere" in the vicinity of "Beowa's enclosure." The *Beowulf* poet's tale of the slaying of horrific monsters by a magnificent hero in ancient Scandinavia, however, probably reflects a myth-making tendency among the Anglo-Saxons more than it reflects their credulity about the world around them.

Theories of Mythic Origin

Sporadic scholarly attempts have been made to link the characters or events of the poem to ancient myths and religious practices. The temptation to read *Beowulf* as a reflex of ancient myth is strong, given that no similar literary work survives in northern Europe from such an early date, but specific links to myth and rite are hard to locate. Nineteenth-century interpretations of the poem as a kind of solar or nature myth are universally dismissed. Scyld Scefing, the founder of the Scylding dynasty of Danish kings, bears a name that translates roughly as "Defender" (from the Old English *scyld*, meaning "shield"), "son of Sheaf" (from Old English *scef* or *sceaf*, denoting "sheaf of grain"), and the poet's allusion to Scyld's mysterious arrival as a foundling links him to what appears to be an ancient fertility myth. But the *Beowulf* poet celebrates Scyld Scefing exclusively as a mighty warrior and father of kings. Herebeald, the elder brother of *Beowulf*'s king Hygelac, bears a name that is reminiscent of Old Norse Baldr, but if the myth of Baldr's death provided some inspiration for the poet's account of Herebeald's death by arrow shot and his father Hrethel's inconsolable grief, then the parallel remains merely suggestive. Hrothgar's gold-adorned queen, Wealhtheow, may ultimately be related to the valkyrie figures of northern myth, at least in a broadly generic sense, but in the poem she functions simply as a gracious queen. Attempts to show an etymological link between her name and the valkyries involve special pleading. Vestiges of shamanism in the poem are equally tenuous. Somewhat like the shamans of northern lands, Beowulf travels "between worlds," as it were, as he descends to a nether region to kill Grendel's mother. But his descent is physical rather than mental; it involves no magic or drums; and its aim is the defense of a kingdom, not initiation or the curing of disease. The hero's name, Beowulf, or "Wolf of the Bees," to accept one etymology, may possibly be a euphemism for "Bear" (that is, a name that avoids using the bear's real name by calling the bear a honey eater, a "wolf of the bees"), and the poem might thus have some connection to a widespread ancient cult of the bear as totemic animal. If so, then the hero's nonhuman attributes have been almost wholly rationalized away.

Attempts have also been made to link the action of the poem's first episode to the Easter liturgy (the climax of the medieval liturgical year) and to the literature of baptism. From a Christian perspective, Beowulf could be thought of as descending, like Christ, into a nether region "to slay the ancient serpent," and the poem could take on aspects of an allegory of salvation. Such approaches have the virtue of explicating the poem in terms consistent with the actual functioning mythology of the Anglo-Saxons. They rightly call attention to the fight against Grendel's mother as the dramatic center of the poem and the site of extraordinary miracles. Still, they are based on arbitrary and predictable connections to a body of doctrine that lies outside the poem. While nothing can stop a devout Christian from interpreting the poem in typological or allegorical terms—for indeed, according to some medieval theological perspectives, the whole natural world and all of human history are open to interpretation through allegory—the poet gives no clear sign that a specific allegory is intended.

Grendel is devilish, but he is not Satan. Beowulf is a great hero, but he is not Christ. In their pursuit of religious symbolism, Christological readings tend to slight the specific contours of the narrative and ignore the poet's sustained interest in the details of German legendry and the ethos of the heroic life.

Beowulf offers a mine of information bearing on Anglo-Saxon folklore, legendry, and popular belief. It also can easily become a minefield for critics intent on searching out elements that are thought to lie beneath its surface. Each such attempt has its interest, and from it something can be learned. At the same time, readers should not be distracted from seeing the poem in its literal narrative as a powerful story whose mood is darkened by Christian pessimism at the same time as its meaning is enriched by ethical concerns. Instead of looking for traces of ancient myth in the poem, current readers are increasingly approaching the poem as a myth; that is, as a work of major cultural synthesis in which the Anglo-Saxons addressed tensions concerning their national or cultural identity in the form of a story set in the ancient past: Are we ethically Christian or pagan, or in some sense both? Are we ethnically Saxons or Danes, or some fusion of the two? Is our cultural heritage to be sought out chiefly in the northern or the Mediterranean world? These are among the questions and controversies that a contemporary audience of Anglo-Saxons would have found posed, if not finally resolved, in the long, complex, and masterfully told story of the deeds of Beowulf, hero and king.

See also: Cædmon; Dragon; English Tradition: Anglo-Saxon Period; Funeral Customs and Burial Rites; Sutton Hoo

—John D. Niles

Berserks. In Old Norse-Icelandic tradition, fierce warriors with animal-like characteristics who are impervious to wounds.

The first attestation appears to be in stanzas assigned by editors to *Haraldskvaedi*, a poem ordinarily attributed to a ninth-century Norwegian skald, Thorbjörn Hornklofi, about whom little is known. The poem is an encomium to King Harold Hárfagri (Fairhair). In its reconstructed form the poem comprises, besides an introductory section, an account of the king's victory at the battle of Hafrsfjörd and a description of various members of his retinue: skalds, warriors, and jugglers. Among the warriors are berserks, "drinkers of blood, battle-bold men who go forth into the army." The next stanza is devoted to *úlfheðnar* (wolf skins), "who carry bloody shields into battle, who redden shields when they come into battle.... the king puts his trust only into bold men who hew into shields." Later, written narrative assigns to King Harold berserks called *úlfheðnar* who wore wolf skins and defended the prow of his ship (*Vatnsdæla saga*, ch. 9).

Elsewhere in the Sagas of Icelanders berserks

sometimes show up as unruly challengers for a woman's hand (*Eyrbyggja Saga* and *Heidarviga Saga*), and the *fornaldarsögur* contain many similar scenes. In many cases the hero overcomes the berserk and himself wins the hand of the woman in an analog to folktales in which monsters threaten princesses and are rescued by heroes who slay the monster and marry the princess (see, e.g., AT 300, "The Dragon-Slayer" and related types). Often, however, berserks operate in groups, most often of 12.

The *berserksgang* (going berserk) is known from *Ynglinga Saga*, the first saga in *Heimskringla*, the compilation of kings' sagas done by the Icelander Snorri Sturluson in the first half of the thirteenth century. In the early chapters of this saga Snorri attempts a euhemerization of the god Odin; that is, he presents Odin as a historical figure, a human king whom men later worshipped and thus elevated to the status of a deity. Among Odin's abilities was that of vitiating the strengths of his enemies, while at the same time, according to Snorri, "his men went without armor and were crazed like dogs or wolves, bit into their shields, were as strong as bears or bulls. They killed people, but neither fire nor iron affected them; that is called going berserk" (*Ynglinga Saga*, ch. 6). By stating that berserks go without armor, Snorri seems to understand the term *berserkr* as "bare shirt," but the parallel with the *úlfheðnar* renders more plausible the etymology "bear shirt." Certainly such an etymology accords with the animal characteristics Snorri associates with going berserk.

Theriomorphic (beast-form) warriors are known from Viking Age iconographic evidence, especially a sixth-century plate from Torslunda, Sweden, and accepting this etymology allows that evidence to be associated with the berserks. More generally, some scholars have seen in the crazed behavior and animal characteristics of the berserks, which are found in many Old Norse-Icelandic sources and in the *Gesta Danorum* (History of the Danes) of Saxo Grammaticus, the reflection of an ecstatic warrior cult of Odin. If the association is made with the etymology of Odin's name as deriving from an Indo-European form meaning "leader of the possessed," the phenomenon must be pushed back to well before the Viking Age, for the etymology is not transparent. Indeed, many scholars see the cult of the ecstatic warrior god as an ancient phenomenon inherited from the Indo-European ancestors of the Scandinavians.

See also: Scandinavian Mythology

—John Lindow

Bestiality. Sexual contact between humans and animals.

The term usually refers to intercourse between humans and animals, but it may include other forms of sexual contact. Medieval texts both describe what may have been actual incidents and tell stories that seem to have derived from folk traditions, making it difficult to determine actual practices.

The early Christian medieval world inherited both texts and traditions that described human/animal intercourse. In the classical Greco-Roman texts, gods in the form of animals had intercourse with humans. For example, Zeus took the form of a bull to carry away Europa and the shape of a swan to seduce Leda. Classical "scientific" writings also told tales of bestial intercourse, probably drawing from folklore traditions. Aelian's *On the Characteristics of Animals* (c. 170 C.E.) is full of tales that describe human relations with goats, horses, baboons, snakes, dogs, geese, and other animals. Pagan Germanic traditions also preserved tales of bestiality, whether between human and animal or between one human and another who took the shape of an animal. Many of the early myths refer to such liaisons, particularly favoring references to intercourse with horse gods and humans transforming into birds to have relations with people.

The Christian tradition did not accept bestial intercourse. During the early Middle Ages most of the references to bestiality were in the form of penitential manuals prohibiting the practice. Yet in some rare tales we can see the tension between old and new beliefs. For example, there is an Old Norse account of the conversion of a household by St. Olaf. Olaf encountered a pagan family worshipping a *völsi*, a preserved horse penis. Olaf fed the ritual item to the family dog, and the family was converted to Christian worship. This tale exemplifies the relationship between Christian and pagan tradition in which the former attempted to eradicate bestial eroticism in the latter.

Tales of bestial intercourse reappear and increase in frequency in Western European literature after the twelfth century. Gerald of Wales, who repeated much folk wisdom he acquired in his travels through Ireland and Wales, related a number of tales of bestiality. Gerald told of men who had intercourse with cows and of women with goats and a lion. He even recounted an incident of a man who passed a calf from his bowels after having been sodomized and impregnated by a bull. In his *Topography of Ireland*, he describes a ritual of kingship in which the man soon to be king has public intercourse with a white mare.

In the later Middle Ages churchmen became more concerned than they had been earlier with the presence of demons interacting with humans. As part of this preoccupation, tales of bestiality increasingly referred to intercourse with demons, the succubi and incubi that seemed ubiquitous. By the thirteenth century, the chronicler Caesarius of Heisterbach (who, like Gerald, delighted in retelling tales he had heard) reported so many stories of demons having intercourse with men and women that he claimed the practice was almost commonplace.

The evidence indicates that over time people

in the Middle Ages changed their opinion about bestiality. Official culture, as expressed primarily in the secular and religious law codes, at first treated the practice as not serious, equating it with masturbation. By the thirteenth century, however, Thomas Aquinas ranked bestiality as the worst of the sexual sins, and the law codes recommended harsh penalties for the practice. Official culture's growing preoccupation with bestiality may have influenced chroniclers recording folktales about the practice, because only after the twelfth century do the sources show an increase in such stories as those of Gerald of Wales. However, it is impossible to tell whether the recounting of incidents of sexual contact with animals reflected a new preoccupation simply on the part of members of official culture, who then chose to notice folktales that were already in circulation, or whether the new preoccupation permeated all of society, which then generated new tales of the practice. Nor is it possible to determine the relationship between the frequency of actual bestial intercourse and the growing popularity of stories about the practice.

In *The Beast Within*, Joyce Salisbury argues that the change in attitudes toward the practice of bestiality reflected a growing uncertainty about the separation of humans and animals. Preoccupation with and legislation against bestial intercourse thus expressed an attempt to secure the separation of species when that separation seemed endangered.

See also: Gerald of Wales; Olaf, Saint

—Joyce E. Salisbury

Bestiary. A book of imaginative and often moralized descriptions of various animals.

It would be unfair to suggest that the Bestiary is a compendium of what passed for natural history in the Middle Ages, or even that it is a handbook of the fauna, real and imagined, that inhabited the medieval world. Indeed, it is misguided of modern scholars to complain of the fantasies recorded about the various animals in these books as if their authors were particularly inept or even mendacious zoologists—it is anachronistic to see these books as handbooks of natural history, even moralized natural history. It was a matter of indifference to medieval clerics whether or not the habits ascribed to the various animals were actually true; what mattered was that these details could be read analogically as so many lessons in the Book of Nature promoting Christian virtues and discouraging vice. Modern scholars have too often, if for understandable reasons, been bedazzled by the Bestiary's illustrations at the expense of inquiring into its textual history.

The earliest extant illustrated Bestiary is the ninth-century Bern manuscript, but its style of illustration shows that it derives from a late-classical model of the fourth century or earlier. The text and illustrative cycle of the Bestiary as written in the central Middle Ages is essentially an English elaboration of a late-classical poem known as the *Physiologus*. Ron Baxter's analysis of the structure of the *Physiologus* reveals that its 36 chapters are divided into eight thematic groups, with the first chapter in each group referring to Christ and introducing the theme of the rest of the chapters in its group; the themes are Avoidance of Vice, the Jews and Gentiles, the Letter and the Spirit of the Law, Human Renunciation of the Devil, the Community of the Faithful, the Avoidance of the Devil's Snares by Turning to Christ, the Power of Christ in the Community of Saints, and Christ's Incarnation. Within groups the succession of animals can sometimes be shown to derive from some biblical prompt: in Group 3, for example, the hedgehog, in chapter 13, follows the siren and centaur, chapter 12, because all three creatures are mentioned in the verse from Isaiah quoted at the opening of chapter 12. The taxonomic principle of the *Physiologus* is shown to be fundamentally theological, based on the moralization to be drawn from each beast, so that even prescientific "commonsensical" categories such as birds, fish, and land animals find themselves jumbled together in any given grouping, to the despair of modern zoologically oriented scholars. Considering the overall structure of the work, the *Physiologus* is thus characterized as a treatise on virtue and vice.

On English soil this text evolved into the peculiarly English genre of the Bestiary. There are now known to be as many as 50 extant manuscripts of the work, and it has recently been suggested that the original English population of this popular work must have been somewhere in the order of 250–350 books. Detailed examination of library catalogs and other evidence proves conclusively that in medieval eyes these works were regarded principally as collections of exempla, handy for use in sermons, and, indeed, not all have illustrations. Careful analysis of the ownership of Bestiaries by the various religious orders shows a marked enthusiasm for them among the Cistercian monks, in whose sermons the creatures are frequently moralized.

Extant manuscripts are conventionally divided into four textual "families." Broadly speaking, First Family manuscripts follow the text of the *Physiologus* most closely; the Second Family, somewhat later, introduces materials from Isidore of Seville and others. The small Third Family uses different supplementary texts, especially the *Pantheologus* of Petrus Londiniensis; rearranges the animal groups of the Second Family; and opens with a discussion derived from Isidore of the so-called monstrous races. These literally marginal races, placed at the edges of *mappaemundi* (world maps), such as that from Hereford, are illustrated in some Bestiaries, such as the late-thirteenth-century York Bestiary. The Fourth Family is represented by only one manuscript, housed in Cambridge University Library and dated about 1425.

When in "The Nun's Priest's Tale" Chaucer compares Chanticleer's crowing to the singing of the "mermayde in the see," his appeal to authority is couched in the words "For Phisiologus seith" (7.3270f.), implying the poet's familiarity with the frequent introductory formula, "*Physiologus dicit,*" of the Latin manuscripts. Though it is clear that the popularity of the Bestiary was on the wane by the date of *The Canterbury Tales*, on the Continent, at least, Theobald's version of the *Physiologus* enjoyed a modest renaissance with the advent of printing, and at least a dozen early printed editions are known.

Some well-known Bestiary stories are in fact only found in the vernacular texts, such as the crocodile's tears in the Anglo-Norman French verse Bestiary of Philippe de Thaon, dedicated to Henry I's queen and composed around 1135 (two of the three known manuscripts of which were written in England). More popular, surviving in more than 20 manuscripts, was the Anglo-Norman *Bestiaire Divin* of Guillaume le Clerc (c. 1210), some manuscripts of which were copied in England and most of which are illustrated. These Anglo-Norman Bestiaries constitute further important evidence for the great popularity of the work in England.

Of course, we must not necessarily infer Bestiary symbolism when confronted with Bestiary imagery, but the evidence of such outside the scriptorium is not without interest and, surely sometimes at least, not without symbolic import. One such case where we may be certain that the artist based his composition on a Bestiary manuscript is the archivolt of the mid-twelfth-century south doorway of the church at Alne, Yorkshire, which includes nine voussoirs (wedge-shaped stones in an arch) whose Bestiary origin are confirmed by their inscriptions.

Baxter has shown that the First Family Bestiary (still a preponderantly *Physiologus* text) was, like its parent, above all a work amenable to oral public performance, whereas the Second and Third Family manuscripts have moved into the study, for private consultation. The celebrated illustrations are also, he concludes, of little or no didactic value; their only value apart from decoration would be as a "finding aid" for a solitary reader looking for a particular chapter, and it is significant that even the earliest First Family manuscripts have already dropped the illustration of the moralizations that can still be seen in the illustrated Brussels *Physiologus*.

However, it is for its—to the modern eye—quirky illustrations and many of the commonplaces of medieval and early modern beliefs about the behavior of real and imagined animals that the Bestiary will be most often remembered. Whether or not it is the earliest source of some of the best-known stories and beliefs about animals, there is no doubt that it was one of the most influential, and several persisted into modern times or modern idiom, such as the statement that the

bear literally "licks into shape" its cubs, or that the fox plays dead in order to pounce on unsuspecting carrion birds, the latter moralized thus: "The Devil has the same nature: with all those living according to the Flesh he feigns himself to be dead until he gets them in his gullet and punishes them."

Another remarkable case is that of the stag, which

> is called *cervus* from its habit of snuffling up the *cerastes* which are horned snakes.... When they feel themselves to be weighed down by illness, they suck snakes from their holes with a snort of the nostrils and, having survived the danger of their venom, the stags are restored to health by a meal of them.

This passage not only typifies the absurd etymologizing (ultimately dependent on Isidore), but it is also typically moralized: "After snuffing up the Devil-snake, i.e., after the perpetration of sin, they run with confession to Our Lord Jesus Christ, who is the true fountain, and, drinking the precepts laid down by him, our Christians are renovated." It is typical, too, in that it presumably alludes to the biblical "panting hart" of Psalm 42 with its very similar moralization of a beast image. It is thus possible that the conjunction of the stag and snake sculpted on the Norman tympanum at Parwich (Derbyshire) is not wholly fortuitous; it might even be that the stag-and-snakes panel picked out in minute gold filigree work on the paten associated with the recently discovered ninth-century Derrynaflan chalice owes its origin to the same late-classical natural history source (but note that the story is also found in Pliny).

It seems likely that the person who carved the bird on a misericord at Denston had the Bestiary story in mind, for he has shown it clutching a pebble in its claw; should it fall asleep while on guard duty, the pebble will drop on its foot and wake it. The elephant allegedly had no joints in its knees and so was obliged to lean up against trees to rest; the hunter would saw almost through such supporter trees so that next time the elephant leaned against it, both would fall down, and the animal, unable to rise again, could be killed. The Bestiary method of capturing a unicorn is similarly unsporting: the unicorn is seduced—and the word does not seem inappropriate in the palpably suggestive context of this fantasy—into laying its horned head in the lap of a naked virgin, whereupon the hunter jumps out from behind a tree and spears it! (See illustration in this volume.) This unlikely method of capture is frequently depicted, as on a misericord at Stratford-upon-Avon. Tiger cubs might be captured by dropping mirrors to confuse the pursuing tigress, who, seeing her own reflection in the mirror, believes it to be her abducted cub.

The whale's appetite for small fish, lured by a sweet odor emitted from its mouth, was compared by the Bestiary to the devil's appetite for men: his attractions lure men of little faith to their destruction, as in the unintentionally humorous scene of the sailors whose ship comes to rest on the back of a whale where they make a campfire. From among the birds, we may single out for mention the eagle, which tests the fearless gaze of its young by obliging them to stare at the sun; those that avert their eyes are cast out. Whether original with the Bestiary or not, its stories and its illustrative tradition undoubtedly had a marked influence on late-medieval art and thought, from such an apparently frivolous image as that of the mermaid (originally appearing in the earliest Bestiaries as a siren of the bird-type but in later manuscripts depicted in the familiar fish-tailed form), to the far more theologically significant icon of the "Pelican in her piety," that is, pecking her own breast in order to feed her nestlings on the blood, a type of Christ's sacrifice for humankind.

See also: Griffin; Iconography; Mermaid; Unicorn

—Malcolm Jones

Black Death. Name given to the catastrophic plague pandemic in late-medieval Europe. The plague raged throughout Europe from 1347 through 1351.

The disease, spread by fleas, has three main forms: bubonic, septicemic, and pneumonic. The bubonic form is characterized by a gangrenous pustule at the site of the initial bite, followed by swelling of the lymph nodes. As the infection progresses, buboes (subcutaneous hemorrhages) appear. Ultimately the disease leads to neurological dysfunction and, in 50–60 percent of victims, death. The pneumonic form is far more deadly, with more than 90 percent of the victims dying. Pneumonic plague occurs mostly in colder climates. In the rarest form of the plague, the septicemic form, bacilli enter the bloodstream, causing a rash, and death follows within a day. The septicemic form is always fatal. The plague bacillus, *Yersinia pestis*, is carried by two types of fleas, *Xenopsylla cheopis* and *Pulex irritans*. The flea bites serve as a primary infection source. In the case of pneumonic plague, secondary infection, from human to human, occurs through bodily secretions, most notably saliva.

The Black Death appears to have sprung up in East Asia, although the plague is known to be native to numerous parts of the world, including Yunnan, China, central Asia, Iran, Libya, East Africa, and the Arabian Peninsula. Well-developed trade routes from East Asia to the Black Sea allowed for movement of goods both overland and by sea to transshipment points serving Europe. The plague reached the Crimean port of Caffa in 1345, spreading from there to the eastern ports of the Mediterranean Sea. In 1347 the plague reached Constantinople. From there it spread quickly to the European continent. The plague arrived in the Sicilian port of Messina in October 1347, and later that same year, the ports of Genoa and Marseilles. Thence it traveled west and north, reaching Paris in the spring of 1348. It skipped over the English Channel into southern England, traveled along the coast, and reached London in the autumn of 1348. In German-speaking lands it went on to both Switzerland and Austria, eventually following trade routes up through Basel, Frankfurt, Cologne, and Bremen.

Mortality rates for the plague were extraordinarily high. Even by conservative estimates, there is strong circumstantial evidence that close to one-quarter of the entire population of Europe died during the Black Death. For example, when the plague reached Holland the mortality was so high that all work on land reclamation along the Zuider Zee stopped. In Bremen, records from the period suggest a mortality rate of close to 50 percent. Some villages, certainly, were completely wiped out by the plague, but estimates of mortality for Europe suggesting close to 90 percent should be considered unlikely. Before the Black Death the plague had reared its head in an earlier pandemic, commonly referred to as the Justinian plague, that ravaged southern Europe from 541 to 544. Later pandemics of the plague also continued to wreak havoc on Europe up through the early eighteenth century.

The extraordinary virulence of the plague, and the huge numbers of victims it claimed, profoundly affected the cultural expressions of many Europeans. The plague became the subject of legends, beliefs, ballads, paintings, and rituals, and it influenced literary works such as Boccaccio's *Decameron*. Recurring plague pandemics and epidemics in Europe ensured the continued relevance of many of these folkloric expressions, and legends concerning the plague could still be collected in the twentieth century.

In plague legends the disease is often portrayed in human form. One of the best-known personifications of the plague from central Europe is the Austrian *Pest Jungfrau* (Plague Maiden), who was said to fly over the land enveloped in a blue flame spreading disease and death in her wake. The celestial nature of the plague figure is also preserved in British tradition. These stories perhaps relate to the common belief that the plague was caused by the wrath of God and portended the end of the world. Other folk belief, reinforced by medieval medical conceptions of disease, maintained that the plague entered the body as a vapor. In postmedieval Scandinavian tradition, particularly from Sweden and Norway, the plague was represented as a traveling couple, often an old man and an old woman carrying a shovel and a broom: "When he [the plague] went forth with his shovel, some people were spared; but where she went forth with her broom, not even a mother's child was left alive."

In the fourteenth century there was very little knowledge of how diseases such as the plague spread. One thing people did know, however, was that the plague came from outside their communities. Numerous plague stories mention ships drifting ashore with dead crews and subsequent outbreaks of the plague. Other traditions mention an unknown animal running through the village spreading the disease. In yet other traditions, wandering mendicants or witches are identified as the disease carrier.

Some of the best-known representations of the Black Death center on the phenomenon of the *danse macabre* (Dance of Death), although the first *danse macabre* was probably not held until August 1424 in Paris. The dance, led by a figure dressed as death, was intended to scare off diseases. Later historians have attempted to link the frenetic dancing associated with the plague to the neurological damage that the disease causes, suggesting that this choreomania was a physiological result of the disease.

The medieval population was generally unable to mount a significant defense against the onslaught of the disease. People felt, however, they had to do something to arrest or at least divert its spread. Fire was often seen as a preventive measure that would divert the plague vapors so they would not reach a village. Others maintained that the plague was unable to cross natural boundaries, such as streams or plowed fields. Numerous rituals sprang up that were intended to halt the plague's advance. Among the more colorful of these rituals is one from Eastern European tradition in which three naked virgins were forced to plow a furrow counterclockwise around the village. In other traditions, young children were buried alive to stop the plague. One of the better-known groups to develop during the time of the plague was the flagellants, a movement that started in Germany. The movement was closely related to the persecution of the Jews, whom some blamed for the plague, maintaining that Jews were poisoning wells and thereby causing the disease. The flagellant movement eventually dissolved into millenarianism and was condemned by the pope.

Numerous postmedieval stories concern the aftermath of the plague. The majority of these stories focus on the extraordinarily high mortality rate during the plague and tell of two lone survivors' subsequent repopulation of the area. Other stories mention the unpredictability of the plague, focusing on the randomness of its distribution in a region. Yet other stories mention the remarkable survival of individuals, often individuals who drove corpses to the cemetery for burial: "She had driven all the dead to the cemetery and had only one jade to drive them with, but she didn't get sick because she smoked a chalk pipe."

Although the plague is not at present a threat, a concern with the unimpeded spread of virulent, catastrophic disease continues to find expression in contemporary folklore. The AIDS epidemic and the emergence of other viral infectious agents, including hemorrhagic fevers such as the Ebola virus, are the subject of numerous contemporary legends and various folk beliefs.

See also: Funeral Customs and Burial Rites; *Memento mori*

—Timothy R. Tangherlini

Blasons Populaires. Generally known stereotypical statements directed against another ethnic, racial, social, professional, or religious group.

While *blason populaire* (signifying "conspicuous generalization") has become the international scholarly term for verbal stereotypes, it has gained no general acceptance, nor has the term *ethnophaulisms* (disparaging statements about any given group of people). The term *ethnic slurs* has become the generally accepted designation for such stereotypes in English. Blasons populaires, or ethnic slurs, are thus verbal statements that have as their topics the generalized characteristics of another group based on stereotypes, national character, ethnocentrism, xenophobia, misogyny, homophobia, prejudice, racism, and so on.

It is impossible to speak of blasons populaires in terms of one genre because they may appear in many forms: single word, phrase, proverb, riddle, joke, or even short narrative. Those that are merely a word usually are nicknames for another group, such as "Krauts" for Germans or "frog eaters" for the French. Examples of short stereotypical phrases are "to go Dutch treat" or "not to have a Chinaman's chance," and two stereotypical proverbs are "Beware of Greeks bearing gifts" and "The only good Indian is a dead Indian." In their longer forms these slurs usually play one ethnic or national group against the other, as in such epigrammatic characterizations as "The Pole is a thief; the Prussian, a traitor; the Bohemian, a heretic; and the Swabian, a chatterbox" or "The Russians act out of terror and compulsion, the Germans out of obedience, the Swiss because they want peace, the Poles in order to have free choice, the French for the sake of their king's glory, and the English for the love of freedom."

Ethnic slurs in the form of riddles are as popular as ethnic jokes—as, for example "What are the three shortest books in the world? *Italian War Heroes, Jewish Business Ethics,* and *Who's Who in Puerto Rico.*" Stereotypical descriptions of outsiders are internationally disseminated, as might best be illustrated by the many traditional phrases alluding to venereal disease in which one nationality chooses a neighboring one to refer to this stigmatized disease: the "French disease" (by the English), the "Spanish disease" (by the Germans), the "Polish disease" (by the Russians), and so on.

Their form does not present a satisfactory basis for typing blasons populaires; rather, it is the function of these traditional insults or mockeries that binds them together as folk expressions. It has been noted in the scholarship on stereotypes that not all of them are necessarily malicious or evil. Stereotypes uttered as self-descriptions by a particular group are especially likely to be employed humorously or ironically. If there is such a thing as national character, then the "kernel of truth" argument would in fact hold that there is some slight validity to some stereotypes. Why would group members otherwise employ derogatory statements, expressed as invectives against them by others, to ridicule themselves? Nevertheless, stereotypes and verbal prejudices become immediately problematic socially and psychologically when directed as ethnic or racial slurs with evil intent toward the outside group. Usually those using such expressions are not aware that they are projecting their own fear, anxieties, and insecurities onto others by calling them names and making them the butts of their jokes.

The scholarly collection and study of blasons populaires went hand in hand with other major collecting projects during the nineteenth century. The two most significant collections of that time are Otto von Reinsberg-Düringsfeld's *Internationale Titulaturen* (1863) and Henri Gaidoz and Paul Sebillot's *Blason populaire de la France* (1884). They have been augmented by Abraham Roback's *Dictionary of International Slurs* (1944) and Hugh Rawson's *Wicked Words* (1989). These dictionaries include texts dating back to classical and medieval times, but many others with more-precise references are contained in the nine volumes of Hans Walther's *Proverbia sententiaeque latinitatis medii aevi* (1963–1986) and in the nine volumes of Samuel Singer's *Thesaurus proverbiorium medii aevi* (vol. 1, 1995). Vincent Stuckey Lean has also included numerous medieval English texts in the first volume of his *Collectanea* (1902–1904), as has Bartlett Jere Whiting in his *Proverbs, Sentences, and Proverbial Phrases from English Writings Mainly before 1500* (1968). For example, the last collection includes medieval expressions such as "Britons are boasters," "Englishmen are changeable," "Frenchmen sin in lechery, Englishmen in envy," "Scots are full of guile," and "The Welsh ever love treachery." This major collection also includes many proverbial invectives against women that reflect the misogynist's attitudes about medieval life: "Woman's words are but wind," "Women are the devil's mousetraps," and "Women can weep with one eye and laugh with the other." Wayland Hand collected numerous medieval slurs against people with red hair in his *Dictionary of Words and Idioms Associated with Judas Iscariot* (1942), and Carolyn Prager, in her article "'If I Be Devil'" (1987), has shown how the proverb "The Ethiopian cannot change his skin" (Jer. 13:23) has been employed as a biblical blason populaire in medieval and Renaissance literature. Yet many more such studies investigating the origin, history, and meaning of ethnic slurs are needed.

Much is known about medieval Latin blasons populaires, but very little systematic investigation has taken place about traditional insults in the vernacular languages of the Middle Ages. There are many in the literary works of such authors as Chrétien de Troyes, Geoffrey Chaucer, Hartmann von Aue, and others. Most of these texts are listed in Singer's multivolume collection of medieval proverbs. For example, under the keyword *Deutsch* (German), he lists 34 texts from various vernacular languages: "Germans are no real Christians and nobody's friends" (Latin); "The angriest people live in Germany" (French); "Nature took good care of us when it placed the Alps between us and the anger of the Germans" (Italian); "We Germans are wild, rough, and angry people" (German); "Germans don't want to do anything else but to drink" (Italian); "A Polish bridge, a Bohemian monk, a Swabian nun, an Austrian soldier, the piety of the Italians and the fasting of the Germans are not worth a bean" (Latin); "A German worries about the damage only after the deed" (German); and "In many ways Germans are beyond any rationality" (French). It is important to note from these examples that traditional insults can also be directed against one's own group. But for the most part ethnic slurs are spiteful invectives against the outsiders or foreigners seen as a collective group, generalizations that are quickly proven wrong when individual members of the ridiculed or aggressively insulted group do not behave in the manner described. Ethnic and racial slurs were ill conceived in classical and medieval times, and they continue to be dangerous verbal weapons today. The fact that many of them together with new invectives are in use to this day is ample proof that they need to be studied historically, comparatively, and critically in their social contexts. A better understanding of the meaning of blasons populaires will lead to a clearer appreciation of ethnic and racial tensions on the local and international level. Many of today's stereotypes and prejudices date back to medieval times, and their longevity is a clear indication of the task that still lies ahead to free the world of such preconceived and ill-founded notions.

See also: Jews, Stereotypes of; Proverbs

—Wolfgang Mieder

Blood. Bodily fluid of fundamental importance in medieval medicine and physiology, with uniquely ambiguous symbolic significance.

Medieval conceptions and uses of blood—including medical, religious, magical, anti-Semitic, courtly, and political ones—are characterized by their combination of opposites. For instance, blood can be both cleansing and contaminating, nourishing and inedible. Blood both reinforces and violates bodily boundaries, and it marks both exclusion and sameness in social groups.

The unique significance attributed to blood is perhaps most obvious in ideas of blood as a life force, ideas found not just in the Middle Ages but also in classical Greek, Roman, Egyptian, and biblical texts. Similar medieval constructions of blood as vital can be observed in the role of Christ's Eucharistic blood signifying his life (a development of classical blood sacrifices); in the medical preoccupation with stemming blood loss; and in magical rituals of bewitchment or of selling one's soul to the devil, where blood could represent the whole person. Traditionally, many scholars have regarded this association of blood with life as nearly universal, and they have explained it by assuming that many cultures establish a connection between blood loss and wounding or death and thus consider blood itself to contain the vanishing life and strength.

At all levels of medieval medicine, blood was commonly conceived of both as the cause of and the cure for many diseases. While learned medicine in the classical tradition had developed elaborate theories that imbalances of bodily fluids, as well as poisonous residues in the blood, were the cause of all illness, folk medicine often seems to have seen diseases quite literally as residing in the blood. Discharging it through bloodletting thus largely sufficed to maintain or regain health. Magical practices often complemented and overlapped with medical uses; the tenth-century Anglo-Saxon *Leechbook*, for instance, requires that the blood extracted to cure spider bites be subsequently applied to a green hazel stick and thrown away over a road.

Nevertheless, medieval medicine was also concerned with avoiding and controlling any spillage of the precious substance. Numerous charms to stanch bleeding in humans and animals survive in Latin and several vernacular languages from throughout the Middle Ages, often mixing pagan and Christian elements. Common types of such charms draw analogies between the stopping of the blood and the river Jordan or Christ's blood. Bloodletting was also subject to various regulations; it was recommended only on certain days of the lunar cycle and considered dangerous on others, as elaborate popular calendars specify.

Human and animal blood was even prescribed as a cure for many ailments, usually by being applied externally to the afflicted body part. Some manuscripts also recommend that magic spells be uttered simultaneously or even written in the blood itself. In literature and legend, the blood of innocent children or virgins could cure leprosy, a disease presented as a punishment for sinfully proud and lecherous behavior.

Menstrual blood, which combined the dangers of blood with those of feminine sexuality, was perceived as especially polluting and destructive. Learned texts claim that, among other things, it causes fruit to fall from trees and grain not to sprout, as well as rabies and a variation of the evil eye. A child conceived during menstruation could turn out to be not only red-haired but also leprous. On the other hand, according to physiological theory, menstrual blood sustained the fetus, and even milk was nothing but processed

blood. Hildegard von Bingen (d. 1179) believed that a mere cloth stained with menstrual blood could protect against blows and fire.

The magical powers ascribed to blood go far beyond healing ones. It was the prime substance used by necromancers to conjure up demons. According to magical recipes, anointing one's eyes with bat's blood could improve night vision, while lion's blood protected against other animals. Bathing in dragon's blood also made the Nordic hero Sigurd's skin impenetrable. Penitentials and books of magic give ample evidence of blood being frequently used as a love potion (e.g., by mixing one's own blood into the beloved's food or drink to arouse her or his love). The widespread belief that a victim's corpse begins to bleed again in the presence of the murderer was even accepted as juridical proof in many late-medieval laws (the so-called bier right).

The Church generally saw blood as a pollutant, which was theologically justified by its association with bloodshed and sin, but nevertheless increasingly encouraged popular devotion to focus on blood, be it the blood of saints, martyrs, or Christ. Such holy blood worked miracles; stayed fresh for years; cured blindness, paralysis, and leprosy; restored severed limbs; and more. A famous example of a saint whose blood worked miracles is Thomas Becket (d. 1170); thousands of pilgrims went in search of healing to Canterbury. Saints' legends also tell of demons and blood being jointly forced out of the body of the possessed.

Christ's wounded body and blood became a similar focus of popular devotion in the late Middle Ages, in the form of his rediscovered relics from the Crucifixion, images of the suffering Christ as Man of Sorrows, and blood collected by the Church from the wound in his side. Mystics describe themselves as drinking blood and milk from Christ's wounds (and the Virgin's breasts) to represent their compassion with him and the comfort and redemption received from his passion.

The blood of the Eucharist became another extremely popular object of devotion in the thirteenth century, as it was made the central rite of Christianity and the key image of Christ's salvation and spiritual nourishment. Eucharistic miracle stories and pictures told of hosts beginning to bleed or even turning into a bleeding body. This typically happened either to reward pious believers, when Jews tried to desecrate stolen hosts by stabbing or soiling them, or when Christians (usually women or heretics) doubted the actual presence of Christ's flesh and blood in the bread and wine (which was declared a dogma in 1215). One of the earliest of these stories tells of the Mass of St. Gregory, a seventh-century legend that became highly popular in the thirteenth century, in which the host turns into a bloody finger in order to convince a doubting woman of the real presence of Christ in the sacrament. Such miracles often initiated major pilgrimages (e.g., in Wilsnack in Germany from 1383).

Witches were associated with blood from the thirteenth century onward and were thought to abuse its powers in their potions (e.g., to cause impotence). The late-medieval idea of witches itself partly derives from classical and perhaps Germanic beliefs in blood-sucking women, as well as from fantasies about cults drinking and worshipping either menstrual blood or that of children (often born of incest). Roman writers were the first to accuse early Christians of such blood drinking in orgies of incest, sodomy, infanticide, and ritual cannibalism. Similar charges were repeated throughout the Middle Ages against several Christian splinter groups. Church and secular laws as well as penitentials frequently condemned but increasingly also shared and even cultivated the belief in such cannibalistic practices and their synthesis in the witch figure.

Jews were accused of and persecuted for similar bloody offenses. In addition to the traditional biblical allegation of having called Christ's blood upon them, Jews were linked with blood in other ways from the thirteenth century onward. At this time there appeared not only many bloody Eucharistic miracle tales but also charges of ritual murder of Christians (usually boys). This belief, the blood libel legend, led to accusations of murder in about 100 cases and perhaps more, mostly in Germany between the thirteenth and the sixteenth centuries; they persisted well into the twentieth century. While allegations of ritual murder go back to at least the case of William of Norwich (d. 1144), the first accusation that Jews had murdered Christians for their blood was probably in a case in the German town of Fulda in 1235, when 34 local Jews were killed as a consequence. The reasons cited for the supposed Jewish need for Christian blood vary, combining tales of cannibalism, crucifixion, ritual, and magic (e.g., blood was said to be required for the healing of hemorrhages or blindness, for circumcision, or for the preparation of unleavened bread). Jews and lepers were also said to have caused the Black Death in Aquitaine by poisoning wells with blood, among other substances.

This tendency of medieval people to think about blood in terms of contrast and opposition can be explained psychoanalytically by the ambiguous stance—comprising a mixture of rejection and desire—toward bodily emissions. It also fits anthropologist Mary Douglas's definition of a pollutant as something that resists neat categorization and is thus both considered dirty and to be avoided and yet given a place in a central ritual of the culture to incorporate its power. Moreover, Douglas sees much of the symbolic value of blood resulting from the analogy between the physical and the social body, where blood represents dangerous margins and transgressions of the social unit.

See also: Eucharist; Evil Eye; Jews, Stereotypes of; Medicine; Vampire; Witchcraft

—Bettina Bildhauer

Books of Hours. Devotional books designed for laypeople, deriving their name from the *Horae beatae Mariae Virginis* (Hours of the Blessed Virgin Mary) and the Marian office contained in them.

Although they were partially composed of liturgical texts contained in the Breviary, they are best known for their extraliturgical prayers, which were widely diffused in the late Middle Ages. From the thirteenth century onward books of hours tended to be physically small, but they often were lavishly decorated and illustrated. These illuminations came to include images of secular as well as religious import, so that in the famous fifteenth-century *Très riches heures* (Very Splendid Hours) and *Belles heures* (Beautiful Hours) of Jean, duke of Berry, there are remarkable pictures of both aristocratic and peasant activities, pictures that provide invaluable evidence about everyday life. Generally books of hours were extremely popular in the fourteenth and fifteenth centuries, especially in France and the Low Countries, and they appear to have survived in greater numbers than any other kind of medieval book.

The first such books had developed much earlier, in the great Carolingian abbeys, with the custom—later diffused through the influence of Cluny, a very famous abbey—of adding to the choral Office of Hours a number of supplementary prayers, such as the seven penitential psalms, litanies, offices of the dead and of the Virgin, and suffrages in honor of God and the saints. Such materials became the main elements of the books of hours, although they were characterized by a rich number of variants. Thus, by the twelfth century the book of hours was conceived of as a supplement inserted at the end of the Psalter (the Psalms of the Bible), sometimes at the end of the missal, or, more rarely, at the end of the Breviary. From the early thirteenth century onward, after its separation from the liturgical books and the introduction of new elements, it constituted an autonomous type of book. The widespread diffusion of the books of hours in the late Middle Ages can be explained as a consequence of new trends in spirituality that by emphasizing personal attitudes in the devotional life stimulated the utilization and circulation of religious objects for private purposes. From the fourteenth century onward, the patterns of pious life provided individuals, rather than just congregations, with a more intense contact with sacred texts, conceived of as means to guide the believer, through meditative reading, to the way of contemplation that came to be known as *devotio moderna*—a form of "modern devotion" fostering very personal, even mystical, approaches to the sacred.

Books of hours were used not only by the educated aristocracy, which undoubtedly provided a model for sumptuous commissions, but also by the middle classes, who exerted an increasingly important role in the intellectual and spiritual life of the period. The popularity of books of hours in France and the Low Countries was a consequence both of the greater interest in the *devotio moderna* in these regions and of the key role played there by the educated middle classes.

In some cases the calendar, the litanies, or the local prayers reveal the destination of the manuscript by their relationship to specific cults. The insertion of special prayers could be owing to the donor's commission, and such insertions might include prayers designed to ask for or take away good or bad weather, to beseech the Virgin's and a special saint's intercession against illnesses and plagues, or to petition for a good death. From the fourteenth century onward Latin texts are often followed by vernacular prayers, especially those in honor of saints whose cults were widely popular, such as Catherine (against afflictions of the tongue), Christopher (against accidents while traveling), Margaret (invoked by pregnant women), and George (against skin diseases). Otherwise the donors could order the transcription of singular or adapted texts: specific references to the donor are often revealed in the litanies or in prayers relating to local contexts. Since they were relatively free from ecclesiastical control, the private use of books of hours stimulated the emergence of a wide range of texts whose decoration and illustration are among their most important elements. The humbler books are decorated by initials, marking the beginning of each text, and frames or borders, characterized on almost every page by vegetal patterns sometimes displaying animals. In the more sumptuous manuscripts, an illustrative cycle is added to the decorations.

The Marian cycle that became standard in the fourteenth century illustrates the office of the Virgin and includes the episodes of Christ's Birth and Childhood, from the Annunciation through the Coronation of the Virgin. Alternatively, the Marian office is sometimes illustrated as a Passion cycle, from the Betrayal through the Deposition, as in the *Hours of William de Brailes*. The penitential psalms could also be illustrated by episodes of David's life or, from the end of the fifteenth century onward, by scenes pertaining to Job. The Office of the Dead was more freely illustrated, sometimes by representing the funeral, the Encounter of the Living and the Dead, or the judgment of a single person, as in the *Rohan Book of Hours*. The calendar was usually illustrated with the labors of the months and the relative zodiacal signs. Portraits and hagiographic scenes often corresponded to the prayers of the saints, while the sections devoted to the Gospels usually displayed the Evangelists' images and sometimes

also their symbols—the angel (or a man) for Matthew, the lion for Mark, the bull for Luke, and the eagle for John. The prayers to the Virgin, accompanied by an image of the Virgin and Child, sometimes displayed (in the most sumptuous exemplars) the portrait of the donor kneeling or being introduced to the Virgin by a holy intercessor. The ateliers that crafted books of hours, especially in great centers such as Paris or Bruges, often engaged in mass production by sharing the work of transcription and decoration or illustration among a number of specialized copyists and illuminators. The display of different techniques and styles reveals the variety of operations adopted in fashioning each manuscript. Since books of hours were usually destined for private use, some parts could be designed to accommodate the insertion of a coat of arms after the purchase of the manuscript.

Although their primary function was religious devotion, in the later Middle Ages books of hours eventually came to depict the social life of the secular world as well. For example, in the *Très riches heures* there is a sequence of illuminated pages accompanying the calendar for each month of the year. For the months of January, April, May, and August, scenes of aristocratic life show men and women in lavish dress feasting, riding, and courting in gestures reminiscent of romances. For the other months, however, we see ordinary farmworkers, both women and men, as they progress through the annual agricultural cycle. Thus, in February the firewood is being cut and the sheepfold tended in heavy snow, while a man and a woman inside raise their garments to warm their legs and feet before the fire, though the woman by the doorway raises her skirt more decorously. March finds the workers digging and plowing, still wrapped against the cold, but June pictures them lightly clad and barefoot for the warmer weather. Here the men cut green stalks with scythes, while one woman uses a pitchfork and another a rake to gather the stalks into piles. In July men harvest wheat with sickles in the background, while a couple shear sheep in the foreground. Dress has become increasingly informal for farmworkers, and some men are depicted here and in other warm months in nothing more than shirt and drawers. Although August foregrounds an outing of aristocrats, dressed in unseasonably warm attire, in the background are peasant men and women openly bathing nude in a pond while nearby workers appear not to notice (nor does the aristocratic party). September and October complete the scenes of working in the fields, while November depicts pig farming and December shows a grisly scene of hunting dogs tearing apart a boar. These depictions of ordinary secular life provide us with extraordinary views of the social life of the time. (See illustrations.)

In theory, the reading of books of hours corresponded to the official liturgical hours; however, their use in private homes and their illustrative programs suggest that they were definitely utilized in private devotions and in the late-medieval practice of meditation, as supported by the contemplation of images. Otherwise, the donors could read them in silence during the Eucharistic celebration. Although the most sumptuous books of hours constituted a minor part of the general production, they were thought of as precious objects to collect and exhibit.

See also: Iconography; Manuscript Marginalia

—Fabrizio Crivello

Boy Bishop, Feast of the. A liturgical feast of misrule and role reversal among the choirboys, held during the Christmas season on St. Nicholas's Day (December 6) or Holy Innocents' Day (December 28).

The earliest mention of the Feast of the Boy Bishop appears in manuscripts from the monastery of St. Gall in 911, when the German king Conrad I visited the monastery during the actual ceremony. The Winchester Troper of about 980 mentions this feast, along with the feasts of the deacons and priests, and all three feasts were commonly known as the Christmas triduum. Whereas the Feast of Fools became very popular in France, it was in England, with its rich tradition of boy choristers and alto choirs, that the Feast of the Boy Bishop had its greatest popularity.

Various locations celebrated this feast either on December 6, the feast day of St. Nicholas, the patron saint of children and scholars, or on December 28, the Feast of the Holy Innocents. By the eleventh century most Boy Bishop celebrations were on Holy Innocents' Day, since it had become the official feast day of students and choirboys, and also because it was closer to the dates of the other feasts of misrule, such as the Feast of Fools.

The boy bishop was chosen by his peers in the cathedral choir, the monastery school, or the grammar school. On Holy Innocents' Day the boys would rise up from their choir stalls during vespers, literally throwing the bishop and his colleagues out of their chairs, and install the chosen boy as their "bishop." Vested in the clothing of a bishop, with miter and staff, he would preside over the ceremonies of the day, at some times and places reading serious sermons and at others participating in the reading of "farcical letters." The boy bishop paraded through the town or parish with his entourage, blessing the people and receiving gifts and alms. Later the alms collected would pay for a party of celebration.

Late-medieval records attest that this feast of misrule grew increasingly distasteful to the clergy and sometimes led to violence. The boys would often ruin church vestments and ornaments and would bully parishioners for money and gifts or vandalize their property. They also sang mocking songs—for example, a record from Hamburg, dated 1304, states that the schoolboys had agreed to refrain from "making rhymes, in Latin or in German, which would stain the reputation of anyone" (trans. E. K. Chambers in his *Mediaeval Stage*, vol. 1 [1903], p. 351).

Because this and other feasts of misrule were perceived as threatening to the clergy, there was a strong movement in the Church from the thirteenth century onward to banish these feasts. On the Continent, in 1431 the Council of Basel restricted the Boy Bishop celebrations to some extent, although they were revived periodically as late as the eighteenth century. In England Henry VIII abolished the custom in 1512; it was revived by Queen Mary during her reign and was finally abolished permanently by Elizabeth I.

See also: Carnival; Christmas; Festivals and Celebrations; Fools, Feast of

—Bradford Lee Eden

Brigid, Saint (d. c. 525) [Saint Brighid]. A female saint who, along with St. Patrick and St. Columba, is viewed as one of the founders of Christian institutions in Ireland and is the subject of numerous, widely popular legends.

Little is known of St. Brigid except that she lived in the late fifth and early sixth centuries and that she founded a famous and powerful episcopal monastery in Kildare that included both women and men. This episcopal see soon came into competition with that of Armagh, whose prestige derived from its association with St. Patrick, for supremacy in the Christian Church of Ireland. Perhaps at least partly to enhance the claims of Kildare, legends of St. Brigid, and especially of her numerous miracles both during her life and after her death, were spread throughout the land. Her cult likewise took root abroad, and there were many churches dedicated to her not only throughout England and Wales but also on the Continent, churches founded by Irish monks. Though her fame circulated mainly in oral tradition, written versions of her life, originally in Latin and Old Irish, were translated into Old French, Middle English, and German, providing evidence of her growing popularity as a universal rather than merely local saint.

The earliest life of St. Brigid was composed in Latin by a monk named Cogitosus in the middle of the seventh century, about 100 years after her death. Although he mentions written sources, Cogitosus evidently depends mainly on popular oral tradition, which, as he says, preserves the wonders she performed "in the memories of the people." According to Cogitosus, St. Brigid was born to noble parents, though that claim may have been no more than a way of giving her elevated status to justify her prominence in the Irish Church. Traditions developing, or at least recorded, somewhat later make her parents more humble. In the ninth century her mother is described as the slave of a druid, and an eighth-century account in Irish has her mother carrying milk to the druid's house at sunrise when she goes into labor and gives birth to the future saint with one foot outside and one foot on the druid's doorstep. We may already see here the associations of St. Brigid with milk and the dairy, with the light and fire of the sun, and with her role in the transformation of pagan Ireland to Christian Ireland.

In the first legend related by Cogitosus, the young Brigid is sent to the dairy to churn butter, but her generous nature impels her "to obey God rather than men," and so she gives away the milk and butter to poor people passing by. Fearing her mother's anger, she then prays for divine help and by a miracle her full quota of butter appears, even more than that produced by her coworkers. According to at least one early life in Irish, when she later decides to become a nun, the bishop who presides over her taking the veil is so "intoxicated" by her holiness that by mistake he reads over her the text for consecrating a bishop, thus giving her a status that is unique among women saints—though other accounts merely indicate that she and the bishop become partners in overseeing the monastery she founds.

There are various tales about her multiplying food, causing a cow to produce an abundance of milk, and even turning bathwater into beer for thirsty lepers. Her most famous legends include her hanging a wet cloak on a sunbeam to dry; her saving the life of a man who mistakenly killed the king's performing fox by producing another, equally talented fox; and her saving a woman's virtue: the woman had been tricked by a man who, lusting after her, had entrusted a brooch to her, stolen it from her, thrown it into the sea, and demanded in payment that she sleep with him; but he was thwarted by the saint, who directed a fisherman to cut open a fish he had caught, and there the lost brooch was found. All of these wonders are related by Cogitosus as signs of St. Brigid's special power, though students of folklore will recognize in them many of the features found in widespread folktales.

Perhaps the best-known legend about St. Brigid comes from a tradition later than Cogitosus. It relates how she received land for her monastery from a chieftain in Kildare, who had refused to give her more land than she could cover with her cloak. When she spread it out on the ground, it miraculously increased in size, covering such a large area that the chieftain begged her to make it stop before he lost all his land.

As in saints' lives generally, narratives of St. Brigid not only include numerous miraculous cures during her life but also after her death, which was commonly understood as the proof of sainthood. As her cult developed, later accounts include even more wonders. For example, in the twelfth century Gerald of Wales, in his *Topography of Ireland*, describes "Brigid's Fire" at the site of her foundation in Kildare, tended by nuns and by the saint herself, surrounded by a hedge that no man may cross lest he suffer the saint's curse. Gerald goes on to tell of one man who crossed it

who was driven mad and suffered a horrible death, and of another who put one foot over the hedge, whereupon his foot and leg perished and he remained a cripple the rest of his life.

This association of St. Brigid with fire appears to be connected to Cogitosus's placing the day of her death on February 1, which became her feast day in the Church and which coincides with the ancient festival of Imbolc, celebrating the beginning of spring and the return of the sun. Although it is still a matter of controversy among scholars, some argue that the saint is connected to the pre-Christian Celtic divinity also named Brigid, who was seen as a protector of her people and who was associated with the sun and light. In this view, legends of St. Brigid would have attributed to her some of the features of the earlier goddess, which would have enhanced the saint's reputation even though at the same time she is represented as distinctively Christian.

See also: Celtic Mythology; Irish Tradition; Patrick, Saint; Saints, Cults of the

—John McNamara

Brutus [Britus, Britto]. Legendary figure who, according to early histories, gave his name to Britain.

The quasi-learned traditions linking the origins of the Britons with Brutus are the Welsh expressions of the common European attempts to explain the origins of nations by reference either to the dispersion of the Trojans after the fall of their city or to the repopulating of the world by Noah's descendants after the Flood. These two accounts could, of course, be combined. The *Historia Brittonum* (History of the Britons, c. 830), attributed to Nennius, is the earliest witness and has three versions of the founding of Britain. In chapter 7, the island of Britain is named for Brutus, a Roman consul, probably derived from a notice in the chronicle of Eusebius-Jerome about the consul D. Junius Brutus (Callaicus) saying that "Brutus Hiberniam usque ad Occeanum subigit" [Brutus subjugated Ireland all the way to the Ocean]. This theme is not developed, and a more common explanation is found in chapter 17, a Welsh form of the "Frankish genealogy of nations" in which Brutus is the son of Hessitio, a descendant of Noah's son Japheth, and is one of four brothers—Francus, Romanus, Albanus, Britto—from whom are descended the Franks, Romans, Albans, and Britons.

But the origin tale that was generally adopted in the Welsh learned historical tradition was that in chapter 10. Here Brutus (Britto) is the son of Silvius, who was the son of Aeneas. The boy accidentally killed his father (as had been prophesied) and was driven from Italy. He and his followers came to the islands of the Tyrrhenian Sea but were driven from Greece because of the killing of Turnus by Aeneas. They came to Gaul, where Brutus founded the city of Tours, and then to Britain, which he and his followers settled. In chapter 18 the classical account is folded into biblical tradition as Brutus is described as a descendant of Japheth.

In his *Historia regum Brittaniae* (History of the Kings of Britain, c. 1138), Geoffrey of Monmouth closely followed the account in *Historia Brittonum*, chapter 10, but elaborated it greatly, bringing Brutus, after a number of adventures, to Albion, then inhabited by a few giants who were defeated by the new settlers. Geoffrey was inspired by the Frankish genealogy to create his own eponymous founders for the nations of Britain. He gave Brutus three sons who inherited the three parts of the island of Britain, Locrinus of England (*Lloegr* in Welsh), Albanactus of Scotland (*Alban* in Welsh), and Camber of Wales (*Cymru* in Welsh, *Cambria* in Latin). Geoffrey's account became the standard historical version of the settlement of Britain. The Welsh bards accepted this version, and in their eulogies to Welsh princes sometimes address them as the descendants of Aeneas. There are a few traces extant in medieval Welsh of native origin tales, but they are very fragmentary.

See also: Geoffrey of Monmouth; Nennius

—Brynley F. Roberts

Burgundian Cycle. Name traditionally attached to texts primarily in German and Scandinavian (but with texts and images all over the Western European medieval world) about the Völsungs and Niflungs/Nibelungen: Siegfried/Sigurd the Dragon-slayer, Brünhild/Brynhild, Kudrun, Günter/Gunnar, Hagen/Högni, and their loves and marriages, jealousies, battles, and final destruction.

The first recording of materials from the cycle is in the anonymous Latin epic *Waltharius* (ninth century), which is associated with the Carolingian court. There are also traces in Old English poetry. However, the principal manifestation is in the German epic *Nibelungenlied* (and its continuation, *Die Klage*, as well as other later texts) and in Scandinavia in the poems of the second half of the *Poetic Edda*, in *Völsunga Saga*, which summarizes these poems, and in *Thidrek's Saga*. The entry *Nibelungenlied* in this encyclopedia gives a detailed summary of the events of the cycle in German tradition, and here only a brief summary of the Scandinavian tradition will be offered, based on the poems of the second half of the *Poetic Edda*.

The gods Odin, Hoenir, and Loki have killed Otr, the son of Hreidmar and brother of Regin and Fafnir, and must pay wergeld. Loki obtains gold from the dwarf Andvari, who curses the hoard. Fafnir kills Hreidmar and changes himself into a dragon to hoard the gold. Regin raises the boy Sigurd (*Reginsmal*). At Regin's behest, Sigurd kills the dragon but learns from birds—whose speech he can now understand, after accidentally swallowing the dragon's blood—that Regin is hostile to him. Sigurd kills Regin (*Fafnismal*).

Riding up to a mountain, he awakens a sleeping woman, who says she is Sigrdrifa, a valkyrie put to sleep by Odin; she advises him about runes and other important matters (*Sigrdrifumal*). At this point the manuscript of the *Poetic Edda* is missing eight pages, which probably told about Sigurd's arrival at the court of Gjuki, oath of blood brotherhood with Gjuki's son Gunnar, marriage with Gjuki's daughter Kudrun, and wooing of Brynhild on Gunnar's behalf by taking on Gunnar's appearance and riding through flames. As the fragment of the next poem (the fragmentary *Sigurdarkvida*) begins, Kudrun has apparently told Brynhild of the betrayal, and Brynhild in turn has demanded Sigurd's death of Gunnar. Gunnar and his brother Högni arrange for Guttorm, a third brother, to kill Sigurd. The following poems take up the aftermath of this killing. Kudrun mourns Sigurd (*Gudrunarkvida* I). The next poem (*Sigurdarkvida in skamma* [The Short Lay of Sigurd]) tells the story up to this point once again.

Kudrun marries Atli (*Gudrunarkvida* II and III). She incites Atli to summon Gunnar and Högni and murder them, but thereafter she murders the children she bore Atli and Atli himself (*Atlakvida* and *Atlamal*; also *Oddrunargratr*). Kudrun marries Jonakr and incites her sons Hamdir and Sørli to avenge their sister Svanhild, who was killed by her husband Jörmunrekk (Ermanaric). On the journey they kill their half-brother Erp, and although they succeed in maiming Jörmunrekk, their attack ultimately fails because they are shorthanded without Erp (*Hamdismal*). So ends the Burgundian cycle in the *Poetic Edda*.

Each of these poems has its own history, and there are numerous repetitions and inconsistencies that a summary cannot suggest. Despite much scholarship on the subject, it is difficult to speak with any confidence of the forms of the individual poems, or of the legends behind them, before they were recorded in Iceland in the thirteenth century. The characters can be derived from actual historical figures of the Migration Age: Günter/Gunnar must be Gundicharius, last king of the Burgundians (whence the name of the cycle), and Etzil/Atil is Attila. Jörmunrekk is clearly Ermanaric. The Huns defeated the Burgundians in 437, though not under the leadership of Attila, and Attila died in bed in 453 with his Germanic bride, Hildico. Sigebert was the name of a Merovingian ruler who was married to the Visigothic princess Brunichildis (d. 613) and was murdered in 575 at the behest of his wife's brother. Because of this historical background and the rich recordings of the cycle in text and image in Germany and in Scandinavia, we know that there must have been extensive oral traditions and that the cycle belongs far more to heroic legend than to history.

See also: *Nibelungenlied*; Scandinavian Tradition

—John Lindow

**Burial Mounds [Barrows, lows, howes, tu-
muli].** Mounds of earth covering the bodies of
prehistoric peoples (Roman and early medieval
barrows are also common), with the corpses frequently interred within a megalithic chamber,
which is often all that survives of the original
denuded mound and thus regarded as a monument in its own right (portal or passage tomb, or
cromlech).

Many of the picturesque names given to these
monuments were not recorded until modern
times, but there are also several that have impeccable medieval pedigrees and show something of
the way in which medieval speculation accounted for their origin.

Mounds and Giants
Just as the Anglo-Saxons, when confronted by
the massive walls of Roman Britain, concluded
that such remains were *enta geweorc* (the work of
giants), they naturally imagined that megalithic
chamber-tombs must be so, too (see, e.g., *Beowulf*, line 2717). Thus, Giant's Grave is a common modern barrow name, sometimes the successor, presumably, of such Anglo-Saxon names as
Thirshowe (from the Anglo-Saxon *thyrs* [giant],
in *Beowulf*, line 1292), preserved in Trusey Hill
(Barmston, in Yorkshire), which probably means
"Giant's Howe," and the *entan hlewe* (Giant's
Low) at Overton, Hampshire. In his *History of the
Kings of Britain* (c. 1138), Geoffrey of Monmouth
gives *chorea gigantum* (Giants' Dance) as the
name for Stonehenge. In late-medieval Germany
the term *hunegraber* (Huns' Graves) reflected a
folk belief that the mounds were connected with
the ancient Huns, who by this date were accorded
gigantic stature. Similarly significantly, Rabelais,
writing in 1532, makes his giant hero, Pantagruel,
pick up a huge rock and plant it on top of four pillars in a field outside Poitiers for the local scholars
to picnic on and inscribe their names, an allusion
to the Pierre Levée dolmen. The same author
took over medieval legends of a giant named Gargantua, who was also associated with megalithic
construction.

Some burial mounds are named after individual legendary heroes who were clearly regarded as
gigantic in stature. About 1540 the antiquary
John Leland wrote, concerning the village of
Barnby in Yorkshire: "The northe hille on top of
it hath certen stones comunely caullid Waddes
Grave, whom the people there say to have bene a
gigant"; although the reference is apparently to a
natural hill on or in which the giant hero Wade is
supposedly buried, it is suggestive (note also the
name Wade's Causeway, given to the nearby
Roman road on Wheeldale Moor). The Germanic smith Weland (Wayland) gave his name
to the barrow called Wayland's Smithy (Oxfordshire) as early as the Anglo-Saxon period, where
it appears in a charter as *Welandes smi|e*. The
several barrow names that seem to commemorate
Germanic gods (i.e., the two Thunor's Lows,

Thor's Howe, the two Woden's Lows, and
Woden's Barrow) were presumably not thought
to be the burial places of these gods but, rather,
perhaps were thought to be under their protection. The Wiltshire Woden's Low is now known
as Adam's Grave, but if this is a deliberate Christianization of a pagan name, it would seem to be
modern.

The *Mabinogi* tale of the burial of the severed
head of the giant Bran in the Gwynfryn (White
Mound) in London is an example of the motif of
talismanic burial, in which the hero is usually (as
in Irish sources) buried in a standing position and
facing the direction of expected enemy attack. In
his late-twelfth-century *De nugis curialium*
(Courtier's Trifles), the gossipy Walter Map relates a tale about a group of three barrows or
cairns in Breconshire, allegedly built over the
severed right hands, left feet, and genitals of
enemy soldiers slaughtered by Brychan and "each
named after the part that lies in it"—this is apparently an onomastic legend (accounting for the
names of the mounds).

In medieval and later Ireland, many a dolmen
was given the name of Diarmaid and Grainne's
Bed, on which these legendary lovers were said
to have enjoyed each other during their year-
and-a-day's elopement. Legendary heroes were
also naturally felt to be buried in some barrows.
For example, the tenth-century Welsh work *Englynion y Beddau* (On the Graves of Heroes) seems
to make the cromlech at Dinorben hill fort
(Denbighshire) the burial place of Hennin Hen-
ben. William of Malmesbury, writing around
1125, refers to the discovery of the grave (*sepul-
chrum et bustum*) of the Arthurian hero Walwen
(Gawain) on the shore at Rhos (Pembrokeshire);
as it is said to be 14 feet long, it may have constituted the inner chamber of a sea-eroded barrow.
The ninth-century *History of the Britons*, attributed to Nennius, presents a list of *mirabilia* (wonders) found in Britain, including the immeasur-
able tumulus of Amr, who was killed by his
father, King Arthur: it is sometimes 6, sometimes
9, 12, or 15 feet long, and it never has the same
dimensions if measured twice in succession. The
same text locates another sepulcher on top of
Crug Mawr mountain (in Cardiganshire); it
shifts its size to accommodate that of whoever
lies down beside it and also conveys lifelong freedom from weariness to any traveler who kneels
three times before it. In the late twelfth century
Gerald of Wales added that weapons left beside
the mound overnight would be found broken to
pieces in the morning; thus, both these mounds
certainly have peculiarities.

Otherworldly Properties of Mounds
Another important *Mabinogi* mound with distinctive properties of its own is that said to be just
outside Arberth (in Pembrokeshire), not specifically stated to be a burial mound (though *gorsedd*,
the term used to describe it, can bear this mean-

ing in medieval Welsh). Its "peculiarity" (*cynneddf*) is that it rewards whoever dares sit upon it with either a blow or a wondrous sight. It is this mound from which Pwyll first sees Rhiannon and Pryderi sees the enchantment fall on Dyfed rendering it a wasteland, and on which Manawydan erects a small gallows. A very similar tradition is found in Old Norse literature, in which a king or seer sits on a burial mound (*haugr* in Old Norse, cognate with *howe*), the clear implication being that they receive inspiration from the interred.

It was only natural that barrows with their imposing portals should be seen as entrances to the otherworld, an especially common belief in early Ireland where the *síd* mounds were believed to be inhabited by an earlier race of divine beings known as the Tuatha Dé Danann (divine beings), whose womenfolk would sometimes lure heroes into the mound. Just as Pwyll's legendary court is located in close proximity to the *gorsedd* at Arberth, so the early Irish kings of Bregha, a branch of the Uí Neill dynasty, had their seat at or near the famous Knowth tumulus, which seems to imply that some of the numen felt to reside in such prehistoric monuments would thus be conferred on the successor court. Two passages in the twelfth-century *Book of Llandaff*, in which the Welsh king transfers land to the church while sitting or lying on the tomb of a former king—Morgan (d. 665), king of Glywysing, does so while lying on the tomb of his grandfather, Meurig—suggest a related and probably derivative rite, by then doubtless made acceptably Christian.

The same sort of transfer of power—poetic inspiration in this case—is recorded in an anecdote in the Icelandic *Flateyjarbók* (c. 1375). According to this account, a shepherd, Hallbjörn, who fell asleep on the burial mound of a poet named Thorleif (interestingly, a man "of great size"), was ever afterward able to compose poetry. Only in recent times has it been said that, should anyone sleep in his mound overnight, he would awake either a poet or an idiot. In a sixteenth-century Welsh tract on the "Names of Giants," by Sion Dafydd Rhys, the same story is told of anyone who will spend a night on the mountain *Cadair Idris* (Idris's Seat).

What may be a related attempt to mobilize the spirits of those interred in a barrow took place on the Sussex shore in 666: as Eddius Stephanus relates in his early-eighth-century *Life of Wilfred*, the saint's party was blown ashore, and prior to engaging the South Saxons in combat, they were ritually cursed by the pagan chief-priest as he was standing on a high mound. Barrows were frequently situated in such a manner as to look out to sea, as if guarding the land from seaborne invasion (cf. Beowulf's cliff-top barrow on the Geatish headland at Hronesness).

Síd-mounds were also regarded as repositories of fabulous treasure. In the eighth-century (?) Irish *Adventure of Art, Son of Conn*, the men of Connacht destroy a *síd* and bear away from it the crown of Brion, one of the Three Wonders of Ireland. The twelfth-century chronicler William of Newburgh tells of a man who witnessed a banquet within a tumulus (identified as Willy Howe at Thwing, Yorkshire); taking care not to drink from the goblet that was offered to him, he stole it and managed to evade pursuit. The vessel, according to William, ended up in the treasury of Henry II! William's contemporary, Gervase of Tilbury, tells an almost identical story (this time, however, located in Gloucestershire) of a golden cup stolen from "a hillock rising to the height of a man." The Yorkshire story suggests derivation from a Scandinavian source, where such tales are common: certain ancestral family "lucks" and talismans are said to have been acquired in similar ways. Bronze Age gold has, of course, been recovered from barrows and cairns in recent times.

Dragons and Mounds

A typically Germanic convention, also appearing in the Welsh tale *Peredur,* is that a barrow contains ancient treasure but is guarded by a dragon (cf. the Anglo-Saxon gnomic verse, "Dragon shall live in barrow, ancient, proud of his treasure"). Beowulf's death is brought about by just such an aggrieved dragon, at what is unmistakably described as a megalithic chamber-tomb. The twelfth-century Latin life of St. Modwenna records an incident of specters haunting Drakelow (Dragon Mound) in Derbyshire; a second life of this saint, written in Anglo-Norman in the thirteenth century, seems to show an awareness of the meaning of the place name, for in one episode concerning the mound, shapeshifters assume the form of a dragon.

Evidence from Old Norse literature, indeed, suggests that the dead man in the mound himself was transformed into a dragon. A story from as early as 858 tells of a fiery dragon that issued from the tomb of the Frankish king Charles Martel (d. 741), blackening the tomb by fire as it left. In Old Norse sources (*Grettir's Saga*, among others), fire is said to issue from howes at night.

There are at least 15 medieval attestations of the place names linking words for "dragon" (drake, worm) with words for "mound" (how[e], low[e]), showing how widespread the belief was. Other names of the "Dragon-hoard" type—for example, Drakenhord at Garsington, Oxfordshire (c. 1230)—probably recall the successful outfacing of the barrow guardian and the recovery of precious grave goods. That these were often of gold is proved by the record of a treasure-trove inquiry held at Dunstable (in Bedfordshire) in 1290, from which we learn that a certain Matthew Tyler earlier in the century had become rich from the treasure he found in the Golden Lowe.

Not only were burial mounds opened by treasure hunters from the very earliest times, as recorded in Anglo-Saxon charter names meaning "Broken-barrow," "Burst-barrow," "Hollow-barrow," and "Idle-barrow" (i.e., "empty-barrow"), but royal licenses were also issued for this very purpose from at least 1237. In his *Chronicle*, Roger of Wendover records that one night in 1178, in St. Albans, the saint himself appeared to a man and miraculously led him to the sight of two *colliculi* (mounds) known as the Banner Hills (*Colles vexillorum*) at Redbourn, Hertfordshire, around which the local populace was accustomed to gather. The monks of the abbey dug into the barrows and were rewarded by finding the miracle-working bones of the martyr St. Amphibalus and nine others.

Mounds in Christian Traditions

Early Christianity clearly recognized the numinous nature of prehistoric burial mounds. One of the strategies it developed for coming to terms with their powerful hold on the popular imagination was occasionally to incorporate them within the church precincts, as at the famous Taplow barrow, which stands within the old churchyard; the former pagan royal site at Jelling in Denmark; Egloscrow (St. Issey, from Cornish *eglos* [church] and *crug* [barrow]); and Ludlow, where in 1199 three skeletons found in a barrow during the construction of the church were immediately identified as the bones of the saintly parents and uncle of the renowned Irish saint, Brendan (d. 577). Other strategies of assimilation were to build the church on top of the monument, as at Mont-Saint-Michel (in Carnac), La Hougue Bie (in Jersey), and Fimber (in Yorkshire), or to Christianize them in some other way: Lilla Howe, a round barrow at Fylingdales, Yorkshire, is still surmounted by a medieval stone cross attested from the early twelfth century; and a presumed late-medieval base crowns the Cleeve Hill barrow (in Worcestershire), as was formerly also the case at the Giant's Grave, the alleged burial place of the giant Tom Hickathrift, in Marshland St. James (in Norfolk). Ty Illtud (St. Illtud's House), a chamber-tomb at Llanhamlach, Wales, has one of its interior walls incised with crosses and other graffiti, including the date 1312.

That such a burial mound might really have been used by a saint is demonstrated by Felix's life of the early-eighth-century St. Guthlac: on a wooded island in the East Anglian fens there was "a mound (tumulus) built of clods of earth that greedy comers to the waste in former times had dug into and broken open, in the hope of finding wealth. On one side of the mound there seemed to be a sort of cistern, and in this Guthlac began to dwell after building a hut over it" (Felix, *Vita Guthlaci*, ch. 28). One of the Old English verses describes Guthlac's *beorg* (barrow) in more detail and states that it had formerly been occupied by the devils before Guthlac, too, broke into it, thus dispossessing them of it. Interestingly, he straightaway erected a cross and then dwelt in the barrow itself, before putting up additional

shelter. The barrow is also several times referred to as his "seat" (*setl*; cf. the etymological sense of Welsh *gorsedd*, and note that Pwyll goes to Arberth mound "to sit"), which the demons are anxious to return to as the sole place in which they had been able to enjoy respite from their torment in hell.

An official record of 1261 shows that a band of murderous brigands used the chamber of a mound called Cuteslowe, hiding out *"in concavitate illius hoge"* [in the chamber of that "howe"], no doubt both taking advantage of such a "haunted" site, which must have helped protect their hideout from the curious, and then adding to its already sinister reputation. The local sheriff ordered it to be leveled to the ground.

The *Life of St. Cadoc*, written about 1100, includes an amusing account of the miraculous provision of grain during a period of famine in the saint's adopted home near Brecon in Wales. By means of a thread tied to its foot, Cadoc (also known as Cadog in Welsh) is able to follow a mouse to a certain tumulus, "under which there was a very beautiful subterranean house, built of old, and filled with clean wheat," which is taken to refer to the megalithic chamber within a tumulus. The bizarre scene, also featuring a mouse, that occurs in the *Mabinogi* tale of Manawydan, in which he erects a miniature gallows on the *gorsedd* at Arberth, from which he intends to hang the mouse he has caught devastating his crops, may well recall the medieval practice of erecting gallows on top of barrows. In 1425, for example, a new pair of gallows was erected in Luberlow field, Haughley (in Suffolk), presumably on the barrow itself, and one of the four Gally Hills barrows at Banstead (in Surrey) had a gallows on it in 1538. Gallows How (Galehoges, 1312) at Dunton (in Norfolk) was presumably the meeting place of the Gallow Hundred. Some of these barrows, at least, were reputed to be the abode of evil spirits, presumably of the interred. The poet of *Beowulf* speaks of *"scuccum ond scinnum"* [devils and evil spirits, line 939], which are said to haunt Heorot and which we may take to be the same kind of demons that threatened the tranquillity of Guthlac's barrow home. The names of these spirits survive in the names of the barrows at Scuckburgh (in Warwickshire) and Scuccanhlau (Horwood, Buckinghamshire), and possibly one at Skinburness, Cumbria (possibly derived from the Anglo-Saxon words *scinna*, "demon," and **burgaens*, "burial place"). Two Yorkshire barrows were named after an Old Norse word meaning "goblin" or "demon": Scratters and Scrathowes. In an Old English charm against a sudden stitch, the spirits that caused the pain are said to have been "loud as they rode over the low"—suggesting, incidentally, an alternative derivation to that usually advanced of the place name Ludlow. Certainly by the late-medieval period, at least, it was felt that these abodes of the ancient dead were appropriate sites on which to dispatch malefactors, whose spirits would be, as it were, in good company. In this connection, it is also worth remembering that Woden was the god of hanged men (cf. the Woden names above).

The Icelandic *Kormak's Saga* describes a sacrifice to the elves who dwell in a burial mound (cf. the thirteenth-century Yorkshire Alfhov, "Elf-howe"); their mound is smeared with the blood of a bull, and the bull's flesh is left for them to feast on. The purpose of this particular sacrifice is to gain the elves' help in healing wounds; other sagas indicate that the mound dwellers could also assist in childbirth. The belief that a barrow is haunted by the malevolent spirit of its occupant, who will attack anyone attempting to dig into the mound looking for treasure, is a commonplace of the Icelandic sagas, and the relatively late Christianization of Scandinavia has preserved tales of the vampire-like *draugr*, an animated corpse that inhabits mounds.

It has often been observed that the Old English element *low*, a common term for "barrow," is a frequent component of the names of places where people met to conduct the business of hundreds (administrative divisions of English counties); for example, the several "Moot-lows," which has led to the conclusion that these moots assembled on and around ancient tumuli. Of 12 such mounds excavated up to 1984, however, only one was positively identified as a prehistoric barrow: Culiford Tree Hundred, Dorset.

See also: *Beowulf*; Dragon; English Tradition: Anglo-Saxon Period; *Mabinogi*; Names, Place

—Malcolm Jones

*C*ædmon (d. 680). Often called "the first English poet," though it would be more correct to describe him as the first person recorded to have composed Christian poetry in English employing a poetic style and form traditional among pre-Christian Germanic peoples.

According to the legend preserved in Bede's *Ecclesiastical History of the English People* (731), Cædmon, whose name indicates he was a British Celt, was an illiterate farmworker of advanced age on an estate attached to the Anglo-Saxon monastery ruled by Abbess Hilda (d. 680) at Whitby. Though not himself a monk, Cædmon, like other laypersons connected to such foundations, participated in festivities of the larger monastic *familia*, which included beer drinking and passing a harp for each person to entertain the others with a song or poem. When the harp approached Cædmon, he fled the feast "for shame" because he did not know how to sing or compose verses. After returning to his own dwelling, he fell asleep among the cattle he was tending and dreamed that a man (perhaps an angel) appeared to him, miraculously bringing from God the gift of singing and composing poems, thus enabling him to produce the famous nine-line "Cædmon's Hymn." The next morning, Cædmon told his reeve (estate manager) about this miracle and was sent to Abbess Hilda, who marveled that he could not only perform that hymn but also compose new poems out of religious (mostly biblical) stories related to him by learned monks of the monastery. She then enlisted Cædmon as a full-fledged monk, and he continued to use his miraculous power to produce further Christian poems using traditional Germanic poetics. Because he composed poems in oral performances after ruminating on the holy texts read to him, and at least one of these poems survives because it was written down as "Cædmon's Hymn," the legend about his poetic gift provides an unusual opportunity for us to glimpse some of the relations between orality and literacy in an early-medieval context.

Bede does not designate Cædmon as a saint, though students of hagiography will recognize in his legend some familiar characteristics of the saints' lives that circulated widely in monastic and popular culture: Cædmon's unpromising youth, his dream vision, his gift of divine speech, his besting of his betters (the scholars who serve to write down his poems), and his ability to foresee the time of his own death. Though our only source for this legend is Bede, numerous manuscripts containing versions of "Cædmon's Hymn" survive as evidence of its wide circulation, and the conclusion of the legend in the Old English translation of Bede in Alfred the Great's time implies that the poem circulated in oral culture before being written down.

See also: Bede the Venerable; English Tradition: Anglo-Saxon Period; Orality and Literacy

—John McNamara

Camlan. Arthur's last battle in Welsh legendry.

An entry in the *Annales Cambriae* (Annals of Wales), under the year 537, states: "Battle of Camlann in which Arthur and Medraut [Medrawd] fell." The site of the battle is unknown. In his *Historia regum Britanniae* (History of the Kings of Britain), Geoffrey of Monmouth locates it on the banks of the river Camel in Cornwall; another possible site, proposed by O. G. S. Crawford, is Camboglanna (Birdoswald), a Roman fort on Hadrian's Wall. However, Camlan, from *camboglanna* (crooked river bank) or *cambolanda* (curved enclosure), is not an uncommon Welsh place name, though none of the places so named appears to have popular Arthurian associations. The annals do not indicate that Arthur and Medrawd were leaders of opposing factions, but Welsh traditions ascribe the cause of the battle to the treachery of Medrawd and to discord at Arthur's court.

According to the Triads of the Island of Britain—allusions to Welsh legendary events, arranged in groups of three—Camlan was one of "the three futile battles of Britain," brought about by a quarrel between Queen Gwenhwyfar and Gwenhwyfach (Triad 84), and "one of the three harmful blows" struck by the latter on the former (Triad 53). Triad 54, which may have a similar context, refers to one of "the three unrestrained ravagings" when Medrawd dragged Gwenhwyfar from her throne and struck her. Geoffrey of Monmouth's account (c. 1138) of the abduction of Arthur's queen by Modred (the form he uses for Medrawd) and the subsequent final disastrous battle derives from the same tradition. The Welsh tale of *Rhonabwy's Dream* does not refer to Medrawd's assault on the queen, but here, too, Camlan is the result of plotting and mischief, as Iddawg Cordd Prydein confesses that he caused strife between Arthur and Medrawd by conveying twisted messages from the one to the other and that Camlan was thus "woven" from his actions. Another early Welsh tale, *Culhwch and Olwen*, refers to the nine who plotted Camlan. Other citations in the Triads and in poetry refer to the three, or seven, survivors of the battle.

The frequency of allusions in medieval Welsh literature and the diversity of the record suggest an active tradition about the battle of Camlan, and its core theme of treachery and internal rivalry leading to the loss of an ordered, harmonious world explains its impact on the popular imagination beyond its strictly Arthurian context. Camlan was a furiously violent, as well as a disastrous, battle. This is the aspect emphasized by many medieval poets, especially Gruffudd ab yr Ynad Coch, who in his elegy to Llywelyn II (the last prince of Wales, killed in 1282) gives that event an apocalyptic significance, "like Camlan." The tradition of Camlan as a furious melee was long-lived, and the word *cadgamlan* (battle of Camlan) is found from the sixteenth century as a common noun for a confused, noisy rabble.

See also: Arthurian Lore; *Culhwch and Olwen*; Triads of the Island of Britain

—Brynley F. Roberts

Candlemas. A feast traditionally celebrated on February 2, which formally marked the end of winter and the beginning of spring in parts of medieval Europe.

Also known as the Feast of the Purification of the Blessed Virgin Mary, Candlemas falls 40 days after Christmas, in imitation of the 40-day period of isolation that Hebrew law imposed upon mothers and their infants. If Christ was born on December 25, then Mary, with her newborn son, would be presented at the temple for purification on February 2.

In the Gospel of Luke a pious man named Simeon sees Jesus in the temple and, recognizing him as the Messiah, says that the infant will be "a light to lighten the Gentiles" (2:32). The early Church seized upon the symbolism of light and promoted the lighting and blessing of candles as an important fixture of this feast, hence its more popular name. The imagery of rebirth and renewal of light during the darkest time of the year, as well as the divine light of Christ appearing to banish the darkness of human sin, led to the ritual of a candlelit procession. The following morning, St. Blaise's Day (February 3), priests would use the burnt-out candles for a ceremony known as the "blessing of the throats": using two candles to make the sign of the cross on the throats of the parishioners, the priests would pronounce their benedictions.

In many regions Candlemas and St. Blaise's Day marked a turning point in the calendar, the beginning of the end of winter. In southern France and elsewhere in Europe, it was said that bears would emerge from hibernation on February 2; thus the Candlemas bear, not unlike the groundhog currently celebrated on February 2, was seen as a harbinger of spring. As the beginning of spring, Candlemas marked the beginning of the Carnival season in many parts of Europe. Candlemas also marked a transition in the rhythms of seasonal work. In England and elsewhere in northern Europe, Candlemas was the date on which cattle were driven off the newly plowed fields, which were fenced so that the work of sowing the seeds for the summer crops could begin.

The feast first appeared in Rome in the seventh century, but it appears to have developed in the Greek world in the fourth century. Surviving records have frequent references to the conflict in the British Isles between the feast of St. Brigid, held with great merrymaking on February 1 by those of Irish, Hebridean, and Manx descent, and Candlemas, which the other Christians celebrated by fasting on the same day.

Due to its focus on the Blessed Virgin, Candlemas was banned from England during the sixteenth century.

See also: Brigid, Saint; Carnival

—Bradford Lee Eden

Cantar de mio Cid. Anonymous epic poem of 3,730 lines on the exploits of Rodrigo (or Ruy) Díaz de Vivar, a low-ranking noble who in the time of Alfonso VI, king of Castile and León, rose through his military talents to become the independent ruler of Valencia.

His epithet in the poem, *Cid*, is an Arabic word meaning "my lord." The poem concentrates on the Cid's campaigns in the valleys of the rivers Henares, Jalón, and Jiloca after he was exiled from Castile by Alfonso, relegating the capture of Valencia to a few lines. The second half is dominated by the story of the marriages of the Cid's daughters, Elvira and Sol, to the infantes de Carrión and the breakup of those unions occasioned by the infantes' criminal treatment of the two women in the oak wood of Corpes. In a magnificent court scene, the Cid obtains from his sons-in-law the return of gifts he has given them, including the swords Colada and Tizón. The two are challenged, along with their elder brother Ansur González, to fight judicial duels with the Cid's champions, who triumph. The poem ends with a celebration of the fact that all the kings of Spain are descended from its hero, an element important in dating the text to around the year 1200.

The portrayal of the Cid that emerges from the poem is one of an extremely capable warrior and military leader who acquires wealth through his martial talents and redistributes it to his retainers, his dependents, and King Alfonso as gifts, and who ultimately transforms the status he has achieved thereby into genealogical value when his daughters contract even more prestigious marriages with the infantes of Navarre and Aragon. Despite this majestic overall design, the poet includes many details of everyday life in his depiction, including the hero's belief in omens.

The *Cantar de mio Cid* survives in its poetic form in a single fourteenth-century manuscript whose first page is missing and that bears a colophon recording that a certain Per Abbat copied the text in 1207, no doubt a relict from an earlier stage of the manuscript tradition. Although the poem was once thought to have been composed around 1140, which would have been a little more than 40 years after the death of the historical Rodrigo Díaz de Vivar in July 1099, most scholars seem to agree, subsequent to the work of Antonio Ubieto Arteta, that the date is much closer to the date given in the colophon.

The poem was incorporated into the vernacular prose chronicles that were initiated by King Alfonso the Wise, beginning in the second half of the thirteenth century; of those prose versions, the one found in the *Chronicle of Twenty Kings* is closest to the Per Abbat manuscript.

The meter of the *Cantar de mio Cid* is highly irregular, with lines varying from 10 to 20 syllables, and the most frequently occurring line, of 14 syllables, only attested in a little more than a quarter of the poem. The lines of each *tirada* (verse paragraph) are linked by a common assonance. The diction is formulaic, just under a third of the half lines consisting of repeated phrases. The text itself refers to its internal divisions as *cantares* (songs), and it was in all likelihood sung. That the irregularities of versification derive from the process through which it was taken down in writing rather than from compositional considerations is a possibility that I believe likely.

Much of the research devoted to the poem has concentrated on the relationship between the occurrences it recounts and the events of Rodrigo's life, about which a fair amount is known for an eleventh-century figure. The poem clashes with recorded historical information in various ways. It combines the Cid's two exiles into one, changes the names of his daughters (María and Cristina in history), ascribes to them unhistorical marriages with the infantes de Carrión, and identifies them incorrectly at the end of the text as the queens of Navarre and Aragon. It fails to mention the hero's service under the Muslim king Mutamin of Saragossa in the period 1081–1085 and plays down his ties with Muslim allies, with the exception of King Abengalbón of Molina, represented as a good Moor. It also omits any mention of the fact that Rodrigo's wife Jimena was a cousin of Alfonso VI and was thus a woman of royal lineage, and of the fact that the king himself led an army against Valencia. Alvar Fáñez, the Cid's right-hand man in the poem, was in history an important military figure in his own right and could not have played the role the poet assigns to him. Bishop Jerónimo, in history the Cluniac Jérôme de Périgord, did not arrive in Valencia until 1097, three years after the Battle of Cuarte in which the poet has him take part. These and many other departures from the historical record make it clear that, contrary to the theories of the renowned philologist and historian Ramón Menéndez Pidal, the poem has no special status as a documentary source.

A number of signs point to the poem's composition in a particular context, in my judgment for an audience of nobles and warriors connected with the milieu of Alfonso VIII of Castile near the end of the twelfth century. The focus on events occurring in the valley of the river Jalón raises the possibility of composition in or near the monastery of Huerta, founded by Alfonso VIII in 1179. María Eugenia Lacarra has pointed out that two powerful Castilian clans of this period, the Laras and the Castros, were linked through genealogy with the principals of the poem—the Laras with the Cid, the Castros with his enemies. Alfonso VIII himself was descended from the hero. The vilification of the infantes de Carrión and their ally García Ordóñez could well derive from the poet's desire to flatter Alfonso VIII and the Laras, especially the Laras of Molina, by reflected praise at the expense of the Castros. The poem's depiction of the processes of enrichment through the acquisition of plunder may have been meant to encourage Christian fighting men to engage in the struggle against the Moors in the perilous period between the Battle of Alarcos in 1095, disastrous for Alfonso VIII's side, and his decisive victory in the Battle of Las Navas de Tolosa in 1212.

One of the themes with which the poem concerns itself is the legitimacy of the Cid's birth. Whereas one would expect only two judicial duels in the climactic combat scene, a third battle matches the Cid's champion Muño Gustioz against Ansur González, brother of the infantes de Carrión, who has launched an obscurely worded and seemingly gratuitous insult at the Cid, implying that he is the illegitimate son of a miller's wife. The motif of the Cid's illegitimacy is referred to clearly from the sixteenth century onward in the corpus of Spanish ballads devoted to him. Muño's victory in the single combat implies that the rumors of Rodrigo's illegitimacy are false, to the benefit of his descendants.

See also: Arabic-Islamic Tradition; *Chanson de Roland*

—Joseph J. Duggan

Carnival. A festival created by medieval European Christians to mark the two or three days (sometimes extended to more than a week) that preceded Ash Wednesday, the beginning of Lenten abstinence.

The festival emerged slowly from the debris of Roman, Greek, Germanic, Slavic, and other ethnic celebrations of the end of winter and approach of spring. The Roman Lupercalia (celebrated on February 15) is documented for 495, which seems to be the latest mentioned of such celebrations, at least by official name. In the early 1140s Canon Benedict of St. Peter's at Rome described for the first time an organized ceremony taking place on Fat Tuesday (Mardi Gras). The pope rode ceremoniously with Roman secular nobility to Testaccio Hill, where a bear, young bulls, and a cock were killed. Benedict interprets the sacrifices as an orientation to Lent and hence to Easter: "so that we may henceforth live chastely and soberly in a testing of our souls, and merit reception of the body of the Lord on Easter."

A seasonal and ludic interpretation of the scene is just as possible as this liturgical one. Records show that Testaccio Hill was used for a bull-killing sport on Mardi Gras for the next 600 years. Equally relevant to the ambivalence of

Carnival's meaning is the presence of the pope together with the prefect of the city, knights, and foot soldiers. Is Carnival "pagan" or "Christian"? It is both, just as it is secular and religious, solemn and playful by turns.

Humanists from the fifteenth century and many others since then have alleged undocumented continuities among Lupercalia, Saturnalia, Dionysia, and any number of other well-authenticated non-Christian practices by European ethnic groups. But the silence between 495 and 1140 remains, broken only by the emergence in the tenth century of family names and place names: *carnisprivium, carnelevare*. The word *carnival* means the end of meat eating. When the word is documented without any reference to ceremonies it is ambiguous, pointing as much to Lent as to the moment just before it, as Rabelais noticed in 1550 to the confusion of single-minded scholars ever since.

More plausible than the humanist idea of a hidden continuity from ancient times is the notion that Christian ideological dominance slowly but successfully dissolved all organized celebrations that possessed non-Christian ideas of spiritual force. By the eighth century, Lenten ritual practices had become well codified. Between the eighth and twelfth centuries the old naturalistic religious practices, which certainly never ceased to exercise their hold on people's imaginations, reclustered at a number of points in the Christian liturgical calendar. Nowhere was this more true than on the days that then acquired the collective name to which Canon Benedict alludes matter-of-factly by describing *"de ludo Carnelevari"* [the Carnival game].

We possess only pinpoints of light about Carnival from 1140 until the early fourteenth century. Only 70 well-authenticated documents mentioning Carnival customs have been found for this period up to now; most are urban, but some are monastic and a few feudal-courtly. The number 70 does not count place names and personal names nor the use of the word as a means of dating feudal obligations. But it does include 15 references to the payment of a "Carnival hen" as a feudal obligation, even though such references may refer only to a practice of private conviviality rather than to any generally shared, public celebration.

From 1250 onward town evidence dominates the records, accounting for 90 percent of the total documented Carnival celebrations found in Europe west of Russia and north of the Balkans. The following sample periods illustrate the rapid increase in documentation now available to scholars in published studies: 1150–1175, 6 documents; 1250–1275, 15; 1350–1375, 35; 1450–1475, 101; and 1550–1575, 146. Before 1500 fewer than three dozen references to village carnivals in the indicated European area have been found; most of them record accidental crimes that occurred during Carnival or describe peasant behavior literally in pejorative and satiric terms. Yet village practices were the basis for the nineteenth-century idea of Carnival as a repository of Indo-European myths and rituals that survived into the nineteenth century in "backward" villages. For ideological reasons as well as because of this scarce documentation, scholars since World War II have generally resisted the earlier tendency to attach the adjectives "age-old" and "customary" to every scrap of evidence about nonelite, popular, and especially "folk" behavior.

Carnival is the most fascinating of medieval festivities. This is not simply because Carnival took form on the edge of a Christian observance rather than beneath it, as in the case of Christmas or Saint John's. Quite apart from the festival's ambiguous ideological overtones, it is naturalistically ambivalent. Does it celebrate the end of winter or the beginning of spring? Young man Carnival (a character in literature from the 1220s onward) is exuberant, noisy, arrogant, and sexy, like spring, but he is also lazy, tyrannical, and fearful, like lingering, self-indulgent winter and like the hibernating bear, sacrificed at Rome in 1140 and still today a popular animal personification of the occasion. Old woman Lent may be ascetic but she is also energetic, enterprising, and forward-looking, like the new season. (The Viennese painting by Pieter Brueghel the Elder called *The Combat of Carnival and Lent* depicts the contrast comically, and in accord with a 300-year-long tradition; see illustrations.)

Carnival is ambivalent, looking forward and backward, toward spring and toward winter, and it is ambiguous, reminding humanity of both the ephemerality and the joyousness of sensuous pleasures. Hence it has proved extraordinarily prolific in modes of festive behavior. By 1500 one can divide European Carnival practices into five clusters, each of them with 20 to 30 modes of expression. Two of the five clusters are primarily concerned with food and three primarily with social organization. Modes and usages within the clusters exhibit the division and ambiguity characterizing the festival generally.

1. Most obviously, Carnival celebrates food consumption in unheeding excess, in total disregard for the future and for one's own body, mind, and intestines. Cakes and doughnuts, pretzels and pancakes, wine and beer, and every manner of beast and fowl, the fattier the better. These must be begged, borrowed, hunted, and stolen; offered to the lord by manorial custom; offered to the city council by public subsidy; given to the poor, to children, nuns, monks, soldiers, and to the family in picnics and banquets; paraded and smeared; and thrown away and thrown about. Most of these practices had serious, ritual forms as well as parodic, ironic, obscene forms.

2. No medieval person needed reminding that the reverse of food consumption is production. The year coming to an end in flagrant excess had simultaneously to be reborn. So the weather signs that moderns associate with New Year's Day, Groundhog Day, or the spring equinox were all consulted at one time and place or another during Carnival. Winter-versus-summer symbolic duels and fracases, usually ending in the victory of fertile, green-garbed summer, were frequent features of the holiday in Scandinavia and the eastern Alps. Greenery appeared on countless costumes. "Burying" winter/death/candlelight in the river or the earth would replenish the soil; bonfires, torches, and fireworks greeted the growing strength of sunlight. Besmearing a person with water or mud, hitching someone to plow or harrow or log, sowing the earth in the middle of town, cracking the trunks of fruit trees with whips and stocks to stimulate their sap—Mikhail Bakhtin's emphasis on the circular meaning of Carnival's inversionary character applies very well here: what goes down will come up.

3. The most prominent aspect of social organization feted in medieval Carnival was political-social hierarchy. Officials paraded or greeted the community at their residences or offices. The military displayed their power in parades and the elites their prowess, above all in jousting. But here, too, mockery and displacement were as evident as confirmation and celebration (not *more* so; in this respect Bakhtin's concept of Carnival errs). There was masking as kings and gods and clergy or conversely as peasants and beggars; indiscriminate public mixing, dancing, singing, and parading of high and low classes and even of women, married or unmarried (notorious in sixteenth-century Venice); and vindictive races pitting Jews and hunchbacks and prostitutes against each other (especially in sixteenth-century Rome). City hall was temporarily taken over; public proclamations condemned all manner of social and political excesses occurring during the previous year; all distinctions between the public and private were abolished; people ran in and out of houses and in and out of the city gates.

4. No less important to social organization than the hierarchies were the conventions separating human from nonhuman worlds. Medieval Europeans necessarily maintained an ambivalent understanding of the conventions separating humanity, nature, and the invisible supernatural world. In this sphere, more than in the case of the preceding three clusters, official edicts condemning masking and costuming as sacrilegious or dangerous to public order produced the most documentation. Because material identifying the wild, demonic, foolish, monstrous, ghostly, and gigantic is more ambiguous in words than in gestures, iconographic evidence is of the essence here.

5. Last but not least, conventions governing and contravening sexual boundaries were put into question; indeed, what could be more pertinent to a winter-spring festival than reproductive relations? Male exhibitionism and male aggression against females were scarcely more in evidence than transvestism, by women no less than by men. Simulating copulation, with all manner of verbal, visual, and gestural obscenities, was commonplace. But so were banquets, parades, and, in northern European areas, sledding parties to honor women. Carnival was a favored time for marriages because copulation was forbidden to good Christians during Lent. But Carnival was also a favorite time to perform charivaris, which ridiculed unseemly marriages by men or women.

All five clusters were celebrated by all social classes and both sexes, although of course individual usages were frequently very class specific. The clusters were by turns elite, official, popular, and "folk" in character, and each of these kinds of cultural identity, chosen and combined by individuals no less than by occupational and economic groups (especially by the urban youth societies, which played central roles in organizing Carnival), borrowed from the others. In the status-conscious medieval and Renaissance framework of European society, Carnival was a time when people could cross social frontiers. It has been fruitfully studied from this perspective by Victor Turner and other anthropological scholars as a ritual process, on the model of Arnold van Gennep's rites of passage.

In the later fifteenth and sixteenth centuries the transgressive role of Carnival customs expanded its place in European culture at elite courtly and scholarly levels through humanist ideology. In the article Masking in this encyclopedia I have cited Dietrich Gresemund's exemplary expression of the new sense of the carnivalesque for those elites elsewhere. This more subjective and ultimately more subversive place of carnivalesque modes of thinking about the human condition is symbolized by the fact that personifications of the festival were presented by three of the most signal figures in European literature: Rabelais gave us Caresmeprenant (*Fourth Book*, 1552); Shakespeare, Sir John Falstaff (*Henry IV, Part I*, 1597, and *The Merry Wives of Windsor*, 1600); and Cervantes, Sancho Panza (*Don Quixote*, 1605).

This analysis has offered an overview oriented sociohistorically. But Carnival studies have always also been concerned with the problematics of representation. During the winter festival period between Christmas and Ash Wednesday, ecclesiastical and state authorities relaxed prohibitions on public theater; the winter season for drama was inspirationally as well as traditionally carnivalesque. Theatrical studies in the twentieth century moved beyond classicist and proscenium-arch prepossessions, inspired in the 1920s by surrealist-absurdist initiatives (e.g., Jean Duvignaud) and in the 1960s by semiotic-structuralist experiments (e.g., Richard Schechner), which in turn have engendered new academic fields like performance and communication studies that have strongly influenced the analysis of medieval Carnival. The observations about Carnival clusters above could be fruitfully supplemented by reformulation in performative, communicational, and representational terms. Such reformulation has already been tried in many particular instances.

See also: Charivari; Festivals and Celebrations; Fool; Martinmas; Masking; Purim; Wild Man
—Samuel Kinser

Carol. A festive combination of song and dance documented broadly throughout the late-medieval period.

The word *carol* finds its source in the Old French *carole*, which indicates both a ring dance and the song that accompanies it—apparently performed with great exuberance, for by the early fourteenth century, *carol* came to mean celebrating in general, as in 1308, when the mayor of London led a group that went caroling (*karolantes*) to the royal court to welcome Edward II upon his return to the city. Toward the end of the Middle Ages, however, the term became more restrictive, denoting only a type of song, usually sung on religious holidays.

As songs, carols are distinguished by their burden (chorus) and stanza structure. The short burden is sung at the beginning of the song and between each of the stanzas. The greater number of carols indicate the stanza as a solo part and the burden as group unison, but about one-quarter of the 474 carols preserved in English manuscripts indicate that sometimes both the stanzas and the burdens were noted for multiple voices.

The most frequent stanza form consists of four four-measure lines rhymed in *aaab*, with the final line serving as a refrain connecting to the burden, most often a couplet of four-measure lines rhymed in *bb*. For example, one of the famous Boar's Head carols, describing a festive meal in which the boar's head is the first course, begins with the burden,

Hey, Hey, Hey, Hey!
The borrys hede is armyd gay.

Then begins the first stanza, whose last line feeds back into the burden:

The boris hede in hond [hand] I bring
With garlond gay in porttoryng
   ["portering," or carrying]
I pray yow all witt me to synge,
Witt hay!

The subjects of surviving carols include not only the celebration of festivals, as in the example above, but also religious and moral counsel, satire, family life, politics, complaint, and love.

Another distinctive feature of the carol is its connection to the folk dances performed by both the peasantry and the aristocracy in the Middle Ages. The dance itself consisted of alternate periods of standing to count time and leftward (sunwise) motion in a ring or serpentine line. Most frequently the dancers would stand during the stanza and dance to the burden, but there are a few carols in which this sequence is reversed and the dance takes place during the stanza. The dance portion consisted most commonly of three steps to the left with accompanying arm motions, sometimes including sexually suggestive gestures. Male and female participants joined hands and followed the directions of the leader, who was usually the soloist of the stanzas.

Nearly all extant references to carols come from religious prohibitions and exempla that link the singing and dancing of carols to sacrilegious activities. In attempting to address cultural resistance against banning the popular secular songs, the Franciscans actively sought to retain well-known tunes, either altering their lyrics to discard lewd or secular subjects or attempting to interpret the words of the song in a religious vein. The carols, however, carried the added offense of being associated with non-Christian cultural practices. And because they were performed at holiday times, they attracted special condemnation from clerics promoting the pious observance of Christian feasts.

Between 600 and 1500 C.E. the Church formally banned the dancing of carols in church houses, on church grounds, and even in church neighborhoods more than 20 times; informally, numerous decrees, sermons, and exempla were written condemning the activity. In such texts as *Liber exemplorum ad usum praedicantium* (Book of Exempla for Use in Preaching) and Robert Mannyng's Middle English *Handlyng Synne* (1303), caroling at the wrong time or place attracts divine wrath. Mannyng, for example, states that anyone who practices caroling in churches or churchyards is in danger of committing sacrilege, especially at holiday times. He then tells a tale of 12 young men and women who congregated in a churchyard to carol on Christmas Eve. They disturb the priest as he is saying mass, and he curses the dancers, praying that they will be forced to dance for the entire following year. The prayer works, and the carolers are trapped in their motions for the next 12 months. While they danced, neither their hair nor their nails grew, they did not soil their clothes, and their complexions never changed. This legend, first situated in the German town of Kölbigk, was retold repeatedly in sermons from the eleventh century to the end of the Middle Ages.

In witchcraft trials of the sixteenth century and later, accused witches often confessed to caroling. The witches' carol was a perverse parody of the secular dance: instead of facing each other, the dancers faced outward from the ring, and in so doing moved "widdershins," or against the motion of the sun.

Nevertheless, caroling thoroughly permeated secular society from bottom to top, appearing in court dances at least as early as the twelfth century. In Wace's Anglo-Norman poem *Roman de Brut* (c. 1155), the women carol at Arthur's wedding, and the fourteenth-century Middle English romance *Sir Gawain and the Green Knight* depicts caroling, both the song and the dance, as a major part of the celebrations taking place in Arthur's hall during the Christmas season.

Most of the carols in existence today are found in fourteenth- and fifteenth-century manuscripts originating from religious houses. Because of their composition in this environment, most carols are anonymous, but it is known that John Audelay, a chaplain from Shropshire, penned 26 carols, and James Ryman, a Franciscan friar in Canterbury, penned more than 100. The most extensive collection of carols is the commonplace book of Richard Hill, which contains 78 carols on diverse subjects. The textuality of these carols is evidenced by their repetition among the late-medieval manuscripts, pointing to the genre's movement from oral folksong to its incorporation into religious uses.

Both religious and secular carols of the later Middle Ages served as entertainment at gatherings in monastic and secular halls. Five of every six of the preserved carols treat religious subjects such as moral counsel, the Nativity, and praises to the Virgin Mary, and most of the religious carols contain prominent Latin phrasing, sometimes written specifically for the piece, sometimes borrowed from liturgical texts or from hymns of the Divine Office.

Carols that emphasize the secular side of such holidays as Christmas include a group celebrating the holly and the ivy, and indicating a festive game in which the men would portray themselves as holly and the women as ivy. The carol "In Praise of Holly" includes these lines:

Her commys holly that is so gent
    [courteous],
to pleasse all men is his intent.…

Whosoeuer ageynst holly do crye
In a lepe [immediately] shall he hang full hye

Note that holly is depicted as male, and that the carol implies in a playfully threatening tone that some people may speak disparagingly of him. Similarly, in "In Praise of Ivy," ivy assumes a female identity, and also states that those who do not praise her adequately are in error:

The most worthye she is in towne—
He that seyth other [says otherwise] do
    amysse—
And worthy to ber the crowne.

The reference to crown suggests that men impersonating holly and women impersonating ivy are competing for a festive prize.

See also: Christmas; Dance; *Sir Gawain and the Green Knight*

—Sandra M. Salla

Catherine of Alexandria, Saint (d. early fourth century) [Katherine].

One of the most popular saints of the Middle Ages; martyred at the beginning of the fourth century, the patron saint of Christian philosophers, women students, virgins, and wheelwrights.

Catherine's legend reached Western Europe in 1020 when Simeon of Treves, a monk of Rouen in Normandy, brought a relic (supposedly a knucklebone of the saint) back from Alexandria. In 1040 a monk at Rouen composed a long Latin account of Catherine's martyrdom. This account, known as the Vulgate version, served as the source for most later versions of Catherine's passion, including the highly influential one in Jacobus de Voragine's *Legenda aurea* (Golden Legend).

St. Catherine's veneration in England began when Robert, the abbot of Rouen monastery, became bishop of London in 1044. *Seinte Katerine*, the earliest Middle English version of her passion, served an instructional or devotional purpose for nuns in the West Midlands. Other tellings, such as the one in the *South English Legendary*, seem to have been intended for the enjoyment of the lay public. The most important English version is John Capgrave's fifteenth-century *Life of St. Katherine*, which includes the story of her early life and of her passion, both in greatly expanded form.

So far as all the versions agree, Catherine grows up in third-century Alexandria, the daughter of King Costus. Beautiful, chaste, serious, and highly educated, she has many suitors, but she wishes to remain a virgin and resists pressure to choose a husband. The Virgin Mary eventually summons Catherine to what is commonly called her Mystic Marriage, in which Catherine recognizes Christ as the perfect spouse she desires, and he gives her a ring. When she awakens from the vision the ring remains on her finger.

The story of her passion begins when Emperor Maxentius orders a sacrifice in honor of a heathen god and Catherine reproaches Maxentius for worshipping devils. Desiring to persuade her rather than kill her, he summons the 50 best rhetoricians in the realm to debate her. She defeats them all, and they confess themselves converted; the emperor orders them burnt. Maxentius then tries to tempt Catherine with promises of gold, power, and status, but to no effect. Infuriated, he has her stripped, beaten, and thrown into prison for 12 days without food. During this time an angel feeds her, and she converts the emperor's wife and his right-hand man, both of whom become martyrs. One of the emperor's minions then designs the "Catherine wheel": four wheels lined with spikes and saws, two moving in one direction and two moving in the other, so that anything put between them would be torn to shreds. Catherine, placed naked between the wheels, prays for God to show the gathered mob his power, and the wheel is smashed with such force that it kills 500 heathens. The emperor finally orders his men to behead her. Catherine, hearing her bridegroom calling, stretches out her neck for the axe. When her head is cut off, she bleeds milk instead of blood and angels carry her body to Sinai.

See also: Saints, Cults of the

—Leigh Smith

Celtic Mythology. Narrative religious and belief traditions of pre-Christian Celts, now known largely through various medieval manuscripts in which the traditions have been Christianized, historicized, or fictionalized to reflect the values and tastes of later times, when myths no longer functioned primarily as sacred narratives.

A wide variety of traditional beliefs, as well as some ancient mythical narratives, survived in the areas of Celtic Western Europe into the medieval period. The inhabitants of these areas were basically farmers, and as one might expect, they had strong and persistent mythical ideas concerning human dependence on the weather and the land and concerning the cyclic relationship between these. This is clear from echoes in the medieval Celtic literatures and to a lesser but not insignificant extent in the folklore of more recent times.

Early Irish literature often identifies the father deity, the Dagdae, with the sun—his name was derived from original Celtic *dago-dévos* (the good god), the term *dévos* being cognate with other Indo-European forms meaning "sky god." In Irish the sun was described as the "horseman" of the heavens, and emanations from the Dagdae are given appellations such as "herdsman" and "plowman." The mother goddess was identified with the land, responsible for the birth of young animals and for the growing of corn and fruit—she was known by many secondary names, but there are indications that her principal name was Danu, derived from that of an Indo-European river goddess. This combination of father deity and mother goddess, with its rich symbolism, can be seen behind many of the mythological narra-

tives that are found in early Irish literature and also, in a less pronounced way, in the old literature of Wales.

It is often remarked that the Celts preserved no cosmological myths, but this may be true only in an overt sense. The Celtic tendency to put night before day and the winter half of the year before the summer half must be based on the movements of the sun, which accordingly was understood to give precedence to the dead ancestors over the living community. The ancestor cult that was so strong among the ancient Celts can thus be viewed as related to the movements of the sun, which sinks in the West, where the otherworld island was situated, and which passes through the underground realm of the dead during the night.

The progression from darkness to light would appear to have been rationalized among the prehistoric Celts into a dialectical relationship between the figures *Dhuosnos* (the dark one) and *Vindos* (the bright one). This emerges in medieval Irish and Welsh narratives in hints at contests (carried out in human, fairy, or animal form) between figures named Donn and Find in Irish narratives, or kindred characters in Welsh such as Arawn and Hafgan or Gwythyr and Gwynn. The ubiquitous Find or Finn (Fion, Fionn) in Irish tradition is a derivative of *Vindos*, while Donn (from *Dhuosnos*) was in persistent Irish lore a lord of the dead whose "house" was a solitary rock off the southwest coast.

The belief that the dead passed to an otherworld island in the West was held by the ancient Celts of the Continent as well as of Britain and Ireland. This realm became known by a variety of names, such as Tír na nog (the land of the young) or Ynys Avallach (the isle of apples), and ancient tradition that envisaged the Isle of Man in this way gave rise to lore concerning a great lord of that island, a magician called in Welsh Manawydan and in Irish Manannán. The idea of an otherworld island off the west coast survived not only in Gaelic areas but also in Welsh, Cornish, and Breton traditions of the Middle Ages. It was often elaborated into legends of a city on the coast or under a lake that had been submerged by a great catastrophe due to some human error or some rash act that brought about the anger of the elements or of God himself.

Early Irish and Welsh sources contain echoes of a mythical contest at a great rock in the western sea, an idea that must have sprung from similar archaic Celtic beliefs. This was developed—probably in the prehistoric period—by associating it with the far-flung plot of a primordial battle between two sets of deities. In its most elaborate form, in the early-medieval Irish text *Cath Maige Tuired*, a great battle is described between the divine Tuatha Dé Danann (people of the goddess Danu) and the sinister Fomorians (Fomoire) (underspirits, who had strong aquatic connections). Such development of mythic symbolism into historical legend is typical of how the detritus of ancient myth came to be treated in medieval lore. The Tuatha Dé Danann are described in the text as inhabitants of Ireland with their royal center at Tara, and the Fomorians as sea pirates who oppress them in a variety of ways. The cast of characters includes several Celtic deities, such the Dagdae himself, his consort the goddess Morrigan (Mor-Ríoghain, "phantom queen"), the smith god Goibhniu, and the polytechnic god Lug (Lugh).

Lug wins the battle for the Tuatha Dé Danann by slaying the Fomorian leader, Balar, who has a terrible eye that destroys all on which it looks. This Balar (from Celtic *Bolerios) dwells on the rocky island of Tory off the northwest coast, and perhaps of equal significance, he is also associated with Mizen Head, the extreme southwest point of Ireland. In fact, the extreme southwest area of Britain was anciently known as Bolerion, a cognate of his name. Balar's connections with both the scorching and the setting sun are therefore clear, and Lug may represent the sun in its more constructive role. Such a basic format was developed into a plot that had Lug as the prophesied son of Balar's daughter, a format that echoes a well-known mythic structure of the eastern Mediterranean region (such as accounts of Sargon, Cyrus, Moses, and Perseus). It seems likely that this plot had been borrowed in antiquity by the Continental Celts from the Greeks and attached to their deity Lugus, of whom Lug is the Irish development. Traces of it have also been argued for Lleu, the Welsh equivalent of the deity, who is described in the *Mabinogi* and other medieval Welsh sources. The plot was further used in medieval Irish accounts of the heroic youth of Finn mac Cumaill, and in the Breton source that Marie de France used for her lay *Yonec*.

Other Celtic deities survived strongly in medieval lore, and in even more human forms. A noted example was the Celtic goddess *Rigantona* (exalted queen), cognate with the above-mentioned Irish Morrigan. In the *Mabinogi* she appears in the guise of Rhiannon, an otherworld woman riding on a large white horse that outstrips all her pursuers. Morrigan was in fact the original name of the otherworld lady known as Macha in the medieval Irish literature. As the goddess of Ulster kingship, she acquired the new name from that of the area that was the center of that kingdom—Macha meaning "plain" or "pasture." Macha was described as a great runner, and her most celebrated achievement was winning a race against horses. Such a *Rigantona*-personage, paralleling the ancestor deity in equine associations, must have been the same as the Continental Celtic goddess of horses known as Epona (exalted horse lady).

Medieval Irish literature relates that Macha warned her husband not to boast of her running skills, but he does so, leading to the tragic end of their union. This exemplifies the process by which suitable narratives were borrowed to underline the importance of mythical personages. The narrative plot here concerns an otherworld woman coming to live with an ordinary man and then leaving him after he breaks a prohibition she had put on him. This seems to have been a floating folklore plot in Western Europe in the early Middle Ages, for it appears later in French legends of Melusine. The floating motif easily attached itself to the goddess of Ulster kingship, as the marriage of the king to the land goddess was an ancient conceit in Celtic inauguration rites. The maintaining of kingship was of course a precarious business, and immemorial tradition had added many types of *gessa* (magical prohibitions) to the ordinary social pressures that a king had to endure.

Lofty personages were made the subjects of floating medieval plots in other contexts also. A popular story in early-medieval Ireland told of how the Daghdha was made to relinquish control of his dwelling in the prehistoric tumulus of Brugh na Bóinne (Newgrange in County Meath) to his son Aenghus. According to this, Aenghus got a loan of the dwelling "for a night and a day" and then kept it forever by claiming that all time is computed as night and day. There are several other ruses of the "tomorrow never comes" type described in Irish tradition, and clearly the plot has been borrowed here from popular lore. Again, however, it underlines the ancient mythic idea of son superseding father or by extension the ritual idea of a king gaining tenure of his realm from the ancestor deity. The name Aenghus meant "true vigor," and the process is again revealed in the name of a character in the Ulster cycle who also relinquishes a kingdom: Fergus mac Roig (or Ferghus mac Ro-éich, literally, "male vigor son of great horse"). The archaic basis of the ritual may further be exemplified by the pseudonym of Aenghus, Maccan Óg, which scholars regard as a development from the archaic Celtic youth deity Maponos, son of Matrona ("exalted mother" or "great mother"). Maponos appears in medieval Welsh sources as Mabon.

As in the case of narrative plots, the mythological personages themselves could gain popularity in comparatively mundane form. A clear instance is the smith god known in Irish as Goibhniu and in Welsh as Gofannon. His memory survived in a Christian context as a marvelous craftsman called Góbán Saer, and legends were told of how this Góbán built monasteries and round towers for saints throughout the length and breadth of Ireland. The images of Celtic deities, particularly Lug, have been deciphered by scholars in the cults of several early Irish saints, while the celebrated St. Brighid (Brigid) of the sixth century c.e. has attracted to her tradition much of the cult of her namesake, the Celtic goddess Brighid (the highest one), and accordingly was portrayed as a patroness of agriculture, of fertility, and of poetry. The cult of St. Brighid, in turn, exerted a large influence on the lore concerning other female saints, not only in Ireland but throughout much of the medieval Celtic world.

The goddess persona persisted into medieval Ireland in two ways: as a convention in the verses of poets, where goddesses were mentioned as consorts and protectresses of great kings and chieftains, and in ordinary folklore, where they were described as fairy queens ruling from palaces within several of the archaeological structures that dot the Irish countryside. One of the most famous of these ladies was Áine (the bright one), patroness of the Eoghanacht dynasty in Munster and later of the Norman family of Fitzgerald. Many folk legends tell of how she appeared from time to time to assist families in need. The patronage of the goddesses, indeed, developed through medieval tradition into one of the most celebrated of all spirits in Irish culture, the banshee (*bean sí*, meaning "woman of the tumulus," or "fairy woman"). She is heard to lament the death of a member of the old Gaelic race, thus showing her special connection with and affection for such a person. Another retention of goddess imagery is exemplified by lore of the Cailleach Bhéarra, an old hag who was said to have lived from time immemorial and was particularly associated in Ireland with farming and harvesting and in Scotland with the wilderness and forests.

Druidic lore did not survive in direct form from ancient Celtic belief, but the learned castes preserved into the Middle Ages and to more recent times much of the mystical and magical functions of their druidic predecessors. It is logical to relate to this context the prophetic and clairvoyant utterances of such figures as Finn and Mongán in Ireland and Myrddin and Taliesin in Wales, as well as the legends concerning the magical powers of many historical poets (resulting in particular from their satires). Aspects of druidic lore persisted in accounts of poets getting their inspiration from otherworld sources and (in a broader narrative context) in the frequent motif in heroic and romantic stories of entry to the otherworld while sleeping or in a trance or through biding at a tumulus. Adventures of this kind concerning Cú Chulainn and Finn in Ireland and Pwyll and Rhonabwy in Wales are the most celebrated, but such visits were a commonplace of the marvelous stories in medieval Celtic literature.

There were many accounts of pseudohistorical or historical ancient kings. The most celebrated of these was Arthur, who bore a Romanized Celtic name, and who probably was in origin a *dux Britanniarum,* a leader of native soldiers in the Britain of the fifth or sixth century C.E. Such leaders, with more or less conventional Roman military skills, tried to defend Britain against the Anglo-Saxon invaders after the imperial legions left. Early sources describe him as the head of a faithful body of warriors and winning several battles, and he was also claimed to have been a great

hunter. From the eleventh century onward, the new Norman overlords of Britain expropriated his memory. Lore about him and his followers developed rapidly, and he came to be portrayed after the manner of a medieval feudal king with his Knights of the Round Table.

The most famous king in Irish medieval lore was Cormac mac Airt, whose origin is lost in remote antiquity but whose connection with the kingship of Tara was exploited by the Connachta or Uí Neill dynasty, predominant in Ireland from the fifth to the eleventh centuries C.E. Legends of Cormac depicted him as a great ancient king who was cared for by a wolf bitch as a child, who came to prominence at 30 years of age, and who delivered many wise counsels and judgments. As the model and claimed founder of Uí Neill kingship, he was thus being portrayed on the lines of the great founders whose fame was becoming known through biblical and classical learning: Romulus, Christ, and Solomon. Much of the regnal and historical lore of medieval Ireland in fact came from sources connected with the Uí Neill dynasty, but it contained within it archaic ritualistic and mythical notions such as the notion that the forces of nature take an active part in the reign of a king and determine his ultimate destiny.

A wide range of migratory motifs and legends circulated within the Celtic world of the Middle Ages. Some of these may have been part of local tradition from time immemorial—such as the cauldron possessed by a deity or magical being that was always full of food and that revived any dead warriors thrown into it. One of the best-known migratory legends had a "three-cornered" plot in which a young hero meets a tragic end through falling in love with a beautiful lady betrothed to a vengeful older man. This is the plot of the tragic stories of Deirdre and Naíse or Gráinne and Diarmaid in Ireland, and of Drystan and Essyllt (Tristan and Iseut) in Cornwall and Brittany. Other migratory motives that were well known in medieval Celtic lore concerned the workings of fate. Examples include the sacrifice of an innocent youth to use his blood in building a fortress, the botched attempt by a man to regain his wife from the fairy realm, the mysterious lake horse that brings great benefit to a farmer until it departs after being hit, and the prophesied death of an individual in an unlikely place or by unlikely means.

These motifs circulated orally, but others may have been spread mainly by literary borrowing. Examples of the latter include a ring being fortuitously recovered from the belly of a fish; a camp or fortress being captured by attackers who gain entry by concealing themselves in baskets or bags, the supernatural lapse of hundreds of years when a hero visits the otherworld, or the false accusation of an innocent young man by the wife of a powerful ruler. Motifs of this kind could be found in Greek and Latin writings, from which medieval Celtic writers borrowed them into their own works. When read out from these more homely sources, the motifs in turn passed into the oral lore of the ordinary people.

With the spread of the Roman Empire, and perhaps from an even earlier date, international tale types entered the cultural zones of the Celts. This process of plot borrowing was much accelerated in the medieval period through trade contacts with other countries; through the travels of clerics, pilgrims, and merchants; and also through the Viking settlements in many Celtic areas. Dozens of such international plots have been identified in medieval Welsh and Irish literature, often being used in association with the names of mythical and historical characters from indigenous tradition. This was another aspect of the tendency to develop detritus of rituals and beliefs into romantic narratives, a process that modern scholars, from their different perspectives, might view either as a confusion of the earlier tradition or as a dramatic perpetuation of it.

One singular example of a very ancient folktale being embedded in early Irish tradition is the story of Mider and his love for Étaín. Both of these characters, as well as several others in the story, were mythical personages, and there are several echoes of ancient ritual and history involved. In the actual story, however, Mider loses Étaín and has to perform stupendous tasks to regain her—this and other motifs in the story possess relatives in AT 313, "The Girl as Helper in the Hero's Flight," one of the earliest and most far-flung international tale types known. It must have been connected with the ancient Irish traditional material sometime in the early centuries of the common era.

A celebrated story in the Welsh *Mabinogi* tells of a male child born to Rhiannon being stolen away by a giant. Rhiannon is accused of killing the baby. A foal is later stolen by the same giant, but the owner of the foal cuts off the giant's hand and manages to recover both baby and foal. Rhiannon and other characters belong to ancient Celtic tradition, but the plot of the story possesses strong parallels in AT 653 ("The Four Skillful Brothers"), AT 712, and other international narrative material. In fact, a similar use of some of the same material occurs in a later medieval Irish story in which Finn mac Cumaill recovers stolen children and puppies from a giant. Finn enlists the assistance of marvelous helpers in his task, a plot based on AT 653; and the related helper tale AT 513 ("The Helpers") is in fact the plot base for another celebrated *Mabinogi* story, that of *Culhwch and Olwen*.

Metamorphosis was a trait often associated with the deities of early Celtic myth, perhaps originating in druidic emphasis on such mystical faculties. By the medieval period it had become commonplace among Welsh and Irish writers when describing the great worthies of old, especially those who had divine names or divine attributes. It was claimed that they could take the forms of various animals and birds and could, when necessary, live for long periods in such forms. To underline and dramatize this belief, narrators made use of episodes and motifs well known elsewhere in international traditions, such as the final episode of the folktale "The Magician and His Pupil" (AT 325), in which two magicians take on various forms as they fight each other. Such tales of transformation influenced the contest of the bulls in the Ulster cycle and the Welsh story of Taliesin. One very popular tradition, frequently used by medieval storytellers in both Wales and Ireland, concerned the great age of particular animals, whose names were celebrated in tradition, and the task of seeking out these animals and comparing their ages. The two principal plots in question—AT 80A* ("Who Gets the Beehive") and AT 726 ("The Oldest on the Farm")—were very old in European lore, but their combination would appear to have been a particular development in the Celtic areas.

Of the many other international narrative plots utilized in medieval Celtic folklore, we may quote one example to show how such material could be at once simple in its structure and pervasive in its influence. This is the story of the king with ass's ears (AT 782), which was well known in classical sources (where the king is often said to be King Midas) and in other sources. A good deal of tradition centered on a king called March, reputed to have been the elderly lover of Essyllt and thus the rival of Drystan (these three characters are commonly known as Mark, Tristan, and Iseut in the Continental literature of the Middle Ages). The name was a corruption of the Latin one, Marcus, borne by a sixth-century local ruler in southwest Britain. It could, however, be interpreted as "horse" by speakers of Celtic. It was natural, then, for the ass's ears, transformed into horse's ears, to be attributed to him. The story was told in Wales, Cornwall, and Brittany that he concealed his ears, but his barber grew sick from keeping the secret and whispered it to a tree or to reeds. A musical instrument was made from the tree or the reeds, and when it was played sang out the dreadful secret! This March was famous in tradition as a seafarer (*llynghessawc*), and thus the story traveled across the Irish Sea and became told of the ancient mythical Leinster king Labhraidh, who was also known as a seafarer (*loingseach*).

See also: Annwfn; Arthurian Lore; Fenian Cycle; Folktale; Gwynn ap Nudd; Irish Tradition; Myrddin; Myth; Taliesin

—Dáithí Ó hÓgáin

Chanson de Geste. Medieval French epic legend.

The chanson de geste (from the French *chanson*, "song," and *geste*, "action, exploit, history") is the medieval French epic legend, written in assonantal or rhymed verse. The earliest extant manuscript is of the *Song of Roland*, written around 1125–1150. Most extant chansons de geste were written down from the late twelfth to the early fourteenth centuries, and the genre remained popular for the duration of the Middle Ages, both in French and translated, and also through imitations in other languages. Most had nationalistic or military themes. Estimates of the number of chansons de geste extant range from 70 to 100, depending on the reasoning behind the estimate.

The French epic tradition has been influential outside France, with works that borrow the form or the content of the chansons de geste appearing in Western European countries into the early modern period. The *Song of Roland* is the most famous.

There are three major ways of classifying chansons de geste: by literary form, cycle, or main character. These forms of classification reveal a great deal about the epics themselves.

In terms of literary classification, the classic, but by no means universal, chanson de geste form is considered to be a *laisse* (irregular-length stanza) comprising decasyllabic lines, each with a caesura after the fourth or sixth syllable. A large number of the earlier chansons de geste use this form, with assonantal *laisses*. Later chansons de geste are more likely to have rhymed alexandrine (12-syllable) *laisses*. There were also prose redactions of the epics in the later Middle Ages.

The most common classification is by cycle. Chansons de geste were often linked in theme or dealt with episodes from a hero's life. A grouping of all the works on Charlemagne or on an epic hero is called a cycle. The earliest known cyclic classification was by the thirteenth-century author Bertrand de Bar-sur-Aube. He defined three groupings: that of the kings of France, that of Doon de Mayence, and that of Garin de Monglane. The first refers to what is commonly called today the *cycle des rois*, or kings' cycle, in which Charlemagne is the chief figure. The second refers to the *cycle des Loherains*, or feuding barons' cycle, and the third features Guillaume d'Orange. More-recent analysts have broken up the works differently, some adding a cycle concerning the First Crusade. The Crusade cycle, however, is seldom dealt with by modern scholars in the same context as other chansons de geste.

Classification by character refers to groupings of works based on the life of a single figure. While the date of writing may not follow the chronology of the epic hero's life, the order of the chansons de geste in the manuscripts invariably starts with the hero's youth, then moves to his early knighthood, then his major battles, followed by his death or retirement to a monastery. Not all heroes have all of these episodes, but the sequence is consistent across the genre. To enable a listener or reader to instantly identify important characters, they were often "marked" by distinguishing traits. Roland had his sword and his horn, whereas Guillaume d'Orange was known by his nose. Major epic heroes included Roland, Oliver, Raoul de Cambrai, Gerbert de Mes, Renaut de Montauban, William of Orange (Guillaume d'Orange), Ogier, and Godfrey of Bouillon.

While Roland is the best known today of the French epic heroes, William of Orange was considered one of the great heroes in the French Middle Ages. He has tentatively been identified with William of Toulouse by several scholars. His exploits were widely known even outside the French-speaking world—for example, he is mentioned in Dante's *Divine Comedy*, as was Godfrey of Bouillon, another great epic hero. The historical Godfrey was born around 1060 and was a key figure in the First Crusade; the legendary Godfrey was said to be the grandson of Elias, the Swan Knight. This gives the hero a mythic ancestry (compare the legend that named the fairy Melusine the ancestress of the French house of Lusignan). Godfrey is a key character in the Crusade cycle of chansons de geste.

Although the tales recounted in the chansons de geste were popular in the Middle Ages, few are well known today. Even the tale of the Swan Knight, made famous through Wagner's opera *Lohengrin*, significantly differs from its epic roots.

While the *Song of Roland* is deservedly famous, there are other epics that are close to it in stature, although very different in literary style. *Raoul de Cambrai*, for instance, is a brilliant treatment of the tragic consequences of injustice and unrelenting anger. The stories dealing with the Mez family build the looming threat of continuing vendettas into a violent series of mesmeric and haunting tales. Not all outstanding chansons de geste were serious: the *Pèlerinage de Charlemagne*, for instance, has brilliant comic sequences as Charles and his lords discover that France is not the center of the cultivated world.

No music has survived for a chanson de geste proper, although a small amount of music does survive for the satirical *Audigier*. Most scholars agree that chansons de geste demonstrate their oral and possibly musical origins through the retention of a large number of oral traits in the works, ranging from their form (division of the text into *laisses*, with a distinct narrative style linked to this, such as the appearance of *laisses similaires*, in which an episode of great importance is dwelled upon through incremental or varied repetition) to phrases that appear in texts (such as comments by the *jongleur* to the audience). Even as the genre became more "written and read" in the later Middle Ages, it retained this sense of being created for live performance.

Scholars are divided on the subject of authors and of the precise oral or written nature of the chanson de geste. One school holds that chansons de geste were written by individuals; another, that they are the product of the collective oral process. Modern scholars are tending toward the view that there may have been an oral or collective gestation period for many chansons de geste but that individual authors were more likely to have written down the extant versions. There are very few named authors for chansons de geste, and most of these are for later works. Interestingly, the *Song of Roland* has a possible named author. The final line names "Turoldus." The jury is still out on whether Turoldus was scribe, author, or performer.

Whether chansons de geste ranked in the Middle Ages as histories or as pure literature is also disputed. While they are not accounted histories by most modern historians and clearly thought of as works of literature by many modern medievalists, it is generally accepted that many works have a core of historical veracity. My work suggests that in the Middle Ages they were regarded as works of history, and internal evidence shows that they were written as a form of history, not simply as entertainment. Most scholarship on the chansons de geste is in French. While no work in English provides a complete introduction to the genre, several bibliographical guides and studies on specific aspects are useful.

See also: *Chanson de Roland*; Charlemagne; Swan Knight; William of Orange

—Gillian S. Polack

Chanson de Roland [Song of Roland]. An epic poem that recounts the battle of Roncevaux, in which Roland, Emperor Charlemagne's sister's son and captain of the rearguard of his army, dies of the effort of blowing his elephant-tusk horn (olifant).

Roland sounds the horn to call his uncle and the rest of the Frankish force back across the Pyrenees into Spain when the rear guard is treacherously attacked by the Saracens under King Marsile. In the preceding battle, Roland's companion Oliver and ten other knights—who, along with Roland, are the leaders constituting the Twelve Peers—and all their followers had been killed. Charlemagne's efforts to capture Saragossa had been stymied, but he returns. Assisted by a miracle that stops the sun in the sky, he succeeds in pursuing the Saracens to the river Ebro, where most of them drown. He then defeats in single combat Baligant, the emperor of Islam, who has arrived to help his vassal Marsile. Charlemagne takes the city of Saragossa and completes his conquest of Spain in its entirety. Upon the army's return to Aix-la-Chapelle, Charlemagne tells Aude, Oliver's sister, who is betrothed to Roland, that the hero has died, upon which she falls dead herself rather than survive him. Roland's stepfather Ganelon, who plotted the ambush during his journey as envoy to Marsile's court and who nominated Roland to lead the rearguard, undergoes a trial at Aix-la-Chapelle in which the jury attempts to reconcile him with Charlemagne. In a subsequent ordeal by combat, his champion Pinabel is defeated by Roland's kinsman Thierry, and as a result Ganelon is executed by being torn apart by horses.

The *Song of Roland* belongs to the genre of the chansons de geste—epic songs that told the deeds of ancestral heroes. These works, ranging in length from 800 to more than 35,000 lines, were sung by itinerant performers, *jongleurs*, who typically accompanied themselves on a stringed instrument, the *vielle*. None of the music of the chansons de geste has been preserved except for that attached to a one-line parody of the genre found in Adam de la Halle's thirteenth-century *Jeu de Robin et de Marion* (Play of Robin and Marion). Over a hundred chansons de geste have been preserved from the Middle Ages. Like a number of older chansons de geste, the *Song of Roland* is based on a historical event, the defeat of Charlemagne's rear guard in a pass of the Pyrenees on August 15, 778. The main historical source for that event is the *Life of Charlemagne* written by one of the emperor's courtiers, Einhard, who lists a Roland, prefect of the March of Brittany, as one of those killed in the battle. Whether Roland was a historical personage is unresolved, however, as only one branch of the manuscripts of Einhard's *Life* mentions him.

The earliest of the seven texts and three fragments of the *Song of Roland* in Old French (the one found in manuscript Digby 23 of the Bodleian Library in Oxford, England; 4,002 lines) is composed in assonance. All but a handful of editions and all translations into modern English and French are based on this version, which was copied in England in the second quarter of the twelfth century and is the oldest manuscript of any chanson de geste. The other texts are in rhyme, with the exception of that found in the Venice 4 manuscript (thirteenth century), which is partly in assonance and partly in rhyme. Of the seven manuscripts, three were copied by Italian scribes, and the legend of Roland gave rise to a thriving tradition of derivative texts in Italy, including Boiardo's *Orlando innamorato* and Ariosto's *Orlando furioso*. The *Song of Roland* was translated or adapted in the Middle Ages into Norse, German, Welsh, Provençal, Spanish, Latin, English, and Dutch. Among its modern derivatives are Roland traditions in the Sicilian puppet theater, in the oral poetry and chapbooks of Brazil, and in Spanish and Faroese balladry.

The longest French version (late twelfth century, 8,397 lines) is found in the Venice 7 and Châteauroux manuscripts. Like the other versions in rhyme, this text adds a series of episodes that appear to satisfy the needs of a different audience from that of the Oxford manuscript. At the onset of those episodes God works two miracles to allow the Franks to distinguish the bodies of their fallen companions from those of the Saracens: the latter turn into hawthorn bushes, but hazel trees grow out of the mass graves dug for the Christians. Biers are constructed from these trees for the corpses of Roland, Oliver, and the archbishop Turpin. Their bodies, as well as those of the Twelve Peers, are taken to Saint-Jean-

Pied-de-Port, whence Charlemagne sends messengers to summon Aude. At this point, Ganelon escapes from his captors and is pursued and taken. Aude and her uncle set out and during the journey she has a series of troubling dreams full of animal and vegetative symbolism. Both the priest who is called upon to interpret the dreams and Charlemagne himself, however, feign that nothing is amiss and that Aude is destined to marry Roland. The emperor initially purports to have lost his nephew to a Saracen princess, but finally he must tell her that Roland and her brother Oliver are dead. After spending time alone with the bodies of Roland and Oliver—whose voice is counterfeited by an angel—Aude confesses her sins and dies. She is buried with her two companions at Blaye. When the army overtakes Ganelon, he undergoes two trials by combat, the first against Gondelbof the Frisian, ending in another attempted escape; the second through his champion Pinabel who, as in the Oxford text, loses to Thierry. Ganelon confesses that he betrayed Roland and after a series of scenes in which the French barons vie in proposing the most gruesome punishment, he is torn apart by horses, again as in the texts in assonance. The French return to their homes, but Charlemagne remains behind. The greatly elaborated episode of Aude's death, the stasis of the final scene, the addition of the miracle scenes, Ganelon's twin escapes, and the debate over punishment change the nature of the *Song of Roland* by diluting its military character with effects of pathos and suspense. This transformation may correspond to the shift from an audience of warriors to one consisting of both men and women.

The early-twelfth-century historian William of Malmesbury mentions that a song about Roland was sung to the Norman army at the onset of the battle of Hastings (1066) so that the warriors might be inspired by the example of its hero. This reference is generally taken to refer to a version of the *Song of Roland* earlier than any now available to us. The Oxford version claims that Charlemagne had conquered England (ll. 372, 2332); had this been true, it would have provided a useful precedent for the Norman invaders. A persistent medieval legend ("Charlemagne's Sin"), to which the Oxford version may obliquely refer (ll. 2095–2098), holds that Roland was not only Charlemagne's nephew but also his son, born of an act of incest with his sister Gisele. God himself subsequently revealed this sin to the emperor's confessor, St. Giles, while the latter was saying mass. Branch 1 of the Old Norse *Karlamagnus Saga*, which summarizes a series of now lost chansons de geste and gives the story of Charlemagne and Roland up to the beginning of the *Song of Roland*, recounts this legend in detail. It also provides a motive for the enmity between Ganelon and Roland, telling how the young hero was seduced by Ganelon's second wife, Geluviz. The Provençal version makes open reference to

Charlemagne's Sin, and it is also narrated clearly in the fourteenth-century epic *Tristan de Nanteuil*. The Charlemagne window in the cathedral of Chartres is dominated by the Mass of St. Giles. If one accepts that the legend of Charlemagne's Sin was known to the poet of the *Song of Roland*, the work may be interpreted as recounting Charlemagne's punishment for his sin by the death of his first-born son, the fruit of that sin. This interpretation has the additional attraction of explaining the location of the earthquake that takes place in the poem (ll. 1428–1429) in anticipation of Roland's demise: not in the Pyrenees where the battle is taking place but in the ancestral land of the Franks, which mourns the coming death of the offspring of the Frankish royal family.

The earliest indication that a *Song of Roland* was in existence comes from medieval documents dating to around the year 1000 that are witnessed by pairs of brothers named Roland and Oliver. Roland is not a very common name in the period, and Oliver is quite rare. Some of the Roland-Oliver brothers are twins. The linking of the two names in this period is seen as an anomaly, one that probably arose from the popularity of a version of the *Song of Roland*. Most Roland scholars accept this conclusion. A note found by Dámaso Alonso in a manuscript copied at the monastery of San Millan de la Cogolla in Spain, dated to the period 1065–1075, contains the summary of a *Song of Roland* that, to judge by the form of the proper names mentioned in it, was composed in Spanish. Some scholars believe on the basis of this "Nota Emilianense" and the onomastic evidence that a French version of the *Song of Roland* must have existed at least as early as the eleventh century. This evidence and arguments from a comparative study of oral-formulaic epic style have led me to conclude that the *Song of Roland* was composed and transmitted orally from a very early period up to the time it was committed to writing in a version close to that found in the Oxford manuscript.

The Oxford text ends with a line that is susceptible to a number of interpretations, the most probable being that the work that Turoldus writes is coming to an end. Some take this name as that of an author, some—as is more likely—as that of a scribe.

See also: Chanson de Geste; Charlemagne; French Tradition

—Joseph J. Duggan

Charivari. A medieval folk custom or ritual consisting of a noisy, masked demonstration, often performed at night, enacted to mortify some wrongdoer in the community, whose transgression was usually social rather than legal.

Both to protect their own identity and to further distress the victims, participants in this ritual of humiliation often concealed their identity by producing bestial noises and wearing animal masks, skins, and costumes or otherwise disguising themselves as animals. They performed raucous songs and made an artificial racket by noisily banging pots and pans like drums, playing other makeshift "musical" instruments fashioned out of household implements, blowing whistles, and ringing bells outside the house of their victim. In the late Middle Ages charivari was an international phenomenon. Practices comparable to the French charivari (even in France, the spelling varied by region, including *chalivali, calvali, chanavari, coribari*) were called *cencerrada* in Spain, *scampanate* in Italy, and *katzenmusik* in Germany. In most cases the names for this ritual allude to this important aural element common in all cultures. The English version of charivari, "rough music," overlapped with similar local folk customs such as the "Skimmity" or "Skimmington," "Riding the Stang," and the "Stag Hunt."

The typical impetus for enacting this ritual was perceived marital disorder. In rural areas remarrying widows or widowers were the most frequent victims of charivari, especially if there was a gross disparity between the age of the bride and groom. The rationales for these youth-driven humiliations varied. Not only was the older partner removing a young person from the local pool of those eligible for marriage, but because remarriages were often conducted quietly and privately at night, the community was deprived of a daylong occasion for festivity and free food and drink. Both in rural and especially in urban centers, other common targets of charivaris were husbands who beat their wives or (more often) husbands who had been beaten by their wives, cuckolded husbands, adulterous wives, people who married foreigners or cultural outsiders, and various sexual transgressors or deviants. What all these offenses had in common was their inversion of the "natural" social order.

In the countryside the groups who enacted the charivaris, referred to as Abbeys of Misrule, were often composed of disorderly local youths who identified themselves as the "abbots" of misrule in mockery of monastic and ecclesiastical rules. The masked, costumed modus operandi of the charivari was designed to divert attention away from the identity and status of these mock abbots. By this means the intended focus could be aimed at (and the onus suffered by) the designated victims, almost scapegoats—the socially transgressive, now shamed newlyweds, cuckolds, husband beaters, and so on. These organized groups secretly conspired to meet at night in costume and to process to the victim's house, yelling profanities, singing raucous songs, and sometimes carrying effigies of the victims. The following day the perpetrators of the charivari would act as if nothing had happened, but the victims had been forced to endure mortification in the community. The Church's official attitude to the charivari was disapproval. Strong opposition to the charivari was expressed in explicit interdictions against the custom at the 1329–1330 Council of

Compiègne and the 1337 Synod of Avignon and continued to be registered in consistent ecclesiastical censure of the practice throughout the fourteenth and fifteenth centuries.

The first extensive medieval literary description of the charivari is found in the early-fourteenth-century *Roman de Fauvel*, a satirical allegory by Gervais du Bus, in which the title character, a donkey who represents disorder, attempts to marry Fortune. When she rejects his suit, he instead marries Vainglory. On the wedding night of this transgressively matched couple, Harlequin the clown and his bestially costumed followers mock the union by performing a *"chalivali"* with makeshift musical instruments. The manuscript of the *Roman de Fauvel* contains three illuminations that offer perhaps the most authentic period illustrations of medieval charivari. One depicts the disturbingly mismatched married couple, with the literally asinine Fauvel approaching the marriage bed of Vainglory, imaged as a human woman. Below this scene are two panels depicting the grotesquely masked and costumed charivari "musicians" who appear to be "serenading" the newlyweds derisively with their own version of rough music (see illustration).

One of the most infamous incidents in the late-fourteenth-century reign of the French king Charles VI, the so-called Bal des Ardents or "dance of the burning men" at a 1393 wedding reception hosted by the king, was interpreted by a royal chronicler, the Monk of St. Denis, as a charivari. Notwithstanding this arguable example (Jean Froissart and other chroniclers do not allude to charivari in other accounts of the event), the charivari generally functioned as an ordered representation of disorder, a means by which the traditional community could express conscious or sublimated frustrations and anxieties, reaffirm social and cultural mores, defend local sexual standards, and release social tensions—all through the "safe" but inverted world of carnivalesque representation that the noise, disguises, and adoptions of animal personae permitted.

See also: Bal des Ardents; Dance

—Lorraine K. Stock

Charlemagne (742–814) [Carolus Magnus, Charles the Great]. The most important monarch of the early Middle Ages.

He was born the son of Pepin III, also called Pepin the Short, and Bertrada on (probably) April 2, 742. With his brother Carloman, he succeeded his father in 768. At Carloman's death in 771 he became absolute ruler of the Frankish realm. In 800 Charlemagne was crowned emperor in Rome by Pope Leo III. He died on January 28, 814. Charlemagne was married four times, and from these marriages he had three sons and five daughters. In his lifetime he waged many wars, against the Langobards, Saxons, Avars, and Arabs, but he also maintained diplomatic relations with Byzantine emperors and with the ᶜAb-basid caliph Harun al-Rashid. He organized the Frankish realm in counties with a strong central administration and was actively involved in Church policy and education. His person and performance were so impressive that Charlemagne lived on after his death, sometimes even larger than life. This process of epic concentration, in which legendary acts are falsely ascribed to a person, can be followed in the extensive medieval literature on Charlemagne, which first appears in Latin within two decades of his death.

The first biography of Charlemagne, Einhard's *Vita Caroli* (c. 829–836), was modeled after Suetonius's *Lives of the Caesars,* especially the chapter on Augustus. Einhard (d. 840), who knew Charlemagne personally, presents him favorably but avoids the poetic exaggerations of later biographies, such as Notker the Stammerer's *De Carlo Magno* (884–887), written for Charles the Fat, Charlemagne's great-grandson. Notker mingles facts with legendary anecdotes relating, for example, how Charlemagne helped a monk who could not sing, and how he "measured with his sword" (decapitated) Norse children. The anecdotes in *De Carlo Magno* are mainly related to persons surrounding Charlemagne, and Notker uses them to convey his criticism of the secular clergy.

Three centuries after appearing in Latin accounts, Charlemagne himself emerges most fully as a folktale protagonist in vernacular literature. The youth of Charlemagne is the subject of the *Mainet* (Old French, twelfth century), which became popular throughout Europe. Here Charlemagne is the son of Pepin and Berte, but the circumstances of his conception are confusing: at that moment King Pepin does not know who his legitimate wife is. Young Charlemagne is threatened by his evil half brothers and flees to Spain, where he adopts the name Mainet and lives at the court of the Saracen king Galafre. On Galafre's behalf Charlemagne subdues the mighty Braiment, after which he has a love affair with the fair Galienne. Charlemagne is now recognized as the best knight in the world, worthy to wear King Pepin's crown. In some versions he then travels to Paris, where he vanquishes his half brothers and receives the crown. Other versions tell of an attack on him by Marsile and an episode in which Charlemagne relieves the besieged town of Rome. J. R. Mien sees at the core of the *Mainet* the archetypal story of a hero, a king's son who is fathered under unusual circumstances, only to be expelled from his own country. In a foreign land the hero must achieve glory by feats of arms to prove himself worthy of the crown. Though *Mainet* has no historical core, it is important that Charlemagne is represented as a worthy king, ennobled by tests of fortune and ruling in harmony and peace.

In *Karel ende Elegast* (Middle Dutch, twelfth–thirteenth centuries, with versions in German, Norse, and Danish), the folktale elements are even more obvious. As Charlemagne sleeps at Ingelheim, God orders him to go out stealing. Reluctantly he obeys, and in the dark woods he meets Elegast, a vassal he had banished. In a joust he vanquishes Elegast, who confesses to being a thief. Charlemagne then recognizes in him a possible help for his mission; presenting himself as the thief Adelbrecht, he proposes to rob king Charlemagne! Filled with indignation, Elegast refuses to do so and instead proposes to rob Eggeric, Charlemagne's wicked brother-in-law. En route to Eggeric's castle, Charlemagne-Adelbrecht takes hold of a coulter (a pointed or cutting implement), which he wants to use as a burglar's tool. Elegast is the first to sneak in, but a cock, whose language he understands by means of some magic herbs, warns him that the king is near the castle. He leaves the castle, but Charlemagne persuades him to go through with their plan. With a magic charm Elegast puts all the inhabitants of the castle to sleep and opens all locks. They gather many treasures and Charlemagne wants to go home. But Elegast wants to steal a precious saddle out of Eggeric's bedroom. There he overhears Eggeric tell his wife that he plans to murder Charlemagne. When Charlemagne's sister reacts with indignation, Eggeric strikes her in the face. Elegast catches her blood in his glove and subsequently informs Charlemagne about the conspiracy. The next day Charlemagne holds court and unmasks the conspirators. Elegast's glove proves Eggeric's guilt, but a trial by combat brings the ultimate decision: Elegast kills Eggeric. Elegast himself is rehabilitated and receives Eggeric's widow as his wife.

The nucleus of the story is formed by folktale traditions of the master thief (particularly AT 952, "The King and the Soldier," but see also AT 950, 951, 1525), combined with the motif of the disguised king who acts as an agent provocateur and discovers a conspiracy against himself (motif K1812.2). The use of magic herbs (to understand animal language) and incantations (to put people asleep and open doors) is well known from folktales, but Charlemagne's use of a coulter as a burglary tool can also be considered a folkloric element. The coulter was actually much used in burglary, to the extent that possessing one could be legally compromising. Because God is the initiator of Charlemagne's adventure, Charlemagne ends up as the just king, under protection of God. The combination of story elements that characterizes *Karel ende Elegast* remains common in many recently collected oral folktales. Modern scholarship has identified postmedieval folktales from Mongolia, Russia, Lithuania, Bohemia, and Poland possessing significant plot parallels to *Karel ende Elegast.* H. W. J. Kroes maintains that the Middle Dutch version represents the root tale from which the others were descended, but he does not explain their transmission history.

The *Pèlerinage de Charlemagne* (Pilgrimage of

Charlemagne), a twelfth-century Anglo-Norman poem with Scandinavian versions, offers perhaps the most coherent example of a Charlemagne text with a folktale structure. Piqued by his wife's taunt that she knows a king greater than he, Charlemagne decides to find this king, Hugo the Strong of Constantinople. He tells his peers, however, that they are going on a pilgrimage to Jerusalem. When they arrive, they are mistaken for Christ and his apostles and receive many relics. After some time, Charlemagne remembers his original goal, and they set off for Constantinople. There the queen's words are justified: Charlemagne and his peers cut a poor figure amid the splendor of the Byzantine court. After being feasted, they make wild boasts, which Hugo learns of through a spy. He obliges them to carry out their boasts, which they do, but only with God's help. Thus Charlemagne's superiority over Hugo is affirmed, but not before he is humiliated: in the final test a flood occurs, which forces Hugo to capitulate but also threatens Charlemagne and his peers. In a procession, Charlemagne's superiority is expressed concretely: he is one foot three inches taller than Hugo. Then the company returns to France, Charlemagne distributes the relics from Jerusalem, and he is reconciled with his queen.

In these medieval stories (as in many more) Charlemagne lives and acts like a folktale hero in a (more or less) folktale setting. He is put to the test, sometimes ridiculed, and sometimes mocked outright, but he always emerges as the great king, a better king than at the outset of the story. One should notice, however, that the magic elements surrounding the "folktale Charlemagne" are always subordinated to or even completely integrated into a Christian conception of him. Charlemagne is always represented as a monarch under the protection of God, ruling in a just and harmonious way. One might wonder whether it is notwithstanding this process of epic concentration or, on the contrary, thanks to it, that Charlemagne was canonized in 1165.

See also: Chanson de Geste; Folktale; Nine Worthies; Romance

—Geert H. M. Claassens

Chaucer, Geoffrey (1344?–1400). English poet and courtier whose early work documents noble festive custom and whose *Canterbury Tales* constitutes one of the richest records of popular storytelling styles to have survived the Middle Ages.

Life and Courtly Context

Nearly 500 records signed by or mentioning Chaucer make his the best-documented life of any English medieval poet's, but it is noteworthy that not one of the records mentions Chaucer's poetry. To the official world, Chaucer is known first as the page of Countess Elizabeth, who was the wife of English prince Lionel (1357), then as a prisoner of war during Edward III's campaign against the French (1359–1360), and later as a member of the royal household (1367), ambassador for Edward III and Richard II (1366–1370, 1372–1373, 1377, 1378), controller of the London Customs (1374–1386), justice of the peace (1385–1390), member of Parliament (1386), clerk of the Works (1389–1391), and deputy forester (1391). Compared to the contemporary French royal court, the English court rewarded its poets informally; whatever their opinion of his poetry, Chaucer's patrons viewed him, formally, as a statesman and public official.

Chaucer's early poetry provides us teasing glimpses of the aristocratic folkways of late-medieval England, a world of festive pageantry in which members of a wealthy merchant class (Chaucer himself was the son of a rich London merchant) provided artistic backdrops for elaborate ritual. A suggestive record, dated April 23, 1374 (St. George's Day, a court holiday celebrating England's patron saint, during which little official business was conducted), granted Chaucer a gallon of wine a day for life; many scholars believe this to have been a reward for a festive poem. Most of Chaucer's early surviving poems were occasional pieces: the *Book of the Duchess* is apparently an elegy in honor of Blanche, the wife of John of Gaunt. The *Parlement of Foules* and *The Complaint of Mars* are the earliest surviving English poems to mention St. Valentine's Day, and they allude to the customary belief that birds chose their mates on this day, while sketching a picture of refined play in which men and women engaged in elaborate courtship rituals. The *Legend of Good Women* mentions two companies of people named Flowers and Leafs, each celebrating the particular virtues of the parts of the plant for which they are named. Reading Chaucer's poems in tandem with such anonymous contemporary works as *The Floure and the Leafe* and *The Assembly of Ladies*, we see his art adorning the pastimes of a noble "folk" who used elaborate, conventionalized, metaphorical "nature" games as part of their holiday celebrations. Real-life festive poetic performances such as the London Puy (popular in the thirteenth century and perhaps continuing into Chaucer's day) and the Parisian Cour Amoureuse (founded on St. Valentine's Day 1400) engaged noble and merchant-class men in song competitions; some of Chaucer's poems may well have been written for similar occasions.

The development of Chaucer's poetic and public careers shows him living in a time of transition during which the merchant and noble classes grew closer together. Unlike his contemporary John Gower—who composed in Latin, French, and English—Chaucer is the earliest known court poet to have written exclusively in English, the language of the great majority, which became during his lifetime the official language of Parliament. His commitment to the common tongue of England signifies the breadth of his association with his audiences, and after his death he was hailed by many poets as the man who "taught" English how to become a respectable poetic language. During and after Chaucer's life, knights, princes, and merchants often met together in London households to exchange verses, indicating the growth of a poetic movement well beyond the confines of the royal court.

Chaucer's allusions to traditional customs make him an important source for medieval English folk culture. If his early work documented noble pastimes, his later poetry—particularly The Canterbury Tales—is rife with accurate references to urban and village rituals and lifestyles. "The Cook's Tale" refers to a prisoner "led with revel to Newgate," thus alluding to the ceremonial procession humiliating criminals in fourteenth-century London. In "The Miller's Tale," John the Carpenter performs a ritual to protect his home from evil spirits. The Miller himself is described as a champion wrestler, also adept at breaking doors with his head, a pastime since recorded at many village fairs. The Wife of Bath refers to the Dunmowe Filch, a slab of bacon awarded to couples who survive a year and a day of wedded life without repenting their marriage; this is a reference to a village tradition later documented in many sources. Such allusions affirm not only that Chaucer was well acquainted with the folk cultures of artisans and villagers but also that his upper-class audience shared his knowledge. Although it was a highly stratified society, Chaucer's England was a place in which the highest and lowest social groups possessed great mutual familiarity.

The Canterbury Tales

Nowhere is the breadth of Chaucer's knowledge of both elite and folk artistry more apparent than in The Canterbury Tales, an ambitious work begun about 1387 and left unfinished at his death, which depicts a mixed social group—ranging from a knight and a prioress to a miller and a plowman (a social mix even broader than Chaucer's audience)—exchanging tales as they ride together on pilgrimage to England's most popular shrine, the tomb of St. Thomas Becket in Canterbury. The various tales borrow from the most-revered international literary figures of the time—Boccaccio, Dante, and Petrarch, for example—as well as from several popular English forms, including the tail-rhyme romance ("The Tale of Sir Thopas") and the Breton Lay ("The Franklin's Tale"), popular with nonnoble audiences in Chaucer's time. As Francis Lee Utley pointed out, nearly all of the tales possess extensive analogs in modern oral tradition. If folktales were defined exclusively by content, the Tales would rank among the greatest early folktale collections.

A close look at The Canterbury Tales reveals, however, that—considered apart from the storytelling frame in which Chaucer puts them—its various narratives are no more or less folktales than are most late-medieval literary productions.

The poem represents a range of entertainment at least as broad as the diverse society of storytellers assembled by Chaucer: "The Knight's Tale" (borrowed from Boccaccio's Teseida) and "The Squire's Tale" (a fragmentary pastiche of "Oriental" romance motifs) reflect the tastes of contemporary gentility. A group of pious romances, including "The Clerk's Tale" (a close reworking of Petrarch's "Tale of Griselda") and "The Man of Law's Tale" (based, like Gower's "Tale of Constance," on an early-fourteenth-century Anglo-Norman chronicle) reflect the more sober tastes of upper-class patrons. Yet Chaucer is equally adept in portraying more popular styles. The poet has the Reeve speak in the regional dialect of Norfolk; the Parson mocks the "ruf, ram, ruf" style of Midlands alliterative poetry; and his own persona, the pilgrim Chaucer, delivers a parodic fragment of a romance, "The Tale of Sir Thopas," in the tail-rhyme style popular among nonnoble audiences in his time. Chaucer's allusions to Arthurian romance are true to the general social status of such stories in the fourteenth century: the Nun's Priest refers to Sir Lancelot in parodic context, and the Wife of Bath, a character of bourgeois background, tells the only Arthurian romance, reflecting the fact that such stories then enjoyed their greatest popularity among the less elevated segments of English society.

More suggestive than the tales themselves is the context into which the poet sets them. Unlike most medieval European frame tales, whose bracketing narratives often serve merely as excuses for authors to present a series of unrelated stories, The Canterbury Tales presents its narratives as extensions of the concerns and social standing of the storytellers. The tales are told as part of a storytelling contest similar in structure to documented fourteenth-century entertainments. In addition to providing a General Prologue that describes the occupation and personal quirks of each pilgrim, the poet supplies links that situate most of the tales in specific performance situations. The tales of the Miller and the Reeve, for example, are not only masterful comic poems but also pointed thrusts in a verbal dual between the two tellers, a duel that brings into play the traditional rivalry between reeves and millers, aspects of social criticism, personal slurs, and oral techniques of indirect insult. Adhering closely to the folklorist's premise that the meaning of a tale is inseparable from its function in context, The Canterbury Tales presents not only a rich sampling of the types of narrative popular in its time but also a vivid, extended lesson in why, how, and for whom such tales might be told.

Like nearly all accomplished medieval tale writers and modern oral folktale tellers, Chaucer did not generally create his stories out of whole cloth; rather, he re-created them from well-worn plots with which his audience was thoroughly familiar. The secret of his art, like that of any great oral artist, lay in making the familiar fresh—

through nuances that first played upon and then surpassed the expectations of his audiences. By first examining other surviving variants of the individual *Canterbury Tales* likely to have been known by Chaucer's audience and then considering how Chaucer changes his tale to reflect the unique circumstances of the fictional teller and performance, folklorists find the pilgrim narrators strikingly similar to modern oral narrators in the way in which they personalize their public art. The best-told *Canterbury Tales* are both thoroughly traditional and brilliantly individualistic, each bearing the stamp of innumerable past tellings as well as the personal imprint of the teller.

A case in point is the Prioress and her tale: in the General Prologue the narrator introduces her as an extremely sensitive person, but one whose sensitivities seem so misplaced that some readers wonder if her cultivated innocence may in fact mask a kind of cruelty. She expresses her "conscience and tender heart" by weeping when she sees mice caught in traps and by feeding her "small hounds," yet she feeds them roast flesh and white bread, better food than the great majority of people ate in Chaucer's England. In the General Prologue Chaucer does not tell us what to think of the Prioress, but her tale—once one compares it to other similar tales known to the poet's audience—points to a distinct interpretation.

After exalting the mercy of the Virgin Mary, the Prioress tells of a pious schoolboy who walks daily through the Jewish ghetto while singing a song in honor of the Virgin. Satan enters the hearts of the Jews. They grow angry at the sound of the song and hire a thug, who cuts the boy's throat and flings his corpse in a latrine. The mother searches in vain for the boy until the Virgin in her mercy causes the child to sing even though he is dead, and his voice reveals his burial place. The local magistrate orders that all the Jews who knew of the murder be rounded up, torn apart by horses, and then hanged as well. The Prioress concludes by praising the mercy of the Virgin.

The tale teller exalts the child's innocence, but she also vividly recounts the torture of the Jews, thus combining naivete with a hint of cruelty. Indeed, in comparing "The Prioress's Tale" to 33 surviving medieval analogs, we find that there is something decidedly cruel about it. These tales, like the Prioress's, were told to exalt the mercy of the Virgin Mary and generally end with the Jews, witnessing the miracle of the boy singing while dead, converting to Christianity; in most versions, no one is executed in retaliation for the boy's death. In only one of the other surviving versions do the angry Christians mercilessly slaughter a whole company of Jews. "The Prioress's Tale," then, would probably have struck Chaucer's listeners as a brilliantly told tale, but one that is so disturbingly selective in its quality of mercy that mercy finally loses its meaning.

The brilliant individual touches that Chaucer puts on this tale do not become clear to us until we, like Chaucer's first audience, immerse ourselves in the traditional tales and expectations from which "The Prioress's Tale" so stunningly departs in its final actions.

Chaucer's influence on subsequent elite literature has been exhaustively documented, but equally noteworthy is the affinity that his works possessed with fifteenth-century popular poetry. After his death he was imitated by many merchant-class and anonymous popular authors; this, and the number and distribution of manuscripts of Chaucer's own work, as well as the fact that his *Canterbury Tales* was the first major English poem printed in England (by William Caxton, in 1478), demonstrate the degree to which Chaucer had earned the status of a truly popular poet by the end of the fifteenth century. The anonymous *Tale of Beryn* provides a conclusion for *The Canterbury Tales* in which the pilgrims arrive at Canterbury Cathedral. Such popular romances as *The Sultan of Babylon* freely borrow from the language of the *Tales*. Comic poems such as *The Wedding of Sir Gawain and Dame Ragnell* and *The Squire of Low Degree* proliferated in the fifteenth century; these anonymous works bear some stylistic resemblance to Chaucer's playful verse. Some critics maintain that the fifteenth-century poems are examples of *gesunkenes kulturgut*, a process in which elite forms "trickle down" to the lower classes. At least as plausible, however, is the possibility that Chaucer's work was popular with the lower classes precisely because he employed the popular idioms of his own time, and did so with such talent that his poems were in essence popular poetry, imbued with folk values from the beginning. As late as the sixteenth century, the anonymous *Complaynt of Scotlande* states that Scottish shepherds told *The Canterbury Tales*, a reference suggesting that many of Chaucer's poems not only grew from but immediately reentered and long survived as part of living British storytelling traditions.

See also: Accused Queen; Folktale; Frame Tale; Loathly Lady; Trickster; Valentine's Day, Saint

—Carl Lindahl

Childbirth. The birth process, with its associated beliefs, practices, and narratives.

Although much more information has come to us from the later Middle Ages than from the early-medieval period, scholars have been able to reconstruct some of the basic premises of Anglo-Saxon obstetrics. Both early- and later-medieval sources tell of predictions of sex, methods for handling a difficult delivery, and herbal remedies. Given the danger that childbirth posed to women throughout the Middle Ages, it is not surprising to find frequent reliance on magic objects, charms, and rituals. From the later medieval period (fourteenth–fifteenth centuries) come many detailed records of both folk medical practices and systematized medicine at monasteries, hospitals, and universities. Manuscripts from this era describe birth positions, fetal development, and disposition of the afterbirth, as well as remedies for such ailments as puerperal fever, abscesses of the breast, and hemorrhage.

Goddesses of Birth

While only fragmentary evidence of goddess worship survives from the early-Christian era, it seems clear that veneration of mother goddesses affected birth rituals in the Middle Ages. Laima, a goddess of birth and fate, is one such deity of Lithuania. The Teutonic goddess Freyja, who protected love and fecundity, was labeled a witch by early Christians, who claimed that she strayed out at night like a female goat among a crowd of bucks—a slur similar to those made against accused witches. As Christianity gained strength, the Virgin Mary grew in prominence as a protectress of mothers and children; however, dangerous goddesses continued to worry some expectant mothers. One greatly feared goddess was Lilith, said to be the first wife of Adam, who had lost her own children. Charms to protect expectant mothers and their babies from the jealous Lilith and her children, the monstrous *lilim* or *lilin*, were common among medieval Jewish women.

Anglo-Saxon Obstetrics

Scholars have debated why there are so few Anglo-Saxon texts on the subject of childbirth. The main manuscripts are Bald's *Leechbook*, *Leechbook III*, and the *Lacnunga*. The first two, separate parts of the same manuscript—London, British Library, Royal 1 2.D.xvii—were written around the year 950 in Winchester. The manuscript from which they were copied dates from the reign of Alfred the Great (871–899). Unfortunately, all that remains of Bald's chapter on obstetrics is an outline of material now missing: remedies for infertility, hemorrhage, and uterine obstructions, as well as instructions for removing a dead child from the womb and predictions of the child's sex. *Leechbook III* is a shorter, simpler assortment of remedies, while the *Lacnunga* (British Library, Harley 585), from a somewhat later time than the *Leechbooks*, provides a good selection of charms. Most of the Old English texts were compiled by Oswald Cockayne in his *Leechdoms, Wortcunning, and Starcraft of Early England*.

One influential text included in Cockayne's collection is the *Herbarium*, attributed to Apuleius, which was written in Latin in the fifth or sixth century. It includes numerous remedies from Pliny's *Natural History*, written in the first century C.E. More than 50 manuscripts of the *Herbarium* from Anglo-Saxon times attest to the popularity of this sourcebook. The *Herbarium*'s remedies include dried comfrey, added to wine, to stop excessive menstrual bleeding; 11 or 13 coriander seeds, held by a virgin against the laboring woman's left thigh, to hasten delivery; and fleabane, boiled in water and placed under a seated woman, to cleanse the womb.

Some scholars have asked whether early-medieval remedies for amenorrhea were actually meant to cause abortion; Anglo-Saxons used wild carrot, parsnip, brooklime, centaury, pennyroyal, and smallage for this purpose. However, Christine Fell has suggested that malnutrition and anemia were common enough to account for most cases of amenorrhea requiring treatment. Marilyn Deegan has attempted to analyze the active principles of Anglo-Saxon remedies, to assess their effects, and to ascertain the complaints for which the remedies were intended.

Certain charms from the *Lacnunga* are highly detailed and ritualistic. For example, a woman who wants to have milk to nurse her child is urged to take milk of a cow of one color into her mouth, then spit it into running water, swallow a mouthful of water, and recite a lengthy charm. A woman who has lost a child and hopes to nourish another is told to wrap dirt from her child's grave in black wool and sell it to a trader. The wording of these charms requires careful interpretation; M. L. Cameron suggests that translators should make no major emendations. While Cameron calls the *Lacnunga* "folk medicine at its lowest level," Deegan finds that many Anglo-Saxon remedies make good sense and that some are still prescribed by herbalists today. Treatments such as the use of fresh horse droppings to control bleeding are no longer common, but their efficacy within their historical period can still be examined.

Late-Medieval Practitioners

Most facilitators of medieval childbirth appear to have been wise women whose skills were recognized, though sometimes mistrusted, by their communities. The *Malleus maleficarum* (Hammer of Witches, c. 1486) tells of murderous midwives who, in harming mothers and their infants, proved themselves to be witches under the influence of Satan. These accounts of death-dealing midwives sound like local legends, but their authenticity is tainted by the book's intended use as a guide for witch-hunting. More-neutral texts tell of both village wise women and more formally trained physicians who assisted with childbirth in the late-medieval period. One of the best-known spokespersons of medieval obstetrics is Trotula, eleventh-century Italian author of *De passionibus mulierum curandarum* (On the Sufferings of Women Patients). Whether Trotula was actually a woman and whether she wrote this treatise on women's diseases are controversial issues; however, it is known that female doctors practiced in Trotula's city, Salerno (during the Middle Ages, the University of Salerno was renowned for the teaching of medicine), in the fourteenth and fifteenth centuries. Both nuns and monks aided women giving birth, as noted in such manuscripts as Sloane 2463 (published as *The Medieval Woman's Guide to Health* by Beryl Rowland). While wise women continued to assist with childbirth through the late-medieval period, formally trained male and female physicians rose in prominence as the Renaissance approached.

Amulets, Predictions, and Guidebooks

The use of amulets was very common in the late Middle Ages. St. Hildegard von Bingen (twelfth century) wrote that pregnant women could protect themselves from evil spirits by holding the magic stone jasper in their hands; Trotula suggested that eagle stone (echinoids, that is, fossilized sea urchins), bound to a woman's thigh, would lessen the pains of birth. A snakeskin or hart-skin girdle was also favored as a talisman for making labor less painful.

Inherited from classical medicine, instructions for fertility tests stipulated that both the man and the woman should urinate upon wheat and bran; if the grain in one vessel became foul, the person who had urinated upon it was barren. Both Trotula and the writer of Sloane 2463 recommended ingesting the sex organs of a hare if one wanted to give birth to a male child. Once a pregnancy had advanced sufficiently, the child's gender could be predicted by the shape and position of the womb. Such predictions are still quite common today.

In contrast to early-medieval manuscripts, midwives' guidebooks of the fourteenth and fifteenth centuries go into considerable detail concerning unnatural birth positions, often with illustrations. These illustrations demonstrate some obstetrical sophistication, although the children in them do not generally resemble infants. Instructions on the removal of a dead child from the womb are sometimes accompanied by remedies, such as myrrh, rue, and dried beaver glands. Remedies for other ailments include such ingredients as herbs, fruits, minerals, animal parts, vinegar, and wine. Fumigation with a fat eel, burned alive, is recommended for curing bloody flux. A live turtledove, burned with its feathers and made into a powder with frankincense and sandragon, is a remedy suggested for a variety of ailments (Sloane 2463). In addition to mixtures and fumigations, the procedures of cupping and bleeding were favored in the late Middle Ages. Manuscripts such as the late-fifteenth-century *The Sekenesse of Wymmen* set a pattern for later, better-known guidebooks, including Thomas Raynalde's *The Byrth of Mankynde* (1552).

See also: Amulet and Talisman; Blood; Lilith; Medicine

—Elizabeth Tucker

Chrétien de Troyes (fl. 1165–1191). The greatest French practitioner of medieval romance and the author most influential in setting the themes and forms of the genre.

We know virtually nothing of Chrétien's life beyond the facts that he composed at least five romances and two lyric poems and that he wrote two of those romances under the patronage, respectively, of Countess Marie de Champagne (1138–1198) and Philippe d'Alsace, Count of Flanders (d. 1191). In all the works attributed to him with confidence, he shows himself to be an adept literary interpreter of the court culture of twelfth-century France; especially notable are his analyses of sentiments and his explorations of the potential conflicts between love and chivalry, between private pleasures and public duties.

The romances known to be by him all set their action in an Arthurian context and make Chrétien one of the most important popularizers of the legend of King Arthur and his knights. Those romances are *Erec et Enide* (Erec and Enide); *Cligés; Lancelot, ou Le chevalier de la charrette* (Lancelot, or The Knight of the Cart); *Yvain, ou Le chevalier au lion* (Yvain, or The Knight with the Lion); and the uncompleted *Perceval, ou Le conte du Graal* (Percival, or The Story of the Grail). The order given here appears to be the order of composition, though there is some evidence that Chrétien was working on *Lancelot* and *Yvain* at the same time.

Chrétien claims authorship also of some adaptations of Ovidian narratives and of a story of Iseut (Isolde) and Marc (and presumably of Tristan), but they have not survived. He may also be the author of a romance titled *Guillaume d'Angleterre* (William of England), a non-Arthurian composition attributed simply to a "Chrétien."

Chrétien de Troyes, the principal creator of medieval romance, is the first author to write of the love story of Lancelot and Guinevere—the former may be a character of his invention—and of the Grail; he is also the first to mention Camelot by name. More important, he allied love themes with an ideal of chivalric endeavor and, specifically, with the notion of a quest. That quest may be a search for the knight's lady or for another character, or it may be for an object. In his final, unfinished, romance (*Perceval*) it is for the Grail.

In the prologue to his first romance, *Erec et Enide*, Chrétien informs us with evident pride that he has drawn his story out of tales that others have regularly garbled. His is the story of a knight (Erec) who wins a bride and then, after their marriage, neglects his chivalric duties. This conflict between chivalric duty and personal inclination, or the potential conflict between chivalry and love, is a theme that Chrétien will develop in several of his romances. In this first one he works it out in a decidedly curious way: others begin to talk of Erec's failings, and Enide, hearing the talk, worries that she will be blamed. When she expresses her concern, Erec overhears her and immediately, without explanation, orders her to leave with him on a journey that will at the same time demonstrate his chivalric worth and test her love.

The second romance, *Cligés*, is written against the background of the Tristan and Iseut story, to which the narrator makes frequent reference. The love of Cligés for Fénice, the wife of his uncle, is reciprocated, but she refuses to duplicate the response of Iseut, whom she describes as having given her heart to one man but her body to two. The solution involves a potion, reflecting the one that bound Tristan and Iseut, but this potion makes Fénice appear to be dead and, until they are discovered by accident, provides an opportunity for Fénice and Cligés to indulge their love.

Lancelot, or The Knight of the Cart is undoubtedly Chrétien's most famous romance, introducing as it does the adulterous love of Lancelot for Queen Guinevere. Indeed, it was in regard to this romance that the term "courtly love" was coined in the nineteenth century. This composition treats the conflict of love and honor overtly and from a perspective unlike that of Chrétien's other romances. When Lancelot, seeking Guinevere, has an opportunity to find her by riding in a cart reserved for criminals, he hesitates for only an instant before concluding that his personal dishonor is nothing compared with his love for the queen. Later, however, she rejects him, not for having disgraced himself but for having hesitated to do so; he briefly put his honor before his devotion to her. He must later expiate this offense by publicly humiliating himself in a tourney.

Yvain, or The Knight with the Lion offers an inversion of the central theme of *Erec et Enide*. Unlike Erec, who neglects his chivalric duties to be with his wife, Yvain is intent on seeking adventure with his friend Gauvain (Gawain) and thus leaves his wife, Laudine, immediately after their marriage. He fails to return at the agreed time and thus loses her love. Accompanied by a grateful lion he had rescued (in an analog of the story of Androcles and the lion), he regains that love by repeatedly demonstrating a newfound sense of responsibility and unwavering devotion to others.

Chrétien's final romance, though uncompleted, was enormously influential: it introduced the Grail into world literature and made this object (which was a marvelous and holy vessel but not yet, in Chrétien, the chalice of the Last Supper) the focus of a quest. Perceval is an appealing character who evolves from a naive Welsh youth to a distinguished and devoted knight. The conflict in this romance turns on a fundamental incompatibility between Arthurian chivalry (at least as Perceval comes to understand it) and a religious ideal. When he first sees a striking procession that includes a display of a bleeding lance and a Grail, he chooses not to inquire about it, having been told that knights should avoid loquacity. He later learns that his silence cost him an opportunity to heal a maimed king and restore his barren land. Perceval eventually embarks on a quest for the Grail, but before the text breaks off Chrétien provides, amid parallel adventures by Gauvain, only a short sequence involving Perceval's spiritual renewal and an exposition of the Grail's meaning.

It was at one time assumed by many scholars that Chrétien drew heavily on Celtic sources—Welsh, Irish, or other—for his themes and motifs. Elaborate theories were offered to explain, for example, the Grail as an analog of a Celtic cauldron of plenty or a cornucopia and the Grail (or Fisher) King as a representation of Bran the Blessed, a Welsh hero or deity wounded with a poisoned lance. Numerous other characters and motifs have been traced to possible sources in Celtic legend. Most current scholars, without entirely denying the relationship of Celtic myth to Arthurian romance, view with skepticism the efforts to offer extensive and precise equivalences between Celtic myths and Arthurian tales. Analogs of a good many Arthurian motifs can also be located in Eastern or classical sources, and moreover it appears probable that stories incorporating material from many traditions were circulating freely, orally or in writing, at the time Chrétien set quill to vellum.

Whatever his sources, Chrétien de Troyes's central accomplishment involves the deft combination of preexisting motifs and stories with material of his own creation and the recasting of the resulting material into a form perfectly fitted to the court culture within which he was writing. Particularly at the court of Marie de Champagne (the daughter of Eleanor of Aquitaine), the literary arts were valued, and the relationships of chivalry to love and of ladies to knights must have been a favored topic of discussion. That is a contention supported by the fact that Chrétien's contemporary at the court, Andreas Capellanus, is the author of *De amore* (On Love), sometimes known as *The Art of Courtly Love*, a treatise that reflects court interest in the subject and even includes, if only tongue-in-cheek, a list of precise rules for lovers. Chrétien's own work is often ironic as well, but it is at the same time a serious effort to fashion an appropriate vehicle—the romance form—for the subtle and most often brilliant exposition of his themes. So successful was he that a good many writers of the following generation appear to have deliberately avoided Arthurian subjects, no doubt understanding that they could not favorably compete with the master on his own literary turf.

See also: Courtly Love; Grail; Knight; Owain; Romance

—Norris J. Lacy

Christmas. A Christian celebration of the birth of Jesus Christ, recorded in the Gospels of Matthew and Luke in the Bible, and whose name was first recorded in 1038 as *Cristes Maessan,* or Christ's Mass.

The New Testament does not provide the slightest indication of the date of Christ's birth. The first recorded date for Christmas is in the calendar of Philocalus in 354, where it is on December 25. From Rome this date appears to have spread to Antioch, Bethlehem, and Constantinople by the end of the fourth century. Both the initial choice of this date and the subsequent enthusiasm with which it was embraced can be accounted for if we examine its traditional pagan origins. From the third to the fourth centuries, December 25 was celebrated as the Birthday of the Sun in imperial Rome. Prior to this period the feast of the Saturnalia, honoring the god Saturn, had been celebrated by ancient pagan cultures on this date.

The Saturnalia was the most popular and lavishly celebrated feast in the Roman world. Moreover, many other cultures featured festivals at about the same time of year, which were known by a variety of names (e.g., winter solstice festivals or midwinter festivals). Apparently motivated by the fact that a major pagan festival was held near a date known from ancient times to be the shortest and darkest day of the year, early Christian leaders placed Christ's birth on this date, thus transforming this holiest of pagan days into one of the greatest of Christian feast days. The emotional and literary precedents inherent in this date were too obvious to be ignored—darkness to light, old order to new order, the junction of the divine and human. The acceptance of this date also guaranteed the quick conversion of pagans to the newly sponsored Christian religion because of the obvious analogies mentioned above. Placing the Nativity at the turning point of winter, therefore, gave Christmas a considerable symbolic potency.

In ancient Rome the Saturnalia was celebrated as a holiday: businesses closed, there was noisy rejoicing, and gambling in public was allowed. Presents were exchanged, especially candles and symbols of light. Some groups would elect a "king" to lead pranks and general merrymaking. Long before Roman times the solstice possessed ceremonial significance in northern Europe. In the prehistoric British Isles a number of megalithic and ceremonial monuments, such as New Grange in Ireland and Stonehenge in England, were built to identify the cardinal points of the sun, apparently for religious festivals that included the winter solstice. Early Irish and Welsh societies placed particular importance upon the power of midwinter mistletoe, a plant that was particularly sacred to their druid priests.

According to medieval legend, as recorded in the thirteenth-century *Legenda aurea* (The Golden Legend) by Jacobus de Voragine, the birth of Jesus took place 5,228 years after Adam, though Jacobus adds that the historian Eusebius of Caesarea reckons the figure at 5,199 years and others at 6,000. Jacobus continues with an account of Joseph and Mary traveling to Bethlehem, where, unable to find lodging, they set up a temporary shelter in a public passageway and "perhaps Joseph set up a manger for his ox and his ass, or as some think, peasants coming in to market were used to tying up their animals there and the crib was ready to hand." The Virgin Mary gave birth, without any pain, at midnight on the eve of Sunday and laid the baby in the manger on hay that "the ox and the ass had abstained from eating" and that was later brought to Rome by St. Helena. The midwife Zebel proclaimed Mary a virgin, but the second midwife, Salome, did not believe it, and when she touched the virgin to find out for herself, her hand instantly withered. But she was then instructed by an angel to touch the child, and her hand was restored. Various signs occurred in the heavens, such as the night turning into "the brightness of day," and at Rome the water from a fountain was changed into oil, which flowed into the Tiber and spread widely over the river.

The new Christian feast of the Nativity engendered an entire string of holy days around December 25. By the fourth century, the baptism of Christ by John the Baptist was celebrated on January 6. It came to be known by its Greek name, Epiphany. By the fifth century, three other feasts had come to be celebrated immediately after the Nativity: the feast of the first Christian martyr, Stephen, on December 26; the feast for Christ's favorite disciple, John the Evangelist, on December 27; and the feast of the Holy Innocents slaughtered by Herod's soldiers, on December 28. In 567 C.E. the Council of Tours established that the time period between the feast of the Nativity and the Epiphany be celebrated as one festal cycle. The addition, in the eighth century, of the feast of Christ's circumcision (January 1) incorporated the ancient festive tradition of celebrating the New Year. Whereas the Eastern Christian lands placed more emphasis on the celebration of Easter, the celebration of the 12 days between Christmas and Epiphany became the major focus of the peoples in northern and central Europe. For the peasantry, this Christmas season marked their longest extended vacation, since during the Twelve Days they generally were exempt from work.

Danish invasions into England during the ninth century introduced the colloquial Scandinavian term "Yule" for Christmas, which explains its use in later medieval and Tudor England. Moreover, the Twelve Days became the major holiday celebration for England and northern Europe during the medieval period. Household accounts in England indicate that large festal entertainments were typical, including extravagant food centerpieces, such as the boar's head that is so well known through the Boar's Head carols. The wearing of festive masks and the presentation of short dramas were common in the English court. These "mummings," as they came to be called, became very popular by the fourteenth century, eventually growing into major theatrical productions. In British towns, mumming often caused problems, as the use of masks and disguises afforded excellent opportunities for crime.

The tradition of the wassail cup or bowl in England is also common during the Twelve Days' celebration. *Wassail* derives from the Old English phrase meaning "be of good health"; it was shouted as a toast by the cup bearer, who drank from the cup and kissed the next participant, who answered with "Drinkhail," and so on, through the gathering. By the fourteenth century the cup had been replaced by a bowl, and the wassail presentation had become an elaborate ceremony among the members of high society.

Feasting during the Twelve Days became increasingly intense throughout the medieval period. Songs and dances were often composed specifically for these festivities. By the end of the Middle Ages the term *carol*—earlier used to signify a dance accompanied by song, with no necessary religious significance—came to be used for songs and dances. Enormous examples of hospitality and generosity were shown toward commoners and the poor by the gentry and royalty during this time of year. It was expected that the gentry would open their houses for feasting and celebrating, and many landowners spent the Twelve Days celebrating in major metropolitan areas such as London and York in order to give alms to the needy and poor.

The religious establishment celebrated the Christmas season with as much revelry as did those in the secular environment. The traditions of role reversal and inverse hierarchy were ingrained in religious festivities. Gestures drawing on these traditions were often precipitated by the words in the Magnificat, one of the prayers from the Office of Vespers: "He hath put down the mighty from their seats, and exalted the humble and meek." In the twelfth and thirteenth centuries four feasts of inversion were celebrated during the Twelve Days: the feast of the deacons on St. Stephen's Day, December 26; the feast of priests on St. John's Day, December 27; the feast of the choirboys, or the Feast of the Boy Bishop, on Holy Innocents' Day, December 28; and the feast of the subdeacons, or the Feast of Fools (Ass), usually held on New Year's Day.

These feasts of inversion were usually celebrated at cathedrals throughout Europe. While the Feast of Fools was observed with greater regularity in France, it was the Feast of the Boy Bishop that was the most popular in England because of the strong tradition of boys' choirs in cathedrals in England. All the feasts emphasized a reversal of authority in the ecclesiastical hierarchy: the bishop and other cathedral canons were literally thrown out of their posts by the lower clergy. While this tradition began as a festive and lighthearted reference to the biblical reading, by the thirteenth century it had taken on a life of its own as an occasion for intense parody, involving

members of both the religious and secular communities in wild celebration.

Gambling, drinking, bawdy singing, and parodies of the liturgy were done openly and often without recrimination by the clergy, usually with the support of the cathedral administration as well as the approval of the general public. The Boy Bishop and his entourage often held an expensive feast, supported by alms and gifts that the boys had collected during processions through the towns surrounding the cathedral precincts. Although many late-medieval ecclesiastics condemned these feasts, their popularity ensured their continuance until well into the seventeenth century.

See also: Boy Bishop, Feast of the; Fools, Feast of; Jesus Christ; New Year's; Virgin Mary

—Bradford Lee Eden

Cockaigne, Land of [French *Cocagne*, German *Schlaraffenland*, Italian *Cuccagna*]. An imaginary land characterized by a paradisiacal inversion of life's harsh realities.

The Land of Cockaigne is a distinctly sensual paradise in which one is paid for sleeping, food and drink present themselves already prepared (a pig, for example, trots up ready-roasted, the carving knife already lodged in its side), and dwellings are built from food (roofs are thatched with pancakes), but the way there is sometimes extremely daunting (in the English poem one must wade seven years through pig shit up to one's chin).

The complex is certainly found in the classical literatures (Athenaeus, Lucian), and the burlesque Old Irish *Aislinge Meic Conglinne* (twelfth century) is an interesting early Celtic example. It is therefore suggestive that the earliest English literary source is an Anglo-Irish poem of the first quarter of the fourteenth century describing the "londe ihote [named] cokaygne," in which the topos is used satirically against the allegedly luxurious lifestyle of the monastic orders. Recently it has been suggested that the Irish abbey of Inislounaght (Island of Sweet Milk) is alluded to in the poem's "riuer of sweet milke."

There is then a considerable gap in the literary record until Hugh Plat's "Merrie tale of Master Mendax to his friend Credulus" from his *Pleasures of Poetrie* (London, 1572). The relevant section opens, "There is within Eutopia, / A house all tylde with tarte [tiled with tarts]," attesting to a quite unwarranted Elizabethan confusion with Thomas More's political vision. From the late sixteenth century onward the name Lubberland was to replace Cockaigne: the Christmas revels at St. John's College, Oxford, in 1607 were to have included an "Embassage from Lubberland."

English onomastic sources, however, attest to the existence of the topos almost as early as the mention (c. 1164) of an "abbot of Cockaigne" (*abbas Cucaniensis*) in the *Carmina Burana*. The name was applied to Cockaynes (Essex) in 1228, presumably implying a spot of great fertility, and a surname, William Cocaine, is found as early as 1193 in Warwickshire.

Although a place named Cuccagna is attested in Italy from 1142, Italian stories employing this name are not found before the fifteenth century. When the fabulous land appears in Boccaccio's *Decameron* (c. 1349–1351), it is named Bengodi and located in the Basque country.

In Germanic literature it appears incidentally in the fifteenth-century Easter plays with the comic character Mercator (e.g., that from Melk, in which it is called Leckant) and the tall tale *Vom Packofen*, where it is called Kuckormurre, the first syllable of which has doubtless been influenced by Latin *Cuccania*, but it is found a century earlier in the form Gugelmiure in the mid-fourteenth-century *Wachtelmaere*, which includes a fairly full description of the paradise. Unlike the English poem, the fifteenth-century Dutch *Cockaengen* appears to be directly dependent on the important thirteenth-century *Cocaigne*. Schluraffen Landt is the name of the country to which Brant's *Das Narrenschiff* (The Ship of Fools; 1494) is bound, but, oddly, this enormously influential work contains none of the traditional Cockaigne motifs such as occur in the derived *Spruch vom Schlauraffenlandt* (c. 1515), and—importantly for the later diffusion of the topos—Hans Sachs's *Schlauraffenlandt* of circa 1530, issued as a woodcut-illustrated broadsheet. It has only recently been noticed that the name that is now standard in German refers to the glutton's paradise as early as circa 1400 in Heinrich Wittenweiler's satire, *Ring*.

In medieval art the complex as a whole does not seem to be found. Even individual, constituent motifs are rare (e.g., the ready-roasted bird about to fly into the open mouth of the lobster-riding fool in the woodcut to chapter 57 of *Das Narrenschiff*). The earliest extant image of the entire Cockaigne topos is Erhard Schoen's woodcut to the Sachs poem, which includes the food house, the sausage fence, the man with open mouth waiting for a ready-roasted bird to fly into it, the ready-to-carve pig, the horse that shits baskets of eggs, and a Fountain of Youth (really an independent motif). The best-known image, however, is Pieter Brueghel the Elder's famous *Luilekkerland*, painted in 1567, after an engraving by Pieter Baltens.

See also: Iconography; World Turned Upside Down

—Malcolm Jones

Courtly Love [French *Amour courtois*]. An elaborately formalized sexual relationship in which a knight worships his lady, enduring torment and performing great deeds in hopes of gaining her love; according to Joseph Bédier, essentially a "cult ... based, like Christian love, on the infinite disproportion of merit and desire, a necessary school of honor which ennobles the lover,... a voluntary servitude ... that finds in suffering the dignity and the beauty of passion."

Courtly love strongly influenced medieval culture in at least two ways: first, as a major theme in lyric poetry and romance from the beginning of the twelfth century, and second, as a leading theme in such social games as tournaments and poetry contests. Some critics have argued that courtly love also effected a change in sentiments such as the world has seldom seen, transforming the nature of love for centuries to come.

The term itself dates back only to 1883, when Gaston Paris coined the phrase *amour courtois* to describe Lancelot's love for Guinevere in the romance *Lancelot* (c. 1177) by Chrétien de Troyes. Medieval literature employs a variety of terms for this kind of love. In Provençal the word is *cortezia* (courtliness), French texts use *fin amour* (refined love), in Latin the term is *amor honestus* (honorable, reputable love). In English *love* is used alone or with qualifiers, some less laudatory than those in other languages. Love *par amour* signifies passionate love, while *derne love* literally means "hidden love." This connotative difference is not surprising, considering that English writers tend to be less interested in love as a literary theme and less tolerant of extramarital amours than their French counterparts. According to Paris, courtly love combines secrecy (necessitated by an illicit relationship) with a quasi-religious devotion of the lover to his lady, a "kind of idolatry."

Literature

This specialized approach to love first appeared in the West about 1100 in the lyrics of troubadours, the poet-minstrels of southern France. While courtly ideals associated the poetic gift with noble birth, the best and most famous love poetry was written by talented professional minstrels. They assumed the personae of knights to satisfy their audiences' expectations and addressed their love poetry to real or fictional ladies. Troubadour poetry reverses medieval social reality by placing the lady above the knightly speaker, whom she dominates completely and often cruelly. He does not ask her love as an equal but prays that his abject devotion will earn her pity. For example, Peire Vidal (c. 1175–1215) hopes that "the submission and humble behaviors I use [will] move thy dear ruth thereto that it shall bring me to thy arms." C. S. Lewis points out the "feudalisation of love" in troubadour lyrics, where the lover vows service to his lady as a vassal would to his lord. Some actually address the lady as *midons*, which does not mean "my lady," but "my lord."

Some troubadours appear to have believed strongly in the ideal of courtly love, and through their efforts to live up to it they became subjects of legend themselves. For example, Vidal, whose poetry is quoted above, addressed certain lyrics to a lady whom he called La Loba (The She-Wolf).

In her honor, one story goes, he had himself sewn into a wolf skin, which excited the attention of a shepherd's dogs; they chased and nearly killed him. La Loba watched, laughing, with her husband and afterward got medical attention for the injured poet. Another troubadour reportedly bought a gown, clapper, and bowl from a leper and waited for alms at his lady's door with the other beggars.

In the mid-twelfth century, themes of courtly love began to appear in the romances, the narrative poetry of northern France. Some associate this development with Eleanor of Aquitaine, granddaughter of the first known troubadour, William IX of Aquitaine. When Eleanor moved north to marry Louis VII of France (1137), some claim she brought with her the courtiers and the tastes that would soon find their way into romance. Whatever the case, Chrétien de Troyes credits Eleanor's daughter, Marie de Champagne, with dictating the plot of his *Lancelot*, and Marie's court became the site where Andreas Capellanus set his treatise on love. Also, it was about the time that Eleanor took Henry II of England as her second husband (1155) that courtly love began to appear in such Anglo-Norman romances as the *Tristan* of Thomas of Britain.

Early critics viewed *Lancelot* and *Tristan* as the major expressions of courtly love in romance form. In many of the *Tristan* romances, the hero's love for Queen Iseut, though adulterous, is idealized and inspires him to great feats of arms. However, the story ends tragically because of the jealousy of her husband, King Mark. Most (if not all) of the authors present the love between Tristan and Iseut as noble because of its constancy. Tristan's love, though adulterous, is apparently justified by the devotion he demonstrates to his lady.

Chrétien de Troyes was the first to connect Guinevere with Lancelot, in the romance that served as the model for Paris's concept of courtly love. The relationship between Lancelot and Guinevere is adulterous but constant in its own terms. Lancelot's worship of the queen is such that he endures her cruelty and obeys her slightest wish. After he rescues her from a ruthless kidnapper, she refuses even to speak to him. She will not tell him why she is angry. In this romance, Lancelot is called "the knight of the cart" because he rides in a cart to reach Guinevere and rescue her. Because, states Chrétien, convicts were conveyed in carts to their place of execution, carts were shameful. Lancelot assumes that Guinevere is angry because she consented to ride in one, and he regards this reason as just. However, she is angry for the opposite reason: because he hesitated to get into the cart, knowing that he had no other way to reach her. When she finally reveals her reason, he regards it, too, as just. To Lancelot all the judgments of his deity are just. Paris's theory would not be controversial if applied only to this story.

However, the term *amour courtois* has been applied to a wide variety of literature, and scholars disagree on whether adultery is an essential part of it. Like Paris, C. S. Lewis considered adultery essential to the concept. In *The Allegory of Love* he considers courtly love an entirely new feeling, one of only three or four "real changes in human sentiment" ever recorded. Its characteristics are "Humility, Courtesy, Adultery, and the Religion of Love." The difficulty and secrecy of an illicit relationship create the agony and ecstasy that characterize *amour courtois*. On the other hand, E. Talbot Donaldson argues that adultery is not essential, noting that this theme receives only "perfunctory treatment" in Middle English romances and that English writers show little interest in it. Donaldson points out that Chaucer's *Troilus and Criseyde*, which Lewis treats at length, "concerns the love of a bachelor for a widow" and does not, therefore, fit Lewis's own definition. Peter Dronke regards adultery as only an incidental feature, arguing that the basic components of *amour courtois* are far from an original contribution of eleventh-century literature. Dronke accepts Bédier's "infinite disproportion of merit and desire" but believes that the lover's adoration of his lady is based on the "feeling that by loving such disproportion may be lessened, the infinite gulf bridged." In Dronke's view, this attempt to bridge the gulf produces the "divine," transcendent feelings that give courtly love its power to ennoble, as when the lover declares that his lady is worth all of Paradise to him, that he would willingly go to hell to be with her. Certainly, the lady's belonging to someone else is one way of envisioning a gulf that must be crossed, but it is far from the only one. Dronke observes that if this feeling is really what characterizes courtly love, then it dates back at least to ancient Egypt, where poetry from the second millennium B.C.E. compares the beloved to a goddess. Furthermore, the feeling is not confined to any particular class, as it appears in Byzantine folksongs of the twelfth century, far from the courtly culture of Provence.

The Social Game

The disagreement about what is essential to courtly love stems partly from debate over the meaning of a particular text: the *De amore* (On Love, c. 1190) by Andreas Capellanus, a contemporary of Chrétien and also attached to the court of Champagne. The *De amore* is a textbook on love. Perhaps written at the request of Marie de Champagne, it expounds a definition of love and rules for conducting an affair. Andreas presents numerous sample dialogues between men and women (usually of different classes) in which the man tries to convince the woman through dialectical argument that she ought to accept him as a lover. Andreas also reports various "Decisions in Love Cases" in which a court of noble ladies, including Marie de Champagne, hands down rulings in disputes over the proper conduct of lovers.

In one of the dialogues the man and woman disagree on whether or not the woman's love for her husband is an excuse for not taking a lover. They submit the question to Marie, who declares that "love cannot exert its powers between two people who are married to each other." Therefore, says the countess, "no woman, even if she is married, can be crowned with the reward of the King of Love unless she is seen to be enlisted in the service of Love himself outside the bonds of wedlock." Such rulings are governed by a set of 31 laws, which Andreas dutifully lists. The first three are "Marriage is no real excuse for not loving," "He who is not jealous cannot love," and "No one can be bound by a double love."

C. S. Lewis, seeking a "professedly theoretical work" on the system that Chrétien showed through example, believed he had found it in the *De amore*. Lewis took it with absolute seriousness, as an authoritative guide to courtly love. From information such as the examples above, he naturally concluded that adultery was essential to love, as understood by the courtly culture of medieval France. But others have argued that Andreas intended his work to be humorous. D. W. Robertson Jr. does not believe that such a social system as we call "courtly love" ever existed. In his view, Andreas is satirizing "idolatrous passion" in the tradition of Ovid's *Ars amatoria*, which is structured so similarly to Andreas's treatise that it could have served as a model.

These perspectives are to some extent reconcilable. Given what we know about the "earnest games" (to use Carl Lindahl's phrase) that were played in medieval courts, Andreas could be referring to a real enough practice that was nevertheless not "real life." As Lindahl explains, there were occasions upon which poets would perform their best love poetry for ladies, who would judge it and select the winner. One such amorous society was the Cour Amoureuse (Court of Love, founded in Paris c. 1400), ruled by a Prince of Love—possibly analogous to Andreas's King of Love, who makes the rules for love affairs. Andreas's "Love Cases" could be referring to similar Love Debates, in which a Queen of Love presided over a mock court and participants would argue, as in a courtroom, how the rules of love should apply to particular cases. Then noble ladies would render decisions, much as Marie and her colleagues do in the *De amore*. As with any game that depends upon the creation of an alternate reality, the fun depends upon all the participants treating that reality with utmost seriousness. Therefore, Andreas's treatise may be understandable as a guide to being a successful courtier in such a Court of Love.

Questions of Social Reality
The controversy about the real meaning of courtly love in literature stems partly from controversy about its application to real life. C. S. Lewis and John J. Parry believe that what Parry calls "that strange social system" was taught and practiced in medieval courts throughout Western Europe. To Robertson the need to tremble in the presence of one's mistress and obey her every wish, no matter how cruel or arbitrary, seems "a terrible nuisance, and hardly the kind of thing that Henry II or Edward III would get involved in." Many have noted that it seems relentlessly, even joyfully, contrary to the rules of official culture, which was Christian and patriarchal. If courtly love was primarily a social game, much of its appeal surely stemmed from the relief it offered from the drab demands of reality, where marriages were made for commercial and political reasons and women were treated as bargaining chips.

The intensity with which some knights played their games argues that, for some at least, courtly love was a sort of social reality. For example, Jean sire de Boucicaut, also noted for his barefoot pilgrimages, founded an order for the protection of ladies. Captured while crusading and imprisoned in Damascus, Boucicaut and his fellow knights passed the time by composing poems focused on a question of love: does constancy in love or promiscuity bring greater pleasure? Once released (1389), Boucicaut and his fellow knights performed their love poetry in Avignon, with the brother of Pope Clement VII acting as master of the revels. This game touched their lives in many contexts, from prison to the papal palace.

Questions of Origin
Lewis asserts that courtly love "appeared quite suddenly at the end of the 11th century in Languedoc" for reasons that he does not claim to know. Investigations into Celtic, Byzantine, Arabic, and Ovidian influences have, according to Lewis, failed to explain the "new sentiment" that we find in Provençal love poetry. More-recent scholars have disagreed, proposing a variety of sources. Dronke argues that courtly love poetry, with all the qualities that characterize it in eleventh-century France, has appeared in many times and places, including ancient Egypt and the Islamic world. Others have suggested that Christian Neoplatonism, which emphasizes the soul's longing to transcend carnality, influenced Provençal love poetry. Still others have argued that traditions of mysticism may have contributed the almost ascetic concern with unfulfilled desire that pervades the poetry. Possibly, as Theodore Silverstein has suggested, each of these operated to some degree on an unbroken tradition of quasi-religious love poetry dating back to the ancient world.

See also: Chrétien de Troyes; Knight; Minstrel; Tristan and Iseut; Valentine's Day, Saint

—Leigh Smith

Cross. Symbol commemorating the Crucifixion of Jesus, and more broadly, the Christian faith.

As the principal symbol of the dominant religion of medieval Europe, the cross pervaded European culture. Its form became incorporated into liturgical art, personal clothing, heraldry, cruciform architecture, and the lived religious experience of medieval Christians. Fitted with an image of a crucified Christ it became the crucifix, an object of progressively greater importance during the medieval era. The cross was pitted in narrative and art against symbols of all other major faiths, especially forms of pre-Christian worship, Judaism, and Islam.

Early Christian works, especially the epistles of St. Paul, stress the cross as a central aspect of Christian identity. It symbolized Christ's brutal sacrifice that had resulted in mankind's redemption and encapsulated the holiness to which each Christian was called. According to St. John Chrysostom (c. 347–407), the Holy Cross had risen to heaven along with the Savior and would play a key role in the Last Judgment. It was a conscious entity, capable of interceding on behalf of humans, much like Mary and the other saints. These concepts became central parts of the spiritual culture of the medieval era and are frequently depicted in religious art.

The gestural sign of the cross (crux usualis), one of the oldest forms of cross symbolism, emerged even prior to the legalization of the faith in the Roman Empire. Small gestural crosses gave way in the fifth century to a large cross traced across head, breast, and shoulders—usually with a formula designating the Trinity (Western tradition) or different aspects of the one God (Eastern tradition). In medieval Europe a gestured cross made large or small punctuated nearly every major act in life, from eating a meal to starting a trip to crowning a king. It was credited with warding off evil, bringing blessing, and even (when performed by a saintly individual) accomplishing miracles. In Odo of Cluny's tenth-century Life of St. Gerald of Aurillac, Gerald (c. 855–909) foils the trickery of an acrobat who is using demonic magic to accomplish his feats. Gerald makes the sign of the cross over the man, who is no longer able to jump as high as before. Writes Odo:

And so it was manifest that this activity of the man's was the result of an incantation, which could no longer aid him, after the sign of the Cross, and that the power of Count Gerald was great, since the power of the enemy [i.e., the devil] had no force against his sign. (Trans. G. Sitwell, in Soldiers of Christ [1995], ed. T. Noble and T. Head)

Soon thereafter Gerald uses the gesture to cure a woman who has been raving. He exorcises the demon inside her by making the sign of the cross over her; she vomits blood and matter and is cured.

Constantine and Helena

The rise of the Cross as an object of veneration owes much to Emperor Constantine (c. 280–337), his mother St. Helena (c. 250–c. 330), and the various chroniclers who transmitted or embroidered upon their experiences in later centuries. On the eve of the Battle of the Milvian Bridge in 312, Constantine was said to have seen a vision of the Cross in the sky accompanied by the inscription "In hoc signo vinces" [In this Sign you will conquer]. The pagan Constantine asked his advisers to explain the vision, and when he learned that the symbol represented Christ, he adopted the new religion for his own. With the new image inscribed on his men's banners and shields, Constantine won the battle and became the first Christian Roman emperor. His symbol, however, is not the usual perpendicular Roman cross but an X-shaped cross in saltire, one of many variations on the cross form common in the medieval period. Constantine's symbol developed into the chi-rho digraph (symbolic of the first two letters of the Greek word Christos) and was later reinvigorated as a symbol of the faith by Charlemagne (742–814).

Legends of St. Helena credited her with the discovery (termed the Invention) of the True Cross in Jerusalem, where it lay buried outside the city. According to legend, St. Helena compelled unwilling Jews to help in her search and eventually recognized the True Cross by its miraculous healing abilities. At Helena's bidding and Constantine's expense, basilicas were constructed in Jerusalem on the sites of the Resurrection and Calvary, and the latter became the home of the Cross relic from the time of its dedication in 325. Ritual kissing of this relic on Good Friday is reported by the Roman Aetheria (Sylvia) around 390, and the ritual became a part of the official office of the day throughout the Christian world during the medieval period. From the seventh century onward the anniversary of the dedication became a feast in the Roman calendar, celebrated on September 13 and 14, and known as the Exaltation of the Cross. Accounts of both Constantine's vision and St. Helena's Invention were immensely popular in the Middle Ages, and numerous Latin as well as vernacular versions survive, including the Anglo-Saxon poem Elene by Cynewulf.

Constantine's miraculous vision was repeated a number of times afterward. Bishop St. Cyril (c. 315–c. 386) reported an apparition of the Cross over the city of Jerusalem in 351. King St. Oswald of Northumbria (605–642) reported seeing a vision of a Roman cross in 634, immediately prior to his battle against the pagan king Cadwallon of Wales. Erecting a wooden cross on the battlefield, Oswald won the battle and claimed his ancestral throne. His cross became an object of veneration in itself, and slivers from it were used in healing elixirs for centuries after. The erection of the cross announced the king's intent to Christianize his realm, an undertaking that was soon carried out by Irish missionaries. The cult of King St. Oswald became popular not only in England but in continental Europe as well.

Relics, Pendants, and Monuments

By the fourth century tiny fragments of the True Cross (many severed from the relic conserved in Jerusalem but others clearly from other pieces of wood) began to diffuse across the Christian world, finding places of honor in churches as well as in personal amulets. St. Cyril of Jerusalem and St. John Chrysostom mention this practice in fourth-century Jerusalem and Antioch, and fragments began to appear in Italy and Gaul during the fifth century. St. Venantius Fortunatus, a famed poet of his day, composed the hymn "Vexilla regis" (The Banner of the King) in honor of the translation of a fragment of the True Cross to Poitiers in the late sixth century. Popes and Eastern patriarchs alike honored royal guests to their courts through the gift of Cross relics: Patriarch George of Jerusalem presented one such fragment to Charlemagne in 799, Pope Marinus I awarded such a treasure to King Alfred of England in 883, and King Sigurd of Norway brought home a fragment from his expedition to the Holy Land (c. 1110). Kings and monastic leaders alike used presentations of fragments to mark important alliances. The churches and cathedrals endowed with relics of the True Cross often became important pilgrimage centers, as the faithful visited in hopes of miraculous cures. Wealthy patrons marked their gratitude through rich gifts and art, and reliquaries constructed to hold Cross fragments were often lavishly decorated. The twelfth-century Irish Cross of Cong, one of the finest pieces of Irish art known from the Middle Ages, was apparently created to hold a piece of the True Cross.

The rise of cross pendants is closely tied to the tradition of obtaining relics of the True Cross. Cross pendants begin to appear in graves often well in advance of the actual arrival of the faith in a given area, indicating that their owners viewed these items at first as merely valuable ornaments or perhaps as significant receptacles of magic power. Pendants vary in form from region to region during the Middle Ages, and certain motifs—such as the cross in saltire (St. Andrew's X-shaped cross) or the T-shaped Mediterranean tau cross—frequently represent Christianizations of prior pagan, often solar, symbols. The St. Andrew's cross motif occurs in Celtic areas such as Scotland and Gaul; a ringed Irish Cross developed in the eighth century, and crosses with arms of equal length became popular throughout the area of the Eastern Church. Crosses decorated with raised bumps or gems on the arms and center represented the Five Wounds of Christ in the Crucifixion, themselves an object of intense devotion in the Middle Ages. Heraldic reworkings of the cross motif led to designs including

notched, flared, or crossed ends, each indicative of a different region or institution.

Christian theologians often treated pictorial art with suspicion, fearing a lapse into idolatry, and this recurrent fear led eventually to the violent iconoclastic controversies of the eighth and ninth centuries, particularly in the area of the Eastern Church, as well as in Gaul. The Roman Church never accepted the arguments of the iconoclasts, however, and in the Second General Council of Nicaea in 787, the use of objects such as crosses and icons was definitively endorsed. In the aftermath of this era, crosses became prescribed parts of the altar and other church sites.

Massive cross monuments of stone are central characteristics of Christianity in the British Isles of the eighth to twelfth centuries. These standing crosses decorated churches, churchyards, and crossroads, and they appear to have served as places of worship and preaching. They could also demonstrate the piety of wealthy patrons, who commissioned them in thanks for supernatural assistance or in the memory of deceased relatives. The earliest such crosses were decorated only sparingly; during subsequent centuries, however, crosses became decorated with ornate inhabited vine-scroll (populated by tiny human and animal figures frolicking in or battling against the tendrils of the foliage) and eventually with carved depictions of biblical events or saints. In their latest development they became crucifixes, depicting a Christ in crucifixion.

The tradition spread with some modification to Scandinavia but is largely absent from the rest of Europe. It is certain that wooden crosses also existed in the British Isles, and some sort of standing-cross tradition may have existed on the European continent as well, where wood was more common. It is difficult to gauge the extent of wooden cross monuments and roadside shrines during the medieval period, however, because of the inevitable decay of such material over time.

Legends and Feasts

Medieval legendry teems with accounts of the Cross or cross symbols, their uses and abuses, and the miracles proceeding from them. These included the apocryphal Gospel of Nicodemus, which details the history of the tree that became the Cross and its relation to the fateful tree responsible for mankind's Fall in the Garden of Eden. The Anglo-Saxon poem known as *The Dream of the Rood* details a wondrous vision of the True Cross and the Cross's own eyewitness account of the Crucifixion. Saints' legends frequently tell of miracles attending the cross pendants of holy men and women after their deaths. In the widespread legend known as the *Flagellatio crucis* (Scourging of the Cross), Jewish persecutors attack a cross, only to find its insides filled with the miraculous healing blood and water of Christ's own body. In the Crusades the cross became a prime symbol of a warrior's acceptance of his holy mission and was emblazoned on shields, helmets, and banners. Some of the oldest flags of Europe reflect this cross symbolism, and many—as in the case of the Danish *Dannebrog* (a red field surrounding a cross of white)—were attributed to divine sources.

Given the centrality of the Cross to the Crusades, it is not surprising that the large relic of the True Cross in Jerusalem was seized by the Persians in 614. Its fate at the hands of Islamic tormentors was recounted in numerous legends until its return in 630. Its reinstallation on May 3 became celebrated as the Feast of the Invention from the eighth century onward, joining the Feast of the Exaltation (September 13–14) and the Good Friday devotions as the principal Cross-related feast days of the Western Church. In the Eastern Church, Cross feast days consisted of the third Sunday of Lent, Good Friday, the Feast of the Apparition in Jerusalem (May 7), and the Feast of the Adoration (August 1). All of these feasts attracted folk as well as liturgical expressions of devotion: for instance, a custom of burying crosses of wood or bread in farm fields on the Feast of the Invention (May 3) is attested in many parts of peasant Europe both in medieval and postmedieval sources.

The Image of Christ Crucified

Although poetry and pictorial art of the early Middle Ages depict a triumphant, heroic Christ on the Cross, the era of the Cistercian St. Bernard of Clairvaux (1090–1153) ushered in a more human, suffering image of the Savior. Crucifixes as well as devotional lyrics from this period stress the human pain of Christ and his mother and direct the faithful toward an intensely physical contemplation of the Crucifixion. This new mysticism spread widely throughout Europe, thanks in large part to the preaching of the Mendicant orders (Franciscans and Dominicans) of the thirteenth century. The Franciscan hymn "Stabat Mater dolorosa" (Stand, Grieving Mother), traditionally attributed to the Italian Franciscan friar Jacopone da Todi (d. 1306), illustrates this new emphasis. The hymn's speaker declares:

Fac me plagis vulnerari
Fac me cruce inebriari
Et cruore Filii.

[Let me suffer the injuries
let me be overwhelmed by the Cross
and the blood of the Son.]

The pained Christ and crucifix soon became the dominant image of the Cross or the Crucifixion in medieval Europe.

See also: Crusades; Jesus Christ; Relics

—Thomas A. DuBois

Crusades. Wars waged by European Christian forces against Islam and other non-Christian religions and cultures, beginning in 1096 and continuing intermittently through the end of the Middle Ages, giving rise to legends and heroic poetry throughout Europe and creating channels for the folk traditions of the Middle East to influence Western culture.

Causes

Many factors combined to bring about the Crusades. The eleventh century witnessed a rejuvenation of the Christian Church, combined with a new religious spirituality affecting the masses. There were numerous pilgrimages to the Holy Land, and biblical learning and preaching dealt intensively with the holy sites in Palestine. Conflicts with the Islamic world intensified as the Muslim Seljuk Turks conquered Syria in 1055 and later attacked Anatolia (1072–1081). In 1071 the Turks defeated the Byzantine army in the battle of Mantzikert and captured Jerusalem from the Egyptian Fatimid caliphs in the same year. As Byzantium was also threatened by Muslim forces, the Greek Orthodox Church and the Byzantine emperor, Alexius Comnenus (reigned 1081–1118), appealed for help from Christians in the West.

Pope Urban II, engaged in a vicious conflict with the German emperor Henry IV, sought help from the European knightly class and from Constantinople, using the conflict in the Middle East to rally troops for a crusade. His goal was to become the leader of a universal Church, uniting Eastern and Western Christianity under his rule. Elsewhere in Europe political and social chaos contended with visions of economic opportunism. In France a multitude of feudal conflicts had led to a form of anarchy and civil war—a disastrous situation that not only drove a vast number of French knights into exile but also caused multitudes of displaced peasants to flee the country. The Italian seaports, on the other hand, looked for military support to safely extend their eastern Mediterranean trade, which the Seljuks had interrupted.

Therefore, buoyed up by his personal ambitions and conscious of the need for remedies to the troubles in Europe, Pope Urban II appealed to European chivalry to take up arms against the infidels in the Holy Land and to recover it for the Christian faith. In preaching the Crusades, Urban drew upon traditional tales and stereotypes to create a mood of fervid animosity against the Muslims, establishing a pattern that other religious leaders would employ for several centuries. Addressing a large crowd in Clermont-Ferrand on November 27, 1095, the pope commented on reports from Constantinople that an evil people in the Persian Empire, bestial and godless, had conquered the Holy Land, killed and abducted people there, destroyed the Christian churches, circumcised the Christians, and tortured them in a horrible manner, raping women and disemboweling men.

The First Crusade and Godfrey of Bouillon

The first army of crusaders, made up of a hysterical mass of peasants and impoverished knights, immediately assembled and marched toward Anatolia. En route to their destination they attacked Jewish communities all over Germany and France. When this ragtag company of would-be soldiers eventually arrived in Anatolia, the Seljuks swiftly crushed them in the first battle (1096). A second Christian army arrived in Constantinople in 1097. It was led by Raymond of St. Gilles, Godfrey of Bouillon, Bohemond of Taranto, and others and included knights from all over Europe. They gained their first victory over the Seljuks at Antioch in 1098 and laid the foundations for making Antioch the center of the first crusader principality. In April 1099 they conquered the abandoned city of Ramlah, and in July they attacked and took Jerusalem. Consequently, the crusader Kingdom of Jerusalem was established under the rule of Godfrey of Bouillon, who died shortly after his victory and was succeeded by his brother Baldwin (reigned 1100–1118). Godfrey instantly became a Europe-wide hero. His stature grew throughout the twelfth and thirteenth centuries, as he was made the subject of heroic poetry. Legendry endowed him with a supernatural origin. A century after his death, French chansons de geste attributed to him a supernatural ancestry. In the poems *Elioxe* and *Beatrix*, Godfrey is the descendant of the Swan Knight, one of seven children born with silver chains around their necks. Six of the children have their chains removed and change into swans. The seventh retains his human form and becomes Godfrey's progenitor. In late-medieval tradition Godfrey became, along with King Arthur and Charlemagne, one of the Three Christian Worthies, a figure of enormous veneration.

Godfrey's Kingdom of Jerusalem did not enjoy the long-lasting glory of Godfrey himself. Conflicts between the Christian rulers and their opponents quickly weakened the kingdom. The Muslims also suffered setbacks, however, so the crusader states retained a weak hold over the Holy Land.

Twelfth- and Thirteenth-Century Campaigns

In the following two centuries many more crusades were organized. When the earldom of Edessa, north of the Syrian crusader states, was lost to the Muslims, the powerful Cistercian abbot St. Bernard of Clairvaux preached in favor of a new crusade. This Second Crusade began in 1144, under the leadership of the German emperor Conrad III and the French king Louis VII. Their goal was to conquer Damascus, but they never achieved it.

In 1187 Sultan Saladin (Salah ad-Din) defeated a Christian army at Hattin and then conquered Jerusalem, triggering the Third Crusade, which was conducted under the leadership of the German emperor Frederick I Barbarossa. When this great leader drowned in a river in Anatolia in 1189, the French king Philip II and the English king Richard the Lion-Heart assumed control of the crusaders. Richard proved to be an excellent strategist and a successful general; he conquered Cyprus and Acre and defeated Saladin, thereby liberating a long strip of the Mediterranean coast and providing Christian pilgrims with access to Jerusalem.

The Third Crusade inspired many legends and romances. Saladin, for example, became a major figure in European lore. The German poet Walther von der Vogelweide (fl. 1200–1220) praised Saladin's generosity in a poem, which the Viennese chronicler Jans Enenkel (late thirteenth century) expanded to a comprehensive song of praise of Saladin's generosity, tolerance, wisdom, and intelligence. Many Arabic poets also glorified Saladin in their works, and the sultan retained his legendary reputation throughout the centuries.

The Christian armies never again equaled the successes of the Third Crusade, and many of the subsequent expeditions were characterized by desperation. The Children's Crusade of 1212, inspired by a popular religious movement, drew upon the biblical concept that children possess greater innocence and godliness than adults. The crusade was made up of approximately 10,000 children, representing all social classes but coming principally from France and the Low Countries. Many died in shipwrecks, and others were sold into slavery, but many returned safely to their homes.

During the thirteenth century the Christians experienced some success—for example, in the Fifth Crusade (1228), when the German emperor Frederick II used diplomacy instead of warfare to regain Jerusalem, Bethlehem, and Nazareth peacefully from the Egyptian sultan al-Malik al-Kamil. Nevertheless, the Khwarizmians, an Iranian-Turkish people, reconquered Jerusalem in 1244, inciting the French king Louis IX to mount the Sixth Crusade (1248–1254), the last major European military effort to recapture and control the Holy Land. Louis was unsuccessful, and despite sporadic victories, Acre, the last Christian fortress in the Holy Land, fell to Islam in 1291.

The Failures of the Crusades

In the long run the Crusades failed because various national interests were constantly in conflict with one another. Byzantium only wanted help from Western Europe to defend its eastern borders; Venice, for economic reasons, was always in conflict with Byzantium; England and France could never agree on the ultimate objectives of the Crusades; and the German emperors and their followers continually experienced religious and political conflicts with Rome.

Other problems were the religious and cultural differences between the Latin crusaders and the Greek Orthodox Church in Constantinople. Members of the Greek Orthodox Church observed rituals significantly different from those of the Western Church and espoused a relatively tolerant attitude toward other cultures and religions.

Despite their idealism and religious fervor, many of the crusaders behaved in a crudely barbaric fashion, lacked discipline, and earned the scorn of both Byzantines and the Muslims. The crusaders who settled in the new kingdoms, ruling over a large non-Western, non-Christian population, had no idea how to carry out their political functions. They seemed genuinely puzzled by the fact that among their subjects there were large groups of Eastern Christians, such as Greek Orthodox, "Syrians," and Jacobites. Although the Crusades had been organized in the name of God, the end result was a ruthless, brutal, and cruel form of imperialism based on a kind of medieval "apartheid" system, as the Christian lords lived in the cities, recognized no real obligations to their peasants, and exploited their lands.

Folkways and Cultural Exchanges

Distinct forms of dress separated the Muslims from the Christians. Although Christians made use of native textiles, they tailored their clothes in accordance with European fashions. The Christians greatly admired and used Eastern architecture for private housing, but not for religious and military constructions. The crusaders did, however, freely use and greatly enjoy the spices and perfumes of the East, which they exported in great quantities to Europe, exerting substantial impact on medieval lifestyles.

The public bathhouses of the East also impressed the crusaders, who established similar bathhouses in Europe. Christian warriors and Italian merchants took home with them new types of weapons, coats of arms, carpets, musical instruments, and paper. In addition, the crusaders copied their opponents' superior military technologies, including armor, siege engines, explosives, special techniques for combat on horseback, and fortification methods.

Perhaps the crusaders' greatest mistake lay in their failure to learn the native language, Arabic. By simply ignoring the culture of the people under their rule, the Christians missed the opportunity to establish a solid foundation for the continued existence of their kingdoms. Eventually their "apartheid" was to turn against them, and as a result of their indifference to the conquered peoples, they lost all the land they had previously conquered.

Some Christian and Arabic sources convey a slightly different picture. According to these accounts, a form of cohabitation was realized fairly soon. The Muslim chronicler Ibn Jubayr (1145–1217), who made a pilgrimage from Spain to Palestine, Syria, Baghdad, and Mecca at the end of the twelfth century, observed with great consternation that the two peoples coexisted rather peacefully and enjoyed the fruits of their work together. He saw both Christian and Muslim merchants carrying out their business peacefully, paying their taxes to their respective rulers, and ignoring the war. Surprisingly, he also reported that the Muslims in Acre were allowed to continue their religious services in their own mosque. Usama ibn Munquidh's *Chronicle* (1095–1188) describes a similar situation in Jerusalem, where the Knights Templar made sure that Christian zealots would not disturb Muslim religious services.

In contrast to this image of tolerance and peaceful coexistence, many Arabic accounts characterize the "Franks," as the crusaders were summarily called, as cruel, dishonest, treacherous, cowardly, and vengeful. These are, however, the same traits ascribed to the Muslims by Western chroniclers. A few of the Eastern chroniclers, such as Usama ibn Munquidh, praised the crusaders for their bravery, heroism, virtues, and strength. Baha' ad-Din ibn Shaddad (1145–1234) portrayed Richard the Lion-Heart as a man of good judgment, great courage, and swift and resolute decisions, and as a highly esteemed leader of his people. Interestingly, some Western sources reflect the dual portrait of Richard by depicting him both as a hero and as a monster. The fourteenth-century English romance *Richard* describes the king as superlatively courageous, but it also characterizes him as serving and eating the heads of Saracens at banquets.

There may have been occasional friendships between Muslims and crusaders, as Usama ibn Munquidh and Gamal ad-Din ibn Wasil (1207–1298) report. Overall, however, the Arabs cared as little for learning about the Europeans as the Europeans cared for learning about them. Each culture tended to dismiss the other as worthless and primitive.

At least one particularly astonishing example of intercultural communication did take place. St. Francis of Assisi, traveling with the Sixth Crusade in 1219, obtained an audience with the Egyptian sultan al-Malik al-Kamil in order to preach to him. Although the sultan listened to Francis, gave him gifts, and provided him with safe passage, this contact led to no lasting peace.

The Crusades led to some positive effects. For a long time, the Crusades inspired European chivalry with new idealism and provided the knightly class with a specific goal. These military enterprises also brought together many people from many different nations and opened their minds to cultures in other parts of the world.

However, the long-term consequences of the Crusades for the West were generally negative, as the high cost of foreign warfare impoverished the aristocracy. The population of Europe was depleted, and the Church lost much of its stature after successive defeats. Nevertheless, the Crusades played a major role in opening routes for major cultural and commercial contacts between East and West.

See also: Arabic-Islamic Tradition; Foreign Races; Hispanic Tradition; Richard the Lion-Heart; Swan Knight

—Albrecht Classen

Cuckold. The husband whose wife has sex with another man; a traditional figure of fun, whose humiliation—in societies that regard the wife as firmly under the husband's control, especially in sexual matters—is the mainspring of countless fabliaux and other comic works; more rarely, a rejected lover.

Iconographically, the "attribute" par excellence of the cuckolded husband is his horn or horns. A misericord in Rotherham Church carved in 1483 depicts a man in a close-fitting hood from which horns emerge: this image may well have been intended to represent a cuckold. In Germany and England—certainly in vernacular literature—the evidence for this convention is relatively late, however. The first English citations unequivocally linked to cuckold imagery are from the fifteenth-century works of the English poet John Lydgate (c. 1370–c. 1450).

Nevertheless, British Latin authors do evidence a familiarity with the cuckold's horns as early as about 1200, in one of the fables of Walter of England, but more significantly, in Geoffrey of Monmouth's *Vita Merlini* (Life of Merlin; c. 1150). In this work Merlin is portrayed as a Wild Man who, mounted on a stag, comes riding up to the house of his former mistress. He finds her enjoying the night of her wedding to his rival, and in a fit of jealous rage Merlin tears off the stag's antlers and hurls them at the couple.

Continental literature features references to the horns of the rejected lover, for example, in a late-twelfth-century poem by the troubadour Bernart de Ventadour. There is reason to believe that the convention evolved in the Middle Ages in regions where Romance languages were spoken. The earliest reference, however, is the expression "to wear the horned hat," which appears in Artemidorus's Latin dreambook of c. 200 C.E. and later appears in the Provençal poetry of twelfth-century troubadours Guilhem de Bergueda (*"porta cofa cornuda"*) and Marcabru (*"porta capel cornut"*). Compare this expression with the punishment meted out to a fourteenth-century Italian who pimped for his wife (thus by definition cuckolding himself) and was subsequently forced to wear a two-horned cap.

A late-fifteenth-century Florentine engraving satirizing cuckolds goes by the title *I Re de Becchi*

(King of the Goats); in this scene, the horns are clearly those of the goat, but a reference to "brow-antlers" by the English poet John Skelton (c. 1460–1529) is late evidence that the stag was often seen as the source of the cuckold's "horns." In fact, a mid-thirteenth-century account by Boncompagno da Signa records that almost any horned animal might figure in this convention, noting that Italian women referred to the deceived husbands as goats, bulls, and stags, as well as cuckoos (*cuculi;* singular *cuculus*). In addition, the women used various jocular phrases involving words beginning with the syllables *cucu,* such as *cucurbita* (gourd), alluding, of course, to the word *cuculus,* which had already acquired the sense "cuckold" by this time. A remarkable miniature in a French manuscript of Gratian's Decretals, circa 1300, depicts a priest marrying a couple while a nobleman looks on. From the groom's temples rise two four-tined antlers; the implication is clearly that he has already been cuckolded by the onlooker.

It is not possible to say whether the various medieval nicknames involving the element *horn* allude to this convention, since horns were common instruments and trophies, but potential English candidates include Panhorn (1251) and, more obliquely perhaps, Bukenheved (Buck's Head; 1301; cf. a stage direction in a *Merry Wives of Windsor* quarto: "Enter sir John [Falstaff] with a Buck's head upon him") and Herteheued (Hart's Head; 1332). There can be no doubt about Uluric Cucuold from Suffolk (c. 1087), and little about the Parisians Guille and Guillaume le Cornu (1292). The well-known two-finger "horned hand" gesture is found in such early works of art as ancient Etruscan and Pompeiian wall paintings; however, such early notices of the gesture are rare. Moreover, even in these wall paintings, the context is not necessarily one suggestive of adultery, although it is often assumed that the positioning of the fingers symbolizes the horns of the cuckold.

The term *cuckold* is usually accepted as deriving from the bird name cuckoo, despite semantic difficulties (for it is not the cuckoo that raises the offspring of others, but they hers). Rightly or wrongly, the connection was certainly made by medieval people. The cuckoo was the cuckold's bird long before Shakespeare. Chaucer's "Knight's Tale," for example, describes Jalousye with "a cukkow sittynge on his hand," and Chaucer's contemporary, the Scotsman Thomas Clanvowe, in his poem on the bird, writes that among lovers, "it was a comune tale, / That it were good to here the nightingale / Rather than the lewde cukkow singe." Jean de Condé (c. 1325) says of the cuckoo, "Ce fu li kuqus de pute aire / Ki a maint home a dit grant lait" [It was the cuckoo, of foul kin, / Who spoke great evil to many men]. In his *Fulgens and Lucrece* (c. 1497), Henry Medwall appears to record an interesting, clearly related folk belief: "Men say amonge / He that throwyth stone or stycke / At such a byrde he is lycke [likely] / To synge that byrdes songe."

The hood seems also to have been part of the folklore of the cuckold (cf. the expression "wered a cukwold hoode" in the fifteenth-century manuscript of *Ipomadon*) for which the coincidence of Latin *cucullus* (hood) with *cuculus* (cuckoo) may bear some responsibility. Pieter Brueghel the Elder's famous *Netherlandish Proverbs* painting of 1559 is also known as *The Blue Hood* (a phrase attested from the late fourteenth century), from the central image, which shows a young wife pulling a hooded cape over her husband's head, clearly symbolizing her intention to hoodwink or deceive him. This particular iconographic motif can certainly be traced back to a late-fifteenth-century wooden carving by a Flemish craftsman in Toledo cathedral, but from at least the late fourteenth century, English sources also record various "hood" expressions in a cuckoldry context. Consider, for example, that in this phrase from Lydgate, "With such a metyerde she hathe shape him an hoode," "metyerde" (literally, "measuring-rod") puns on the combination of "meat" and "yard" to signify a penis.

In a glossary of circa 1440 the word *cockney* (coken + ey = cock's egg) is defined as *cornutus* (cuckold, literally "horned") and probably already has this sense in Chaucer's "Reeve's Tale." The German name for the cuckold, *Hahnrei*, might also seem to be composed of *hahn* (cock) and *ei* (egg), but the second element is *-rei*, explained as meaning "castrated," so that the word means "castrated cock," that is, capon. The word *capon* is itself similarly used to mean "eunuch" in thirteenth-century English, and a most interesting early-fifteenth-century gloss on the Latin word *gallinacius* reads "*homo debilis* [weak man], a malkyn [otherwise a nickname for a promiscuous young woman] & a *capoun*." This is of particular interest, as Konrad Gesner, in his *Vogelbuch* (Bird Book) of 1557, records that one method of contemporary caponization was to excise the cock's testicles, comb, and one of its spurs, grafting the spur in place of the comb, where it continued to grow, resembling a small horn. This grafting of a "horn," it is suggested, then served as a sign by which to identify the caponized birds.

The cuckold is naturally assimilated to the "hen-pecked" husband or effeminate man. The *hennetaster* (hen groper), a type of the effeminate man, is depicted circa 1500 in stallwork at Emmerich, Kempen, and Aarschot. The earliest English reference (contemporary with his appearing in Brueghel's *Netherlandish Proverbs*) is Dame Chat's insulting insinuation that Hodge came "creeping into my pens, / And there was caught within my house groping among my hens" (*Gammer Gurton's Needle*, c. 1563). It is notable how so many of these terms concerning dominant and subservient sexual roles revolve around the barnyard relations of the cock and hen.

A late but interesting instance of the public ridicule of cuckolds is recorded in Henry Machyn's diary for May 15, 1562: "The same day was set up at the Cuckold Haven a great Maypole by butchers and fisher-men, full of horns; and they made great cheer." That derisive horns were a constituent of the mocking rituals known as charivaris, when aimed at cuckolds, may be gathered from early descriptions and depictions (e.g., Joris Hoefnagel's drawing of 1569). The apprentices of a goldsmith insulted their master by "making a horned head upon his dore sett betwene the lettres of his name and other lyke villanyes" in London in 1558. Throughout the Elizabethan era, court records make frequent allusion to the setting up of horns at the doors of houses where the husband was believed to be a cuckold. An especially elaborate instance occurred in Wiltshire in 1616, when a buck's horn stuck with a wisp of hay and "a picture of a woman's privities" was used.

See also: Charivari; Fabliau; Trickster

—Malcolm Jones

Culhwch and Olwen [Culhwch ac Olwen]. Welsh prose tale, extant in two fourteenth-century manuscripts, probably composed in its present form somewhere in southwest Wales in the last decades of the eleventh century.

Culhwch and Olwen shares its plot with an internationally distributed folktale known as "Six Go through the Whole World" (AT 513A), in which the hero gathers a number of companions, each possessing some remarkable skill or extraordinary power, and sets out to find and win a giant's daughter as his bride. Her father sets a series of difficult tasks, which the hero accomplishes with the essential aid of his companions. In *Culhwch and Olwen* the core plot is greatly elaborated by incorporating a number of other story elements and Celtic legends into its narrative and, most strikingly, by placing the entire story into the framework of Arthurian legend, so that King Arthur and his warrior band perform for Culhwch the difficult tasks required to win Olwen, the daughter of the giant Ysbaddaden. The earliest developed picture in European literature of an established Arthurian court is seen in this work.

Another distinctive departure from the traditional oral tale in *Culhwch and Olwen* occurs in two extended catalogs that interrupt the narrative, first when Culhwch appears at Arthur's court to ask for help in his quest and then when Ysbaddaden specifies the tasks required to win his daughter. Invoking the aid of Arthur, his cousin, in the name of Arthur's court, Culhwch proceeds to name all the men and women who belong to that court. In that extensive list of names, many with epithets and allusions to marvelous exploits attached to them, we hear the echoes of a world of traditional story lost to us—of Teithi Hen, whose kingdom was inundated by the sea, of Hueil, son of Caw, who never submitted to a lord's hand and who stabbed his sister's son, and of many others. In the other catalog, the three tasks demanded of the suitor in the traditional tale are expanded by Ysbaddaden to a list of 40 *anoethau* (wonders, things difficult to obtain), which Culhwch and the Arthurian band must accomplish. The fulfilling of each task is a potential tale, but we actually hear the stories of only ten and brief references to the completion of a few others. Here, especially, we see drawn into the story motifs and tales known elsewhere in Celtic tradition and international folk narrative, such as the "unending battle" motif (A162.1.0.1), a tale of progressively older animals aiding in a quest (B124.1; B841.1; F571.2; H1235), and the ancient and widespread story of grateful ants who perform the task of sorting seeds (B365.2.1; B481.1; H1091.1).

The language of *Culhwch and Olwen* is consciously archaic, but the narrative style is energetic and richly varied, in turn heroic, comic, lyrical, boisterous, and learned. The stirring climax of the story is the hunt of a great boar, named Twrch Trwyth, an epic chase across the landscapes of Ireland, Wales, and Cornwall. Two descriptive set pieces, one describing Culhwch and the other Olwen, seem to depend on oral delivery for their full effect. They are early examples of Welsh *araitheu* (rhetorics), rhythmical and alliterative passages of extravagant prose analogous to the "runs" in Irish oral storytelling, and are perhaps the clearest examples of the many strong suggestions of performance running through *Culhwch and Olwen*. It is generally believed, however, that this tale is a literary composition, the product of an unknown author, and not a transcribed example of the art of the *cyfarwydd*, the Welsh oral storyteller. Side by side with the folktale elements and the performance style are the formal structuring, internal cross-references, allusive language, and ironic voice of literary composition. *Culhwch and Olwen* appears to be one of those interesting medieval works that is a mimesis of traditional style by an individual author, blending oral and written ways of telling a story.

See also: Arthurian Lore; Folktale; *Mabinogi*; Welsh Tradition

—Andrew Welsh

*D*ance. The performance of a succession of rhythmic and controlled or patterned bodily movements, usually within a predetermined framework of time and space, and often to music.

Such a generic definition is admittedly inadequate for "dance" in its broadest sense. There is a tendency for such definitions to be too exclusive or too all-inclusive; for instance, emphasizing bodily movement, in an attempt to evoke a concrete image, disregards other dimensions of the activity. George S. Emmerson states that "dance draws energy from something deep in the human spirit or psyche and shares the mystical powers of all the arts, music, poetry, and sculpture in particular. It is a vehicle of ecstasy, liberating the body from the mind, the body's mass from gravity, and inspiring with ritualistic power." Thus, dancing is physical action, but action that has meaning, generally on multiple levels of consciousness, and invites interaction and evokes response. The use of rhythm, gesture, and movement as a means of externalizing feelings and conveying messages appears to be one of the basic human needs. Its origins, therefore, are lost somewhere in humankind's prehistory, which fact in itself makes definition and interpretation difficult.

Evidence of Medieval Dancing Practices
The key words for dance used by the early Church fathers in the early Middle Ages were *saltare*, *ballare*, and *choreare*. *Saltario*, or pantomime, was representative dance by professional performers. From this word came the dance term *saltarello*. *Ballare* was the most general term used for dance in the Middle Ages, while *choreare* became associated with group dancing in circle or line patterns. *Danzare* (and later, *dancier*, *danser*, and *tantzen*) did not appear in the vocabulary until the late Middle Ages. Proper names for specific dances began to appear in the twelfth century: *estample*, *trotto*, *cazzole*, *carole*, *reien*, *hovetantz*; German peasants danced *hoppaldei*, *firlefanz*, and *ridewanz*. The *carole*, a circle dance, became the form most often described by medieval poets. It was the ancestor of the *branle* and the *farandole*. Sometimes it was contracted into a closed circle and was accompanied by musical forms like the virelai, rondeau, and ballade. The more formal *danse* referred to couples or groups of three people and was usually mentioned in relation to nobility. These formal dances eventually led to the Burgundian *basse danse*, the Italian *bassadanza*, and the early modern *pavan*.

We lack concrete evidence for the prehistories of both music and dance, although mythic tales of their origins abound in almost every culture. While there was a change in the style, technique, and development of dance during the Middle Ages, it is difficult to provide more than the barest description of the whole period. The reason is the absence of primary dance sources. Most dance information must be gathered from iconographic sources, literary references, and musical evidence. Ironically, a significant portion of the limited concrete information available about dance in the medieval period comes not from the folk who engaged in dancing for whatever reason but from entities opposed to and critical of the practice, representing generally the medieval Christian Church. When Christianity replaced the so-called pagan belief systems of Europe, worship of the new deity was superimposed on the old cults, and through the influence of tolerant churchmen such as Pope Gregory the Great—who directed the Christianization of England beginning in 597—ancient religious practices were perpetuated in a new guise. Although devout ecclesiastics never came to terms with practices such as dancing, playing, and masquerading, the people of Europe were deeply attached to their ancient customs and heedless of their pagan implications. The two great cultural divisions of northern Europe—Celtic and Germanic—celebrated such festivals as Samhain (November 1), the beginning of the winter feast; Beltane (May 1), the beginning of the summer feast; and Lugnasa (August 1), the harvest feast. The Church superimposed its own festivals these, with the result that in the winter celebrations extended from All Souls' Day to Twelfth Night, in the summer from Palm Sunday through May Day and Whitsun (Pentecost), and the harvest feast, Michaelmas (September 29), which took place all over Europe, might likewise involve protracted periods of festivity. While dancing was not a part of official Christian ritual, it retained its festive function despite ecclesiastical opposition. For instance, though the May Day festivities differed from place to place and from century to century, during the Middle Ages the aristocracy generally engaged in such martial activities as archery, minstrels performed, and villagers danced, often around and in the churchyard and sometimes in the church itself. Bishops throughout the Middle Ages denounced the use of the church and churchyard for secular pursuits, but with little effect. In 1210 Jacques de Vitry declared that the "woman who leadeth the dance [may] be said to have the devil's bell on her." A thirteenth-century statute of the Diocese of Aberdeen decrees that neither "choree" (from the Greek, indicating song and dance) nor "turpes et inhonesti ludi" be permitted in the church or churchyard. Even Robert Mannyng's use, in *Handlyng Synne* (1303), of the widely known legend of the sacrilegious dancers of Kölbigk implies a warning against the excesses of dance that interfere with the services of the church.

In addition to edicts from the Church and ecclesiastical commentaries, historical and literary references, paintings, manuscript illuminations, and carvings offer piecemeal information about medieval dance. As early as circa 98 C.E., Tacitus in his *Germania* commented on a dance of the Germans, performed by "naked youths ... among swords and spears," perhaps a pyrrhic dance or rhythmical weapon drill of the sort used by special groups such as the trade guilds during the medieval period. The author of the fourteenth-century English romance *Sir Gawain and the Green Knight* describes a carol, or song and dance combination, performed at Christmas. Chaucer, especially in the *Legend of Good Women* (c. 1385) and portions of *The Canterbury Tales* (c. 1387–1400), and Gower in *Confessio Amantis* (c. 1390) refer to ring dances performed mostly by the lower classes. In the fourteenth-century *Stanzaic Life of Christ* the word *ring* is used to indicate a closed round dance, and in the fifteenth-century rhymed ecclesiastical calendar (presumably by John Lydgate), a whole company of saints is depicted as dancing a joyous carol or ring dance. Carols, or ring dances, figure repeatedly in French romances of the medieval period, such as *Le roman de la rose*, *Guillaume de Dole*, and *Le roman de la violette*.

Dancing Patterns
European folk dances combine the elements of pattern, steps, and sometimes costume. Common patterns are the circle or ring, the chain, and the processional; more-complicated patterns developed in some countries. The simplest and perhaps earliest form, the closed circle, is found everywhere in postmedieval Europe. In its most elemental state—examples of which are the Yugoslav, Romanian, and Bulgarian Kolos and Horas and the Breton Bondes—the dancers are equal and sex is immaterial because all must join in; often there is no progression, or at most a gradual movement to left or right; the dancers hold each other's hands, wrists, shoulders, elbows, or belts and face the center. In the more complex ring dances, such as the Celtic Sellenger's Round and Circassian Circle and Russian and Yugoslav dances like the Moonshine and Neda Grivny, the dancers move in and out of the circle, and though maintaining contact with each other during most passages, they open out to perform individual movements. Many of the dances associated with work, such as the Armenian Carpetweaving Dance and the Hebridean Weaving Lilt, utilize this more complicated circle pattern, with the individual movements representing the motions of the particular labor involved. In the Middle Ages the trade guilds, which had to teach their apprentices the secrets of their craft, made several of these dances their particular property. The dances of the guilds were pyrrhic in nature, that is, they were rhythmic drills employing the tools of the particular craft.

The many morris dances and the point-and-hilt sword dances also employ the circle or ring and are sometimes confused with each other.

These dances are ritualistic rather than communal or social and are performed either by professional dancers or by amateurs representing a particular brotherhood, organization, or guild. In the morris dance, six morris men carry sticks or handkerchiefs and are dressed in ritual costume, with bright-colored ribbons, flowers, and greenery as well as a pad of bells on each leg. Unlike the sword dances, the morris—as known in postmedieval times—is a step dance with highly developed foot, hand, and body movements. It is danced in the spring, usually during Whitsun week. The dance may have got its name from the custom of blackening the faces of the dancers so that they looked like Moors or Moresco—hence morris. The point-and-hilt sword dance, sometimes confused with the morris, was performed primarily during the Christmas season and was familiar in all European countries during the late-medieval period. In this dance the participants are linked together in a circle joined by swords held hilt and point; they dance to a drum or fiddle through a series of evolutions, ending with swords in a locked formation about the neck of one of the dancers. In the fifteenth century and later, certain dramatic personages became a part of festival celebrations and were incorporated in the morris dance—Robin Hood, Little John, Friar Tuck, and others. Consequently, also associated with the morris dance and the sword dance are guisers and grotesques, fundamentally of two kinds: those wearing the skin or tail of some animal and those masquerading in the dress of the opposite sex, usually men dressed as women.

Some of the more social or communal ring dances involve forming double circles, often an inner circle of men and an outer circle of women.

Interestingly, the carol or carole, generally described as a circle or ring dance, also contains elements of the chain. The word *carol* occurs in extant British literature about 1300 in the *Cursor Mundi* in the exact sense of the Old French *carole*, meaning a ring dance in which the singers-dancers themselves sing the governing music. Throughout the medieval period the carol enjoyed enormous vogue as a pastime, figuring repeatedly in the medieval French romances already mentioned and in other medieval literature. It consisted of a chain, open or closed, of male and female dancers moving to the accompaniment of the voice or instruments. The movement was usually three steps in measure to the left, followed by marking time in place. Though the dancers joined hands, the clasp had to be broken for the frequent gestures. It was the duty of the leader not only to direct the proceedings but to sing the song to which the carol was being danced, and during the singing the ring moved to the left. The company of dancers would then stand in place while they responded to the leader's stanza with the refrain, or burden, of the song. The popular dance inspired the legend of the cursed carolers recounted in the Middle English *Handlyng Synne* of Robert Mannyng, among other sources. The legend tells of a group of boisterous dancers of Kölbigk who, for disturbing mass, were condemned to continue their round for a year without stopping.

Many Scandinavian and German dances open with the processional or promenade, another common pattern. Modern England retains two such processionals, the Helston Furry Dance and the Abbots Bromley Horned Dance, the latter of which dates back at least to the seventeenth century. The whole community took part in these processionals, dancing in and out of the houses and through the town, sweeping everything with branches of May or green broom and sometimes being led by a hobbyhorse or other animal. The Irish Rinnce Fada is also of this form and was probably familiar during the medieval period, though the first literary description of it is given in James Boswick's *Who Are the Irish?* in connection with a visit by James II to Ireland in the seventeenth century. In this dance, three leaders were followed by a line of dancers in couples joined by holding white clothes or handkerchiefs. Certain of these dances involved a single file of men and one of women and are akin to the popular couple dances that became the principal feature of many Scandinavian, Teutonic, and Alpine traditions. The more-complicated patterns involving circle and longways dances developed from the early court and social dances, and many of these innovations were not available to medieval dancers, particularly the lower classes. The actual steps of these figured dances were often simple, but different ways of holding a partner or of changing places were introduced: Inside Hands Joined, Two Hands Hold, Cross Hands Hold, Arming, Double Ring Grasp, and others.

Emotional and Social Dimensions

It is impossible to know with any certainty what emotional, intellectual, social, and spiritual dimensions the various folk dances possessed for medieval dancers. It is very likely that some of the dances retained remnants of their pre-Christian association with magic and supernatural ritual; for instance, ecstatic dances, associated with the fear of death, gave rise to the *Danse macabre* (Dance of Death). This dance madness was associated with the plague and other diseases. Certainly, there were dances that were used in connection with Christian festivals and activities—dances such as the carol, depending on the contents of the dance song, and the war-like dances of the trade guilds in conjunction with morality plays. The medieval Church steadfastly imposed strong restrictions against the use of dance in the liturgy, but this did not curtail its popularity in secular society. From a political and social standpoint, dance provided a means of communication and interchange between different nations and cultures and for a time at least between the privileged and lower

classes. The dances of Scotland were transmitted to France, for instance, and the dances of France were influential in England. Likewise the dances of the peasants were appropriated by the courts, where they were changed by the nobility, and these changes were often then adopted by the lower classes. However, during the medieval period a countermovement was already under way, and dance became a vehicle for exhibiting and defining class distinctions (the dances of the elite prioritized rigid posture, impassive countenances, emotional containment or withdrawal, and graceful movement while the dances of the lower classes invited spontaneity, vigorous action, rudeness, and awkwardness) and for training the privileged in the qualities that set them apart as superior and excluded the poor. The basse dances (which flourished from about 1350 to 1550) and the pavaynes (from 1450 to the middle of the seventeenth century) were slow, dignified, stately dances with intricate steps better suited to hall and castle than to the village green and peasant revelry. The introduction of dance masters and the self-conscious practice of dance as an art form peculiar to the socially elite created an ever-widening gap between how dances were performed by the rich and the poor and what the dances meant for the performers. The dances appropriated and modified by the court elite thus differed significantly from the lower-class dances in nature and function.

See also: Carol; Hungarian Tradition; Sword Dance

—Bradford Lee Eden and Lee Winniford

Dance of Death [French *Danse macabre*, German *Totentanz*].

A late-medieval topos apparently owing its popularity to a series of paintings of 30 men led off by skeletal apparitions of themselves.

Accompanied by verses, these paintings were done on the walls of the Cimitière des Saints Innocents (Cemetery of the Holy Innocents) in Paris in 1424–1425 and recorded in Guy Marchant's illustrated book, printed in Paris in 1485. The earliest surviving printed versions of the *Danse*, however, are block-books depicting both males and females issued with German texts in 1465 and about 1480.

Very shortly after the appearance of the text from the Cimitière des Saints Innocents, the poet John Lydgate translated it into English, and this accompanied copies of the paintings made on the cloister walls of Old St. Paul's in London soon after 1430; hence its English vernacular name, "the dance of Paul's." Other early derivatives were the paintings at Basel (c. 1440), Ker-Maria, Brittany (c. 1460), Lübeck (1463), and Berlin (1484), and a *Danse* sculpted in snow in Arras in 1434. Processional and dramatized *Danses* are also attested—one performed before the duke of Burgundy in Bruges in 1449, another in Besançon Cathedral four years later, and in England, in St.

Edmund's Church, Salisbury; even one in the church at Caudebec in 1393, a generation *before* the Innocents murals. Kenneth Varty has recently noted that an altarpiece painted for the Abbey of St. Omer in 1458 by Simon Marmion includes a view of a Benedictine cloister painted with the *Danse*. A *horae* (book of hours) that he illuminated in the late 1470s (now in the Victoria and Albert Museum) includes marginal figures of a skeletal Death seizing, for instance, a fashionably dressed young woman, the immediate precursor of the *Danse*-derived images found in the earliest Parisian *horae*.

English cycles include the murals formerly in the Guild Chapel at Stratford-on-Avon (c. 1500) and the late-fifteenth-century misericords of Coventry Cathedral (destroyed in World War II), but the best extant complete example of the theme is a series of carvings on the roof ribs of the mid-fifteenth-century chapel at Roslin in Scotland, based on French models. It has also only recently been pointed out that verses on a rudimentary *Dance of Death* (independent of Lydgate's) are found in the earliest London editions of the *Kalender of Shepherdes* (1506, c. 1510, and later) along with a few woodcuts first used in Marchant's late-fifteenth-century *Danse macabre* editions. The Dance series proper appeared as border decorations in Parisian printed *horae* from the 1490s on, but it was not until 1521, apparently, that they appear as a sort of appendix to a Parisian *horae* printed for the English market accompanied by the Lydgate verses.

Some impression of early-sixteenth-century England's familiarity with the paintings of the *Danse macabre* is suggested by the thirty-third *demaunde* in the earliest printed English riddlebook, Wynkyn de Worde's *Demaundes Joyous* of 1511: "Wherefore be there not as many women conteyned in the daunce of poules as there be men?"—"Bycause a women is so ferefull of herte that she had leuer [rather] daunce amonge quycke [living] folke than deed!" Although not found in the extant late-fifteenth-century French incunabula from which roughly half of the other *demaundes* were taken, the same *demaunde* does occur in a manuscript text of about 1470: "Pourquoy en la danse macabree ne dansent nulles femmes mais ung mort et ung homme vif?" "Pour tant que les femmes n'ont cure de danser aveuc les mors mais tres bein aveuc les vifs!" The obscene pun on *vits* (penises) is lost, of course, in the literal English translation.

See also: Black Death; Funeral Customs and Burial Rites; Memento Mori

—Malcolm Jones

Dante Alighieri (1265–1321). The greatest Italian poet, whose works, particularly *La divina commedia* (The Divine Comedy, 1308–1321), draw extensively upon the folk traditions of his time.

Dante titled his masterpiece simply the *Commedia;* only much later, in the sixteenth century, did readers christen it "Divine." In choosing the term *commedia* (from two Greek words, meaning "rustic song"), the poet was following classical literary tradition of casting comedy in language less elevated and more accessible than that of tragedy. Dante, intending his work to be accessible to all his compatriots, wrote it in Italian rather than in Latin. The *Commedia* describes a journey through the three otherworlds of Catholic doctrine: *Inferno* (Hell), *Purgatorio* (Purgatory), and *Paradiso* (Paradise).

Dante's earlier Italian works—such as *La vita nuova* (The New Life, c. 1292–1294), *Il convivio* (The Banquet, c. 1304–1308), and the *Rime* (Rhymes, 1293–c. 1310)—serve as introductions to the *Commedia*. Several of his Latin works, especially *De monarchia* (On Monarchy, c. 1310–1317) and *De vulgari eloquentia* (On the Eloquence of the Vernacular, or Common, Language—i.e., Italian, as opposed to Latin, c. 1304–1305), add to an understanding of the *Commedia*. In all these writings of lofty content and erudition, there is always a certain presence of popular traditions and folkways, especially in the vernacular works and above all in the *Commedia*. Popular and learned traditions enjoy a parallel development in Dante's work. The former does not diminish the latter; on the contrary, it enhances and enlightens the text. Dante intended the *Commedia* as an exemplary poem in the vernacular, in imitation of its most immediate model, Virgil's *Aeneid*, as well as Homer's *Iliad* and *Odyssey*. He also employs folklore abundantly as a reflection of his world and times, thus enriching his work with concrete realism and imagination. The author is the perfect example of an intellectual who creates a symbiosis of erudite and popular culture to portray his world in colorful and dramatic ways. As Dante himself said, this is "the sacred poem to which heaven and earth have so set hands" (*Par.* 25:1–2).

Dante's Documentation of Folk Traditions
Numerous folk traditions appear in the *Commedia*. Life-cycle customs include calling out the name of the Virgin Mary upon giving birth (*Purg.* 20:19–21; *Par.* 17:34–37), betrothal and wedding traditions (*Purg.* 5:130–136, 24:43; *Par.* 10:140–141, 15:104, 25:105), and death and burial rites (*Purg.* 3:112–132, 33:35–36). In referring to the *ninna-nanna* (lullaby, *Purg.* 23:111) and a child's toy, *il paleo* (spinning top, *Par.* 18:41–42; see also *Aeneid* 7, 378), Dante draws upon lore surrounding children. He also refers to feasts, festivals, tournaments, and races (*Inf.* 15:121–124, 22:1–12; *Purg.* 28:36; *Par.* 16:40–43), as well as proverbs and sayings (*Inf.* 15:95–96, 18:66, 22:14–15, 23:142–144; 28:107; *Purg.* 16:113, 22:149, 33:97; *Par.* 16:58–59, 18:52–53, 22:16). The *Convivio* features the proverb "Una rondine non fa primavera" [One swallow does not make a spring].

Dante also depicts traditional beliefs, clothing

customs, dances and songs, legends and tales, fables, gestures, astrology and numerology, and metaphors and metaphorical language. His keen observations of daily life, combined with his purpose of portraying a realistic society, account for the richness and precision of his descriptions of popular customs and his use of diverse—and appropriately employed—linguistic registers (some drawn from traditions of the grotesque and low comedy), as in the cantos of the barrators and the devils (*Inf.* 21 and 22).

In his early work *The New Life* Dante describes the wedding custom (14:1–15) in which the bride's young female friends attend a banquet at the groom's house. The young men present initiate the custom of *corteggiamento, donneare*, courting the young women. Traditionally, the groom's banquet lasted three days and then moved to the bride's house, where it could last for several more. *The New Life* also depicts *corrottos* (chs. 8 and 22), funeral laments, performed by women and men in different groups.

Use of Numerological and Calendar Traditions
In *The New Life* Dante also describes his obsessive love for Beatrice, who would later appear in the *Commedia* (*Purg.* 30) as the poet's guide to Paradise. Significantly, Beatrice first appeared to Dante on the calendar feast of Calendimaggio (May Day) 1274, when he was almost nine and she was entering her ninth year. She died on June 19, 1290. Nine would become Beatrice's symbolic number. Nine comprises three 3's, thus evoking the Christian Trinity. Dante also draws upon the learned lore of the Syrian, Latin, and Arabic calendars (*Vita nuova* ch. 29) to lend significance to the number 9; he identifies the death of Beatrice with the numbers 9 and 10, the latter being the perfect number. Indeed, numerology and astrology (which in the Middle Ages was equivalent to astronomy) are very much part of Dante's intellectual tradition and play an important role in his art, as demonstrated by the structure and form of the *Commedia*. The *Commedia* comprises 100 cantos composed in three-line stanzas, subdivided into four groups—1 + 33 + 33 + 33—one canto for the prologue and 33 each for the three realms, a structure based on the trinitarian 1 and 3. Symbolic numbers also structure each of the three realms: the ten circles of the *Inferno*—whose eighth circle contains ten pouches encasing the sins of fraud; *Purgatorio*, with its seven terraces, its Ante-Purgatory, and the Earthly Paradise; and the ten spheres of the *Paradiso*. There are several strategic places in which numerology plays an important role, as in the appearance of the three beasts encountered by Dante as he begins his journey: the *Lonza* (leopard), *Leone* (lion), and *Lupa* (she-wolf). The three *L*'s represent the evil trinity (Lucifer); in canto 34 Lucifer will appear as a three-headed monster, described as "the Emperor of this dolorous kingdom." In *Paradiso*, the Heaven of the Sun (cantos 10–12)

possesses two groups, with 12 figures in each, bearing a direct correspondence with the 12 signs of the zodiac, the 12 tribes of Israel, and the 12 apostles.

Dante structures the chronology of the *Commedia* in close correspondence with the Christian calendar. He begins his journey on the evening of Holy Thursday, April 7, 1300, as he becomes lost in the forest. On Saturday night, the traveler emerges from hell, having spent 24 hours there. By crossing the equator into the Southern Hemisphere, he finds himself on the shore of purgatory at the dawn of Easter Sunday, April 10. He enters Paradise on the Wednesday after Easter at noon, and the journey ends seven days later, when on the evening of Thursday, April 14, the *viator* (wayfarer) enjoys the final vision of Paradise. Dante's journey, then, coincides ritually to Christ's death and resurrection.

La vita nuova and the *Commedia* also register religious customs and popular piety: Dante sees Beatrice in church probably on the Feast of the Visitation (May 31), when *laudes* for the Virgin Mary were sung (*Vita nuova* ch. 5); later, as Dante laments Beatrice's death, he describes pilgrims on the way to Rome to see the famous Veronica's veil. In chapter 40 the narrator offers a definition and classification of pilgrims and pilgrimages, naming those who go to Jerusalem *palmieri* (bearers of palms), those who go to Rome, *romei*, and those who go to Santiago de Compostela in Galicia *peregrini* (pilgrims). The terminology is determined by the pilgrim's insignia: two crossed keys, symbolic of St. Peter, for the *romei*; two crossed palms from Jericho for the *palmieri*; two crossed walking canes for those going to the shrine at Santiago and a shell for them on their way back. In a previous chapter the narrator tells us that Love appeared to him like a pilgrim dressed humbly, "without pomp" (*Vita nuova* ch. 9), mirroring the medieval image of the pilgrim as *homo viator* (man the wayfarer), one who journeys for the expiation of sins. Dante himself is a pilgrim in the *Commedia*, as he is reminded in *Purgatorio* 13:96.

Dream and Color Symbolism
Dreams (*Vita nuova* chs. 3 and 13), oneiric (dream) literature, and oneiromancy (divination through dreams) play a significant role in *La vita nuova*, predicting such future events as Beatrice's death (ch. 23). Dreams are also vital and meaningful components of *The Divine Comedy*. In *Purgatorio* 9, the pilgrim Dante dreams that a golden-winged eagle has flown him to the sphere of fire; dreaming that he and the eagle are burning, he awakes. In canto 19 he dreams of a *femmina balba*, a stammering, pale, cross-eyed, club-footed woman, who transforms into a beauty and tells him in a song that she is the siren who confounds mariners like Ulysses. She turns out to be the symbol of incontinence or the sins of the flesh, and her ventral stench awakens the pilgrim. In

canto 27 (91–109), the poet, having reached Earthly Paradise, dreams of Leah and Rachel, who traditionally represent, respectively, the active and the contemplative life. All three oneiric visions occur just before dawn—a time at which, according to medieval traditions, the most truly prophetic dreams occur.

Another element present in both *La vita nuova* and *The Divine Comedy* is the symbolism of colors, often represented through clothing customs. Beatrice first appears to the narrator dressed in red, a color of the highest dignity, and wearing a belt stylish in Dante's time. The second time she appears dressed in white, a color worn by both angels and brides. The *cinta*, or belt, was a customary part of dress codes for both sexes in Dante's time. In *Paradiso* 14 we learn through Dante's predecessor Cacciaguida (c. 1091–1147) that Florentine women wore highly prized belts adorned with precious metals and stones. Indeed, the cantos of Cacciaguida (15–18) are a mine of information regarding popular traditions, as, here, Cacciaguida is reminiscing about the Florence of old. In canto 15 there are references to both male and female dress codes (100–102). When Beatrice reappears in *Purgatorio* 30, she wears the colors of the three theological virtues: a white veil crowned with olive boughs, a green cape, and a red dress. Other examples of dress traditions occur in *Purgatorio* 23, which calls the shameless Florentine women less chaste than the women of Barbagia, a wild region of Sardinia (94–96), and *Purgatorio* 8 and 24, which describe the band or veil that distinguished married women or widows.

Inferno 21 and 22 treat magicians, astrologers, necromancers, and diviners from such ancient seers as Tiresias and Calchas to relatively recent figures legendary in Dante's time: Guido Bonatti of Forlì, who practiced in the court of Frederick II; Asdente, a poor cobbler of Parma; or the renowned Michael Scot, who enjoyed a great reputation as a sorcerer and prophet at the court of Frederick II. All have their heads twisted backward and shed tears of anguish, because of the law of *contrapasso*, punishment that fits the crime, that Dante applies in his *Inferno*. This particular canto is rich in an atmosphere of magic, evoking witches and witchcraft (20:121–130), even mentioning "the man on the moon," which in Italian folklore is Cain carrying a bundle of thorns: "See the wretched women who left the needle, the spool and the spindle, and became fortune tellers: they wrought spells with herbs and with images. But now come, for already Cain with his thorns holds the confines of both the hemispheres, and touches the waves below Seville; and already last night the moon was round" (Singleton translation). It is well known that witches congregate under a full moon and that traditionally one should not begin anything new under a full moon.

There are devils whose names are derived directly from popular beliefs and early theatrical representations. These devils are assigned to hook, massacre, and quarter the lawyers. Malebranche (Evil Claws) leads the others, whose names indicate their popular origin: Malacoda (Evil Tail), Scarmiglione (Rougher Up), Alichino (Bent on Wings?—the French Hallequin, a predecessor from popular farce of the Arlecchino of the commedia dell'arte), Calcabrina (Frost Trampler), Cagnazzo (Doggish, or Bad Dog), Barbariccia (Curly Beard), Libicocco (from two winds "libeccio" and "scirocco," thus Blaster), Draghignazzo (Dragonish, or Bad Dragon), Ciriatto (Hoggish), Graffiacane (Dog Scratcher), Rubicante (Rabid Red). Dante also relates the beliefs about the devil traditional in his time, for example, that the bodies of those who betray guests are seized by the devil while still alive on earth, as their souls lie in hell (*Inf.* 33:121–126).

There are games such as chess (*Purg.* 28:93) and a dicing game called *zara* (*Purg.* 6:1–3), and dances such as the *ridda* (*Inf.* 7:24) and *tresca* (*Inf.* 14:40; *Purg.* 10:65). There are references to dolphins who warn sailors of approaching inclement weather (*Inf.* 22:18), the swallow's appearance in January as a false sign of spring (*Purg.* 13:123), boar hunting (*Inf.* 13:113), and falcons and falconry (*Inf.* 17:127–129, 22:130; *Purg.* 19:64; *Par.* 18:45, 19:34). Traditional gestures occur: A usurer sticks out his tongue out as a sign of mockery (*Inf.* 17:74–75), and a thief turned into a serpent spits as a sign of scorn or disdain (*Inf.* 25:136–138).

At the end of *Purgatorio* there appears a tableau that evokes the urban festivities of Dante's time: a cart representing the Church, pulled by a griffin (Christ), leads a procession of many figures representing the Old and New Testaments, imitating the form of medieval pageants.

Two examples epitomize Dante's proximity to popular culture. First, at the end of *Purgatorio* Beatrice says *"che vendetta di Dio non teme suppe"* [that God's vengeance fears no soups (that is, hindrances)], referring to those who are to be blamed for the corruption of the Church and who should expect imminent punishment (*Purg.* 33:36). This refers to the popular belief, probably of Greek origin, that a murderer who consumed a wine soup within nine days of the homicide, either on the body or on the tomb of the victim, would be safe from the relatives' revenge. For this reason the family of the deceased would guard the body for as many days. Dante's expression is equivalent to an Italian proverb saying that God does not pay on the Sabbath, "Dio non paga il sabato," meaning that his vengeance can occur at any time. In his study of popular tradition in *The Divine Comedy*, Giuseppe Pitrè has shown that this tradition was widespread throughout Europe.

The second example alludes to the custom of throwing stones on the unburied body of a slain enemy, thus creating a stone burial. It is part of a well-known ancient custom in which stone throwing signifies sympathy or respect. This same passage also records the practice of burying excommunicated people or heretics outside the church grounds and the symbolism of unlit candles, in which burials are conducted "*sine luce et cruce*" [without light and cross]. In this passage King Manfred of Sicily narrates his own burial, while telling Dante how he died, saved by his last-minute repentance, unbeknownst to the pope, who had excommunicated him.

Popular tradition finds its way into all of Dante's works in varying degrees, of course, but always as an integral part of the whole and essential to the vision of the author. Along the way in Dante's poem one encounters so many references to folkloric tradition that Benedetto Croce labeled Dante "a poet of his people." In other words, Dante's poem should be considered a national poem, as Jacob Grimm viewed national epics—as works belonging to a whole people and not to a specific author.

See also: *Decameron*; Dreams and Dream Poetry; Hell; Italian Tradition; Purgatory

—Giuseppe C. Di Scipio

David, Saint (d. c. 589) [Dewi Sant]. Sixth-century monk and missionary, patron saint of Wales.

David's feast day, commemorating his death, is March 1. Tradition credits him with founding 12 monasteries, including Glastonbury, before he settled in his own religious foundation in Vallis Rosina (Glyn Rhosyn) or Mynyw, the eventual St. Davids in southwestern Wales. We have no contemporary reports of his life, though Irish annals note his death, and the Irish *Catalogue of Saints* (c. 730) and *Martyrology of Oengus* (c. 800) also refer to him, but traditions about him were recorded in a number of Latin *vitae*, mainly deriving from Rhigyfarch's *Vita Dauidis* (c. 1095). A Welsh life, the *Buchedd Dewi*, closely related to a twelfth-century Latin text, was compiled about 1346, and Gerald of Wales composed *Vita Sancti Davidis* about 1194. David also appears in the legends of other saints (including that of St. Paul de Leon, c. 884). Poets of the twelfth to fifteenth centuries (most notably Gwynfardd Brycheiniog, Iolo Goch, Ieuan ap Rhydderch, Dafydd Llwyd o Fathafarn, Lewis Glyn Cothi, and Rhisiart ap Rhys) also recorded traditions about David.

Many of the motifs in the traditions about David are common to the Welsh saints, fitting the heroic biographical pattern (in religious form), but appear in specific forms that are also distinctively David's. For example, his conception and birth are accompanied by miracles: his birth was prophesied 30 years in advance (to his father Sant, a king, who raped the virgin Non when he met her on the road); St. Patrick and St. Gildas gave way before him; from the time of conception he (and his mother) ate only bread

and water (and sometimes cress), perhaps contributing to his epithet *Dyfrwr* or *Aquaticus* (Waterman); at his baptism he healed a blind *wynepclawr* (flat-face). Though many saints work wonders with water, only David depoisoned and heated the waters of Bath, giving them their healing properties. Like most of the saints, David came into conflict with a secular power, in his case the prince Boya, but the form of the conflict is unusual: threatened by David's increasing authority (demonstrated by the smoke from his fire covering the land), Boya and his wife send first armed men and then naked women against David and his followers, and Boya's wife, in a last wicked step before madness, kills her stepdaughter. David prevails, and in the end Boya is killed and his tower destroyed by a fire from heaven.

When or how David came to be considered the patron saint of Wales is unknown. The tenth-century *Armes Prydein* prophesies that David's banner will lead the united Celtic forces and calls on him to lead the warriors against the Saxon intruders, sentiments echoed over the centuries by other prophetic poems invoking his name. We have later evidence of the political struggles for his supremacy, both as the leading saint in Wales and as archbishop of a see having status equal to that of Canterbury. Rhigyfarch, while drawing on local traditions about David, was also responding to ongoing disputes between the dioceses of St. Davids and Llandaff, represented by St. Cadog. In David's *vitae*, the simplest statement of his supremacy is in the Synod of Brefi, which was convened to select an archbishop through a contest in preaching. David did not attend, but after none of the contenders could make themselves heard even by the closest audience, messengers were sent for him. As David preached the ground rose under him (forming the hill on which the church of Llanddewibrefi now stands), and he could be heard clearly by everyone even at a great distance. According to tradition, David's right to his position was also established while he was on pilgrimage with St. Teilo and St. Padarn to Jerusalem, where the patriarch of that city consecrated him archbishop or, in an alternate tradition (possibly owing to the narrators' need to align the Welsh Church with Rome), while on pilgrimage to Rome, where he was raised to the archiepiscopate. David's archiepiscopacy was further guaranteed in tradition when St. Dyfrig, archbishop of Caerleon, passed his mantle to David, who transferred it to his own city, Mynyw. This tradition was influenced by Geoffrey of Monmouth, who apparently introduced the Caerleon element, and was used by Gerald of Wales in his own twelfth-century attempts to have the metropolitan status of St. Davids recognized by the pope in Rome.

The importance of St. David and his church is apparent, moreover, in the way other saints are measured against him, either as associates or as competitors (*Vita Cadoci* repeatedly stresses

Cadog's superiority over David), in the 53 churches and 32 wells dedicated to him, and in the medieval mathematics of pilgrimages (two journeys to St. Davids equal one to Rome, and three equal one to Jerusalem). In the early twelfth century, David was recognized as a saint by Pope Calixtus II, unlike all the other Welsh saints who acquired their titles from their roles as hermits and ecclesiastics, which was the meaning of the word *sant (sanctus)* in the early Middle Ages. Allusions to David in medieval poetry show that the audience could be expected to know many traditions about him, including some not recorded in the various *vitae*. The poetry also shows him associated with the prophetic tradition.

Although his religious role was affected by the Protestant Reformation, David has remained a national figure—one whose Church could be used to vie with Canterbury, one who represents Welsh spiritual independence from the period before influences of the Roman Church, and one who can be honored by even the most secular as an early Welsh leader and symbol of Wales.

See also: Geoffrey of Monmouth; Gerald of Wales; Saints, Cults of the; Welsh Tradition

—Elissa R. Henken

Decameron. One of the most important frame tale collections of the Middle Ages, in which ten young people, having fled Florence to escape the Black Death, pass time during their exile by telling stories, each a tale a day for ten days, for a total of 100 tales.

The author, Giovanni Boccaccio (1313–1375), was born in Certaldo, near Florence—surroundings that provided the stage for the 100 tales told in his *Decameron* (c. 1349–1351) by seven well-bred young ladies and three young men. The tale tellers' number (the perfect number 10) and names conceal symbolic meanings: Neiphile, for example, means "new in love" and Dioneo "a new lustful god," Venus being the daughter of Dione by Jupiter. As the author's mouthpiece, Dioneo is the most daring storyteller among the ten and has the freedom to choose any topic, while the others must stick to the theme of the day.

The *Decameron*, "an epic of the merchant class," describing people from all walks of life, is rich with folkloric traditions, containing, for example, folk beliefs from fourteenth-century Tuscany, where the action unfolds. Though the storytellers are from the elite class, they show familiarity with folkways from both oral and literary traditions, from both the countryside and the city. This is also due to the author's own inclination, his studies, and his practical worldly experience, especially in the 1320s at the court of King Robert of Sicily. Boccaccio trained to be a banker in Naples and came in contact with merchants, sailors, adventurers, and people of various social classes, as is attested in the *novella* (tale; plural

novelle) of Andreuccio of Perugia (2, 5), a horse trader whose misadventures and final fortune are re-created in an atmosphere of complete realism depicting the places and people of Naples. In his tales Boccaccio alludes to cults of false relics and false saints (2, 1; 3, 10; 6, 10), prophetic dreams (4, 5; 7, 10), powders, plants (4, 7), and specters and phantasms (3, 8). He also treats many of the most important legendary figures known in fourteenth-century Italy, some of whom were known throughout Europe and some of whom were celebrated principally in his native Tuscany; for example, Saladin (Salah ad-Din, 1138–1193), whose legendary munificence earned him a place in Dante's Limbo (*Inf.* 4:129) (1, 3 and 10, 9); the sultan of Babylon (2, 7); Ghino di Tacco, a famous thief (10, 2); and Calandrino, a legendary fool and object of pranks by the notorious painters Bruno and Buffalmacco (8, 6; 9, 5). There are contemporary figures, such as Cangrande della Scala, the famous Ghibelline lord of Verona (1, 7), to whom Dante dedicated *Paradiso;* Ciacco, a notoriously witty glutton of Florence (9, 8), known also to Dante (*Inferno* 6); and many other colorful personages. The text also includes songs, dances, and the playing of musical instruments such as the lute (at the end of Day 1) as a part of the daily routine of entertainment, along with the narration of stories often derived from oral tradition.

Folklore has therefore a tremendous role in Boccaccio's work, where it represents the sum of a cultural era; this is especially true of the *Decameron,* which represents the bourgeois society of fourteenth-century Italy and was supposedly written primarily for women of that class.

From the very beginning, through the description of the plague that provides the frame of the work, the reader is alerted to the customs of this society and how they are altered by a calamitous epidemic that afflicted Italy and Europe in 1347–1351. Boccaccio, perhaps in jest, attributes the plague either to the "works of the stars" or to divine punishment for human iniquity. As a result of the Florentine outbreak of 1348, the most common societal practices, such as wakes, burials, and religious rites for the dead, were all suspended; instead, hundreds of bodies were thrown in common graves as if they were merchandise on a ship. There were those who engaged in eating, singing, and drinking excessively, believing that this would ward off the plague, and those who decided to lead a moderate or even Spartan life in order to fight off the disease. Others, following vernacular medical practices, would go around the city with flowers in their hands, carrying odorous herbs or spices, believing thus to escape the plague. Yet others abandoned the city and their property. In this fashion laws and customs totally disintegrated, not only in the city but also in the *contado,* the countryside, where animals roamed as they pleased, even returning home at night as if they were rational beings, ironically doing what humans did not do in these circumstances. Boccaccio tells all this with a sense of wonderment, of play, rather than in a dramatic tone. The introduction, however, is very important because it sets the stage for the entire work, so that the tales told by the ten narrators are in a sense a reconstruction of this same society with the customs and beliefs that had dominated normal everyday life, as well as an echo of an ideal multifaceted life.

Popular Beliefs

Another important characteristic of the *Decameron* is the oral nature of many of the *novelle* dealing with personages who peopled the city-state of Florence and other cities and the merchants whose business took them throughout the Mediterranean, France, Flanders, and elsewhere. The very first *novella*, in fact, tells the story of one Ser Cepparello of Prato who has gone to Burgundy, charged with collecting money owed to Musciatto Franzesi, a Florentine merchant. Ser Cepparello is a wicked, immoral being who through a false confession on his deathbed ends up being declared a saint: the people readily believe his confessor's near-beatification of Cepparello and contrast his life to their sinful ways. The tale parodies the superficial, customary way in which saints were sometimes created, and it also presents references to folk customs, portraying the ready acceptance of relics, miracles, and newly created saints in popular religion.

The same popular religious practices are shown in the boisterous *novella* of Frate Cipolla (Brother Onion), in which the author reaches a height of comic inventiveness when describing Cipolla's ability to convince the common folk of the existence of false relics while at the same time collecting their money and saving his own skin. The central characters of this *novella* (6, 10) are really the people of Certaldo, Boccaccio's hometown (a town famous for its onions, says its native-born narrator). The townspeople, whose faith and devotion must rely on something concrete and tangible, are easily duped into accepting Brother Cipolla's claim that he possesses a feather from the wings of the Angel Gabriel or the coals with which St. Lawrence was roasted in martyrdom. Boccaccio has Brother Cipolla speak of the many relics shown to him by the most reverend patriarch of Jerusalem, whom he names Nonmiblasmete Sevoipiace (Don't-blame-me If-you-please), including the finger of the Holy Spirit and a lock of hair of the seraphim who appeared to St. Francis.

Another major theme in Boccaccio is the belief in ghosts, apparitions, and other supernatural phenomena, as in the *novella* of Nastagio degli Onesti (5, 8). Nastagio, rejected by his beloved, wanders in the woods. There he sees a terrifying vision of a woman hunted down by dogs followed by a knight threatening to kill her as punishment for her unwillingness to return his love. The knight catches up with the woman, kills her, and throws her heart to the dogs. Then the woman comes back to "life" as if she had never been injured. Nastagio learns from the spectral knight that the woman's murder is reenacted in the same spot every Friday morning, and he invites his beloved to that spot. She witnesses the same vision and is driven by fear to accept Nastagio as her husband.

Magic and Incantations

Day 7 of the *Decameron* is devoted to stories based on the tricks women play on their husbands either for self-preservation or out of erotic passion, a theme common in medieval popular traditions. In the first tale, Gianni Otterighi is led to believe by his wife that the person tapping on the door is a werewolf; she knows quite well that it is her lover, and she convinces Gianni to exorcise the werewolf with an incantation filled with sexual innuendo. She then orders her husband to spit, an act that according to contemporary folk belief is effective in incantations.

Tale 7, 3 also contains incantations, as well as the custom of *comparatico*, which prohibits sexual union between a godfather and his *comare* (the mother of his godchild) on the ground that it is incestuous (see also 7, 10), a rule that Brother Rinaldo easily ignores. The use of wax images as votive offerings is also recorded here. Popular religion is present in 7, 2, a tale derived from Apuleius (*Metamorphoses* 9, 5–7), and in the "Lover in the Cask" (the fabliau "Du Cuvier"), in which the husband goes home because it is the feast of St. Galeone (the Calendar of Saints, in which every day is a holiday, is a frequent narrative device) just as Peronella, his wife, is receiving her lover. An incantation appears in *novella* 7, 9, in which Lydia makes love to Pyrrhus in a tree and persuades her husband, who witnesses the event, that what he saw with his eyes was a deception caused by the enchanted tree; this is a classic fabliau plot with Eastern sources (AT 1423, "The Enchanted Pear Tree"), also reworked by Chaucer in "The Merchant's Tale." Supernatural elements and the return from the dead are the subject of the last tale of Day 7, in which Tingoccio returns from purgatory to inform his friend Meuccio about conditions in the otherworld. Meuccio learns that there is no special punishment for violating the custom of *comparatico*, that is, for making love to the mother of one's godchild. The incantation element is also found in the *novella* of Donno Gianni (9, 10), who makes his *compare* Pietro believe that by casting a spell he can turn a mare into a fair young maid and vice versa. As the priest proceeds to do this to Gemmata, the fool's wife, by attaching his "tail" (member) to her, Pietro protests and the spell is broken.

Another tale of magic and incantations is that of Diadora and Messer Ansaldo (10, 5), an analog to Chaucer's "Franklin's Tale." Exemplary for the presence of magical beliefs, as well as for allusions to Sabbats, witches, and the cult of Diana, is the *novella* of the tricksters Bruno and Buffalmacco and the prank they play on Master Simone, telling him that their jovial mood and good luck are due to their "going on course," which means "to meet with the witches" (8, 9). Such details demonstrate Boccaccio's familiarity with lore about witches.

Though Boccaccio may seem to ridicule magical practices, he is also a product of an age in which they were part of life and admired by intellectuals, such as Dante and himself. There is a legend, perhaps born from these tales of magic, concerning Boccaccio himself: according to legend, Boccaccio's tomb was demolished and his ashes thrown to the wind. As a necromancer he had a devil that would periodically transport him to Naples to visit his beloved Maria D'Aquino and return him to Certaldo within two hours. On his last flight, hearing the Ave Maria sung at vespers, he gave thanks to God, and the devil dropped him near Certaldo, where he died. There is another popular belief that Boccaccio had the devil build a hill near Certaldo in one night with a bushel of dirt. Then Boccaccio requested a crystal bridge connecting his castle to the hill. The devil found this impossible and instead strangled him the night before the bridge was to be built.

Perhaps the young Boccaccio, author of the *Decameron*, ridiculed and spurned such beliefs, but the older one did not, as can be seen in such later works as *Commento* and the *Corbaccio*. Boccaccio remains constant in his admiration for intelligence, reason, and wit, but also in his wish to represent the nature of medieval people, with all their fears, customs, and beliefs—and that is what he did in narrating these 100 tales, or as he says, "stories or fables or parables or histories or whatever you choose to call them."

See also: Chaucer, Geoffrey; Frame Tale; Italian Tradition; Novella

—Giuseppe C. Di Scipio

Dragon. A fabulous creature usually described in medieval narratives as a serpent of great size, with wings and a tail, two or four feet, sharp talons, and (often) impenetrable scales and fiery breath.

The dragon figures most prominently in medieval narratives as an opponent or assailant of human heroes, who typically vanquish the monster. The origins of the dragon are to be found in creation stories and other myths that feature a chthonic monster—that is, a beast born from the earth or living underground. In the ancient Middle East the dragon is associated with life-giving waters; in early-medieval northwest Europe the world-encircling Midgard Serpent (*Midgardsormr*) demarcates between primeval chaos and the inhabited world. In narrative terms, the dragon of medieval folklore exists principally as a monstrous serpent, acting as a vicious opponent of human saints, warriors, and heroes of popular culture. The slaying of a dragon is a desideratum

in the careers of many heroic and chivalric figures in medieval literature; though most dragons' human opponents are male, some females—especially female Christian saints—also play a role as slayers or tamers of dragons.

Narratives of the dragon-slayer have been regarded by Joseph Fontenrose and Calvert Watkins as fundamental expressions of an underlying theme in Western mythology—the theme of heroic combat—and Vladimir Propp treated the structure of the folktale version of this myth as basic to the narrative structure of all European märchen, or wonder tales. Motifs associated with the figure of the dragon are indexed as B11, dragon, under the general heading of Mythical Animals. The most important narratives are indexed as tale type AT 300, "The Dragon-Slayer," a plot closely related to AT 301, "The Three Stolen Princesses," some variants of which—notably, in *Beowulf*—include a dragon as one of the monstrous adversaries faced by the hero.

Whereas the etymology of the other Indo-European words for snakes, adders, and other similar creatures derives from their length or means of locomotion, the word *dragon* (Old English *draca*, Middle English *drake*, Old Norse *dreki*, Old High German *trahho*, deriving from Latin *draco*, Greek *drakon*) has been associated with the Indo-European root **derk*, "see," and this is assumed to refer to the dragon's glittering eyes or its sharpness of sight. This may explain the origin of the motif, attested frequently in Hellenic, Italic, and Germanic dragon lore, whereby the dragon functions as the sharp-sighted guardian of something of value, normally a golden object or hoard of objects. The hoard-guarding dragon is commonplace in Germanic folklore, and dragon-slayers' fights with dragons are often part of an attempt to seize the monster's treasure.

Classical Dragon Lore

Sources of medieval dragon lore are to be found in its classical antecedents, where dragons were treated both as supernatural creatures of legend and mythology and as subspecies of the serpentine order. In the classical cosmographies and natural histories of Aelian, Solinus, Pliny, and others, dragons are said to inhabit the known—albeit usually remote—locations in the natural world. They appear frequently in bestiaries and encyclopedic, geographic, and travel literature and also as characters in Greek and Roman fables. Giant worms and winged snakes are described in Herodotus's *Historiae* and in the descriptions of India by Ctesias and Megasthenes (fifth and fourth centuries B.C.E.). Dragons proper are described in numerous works, including Pliny's *Natural History*, Lucan's *Pharsalia*, Isidore of Seville's *Etymologies*, *The Wonders of the East*, Brunetto Latini's *Li livres dou tresor*, Pierre Bersuire's *Ovidius moralizatus*, Mandeville's *Travels*, and Guillaume du Bartas's *Devine Weekes and Works*. Bestiaries compiled by Gervase of Tilbury,

Guillaume le Clerc, Pierre de Beauvais, and Richard de Fournival all contain a section on the dragon; the Old English *Wonders of the East* includes a description of 50-foot-long dragons, and the *Liber monstrorum* (Book of Monsters) includes a description of a giant serpent.

Elaborate narratives of dragons and dragon-slayers in classical mythology include the stories of Jason, Cadmus, Perseus, Hercules, and Apollo; biblical material paralleled in ancient Middle Eastern mythology contributed significantly to the popularity of the dragon in the learned Latin culture of medieval ecclesiastical literature. Texts in all these genres were known throughout Europe in the Middle Ages, and, translated into most of the European vernacular languages, they contributed significantly to the medieval figure of the dragon appearing in folklore and popular literature. Indeed, one of the vexed questions in the study of medieval dragon lore is that of the relationship between learned, classical, and sacred traditions—which were mediated to medieval European culture through written sources—and indigenous, vernacular traditions emerging through oral transmission. The diversity both of the sources of dragon motifs and of the genres, themes, and linguistic and national traditions within which these motifs were elaborated in the Middle Ages has led Lutz Röhrich to conclude that no single unifying formulation can possibly summarize medieval folklore related to the dragon. As a figure of folklore, then, the medieval dragon should be regarded as an amalgamation of indigenous Germanic and Celtic motifs with Christian biblical theological symbolism laid on a foundation of Middle Eastern, Anatolian, and Illyrian cosmogonic and mythographic concepts.

Christian Dragon Lore

The dragon's importance as a medieval popular motif derives in no small part from biblical associations of the dragon with the arch-figure of diabolical evil in the Christian tradition. By a series of mistranslations, three Hebrew words for sea and land monsters hostile to God or the people of God were rendered into various Greek terms by the translators of the Greek Bible and later into Latin by St. Jerome, with the result that medieval readers and hearers of the Bible, particularly of the Psalms and the prophets, interpreted the dragon as a symbol of pride. A fourth term, the Hebrew word for "jackal," was mistranslated as "dragon," and this error is the origin of the long tradition, culminating in the medieval bestiaries, in which the dragon appears as an allegorical symbol for the sin of pride and thus for the original author of pride, Satan. This error lies behind the repeated designation of the "desert wastelands of foreign enemies" as the habitation of dragons in medieval literature, standing for the desolation resulting from a people's wandering from God. The Authorized version of the Bible contains 20 readings of Hebrew words as "dragon."

Dragons appear frequently in medieval saints' lives, the earliest popular narrative genre in the Western European tradition. By the end of the Middle Ages well over 100 saints had been credited with critical encounters with diabolical foes manifest in the form of a dragon or monstrous serpent, including such influential figures as St. Perpetua, St. Anthony of Egypt, St. Margaret of Antioch, St. Gregory, St. Martin of Tours—and of course St. George. Although many such saints were venerated in local, relatively isolated cults (e.g., in Cornwall, Ireland, and Scotland), a significant number are canonical saints with genuinely international reputations and associated paraphernalia—visual, ritual, votive, and literary—indicating the widespread influence of the dragon as a figure of popular belief not only within the culture of ecclesiastical learning but also in the lay population. Among them, St. Martha seems to have been quite popular in early-medieval Provence, where a body of legend and Rogation-tide (i.e., the three days before Ascension Day) ritual surrounding the saint survived into the twentieth century in the form of an annual procession in which the vanquished monster was displayed amid celebration.

By far the most famous dragon-slaying saint is George of Cappadocia, whose rescue of a condemned maiden was translated again and again in late-medieval literature largely as a result of the immensely popular thirteenth-century *Legenda aurea* (The Golden Legend) of Jacobus de Voragine. George's adventure against the dragon, set in Libya, is a relatively late (probably late-eleventh- or early-twelfth-century) addition to the martyr's legend. Scholars have not determined precisely how the episode of the dragon became attached to the martyr, but it would appear that St. George's legend was amalgamated either with the figure of the dragon-slayer from medieval romance or with the figure of Perseus, whose seaside rescue of Andromeda bears an unmistakable resemblance to George's rescue of the doomed maiden from the dragon.

Germanic and Celtic Dragon Lore

The richest vein of medieval dragon lore is to be found in the epic/heroic and romance traditions that flourished in northwest Europe in the Germanic languages, where the legendary figure of Sigurd/Siegfried is regarded as the most renowned of the dragon-slayers. The earliest reference to this legend appears in Old English, in a digression early in *Beowulf*, whose date has been placed by scholars anywhere from the eighth to the tenth century: the hero—himself a dragon-slayer in his final adventure—is compared favorably with Sigurd's father, Sigemund, said by the poet to be the supreme hero of the north. Later literary accounts ascribe the dragon adventure to the more famous son, whose unsurpassed reputation for heroic valor is echoed in *Völsunga Saga*. A different version of the story is extant in *Thidrek's Saga*, which contains Continental Germanic legend and folklore of a provenance almost as early as that of *Beowulf*. A large number of poetic allusions to Sigurd, slayer of the dragon Fafnir, in Old Norse skaldic verse attests to widespread familiarity with the legend, as do a similar number of runic and monumental stone and wood carvings from medieval Scandinavia and the British Isles. Besides Sigurd and Beowulf in the Old Norse and Old English traditions, dragon-slayers and associated dragon lore may be found in scores of Old Norse prose and poetic narratives in addition to those mentioned above, especially the *Poetic Edda* and the *Prose Edda* of Snorri Sturluson. The Latin narratives in Saxo Grammaticus's *Gesta Danorum* give accounts of the dragon fights of Frotho, Fridlevus, and Harold Hardraada. The last of these, the Norwegian King Harold, is associated with dragons in several episodes not included by Snorri Sturluson in the *Heimskringla*—including the Icelandic tale of "Thorstein the Over-Curious" and two adventures of Prince Harold in Byzantium.

Dragons appear under Vortigern's castle in the works of Geoffrey of Monmouth and Gervase of Tilbury, in the work attributed to Nennius, in Ranulf Higden's *Polychronicon*, and in the *Roman de Brut* as well as in the *Alliterative Morte Arthure* and Malory's *Morte Darthur*, where Lancelot, Tristram (Tristan), and Yvain all are described as dragon-slayers. King Arthur's dream of the airborne battle between a dragon and a boar is interpreted by "a wise philosopher" as representing the conflict between Arthur's Welsh forces and "some tyrant." Other dragon-slayers in medieval English romance include Beves of Hampton, Guy of Warwick, Sir Torrent of Portyngale, Sir Degaré, Tom a Lincolne, Sir Eglamour of Artois, and the Knight of Curtesy as well as St. George, whose sacred legend was revised repeatedly along the generic lines of medieval romance. Dragons appear in all major vernacular manifestations of the Tristan legend. In *Sir Gawain and the Green Knight*, the eponymous hero fights "with wyrmes" [against dragons] among the other malevolent beings set to waylay him in his journey through Logres (line 720).

The motif indexes typically catalog various elements of dragon lore under several main headings, including the origin, form, habitat, and habits of dragons. As to form, dragons appear generally as serpentine creatures of immense size, capable of swallowing human beings and large animals whole. Their origins are seldom described, though several Old Norse sagas refer to broods of young dragons reminiscent of the offspring of nesting birds. The dragon is generally described as a large serpent with two wings, two clawed feet, and a lashing tail. The dragon in the legend of St. Martha is a composite of physiognomic features of bird, bear, fish, ox, lion, and

viper. The medieval encyclopedic tradition (represented, e.g., in Isidore of Seville's *Etymologies*) ascribes the dragon's main offensive strength to its tail; in other sources, however, either poisonous or fiery breath constitutes the monster's main offensive weapon. For defense the dragon relies on its horny or scaly hide; in some instances its imperviousness to iron weapons is attributed to supernatural or magical power. In a number of instances, including the Sigurd texts and episodes in *Gull-Thorir's Saga*, *Ector's Saga*, and *Ragnar's Saga*, the dragon is a human who has been transformed into monstrous shape either through greed or through a curse placed upon the treasure that the dragon possesses. This feature seems to suggest the influence of Old Norse folklore concerning the *draugar* or *haugbúar*—otherworldly human revenants appearing sometimes as the inhabitants of grave mounds in repose with priceless burial goods.

Dragons as Guardians of Treasure

The motif of the dragon guarding treasure is found in ancient Greek mythology and classical Latin legend, and it seems to be central to the Germanic folklore concerning the creature: Fafnir, the dragon slain by Sigurd, is the greedy possessor of a cursed treasure seized by Loki, Hœnir, and Odin from the hoard of the dwarf Andvari; so also is the dragon slain by Beowulf—Sigurd's counterpart among the legendary northern heroes. Fafnir, Sigurd's draconian enemy, is motivated by greed to murder his father and take the treasure his father had extorted from Loki for the murder of Fafnir's brother Otr. The treasure is cursed by its original owner, and whoever comes to possess it dies violently—until the Nibelungs cast it into the Rhine forever.

Beowulf's treasure also seems to have this same sort of curse on it. Even though he possesses it only briefly, it seems to have something to do with his death and with the decline of his people the Geats (who wisely bury most of it and burn some of it on Beowulf's pyre). An Anglo-Saxon proverb from the Old English poetic Cotton Maxims says "the dragon shall [be] on the mound, old, exultant in treasure," and a similar gnomic passage in *Beowulf* repeats the observation; a marginal gloss in a fifteenth-century codex of Icelandic law says "Just as the dragon loves the gold, so does the greedy love ill-gotten gain." Treasure-guarding dragons appear twice in *Ector's Saga*, and in the fourteenth-century *Konrad's Saga* the hero undertakes a quest to an otherworldly castle filled with treasure-guarding dragons in order to acquire jewels as part of a bride-price.

Combat with Dragons

Motivations for the hero's fight with a dragon are various, deriving from characteristic attributes and habits ascribed to dragons themselves. Friedrich Panzer divides these into two broad categories: fights with dragons to relieve a people or nation from the dragons' attacks; fights to acquire treasure. The dragon episode at the end of *Beowulf* represents a combination of these two motifs. Dragon-slayers achieve their goal through a variety of methods and instruments. In the St. George legend the episode is typically depicted in iconography with the saint impaling the monster with a lance or spear through its mouth; in the Sigurd narratives and in stone and wood pictographs throughout Scandinavia and the British Isles the hero—sometimes instructed by Odin—digs a trench in the dragon's path and from this position stabs the dragon's underbelly with a sword. Elsewhere in Germanic legend the dragon is impervious to weapons except for a special spot on the underside of its torso; this is the point of entry where Wiglaf's ancient, giant-made sword penetrates the dragon in *Beowulf*. A number of Old Norse sagas identify a vulnerable spot on the left wing or along the spinal ridge.

In the Middle English *Sir Degaré*, the hero beats the monster to pieces with a wooden club. In Icelandic hagiography, Bishop Gudmund sprinkles holy water on a dragon/sea monster, which then bursts into 12 pieces and washes ashore. In later Icelandic popular romance, heroes and their helpers engage in elaborate machinations to reach dragons in their remote places of habitation. Rewards for slaying dragons often include not only treasure but also a bride and possession of part of an afflicted kingdom. The Welsh narrative *Owain*, the Old French *Yvain*, and the Old Icelandic *Iven's Saga* share an episode in which the hero slays a dragon that has a lion gripped in its claws and the coils of its tail. Afterward the lion becomes a sort of mascot and traveling companion of the hero, accompanying him on subsequent adventures. In Old Icelandic this story found its way from *Iven's Saga* into several other sagas as well. While most medieval heroes slay the dragons they encounter, the saints of medieval hagiography frequently banish the monster to deserts or wastelands. Jacques Le Goff regards this as the narrative expression of ritual cleansing of a pagan geographical site for Christian occupation. Paul Sorrell applies this insight to *Beowulf*.

In *Thidrek's Saga* the king is captured by a dragon, flown to the dragon's nest deep in a remote forest, dropped among the dragon's brood, dismembered, and eaten. Beowulf is successful only with the help of his retainer Wiglaf and is himself mortally wounded. Dragon-slayers protect themselves from dragons' fire and poison by various means, including sable-lined cloaks, shields covered with ox hide, and tar-soaked fur breeches; in *Ector's Saga*, Fenacius receives a magical ointment from a cave-dwelling dwarf, which protects him from injury. The swords with which heroes slay dragons are sometimes legendary or magical swords; the one with which Wiglaf delivers the strategic blow in *Beowulf* is an *ealdsweord eotonisc* (giant-made ancient sword),

required to penetrate the monster's otherwise impervious scales.

The great body of traditional lore and legend surrounding dragons waned at the end of the Middle Ages even as the figure of St. George the dragon-slayer came to be an extremely popular embodiment of Renaissance chivalric and aristocratic ideals. Ulisse Aldrovandi's *Serpentum et draconum historiae libri duo* (Two Books on the History of Serpents and Dragons, 1640), though postmedieval, is the last great compendium of popular and learned lore passed down through the Middle Ages.

See also: *Beowulf*; Bestiary; George, Saint; *Nibelungenlied*; Scandinavian Tradition

—Jonathan Evans

Drama. A performance genre that in the Middle Ages included popular mystery cycles and morality plays, both drawing heavily on traditional character types and comic rituals.

Earlier scholars of medieval drama tended to perpetuate a rather simple evolutionary model of development, according to which a simple speech in the Easter matins liturgy marked the birth of the genre. In the tenth century, church performances began to elaborate upon the words spoken by the angel in Christ's tomb: *"Quem quaeritis?"* [Whom do you seek?]. From these elaborations, more-complex liturgical dramas evolved and eventually passed into the vernaculars, yielding the great Mystery Cycles and Passion, and saints, plays of the fifteenth and sixteenth centuries. Like its biological equivalent, this evolutionary model has been replaced by one of greater complexity and more discontinuity. Instead of a smooth line of upward development, we now recognize a pattern of radical bursts of activity followed by periods of relative inactivity. We must also give far more attention to various secular (i.e., nonclerical) influences, obscure though they tend to be, upon the growth and development of medieval sacred drama and eventually the Renaissance professional stage.

Foundations of Profane Drama

One must begin with the fall of the Roman Empire and the end of a vast "entertainment industry" that had penetrated to every corner of the empire. Numerous theaters, amphitheaters, and circuses existed even in frontier regions such as Britain. What happened to the myriad personnel of this entertainment industry in the so-called Dark Ages? It is quite likely that a substantial proportion of these performers continued their trade in some fashion in the new barbarian regimes and created future generations of entertainers. We have a thin but constant stream of references to *mimi*, *ioculari*, and *histriones* for the early Middle Ages, a good number of these gathered by E. K. Chambers in his magisterial *The Mediæval Stage* (1903) and by Allardyce Nicoll in *Masks, Mimes, and Miracles* (1931).

These predominantly clerical records are, of course, of a negative sort, and we can also find a constant theme in later exemplum literature of saintly opposition to popular entertainers. How these shadowy professional entertainers related to the bards, minstrels, and jesters of the indigenous Celtic, Germanic, and Slavic traditions is a matter of almost total speculation, but some interaction, some coalescence there must have been. Attempts to prove the existence of fully developed theater (ritual dramas of combat or wooing, the antics of "sacred clowns," etc.) for the pagan cultures of Europe have not been very convincing. Yet the clerical record also reveals the persistence of uproarious animal masquerades (particularly horse, stag, and bull), especially during the midwinter season, which may well be pagan survivals. (The well-known illuminations for the *Roman de Fauvel* show a range of such animal masks in performance.)

Even if we cannot point to very much in the way of pagan Celtic or Germanic performance directly influencing the dramatic traditions of early-medieval Europe, it is quite clear that by the tenth century—that is, when the dramatic molecule of the *Quem quaeritis* trope was supposedly re-creating drama all over again out of nothing— there was a considerable body of popular theater (if not of scripted dramatic texts) that began almost at once to interact with the so-called liturgical drama. In this fusion we can perhaps detect two separate if intertwined types of profane dramatic activity: (1) that bearing the earmarks of professional itinerant players, and (2) that rising more directly from community needs and a communal theatrical/mimetic impulse geared to the yearly cycle and not dependent on professional performers. Thus, there existed a "professional" and a "folk" popular theater, both of which interacted with and influenced the sacred drama of the Church and later that of lay organizations.

We must also bear in mind, however, the existence of certain universals of popular theater and physical comedy, based on deprivation (especially hunger), pain, and physical or symbolic humiliation; these can crop up in just about any context, including the sacred. After all, the Christian liturgy itself (particularly the Magnificat verse "He has put down the mighty from their thrones, and has raised high the lowly" [Luke 1:52]) gave rise to such quasi-dramatic, *monde renversé* events as the Feast of the Ass or Feast of Fools in certain French cathedrals. If we examine the play texts of Hrosvitha (c. 1000), the Saxon nun who produced edifying "dramatic" works for her convent of Gandersheim, we notice not only the literary influence of Terence but also certain elements of low comedy. In *Dulcitius*, for example, the evil governor on his way to violate his female Christian prisoners winds up befuddled in the kitchen, hugging and kissing the sooty pots and pans, and presenting a ridiculous spectacle to his own astonished guards. Some 400 years later

in one of the earliest vernacular farces, the Dutch *sotternien* (sot play) entitled *Die Buskenblaser* (The Boxblower), a dumb peasant, returning from the sale of his cow, is tricked by a mountebank into trading his silver for a magic box that will restore his wife's desire for him. He must blow into the box, which is full of powdered charcoal, and he thus renders himself a sooty "devil" when he believes he has become irresistibly handsome. There is no need to speculate on influence here, from Hrosvitha's book Latin to the vernacular Dutch, as we are clearly dealing with a kind of "universal grammar" of the laughable. Sooting up, moreover, remains one of the most available disguises (as well as a threat to spectators) for folk masqueraders of all sorts up to the present time. Its associations with the demonic, anarchic, or the sexually "dirty" are what we might call archetypal.

"Professional" Influences

The influence of professionals may be detected quite early on in the liturgical drama. We have the curious example of the Mercator episode in that most central and sacred of the sacred dramas, the Easter play. On the slim basis of Mark 16:1 ("When the Sabbath was over Mary Magdalene, Mary the Mother of James, and Salome bought aromatic oils so that they could come and anoint him [Jesus]"), an unguent seller entered the Latin liturgical drama. By the fourteenth century, in the German Easter plays, the figure had acquired a brace of servants and a wife, and his dramatic action had evolved into a virtually independent farce. The Mercator scene, for example, takes up at least 40 percent of the Easter play from Innsbruck (c. 1390), and it has little thematic justification for so dominating the sacred story (unlike the Mak episode in the Wakefield Master's *Second Shepherd's Play*, for example). This irrepressible mountebank scene, moreover, must surely have reflected something of mercantile performances in real life. In other words, theater and life were already influencing each other through the figure of the itinerant "professional."

Mercator and his servant Rubin in the Easter play are paralleled by a similar pair in the earliest recorded vernacular farce, *Le garçon et l'aveugle* (The Boy and the Blind Man) of late-thirteenth-century France. The physical demands of this piece are minimal, and its story line is absolutely basic—the victimization of the testy blind man by the cheeky servant. It probably represents part of the repertory of an itinerant, nuclear acting company: the *histrion* and his boy apprentice. By the late fifteenth century, we can be certain of full acting companies responsible for such pieces as the famous English morality play *Mankind* (c. 1470). Scholars of early English drama have often remarked on the seriously competing aspects of moral teaching and popular entertainment in this work. A strong vein of decidedly low comedy centers upon the three outrageously costumed vices, New Guise, Nowadays, and Nought, who stage what appears to be a mock bear-baiting-*cum*-dance, then a scatological Christmas carol involving audience participation, and finally a collection from the audience before bringing on the final "thrill" of the performance, the appearance of the devil Titivillus himself. With these obvious "crowd-pleasing" shenanigans, the play was evidently the property of a wandering company of five or six professional actors. Scholars have pointed out that the demanding roles of Mercy and Titivillus could well have been doubled by the lead actor of the troupe. In the Elizabethan play *Sir Thomas More* (c. 1595) we have a scene reflecting this earlier practice. A small troupe of Moral Interlude players, "four men and a boy" (for all the female roles), present themselves and their repertory to the chancellor. A similar scene, of course, occurs in Shakespeare's *Hamlet*, but there the company has a decidedly Renaissance repertory.

"Folk" and Communal Influences

Shakespeare's other famous play-within-a-play is also our touchstone for early amateur theatricals. Although Pyramus and Thisbe is a tragic Renaissance theme, the "rude mechanicals" who perform the story in *A Midsummer's Night Dream* reflect something of medieval practice, although the naivete of their representation no doubt reflects the later professional theater man's sense of easy superiority. Medieval Latin liturgical drama (monastic or ecclesiastic) reached its peak of development in the late twelfth century, but only in a relatively limited area, and it can be argued that it represented an evolutionary dead end. The thirteenth century is relatively bare of dramatic texts, but when a vibrant literary theater reemerges in the fourteenth century it is in the new vernaculars and for the most part in the hands of the laity. Various organs of urban lay power became the producing agents for this second wave of medieval drama. Craft guilds were crucial in the development of the extended cycles of mystery plays in the English cities of York, Chester, Coventry, and elsewhere, whereas lay religious confraternities were more often responsible for theater production on the Continent. Both infused into religious drama artisanal and bourgeois values and interests, including substantial elements of low comedy and folk material. Comic figures, partly based on realistic observation, partly on venerable types of the folktale, are found throughout the sacred vernacular plays. The Wakefield Cain, a foulmouthed, miserly, malcontented plowman, acquires a lovable wacky servant, Garcio; in a sense, the play gives us the two faces of the Trickster figure. Other contemporary workmen bitch and moan for grotesque effect, for example, the clumsy, incompetent carpenter-soldiers of the York Crucifixion. Shrewish women are everywhere, from Noah's wife, who exchanges blows with her husband, to the Chester alewife hauled off to hell in the Last Judgment for her short measures, to the blacksmith's wife in a Parisian Passion play who, in order not to lose a sale, takes it upon herself to forge the nails of the Crucifixion. Even saints could be handled popularly (and ambiguously). St. Joseph, almost always portrayed as a *senex* (old man) in the medieval period, might rant and rave like the cuckolded husband of a fabliau, or, as in the German tradition, he might behave like a doddering fool, blowing on the fire and stirring up porridge for Baby Jesus or rinsing out his diapers.

Marginal types are also common. A whole tavern full of thieves and gamblers is vividly presented in Jean Bodel's *Jeu de Saint Nicholas* (c. 1200). Mak in the Wakefield Master's *Second Shepherd's Play* with his larcenous nocturnal lurkings, his wolf-skin clothing and magic spells, together with his fecund "dirty bride," Gill, represents a kind of residual pagan of the medieval hinterlands. On the other end of the spectrum, lordly figures—Herod, Pharaoh, and Pilate particularly—pushed tyrannical language to near-absurd extremes and approached the intensity of the *diableries*, the comic performance of the devils themselves. These latter were immensely popular, with their roaring, obscene speech, "rough music," acrobatics, pyrotechnics, and periodic assaults upon the audience. They were prime examples of the "threat-deflated" model of the laughable and were no doubt related to and perhaps influenced by archaic rural performances of the winter season, which featured the intrusions of anarchic, ugly, masked figures, whether these were imagined as the "old gods" demonized or more purely biblical figures of evil. Extensive *diableries* were characteristic of many French and German religious dramas, whether appropriate or not to the action. Generally, however, the comic figures and episodes in the vernacular religious drama were subsumed in the larger purpose of presenting sacred history. They might be used for sophisticated iconographic play (for example, Mak's stolen lamb in the cradle parodies the *Agnus Dei*), or to make a wry theological point vis-à-vis unredeemed humankind (for example, Noah's wife, dragged kicking and screaming into the safety of the Ark), or simply as negative exempla in more generalized moral teaching.

While this comic leavening was rising in the vernacular sacred drama, purely secular plays were, not surprisingly, also developing, and under similar circumstances. Paralleling the lay religious confraternities were a variety of secular organizations, often related to them, that turned out seasonal and other occasional entertainments such as greetings to noble visitors. A remarkable body of early plays emerged from the Confrérie des Jongleurs et des Bourgeois d'Arras. One of these, Adam de la Halle's *Jeu de la feuillée* (Play of the Leafy Bower, c. 1280) was evidently a Maytide entertainment in which a cross section of

Arras townspeople, including the author himself, set up a bower to entertain the Queen of the Fairies. Morgan le Fay and her entourage duly arrive and interact with the mortals. A raving idiot also weaves in and out of the scene, supplying a different kind of entertainment. The play is an intriguing intersection of bourgeois lifeways, aristocratic romance, and rural folklore.

Secular drama was more frequently found indoors, however, during the winter or "festival" half of the year (roughly November to March). The societies of French law clerks, the Basoche, were responsible for many of the classic early farces (and particularly that masterpiece of legal double-dealing, *Pierre Pathelin*), all probably entertainments for holidays in term time. Such organizations also spawned actual fool societies, such as Les Enfants sans Souci, which developed not only parades of motley antics but also a type of very topical satirical review called the *sottie*. Similar developments occurred in the Low Countries, leading to a wide variety of dramatic forms there—farces, romances, moralities, even experiments with the play-within-the-play—and the development of important performance-oriented literary guilds, the Chambers of Rhetoric.

Drama at Christmastime was particularly popular in cathedral schools and the later colleges and universities, as were such parodic ceremonies as that of the Boy Bishop, which arose from the feast of the patron of children, St. Nicholas (December 6) or the Feast of the Holy Innocents (December 28). A late example of such school drama embodying the mock-king motif is *The Christmas Prince* staged at St. John's College, Oxford, in 1607.

Carnival was another, relatively late focus for communal theater. The French were fond of *sermons joyeux* praising mock saints based on festival foods—Saint Jambon (Ham), Saint Andouille (Chitterling), Saint Oignon (Onion), and so on. The Italian tradition had dramatized Combats of Carnival and Lent, for example, the fifteenth-century *Rappresentazione et Festa di Carnasciale et della Quaresima*. Several German cities evolved their own bodies of Carnival drama, Nuremberg being the most prolific among them. Members of the prestigious Nuremberg Meistersinger guild, such as Hans Rosenplüt or Hans Folz, would also toss off crude sketches (*Fastnachtspiele*) for the Carnival season. Apart from the occasional literary themes essayed, these dramatic efforts directly reflected the festival process itself. Overindulgence and uproarious behavior were the subject matter, with the dramatic situations typically involving diagnoses by quack doctors, mock trials, or ridiculous competitions. The plays were dominated by the figure of the violent, stupid, and gluttonous *Bauer* (peasant), a favorite festival disguise of the urban-dwellers. In the following century Hans Sachs attempted to tame the often wittily obscene and scatological *Fastnachtspiele* in the interests of the new Reformation. His *Das Narrenschneiden* (Fool Surgery) of 1536 delivers a serious sermon on the seven deadly sins, who are imagined, however, as embryonic Fools, a kind of worm infestation, in the bloated belly of a Carnivalist. The Fools (evidently little puppets) are removed in a slapstick surgical operation by a traditionally extravagant quack doctor and his cheeky servant. The piece thus exemplifies the tensions between moral teaching and untrammeled festival entertainment in the theatrical life of the early modern city.

It is harder to trace the forms of popular theater in the medieval countryside, given the limitations and fragmentary nature of the evidence. Pieter Brueghel the Elder's painting *The Combat of Carnival and Lent* (1559; see illustration) is set in a Flemish village and is a major piece of visual evidence in this area. The central figures of Carnival and Lent and their burlesque combat may be more fantasy than strict reportage, but the surrounding figures evidently accurately reflect the masking and theatrical practice of the folk. We notice bag and other improvised masks, false noses made of hollowed-out tubers, the wearing of food items (waffles) and cooking utensils, and "rough music" on gridirons and rummel pots (rummel is a mixture of grains). On the peripheries of the crowded canvas one notices actual play scenes. One is a procession of a Warrior, an Emperor, and a shaggy Wild Man, identified as the story of Orson and Valentine, which also shows a collection being taken up among the spectators. Another scene, identified as "The Marriage of Mopsus and Nissa" or "The Dirty Bride," features a pair of grotesque lovers and a very makeshift "set," evidently the shelter in which they consummate their love. Other scenes of rural folk performance can be found in other Brueghel works, particularly his *Kermis* (church anniversary) scenes. The *Fair at Hoboken* engraving shows a small booth stage on barrel tops for a cuckolding farce performance, and *The Fair of St. George's Day* (i.e., April 23) shows an enactment of the dragon-slaying, with the smallish monster built on a kind of wheelbarrow.

England provides an example of actual folk-play texts in the Robin Hood plays performed as part of parish fund-raising May games in the early sixteenth century. These were directly derived from the medieval Robin Hood ballads, evidently through the new medium of print. They involved few impersonations, but they featured large set combat scenes and morris dances. Despite extravagant claims for the antiquity of the English mummers' play, another combat-based sketch performed as a perambulation at Christmastime, its origins cannot be pushed back much beyond this first age of popular print culture.

Keeping the Brueghel scenes in mind, it should be clear that rural folk drama and the more sophisticated artistic expressions of the urban centers were not mutually exclusive; rather, they influenced each other constantly.

The countryside was not remote from the medieval town, either in physical distance or in outlook. The *Romance of Valentine and Orson* could "devolve" into a village play at holiday time. But conversely, the figure of the Wild Man in the romance might well have been influenced by earlier folk enactments. In that quintessentially urban farce *Pierre Pathelin*, with its drapers and law courts and fast-talking shyster hero, the last word is given to a smelly shepherd who turns the tables on the trickster by resorting to his "natural" language, the baa-ing of a sheep.

Folk material, or more narrowly the popular character type and the grotesque comic situation, passed into the religious drama of Europe in large doses through many conduits over the centuries. At the same time, and under the same impulses, a profane drama flourished and gradually became professionalized. Both streams merged (as in the *Mankind* example) and helped create the glories of the professional Renaissance stage. The religious drama, in turn, was taken up by the folk when it faded in the centers of power in the Early Modern period, and it remains today one of the living legacies of the Middle Ages. From the Mexican *Pastores* (Shepherds' play) to the Tyrolean *Nicholausspiele* (St. Nicholas play), an essentially medieval drama lives, as it has always done, with its complement of Wild Men, demons, tricksters, dolts, and capering fools. Even in urban America one can find the phenomenon. The Hungarian neighborhood church of St. Stephen in Toledo, Ohio, annually stages a Bethlehem play on Christmas Eve in which an axe-wielding, fur-clad monster also raises his ugly voice in the sanctuary but is ultimately brought tamely to the crib of the Christ Child.

See also: Carnival; Festivals and Celebrations; Fool; George, Saint; Robin Hood

—Martin Walsh

Dreams and Dream Poetry. Often interpreted in the Middle Ages as supernatural messages or as forecasts of future events; frequently represented in poetry, or even as a poetic form in its own right, throughout medieval literature.

According to modern psychology, dreams arise from the unconscious and have reference to the dreamer's past. Medieval thinkers knew of such dreams, but these were only one kind in a hierarchy of dream types, and not a particularly valuable one at that. The dreams that were valued in the Middle Ages were those believed to come from supernatural sources and to have reference to future events. There were some who were skeptical of divination by means of dreams on philosophical grounds, but most medieval thinkers who mistrusted dreams did so because they believed the supernatural source of dreams to be the devil far more often than God. The interpretation of dreams was also a cornerstone of medieval medicine, and the value that was placed on the phenomenon of dreaming at the

time is reflected in the frequency and importance of dreams in medieval literature as a whole.

Sources

Medieval Christian attitudes toward dreaming have roots in several sources, including the Bible, Greco-Roman antiquity, and Celtic and Germanic cultures—as well as influences from beyond Europe itself. The notions inherited from these sources were contradictory, and medieval speculation on dreams is characterized by an attempt to reconcile them.

Dreams are an important aspect of biblical narrative, in which they are portrayed as the sacred breaking into the profane realm, as a major means by which God talks to or makes his will known to his people. The majority of references to dreams and dreaming in the Bible are positive, but there are also passages critical of dream interpretation, particularly in those books traditionally called Wisdom literature. Medieval exegetes struggled to reconcile the examples of Daniel and Joseph with specific prohibitions and condemnations of dreams, such as that in Lev. 19:26.

Dream interpretation, or oneirology, was such a highly valued art in the Greco-Roman world that the Church, especially in the early-medieval period, tended to regard it as a pagan trait and was suspicious of the practice. Dream incubation, or sleeping in a temple to induce dream visions, was condemned, but the practice continued through the Middle Ages at the shrines of saints. Moreover, much pagan philosophical speculation about dreams remained important, and the classification of dream types in general use in the Roman Empire was held throughout much of the Middle Ages. Antique oneirology reached its acme and was crystallized in the writings of Artemidorus (second century C.E.) and the Neoplatonic Macrobius (c. 360–422), which were of crucial importance in medieval dream theory. Artemidorus was known only indirectly, so much of the practical and theoretical material in his *Oneirocritica*, a manual of dream interpretation, may not have been known, but the symbols found in this book form the ultimate source of medieval dreambooks such as the *Somniale Danielis* (Dreambook of Daniel), though in a vastly simplified alphabetical listing. Macrobius's *Commentary on the Dream of Scipio* was the most important work on dreams known and used in the Middle Ages, and in it can be found the authoritative fivefold classification of dreams used through the period: the *somnium* (symbolic dream), the prophetic *visio* (vision), the *oraculum* (oracular dream), the *insomnium* (nightmare), and the *visum* (apparition). Apparitions and nightmares were not deemed worthy of notice, but the other three kinds of dreams were believed capable of foretelling the future. Oracles and visions do this directly, but enigmatic or symbolic dreams require interpretation.

Early Christian Transformations

According to Jacques Le Goff, there are two crucial periods in the formation of medieval Christian dream theory—the second through seventh centuries, and then again in the twelfth—and only after the first period were Celtic and Germanic influences felt. Of the two influences at play in the earlier period, the classical seems to have been stronger than the biblical. Angels appeared in biblical dreams, but there were no demons or dead people, and these are very common elements of many recorded early-Christian dreams. Furthermore, Christian dreams were used to interpret the future, whereas biblical ones served only to put the dreamer in contact with God. In oneirology, as in many other areas of thought, the Church Fathers simply put a Christian cloak on pagan philosophy. By the time of Pope Gregory the Great (540–614), however, there is evidence of a belief not present in pagan philosophy, that of a general correspondence between the truth value and the source of a dream. Gregory warns that only saints can tell if a dream is sent by God or by demons. This important development in Christian dream theory was a moral one. It was now necessary to know not just whether a dream was true or false but whether it was a revelation or a temptation. Earlier thinkers, including Augustine, had held that individuals were not morally responsible for the content of their dreams, but this had changed by the time of Isidore of Seville (c. 560–636), who believed demons had God's permission to drag dreamers through the terrors of hell, both to punish and to test them. Irish penitential manuals of the seventh century also indicate that from this time on dreamers were held culpable for the sexuality of their dreams.

In sum, Christian thinkers' faith in dreams tended to weaken in the early Middle Ages. Part of the establishment of the Church in the fourth through the seventh centuries was an attempt to turn Christians away from their dreams. Dreams were mistrusted because of a developing notion of demons actively tempting the sleeper; because of their links to heresy, individuality, and sexuality; and because of a strengthening theological notion that divination was wrong even if possible, as the future belongs only to God. By decree of Pope Gregory II (reigned 715–731), dream interpreters were to be avoided. Such decrees were common in the time and realm of Charlemagne (reigned 771–814).

Official condemnation notwithstanding, dream theory developed, and dreambooks and interpreters circulated unabated. While theologians had to reconcile contradictory attitudes toward dreams and thus sometimes mistrusted them, there is no evidence that the common people shared their doubts. In fact, dream narratives in both hagiography and historical works such as those of Bede and Gregory of Tours multiply and become more detailed as time goes on. In Bede's *Ecclesiastical History of the English People* (731), one of the most famous early medieval accounts of a dream vision relates the story of Cædmon, a farmworker attached to St. Hilda's famous monastery at Whitby. One day he flees the company of those who share in singing tales out of embarrassment over his inadequacy, but later that night he is visited by an angelic figure who teaches him to sing of God's creation. The next day, Abbess Hilda and her learned monks marvel at Cædmon's newfound ability to turn biblical narratives into traditional Old English poetry, and Bede records the event as a miracle.

The Twelfth Century and Beyond

Dream theory underwent no fundamental changes or developments until the twelfth century. The fullest treatment of medieval dream theory at this time, before it underwent substantial changes, is found in Book 2 of the *Policraticus* of John of Salisbury (c. 1115–1180). John clearly finds himself in a dilemma over what to believe about the phenomenon of dreams and the issue of their interpretation. He knows the dream to be both a psychological and a physiological phenomenon, but more than either of these, it can sometimes be an experience by which the human soul can access the realm of the divine and gain knowledge about the future. The problem is one of certainty. On the one hand, Christ is known to work through *somnia*, or dreams, yet on the other hand, the attempt to interpret the symbols found therein is not only vain but wrong without Christ's own illumination. In her *Causae et curae*, Hildegard von Bingen (1098–1179) ascribes greater moral significance to dreaming than others had done, as she correlates the dreamer's moral status directly with the quality of the dream, stating that both God and the devil evaluate the moral fitness of a dreamer's thoughts.

The main twelfth-century development was the increasing availability and prestige of Aristotelian philosophical and medical works. The integration of Aristotelian thought on dreams with Christianity was a difficult task, as Aristotle said that dreams had no divine significance and the Church said that they did. The notions that dreams are a natural medical phenomenon and that they are realms of interaction with the divine are fraught with potential conflict. In the Middle Ages, though there may have been a few theologians who argued for one extreme or the other, the majority of thinkers managed to find a middle path according to which dreams could have natural causes and at the same time be the realm of supernatural influences.

The new teachings brought on increased interest in the physiology of the "lower" kinds of dreams and their relation to bodily health, and the net result was an overall increase in interest in dreams, as those thought insignificant before were now held to have as much meaning as those that had been believed powerful all along. Medieval doctors came to hold that dreams were expressions of the condition of the "virtues" that regulate the functions of the body and that any disturbance in the normal balance existing in a healthy person among the bodily humors was reflected in dream images. All humans contained the four "humors"—the sanguine, which produced an optimistic, perhaps a foolishly optimistic, outlook; the choleric, which made for hot tempers; the melancholic, characterized by introspection, even depression; and the phlegmatic, with its tendency toward withdrawal and inaction. This general theory influenced thought on dreams in two ways. First, there was a general correspondence between the seasons and the most common type of dream: sanguine in spring, choleric in summer, melancholic in fall, and phlegmatic in winter. Second, people of a certain humor or temperament were believed to dream in a certain way.

Another important development in dream theory was the increasing importance of astrology in the central Middle Ages. The connection with oneiromancy and astrology is the cornerstone of *De prognosticatione sompniorum* (Forecasting through Dreams, c. 1330), attributed to Guillelmo de Aragonia, in which the most salient feature of dream interpretation is found to be in the stars.

Despite all the schemes of categorization and hierarchization, at no point in the Middle Ages is there any clear distinction between dreams and visions. In his *De probatione spirituum* (The Examination of Spirits, 1415), Johanes Gerson writes that many who in good faith have regarded themselves as visionaries have really only seen dream images. A millennium earlier, the early Christian martyr Perpetua recorded a whole series of narrative visions in her diary, but only at the end did she mention that she awoke, indicating for the first time that she had been asleep during all that preceded. Many other Christian visions may have been received and recorded without knowledge or indication of awakening.

A number of recent studies have suggested that it is possible to know how and about what medieval people really dreamed. Medieval writings are peppered with personal dream narratives accompanied by background circumstances, and autobiographies proliferated in the twelfth century. The most prominent examples of this are the autobiographical *Monodiae* of Guibert de Nogent (c. 1115) and the *Opusculum de conversione sua* (Little Book of His Conversion) of Hermann of Cologne, a twelfth-century convert from Judaism to Christianity.

Dreambooks

Medieval dream interpretation was founded upon analogical thinking. The language of dreams is a symbolic language, and the popularity of dreams in the Middle Ages is due to the fact that they were a normal expression, a part of the cycle of medieval symbolic thought. The most common way of interpreting dreams was through use of "dreambooks." Physiological dreambooks, such as that of Hans Lobenzweig (thirteenth century), were used by doctors and reflected medical teachings. They were a later development and did not challenge the popularity of symbolic dreambooks, which remained far more numerous throughout the medieval period and which can be classed into three other kinds of dreambooks according to the way they assign meanings to symbol. All three faced some official prohibition but were openly and commonly used throughout the Middle Ages.

The first kind was the "dream alphabet" or "chancebook," an alphabetical list of possible dream interpretations that used only the fact that a dream had occurred and had nothing at all to do with the content of the dream. To use it, one would pray, open the psalter, and compare the first letter seen with the list in the dream alphabet. The most common chancebook was known as the *Somniale Joseph* (Manual on Dreams Associated with Joseph), which is found in both Latin and in many vernacular languages. The second kind of dreambook was the "dreamlunar." As with the chancebooks, the interpretation of dreams by means of the dreamlunars had nothing to do with the specific content of any given dream. Rather, all dreams on a given night have the exact same meaning, which is assigned by the dreamlunar on the basis of the phases of the moon. It is the date of the night that determines the meaning, not the dream itself. This kind of dreambook is found only in Latin, and its circulation was more limited than the other kinds of dreambooks. The "interpretation of dreams" by means of these two kinds of books was really nothing of the sort; rather, the occasion of a dream was used as an excuse for practicing divination.

The lists of interpretations of dream symbols found in a third kind of dreambook, or "dreambooks proper," are keyed to the images of specific dreams. Symbols in these dreambooks proper were grouped according to class. The order was alphabetical in Latin, but this was usually lost in vernacular translations. These books were meant as an aid to the universal and quotidian experience of dreaming. They have prefaces indicating the importance of such factors as individual station and disposition, time of year, time of night, and so on in the interpretation of dreams, but in the works themselves they ignore this complexity and give only one interpretation per symbol. These books are all indebted to Artemidorus's *Oneirocritica* (Judgment of Dreams). Works in this category include Pascalis Romanus's *Liber thesaurus occultus* (Treasury of the Occult, 1165), Arnald of Villanova's *Expositiones visionum* (Explanations of Visions), and the Byzantine/Arabic Achmet's *Oneirocritica* (Judgment of Dreams; Latin translation c. 1170).

However, the dreambook known as the *Som-*

niale Danielis (attributed to the biblical Daniel) was without a doubt the most important and famous work of this type in the Middle Ages. It was also the most widely circulated medieval dreambook, with hundreds of extant manuscripts dating from the ninth to the fifteenth centuries. These are found in Latin as well as in translations into many vernaculars. Indeed, the *Somniale Danielis* had such a wide circulation that it seems safe to assume that its dream topoi, or commonplaces, were general property in medieval civilization. Stephen Fischer, the scholar who has done the most work on it, considers it to be the medievalist's primary source for understanding the significance of dream topoi.

Dream Poetry

The interpretation of medieval literary dreams is not always given with their depiction, and so their meaning can be missed by modern readers. Contextualization and knowledge of medieval Christian imagery may sometimes reveal the meaning of a symbol, but when they do not, dreambooks such as the *Somniale Danielis* may be valuable aids to interpretation. However, not all medieval literary dreams draw their symbols from Christian imagery, and Celtic and Germanic dream lore also appears throughout much medieval literature. While the old sagas of the North often contained rich and complex dreams, as in *Gisli's Saga*, they did not consist entirely of dreams. The old northern and the Christian dream symbolism may, however, be joined, as in the Anglo-Saxon poem *The Dream of the Rood*, which provides striking imagery of Christ's cross in the language of Germanic heroic poetry.

This poem is an example of dream poetry, a whole genre of allegorical literature in which narrative material is structured as a dream or is presented as having occurred in a dream. The genre can be found throughout the Middle Ages, but it flourished most in the twelfth to fourteenth centuries and is generally acknowledged to have reached its acme in Middle English literature. Not surprisingly, much of this poetry is religious. Thus, specifically Christian imagery may be found in the fourteenth-century *Pearl*, in which a grieving father has a dream vision of his dead daughter in the heavenly Jerusalem, described in images that clearly derive from biblical and patristic tradition. Even so, the late-medieval dream vision can, as in the earlier *Dream of the Rood*, combine the religious and the secular in such a work as the fourteenth-century *Piers Plowman*, which depicts the dreamer searching for spiritual truth while passing through a world that provides vivid images of the society of the time.

Dream poetry, however, also depicted many nonreligious visions, and from the thirteenth century onward it dealt frequently with themes of quite earthly love. The single most important work of the form is the *Roman de la rose* of Jean de Meun and Guillaume de Lorris, with its focus on the God of Love and on inner emotions of the dreamer, named only the Lover, who in a garden impetuously approaches the Rose, the object of his desire, is rebuffed, and must go through a long education in the rules and art of love before finally achieving his quest. This work was immensely popular during the later Middle Ages and was the model for much subsequent medieval French dream poetry, such as Deguile-ville's *Pèlerinage de la vie humaine*, Froissart's *Paradys d'amours*, and Machaut's *Dit dou Lyon*. Chaucer translated at least part of the *Roman de la rose* into Middle English, and his own dream poetry was also directly indebted to it. His *Book of the Duchesse, House of Fame, Parlement of Foules*, and *Legend of Good Women* are among the most masterful dream poems written in England, and largely through his influence the form proliferated and was still popular in the sixteenth century.

See also: English Tradition: Anglo-Saxon Period; French Tradition; Medicine

—Alexander Argüelles and John McNamara

Druids. Priestly class among the ancient Celtic peoples.

As the priests of the pagan Celts, the druids evidently ceased to exist in Gaul after the conquest by Caesar in 58–57 B.C.E., and in Roman Britain after the defeat by Suetonius Paulinus of their rebellion on Anglesey in 61 C.E. It is uncertain how long they continued in Ireland and lowland Scotland, since written history begins in these areas only after conversion to Christianity from the fifth century onward. Nonetheless, it is safe to assume that during the Middle Ages the druid proper was by and large a figure of legend rather than a living reality. What is known about druids from medieval times comes almost solely through the medium of writings by Christian monks, who had a vested interest in portraying them as the defeated opposition, and certainly as figures of the past.

The druids of the free Celtic era were organized in colleges of three possibly overlapping classes: the *druides*, who were in charge of justice and the observation of ritual as well as being the counselors of kings; the *vates* or *ovates*, who were prophets; and the *bardoi* or bards, in charge of the preservation of history and lore through the medium of poetry and story. After the demise of the druidic institution, it seems probable that the bards continued to operate in a secular forum as poets and storytellers, and if the ethnographic observations of medieval and early modern researchers are correct, they assimilated the prophetic role of the *ovates* as well. The druids' function as both priests and regal advisers was taken over by the priests of the Christian Church. The judicial function was partly taken over by practitioners of canon law, but the *brehon* judges in Ireland may have preserved the remnants of druidic precepts in their administration of secular law (known as *brehon* law, which circulated in oral tradition until first written down by direction of St. Patrick in the fifth century). Classical commentators noted that druids were skilled in natural science and medicine, although it is unclear which of the three classes was in charge of these disciplines.

The first representations of druids in medieval Celtic literature come in the early Irish saints' lives. The druidic antagonists of Irish saints usually engage in magical contests with the holy men and women, illustrating that the pyrotechnics of their false religion are inferior to the simple power of the saint's faith in the true God. For instance, Luccet Mael, adviser to the pagan king Lóegaire, can create a huge snowfall by his magic, but only St. Patrick can cause the snow to melt away. St. Brigid, in most accounts, is the daughter of a druid's slave girl, and one of the first signs of her Christian holiness occurs when she finds she can no longer eat the food of the druid's household; she must be fed only from the milk of a pure, Christian cow.

In the medieval Irish tales set in the pre-Christian past, representations of druids going about their daily lives compare well with the depictions found in the Greco-Roman writings. Cathbad the druid, a major figure in the Ulster cycle of tales, is a counselor to kings, an educator of youth, and a prophet. However, in contrast to Caesar's statement that druids were exempt from military service, Cathbad is also the leader of one of the *fianna*, or warrior bands. The druid Mug Ruith, Slave of the Wheel, is depicted as one-eyed or blind, clad in a bird-skin cloak, and driving a gleaming metal chariot. He engages another druid, Ciodruadh, in aerial battle. Other druids in the sagas are healers, shapeshifters, dream interpreters, stargazers, and magicians.

In the tales of *The Destruction of Da Derga's Hostel* and *The Love-Sickness of Cú Chulainn*, druids are depicted engaging in a kind of prophesy called the *tarb-feis*, or bull feast. A white bull was sacrificed and skinned and a broth made of the flesh. One druid would drink the broth and go to sleep on the skin, watched over by four other druids. In his sleep he was supposed to dream of the appearance of the next king. Martin Martin, in his *Description of the Western Islands of Scotland* (1716), tells of a similar practice still being carried out in the late seventeenth century, and the elaborate *Dream of Rhonabwy* may be a fourteenth-century Welsh literary reflex of the same ritual.

In these stories about the conversion of Ireland to Christianity, the druid appears in order to show how Christianity surpasses paganism. The druids themselves are depicted as knowing through their prophetic powers that their time is over. In the story of the death of the king Conchobor mac Nessa, the son of Cathbad the druid, the king is incapacitated when an enemy hurls the calcified brain of the warrior Mes Gegra so that it lodges in Conchobor's skull. Druid doctors

tell him that he must live quietly, without excitement, without drinking, without having sex. Conchobor lives like this for seven years, until one day there is an earthquake. His druids inform him that this is because, off in Palestine, the Son of God—who coincidentally shares Conchobor's birthday—is being crucified. Conchobor springs to his feet in a passion and dies as the embedded brain ball explodes from his head, baptizing Conchobor in a gush of his own blood. This, we are told, is how Conchobor became one of two men in Ireland to believe in Christ before the coming of Patrick. Conchobor only acquires the requisite knowledge through the skills of his druids, but his baptism is accomplished through the expulsion of a literally concrete symbol of the pagan Celtic way of life, which was, as the classical ethnographers noted, marked by the practice of head-hunting.

What survived of Druidism after its defeat by Romans and Christians, then, is found in the narrative, legal, and medical lore of the medieval Irish and Welsh and in the less abundant material in Cornish, Scots, and Breton. However, since the poets, storytellers, lawyers, and doctors—not to mention monks—of medieval Wales and Ireland did not live frozen in a time capsule like Merlin in his Crystal Palace, we cannot assume that the medieval Celtic literatures present a shattered jewel of pagan thought that merely needs to be reassembled into wholeness. Particularly in Ireland, the druid became, in medieval times, an active folkloric figure whose narrative deeds and symbolism provided a dynamic forum in which the medieval Irish might explore the relationship between their pagan past and Christian present.

See also: Irish Tradition

—Leslie Ellen Jones

Dwarfs. A supernatural race of master artisans who serve as donor figures to the gods in Scandinavian mythology and as donors or servants to knights and heroes in Old French, Middle High German, and medieval Scandinavian chivalric and heroic literature.

Scandinavian mythological sources depict *dvergar* (dwarfs) as an all-male race of supernatural beings, residing in cliffs and stones, created asexually from the bones and blood of giants. Though in most instances dwarfs appear to be quite separate from other mythical races, Snorri Sturluson, in his thirteenth-century mythological manual, the *Prose Edda*, conflates dwarfs and "black elves," a subcategory of beings that appears only in his writings.

In the grand dichotomy of the mythology, dwarfs are aligned with giants in opposition to gods and humans. Nevertheless, their most important role in Scandinavian sources is that of donors to the two latter races. Dwarfs are said to have created the most powerful weapons and prized possessions of the gods. They are reluctant donors, however, and the gods generally obtain the goods through deceit, threats, or bribery.

Some Eddic poems, recorded in the thirteenth century, attribute occult knowledge to dwarfs, yet they seem rather gullible and are always short-changed when dealing with the gods. However, dwarfs can get the better of humans; consider King Sveigdir, who, according to Snorri Sturluson's thirteenth-century *Ynglinga Saga* (Saga of the Ynglings, ch. 12), was lured into a stone by a dwarf, never to emerge again.

While dwarfs hardly figure in the Norse family sagas at all, they abound in the more fantastic, heroic genres of the *fornaldarsögur* (sagas of antiquity) and the *riddarasögur* (sagas of knights). However, in these sagas the dwarfs usually appear as servants to knights and heroes and do not present a threat to their masters. Dwarfs of this bent are also encountered in some Scandinavian ballads. They are cognate with their kinsmen in medieval romances from the European continent, the German dwarfs and French *nains*.

Dwarfs frequently appear in Middle High German literature, particularly in the cycle of Dietrich von Bern, preserved in the thirteenth-century *Heldenbuch* (Book of Heroes) and in other romances. The earliest reference to a *nanus* (dwarf) is from an eleventh-century fragment, but most are encountered in works from the twelfth to fourteenth centuries. As in Scandinavian sources, they are master artisans, unsurpassed in the art of forging weapons. They are said to be small and are often dressed according to chivalric fashion. Female dwarfs are attested, but their importance is negligible.

The role that dwarfs fill in Middle High German literature is most often that of the knight's sidekick or servant. In this they closely resemble the *nains* of the Old French romances. Though the *nains* are often uglier and more conniving than their German cousins, they, too, are sharp dressers of diminutive size. More consistently than German dwarfs, the *nains* are always cast as servants to knights, and they habitually accompany them in their adventures.

Most of the scholarly literature on dwarfs centers on questions of origins. In 1906 Fritz Wohlgemuth hypothesized that the *nains* were modeled on historical court dwarfs. August Lötjens, in a work from 1911, refuted this literal-historical explanation, citing a lack of evidence for the existence of court dwarfs, and suggested that the dependence of French romances on Celtic folklore might provide a better context in which to seek the origin of the *nains*—a view echoed by Vernon Harward in 1958, in his book on dwarfs in Arthurian romance. As to the dwarfs of Middle High German literature, Lötjens is of the opinion that they are literary hybrids of the chivalric *nains* and the more earthy dwarfs of Germanic folk tradition.

In a book on medieval dwarfs and elves in Europe, Claude Lecouteux claims that dwarfs are closely related to the dead, a hypothesis previously argued in the Scandinavian context by Chester Gould in 1929. Lecouteux also refers to the theories of Georges Dumézil about the tripartite system of Indo-European mythologies and suggests that dwarfs should be seen as third-function (i.e., fertility) beings, since they work the riches of the earth through their metalwork.

In a number of works from the 1970s and 1980s Lotte Motz proposed another theory of the origin of dwarfs: that dwarfs harken back to an Indo-European class of artisans, preserved as a faded memory in folklore and also in the Greek Hephaestus (blacksmith of the gods). According to Motz, the main characteristics of this class are craftsmanship and physical deformity, and she claims that its historical achievements may be observed in the megalithic stone structures of Europe.

Though Motz, like many before her, is confident that the dwarfs of medieval literature derive immediately from contemporary folk belief and legend tradition, there is good reason to think otherwise. The *nains* of chivalric romance are a clearly defined, formulaic literary type, perpetuated through literary borrowings. They bear a much closer resemblance to helper figures in fairy tales than to supernaturals from legend tradition. Although the dwarfs of Middle High German tradition are more diverse, they too usually function as helpers or donors. In an article from 1924 on Scandinavian dwarfs, Helmut de Boor made a similar claim when he contrasted elves and dwarfs, arguing that the former belong to legend and belief whereas the latter inhabit the enchanted world of the fairy tale. Elves, he notes, appear in historical works and the more realistic family sagas, but dwarfs are mostly confined to more fanciful genres, such as the *fornaldarsögur*, on the one hand and to learned, speculative reworkings of folk tradition, like the Eddic poems and Snorri's *Prose Edda*, on the other.

Nonetheless, de Boor acknowledges a trace of folk legend tradition in two motifs associated with Scandinavian dwarfs, namely, their supernatural craftsmanship and their living quarters in stones. Scandinavian place names like Dvergaberg (Dwarf-Rock) and Dvergasteinn (Dwarf-Stone) lend support to the latter, as does the Sveigdir episode cited above, which has countless analogs in more recent folk legends of stone dwellers. It may be added that in this respect dwarfs are hard to tell from other nature beings of folk tradition, such as elves and fairies, and by the time of the folklore collections of the nineteenth century dwarfs are interchangeable with these beings in a number of supernatural legends from northern Europe.

See also: Eddic Poetry; Scandinavian Mythology; Snorri Sturluson's *Edda*

—Valdimar Tr. Hafstein

$\mathcal{E}$**ddic Poetry**. The mythological and heroic poetry of medieval Scandinavia.

These poems concern themselves with three main topics: mythology, particularly the exploits of the gods and their relationship with other groups such as giants; ethics and codes of behavior; and the heroic North. One can divide the Eddic corpus into three groups. There are 29 main Eddic poems found in the primary manuscript, and a thirtieth, *Baldrs draumar* (Baldr's Dreams), is often added to this central corpus. Most Eddic compilations include other poems as well in what is known as the "Eddic Appendix," such as the *Rigsthula, Hyndluljod, Hlödskvida,* and *Grottasöngr*. Finally, a group of poems and stanzas taken from the *fornaldarsögur* (legendary sagas) is called the Eddica Minora.

The primary manuscript for the Eddic poetry, containing the main 29 poems, is the *Codex Regius*. Codicological evidence suggests a date of 1270 for the composition of this work. This manuscript, discovered by Bishop Brynjolf Sveinsson in 1643, was originally attributed to Saemund Sigfusson, thus explaining the frequently confusing allusions to both the *Poetic Edda* and Saemund's *Edda* for the Eddic poems. This attribution has been abandoned. The *Poetic Edda*, or *Elder Edda* as it is also known, is distinct from *Snorra Edda*, or the *Prose Edda* as it is known in English. This latter text, written by Snorri Sturluson in the early part of the thirteenth century, includes an elaboration of many of the myths found in the *Poetic Edda*. Indeed, there has been considerable debate concerning the relationship between Snorri's work and possible earlier written Eddic poems.

A general logic governs the placement of the poems in the *Codex Regius* manuscript. Poems in the first section recount stories about the gods, the Aesir. The work is introduced by the *Voluspa* (Sibyl's Prophecy), which chronicles the fate of the gods, detailing the events at the end of the world. Next follow three poems about the god Odin, a poem about the god Frey, and then five poems about the god Thor. The second large section of the manuscript deals with the heroic lays of Sigurd, and these poems generally follow a chronological pattern. They are joined together by short prose interludes.

The word *edda* used to describe these poems is actually borrowed from the title of Snorri's work. The origins of the word are somewhat obscure, and several etymologies have been suggested. Some contend that the word derives from *óðr*, meaning "poetry" and by extension "poetics." Another suggestion is the word *Oddi*, the name of a farm and literary center where Snorri received some education. And yet a third suggestion is *edda*, a word meaning "great-grand-mother." The myths would then be stories of a great-grandmother. A final suggestion is the derivation from the Latin *edere*, "to produce," much like the derivation of *kredda* (creed) from *credere*, "to believe."

There are four main meters of the Eddic poems. The most common of these is *fornyrðislag*, or "old way meter." In this meter each stanza consists of eight half lines (four long lines) of four or five syllables each. The stanzas, in turn, are broken into two equal units of four half lines, the *helmingar* (singular *helmingr*), each of which forms a syntactic unit expressing a complete idea. The first half line of each long line has one or two syllables referred to as the *studlar*, or supports, followed by a single alliterating syllable that generally falls on the first stressed syllable of the second half line. This syllable is known as the *höfuðstafr*, or main pillar. Alliteration occurs either in consonants with like consonants or any vowel with any other vowel. The stanzaic form of the *Edda* contrasts notably with the stichic forms in early Indo-European and Germanic verse, such as the *Hildebrandslied* (Lay of Hildebrand) or *Beowulf*. The earliest Eddic poems have varying stanza lengths, possibly marking the transition from stichic forms to stanzaic forms. The *ljóðaháttr*, or song meter, is also stanzaic but consists of stanzas of six lines. Each *helming* consists of two half lines, followed by a full line that alliterates with itself. The *galdralag* is a variation on *ljóðaháttr* and is associated with magic. It includes a repetition of the long line in each *helmingr*, often incorporating a variation of that line. The final, and least frequent, of the Eddic meters is *málaháttr*, or speech meter. Generally similar to the *fornyrðislag*, it has a longer half line. While scholars often try to make clear distinctions between Eddic verse and skaldic verse, it is not clear that such a distinction was made by medieval Scandinavians. In general, however, Eddic poems tend to have a more distinct narrative component, do not follow the strict rules of syllable counting that characterize the skaldic forms, and make far less use of kennings—metaphors forged from compounding words (e.g., "whale-road" for the tempestuous sea).

There has been significant debate surrounding the composition and transmission of the Eddic poems. Since they are considered to be of considerable value in the study of pre-Christian Scandinavia, a great deal of effort has been expended on determining the oral roots of the poetry. The Parry-Lord model of oral-formulaic composition had significant influence on the theorizing of these oral origins for the Eddic corpus in the pagan period. Because of the lack of significant variants of many of the Eddic poems, much of this type of investigation has been inconclusive. It appears that, rather than showing the significant variation characteristic of oral epic forms, such as those studied by Albert Lord and Milman Parry, the Eddic poems had a rather stable form and were quite likely learned and performed from memory, with little if any formulaic recomposition.

See also: Burgundian Cycle; Scandinavian Mythology; Snorri Sturluson's *Edda*

—Timothy R. Tangherlini

English Tradition: Anglo-Saxon Period. The folkloric culture of the English before the Norman invasion of 1066.

Historical Context

Anglo-Saxon folk culture has its origins among the Continental Germanic peoples of northern Europe, but its specifically English tradition begins with their migration to Britain. Historians now think this migration may have begun as early as the fourth century, though an older tradition has it that the Angles, Saxons, and Jutes came to this former Roman province in 449. Soon afterward the migration inspired myths of origin that persisted throughout the Anglo-Saxon period in lore and literature. The pagan Anglo-Saxons eventually overran England (from *Engla-lond*, "land of the Angles"), wiping away most of Roman Christianity until they were converted by missionaries coming separately from Ireland and from the Continent. As related by the historian Bede writing in 731, the conversion of Anglo-Saxon England was for the most part slow, uneven, halting, and even at times reversed. Gradually, however, churches were consecrated throughout the land, and great monasteries were founded, monasteries that became some of the most important centers of learning in Europe. Consequently, Anglo-Saxon culture became an increasingly diverse mixture of the older lore and customs of the North combined, at least among the educated, with the Latin culture from the South consisting mainly of classical and Christian writings.

This early English culture was disrupted in 793 when the Vikings began raiding, and later invading, throughout the British Isles. Their advance was eventually halted by the military victories of Alfred the Great (849–899), who then labored to restore the high level of learning that England had enjoyed before these invasions. And even though Viking raids resumed in the late tenth and early eleventh centuries, the periods of peaceful relations were sufficient for an Anglo-Scandinavian culture to develop in the North. The conversion of the Vikings to Christianity encouraged their assimilation, and by the time of the Norman Conquest (1066) there was little to distinguish between English and Scandinavian elements at the level of folk culture.

Social Context

Even with persistent warfare, the essential ordering and rhythms of the predominantly rural society remained fairly constant, as indicated by comparison of early settlement and landholding patterns established by archaeological research with those found, often centuries later, in the great Domesday Book survey of 1086. Dwellings were not large compared to those of the later Middle Ages. Surviving foundations of an apparently typical longhouse measure twenty-four to twenty-seven meters in length by about five meters in width, while many smaller houses measure around eight and a half meters by five and a half meters, as found on small farms or in villages of 50 to 150 inhabitants. Compared to such modest structures, the Old English poem *The Ruin* expresses awe at the "race of giants" that Anglo-Saxons believed must originally have erected the old (Roman) stone structures—or even more ancient Neolithic monuments—that they sometimes encountered in their midst. Besides kings and a few powerful nobles, most of the population consisted of free farmers, each of whom had a holding, called a "hide," deemed sufficient to feed an average family, though the size of the holding would vary from region to region according to the quality of the land. As the population grew, farming tended to shift from three-field to two-field rotation, which diminished the productivity of the soil. Their diet, primarily grains, was supplemented by dairy products and some meat, mostly from sheep, whose wool also became a major product for export, particularly toward the end of the period. Women and men shared in agricultural labor, and although grave goods for women include objects associated with spinning, weaving, and household economy, there does not seem to have been as clear a line between the "women's sphere" and the "men's sphere" as appeared at a later time. Indeed, laws and wills show that women had considerable status and legal rights alongside men, and the literature of northern Europe abounds with powerful female figures. Evidence from paleopathology indicates that hard work in the fields contributed to widespread osteoarthritis, along with numerous injuries, especially to the ankles and feet. Although precise figures on life expectancy are unavailable, and would in any event vary according to local conditions, life was precarious for members of all classes. Infant and early childhood mortality was high: Excavations at Thetford show that 87.5 percent of child deaths had occurred by age 6, though that figure seems high compared with other sites. Research in some areas suggests a 50 percent mortality rate by age 30, rising to about 90 percent by age 50. Life expectancy for the average person would therefore have been in the early thirties, with a slightly lower figure for women than men because of the dangers of childbirth. The very few persons recorded as reaching their seventies or beyond were typically from the upper nobility or clergy, who probably enjoyed the healthiest diet and hygiene. Yet even with some stratification of society, no sharp division between folk and elite culture existed among the Anglo-Saxons, so that even their "sophisticated" art and literature were permeated by folkloric patterns and materials.

From these social conditions emerged the traditional worldview of the Anglo-Saxons. As elsewhere in the literature of the North, Old English poems stressed the power of fate, or *wyrd*, as the "most powerful of forces" (*Maxims II*: 5). The individual's identity was so inextricably tied to that of the group that the greatest terror was to be isolated from community (as in the poem *The Wanderer*), and the bonds of loyalty between lord and retainer could not be broken without the greatest dishonor (as in the heroic poem *The Battle of Maldon*). The very shortness and uncertainty of life implied that the greatest virtue lay not so much in living a long and prosperous life as in living and, if need be, dying so as to live on in communal memory with honor (as throughout *Beowulf*). Wealth was valuable to the extent that it was shared, thereby strengthening communal bonds, and the ending of *Beowulf* sings of the uselessness of riches amassed but unshared.

Sources for Anglo-Saxon Folklore

Though Anglo-Saxon folklore generally circulated orally, most of it comes to us in texts written by the literate fraction of the population, whose education took place either in or under the influence of the monasteries. Yet in many cases the traditional folk culture and the newer Christian (and to some extent classical) learning became so intertwined that for us to try to separate these elements analytically would distort the mental and social world that the Anglo-Saxons themselves experienced.

A case in point is the great scholar Bede's work on computing the calendar, *De temporum ratione* (725). After discussing the Hebrew, Egyptian, Roman, and Greek systems, he writes a chapter on the Anglo-Saxon year, which began on December 25 and consisted of 12 lunar months: (1) Giuli, or "Yule"; (2) Solmonath, for offering cakes; (3) Hrethmonath, for the goddess Hretha; (4) Eosturmonath, for the goddess Eostre; (5) Thrimilchi, when cows are milked three times a day; (6 and 7) Litha, possibly for the moon or for the "calm time"; (8) Weodmonath, month of the weeds; (9) Halegmonath, month of holy offerings; (10) Winterfyllith, first full moon of winter; (11) Blotmonath, month of slaughter or sacrifice; (12) a repetition of Giuli, apparently the beginning of "Yule," leading again to December 25, which was known as Modranect, or "Night of the Mothers." Bede goes on to offer a prayer of thanks to Christ for being delivered from these "vain" matters, but he nevertheless has provided us with invaluable evidence of one aspect of the popular culture of his time.

Other works comfortably mix folklore with bookish learning. *The Exeter Book*, which contains some of the most sophisticated Old English poetry, also contains numerous riddles to tease the wits with images of such commonplace objects as horns, fish, cuckoos, beer, and bows—alongside riddles about a book and a pen and fingers. Only someone familiar with the village market could have a fair chance at "A One-Eyed Seller of Garlic," and only someone who had long observed the creatures of the woods could solve "A Badger." Yet these riddles survive only because monks took great delight in collecting and preserving such folklore at the same desks where they carried out the more "serious" tasks of writing and transcribing commentaries on the Psalms and the Gospels.

So also with the many charms that fill the leechbooks, or medical manuals, together with other lore about illnesses, injuries, and their treatments. These manuals often combine information from classical works on medicine with incantations "For a Sudden Stitch," "Against Wens," or even "Against a Dwarf" (apparently one who causes disease). Charms were often filled with references to pre-Christian beliefs and rituals associated with ancient folk medicine, and it seems remarkable that monastic scribes copied them even into the margins of such a Christian classic as Bede's *Ecclesiastical History* (e.g., in a manuscript now at Corpus Christi College, Cambridge). In "The Nine Herbs Charm" a passage in which Woden used plants to cure snakebite and defend human habitation against poison is immediately followed by a passage in which Christ is credited with creating thyme and fennel, endowing them with great power, and giving them to aid poor and rich alike, all while he hung on the cross. Some charms offer power over nature, as in "For a Swarm of Bees." "Land Remedy" promises to cure fields that failed to produce or had been harmed by sorcery or witchcraft. It combines the Christian power of chanting in Latin the Benedicite, the Magnificat, and the Pater Noster with boring a hole in the beam of the plow and inserting incense, fennel, holy soap, and salt and placing the seed to be planted on the body of the plow, all the while chanting an incantation to "Erce, Erce, Erce, mother of earth." Then, while making the first furrow, the plowman is to chant "Hail to thee, Earth, mother of men! Be fruitful in God's embrace, Filled with food for the use of men." It may seem curious to us that medical manuals dealt with nonphysical causes of disorders in humans or in nature, but it was evidently extremely important for Anglo-Saxons to protect themselves by charms, potions, and the like against sorcery and witchcraft. When witchcraft or sorcery was discovered, terrible punishment could be exacted, as is recorded in a tenth-century document declaring that a widow and her son must forfeit their land for driving an iron pin into the image of a man. The woman was then denounced as a witch and drowned at London Bridge, and her son was made an outlaw.

Perhaps less ominous but equally mysterious are the diagnoses in Bald's *Leechbook*, a collection of medical lore, for disorders resulting from "elfshot," though the book also offers more straight-forward cures for everything from poisonous spider bites to potions "for a man who is over-virile" or "for a man who is not virile enough." We may also infer from this work and *Lacnunga* that their frequent references to dysentery, toothache, and various forms of bleeding suggest that these were of particular concern at the time. Yet the distance from practical advice on such matters to something approaching folk magic was never very great. *Lacnunga* elsewhere recommends that a woman trying to avoid a miscarriage should first step three times over the grave of a dead man while reciting a certain incantation, and next she should step over her (live) husband's body in bed while reciting, "Up I go, I step over you, with a live child, not a dying one, with a child to be fully born, not with a doomed one." Those who think that there was a sharp division between elite culture and folklore in Anglo-Saxon England would do well to consider that such prescriptions were commonplace in learned works at the time.

Another area for research is the complex body of law through which the Anglo-Saxons sought to define themselves as a people. Of the legal codes that survive, Aethelberht's Laws (c. 602–603) is by far the oldest. It not only lists prohibitions against various actions, along with fines appropriate for the violations, but it also provides an elaborate system of compensations—payments that must be made to an offended party for injuries to different parts of the body or for sexual violations against a spouse or servant. Each payment is measured according to the severity of the injury, so that cutting off someone's thumb requires a higher compensation than removing a little finger, and wounding a man's sexual "branch" so badly that it is ineffective demands a recompense three times his wergeld, or the amount of compensation due for taking his life. The laws give us insight into social practices and values, and despite the impression that acts of violence were commonplace, these laws actually stress the ways people attempted to settle conflicts peaceably once they had arisen.

Still other sources for folklore are the penitentials, manuals listing and defining the penances for various sins requiring confession to a priest. Penitentials offer us a vivid view of folk culture, at least as presented by the ecclesiastical writers who filled them with an amazing host of sins, defining their seriousness relative to one another and the penance to be meted out for each offense. Both the penitential of the great Archbishop Theodore and the penitential ascribed by Albers to Bede list numerous forbidden sexual practices—from adultery and fornication to various homosexual activities and even "unnatural intercourse" between a married couple "from behind." Ejaculating semen in another's mouth is "the worst of evils," far worse than incest between parent and child or brother and sister. Yet beyond

this clerical fascination with sexuality there are numerous references to folk practices that threatened the official Church. There are specific prohibitions against sacrificing to demons, engaging in auguries or divinations, consulting omens from birds or dreams, conjuring up storms (presumably against enemies), and "seeking out any trick of the magicians." (Compare the horror at *helrunan*, those who know or can "read" the mysterious runes of hell, in *Beowulf* 163.) Also intriguing are the injunctions against any woman who "puts her daughter upon a roof or in an oven for cure of a fever," a man "who causes grains to be burned where a man has died, for the health of the living and of the house," or a woman who mixes her husband's (or lover's?) semen in food to increase his ardor for her.

Yet another source of folklore is the large body of saints' lives from this period. Saints' lives naturally had the full endorsement of the official Church, but they are also filled with folkloric elements and suggest a point at which ecclesiastical and popular beliefs could mingle freely. Consider Ælfric's *Life of St. Edmund*, the Christian king of East Anglia slain by "heathen" Vikings in 869. Within a quarter of a century his cult was flourishing and he was widely revered as a martyr-saint whose passion and death became the subject of traditional legend, first as popular oral narrative and then in a Latin account by Abbo of Fleury, followed by Ælfric's Old English adaptation of Abbo. Ælfric's version generally follows the generic conventions of hagiography, yet it derives its main interest and memorability from strong folkloric elements: the king's body pierced by so many Viking javelins that it resembled a hedgehog with bristles sticking out in all directions; the decapitated head protected in the deep woods by a wolf that despite its hunger would not eat of it; the head calling out directions to the folk searching for it; the uncorrupted flesh and miraculous cure of Edmund's neck wound even after having been buried for a long time; his corpse continuing to grow hair and fingernails so that a widow had to trim them every year; the dead saint's power to freeze in their various positions the would-be grave robbers of his tomb until they could be apprehended and punished the next morning; and of course the conventional note that numerous miracles—especially cures—occurred at his burial site. Ælfric comments at the end of his story that the saint's miracles preserved "in the speech of common folk" were far more numerous than he could write down in his book. The presence of these elements in the work of such a scholarly monastic writer suggests the extent to which folk culture permeated the mental world of the monastery.

Such evidence demands that we not only recognize the enormous importance of Latin learning in Anglo-Saxon monastic communities, but also that we accord equal importance to the fact that these communities were not sealed off from the larger social world. Monasteries not only recruited members from the surrounding folk culture but also incorporated many folkloric elements in their own oral lore, which provided material for many of their writings. After the Vikings sacked Lindisfarne in 793, a monastic author noted in the *Anglo-Saxon Chronicle* that this catastrophe had been forecast by various portents, including the "fiery dragons" that "were seen flying in the air" (cf. *Beowulf*).

See also: Bede the Venerable; *Beowulf*; Cædmon; German Tradition; Medicine; Scandinavian Tradition; Sutton Hoo

—John McNamara

English Tradition: Middle English Period. The folkloric culture of England following the Norman invasion of 1066.

Conquest
The line traditionally drawn between the Old and Middle English eras is 1066, the date of the Norman invasion. Yet there was a long, slow period of transition during which the native English culture absorbed that of the Norman conquerors and transformed itself in the process. The most obvious changes occurred at the top. Though Anglo-Saxon government had become increasingly organized from the time of Alfred, England was largely a culture of chieftains and family-centered communities before the Normans imposed their strongly centralized government. More than 4,000 Anglo-Saxon thanes had served Harold Godwinson in 1066. After William the Conqueror defeated Harold, the thanes' roles at the top of a tighter power structure were filled by fewer than 200 Norman barons.

The move away from familial communities and toward centralized government would take centuries to complete, but from the beginning it caused major changes in upper-class pastimes. Old English heroic verse, enjoyed by a now decimated aristocracy, disappeared from writing, replaced by French chansons de geste. The most famous of the new French poems celebrated Charlemagne's nephew, Roland. Chronicles report that during the Battle of Hastings the Norman minstrel Taillefer rallied the invading troops by singing a version of Roland's story. Although some question these accounts, they demonstrate that Roland was well known to twelfth-century Anglo-Normans.

Because the Anglo-Saxons lost control of most of the centers of education and means of preserving writing, we do not know much about the legendry of the losers. Yet chronicles and other sources mention English heroes who battled the Normans. The most celebrated resister was Earl Hereward the Wake. According to the *Book of Ely*, peasants were still singing songs in praise of Hereward a century after his revolt. Hereward's legends trace the fortunes of Anglo-Saxon warrior culture. Accounts of the young hero in *Gesta Herewardi* present a figure resembling Beowulf who fights a Cornish giant and a magical bear. Stories set after the conquest depict Hereward as an outlaw like Robin Hood, living among commoners. Young Hereward is an aristocratic warrior hero; the adult is a guerrilla. The popularity of Hereward's stories in East Anglia was no accident, for in this region the Norman administration was forcing free people into bondage.

Farming and Housing
Political changes in England were swift and momentous, but country life proceeded by slow turns. The open-field system of agriculture, allowing crop rotation, preceded the Normans, but importations soon after the Norman invasion such as the leather harness for horses enabled each peasant to plow more land and the land to sustain a denser population. There were two agricultural regions in medieval England, corresponding with the two major topographical patterns. The west and north were relatively heavily wooded and sparsely populated. Here, as in Celtic Scotland and Wales, agriculture, herding, and hunting combined to create a subsistence economy for noncentralized tribal societies. Central England, however, was flat and not heavily forested—well suited for the new farming technology.

As the villages grew, so did the distances between the rural lords and the local peasantry. In Old English architecture most dwellings had been similar in design: although structures varied in size and quality with the status of the occupants, the wood-framed longhouse had served the earls, the peasants, and the farm animals alike. Now the Norman barons, more powerful than their Old English predecessors, began to occupy stone castles, creating obvious and visible distances between the classes. Castle dwellers attained a degree of privacy unheard of in earlier society. Such twelfth-century romances as Thomas of Britain's *Tristan* made much of this newfound sense of privacy, as heroes and heroines began to cultivate fantasies of secret lives. Isolation from one's lord and fellow warriors had been one of the greatest curses of Old English poetry, but for Tristan and other romance heroes such separation is desirable, as long as the hero can share his privacy with his lady.

Rural Seasonal Customs and Ceremonies
Daily life was driven by seasonal change. Both lower-class and upper-class celebrations were firmly rooted in the agricultural calendar, and both retained aspects of "natural religion," beliefs in supernatural links between society and nature retained from Anglo-Saxon times. Some traditions (such as folk celebrations of All Hallows' Eve) incorporated elements of Celtic ritual, re-

flecting the combining of Celtic and Anglo-Saxon traditions that had occurred in the monasteries centuries before. The peasant's work year is neatly summarized in this fifteenth-century poem:

Januar	By this fire I warme my handes;
Februar	And with my spade I delfe [dig] my landes.
Marche	Here I sette my thinge to springe;
Aprile	And here I heer the fowles [birds] synge.
Maii	I am light [happy] as birde in bow [bough];
Junii	And I weede my corne well ynow.
Julii	With my sythe [scythe] my mede [meadow] I mowe;
Auguste	And here I shere [shear] my corne full lowe.
September	With my flaill I erne my bred;
October	And here I sowe my whete so rede.
November	At Martynesmasse I kille my swine;
December	And at Cristesmasse I drynke redde wyñe.

("The Months," quoted from *The Oxford Book of English Medieval Verse* [1970], ed. C. Sisam and K. Sisam)

Work dominates the year. Recreation is mentioned for only those four months—December, January, April, May—when peasants were granted vacations of a week or more by their lords. The greatest amount of social ritual took place when the least work was required: the colder months, otherwise intolerably dark and dull. After the harvests were gathered and the grain tallied, villagers determined how many animals could be sustained by their grain. The remaining stock was slaughtered, and many animals were consumed in the autumn feasts, which combined extravagance and necessity. Because summer work had left little time for socializing, the cold months featured intensive visiting and courtship, during which neighbors reasserted communal bonds and began new families. Winter celebrations began after Michaelmas (September 29), the traditional date of the final harvest. November 1, the new year of Celtic tradition, and Martinmas (November 11) marked the beginning of winter, as communities gathered for slaughtering, feasting, and courtship. The next great holidays fell on Christmas (December 25) and the following Twelve Days, ending at Epiphany (January 6). These Christian celebrations were marked with feasts, gifts, and processions, as people normally separated by their work would travel to neighbors' homes. Peasants were expected to provide their lords with additional holiday food, but they were usually released from labor during the Twelve Days. Winter ended with the candlelight procession of Candlemas (February 2) and the wild games of Shrove Tuesday, when the last of the meat set aside for winter was consumed and the fasts of Lent began.

Another work break occurred at Easter, when lords granted peasants a week off. Easter week ended with Hocktide, which probably featured courting games. May Day (May 1), based on the Celtic holiday Beltane, was another lovers' day: young men and women gathered greenery, paired off, and spent the evening in the woods. Rogation, a men's festival, occurred on the days preceding Ascension Day (40 days after Easter). Led by a priest, men went "ganging"—walking the borders of their villages and initiating boys by throwing them into the creeks and against the trees that marked those boundaries. The ritual stressed community solidarity, male bonding, and prayer for the fertility of the fields. The final spring festivals fell during the week of Pentecost, when again peasants were released from labor, and the processions and plays of Corpus Christi (the Thursday following Pentecost, which fell 50 days after Easter) were enacted.

Because summer work was so demanding, little ceremonial took place then, but one important feast was St. John's Day (June 24), or Midsummer, marking the summer solstice. Peasants tended fires through the night, and young men leaped over the fires, presumably to assure virility, certainly to impress watching women.

Urban Celebrations

From the twelfth century forward, with the rise of the merchant class, urban celebrations took on increasing importance. Towns grew as rural people arrived to take on craft work and as merchants from the Continent swelled the ranks of wealthy commoners. The most successful merchant families imitated the nobility, sometimes adopting aristocratic dress and heraldic arms. Craftspeople in effect created a middle world that drew some of its traditions from the peasantry and some from the nobility.

Urban and noble ceremonial constituted a sometimes refined borrowing of the agricultural calendar. During the major seasonal festivities, nature "visited" the city. In a twelfth-century description of Christmas in London, William Fitzstephen reported that houses and churches were filled with holly, ivy, bay, and other evergreens. Rural holiday processions were echoed by city mummings. In 1377, 130 mummers visited Richard II, played dice with him, and gave gifts to his court. Not all mummings were so staid; numerous London ordinances forbade masks and rioting during the Twelve Days.

Like the peasants at Rogation, urban groups

possessed rituals of community definition; like city life in general, these tended to be specialized and factional in comparison to the rural. Norwich observed the day of England's patron, St. George (April 23), by sending the entire hierarchy of the town on a procession to the country, where an actor playing George slew a mock dragon. Corpus Christi celebrations included torchlight parades representing the city's hierarchy; a group's place in the parade was so important that guildsmen fought violently for choice positions.

Londoners observed at least ten annual processions, most including stops at the church of Thomas Becket, the most popular English saint, and with visits to the graves of Thomas's parents. Among the most elaborate noble ceremonies were celebrations of love. The poetry of Geoffrey Chaucer provides the earliest mention of St. Valentine's Day (February 14) as a time when men and women paired off. Chaucer and other court poets also mention lovers' games in May; these rituals seem to have differed from the rural customs mainly in their lavishness. Merchants imitated noble courtship patterns in such festivals as the London Puy, a song competition founded in the thirteenth century for the celebration of love.

Romance and Folktale

In the process of colonization the Normans capitalized on ethnic conflicts in Britain. In order to conquer Wales the Normans befriended elements of the Welsh aristocracy. Neither the Romans nor the Saxons had conquered Wales, but the Normans came much closer, largely by intermarrying with Celts, settling Bretons and Flemings from across the English Channel, and playing upon the Welsh hatred of the English. The new aristocracy developed a mythology that served as a charter for their conquest. Histories and romances combined French aristocratic values with elements of Celtic folk tradition. Stories of King Arthur, long popular with the Welsh and Bretons, were reworked and made part of an elite history. About 1138 Geoffrey of Monmouth, drawing upon British literary and oral tradition and his own imagination, completed his *History of the Kings of Britain*, which inspired writers to tell Arthur's stories in Latin, French, and ultimately English. From their earliest appearance in the mid-twelfth century, romances based on Celtic legend resembled postmedieval märchen in content and form. Beginning in a courtly world of kings and queens, the stories proceeded to relate supernatural encounters. An otherworldly visitor (such as the bird-knight in Marie de France's *Yonec*), or a journey into an enchanted woods (as in Chaucer's "Wife of Bath's Tale" and the Middle English *Sir Launfal* and *Sir Orfeo*), would bring the everyday and the otherworldly face to face. As do most märchen, many romances told

the story of a single young hero, beginning with a series of initiatory tests and ending with that figure's coming of age or marriage: the Middle English *Sir Degaré* and *Perceval of Galles* demonstrate this pattern.

Overlapping the supernatural romances was a group of feudal tales celebrating legendary heroes: *King Horn, Havelok the Dane, Guy of Warwick*, and *Beves of Hampton* exist in both Anglo-Norman and English versions. They tell of young men whose valor gains them kingdoms and royal wives. Unlike the Celtic-inspired tales, these works build upon English and Anglo-Scandinavian heroic legendry, and they also possess their share of marvels: Guy of Warwick, for example, battles giants, a dragon, and an impressive bovine, the Dun Cow.

Like the postmedieval oral tales to which they are clearly related, romances varied according to the status of the groups that shared them. The Anglo-Norman *Romance of Horn* extols kingship and the male world of knighthood; Marie's *Yonec*, written at nearly the same time, presents women's negative response to the male world and introduces a supernatural lover who saves an oppressed woman from her cruel lord. *Guy of Warwick*, perhaps the most popular Middle English romance, introduces a common hero, a steward's son, whose deeds elevate him and make an earl's daughter his wife. Elite romance celebrates hierarchy; popular romance, more directly related to the modern folktale, presents a compensation fantasy in which the lowly find power.

The deeds of romances—even the supernatural romances—were presented as true, sometimes with corroborating evidence. Although contemporary critics tend to dismiss such truth claims as mere conventions, the complex interaction between romance and historical legendry cannot be overlooked. In 1191 monks at Glastonbury claimed they had found the grave of Arthur, while for centuries, others claimed that Arthur lay asleep in a cave. As late as 1485, in his introduction to Malory's *Morte Darthur*, William Caxton states that seeing such relics as Gawain's skull and Cradok's mantle convinced him that the tales of Arthur were true.

Whether or not we believe that medieval listeners believed these tales, there is no doubt that the romances presented models for society to emulate. Around 1300, an English king, perhaps Edward I, had a Round Table built; like English kings before and since, he played the role of Arthur. Guy of Warwick's battle with the dragon became the subject for sermons on courage. By the end of the fifteenth century knighthood was essentially dead as a military phenomenon, but it continued to thrive in aristocratic play.

Religious Lore

Religious lore took on new shapes as society changed. Parish guilds, created as congregants banded together for mutual security and recreation, participated in pilgrimages, processions, and annual feasts that embraced music, gaming, and speech making. In urban centers such as York, Beverley, and Chester, craft guilds combined their talents to stage Corpus Christi cycles, enacting in as many as 40 different plays the important scenes of Christian history. Such works as the Wakefield Master's *Second Shepherd's Play* borrowed from folktale to create an energetic blend of popular culture and religious doctrine. The *Second Shepherd's Play* utilizes a humorous narrative ("Mak and the Sheep," AT 1525M) widespread in medieval and postmedieval tradition—in which a man who has stolen a sheep disguises it as a baby in order to escape arrest and punishment—and turns it into a comic echo of the birth of Christ, the biblical event celebrated in this drama.

Folktale and Christian doctrine also met in the pulpit. From the twelfth century onward sermon collections were filled with popular narratives adapted to moral and religious purposes. Such legends as "The Spider in the Hairdo" were localized and used to warn parishioners of the consequences of ungodly behavior: an Oxfordshire woman took so long to adorn her hair each Sunday that she began arriving later and later at church. One week she entered church just as the mass was ending, and the devil, disguised as an enormous spider, descended upon her head and would not leave until a priest administered communion to the woman.

The popularity of exempla is attested in verse treatments like Robert Mannyng's *Handlyng Synne* (1303), which provides a wealth of belief narratives, such as the tale of the couple that became stuck together while having sex on holy ground; only the prayers of monks could separate them. Also popular were Middle English saints' lives, which reinforced Christian values through heroic models rather than through the scare tactics of the exempla. Late-medieval England saw the rise of pilgrims' processions, especially to the shrine of St. Thomas Becket in Canterbury. Murdered by servants of his king in 1170, Thomas became the center of a popular cult. Visits to his shrine were supposed to cure all manner of physical and spiritual ills. As the Middle Ages wore to a close, the pilgrimage to the shrine of the Virgin of Walsingham eventually superseded the Canterbury pilgrimage in popularity.

The great cathedrals present concrete proof of the blendings and tensions of elite and folk cultures. At Canterbury folklore was enlisted to support official fund-raising efforts through stained-glass panels depicting popular legends of people saved by St. Thomas or punished for failing to honor him. Throughout England, misericords, the carved undersides of bishops' seats, depicted folk themes. As the bishop promoted the official order, the carvings beneath his buttocks challenged that order, presenting a world turned upside down in which mice hanged cats, carts pulled horses, and wives beat their husbands.

See also: Becket, Saint Thomas; Carol; Drama; Festivals and Celebrations; Folklore; Folktale; Misericords; Outlaw; Romance; Valentine's Day, Saint; World Turned Upside Down

—Carl Lindahl

Eucharist. Both an object and a ritual, enfolded within the sacrament that was raised above all others in the central Middle Ages, circa 1200.

The Eucharist was the ritual of remembrance of Christ's sacrifice as presaged and offered by Jesus to the Apostles at the Last Supper and celebrated in a variety of forms by early Christians. Throughout the twelfth century its significance and the details of the procedures attached to it became increasingly clarified and codified by theologians and canonists. During the celebration of the Mass, the words of consecration were pronounced by the priest at the altar over an unleavened wheaten disc of bread (the Eucharistic host, the Eucharist) and a chalice of wine; these words in turn summoned Christ as his body became present in the bread and wine. The nature of this "presence" was the subject of heated debate in the central Middle Ages, but it was strongly formulated in 1215 as being a substantial presence—a real one, in the sense that the bread and wine had been transformed into Christ's flesh and blood through the operation of "transubstantiation" at the pronouncement of the priest's words, the very words that Christ had enunciated at the Last Supper. The wheaten disc of bread thus became Christ's body, the real historical body of the Passion, even as the external appearance of bread (and wine) remained on the altar. This statement dictated highly ritualized treatments of the host-Christ and also prompted a barrage of investigation into the consequences of the theological claims about it: Was Christ there in flesh and blood? Did he exist on the altar and in heaven simultaneously? Could even a sinful priest effect the transformation of transubstantiation? Believers were encouraged to participate in the Eucharistic Christ by receiving the Eucharistic host at communion at least once a year, as the final stage of an annual self-examination, following confession and penance. Following the pastoral rulings of the Fourth Lateran Council of 1215, communion became the annual touchstone of Christian virtue, of membership in the community of the Church, and of social acceptability. Monks and nuns were allowed to take communion more frequently, and priests could celebrate it daily and twice on Christmas Day.

The enormous power attributed to the simple wheaten disc that was the host gave rise to problems related to the manner of its handling and containment. It was to be contained in precious metal vessels and locked away in the church; it was to be put into transparent containers for occasional viewing by the populace; it was to be carried out of the church in procession only with the utmost care and decorum, held by the priest and accompanied by a retinue of clerical servers and adoring believers. The very marking out of the Eucharist and its space evoked desires to increase the frequency of occasion for gazing at it. In response, Church authorities from the Middle Ages and later inveighed against too frequent display of the Eucharist or too frequent reception of communion by lay people. The world of exemplary religious tales known as exempla, which reflect popular understandings and widespread practice, repeatedly dramatized the many ways in which laypeople attempted to appropriate the host to themselves for private use. Most often this was achieved by taking the host out of the mouth after communion, and less frequently through theft from a church. A layperson may have procured the host for use in the pursuit of health, love, or prosperity. One of the most famous tales of the period is that of the woman who sprinkled her beehive with crumbs of the host to encourage the bees' productivity, only to find that her bees had erected a waxen altar and adored the Eucharist on it. Another common tale had the host used in the pursuit of love as a wife held it in her mouth while kissing her husband in the hope of rekindling his affection. When employed in magic, the useful Eucharist could also effect harm: poison could be concocted with the host as an important ingredient, like that which the Jews were claimed to have prepared for the poisoning of the wells in 1321 and 1348.

Eucharistic ideas and practices offered scope for the development of a wide range of related beliefs. Groups that came to be considered dissenting, aberrant, or heretical (e.g., the Lollards, Cathars, and female Beguines of northern Europe) often developed critiques of Eucharistic lore. As a central symbol of Christian orthodoxy, the Eucharist became a focus for fantasies of abuse and labeling of difference. Thus, in the later Middle Ages, marginal groups, especially the Jews, were accused of desecrating the host. Such accusations often inspired violent mob actions. In the anti-Semitic narratives, which are to be found both in guidebooks for preaching and in chronicle reports of rumors and actions of communities, the Eucharist is said to have been tested or abused by Jews and to have reacted potently: by turning into a crucifix, into flesh, or into a wounded child (Christ).

See also: Blood; Jews, Stereotypes of

—Miri Rubin

Eulenspiegel. German trickster figure whose pranks were first published circa 1510, in a form recently discovered to have been codified by Hermann Bote of Brunswick.

It seems certain, however, that the anecdotes that Bote recorded had circulated in oral tradition since about 1400. Eulenspiegel's name, conveyed in early woodcuts by a rebus of an owl (*Eule*) and mirror (*Spiegel*) that he holds aloft (hence the c. 1519 English translation as Howleglass; see illustration), seems actually to be composed of *ulen* (to clean) and *Spiegel* (in hunter's terminology, an animal's rump). The name is thus originally a scatological joke at the hearer's expense, meaning something like "Wipe my arse," a fitting sobriquet for a figure with such a pronounced penchant for scatology.

Even as a child, riding behind his father on the same horse, he deliberately exposed his bare bottom to passersby, who were duly scandalized. His first recorded exploit as a young man derives from a characteristic linguistic perversion of a task commanded by his lord: he was always to defecate on any hemp (*Henep*) he might find growing by the wayside, in order to fertilize this valuable plant from which the ropes that hang thieves were made. He pretends to have become confused and treats the mustard (*Senep*) he brings up to the lord's table in the same manner as he treats the hemp. This behavior is curiously reminiscent of an actual incident that took place during the early days of the Swiss Reformation: upon his arrival in Zug in 1523, a mustard dealer was told that all his mustard came from Zurich and that *hette der Zwingli darin geschissen* (Zwingli had shat in it); here we see the Swiss Protestant leader Huldrych Zwingli (1484–1531) portrayed as Eulenspiegel.

Eulenspiegel even obtains rewards by eating his own excrement, and in this manner succeeds in outdoing the king of Poland's court jester. On another occasion, by substituting his own excrement for that of a constipated child, Eulenspiegel earns the thanks of the child's mother. He tricks a cobbler into thinking that frozen excrement is tallow, drives away his employer with a particularly noxious fart, and introduces a pile of his excrement into a tavern, thereby driving out the company. He defecates in a bathhouse, pretending that he had thought it was a latrine; he imitates an innkeeper's small children, relieving himself in the middle of the floor, and tricks another innkeeper's wife into sitting on hot ashes with a bare bottom; he soils his bed in another inn and claims a priest did it (this last episode is perhaps the subject sculpted on a corbel in the staircase tower of the Hotel de Ville in Noyon). He "moons" a messenger, and so on. Even on his deathbed, the arch-trickster contrives to fool the avaricious priest who comes to hear his confession, causing him to thrust his hand into a pot full of excrement covered with a layer of coins! It is noticeable, however, that Eulenspiegel's scatological pranks are directed against aristocrats, priests, burghers, and tradesmen, but never against the lowliest stratum of society, to which he himself belongs.

There seems to be little iconography that can be indisputably linked to Eulenspiegel before the first woodcut-illustrated editions of the early sixteenth century. However, one such presumed reference is that of a wooden carving in the shape of his rebus (i.e., an owl holding a mirror) at Kempen (1493).

See also: Fool; Scatology; Trickster

—Malcolm Jones

Evil Eye. The ability to inflict death, disease, or destruction by a glance.

Belief in the evil eye is widespread throughout Christian, Jewish, and Islamic cultures and shows remarkable similarities of detail wherever and whenever it occurs. This belief is also ancient; it is found in Sumerian and Egyptian texts and throughout the Greco-Roman world. In the folk belief of recent centuries, it is strongest in countries bordering the Mediterranean, whether Christian or Islamic, and it also exists in Ireland and Gaelic Scotland, though not quite so intensely. More sporadic allusions occur in the folklore of virtually every European country. The evil eye is regarded as a natural, inborn power, unlike witchcraft or sorcery, but there are divergent traditions as to whether it is under the control of its possessor. Sometimes it is spoken of as a force deliberately projected in a spirit of envious malice; sometimes, as something automatic and unconscious.

The actual term *evil eye*, together with its equivalents in other languages (Italian *malocchio*, French *mauvais oeil*, German *böser Blick*), derives ultimately from biblical references to envy and malice: "Is thine eye evil because I am good?" (Matt. 20:15); Christ's listing of "an evil eye" among sins that "come from within" (Mark 7:22–23); and "Eat not the bread of him that hath an evil eye" (Prov. 23:6–7). In southern Italy, the power is commonly called *jettatura*, alluding to its being "cast" upon the victim. A learned Latin-based term, found in several languages, was *fascination*. In more colloquial English, from the Middle Ages to recent rural dialects, the concept was conveyed through a verb: people said their children, or their cattle, had been "overlooked." This was Shakespeare's usage: "Vile worm, thou wast o'erlook'd even in thy birth" (*Merry Wives of Windsor* 5.5.87).

By medieval criteria, belief in the evil eye was not a superstition, for its existence was a theory endorsed by the best authorities: not only Scripture but also many respected writers of antiquity. In his influential *Natural History* (7,2) Pliny says that among the Triballi and Illyni there are enchanters who can kill anyone they stare at, especially if the look is an angry one. They can be recognized because they have a double pupil in one eye. Cicero likewise held that the glance of any woman who has a double pupil is harmful. Moreover, medieval science held that vision was an active power, in which eyes emitted rays; the evil eye could therefore be a natural force, not a magical one, as the lawyer Bartolo of Saxoferrato pointed out in the 1330s. Thomas Aquinas refers casually to old women who harm children by

looking at them. Francis Bacon, in his essay "Of Envy," says love and envy are passions that can "fascinate or bewitch" and that envy is accompanied by "an ejaculation or irradiation of the eye" that becomes a harmful "stroke or percussion" to the person envied.

There is such similarity between classical sources and recent folklore about the nature and effects of the evil eye, and even what amulets, words, and gestures to use against it, that one can safely assume continuity of tradition across the centuries. The beliefs and practices of an Italian in Dante's time can hardly have been very different from those of a Roman in Pompeii or a Neapolitan of the nineteenth century when these latter have so much in common. This is fortunate, since direct evidence from the Middle Ages is curiously scarce—much scarcer than in either the preceding or the later periods. In some Italian paintings of the fourteenth and fifteenth centuries, the infant Jesus is depicted wearing coral beads, probably because, as Reginald Scot says, "The corall preserveth such as beare it from fascination or bewitching, and in this respect they are hanged about children's necks" (*Discoverie of Witchcraft*, 1584: 13, 6). Similarly, many lead badges from Flanders, France, and England, dating from around 1400, are blatantly sexual and may be meant to avert the evil eye, as were Roman phallic amulets.

Allusions in medieval literature are few but striking. Irish mythological texts tell of the giant Balar (also Balor) Birug-derc (Piercing-Eyed), whose eye is kept covered by a metal lid except on the battlefield; once opened, it destroys whole armies by its poison. In Icelandic sagas there are several mentions of wizards or witches whose glance could blunt weapons, drive men mad, cause any living creature to drop dead, and "make the land turn over" so that nothing ever grew there again. Before killing such a wizard, it was necessary to put a bag over his head to guard against the power of his dying glance. As these literary sources are concerned with heroism, possessors of the evil eye are then defeated in combat, not thwarted by amulets.

See also: Amulet and Talisman; Phallic Imagery; Witchcraft

—Jacqueline Simpson

Exemplum [Pl. exempla]. A story told to illustrate a moral lesson.

Stories with morals have been told since ancient times, from Aesop's fables in ancient Greece, through the long traditions of fables and animal tales with morals in the Middle Ages, and even beyond into modern times. However, the most distinctive form of the medieval exemplum is found in sermons preached to popular audiences, though the term has sometimes been used more loosely in modern literary studies to designate exemplary stories in general.

In preaching aimed at lay audiences, exempla

functioned to bridge the gap between a more or less theologically educated clergy and the popular religion of ordinary people, and therefore many exempla either came from or became widespread in the folklore of town and country alike. In the early Middle Ages, exempla for sermons tended not to be available in highly schematized form. There are numerous accounts of exempla in the preaching of St. Patrick, St. Cuthbert, and St. Boniface, all of whom traveled widely to bring their message to the common people. In Bede's *Ecclesiastical History of the English People* (731) there are numerous stories related as exempla— such as the blacksmith monk who dies unrepentant and is carried by devils to hell—with the observation that the circulation of such stories has confirmed many in the faith and brought them to amend their lives. While Bede does not always describe the precise way these stories circulate in oral tradition, it is clear they are functioning as exempla whether they are presented in sermons or in more informal storytelling events. Evidence of more formal presentation of exempla in sermons is available, however, as indicated by the Anglo-Saxon *Blickling Homilies* (c. 970), which, like the contemporary homilies of Ælfric, were composed in the language spoken by ordinary people. Here, in the Blickling sermon for Easter, we have an account of Christ's triumphant Harrowing of Hell, based on the popular apocryphal fourth-century Gospel of Nicodemus, complete with Christ loosing Adam from his bonds but leaving Eve still bound, and being persuaded by Eve to release her as well by reminding him that, however remotely, she is the mother of his mother. Like most exempla set in hell, the story is filled with vivid and terrifying images of punishments that await unrepentant sinners. In the sermon for Michaelmas, the Blickling homilist recounts a vision of St. Paul, who was

gazing towards the northern part of this world, where all waters pass below, and saw there above the water a certain gray stone. And to the north of the stone there had grown very frosty groves; and there were dark mists; and beneath the stone was the dwelling place of water-monsters and evil spirits. And he saw that on the cliff many black souls bound by their hands were hanging in the icy groves; and the devils in the shape of water-monsters were clutching at them, just like ravenous wolves. And the water under the cliff below was black; and between the cliff and the water was about twelve miles. And when the twigs broke, the souls which hung on the twigs dropped below and the water-monsters seized them. These were the souls of those who had sinned wickedly here in the world, and would not turn from it before their life's end. But now let us earnestly beseech St. Michael to lead our souls into bliss, where

they may rejoice in eternity without end. Amen.

Here the Anglo-Saxon preacher invokes the horrors of the frozen North for the damned, and scholars have often noted the similarity between this description and the mere in *Beowulf*, showing the kind of link that could exist between the sermon exemplum and heroic poetry in popular culture of the time.

During the twelfth and thirteenth centuries the Church became increasingly anxious about heresies spreading among the laity, so various efforts were undertaken to ensure the orthodoxy of lay Christianity. Thus, in 1215 the Fourth Lateran Council legislated annual participation in the sacraments of penance and communion for everyone, and this promoted the spread of penitential manuals among priests hearing confessions or preaching against the sins described in them. In 1235 Robert Grosseteste, bishop of London, required clergy in his diocese to preach sermons specifically in English on the seven deadly sins, the Creed, the sacraments, and similar subjects. In 1281 John Peckham, archbishop of Canterbury, in the Constitutions of Lambeth extended the list for required preaching in English to include 14 articles of faith, the Ten Commandments, the seven sacraments, and so forth.

Since many of the clergy were unprepared for this new requirement, numerous manuals on preaching began to appear in the thirteenth century, complete with compilations of numerous exempla to be used in sermons. For example, Jacques de Vitry (c. 1170–1240) produced *Sermones vulgares* (Popular Sermons), a collection of model sermons filled with exempla drawn from literature and from personal experience, which did much to popularize their use in preaching. Some manuals were organized around lists of virtues and vices arranged alphabetically, as in the *Summa predicantium* (Compendium for Preachers) by John of Bromyard (d. 1352), which contained numerous stories to illustrate the moral lessons. Still others could be organized around a particular theme common in preaching. A well-known example would be Chaucer's "Monk's Tale," which presents a long series of stories, all of which exemplify the fall of the mighty and the theme of mutability, guiding the audience to look beyond the transient glories of this world to the eternal ones of the next.

Of particular interest were the founding and flourishing of the new preaching orders, especially the Franciscans and the Dominicans, in the thirteenth century. They were specifically trained for popular preaching, and they seem in some cases to have outshone the local clergy in their ability to attract popular audiences, along with the donations that went with such popularity. These friars spiced their sermons with fables and animal tales as well as with more conventional fare. They brought many of these out of the Latin classroom, where they had been used in text-books for monastic students, and gave them wide circulation in popular culture. In turn, these friars also drew upon much folkloric material already circulating in oral tradition, as the research of Frederic Tubach suggests.

In 1312 the Council of Vienne gave Dominicans and Franciscans license to take their preaching out of the churches and into the streets (*in plateis communibus*). In addition, they directed the hierarchy and parish priests not to criticize them for this activity. Nevertheless, criticism of the friars did spread, as the case of Chaucer's Friar suggests, and in Florence one critic noted that after the popular Bernardino of Siena had finished his sermon and left, the people, no longer inspired by his preaching, "like snails in flight that had drawn in their horns ... [now] shot them out again as soon as the danger was over," giving themselves over to "cards, dice, false hair, rouge pots, and ... even to chess boards."

Popular sermon exempla ranged from the fearful to the humorous. In one, a bishop hears from a recently dead hermit that of the 30,000 people who died that day, only he and St. Bernard went to heaven, while three went to purgatory, and all the rest went to hell. In another, a con man offers to ornament a king's palace with paintings, telling him that no one who is a cuckold, a bastard, or a traitor will be able to see them. When the king and his entourage come to see the paintings, they all exclaim their pleasure at the art even though they do not see anything. Finally, of course, one knight among the court has the courage to point out that there are no paintings on the walls. But perhaps the most famous exemplum of them all is Chaucer's "Pardoner's Tale," in which three drunken revelers set out to kill Death in the midst of a plague, but ironically they all meet their own deaths through their greed. In Chaucer's fourteenth-century *Canterbury Tales*, this exemplum is itself ironic in that it is presented in a sermon directed against greed by the very pilgrim who uses his skills as a popular preacher to fulfill his own greed.

See also: Animal Tale; Chaucer, Geoffrey; Fable; Folklore; Judah the Pious

—John McNamara

*F*able. A short narrative, often but not always with animal characters, to which memorable bits of wisdom, often proverbs or moral lessons, are appended.

The Western fable tradition traces its origin back to Aesop, a Greek living in the sixth century B.C.E., though it is likely that at least some of his fables circulated orally much earlier. Aesop himself appears not to have written them down, but very ancient tradition claims that the form in which they were eventually put in writing is faithful to the way Aesop himself told them. Little is known of this Aesop; legend has it that he was a clever slave, but that may simply be a way of explaining why his fables often favor underdogs. In any event, Aesopic fables became very popular in antiquity, eventually becoming a part of the Roman curriculum for teaching grammar and rhetoric in the schools, as recommended by Quintilian and Priscian.

Broadly speaking, the history of the fable in the European Middle Ages is the history of two fable collections: the first-century Latin prose and verse versions of Phaedrus and the fourth-century Latin prose translations of Babrius's earlier Greek collection. Both collections included fables that circulated in both written and oral traditions, but neither was associated with its original author: the Phaedrus collection traveled under the name of Aesop, Romulus (after a fourth-century popularization with that name), and others; part of Babrius's collection came through the Middle Ages under the name of the fourth- or early-fifth-century Latin translator Avianus. Both collections eliminated some of the fables in their sources—Romulus contains about half of the Phaedrus material and Avianus about one-third to one-fourth of Babrius—and together they constituted the essential corpus of Aesopica through the Middle Ages. To this must be added some of the Indian fable tradition that arrived in the West during the thirteenth century along with Arabic-Persian fables encountered by Europeans during the Crusades. Fables in Greek appear not to have been known in the West, though they continued to flourish in Byzantium.

The Avianus collection retained its integrity throughout the Middle Ages, and it was used as a standard textbook for young Latin students to the thirteenth century. The Romulus collection underwent a much more complicated history, producing different versions of individual fables as well as different versions of the collection itself. Even so, the Romulus tradition gradually replaced Avianus in the schools during the later Middle Ages, largely through the success of the twelfth-century collection by one "Gualterus Anglicus" (Walter of England, the same person called by German scholars the "Anonymous Neveleti," the name of a seventeenth-century editor of the work). Also in the twelfth century, but without any direct connection with Walter, Marie de France produced the first vernacular collection (in French). The first 40 of her 103 fables are from a branch of Romulus and thus go back to classical antiquity, but her remaining 63 appear to come from other sources, including folk tradition, and some may very well be original with her. Later, in the fifteenth century, the Scottish poet Robert Henryson wrote his famous *Moral Fables*, which were based partly on the Romulus version of Walter but also contained much new material.

Only at the very end of the Middle Ages did the romance of the *Vita Aesopi* (Life of Aesop), with its ten or so fables, arrive in Western Europe. The first Latin versions arrived in Italy perhaps as early as the end of the fourteenth century, and its first vernacular translation (into French) seems to have been Heinrich Steinhöwel's *Esopus* (1476–1477). Though typical of medieval Aesopica, *Esopus* also marks the beginning of the new humanistic collections, which would swell the number of fabular motifs from the medieval corpus of roughly 125 to well over 500. Steinhöwel's work was immensely popular and served as the basis for the famous English translation by William Caxton in 1484.

There are several features that contribute to the popularity of fables. Typically they are short, develop characters and action rapidly, and come to conclusions that often involve paradoxical twists of plot. They often use animals as characters, though they also may use humans (about one-third of Marie de France's fables include humans), and they are thus similar in some respects to the animal tale, such as that found in the famous Reynard cycle (discussed in the entry Animal Tale in this encyclopedia). But perhaps the main feature that distinguishes the fable from other narrative forms is the pithy statement of folk wisdom, often amusing, appended to the story as its "moral" or, in the later Middle Ages, the elaborate allegorical exegesis of the story that precedes it.

Take, for example, the fable that appears first in the works of Walter of England, Marie de France, and Robert Henryson. In Walter this is "De gallo et lapide" (The Cock and the Gem), a simple story told in 10 lines about a rooster digging for food, uncovering a precious jewel, rejecting the jewel because he cannot eat it, and therefore described as foolish at the end. What is remarkable is the 35-line allegorical interpretation that follows, in which the rooster becomes a figure for foolish persons who reject the grace of the Holy Spirit. Walter goes on to cite such authorities as Cicero and Seneca in a discussion that shifts attention away from the fable and focuses entirely on the commentary for its own sake. In Marie's version, "Del cok e de la gemme," she relates the same basic story but with a simple

4-line conclusion, noting that for some men and women, "The worst they seize; the best, despise." Henryson lengthens the fable itself, stressing the plight of the poor who need food rather than beautiful things. Yet in the moral commentary he shifts to blaming the rooster for being more concerned with worldly than spiritual needs. Even so, he does not abandon the fable itself in the manner of Walter.

There are, of course, more complex and interesting fables. For example, in some of Marie's fables that are not part of the Romulus tradition, she produces something very close to fabliaux. In "Del vilein ki vit un autre od sa femme" (The Peasant Who Saw Another with His Wife), a peasant actually sees his wife in bed with another man. When he confronts her, she makes him gaze upon his own image in a vat of water, noting that what he sees there is not the reality it appears to be, and concluding therefore that seeing is not believing. The gullible husband agrees and apologizes to his wife for accusing her of infidelity. Marie's "moral" is very simple, stressing the importance of using one's common sense.

More typical of the medieval fable is Henryson's "The Wolf and the Wether." The fable begins with a shepherd's loss of his sheepdog, which causes terrible fear and lamentation. We hear in the shepherd's words that this man of the country, whose livelihood is now threatened by the loss of his dog, not only fears the prospect of becoming a penniless beggar in the town but is genuinely touched by the loss of his "darling deid." Touched in turn by this lament, the wether replies with proverbial wisdom, enjoining him not to grieve. The wether then proposes the deception of putting the dog's hide on himself, and in his new guise he simulates the dog's ability to chase off enemies with great success. Thus, when a wolf snatches one of the sheep and the chase ensues, Henryson describes the wolf fleeing what he thinks is the dog, letting out "his taill on lenth," ignoring the dangers of "busk" and "boig" in his panic to escape. Inevitably, the wether-dog's pelt is stripped off by his mad pursuit of the wolf through the briars. In the final exchange between the wolf and the wether, we have vivid details of the wolf's humiliation at having befouled himself ("schot behind") three times through fear in the chase. The exposed wether tries to pass it all off as a game, but the wolf seizes him by the neck and kills him. It is worth noting that Henryson expands the exchange beyond earlier versions, thus heightening the comic, if rather brutal, realism of his narrative.

But then comes the "moral." As the *moralitas* would have it, the wether deserves his fate because through pride he presumed beyond his proper station. However, if we look back at the fable itself, it would appear that while the wether does exceed his proper sphere, he does so not by pretending to be a dog, nor by presuming to wear the dog's hide, nor even by chasing the wolf. His mistake lies in pursuing the wolf beyond the limits of his responsibility, beyond his agreement with the shepherd, and certainly beyond what is necessary to protect the sheep. It is in carrying out his mad pursuit that he forces the wolf to befoul himself out of fear no less than three times. Clearly the wolf punishes the wether for humiliating him, not for presuming above his station. None of this appears in the *moralitas*, of course, and it is easy to see how the details of the wolf befouling himself—a common motif in folk humor—could resist the control of an "official" interpretation.

See also: Animal Tale; Marie de France

—Pack Carnes and John McNamara

Fabliau [Pl. fabliaux]. A distinctive type of short tale, centering on a trick or deception, that usually leads to, although occasionally it thwarts, a misdeed.

Fabliaux are comical—often darkly or ironically so—and normally feature bawdy, scatological, or criminal activities, often in combination. They are a significant feature of the medieval literature of several Western European vernaculars.

The term *fabliau* is French, a diminutive of *fable,* and derives from northeast France, where it appears as a dialectal form in Picard in the twelfth to fourteenth centuries. Of at least 127 fabliaux known in French literature of this period, a high proportion are set in this region, and several of these explicitly label themselves fabliaux, as in the first line of "Le prestre qui ot mere a force" (The Priest Who Had a Mother Forced upon Him): "Icil fableau ce est la voire" [This fabliau is the truth]. Although Old French literature offers the greatest range of fabliaux, they were also strongly represented in Middle English, Middle High German, Middle Dutch, and medieval Italian.

Fabliaux often share characteristics with the exempla, to the extent that the same tales sharing the same plot appear in both genres. Exempla are also short narrative tales; they were used to demonstrate or emphasize a moral argument or an accepted truism and were intended to be affective and didactic, to guide the audience toward morally virtuous behavior. Fabliaux are not lacking in morality—indeed, many of them end emphatically with a moral pronouncement—but they are considerably more tolerant of immoral conduct, both within the narrative (such as adultery between two characters) and in the form of telling the stories (as, for example, when Chaucer's Miller drunkenly upsets the prescribed social order to tell his fabliau in *The Canterbury Tales*). The relaxed attitude of the fabliaux to immorality is apparent in their use of marked language, either through the blunt use of crude or improper terms or through the use of euphemisms that clearly signify a vulgar action or object. This is particularly noticeable in fabliaux with a sexual theme. Exempla, however, uphold conventional propriety in every respect.

The apparent knowingness of the fabliaux—implicit in their carefully crafted plots—suggested to Joseph Bédier, among others, that their social and cultural origins lay with the bourgeoisie and that they should be viewed as the literary expression of that particular social class. The informal style, colloquial speech, and urban settings that are common to many fabliaux can be seen as supporting this theory. However, Per Nykrog suggested, rather, that fabliaux represent the antithesis of romance, a subtle parody that only an aristocratic audience would have recognized and appreciated. More recently, John Hines has argued that the focus of such speculation is misplaced and that a more pertinent focus is on the tone and content of the fabliaux. Many authors of fabliaux drew attention to themselves in their texts, and the most common persona adopted was that of the *jongleur* (the typecast figure of an itinerant minstrel), who has many parallels with the narrative figure of the clerk (student). Both of these figures are presented as being able to obtain all of their needs and desires (food, sex, etc.) by using their wits, and indeed they appear to delight in doing so, outwitting figures from every social stratum from peasant to knight. The most famous fabliau writer in Middle English, Chaucer, provides useful examples of this sort of tone in his "Miller's Tale" and "Reeve's Tale" in *The Canterbury Tales*. In both of these tales clerks outwit artisans. They are juxtaposed with "The Knight's Tale" (a romance) and are deliberately introduced as "cherles tales" (tales told by lower-class men), yet the sophistication and erudition displayed in the tales seems to preclude such lowly and uneducated origins. Such a focus on wit, combined with the connections between fabliaux and the medieval satirical tradition (as discussed by Peter Dronke), suggests that locating the fabliau in a wide-ranging scholarly milieu is more productive than trying to precisely define its exact source and intended audience.

Although putting forward the Miller's and Reeve's narratives as "cherles tales" is a device for Chaucer to suggest that conventional propriety and morality may be bypassed here and that he cannot be held responsible as author, fabliaux are neither immoral nor amoral. Many fabliaux end with an explicit moral, although the exaggerated and absurd nature of many fabliaux means that a conventional moral can seem inadequate, if not facetious. The actual moral message of a fabliau is more likely to be found in poetic justice, in a down-to-earth aside that balances the excesses of the narrative, or in the implicit warning found in the consequences of foolish or unlawful conduct—that is, as part of the narrative itself rather than in the conventional moral that is appended.

Although the term *fabliau* derives from Old French and the majority of extant examples of the genre is French, there is some evidence (adduced in the work of Jan de Vries and John Hines) that their original derivation was more widely rooted and that French authors (particularly in the Picard region) were probably involved in mutual exchange of material with the Middle Dutch authors of fabliaux, which were known in their native language as *boerden* (sg. *boerde*). There is also some evidence of similarly close relationships among European fabliaux. However, France remains the center of fabliau production, and many of the early French fabliaux name their authors; Jean Bodel and Rutebeuf are among the best known. The willingness of the authors of these narratives to name themselves suggests that despite their typical content and language, the tales would probably have been regarded as socially acceptable and valid literature—one only has to look at the fabliaux from such well-known and respected authors as Chaucer and Boccaccio (whose narratives in the *Decameron* are, interestingly, told by a mixed-gender group of aristocrats) to see that this was clearly the case by the later Middle Ages.

The acceptability of the genre is further demonstrated by the fact of its survival and circulation in the postmedieval period. In the early sixteenth century, jestbooks (collections of amusing prose narratives) began to be compiled, often featuring narratives that are recognizable as fabliaux. Interestingly, however (as the first English translation of Boccaccio's *Decameron* was not available until 1620), the primary source for these was Boccaccio rather than Chaucer. The postmedieval fabliau tradition flourished most extensively in the form of ballads, many of which feature the sexual, scatological, or criminal behavior associated with the fabliau and draw either on literary material from Chaucer, Boccaccio, and early French fabliaux or on more-localized traditions.

Undoubtedly the fabliaux are closely allied to the oral traditions of medieval and postmedieval Europe. This relationship, suggested by the fictional storytellers of the *Decameron* and *The Canterbury Tales*, is demonstrated by Boccaccio and other medieval novella writers such as Sercambi who often name their oral sources and make it clear that the plots and storytelling contexts themselves were distributed through a wide social range, embracing the merchant classes, artisans, and peasants. The social breadth of the fabliau is also indicated by the huge number and variety of surviving texts. For example, Chaucer's "Friar's Tale," a narrative that like many others can function either as an exemplum or a fabliau, exists in well over 60 late-medieval versions, in Latin as well as German and English and several other vernaculars, and persists in later oral tradition as "With His Whole Heart" (AT 1186), vastly popular in twentieth-century Europe. The written medieval fabliaux demonstrate the same fluidity of plot and style found in later oral story-telling contexts, in which the narrator freely re-shapes the received traditional material to fit his or her personal rhetorical stance and the tastes and expectations of the audience.

See also: Chaucer, Geoffrey; *Decameron;* Folktale; *Novella;* Trickster; *Unibos*

—Nicola Chatten

Fairies. Supernatural beings of medieval legendry and romance who maintain their own realm, sometimes venturing into the human world or drawing mortals into theirs.

Some classes of supernatural beings belong to the realm of mainstream religion: gods, angels, demons, devils. Other classes belong to the secular realm of the supernatural, and these may conveniently be termed *fairies,* although every language and culture area has its own names for these beings. Yet while fairies represent the secular supernatural, both scholarship and various folk traditions suggest that many fairies are descended from pagan deities.

Fairies and Witches
While fairies are the secular complement to the angels and demons of the religious sphere, fairies can also be seen as the supernatural complement to the witches of the mundane realms. As several scholars of early modern witch beliefs have pointed out, fairies and witches are both blamed for causing sudden and otherwise inexplicable illnesses in humans and animals (a stroke was originally a fairy stroke) or changes in the weather (whirlwinds are troops of fairies passing by), for affecting the fertility of fields and livestock, and for having a particular interest in human children, whom they may kidnap or otherwise harm. Both fairies and witches are believed to be predominantly female, and congruent with their association with matters of fertility, many stories deal with the consequences of a man marrying a woman who turns out to be a fairy (positive) or a witch (negative). In some cases in early modern Europe it appears that human women may have formed groups that were believed to mirror in the mundane realm the groups of trooping fairies believed to inhabit the supernatural realm. These trooping fairies are headed by a figure known as Herodias, Herodiana, Perhta, or Holda, suggesting a continuity with classical and northern goddess figures. Fleeting references in medieval texts, such as Regino von Prüm's tenth-century *De ecclesiasticis disciplinis* and Burchard of Worms's eleventh-century *Decretals,* to groups of deluded women who followed "Diana" suggest that this belief may also have existed in the Middle Ages.

Fairies are believed to inhabit liminal zones: in the wilderness they are encountered in the parts of the forest where people go to pick berries or gather firewood; in the domestic realm they live in barns and outbuildings or enter the house at night when humans sleep. Many fairies are found living in or near water: wells, lakes, fountains, streams, or the ocean. Other fairies are found in mountains or dwelling within the "hollow hills" that often are Neolithic burial mounds. Thus, fairies belong not to places that are completely shut off from human access but to places that are incompletely incorporated into the mundane world, places where animals or fish (sources of food) dwell, places where humans no longer dwell, places where humans venture to collect goods (such as berries and firewood) that are not cultivated but found by the bounty of nature.

Names and Traits of Fairies
The names of fairies vary from locale to locale. Perhaps the most famous are the Irish Tuatha Dé Danann (Tribes of the Goddess Danu) or people of the *sidh,* or fairy mound. In Wales they are the Tylwyth Teg (the Fair Tribe) or Plant Rhys Ddwfn (Children of Rhys the Deep). English fairies have more names that can be listed in one breath: boggarts, brownies, greenies, pixies, knockers, lobs, hobs, and lubberkins. The French call them *fées,* the Bretons *Korrigans.* In Sicily there are the *donas de fuera* (ladies from outside). In the Balkans the main word is *vila;* in Russia *rusalka;* in Greece the classical *nereid,* originally a water sprite, has expanded to cover all fairylike beings.

Many of the names of fairies are euphemistic, often translating merely as "they." Other euphemisms mean things like "the Gentry," "the Fair Ones," "the Good Ones," "the Mothers." Tomás Ó Cathasaigh has pointed out that in Irish, *sidh* is the term used to name both "dwellings of the fairies" and "peace." He proposes that the name for the otherworld and those who live there is a reflection of the state encountered there, for the land of the Irish fairies is preeminently a land of peace and plenty. Good relations with the otherworld on the part of the king extend this state to the mundane realm. Likewise, the Welsh Tylwyth Teg may be "fair" in the sense of "beautiful" or "light-skinned and blonde," but *teg* also has the sense of "fairness, justice," qualities that are believed to mark the otherworld and its inhabitants. At the same time, names of fairies often refer to "fairness" in the sense of whiteness, and whiteness and luminescence are typically associated with the alternate reality of the otherworld.

The fairy realms are also marked by temporal distortions. An hour with the fairies is a century at home. Many mortal heroes, such as the Irish Oisín, tarry with fairy women only to discover, when their homesickness grows too much to bear, that they themselves have become the stuff of legend. Either eating mortal food or setting foot on mortal soil returns them from eternity to chronology, and their bodies crumble to the dust that they should have become.

Fairies are shapeshifters. In Celtic traditions

their most common guise is as water birds: Caer, the love of the god Oengus, spends alternate years as a swan or as a maiden; Mider and Étain become swans as they escape the mortal Eochaid; the father of king Conaire Mór appears as a bird but takes off his bird skin and assumes the shape of a man to sleep with Mes Buachalla; and his "people" are birds who ride on the waves of the sea. Water birds, like fairies, are multivalent creatures since they can live on land, air, and water. But fairies also take the forms of deer, bulls, wolves, dogs, eels, worms, or even flies.

Fairies, then, are preeminently Other. They are tiny or huge, compared with humans. They are primarily female, when seen through the eyes of a male-dominated society. They live in all the places where humans go but do not stay and are most active at the times when humans are asleep or in a liminal state (giving birth, about to be married, intoxicated). Yet they also look like humans, can mate with humans and produce viable offspring, and live socially under a monarchy. They enjoy food and drink and music, nice clothes and jewels, and value gold as highly as any human. They are both more and less, both seen and unseen, both canny and uncanny.

Most material collected on fairies dates from the early modern period. Medieval sources are patchy at best, but every element of modern fairy lore seems to make at least a cursory appearance in the medieval period. There are references to the Wild Hunt as early as the *Anglo-Saxon Chronicle* in 1127, a troop of unhallowed souls led howling through the night sky by the fairy king (Gwynn ap Nudd, Odin, Herla, Wild Edric). The great French romances of the twelfth century draw upon fairy beliefs for literary ends but probably do not tell us as much about folk belief as they do about elite concerns. Fairy women in the romances can be seen as anima figures, initiating the hero into his proper place in society. They may also be seen as "shattered jewels" of former goddesses, classical or Celtic.

Fairy Women

Many of these medieval fairy women are ancestor figures. Melusine, half woman, half snake, whose legend predates the fourteenth century, was the progenetrix of the French house of Lusignan and was said to appear to announce the death of each lord until the castle itself was destroyed (see illustration). The Lady of Llyn-y-Fan-Fach in Wales was the mother of the famed Meddygyon Myddfai, a family of physicians who claimed to have learned their healing skills from their fairy ancestress in the twelfth century. Both Melusine and the Lady were typical fairy brides, who married a mortal under certain conditions that he must not break under pain of losing her. Inevitably the conditions are broken (Melusine is seen in her snaky form, the Lady is struck three times without cause), and the fairy must return to her otherworldly habitation. Nonetheless, the fairy bride

still visits those she left behind her, to announce a death or to teach her children, becoming a medium of communication between the supernatural and the mundane worlds. A similar fairy bride is the woman Macha in the Irish story of the "Debility of the Ulsterman," a precursory tale to the epic *Táin Bó Cúailnge* (Cattle Raid of Cooley). Here the taboo is against her husband speaking of her; when he boasts of her swiftness before the king of Ulster she is forced to run a race against the king's fleetest horses even though she is heavily pregnant. She wins the race but dies giving birth to twins and puts a curse on the Ulstermen: in their times of greatest need they will be afflicted with pangs of childbirth for nine days. This Macha is perhaps closest to an identifiable goddess, for Macha is also a name of one of the three forms of the Irish war goddess, the Morrigan. It should be noted that all these tales of fairy brides are marked by a state of "either/or": Melusine is both woman *and* snake and gives birth to deformed children; the Lady of Llyn-y-Fan-Fach is won through an offering of bread that is neither raw *nor* cooked; and Macha curses men to feel the pains of women in labor, placing them in a status between genders.

Fairy Realms

The land of the fairies is often represented as being within or under the earth. The Tuatha Dé Danann are closely associated with the fairy mounds of Ireland, and whereas stories set in the earliest days locate gods in the mounds—Oengus with Brugh na Boyne, Mider with Brí Léith—later stories call the mounds' inhabitants fairies. The fourteenth-century romance of *Sir Orfeo* represents the fairies who have kidnapped Queen Meroudys as living within the earth in a fair country reached through a cave. Gerald of Wales, in his *Itinerarium Cambriae* (based on a journey through Wales in 1188), tells the story of Elidyr, a priest who as a young man was met by two small men who took him underground to a wealthy country where the sun never shone but the people were beautiful and fair—both blonde and just. They worshipped nothing but the truth. Elidyr traveled happily back and forth between his land and the fairies' until his mother incited him to steal some gold for her. He tried to make off with a golden ball but was caught in the act, chased out of fairyland, lost the ball in his escape, and was never able to find his way back. The green children, said to have appeared during King Stephen's reign and recorded in the chronicles of Ralph of Coggeshall and William of Newburgh, claimed to have come from a subterranean land where there was no direct light and the people were all of a light green color. The boy and girl, who were found in a pit in Suffolk, lost their greenness over time. Like the fairies met by Elidyr, the green children seemed to be vegetarians, living only on beans. Elidyr's fairies spoke a language like Greek, and the green children initially spoke an unintelligible tongue. The boy eventually died, but the girl lived and learned English and was able to tell their story.

Though the green girl claimed that her native land was called "St. Martin's Land" and its inhabitants were Christians, as a general rule fairies are not believed to subscribe to the Christian faith. Chaucer, in "The Wife of Bath's Tale," depicts the fairies as being driven out of their haunts by the prayers and incessant blessings of itinerant priests. Indeed, from the earliest mentions of fairies, they are always already on their way out, whether driven by ethnic invasion in the legendary history of Ireland, religion in the medieval and early modern ages, or technology in the industrial and postindustrial eras. But they have never disappeared altogether.

See also: Annwfn; Celtic Mythology; Fairy Lover; Gerald of Wales; Map, Walter; Maxen Wledig; Wild Hunt

—Leslie Ellen Jones

Fairy Lover. A supernatural figure of medieval legend and romance, who engages a mortal in sex, love, or marriage (motifs F300–F305).

Occasionally the male fairy is a rapist—like the fairy knight in *Sir Degaré* (English, fourteenth century), who forces himself upon a king's daughter when he finds her alone in the woods—or an abductor, like the king of Faerie (the fairy realm) in *Sir Orfeo* (English, fourteenth century), who seizes Orfeo's wife as she sleeps beneath a tree and spirits her off to his otherworld. Occasionally the female fairy is at least at first the unwilling target of a mortal man's advances, as in *Thomas of Erceldoune* (Scottish, fifteenth century). But most often, in the romances at least, a strong mutual attraction binds mortal and fairy.

Many fairy-lover tales feature a command or taboo that the mortal must obey in order to preserve his or her relationship with the fairy. The greater number of taboos entail secrecy and involve the speech of the mortal (motif C400). In Marie de France's twelfth-century poem *Lanval* the hero is forbidden to speak of his fairy mistress to King Arthur's court; Wild Edric, central figure of a twelfth-century British legend, must promise never to reproach his fairy wife because of her sisters; and Thomas of Erceldoune is forbidden to talk to the inhabitants of Elfland save for the Fairy Queen (C715.1). Other conditions imposed by otherworldly lovers include time or place taboos, such as Melusine's restriction on her husband never to visit her on Saturday, and conduct taboos, such as the restraint on the mortal husband in Walter Map's "The Fairy of Fan y Fach," who is forbidden to strike his fairy bride with a bridle. Other types of tests and restrictions also appear in the fairy-lover tales. For example, Sir Orfeo wins back his wife from the Fairy King by impressing the king with his harp-playing skills.

The fairies of the fairy-lover tales generally take one of two forms. They are either fairy nobility (such as a fairy king or queen) or they appear at times to be part animal or monster and part human. Tales involving a fairy king or queen center on the abduction (whether voluntary or involuntary) of a mortal, who generally possesses some extraordinary quality. The abductees tend to be nobles—for example, the wife of Sir Orfeo—or bards who excel at their craft, as in *Thomas of Erceldoune*. When the fairy is part monster or animal, the mortal lover is also often noble—for example, the king who marries the monstrous Melusine (French tales call her half serpent; Norman versions call her half dragon).

Except in Irish tradition, where male fairies abound, female fairies significantly outnumber males in surviving medieval texts, romances in particular. This may offer some explanation of the generalized gendering of fairies as female in the Middle Ages, as in the Arthurian legends' classifications of Morgan le Fay as "fairy" and Merlin as "demon." Even the Wife of Bath, in the introduction to her tale in which she laments the disappearance of the fairies of King Arthur's day, distinguishes the fey "elf queen" from the masculine-gendered "incubus."

Also revealed in the fairy-lover variants is the apparent belief that the contact between a fairy and mortal may produce children (F305, offspring of fairy and mortal). Belief in the generation of "fey blood" in mortals led a number of families, such as the Lusignans of Poitou and the Meddygyon Myddfai of Wales, to claim fairy ancestresses for their line. Most notable and far-reaching is the tale of Melusine, the grande dame of the house of Lusignan:

King Elinas of Albany (Scotland), after the death of his wife, found refuge in hunting alone. One day, he approached a fountain where he found a woman named Pressia singing. He at once fell in love with her, and she consented to marry him on the condition that he never visit her at the time of her lying-in. Later, she gave birth to triplet girls, Melusine, Melior, and Palatina, and the king, forgetting his promise, rushed to her side, where he found his wife bathing the babies. The moment she realized he was there, she snatched up the daughters and vanished. Taking refuge at Cephalonia, the Hidden Island, Pressia showed Albany to her children every day, explaining that had their father kept his word, they would be happy there together. The triplets swore revenge, and led by Melusine, they enclosed King Elinas's holdings. Pressia was displeased and punished Melusine by turning her into a serpent from the waist down. The infliction would periodically plague her until she could find a man who would marry her under the condition of never seeing her on a Saturday. Raymond of Poitou agreed to marry her under these conditions, and the couple fell deeply in love. With her fairy wealth, Raymond built the Castle of Lusignan. The couple had a joyful marriage. Their children, however, were always deformed at birth. Raymond's cousin suggested to him that Melusine had another lover, whom she met on Saturdays when he was forbidden to see her. To prove or disprove her loyalty, Raymond hid behind the arras the following Saturday, only to see Melusine emerging from her bath with the body of a serpent. He decided that he would keep his knowledge a secret. When Melusine tried to comfort her husband after one of their children set fire to the Abbey of Melliers, however, Raymond reproached her: "Get out of my sight, you pernicious snake! You have contaminated my children!" Melusine fainted. When she recovered she cursed the lords of Lusignan to hear her wailing voice before their deaths, and she disappeared through a window. (See illustration.)

This tale, the *Chronique de Mélusine*, composed by Jean d'Arras at the end of the fourteenth century, features not only sexual contact between a mortal and a fairy but also the fairy's half-human, half-animal form and the common taboo pattern. Jean ends his tale with reports of recent sightings of Melusine, who reappears whenever the Lusignan's castle is about to change hands.

Mélusine was preceded by many similarly structured legends dating back to the twelfth century, although the earlier tales tended to give the "fairy" a demonic character. For example, "Long-Toothed Henno" in Walter Map's *De nugis curialium* tells of Henno's marriage to a beautiful young stranger he has found on the coast of Normandy. The couple have several children and live in happiness until Henno's mother notices that the mysterious bride avoids holy water and does not take communion. Henno spies on her and sees her in the form of a dragon. He then joins forces with a priest, and the two sprinkle her with holy water, which causes her to disappear shrieking.

In both romance and legend a love relationship with a fairy could bring special powers to a mortal. When Thomas of Erceldoune must depart from Faerie, his fairy lover endows him with the gift of prophecy. The prophecies ascribed to Thomas, like the prophecies of Merlin (also inspired by the love of a fairy), discuss the political and social climate of the British Isles and were upheld as inspired revelations of the future throughout and beyond the Middle Ages.

See also: Fairies; Map, Walter; Romance

—Sandra M. Salla

Fenian Cycle [Fianna Cycle]. Stories of Finn (Fion, Fionn) mac Cumaill and his Fianna warriors, extremely popular in Ireland, Scotland, and the Isle of Man during the Middle Ages and later.

The cycle has its roots in antiquity. The name *Finn* (written *Find* in medieval literature) is the modern form of the ancient Celtic name *Vindos* (The Bright One), and the character known to tradition seems to have developed from a general Celtic cult of a bright deity reflecting wisdom. The cult further appears to have been part of the druidic lore that centered on the Boyne River in prehistory. The warrior band called Fianna, on the other hand, derives from early young men's groups of hunter-warriors, groups that were common in Celtic culture as in the early history of many other peoples.

The words *Finn* and *Fianna* are not etymologically related, and it is therefore necessary to explain how Finn in tradition came to be the leader of such a band. There is no real evidence that such a connection existed in archaic Celtic lore. It is significant that Finn occurs in the earliest literary sources (beginning in the sixth century C.E.) in a distinctly Leinster context, and it has therefore been suggested that the loss of the Boyne valley by the Leinstermen caused them to use the seer cult of Finn as a spur to their young warriors to attempt to regain that rich and fertile territory. This would have caused the personage Finn to be intimately linked to Fianna lore in the Leinster of that period. It is significant that tradition always claims that Finn's headquarters was on the Hill of Allen in County Kildare, which was probably a sacred site of the pre-Christian Leinstermen. The sources show, nevertheless, that by the eighth and ninth centuries stories of Finn and his Fianna had already spread to other parts of Ireland, and we may surmise that accounts were reaching Scotland and the Isle of Man by that time also. There are also traces of Finn in medieval Welsh literature, which in several cases exhibits early Leinster influence.

Finn is at all stages of tradition as much a seer as a warrior, and he has a distinctive way to gain knowledge of past, present, and future: by placing his thumb in his mouth and chewing it. This, and the perpetual theme of youth in the lore concerning him, may have their origins in ancient druidic lore of a child deity. The Fianna focus of the lore is also clear, however, from the early stories, in which he features as a typical youth, frequently engaging in armed combat with other young men, especially concerning women. As the lore gained impetus from repeated oral telling, particular companions became the highlighted members of his troop: these included the swift runner Caoilte, the handsome young warrior Diarmaid, and Finn's son Oisín. The twelfth century was a watershed in the development of this lore, for at that time biographies of Finn were assembled and a whole new format was given to the corpus of the lore.

The accounts of Finn's youth record that he was born after his father Cumall was killed in battle, that as a boy he had to be reared in the wilderness for fear of his father's enemies, that he obtained wisdom by accidentally gaining the first taste of the Boyne salmon, and that he regained his father's position of leader of the Fianna of Ireland by saving the royal citadel of Tara from a ferocious fire-breathing phantom. When he ascended to the position of leadership, he was reconciled to Goll mac Morna, the incumbent leader who had slain Cumall. Goll proved to be a brave and honorable colleague to Finn, but the fact that he had killed Finn's father was a continuing source of insecurity within the Fianna. Storytellers exploited this dramatic tension to the full, describing many savage outbreaks of fighting between the two and their supporters.

The new format for the lore came from a long and varied text entitled *Acallam na Senórach* (Dialogue of the Ancients, or Conversation of the Old Men). This used the popular medieval theme of pagan worthies being posthumously baptized by Christian saints, but in this case Oisín and Caoilte were described as survivors after all the rest of the Fianna had died. They met the missionary St. Patrick and brought him on journeys throughout Ireland, describing the deeds performed at the different sites by Finn and his warriors of old. The text used much earlier material but did not hesitate to invent where necessary, and it thereby gave impetus to the growing fashion of composing new Fianna narratives. Nature poetry had already become a staple of Fianna lore, reflecting the fact that Finn and his companions often lived in the wilderness, and in the twelfth century this poetic impulse was developed into the composition of narrative lays consisting of loosely rhymed quatrains. These lays were usually couched in terms of the debate between Patrick and Oisin, and they told of great single combats, hunts, and adventures of the Fianna abroad as well as in Ireland. The composition of Fianna lays continued all through the later Middle Ages and down to recent times. They were chanted and frequently passed into oral tradition. They were particularly popular in Scotland, where they were in greater demand than even the prose stories.

It is remarkable how certain basic themes are continually reworked within the Fenian cycle. Such themes as the conflict between youth and age; the restoration of ladies, children, or even warriors abducted by human enemies or by supernatural beings; and the personal conflicts between members of the Fianna were played upon by storytellers with a great range of variety and with elaborate background detail. Tales of massive battles fought by the Fianna against foreign invaders owe much to the Viking wars of the Middle Ages, while accounts of Finn's adventures in love were indebted to late-medieval accounts in other languages of Arthur and Charlemagne.

Certain stories, however, were transmitted through the centuries in comparatively stable form. The story of Finn's betrothal to Grainne and of her love for the younger Diarmaid was being told as early as the eighth century C.E. and continued to be popular throughout the whole Gaelic world, as medieval storytellers made much of the tragic death of Diarmaid brought about by Finn's rather uncharacteristic jealousy and lust for vengeance. Another story, which appears to have been current from the tenth or eleventh century, is allegorical and is thought to have influenced (through Viking contacts) the medieval Norse myth of Thor's visit to the dwelling of Utgarda-Loki. We are told that Finn and some of his men once visited a strange house, where they failed to control a vicious ram and where a beautiful young lady refused Finn's advances. The ram could only be subdued by a doddering old man who lived there, and it was later explained to Finn that the ram was the world, the old man was time, and the beautiful maiden was youth.

The cycle was enriched in the Middle Ages by several plots borrowed from international folktales. Whereas the story of how Finn gained wisdom from the Boyne salmon belonged to ancient lore of seer-craft, the actual plot—which has him unwittingly getting the first taste of the salmon intended for another person—closely parallels episodes of AT 673 (an international plot concerning the eating of a white serpent). Most influential was a series of international plots concerning marvelous helpers (AT 513, AT 570, and AT 653). These plots must have been attracted to Finn by accounts of his companion Caoilte, who was a stupendous runner. The helpers, portrayed as members of the Fianna or as visitors to the celebrated troop, assist Finn in such matters as gaining a wife, winning his freedom from captivity, or recovering babies stolen away by a giant.

The ultimate origins of the Finn persona in druidic practices exerted its influence on stories of him at all stages. One early source describes him as having a multicolored cloak enabling him to change his shape at will, and others tell of his visits to tumuli, cairns, and underground caverns in which he either gains special information or overcomes monstrous beings. From the thirteenth century onward such traditions developed, through combination with accounts of great battles won by the Fianna, into stories of how Finn and his companions had to attack and destroy sinister dwellings where some of their people had been enticed to a feast and then made captive. Folklore further rationalized this by claiming that the Fianna, though confined to hell as war-like pagans, conquered the devils and fought their way to freedom from that terrible place!

In later centuries folk traditions portrayed Finn as a vanquisher of giants, and many hills and rocks in the landscape are associated with him and his adventures. The scope and diversity of the lore has led to his being regarded as a mirror of human character, and this is echoed by many folk saws that refer to his experiences and behavior. The influence of the cycle on modern international culture is for the most part due to the sensational but inaccurate prose-poems composed in English in the late eighteenth century by James Macpherson.

See also: Celtic Mythology; Folktale; Irish Tradition; Ulster Cycle

—Dáithí Ó hÓgáin

Festivals and Celebrations. Events, feasts, rituals, and performances enacted annually for religious purposes and to mark the rhythms of seasonal agricultural work.

The Two Calendars
The annual celebrations of the medieval laity were determined by two interlocking but by no means identical calendars, the liturgical calendar of the Church and the pre-Christian calendars of the agricultural year. When Christianity became the official religion of the Roman Empire in the fourth century it was in a position to either eliminate altogether or modify and Christianize the major Roman festivals. A most conspicuous example is the Saturnalia (December 25–31), which was absorbed into celebrations of events surrounding Christ's Nativity, along with the Kalends of January (New Years' Day), to become by medieval times the Twelve Days stretching from December 25 to January 6.

With the fall of the Roman Empire it was in the Church's interest, in its gradual conversion of Celtic and Germanic Europe, to translate important aboriginal calendar dates into Christian terms as well. Pope Gregory the Great, in a famous letter to Mellitus of Canterbury, as recorded in Bede's *Historia ecclesiastica*, outlines such a policy of appropriation and transmutation. It would be a mistake, however, to view this Christianization of the pagan calendar as a straightforward process, the product of a continuous, rational campaign. Rather, we should speak of an evolving rapprochement of the two calendars, liturgical and traditional, over the early-medieval centuries, resulting in a rich mix of festival practice wherein one might occasionally glimpse a less-than-thorough Christianization of the pagan underlay.

Such nineteenth-century German mythographers as Wilhelm Mannhardt and Jacob Grimm, early-twentieth-century British folklorists of the Cambridge School, and followers of James G. Frazer, author of *The Golden Bough* (1890), are all too ready to find fully intact "pagan survivals" in medieval and Early Modern annual celebrations. More recent titles, such as *Saints, Successors of the Gods* (1932), by Paul Saint-Yves, betray an almost romantic attachment to the idea of an undying paganism. Today, however, only the most uncritical New Age enthusiast can subscribe to the theory of a vibrant, coherent paganism existing in the Middle Ages in opposition to the "official culture" of the Church and the landlords. The reality is far more complex and elusive, resisting such easy generalizations.

Our model for European popular belief of the early Middle Ages should be the hybrid and eclectic Christianity readily observable in the indigenous populations of Mexico or Peru. There one cannot speak of "Aztec," "Mayan," or "Inca" survivals as absolutes, within an essentially baroque Christianity, but merely as components of a new, "third-term" spirituality.

Recent scholars of late antiquity/early Christianity, such as Peter Brown, have restored to a certain extent, and on a firmer historical basis, the Church's role as creative transformer of European culture rather than as simply the exterminator of pagan practices and outlook. The cult of the martyrs, for example, expanded the festival calendar without any necessary reference to the year cycle. Paulinus of Nola gives a vivid account of a fifth-century "secular" festival achieved within such a religious commemoration, that of his patron saint, Felix, whose *dies natalis*, or "birth into a higher life" (i.e., date of death) was celebrated on January 14:

> They now in great numbers keep vigil and prolong their joy throughout the night, dispelling sleep with joy and darkness with torchlight. I only wish they would channel this joy in sober prayer, and not introduce their winecups within the holy thresholds.... I none the less believe that such merriment ... is pardonable because ... their naivety is unconscious of the extent of their guilt, and their sins arise from devotion for they wrongly believe that saints are delighted to have their tombs doused with reeking wine. (Poem 27)

It might not be an exaggeration to say that the most conspicuous festival of the calendar year for the average medieval agriculturalist was the parish anniversary, or *kermis*. Again, this did not necessarily have any connection with the year cycle, being simply the feast day of the patron saint to whom the parish church was dedicated. It should be pointed out, though, that the majority of these took place in mild weather, taking advantage of a saint's multiple feast days for optimum community participation. Martin of Tours, for example, who was buried on November 11, also had a convenient summer feast day—July 4—that commemorated the translation of his relics. Moreover, some medieval saints of minimal historicity, such as George and Nicholas, could develop genuinely mythic dimensions without, it would seem, any "source" in a pagan pantheon. Their festivals—April 23 and December 6, respectively—often featured secular enactments, thus expanding the festival calendar. Even such a festival as Corpus Christi (Thursday after Trinity Sunday), established by the Church as late as 1311 for theological purposes, could be easily absorbed by the populace. It became the occasion for one of the most vibrant expressions of vernacular culture, the Corpus Christi pageant cycles.

The Two Halves of the Year

Though it is important to emphasize the historical as opposed to the seasonal nature of many Christian feasts, it is nevertheless also true that the Church's calendar responded at a fairly deep level to the year cycle. Advent, symbolizing the benighted era of the Old Law, took place at a time of dying back into the earth. Christ's Nativity was coterminous with the sun beginning to regain its strength after the winter solstice. Christ's death and resurrection paralleled the season of germination and flowering, and so on. Certain conspicuous saints, moreover, appear to occupy positions of importance on the year wheel—John the Baptist (June 24) at midsummer, Michael the Archangel (September 29) near the autumnal equinox, and so on. The Irish St. Brigid's multiple parallels with the ancient Celtic fire festival of February 1 seem more than just coincidental, and All Saints' Day and All Souls' Day (November 1 and 2) occupy the place of Samhain, the Celtic new year and feast of the dead. Europe's pagan past, then, certainly cannot be dismissed entirely from the equation, however difficult it might be to prove "survival" in specific instances.

The Church year, moreover, breaks into two large segments in roughly the same way the agricultural year does. After Pentecost or Whitsun (40 days after Easter) the liturgical year no longer paralleled the career of Christ on earth. The 23 Sundays after Pentecost, a period relieved by very few major feast days, corresponded to the months of intensive labor in the agricultural year, when major secular festival activity was likewise minimal. We can thus speak, in gross terms, of two half years, the "working" half and the "holiday" half. This distinction has recently been developed by French scholars, such as Claude Gaignebet and François Laroque. Within the interweaving of the two calendars we can perceive, then, areas of tension (not the same as outright opposition between "popular" and "elite") between the Church's concerns and those of the country folk.

The harvest season heralded the beginning of the holiday half of the year. A "harvest home" would feature a church service of thanksgiving, but often in tandem with archaic rituals of weaving anthropomorphic and other figures (corn dollies) from the final sheaves or felling the last sheaf by means of thrown sickles. With the grain processed and stored or brewed, and later, in November, with the herds culled, the animals slaughtered, and their meat preserved, the work of the year was over. It was a time then for feasting and particularly for recognizing the obligations of masters to men in view of their control of the winter food supply and shelter. In later medieval centuries the late autumn was the principal turnover period for hired agricultural labor and involved many such welcome or farewell feasts.

This period of plenty, however, soon had to accommodate the penitential season of Advent in preparation for Christmas, as well as the more general phenomenon of the dying of the year. Special commemoration of the dead, with consequent close proximity of ghosts and wraiths, only partially ameliorated by the Church's feasts of All Saints' and All Souls', perhaps retained a sense of the dangerous threshold represented by the pre-Christian Celtic and Germanic new years. Our Halloween is a dim survival of this period.

The conjunction of the Nativity with the winter solstice and such pagan midwinter festival periods as the Germanic Yule produced a very complex pattern of celebrations. Folkloric activity certainly flourished within the Christian mythos, from Francis of Assisi's first crèche at Greccio to the German cradle-rocking ceremonies and Epiphany star-singers. But also within the Yuletide season of feasting, storytelling, and gambling, masquerades could take on a decidedly non-Christian character. Repeated early Church prohibitions, evidently unsuccessful, against animal-masking (stags and bulls particularly) at the New Year have been conveniently collected by E. K. Chambers in his *Mediaeval Stage*. Wild Men and other menacing grotesques were popular in later medieval Yuletide assemblies. The late-medieval development in German-speaking areas of a *Ruprecht* figure— a devilish figure dressed in black—as shadow to the gift-giving, child-oriented St. Nicholas epitomizes the dichotomies of the Season of Peace. The piquant "sport" of King Arthur's Christmas was, we might recall, the beheading game of a gigantic Green Knight.

The Twelve Days of the Christmas–New Year–Epiphany season, moreover, developed pronounced "rituals of inversion" for which we may legitimately use the Bakhtinian adjective *carnivalesque*. These cannot be solely accounted for by reference back to the Roman Saturnalia festivities in which masters and slaves switched places. They appear rather to be sui generis, developing even within the walls of the Church itself in the famous *festa asinorum* (Feast of the Ass) or *festa stultorum* (Feast of Fools), which were in the hands of the minor clerics, especially in some French cathedral hierarchies. A less raucous but seemingly related phenomenon is the Boy Bishop ceremony in which youth and innocence invert with age and experience for a good stretch of the Christmas season, beginning either on St. Nicholas's Day or on Holy Innocents' Day (December 28). A late-medieval, bourgeois example of the type was the "King of the Bean" ceremony on Twelfth Night (January 5–6). Inverted kingdoms continued to be part of medieval school and university celebrations, with their "Christmas Princes," and so on.

Rituals of inversion reached their most intense expression in the span of three or more days known as Carnival or *Fastnacht* preceding the penitential season of Lent. Since Lent was calculated back 40 days from the movable feast of Easter (which was in turn calculated by the lunar Hebrew calendar), Carnival had no specific dates but nevertheless clearly represented an end-of-winter celebration. At the same time, however, the withered, deprived figure of Lent, a personification almost of "back winter," always triumphed over the bloated King Carnival in the mock combats so typical of the festival (see illustration). Rather late in development compared to other medieval festivals, Carnival grew to be the most conspicuous and influential manifestation of European popular culture in the period. No doubt the improvement of agricultural technology partially accounts for the development of this festival of "conspicuous consumption" at a time, in earlier centuries, when winter supplies would have been at a point of near exhaustion. It may also have expressed, indirectly to be sure, some of the accumulating spiritual tensions that would result in the Reformation. In any case, the influence of Carnival upon early modern culture is undeniable, and it remains the principal focus of contemporary scholars of popular culture. The precise *meaning* of Carnival, however, remains very much in contention between the "pagans," who follow Mikhail Bakhtin's antiestablishment bent, and the "Christians," exemplified by Dietz-Rüdiger Moser, who find it a relatively unambiguous expression of an essential Christian culture. In such a widespread and complex phenomenon, no doubt both points of view need to be creatively synthesized.

Eastertide, by contrast, is rather anticlimactic from the popular cultural point of view. The season's playful festival release from the pressures of Lent was certainly not comparable to Carnival. Nevertheless, the period is rich in festival activity involving fertility and renewal of the growing earth, quite apart from Easter-egg ceremonies, relatively late arrivals from the East. Plow processions had begun as early as the end of the Twelve Days of Christmas, and agriculturally oriented ceremonies and sports naturally dominate the spring months of March, April, and May. With the opening up of travel routes after winter we get events like the beating of the (parish) bounds, various "ridings" and local pilgrimages, and mass gatherings on hilltops. Maytide was conspicuously celebrated by the landed aristocracy in outdoor fetes with boating and music, dancing about the first violet of the spring, and various forms of dalliance, all celebrated by the great secular poets of the Romance and Germanic languages, the troubadours and minnesingers. Dalliance was also practiced on the commoners' level, with Lords and Ladies of the May and various nocturnal woodland jaunts. Rustic sports, often with a combat motif, were also a conspicuous feature of outdoor celebrations: enactments of Robin Hood and St. George and the dragon, water jousts, and so on. The creatures of the "third way" between heaven and hell, the fairies, satyrs, and so on, were also more benevolent in this season than their rough counterparts of the late autumn and winter impersonations. Adam de la Halle's late-thirteenth-century play *Jeu de la feuillée* shows an easy mingling of the fairy bands with the good burghers of Arras in their May bower.

With the great midsummer bonfires of St. John's Day (June 24), this "green" phase of the festival half year may be said to come to an end. The months of July, August, September, and October are clearly given over to the "working" half year with very few festivals of note, apart from the locally determined *kermis* celebrations, as mentioned above. In their toil, medieval agriculturalists could look forward again to a rather crowded procession of saints, Wild Men, infant saviors, were-animals, fools, cannibals, and fairies as festival "objectifications" of their complex and often conflicted worldview.

See also: Candlemas; Carnival; Christmas; Harvest Festivals and Rituals; Midsummer; Peasants

—Martin W. Walsh

Finno-Ugric Tradition. The folkloric culture of the Sámi (Lapps), Finns, Karelians, Estonians, and related peoples of the Baltic region.

Speakers of Finno-Ugric languages were well established in northeastern Europe by the Middle Ages. Occupying a vast area from central Scandinavia to the White Sea and south to the Volga, these peoples formed a wedge between the expanding settlements of Scandinavians, Slavs, Balts, and Tartars. They figure in medieval texts first as unrepentant heathens and later as subjugated tribes. Although Cheremis, Permian, and Mordvin peoples all figure in medieval sources, this entry focuses on Sámi and Baltic Finns (i.e., those Finno-Ugric peoples best attested during the medieval period).

The Sámi (Lapps) of Scandinavia and Finland lived by hunting and fishing, supplemented with small-scale sheep or reindeer herding. Life revolved around the *siida*, a collective organization of extended families residing on common lands. Families tended to migrate seasonally, sometimes congregating in a single place for winter. Clothing was made of wood, leather, fur, and birch bark.

Many Sámi legends center on outside threats to the *siida*. Accounts of marauding demons, the *Chudit*, and their defeat and legends of a vengeful creature named Staalo probably reflect early-medieval contacts with non-Sámi traders and Vikings.

The Baltic Finns (Finns, Karelians, Estonians, Ingrians, Vepsians, Votes, and Livonians) practiced shifting agriculture along the coasts of the Baltic, Lake Peipus, and Lake Ladoga. Typical crops included barley, rye, roots, flax, and hemp. Hunting supplemented the diet. No kingship system existed, but tribes banded together in times of war and maintained hill fortresses in some regions.

The ancient house was conical, made of logs inclined inward toward a central ridgepole. Rectangular log homes became the norm by the early-medieval period. During the twelfth and thirteenth centuries a Swedish-derived house type replaced the earlier Slavic cabin in western Finland and Estonia. The sauna played an essential role in both practical and ritual life.

Both the Sámi and the Baltic Finns possessed epic songs that related myths and detailed the adventures of heroes. A regular meter and alliteration stabilized texts over generations. During the Viking Age and later, songs of seagoing heroes, wanderlust, and sexual exploits arise in the genre as well. After Christianization the genre became adapted to European ballad themes and peasant pastimes. A west Finnish song details the martyrdom of the English missionary St. Henrik; an Orthodox Karelian song cycle relates the life of Christ. Lyric songs concerning the plight of orphans, daughters-in-law, and shepherds voice protest. Courtship and game songs abound as well. Advice songs codify traditional wisdom with regard to weddings. The formal features of balladry (e.g., rhyme and refrains) were not adopted until the seventeenth century. Most church music, many dances, and the violin were also postmedieval arrivals.

Pre-Christian Religion

Evidence from folksongs, combined with mentions of vanquished deities in medieval chronicles, Mikael Agricola's catalog of Finnish and Karelian gods (1551), Lutheran accounts of Sámi religion, and insights from comparative Finno-Ugric mythology shed light on the gods, cosmology, and rituals of these peoples.

In general, Finnic peoples worshipped a variety of celestial deities, most of them male, including a thunder god (e.g., Sámi Dierpmis, Finnish Ukko) and a god of the sky (e.g., Sámi Radien, Finnish Ilmarinen). In addition, people worshipped "lower-order" deities, most of them female, associated with water, forest, and home. Proper appeasement of these spirits guaranteed health and prosperity. Generalizations are difficult, however, since many gods seem to have been particular to a single community and others go by multiple names. In many cases it is unclear whether the object worshipped is a natural entity itself (e.g., the sun) or a personified deity. The Finno-Ugric practice of naming demons after the supreme deities of neighboring peoples adds further confusion.

The cosmos was formed of the earth, a celestial realm, and often multiple underworlds inhabited by deities, demons, and the dead. Dead relatives were buried in groves, and their spirits were venerated as sources of help and guidance. Women's lamentations formed part of Ingrian

and Karelian funerals and may have occurred elsewhere as well. Ritual sacrifices of livestock and bears were common to all Finno-Ugric peoples, as were beliefs in various forms of losing one's soul or of the soul's traveling. Among agrarian populations planting and harvest rituals ensured good fortune.

Shamans (Finno-Ugric *nojta, Finnish noita, Estonian noid, Sámi noaide) played important roles. Through drumming, song, or intense physical activity they induced a death-like trance, during which their soul, freed, could wander the cosmos to discover valuable information (e.g., the origin of a disease) or retrieve a lost soul. Shamans also served as cult leaders, overseeing sacrifices at sacred places and prophesying. Such activities earned the Sámi and Baltic Finns a reputation for sorcery among their Scandinavian neighbors. Adventures of shaman heroes, such as the Finnish Lemminkäinen and Väinämöinen, were preserved in folksongs. Hundreds of incantations relating the origins of iron, fire, rickets, snakes, and so on survived Christianization.

From Contact to Conquest

Sources such as Ohthere's report to the English king Alfred (892) indicate early Scandinavian trading ties with both Sámi and Finns. Finnic grave finds from the period indicate familiarity with trading centers such as Birka and with worshippers of both Thor and Christ.

As the Viking Age subsided, Finnic peoples were drawn into wider political unions. During the 1140s western Finns—the Häme people—became allied with the Swedish crown, while Karelians allied themselves with the Novgorod Empire. These alliances led to the Swedish crusade against Finland in the 1150s. Real Christianization was aided by the arrival of the Dominican Order in 1249. Dominican monasteries and convents became important channels for the spread of European saints' legends and exempla and were instrumental in recording native Finnish herbal lore.

After a series of Swedish crusades, the Karelians were finally converted to the Eastern rite through mass baptisms imposed by Duke Jaroslav of Novgorod in 1227. A thirteenth-century birch-bark text contains a Karelian prayer to Jumala (God), also called Bou (from Russian Bog, "God") and associated with jumalannuoli (God's arrow)—apparently a thunderbolt. This text reflects the syncretic nature of postconversion Christianity. By the Peace of Päkinäsaari in 1323, however, Karelia was firmly established as an Orthodox realm. Monasteries such as the one at Vellamo spread the traditions of the Orthodox church and the "northern style" of icon painting—characterized by bright colors and folk elements—developed among Slavs and Finnic Christians of the region.

Parts of western Estonia were Christianized by

the Danes in 1218. Christianity came to the rest of Estonia through the efforts of the crusading Fratres Militae Christi, or Swordbrothers, an order of German monastic knights who built castles at Tallinn (Reval) and Tartu (Dorpat). The Swordbrothers depended on taxation of the subjugated for their survival and bent the Finnic peoples of Estonia into feudal serfdom.

That the Sámi were spared such ruthless conquest during the Middle Ages probably stems from their location and willingness to comply with outside demands for trade and taxes.

With Christianity came a host of folk traditions, including etiological legends—belief tales explaining the origins of natural features, animals, and personal and places names—as well as saints' legends, witch lore, and saints'-day festivals. Their celebrations contained elements typical of Europe in general, but unique customs existed as well, some of which may reflect earlier beliefs and practices.

See also: Baltic Tradition; Shamanism

—Thomas A. DuBois

Flyting [Fliting]. An exchange of vituperation or ad hominem verbal abuse.

Descending from the Old English *flit* (strife, contention) and *flitan* (to dispute, quarrel), the word *flyting* entered into the dialect of Middle Scots popular culture, where it designated abusive speech or quarreling that sometimes culminated in legal action. Scottish court poets of the fifteenth and sixteenth centuries used "flyting" as a generic term for their poetic duels, of which *The Flyting of Dunbar and Kennedy* and *Polwart and Montgomerie Flyting* are outstanding examples. Featuring flamboyant hyperbole, verbal pyrotechnics, and vitriol not untempered by a sense of the comic, these poetic exchanges stand at the head of an enduring Scottish tradition and are responsible for the currency of the word "flyting" as a general designation for verbal duels of this kind.

The term has also been applied by scholars to an assortment of quarrels in early Germanic literature. The flyting between Beowulf and Unferth in the Old English epic *Beowulf* features heroic adversaries in the hospitable setting of a mead hall, whereas the flyting between Byrhtnoth and the Vikings in *The Battle of Maldon* pits enemies about to commence battle. Flytings in Icelandic saga, such as that between Skarphedin and Flosi (and others) at the Althing in *Njal's Saga*, belong to the feuding process around which the legal institutions of medieval Iceland were in large part built. More extravagant are the quarrels between the gods in the *Poetic Edda*, such as the squaring off between Thor and Odin in *Harbardsljod* or between Loki and the other gods and goddesses in the Lokasenna; or again, in early Celtic literature, as in the seriatim contests between Cet mac Matach of Connacht and the men of Ulster in *Scéla Mucce Meic Dathó* (The Tale of Mac Dathó's

Pig). Nomenclatures vary: Old Irish provides the word *comram*, while some scholars prefer the indigenous terms *senna* and *mannjafnaðr* in discussions of Norse literature. Whether "flyting" will win acceptance as an inclusive, cross-cultural rubric remains to be seen. In any event, the generic and historical relations between flyting and other medieval debate forms, such as the *débat* or *tenso*, still need elucidation.

Other works of medieval literature, such as the Middle High German *Wartburgkrieg*, the Middle English *The Owl and the Nightingale*, and pairs of tales in Chaucer's *Canterbury Tales* (such as "The Miller's Tale" and "The Reeve's Tale"), might productively be characterized as flytings. Similarities have further been noted between medieval flytings and the verbal dueling practices that flourished in the literatures and civilizations of the ancient Greeks, Chinese, Indians, Turks, Mayans, and others. Of contemporary relevance is the practice of "playing the dozens" among inner-city African Americans or the highly formalized poetic dueling still cultivated in the Arab world and recently transmitted through the airwaves between Saudi and Iraqi adversaries during the Iraq war of 1991.

In this heterogeneous mass of material, several fundamental definitions and distinctions can be offered. Despite its untamed appearance, flyting represents a contest mode whose rules, though usually unstated and shaped by local practice and convention, are known to the participants. As with most games, flyting as an originally oral activity (even when represented in written texts) typically transpires before witnesses and often contains mechanisms for self-evaluation, that is, for the determination of who has won and lost. What differentiates flyting from other forms of disputation, such as intellectual debate, is its personal orientation: flyting insults and boasts are targeted at the flyters themselves or at other persons (such as ancestors or kinsfolk) with whom their reputations are intertwined.

A flyting can be linked to some performance, usually martial or athletic, that is itself external to the verbal disputation, or it can be self-contained and self-fulfilling. Into the former category fall most flytings of the "heroic" type, in which warrior boasts or insults are intended to carry a contractual and predictive value on an upcoming heroic test. The dispute between Beowulf and Unferth is resolved not in words but in deeds, as Beowulf proves his heroic mettle in hand-to-hand combat with Grendel. In this way the Beowulf-Unferth flyting represents just one stage in a larger contesting process. By contrast, the "ludic" flyting—that is, one in which poetic proficiency and wit under pressure are cultivated and prized—of Dunbar and Kennedy proposes no material test by which the quarrel can be adjudicated; rather, it consummates itself as verbal display. "Heroic" flyters in combat situations, on the other hand, assign greater value to manly prowess, to whose demonstration the flyting is an elaborate preliminary.

See also: *Beowulf;* Chaucer, Geoffrey; Scottish Tradition

—Ward Parks

Folklore. The traditional, unofficial culture of communities (folk groups); the academic discipline that studies such culture.

When British antiquarian William John Thoms coined the term *folklore* in 1846 he was seeking a new name for "popular antiquities": the customs, beliefs, stories, and artifacts shared by the old-fashioned and poorer segments of society as part of their communal legacy.

To early scholars folklore was first and foremost an *item*: a proverb, riddle, song, tale, dance, custom, ritual, design, tool, or building. Items of folklore were assumed to be of great antiquity, passed down from generation to generation with little change. A second trait that early definitions focused on was folklore's strong association with certain *groups*: ethnic (for example, the Germanic Jutes who settled southeast England or the Basques of the Pyrenees, both culturally distinct from surrounding populations), religious (the southern French villagers who formed the folk cult of St. Guinefort; or Irish monks, who established a lifestyle distinctly different from monks trained by the Roman Church), regional (Scandinavia, where numerous north Germanic tribes shared many cultural traits derived from social interaction and common geographical conditions), occupational (blacksmiths, friars, minstrels), social (the upper aristocracy of northern France, or the peasants of the same region), or national (English or French, though the concept of nationhood did not become a major cultural force until the late Middle Ages).

More recently folklorists have stressed a third trait: folklore is a community-based *process*, most often involving word-of-mouth and face-to-face communication in close-knit groups, through which people express and negotiate their shared understandings, values, beliefs, and concerns. Folklore is constantly changing to reflect the changing circumstances of those who share it. Thus, contemporary folklorists reject the old assumption that lore is a fossil, passed on unaltered for generations. In any vital folk group, old traditions are continually remade in response to current conditions.

Today's folklorists also view folklore as the unofficial culture of *any group*, not just the poor or old-fashioned. No matter what their social background, such groups as families share beliefs, attitudes, gestures, and behaviors—as well as such material traditions as food preparation and crafts—that they create and reshape as unofficial expressions of group identity.

The process of folklore is both conservative and dynamic. Because such folk performers as storytellers must meet the expectations of a live audience, they present their hearers with familiar, time-tested plots, themes, and styles, ensuring that each performance owes much to the norms established by past performers and audiences. Yet because no two storytelling sessions are identical, each performance is also new and unique, reflecting the concerns of its immediate context as well as the special artistry of its teller.

Thus, to know the folkloric meaning of a tale, for example, nothing is more important than, first, knowing the community that shares it and, second, experiencing (not merely witnessing) the actual performance: the moment at which the "item" comes to life, both as the personal expression of the teller and the shared experience of the group. For this reason fieldwork—the intensive immersion in a community, through which the folklorist gets to know and share its daily life, not just its performative moments—is the single most important requirement of contemporary folklore studies. Without such firsthand experience, anything—no matter how thoughtful or how long considered—that a folklorist says about a community is guesswork. (Even with such experience, the best efforts of the most dedicated and sensitive fieldworker still cannot do justice to the complex realities of even the smallest community, but that is a limitation that anyone who studies human groups, from any perspective, must live with.)

Today's specialists in medieval folklore are denied the most important experience a folklorist must have: every single member of every community from which they may wish to learn has been dead for many centuries. There are no performances to witness, no one to listen to or watch. We have only a fraction of the material remains of these communities, and those remains heavily favor the official culture of the most powerful and wealthy. Hundreds of medieval cathedrals still stand today, but the average peasant's house stood for no more than 30 years. Thousands of papal bulls and royal edicts survive, but not one oral performance of a folktale. For most of the Middle Ages, writing—the only medium through which we can know the words of medieval people—was reserved for a relatively small and specialized segment of the population comprising principally those trained and indoctrinated in official Christian culture.

Recovering the Contexts of Medieval Folklore
Fortunately, because the folkloric process is the day-to-day, unofficial, community basis on which most other culture is based, its influence on society is pervasive. Folklore does not exist simply in oral documents; it also permeates many written sources, even within the universities, monasteries, and palaces of the Middle Ages. And occasionally even the frozen text of a dusty document will display something of the vividness of a live performance. In the late twelfth century an

anonymous monk in Cambridgeshire took the time to write a satire on the people of the neighboring shire of Norfolk, a poem in Latin, the *Descriptio norfolciensium* (Description of the Norfolkers). Anything but an official document, the *Descriptio* presents a series of numskull jokes that stereotype the Norfolker as an irredeemable idiot. This manuscript represents some of the earliest occurrences of jokes still widely told today—for example, one about a Norfolker who felt so sorry that his horse had a heavy load to bear that he shouldered the load himself—and then mounted the horse, so that it would have to carry him as well (AT 1242A, "Carrying Part of the Load"; see illustration).

We have some complete copies of this priceless expression of regional folk rivalry. But even more impressive is a partial copy of the same poem, written by a monk from Norfolk. Up to a point, the monk dutifully copies these diatribes against his own shire, but then he can take it no longer, breaks off the tale, and launches into his own performance, blasting the author of the *Descriptio* and singing the praises of Norfolk. It is possible that this response was composed at the very moment it was written down, just as a folktale is re-created anew during an oral artist's performance. The Norfolk monk may have been alone, writing silently as he composed it, or he may have spoken it as he wrote, in the company of other monks who urged him on and otherwise contributed to the performance. (Or—perhaps more likely—the performance was shaped not by the creator of either text but by the audience, a Norfolk copyist who had both complete works in front of him and who grew so angry reading the *Descriptio* that he refused to write down any more of it and proceeded immediately to copy the response. Yet even this more prosaic explanation would demonstrate the audience's enormous power in folk tradition, the power either to sustain a performer's work for generations or to consign it to oblivion.) We will never know exactly how this text came to be. The performance preserved on paper remains just a shadow of an actual folk performance, but it is nevertheless a particularly rich and deep one.

Much more often, however, medieval records of folk performance offer one sort or another of negative evidence. For example, the great majority of the copious records of the famous medieval Feast of Fools celebration are either sets of rules ordering that certain playful activities not be performed (thereby giving us good reason to think that they were indeed performed, and in defiance of the authorities) or pronouncements banning the festival altogether. Only rarely do we get an eyewitness account of an actual performance, and in not one case is the festival described by someone who approves of it.

Folkloric Studies and Sourcebooks

Because the contexts essential to understanding medieval folklore are most often fragmentary,

folklorists must be resourceful, eclectic, and rigorous. They must collect as much information as they can find and use it carefully to reconstruct as fully as possible the lifestyles and value systems of past societies. Historians of unofficial culture, some identifying themselves as folklorists and some not, have marshaled diverse written records and archaeological evidence to supplement or substitute for oral traditions. In *Montaillou: The Promised Land of Error* (1978) Emmanuel Le Roy Ladurie artfully rereads testimony from the trials of accused heretics and finds beneath the official veneer of these documents a wealth of evidence from which he is able to describe the home life, social relationships, sexual practices, funeral customs, and folk religion of a thirteenth-century French village. In *Medieval Popular Culture* (1988) Aron Gurevich sifts through saints' lives, penitential manuals, clerical tracts, and other Latin sources to find evidence of a folk culture (possessing unique conceptions of time, symbolism, morality, and the afterlife) alive in the midst of elite clerical culture. In *Medieval Marriage: Two Models from Twelfth-Century France* (1978) Georges Duby examines annulment proceedings, clerical tracts on marriage, family histories of noble houses, and archaeological records to reconstruct the attitudes and customs surrounding sex, marriage, gender roles, and family values shared by the upper aristocracy of northern France. In *Earnest Games: Folkloric Patterns in The Canterbury Tales* (1987) Carl Lindahl employs slander records, courtesy books (that is, a manual teaching appropriate behavior), coroners' rolls, and Chaucer's poetry to reconstruct folk techniques of indirect insult employed in fourteenth-century England.

As a rule, it is far easier to recover a broad social context for a medieval song or tale than to situate an actual performance. To get a sense of the style, content, and meaning of any one poorly described festive enactment or written approximation of a folktale, it is especially important to look at as many related examples as possible. Items of folklore are available to medievalists in many extensive collections. E. K. Chambers's *Mediaeval Stage* (1903)—though outdated as a theoretical statement—remains useful as a compendium of records related to minstrel performances, mummings, interludes, Feast of Fools enactments, and other medieval rituals and entertainments. Lütz Röhrich's *Erzählungen des späten Mittelalters* (Tales of the Late Middle Ages, 2 vols., 1962) brings together late-medieval folktales from Latin and vernacular prose and verse and sets them alongside oral tales collected centuries later from peasant narrators, allowing readers to learn something of the continuities and differences between these two vastly different cultural contexts. Roger Vaultier's *Folklore pendant la Guerre de Cent Ans* (Folklore during the Hundred Years' War; 1965) presents a catalog of pilgrimage activities, seasonal festivals, and rites of passage mentioned in certain French legal documents. Though it presents many unsupported theories, Claude Gaignebet's and Jean-Dominique Lajoux's *Art profane et religion populaire au moyen âge* (Secular Art and Folk Religion in the Middle Ages; 1985) is a virtual encyclopedia of the secular beliefs, tales, gestures, and customs represented in visual form in French sculptures and carvings.

Although any one of these records, taken alone, may reveal little about the meaning of a folkloric performance in its original context, we can nonetheless learn much by viewing the records together, creating a multitextual context, allowing us to discover what is especially important or unique about any given text by learning how it differs from the others. Medievalists can best benefit from such sources by first considering some of the leading premises, methods, and tools developed by folklorists.

Patterns and Variations

Because folklore tends to combine stable, long-lived patterns with the needs and nuances of its immediate context, such forms as folktales present an excellent medium for studying intercultural variation as well as change over time. For example, certain British stories of outlaw heroes spanned a period of centuries, during which time they told of the Anglo-Saxon resister Hereward (eleventh century), the Scottish rebel William Wallace (thirteenth century), and the legendary yeoman Robin Hood (fourteenth century or earlier). The plot of one of the tales told about Hereward in the twelfth century is also found in fifteenth-century tales of Wallace and Robin Hood: the hero befriends a lowly potter, borrows his clothes, and uses this disguise to infiltrate enemy territory, where he embarrasses his chief enemy (William the Conqueror, for Hereward; Edward I of England, for Wallace; and the Sheriff of Nottingham, for Robin Hood).

The traits shared by all three groups of stories allow us to say something about the nature and function of medieval English outlaw legends in general. In all cases the stories arose in the midst of domestic unrest, and the outlaw hero emerged to represent the values of groups alienated from and threatened by the dominant power structure. By aiding the oppressed at the expense of the oppressors, the outlaw hero represents a rejection of the dominant culture and the assertion of the moral superiority of the underdog.

Yet, more specifically, the differences between the outlaw heroes reveal something of the social climate in which each emerged. Hereward is an Anglo-Saxon earl allied with Anglo-Saxons of lower social standing against the Norman occupation. His stories show the English side of an ethnic conflict and a rejection of the values of the new French-speaking rulers. William Wallace plays a similar role for Scottish patriots resentful of English rule, as the hero and his poor followers

continually outsmart and embarrass the numerically superior English. Robin Hood unites yeomen and dispossessed nobles against Church leaders and corrupt members of the upper aristocracy, thus revealing the common concerns of minor landowners and tradespeople threatened by the entrenched interests of the most powerful landlords and lawmakers.

As similar as these groups of outlaw legends are, each can be located in a different general social context, a context that is "truer" than the events of the story. Hereward and Wallace were flesh-and-blood outlaws; Robin Hood probably was not. The specific legends just discussed almost certainly do not represent actual events. Like so much folklore, these tales are older than the events portrayed; their truth lies in the ways in which they are molded to reflect the concerns of the tellers.

Medievalists using tales to document social contexts should know as many intercultural versions of a tale as possible. That knowledge will help them discover what is unique to the region, period, group, or individual performer under study. Such international catalogs as Antti Aarne's and Stith Thompson's *Types of the Folktale* (1961) and Thompson's *Motif-Index of Folk-Literature* (6 vols., 1955–1958) help researchers find variants of internationally distributed narrative plots. Although both indexes incorporate a great deal of pre- and postmedieval folklore, they are invaluable tools for the study of the traditions of the Middle Ages.

Other indexes present exclusively medieval material, although these tend to be limited to one specific genre or culture. Among the most important for their respective areas are Gerald M. Bordman, *Motif-Index of the Middle English Metrical Romances* (1963); Tom Peate Cross, *Motif-Index of Ancient Irish Literature* (1952); D. P. Rotunda, *Motif-Index of the Italian Novella* (1942); and F. C. Tubach, *Index Exemplorum* (1969), a catalog of 5,400 late-medieval exempla (tales told for moral purposes) circulating in clerical communities throughout late-medieval Europe.

Close Comparative Studies

In comparative folklore studies, the more similar two items of lore, the more significant the differences between them. For example, any item of folklore will possess at least three kinds of style: generic, cultural, and individual. In order to identify significant differences in the cultural styles of two different groups or periods, one must first minimize the generic and individual variables of the texts under study.

To illustrate: different forms, or genres, of folklore are told for various purposes and according to differing rules (their "generic styles"). The exemplum, for instance, is a moral tale—sometimes fictional, sometimes believed to be true—told most often by religious specialists to reinforce moral and spiritual precepts. The belief legend, on the other hand, is a narrative or a debate that tests the limits of belief. The contents of exempla and legends overlap considerably, and the two forms often blend together, yet they tend to differ significantly in function and style. In the second half of the thirteenth century, in the north of England, an Anglo-Norman author composed *Manuel des pechiez* (Manual of Sins), a collection of exempla, each of which concludes with a moral illustrating appropriate Christian behavior. The tales of the *Manuel* are told as true, but the truths that it intends to illustrate are moral and doctrinal truths. On the other hand, in his *Journey through Wales* and *Description of Wales*, Gerald of Wales (c. 1146–1223) relates many belief legends concerning strange events that defy orthodox explanation. We learn from Gerald that such tales actually circulated among his Welsh contemporaries, who told them to illustrate their notions of ways in which the supernatural was manifested in their lives. Although the received Christian doctrine of Gerald's time denied that humans had the power to foretell the future, Gerald told legends about Welshmen with prophetic powers and attempted to reconcile these stories with official Church precepts. Gerald's stories and explanations tell us much about the overlaps, differences, and conflicts between Welsh folk belief and Christian orthodoxy in the twelfth century.

Both the *Manuel des pechiez* and Gerald's stories are valuable sources of medieval folklore, but to compare them with the intent of finding differences between twelfth-century Welsh and fourteenth-century English folk beliefs is to compare apples and oranges: the *Manuel*'s exempla are framed and presented as spiritual truths, while Gerald's legends are actual records of orally circulating legends that show us much about how the people of twelfth-century Wales used stories to express and negotiate their concerns about the nature of their world and the supernatural forces believed to inhabit it. These generic differences are too great to allow significant cultural distinctions. Robert Darnton's *Great Cat Massacre and Other Episodes in French Cultural History* (1984) commits a similar error in trying to reveal differences between French and English folk cultures through a comparison of French märchen and English nursery rhymes.

Yet by comparing two more-similar texts, a folklorist can learn a great deal. In 1303, about 40 years after the *Manuel des pechiez* appeared, the Englishman Robert Mannyng wrote *Handlyng Synne*, a direct translation of the *Manuel* yet at the same time an entirely new work, which addresses a lower-class English-speaking audience rather than the elite French-speaking community of the same district, for whom the author of the *Manuel* wrote. Here are two texts from the same area, between which we can establish a direct connection, and the contrasts between them are very striking. Yet in comparing just two texts it is important to ask if the differences between the two represent something more general than the individual stylistic differences between the two authors.

Mannyng relates many tales not told in his original; in many cases he states that he has heard them told in his community. In other cases he translates tales from other sources, such as the famous legend of the "cursed dancers" (motif C94.1.1). This tale, which first emerged in eleventh-century Germany, tells of a raucous group of young people who one Christmas violated the sacred space of a churchyard and became stuck together, forced to dance incessantly for the following year. Mannyng expressly writes *Handlyng Synne* to appeal to "lewde" (unlearned) speakers of English, especially for those who love listening to tales while at play, feasting, and drinking ale. Thus, when Mannyng changes his Anglo-Norman source material in certain ways, we have reason to think he may be doing so not merely to express his individual style but, more important, to accommodate a different audience from the *Manuel*'s, a lower-class audience. We might thus conclude his version reflects the oral styles current among this group in his time. A close look at his changes supports this interpretation. To give just one example: Mannyng's Latin sources clearly indicate that the events related in the legend of the cursed dancers took place in Germany. But Mannyng first says this tale is as true "as the gospel" and then goes on to situate it "in this land, in England." The truth that Mannyng imparts by changing the locale is definitely not a literal truth (indeed, literally, Mannyng could be charged with lying) but an important "social truth" for legend tellers, who in medieval times, as today, intensify their stories by localizing them, making them more immediate, as if to say, "not only did this event happen, but it happened here, and it could happen to you." Localization is a widespread generic marker through which members of a legend-telling community express the idea that the story "belongs to us, and is about us."

Read against each other, the *Manuel des pechiez* and *Handlyng Synne* do indeed tell us much about medieval oral traditions, but even so, it is important to note that they *still* do not tell us about the differences between the beliefs of upper-class Normans and those of lower-class English people in northern England in the later Middle Ages, because the works accent different types of belief, in two different generic styles.

Again, finding the real cultural differences embedded in diverse folkloric texts requires researchers to take into close account variations of genre, plot, theme, context, and function and to recognize that the most telling differences are likely to emerge from comparisons of those texts that are most similar (here is where such works as *The Types of the Folktale* are particularly valuable).

Moreover, in efforts to use folklore to characterize general cultural trends, it is important to compare as many such texts as possible because every storyteller has an individual style. Cultural style becomes apparent only after one has examined the shared traits of many different tellers from the same group.

Historical Fact and Social Truth

Folklore combines two types of truth: actual historical fact and "social truth." Both types are valuable for different purposes, but they are often difficult to distinguish. For example, William Camden's *Britannia* (1586) records an oral tradition about a giant named Jul Laber buried in a mound in southern England. Camden noted that the mound stood near a battle site from Julius Caesar's invasion of Britain and deduced that it was the burial place of the Roman tribune Laberius Durus, killed in Caesar's invasion. If so, a tenacious oral tradition helped preserve the name of the tribune for more than 1,600 years. Yet this "actual fact" was combined with the social fact that the tribune had been converted to a giant, adapted to an English folk tradition of ascribing ancient Celtic and Roman ruins to giants—thus expressing a social truth important for the tellers of these tales, and for folklorists as well.

Distinguishing social truth also requires consulting as many sources of as many different kinds as possible. For example, there are five separate medieval accounts relating that the Norman jester, Taillefer, entertained the troops of William the Conqueror during their battle against the English at Hastings (1066). Only the two latest of the five accounts, beginning with William of Malmesbury's (1125), claim that Taillefer sang the *Chanson de Roland* (Song of Roland) to inspire William's army. The late date of these accounts leads us to believe that Taillefer probably did not sing the *Chanson* at Hastings, but the claims that he did may tell us something significant about the social truth of twelfth-century English aristocrats: their adoption of the *Chanson de Roland* demonstrates their continued identification with mainland French aristocratic culture long after their initial occupation of England.

Folklore as a Reflection of Its Tellers and Its Time

Folklore—though a strong indicator of the teller's worldview—may provide a very skewed version of someone else's reality. For example, legends told during the fourteenth and fifteenth centuries and summarized in such documents as the *Malleus maleficarum* (Hammer of Witches, c. 1486) claim to describe the actual practices of witches, but they are in large part retellings of older stories once used by monks to stereotype Jews and heretics. These stories tell us little about the folk practices of accused witches, but they reveal much about the fears and folk beliefs of the accusers. Again, only a thorough knowledge of earlier and international legends about witches can help

separate the claims of the inquisitors from the reality of the accused. Studies like Carlo Ginzburg's *Night Battles* (1983) apply such knowledge to transcripts from Italian witchcraft trials to peel away the outsiders' lore and to recover important information about the actual practice of folk magic and religion buried in surviving records.

As ancient as much folklore appears, the fact that it changes over time makes it a much better indicator of the present than of the past. Folklore collected in one era will not necessarily reveal the beliefs of an earlier time. This last point deserves special stress, as some of the greatest early folklore studies are based on the premise that current folklore can explain the worldviews of long-dead peoples. Jacob Grimm's *Teutonic Mythology* (1835), for instance, presents a wealth of medieval and postmedieval stories, rhymes, and customs, from which he attempts to reconstruct ancient Germanic religion. Grimm's study remains extremely valuable because it brings together so many important sources for the study of medieval Germanic folklore. Yet twentieth-century folklorists do not share Grimm's conviction that a nineteenth-century folktale can reveal much about medieval folk belief. To the contrary, the great value of folklore lies in its living, changing qualities—the ways in which it adapts received traditions to new conditions, becoming in the process both the personal expression of the individual performer and the communal property of those who share those traditions.

See also: Folktale; Legend; Motif; Myth

—Carl Lindahl

Folktale. An oral prose narrative shared by a traditional community, relatively stable in plot but varied at each telling to suit the artistic and rhetorical purposes of the teller, as well as the tastes and expectations of the immediate audience.

Some scholars use the term *folktale* very generally and literally, to designate any tale shared orally in folk communities. More commonly, however, folklorists use the term for works of oral fiction told to entertain or educate, thus separating them from *legends*, tales in which belief is a major factor and which are usually told as true, even if their truth is often debated.

This characterization of folktale presents two major difficulties to students of medieval folklore. First, as oral performance is a defining trait of the folktale, and as we cannot say for sure that any surviving written versions are verbatim transcriptions of oral performances, we could easily conclude that there are no medieval folktales available to us. There is plenty of evidence that oral storytelling was rife in the Middle Ages, but most of it is negative evidence. The pious authors of saints' lives tended to trivialize folktales, and they did not repeat them. Felix, the author of a Latin *Life of St. Guthlac* (eighth century), says of the saint, "He did not imitate the chattering nonsense of matrons, nor the vain fables of the common people, nor the stupid whining of the country folk"—a strong suggestion that there is a vital storytelling tradition in early-medieval England, but the author's scorn for the contents of these stories prevents him from telling any. More rarely, writers intimate that they enjoy oral tales: Alvar of Cordova, a twelfth-century Spanish Christian, laments the fact that his country is under the control of the Arabs, then adds "and yet we are delighted by a thousand of their verses and tales"—but note that even this satisfied listener did not retell the Arabs' stories. So we are left with certain knowledge of the importance of oral narrative in medieval Europe but great uncertainty about what the tales were or how and why they were told.

The second problem has to do with fiction. If we choose to define folktales not simply as narratives but particularly as fictional narratives, we must establish that such tales were considered fictional by the *medieval* narrators and their listeners. We seldom get such precise information. For example, in the passage cited earlier from the *Life of St. Guthlac* the author considers the country tales to be "vain fables," but it is altogether possible that the folk themselves believe them true even if the writer does not. Folklorists may—and often do—identify a medieval narrative as a folktale simply because it shares its plot with well-known oral fictions from more recent times. A classic märchen such as "Red Riding Hood" (AT 333), considered an entertaining fiction by modern readers familiar with the literary versions of Charles Perrault (1697) and the Grimm brothers (1812), may appear in a medieval manuscript, but the fact that the medieval tale resembles the modern is no guarantee that it was performed as fiction in the Middle Ages. Indeed, the earliest surviving version of "Red Riding Hood," in Latin in the eleventh century, seems to have been told as a true story. The German author, Egbert of Liège, introduces it as follows: "What I have to relate, the country folk can tell along with me, and it is not such a wonder to believe the truth."

Consider the plot of one of the most popular tales in European tradition, known and endlessly repeated from ancient Greece to twentieth-century Scotland: a monster terrorizes a kingdom, demanding an annual tribute of virgins, chosen by lot, to fulfill his lust and hunger. One year the lot falls to the king's daughter, and the desperate king offers her in marriage to anyone who will slay the monster. A hero appears, kills the monster, and then cuts out its tongue. An impostor, intent on marrying the princess and inheriting the kingdom, finds the dead monster, cuts off its head and presents it to the king, and is about to marry the princess when the hero suddenly reappears to produce the tongue and prove that he is the rightful husband of the princess.

This plot, known to folklorists as "The Dragon-Slayer" (AT 300), appears, fully or partially, in Greek myth (the story of Perseus), medieval saints' lives (including the story of St. George and the dragon) and romances (for example, the *Tristan* of Gottfried von Strassburg), as well as postmedieval märchen—for example, as the tale of the "Two Brothers" in the Grimms' *Kinder- und Hausmärchen* (Children's and Household Tales), better known as the *Grimms' Fairy Tales*. This simple plot runs a long generic gamut, from classical myth to medieval Christian legend and adult entertainment to bedtime stories for twentieth-century children. Many medieval and postmedieval narrators have presented the tale of St. George as a true story, but few if any listeners believe the Grimms' version of the same plot to be a factual account. Thus, plot outline and content alone simply cannot establish whether a surviving medieval tale is a work of fiction.

With no extant medieval oral tales and precious few written ones that we can clearly identify as fiction, today's students of medieval folklore must ask themselves what we *do* have to work with. The answer is not disappointing.

First, there is the fact that even the most sophisticated medieval writers lived in a world in which oral entertainment was the norm. Because they heard tales both told and read aloud, they tended to rewrite their literary sources much as an oral artist would retell them, changing details and emphasizing styles suitable not only to their own tastes but to the audience that would hear the tale performed aloud. For example, the fourteenth-century English poets Geoffrey Chaucer and John Gower both wrote versions of a story known to folklorists as "The Maiden without Hands" (AT 706). The two men both wrote in medieval London, for members of the court of Richard II (reigned 1377–1399). Both, unquestionably, drew upon the same source, Nicholas Trivet's *Anglo-Norman Chronicle*, written nearly a century earlier for Richard's royal ancestors. The two men's stories—Chaucer's "Man of Law's Tale" and Gower's "Tale of Constance"—resemble each other more than either resembles Trivet's. Trivet told his story as history; Chaucer and Gower told theirs more as exempla, stories shaped to fit a moral purpose. That Chaucer's and Gower's versions are so similar no doubt has much to do with the fact that they lived at the same time and in the same place and shared the same courtly audience. Yet Chaucer's and Gower's versions, though much alike, are in many ways radically different.

The supremely educated Chaucer and Gower, two of the most respected artists and thinkers of their time, have this in common with the tellers of oral folktales: both believe that *familiar stories are always the best*, that the art of storytelling lies not in surprise, surface variation, or superfluous innovation but in retelling a well-known story so well that an audience thoroughly familiar with its contents will still respond with excitement, experiencing it as if for the first time.

Another way in which Chaucer and Gower resemble oral folktale tellers is in the social breadth of their sources. In addition to their retellings of "The Maiden without Hands," both tell versions of the tale of the Loathly Lady (AT 406A, "The Defeated King Regains the Throne"). Whereas they drew their separate versions of the former from a royal chronicle, it is much more likely that they derived their versions of the Loathly Lady tale from oral traditions. Here the differences between Chaucer's and Gower's versions are intense. Their common plot rests on the question "What do women most desire?" In both tales a male protagonist must forfeit his life unless he can answer this question. In both, a Loathly Lady, an abominably ugly woman, supplies the correct answer—that women desire sovereignty in love (in Gower's tale) or unqualified sovereignty (in Chaucer's)—but the monstrous woman demands compensation for sharing her secret: the knight must marry her.

Gower presents a gentrified version of the story, with a supremely chivalrous knight as hero. Sir Florent kills a rival in fair combat and then is sentenced to his quest by the villainous mother of the slain knight. The Loathly Lady provides Florent with the answers he needs—that women desire sovereignty in love—and on their wedding night she transforms herself into a beautiful woman. Gower's story asserts that women who rule in love are beautiful and good, but women who attempt to rule in other respects—as did the villainous mother of the slain knight—are morally ugly. Gower uses the story of what women most desire to convey a predictable message of male social dominance.

Chaucer's Loathly Lady tale is told to an entirely different purpose. He places his version in the mouth of his fictional character, the Wife of Bath, an outspoken advocate of female dominance. In her tale the knight is a rapist, a criminal so unheroic that the Wife does not even deign to give him a name. King Arthur condemns the knight to death, but Guinevere and the ladies of Arthur's court intervene to teach the knight a valuable lesson rather than to kill him (the narrator's way of pointing out the greater mercy and wisdom of female rule). On their wedding night, after the Loathly Lady has saved and married the rapist, she delivers a long lecture to the effect that nobility is not a birthright but must be earned. She then asks the knight if he would rather have her be ugly but faithful to him or beautiful and unfaithful. The knight puts the decision in her hands, and when granted sovereignty, the Loathly Lady becomes beautiful at all times and rules over the knight in happiness and harmony. In this amazing performance Chaucer makes his tale suitable for the nonnoble Wife of Bath by rejecting courtly storytelling styles and values. He presents instead a popular romance in which women turn the male-dominated world upside down and establish a better one.

Chaucer is an acute practitioner of lower-class storytelling styles. His "Wife of Bath's Tale" is in some ways remarkably similar to another version of AT 406A, *The Wedding of Sir Gawain and Dame Ragnell*, a popular romance of the mid-fifteenth century. Here, Sir Gawain is the hero, and by showing himself braver and truer to his word than the cowardly King Arthur, he saves the king. Gawain's "reward" for bravery is to marry the Loathly Lady, but folktale justice prevails when she transforms into a beautiful woman. It is the heroine who provides the rewards that Gawain truly deserves, and she effectively supplants King Arthur as a fair and rightful ruler.

Thus, surviving written tales do tell us something about medieval storytelling. Though deprived of the voices of medieval narrators, we still have the means of comparing their plots and styles to illumine aspects of the artistry and worldviews of the long-dead tellers and their listeners.

Comparative Studies

Since the early nineteenth century, when the Grimm brothers pioneered the study of folktales, scholars have been intrigued by a pervasive paradox in traditional narrative: how a given plot can be simultaneously so stable and so fluid. For all their differences, oral tales current in traditional cultures throughout Europe, the Middle East, and India resemble each other remarkably. Folklorists, assuming that these widespread tales were ultimately related, devised means of classifying their plots for comparative study. One of their basic assumptions—that a plot as varied and complex as the "Dragon-Slayer" or "Red Riding Hood" would not have been independently invented but instead spread orally from teller to teller over long periods of time—is broadly supported by today's folkloric research. The more complex the plot of a tale, the more likely that the different versions share a common history and were passed on in chain-like fashion from teller to teller (although the chains are many and tangled).

Building on the assumption that all the tales of a shared plot had an ultimate oral source, folklorists further reasoned that if they amassed enough variants of a single plot, grouping the oral versions by the language in which they were told and the written versions by date, they would discover the tale's original form (urform), age, and place of origin. Investigators sharing these assumptions and methods came to be identified as the Historic-Geographic School, or the Finnish School, because the Finns Kaarle Krohn and Antti Aarne were instrumental in its development. They used the term *Märchentyp*, "tale type," to designate plots with significant international distribution. In 1910 Aarne published the first numbered catalog of such plots, *Verzeichnis der Märchentypen* (Catalog of Tale Types), which the American folklorist Stith Thompson expanded in two English editions, renaming it the *Types of the Folktale* (1928, 1961).

Using the methods and cataloging principles outlined above, folklorists began assembling versions of a given tale type and attempting to reconstruct its life history. Kurt Ranke, for example, examined more than 800 variants related to the Grimms' tale of "The Two Brothers" (AT 303), which incorporates the "Dragon-Slayer" tale type. Ranke concluded that the ultimate source of the complex tale was medieval France and that its plot has preserved a remarkable continuity in oral storytelling communities without significant influence from written versions.

Scholars now generally discredit some of the premises of the Historic-Geographic method. First, many early folklorists assumed that the tales were primarily oral and evolved independently of written versions. In their view, the medieval stories that survive in writing would be considered more or less incidental to the history of the tales. Yet from the 1920s onward Albert Wesselski and others have demonstrated that written and oral tales interacted and influenced each other significantly in the Middle Ages, a finding fully supported by twentieth-century field research by Linda Dégh and others, who observed that even illiterate narrators readily seize upon written tales read aloud to them and work such writings into their repertories, though of course they recast such narratives to suit their personal aesthetics and the tastes of their audiences.

A second objection to the Historic-Geographic School has to do with its assumption that we can establish, even approximately, the date, place, and form of origin of a given tale. Close observations of living oral traditions work against this proposition. Individual narrators are often so creative in adapting new tales that even one retelling can make certain unpredicted changes, disguising the shape of the received tale. Thousands, even millions of retellings, such as medieval tales experienced, would probably disguise the original beyond recognition or recovery. Similarly, individual communities often possess such distinctive tastes and expectations that they will demand a tale be told their way from the beginning, or they will simply refuse to listen to it again.

Swedish folklorist Carl von Sydow was among the first to reject the assumptions of the Finnish School, but he argued that their catalogs and methods were still valuable because even if they could not reveal the urform of a given tale, they could reveal much about the oikotype, literally the "home type," of a tale—a distinct form adopted to the aesthetics and values of a given culture or community. Building on von Sydow's ideas, recent folklorists have shown that significant shifts of style and structure occur as a plot shifts from culture to culture, genre to genre, or class to class. Thus, one may view Gower's and Chaucer's versions of the Loathly Lady tale as expressions of two social oikotypes, the aristocratic and popular versions of the same basic plot.

The Types of the Folktale

There are three broad subdivisions of oral prose fiction: AT 1–299, Animal Tales (treated in a separate article of that title in this encyclopedia); AT 300–1199, Ordinary Folktales; AT 1200 and above, Jokes and Anecdotes.

Ordinary Folktales are far from ordinary in content: they generally concern objects such as cloaks that render the wearer invisible, supernatural beings such as dragons, witches, and talking animals; wondrous events such as transformations of humans into animals; and extraordinary landscapes containing glass mountains, trees that stretch to the stars, rotating palaces, and so on. Such tales are generally identified as "fairy tales" by nonfolklorists because the literary adaptations of their plots—by Charles Perrault, Madame de Beaumont, and Hans Christian Andersen—are generally known by that name. But folklorists identify the oral versions as märchen (German for "little story"), or sometimes magic tales (*Zaubermärchen*) or wonder tales.

Most often the märchen focuses on a single protagonist, a boy or girl, who becomes separated from his or her family and becomes an adult through a series of adventures involving wanderings through otherworldly landscapes and encounters with supernatural beings. Such popular postmedieval tales as the "Dragon-Slayer," "Jack and the Beanstalk" (AT 328), and "Beauty and the Beast" (AT 425C) follow this general form. In many oral traditions still active in the late twentieth century, from Eastern Europe to the U.S. Appalachians, such folktales are still told with a distinctly medieval frame of reference: The hero is a knight, the heroine a princess, and combats are conducted by "champions" in armor, bearing swords.

The medieval narratives that have most in common with these recent oral tales are romances, appearing first in rhymed form in France in the second half of the twelfth century and spreading to Germany, England, Italy, and other cultures through the following century. Innumerable romances follow the general sketch given above, and a substantial number have exact analogs or major parallels in recent oral traditions: to name a few, the Middle Dutch *Torec* (cognate with AT 301, "The Three Stolen Princesses"), Chaucer's "Wife of Bath's Tale" (AT 406A, "Defeated King Regains the Throne"), the French *Yonec* (AT 432, "The Prince as Bird"), the French *Eloixe* and the Middle English *Chevelere assigne* (AT 451, "The Maiden Who Seeks Her Brothers"), the German *Rittertreue* and the English *Sir Amadas* (AT 505–508, "The Grateful Dead"), Latin and French versions of Amicus and Amelius (AT 516, "The Faithful Servant"), and the French *Belle Helene* and the English *Emare* (AT 706, "The Maiden without Hands").

Postmedieval märchen are generally identified by their formulaic frames, verbal cues at the tale's beginning, to alert the listener that the story to follow will be fanciful (for example, the English "Once upon a time …"), and end, to close the tale with a similar marker (such as "They lived happily ever after"). The closing formula often playfully suggests that the story just told may be true: "They are still alive today; this is all, and tomorrow you can have them call" or "And that is all there is to the story. Take it, or, if you don't believe it, leave it."

Medieval tales resembling märchen sometimes possess similar but briefer opening formulas: Middle English "whilom" and Latin *"quondam"* (both meaning "once") or the slightly more elaborate *"Ein man sprach ze sinem wibe …"* [A man said to his wife …], used by the thirteenth-century poet Der Stricker to begin most of his rhymed tales about marital situations. Some medieval tales play more intensively with the frame. For example, the Old Icelandic *fornaldarsaga* (saga of former times) the *Saga of Hrolf Gautreksson* ends with a formula evocative of those in modern tradition: "I think you shouldn't find fault with the story unless you can improve on it. But whether it's true or not, let those enjoy the story who can, while those who can't had better look for some other amusement."

In addition to the princesses, kings, and knights common to both medieval romance and modern märchen, the two forms also share a number of villains: giants and dragons, for example, are as easily found in romance as in märchen. Fairies abound in both medieval and modern versions, playing more varied roles: they may be lovers, villains, or helpers.

In addition to tales of magic, Ordinary Folktales embrace two other categories. In Religious Tales (AT 750–849) supernatural aid comes from figures such as Christ or St. Peter rather than from fairies, and supernatural adversaries tend to be demons rather than giants. These oral tales greatly resemble medieval exempla, and it is indeed in exempla collections that we tend to find their medieval predecessors. In the widespread modern versions of "The Wishes" (AT 750A), Christ and St. Peter walk the earth, dispensing three wishes to a pious peasant, who uses them well, and three more to a foolish one, who uses the first two poorly and must then use the third to undo the others. Medieval predecessors of this tale often include only half of the modern plot: pious exemplum literature tends to focus on the three good wishes granted the pious man, while medieval fables and jokes often develop the plot of the three foolish wishes, which are sometimes the "gifts" of a demon rather than God. A variant of the latter occurs in "Del vilein e del folet" (The Peasant and the Goblin), a rhymed tale told by Marie de France in her *Fables* (no. 57, twelfth century): a goblin visits a peasant and gives him three wishes; the peasant gives two to his wife and keeps one, a secret, to himself. They come upon a cooked sheep with its marrow bones dripping fat. The wife craves to eat the fat but

can't get hold of it, so she wishes that her husband would have a giant bird's beak so that he could get it for her. As soon as he realizes that he has been deformed through his wife's wishes, the husband uses his only wish to regain his human face. The tale ends with the third wish still unused, but Marie seems to imply that with only one wish remaining, and that in the hands of the foolish wife, the couple's future does not look good.

A third category of Ordinary Folktale is the Novella, a tale in which the magic elements of the märchen are generally missing or at least subdued. Thompson groups a good many novellas together as romantic tales; they concern themselves with situations of courtship, marriage, and love. One variation on the courtship theme is "King Thrushbeard" (AT 900), known from a thirteenth-century German poem and in other medieval texts ranging from Iceland (*Clarus's Saga*, fourteenth century) to Italy (where several versions appear). The plot concerns a haughty princess who humiliates a noble suitor; she is punished by having to marry or live with a wretched beggar or tramp. The beggar turns the tables on her by making her do degrading work until she is humbled. The beggar ultimately turns out to be the suitor (or his ally) in disguise, and the tale ends with the reconciliation and marriage of the princess and the suitor.

Many of the oral tales now known as novellas appeared first as medieval Italian *novelle* (singular *novella*, a term that in Italy referred not only to realistic tales but to legends and märchen as well). These short prose fictions began to appear in collections at the end of the thirteenth century, and in the fourteenth they gave rise to such masterful frame tales as Boccaccio's *Decameron* and Sercambi's *Novelle*. Whereas the rhymed romances of northern Europe most strongly suggest the imagery and magical atmosphere of today's oral märchen, the Italian *novelle* are the medieval tales that best evoke the oral prose styles found in today's more realistic oral fictions.

Typical of the Italian *novella* are acts of romantic deception and its inverse, steadfast love, both of which are combined in "Which Was the Noblest Act?" (AT 976), a plot rendered into writing twice by Boccaccio (in *Il Filocolo* and the *Decameron*) and once by Chaucer (in "The Franklin's Tale"). A suitor pressures a married woman to become his lover. To put him off, she says that she will sleep with him if he can perform an act that she believes impossible—such as creating a garden in the midst of winter (*Filocolo*) or making the rocks disappear from the Breton seacoast ("The Franklin's Tale"). With the help of a magician, to whom he has promised an enormous payment, the would-be lover actually accomplishes the impossible (or creates the illusion that he has). The wife resists her suitor, but her husband, discovering that she has made a promise, tells her that she must keep her word. Upon hearing of the husband's nobility, the suitor releases the wife from her promise, and when the magician hears of the suitor's nobility, he in turn refuses payment for the magic he has performed. The tale ends as the narrator asks the audience which of the characters was noblest. In Chaucer's tale no answer is given—listeners, or readers, must decide for themselves. In Boccaccio's *Filocolo*, the Lady Fiammeta delivers a judgment, finding the husband the most noble because he made no promises or bargains, yet enjoined his wife to keep hers even at the cost of his own honor.

In addition to being a *novella*, "Which Was the Noblest Act?" is also what folklorists call a dilemma tale, a story that ends with a riddle-like question that the audience must solve. Like the version of "Which Was the Noblest Act?" presented by Boccaccio in *Il Filocolo*, many medieval dilemma tales took the form of "questions of love," tales that posed romantic problems, leading to audience debates and judgments concerning the relative merits of the fictional lovers and their actions. Dilemma tales have enjoyed enormous popularity in Arabic-Islamic traditions from the Middle Ages to the present, and it is reasonable to assume that Islamic influences lie behind the dilemma tales that influenced both storytelling traditions and courtly love games in Europe from the twelfth century onward.

Jokes and Anecdotes

In this catchall category can be found a host of tales, some of them quite realistic, many obviously humorous in intent. Some, such as *Unibos* (AT 1535) and "The Master Thief" (AT 1525), exist in lengthy and complex medieval forms, but most are short fictions. Their brevity made them extraordinarily popular for use in sermons and fables, where they could summarize moral points briefly and entertainingly, as well as in the tale collections that became increasingly popular in the later centuries of the Middle Ages.

These tales generally involve trickery, concentrating on extremes of cleverness (AT 1525–1629) and stupidity (AT 1200–1349, 1675–1724), often ridiculing religious orders (AT 1725–1829) or other groups or professions (AT 1850–1874).

Typical of such short narratives is "With His Whole Heart" (AT 1186), told in diverse ways by various tellers to ridicule the greed of either lawyers, judges, bailiffs, knights, or peasants. In one fifteenth-century Swiss version, appearing in a Latin exemplum collection, a lawyer makes a pact with the devil, who has assumed a human form. They will travel together, each taking what is freely offered him, and see who gets the most. They pass a poor man trying to drive a troublesome pig. When the pauper screams at the pig, "Devil take you!" the lawyer turns to the devil and tells him to take the animal. But the devil responds that the pig wasn't really offered "from the heart." Next the travelers pass a mother berating her child: "Devil take you!" But again the devil does not take the offering, because the woman was merely speaking in anger and her words did not come from the heart. Finally, the devil and lawyer enter a town, and the lawyer is surrounded by villagers screaming, "Devil take you!" Because the villagers meant what they said with their whole hearts, the devil drags the lawyer off to hell.

This tale appears in dozens of versions. Though the writer of the above version claimed it was true and presented it as a legend, the tale most often appeared as an exemplum or as a joke. In Chaucer's "Friar's Tale," the most famous example of this plot, the Friar shapes the story as a narrative weapon to ridicule the person and profession of his enemy, the Summoner.

A substantial number of the jokes and anecdotes about married couples (AT 1350–1439) concern adultery and other sexual exploits, and they find many medieval examples in the Old French fabliaux (twelfth and thirteenth centuries) and the Italian *novelle*. Typical is "The Enchanted Pear Tree" (AT 1423), versions of which appear in thirteenth-century Latin verse fables, Boccaccio's *Decameron*, and Chaucer's *Canterbury Tales* ("The Merchant's Tale"). The following version of the plot appears in the anonymous *Novellino* (c. 1280), the oldest surviving collection of Italian prose tales: a blind man, deeply jealous of his beautiful wife, holds her near at hand. Another man, smitten by the wife's beauty, begins courting her with silent gestures in the presence of her husband. The woman concocts a plan to have sex with her suitor. He climbs into a pear tree and waits for her, she tells her husband that she has an overwhelming desire for pears, and the husband helps her into the tree. As he stands at its base, with his arms around the trunk to keep his wife from wandering off, she connects with her lover. They zestfully enjoy their long-deferred pleasure, shaking the boughs of the tree, which rain pears on the head of the husband. Christ and St. Peter look on at the scene. Peter is outraged and asks Christ to restore sight to the man so that he can see what his wife is doing. Christ replies that as soon as the husband's sight is restored, the wife will find a way to escape the consequences of her actions. When Christ allows him to see again, the husband yells angrily at his wife, but she answers immediately, "If I had not done thus with him, you would never have seen the light"—a true statement. The tale concludes with a terse moral: "And thus you see how faithful women are, and how quickly they can find an excuse."

This short tale, brief as a fable, illustrates a major difficulty in classifying folktales. If we analyze folktales according to both plot and content, as the *Types of the Folktale* does, we soon discover that individual narrators are far too flexible and creative to observe such arbitrary boundaries.

Marie's "The Peasant and the Goblin" (summarized in the previous section) is classified as a religious tale, but no representatives of Christian religion appear in her narrative, nor is a religious moral drawn. The Italian *novella* just summarized features Christ and St. Peter, and—at least in terms of its content—it is more worthy than Marie's narrative to be classified as a religious tale. However, Chaucer's version of the pear tree story places the Greek gods Pluto and Proserpine in the roles of Christ and Saint Peter and would not therefore be classified as a religious tale.

Every folktale follows some sort of generic conventions, but those conventions vary widely from group to group, place to place, time to time. Moreover, every folktale possesses a cultural style adapted to the values of the audience that enjoys it. And every well-told folktale is largely shaped by the individual style of the narrator—a fact as demonstrable for oral artists as for writers—giving rise to a variety of styles as numerous as there are great narrators, a variety that could never be captured by any catalog that folklorists could devise.

Much more knowledge of oral folktales is available from the end of the medieval period than from its beginnings. There are still no verbatim oral folktales from these later times, but there is some remarkable documentation of the sorts of stories told by common folk. The *Complaynt of Scotlande* (1547) presents a catalog of the tales told by Scottish shepherds in the first half of the sixteenth century. More than 40 specific titles appear. These poorer members of the social order are decidedly tale-rich. Some of their tales come from classical mythology: "the tale where Perseus saved Andromeda from the cruel monster," "the tale where Hercules slew the serpent Hydra that had vii heads," "the tale where Jupiter transformed his dear love Io into a cow." Some derive from the literary masterpieces and popular romances of the late Middle Ages: "the tales of Canterbury," "Lancelot du lac," "Bevis of Southamtoun." Others suggest (indeed, bear the same titles as) the oral folktales told in Scotland up to the present day: "the tale of the red etin [giant] with three heads," "the tale of the three-footed dog of Norway," and "the tale of giants that eat quick men." The world of the medieval folktale continually blurs the boundaries of oral artistry and literature, Christian religion and classical myth, realism and fantasy, belief and love of fabulation.

See also: Accused Queen; Amicus et Amelius; Animal Tale; Folklore; Frame Tale; Marie de France; Motif; Myth; Novella; Seven Sages, The; Swan Knight; Trickster; Unibos

—Carl Lindahl

Foodways. Traditional styles of food preparation and use.

What food a family (or other group, such as a monastery) ate in medieval Europe depended on a number of factors: principally religion, income, and social level; whether they lived in the country or the city; and whether their region was southern—that is, near the Mediterranean—or northern. But in general the diet was not basically very different from today's—or at least yesterday's. Bread of one sort or another, whether hearth-baked "cakes" or loaves purchased from a baker or baked in a manor house, was the staff of life everywhere. It was washed down preferably with wine in the South and by those who could afford it in the North, and otherwise with ale or, in some areas, cider or other mildly alcoholic fruit-based drinks. Milk was an alternative for those who kept cows, but it was of dubious quality in the cities, and water was a last (and sometimes unhealthy) resort.

With the bread, at least for the main meals of the day (dinner and supper), went meat, fish, eggs, cheese, or legumes such as fava beans (listed in descending order of prestige and price); they were often accompanied by such vegetables as onions, leeks, and cabbage or by salads in the summer. Pasta was popular in Italy and was sometimes served in England. Rice was grown around the Mediterranean, and during the later centuries it was imported as a luxury in the North. But pasta was not served with tomato sauce, and the available vegetables did not include peppers, both tomatoes and peppers being among the New World imports that were later to transform eating habits in Europe and elsewhere.

Regional and Seasonal Cuisine

Regional differences in food choices were similar to those found today. Pork was, of course, forbidden to Jews and to Muslims—who had a considerable impact on the culinary habits of the parts of Spain and Italy they inhabited in the early Middle Ages. For example, it was they who introduced carrots and spinach to the Western world. Olive oil was central to the cooking of southern Europe, and butter was widely used in Scandinavia and the Low Countries. Elsewhere, animal fats such as lard were more used than either butter or olive oil. Walnut oil was a possible alternative on days when animal products were forbidden, which meant *all* of Lent, including Sundays. Thus, eggs, butter, and cheese were forbidden during this period, although they were permissible on ordinary "fast days." We may well doubt, however, that the peasants whose normal diet depended on eggs and dairy products (such as the poor widow of Chaucer's "Nun's Priest's Tale") took this Lenten prohibition seriously: the hens' best laying season would often have coincided with Lent.

There were a great many fast days for Christians, who were the vast majority of the population. In monastic communities, often only the very young or the infirm were allowed to eat meat. While the fasts decreed by the Church for the general population varied somewhat over the approximately ten centuries of the Middle Ages, typically Wednesday, Friday, and Saturday were meatless every week; to these were added the "vigils" before various feast days. For example, the English household of Dame Alice de Bryene, from which we are fortunate to have a record of all purchases for the kitchen for a full year, abstained from meat on Thursday, October 27, 1412, because it was the Vigil of St. Simon and St. Jude, and on six other days of the year that would ordinarily have been "meat" days but that in that year were the vigils of feasts.

Dame Alice's household also fasted on the three Rogation days preceding the Ascension Day feast, but they did not observe a fast resembling that of Lent during Advent, the pre-Christmas season beginning four Sundays before Christmas. At some other times and places, Advent was also a continuous fast. Even without a rigorous four-week fast before Christmas, obviously meatless days generally amounted to considerably more than half of the year. We might envy the fish-day diets of those who lived near the sea: Dame Alice's household and guests were frequently fed Dover sole, shrimps, and oysters, among other fresh fish. But most people had good reason to get very tired of the dried salt cod known as stockfish and an endless parade of smoked ("red") and pickled ("white") herring.

The most common method of cooking was boiling in a pot. Thus, the majority of medieval dishes for which we have recipes are "pottages," usually soups or stews. But a well-equipped kitchen would also have had frying pans, often used for cooking fresh fish, and a spit for roasting. Ovens were built into the walls of the kitchens of greater houses, but most residents of towns and cities did not have ovens, even in a prosperous household. Instead, they took their pies or other food requiring baking to a cookshop or to a community baker. Alternatively, they could buy pastries of various sorts, especially pieces of meat or poultry enclosed in a leaf of pastry and known as pasties, from a cookshop or a specialized pasty maker.

Throughout the period and all over Europe the peasantry subsisted primarily on pottages made from what could be grown in their kitchen gardens, plus whatever fish, game, or meat from domestic fowls or animals they could spare, and, of course, coarse bread and dairy products. What is still known in English pubs as plowman's lunch—bread and cheese with (usually) pickled onions—is pretty close to what a medieval plowman got to eat, except that no peasant would have had the white bread generally supplied by pubs today. Dame Alice's steward records a quantity of cheese for "certain laborers" in his 1419 account book, and he frequently records a number of loaves of "black" bread distributed to outdoor workers. Of course, a plowman in the Mediterranean area would have been likely to supplement his bread and cheese with olives rather than onions.

Recipes

A few culinary recipes can be found in early medical texts, and there are accounts of food served on various occasions in many works of literature, but most of these are of the later period. It is probable that food gets less attention in works of the early Middle Ages because it was so basic as not to seem of special interest. The bulk of the recipes that have survived are from the later centuries, that is, from the late thirteenth century through the fifteenth. And they are all from upper-class or clerical households, naturally enough, since only such establishments would have had a literate clerk to write out recipes. But that does not mean they do not contain recipes that would have been thoroughly familiar to much humbler people.

Many recipe collections begin with basic vegetable pottages, which were no doubt what everyone had been eating for centuries and which the peasantry still relied on, such as stewed cabbage with onions or leeks and dried beans, with or without bacon. Pieter Brueghel the Elder's sixteenth-century paintings of peasant festivities show peasants eating bowls of what seems to be either a thick pea soup or the wheat porridge known as frumenty. There are also recipes for these dishes in collections emanating from such distinguished households as that of Richard II (reigned 1377–1399). Later in such recipe collections we often find directions for roasting a variety of meats and poultry; there would be nothing very new about this, either. We can see similar roasts (as well as bowls of pottage) in one of the dining scenes on the Bayeux Tapestry (c. 1100).

But most of the recipes found in medieval culinary collections are far from being peasant fare. By the late thirteenth century a new and more sophisticated cuisine, ultimately of Middle Eastern origin, had spread across Western Europe, and truly luxurious cooking had become a mark of prestige. The most obvious feature of this cuisine was the use of imported (and thus expensive) spices. Dame Alice paid 25s. 1d. a pound for pepper in 1419—more than 25 times the price of a *bushel* of mustard seed, 12d. Pepper and cumin seem to have been the only widely used imported spices in the early Middle Ages, but by the fourteenth century cinnamon, ginger, nutmeg, mace, and a number of other spices (some of which, such as cubebs, are rare today) were widely used in sauces and in pottages with a base of meat, poultry, or fish.

Spices and Food Preservation

Spices were used partly *because* they were expensive—the twentieth century did not invent conspicuous consumption—but also because they were supposed to have medicinal benefits and, probably most important, to make the food more interesting. Many people think that spices were used to cover up the "off" flavors of none-too-fresh meats. That this was not the case should be obvious, when we consider that refrigeration was not invented until a number of centuries after Western cooks had largely relegated most spices to sweet dishes, retaining only pepper as a common seasoning for meats and fish. Any meat or fish that had to be kept for longer than it would stay fresh was preserved by salting or smoking: ham, bacon, smoked sausages, dried cod, and pickled herring were eaten in most parts of Europe, and in areas where beef was a common food, it was apt to appear as corned beef.

But there must have been cool storage areas where cooked food could be safely stored for a day or more. One of the reasons for the popularity of jellied dishes was that they were regarded as a safe way to keep fish or meat from spoiling for a number of days; many of the directions for such dishes tell us to keep them in a cool place. On some days, Dame Alice's provisions seem to have been especially generous for no particular reason. For example, "one quarter of bacon, one lamb, one heron, seven geese, eggs" to serve 20 people at dinner and 8 at supper. But almost invariably, the following day shows so little provided that the kitchen must have been depending on leftovers, some of them probably presented as entirely different dishes, since many medieval recipes call for already-cooked meats.

Another new feature of medieval haute cuisine was a love of food colorings. The most ubiquitous was saffron, which gave many a dish a golden color. But there were also red food dyes, such as "sanders," and blue ones. These, however, were not used as frequently as was ground parsley or other green herbs, to give a "gaudy green" color, and blood, to give a deep, almost black, shade of brown. Some of the fancier dishes were parti-colored: one side of a pudding-like dish might be dyed pink or yellow and the other side left white. Pure white was also regarded with favor: one of the internationally famous dishes of the period was *blancmanger* (white food), which usually got its white base from the use of rice (another food introduced by Muslims in the Mediterranean area).

One very important ingredient in this style of cooking was almond milk. It was used instead of cow's milk as a basis for many sauces and thickened pottages, especially during Lent, when milk was forbidden, but also by preference in a great many dishes even on "meat" days. No doubt this was partly because town dwellers could not trust the freshness of the milk, but since almonds were expensive, at least in the North, it was also no doubt a prestige ingredient like spices. And anyone who has tasted dishes made with almond milk knows that it has an interesting flavor of its own.

The almonds to make this "milk" were ground in a mortar. The mortar and pestle were in constant use in a sophisticated medieval kitchen. For example, meat and fish, usually cooked, were turned into various specialties, including one

named for the mortar itself, *mortreux* in English, *mortereul* in French, *morterol* in Catalan, and so forth. Spices, herbs, and many other things were also ground in mortars. No professional cook could conceivably have done without one.

One more important "new" ingredient introduced from the East was sugar. It was thought to be especially good for sick people and sickly children, but it was not the only sweetener in wide use in the late Middle Ages. Honey, produced domestically, was cheaper. Dried fruits were also much used, especially in England, where some of the later collections seem to call for at least two of figs, dates, or raisins in one recipe after another. But sugar was considered to be a spice and was usually used in small quantities, like salt, except when it was sprinkled over fritters or made into sugar candies. The dishes intended to be really sweet generally specify "a large quantity" of sugar; we can infer that sparing use was otherwise the rule.

Feasting
Those who have seen some of the menus for great historical feasts—for such occasions as coronations, royal weddings, and the installations of bishops—may have been surprised (or appalled) at the length of these menus. Many of them run to three courses, in each one of which there may be as many as 20 different dishes. Spicy pottages have their place in this array, but the majority of dishes listed are usually plain roasts and simpler dishes. Few vegetables appear on feast menus; they were so commonplace they simply were not treats worthy of a formal occasion. And it must be remembered that these were very special occasions. Most people had far less to choose from (if they had any choice at all) as a general rule, even in well-to-do households.

Still, a fair proportion of the population must have been able to partake of a pretty lavish "feast" on occasion: on Sunday, January 1, 1413, 160 people were recorded as being present for dinner at Dame Alice's manor, including a harper, servants, tenants, "and other strangers." It would be nice to know what the kitchen did with the 12 gallons of milk purchased for that occasion. That would have made an enormous amount of junket, sweet tart filling, or other special dishes requiring a very skilled cook, such as "larded milk," a savory custard containing bacon. But this lavish feast menu does not mean that the humbler members of such a gathering got their choice of the swans, geese, capons, rabbits, mutton, beef, veal, and pork: two swans would not have gone very far among 160 diners.

Invariably the choicest foods were served to the head of the household and to honored guests of high rank. Nevertheless, almost everyone must have had a share of the white bread, of which the supply for the day was 314 loaves. This was 82 more than had been baked and used in the entire preceding month. That would probably have been in itself a treat for most of the lower-ranking "guests." Presumably, those low-ranking guests, however, were not so naive as to think they could toss bones around, and generally behave as Hollywood would have us think people acted in this period. Medieval standards for table manners and associated rituals for serving food were in fact a lot stricter than are accepted manners today.

See also: Wine

—Constance B. Hieatt

Fool. Not only one of the most important cultural figures of the late Middle Ages but also perhaps the most interesting, a paradoxical figure who at his most servile merely uses empty, puerile buffoonery to entertain the society that patronizes him, but who at his most heroic challenges the very assumptions on which that society is founded.

The fool vacillates between simpleton and satirist, between Vice and "fool for Christ's sake," between whipping boy and scourge; he is both the problem and the commentary on that problem—all these are encompassed in the term *fool*. He is especially a key figure in any understanding of the transitional period between the end of the Middle Ages and the beginning of the early modern era; this is nowhere better demonstrated than in the Germanic region, where Sebastian Brant's *Das Narrenschiff* (The Ship of Fools), published in Basel in 1494, rapidly became a Europe-wide best-seller. It was translated into Latin, the lingua franca of scholarship, in 1497 and into the various vernaculars in the years following (two English translations appeared in 1509), inspiring various imitative ships-of-fools, such as the English *Cock Lorelles Bote* (1518). It is important to note that Brant's innumerable oceangoing fools— "*stultorum infinitus est numerus*" [the number of fools is infinite], from the Latin Vulgate Bible, Eccles. 1:15, is a favorite quotation in folly literature—are not funny men (despite the caps and bells given to them by the illustrator) but a company of Vices, and they are sailing to perdition.

The Iconography of the Fool

The particular *insipiens* (fool) to whom we owe much of our knowledge of fool iconography is the one who, in the opening words of both Psalm 52 (Authorized Version 53) and Psalm 13 (Authorized Version 14), "hath said in his heart, 'There is no God.'" From the early thirteenth century on, the illuminated "D" of the opening of the psalm ("*Dixit insipiens*" [The fool said]) becomes a circular frame displaying the atheistic fool, often disputing with King David, reputed author of the Psalms, so that in later manuscripts he is visualized very much as David's court jester.

Sometimes he is completely naked, a madman who has thrown off his clothes in his frenzy, and he carries only a club for his protection and perhaps he chews on a stone. (Interesting evidence that nudity played a part in real-life fooling

comes from the Wardrobe Accounts of Edward I, which record a payment made to Bernard the Fool and 54 of his companions, who came before the king at Pontoise near Paris, "naked and with dancing revelry," c. 1300.) The simple stick type of club was perhaps a staff allowed the fool, for his own protection as much as anything else in an age that exposed many unfortunates, "natural" as opposed to "artificial" fools, to public humiliation. In the *Prose Tristan*, for example, the hero, having lost his reason, having become a real fool, takes a shepherd's cudgel to fend off those who torment him. The fool's club is perhaps also implicit in the matronymic of Edward II's court fool, Robert, who is named in the royal accounts for 1310–1311 as the son of one Dulcia Withastaf (With-a-Staff).

By the late thirteenth century the club had been transformed into the familiar fool's-head-on-a-stick, or *marotte* (bauble), which is sometimes made to deliver the fool's speeches, as in a Dutch play of circa 1500, in which the fool repeatedly punches his marotte whenever it criticizes abuses committed by the clergy and the better-off burghers, thus ostensibly dissociating himself from the criticisms of these powerful groups voiced by the marotte.

Other types of marotte are also represented: the bladder-on-a-stick, for example, and the sometimes distinctly phalli-form padded leather cosh. A phallic marotte is carried by the preacher of the *Sermon joyeux* [parody sermon] *de Saint Velu*, a burlesque phallic saint. In addition to exhibiting to his congregation the "tomb" of the martyred St. Velu (Hairy), in the shape of a *brayette* (codpiece), the sermon's editor suggests that at the sermon's climax, the fool-preacher held aloft the pseudosaint himself, in the form of a phallic marotte. In his *Traité contre les masques* (1608), Jean Savaron recorded that in Clermont during the year-end festivals, young men, masked and disguised as fools, ran through the streets armed with clubs "in the form of codpieces stuffed with straw or padding, striking men and women." Another widely represented aspect of fool phallicism is the suggestive use he makes of the bagpipe.

An important non-Psalter court fool appears in one of the mid-thirteenth-century English Apocalypse manuscripts: he is partially nude and his perhaps crippled legs parody Domitian's *attitude royale*, as his phalli-form marotte similarly parallels the emperor's scepter. Two other features of this careful image deserve consideration, for this fool is tonsured and has his fingers in his mouth.

A homily "Against Contention," intended for preaching throughout the churches of Henry VIII's realm in 1547, includes the question "Shall I stand still, like a goose or a fool, with my finger in my mouth?" This quotation significantly combines all three of the elements that go to make up a misericord in Beverly Minster, carved in

1520—the fool, the goose, and the finger in the mouth—and constitutes valuable proof that the misericord's goose "supporters" are not merely whimsical, decorative additions (the goose has been a proverbially foolish bird since circa 1500, at least). The finger in the mouth gesture perhaps originally betokened the drooling nature of the fool, the village idiot, rather than the "artificial" fool or jester.

Fools' heads seem either to have been completely shaved—"lette the madde persons hed be shauen ones a moneth," recommends Andrew Boorde's *Dyetary of Helth* (1542)—or to have been shaved in some special manner. Double and triple tonsures are commonly illustrated. In the late Middle English romance *Ipomadon* the hero disguises himself as a fool by having a barber shave his head in an "indented" pattern, and "half his chin" shaved as well.

Another distinctive fool attribute, his attire, classically includes the ass-eared hood and the cock's comb (English coxcomb, "fool"): while the former is certainly in evidence by 1350, the latter seems not to have made its appearance for another century. The ass had long been associated with foolishness, of course, but where did the notion of adorning the fool's head with the comb or head and neck of a cockerel come from? One of the common features of descriptions of the classical fool is the insistence that—when not shaved completely bald—he wore his hair in some distinctive manner. St. Augustine, writing around 400 C.E., referred to the "*excordes cirrati*" [crested fools] of the late Roman Empire, a description seemingly applicable to the Greek "laughter maker" who entertained Lucian's Philosophers' Banquet some three centuries earlier: his head was shaved except for a few hairs that stood up straight on his crown. A sixth-century B.C.E. vase painting shows two actors masked as cockerels with crests and wattles. Allardyce Nicoll claimed that "all through the course of the mimic drama [the cockerel-type] held its popularity, and it is not fanciful to see in the cockscomb of the medieval fool the remnants of this character" (*Masks, Mimes, and Miracles* [1931], p. 365).

Court Fools

Although more archival research remains to be done on real-life fools, much of significance has already been uncovered, including the names of household fools—such as the "John Goose, my lord of York's fole," recorded in the Privy Purse Expenses of Henry VII's queen, Elizabeth of York (1465–1503), or the early "Tom-fool," whose funeral expenses are recorded in the Durham Cathedral Accounts in 1365.

The saintly fourteenth-century Fra Jacopone da Todi, "the Fool of God," "in a fervour of spirit and on fire with disdain for the world," it is said, "took off all his clothes, then taking a pack-saddle put it on his back, set a bit in his mouth, and went about on all fours just as though he were an ass."

A similar—but involuntary—humiliation seems to have delighted Tudor monarchs. The accounts detailing court entertainments during the reign of Henry VII reveal that one of the king's favorite jests was to dress the fool as a horse, with shoes, saddles, and bridles provided for by the royal Privy Purse. Both Jacopone and Henry's court fool perhaps ultimately owed their equine capers to one of the rites of inversion that made up the extraordinary Feast of Fools. Writing circa 1289, the French theologian, Guillaume Peraldus, attacked the nakedness of both clerical and lay revelers, referring significantly to the cleric who clothed his horse in scarlet and himself with his horse's blanket.

The hobbyhorse is another of the fool's attributes seen in Psalter illuminations and elsewhere. The Wardrobe Accounts of 1334–1335 for the court of Edward III interestingly mention "xiiij hobbihorses pro ludo Regis." The Christmas revels in which these hobbyhorses may have been used in a mock joust, in 1347–1348, mention a similar number of "viseres" and "crestes" as part of the entertainers' festive costume, including a set of the latter in the form of upended legs wearing shoes. An interesting parallel is the arms of the Foljambe family, displayed on an alabaster panel of the 1370s, which includes a helmet with just such a crest, a *folle jambe* (crazy leg), the leg being "mad" or "foolish" because, in classic *monde renversé* fashion, it springs from the head! Similarly, in a *Proverbes en rimes* manuscript of circa 1500, the illustrated proverb depicts a fool with marotte in one hand wearing only one shoe; the other he holds on his head with his free hand!

Fools' Dress

The fool depicted in the woodcut to the Venetian Malermi Bible printed in 1490 (the *insipiens* of Psalm 52 again) wears only one shoe. At the same point in a mid-fourteenth-century Scandinavian Bible, the fool is also so shod. Indeed, as early as 1209 a goliard (composer of satirical poetry in Latin) named Durianus—who styled himself "long favoured with the fools' dementia, bishop and archpriest of the wandering scholars of Austria, Styria, and Bavaria"—composed a parody in which he describes how all the members of that "sect," "impelled by sheer simplicity and sluggish folly," wander about "with one bare foot."

German and Welsh medieval legal codes, among others, prescribe the cutting short of a garment as a punishment for certain crimes, and this may parallel the characteristic short tunic often worn by the fool. In her spiritual autobiography the English mystic Margery Kempe states that while en route to the Holy Land on her pilgrimage of 1413, she so irritated her traveling companions in the neighborhood of Konstanz that "they cut her gown so short that it only came a little below her knee, and made her put on a piece of white canvas like a sackcloth apron, so that she would be taken for a fool." In Wolfram von Eschenbach's romance *Parzival* (c. 1210), the hero's mother uses sackcloth to make him a disguise of *toren kleit* (fool's clothes). Similarly, it seems that Margery's German tormentors were deliberately intent on making a fool of her, but she was doubtless not entirely unhappy to find herself made "a fool for Christ's sake."

Nothing in the costume of the fool is accidental. Everything is symbolic of his folly, of his derangement, including the familiar "motley": the checkered, tattered, or diagonally opposed colors of his tunic, especially the yellow and green, which Michel Pastoureau has termed the "colors of disorder." It is a red and blue check, however, that covers a most interesting entertainer in the famous Luttrell Psalter; the same pattern appears on the bishop's miter that the fool wears. Precisely contemporary, the Durham Cathedral Accounts for 1338–1339 record the purchase of four ells of checked "burel" (*burelli scacciati*) for clothing Thome Fole.

A most important portrait of a jester, containing several common iconographic features, is attributed to Quentin Massys (c. 1515). The figure is physically deformed (hunchbacked), has an abnormally long nose (phallic symbol), wears a hood through which ass's ears poke (and on top of which are the head and neck of a cockerel), and has a scalloped edge to his short tunic, which is kept in place by a belt hung with bells, and he shoulders a marotte that terminates in a grinning armless fool who has pulled down his trousers, exposing his bare bottom to the viewer. But still the picture is not exhausted. The fool himself places his finger on his lips and says, mysteriously, *Mondeken toe* (Mouth shut)! Werner Mezger was the first to note that the apparent bulge visible in his forehead alludes to another well-known motif, the "stone of folly." The burlesque operation in which this "stone," held to be the cause of all the foolishness in the fool's head, is surgically removed was illustrated by Hieronymus Bosch and Pieter Brueghel the Elder, among others.

An important aspect of fool iconography is his commentary function; if the man depicted is not designated a fool by the placing of an ass-eared hood on his head, then his folly is often quite literally pointed to by an accompanying fool.

Proverbial follies are many and various, and sometimes their representation in medieval art demonstrates a strange kinship between the fool and the saint, the "fool for God," who can, indeed, achieve the impossible. When the late-medieval "foles of Gotam" (later, ironically, the "Wise Men of Gotham") attempt to prolong the spring by "penning the cuckoo" (cf. the many English fields that recall this folly with the names "Cuckoo Pen" and "Cuckoo Bush"), it simply flies above the fence they have hastily erected around the bush on which it has alighted.

In late-medieval art the fool is ubiquitous, not just in the graphic arts but in every conceivable applied or decorative art. He appears on ornamental garden fountains, public town fountains, bronze candelabra, wooden towel rails, jewels, and the finials and feet of precious vessels.

It is important to emphasize that the fool and fool literature are Europe-wide phenomena; they reach their climax around 1500, in the wake of Brant's *Das Narrenschiff*, with Erasmus's *Praise of Folly* (c. 1511) and Thomas Murner's two books of the following year with their important woodcut illustrations. In France, the land of *sociétés joyeuses* (fool societies) such as the Infanterie Dijonnaise or the Parisian Les Enfants sans Souci, there is an explosion of fool literature throughout the fifteenth century, with farces and *sermons joyeux*, and contemporary Germany had the *Fastnachtspiele* (Carnival plays). In England, Lydgate's *Order of Fools*, cataloging 63 types of fools, predates *Das Narrenschiff*, which to some extent it anticipates, as does the Scots poem "The Foly of Fulys," and French lists from the early fourteenth century, which catalog 32 types of fools.

See also: Carnival; Fools, Feast of; Masking; Names, Personal; Trickster

—Malcolm Jones

Fools, Feast of. A festival of misrule and role reversal among the clergy, usually held during the Christmas season (most commonly on New Year's Day) and famous as an occasion for celebration and wild parody among the population at large.

The earliest accounts of the feast, emerging at the end of the twelfth century, refer to it as the "feast of the subdeacons." During the celebration, members of the lower clergy in cathedral chapters would switch places with their superiors and take control of cathedral functions. The practice of turning a lowly person into a "king for a day" or "lord of misrule" was extremely common in medieval celebrations of the Christmas season. Writing circa 1180, Joannes Belethus, a Parisian theologian, mentions four such role-reversal festivals held "after Christmas": "those of the deacons, priests, and choir-children [later known as the Feast of the Boy Bishop], and finally that of the sub-deacons, which we call the Feast of Fools."

All of these celebrations possessed a degree of official support from the Church, which generally marked holidays with a certain measure of festive equality, in which lowly people would temporarily and playfully assume roles of power. Yet from the earliest allusions to the Feast of Fools, it is clear that Church officials wished to limit the powers of the subdeacons, at the same time that the subdeacons were clearly pushing to extend those powers. The first extensive record bears witness to this conflict: it is a document, dated 1199, in which Eudes de Sully, bishop of Paris, attempts to reform the festival as practiced in the Cathedral of Notre Dame. Eudes give us an idea of the Church's view of how the festival should ideally be performed: the subdeacon chosen as ruler for a day would receive the *baculus,* or baton, normally used by the choir director to lead the singing, and he would lead part or all of the divine service for the day, including verses from the biblical passage "He has put down the mighty from their seats and exalted them of low degree" (Luke 1:52)—words referring to God's exaltation of the Virgin Mary but obviously important to the lower clergy because it gave them a script for temporarily unseating their superiors. Near or at the end of the service, the *baculus* was to be passed back to the director.

Eudes's document, however, makes it abundantly clear that the activities of the day went far beyond the minor symbolic revolution that the bishop had in mind. His letter implies that the subdeacons sang "He has overthrown the mighty" repeatedly and with particular zeal and pulled the higher clergy from their customary seats, seating themselves in their places. Further references indicate that the festival not only had spread beyond its prescribed limits in the church but had spilled into the streets. Eudes states that there was to be no masking, no songs, and no processions accompanying the mock leader to the cathedral or back to his home.

Eudes's attempts at reform met with only temporary success at best, for during the following decades a host of further orders and prohibitions appeared, attempting to rein in a festival that had clearly taken on a life of its own. In 1212 a French national church council directed the clergy to abstain from the feast, and in 1234 a decretal from the pope himself banned masking and performances in churches during the Christmas season. After this date the references to the feast multiply: nearly every account is negative, and many are attempts to ban it. About 1400 the Paris theologian Jean-Charlier de Gerson—who found the festival filled with cursing and "almost idolatrous" activities, "more execrable" than the excesses of taverns—despaired that only an order from the king of France could stop it. In 1438 Charles VII issued just such a decree, but the Feast of Fools persisted nonetheless, surviving well into the seventeenth century in some places before it was fully suppressed.

The richest records, from the thirteenth and fourteenth centuries, indicate that the festival was most popular in northern France, but it was also celebrated extensively in Germany and was further recorded in Bohemia, Italy, and England. Although the Feast of Fools may have been at one time specifically the property of the subdeacons, the canons and other secular clergy were in charge of most of the events for which we have records; more important, the feast possessed an enormous appeal for the public at large and no doubt drew upon certain folk customs associated with winter revelry. The celebration assumed the character of a major spectacle—a citywide New Year's party—both within and without the walls of the church.

Inside the church a full-scale religious parody developed, as the lower clergy burned old shoe leather or even dung instead of incense, played dice on the altar, jangled the bells of their fools' costumes, and dressed their leader in full ecclesiastical regalia—though sometimes the fool bishop wore the bishop's holy trousers on his head. In the streets there were massive costumed processions, in which some of the clergy wore their garments inside out or traded clothes with townspeople, dressed up as women, wore grotesque masks, and even paraded nude, sometimes whipping each other.

Much of the festivity centered upon the actions and ritual mockery of the ruling fool himself. Depending on the location, the ruler for a day was known variously as the "lord," "king," "prelate," "bishop," "archbishop," or even "pope" of fools. Sometimes he was ceremonially shaved in front of the church before the service began, a spectacle that occurred as part of the public feast in Sens in 1494. In other ceremonies he pronounced benedictions and passed out mock indulgences.

Central to many enactments was the celebration of the ass, or donkey. The image of the ass emerged in two major and overlapping manifestations: first, as the beast that carried the Virgin Mary and her newborn son on their flight from Jerusalem and, second, as the emblematic animal of the fool, for fools wore ass's ears as part of the costuming and were generally associated with the ass. Indeed, the Bishop of Fools would sometimes ride a donkey. A French manuscript of circa 1280 shows him making the gesture of blessing while riding backward on a donkey. The reformer Jan Hus described a Feast of Fools in which he had himself participated in late-fourteenth-century Prague: a "bishop" had been chosen and seated backward on a she-ass, being led like that into mass, whereupon the animal had brayed and even polluted the very altar itself. In some places the clergy and congregation would bray like asses during the performance of the parody service.

Although the Feast of Fools did not survive into modern times, it currently persists in popular imagination as one of the defining images of medieval culture through such fictional treatments as Victor Hugo's novel *Notre Dame de Paris*—adapted in drama, film, and cartoons as *The Hunchback of Notre Dame*—and in such influential scholarly studies as Harvey Cox's *Feast of Fools* and Mikhail Bakhtin's *Rabelais and His World*, which, respectively, view the feast as a master symbol of religious playfulness and as the ultimate expression of folk creativity.

See also: Boy Bishop, Feast of the; Carnival; Christmas; Fool; Masking; New Year's

—Bradford Lee Eden and Malcolm Jones

Foreign Races. Unknown, little-known, and sometimes imaginary peoples beyond the borders of the Christian world.

Xenophobia and curiosity led medieval Europeans to react to these strangers in various and sometimes contradictory ways. In the early part of the Middle Ages, encounters with strangers were generally hostile, as the Huns threatened the European heartland in the fourth and fifth centuries C.E. and were finally defeated during an attempt to invade Gaul in 451. In the ninth century the Magyars (ancestors of the modern Hungarians) attacked the West and were only defeated in 955, near Augsburg, after the Germans had established a new force of horsemen equipped with chivalric armor.

The next major contact with non-Europeans occurred during the age of the Crusades (beginning in 1096), when huge Christian armies went to the eastern Mediterranean to liberate the Holy Land from the Arabs. Although some of the Crusades were simple military enterprises, many European knights found themselves not only settling in Palestine at the end of some of these conflicts but also establishing surprisingly close relationships with their Muslim neighbors.

Although his birth and rank placed him well above the knightly class, Holy Roman Emperor Frederick II (1194–1250) shared these knights' affinity for Saracen culture. Perhaps it is not surprising that Frederick, who also preferred his residences in his southern lands in Sicily to his northern estates in the area of present-day Germany, enjoyed great familiarity with the Arabic world. His enthusiasm for the lands of the Crusades was such that his nonmilitary crusade to the Holy Land (1228–1229) quickly took on the trappings and pomp of a state visit.

Perhaps because of Frederick II's extreme fascination with "infidel" territories—a fascination that might have been considered unseemly in a Christian ruler—or perhaps for other reasons, the pope excommunicated him in 1228. In spite of the pope's protests, Frederick also established a Saracen colony at Lucera in southern Italy, and he further enraged the pontiff by refusing to try to forcefully convert the Muslim inhabitants to Christianity.

In a few cases such contacts led to early forms of tolerant behavior and thinking. In most other cases, however, they led to rejection and stereotyping, not because of a dearth of information but because many Europeans were stubbornly certain that Christianity was superior to Islam and all other religions. Nevertheless, we need to distinguish between personal concepts about foreign races, as they have been expressed in literary works, for example, and theoretical discussions about races, such as those found in religious texts and theological treatises. Both in the Old Testament and in the writings of the Church Fathers there are statements indicating that God has the power to create many races, miracles, and phenomena.

The vast majority of medieval people knew nothing at all concrete about foreign races, and they viewed them with great suspicion and fear— an uneasiness best represented by the many images of grotesque monsters carved into capitals and by the strange beings portrayed on maps of the world. In most cases "monsters" have to stand in for "foreign races," as the classical Greek tradition, established by Ctesias (fl. c. 400 B.C.E.), a court physician in Persia, and reemphasized by Pliny the Elder (23–79 C.E.), had a profound impact on medieval people. Alexander the Great's experience in India became a highly influential source of material for medieval writers, and it preconditioned their minds about foreign races in that part of the world. In *The City of God* St. Augustine (354–430) wrote of "monstrous races" as proof of God's providential power and as an indicator of how little Christians actually know about the universe. In his important work *Etymologiae* the Spanish scholar Isidore of Seville (c. 560–636) shows that he is fully convinced of the existence of monsters, and he lists all their characteristics in detail. But these arguments all clearly represent theoretical speculation and mirror popular beliefs. The first real contacts with foreign races occurred when Europeans traveled to the East. The pilgrim Egeria was the first to write about her experiences on her travels (sometime between the fourth and the sixth centuries); however, she paid little attention to things non-Christian.

It was not until the fourteenth century that travel accounts would actually pay attention to native populations. During her tour of the Holy Land the English mystic Margery Kempe (c. 1373–c. 1440) experienced bad treatment and indifference from her fellow pilgrims, but a friendly and beautiful Saracen man helped her climb up the mountain where Christ had fasted. One of the earliest German travel accounts—a 1336 work by Ludolf von Sudheim—indicates, however, that these pilgrims were like modern travelers, accompanied and guided by Franciscan friars who blocked their view of foreigners and foreign culture and directed their attention toward the holy sites.

One of the most important testimonies about foreign races was that of the Venetian merchant and traveler Marco Polo (1254–1324), who undertook a major trip as far as China (1271–1295) and returned with a book filled with highly exotic but—to a certain extent—accurate information about foreign races. Because his contemporaries did not believe his account, the book was called *Il milione* (Millions of Lies). By contrast, John Mandeville, who composed an entirely fictional travel report (c. 1356)—one in which the monstrous and the miraculous play a much greater role—appealed to his audience and met with resounding success, probably because during this time contacts with the East had been cut back dramatically and any fanciful account could easily claim to present authoritative information. The more medieval Europeans knew about foreign races, and the less threatening the latter appeared to them, the more likely it was that Europeans acknowledged their common humanity, even though the foreigners might practice a different religion.

Sir Jean de Joinville (1225–1317), who composed a comprehensive crusade chronicle, indicated that to his mind the caliph of Baghdad had the same rank as the pope. In this way Joinville was insinuating that neither Christianity nor medieval Europe was the only force in this world. Fulcher of Chartres (d. 1127), who had stayed in the Holy Land after the First Crusade, writes that all the Occidentals living in the East had adapted so well to the new world that they almost could be considered natives; this is a remarkable statement about ethnic acculturation.

The most impressive observation about foreign races can be found in Wolfram von Eschenbach's *Willehalm* (c. 1218–1220), wherein Giburg, the formerly heathen wife of the protagonist, appeals to the court council not to forget that despite their different religious beliefs, the enemies besieging their castle are part of God's creation and should paradoxically be treated kindly, even in the middle of deadly combat: "Spare the creatures of God's Hand!" Furthermore, she points out that all Christians were once heathens and that they should have pity on their adversaries in battle, because Christ also forgave those who killed him. At the end of the story the Christians win a resounding victory over the Saracens, but Willehalm acknowledges their worthiness as warriors and helps them prepare their dead for burial, thus honoring the human quality of his opponents and accepting them as members of this universe. Although Wolfram did not succeed in changing the prevailing medieval attitudes about foreign races, he was a remarkable observer and a deeply humanistic thinker for his time.

In this respect we can also refer to many of the Byzantine verse romances, such as the Middle High German *Herzog Ernst* (1180–1220), in which the protagonist spends a long time among foreign races, whom he treats like any other people. These people, in turn, acknowledge him for his chivalric virtues. They are clearly depicted as monsters, but in evaluating them this does not matter at all; instead what counts are their character and inner nobility. The Old French romance *Aucassin et Nicolette* presents a prince who is in love with a Saracen slave girl, although his parents object to this mésalliance. Despite the profound racial conflict, the lovers overcome all difficulties, eventually marry, and rule over their inherited lands. The most famous marriage between a Christian and a person from a different race can be found in Wolfram von Eschenbach's *Parzival* (c. 1205–1210). In this romance Gahmuret marries the black queen, Belakane. Their child, Feirefiz, although checkered black and white, emerges as an admirable figure who is the absolute ruler of the entire world of Asia. He arrives at Arthur's court at the moment when his brother Parzival is about to embark on the adventure of bringing back the Grail.

In later centuries European travelers began to make explorations farther and farther into the unknown East. Odoric of Pordenone went to Asia from 1314 to 1330, and Niccolò de Conti went as far as Indonesia. Bertrandon de la Brocquière, who visited the Holy Land (1432–1433), expressed great admiration for the civility of the Turks. Others, however, sharply criticized them and portrayed them as monstrous and cruel. This ambivalence was characteristic of medieval attitudes, inasmuch as foreigners were perceived either as evil or as part of God's creation, depending on the function they were assumed to occupy within each specific context. It would be problematic to charge the European peoples of the Middle Ages with outright racism in the modern sense of the word. On the other hand, it does seem appropriate to credit some people from that time period with having tolerant opinions regarding foreign races. There were many contacts with foreign peoples, and some of these contacts were of quite a positive nature.

See also: Crusades; Giants; *Mandeville's Travels*; Travel Literature

—Albrecht Classen

Frame Tale. A fictional narrative composed primarily for the purpose of presenting the other narratives that it surrounds.

A frame tale depicts a series of stories whose narrators are characters in the frame. While frame tales vary considerably in length and complexity, each provides a context for reading, listening to, and interpreting the interior tales. A frame tale derives its own meaning largely from what it contains and does not stand independently from the tales enclosed within it. The interpolated tales can appear independently, however, or in a different frame with a different connotation.

Frame tales have also been called *novellae*, boxing tales, or stories within stories. The genre appears to have been an Eastern invention, most likely originating in India, where it can be traced back at least three millennia. By the tenth century it had reached the Middle East, and by the twelfth, Europe. The frame tale gained the height of its popularity in Europe in the fourteenth century but faded in most areas in the early-modern period.

Some of the best-known and most-studied frame tales appear here in the approximate order of their creation. It is impossible to date the origin of many of these works or the longevity of many others. For example, estimates of the date of origin of the *Panchatantra*, generally accepted as the earliest surviving frame tale, vary by 700 years and more. Other frame tales had different periods of influence in the East and West. For example, the famed *Thousand and One Nights* has exerted a continuous influence in the East from about 800, but it had a relatively slight effect on Western narrative traditions until after 1300, when its influence became substantial. After the Sanskrit *Panchatantra*, there appeared the *Book of Sindibad* (c. 800), which spawned many versions in the East and found its way to the West in the form of *The Seven Sages of Rome*, in which seven wise men tell stories to dissuade a king from executing his own son. Then followed the Arabic *Alf Layla wa-Layla* (Thousand and One Nights), in which Shahrazad narrates a story each night so that her tyrannical husband will not kill her as he has all his former wives; *Kalila wa-Dimna*, an Arabic version of the *Panchatantra*, in which two jackals trade stories about ethics and behavior; Petrus Alfonsi's *Disciplina clericalis* (twelfth century); the Persian *Tuti-Nameh* (c. 1300), the story of a parrot who tells stories night after night to keep his mistress from an adulterous rendezvous; Juan Manuel's *Conde Lucanor* (1335), in which Patronio, a counselor, answers the count's questions, illuminating each with an exemplum; Boccaccio's *Decameron* (c. 1349–1351), the story of seven young women and three young men who flee to the country to escape the plague and entertain each other with stories of love and lust; John Gower's *Confessio Amantis* (The Lover's Confession, c. 1387–1393), in which Genius tells tales illustrating the seven deadly sins; Chaucer's *Canterbury Tales*, which depicts a variety of characters, of varied classes, on a pilgrimage to Canterbury during which they compete to tell the most edifying and entertaining tale; and Marguerite de Navarre's *Heptameron* (first printed edition, 1558), similar to the *Decameron* but with fewer narrators, who are apparently based on Marguerite's own acquaintances. Certain wisdom books, or "mirrors for princes," may also be included in a broad definition of the frame tale.

The frame tale covers a spectrum from the primarily diverting to the primarily didactic. The structures also vary from loose to tight, a tight structure being one where the frame tale strictly limits the type of story that can be interpolated in any given position. The *Thousand and One Nights*, for example, has a loose frame because Shahrazad can theoretically tell any kind of story as long as it is entertaining. Gower's *Confessio Amantis*, on the other hand, links its stories tightly to their contexts. When Genius is presenting a lesson on pride, he tells tales in which this emotion is highlighted. This type of structure also allows for irony in texts such as Juan Ruiz's *Libro de buen amor* (1330, 1343), in which a character presents a lesson and then tells a story that contradicts it.

Most of the earlier frame tales are of anonymous authorship and probably descend from an oral storytelling tradition. Later texts, particularly in the European tradition, have named authors, but they still appear to draw heavily on both oral traditions and earlier frame tale texts.

Different frame tales may have interpolated tales in common. For example, tales in Boccaccio's or Chaucer's works may have made earlier appearances in the *Thousand and One Nights* or *The Seven Sages of Rome*. Stories in common among frame tales have led some to conclude that medieval authors read earlier texts. That frame tales both in oral and written form worked as conduits transmitting tales across linguistic and cultural boundaries seems certain; however, it has been difficult to determine which frame tale a particular author might have read or heard.

The frame tale depicts the oral storytelling tradition and works as a bridge between oral and literate narrative. Along with exempla collections that do not have frames, framed collections present traditional tales to a literate audience. An audience is written into the frame tale, allowing an author or compiler to guide the reader's interpretation. Different frame tales thereby contain different narrator/audience dynamics. Some have a sole narrator for the interpolated tales, indicative of storytelling by teachers and parents; others have several narrators, thus leading to an agonistic environment characteristic of public storytelling. A frame tale is thus a self-reflexive form, a story about storytelling in all its variety.

See also: Chaucer, Geoffrey; *Decameron*; Folktale; Novella; Seven Sages, The; Thousand and One Nights

—Bonnie D. Irwin

French Tradition. The folkloric culture of France.

History and Context

At Charlemagne's death in 814 the empire of the Franks covered not only present-day France but also Germanic lands north to Hamburg, including the Netherlands, and east to Regensburg and Salzburg; its southern borders stretched down the Italian peninsula and across the northern quarter of Spain. However, by the time of the First Crusade (1096–1099) the kingdom of France had been considerably pared down, extending to the north only to Flanders, and to the east to an axis from Champagne down the Rhone valley to Arles. Burgundy contained, along with most of its present territory, the region of Besançon and part of Provence. By 1494 France's borders had not stretched much: they now extended to the tip of Lombardy but still fell just short of Metz and did not include Franche-Comté or Savoy.

The fluctuations of the French kingdom's borders during the Middle Ages pose specific problems in understanding French history: today, in referring to "French" history, customs, or folklore, we could easily be speaking of something found in an area that was part of a separate kingdom at a given time in medieval history. Thus, there are considerable differences between the political history of France and its cultural history, which is defined by language, commercial intercourse, family and vassalic ties, and social interaction based on common natural borders.

At the dawn of the Middle Ages, Gaul (as France was called during the Roman period) was already a mix of religious and customary traditions. Roman feasts, calendar systems, popular beliefs, and rituals added a layer of folk religion to the Celtic substratum, and a third layer, Christian traditions, followed. Some Roman ceremonial complexes became important components of later folk culture, such as the rituals of winter solstice, or aspects of Fevralia present in the February Carnival.

During the great invasions that followed the withdrawal of Roman forces in the fifth century, numerous Germanic tribes brought with them a new input of mores, customs, and beliefs. Around 526 the territory of France was crisscrossed by Barbarian invasions. The Franks, from north of Cologne, migrated along a northeast-to-southwest axis, through Tournai, Paris, Orléans, and Bordeaux. The Burgundians traveled south from around Mainz to their future territory down the Rhone valley. Visigoths covered the southernmost areas, from Toulouse to the old Roman Narbonensis (later Narbonnaise) and Provence. The Vandals swept across the eastern plains, parallel to the Frankish axis but stretching further down, to Toulouse, and the famous Huns reached Paris and Troyes.

The cultural history of these invasions remains incompletely understood, and their impact is very difficult to determine. Fragments of symbolic iconography point to a spreading of solar cults across Europe during this period. The last wave of Germanic invaders left linguistic traces: the dialect of today's Normandy bears the imprint of the marauding Viking armies that invaded northern France in the ninth century and eventually, in 911 under Rollo (known in Denmark as Hrolf the Walker), became the rulers of Normandy. The northmen's incursions were not, however, limited to Normandy. They also set upon the entire Atlantic coast, from Nantes to Bordeaux and the Pyrenees, and along the Mediterranean, upon the regions of Narbonne and Provence.

Although the Muslim invasions were pushed back at the dramatic encounter of Poitiers in 732, small groups were said to have remained in France. Some were settled as populations of prisoners, for instance in the silver-mining region of Largentière (Ardèche). Chronicles tell of Saracen strongholds controlling the Alps as late as 927. In fact, Muslim garrisons did not evacuate from Grenoble until 965 and from Provence until 973. Some Saracens, according to local oral traditions, settled even in northern villages, dubbed "Saracen" in the region, such as the little town of Uchizy, near Mâcon.

Miracles of the French Monarchy

Several legends arguing for the divine origins of French kingship began during the time of these invasions with the conversion of the Frankish king Clovis to Christianity in the late fifth century. However, some of the legends did not come into being until considerably later than this, and all of them changed during the course of the Middle Ages, reaching their final form by the end of the fifteenth century.

Perhaps the most famous is the legend of the Holy Phial, which says that on the day when Clovis was baptized the priest responsible for bringing the sacred oil was delayed by the crowd and did not arrive at the proper time. However, a dove came down from heaven bearing a small phial of the necessary oil, which was used for the ceremony. The phial was preserved at the Abbey of St.-Rémi and used for the anointing of the kings of France from 869 forward. No matter how many kings were anointed, the container never ran dry. The miracle of the dove and the oil was interpreted as giving divine sanction to the French monarchy. The practice of anointing French kings, which began with Clovis and became de rigueur in the ninth century, also explains the sacerdotal powers that kings of France enjoyed in addition to secular powers throughout the Middle Ages and beyond.

The legend of the fleur-de-lis also centers on Clovis, though it dates only from the fourteenth century. Before Clovis's conversion to Christianity he married Clotilda, a Christian who tried in vain for many years to convert him. Queen Clotilda made a habit of visiting a holy hermit, and she prayed with him shortly before an important battle that Clovis was expected to lose. After they prayed, an angel appeared bearing an escutcheon with armorial bearings in the form of golden fleurs-de-lis on an azure background. The angel told the holy man that if Clovis wore this coat of arms in place of his usual crescent, he would win the battle. Queen Clotilda quickly contrived to have the crescents removed from all of Clovis's equipment and replaced by fleurs-de-lis. When Clovis called for his armor, he was astonished to find the "wrong" coat of arms on it and sent it back for another. Of course, the next suit of armor also bore the fleur-de-lis. Four times Clovis sent his armor back, and four times he was brought armor with the new pattern. Finally, having graver concerns than the appearance of his armor, Clovis wore the fleur-de-lis into battle and won a miraculous victory at the battle of Montjoie. When Clotilda afterward revealed the subterfuge, Clovis finally became a Christian.

The legend of the oriflamme inevitably came to focus on Clovis as well because of his role in the other two miracles. In this one, the emperor of Constantinople dreamed that he saw a knight holding a flaming lance standing by his bedside. An angel then told him that this knight would free Constantinople from the Saracens. In earlier versions the knight turns out to be Charlemagne, but in a later form he becomes Clovis. The flaming lance is the oriflamme, the red standard of the Capetian kings.

Beginning in the eleventh century with Philip I, French kings were believed to have healing powers, another powerful claim to divine sanction of their rule. Scrofula, an inflammation of the lymph nodes, was a very common disease in the Middle Ages, owing largely to unsanitary living conditions. Scrofula produces sores and swellings about the face and can be badly disfiguring, but it is hardly ever fatal and often goes away on its own. The kings of France claimed to be able to heal this disease, which came to be called the king's evil, by ritually touching the sores. As scrofula often does vanish as suddenly as it comes, numerous "cures" were recorded, and the French government kept careful records of them. Philip I and his successors would touch for scrofula in elaborate, very public rituals, to which sufferers would flock in hopes of a miracle. As Marc Bloch observes in his classic study of sacred monarchy, French kings must have gained great prestige from this healing touch, because in the twelfth century their English rivals began also to touch for scrofula. In the thirteenth century St. Louis (Louis IX) expanded the ritual, adding certain holy words to the traditional sign of the cross. He taught these words to his grandson, Philip the Fair, who despite being far from saintly also spoke them when he touched for scrofula. Another indication of the hold of this ritual on popular imagination is that it continued long past the Middle Ages, into the nineteenth century.

The Folk Calendar

Folk time is increasingly recognized as an all-encompassing worldview that translates daily experience onto a sacred plane. Arnold van Gennep's approach to French folklore has provided a temporal framework of specific calendar cycles throughout the year that proves useful for the study of medieval French folklore. Van Gennep's delineation of "minicycles" completes the year, extending past the vast cycles of Christmas, Carnival, and Easter to embrace, for instance, the late-fall festival, St. Martin's Carnival (November 11), and such end-of-summer celebrations as the feasts of St. Margaret (July 20), Mary Magdalen (July 22), St. Anne (July 26), and St. Sixtus (August 6).

Folk calendar symbolism emerges in the dramatization of crucial calendar moments, acted out, for instance, through recitations of the Combat between Sir Carnival and Lady Lent or, as is frequent in France, a gaunt, irascible male figure named Caresprenant (Lent). In these combats, each side mobilizes vast quantities of foodstuffs, raw, still alive and kicking, as well as prepared, to engage in a mock battle that ends—nonrealistically—with the victory of the infinitely more popular Carnival. The medieval poetic tradition of the *débats* between seasons (summer against winter) or months (April against May) can be

seen as another expression of ritualized calendar behaviors.

Local traditions exemplify the link between crucial calendar points and nature lore, in forms often maintained by modern French folklore. For instance, Gervase of Tilbury tells us of a walnut tree in Barjols, near Arles, that does not regain its leaves in spring but remains fallow and bare until the feast of St. John the Baptist (June 24), when it suddenly "celebrates" the Precursor's birth and is covered with leaves and fruits. He also recounts the tradition of a deadly battle waged for eight days around the feast of St. John the Baptist by armies of gigantic horned scarabs in the two towers of the castle of Remoulins, near Uzes, a version of the tradition, common in France, of a supernatural battle of animals (usually cats or birds).

Folk Rituals and Beliefs

In France, as elsewhere in Western Europe, many folk beliefs centered on the popular saints of a particular locality. After the Virgin Mary in a variety of guises (such as Notre Dame des Neiges), the most venerated were the Baptist, St. John the Evangelist, Mary Magdalen, Margaret, Anne, Catherine, Blaise, Nicholas, George, and Christopher. However, every region and even subregion had its focal saint, whose cult attracted a wide range of ceremonial behavior, hagiographical tradition, and folk belief: Martin around Limoges, Yves and Anne in Brittany, the child Foix around Conques. Outstanding in Provence were Mary Magdalen and the local cult of the "Three Marys." Curiously, sometime in the twelfth century in Corbeny, St. Marcoul became associated with the healing of the king's evil. The monks of Corbeny duly began selling small bottles of water sanctified by having Marcoul's relics immersed in it. Sufferers would then purchase this water and use it for washing their sores. Some would even drink it. The perceived power of saints' relics was so great that some holy people were assaulted on their deathbeds by crowds of believers; such was the fate of the Joachimite Beguine Douceline of Digne, whose clothing and body were torn to pieces.

Facetious folklore also created its own imaginary saints who people the folk theater, the fabliaux, and popular sayings: St. Caquette, patron of talkative women, and the obscene or profane saints Couillebault (Boldball), Jambon (Ham), and Andouille (Chitterling), to name a few.

Localized folk worship easily crossed the line into heresy. For example, in the thirteenth century the Dominican friar Stephen of Bourbon was appalled to learn that the people of the Dombes, near his convent at Lyons, worshipped a greyhound, whom they called St. Guinefort. According to the local legend, this "Holy Greyhound" had saved an infant from a snake. The child's guardians, however, killed the dog, mistaking the snake's blood on the dog's muzzle for the child's blood and assuming the dog had hurt the child. Afterward, realizing their mistake and overcome with remorse, the lord and lady placed the dog in a well, filled the well with stones, and planted trees around it. Apparently the local peasants treated the Holy Greyhound as a martyr, praying to him in times of sickness or need.

Women with sick children would bring offerings to the well and perform various rituals that provide a fine illustration of the melding of Christian traditions with local pagan practices. After passing the naked infants between the trees nine times, they would hang their swaddling clothes on the surrounding bushes and place the babies at the feet of the trees. They would then ask the fauns of the forest to take back their sick children and leave the mothers their own children, whom they said the fauns had taken away. They left the children lying on straw, with burning candles on either side of their heads. Naturally, the straw often caught fire, and many of the babies burned to death. As soon as Stephen discovered this ritual, he outlawed it and had the dog disinterred. He also had the trees chopped down and burned along with the remains of the dog. However, local belief in the Holy Greyhound and his healing powers did not die out so easily; it continued for several centuries longer, as Jean-Claude Schmitt shows in his folkloric study of St. Guinefort.

A larger and more influential heresy was that of the Albigenses, or Cathars, which sprang up in parts of the Southwest, in particular around Foix. The Dominican Order of friars was founded to combat this heresy, more by argument than by physical means. However, in 1209 Pope Innocent III declared a crusade against them, and the northern armies crushed them brutally, as in Béziers, where the entire population, Catholic and heretic, was put to the sword. "Kill them all; God will know His own," the papal envoy was reported to have said. This grisly victory was followed by a process of religious reconquest, with Inquisitors pressing local populations to reveal the extent and manner of their contamination by heretical practices and beliefs.

Such was the task of Jacques Fournier, who centered his inquiry on Montaillou, a small village whose inhabitants were intensely concerned with salvation and a spirituality that resembled Manichaeism in its conception of the universe as divided between equal and opposing forces of good and evil. The elite of this sect, the *parfaits* (perfect ones), sought to imitate the Twelve Apostles as far as possible, and they met high standards of poverty and chastity—apparently higher than the officials of the established Church. They were also very learned and skilled in disputation. In order to meet their adversaries on an equal footing, St. Dominic's order also had to become well educated and to eschew personal property.

Fournier was a thorough and conscientious Inquisitor. His records of the villagers' testimony are so detailed that Emmanuel Le Roy Ladurie, a twentieth-century historian, was able to use them to conduct a thorough analysis of village life: hearth-side customs, child rearing, social networking, traditional gestures, magical beliefs, and many other aspects of local folk culture. Because religious conversation so thoroughly penetrated everyday life, the trial testimony revealed many aspects of local custom. For example, in one of the Inquisitorial transcripts, we learn from villager Vuissane Testanière:

> At the time when the heretics dominated Montaillou, Guillemette "Benete" and Alazaïs Rives were being deloused in the sun by their daughters.... All four of them were on the roof of their houses. I was passing by and heard them talking. Guillemette "Benete" was saying to Alazaïs, "How can people bear the pain when they are burning at the stake?"
>
> To which Alazaïs replied, "Ignorant creature! God takes the pain upon himself, of course!" (*Montaillou: The Promised Land of Error* [1978], p. 141)

From this and similar records, Le Roy Ladurie concluded that delousing—picking lice from the hair—was an important social ritual, was always conducted by a woman, and was often but not always practiced on a male lover, and that a favorite site for delousing and gossiping in Montaillou was on the flat rooftops of the village houses.

The interpenetration of official and folk belief found in Montaillou also existed in urban areas. French cities produced an abundant civilian architecture, which, along with Church monuments, provided an extensive surface for the inscription of the motifs, themes, and legends of folk culture. The cities of France were richly adorned with an iconography that was both symbolic and functional. For instance, the referential language of street signs is an expression of folklore. Saints and the emblems of their martyrdom signaled shops and taverns to passers-by, such as St. Lawrence and his grill for rotisseries, St. Catherine and her razor-laden wheel for barbers or potters. The corner pillars of houses, beams, lintels, and fountains all offer traces of a folk culture in which the saints coexist with the Wild Men; mermaids; the misogynist Bigorne, who feeds on harried husbands, and Chicheface, who feeds on good wives; the Four Sons Aymon on their horse Bayard; the bear doing the morris dance; the dragon; and the man who wants to shoe a goose.

Such was the lively and colorful late-fifteenth-century world of François Villon, the quintessential Parisian poet. His work reflects not only his Sorbonne education but also his active participation in urban folklife. Villon's poetry features not the enchanted forests of courtly romance but the taverns, brothels, and even prisons of late-medieval Paris. His often painfully realistic characters include thieves, prostitutes, policemen, and of course a full complement of corrupt clerics, who according to Villon assist the husbands of their parishes by giving pleasure to their wives. An important source of the poet's famous irony is the easy coexistence of the sacred and profane, as apparent in Villon's Paris as in his poetry. In compact universe of the medieval city, iconography, myth, and custom weave a complex texture of signification that underpins folk life.

As the representations described above suggest, medieval French folklore knew many supernatural or supranatural beings. The most prominent may have been the devil himself (Satan, Sathanas, Lucifer), often personified as the Master Builder who commandeers bridges and steeples in particular and puts sinners to sleep "with his viola." Others include dwarfs like the famed Oberon, elves such as the later Pacolet, giants and ogres from Geoffroy à la Grande Dent to Gargantua, mermaids or "serpent women," Wild Men and Women, fairies and ghosts, and the premier magician Maugis, cousin to the Four Sons Aymon, who was protected by the magical horse Bayard. We might include what Nicole Belmont calls verbal beings: bogey men whose mere name frightens children—for instance, the Barbo or Babou (thirteenth century), subject of a rich 1982 essay by Jacques Berlioz, who shows its link to a werewolf called Barbeu.

Many French folk narratives are associated with particular places. Place names are witness to important legendary figures whose names are attached to hills and mountain passes. Among them stand out figures from the chansons de geste: Roland, the ill-fated nephew of Charlemagne, or the horse Bayard, mount of the Four Sons Aymon.

Places all over France are connected to stories of the supernatural. Gervase mentions the high tower of the castle of Livron near Valence, still called the devil's tower in the nineteenth century, which does not tolerate a night watchman and mysteriously deposits any intruder at morning down in the valley, or the rock of the Annot castle, in the same region, which can be easily moved by the little finger but not the whole body. Other localities are attached to legends concerning historical figures, such as Pepin the Short, father of Charlemagne, slaying a lion at Ferrières-en-Gatinais, represented on a capital of the twelfth-century church. Numerous legends concern the fairy-mermaid Melusine, a serpent-tailed woman who is linked to the origins of the noble family of Lusignan, from whom Eleanor of Aquitaine descended, and to the regional histories of Poitou. (One English legend identifies the serpent-tailed woman as Richard I's mother, al-though no legends go so far as to claim that Eleanor herself was half serpent.)

Other legendary beings seem not to be connected with a particular locale. The Wild Hunter is known through numerous local traditions: Hellekin, a figure of Germanic origin first documented by Ordericus Vitalis, was reputed to ride down lonely roads followed by hordes of noisy, disheveled ghosts, who played dissonant metallic music and seized any unfortunate passerby. The Wild Man spawned an entire family in the decorative arts of the Middle Ages; they appear on tapestries, engraved chests, and coffers. In festive folk traditions, the Wild Man—sometimes conflated with the bear—was a frequent figure in costumed Carnival celebrations. In female form, the Wild Woman is linked to fear-producing beliefs in children and to populations of wild animals.

In short, every area of folklore as we know it in the West has been represented in the French Middle Ages and invites continuous unearthing of what the French call the "archaeology of knowledge."

Literature and Folklore

Folklore and folk culture have provided the inspiration and context for much of France's most memorable literature, including *lais*, romances, ballads, and chansons de geste. The *Chanson de Roland* tells of a disastrous battle, which actually occurred at Roncevaux in 778, in which the Moors surprised and annihilated the rearguard of Charlemagne's army, led by Roland. The story of his final stand was probably passed down through heroic songs performed in French by *jongleurs* until the time of the First Crusade (1096–1099). When the *Chanson* as we now know it was written down, around 1100, Roland was the ideal hero for French knights, who had been inspired by the idea of fighting the Muslims in the Holy Land. This may be the reason that the *Chanson* was put into literary form and began a long tradition of Roncevaux legends.

The figure of the *jongleur* plays an important role in the *Roman de Silence*, an unconventional thirteenth-century romance. In this story, a beautiful, aristocratic girl is disguised as a boy and trained for knighthood. Because the king has decreed that women cannot inherit property and her parents have no sons, they resolve to pass her off as a male and raise her as they would raise a son. As the girl grows up, Nature and Nurture begin to argue over her proper condition, but Nurture, with the help of Reason, exerts power over the young Silence, and the ruse works. Nevertheless, Silence lives in constant fear of discovery, and she worries that even if the law changes, she possesses no skills that would enable her to survive as a woman. She therefore assumes another disguise and leaves her parents with a troop of *jongleurs*, from whom she resolves to learn their trade. Minstrelsy was one of the few professions open to women, and if she mastered it she could always support herself. Difficulties naturally ensue, the most delicate of which begins when the disguised Silence enters the royal court, and the queen, believing her to be a boy, tries to seduce her. When Silence refuses her advances, the queen accuses "him" of rape, a charge that Silence can, of course, prove false, but only by revealing who she really is. The "happy" ending, which troubles some modern readers, includes the execution of the queen and the marriage of Silence to the king, solving her inheritance problem. Nature, the reader is encouraged to assume, will enable her to live as a woman from this point forward.

Strong female characters, good and evil, appear in the late-twelfth-century *lais* of Marie de France, who claims to have derived her poems from Breton oral traditions. For instance, her *lai* of *Bisclavret* features a werewolf similar to Barbeu. The beginning of *Bisclavret* finds the title character happily married to a beautiful woman. Although she loves him, she insists on knowing why he is absent from home for three days every week; the worst she can imagine is that he is seeing another woman. When he reveals that he goes to the forest, sheds his clothes, and becomes a werewolf, she is horrified and ceases to love him. With the help of another man, who wants her to become his mistress, she follows Bisclavret to the forest and steals his clothes. Without them he cannot regain the form of a man, and she is able to live with her lover while Bisclavret remains a beast in the forest.

After a year or so the king, on a hunt in this forest, sees a wolf that bows before him. Flattered, the king adopts him and takes him back to the palace, where his docility makes him a great favorite. He attacks no one—except a certain knight and his lady, who, of course, turn out to be his wife and her lover. Puzzled by this selective fierceness, the king subjects the lady to torture until she reveals what she did to her husband. Fortunately, she still has the clothes. Bisclavret regains his former shape, and the scheming couple is exiled.

Marie's *lais* are known for their lively style and economy of words—*Bisclavret* is not much longer than the summary above. An example of the opposite approach is the work of Marie's contemporary, Chrétien de Troyes, who like Marie based much of his work on Celtic legendary traditions. Chrétien is known for his creative Arthurian romances, which are as elaborate and highly developed as Marie's *lais* are efficient and concise. Like Marie, Chrétien makes use of magic and the supernatural. For instance, *Yvain, ou Le chevalier au lion* (The Knight with the Lion) includes the figure of the Wild Man, along with a magic spring, a magic ring, an evil giant, and a salve that cures madness (prepared by none other than Morgan le Fay).

Yvain initially sets out to find the magic spring to avenge the humiliation of his friend, who was put to flight by its owner. As his friend tells him, if one pours some of the water from the spring onto a nearby slab, such a tempest ensues that no animal can stay in the forest. The owner, angry at the wreckage of his forest, comes out ready to fight, and he is too big and strong for most knights to withstand. Yvain, however, fares better than his friend. He mortally wounds this knight, whom he pursues into his castle. The castle's portcullis comes down, killing Yvain's horse and trapping Yvain inside. In the manhunt that follows, Yvain is saved from capture by Lunette, maid to the lady of the castle. Lunette reminds Yvain that she once visited Arthur's court and that of all the knights, only Yvain treated her with courtesy. In gratitude, she makes him invisible and offers to let him escape. However, Yvain hesitates to return to court without proof of his exploit, and when he sees the knight's beautiful widow, Laudine, he no longer wishes to escape. Yvain realizes that wooing the widow of the man he has killed will be no easy matter. Therefore, Lunette does the wooing for him, and she prevails quickly. Meanwhile, Arthur, believing that Yvain has been killed, brings an army to avenge him, but by the time his forces arrive at the spring, Yvain is lord of the castle.

The story might have ended happily at this point, but Yvain's old friend Gawain criticizes his retirement from athletic chivalry, including jousts and tournaments. Reminding Yvain of his reputation, Gawain persuades him to leave home for a while. Laudine consents to this, giving Yvain a ring that will protect him from harm as long as he is true to her, which means, among other things, returning to her within a year. Yvain, enjoying the sport and the company of his old comrades, loses track of the time and overstays his leave. When he realizes that he has incurred eternal banishment from Laudine's presence (and an emissary of Laudine's comes to take back the ring), Yvain goes mad. He lives as a wild man in the woods until he is found and cured with Morgan's salve. After regaining his wits Yvain vows to regain his wife. Before he can do so, he must meet a number of challenges, including killing a giant and rescuing Lunette from the stake. Lunette once again applies her considerable verbal talents to the reconciliation of her mistress with Yvain. Again she prevails, and the romance ends happily.

Like Chrétien's other romances, *Yvain* not only borrows magical elements from Celtic tradition but adapts them to his particular audience, the northern French aristocracy of the late twelfth century, which included a large proportion of bachelor knights, landless young warriors who stood little chance of marrying well or acquiring castles and lands. Yvain is himself a bachelor knight, attached to a royal court but apparently landless, whose sheer skill at arms allows him to gain a fairy-like lover and the rulership of an otherworldly realm. Chrétien, in bestowing Yvain with wife and lands, creates an ideal compensation fantasy for the bachelor knights in his audience. Like the master narrators of oral tradition, even this most refined of medieval French writers crafts his poems to embody the unofficial values and aspirations of his community.

See also: Chanson de Geste; Chanson de Roland; Charlemagne; Chrétien de Troyes; Courtly Love; Fairy Lover; Guinefort, Saint; Marie de France; Mermaid; Romance; William of Orange

—Francesca Canadé Sautman

Funeral Customs and Burial Rites. Ceremonies and rituals performed after death to aid the soul of the departed and to give comfort to the living.

Funeral rituals are a rich source of information on folk beliefs surrounding the human body, social identity, and life after death in the Middle Ages. St. Augustine, in a famous passage in his tract on the care of the dead, suggested that funeral ceremonies are "rather solaces for the living than furtherances to the dead"—a sentiment that no doubt contains an element of truth. Medieval funerals operated as markers of social status, and their ritual structure afforded elements of psychological therapy for the living participants. It is also possible that many of the ritual forms, though nominally Christian, were dictated by long-standing superstitions regarding vampires, evil spirits, and vengeful ghosts. At the same time, it should not be forgotten that most medieval customs were predominantly religious in purpose, aimed at helping the soul of the deceased in its journey to the next world.

Funeral customs are best characterized as *rites of passage*. In Arnold van Gennep's classic formulation, they comprise rituals of separation (preliminal), transition (liminal), and incorporation (postliminal). For the medieval Christian, this ritual process embraced (1) the separation of the soul from the body, (2) a transitional phase during which the soul's fate was decided, and (3) the soul's eventual incorporation into heaven. A similar pattern awaited the body: separated from the land of the living by death, the corpse underwent a liminal stage during which it was prepared for burial, before submitting to postliminal rites of incorporation in the cemetery.

Unlike modern Western attitudes, however, which focus on death as a rupture rather than a passing, medieval society afforded more significance to rites of transition and incorporation than to those of separation, reflecting the close ties between living and dead in this period. The emphasis on passage and transformation also reflects a loss of certainty in the period regarding the fate of the human soul. Whereas the Christian communities of Roman antiquity tended to celebrate death as the passage of the triumphant soul to celestial bliss, by the early Middle Ages salvation no longer seemed assured. Humankind's fallen condition required penitence, and death rituals consequently focused increasing attention on the state of the dying person's soul as it passed from one world to the next. In the years before 900 a complex of prayers, gestures, and actions emerged that formed the basis for a rite of passage that was to see the vast majority of Christians from deathbed to grave for many centuries thereafter. Although such rituals were as yet largely confined to the cloister, they became generally available to most members of the laity by the twelfth century.

From Deathbed to Funeral

The first stage in the traditional medieval death ritual began in the last hours of life. When the family, doctor, or friends sensed that death was near, it was their duty to call for the priest. After performing mass in church, the priest would solemnly transport the consecrated host to the home of the sick person. His ministrations began by holding a crucifix before the face of the dying person to provide comfort and to drive away demons. After testing their faith, extreme unction was administered (anointing with holy oil), followed by the sacrament (called the *viaticum*, Latin for "one for the road"). In the fifteenth century printed instruction manuals on the art of dying well (called *Ars moriendi*) became popular in Western Europe, and illustrated versions contain a final woodcut depicting the deathbed ritual. *Moriens* (the dying man) still grasps a lighted candle, supported by the cleric who conducts the last rites. The soul escapes from the body, to be caught by angels above, while angry demons seethe with disappointment on the floor below.

The onset of death was tested by various methods, such as holding a feather or mirror in front of the mouth to determine whether a person was still breathing. Middle English lyrics recounting the signs of death listed the visible indications that might be perceived:

When the head trembles,
And the lips grow black
The nose sharpens
And the sinews stiffen
The breast pants
And the breath is wanting,
The teeth clatter
And the throat rattles,
The soul has left
And the body holds nothing but a clout.

After death, the first action was to lay out the body and wash it. The corpse remained in the location where death had taken place, usually at home. If the body was to be kept in the house overnight, a wake, or "night watch," might be organized and candles might be lit around the corpse. In her will of 1434 the London widow Margaret Ashcombe requests "two tapers to stand at my head while my body resteth in my house of dwelling." Lit candles and tapers were commonly depicted around bodies awaiting burial in medieval manuscript illuminations, and though conventionally understood in Christian contexts as representing the "light of faith," these possibly fulfilled an apotropaic function by warding off evil spirits.

Before the body could be moved, it had to be appropriately dressed in a shroud or winding sheet. In the early Middle Ages the body was usually exhibited uncovered on a bier, both at home and on its way to the cemetery. However, by the thirteenth century in northern Europe, it was commonly sewn in a shroud and enclosed in a coffin. Once covered, the corpse might also have been laid out on a hearse. Unless the departed was wealthy, the coffin was usually only for the purpose of conveying the corpse from the place of death to the graveside, so that a reusable coffin and a public hearse were normally standard parish equipment. *Herse* is a French word signifying "harrow," and the fifteenth-century hearse simply took the form of an iron stand, with harrow-like spikes adapted as candle holders.

Once the corpse had been properly prepared, the next stage in the funeral ritual was the procession. This was a symbolic journey with both social and religious significance. Usually made up of priests, monks, friends, and relatives, it was also followed (if the deceased was wealthy) by a group of poor people who would pray for their superior's soul. At the front of the procession or at the church a bell might be sounded: this "passing bell" announced the passing of the soul into the next world, frightened off devils, and requested the prayers of those who heard it ring; sometimes it also indicated the social status of the departed by the number of tolls. The funeral ceremony was thus an important status symbol for the rich, an outward sign of the power and prestige of the deceased and the family to whom he or she belonged. But it also functioned on an eschatological level, generating prayers for salvation and providing an opportunity for good works; the poor were crucial elements in funeral pageantry and were usually rewarded with small gifts of alms in return for their attendance.

The religious function of the funeral procession is demonstrated by the fact that it was accompanied by the recitation of verses from the *Ordo defunctorum* (Office of the Dead), a collection of prayers and hymns modeled on the monastic timetable of hours. The office comprised two major components: first, the evensong of the dead known as the *placebo* (after the opening word of the service, from Psalm 116:9) and, on the next morning, the *dirige* (the opening word of Psalm 5:8, from which the English word "dirge" derives).

Depending on the status of the deceased, a funeral sermon might be delivered. An important death presented an ideal opportunity to remind the living of the transitory nature of life, and John Mirk started his sermon for burial with a salutary *memento mori*: "Good men, as ye all see, here is a mirror to us all: a corpse brought to the church." In addition, the deaths of the wealthy might be accompanied by funeral feasts (which are sometimes mentioned in wills).

Rituals of Mourning

During the funeral ceremony participants would often wear specific outfits to express their grief. In the later Middle Ages mourning dress was subject to strict sumptuary laws. The restrictions imposed by these laws guaranteed that dress was used to define and enforce social distinctions. The strict regulations of Margaret Beaufort, mother of Henry VII of England, make this clear. Issued in 1495–1510 these dictate the etiquette of mourning dress to be worn by each rank. Those of "greatest estate" had the longest trains, held by train bearers; they were also permitted the lengthiest tippets (thin, narrow attachments to the hood). In contrast, chambermaids were to have "noe manner of tippetes" at all. Books of hours reflect similar sentiments: the late-fifteenth-century *Grimani Breviary* contains a full-page miniature depicting a funeral ceremony, at the base of which is a burial scene clearly demarcating social boundaries. The chief mourners wear the deepest mourning and longest tippets, and the young boy at the front (possibly heir to the deceased) wears a tippet that extends from his hood to the back of his heels.

During the fourteenth century black became the predominant color of mourning for the wealthy, reviving the classical traditions of ancient Greece and Rome. Before this time black was probably not the norm. The Bayeux Tapestry shows Edward the Confessor's shrouded corpse being carried to Westminster Abbey on a bier by men wearing ordinary colored clothing. However, a glance at illustrations of the Office of the Dead in fifteenth-century books of hours confirms that black was the most popular color of mourning in northern Europe in the later Middle Ages, at least for the well-to-do. Indeed, in 1451 a wealthy testator commanded that the church at Somerby by Brigg be put into mourning and that "the priests array the altars and over sepulchers with black altar cloths."

Black's associations with death are ancient. Its oldest meanings are predominantly negative: darkness and night, evil and misfortune, the dark depths of hell and the unknown. Its use is also possibly connected with a deep-rooted dread of ghostly return, since it purportedly renders human beings invisible to spirits and thereby protects them from harm during the period of mourning, which corresponded to the length of time during which the corpse was thought to be dangerous. In addition, black was the color of the ascetic life, and Benedictine monks were known as *nigri monachi* (black monks) by the eleventh century. Lepers were required to wear gray or black in the fourteenth century, symbolizing the fact that they were "dead to the world." Significantly, living lepers were sometimes separated from society with elaborate funeral-like rituals: the diseased individual was led to the church chanting the penitential psalms of the funeral service, and a requiem mass was performed before the leper was taken to the cemetery to be sprinkled with a spade of earth. Thus, the color black had a long tradition of marking certain members of society off from others through its associations with humility, penance, and death.

Other than the adoption of mourning dress, grief was expressed through various bodily signs. The history of gestures in the Middle Ages is difficult to gauge, for the very reason that body language is inherently folkloric—passed down from generation to generation by ritual repetition rather than textual transmission. Nevertheless, cautious use of visual representations and textual anecdotes allows a degree of insight into the medieval language of emotion. Evidence suggests that control over one's emotions was revered for much of the Middle Ages, and uncontrollable gestures were connected with sin. Violent acts of grief such as wailing, tearing of the hair and beard, the clawing of the face and breast, and the kissing of the dead were condemned by early Church Fathers, such as John Chrysostom, who described the lamentations of women at funerals in the fifth century as "diabolic trickery." However, by the thirteenth century the appearance in art of apocryphal scenes such as the Lamentation over Christ testifies to a greater emotional tendency in art and religion. Normally in such contexts male figures, when they appear, are models of self-restraint and stoical resignation, whereas the female mourners perform dramatic acts of grief. The gender polarity is repeated in funeral and burial scenes in books of hours, which commonly depict exclusively male mourners and are consequently free of violent gesticulation. It should be stressed that manuscript images represent ideals, not social realities, and they cannot be taken as direct evidence of everyday folkloric practice, although they are clearly related.

The dead body awaiting burial was subject to various folkloric beliefs, including the idea that the corpse of a murder victim would bleed to reveal its killer. When the duke of Burgundy was present at the funeral of the duke of Orléans in 1407, dressed in black and "showing very great mourning, as it seemed," legend has it that spectators saw blood flow from the corpse, indicating foul play; it transpired that the duke of Burgundy had indeed ordained the murder.

Cemeteries and Burial

The burial of the shrouded body marked the next stage in the ritual process. The corpse was blessed in the cemetery before burial to ward off demons. Visual images of interment in manuscripts do not usually depict the presence of mourners, only a priest and his assistant. Graveyard scenes show people at their most desolate, abandoned by fellow humans and God. This reflects the liminal status of the unburied corpse—neither of this world nor yet of the next. Nowhere is this sense of desolation more striking than in the *Rohan Book of Hours* (c. 1420), where the dying man of *Ars moriendi* illustrations is famously transported to the cemetery, his naked corpse laid out on the ground amid skull and bones, as St. Michael and Satan battle it out over the fate of his soul—a surreal juxtaposition of deathbed rituals with the desolation of the grave.

Burial was one of the seven corporal acts of mercy, and it is depicted in one of the painted glass roundels from Wygston's House, Leicester (c. 1500), representing the theme. These portray a shrouded cadaver being lowered into a freshly dug grave, bones all around. A priest touches the corpse with a cross as it enters the grave, and clasps a sprig of hyssop with which he sprinkles holy water. The symbolism of hyssop relates to Psalm 51:7, "Purge me with hyssop, and I shall be clean." The widow is also in attendance, and behind the priest stands the benefactor who holds a lit candle and a rosary.

In ancient Mediterranean cultures the dead were buried outside the precincts of the living in burial complexes, or *necropoli* (cities of the dead). However, unlike Jews and pagans, for whom contact with corpses was strictly taboo, Christians regarded the bodies of martyrs as sacred and holy—intercessors between living and dead. This eventually gave rise to the burial of the sainted dead within the city walls, in basilican churches, so that between the fourth and sixth centuries the creation of holy sites dedicated to "the very special dead" completely transformed the urban topography of pagan antiquity. The desire to be buried *ad sanctos* (near the saints) led to the eventual admission of the dead bodies of the whole Christian populace into the communities of the living.

Grave goods are not normally discovered in Christian graves, with the exception of members of the Christian hierarchy such as clerics, bishops, and kings, who were buried with the insignia of rank. A good example is Archbishop Walter de Gray (d. 1255), whose tomb in York Minster was opened in 1968. His coffin contained a pastoral staff, ring, chalice, paten, and fragments of fabric. Such adornments were probably worn "in readiness to meet Christ." In contrast, the bodies of normal people were usually buried naked in the shroud, and excavations of Anglo-Saxon cemeteries indicate that pagan-style burials, in which the body was clothed and buried with grave goods, ceased in England during the early eighth century. Notable exceptions include pilgrim burials, such as the one discovered at Worcester Cathedral, where the body was found complete with boots, coat, staff, and scallop shell.

By the later Middle Ages the orientation of graves was consistent: head points west, feet east, in anticipation of resurrection. Excavations of cemeteries for criminals, however, suggest different orientations: at St. Margaret in Combusto, Norwich, "where those who have been hanged are buried," bodies were buried east-west, north-south, or south-north, and some were thrown into the grave facefirst (an example of the phenomenon of *widdershins*, or ritualistic reversing). Such treatment suggests that old ideas died hard regarding the life of the body after death. Indeed, excavations of Anglo-Saxon cemeteries from the seventh century suggest a transition period when pagan practices still lingered among ostensibly Christian communities: superstitious behaviors, from decapitating corpses to providing pagan amulets, suggest that people had their doubts about the power of the new religion over the potentially revenant dead who had been denied traditional pagan burials.

R. C. Finucane has shown how the different forms of burial accorded to various social groups reaffirmed "the secular and spiritual order by means of a corpse." The ceremonial burial of kings was poles apart from the disrespect shown to criminals; the enshrinement of saints in the holiest part of the church contrasted wildly with the refusal of Christian burial to heretics, excommunicates, pagans, Jews, and unbaptized infants. Women who died in childbirth and suicides were also technically condemned to burial outside the perimeter of the churchyard for most of the Middle Ages, though in practice it seems that these regulations were rarely adhered to. Strict punishment of suicides after death, which could entail stakes through the heart and burial at crossroads, was only strictly enforced in the late fifteenth century.

After the church, the medieval cemetery was the most sacred place in most towns and villages, and if it was polluted by bloodshed, no one could be buried there for months or even years after. A special ceremony had to be performed—usually consisting of public penance by the perpetrator— to remove the pollution.

Burial grounds were also important social spaces, used for games, markets, and even the pasturing of animals. This reflects the close ties between living and dead in the Middle Ages. In the twelfth century, according to the *Chronicle* of Jocelin of Brakelond, on Boxing Day (December 26) there were gatherings in a cemetery in Bury Saint Edmunds: there were "wrestling bouts and matches between the Abbot's servants and the burgesses of the town; and from words they came to blows, and from buffets to wounds and bloodshed." By way of punishment the people involved were stripped naked and scourged, and the abbot "publicly forbade gatherings and shows in the cemetery."

Remembrance

Commemoration of the deceased marked the final stage in the funeral ritual. Strictly speaking, "funeral" in the Middle Ages did not denote a single event pinpointed in time but a process that might be drawn out over weeks or even years. The section of the Office of the Dead known as the "dirge" continued to be recited at the week, month, and year anniversaries of a person's death, and a requiem mass might be performed for a period after burial, according to the individual wishes of the deceased. This continued performance of the requiem mass stimulated the foundation of chantries, which, while of direct benefit to the soul of the deceased in purgatory, also allowed the bereaved to be constantly involved in the welfare of the dead.

For those who did not have the means to pay for the endowment of a chantry, the parochial bederoll served a similar purpose, listing members of the parish for whose souls prayers were to be said. That this form of remembrance was not beyond the means of the poor is suggested by the fourteenth-century poem *St. Erkenwald*, which states: "Yet plenty of poor people are put in graves here / Whose memory is immortally marked in our death-lists."

The wish to attract intercessory prayer also affected the design of tombs, which were often erected in the same space as chantry chapels. The exact function of tomb iconography is a matter of some controversy. Whereas Erwin Panofsky argues that tombs were concerned primarily with looking forward to the afterlife and promoting the rank and family name of their inhabitants, Philipe Ariès sees after the eleventh century "a return to the individuality of the grave," speaking of the stark contrast between the later period and the anonymity of the early Middle Ages, where only the graves of saints and very great persons were identified.

See also: Blood; Memento Mori; Purgatory; Spirits and Ghosts

—Robert Mills

The Combat of Carnival and Lent; sixteenth-century oil painting on oak wood by Pieter Brueghel the Elder. In the foreground a fat man, playing the role of Carnival, straddles a barrel and faces off with an emaciated old woman impersonating Lent. (Ali Meyer/Corbis) See *Carnival; Drama; Festivals and Celebrations*

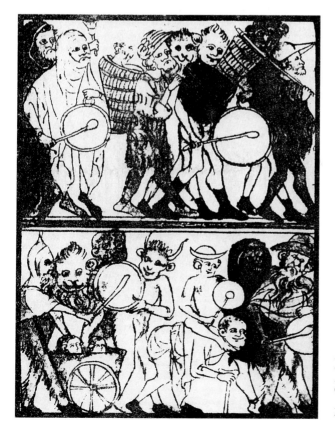

A charivari, as depicted in the early-fourteenth-century French *Roman de Fauvel*; illustration by Gervais du Bus. (Paris, BN MS Fr. 146, fol. 36v) See *Charivari; Wild Man*

The Legend of the Three Living and the Three Dead, a thirteenth-century fresco located in the Monastery of St. Benedict, Subiaco, Italy. (Corbis/Archivo Iconografico, S.A.) See *Funeral Customs and Burial Rites*; Memento Mori

A German depiction of the Dance of Death involving a usurer, a mayor, and a landowner. (Foto Marburg/Art Resource, NY) See *Dance of Death*; Memento Mori; *Misericords*

Wild Woman depicted in the lower margin of an antiphonary. (The Pierpont Morgan Library, New York, M. 905, vol. 2, fol. 122) See *Drama*; *Iconography*; *Wild Man*; *Wild Woman*

Wild Man depicted in the lower margin of the same antiphony. (The Pierpont Morgan Library, New York, M. 905, vol.2, fol. 205) See *Drama*; *Iconography*; *Wild Man*; *Wild Woman*

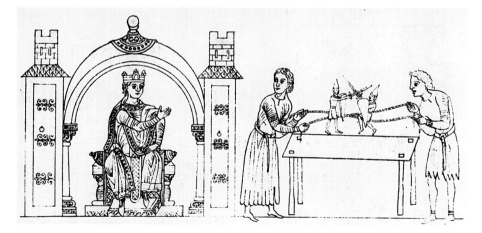

The earliest known drawing of puppets; two men manipulate figures of knights in this twelfth-century illustration from Herrad of Landsberg's *Garden of Delights* (Reproduced from Gérard Cames, *Allégories et symboles dans* l'Hortus deliciarum, Leiden, 1971) See *Drama*; *Masking*; *Puppets and Puppet Plays*

Two-tailed mermaid, printed by Juan Joffre, Valencia, Spain, 1520. (North Wind Picture Archives) See *Mermaid*

A captured unicorn, on a lady's lap, wounded by a knight. Ormesby Psalter, English, fourteenth century. (Oxford, Bodleian Library, Douce MS 366, fol. 72r) See *Bestiary*; *Unicorn*

The fairy Melusine takes on the traits of a serpent and flies from her locked chamber; from a fifteenth-century French woodcut. (Dover Pictorial Archives Series) See *Fairy*; *Fairy Lover*; *Mermaid*

Left: Gargoyle as a caricature of a nun on Horsley Church, Derbyshire, circa 1450. (Archive Photos) See *Gargoyles*

Below: Hans Baldung Grien, *The Witches' Sabbath*; Chiaroscuro woodcut, 1510. (Museum of Fine Arts, Boston, bequest of W. G. Russell Allen) See *Witchcraft*

A mounted devil carries off a woman. This legend theme, well known as early as the eleventh century, became popular toward the end of the Middle Ages; this depiction is a woodcut from Olaus Magnus, *Historia de gentibus septentriolanibus*, printed in 1555. (Dover Pictorial Archive Series) See *Satan*; *Spirits and Ghosts*; *Witchcraft*

A vain woman looks for herself in a mirror and sees a devil's anus instead; woodcut by Albrecht Dürer, 1493. (Dover Pictorial Archive Series) See *Satan*; *Spirits and Ghosts*

Ape nurses fox in bed; misericord supporter, Beverley
Minster, Yorkshire, 1520. (Photograph by Malcolm Jones)
See *Misericords*

Illumination for February, from
the *Très riches heures de Jean duc
de Berry*. (Fol. 8v; Musée
Condé; Giraudon/Art Re-
source, NY) See *Books of Hours*

This misericord presents a folly popular in numskull jokes from the Middle Ages to the present: to spare his horse, a man shoulders the horse's load himself—but rides the horse, so that it will have to carry him as well; this is folktale type AT 1242A, "Carrying Part of the Load"; fifteenth century, La Guerche de Bretagne, France. (Photograph by Elaine Block) See *Folktale; Misericords*

Illumination for August, from the *Très riches heures de Jean duc de Berry.* (Fol. 8v; Musée Condé; Giraudon/Art Resource, NY) See *Books of Hours*

Hell-mouth, a fifteenth-century German woodcut. (J. de Teramo, *The Book of Belial*, Augsburg, 1475; Dover Picture Archives) See *Hell*

Illumination of Jesus Christ confronting Satan, from a fourteenth-century Italian manuscript. (Corbis/Archivo Iconografico, S.A.) See *Satan*

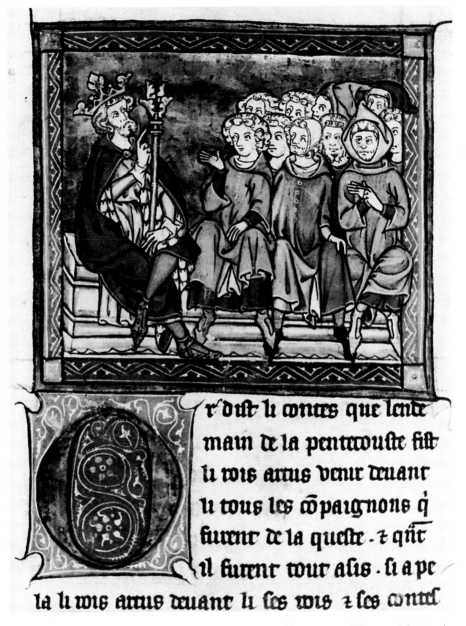

r̃ dist li contes que lende
main de la pentecouste fist
li rois artus venir deuant
li tous les co̅paignons q́
furent de la queste . τ q̃t
il furent tout asis . si a pc̃
la li rois artus deuant li ses rois τ ses contel

King Arthur convokes the Grail questers. (Reproduced by courtesy of the Director and University Librarian, the John Rylands University Library of Manchester; French MS 1, fol. 114v) See *Arthur; Arthurian Lore; Chrétien de Troyes; Grail*

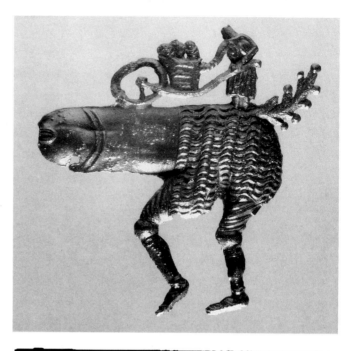

A fifteenth-century Dutch lead badge. (Reproduced with kind permission of H. J. E. Van Beuningen, photo by Tom Haartsen) See *Phallic Imagery*

An early-sixteenth-century German representation of Eulenspiegel; note the owl and the mirror from which his name is derived. (North Wind Picture Archives) See *Eulenspiegel*; *Trickster*

Portal tomb on the Burren, in the west of Ireland, built circa 3500 B.C.E. Such tombs and the mounds that often covered them are sometimes depicted as entryways to the otherworld in medieval Irish mythological traditions. (Photograph by Peter McNamara) See *Annwfn*; *Burial Mounds*; *Celtic Mythology*; *Fairies*

The legend of St. George and the Dragon was the most popular medieval version of the plot identified by folklorists as AT 300, "The Dragon-Slayer." (Dotted print, upper Rhine, 1460; Bettmann/Corbis) See *Dragon*; *Folktale*; *George, Saint*

St. Francis of Assisi preaching to the birds, from Matthew Paris's *Historia Major*, circa 1240 (Corpus Christi College, Cambridge, MS 16, fol. 66v; reproduced from Elizabeth Hallam, *Four Gothic Kings*, New York, 1987) See *Italian Tradition*; *Saints, Cults of the*

Altarpiece from Ardal Church, Sogn, now in Bergen Historisk Museum, depicting the Church's reinterpretation of Olaf's death. Contradicting saga reports that he died in battle, sword in hand, ecclesiastical sources portray Olaf finding death as a gentle Christian martyr. (Courtesy of Kathleen Stokker) See *Olaf, Saint*; *Scandinavian Tradition*

Foreign races, as depicted in Konrad von Megenberg, *Book of Nature*; Augsburg, Germany, 1475. (Dover Pictorial Archive Series) See *Foreign Races*

A late-fifteenth-century French *proverbes en rimes* [rhymed proverbs] manuscript, illustrating the proverb known to modern English speakers as, "Don't look a gift horse in the mouth." (Walters Art Gallery) See *Proverbs*

An image from a medieval German print of a woman being drawn and quartered. (Archive Photos) See *Punishments*

G ames and Play. Pastimes either planned or spontaneous, operating in a space and time set apart from the routine, subject to their own rules, and involving any or all of the elements of mental or physical competition, display, or imitation.

Like our modern word *play*, the Latin word *ludus* (play) and its vernacular equivalents, including the word *game*, could refer to a wide range of activities in the Middle Ages: a seasonal festival, a theatrical drama, a board game, an outdoor sport, a joke, or almost any form of amusement.

Throughout the Middle Ages games were both condemned and defended. Preachers frequently discussed idle pastimes as part of the deadly sin of sloth. Late-medieval woodcuts show demons encouraging gamesters to play dice, and sermons and educational treatises warn against overindulging in summer games and other entertainments. Monarchs, religious authorities, and town officials issued numerous prohibitions of games, sometimes mandating severe penalties such as imprisonment and even death. Yet there is ample evidence that people continued to indulge in traditional pastimes despite urban and clerical bans, and arguments for the psychological and social benefits of play are found throughout the period. For example, the fifth-century monk John Cassian recorded a story comparing the human mind to a bent bow, which must occasionally be released to avoid its becoming lax and ineffective. In 1444 a Parisian cleric similarly defended the Feast of Fools, an annual ceremony that parodied the religious service. After likening devout Christians to wine barrels about to burst with the pressures of piety, he argued that play was an essential release valve: "We permit folly on certain days so that we may later return with greater zeal to the service of God."

Medieval games—as the historian Thomas S. Henricks puts it, "who gets to play what with whom before whom (and in what ways)"—can tell us a great deal about social relations in the Middle Ages. Some games were limited, by custom or by strict regulation, to participants of a certain age, gender, or social level. For example, noblemen competed against one another in exclusive jousts and tournaments, where entry depended on status. On the other hand, many games were enjoyed by a large portion of medieval society. Men and women, monarchs and peasants alike, indulged passionately in dice games, whose popularity is attested by accounts of court cases, records of gambling debts, and the large number of dice found at archaeological sites.

Just as important as who played certain games

were the social functions these games performed for participants and spectators. Leisure pastimes could reinforce social hierarchies, a role that the historian Mervyn James has posited for the Corpus Christi celebrations of medieval English towns, in which citizens processed in order of status. Or games could seemingly turn social hierarchies upside down, as did Hocktide, a spring celebration that involved women pursuing and capturing men. Some pastimes, such as annual football matches between neighboring villages, could regulate potentially deadly rivalries, but games could also cause tensions to erupt in violence. In the 1260s in London a man killed a woman during a quarrel arising from a game of chess, and in Basel in 1376 Carnival celebrations caused a riot. Thus, although games occurred in a time and space separated from the everyday (a holiday afternoon, a field temporarily given over to sport), they could also reinforce or even amplify the everyday conflicts and bonds of the medieval community. In fact, games were sometimes used as symbolic representations of society: medieval scholars wrote chess moralities in which each social class (pawns, knights, king, and so on) performed its own particular function in a common battle against the devil.

Village and Urban Games

Village and urban games and festivities most frequently occurred on Sundays and holidays, particularly during the Carnival season (the days preceding Lent) and during the spring and summer months. In his account of London life written around 1180 William Fitzstephen lists numerous carnival and warm-weather diversions: young men occupied themselves with football, horse racing, cockfighting, mock battles, leaping, archery, wrestling, stone throwing, and javelin throwing; young women occupied themselves with dancing. Fitzstephen also mentions winter games: bull and bear baiting, ice skating, and ice tilting (mock combat using poles). These pastimes, along with many others, were enjoyed not only in twelfth-century London but throughout medieval Europe.

Competitive games added to a sense of community, and whole villages or urban neighborhoods might turn out to support the participants. In England annual football matches took place between neighboring villages by at least the fourteenth century, and in the fifteenth century married and unmarried men played against one another at weddings. Medieval football (an ancestor of soccer) involved two teams, of unspecified and sometimes quite large size, attempting to move a ball across a boundary. Judging by court records, the game was loosely organized and often brutal. Though it provided an alternative to (and may have even developed from) unregulated fighting, it sometimes led to riots, accidental deaths, and even homicides.

Bowls (*boules*), another ball game, was exceedingly popular, especially in France. In a common version, competitors tried to throw their balls closest to a target, either a stake or a smaller ball, while at the same time attempting to knock their opponents' balls away. Variants of bowls eventually evolved into modern croquet and bowling.

In addition to competitive games, holiday festivities in the Middle Ages included such other forms of play and spectacle as mumming, theatrical performances, processions, puppet shows, acrobatics, minstrelsy, performances of trained animals, and elections of mock rulers.

Medieval villagers and townspeople also engaged in more sedentary pastimes, both indoors and outdoors. Men and women played dice, backgammon (or tables), morris (or merels), and—to a lesser extent—chess. Morris, an expanded version of our tic-tac-toe, involved creating rows of pieces and capturing the opponent's rows. Wooden morris boards survive from the tenth century, and morris boards have been found scratched into the floors of cloisters and watchtowers. Card games became popular only in the late fourteenth century.

Almost all medieval games involved gambling, with both participants and spectators wagering on the outcomes. Money was the most common wager, though *boules* games in France were frequently played for wine. Dice, the quintessential betting game, was repeatedly and unsuccessfully banned. Some gaming laws were more concerned with cheating and swindling than with gambling or the game itself: in medieval Hungary those found using fixed dice could be punished by being dunked in hot water or having a die struck through their palm.

Medieval authorities occasionally mandated participation in village and urban games, a command blurring the line between work and play. During the Hundred Years' War the king of England ordered that men making less than a certain income practice archery during their free time. To ensure cooperation, many other holiday pastimes, such as handball and football, were banned under pain of imprisonment. At the same time the king of France also promoted archery practice and prohibited popular games such as dice and *boules*. In the minds of these rival monarchs, the safety of their realms depended on the control of village pastimes.

Courtly Games

The perceived link between play and military prowess was made even clearer in the case of courtly pastimes. Furthermore, just as village games could contribute to camaraderie and a sense of local identity, so some courtly games were a way for noble men and women to confirm their membership in the aristocracy.

Hunting was one such elite sport; it was thought to refine military skills and noble virtues. Kings and noblemen hunted on restricted land—the most extensive was the king's forest estab-lished by William the Conqueror in England—and had exclusive rights to certain prey, such as the stag and the boar. Trespassers and poachers could be severely punished. Interestingly, poaching itself became a risky and prestigious game for the lower classes, who were legally permitted to hunt only vermin, such as wolf, fox, and badger.

Another activity important to upper-class identity was chess. The game penetrated Western Europe sometime before the year 1000, probably through the Islamic cultures of Spain and Sicily, and is first recorded among churchmen. After early and unsuccessful attempts by Church officials to control its popularity, chess spread to lay society through the monasteries, schools, and universities of the twelfth century. Although chess was played in towns and villages as well as in noble homes, the mastery of chess remained a sign of courtly refinement for noblemen and -women. Manuscript illuminations depict chess games in gardens, and medieval romances portray chess as a typical aristocratic pastime.

Despite these examples it is often difficult to draw a clear distinction between high and low culture in the Middle Ages. Nobles and peasants observed the same religious holidays and frequently attended the same celebrations. Entertainments such as minstrelsy, mumming, dancing, and dramatic performances were enjoyed both in towns and at the royal court. Furthermore, many courtly pastimes differed from village ones only in the playing space and in the quality and availability of specialized equipment. Tennis, a game that originated in France and swept Europe during the fourteenth century, is a good example: while the upper classes played with expensive rackets on standardized courts and used an elaborate scoring system, the lower classes played handball—an earlier version of the game—in streets and fields. Even the elaborate tournaments of medieval knights were mirrored in the sword-and-buckler play of the towns and villages.

Children's Games

Like children of other time periods, medieval children of all classes engaged in imitative and competitive play, sometimes involving special toys. As spectators or participants, children were fully involved in the festive life of their communities, and in their play they copied not only the work but also the leisure activities of their elders. For example, the game of marbles—whose popularity is demonstrated by the hundreds of marbles uncovered at archaeological sites—was probably a miniaturization of the adult game of bowling.

Children's Games (1560), a famous painting by Pieter Brueghel the Elder, depicts more than 80 children's games, many of which date to the Middle Ages. Medieval manuscript illuminations show infants being amused with rattles and toddling with wheeled walkers and older children playing with balls, tops, hobbyhorses, whistles, drums, cymbals, hoops, jump ropes, kites, and marbles.

Some toys, such as dolls, were designed for imitative play and reflected the world that medieval children grew up in. Archaeologists in France and Germany have discovered small clay knights, women, and animals dating from the thirteenth century, along with tiny clay vessels that might have been toy dishes. Figures of knights on horseback and other military toys were probably used to fight mock wars and tournaments. An illustration in a twelfth-century German manuscript shows two children manipulating toy knights with strings, and in 1383 the young Charles VI was given a wooden cannon to play with.

Like adult games, children's games could involve an element of violence. In hoodman-blind, a medieval version of blindman's bluff, the child who was "it" was "blinded" by a hood and tried to catch the other children, who hit at him or her with their own knotted hoods. Children also engaged in animal sports, hunting small game with child-sized crossbows, and holding their own cockfighting matches. On Shrove Tuesday, the day before Lent, medieval English schoolboys brought their cocks to school, where the birds would fight to the death.

See also: Carnival; Festivals and Celebrations; Fools, Feast of; Harvest Festivals and Rituals; Masking; Puppets and Puppet Plays; Sword Dance
—Karen Bezella-Bond

Gargoyles. Stone, marble, or (rarely) metal waterspouts found on medieval ecclesiastical and secular buildings.

From the late twelfth century onward gargoyles served to drain rainwater from roofs and direct it away from walls. Their practical function was usually masked by decoratively carving the gutter's top surface and by making the exit hole correspond to an anatomically correct hole on the figure's body. Though gargoyles are generally carved as whole sculptures, less frequently they consist of two halves fit together, as seamlessly as possible, around the central gutter (e.g., at Laon Cathedral, c. 1210).

Generally overlooked in art history studies, gargoyles are occasionally cited in research on single folkloric themes. Gargoyles can be considered only in part a kind of medieval marginalia: situated on the upper edges of tall walls, they bear comparison to manuscript margins' decorations, misericords, keystones, and other elements adorning the peripheries of buildings, books, and furniture; yet the subjects that carvers and architects chose for gargoyles overlap only slightly with the subjects depicted in other medieval marginalia. It is also difficult, given the present state of research, to identify thematic relationships among gargoyles belonging to the same building. Thematic studies have been limited to isolated figures or sometimes to types of gargoyle. Particular care must be taken when making a folkloric interpretation of gargoyles, as those that appear in published studies constitute only a small percentage of the actual total, and there is great uncertainty about their chronology. Furthermore, postmedieval restorations (for example, Eugène-Emmanuel Viollet-le-Duc's restoration of Notre-Dame in Paris in 1845–1864) have drastically changed the original appearance of certain gargoyles and replaced others altogether, so that many of the most famous "medieval" gargoyles were in actuality carved long after the Middle Ages. The literature on gargoyles seldom refers to such restorations. An attempt at a thematic classification can therefore be no more than a working hypothesis until art history research provides surer grounds for interpretation.

Gargoyles frequently appear in animal form. There are animals belonging to real species native to Europe, dogs being the most popular (the sculptures on the cathedrals of Laon in France and Mechelen in Belgium are particularly noteworthy), but goats, donkeys, cows, pigs, and birds also abound. Among the most popular nonnative species are lions (for example, the thirteenth-century figures, largely restored, on the eastern end of Rheims Cathedral or the fourteenth-century compositions on Saint Mary's Church, Over, Cambridgeshire) and monkeys (on the Hauptmarkt fountain in Nuremberg or the fourteenth-century monkey-like beings at Vincennes castle). Particularly common are fantastical species, such as dragons and unicorns. Medieval bestiaries, which provide moralizing and allegorical descriptions of both real and imaginary animals, provide a good key to the basic symbolism of all these species. Motifs overtly recalling specific folkloric themes seem to be more rare: for example, the folktale motif of the animal musicians (motif B297.1), which appears as a sow with a harp at Notre-Dame-de-l'Épine, France (sixteenth century).

Hybrid animal types are especially common: creatures constructed of parts of different animals, like the thirteenth-century bird with four legs on Burgos Cathedral, Spain, or the figures at Ely Cathedral. Particularly common are four-legged animals equipped to fly: cows (Utrecht, Netherlands), dogs (Milan, Italy), fish (Lier, Belgium), lions (den Bosch, Netherlands), and goats (Mechelen, Belgium) all appear with wings. According to some interpretations, these composite creatures have an overtly negative, if not a precisely diabolical, significance, representing confusion and disharmony.

Along with nonhuman animal hybrids, there are hybrids composed of human and nonhuman parts. Only seldom do these partly human gargoyles represent creatures known from classical and medieval mythology, that is, such figures as sirens, centaurs, mermen (Milan), or harpies (e.g., Brussels town hall, sixteenth century). More often they appear as "disordered" combinations. Many of these grotesque creatures display features—such as horns, pointed ears, and fangs—belonging to the iconography of the devil, and they have frightening expressions; see the fourteenth-century gargoyles of the church of Saint Ouen in Rouen or the gargoyles on the facade of the twelfth-century church of Saint Martin in Laon.

Fairly common are images of human beings covered with scales or hair, identifiable as Wild Men or as their close relatives, Green Men—for example, the gargoyle apparently converted into a wall spout in the courtyard of the Hôtel de Cluny in Paris. The Wild Man, especially, is a pervasive folkloric figure in other contexts; it appears often in festivals, pageants, and carvings as well as in the form of gargoyles.

Human beings are rarely represented as physically handsome. A few such good-looking gargoyles are found on the thirteenth-century facade of Salisbury Cathedral, the fourteenth-century cathedral of Freiburg im Breisgau, and the thirteenth-century church of Saint Ursin in Troyes. More often the human figure undergoes various deformations. These can consist of a grotesque alteration of the face or of other parts of the body, resulting in general somatic ugliness, or of gestures considered indecorous because they are exceedingly expressive, overtly mocking, or obscene. Among the first we find expressions of terror or rage; among the second, figures pulling their mouths to grotesque widths or sticking out their tongues. Among the most famous obscene creatures are the men exposing their anuses and apparently defecating—for example, outside the cathedrals of Autun (thirteenth–fourteenth centuries) and Freiburg im Breisgau (fourteenth century).

Because of their pronounced ugliness, these figures have been seen as general depictions of sin and its punishment or as representations of particular sins. This latter hypothetical interpretation is perhaps based on a reading of the gargoyles' nakedness or of certain gestures the gargoyles eternally assume—for example, touching their throats with their fingers in a gesture that could be interpreted as representing the deadly sin of *gula*, or gluttony. Sometimes gargoyles are seen as generic representations of vice—vice embodied in the physical deformity of the human figure, a sort of "reverse image" of the well-ordered harmony of creation. Moreover, the deformed human figure in gargoyles would be a reminder of punishments awaiting the sinner after death; thus, such figures would have been seen by contemporaries as damned souls, changed into hideous stone figures and forbidden from entering the church.

There are many more interpretations of monstrous gargoyles, which are based on the relationship between the inside and the outside of the building: that these are apotropaic demons keeping guard over the church or diabolical beings or worldly temptations waiting outside the church.

The apparently scatological gargoyles—for example, the defecating men at Autun and Freiburg—have generally been interpreted as functioning apotropaically (that is, to ward off evil) or simply as being gestures of mockery. They have been related to the many similar examples known from medieval folklore and iconography. Yet more complicated interpretations have seen these figures as conveying initiatory meanings related to ritual anal presentation and kissing.

More clearly connected to folklore are rare complex scenes, such as that of a woman copulating with a goat (a well-known embodiment of the devil)—an act commonly attributed to witches throughout the last centuries of the Middle Ages and beyond—at the church of Notre-Dame-de-Marais in Villefranche-sur-Saône (France, sixteenth century). There is also a group apparently representing a deer-hunting scene, transposed in a vertical sequence at Freiburg im Breisgau Cathedral, that evokes not only representations of hunting from Roman art but also episodes of medieval literature, folktales, and hagiography. Consider as well the male figure carrying a fool on his shoulders at Saint-Germain-l'Auxerrois in Paris (fifteenth century).

It is also a difficult task to establish thematic connections between the gargoyle and the sculpted console that sometimes supports it because the two are not always contemporaries. This is the case with the facade of Poitiers Cathedral (thirteenth century) or with Saint-Père-sous-Vézelay (fourteenth century).

Even if we concede the difficulty of evaluating medieval gargoyles as a repertory of folkloric themes, we can still see them as an expression of a certain medieval taste for deformity and the grotesque—terrifying and comic at once. This taste has been much examined in a large variety of studies of medieval culture. Meanwhile, great care should be taken in interpreting gargoyles as a space freely given to sculptors' imagination on the margins of Gothic buildings—buildings that are otherwise carefully mapped out to the last detail. In approaching gargoyles, we should follow the lead of those who have studied the grotesque figures of manuscript marginalia and consider the degree of conventionality of certain themes, the possible existence of a tradition internal to the genre that probably carried far more weight than is presently thought. Such a tradition certainly had its roots in what we call popular culture, but precisely detecting and classifying its themes and their significance and origins seems a particularly difficult undertaking, at least for the moment.

See also: Green Man; Iconography; Manuscript Marginalia; Mermaid; Misericords; Wild Man; Wild Woman

—Chiara Piccinini

Gawain [French Gauvain]. Nephew of King Arthur and a paragon of Round Table chivalric virtues.

Some scholars speculate that the character of

Gawain is linked to that of a Celtic solar deity (given that his strength sometimes waxes and wanes with the energy of the sun) or with the Irish hero Cú Chulainn. However, he first appears in Arthurian literature in the early twelfth century as Walwanus, a warrior and kinsman of Arthur in the chronicles of Geoffrey of Monmouth, *Historia regum Britanniae* (History of the Kings of Britain).

By the time he appears in France in the mid-twelfth-century *Roman de Brut* of Wace, Gauvain (to use the French version of his name, appropriately, here) has become an exemplar of courtliness. Chrétien de Troyes portrays him as a model for his central heroes, Erec, Lancelot, and Yvain. Although he begins these romances in a position of preeminence, his role in many romances becomes secondary when he is surpassed by the central hero. Gauvain becomes associated with certain flaws, especially a tendency toward dalliance with female admirers. Gauvain's worldliness disqualifies him from the spiritual quest for the Grail in Chrétien's *Le conte du Graal* and its continuations. In the later Grail romances, particularly the Vulgate cycle, Gauvain's wantonness and other faults are increasingly apparent. Though Gauvain is the hero of other French romances, such as *La mule sans frein* (The Mule without a Bridle) and *Le chevalier à l'épée* (The Knight of the Sword), his dignity is undercut by humor in these works.

Gawain remains popular in Arthurian literature throughout Europe. In Germanic cultures he is a less flawed and more exalted hero. He has a major role in German romances, including Wolfram von Eschenbach's *Parzival* and Hartmann von Aue's *Erec*. Heinrich von dem Türlin gives him the central role in *Diu Crône* (The Crown), where he finally succeeds in the Grail quest. The Middle Dutch *Roman van Walewein* offers further evidence of his widespread appeal.

Late-medieval English romances seem to retain an awareness of Gawain's reputation for dalliance, as the hero is tempted by a lady in *Sir Gawain and the Green Knight*, and he weds or beds a variety of uncourtly maidens in the tail-rhyme romances *The Wedding of Sir Gawain and Dame Ragnell*, *Sir Gawain and the Carle of Carlisle*, and *The Jeaste of Sir Gawain*. Nevertheless, in these tales Gawain proves loyal and monogamous. Here, as in the alliterative romances *The Awntyrs off Arthure* and *Golagras and Gawaine* and in the final books of Malory's *Le Morte Darthur*, Gawain emerges primarily as a warrior supremely devoted to his uncle Arthur and other members of his family.

Thus, medieval romance presents two Gawains, reflecting two distinct cultural perspectives. The French Gauvain serves as the flawed foil for greater knights, while the Germanic Gawain upholds values of warrior prowess and tribal loyalty. Gawain particularly excels in such nonnoble creations as *Gawain and Ragnell*, where

his courage far exceeds Arthur's—an indication that Gawain probably served as a model for England's less exalted social groups as the Middle Ages drew to a close.

See also: Arthurian Lore; Loathly Lady; Romance; *Sir Gawain and the Green Knight*

—Cathalin B. Folks

Geoffrey of Monmouth (c. 1090–1155).

Anglo-Norman writer whose *Historia regum Britanniae* (History of the Kings of Britain, c. 1138) professed to present a continuous historical narrative of the kings of Britain from the eponymous Brutus, great-grandson of Aeneas, to the Britons' loss of sovereignty to the English following the death of Cadawallader in 689 C.E.

Geoffrey traces the fortunes of the "ancient Britons," the forefathers of the Welsh, Cornish, and Bretons, through a succession of some 120 kings and queens over a period that extends from the sack of Troy to the seventh century. Brutus, son of Silvius, grandson of Aeneas's son Ascanius, together with his followers, flees the sack of Troy and, exiled from Rome, spends years living in Greece and wandering the Mediterranean Sea and southern Gaul before settling on the island of Albion, which is renamed Britannia. Geoffrey's narrative moves swiftly over the period of British hegemony and gives vivid accounts of wars, conquests, invasions, and civil discord. But the central figure in the history is Arthur, and the account of his antecedents and reign takes up almost half the story. The wars with the English and Arthur's temporary success—ultimately undermined by his betrayal by his nephew Modred and the resulting civil war, in which Arthur is killed—prove to be the turning point in the narrative. The years following Arthur's passing are years of final decline, and Geoffrey brings the book to a close quickly.

Geoffrey claimed to have translated his history from "an ancient book in the British language," which his friend Walter, the archdeacon of Oxford, had brought out of *Britannia* (which can mean either Wales or Brittany). But the strong thematic structure of the *Historia* (which plays recurrently on the relationship between Britain and Rome) and its firm composition (which varies periods of internal strife, wise rehabilitation, and foreign threats and which gives some prominence to the role of women leaders) preclude our taking the book to be a translation of an old Welsh or Breton chronicle. Its literary qualities and historiography suggest, rather, that its context is to be found in twelfth-century English historical writing, but that Geoffrey's book, unlike his contemporaries' work, is largely an imaginative narrative, a "prose epic" rather than a *historia*. As such, it can be read at different levels—as an outrageous forgery, a satire of contemporary historians (especially William of Malmesbury and Henry of Huntingdon), or a "British" version of the Anglo-centric histories being produced—but in terms of content it is a pastiche made up of material from a variety of sources: the Bible, Bede, *Historia Brittonum* (History of the Britons), and British legendry.

As with any other composed literary work, it is not easy to trace the *Historia's* sources precisely, as Geoffrey freely used and adapted his reading, his general culture, and contemporary ideas. There is no doubt that he drew upon popular folkloric elements, but these may differ significantly in their status as sources and in the way in which they were utilized.

Some episodes are popular elements that Geoffrey appears simply to have taken from the general stock of themes and stories that were familiar to him and that he used in his own narrative context. Thus, the sea monster that attacks Northumbria and is killed by Morvidus need not have had any such specific existence prior to the *Historia*. The claim that Albion was inhabited by giants before the coming of Brutus may be not traditional but, rather, Geoffrey's adaptation of Genesis or perhaps of Ovid's *Metamorphoses*. If so, Corineus's combat with the most notable of these giants, Gogmagog, is not traditional but a reflection of the popularity of Cornish wrestling. Brutus himself had received a prophetic dream vision of his coming to Albion when he offered a sacrifice to the goddess Diana before sleeping in front of the altar on the skin of a hind. Dream visions during sleep on an animal skin are part of medieval folklore, but they have a wider context in medieval dream literature and belief, and Brutus's dream is another example of Geoffrey's use of contemporary themes (or of a literary source such as *Aeneid*, Book 7) to give verisimilitude to his account. Geoffrey includes a number of other prophetic dreams in the *Historia* (though not occasioned by any divinatory practice), and it is interesting that Geoffrey displays a degree of skepticism about their significance.

Other popular themes, taken either from literary or general oral sources and used by Geoffrey for his own purposes, are fraternal discord, donning an opponent's arms to deceive an enemy, and disguising oneself as a servant to gain access to an enemy to kill him (often by poison).

Geoffrey has used Welsh legendry whenever he could and within the limits of his own knowledge. His prime source appears to have been *Historia Brittonum*. His account of the coming of the Saxons under Hengist and Horsa, their duping of Vortigern, and the "treachery of the long knives" is an elaboration of the Nennian narrative, which appears to have been an established traditional legend with a number of popular themes. It came to Geoffrey, however, from a literary, not an oral, source. Part of the narrative is an account of Vortigern's tower and its sinking foundations. Vortigern's sages advise the king that the blood of a boy born without a father must be sprinkled on the foundations. Geoffrey draws on popular beliefs—that the boy was born of a nun and an in-

cubus—to elaborate the account, and, in one of his favorite ploys, he gives the boy the name Merlin or Myrddin (instead of Nennius's Ambrosius) so that he may be eponymously associated with Caerfyrddin (modern Carmarthen), which could be popularly understood as "stronghold of Myrddin." From Nennius, too, comes Geoffrey's descriptions of two lakes possessing remarkable natural features. These form part of Nennius's list of *mirabilia* (marvels) and derive from popular tradition. Geoffrey, however, uses them to enliven his narrative and gives them an Arthurian context. Geoffrey's knowledge of Arthur's early campaigns comes from Nennius, but he has also some independent information about the king: his special weapons, the shield Prydwen, the lance Ron, and the sword Caliburnus, and his closest followers and family, Guinevere, Kay, Bedivere, Gawain, and Modred. Geoffrey also knows of a traditional tale about the passing of Arthur to the Isle of Avalon after the battle of Camlan, though he is careful not to prophesy his return. This section of the Arthurian narrative is given its own introductory paragraph, which may suggest that Geoffrey knew of it as a particularly significant episode in the legend of Arthur.

Geoffrey has a unique account of the begetting of Arthur. The love-stricken Uther Pendragon comes to Ygerna and seduces her in the shape and form of her husband Gorlois. Forms of this story are found elsewhere; for example, the myth in which Jove sleeps with Alcmene in the form of her husband Amphitryon and begets Hercules; or the late-Irish story of the begetting of Mongan by Manannán mac Lir in the form of Fiachna. The same plot may underlie the shapeshifting of Pwyll and Arawn in the First Branch of the Welsh Four Branches of the Mabinogi. Whether the tale of the begetting of Arthur is traditional or Geoffrey's creation cannot now be established.

Other examples of Welsh historical legendry that Geoffrey does not appear to have drawn from literary sources, but that are reflected in Welsh texts, are the role of Cassivelaunus (in Welsh, Caswallawn) in the reception of the Romans, and the story of Maxentius (in Welsh, Maxen Wledig), Conanus Meriadocus (in Welsh, Cynan Meiriadog), and the founding of Brittany.

Apart from his personal use of nonspecific popular elements and his knowledge of Welsh historical legendry, Geoffrey has a few examples of what may be genuine folk narratives, embellished and adapted to his own purposes. One such tale may be the story of Lear and his daughters; another may be the ruse by which Hengist, offered as much land as a hide might cover, cuts the skin into a single thong to mark the bounds of his citadel, thereafter called "Thanceastre." This may be a genuine etymological tale (though "Thanceastre" has not been identified), but a similar story is found in the *Aeneid*, Book 1, about Dido and Carthage. The story of the removal of Stonehenge (Giants' Dance) from Ireland to Salisbury Plain has no clear parallels (though the idea of stones with medicinal properties is familiar). Their actual removal is accomplished by Merlin's skill and contrivances, not by his magic, but that Geoffrey should have envisaged the transporting of such a huge monument from one part of Britain to another is striking in view of the now accepted opinion that these massive stones were somehow moved from Pembrokeshire. Whether some story about the erecting of Stonehenge was current in the twelfth century cannot be confirmed, but Geoffrey's account is intriguing.

Geoffrey has other giants—*ogres* is a better term—whose stories appear to be unreconstructed folktales. The fierce monster of Mont-Saint-Michel sank ships with rocks and devoured their crews and raped and killed Helena, niece of the king of Brittany. He is challenged by Arthur and slain in single combat. Arthur may not have been the original hero, but it seems probable that Geoffrey is drawing on a local folktale that explained the name of a small adjacent island, Tombelaine, as *Tumba Helene* (the tomb of Helen). After killing this monster, Arthur recalls an earlier combat on Mount Arvaius with the giant Ritho, who had demanded the king's beard, promising to make it the prized part of his cloak of royal beards. Arvaius was taken by Welsh translators to be Eryri, Snowdonia (in north Wales), and they render the giant's name as *Rhita* or *Rhica*. The tale is not found prior to the *Historia*, and at least some of the later Welsh stories about Rhita Gawr (the giant) owe something to Geoffrey, but the story of *Culhwch and Olwen* has an episode in which Arthur seeks the beard of the giant Dillus Farfog (Dillus the bearded) to make a leash for one of his hounds. In Welsh law and folk custom, beards were symbols of status and vitality, and Geoffrey's story fits a Welsh cultural context very well. Both of these giant stories portray an Arthur less sophisticated than the Norman king-emperor characteristic of the *Historia* but more like the leader found in early Welsh poetry, and they may be genuine pieces of folk narrative.

Geoffrey of Monmouth does not appear to have drawn heavily on popular tradition. He intended his history to be readable but acceptable, and it does not contain many fantastic episodes. His use of popular elements is judicious and is intended to enliven his narrative.

When trying to determine the relationship between the *Historia* and folk tradition, it can be just as confusing to consider texts compiled after Geoffrey as to consider his possible sources. The *Historia* was so well received that it became in effect the official history of Wales and influenced subsequent views of history and tradition. As a result it is very difficult to determine whether an item that first appears in the *Historia* and then in later texts existed orally before Geoffrey, was passed as literary text from Geoffrey to the later

sources, or passed from Geoffrey into oral tradition, whence it was picked up by later writers. Sometimes one can discern folklore in the translations of the *Historia*, in which translators-copyists have changed or added to Geoffrey's work in accordance with the story as they knew it. The most striking example of this is the addition of the story of *Lludd and Llefelys*, in which the wise Llefelys advises his brother Lludd on how to rid the Island of Britain of three plagues that infest it.

See also: Arthur; Arthurian Lore; Brutus; Lear, King; Maxen Wledig; Merlin; Myrddin; Nennius

—Brynley F. Roberts

George, Saint (d. 303?).

An early martyr, probably a Roman soldier, reputedly killed in 303 C.E. at Lydda (Palestine); later, the patron saint of England.

All further stories told of St. George are unhistorical. Beginning in the sixth century, he was regarded as a patron of the Byzantine army, but to Western Europe he was only a minor figure until a reported vision of him before the capture of Antioch in the First Crusade was taken as a sign of victory. A military and aristocratic cult rapidly developed. His feast day (April 23) was made a holiday in England in 1222, Edward III chose him as patron of the Order of the Garter in 1343, and Henry V invoked him at Agincourt; by the close of the Middle Ages he was regarded as the patron saint of England and a model of chivalry. He was also the patron of Venice, Genoa, and Portugal and was venerated in Germany as one of the "Fourteen Holy Helpers." In postmedieval times his cult declined steadily, and in its calendar reforms of 1969 the Catholic Church reduced his ranking from that of a "universal" saint to an optional local one.

Early accounts (Greek, of the sixth century) concentrate on his martyrdom; for eight days he miraculously survived various tortures, including being speared, scourged, forced to run in red-hot shoes, broken on a wheel, thrown into quicklime, and poisoned, but he was finally beheaded. Later Latin texts multiply the tortures to extend over seven years, interspersed with equally astounding miracles. But it was the tale of his combat against a dragon that ensured his popularity. This tale first appears in the *Legenda aurea* (The Golden Legend), compiled by Jacobus de Voragine in the thirteenth century. It tells how George came to a pagan city whose inhabitants, terrorized by a dragon from a nearby lake, were forced to feed it a human being daily; the lot had fallen on the king's daughter, but George pierced the dragon with his spear, bound it with the princess's girdle, and led it into the city before beheading it. All then became Christians.

The dragon fight was a popular subject for icons and paintings. George's deeds and his prolonged martyrdom are also shown in a series of murals in the cathedral of Clermont-Ferrand and the chapel of San Giorgio in Padova (Padua,

Italy), and a set of sixteenth-century windows in the parish church of Saint Neots (Cornwall).

In England in the late Middle Ages his feast day was celebrated by processions in many major towns, including Leicester, Coventry, Reading, and King's Lynn, as well as in many smaller places. A magnificently dressed rider impersonated the saint, and an effigy of the dragon was paraded and "slain." Though ostensibly religious in intent, these events were also occasions for displays of communal pride by guilds and civic officials and for popular delight in pageantry; some therefore survived the Reformation as civic events, transferred to some other date. One of the best documented took place at Norwich from 1408 onward, organized by the local St. George's Guild; after the Reformation it became a Mayor's Show, in which saints or religious symbols were forbidden but the dragon was still allowed "to show himself, for pastime." The last of these dragon effigies, known as "Snap" and made in about 1795, can still be seen in the Castle Museum at Norwich. It is made of painted canvas over a wooden frame, designed to rest on the shoulders of a man walking inside it; its neck can retract, shoot out, and turn, while its iron-clad jaws are opened or snapped shut by a cord.

A versified charm preserved in a fifteenth-century manuscript shows that St. George was not only the patron saint of fighting men but could also be invoked as a protector against more homely evils—and, interestingly, that he was thought of in chivalric imagery as "Our Lady's knight." Anyone whose horses are "hag-ridden" (i.e., suffering from night sweats, ascribed to being ridden by a supernatural witch) is instructed to

Take a flynt stone that hath an hole thorow
it of hys owen growynge, & hange it ouer
the stabill dore, or ell [else] ouer ye horse,
and writhe this charme:

In nomine Patri &c. [the words recited in
  a blessing or when making the sign of
  the cross]
Seynt Jorge, our ladys knyght,
He walked day, he walked nyght,
Till that he fownde that fowle wyght [foul
  creature];
And when he her fownde,
He her beat and her bownde,
Till trewly ther her trowthe sche plyght
  [gave her word]
That sche sholde not come be nyght
With-inne vij rode [seven rods] of londe
  space
Ther as Seynt George i-namyd was.
In nomine Patri &c.

And wryte this in a bille and hange it in the hors' mane. (MS Bod. Rawlinson C506 f.297)

The legend of George was remodeled after the Reformation, first in Spenser's *Faerie Queene*, where, as the "Red Crosse Knight," he represents the struggle of Protestant truth against popish error, and later by Richard Johnson in 1596 in a popular work, *The Most Famous History of the Seaven Champions of Christendome*. Johnson strips the Christian elements from the lives of the patron saints of seven countries, replacing them by chivalric and magical adventures imitated from medieval romances. George is born to noble English parents but is stolen soon after birth by an enchantress, whose power he eventually outwits. Not only does he save Sabra, the king of Egypt's daughter, from a dragon, but after further adventures he encounters a second dragon (in England) and kills it, but himself dies from its poison and is buried in Windsor Chapel. This patriotic and secularized story proved immensely popular, and together with Spenser's work ensured George's continued status as patron of a Protestant England.

See also: Dragon; Saints, Cults of the
—Jacqueline Simpson

Gerald of Wales (c. 1146–1223) [French Gerald de Barri, Latin Giraldus Cambrensis].

Norman-Welsh scholar (educated in Paris; taught canon law), cleric (archdeacon of Brecon; twice rejected as bishop of St. Davids, for whose independent status he ardently fought), royal clerk (in the court of England's Henry II), ecclesiastical reformer, and monarchical critic.

Gerald wrote some 20 books presenting his arguments, his philosophies, and accounts of his travels and in the process recording innumerable items of folklore—oral, customary, and material—much of it in an autobiographical context and deriving from personal experience.

Certain of Gerald's books are marked by their inclusion of folklore. *Topographia Hibernica* (Topography of Ireland, 1188) draws on materials gleaned during two trips to Ireland: in 1183, accompanying his brother to recover family lands, and in 1185–1186, accompanying Prince John and then staying on for his own studies. The book treats nature lore (the crane responsible for guarding the flock holds a stone in its upraised foot so that if it dozes off the falling stone will wake it; barnacles on logs turn into birds), migratory legends (a lake resulting from a well overflowing when momentarily left uncapped), saints' legends (a duck belonging to St. Colman cannot be cooked; St. Ninnan banishing fleas from a certain village), material culture (hooded capes and trousers made of wool; the reins and crooked sticks used to guide horses; midwives not swaddling infants or shaping their limbs but, rather, letting nature take its course), music (fast, lively airs on harp and timpani), and customs (ritual union of a king with the land through intercourse with and ingestion of a white mare). *Itinerarium Cambriae* (Journey through Wales, 1191), which reported a journey with Archbishop Baldwin of Canterbury in 1188 to enlist volunteers for the Crusades, and *Descriptio Cambriae* (Description of Wales, 1194) detail a similar range of items, including nature lore (how beavers escape hunters), material culture (techniques for leading plowing oxen, fishing with coracles, design of reaping knives, foodways, communal beds made from rushes and covered with a *brychan*, a woven, usually woolen coverlet), music (on harp, pipe, and *crwth*—a stringed instrument—and singing in multipart harmony), and customs (young people celebrating St. Eluned's feast day by singing and miming work forbidden on Sunday). In addition to saints' legends (a boy sticking to St. Davids Church when he would have defiled it, dogs refusing to shelter in St. Caradog's cell until invited by him, St. Curig's staff healing those who offer proper payment at his shrine) and *memorates* (first-person accounts of supernatural experiences), such as the tale of the child named Elidyr who claimed to have been taken to a beautiful underground otherworld by two tiny beings, the *Descriptio Cambriae* also contains historical anecdotes, such as the tales of birds bursting into song in recognition of Gruffydd ap Rhys ap Tewdwr as rightful ruler of the land, or of Henry II testing Merlin's prophecy that an English king who had conquered Ireland would die upon crossing the stone known as Llech Lafar; Henry crossed and lived.

Gerald's descriptions of Ireland and Wales, fraught with an outsider's view of native and therefore perceivably primitive cultures, reflect his own peculiar cultural status and expectations as a member of Marcher society, the product of intermarriage combining the lines of Welsh princes and Norman aristocracy, trained in Paris at the center of urban, urbane Europe, and employed in the English court. When he looked at the Irish he recognized some of the qualities of the "noble savage," but he also saw a culture devoid of the hallmarks of civilization—settled agriculture, cities, industry, commerce, and the preferred form of Christianity—and he accepted all his culture's stereotypes of the "barbarian."

He traveled to Ireland, the western edge of the known world, expecting to find wonders comparable to those of the East. His readiness to accept marvels, combined with his failure to understand the full cultural context of everything he learned, meant he was not always able to assess the accuracy of his material, making him appear ingenuous at times. Nevertheless, his descriptions, if not always his interpretations, are considered generally reliable, and he did attempt to write rounded ethnographies, describing a people by recording various interrelated aspects of their lives: their appearance, environment, history, customs, entertainments, warfare, and daily practices.

In both Ireland and Wales, where he was only a little less the outsider, Gerald proved a keen and curious observer providing otherwise lost information and simultaneously revealing bits of his own folk culture and belief system. He displays, for example, a fascination with and acceptance of prophecies, and he shows himself an able manipulator of folklore. He uses the story of Meilyr, for example, to denigrate a rival author: Meilyr would be relieved of his demons whenever St. John's Gospel was placed in his lap but be immediately overcome by the demons when touched with Geoffrey of Monmouth's *Historia regum Britanniae* (History of the Kings of Britain), a book that in Gerald's opinion was filled with falsehoods. Gerald also drew extensively on folk traditions about St. David to support his fight for metropolitan status for the see of St. Davids.

When Gerald writes about the Church he writes as an insider, although still from the position of one observing the strange behavior of the "locals." As an archdeacon (the "eye" of the bishop) Gerald would have been responsible for discipline, spotting irregularities, border disputes, and other assorted problems; as someone trained in the Roman Church, he would have had difficulty accepting some of the vestiges of ecclesiastical custom of the earlier "Celtic" Church. Accordingly, in addition to tales of Christian marvels, he also repeats narratives critical of ecclesiastical misbehavior and hypocrisy, especially when involving his personal villains, the monks. Gerald's *Gemma ecclesiastica* (The Jewel of the Church, 1197), for example, draws many exempla from patristic, classical, and hagiographic writings (which were themselves ultimately drawn from oral tradition), but it also records many oral narratives: exempla about images of Jesus or the Virgin Mary bleeding when struck, fabliaux about various monks and clerics sexually tempted by women, anecdotes involving incubi and succubi (male and female sexual predators), and contemporary legends about spiders accidentally drunk in the sacramental wine crawling out through the drinker's toe, arm, or tonsure. *Speculum ecclesiae* (A Mirror of the Church, 1220), with a more embittered and critical tone for the monastic orders, contains contemporary anecdotes and fabliaux about lax morals of monks, gluttony and love of drink, and covetousness. *De jure et statu Menevensis ecclesiae* (The Rights and Status of St. Davids, 1218) includes, along with its accounts of conversations with Pope Innocent III and other prelates, narratives such as the ribald tale of the stolen horse shown to be a gelding upon examination.

See also: Celtic Mythology; David, Saint; Exemplum; Folklore; Geoffrey of Monmouth

—Elissa R. Henken

German Tradition. The folkloric culture of the West Germanic peoples.

Medieval folk tradition and its customary transmission in Germany were the result of thousands of years of development. Thus, both the tradition and its lines of transmission consist of many highly varied elements, of diverse historical and cultural origins. This great diversity manifests itself in many folkloric forms, including sacred and secular rituals, life-cycle customs, magical beliefs, folk wisdom, folk medicine, sayings about the weather, and both the written and oral traditions of märchen, legends, saints' lives, proverbs, riddles, jokes and anecdotes, folk sayings, and beliefs about ghosts and demons, angels and saints, and witches and devils. In addition, it manifests itself in material culture in the forms of houses and settlements, utensils and tools, the material products of religious and secular folk art, clothing, costume, and food. All of these have undergone thousands of years of development, shaped by many and various intellectual, cultural, material, and socioeconomic influences. Stemming from a variety of sources, these elements of folklore differ widely even in their respective ages.

Even today the various tribal divisions of the German people continue to play a fundamental role. For almost 2,000 years the Germanic homeland consisted of the north German plains, the region of lower Saxony between the Ems and the Elbe Rivers. Expanding to the south and west, West Germanic tribes settled lands originally inhabited by Romano-Celtic peoples; migrating to the east, they took over Baltic and Slavic territory. Despite the fragmenting effect of centuries of territorial movements, traditional tribal divisions remained intact even at the end of the Middle Ages: Bavarians, Swabians (Alemanni), and Franks occupied the South; Wesphalians and Lower Saxons, the North; Saxons, central Germany; and Frisians, the North Sea coast. This geographic and tribal diversity played a fundamental role in determining traditional German folk culture at least up to World War II.

In the Middle Ages tribal differences were reflected in the very layout of fields and villages. Fields were worked according to the three-field system of crop rotation—that is, every year the soil was prepared for a different crop. In the north German and lower Alpine regions single farms predominated, while Franks and Hessians preferred to settle close together in villages. During the Middle Ages nearly every region developed its own characteristic type of house; for example, the *Hallenhaus*, a type of longhouse popular in lower Germany; the two-story Swabian *Einhaus*, built on a stone foundation; and the typical *Schwarzwald*, or Black Forest house, which like the other two house types provided lodging for both people and livestock, but which unlike the others contained a wall to separate the animals from the people.

Within village society the smith and the shepherd have played special roles since time immemorial. In the eyes of the common people they possessed mysterious powers to heal sick cattle or to recover stolen livestock. Bee culture was common on the outskirts of the villages, where wild bees were smoked out of their hives in order to get the honey. Villagers drove swine into the forest to fatten on acorns. Charcoal was produced in forest kilns. Peasants mowed grain with sickles and cultivated spelt, millet, flax, and poppies along with rye to increase self-sufficiency. Clothing was strictly regulated, especially in the cities, where every level of society—peasant, middle class, nobility, or clergy—possessed its own particular costume that made it instantly recognizable. During the eighteenth century regional variations in costume developed from the more formal urban models and gradually reached rural areas.

Celebrations and customs also underwent changes over the course of centuries. The first major turning point was the Christianization of the German tribes in the eighth century. Christian missionaries, especially St. Boniface among the Frisians and St. Columban, St. Gall, and St. Pirmin in the South, declared the Germanic gods to be *unhold* (*hold* meant "friendly" or "good-natured"; thus the negative *unhold* was roughly equivalent to "diabolical"). Ideas and concepts that sprang from tribal and folk origins were animistic and presumed that natural occurrences, as well as the fate of the individual, were governed by supernatural powers. Those powers could in turn be influenced by resorting to magical and, especially, religious means. There is surely no people that does not populate its world with supernatural beings, which serve the function of explaining the unexplainable in human life. The oldest documentary evidence of German folk custom, after the *Germania* of Tacitus (c. 100 C.E.), is the so-called *Indiculus superstitionum et paganarum* (Letter Concerning Superstitions and Pagan Practices), written in 743 C.E. but only rediscovered in a manuscript in the Vatican in 1652. It originated during the period of the conversion of the Saxons and contains brief descriptions of stone- and tree-worshipping cults, magical spells and predictive sayings, traditions honoring the dead, annual ritual fires, image magic (charms), and vegetation cults. The manuscript bears witness to a syncretic blending of heathen cult forms with those that are, on the surface at least, Christian. Vestiges of such customs and magical beliefs have continued essentially into modern times: fires lit to celebrate the winter and summer solstices, stone- and spring-worshipping cults on sites of Christian pilgrimage, and even the Christian tradition of relics. Many such customs were preserved, if in modified form, into early modern times—for example, ringing bells and intoning blessings during storms and employing other blessings to ensure good weather.

The various genres of folk narrative are attested only in the later Middle Ages. The oldest documentation is found in the jokes and student songs of the *Cambridge Song Manuscript*, a Latin collection copied by an Anglo-Saxon hand about 1059. Alongside sacred songs, the manuscript contains comic poetry originating on German, English, and French soil. Toward the end of the Middle Ages can be found numerous collections of humorous tales, intended primarily for casual amusement. Often they present stereotypical characterizations ridiculing unfaithful wives, unscrupulous innkeepers, greedy merchants, miserly bourgeois, and fat, naive peasants. Also common in these stories is the mockery of the lower orders of the clergy, lecherous village priests, and mendicant friars. These tales possess parallels in the Italian *novella* tradition, in Boccaccio for example, as well as in Chaucer, demonstrating how commonly medieval tales crossed national boundaries.

Texts of exempla and sermons from the Middle Ages are also excellent sources of popular humor, saints' lives, fables, märchen, and legends. By injecting anecdotal, edifying, and cautionary tales into his sermons, the preacher sought to instill Christian precepts in the faithful as he engaged their interest by entertaining them.

Medieval comic tales, with their didactic, moralizing, and religious functions, constitute an exceptionally rich source for cultural history, providing information on the acceptable and unacceptable folk customs of the time and illuminating the ways of life of various levels of society, from the clergy to the peasant and the mercenary soldier. A further source of folk narrative is provided by the so-called *Gesta Romanorum* (Deeds of the Romans, 1342), a collection of tales, legends, and anecdotes recorded by priests and later translated into all the European languages, disseminated throughout the Continent for entertainment and edification.

In medieval times written and oral transmission were already interacting in mutually enriching ways, although heroic legends such as those of the Nibelungs, Alexander, and Roland, which were fixed early on in written form, possessed very few parallels in popular oral tradition. It was not until the beginning of the nineteenth century that märchen and legends were first collected and written down. Famous as pioneers in this endeavor, the brothers Jacob and Wilhelm Grimm published the first edition of their *Kinder- und Hausmärchen* (Children's and Household Tales, better known as *Grimms' Fairy Tales*) in 1812, followed by their extensive collection, the *Deutsche Sagen* (German Legends), in 1816 and 1818. They drew the märchen predominantly from the contemporary oral tradition, while for the legends they utilized the widest-ranging written sources: chronicles, travel literature, sermons and exempla, topographical and statistical works, classical works, medieval manuscripts, and calendars.

Most German folk legends had been transformed over the centuries by Christianity. This Christianization of legendary material occurred in two phases. In the first phase, *interpretatio Christiana* (Christian interpretation), which occurred during the period of the conversion of the

Germanic tribes, their gods and sacred objects were reinterpreted as the works of the devil; the "heathen" beliefs and magic practices and rituals, such as those preserved in the above-mentioned *Indiculus superstitionum*, were the most affected. The second phase began in the twelfth century with the development of the concept of purgatory as the "third realm" between heaven and hell. It is scarcely possible to comprehend the Western medieval transmission of legendary material without recognizing the importance of the Christian doctrine of purgatory, which was first fixed as a dogma toward the end of the twelfth century. Priestly logic demanded that there be a place that would serve as the abode of those deceased persons who were not to be consigned directly to hell but who were also not so free of (original) sin that they could be accepted immediately into heaven. Thus, they conceived of a temporary residence, a place where souls of the sinful atoned for venial sins and were purified. Picturing their suffering powerfully stimulated the fantasies of the faithful. Many legends tell of apparitions of those tortured souls seeking redemption. As a tangible or visible sign of their existence they might leave behind an imprint of a hand, stamped in fire on wood or other surfaces. Such signs persist into present times, strengthening the popular conception of poor sinners as worthy of mercy and deserving help through the donation of masses, offerings, and prayers. A Christian ethos manifested itself not only in the obligation of almsgiving but also in the doctrine that words of forgiveness from survivors can help the newly deceased find salvation.

Alongside legends of the dead, which were rooted primarily in the popular religious conception of the tortured soul, Christian motifs are also found in the legends of sin and its punishment. One of the earliest of these is the tale of the dancers of Kölbigk, mentioned around 1075 in the chronicle of the monastery of Hersfeld: during the Christmas matins (morning prayers) of the year 1012, 16 men and women dance in the cemetery by the church. As the pastor admonishes them to take part in the matins, they ridicule him. In response he places a curse on them, requiring them to dance for the next coming year. Eventually their dancing feet dig a deep trench in which they stand up to their hips. At the end of the year, Bishop Heribert of Cologne releases them from the curse, at which point most of the dancers either die or become incapacitated. The tale is based on an epidemic of dance mania that under priestly influence was turned into a moralizing exemplum. Diffusion of the story during the Middle Ages was aided by the fact that travelers and beggars claimed to have been participants in the blasphemous dance and produced petitions that reinforced their claims by stating that the tale was an actual account of their experience.

Among the oldest legends that we know, even

from pre-Christian times, are those concerning the crossing of the dead into the world beyond, already attested by Procopius of Caesaria (sixth century). They originate from a concept of a kingdom of the dead separated from the world of the living by a body of water. These legends turn up in nineteenth-century tradition as does the story of subterranean beings or dwarfs crossing a river at nighttime; the ferryman cannot even see his passengers and notices that they have filled his boat only as it sinks. This tale belongs to a body of legendry that transmits knowledge of the beyond. The souls of the dead are ferried over to the Isles of the Dead, which, according to Procopius, is Britain. The author maintains, "These events are verified by statements of the people of that region." The narrative undoubtedly points to archaic strata of popular belief that have not yet been Christianized.

A similarly ancient tale is that of the Wandering Soul (the legend of Guntram), told by the Langobardian historian Paulus Diaconus in his *Historia Langobardum* (History of the Lombards, 787–797). According to the story, the Franconian king Guntram takes a rest while out hunting and falls asleep. A servant attending the king watches as a small creature, probably a snake, crawls out of the king's mouth and attempts to cross a small stream flowing nearby. The servant lays his sword across the stream, enabling the creature to crawl over and disappear into a mountain. After a short while, it returns and slips back into Guntram's mouth. On awakening the king tells of a dream in which he crossed a river on an iron bridge, reaching a mountain where he found wonderful treasures. Excavations in the mountain across the stream turn up a quantity of gold. This story, which Paulus Diaconus wrote down toward the end of the eighth century, is the oldest written documentary evidence of the concept of the separable soul. The story of a man's wandering soul, or alter ego, taking on animal form presents relics of an archaic and very widespread belief that has an extensive oral and literary tradition and was even included by the Grimm brothers in their legend collection.

The monk Notker the Stammerer of St. Gall (d. 912) tells of a goblin that steals wine for the bishop. When he permits the barrels to run empty, the bishop curses him and flogs him unmercifully. The goblin screams, "Woe is me, that I lost the bottle of my godfather." Stories of goblins are also told by Thietmar of Merseburg (975–1018) in his chronicle, which states that in the year 1017 he and other residents of his monastery actually experienced these supernatural events. The pious bishop recognizes the goblins to be ungodly demons and attributes the events to his lack of success in converting the Saxon populations: "Moreover, it is not surprising to see such a sign and wonder in these regions. For the inhabitants seldom go to church and care nothing of the visits of their pastor. They worship their own household gods and sacrifice to them, believing they can be of help to them."

For centuries the Roman Church waged intense war with werewolves and Wild Women, fairies and witches, norns and goblins. But its struggle with the belief in spirits and magical concepts, all deeply rooted among the populace, made scarcely an impression on the popular attitudes and conceptions of the surrounding world. Again and again one is astonished to see the range of sources upon which German narrative tradition draws. Sometimes individual motifs, such as the Polyphemus motif from the *Odyssey* or the Sisyphus motif, separated from their ancient narrative framework, reemerge in the tales of a completely different culture, in this case that of Alpine legends. Polyphemus complains to his cyclopean companions that "Nobody" has wounded him (Odysseus assumed the name "Nobody" to trick the Cyclops), but the other Cyclopes retort that they can do little for someone who has hurt himself and decline to come to his aid. In the analogous German legend, a forest demon is caught in the crook of a tree by a clever peasant who gives as his name "Did It Myself"; when the demon's fellows rush to his aid and ask who trapped him, he can only answer "Did It Myself." In another tale, similar to that of Sisyphus, a shepherd who let a cow fall to its death must spend his afterlife forever hauling the cow back up the mountain, only to have it slip from his hands and fall back down just before the goal is reached. It is of course difficult to establish solid theories about the transmission of such motifs from antiquity or from the East. The interrelationships have not been sufficiently investigated and are not always even clear, owing to a lack of knowledge of intervening stages in the process of transmission. For now, we can only state that such motifs can derive from other cultures and earlier epochs and can live on into the present.

See also: Eulenspiegel; Legend; *Nibelungenlied;* Peasants; Tannhäuser; *Unibos*

—Leander Petzoldt

Giants. Monstrous supernatural beings in Scandinavian mythology; also, the subject of local legend throughout medieval Europe, represented in medieval pageants, and appearing in many medieval romances and more recent folktales.

The fullest picture of giants in northern mythology is found in Old Norse literature. In the mythological poems of the Icelandic *Poetic Edda*, they are in conflict with the gods and are represented as an older race of beings, who know of the beginning of the worlds. Even Odin, wisest of the gods, consulted the giant Vafthrudnir when he wished to discover hidden knowledge. In the thirteenth-century *Prose Edda* of Snorri Sturluson the world was said to have been formed from the body of an ancient giant, Ymir, from whom both giants and gods were descended after he was slain by the creator gods.

The giants, who dwelt in Jötunheim (literally, Giant World), were dangerous neighbors to the gods in Asgard, and Frigg warned her husband against making a visit to Vafthrudnir, because if Odin could not outdo the giant in a riddle contest he could be destroyed. The enmity between gods and giants was like that between gods and Titans in the mythology of ancient Greece, and Thor, with his mighty hammer and power over the lightning, defended the gods from the threat of cold, darkness, and sterility.

The giants are sometimes called "frost giants." Their aim was to carry away Freyja, goddess of fertility, as well as the golden apples that gave the gods perpetual youth, and the sun and moon, thereby causing the return of chaos. Surviving myths show the constant threat the giants posed to the gods. They sought to obtain Thor's hammer, the weapon they feared most, or else to lure him unarmed into Jötunheim. One giant, Hrungnir, made his way into Asgard, but was slain by Thor in a duel. Another giant built a wall around Asgard, but demanded Freyja and the sun and moon as payment, so Loki prevented him from completing his work, and he was slain.

Myths recounting Thor's, Odin's, or Loki's entrance to the realm of the giants are found in some of the earliest surviving poems from pre-Christian Iceland, and some are illustrated in carvings considerably older than the literary sources. One such journey, ending with the battering to death of the giant Geirröd and his two daughters after they attempted to destroy Thor, was known to Saxo Grammaticus, the thirteenth-century Danish historian.

A long comic tale of about the same date in the *Prose Edda* relates how Thor was humiliated when he visited the hall of the huge giant Utgard-Loki, skilled in deceptive magic. Thor only discovered too late how he had been hoodwinked, but he had terrified the giants by his divine strength. When Thor went fishing for the Midgard serpent, he was accompanied by a sea giant, Hymir, who was so frightened when Thor hooked the monster that he cut the line at the crucial moment of the catch. Thor went to the hall of the giant Thrym to recover his stolen hammer, disguised by Loki as the goddess Freyja, coming to be wed, and once he got his hammer back he slew the giant and all the wedding guests.

Odin overcame the giants by disguise and cunning rather than by brute force, and a famous and possibly ancient myth relates how he recovered the magic mead of inspiration, which the giant Suttung had taken and kept within a mountain. In serpent form, Odin crawled through a crack in the rock and then made love to the giant's daughter in return for three drinks of mead. He emptied the three vessels that held it and flew back in the form of an eagle, to vomit up the precious liquid when he reached Asgard. In another tale Loki rescued the stolen golden apples, along with the goddess Idun, and flew off in bird form, pursued by the giant Thjazi in the form of an eagle, but the gods prepared a fire that singed the giant's wings when he flew into Asgard, and he was slain by Thor.

Thus, it can be seen that a number of early and powerful myths are concerned with the struggle of gods against giants to preserve the culture that they had created, until the end comes at Ragnarök. In this battle the giants at last gain entrance to Asgard, accompanied by the monsters that also threaten the gods, and by the treacherous Loki, sometimes represented as a giant. In the final battle both gods and giants perish, while the earth is destroyed by fire and sinks into the sea. But it is fated to rise again from the cleansing waters, to be ruled by the sons of the gods in a new age.

A different relationship between supernatural beings is indicated by marriages between the gods and the daughters of giants. In the poem *Skirnismal* (The Lay of Skirnir), Skirnir woos the fair maiden Gerd on behalf of Frey; she is the daughter of a giant in the underworld and can only be reached by a long and perilous journey. Skadi, daughter of the giant Thjazi, married the god Njord, although the marriage failed because she belonged to the world of mountains and he belonged to the world of the sea.

These northern giants possess a certain power and dignity not retained in later medieval literature. There are traces of a powerful giant race among the Germans. Weland, known to the Anglo-Saxons as a supernatural smith and associated with an ancient burial mound on the Ridgeway in southern England, was a member of a family remembered in heroic poetry. His father was the giant Wade, remembered in English local tradition, and his son was the famous hero Widia. In the romances and folktales, however, giants appear as powerful but rather stupid unnamed beings who wreak havoc in the land, capture maidens and imprison them in their castles, feast on human flesh, and hurl stones and boulders about the landscape. They are overthrown by valiant knights or deceived by intelligent young heroes. In postmedieval folktales the giant's wife often assists the hero by concealing him from her husband, as in the widespread tale of "Jack the Giant-Killer."

Much local tradition throughout Europe associates giants with impressive ruins or spectacular rocks and hills, while long mounds may be known as their graves. The Anglo-Saxons described the ruins of Roman buildings as the work of giants, as in the poem *The Wanderer*.

The builder of Asgard was a giant, and there are many later legends of two giants flinging stones or a shared hammer from one to the other as they made roads or piled up rocks, and sometimes the giant's wife helped in such operations, carrying stones in her apron until the strings broke. Dropped stones or loads of earth were said to account for certain hills and isolated boulders.

Sometimes the giant in such legends was transformed into the devil, but many giants survived in local tradition. They were particularly popular in Cornwall, and according to Geoffrey of Monmouth this was the case as early as the twelfth century.

Local giants of postmedieval legendry were by no means always hostile figures; many were remembered with affection, and humorous tales were told of them. Some seem to have been local men of outstanding size and strength rather than supernatural figures. Tom Hickathrift is still remembered in East Anglia, where a long piece of granite in a churchyard is identified as his grave and columns of broken memorial crosses are declared to be his candlesticks. He is recalled as a friendly neighborhood giant, whose great exploit was that of overthrowing another giant by using the wheel of the wagon he had been driving as a shield and its axle as a weapon. A similar tale is told of another Tom, known as the Hedger, a Cornish giant remembered as a man of great strength, eight feet tall. Their powers, however, were liable to increase in popular tradition; Tom Hickathrift was said in a rhyme to devour church and steeple, and all the people, and still remain hungry, and his name was used to frighten naughty children.

A custom that kept giant figures alive in popular imagination was that of carrying giant figures in procession in various towns and cities; they were regarded with pride and affection by the townspeople. Most of the English processional giants were destroyed at the Reformation, but one survives at Salisbury. Originally 14 feet high, he is supported on a light wooden frame that can be carried by a succession of men, and he was provided with new clothes from time to time. He was the pageant figure of the Guild of Tailors, mentioned in their records as early as 1570, and was known as St. Christopher since the Middle Ages. He was brought out on June 23, St. John's Eve, and July 15, the eve of St. Ogmund's festival, and he still appears on such special occasions as the Silver Jubilee of Queen Elizabeth II.

Two London giants housed in the Guildhall are figures carved in wood, now known as Gog and Magog; in Tudor times they were Gogmagog and Corineus, from Geoffrey of Monmouth's twelfth-century account of the giants of Britain. Earlier still, they were Samson and Hercules. They welcomed Philip of Spain when he married Queen Mary in 1554 and saluted Elizabeth I from Temple Bar when she became queen in 1558. There are also references to two giants welcoming Henry V in 1415 after his victory over the French in the battle of Agincourt. The present figures replaced eighteenth-century ones—14 feet, 6 inches high—burned in the London Blitz. They were successors to an older pair, destroyed in the Great Fire of London.

Processional giants have fared better in continental Europe and flourished in the Netherlands, Belgium, and northern France, where many are still paraded at festivals. Some are accompanied by dragons and monsters of various kinds, like the Salisbury Hob-Nob, a horse-like figure with snapping jaws that might tear the clothes of people in the crowd.

The folklore of giants is a mixture of horror and comedy, with the latter element predominating. Tales of a local giant getting the better of a villain or of a powerful but simple giant overcome by a quick-witted young opponent are popular because they are amusing. The various landmarks and objects associated with giants are shown to children and thus keep their memory alive. Jesting tales of their exploits, however, are still told among adults, as well as among children, and so it must have been in medieval times.

See also: *Anglo-Saxon Chronicle;* Burial Mounds; Eddic Poetry; English Tradition: Anglo-Saxon Period; Geoffrey of Monmouth; Scandinavian Mythology; Snorri Sturluson's *Edda;* Thor

—Hilda Ellis Davidson

Gildas (c. 495–c. 570). British cleric, Welsh saint, and author of the earliest surviving history of Britain.

Born, it is believed, in the northern British kingdom of Strathclyde, Gildas probably trained in the Church in south Wales and may eventually have settled in Rhuys in Brittany. He is credited with giving essential impetus to the monastic movement in Wales through his writings and his own religious activities. He wrote *De excidio et conquestu Britanniae* (On the Ruin and Conquest of Britain, c. 547) and probably a penitential, and he is the subject of a ninth-century Breton *vita* (saint's life) and a twelfth-century Welsh *vita* compiled by Caradog of Llancarfan. Gildas both preserved traditional lore and was the subject of it, appearing as a character in both secular and hagiographic tradition.

In *De excidio,* composed principally as a diatribe against the excesses and improprieties of his society and its rulers, secular and ecclesiastical, Gildas relates in an introductory section the history of Britain—its founding, conquest by Rome, and conflicts with the Saxons. Gildas's application of the biblical notion of history as a record of God's dealings with peoples (*gens*) and his interpretation of Britain's losses to the Saxons as God's chastisement of the people's waywardness and sin are his own, but his history, the earliest extant written history of the British, appears to be based on oral history. Though his history has very few specific dates or names, it does include report of the "supreme ruler/proud tyrant" (*superbo tyranno*), identified in later texts as Vortigern, who invited the Saxons into the land and whose name could be interpreted as "supreme ruler"; reference to a decisive British victory at Badon Hill (later associated with Arthur); and contemporary anecdotal criticism of the British king Maglocunus (Maelgwn Gwynedd) for killing his uncle the king, listening to the praises of poets, and incestuous union with his nephew's wife. De excidio is significant in medieval folklore not only for the hints of oral tradition it contains but also as the first link in a chain of histories that laid out the Welsh national historical myth with its understanding that the British once ruled the whole island and will one day do so again.

In the vitae, in eleventh- and twelfth-century genealogies, and in the eleventh-century prose tale Culhwch and Olwen, Gildas is depicted as one of many (20, 21, or 24) sons of Caw, a king (and possibly giant) in Scotland. Gildas is associated with Arthur through his brothers. According to his Welsh vita, Gildas's brother Hueil kept harassing Arthur until the king was finally forced to kill him. Gildas imposed a penance on Arthur, and the two made peace with each other. The conflict of Hueil and Arthur seems to be a well-established tradition that reappears later in Welsh texts. In Culhwch and Olwen Hueil's stabbing of Arthur leads to a feud between them, and in Elis Gruffudd's chronicle (c. 1530), Hueil again wounds Arthur, this time after stealing his mistress, and the whole affair ends when Arthur beheads Hueil. Caradog's Vita Gildae also reports the earliest abduction tale about Gwenhwyfar (Queen Guinevere). When Arthur lays siege to Glastonbury where Melwas is holding Gwenhwyfar, Gildas intercedes and effects the safe return of Gwenhwyfar. Gildas is probably a late addition to this Arthurian tale, either as a foil to subdue Arthur or in the role of an existing character, perhaps the wise intermediary, but this provides a good example of how a figure can be incorporated into an already existing oral tradition, either for political reasons or because of his own increased importance.

Another example where Gildas is drawn into another's tradition involves St. David. According to several of St. David's vitae and to Vita Gildae, Gildas was unable to preach in the presence of the unborn David, a sign that all would give way before David, who would become the preeminent Welsh saint.

Other traditions about Gildas include relatively common hagiographic motifs of healing, raising fountains, driving off or confining birds through prayer, and causing thieves to stick to the ground, but he is specially noted for making bells (given specifically to St. Brigid, St. Cadog, and St. Illtud) and writing books (the De excidio and a splendid, miracle-working copy of the Gospels).

See also: Arthurian Lore; Culhwch and Olwen; David, Saint; Geoffrey of Monmouth; Maelgwn Gwynedd; Nennius

—Elissa R. Henken

Godiva, Lady (d. 1067). Arguably the most famous citizen of Coventry, known for her legendary naked horseback ride through the town's streets, covered only by her body-concealing long hair, an incident that has made her an instantly recognizable figure of medieval folklore.

The ride was provoked when, on behalf of the citizenry of Coventry, Godiva importuned her husband Leofric to lower taxes, and he promised to do so only if she rode naked through the town. Her long hair allowed Godiva to fulfill her husband's "impossible task" or ultimatum and thus intercede for the citizens while still protecting her wifely chastity from the shame of revealing her nakedness to the public.

Although Godiva and Leofric are historically documentable figures (he died in 1057; she died in 1067), her ride was not mentioned in records concurrent with Leofric's eleventh-century earldom of Coventry. Contemporary chroniclers Florence of Worcester and Roger of Hoveden merely report that this Anglo-Saxon earl and his wife enjoyed a shared reputation for piety and charity, and William of Malmesbury notes Godiva's special devotion to the Virgin Mary. The earliest narration of her ride through the streets of Coventry occurs in Roger of Wendover's early-thirteenth-century chronicle Flores historiarum (Flowers of History), produced at the Abbey of St. Albans nearly two centuries after the purported event. Another similar account occurs in the mid-thirteenth-century Flores historiarum, reputedly by Roger's successor at St. Albans, Matthew Paris. Both Roger and Matthew begin by attesting the various endowments to religious houses made by the earl and his wife, and they continue the tradition of Godiva's devotion to the Virgin Mary.

According to these thirteenth-century chroniclers, who provide the most detailed versions of the Godiva legend, Godiva spoke to her husband about Coventry's citizens' disgruntlement with high taxes he had imposed, begging him, in the name of Christ and his mother the Virgin Mary, to release his people from these onerous financial burdens. Angered by his wife's insistence on an issue that was against his financial interests, he forbade further discussion. When she continued imploring him on behalf of the people, he promised to lift the taxes only if she would ride naked through Coventry's marketplace. She loosened her long hair, "veiling" her naked body from public view "except for her beautiful white legs," and rode, accompanied by a pair of knights, through the town's center. Leofric then upheld his pledge and canceled the high tolls.

Both accounts indicate that Godiva's ride took place immediately after her argument with Leofric, while the entire town was assembled in the marketplace. Matthew Paris's version differs from Roger's by placing the outcome in a more hagiographical framework. Matthew attributes the fact that Godiva's nakedness was not seen by the townsfolk to a miracle, and he views the town's deliverance from taxation as a divine sign. Later medieval chroniclings of the legend reduce the tale to its essentials, briefly covering how the town got financial freedom and leaving the time frame between Leofric's challenge and Godiva's ride vague.

The abbreviated account in the fourteenth-century *Polychronicon* by Chester-based Ranulf Higden adds a new detail, perhaps derived from oral versions of the now-spreading legend: despite Godiva's ride horses were still subject to Leofric's tolls. Higden's popular history was a source for other chroniclers writing throughout the fourteenth and fifteenth centuries, which may account for the inclusion of the Godiva legend in Henry Knighton's *Chronicon*, John of Tynemouth's *Historia aurea* (Golden History), John Brompton's *Chronicle*, and the *Chronicle* of John Hardyng.

By the fifteenth century Godiva's ride had eclipsed any other events in Leofric's reign. Local reference to the story began in the fourteenth century when a stained glass window was erected in Coventry's Holy Trinity Church, honoring Godiva and Leofric and bearing an inscription saying that Leofric made Coventry toll free for his wife. Faced with the threat of an increased toll on wool in 1495, the Coventry townsfolk nailed a verse to the door of a local church reminding all of how "Dame Good Eve" once made Coventry toll free and calling for similar freedom now from the wool custom. In the sixteenth century Coventry celebrated a mass in her honor, and in later centuries her picture was placed in St. Mary's Guildhall, processions were held in her honor, and she became an important feature of the annual St. Michaelmas town fair. In the seventeenth century another element was added, the story of the town tailor, Peeping Tom, who wanted to see Godiva's nakedness as she rode by but was blinded when he looked at her.

The power of the symbols and images that inform Godiva's legend are more significant than questions of its historical accuracy. Godiva, called Dame Good Eve by fifteenth-century inhabitants of Coventry, incorporates the sometimes contradictory aspects of three powerful and archetypal female figures from medieval hagiographical or religious symbolism: Eve, the Virgin Mary, and Mary Magdalen. Her nakedness and the importuning of her husband suggest the shame of Eve, the most negative female stereotype in medieval iconography, at the Fall in the Garden of Eden. Her intercessory function as spokesperson for the oppressed citizenry of Coventry suggests the special object of Godiva's devotion and her probable model, the Virgin Mary, in her role as intercessor for or mediatrix between all humans and her son Christ. Godiva's long, body-concealing hair suggests Mary Magdalen, a reformed penitent and patron saint of prostitutes, whose medieval iconography depicted her naked body completely concealed by her long, luxuriant hair. The Virgin Mary and Eve were antithetically opposed in medieval biblical typology: Mary was the "new Eve" who

through her role in the Incarnation of Christ canceled Eve's sinful legacy to humanity. The unreformed Mary Magdalen recapitulates Eve's sensuality and sinfulness; the reformed Magdalen's ultimate attainment of grace and sanctity in the life of an anchorite also reverses Eve's sinful fall while at the same time suggesting affinity with her namesake, the Virgin Mary.

In every respect, Lady Godiva, or Dame Good Eve, literally embodies the saintly models of the two Marys, her avowed patroness Christ's mother and Mary Magdalen, who also covered her naked body with long hair. In medieval typology, both Marys were "good" versions of postlapsarian Eve, rendering Godiva another Good Eve for her transgressive but sanctified ride through the marketplace to attain financial freedom for the oppressed people of Coventry. Many visitors are drawn to present-day Coventry by Godiva's legend. As they exit or enter the train station in the heart of the commercial center, they encounter a larger-than-life equestrian statue of Godiva's ride, which attests Godiva's past and, through increased tourism, ongoing importance to the market economy of Coventry.

See also: Mary Magdalen, Saint; Virgin Mary

—Lorraine K. Stock

Gododdin, Y [The Gododdin]. Welsh poem ascribed in its original form to the poet Aneirin (fl. c. 600) and found in thirteenth-century manuscript *Book of Aneirin* (Cardiff Central Library).

The text as found in the manuscript consists of 103 stanzas, some of which are found in variant forms, and it is clear that the poem existed in more than one version. Many of the stanzas mourn the death in battle of individually named warriors of the war band of the Gododdin (the earlier Votatini tribe) around modern-day Edinburgh. Some 300 in number, they had been feasting for a full year at the court of Mynyddog Mwynfawr the king but were annihilated in a disastrous foray against Deira and Bernicia at Catraeth, usually taken to be Catterick in Yorkshire. There is no historical record of the battle (nor of the king), and the circumstances for the composition of the poem must be inferred from the text itself. The poem shows mature literary skills and is a classic example of the ethos of heroic verse. There is some evidence for a written version of the poem in the ninth century, but it is clear that the extant text contains later accretions to whatever may have been first composed. The extant text also provides evidence that the poem was a highly regarded part of the curriculum of bardic training, and medieval poets refer to it both as a model to be emulated and as an element in bardic contests. The poem was part of an active literary tradition from its first composition, so that it is not surprising that narrative features in the text should show folkloric developments. Typical of "the epic of defeat" (a martial tale celebrating the heroes of lost battles) is the comment that only the poet, "on account of his fair song," and three others escaped from the battle; another stanza claims that there was only one survivor.

The poem has always been ascribed to Aneirin, named in the *Historia Brittonum* (History of the Britons) as one of the British poets who "flourished" in the time of Ida of Northumbria (c. 558–570). The text, however, has some indications of the development of the historical poet into a saga character. One stanza refers to his being imprisoned and rescued or ransomed with gold, silver, and steel. This allusion to imprisonment in an underground cell has been interpreted as being a reference to the custom (attested in Irish literary tradition) of inspired bardic composition in a darkened room.

Later Welsh tradition gives to Aneirin the role of a sage and seer, attributing to him gnomic and prophetic verse. Another stanza in *The Gododdin*, obviously later than the original poem, refers more explicitly to Aneirin's violent death as the result of a blow; this is again referred to in two related triads, which note the killing of "Aneirin of Flowing Verse, Prince of Poets," by Heidyn son of Enygan as one of the three unfortunate assassinations of the Island of Britain, and as "one of the three unfortunate hatchet-blows of the Island of Britain." The narratives that developed around the poem and its author are not as well recorded for Aneirin as for his contemporary, the poet and prophet Taliesin, but that the historical and folkloric personae were becoming merged in his case also cannot be doubted.

See also: Nennius; Taliesin; Triads of the Island of Britain

—Brynley F. Roberts

Golem [Hebrew "body without soul"]. Homunculus or anthropoid; a human-like creature created by mortals using mystical or technological means.

In the ancient cultures that once flourished in the areas of present-day Egypt, China, and Greece there is much evidence attesting to traditions of statues that became animated. Well known is the statue of a woman created by Promotes, which was called Veritas (Truth), and the one created by his apprentice, which was called Mendacio (Lie); both became living creatures. In these ancient traditions the creation of anthropoids was connected to the worship of idols and to the need to prove that these objects of worship are not only material objects but also have life of their own. In a Jewish tradition of late antiquity, Enosh, a grandson of Adam, was asked to demonstrate how God had created the first man. He took dust and water, shaped out of it a form of a man, and blew life into its nostrils. But Satan entered into it, and people started to worship it as God. This was the beginning of idolatry.

The word *Golem* appears only once in the Hebrew Bible (Psalms 139:16), where it refers to the creation of the first man. Later interpretations of this text, especially in the Talmudic literature, present the Golem as one stage in the 12-hour process through which God created Adam (Babylonian Talmud tractate Sanhedrin 38b; Midrash Genesis Rabbah 24:2). The affiliation of the Golem with the creation of Adam continues to be one of the most widespread traits in Jewish traditions throughout medieval and later periods.

Another important element of the Golem traditions is the function assigned to the mystical book *Sefer Yetzira* (Book of Creation) in the process of its creation. This small and most influential Hebrew composition was created in late antiquity, and it presents the letters of the Hebrew alphabet as the foundation God's deeds—the creation of the world and of human beings. According to this composition God created Adam by means of the letters of the alphabet; thus, the mystics could imitate God's manipulation of the letters and create a man in the same way. Thus, *Sefer Yetzira* became the most important source of magic knowledge used in the attempts to create humans in late antiquity and in the Middle Ages.

The most influential passage in the Babylonian Talmud (tractate Sanhedrin 65b) tells of the learned Rava who created a Golem as an intellectual practice; it was returned to dust. Other rabbis, while studying *Sefer Yetzira*, on every Sabbath eve used to create a calf and then eat it. Such legends, which medieval Jews accepted as factual, were the proof that proper knowledge of the practices described in *Sefer Yetzira* is the key for the mystery of creating humans, and so it was studied in depth and followed intensively by magicians and mystics.

Almost all Jewish mystical and magical trends of the Middle Ages connected the creation of the Golem to their systems and practices. From a folkloristic point of view, the narrative traditions developed by and around the German Pietists of the twelfth to thirteenth centuries are of special significance. The Pietists' interest in all magical aspects of everyday life and their deep beliefs in the possibility of changing reality by means of mystical practices involved them deeply in attempts to create humanoids. In the cycles of legends told about the central figures of the movement—Rabbi Samuel the Pious and his son Rabbi Judah the Pious—they participate deeply in the creation of the Golem. A typical legend is that of Rabbi Elijah of Chelm, a folk healer and mystic of the sixteenth century. He

> made a creature out of matter and of form and it performed hard work for him for a long period, and the name of 'emet was hanging upon his neck, until the Rabbi saw that the creature of his hands grew stronger and stronger.... R. Eliyahu the master of the name was afraid that he would be harmful and destructive. He quickly overcame him

and removed the name ['emet] from his neck, and it turned to dust.

This narrative appears in many and various forms in Hebrew manuscripts and early prints, which attests to its popularity in oral and written traditions. It also raised, for the first time explicitly, the moral question of the legitimacy of repeating the most important deed of God—the creation of man—for personal benefit. As in the Talmudic legends mentioned earlier, when the Golem was created as an intellectual exercise, as an act of pride, or for personal benefit (to be eaten or to serve the master), it gets out of hand, becomes dangerous, and has to be eliminated.

The most popular Golem legends, which connect him to the sixteenth-century Rabbi Judah Löw of Prague (the Maharal of Prague), attempted to resolve the moral dilemma of creating the Golem. The legends appear only in late sources of the eighteenth to nineteenth centuries, but they started much earlier as oral local legends of the Jewish community of Prague and were adapted quickly in the folklore of many Jewish communities, and ultimately by general, non-Jewish folklore and popular culture as well. According to these legends, the great scholar and mystic Rabbi Löw created the Golem, following the ancient Jewish practices, in order to save the Jews of Prague from the blood libels they were accused of at that time. The Golem, an invincible creature that no weapon or fire can harm, was used by the rabbi as the only soldier and guard of the Jewish community. After the danger passed, Rabbi Löw took him to the attic of the Altneuschul—the ancient synagogue of Prague—and there removed the sacred name from him (as Rabbi Elijah of Chelm had before), and the Golem became a pile of dust that exists in the closed attic of the synagogue to this very day.

The message of these legends is that one can exceed the limits of one's humanity and imitate God only when one does so for a moral cause. Any other motivation, such as pride or greed, leads to punishment. This cycle of legends was developed in the late nineteenth century, and it reflects attitudes and concerns of Jewish culture of the time, but its roots and beliefs are earlier and can throw light on the folklore of the Golem in the Middle Ages.

See also: Jewish Tradition; Judah the Pious; Magic; Magic Manuals

—Eli Yassif

Grail. An object sought by King Arthur's knights in perhaps the most famous quest in legend and literary history.

The grail is almost invariably associated with nourishment or feasting and is generally capable of producing any desired food or drink; its power often sustains life itself. At first a mysterious object with certain marvelous properties, the grail was soon transformed by writers into a sacred object associated with Christ's death and with the Church's sacraments.

The word *grail* itself (Old French *graal*, derived from Latin *gradalis, gradalem*) originally meant simply a serving dish or platter and had no religious or other special significance. It was first given a specialized meaning by Chrétien de Troyes in his romance *Perceval, ou Le conte du Graal* (Perceval, or The Story of the Grail, c. 1190). Perceval, a guest in the Fisher King's castle, witnesses a strange procession that includes a mysterious bleeding lance and a grail radiating light and set with precious stones. Much later in the story, he and we learn that the grail is a "very sacred object" and that it is associated with a genital wound that has disabled both the Fisher King and, by extension, his land. Chrétien informs us that the grail contains a single Mass wafer that sustains the life of the king's father. By neglecting to ask about the grail, Perceval fails to restore the king's and the land's health, and his failure necessitates a quest to find the grail and ask the appropriate question. Chrétien's romance is incomplete, and thus it is left to later writers both to define the grail further and to bring the quest to a successful conclusion.

The Welsh romance *Peredur*, related to Chrétien's romance, features a platter that is an obvious analogue of the French author's grail, but it is not designated by that name: it is called simply a *dyscyl* (platter). In addition, it contains not a Mass wafer but a human head, reflecting perhaps the John the Baptist story as much as a pagan myth. It was once assumed by some scholars that the Welsh text was Chrétien's model, but *Peredur* probably dates from the thirteenth century, and it is more likely that the two romances had a common source.

In Chrétien the grail is, as noted, a wondrous and marvelous object, but it is not yet the Holy Grail that it would soon become—the chalice of the Last Supper and the vessel in which Christ's blood was collected after the Deposition. That identification was made soon after Chrétien by Robert de Boron, in his *Joseph d'Arimathie* (Joseph of Arimathea, c. 1200). Robert thus completed the refashioning of the mysterious grail into the Holy Grail, a symbol of Christ's real presence. He also offered a fanciful etymology for the word *graal*, deriving it from French *agréer* (to please) because of its ability to provide pleasure.

At about the same time, several authors continuing Chrétien's romance further develop the theme of the bleeding lance, identifying it as the spear of Longinus and leading to the association of both Grail and Lance with the mass. Both objects also play a central role in Wolfram von Eschenbach's great romance *Parzival* (c. 1200), but Wolfram writes of a Grail that is neither a platter nor a chalice but, rather, a stone. Identified as *lapsit exillis*—a puzzling term that suggests "fall" and "exile"—this Grail is guarded by Templars. The castle's king, Anfortas, suffers from a wound in the groin but is kept alive by the Grail. He can be released from his suffering only by a youth who will ask the appropriate question about his condition. That youth, Parzival, initially fails to make the inquiry and must undergo chivalric tribulations and religious renewal before he can return to the castle to heal Anfortas.

Despite Wolfram's innovation, the Grail remained, for most writers, the chalice associated with the Last Supper. A major development of the Grail theme occurs in the vast French Lancelot-Grail (or Vulgate) cycle, composed between about 1215 and 1235. Consisting of five interconnected romances, the cycle relates the history and prehistory of the Grail (the vessel from which Christ and his disciples ate the paschal lamb) and that of the Arthurian world. In the fourth of the Lancelot-Grail romances, *La queste del saint Graal* (The Quest for the Holy Grail), the quest is preceded by the mysterious appearance of the Grail at Arthur's court. The vessel enters the castle (without being carried) after a thunderclap and a great light; accompanied by a wonderful fragrance, it moves through the room producing the food and drink most desired by each person there.

Although some manuscripts identify Perceval as the Grail knight, that role generally falls instead to Lancelot's son Galahad, the only knight who, perfect and pious, is spiritually qualified to achieve a full Grail vision after transporting the Grail to the holy city of Sarras. In *La queste del saint Graal*, the final Grail vision is a mystical experience during which the figure of Josephus, the first Christian bishop, conducts the Grail mass; the latter is a literal transubstantiation in which Christ himself appears and speaks to Galahad and his companions. Galahad dies immediately afterward, and the Grail is taken up into heaven.

These and other French sources inspired numerous writers and were translated or adapted into a number of languages. The most notable was Sir Thomas Malory, whose *Le Morte Darthur* (completed in 1470) largely established the model for the Grail and other Arthurian themes in modern literature and art. The Grail itself is the same object for Malory that it had been for the Vulgate authors: the cup used at the Last Supper. Malory, however, alters the rigorous moral test that in the French version had ultimately excluded all but Galahad. In the process Malory appears to be offering hope of accomplishment to any Christian person of proper virtue and devotion.

Perhaps curiously, the medieval Church remained silent on the subject of the Grail and the quest, and it is largely in the postmedieval period that speculation has flourished about the object itself, its origin, and its possible survival and location. In popular lore a number of objects—a wooden cup in Wales, a green bowl in Genoa, and so on—have been identified as the Grail. In addition to seeking sources or prototypes of the Grail itself, scholars have investigated in detail possible models for the procession in which the Grail appears. Theories are numerous and complex but inconclusive. The major approaches can roughly, if simplistically, be divided among Christian, ritual, and Celtic theories: in the first, the objects in the Grail procession (in Chrétien's romance) are considered to be related to the liturgy and perhaps in particular to the St. John Chrysostom mass.

The theory of ritual origin, most popularly associated with the work of Jessie Weston, hypothesizes that a link exists between the Fisher King story and the Eastern religions (of Attis, Osiris, and Adonis) associated with death and rebirth. Related theories tie the story of Perceval to that of the Egyptian god Horus. In general the ritual theories attempt to link fertility or vegetation rites to the idea of a Waste Land that lies sterile until its king is healed by circumstances or actions (such as the asking of a particular question) related to the Grail.

The names most closely linked to the theory of Celtic origin are doubtless Roger Sherman Loomis and Helaine Newstead; they and others sought Celtic analogues of numerous themes and motifs from Grail romances. One of these theories connected the Fisher King (named Bron in Robert de Boron's work) with the Welsh hero Bran the Blessed, who in legend was wounded by a poisoned spear. The Grail itself, with its capacity for producing abundant food and drink, is seen as a representation of a magical cauldron of plenty (or cornucopia), of which many exist in Celtic legend.

During the late twentieth century yet another theory has received a great deal of popular exposure, though without gaining any significant scholarly acceptance. That is the Holy Grail–Holy Blood theory, the notion that the Grail is associated with (or simply is) the bloodline of Christ, a notion sometimes tied into suggestions that the Cathars were—and that a secret society still may be—the Grail's guardians.

See also: Arthurian Lore; Chrétien de Troyes

—Norris J. Lacy

Grain Miracle. Legend associated in the Middle Ages with the Virgin Mary and a variety of female saints, who, by passing through or around a field, cause grain that has just been sown to grow miraculously to its full height.

Examples of the grain miracle legend appear in writings, paintings, and sculpture throughout the Middle Ages and beyond. Sometimes the legend is associated with the Virgin Mary. Carrying the child Jesus, she flees toward Egypt with Herod's soldiers in pursuit and passes by a man in the act of sowing seeds (or sometimes plowing his field). The Virgin instructs the farmer that if soldiers come looking for her, he should tell them that he saw a woman pass by while he was sowing. As soon as Mary leaves, the freshly sown seeds sprout and grow tall. Immediately Herod's soldiers arrive and ask the farmer if he has seen a mother and child pass by. He answers, "Yes, when I first began to sow this seed." Assuming the seed had been sown months before, the soldiers turn away, and Virgin and Child are spared.

When the basic plot is adapted to a female saint, she is typically a virgin who is fleeing a would-be rapist. This tale appears as a featured event in the lives of early-medieval saints— Radegunda (French, sixth century), Macrine (French, ninth century), Walpurga (English and German, eighth century), and Milburga (English, d. 715)—whose veneration is associated with the agricultural cycle. For example, in England in the eleventh century, Radegunda's feast day was observed on February 11, the day "the birds begin to sing," as spring and the plowing season begin. Similarly, a fourteenth-century story about Milburga relates how she kept the peasants' fields free from geese and worms during sowing season and in this way preserved the crop from predators. Thus, the virgin saints associated with the grain miracle can be seen as grain protectresses.

These legends have roots in the magico-religious ideas going back to the Bronze Age and are manifest in diverse goddesses worshipped among disparate agrarian peoples of the Mediterranean. There is archaeological, textual, and art-historical evidence that points to the ongoing veneration, in a variety of cultures, of a female figure propitiated by special rites when the ground was first "awakened." It was at this time, before the seed was placed in the "belly" of the earth, that the land was "purified" and an earth mother goddess was invoked as protectress of the grain. One of the earliest pictorial examples of this vegetation protectress is found on a pithos (a large earthenware jar for storing grain) from the ninth century B.C.E. in Crete. This goddess, riding atop her cart, arrives to promote the growth of vegetal life in the spring.

The concept of a grain protectress is found in pagan Roman and Celto-Germanic agrarian cultures as well. Textual accounts from the Roman world describe the *Feria sementiva* (Seeding/Planting Festival), celebrated in the very early spring when the new agricultural cycle began. Ovid (*Fasti*, 1.655–704), Tibullus (2.1.5.–8) and Virgil (*Georgics*, 1.337–350) describe a seeding festival that invoked the mother goddess of grain. Participants asked her to provide abundant growth and to protect the fields. The ritualized enactment of this ceremony included a purification rite and a sacred circuit around the fields, a circuit that was to provide a barrier against any evil spirits that could harm the grain.

The festivities associated with *sementiva* persisted well into the Christian era, as peasants were reluctant to abandon customs so intimately connected with the growth of vegetation and therefore with the sustaining of life. In the Germanic north as well as in Romano-Celtic Gaul, literary and art-historical evidence reveals the imagery of a grain protectress who promoted crop fertility by her symbolic passage through the countryside. In his *Liber in gloria confessorum* (Book in Praise of the Confessors) Gregory of Tours (538–594) supplies a description of the statue of the earth mother goddess of sowing venerated by the Franks. He describes how she was drawn around in a cart to enhance the prosperity of the fields but reports that when the cart got stuck, the people turned away from her and converted. This Christian text provides an example of how the early spring seeding ritual was taken over by the Church so that it could redirect peasant veneration from the pagan earth mother goddess to early-medieval female saints.

See also: Brigid, Saint; Peasants; Virgin Mary

—Pamela Berger

Green Man. The somewhat whimsical name for what are less romantically termed "foliate heads"—carved faces (usually male) from whose mouths foliage emerges.

A variant type is a human face formed of foliage, framed by hair depicted in a foliate manner, as found, for example, in Villard de Honnecourt's famous mid-thirteenth-century sketchbook. Unfortunately, much nonsense has been written about these motifs—precisely the sort of thing that has given the study of folklore a bad name in academic circles—and some of it by scholars who should have known better. M. D. Anderson, for example, sees them as relics of pre-Christian tree worship, personifications of the spirit of the tree, and makes the inevitable reference to *The Golden Bough*. Highly dubious comparisons are regularly made with the attested druidic reverence for the oak and with folk customs, such as the Jack of the Green (a character in postmedieval May Day pageants, who dressed in greenery and sometimes took on the appearance of a walking tree), first attested in the late nineteenth century, or with other exotic cultures. Extremes of idiocy are reached by those writers who plot the occurrences of the popular pub name "The Green Man" as if this reflected the former prevalence of a pre-Christian tree-worshipping cult.

Conventionalized leaves emerge from the mouths of stone capital heads as early as the Norman period in England (e.g., at Kilpeck) and are also found in contemporary Continental sculpture. By the later Middle Ages, however, the motif is preeminently an English decorative taste, enjoying great popularity in sculptural media and especially common on roof bosses, corbels, and misericords. In fact, heads emerging from or above stylized acanthus leaves can be found in Roman sculpture (as on the third-century B.C.E. so-called Jupiter columns at Cirencester and elsewhere). By the eighth century the "inhabited vine-scroll" populated by tiny human (and animal) figures frolicking in or battling against the tendrils of the foliage has become a decorative commonplace.

See also: *Sir Gawain and the Green Knight*
—Malcolm Jones

Griffin *[Griffon, gryphon].* A fabulous winged creature with an eagle's beak and lion's body.

Bird mammals existed in the lore of Mesopotamia and other ancient cultures, but the medieval griffin was chiefly inherited from Greco-Roman art and literature. The classical griffin originated in oral travelers' tales from Scythia first recorded by Herodotus, Pliny, and other ancient writers. Griffins were believed to live in remote deserts of central Asia, where they guarded gold, made nests on the ground, and preyed on horses, deer, and humans. Although travelers in the Middle Ages continued to describe griffins as real fauna of Asia or India, no author ever claimed to have seen a live griffin.

By late Roman times griffins had come to be associated with Nemesis, goddess of divine retribution. By 500 C.E. the classical griffin's strength, ferocity, and guardianship over gold were integrated into Christian imagery. Medieval bestiaries drew on Greco-Roman natural histories to describe the enigmatic griffin's appearance and behavior, and the creature assumed layers of ambiguity, fantasy, and symbolism. Medieval additions to the griffin legend included eggs of agate, the ability to fly, tremendous strength, and magical powers.

Griffin designs decorated a wide range of secular and religious objects of the Middle Ages: caskets, jewelry, tapestries, game pieces, coats of arms, manuscript margins, architectural details, and liturgical lamps. The variety reveals how versatile the motif could be for elites and ordinary folk alike. For example, ornate Italian and English chests for precious jewels and valuables were often adorned with griffins, recalling their traditional role as defenders of gold. Griffins also stood guard on elaborately carved coffins and saints' reliquaries. On the other hand, series of plain bronze griffin buckles (Byzantine, eighth–tenth centuries C.E.) were definitely not luxury items; art historians believe that these everyday items warded off evil spirits for less affluent wearers. In the complex symbolism of bronze lamps cast in fantastic griffin shapes and decorated with crosses and other Christian symbols, the griffin represented violence and temptation subdued by the Church.

The griffin's exotic nature suited the bizarre zoology of Romanesque and Gothic art. Along with other real and imaginary fauna, griffins abounded on cathedrals and monasteries from Italy to Ireland. Naturalistic griffins are included in Adam and Eve's earthly paradise on ninth-century French ivories, and the border of the Bayeux Tapestry (c. 1100) teems with griffins. Some scholars argue that the griffin's popularity in European art and architecture must have been influenced by the development of bestiaries, but it is more likely to be evidence of the continuous survival of a very ancient cross-cultural tradition, as Asian, Middle Eastern, and African decorative goods and beliefs were integrated into medieval Europe.

Compilers of bestiaries provided a vivid illustration and appended a Christian allegorical meaning for each creature. Greed and bloodthirsty antipathy toward humans were the griffin's standard "moral" traits. Yet the rich tradition of griffins and their composite, dualistic nature meant that they were never simply purely evil monsters; they could also be seen as vigilant guardians, relentless avengers, and even gentle protectors.

The griffin was a natural emblem in heraldry. The earliest griffin coat of arms, attested in 1167, was that of Richard de Revers, earl of Exeter. The griffin device became especially prevalent in the 1400s and accounts for the many Germanic and English family names derived from the word *griffin.* One ingenious explanation for the origin of medieval griffins proposes that it is the result of an early instance of the heraldic process of dimidiation, in which the left and right halves of two different coats of arms (in this case, an eagle and lion) are conjoined by a diagonal bend (diagonal band from upper right to lower left) or vertical pale (stripe). The result would be an eagle-headed lion. But as we have seen, griffins preceded heraldry by millennia.

Numerous medieval romances describe fierce griffins carrying off strong men: *Herzog Ernst* (c. 1180–1220) and *Kudrun* (c. 1230) are two German examples. Medieval traditions associated griffins with Alexander the Great (356–323 B.C.E.). In some versions, the ambitious Alexander harnesses four flying griffins to carry him aloft to triumph over the heavens, but God forces the heathen conqueror back to earth. In the early fourteenth century, Griffin symbolism inspired a very different climax in Dante's *Divine Comedy,* in which the triumphal chariot of the Church is drawn by a Sacred Griffin. Its golden head and wings represent Christ's divinity, and the red-and-white limbs signify the Savior's earthbound nature. The Sacred Griffin restores the Tree of Knowledge, withered since the Fall, and returns to heaven.

People expected to learn more about mysterious griffins in travelers' lore about faraway lands. Marco Polo (1254–1324) identified the griffin with a monstrous bird of Madagascar. According to another highly popular fourteenth-century work, the *Travels of Sir John Mandeville,* one griffin was as strong as eight lions and 100 eagles, able to carry a horse or two oxen to its nest. The talons were so huge they served as drinking cups. Around this time so-called griffin's claws (typically, polished ibex or rhinoceros horns or the tusks of extinct mammoths) elaborately set in gold and encrusted with gems began to circulate in Europe. These claws, as well as griffin "feathers" and "agate eggs," were alleged to reveal the presence of poison, confer magical power, and cure blindness and infertility.

Prehistoric fossils may have influenced the griffin's image. In 1993 I proposed that the ancient Scythian-Greek legend was inspired by observations of the remains of beaked, egg-laying, quadruped dinosaurs about the size of lions. These well-preserved skeletons and nests with petrified eggs are ubiquitous along the caravan routes through the central Asian deserts where gold has been mined since the Bronze Age. Continued sightings in the Middle Ages of fossils along the Silk Road (a trade route stretching from China to the Middle East) would perpetuate the tale, and souvenir bones, horns, and eggs would convince European travelers of the griffin's existence. This scenario has been generally accepted by paleontologists and classicists, but other cultures' bird-mammal folklore also nourished medieval European beliefs about griffins. As scholars of many fields have shown, in the Middle Ages the venerable griffin was a powerful multicultural image of great age, depth, and profound symbolic potential.

See also: Bestiary; Mandeville's Travels

—Adrienne Mayor

Guinefort, Saint. A greyhound celebrated in thirteenth-century legends and rituals near the French city of Lyons.

Although the name St. Guinefort was also applied to several human figures (notably Guinefort of Pavia, Italy), it is the dog that has become the focus of folkloric interest because its story and cult were unusually well documented and have been studied at length by Jean-Claude Schmitt.

The legend and cult of the greyhound came to ecclesiastical attention through Stephen of Bourbon (c. 1180–1261), a Dominican friar attached to the convent of Lyons, whose descriptions are recorded in a treatise left unfinished at his death. Stephen heard the legend and testimony concerning the cult about 1250 in the course of preaching against sorcery and hearing confessions in the diocese of Lyons. Many women confessed that they had taken their children to St. Guinefort. They related this legend about the holy dog:

The greyhound Guinefort belonged to a lord and lady, who one day left their baby boy in the care of a nurse. When the nurse left the baby unattended, a huge serpent entered the house. The faithful greyhound killed the serpent and tossed its body a safe distance from the infant. But when the nurse returned to the house to find the cradle upset and cradle and dog covered with blood, she shrieked; the lord entered and instinctively slew the dog with his sword before finding the baby unharmed.

This narrative of the faithful dog is a widespread exemplum and legend type, classified as B331.2 in Stith Thompson's *Motif-Index*. The tale is recorded in no fewer than 11 Latin versions written throughout the late Middle Ages and in many more-recent accounts. Perhaps the most famous variant is the story from which Thompson takes his title: "Llewellyn and His Dog," in which a Welsh prince kills his faithful dog Gelert before discovering that the hound has saved his child from a snake. Although the earliest recorded Gelert narrative dates only to 1800, a manuscript illumination dated 1484 pictures the prince of Wales with a helmet surmounted by a cradle in which a greyhound stands—this iconographic flourish, unique in medieval heraldry, is taken as evidence that the story of Llewellyn and his dog was well established in Britain by the end of the Middle Ages.

The French version, however, is of particular interest because it bears evidence of oral circulation among a peasant population. Unlike the numerous elite versions of the exempla collections, the folk story recorded by Stephen has no appended moral. It is also the most economical account, mentioning, for example, one female servant assigned to the infant instead of the two or three women mentioned in exemplum accounts. Schmitt interprets this narrative economy both as an indication of a tale streamlined through the process of oral narration and as an indication of a peasant's view of a noble household, in which one servant is more than enough to mind the manor.

The importance of Stephen's narrative extends well beyond its possible indications of peasant narrative styles because the friar proceeds to contextualize the legend by explaining how village women used it as a justification for their healing rituals. His account continues:

Discovering the loyalty of the dog, the people of the household threw it into a well near the manor house, heaped stones upon the grave, and planted trees nearby. After the manor fell into abandon, peasants, preserving the memory of the dog's heroics, began to honor it as a martyr. They made the grove and grave the site of a ritual in which mothers would take their ailing infants. Under the guidance of an old woman, they brought offerings of salt and other things to the grove, removed their babies' swaddling clothes and hung them on bushes, drove nails into the grove's trees, and passed their naked babies between two trees. The mother would toss the child nine times between the trees into the arms of the old woman, invoking the "fauns of the forest" (i.e., the spirits of the woods) to take the ailing child and to replace it with a healthy one. Then the child was placed naked on a bed of straw between two lit candles and left alone. If the child was alive when the mother returned, she plunged it nine times into the waters of a nearby river, which action was supposed to ensure that the child would be healthy.

This complex ritual contains many elements—such as purification by fire and water—that have been documented not only in the Middle Ages but also among French peasantry into relatively recent times. The significance of the trees as agents in the healing process, for example, evokes a religious practice documented in the region of the Guinefort cult in 1158: a shrine containing the relics of St. Taurinus, when set at the foot of an oak tree, instantly cured a paralytic. The tale and the ritual, read together, offer unusually rich testimony of a living legend complex through which peasants used narratives to explain their ritual activities. The ritual itself reflects a belief in changelings: the ailing infants brought to Guinefort's grove were apparently believed to be not human children but spirit children that had been substituted for babies. The ritual was designed to induce the spirits to take back the substitute children and to return the human babies.

As an orthodox churchman, Stephen regarded this cult practice as misguided and demonic. His account emphasizes that he had the remains of the dog disinterred and the grove destroyed by fire. As Schmitt points out, Stephen's response is patterned according to a major topos in ecclesiastical folklore, a narrative pattern in which a holy man visits the site of a cult and debunks the central cult figure. Both the peasant women and Stephen of Bourbon could thus be said to be acting according to ostention—the process through which people use legend as a script for their own actions. The women used the story of the greyhound, as Stephen used saints' lives, as inspirations to guide their own activities.

See also: French Tradition; Legend

—Carl Lindahl

Guy of Warwick. Hero of romance, legend, and history, popular from the thirteenth-century Anglo-Norman poem, with international repute by the fifteenth century, widely known during the Renaissance and to the present day.

Guy's story combined chivalric high sentiments and dedication to preserving order in this world with the idea of withdrawal from worldliness to serve God in expectation of union in eternity; these combined ideals help render Guy such an appealing hero. His story, which celebrates chivalric ideals and recognizes their real limitations, has been adapted across the centuries to reflect current religious, social, and political values. The composite romance has attracted a wide audience and includes many traditional elements that persist in increasingly abbreviated versions of the original long narrative.

A Saxon of the tenth century, in the reign of Athelstan, Guy begins life as a steward's son, receives knightly training, and falls in love. In order to win Felice, daughter of Rohalt, earl of Warwick, he achieves fame as the finest knight by winning tournaments, assisting many in distress, becoming a sworn companion of the earl Terri, and slaying the Irish dragon in Northumberland. Forty days after their marriage, and the begetting of a son, Reinbrun, Guy has a moment of religious understanding that leads him to forsake his worldly seeking and dedicate himself to God.

He begins a second series of adventures as a pilgrim knight in the Holy Land, where he slays the pagan giant Amorant. As a pilgrim champion, announced to Athelstan by an angel, Guy defeats Colbrond, the Saracen giant of Anlaf, king of the Danes. Refusing public honors, Guy retires to Warwick to live as a hermit. He is reunited with Felice, who has performed many deeds of charity in his absence, only moments before he dies. Felice soon follows, and they are buried in Lorraine.

Heralt d'Ardern, Guy's mentor and friend, goes to Africa and finds Reinbrun, who had been stolen when a boy. After Reinbrun rescues one of his father's old companions from a fairy knight and encounters Heralt's son Aselac, all return home. The poem's prologue and epilogue identify Guy as an ideal figure, worthy of emulation.

The original Anglo-Norman romance *Gui de Warewic* (12,926 lines) was written for a baronial society that sought respectability through ancient lineage and a sense of belonging in a conquered land. The first romancer drew upon the historical characters of Athelstan and William Marshall, the hagiography of St. Alexis, the exploits of William of Orange, and episodes and stylistic traits of Chrétien de Troyes. There are two complete fourteenth-century translations into Middle English romance and one in French prose. Peter Langtoft introduced Guy into history as the savior of Britain in his *Chronique d'Angleterre* (Chronicle of England), translated into Middle English by Robert Mannyng of Brunne in 1338. Here, Guy's victory over Colbrond gives the account of Athelstan an emphasis analogous to the Anglo-Saxon poem *The Battle of Brunanburh*. Guy's place in history as the savior of England expands with chroniclers like Gerald of Cornwall and Henry Knighton, and his exemplary character is deployed in *Speculum Gy de Warewyke* and as a subject for sermons in the Latin *Gesta Romanorum* (Deeds of the Romans), where Tale 172 combines episodes from the romance to make Guy an example of constancy.

Pictorial representations most frequently show Guy as the slayer of giants and dragons (Taymouth *Hours* and Smithfield Decretals, a Gloucester misericord, a mazer [large drinking cup]), apt icons for the favorite medieval English hero, whose fame at times exceeded that of

Arthur and Robin Hood. Guy shares traits with the later English folktale hero Jack the Giant Killer, and with St. George, the patron saint of England.

Illuminations in the fourteenth-century Smithfield Decretals give evidence of popular, oral tradition; they depict Guy slaying giants and dragons, as well as the Dun Cow, a local folk episode that becomes part of written texts only in the sixteenth century.

With the increasing influence of the Beauchamp earls of Warwick in the fifteenth century, Guy continues in Chronicles of Thomas Rudborne and John Hardyng and a poem of John Lydgate. He is featured in the Rous Rolls and Beauchamp (Warwick) Pageants, in which Guy is recognized by the Soldan's lieutenant in the Holy Land. At Guy's Cliffe, already tied to the legend because of a cave where Guthi's (Guy's) prayer is carved in Roman and Saxon runic characters, a larger-than-life statue is carved from the rock. Richard de Beauchamp modeled his life on Guy, and his funeral effigy emulates his ancestor. There is a less sophisticated Middle English romance and a short metrical romance, Guy and Colebrande. Guy's international repute is evident in a Celtic Irish Life of Sir Guy of Warwick; Gydo und Thyrus, a German retelling and romanticizing of the tale from the Gesta Romanorum; and the frame story of William of Warwick in Joan Martorell's Tirant lo Blanc (begun 1460, pub. 1490).

The legend of Guy of Warwick contains many traditional elements found in medieval romances and saints' lives, as well as later oral folktales; these are among the most common motifs: proud princess rejects low-born suitor (L100), knight becomes hermit (*P56), husband in disguise visits his wife (K1813), winning of a princess (Blanchflour) in a tournament (H331.2), sworn brotherhood (P311), false steward (Morgadour; K2242), slaying of giants (*F531.6.12.6), fight with dragons (B11.11), decision of victory between armies through single combat (*H217.5).

See also: George, Saint; Romance

—Velma Bourgeois Richmond

Gwynn ap Nudd [Gwynn, Son of Nudd]. King of the otherworld, later king of the fairies, in Welsh folklore.

His name suggests his mythological origins. Gwyn (white) is frequently associated with otherworld figures, and Gwynn's father, Nudd, who sometimes has the epithet Llaw Ereint (Silver Hand), is cognate with Irish Nuadha Airged "silver hand or arm," king of the otherworld race, the Tuatha Dé Danann. Both the Welsh and Irish names are etymologically related to Nodons, a god, to whom dedications have been found in a Romano-British temple at Lydney Park, Glouces-

tershire. A tale about Gwynn ap Nudd is outlined in Culhwch and Olwen, a Welsh story dating from about 1100 in its surviving form. Gwynn had abducted Creiddylad, daughter of Lludd, from Gwythyr ap Greidiol, to whom she was to be married. Arthur reconciled Gwynn and Gwythyr, decreeing that they should do battle for her each May Day until Doomsday, when the victor on that day should have the right to claim her.

Gwynn's Irish counterpart is Finn (Fionn), who is, however, the husband who loses his wife Grainne to the young Diarmaid, with whom she elopes on the night of their wedding feast. The Welsh and Irish tales are obviously analogous stories of love triangles and elopements (or abductions), though the roles of Gwynn and Finn have been reversed. In the Irish story, Diarmaid and Grainne take refuge in a clearing in a wood but succeed in escaping when Finn and his men surround them. A similar episode may be referred to in a fragment of Welsh folklore conserved in a fourteenth-century Latin treatise condemning soothsaying: the author notes the foolish actions of those who call upon the king of the spirits and his queen ("ad regem Eumenidium et reginam eius") saying, "Gwynn ap Nwdd qui es ultra silvis pro amore concubine tue permitte nos venire domum" [Gwynn ap Nudd, (you) who are yonder in the forest, for the love of your mate, permit us to enter your dwelling]. Culhwch and Olwen assigns a special place to Gwynn as a huntsman, and there are other references to his horsemanship and hunting skills. He later appears in Welsh folklore as the leader of cwn Annwn (hounds of Annwfn), the devil's pack hunting their prey of doomed mortals. The shift from king of Annwfn to king of the fairies or of the devils and the identification of Annwfn with hell are found in Culhwch and Olwen, where Gwynn is described as he "in whom God has set the spirits of the devils of Annwn lest this world be destroyed."

Gwynn's hellish associations are expressed unequivocally in the sixteenth-century Life of St. Collen, wherein the subjects of Gwynn, "the king of Annwfn and the fairies," are dismissed as merely devils. The saint visits Gwynn's court on Glastonbury Tor, "the fairest castle he had ever seen." He is not deceived, however, and he makes the illusion disappear by pouring holy water over the gathering. Both late-medieval poets and later folklore stress the fairy aspects of Gwynn's legendry, focusing on the stories of his leading unwary travelers into his marshes and pools and causing them to lose their way on the misty hills, and the more gloomy, frightening features of Gwynn's character disappear.

See also: Annwfn; Celtic Mythology; Culhwch and Olwen; Fairies; Wild Hunt

—Brynley F. Roberts

Hamlet. Protagonist of a Danish legend.

The principal source for the medieval legend is the biography composed in Latin by Saxo Grammaticus around 1200 as part of his *Gesta Danorum* (History of the Danes; 3.6.1–4.2.2). Other accounts are found in Danish annals and in Icelandic literature. His name appears in such forms as Amleth, Amblet, Amlæd, Ambluthe, Amblothæ, Amlóthi, and Ambáles but never as Hamlet, a similar-sounding but etymologically unrelated English name that Elizabethan playwrights adopted when they reworked the medieval Danish story for the tragic stage.

According to Saxo, Amleth's father and uncle were corulers of the Danish peninsula of Jutland, but the latter grew envious of the former, openly slew him, and wed his widow Geruth. Sitting at the filthy hearth and carving wooden crooks for no obvious purpose, Amleth played the fool so that his uncle would not take him seriously as a potential avenger. Suspecting that Amleth's apparent folly might conceal cunning, the king's men subjected him to a series of tests. First they brought him together with a beautiful woman in a secluded spot to see if he would have sexual relations with her; Amleth did so, but only after eluding his spies. Next they brought him together with his mother in her bedroom to see if he would speak openly with her; again Amleth did so, but only after slaying the eavesdropper. When eventually the suspicious king dispatched him to Britain with two escorts and a runic letter instructing the British monarch to put him to death, the youth secretly rewrote the letter during the voyage, calling upon the king to execute the escorts and to give his daughter in marriage to Amleth. Returning to Denmark just as the king's men were celebrating the funeral, Amleth plied them with drink, tied them up, and set fire to the king's hall. Amleth became ruler of Jutland and went on to have other adventures before eventually falling in battle.

The narrative is enlivened with a good deal of humor, especially in the hero's punning responses to the interrogations of the king's men by means of which Amleth manages to tell the truth while cheerfully maintaining an appearance of imbecility.

The other major treatment of the Hamlet of tradition is the Icelandic *Ambáles Saga*, a romantic saga of the sixteenth or seventeenth century, composed at a time when evidently the story still circulated in Icelandic oral tradition. There is little trace of the oral story after this work.

Numerous scholarly attempts have been made to discover the origin of the Hamlet legend or the etymology of the hero's name on the assumption that they contain the key to understanding the story. These attempts have not found a consensus, although they have called attention to various other legends that resemble that of Hamlet, whether closely or distantly. In my opinion, the Scandinavian legend of Hróar and Helgi (also called Harald and Halfdan) and the ancient Roman legend of Brutus are so similar to the Hamlet legend that a genetic connection must be assumed. If this is correct, the Hamlet legend is one of several realizations of an old migratory legend.

Saxo's work was first published in 1514. Later in the century the Frenchman François de Belleforest retold the story of Amleth in a popular collection of tragic stories, *Histoires tragiques*, and soon afterward there was an English play, now lost, on the subject. Around 1600 Shakespeare reworked the story for the company to which he belonged.

See also: Scandinavian Mythology

—William Hansen

Harp. Musical instrument consisting of strings—framed in wood—that are plucked by the artist.

The European harp of the early Middle Ages is distinguished from the ancient Mediterranean harp by its three-part construction of sound chest, string arm, and column, which together create a triangular frame. The origin of this Western frame harp is uncertain; various sources credit its creation to either Irish, Anglo-Saxon, or Norse cultures. Scholars must rely on the visual arts in researching the medieval harp, for there are no extant instruments that predate 1400 C.E. A tenth-century Anglo-Saxon manuscript is cited as the earliest example of a frame harp in an English drawing. The continental European Utrecht Psalter, written and illustrated between 816 and 835, depicts David the psalmist with a frame harp. Sometimes David carries an ancient Greek lyre, and this has led to some confusion as to whether the Latin *cithara* refers specifically to the frame harp. The ambiguity is also reflected in several Germanic languages, in which the verb "to harp" meant "to play a stringed instrument" and did not necessarily describe the Western harp. Depending on the time and place, the harp was called by many names—*hearpe, cythara, cruit, chrotta, rottae, lyre,* or *telyn*—but whether these names referred exclusively to the frame harp continues to be debated.

The harp is described as the "joywood" or "gleewood" in *Beowulf*, and it is the singing and harp music that maddens the monster Grendel and leads to Grendel's attacks on Hrothgar's hall. The discovery of the Sutton Hoo ship burial in Suffolk, England, provided archaeologists with the remnants of a stringed instrument. However, a 1969 reconstruction of the Sutton Hoo instrument resembles more a rounded lyre than the triangular frame suggested by the name *hearpe* or *harpa*.

In the Norse sagas not only do harpers play songs of heroes, but heroes themselves play the harp. Gunnar, a hero of the thirteenth-century Icelandic *Völsunga Saga*, displays great skill as a harper. When thrown bound into a snake pit, he plays a harp with his toes. Witnesses find the performance better than most performers could accomplish playing with their hands. Gunnar's music charms all but one of the poisonous snakes to sleep; that one snake eventually kills him.

Other major harper heroes of medieval traditions include Tristan and Orpheus. In Gottfried von Strassburg's romance, *Tristan* (c. 1210), the famous lover astounds King Mark's court by playing the harp in "Breton style" so well that "many who stood and sat there forgot their own names." Orpheus, the famous musician of classical tradition, is transformed into a minstrel king in the fourteenth-century Middle English romance, *Sir Orfeo*. Orfeo's wife, Dame Heurodis (i.e., Eurydice), is abducted by the king of the fairies, and Orfeo follows her to the otherworld, where he plays the harp so enchantingly that he induces the fairy king to relinquish her.

Traditionally, gatherings of the early Irish Parliament, or *Feis*, at Tara, County Meath, were followed by minstrelsy and harping in the banquet hall. According to legend, St. Ruadhan cursed the gathering in 560 C.E. and the harp was mute thereafter, as Thomas More related in his poem "The Harp That Once through Tara's Halls." Early Irish ecclesiastics, such as St. Kevin and St. Columba, are reported to have played the Irish *cruit*, and Alfred the Great was said to have disguised himself as a harp player in order to enter the Danish camp. St. Aldhelm, the eighth-century bishop of Sherborne, played his harp at a bridge crossing and then preached a sermon to the crowd that gathered. In 1183 Gerald of Wales, court chaplain to Henry II, wrote in praise of the musicians he had heard in Ireland, and he states that both Wales and Scotland were influenced by the Irish harpers.

The harper was singled out from earliest times for special recognition in northern Europe, and especially in the Celtic-speaking areas of the British Isles. The harpist was accorded the status and privileges of the highest-ranking commoner in society. The harper's chief function was to accompany the poet's recital of panegyric poetry, and the harpist was given a place of honor beside the poet, although the harpist was not of noble birth. Harpers were also liable to persecution because of their association with nationalist feeling. The Welsh harpers were persecuted after the conquest of Wales by Edward I in 1284. Although one of the most magnificent surviving Irish harps dates from around 1500 (now in the National Museum of Ireland), Irish harpers were placed under threat of death by the mid-1500s. By 1600 the harping tradition was almost extinct in Ireland although harping still continued in isolated areas throughout the Celtic world. The harp itself continued to evolve into the frame-pedal harp familiar to most people today, but harping as a pastime associated with the communal merriment of the early Middle Ages had ceased by the early seventeenth century.

See also: Cædmon; Minstrel

—Cynthia Whiddon Green

Harrowing of Hell. A widespread and popular narrative relating what Christ did after his Crucifixion and before his Ascension into heaven.

According to a myth circulated in the Middle East, a deity goes to the underworld and conquers its prince. Motivated by the belief that Christ also descended into hell during the three days after his death, early Christian communities added it to the topography of the hereafter to which Jesus had descended after his death. Even so, it is only between the fourth and eighth centuries that this idea became an obligatory part of religious faith and was taken up in the creeds. The place of the descent into the underworld—limbo—was referred to as *limbus patrum* (borderland of the fathers), as the Fathers of the Old Testament dwelled there (cf. *limbus puerorum* [borderland of unbaptized children]). Especially important here would be the apocryphal Gospel of Nicodemus (third to fifth centuries), a widely popular "eyewitness account" that describes how Christ breaks open the gates of Hades and has the prince of the underworld bound. Then he leads Adam, Eve, and the other righteous souls of the old covenant out of limbo. In the early phase of the Reformation there was embittered discussion as to whether or not Christ himself had also experienced the sufferings of hell during this descent into the underworld.

In visions of the hereafter, in scholarly literature, and in religious poems and prayers, the descent of Christ into limbo is scarcely found as a separate theme. Limbo, however, did appear frequently in Romanesque and Gothic representations of the life of Christ (e.g., on Lent cloths); it was commonly portrayed as the jaws of hell, with the souls contained therein, and was held open by a pillar to which Christ had bound Satan. Limbo also appeared as a prison or a burning fortress.

The descent of Jesus into hell was present in the general consciousness mainly through Easter plays. The devils' fear of God's arrival, their attempts to keep some of the souls for themselves, and their later efforts to repopulate hell were expressed in thoroughly burlesque scenes. The gratitude of the released souls, whom Christ leads into heaven, was forcefully depicted. For all of them, including the innocent, had been previously handed over to the devils to be tortured. Although an authority such as Pope Gregory the Great had believed that the righteous among the Fathers had been held in confinement in a darkened cell without being tortured, the Middle Ages frequently made no distinction at all between torture in the real hell and torture in this limbo. This can be clearly seen in the wording of religious drama. Thus, for example, Jesus says to the devils in the so-called Easter play of Muri (mid-thirteenth century), as he liberates the souls from limbo, "You have destroyed them in a wretched and horrible fashion through the fire and fierce agonies of hell." And the souls reply that they called for the Savior "in the fierce agony of hell." Judas, Annas, Caiaphas, and Herod, however, must remain there forever.

See also: Dante Alighieri; Hell; Purgatory

—Peter Dinzelbacher

Harun al-Rashid (763 or 766–809) [Haroun al-Raschid, Harun ar-Rashid]. ᶜAbbasid caliph who ruled Baghdad from 786 to 809 C.E., when the city was at its cultural and commercial peak, and who subsequently became a major figure in Arabic storytelling traditions.

As ᶜAbbasid leader, Harun al-Rashid led the pilgrimage nine times during his reign and led Muslim troops against the Byzantines. He is perhaps best known in Western tradition as the caliph who presented Charlemagne with an elephant. In Baghdad the caliph surrounded himself with poets, musicians, and scholars. Harun's era has thus come to represent both the golden age of ᶜAbbasid rule and its attendant decadence and luxury.

Developing parallel to the historical record of Harun al-Rashid's character and accomplishments was a flourishing legend tradition, both written and oral. In addition, Harun al-Rashid, his wife Zubaida, and his vizier Jaᶜfar figure prominently in the *Thousand and One Nights*. Even historians such as al-Masᶜudi (896–c. 956) relied heavily on anecdotes and stories when describing him, and it is now widely agreed that what is known about Harun is largely derived from fiction and legend. The folk traditions of Harun al-Rashid tales are based loosely on actual events and circumstances, but the popularity of the fictional accounts has allowed them to subvert the authority of even the most reliable historical records.

One series of legends and tales about Harun al-Rashid concerns his relationship with Jaᶜfar the Barmaki. The Barmaki (also known as the Barmecides) had been for generations advisers to the ᶜAbbasid caliphs. Harun's execution of his adviser and boon companion Jaᶜfar in 803, however, substantially lessened the Barmaki's influence over the ruling family. Jaᶜfar's political influence had become a threat to the caliph's authority, but the more prevalent story was of romantic intrigue. Popular legend has it that Harun married his sister ᶜAbbasah to Jaᶜfar so that he would not have to be without either of them. While Harun purportedly saw the marriage as platonic and chaste, Jaᶜfar and ᶜAbbasah had other ideas. Many women's tales (*amr al-mar'ah*) tell this version of events, and although most historians rejected the story, they continued to include it in their histories of the ᶜAbbasid caliphate as evidence of the ruler's fiery temper.

Tales also attribute to Harun a social nature, despite the fact that he moved out of Baghdad to a country estate as soon as it was politically expedient. Harun al-Rashid's reputation as wine drinker—wine was forbidden to Muslims—and party-goer persisted largely due to his patronage of Abu Nuwas (d. c. 810), a poet famous for wine songs. Like his relationship with Jaᶜfar, Harun's friendship with Abu Nuwas was inconsistent. He paid the poet handsomely but imprisoned him several times as well. Harun al-Rashid's erratic behavior led to numerous tales of a caliph who drank and who would then feel remorse and punish his party companions. Legends indicate that the caliph tolerated unlawful drinking, and tales in the *Thousand and One Nights* show him participating in these illicit activities. The popularity and supposed credibility of these accounts led the historian Ibn Khaldun (1332–1406) to attempt to rehabilitate Harun al-Rashid's reputation. A caliph as renowned for his piety and as interested in theology as Harun al-Rashid was could not, reasoned later historians, also participate in drinking and revelry.

Harun al-Rashid's distrust of his advisers and his intellectual curiosity are well documented. Storytellers, aware of these traits, also endowed the caliph with insomnia and composed tales of him wandering the streets of Baghdad in disguise in order to monitor the activities of his subjects. The night wanderings of Harun al-Rashid are not a commonplace of the histories but are widely accepted as part of his biography. In the *Thousand and One Nights* he is depicted as rash and adventurous, often getting himself into trouble, and certainly not acting with the dignity expected of the commander of the faithful. In "The Porter and the Three Ladies of Baghdad," he almost loses his life because he speaks out inappropriately at a party, and in "The Slave Girl and Nur al-Din," he climbs a tree to investigate an illicit affair taking place in one of his palaces. These incidents are typical of the way in which Harun is depicted in the *Thousand and One Nights*. A discerning Jaᶜfar often accompanies him on his journeys in order to temper the caliph's impulsiveness. In these stories, too, Jaᶜfar patiently suffers Harun's wrath.

The importance of Harun al-Rashid to medieval folklore extends beyond his role as subject of legend. Harun's reign was also the golden age of ᶜAbbasid storytelling, and many of the medieval Arab tales still extant were recorded during his reign. In both oral and written forms, the stories of the ᶜAbbasid period have perpetuated and enhanced the reputation of Harun al-Rashid as ruler and patron of the arts.

See also: Arabic-Islamic Tradition; *Thousand and One Nights*

—Bonnie D. Irwin

Harvest Festivals and Rituals. Events, feasts, and performances marking the culmination of the agricultural year.

The Labors of the Season

The end of the agricultural year in medieval Europe was an incredibly busy period for rural workers. From roughly the beginning of August through early November there were the multiple tasks of cutting, drying, and storing animal fodder; harvesting grain for human consumption; and processing this grain by threshing, winnowing, milling, and storing or brewing. The harvest stubble was then grazed by domestic beasts and fowl, outlying herds were driven in, and a portion of the livestock was slaughtered and preserved by smoking or in brine. In particular areas there was the special case of grape harvesting and wine production as well. Naturally the time frames for these many activities and their attendant festivals of thanksgiving would vary greatly from the Mediterranean regions to the northern realms of Scandinavia and Scotland.

Harvest Celebrations

Celebrations at the end of the reaping of rye, wheat, barley, and oats are no doubt as old as agriculture itself. Sir James Frazer and the Cambridge School of comparative religion made much of early modern European harvest rituals in the interest of establishing connections with an aboriginal worldview and particularly with an all-pervading Corn Spirit. This numen (that is, spiritual force) would be represented and indeed concentrated in the last standing stalks of the field. Sickles might be thrown at them until they fell, or the last stalks might be trampled into the earth, indicating an accreted and dangerous power in this unharvested remnant. German folklore has a *Roggenmuhme,* or harvest bogey woman, for example. The last sheaf particularly had to be removed in special ways and was especially honored and woven into anthropomorphic or abstract shapes that might have any number of local designations: "harvest doll," "kern baby," "old man," "cripple goat," or "harvest queen" (which British antiquarians liked to identify with the Roman goddess of grain, Ceres). Such practices appear to be pan-European. Poland, for instance, has both a *pszenna baba* (old wheat woman) and a *dziad* (old man). The figure is brought out of the fields in triumph, usually on a decorated "hock cart," to serve thereafter as a focus for festivities. These large anthropomorphic figures are evidently the ancestors of the decorative "corn dollies" hung up in individual houses in more recent times in Britain and elsewhere. The fundamental notion of the dying and reviving god was thus thought to be very much alive in rural Europe up to the Industrial Revolution and even beyond. Such early modern folksongs as "John Barleycorn" were quite self-conscious celebrations of this very Corn Spirit. Such perennialist notions were widespread in late-nineteenth- and early-twentieth-century scholarship, for example, in the work of Heino Pfannenschmid.

While a connection to the Corn Spirit remains an attractive, even a logical thesis given the general conservatism of the rural people, there is very little in the way of hard evidence to corroborate it from the early-medieval period. To be sure, one can argue, as did Maire MacNeill in her magisterial study *The Festival of Lughnasa,* that in the ultraconservative west of Ireland there was a real continuity with the pagan Celtic past in the bonfires on mountaintops on the first day of August. These celebrate the first fruits and, obliquely, the ancient solar and fructifying deity Lug (Lugh). Elsewhere in the British Isles the day is Lammas (from the Anglo-Saxon *hlafmaesse,* "loaf-mass") and lacks this pagan coloration. There are intriguing hints in the medieval record for England, however. William of Malmesbury passed along a bit of Anglo-Saxon lore that appears to be the remnant of an etiological myth for the arrival of agriculture in the North: the magical child Sceaf (Sheaf) was said to have arrived off Scandia asleep on a sheaf of grain in an oarless boat. He would later become an ancestor of the Anglo-Saxon kings. And what are we to make of this report from the reign of King Stephen (1135–1154) by the chronicler William of Newburgh?

> At harvest-time, when the harvesters were busy in the fields gathering crops, two children, a boy and a girl, emerged from these ditches [Wolfpittes, near Bury Saint Edmunds]. Their entire bodies were green, and they were wearing clothes of unusual colour and unknown material. As they wandered bemused over the countryside, they were seized by the reapers and led to the village.

The green children refuse all human food until they are given newly shelled beans, upon which they subsist until they learn to eat bread. Having then learned "our language," they describe their twilight homeland across a wide river, a typical description of Faerie (the fairy realm). Is this an embroidered account of the discovery of actual feral children, or is it a garbled account of an archaic harvest ritual translated into legend form? It could be either, but it may well be that the Corn Spirit, here as in the William of Malmesbury passage, is peeking through as a palimpsest in the records of elite culture.

An unbroken chain of celebratory harvest practices going back to the Neolithic is certainly possible for much of medieval Europe, but throughout the region these customs were altered by at least a certain degree of Christian influence, which no doubt varied widely from region to region. Thanksgiving for the harvest is of course biblical as well, and we must imagine a range of practices, some more pagan in feel, some perfectly Christian and acceptable even to many of the Reformed, like the more recent display of the fruits of the harvest in church, or the tamer harvest wreaths and simply decorated sheaves.

In the special case of wine production, it

seems that medieval practice had little or no connection with or recollection of Dionysus comparable to the Corn Spirit phenomenon, probably because of the dominating influence of monasticism in the spread of viniculture in the early-medieval period. Early Modern images of the reveling Bacchus in wine-drinking cultures are clearly popular reflections of Renaissance learning. Medieval viniculture, by contrast, was under the patronage of such demure saints as the martyr St. Vincent in France or the pope St. Urban in German-speaking areas.

If we can extrapolate backward from more recently documented folk practices, all the end-of-labor celebrations, the singing of the "harvest home," the thanksgiving and conspicuous feasting, the final rounds of fairs and parish gatherings known as church ales must certainly have occasioned a high degree of revelry and afforded opportunities for creating solidarity between the owners and the workers of the land in the central Middle Ages. (The visual record of harvest time when it emerges—in the illuminations of aristocratic books of hours, for example—invariably shows the work of the season and little of the celebration.) Although there might be local practices, such as the two principal reapers being designated Harvest Lord and Harvest Lady, harvest festivals do not seem to have developed very strong rituals of inversion, mock kingdoms, and so forth. They might be extremely egalitarian, but they were not quite fully carnivalesque in spirit.

Robert Herrick, a poet of the seventeenth century, probably gives us the best window on earlier harvest celebration in his "The Hock-cart, or Harvest Home," dedicated to the earl of Westmorland:

Come forth, my Lord, and see the Cart
Drest up with all the Country Art.
See, here a *Maukin*, there a sheet,
As spotlesse pure, as it is sweet:
The Horses, Mares, and frisking Fillies,
(Clad, all, in Linnen, white as Lillies.)
The Harvest Swaines, and Wenches bound
For joy, to see the *Hock-cart* crown'd.
About the Cart, heare, how the Rout
Of Rurall Younglings raise the shout;
Pressing before, some coming after,
Those with a shout, and these with laughter.
Some blesse the Cart; some kisse the
　　sheaves;
Some prank them up with Oaken leaves:
Some crosse the Fill-horse; some with great
Devotion, stroak the home-borne wheat:
While other Rusticks, lesse attent
To Prayers, then to Merryment,
Run after with their breeches rent. (*The Complete Poetry of Robert Herrick*, ed. J. M. Patrick [1968], p. 141)

While Herrick might have been influenced by classical descriptions of revelry here, there are many valuable close observations of contemporary rural celebration in the passage: the white linen caparisons for the horses; a female image (the *Maukin*) made of the last sheaf, and particularly the festival behaviors of the folk. The poem's expression of a high-spirited agricultural piety is probably quite accurate. Later folkloric descriptions mention liberally drenching the cart and revelers with water and occasional cross-dressing, which could also be archaic features of the ceremony. After this passage Herrick describes a massive feast given by the lord of the manor in which the agricultural tools are freely toasted by the laborers: "the Plough ... your Flailes, your Fanes, your Fatts ... the rough Sickle, and crookt Sythe, / Drink frollick boyes, till all be blythe."

Harvest was the period for adjusting manpower needs as well. As feudalism broke down, and especially after the Black Death, when agricultural laborers became a more fluid commodity, the old quarter days for rent payments (Michaelmas in England and Martinmas in Scotland, for example) would also mark the time for renegotiating arrangements of employment and securing winter quarters. Harvest feasts thus served as earnest or severance pay for this new rural working class. In Yorkshire, for example, these "mell suppers" would become foci for dramatic sketches and class satire. But again, such developments nowhere approached the rich theatricality of the Christmas season or the days of Carnival.

Christian Feasts of Harvesttime
Rituals and celebrations during the harvest season, then, varied in time from region to region, and indeed from crop to crop, but were fairly consistent in their celebratory form and content. Particular feasts in the Christian liturgical calendar served to fix some features of the seasonal celebration to specific dates. The Western Church's Feast of the Archangel Michael on September 29 arose from a Roman Church dedication in the sixth century, but it also approximated the autumnal equinox. As conqueror of the fallen angels, Michael would be an ideal protector against the forces of darkness at the time when day began to lose out to night. His cult places were usually on high ground and often overlooked the sea-lanes, as with Mont-Saint-Michel in Normandy and Mount Saint Michael in Cornwall. Mountaintop St. Michael fires were common, especially in Germanic-speaking territories. Michaelmas was more prosaically a quarter day in England, but it was also the prime time to dine on geese fattened on the post-harvest stubble. The Michaelmas goose, often sold at special "goose fairs," was often relegated to St. Martin's Day (November 11) in other parts of Europe. Special large loaves, such as the St. Michael's Bannock of the Isle of Skye, are also characteristic of the archangel's feast day and of the season in general.

Michael's function as psychopomp (guide of souls to the otherworld) in medieval culture is more properly represented a month later in the joint feasts of All Saints' Day and All Souls' Day (November 1 and 2), festivals instituted by the Church in the ninth century to appropriate the two pre-Christian festivals—Celtic and Germanic—celebrating the new year. These pagan festivals, and particularly the Celtic Samhain, marked the dying of the earth into itself and were powerful periods of liminality when the dead—and assorted spirits—were likely to intersect with the now sedentary, and hopefully well-provided-for, human population. Particularly archaic elements clustered at this turning of the year, especially in regions of Celtic influence. There were large bonfires with their attendant sports, such as leaping the fire and scattering the firebrands. All Hallows' in Celtic territories also marked the first appearance of masked performers with their village perambulations and Mischief Night acts of chaos. It is not too difficult to see in these guisers prophylactic impersonations of ancestors or otherworldly figures. "Punkies," hollowed-out turnips with carved features and candles inside, carried on high poles (ancestors of the American jack-o'-lanterns), may have been another way of representing these liminal personages. Indoor games of prognostication were also common to the season—predicting how one would fare during the year, ones' future love life, and so on—and might well have been a degeneration of darker and more serious divination practices. These often involved fruits of the harvest, such as apples.

Church influence on the All Hallows' period can be seen in such practices as "souling" or "soul-caking" in Britain and elsewhere, in which a begging procession sings (to some degree as surrogates for the departed souls) and receives money or a special bread, the "soul cake." Bell-ringing for the departed souls was another widespread practice, documented by Roger Vaultier for fourteenth-century France. We can see in the harvest festivals a general movement of wider and wider inclusion, from celebrating the land laborers at the harvest home to incorporating even more marginal elements of society—the beggars, the homeless, the "poor souls"—at the gate of November. The two halves of the festival, the pagan and Christian, thus served simultaneously both to placate the elemental or chthonic forces and to honor the unseen members of the universal Church. The Church's control over this process was by no means complete. Indeed, it could be argued that Halloween became one of the most resistant of the "pagan" festivals originally appropriated by the Church. In America the holiday, after generations of confinement to children, is rapidly growing among the adult population in a carnivalesque direction. In the case of the Mexican Los Dias de Muertos (Days of the Dead) we can see another example in which a different pagan inlay breaks uproariously though the Church's solemn festivals of the saints and souls.

The onset of winter was also a time for particular attention to domestic animals. In Bavaria the feast of the animal patron St. Leonard (November 6) marks the last processional "riding" of the year and the blessing of the horses against the winter season. Elaborate decoration of herd animals is common in Alpine regions in the earlier events of the *Almatrieb* or *Kuhreihen* (cow dances), which brought the stock down from their high summer pastures. Some herd animals were so honored in the harvest season, but others were subject to blood sports in conjunction with their slaughter for meat, particularly in November, known as the "blood" or "slaughter" month in all the Germanic languages. "Goose pullings" involved riding under a suspended goose with the intent of pulling off its head. Village-wide bull-runnings were not confined to the Iberian Peninsula in the Middle Ages: they could be found as far north as Lincolnshire. From early Norman London to late-medieval Würzburg, combats between wild boars were also common holiday fare during the late harvest season.

Martinmas (November 11) was the final harvest festival. "Inter festum S. Michaelis et S. Martini venient cum toto ac pleno dyteno" [between the feasts of St. Michael and St. Martin they sing harvest home] reads a medieval record from Hedington in Oxfordshire. In many parts of Europe the day signaled the slaughtering of animals (cattle, pigs, and geese especially) that were not to be kept over the winter. It was also a common date for broaching the new wine in France and central Europe. The surplus meat, the perishable innards, and the new wine afforded another opportunity for conspicuous feasting. The Martinmas carouse, particularly in the German-speaking areas, laid more emphasis on verbal arts (drinking songs, comic tales, and so on) than did earlier harvest feasts and in this respect was more like a winter revel. As with the "poor souls" of November 2, the famous icon of the "Charity of St. Martin" (in which St. Martin splits his cloak to share it with a naked beggar) served to underscore obligations downward to the underprivileged at the onset of winter, especially the obligations to share harvest and slaughter largesse. Since Merovingian times Martin's feast also marked the beginning of the penitential season of Advent. Martinmas thus served as a kind of brief Carnival to this lesser Lent.

See also: Advent; Festivals and Celebrations; Martinmas; Samhain

—Martin W. Walsh

Hell. An underworld place of punishment for those dead who had led wicked lives.

The descriptions of hell in classical literature (Virgil, *Aeneid* 6) were seen as poetic fictions in the Middle Ages, and like those of the Germanic and Celtic traditions they played a rather minor role in Christian beliefs concerning the hereafter. Considerably more important was the biblical tradition, and even more important was the tradition of the Apocrypha, above all the Apocalypse of Saint Peter and the *Visio Pauli* (third century) with their lengthy descriptions of the punishments of the hereafter.

According to general medieval opinion, hell was created by God in the center of the earth especially for those angels who, under Lucifer's guidance, had fallen from God. For that reason in many legends (e.g., about Theodoric the Great) volcanoes were considered entrances to the underworld. Occasionally it was thought, however, that one could locate special regions of hell also on the surface of the earth. In the legend of St. Brendan, for example, we hear of islands whose cliffs are burning or where gigantic forges are housed, where the souls of the sinners are tortured in perpetuity. There were also local traditions about specific hellish regions, as numerous place names for particularly desolate regions demonstrate in all of Europe. That the distinction between hell and purgatory was not always clear often becomes evident, for example, when it is stated in the *Prick of Conscience* concerning hell, purgatory, and limbus that "Alle thes places me mai helle calle, / For hei beth y-closed withinne the eorth alle" [All these places men may call hell, for they are all enclosed within the earth].

Today it is surprisingly little known that the Church Fathers and teachers of Christianity, from late antiquity to the early modern period, considered it an established fact that by far the greatest part of mankind is predestined by God for hell. The most influential of the Church Fathers, St. Augustine (d. 430), formulated this in writing: because of original sin, mankind became a *massa damnationis* or *massa damnata*, a throng foreordained to hell, from which only very few are pardoned by the mercy of God. All others are "predestined," that is, designated in advance, "to perpetual death," "to perpetual ruin," "into the eternal fire." This teaching was transmitted to the people through sermons. Johannes Herolt, a popular German preacher of the fifteenth century, calculated that of 30,000 dead, only 2 attain salvation and only 3 may atone for their sins in purgatory; all 29,995 others are damned. According to Church lore it was completely clear: *extra ecclesiam nulla salus*—outside the Catholic Church there is no salvation. The Council of Florence (1438–1439) declared unequivocally: "The souls of those who die with a mortal sin, or even only with original sin, descend immediately into hell, where they are, however, punished with different types of tortures." Since only baptism redeems one from original sin, the fate of all non-Christians, including unbaptized Christian children, was thereby sealed. The latter were thought to be in eternal darkness in a limbo, *limbus puerorum* (literally, a borderland of children). Neither did

the Church recognize the circulating legends in which a heathen such as Emperor Trajan was freed from hell through the prayers of Pope Gregory I or a man who murdered his son, such as the father of St. Odilia, was freed from hell by the prayers of his daughter.

In hell an accumulation of the most unimaginable tortures exists in perpetuity. In the vision of the English layperson Ailsi (died c. 1120), for example, hell is an infinitely large house in which the souls are bound with red-hot chains on that part of the body with which they sinned. The lawyers, advisers, liars, flatterers, slanderers, and all similar people are fastened with chains of fire through their tongues. Other souls are cooked in lead, pitch, and brimstone baths and liquefied into nothing; they take shape again, however, for further tortures and go from one torment to the next. In addition, there are hundreds of similar depictions of hell from monks and laypersons, as well as from famous female mystics, such as Hildegard of Bingen, Birgitta of Sweden, or St. Frances of Rome. These fantasies were proliferated through the sermon and were captured in the plastic and graphic arts.

While the representations of hell prior to the central Middle Ages intensively occupied the intellectual upper stratum, at that time primarily monks, the average believers were for the most part not yet exposed to them in detail. Not until they were confronted with Romanesque art, with its depictions of the Last Judgment on churches, outside on the west facade and inside on the arches and walls, and with the increased rigor of the sermons, primarily by the friars of the early thirteenth century, were the people more intensely injected with the fear of hell. Even when the form given to hell or to the jaws of hell in the depictions of the Last Judgment referred to the eternal dungeon at the time of the resurrection of the bodies, one still did not imagine this place differently. The representation of hell, for example, that the sculptor Erhard Küng (d. 1507) created for the tympanum of the cathedral in Bern shows the damned hung on hooks by their widely stretched-out tongues while they hopelessly attempt to pull up their legs, which are being burned from below by leaping flames. A monk and a prostitute are forged together with a heavy chain; a demon crushes the monk's penis with tongs. A naked pope still wearing his tiara is pushed head over heels by a biting devil into the abyss of hell, and so on.

The citizens of every medieval city were confronted daily with these and similar scenes in public spaces. And in how many churches was hell not also painted behind the high altar, so that persons doing penance there had their fate before their eyes in the event that they concealed a sin! Religious drama brought the jaws of hell to life on the stage through Easter plays and Last Judgment plays; usually, as in Gothic art, these terrible jaws were given the form of a lion's mouth, which could be opened and closed through a mechanical apparatus, in which it thundered and out of which fire shot forth. An analysis of pictures and texts available to the common people shows that the fear of hell occupied the Christians of the Middle Ages significantly more than the pleasure of anticipating heaven.

See also: Dante Alighieri; Harrowing of Hell; Purgatory

—Peter Dinzelbacher

Hispanic Tradition. The folkloric culture of the peoples of the Iberian Peninsula.

Numerous aspects of Spanish and Portuguese folk literature and folklore are well documented in medieval sources, though there are many gaps in our knowledge, gaps that can only be very partially filled by analogous evidence from post-medieval traditions. Lyric poetry, epic, ballad, drama, folktales, proverbs, riddles, folk speech, legends, music, children's rhymes and games, folk belief, cookery, and material culture are substantially attested and will be discussed in this entry.

History, Context, Worldview

Before the Roman conquest—a gradual process not completed for some 200 years (214–219 B.C.E.)—the Iberian Peninsula was inhabited by numerous peoples of diverse origin and unrelated linguistic affiliation, about whom, in many cases, we know relatively little. Pre-Roman Iberia can be seen as two distinct regions. On the one hand, the southern and eastern coasts, from the Pyrenees to the Portuguese Algarve, had long been receptive to commercial contacts and cultural exchanges and early on saw the establishment of trading posts and even foreign colonies along their shores. On the other hand, the less accessible center, west, and north attest to a complex of tribal societies bitterly opposed to outside intervention. The southern coasts were occupied by the Tartessians; their land and capital, Tartessos (of unknown location, but possibly near the mouth of the Guadalquivir), corresponds to the biblical Tarshish, whence, every three years, ships came to King Solomon: "Bringing gold and silver, ivory and apes, and peacocks" (2 Chron. 9:21). Along the northeastern coast lived Iberians, who gave their name to the entire peninsula, as well as to the Ebro River. Both peoples spoke non-Indo-European languages. The southern coasts and the Balearic Islands were colonized by Phoenicians at an early date (1100 B.C.E.), while the east and northeast saw the establishment of numerous Greek trading posts. The Carthaginians, colonizers of what is now Tunisia and heirs to Phoenician language and culture, occupied the southern coasts and the Balearics during the fifth through third centuries B.C.E. These three eastern Mediterranean colonial initiatives left various place names (Cadiz, Alicante, Cartagena) but otherwise had no effect on modern Hispanic languages. The center and north-northwest were inhabited by a linguistically diverse population: pre-Indo-Europeans on the one hand and various consecutive invaders from central Europe on the other: Indo-European pre-Celts, proto-Celts, Celts (Celtiberians), and some early Germanic peoples. The Lusitanians, one of the pre-Roman peoples of Portugal and western Spain, were probably, at least in part, of Celtic origin. The various dialects of Basque represent the only modern survival of Spain's pre-Indo-European language stock. Basque, which in medieval times extended south to the environs of Burgos and east along the Pyrenees as far as Andorra, has given a number of loanwords to Castilian and, to a lesser extent, to the other languages and has perhaps also influenced Castilian phonology. Basque, for its part, has accepted a massive lexicon of borrowings from Latin and from medieval and modern Spanish. Basque is probably distantly related to the Caucasian languages (though rival origin theories compete for serious consideration). Gradual Romanization established a form of colloquial, or "vulgar," Latin as the common language, except for the Basque-speaking regions and possible pre-Roman speech islands that may have persisted into the early Middle Ages. Hispanic Latin was somewhat archaic by comparison to more central and more innovative areas of Romania (Gaul and Italy), and it embodied a substantial number of pre-Roman loans in its lexicon and morphology.

Like other regions of the Western Roman Empire, Iberia experienced massive invasions by various Germanic peoples during the early years of the fifth century C.E.: Suevians occupied Galicia in the northwest; Visigoths came to control all other areas and eventually, after defeating the Suevians (585), the entire peninsula; Alans (Iranians associated with the Germanic migrations) were soon annihilated by the Visigoths; their remnants joined the Vandals, who, after briefly settling in southern Spain (perpetuating their name in Andalusia), elected to cross to North Africa to found a powerful Vandal kingdom in Tunis. The Visigothic presence on the peninsula lasted from 413 until the Islamic invasion of 711 C.E. When they reached Hispania, the Visigoths had already experienced many years of association with Roman language and culture; many were probably bilingual in Gothic and Latin, and the Gothic language was doubtless already fighting a losing battle for survival. Even so, Gothic has given Spanish and Portuguese many loanwords (often referring to war and to material culture), as well as numerous personal names and place names. When they arrived in Spain the Visigoths were already Christians, but their Arian creed contrasted with the Hispano-Romans' Catholicism. Motivated more by political expediency than religious sentiment, Recared I, together with many of his subjects, converted to Catholicism in 587, but religion did not play the all-important role within the value system of Visigothic Hispania that it was to have in Hispanic life in subsequent centuries.

Hardly 80 years after the death of Muhammad (632 c.e.), the armies of a victorious, rapidly expanding Islam had swept across North Africa and stood at the Straits of Gibraltar, on Hispania's southern threshold. In 711 an expeditionary force of 7,000 men, made up mostly of Berbers and a few Arabs and commanded by a Berber warrior, Tariq ibn Ziyad (whose name is remembered in *Gibraltar* [*Jebel Tariq*, or "Tariq's mountain"]), crossed the straits and defeated the forces of Roderick, the last Visigothic king. In 712 Tariq was joined by the Arab governor of North Africa, Musa ibn Nusayr, with a mostly Arab army of 18,000 men. Within 6 years the entire peninsula, except for a narrow northern fringe along the Cantabrian coast and the Basque Pyrenees, was under Muslim control. These momentous events and the subsequent eight centuries of Christian Reconquest are the two most important factors in medieval Hispanic history and were crucial in shaping the distinctive character of Hispanic peoples, leaving a significant imprint on essential features of their culture. Spain and Portugal during the Middle Ages were complex, multiethnic, tri-religious societies in which Christians, Muslims, and Jews lived side by side and interacted, influencing one another's cultures. As the Reconquest gradually moved southward, the Christian north came to be divided into a number of small, independent, rival regions, none strong enough to prevail against the Muslim south. From east to west, Christian Hispania consisted of Catalonia, Aragon, Navarre, the Basque area, Castile, Asturias-Leon, and Galicia, each with its separate language and its distinctive culture—distinctions that persist to the present day. Medieval Spaniards thought of themselves in religious rather than in national terms. The adjective *español* is a borrowing from Provençal. The frontier society that evolved out of the Muslim Conquest and the Christian Reconquest comprised a variety of ethno-religious minorities. In the Muslim south many descendants of Goths and Romans had accepted Islam but were initially thought of as a distinctive group, while others maintained their Christian faith and were known as *mozárabes* (Arabized). Christians, Muslims, and Jews all spoke as their everyday language the archaic Mozarabic dialect, a highly conservative form of Ibero-Romance, while Arabic was the language of government and literature. As the Christian kingdoms slowly advanced southward, a large Muslim population came to live under Christian domination. These conquered Muslims were called *mudéjares* (Arabic for "those allowed to remain"); after the Reconquest was completed in 1492—followed by their forced, though superficial, conversion to Christianity—they were known as *moriscos*

(Moor-like). Along the changing *frontera* between Christian and Muslim territory there lived a small, culturally flexible, and religiously ambivalent group known as *enaciados* (from two Arabic terms meaning "stranger; deserter; turncoat" and "distant, removed"), whose livelihood—as scouts, messengers, smugglers, spies, and translators—depended essentially upon the peculiar circumstances of a frontier society. In the late fourteenth century many Spanish cities witnessed violent anti-Jewish pogroms, leading to a progressive decline in the Jewish communities and culminating in the exile of all unconverted Jews in 1492. Consequently, the late Middle Ages and the sixteenth century saw the formation of yet another ethno-religious minority, *conversos* (or *marranos*), Jews who had converted to Christianity (and their descendants). The medieval Hispanic symbiosis of Christians, Muslims, and Jews is reflected in numerous cultural exchanges: the rich poetic tradition developed in Muslim Spain and creatively imitated by Hispanic Jews undoubtedly patterned its distinctive stress-syllabic metrics on Hispano-Romance models, as opposed to classical Arabic poetry. One of the Hispano-Arabic poetic genres was the strophic colloquial Arabic *zajal*, which was also used in Castilian compositions of the late Middle Ages. Several Hispano-Christian institutions were doubtless patterned on Islamic models: the pilgrimage to the tomb of St. James in Galicia, initially conceived as a means of spiritually uniting all the peninsular Christian peoples (and ultimately a major cultural link between Hispania and the rest of Europe), was surely suggested by the Muslim hajj, the pilgrimage to Mecca. The Spanish military orders, which combined war-like and religious functions, were probably based (like their crusader counterparts in Palestine) on the analogous Muslim institution of the *ribat*, border monastery fortresses manned by religiously inspired warriors devoted to the territorial expansion of Islam. Indeed the Reconquest itself can be seen as a response to the Muslim holy war (jihad). Hispano-Arabic gave to medieval Spanish, Portuguese, and Catalan numerous place names and an abundance of lexical borrowings—pertaining especially to agriculture, architecture, commerce, science, war, and material comforts—many of which continue in modern use. Particularly striking are semantic calques, which attest to the syncretic character of medieval society: Old Spanish *casa*, like Arabic *dar*, comes to mean both "house" and "city," while *correr*, on the model of Arabic *gha-wara*, means not only "to run" but also "to pillage." Such Spanish expressions as *Esta es su casa* (This is your house), said to welcome a guest, *Hasta mañana, si Dios quiere* (Until tomorrow, if God wills it), and *Que Dios te ampare* (May God protect you), said to avoid giving alms, all have exact Arabic counterparts. The religious totalism of Spanish Islam, combined with similar values in medieval Christianity, was to leave its distinctive mark on Spanish Catholicism.

Lyric Poetry

Hispanic lyric poetry is first documented in brief Mozarabic-dialect stanzas, known as *kharjas* (Arabic for "exit"), appended to learned compositions in classical Arabic and Hebrew, written by Muslim and Jewish poets from the eleventh to the fourteenth centuries. The exact nature of the *kharjas* has inspired heated polemics, but numerous agreements in style, themes, metrics, and formulaic diction between the Mozarabic *kharjas* and later lyric genres—Castilian *villancicos* (peasant songs) and Portuguese *cantigas d'amigo* (lovers' songs)—assure us of the *kharjas'* ultimately traditional character, though known texts have doubtless been distorted by the learned context to which they were adapted. The *kharja* "What shall I do, Mother? My lover is at the door" embodies not only the same protagonists and the same situation, but also the same á-a assonance as a *villancico* documented in the early 1600s: "Gil Gonzalez is knocking at the door. I don't know, Mother, if I should open it for him." Thematically the *kharjas* are extremely limited: most are attributed to amorous girls who lament the absence or faithlessness of their lovers. The *villancicos* and *cantigas d'amigo,* usually represented as women's poetry, are thematically much more variegated, covering a rich panoply of topics and perspectives. Surviving medieval lyrics are only a vestige of what once existed: Catalan Jewish wedding songs have uniquely survived in two fifteenth-century Hebrew-letter manuscripts. Competitively improvised lyric poetry can be substantiated in tenth-century Hispano-Arabic and later on in Castilian. Funeral dirges were sung in Castilian and almost certainly in the other languages as well. Doubtless various lyric genres have been totally and irretrievably lost.

Traditional Heroic Poetry

In Castilian traditional heroic poetry was devoted to various national themes, as well as to numerous Spanish adaptations of Old French *chansons de geste*. Only three epics have survived in poetic form: the *Cantar de mio Cid* (Poem of the Cid), *Las mocedades de Rodrigo* (The Cid's Youthful Adventures), and *Roncesvalles* (a Spanish adaptation of the *Chanson de Roland*). All three survive in unique, incomplete copies. A number of other narratives, both national and French, can be partially reconstructed on the evidence of chronicle and clerical adaptations, ballad derivatives, and lyric references. There were undoubtedly also epic poems in Aragonese and Catalan, though they survive only in chronicle prose. A thirteenth-century Portuguese parody echoes the *Chanson de Roland,* suggesting that the epic circulated in Portugal either in Old French or in a Portuguese adaptation. The *moriscos* also cultivated heroic prose narratives in

their distinctive Spanish dialect, following Arabic models. Debate concerning the essentially traditional or learned nature of medieval epic has generated an ongoing polemic between advocates of traditionalism and individualism.

The Hispanic Ballad

With origins in fourteenth-century Castile, the Hispanic ballad (romance) soon spread to all areas of Spain and Portugal. It was sung in Spanish, Portuguese, and Catalan and by Christians, Muslims, and Jews. We have a few Castilian ballads in fifteenth-century manuscripts, and many were selectively printed in sixteenth-century chapbooks and poetry collections. There is less evidence from Portugal, though it is still very substantial, existing in a few sixteenth-century manuscript copies and in many contemporary allusions. There is much less from Catalonia, though the very first ballad text preserved is in a mixture of Spanish and Catalan (1421). We have indirect evidence that ballads were sung by exiled *moriscos* in Tunis, while substantial modern documentation from Sephardic Jewish communities in North Africa and the Balkans abounds in medieval text-types and assures us that the ballad genre *(romancero)* was cultivated by all Hispanic peoples, regardless of religion. The ballads originated as fragments of epic poems. Numerous epic-based songs were printed in the sixteenth century, and some survive in the modern tradition, but the eight-syllable assonant ballad verse was also used early on to compose historical and novelesque narratives having nothing to do with the epics. The genre is characterized by great diversity of themes and postmedieval pan-Hispanic diffusion; it has survived, from its medieval origins to modern times, in essentially all communities where Hispanic languages are spoken.

Popular Drama

With its close connection to liturgy, popular drama is surely the least exclusively oral of medieval folk-literary genres. Vernacular religious drama is poorly documented in Castilian, with the twelfth-century *Auto de los Reyes Magos* (The Three Kings) as the lone testimony from before the 1400s. By contrast, there is evidence of a rich medieval liturgical drama in Catalonia. Previously unnoticed documentation has recently emerged for Portugal. Though they have not come down to us, there must also have been other, secular types of popular representations, such as the scandalous *juegos de escarnios* (games of mockery), condemned in laws compiled by Alfonso the Wise (late thirteenth century). Popular religious dramas, heirs to the medieval tradition, have survived down to the present in various regions of the Hispanic world.

Folktales

Folktales as such cannot be documented, but there are numerous compilations of exempla (moralistic stories) in Castilian. Though many have a long written ancestry, going back to Latin and Arabic sources, others doubtless were drawn from oral narrative, and in some cases their structure agrees with that of folktales current in modern tradition. Some can be shown to have been orally transmitted from Hispano-Arabic origins. Golden Age Spanish literature (sixteenth and seventeenth centuries) attests to a rich corpus of traditional stories and anecdotes, many of which undoubtedly began to circulate in medieval times.

Proverbs

From the very beginning proverbs have been incidentally cited in such literary works as the Castilian epic, clerical poetry, and historical and didactic prose writings. They are also an essential part of other genres: proverbs became songs and songs became proverbial; particularly apposite ballad lines came to be used as proverbs and proverbs were absorbed into ballad narratives; and stories were based on proverbs and their lessons became proverbial. Proverbs are also frequently cited in Portuguese, Catalan, Hispano-Arabic, and Hispano-Hebraic writings. They continue to be a vital and dynamic part of Hispanic folkspeech today, as they have been for centuries. The first systematic collections date from the fifteenth century, and numerous lengthy compilations, embodying much medieval material, were brought together in the 1500s and 1600s. Some proverbs can be traced to Middle Eastern sources: "El polvo de la oveja, alcohol es para el lobo" [The dust of the sheep is balm to the eye of the wolf]. Many proverbs first recorded in the 1400s are still in modern use: for example, "Cria cueruo e sacarte ha el ojo" [Nurture a crow and it will pluck out your eye], and "Más vale paxarillo en la mano, que buytre volando" [A little bird in the hand is worth more than a vulture flying].

Riddles

Though there are no medieval riddle collections per se, medieval oral riddles can be documented in Castilian in various literary sources. Some are picked up by proverb compilations, as in the following postmedieval example from Hernán Núñez (1555): "Cien dueñas en el corral, todas dicen un cantar—Que es cosa y cosa de las ovejas" [A hundred ladies in a pen, all sing the same song—A riddle about sheep]. The following riddle, traditionally concerning the sun, was given a new, pious interpretation and published in Dámaso de Ledesma (1605): "Que es cosa y cosa, que pasa por el mar y no se moja?" [A riddle: What passes through the sea and doesn't get wet?] (no. 414). Eastern Sephardic Jews had a substantial riddle tradition. About half the repertoire is of Turkish or Balkan origin, but other examples can be traced to peninsular analogs, and thus some at least may predate the 1492 exile. We lack early

documentation from Portugal. There is a short fifteenth-century Catalan list, which, however, seems more literary than oral.

Folkspeech

Medieval texts abound in conventional phrases, often binary in structure: *en invierno y en verano* (in winter and in summer, i.e., "always"); *ni de dia ni de noche* (neither by day nor by night, i.e., "never"); *nin en yermo y nin en poblado* (neither in uncultivated land nor in populated places, i.e., "nowhere"); *moros y christianos* (Moors and Christians, i.e., "everyone"); *grandes y chicos* (grown men and youngsters, i.e., "everyone"); *de voluntad y de grado* (with goodwill and willingly); *non vale un figo* (it's not worth a fig). Just as Middle English used binary expressions combining Anglo-Saxon and Norman French synonyms (*huntynge* and *venerye*), so—particularly in *morisco* texts—we find Spanish-Arabic doublets such as *sunna i regla* (doctrine and law). Traditional comparisons, such as *commo un bravo leon*, ... *oso ravioso*, ... *lobo carnicero* (like a wild lion, ... a raging bear, ... a ravening wolf), occur in heroic poetry and respond as much to traditional formulaic diction as to colloquial usage. Curses and insults—some startlingly severe—are well attested in medieval law books. Francisco del Rosal documents many contemporary expressions that probably differ little from late-medieval counterparts.

Legends

Medieval texts are replete with legends: the Goth Teodomiro, lacking warriors, puts women holding reeds on the battlements of Murcia to deceive the Muslim invaders. At Covadonga the Moorish arrows shot at Asturian defenders miraculously turn back against the attackers. King Ramiro II of León, betrayed by his Muslim queen, ties her to an anchor and throws her into the sea, thus explaining the Portuguese place name Fozde-Ancora. The city of Zamora supposedly derives its name from the founders' encountering a black cow (*vaca mora*) at the location of the future town and shooing it away, using the exclamation *aza!* (scat!). The birth of King James I of Aragon is connected to the traditional motif of the substitute bed partner. Some legends are surely of Islamic origin: King James I, just like ꞎAmr ibn al-ꞎAsi, the seventh-century conqueror of Egypt, orders his tent left standing because a swallow has nested atop the tent pole. Legends often form part of epic narratives, but they need not be used to explain their origin: Spain's betrayal to the Muslims; Fernán González's purchase of Castile; the Cid's illegitimate birth.

Music

Many medieval tunes were notated. Alfonso the Wise's vast late-thirteenth-century Galician-Portuguese compilation, *Cantigas de Santa Maria* (Songs of Holy Mary) embodies a rich assemblage. The presence of Arabic and Jewish elements is hotly debated. The music of St. James pilgrim songs has survived in medieval Catalan notations, as have transcriptions of *cantigas d'amigo* by the Galician minstrel Martin Codax and *cantigas d'amor* (love songs) by the Portuguese King Dom Dinis (the latter brought to light, in a dramatic discovery, only in 1990). A good number of ballad and lyric tunes are also available, particularly in the massive *Cancionero musical de Palacio* (Palace Song Book); others, subjected to the polyphonic tastes of sixteenth-century court composers and guitar masters, must be approached with great caution if viewed as authentic medieval witnesses. No Hispano-Arabic music was notated, but a good number of medieval songs are still sung in North Africa, and their music doubtless also originated in the Middle Ages. We know a good deal about musical instruments from contemporary allusions and iconography. Their designations, reflecting the eclectic character of the music itself, embody a mixture of Western and Arabic terms. A tenth-century penitential gloss (*Glosas silenses*) warns against participating *ena sota* (Latin *in saltatione*), which corresponds etymologically to the *jota*, a modern Aragonese folk dance—allowing us a rare glimpse of some sort of ritualized dance or mime, involving disguise in women's clothing, grotesquely painted faces, and the brandishing of bows (and arrows?), spades, and similar implements. There are other medieval allusions and iconographic representations of dances, but little detailed description. For the Golden Age (sixteenth and seventeenth centuries) we are better informed, though many—but surely not all—patterns may have changed. Central to medieval music and its performance were professional minstrels (Spanish *juglar*; Portuguese *jogral* and *segrel*; Catalan *joglar*), a diverse, multilingual, and widely traveled company that included Christians, Muslims, and Jews. Some journeyed abroad, and at home they were joined in providing entertainment by numerous foreign colleagues, especially from Provence but also from northern France, Italy, Germany, Flanders, England, Scotland, Bohemia, and even Cyprus.

Children's Rhymes and Associated Games

A Spanish counting-out rhyme—*De vna, de dola, de tela, canela*—was printed in 1596 and may well be of medieval origin, as more certainly is a cumulative song about the consecutive aggressions of dog-cat-rat-spider-fly, probably alluded to in Fernando de Rojas's Celestina (1507) and indisputably attested in an early-seventeenth-century citation (Gonzalo Correas). An illumination in Alfonso's Cantigas depicts boys playing a medieval form of baseball, and Catalan children's games are nicely illustrated in a fifteenth-century book of hours. Rodrigo Caro's learned treatise, comparing mid-seventeenth-century games with their classical analogs, doubtless also documents medieval practice.

Folk Belief and Custom

Elements of pre-Christian mythology survived into medieval times (and indeed, to the present): the huntress Diana lives on in the *xanas*, supernatural denizens of springs, caves, and forests. Orcus, god of the classical underworld, came to be seen as Death personified, known in medieval Spanish as Huerco. The mysterious Elpila, alluded to in the *Poem of the Cid*, may be a Germanic elf. Juan Ruiz's *Libro de buen amor* (Book of Good Love; 1330–1343) refers to *mozas aojadas* (girls affected by the evil eye) and Ibn Quzman in the twelfth century likewise mentions the evil eye. Beliefs in magic, witchcraft, auguries, the flight of birds, and other practices are well attested. There are various references to soothsayers *(adevinos)*. Folk medicine, popular prayers, and incantations *(ensalmos)* can be documented or inferred from sixteenth-century and modern examples, just as a rich corpus of modern agricultural rituals surely embodies much medieval material. A modern Judeo-Spanish rain prayer agrees exactly with an early seventeenth-century counterpart: "*Agua, O Dio! Que la tierra la demanda*" [Water, O God! The earth requires it]. Francisco del Rosal's late-sixteenth-century compilation doubtless records many medieval beliefs and customs.

Cookery

Ruperto de Nola's *Libro de guisados* (Cookbook) was translated into Castilian and printed in 1525, from a Catalan original probably written in Naples in the 1470s. It thus reflects eastern peninsular usage, offering detailed instructions for preparing *caldo lardero de puerco salvaje* (fatty wild boar's broth), *escabeche de conejos* (marinated rabbits), *gato assado como se quiere* (roast cat as you like it), *lobo en pan* (breaded wolf), *morena en parrillas* (grilled moray eel), and *potaje de calamares* (squid stew), among a host of other delicacies. Medieval cookbooks catered to the tastes of royalty and the high nobility, and aside from the generally traditional character of medieval society, we should be cautious about seeing these recipes as folk cookery. There is similar aristocratic information for Portugal. We are also well informed about Hispano-Muslim cuisine, for which, among other sources, there is a thirteenth-century treatise. Abstention from (or willingness to eat) pork products was very much on people's minds in Christian Spain. Ruperto de Nola's recipe for *berenjenas a la morisca* (*morisco* eggplants)—still famed in Cervantes's time as a typical *morisco* dish—insists on the use of olive oil rather than bacon grease. The fifteenth-century *converso* poet Antón de Montoro laments that despite attending mass, crossing himself, saying the credo, and eating bowls of fatty pork and half-cooked bacon, he has never been taken for a Christian. Inquisitional records tell of individuals denounced for refusing to eat pork. A *morisca* and her family come to grief because of their distinctive and obviously Muslim eating habits: "They ate couscous with their hands, rolling it into little balls like the Moors do." Juan Ruiz's *Libro de buen amor* documents the word *adefina* (from Arabic *dafana*, "to cover"), showing that the classic Hispano-Jewish stew *(adafina)*, still eaten on the Sabbath by modern Sephardim, was also enjoyed in the Middle Ages.

Material Culture

Medieval iconography and modern analogs suggest what rural houses must have been like. Some types, such as the modern northwestern *pallozas* (round thatch-roofed houses), even perpetuate premedieval patterns. Medieval furnishings were sparse and austere. Items implying comfort and luxury—including the words for "pillow" and "bedspread"—in several cases have Arabic names. In the realm of dress—about which we know a great deal, thanks to iconography (though mostly in reference to the nobility)—and fabrics, Hispano-Muslim and northern European products competed in popularity. In the twelfth- to thirteenth-century Castilian pantheon of Las Huelgas, Catholic kings, queens, princes, and princesses were buried in luxurious Hispano-Muslim robes and rested on pillows decorated with ornate Koranic inscriptions. In fifteenth-century Burgos stylish ladies were still dressing in Moorish garb. We have substantial knowledge of medieval agriculture and of the implements and technologies it involved, many of which can be traced to Middle Eastern origins.

See also: Arabic-Islamic Tradition; *Cantar de mio Cid;* Chanson de Geste; *Chanson de Roland;* James the Elder, Saint; Jewish Tradition

—Samuel G. Armistead

Homosexuality (male). Condition and behaviors most often referred to in medieval texts as *sodomy* and *the sin against nature.*

Such terms derive from moral theology and canon (church) and civil law and suggest freely willed actions, almost always without any modern notion of sexual orientation as a genetic or psychologically fixed condition. Contemporary scholars of the Middle Ages will use all of these terms in qualified ways, adding on occasion the more theoretically tendentious *gay* or *queer.*

Whatever the term, there is plenty of evidence of homosexual male activity in the Middle Ages. Yet paradoxically, medieval discussion of male-male relations is characterized by intentional silence, rumor, and innuendo. These form part of a largely negative strategy of canon and civil law against homosexuality that intensified from the beginning of the twelfth century. More neutral medical writings on homosexuality were less widely known or applied. At the same time, same-sex desire seems to have its own literature, particularly in the earlier Middle Ages.

The problem with the so-called sin against nature or sodomy (a name derived from the story of the destruction of Sodom in Genesis 19) is that authorities were often divided about what it actually comprised. Often no clear explanation of it existed. Law codes and penitential manuals (handbooks for priests hearing confession) may condemn sodomy but may either not explain exactly what it is or even warn priests not to explain it, lest repenting sinners become tempted. M. Jordan notes that no other sin or class of sinners was treated in such a contradictory manner.

More rumors abounded about sodomy than outright depictions of it. A type of rumor-insult has a number of documented sources, such as in certain Galician Portuguese poems. Much further north, the rumor-insult warranted peculiar attention over centuries in Scandinavia. The major god Odin accuses the trickster god Loki of being a "lactating cow" and a passive homosexual *(argr),* an insult also associated with cowardice. By contrast, some sources also depict Odin drinking the semen of hanged men in order to regain or replenish masculine power. In later Norse culture even an accusation of effeminate homosexuality (as in *Njal's Saga)* could result in permanent outlawry (i.e., lifetime banishment).

In the urban centers of Europe priests and students were commonly thought to practice sodomy. Walter Map, who studied in Paris in the twelfth century, decried the prevalence of sodomy there. Certain kings were believed to be sodomites or known to have same-sex lovers (such as Frederick II of Sicily and Edward II of England), and the late-eleventh-century court of the Norman English king William Rufus was criticized for its fashionable, long-haired young male retinue. More ominous were the rumors that began with Justinian's *Corpus juris civilis* (The Body of Civil Law), which held that sodomy was responsible for famines, plagues, and earthquakes. Peter the Chanter declared that when the Virgin Mary gave birth to Jesus, all of the sodomites in the world died instantly. Greed for the wealth of the Templar Knights as well as rumors of sodomy led to the arrest of all Templars in 1307.

Such intolerance drew in no small part from the writings of St. Paul in the New Testament and especially of such early Church Fathers as Augustine, who regarded all nonprocreative sex as sinful. Augustine opposed same-sex activity, though not with detailed articulation. But the connection between theological pronouncement and actual practice varied according to time and circumstances. Scholars such as John Boswell argue that intolerance against sodomy grew out of social anxiety rather than ecclesiastical repression; others adjust this thesis by accentuating the Church's complicity. D. F. Greenberg sees the rise of intolerance as part of a struggle between Church and state for lands and wealth; to put up a united front in the process, the Church reinforced the discipline of both married and "sodomite" clergy. Greenberg does point out that an in-

creased focus on sacramental theology emphasized the purity of priests.

Intolerance can also be traced at least in part
to theology and canon law. Before the eleventh
century most canon law on sodomy was relatively mild, calling for only temporary excommunication for offenders. With increased attention in penitential manuals for confessors and
the invective of antisodomites such as Peter
Damian (who seems to have invented the term
sodomy), penances for sodomy increased. Compared to other sexual sins, sodomy received the
most severe penalties (as much as 7–15 years of
penance).

Moral theologians and canonists appealed to
the developing notion of the "natural" that received greater definition by the later eleventh
century. Arguments from nature were seldom
based on observation but relied, rather, on the
Stoic and Aristotelian writings that became
more available in the twelfth century. Sodomy,
for example, was considered particularly "unnatural" since it was believed that not even animals
engaged in it (except for male hyenas, who were
believed to change their sex to suit male partners). Gratian's code of canon law, completed
circa 1150, condemned as unnatural the inappropriate, nonprocreative use of the sex organs, including sodomy, fornication, adultery, and incest.
In the thirteenth century St. Thomas Aquinas
developed a hierarchy of four major categories of
unnatural sexual sin: masturbation, bestiality,
homosexual sodomy, and heterosexual sex not
directed toward procreation (for example, coitus
interruptus).

Civil law in Byzantium, developed by Justinian, instituted the death penalty for sodomites,
though there was apparently no popular support
for such punishment. Other than the Visigothic
penalty of castration for sodomy, Western European civil law did not impose serious penalties
until after the eleventh century. Charlemagne's
edicts against sodomy and unnatural acts contained no actual penalties, only an appeal for repentance. In the later Middle Ages, Greenberg
argues, pressure from middle classes in autonomous towns of the Low Countries, Germany,
and northern Italy led to harsh municipal laws; in
1260 Orléans called for castration, amputation of
the penis, and burning at the stake.

Both ecclesiastical and civil control had become more organized and centralized by the later
Middle Ages, and both sources of repression
linked various marginal groups together: sodomites, heretics, witches, Muslims, Jews, and usurers.
Heretics were often assumed to be sodomites. In
fact, the word *bougre* (either from the Bulgarian
source of the Catharist heresy or from heresy opponent Robert le Bougre), ancestor of the modern word *bugger*, was not only applied to heretics
but also to the usury and deviant sexuality they
were believed to promote. Heretics appear with
usurers and sodomites in the literature of the pe-

riod, notably in the Circles of the Violent in
Dante's *Inferno*.

In contrast to condemnation in theology and
secular authority or literature, medical writings
presented a dispassionate description of the
causes and nature of same-sex desire or activity.
The *Problemata* (attributed to Aristotle) specu-
lates that men desire passive homosexuality because retention of semen in the anus requires
friction of the anus to release it. Later in the
Middle Ages the widely circulated *Canon of Medicine* by Avicenna dismisses earlier physiological
explanations, proposing a cure of beating, fasting, and imprisonment that is penal rather than
medical. Jordan notes that Albertus Magnus (c.
1200–1280) had access to medical writings by
Avicenna (980–1037) and other sources, yet he
used them selectively and omitted medical explanations of sodomy when it was convenient to
do so.

It is possible, nonetheless, to speak of a homo-
erotic literature in the Middle Ages. From the
Carolingian era (late eighth century) and for the
next few centuries homosexual erotic poetry can
be found, though it is not clear how widespread
this poetry was even in learned, most likely ur-
banized ecclesiastical circles, and some scholars
have argued that medieval writers are echoing
classical Latin rhetorical commonplaces rather
than actual feelings. In the twelfth century a debate poem pitting Ganymede against Helen
weighed the merits of loving boys or women.
Aelred of Rievaulx, a twelfth-century Cistercian,
encouraged a tender, singular affection for other
monks that was based on his theological premise,
"God's friendship," and referred to John and Jesus
as "married."

Saints' legends include negative exempla—for
example, the martyrdom of the beautiful young
Pelagius, who resisted the sexual advances of an
evil caliph. On the other hand, stories of paired
saints, such as the martyrs Sergius and Bacchus
(d. 290), express such a passionate and exclusive
devotion that they have recently been interpreted as lovers. John Boswell, in *Same-Sex
Unions in Premodern Europe*, has studied rites of
brotherhood in Greek and Slavonic texts, suggesting cautiously that they might have had an
erotic meaning under certain circumstances. (Indeed, some Slavic peoples were notable for a relative lack of concern about homosexuality well
into the early modern period.)

Boswell's thesis, however qualified, remains
controversial among other scholars. But as with
the study of sexuality in general in the Middle
Ages, a certain amount of speculation is inevitable. The inconclusiveness of sources and the
dialectic of rumor, silence, punishment, and
class-based popular literature continue to make
medieval homosexuality a fertile field for the approaches of folklorists.

See also: Knights Templar; Lesbians

—Graham N. Drake

Hungarian Tradition. The folkloric culture of the Hungarians, who settled in their present-day country and converted to Christianity in the tenth century.

Before the tenth century, during their wanderings from the East, from the southern Russian steppes, and to the Carpathian basin, the originally Finno-Ugric Hungarian language and culture were subjected to Turkic, Iranian, and later Slavic influences. Slavic influence continued to play an important role during the centuries of settlement and afterward, together with later Italian, French, and German impact. During the eleventh to thirteenth centuries, pre-Christian religion and culture coexisted with Christian culture, and popular culture with "pagan" roots went through a process of Christianization. We cannot really speak of folklore as separate from an also primarily oral popular culture. In the thirteenth and fourteenth centuries, aspects of pre-Christian culture and poetry survived in the traditions of rural populations rooted in agriculture and animal husbandry. At the same time, the traditions of the peasantry gradually integrated into the framework of Church culture, merging with and transformed by newly arrived European literary and folkloric influences. New medieval European genres and forms developed and spread in Hungarian folklore; most of these genres only incidentally contained archaic, pre-Christian features.

Although the Latin literature of the Church was present from the beginning of the period, most of the potential written sources for the study of medieval folklore were destroyed in wars and migrations in the Middle Ages and in later times. Surviving sources allow us only an indirect view of oral folklore from occasional notes and allusions by royal chroniclers and monastic historians, the folkloric elements of sermon literature, chance remarks by travelers, and surviving data of urban, semifolkloric genres. At the same time, certain elements of modern folklore that are archaic or probably of medieval origins, linguistic evidence, and, sometimes, analogs of European lore preserved in medieval literature also make it possible to infer the existence of a genre or a work of art in Hungary at the time. The primary sources for the study of popular religion, rites, and beliefs are Church regulations, laws, notes, and prohibitions of certain "pagan" rites.

Religion

Probable traditions in the pagan religion of ninth- and tenth-century Hungarians, some of which were later assimilated into Christian mythology and cults, include a god of the sky and a creator deity (which were assimilated in the Bogomil Christian beliefs of the dual creation of the world), a goddess of childbirth and fate, nature spirits, a weather demon (dragon), helpful and harmful spirits, and demons of diseases. Linguistic evidence points toward the existence of cults of bears and wolves. The pantheon of gods and demons survived partly in beliefs eclipsed by Christianity and partly in myths and legends. Some of these narratives later merged with apocryphal etiological Christian legends related to the Old and the New Testaments, which were also widespread in folklore. Royal laws and linguistic data hint at the activities of magicians, diviners, and healers, and we have linguistic evidence for the existence of a *táltos* (shaman) during the Hungarian settlement period. The ancient Hungarian shaman continued to exist in a form and with a function similar to those of the mediators of the Christian Slavs. Driven to the periphery by the Christian clergy, his main task became the securing of agrarian fertility.

As for cult activities, very early sources give information about the sacrifice of a white horse to the god of the sky. However, the cult of the dead and the sacrifices to the dead have survived to the present in an altered form. Originally a propitiatory sacrifice, the funeral feast had become a memorial charity feast by as early as the first centuries of Christianity. The rites of church culture, the cults of saints, dead heroes, holy places, and relics imbued with Christian symbolism and the Christian forms of communication with the otherworld, visions, and apparitions quite soon gained a central position in folklore.

One of the most important forms of the folklore surviving from the pre-Christian times was the "magical poetry" that accompanied individual and collective magical rites. Incantations were used to heal, to ward off diseases, and to bring abundant harvests or good luck to the house. The folkloric incantations merged with the official formulas of benediction and exorcism used by priests and monks; thus, the texts contain pagan magical elements to drive away sickness as well as Christian elements of prayer and blessing. The first known Hungarian written example, the "Incantations of Bagonya," dates from 1488.

Related to magical poetry is a specific, archaic, paraliturgical verse form of prayer. Its existence in the Middle Ages can be inferred from some stylistic elements of modern texts, but examples are known from twelfth-century Italy and Germany as well. It is characterized by free rhythm, lack of stanzas, a recitative performing style, and contents that differ from the topics of official prayers: the magic defense of the individual and the home, the magical enforcement of salvation, or apocryphal elements of the Passion of Christ.

Rites, Plays

We have no information on the rites of the shepherds' feasts, probably held in the spring and fall. All our medieval data refer to calendar holidays. From the beginning of the Middle Ages, collective rites and related rite songs (magic poetry) were part of the rituals of Christian holidays, or at least they were related to Christian calendar holidays. Due to the links with Byzantium in the first centuries of the Hungarian kingdom, some of the holiday rites have Byzantine, Orthodox, or Slavic parallels. Later elements show characteristics that are predominantly central European, related to Western Christendom. Among the agrarian population, the holidays of the winter and summer solstices (St. Lucy's Day, December 13; Christmas; St. Stephen's Day, December 26; New Year's Day; Midsummer or St. John's Day, June 24) as well as the spring holidays (Palm Sunday, Whitsun) were accompanied by magic words influencing the fertility of animals, crops, and families. These were sung by processions of groups wearing animal or demon masks. The *regösének* (*regös* song) of the winter solstice and the *szentiváni ének* (Midsummer Day song) had certain elements that referred to the solstice and a cult of the sun (deer masks with astral symbols, lighting bonfires). The main themes of spring rites, performed with green twigs, were the expulsion of winter/death (cf. Central and Eastern European *morena*) and the bringing in of reviving vegetation. The racing tournaments and king-making games at Whitsun contained elements of initiation into adulthood. Festival songs often contained Christian references related to the day in the calendar (e.g., Midsummer Day's songs invoked St. John the Baptist). Pre-Christian motifs of fertility magic were now complemented by genres and motifs of love poetry, itself just developing in Europe. *Párosítók* (pairing songs) were performed at ceremonial rites and weddings, and nonliturgical religious poetry such as the *Certamen* (Contest of Flowers) were sung at Midsummer, while moralities and allegorical plays were enacted in carnivals. Some elements of the customs of reciting greetings by masked men at Carnival time were connected to world-turned-upside-down symbolism. In the celebration of carnivals, a custom taken over from Italy and Germany, motifs of the lay popular theater of medieval Europe were present: contests, tournaments, sword dances, and *moresca* (morris dances).

In the genre of the church drama, we have data on the activities of liturgical singing groups, performing students, craft guilds, and confraternities, as well as performances in towns, where the ordinary citizens also participated at Christmas and Easter with songs in the vernacular (eleventh- to thirteenth-century Corpus Christi processions included *tableaux vivants*). At Christmas there were *betlehemezés* (Nativity plays); at Epiphany, *tracti stellae* (star-plays); and at Easter *ludi paschalis* (Easter plays). Toward the end of the Middle Ages villagers were probably also performing folkloric plays (e.g., the *Quem quaeritis*, which later became a separate Easter play). Folkloric variants of *betlehemezés* were accompanied by shepherds' plays and shepherds' dances in which the performers wore animal-shaped masks. The folklore forms preserved archaic, pre-Christian European musical material (recitatives, forms of cries, twin-bar structures). Impor-

tant genres were the musical greetings of students on various holidays, which were based on plain chants of the liturgical repertoire, and the ceremonial *recordation* where carols were sung (e.g., on St. Blaise's Day—February 3).

As for the folklore of rites of passage, we can infer musical material connected to weddings and funerals. Beside love songs (pairing songs preserving the memories of magical "pairings" of marriages), traces of religious dramas connected to wedding feasts (e.g., the "Wedding of Cana") are discernible. The rites and textual and musical materials of funerals are mainly of church origin, with the exception of the *sirató* (lament). The lament genre flourished throughout the Middle Ages. Performed by women, it was connected to several elements of the funeral rites, and repeated parts alternated with improvised lyrics.

Music, Dance

We have data not only on music as an accompaniment for ritual and liturgical forms but also on instrumental music performed at revels by Hungarians on foreign raids. Individual players of various instruments are mentioned in several sources. From the end of the Middle Ages we consider data on musicians at fairs, weddings, and dance parties; wandering musicians in villages and towns; court musicians; and even wandering Hungarian musicians in other parts of Europe. Probable instruments included the *furulya* (whistle), a horn-like instrument, and a one-sided drum. The Hungarian *hajdu* dance was already popular in Poland before 1500. In the court of the prince of Milan in the fifteenth century a dance "after the Hungarian style" is mentioned. Some of the more modern forms of dances offer hints about the nature of late-medieval dances. Shepherds' dances and skipping dances are somewhat undeveloped in form and genre. Lads' dances, old dances in pairs, and girls' roundels performed at Lent are more elaborate.

Lyric Poetry, Songs, Hymns

In addition to the "flower songs," a new medieval genre, the "dawn song" (French *aube*; German *Tagelied*), in which lovers recall their night spent together, was known in Hungary as well. Dance songs, drinking songs, swineherds' songs, goliardic poetry, *nefanda carmina* (cursing songs), and mocking songs were probably also known at this period. Wandering minstrels and, especially, itinerant students had an important role in performing and spreading these songs. Besides performing theatrical plays and epic poetry, students had another function as singers of holiday and family greetings: performing satirical and parodic genres.

Popular hymns came to Hungary with the Gregorian style. The chants, translated from Latin to Hungarian, appeared first as tropes within the liturgy and later as independent forms sung on church or lay communal events, holidays, and family feasts (e.g., Christmas and Easter carols,

Holy Thursday hymns, songs to the Virgin Mary, lamentations of the Virgin Mary). Musically they represented the style that had become universally popular in Europe by the fourteenth century.

Epic Poetry

Epic poetry continued the traditions of pre-Christian times and the first centuries after the settlement of Hungarians. Although no lyrics survive, the content of these songs can be reconstructed from thirteenth- and fourteenth-century chronicles. Important topics include the "Legend of the Wondrous Stag" (Kézai's *Chronicle, Illustrated Chronicle*) about the origins of the Hungarian people. In the legend, Hunor and Magor (the personifications of the Onogur and Magyar ethnic names) arrive in their new land while chasing a stag. The motif of stag hunting and the name of the *progenitrix ünő* (female stag) suggest a totemic heritage. The motif of intercourse with a male bird of prey appears in the "Legend of Álmos," the totemic origin myth of the first royal family. The Christian version of the legend of the Wondrous Stag is related to St. Stephen, the first Hungarian king: the stag, wearing a cross between its horns, leads the Hungarian people into their new homeland and converts its pursuer, the pagan hero. The story of the killing of Prince Álmos, who led the Hungarians into the Carpathian basin, suggests a system of dual rulership and the sacrificial murder of the king. According to the story of the "Country Bought for a White Horse," the Hungarians bought their new land from the Slavic peoples already living there; this is a well-known theme in more-recent Hungarian folklore. Several chronicle tales recount the feats of the heroes conquering the new land and the adventures of the first kings—for example, the conflict between King Endre and his brother, Béla, when the latter had to choose between the crown and the sword. Other legends center on exploits of the chieftains leading Hungarian raids on the West—for example, how the short Botond killed a Greek giant, or how the chieftain Lehel, by blowing his horn at the scaffold, made the German emperor who had ordained his execution become his servant in the otherworld.

Many earlier songs concerned the eleventh-century king St. László. Stories about him became legends, and scenes from these legends often appear on the frescoes of fourteenth-century Romanesque churches. The most important motifs include the mythical, invulnerable hero wrestling; the king releasing the girl carried away by a Cumanian warrior; and the motif of "searching for lice on the head of the king," known from the Bluebeard story cycle.

These song cycles centered on individual heroes contained in motifs with Asian (that is, Mongolian) parallels (e.g., mythical combats), as well as common European folklore motifs of heroic tales and Christian legends.

After the thirteenth century ancient Hungarian epic poetry partly integrated into the emerging Latin literature and into the court epic tradition, which began to develop in Hungarian in the thirteenth and fourteenth centuries. At the end of the twelfth century and in the first half of the thirteenth century, French chansons de geste and romances—including poems about Troy and Alexander the Great—began to spread among the top layers of Hungarian cultural life, but presumably written examples have all been destroyed.

Certain themes of the declining heroic epic lingered on in a new, late-medieval genre, the ballad, which became fashionable and displaced the heroic epic songs from Hungarian culture. The ballad came from France to Hungary through cultural relations with thirteenth-century Anjou and through French-Walloon settlers moving into Hungary in the thirteenth and fourteenth centuries. Ballad topics include love tragedies, adultery, incest, conflicts between husband and wife or between children and parents, child murder, and social antagonism. We also know of some humorous ballads and legendary religious ballads, the latter showing a close connection with apocryphal legends and ancient mythological topics (e.g., songs to the Virgin Mary, Jesus looking for shelter, the girl carried off to heaven). Some ballads continue the Hungarian heroic epic tradition, containing Eastern European Turkic and Caucasian elements (e.g., the ballad of Izsák Kerekes, containing the motif of a magical sleep before battle, or the ballad of "The Walled-Up Wife"). Although Western European, especially French, influence has a strong mark on the musical material, the tunes of the ballads primarily bear medieval Hungarian and some archaic pre-settlement characteristics.

The other important developing epic genre in the Middle Ages was the tale. We do not know when the shift from heroic epic to heroic tale took place, or whether it took place at all, but part of the European wealth of tales already well documented at the time must have been known in Hungary. Codices written in Latin and later in Hungarian, as well as sermons, sometimes refer to legends and tales related to the Golden Legend. For instance, we know of the tale of "Truth and Falsehood" (AT 613) from the records of a fifteenth-century preacher, who got it "from the mouth of the folk." Heroic tales probably preserved some pre-Christian Eastern themes: celestial bodies obtained by a demiurge (creator god), voyages to the realms of the dead, and the like.

See also: Baltic Tradition; Finno-Ugric Tradition; Slavic Tradition, East

—Éva Pócs

*I*conography. Conventional, symbolic representations in the visual arts, conveying information of interest to folklorists in almost every conceivable artistic medium, in monuments of "high art" as much as in humbler media such as lead badges and biscuit molds.

While the modern distinction between the religious and the secular is not valid for the Middle Ages themselves, it is nevertheless of practical use in discussing medieval iconography here, especially as, historically, nonreligious imagery has been neglected. The exceptions have been those categories of secular iconography that pertain to the aristocratic strata of medieval society (e.g., Arthuriana and other romances of chivalry, such as the Charlemagne and Alexander cycles).

Scholars have adequately surveyed the illustration of fables (e.g., in the borders of the Bayeux Tapestry), of beast epics (especially that of *Reynart*), and of the fauna of the Bestiary and "monstrous races" (insofar as these last have entered the popular consciousness). However, such ready-made collections of folkloric material are the exception. For the most part there is no substitute for combing the published catalogs of the various categories of artifacts, and there is still much of interest to be extracted from them. Nor, indeed, is there any substitute for original observation and research: of all the areas of medieval studies, this is perhaps the least well quarried.

Badges, Seals, and Molds

Religious folklore and popular Christianity, especially the lore of saints, have received considerable attention in recent years, particularly via the evolving study of "pilgrim badges." Colorful folktales are summarized in such lead images as the devil being conjured into the boot held by the Berkshire "saint" John Schorn, or the greyhound badges inscribed "Bien aia qvi me porte" [May he who wears me have good luck]. This auspicious phrase probably alludes to the cult of the French greyhound, St. Guinefort, invoked to protect infants. The same little lead souvenirs commemorate other equally remarkable saintly deeds—for example, the miracle through which St. Werburg miraculously contained geese within their wattle pen; unlike such proverbial fools as the Wise Men of Gotham, who sought in vain to pen the cuckoo, the saint as a "fool for Christ's sake" achieves the folly. Even the organizers of St. Thomas Becket's cult did not disdain from issuing a lead memento in the form of their saint's initial at the center of a four-leaf clover, a classic example of the "reinforcement" of a religious amulet by a secular good luck charm. The festivities of popular religion are also alluded to in such fifteenth-century badges as the crowned plows that commemorate the festival of Plow Monday.

The lead badges of secular content have perhaps an inordinate degree of importance for the study of popular attitudes, because sexuality, in particular, is rarely so explicitly expressed in any other medium. The Salisbury badges (fourteenth and fifteenth centuries) include milkmaids celebrating May with their vessels piled on their heads some three centuries before such dances are recorded in writing. A holly sprig is plausibly interpreted to be an allusion to the folk game played between the partisans of holly and ivy (this game can be inferred from contemporary carols). Lovers' badges embody a mixture of popular and more courtly motifs. Prominent are hearts and flowers—especially the quatrefoil (fourleafed) flower known as the "truelove"—bearing such inscriptions as "herte be true" and "veolit in may lady." A unique Dutch badge depicts the arm of a lover who literally "wears his heart on his sleeve." Miniature openwork purses in which imitation "coins" are trapped are doubtless "good luck charms" to attract (monetary) fortune. One inscribed *grommerci* (thank you) bears comparison with the fifteenth-century carol refrain, "Gramercy my own purse." The ape who stands on a fish and urinates into a mortar that he simultaneously works with a pestle is perhaps a satire on the dubious ingredients used by apothecaries. Religious satire is certainly present in the badge of the fox friar who preaches to the geese, his intentions made clear by the dead goose tucked out of sight under his belt.

Unlike lead badges, personal seals were not available to the humblest pockets, but by the later Middle Ages they had descended quite far down the social scale from the earliest royal and aristocratic types. There is a frequent use of the rebus to represent the owner's surname—for example, a ginger jar above the words *grene ginger*, the seal of John Grene (1455), confirming the medieval delight in punning humor. Other seals refer to folktales. Despite its Latin motto, "Te waltere docebo cur spinas phebo gero" [I will teach you, Walter, why I carry thorns on the moon], the seal of Walter de Grendon (c. 1330), depicting a hooded man bearing a double bundle of thorns hanging from a stick over his shoulder inside a crescent moon, with a little dog at his feet in front of him and two stars, alludes to the popular notion of the Man in the Moon, banished there for gathering firewood on a Sunday. There seems no obvious reason why Walter chose this seal for himself; how much more appropriate it would have been for Richard Moneshine, whose seal is dated 1394. Other motifs include the world-turned-upside-down theme of the hare riding the hound, popular on fourteenth-century seals.

The stone and earthenware molds in which biscuit and cake dough were formed had assumed a degree of complexity by the later Middle Ages, especially in Germany, and, like seals, they frequently combine text and image. An inventory made in 1521 of molds mostly dating from the previous decade and belonging to one Claus Stalburg of Frankfurt will serve both as a representative list of such popular imagery, in its mixture of the sacred and the profane (including erotica), and also as a timely reminder that the iconographic record is not necessarily dependent on the survival of the images themselves.

The 40 molds enumerated bear 52 representations, including Pyramus and Thisbe; St. Christopher; Romulus and Remus; the Death of Lucretia; the Baptism of Christ; Venus and Cupid; the fabliau of the widow's son killed by the king's son's horse, and the king's sentence on him; women and fools playing; a young man and a woman on a bed; a peasant and wife threshing hens out of eggs (a proverbial Gothamesque folly); an old man with a young woman, the folly of whose unequal relationship is pointed out by both the presence of a fool and a swarm of hornets who sting the man; three naked women fishing; Christ's Passion; a morris dance; a fool in a basket being dragged along by an old woman; a young woman who offers a hermit a love potion; Samson and Delilah; Adam and Eve; and a peasant trying to force an outsized caltrop into a sack (showing incidentally that this design must derive from a woodcut in the enormously influential early printed book *Das Narrenschiff* [The Ship of Fools, 1494]).

Images in Cloth, Wood, and Stone
Tapestry and embroidery remain two of the most valuable media for the study of secular art, but—because of their costliness—the themes they illustrate seem to reflect the aristocracy's taste for the tales of chivalry or courtly love; many subjects are now only known to us through inventories: Sir John Fastolf (d. 1459) owned a bench covering of "a man scheyting at j blode hownde" [a man shouting at a bloody hound], which looks very like an illustration of the tale "Llewellyn and His Dog" (motif B331.2), in which a dog saves a child from a snake and is seen leaving the child's room with blood on its mouth; a man, thinking the dog has killed the child, kills the dog before discovering his error. If this image indeed refers to the tale, it significantly predates the German woodcuts illustrating the story, which appeared in the 1530s.

The humbler painted cloth—the "poor man's tapestry"—is perhaps of greater relevance, as it reflects more popular taste; unfortunately, however, very few survive. Once again, though, the evidence of inventories is of help here: particularly interesting is the mention of "a paynted cloth of Robyn hod" hanging in the parlor of Robert Rychardes of Dursley (Gloucestershire), according to an inventory taken in 1492. Even erotica seem to have appeared in this relatively transient medium, for according to an inventory of the ef-

fects of a Brussels official who died in 1505, among the four secular pictures he owned were two paintings on cloth representing *amoureusheyden* (lovers or loving). Upon her death in 1448 Alice Langham of Snailwell, near Newmarket, left her son a cloth painted with the history of *King Robert of Sicily*, a pious romance; in 1463 John Baret of Bury Saint Edmunds left his nieces "the steyned cloth of the Coronacion of Oure Lady" and another one featuring the "Seven Ages of Man." The latter was no doubt a far humbler version of the "VII Aages" tapestry series that Jean Cosset of Arras produced for his lord in 1402. It was perhaps familiarity with such stained cloths that led Sir Thomas More "in his youth ... in hys fathers house in London" (c. 1490) to devise "a goodly hangyng of fyne paynted clothe, with nyne pageauntes, and verses over of every of those pageauntes" on the same Ages of Man theme. The poet John Lydgate (d. c. 1450) similarly "deuysed" a "peynted or desteyned [stained] clothe for an halle a parlour or a chaumbre ... at the request of a werthy citeseyn of London." This cloth is of particular iconographic interest, for it depicted the satirical misogynistic motif of the mythical beasts "Bycorne," who grows fat on a diet of submissive husbands, and "Chichevache," who grows skinny preying on faithful wives. Chivalric themes were also represented in the late fifteenth century: one of the members of the Clarel family of Aldwarke in South Yorkshire bequeathed to the Church of All Saints in Rotherham a stained cloth depicting the celebrated joust between Anthony Woodville and the Bastard of Burgundy, which took place before Edward IV at Smithfield in 1467.

Although it survives for the most part in ecclesiastical contexts, sculpture in wood and stone contains much of folkloric relevance. In wood it is misericords, in particular, that are of interest to us. In stone the primary sites of interest are roof bosses, capitals, and corbels. The roof bosses are fascinating both because of their location—in this respect, they are similar to misericords—and because they are not easily visible. Their carvers seem sometimes to have been granted considerable license, perhaps because the roof bosses were rarely seen. Bosses, in particular, make use of phallic imagery and scatology and illustrate exempla (e.g., the Clever Daughter at Exeter) and other popular motifs (e.g., the preaching fox and the bagpiping pig at St. Mary's, Beverley; a doghead at Bristol). They also attest such folk amusements as "gurning" (making ugly faces) through a horse collar (Lacock, Wiltshire). At Meavy (Devon), a mouse emerges from one ear of a human (?) head, while its tail is visible in the other; perhaps this image is a humorous portrait of some "empty-headed" local.

Individual capitals and corbels reflect the same range of imagery: the Aesopic fable of the ass who tried to imitate his master's lapdog was carved on a capital at Westminster Hall as early as circa

1090 (it does not appear again in English art until the late-fifteenth-century Reynard woodcuts). Proverbs are also illustrated in stone, especially in late-fifteenth-century Flemish art.

One of a series of bas-reliefs decorating the Brussels town hall depicts the man who is so churlish that he cannot bear to see the sun shining in the water as well as on him! In addition to its being represented appropriately in snow, this is one of more than 100 proverbs illustrated in Pieter Brueghel the Elder's famous painting *Netherlandish Proverbs* (1559). This work represents the culmination of the late-medieval enthusiasm for proverbs and their representation in the arts; the late-fifteenth-century French illustrated *Proverbes en rimes* (Rhymed Proverbs) manuscripts are but one manifestation of this interest.

Snow, Metals, Printing, and Illuminations

Snow was undoubtedly the most ephemeral sculptural medium, however! It seems incredible that any record of such spontaneous sculpture should survive, and yet we know that a *danse macabre* (dance of death) was made at Arras in 1434. Moreover, a 400-line poem published in Brussels in 1511 describes in some detail the fascinating series of sculptures made throughout the city during the hard winter of the previous year. These include Christ and the woman of Samaria; a preaching friar with a dripping nose; a cow "manuring" the ground; Adam and Eve; St. George rescuing the princess from the dragon; Cupid with drawn bow atop a pillar; Roland blowing his horn; Charon's ferry; a *mannekin-pis* (pissing mannequin) whose rosewater "urine" fell straight into the mouth of a gaping man below; a mermaid; a fool and his cat washing its bottom; a unicorn resting its head in a virgin's lap; the King of Friesland (Freeze-land); a tooth-puller; the Man in the Moon; a woman naked but for a rose held before her genitals (cf. the symbolism of the flower in the *Roman de la rose* [Romance of the Rose]); an armed merman; a man astride a keg of real beer; and two motifs from the extremely popular late-medieval power of women topos: Sardanapalus, with his head in Venus's lap, and so "unmanned" by her that he is portrayed with distaff in hand (Hercules is much more common in this role), and Aristotle ridden by Phyllis, brought to grief by her *quoniam* (genitals), as the text has it.

Bronze statues would have been visible to the populace in such public media as tomb sculpture, candelabra, and fountains: fools from each medium, respectively, exemplify the motifs of whipping a snail in order to make it go faster (a Gothamite folly found also on a Bristol misericord), standing foolishly with finger in mouth, and wearing only one shoe.

Because of their taste for depicting everyday urban life, aristocrats' metalwork (known to us mostly from inventories) sometimes includes motifs of folkloric interest. One such example is an enameled goblet owned by Louis d'Anjou with the figure of a knight handing a lady up some steps; at the top of the steps there was a blind beggar, together with his dog, holding a basin and the inscription: "Donnez au povre qui ne voit" [Give to the poor man who cannot see]. Another example is the table ornament enameled with all the various street cries of Paris (inscribed on banderoles held by the traders).

Wall paintings are another vast area of interest, and those late-fifteenth-century examples still extant in the Swedish churches of Osmo, Tensta, and Kumla, among others, are perhaps of greatest value to students of medieval folklore. Subjects include a witch's familiar, a "milk hare" draining a cow of its milk (Osmo), and the antifeminist exemplum of the devil who is so afraid of an old woman (who has succeeded in splitting up a married couple where all his efforts had failed) that he dare not hand her the pair of shoes that are her reward; instead, he holds them out to her on the end of a stick (there are several examples of this image). World-turned-upside-down subjects can also be found, such as the ox butchering the butcher (Tensta), and hares capturing the hunter (Kumla). Woodcuts and engravings make their appearance in the late Middle Ages. Although they often illustrate works of interest to the folklorist, they rarely possess a value independent of the text. At times, however, one can gain valuable insights into the popular attitudes of the period by examining such motifs as the one on the title-page cut to *Neu Layenspiegel* (New Mirror for Laymen; Augsburg, 1511), where the young witch copulating with a man is shown "unnaturally" on top.

A 1479 woodcut of a schoolroom, in a book published in Augsburg, shows one of the pupils wearing an ass's head—an actual contemporary punishment for dunces. This piece reminds us of the proverbial stupidity of that animal, according to medieval (and indeed, later) popular belief. Compare this with a marginal scene in the Rutland Psalter (English; c. 1260) that depicts two monks quarreling—the one who is about to draw his dagger says to the other (in mirror writing), "Tu es asin[us]" [You are an ass].

The earliest broadsheets extant are equally valuable. There is the French sheet published by Guy Marchant (Paris; c. 1495), in which the monstrous cow Chicheface—who lives off faithful wives—complains that there are so few that it is reduced to the skinny state in which the artist has drawn it. Other examples are given by the German spinning sow, which is also pressed into the service of antifeminism, and the fragmentary English sheet of King Henry VI, venerated as a saint, being adored by kneeling suppliants who pray to him to ease their wounds; it shows the little votive limbs hanging up at the shrine left as offerings. Of equal interest is the German woodcut (c. 1420–1440) of St. Gertrude, plagued by mice as she spins. Similarly, the early woodcut

Pestblätter (plague sheets) invoke the protection of various saints against a more serious plague.

Images depicting those beliefs and practices that some religious authorities condemned as superstitious even before the rise of Protestantism (apart from the pilgrim badges discussed above) are to be found in all types of saints' lives. Many "religious" scenes in miniatures and paintings offer important opportunities for students of medieval folklore. "The Reviling of Christ before the Crucifixion," for instance, is a most valuable record of contemporary (insulting) gestures: the tongue out, the mouth distorted by the fingers, the "fig" gesture, the teeth flicking, the goitered appearance of the torturers. Scenes of hell are similarly valuable as a source of motifs of demeaning popular punishments (e.g., barrowing).

A twelfth-century manuscript illustrating the life of St. Amand depicts a blind woman whose sight is mysteriously restored once she takes an axe to the tree she had worshipped before she was converted by the saint. The artist has depicted two very human-looking heads representing the tree spirits in the top of the tree. On a happier note, newborn babies are sometimes accompanied by a seemingly irrelevant stork in attendance (e.g., the cradled baby in the border of the "Judgment of Solomon" page in the *Hours of Catherine of Cleeves*).

There are many other categories of decorative material that are not considered here—among them, stained glass, ceramics (including floor tiles), ivories, the so-called *Minnekästchen* (love caskets), the earliest woodcut playing cards, and pictorial graffiti.

See also: Cockaigne, Land of; Cuckold; Fool; Manuscript Marginalia; Misericords; Phallic Imagery; Sheela-na-Gig; World Turned Upside Down

—Malcolm Jones

Inns and Taverns. Establishments selling wine and sometimes lodging, food, and ale, located mainly in England.

Although the distinction between inns and taverns was sometimes blurred in the Middle Ages, inns offered lodging to their customers but taverns did not, and inns were generally larger in size and served customers of a more elite class than taverns. Inns first arose in England in the twelfth and thirteenth centuries, and by the fifteenth century inns were a prominent feature of the medieval town. Late-medieval inns were very large, capable of housing between 200 and 300 guests, and their facades extended across wide sections of a town's main thoroughfare. Although innkeepers sometimes brewed their own ale and beer, they primarily served wine. At an inn a guest would also be served elaborate meals including several courses of meat and fish. Taverns began to appear sometime in the twelfth century. By the fourteenth century the number of taverns had increased significantly, though they were mostly concentrated in England's southern coun-

ties. Taverns had expanded in size, often encompassing several rooms, and were the main social centers of urban life. Late-medieval taverners, especially those who were also vintners, were oftentimes prominent members of society. Most taverns served no beverages other than wine, and, indeed, some scholars believe that during certain parts of the Middle Ages taverners were prohibited from selling ale. Since the price of wine was very high throughout the Middle Ages, taverns were frequented only by the middle to upper classes; even when the cost of wine was at a relative low during the thirteenth century, it was still not affordable for the lower classes, and after England's loss of Gascony during the Hundred Years' War the cost of wine soared. Some taverns also sold food, but only basic and simple meals; elaborate feasts were only to be had at inns.

As roads improved and more and more Christians began to go on pilgrimages to visit shrines containing holy relics, abbeys and monasteries began to establish adjacent hospices in which they offered shelter for pilgrims and other travelers for two or three nights. The abbeys and monasteries required no fee from their guests, but a gratuity for the guest-master, the elder monk or friar who supervised the hospice, was expected from those who could afford it. Eventually inns arose along merchant routes and pilgrimage ways to ease the crowding of monasteries and to offer travelers the option of longer stays. Located on the main road of the town, inns were also more convenient for the traveler than were the abbeys and monasteries, which were usually far from the main roads. Inns served traveling clerics and wealthy wool merchants as well as pilgrims, and they offered their guests entertainment as well as food, drink, and lodging: the communal rooms in the lower level of the inn would often be filled with players, acrobats, jugglers, and mummers. The innkeeper's obligation to entertain his guests, it is thought, is related to the emphasis on entertainment at abbeys and monasteries, where monks entertained the travelers with music, singing, and storytelling at the guest-master's request.

The earliest ancestors of taverns were the *tabernae* (small shops or booths) that sold drink alongside the Roman roads in the Anglo-Saxon period. The *tabernae* were identified by a long pole (later termed an "ale-stake") outside the front door; a vine or evergreen branch hanging from the top of the pole indicated that the shop sold wine as well as ale. The green branch or bush was supposed to be suggestive of ivy leaves, the symbol of Dionysus, the Roman god of wine. It has been conjectured that the symbols of the pole and the bush were adopted from the Romans, who probably introduced early *tabernae* along with the roads they constructed in the 100 years after Julius Caesar's invasion of England in 55 B.C.E. We know that taverns proper first arose sometime before 750 C.E., because it was approximately then that Ecbright, archbishop of York, issued Canon 18 forbidding priests from eating or drinking in taverns.

Ecbright's was the first of many such regulations established as the number of inns and taverns rose. In 1175 Archbishop Richard decreed that clerics might stop at taverns if their travels necessitated it but that they could not do so only for pleasure, and in 1195 Archbishop Walter ordered that priests should abstain from taverns and public drinking. That the prohibition was repeated suggests that priests and clerics were frequent patrons of taverns. In 1329 a civic proclamation in London ordered that "whereas misdoers, going about by night, have their resort more in taverns than elsewhere, and there seek refuge and watch their hour for misdoing, we forbid that any taverners or brewers keep the door of his tavern open after the hour of curfew." Moreover, lawmakers of fourteenth-century London were as wary of taverners themselves as they were of their customers, for in 1311 they issued a charter dictating that taverns must always have their wine cellar doors open, so that customers might see their wine being drawn, to ensure that it was not being watered down. In the later Middle Ages Taverners and Innkeepers assizes, such as those passed in Coventry in 1474, restricted the profits that could be made on wine. Fifteenth-century London taverns were prohibited from selling drink on Sundays until high mass had ended, but inns, interestingly, were exempt from this rule. H. A. Monckton suggests that the exemption "is an interesting example of the way in which inns attempted to give their guests the same sort of freedom which they could enjoy in the privacy of their own houses," but perhaps, I would suggest, the exemption also reflects the higher social status of the inn's patrons.

There is evidence that some taverns offered what were considered objectionable forms of entertainment: John Wycliffe, the fourteenth-century theologian and reformer, condemned the habits of clergymen who idled their time in taverns among "strumpets," and in 1393 London magistrates reported that "many and divers broils and dissensions [arose] by reason of the frequent ... consorting with common harlots at taverns." Gambling with dice and cards was common at many taverns, and by the later Middle Ages backgammon had become a popular tavern game.

Taverns consisted of several rooms, usually on the ground floor of a building with a wine cellar on the same floor. Some taverns also had kitchens where simple meals were cooked; if there was no kitchen a taverner might order food for his customers from a neighboring cookhouse. Inns were generally much larger buildings. They had their kitchen, parlors, stabling, halls, and communal rooms on the ground floor and guest chambers on the first and second floors. Most inns conformed to one of two architectural styles: the courtyard style, in which the inn surrounds a courtyard and has galleried upper floors accessible by stairs on either side of the courtyard, or the gatehouse style, in which the courtyard is at the rear of the inn. Because players often performed in the inn courtyard while guests watched from the galleried upper floors, it is thought that the courtyard-style inn suggested the design of early modern theaters like the Globe, where higher-class patrons seated behind the balustraded galleries watched performances on the stage below.

Inns and taverns had elaborate and interesting signboards whose pictures symbolized their establishment. A signboard might portray a bush, representing the wines of Dionysus, or the heraldic shield of the family on whose land the inn was, or certain animals (lions, bulls, greyhounds, or white harts) that represented the crests of different kings of England. Some signboards represented trades and vocations, aligning the inn or tavern with a certain trade organization; for example, a sign might portray a wheat sheaf to represent the Bakers' Company or three compasses to refer to the Carpenters' Company.

One of England's most famous inns is the Tabard in Southwark, built about 1304. The Tabard is known to many as the initial meeting place of the pilgrims in Chaucer's *Canterbury Tales*, and in the late Middle Ages it was a well-known point of departure for pilgrimages. In *The Canterbury Tales* the inn creates a community out of a disparate group of people. Chaucer's contemporary, John Gower, provides a less favorable portrayal of a drinking establishment in his *Mirour de l'omme* (Mirror of Man). Gower describes a taverner who deceives his customers by allowing them to sample fine-quality wines and then selling them poor-quality or watered-down bottles of wine instead. The deceitful taverner also bandies about the exotic names of different kinds of wine while serving ladies, inciting them to drink more by pretending to give them samples of these different wines while really selling them several glasses of the same cheap wine.

See also: Foodways; Pilgrimage; Wine

—Tara Neelakantappa

Irish Tradition. Medieval Irish tradition, reflected in an enormous corpus of literature produced in Latin and Irish by the literati in the period from the sixth to the seventeenth centuries C.E.

In this article, the intimidatingly large load of information about a wide range of folkloric genres presented by medieval Irish literature of this period will be divided into smaller corpora, and an indication will be given of what kinds of "folklore" or data useful to folklorists can be gleaned from them.

First, let us consider the roots of and motivating factors behind the remarkable literary productivity of medieval Ireland, for without a sensitivity to the agenda of Irish writers, the folklorist, like the Celticist, is liable to underestimate the cultural value of this literary evidence. While we have no incontestably fifth-century vernacular literature surviving from Ireland (in general, I should note, the dating of Irish texts is a hazardous and risky business), given the sophistication of the earliest attested literary Irish it is reasonable to assume that the project of rendering a written form of the native language using the Latin alphabet was launched shortly after the introduction of Christianity in the fifth century. (This project was arguably already afoot in the pre-Christian development of *ogam*, a system for writing Irish, primarily for inscriptional purposes, that was based on the sounds represented by the Latin alphabet.) The invention of a written vernacular, or of what scholars call "Old Irish" (essentially the literary language of pre-Viking Ireland, evident in texts whose original production can be dated to between the sixth and ninth centuries), took place in the setting of the scriptoria, that is, copy rooms, of the monasteries and churches of Ireland and of those ecclesiastical institutions on the Continent established by peripatetic Irish clerics. These scriptoria, however, were not insulated, strictly "religious" environments. Rivaling the courts of local kings (whose family members were in many cases deeply implicated in the religious life), monasteries became the major political, social, and cultural centers of medieval Ireland, and the perspectives of the producers of early Irish literature clearly reflect this centrality and the monasteries' interdependence with the secular world around them. Early on in the history of Irish Christianity its representatives made peace (easy or uneasy, depending on which scholar is consulted) with some key "native" institutions that had played (and with this new rapprochement with, or co-optation by, the Church continued to play) key roles in the transmission of tradition. These institutions included kingship, whose possessors patronized the Church and in turn could at least in theory turn to churchmen for the preservation (in written form) of traditions that validated their kingship; the localization of religious cult, which, translated into Christian terms, generated the extraordinary proliferation of saints in early-medieval Ireland, along with their cults' intimate associations with particular monasteries or churches and federations of such units; and poetry, whose practitioners were dramatically reinvented within the Christian milieu, with the result that the *fili* ("one who sees," the standard word for "poet" in Irish, designating a figure whose range of expertise and functions extended far beyond the composition or performance of poetry) became a staple member and welcome guest of the monastic community.

Thus, while their religious orientation and strong interest in the literatures of early Christianity and the classical world may have diminished or affected their sympathy for certain aspects of their native culture, the learned producers of early Irish literature were by no means cut off from their society (or at least, not from the upper echelons of their intensely hierarchical society), and literary composition, like the project of devising a written form of the vernacular, was clearly motivated at least in part by a desire to record current, receding, and past oral traditions and in "capturing" them in writing to reformulate their authority in terms of new cultural politics. While it would be going too far to describe medieval Irish literature as ethnography, it nevertheless contains a strong impulse to preserve as well as to create. Even if in many cases texts present us with invention or reinvention rather than preservation of tradition, they provide us with valuable clues as to what tradition was supposed to be like.

We actually do have Latin compositions that were probably written in Ireland in the fifth century, but these hardly constitute "Irish literature," although they did wield considerable influence. The texts in question are the *Confessio* (Confession) and *Letter to Coroticus* attributed to Patrick, a missionary to Ireland celebrated in legend in oral and written tradition down to the present day. In his tantalizingly brief references to the Irish, among whom he lived as a slave before he returned to convert them, the Briton Patrick mentions some "pagan" customs of interest to a folklorist, such as the sucking of the breast as a traditional sign of supplication and the offering of a portion of one's food to supernatural forces in order to turn away evil. Scholars of Patrician legend little appreciate the fact that the very narrative framework that Patrick constructs for his life by way of the personal experience narratives he strings together in the *Confessio* is folkloric, evoking the "heroic biography" pattern studied by many scholars, notably Tomás Ó Cathasaigh.

Beyond Patrick's own writings, some of the earliest literature to have survived from Ireland are the saints' lives written in Latin in the seventh century. Chief among these are the lives of Patrick written by Muirchú and Tírechán, the life of Brigid by Cogitosus and some other early Latin lives of this popular female saint, the life of Columba written by Adomnán, and the account of the voyage of Brendan, possibly authored by a non-Irishman. In these texts, which to some extent exerted an influence on Continental hagiography as well, we have the earliest attestations of certain legends that live on in the oral traditions of twentieth-century Ireland and Scotland, such as the stories of Patrick's reviving the wicked pagan's bull and Brigid's loss and miraculous recovery of her eye, as well as of important elements of saints' cults alive and well in the present day, such as the importance of wells for healing and of elevations for pilgrimage. In his introduction to a collection of Latin lives of the saints, Charles Plummer cataloged the "pagan" elements and other matters of ethnographic interest to be found in these texts, as did Whitley Stokes in his introduction to an edition and translation of the Irish saints' lives from the Book of Lismore.

Constituting, at least in some of their more archaic layers, our earliest corpus of vernacular literature from Ireland are numerous law tracts, which cover a wide range of topics, including the maintenance and curing of the sick, the procedures of satire, the rituals of contract, and beekeeping. Fergus Kelly's massive study of early Irish farming, based primarily on the law tracts, shows how many of the "folkways" of medieval Ireland can be reconstructed on the basis of these difficult texts, which have proven invaluable to linguists and cultural historians alike. The legal aphorisms with which these tracts are peppered clearly constitute an important subgenre of proverb, and the occasional references to narratives provide us glimpses of the multiformity of the storytelling repertoire, as well as witnessing to the function of story as paradigm and precedent. Complementing and clearly closely connected to the secular law tracts in Irish (produced and elaborated upon by Irish legal specialists throughout the medieval period) are surviving collections of ecclesiastical legislation in Latin or Irish—such as the *Law of Adamnán*, whose preface presents a bizarre account of what Daniel Melia has described as shamanic initiation—and penitentials (the genre is an Irish invention), which catalog sins that in many case pertain to folk custom and belief.

While poems surviving from the Old Irish period (including the many poetic passages in the law tracts) typically evince their learned origins and in some cases even represent innovative extensions of the poetic function, these texts, and their prose introductions or frames, offer valuable clues as to particular oral performative genres and ritual activities, such as inspired prophetic utterance (e.g., the archaic, or archaized, *roscada* attributed to characters in heroic saga), keening or lamenting the dead (e.g., Bláthmac's poem on the death of Christ), work songs (e.g., *Tochmarc Étaíne* [Wooing of Étaín]), and lullabies (e.g., the poem to the baby Jesus attributed to St. Íte). The genre of praise poetry, the basic product of the poet operating outside the scriptorial milieu but perhaps deemed subliterary by the producers and guardians of literature, is only rarely represented, or only indirectly, in the earliest manuscripts, except for the purpose of demonstrating metrical forms in learned tracts on such matters. Although most medieval Irish prose tales also include poetry, and poetry often comes equipped in manuscripts with a prose introduction that sets up the premise, poetic language and prose obviously serve different ends, and the marked language of poetry is typically more embedded in particular ritual or social situations. (This is not to say that prose tales or their performance in medieval Ireland were not sensitive to context—see, for example, the epilogues to the late Middle Irish *Altrom Tige Dá Medar* [Fosterage of the House of Two Cups] and to the parodistic *Aislinge Meic Conglinne* [Vision of Mac Conglinne].)

For only a few secular tales have incontestably Old Irish versions survived; a marked number of these have to do with encounters with the (non-Christian) otherworld, such as the *Immram Brain* (Voyage of Bran), which tells of marvelous transmarine realms and beings encountered by the Odysseus-like Bran and his crew, and the cycle of stories about the legendary Ulster king Mongán, who leads a curious double life as both mortal and supernatural being. These narratives affirm the venerability of the beliefs widely attested in modern Irish and Scottish folk traditions that the otherworld presents a mirror-image (although often with some crucial difference) of this world and that a human who travels to an otherworld will experience, like Rip van Winkle, a dislocation in time—a theme most vividly exploited in the Middle Irish tale *Echtrae Nerai* (Nera's Supernatural Adventure).

It was during the period between and including the tenth and twelfth centuries, in the phase of the literary language referred to as Middle Irish, that the bulk of the surviving literature of medieval Ireland was produced, at least in its original form. This is an era of ambitious literary undertakings, including the compilation of the *Lebor Gabála Érenn* (Book of the Invasions of Ireland), commonly referred to as the masterpiece of Irish pseudohistory, that is, the attempt of the literati to construct a history comparable to existing Continental literary models that would fit native Irish traditions about the past into a larger "learned" (including biblical) historical framework. In fact, this pseudohistorical project, including such other ancillary texts from this period as the *Cath Maige Tuired* (Battle of Mag Tuired) (an account of the ambivalent relations between the Tuatha Dé Danann, one of the primeval invading peoples of Ireland, and the demonic Fomorians [Fomoire], would-be possessors of the island) and the *Suidiugud Tellaig Temrach* (Settlement of the Territory of Tara), comes close to mythography, along the lines of what Hellenistic authors such as Apollodorus and the medieval Icelander Snorri Sturluson fashioned out of their own traditions. The introductory passages of Middle Irish tales from the so-called Ulster cycle (which I discuss below), such as the *Serglige Con Culainn* (Sickbed of Cú Chulainn) and the *Mesca Ulad* (Drunkenness of the Ulstermen), make it clear that the Tuatha Dé Danann and other residents of the *síd* ("otherworldly dwelling," the standard term in both early and later Irish for the sites of the supernatural) constituted the pantheon or recipients of the worship of the preChristian Irish. Perhaps not surprisingly, it is to these later texts that we have to turn to find some (occasionally dubious) indication of who the gods and goddesses of the ancient Irish were, and what stories were told about them, instead of to the earlier saints' lives, which are in general tight-lipped or dismissive about just what it was that Christianity was replacing (although the word *síd* is to be found in the text of Tírechán's *Life of Patrick*, a rather conspicuous vernacular import into the Latin text).

Arguably the most intriguing pieces of evidence provided by Middle Irish literature to the student of traditional narrative are the tale lists, one of which is embedded in a narrative text. These purport to be inventories of the storytelling repertoire of the *fili*. (The poet in Irish tradition, as in Welsh tradition, is assigned the function of storyteller or guardian of narrative lore.) Among the repertoire the list presents us with approximately 200 titles, of which only a fraction is actually represented in the surviving literature. Of particular interest in these lists is the organization of the narrative material according to generic titles that index the main action or event in the story—such as *aithed*, "elopement"; *aided*, "violent death"; *táin*, "cattle raid"; *togail*, "destruction"; and *serc*, "love." Conceptualizing stories in terms of what happens in them is a traditional procedure also in evidence in the titles actually assigned to narrative texts in manuscripts, although the latter also feature a different taxonomic principle, commonly used by scholars of medieval Irish literature as well, whereby stories are organized on the basis of their cast of characters or setting. The twelfth-century manuscript known as the *Book of Leinster,* for example, contains, among many other items, not only a recension of the *Táin Bó Cúailnge* (Cattle Raid of Cooley), the massive centerpiece of the Ulster cycle of stories having to do with Cú Chulainn, Conchobor, Fergus mac Roig, and other heroes associated with Ulster of a particular era, but several additional stories from this cycle as well. Moreover, some of the titles assigned to narrative texts by scribes (e.g., *scéla*, "news [about]") do not highlight a particular action or event at all but, instead, function as the equivalent of "other" among responses to a multiple-choice question. Still, there is much of narratological value to be gleaned from these designations of "native genres," whether or not they stem from popular or learned tradition, and the studies of Vincent A. Dunn and Daniel Melia show that examining medieval Irish narratives grouped according to their designations uncovers key recurring structural patterns.

It has often been asked whether the Ulster cycle of tales (which in the historical arrangements of medieval Irish scribes comes after the primeval period of what scholars would call the "mythological cycle," featuring the successive invasions of Ireland, but before the periods of the kings' cycle and the Fenian [Fianna] cycle discussed below) reflects an earlier, Iron Age phase of Irish society and culture, comparable perhaps to the civilization of the ancient Continental Celts. The archaeologist James Mallory has demonstrated that the artifacts and technologies on display in the Ulster cycle do not point to any one era but, rather, form a synthesis of the contemporary and the anachronistic. Dating problems aside, these texts contain a wealth of information about traditional dress, foodways, crafts, and medicine. The stories themselves supplied Hector Munro Chadwick and Nora K. Chadwick with an important Celtic pillar for the construction of their idea of a Heroic Age perpetuated in epic, even though the application of the term "epic" to the Ulster tales is problematic. Still, given details such as Cú Chulainn's divine paternity (some of our texts make him out to be the son of Lug, one of the great gods of the Irish as well as the Continental Celtic pantheon); the barely sublimated supernatural qualities of important players such as Medb, the queen of Connacht; and the larger-than-life quality of the characters in general, including Conchobor, the king of Ulster, one could reasonably set these tales alongside the Homeric and Indo-Iranian epics as reflecting an Indo-European tendency (studied most productively in the Irish context by Elizabeth Gray) to transpose the mythological dramas of the gods onto the level of heroes and heroic tale.

Another compelling question that has been asked about these texts is: by whom or in whose interests were the literary compositions featuring Ulster tales (which, one should note, often feature non-Ulster characters and places) produced or collected? Various theories having to do with the political, familial, and cultural agendas of medieval Irish literati and their ecclesiastical and secular patrons have been proposed. Doubtless also contributing to the seeming popularity of these narratives and characters in pre-thirteenth-century Irish literary tradition, which was based primarily outside Ulster, is their otherness. Perhaps playing a role comparable to that of stories about cowboys and Indians in modern U.S. culture, these tales about the struggles between the heroes of Ulster and those of Connacht and the other parts of Ireland simultaneously evoked nostalgia from the audiences of medieval Ireland and satisfied their appetite for the exotic.

An intriguing miscellany of texts having to do with kings, reigning from the pre-Christian era to the eighth century, is also to be found in the corpus of Middle Irish literature. Examples include the *Togail Bruidne Da Derga* (Destruction of Da Derga's Hostel), *Fled Dúin na n-Géd* (Feast of the Fort of the Geese), *Cath Almaine* (Battle of Allen), and *Aided Muirchertaig meic Erca* (Death of Muirchertach mac Erca). While this kings' cycle has nothing like the recurring cast of characters that we find in the mythological or Ulster cycle, and the kings in question are from various parts of Ireland, there is a certain thematic consistency to these tales, which typically dwell on the difficult, often deadly decisions kings have to make. The assertion of historicity that often informs these tales (which sometimes find their way into annalistic literature as well) and their cautionary overtones (the message that kings should not overstep their bounds, and the morbid glee evident in the depictions of what happens to them when they do) remind the folklorist of the legend, a genre to which these texts are clearly indebted. Worth mentioning in connection with the kings' sagas are the numerous references in a variety of texts to the rituals and ideology of kingship, including the genre of wisdom literature putatively addressed by traditional figures of authority to kings or kings-to-be—for example, the Old Irish *Audacht Morainn* (Testament of Morann) and the Middle Irish *Tecosca Cormaic* (Instructions of Cormac)—and a list of the prohibitions (*geisi*) placed upon the king ruling in the ancient site of Tara. (The motif of the *geis* survives into modern Gaelic heroic tales.)

A Middle Irish masterpiece that deserves a separate mention in a survey of this kind is the *Aislinge Meic Conglinne* (Vision of Mac Conglinne); though it is a parody (or perhaps precisely because it is a parody), it sheds light on all the folkloric features of medieval Irish literature that have been mentioned so far, including the legendry and cult of saints, stories of the deeds of heroes and the perils of kingship, generic distinctions among narratives, the performative contexts of prose and poetry, and the inclusion of ethnographic detail as a stylistic device. Additionally, the author has provided us with an extraordinary inventory of foods and food preparation to go along with the text's over-the-top verbiage, setting up in effect a fascinating equation between food and words as parallel items of social exchange. The figure of Mac Conglinne himself—his gluttony, avarice, craftiness, and gift of the gab—is worthy of inclusion in any rogues' gallery of Greatest Tricksters, and the text's allusions to other "vulgar" characters of story like Mac Conglinne, and to the class of roving performers/rhymesters/satirists whose ranks the clerical student Mac Conglinne joins at the beginning of his adventures, provide us with a glimpse of types of popular entertainment and entertainers at a considerable remove from the learned and perhaps old-fashioned repertoire and persona of the *fili* usually featured in literature of this period. Other Middle or Early Modern Irish texts that intimate this wider world of performance and performers are the *Loinges Mac n-Uislenn* (Exile of the Sons of Uisliu), the famous story of Derdriu, a storyteller's daughter whose beauty and poetic voice provoke a testing of gendered power structures; *Tromdám Guaire* (Heavy Hosting of Guaire), in which the whole array of the medieval Irish entertainment profession is comically and embarrassingly on display; and the *Buile Shuibne* (Frenzy of Suibne), the account of a truly offbeat poet.

Folklore is to be found not only in the great narrative compositions of Middle Irish literature. Rife with bits of lore—including popular belief and custom, traditional explanations of the origins of names, proverbs, and allusions to narratives mentioned nowhere else in the corpus—are learned compilations such as the *Sanas Cormaic*, commonly known as *Cormac's Glossary*, the *Cóir Anmann* (Fitness of Names), the *Triads*, and the *Auraicept na n-Éces* (Scholars' Primer). In *Cormac's Glossary*, for example, we find a famous description of the mantic rite known as *imbas forosnai*, "the great knowledge that enlightens," and other techniques for obtaining esoteric knowledge. An invaluable resource for scholars researching Irish place names and the traditions associated with them is the voluminous *Dindshenchas* (Lore of Places), which exists in both poetry and prose. Even though many of the etymologies and etiologies presented herein are the products of learned invention, this compilation constitutes the apex of the pervasive medieval and modern Irish fascination with toponymy.

Also redolent of this fascination are the earliest major texts that have survived from medieval Ireland having to do with the adventures of Finn (Fion, Fionn) mac Cumaill and his hunting-warring band (*fian*, often referred to in the plural, *fianna*). (Marie-Louise Sjoestedt, Kim McCone, and others have argued that Finn and his men derive from the Indo-European complex of ritual and myth having to do with the *Männerbund*, an ancient initiatory institution for young men, which is also reflected in, for example, the "Wild Huntsmen" legends and beliefs to be found among other Western European peoples.) Unlike the Ulster heroes and kings who figure in most earlier narrative compositions, Finn the *rígfhénnid* ("chief *fénnid*," i.e., member of a *fian*) and his comrades range freely over Ireland, exhibiting a remarkable familiarity with and freedom in all of its wildernesses, which constitute their turf. The knowledge and love of the landscape regularly exhibited by the so-called Fenian heroes go hand in hand with the literary compulsion to account for place names and to record antiquarian lore, as is evident in the medieval masterpiece of Fenian literature, the *Acallam na Senórach* (Dialogue of the Ancients), in effect a frame tale, whose earliest recension probably dates from the twelfth century. St. Patrick plays a starring role in the *Acallam*, in which the missionary saint meets the miraculously surviving members of Finn's *fian* and, like a folklorist or oral historian, coaxes them to tell him and his scribes all that they know about the past, particularly their own. The ancient Fenian heroes, particularly Caílte and Oisín, the son of Finn, oblige Patrick happily and provide him with a veritable archive of lore, including stories and poems, Fenian and otherwise. The *Acallam* is one of the most popular (that is, widely copied and redacted) texts of the later medieval and early modern period. Like another Fenian composition from the twelfth century or later, the *Feis Tighe Chonáin* (Feast of Conán's House), it demonstrates the centrality of the trope of dialogue to the medieval Irish literary project—the conceit that literature is produced as the result of a conversation, sometimes made possible by supernatural intervention, between "contemporary" and "ancient" interlocutors, or a conversation among just the "ancients" that is recorded for posterity. This stereotypical casting of literature as the product of fieldwork is especially suggestive in its application to these and the other Fenian texts that start to appear in profusion in the twelfth and later centuries, since quite possibly Fenian story actually was a literary import from more popular traditions. (Stories about the Fenian heroes were collected from the Gaelic-speaking storytellers of Ireland and Scotland, and even of Nova Scotia, well into the twentieth century.)

Not only did the Fenian tradition contribute a new source of story to medieval Irish literature, but it also provided a context for a heretofore uncharacteristic use of poetic language in Irish literature—namely, to tell a story in a style and form that can be described as "balladic." The earliest surviving Fenian *laídi*, "lays," are to be found in the twelfth-century *Book of Leinster*, and these are of a piece with the Fenian narrative poems to be found in later manuscript collections, such as the sixteenth-century *Book of the Dean of Lismore* from Scotland and the seventeenth-century *Duanaire Finn* (Finn's Songbook), based on Irish sources. The singing of such "ballads," featuring the adventures of Fenian or other heroes, was still attested in Gaelic-speaking areas in the twentieth century. More study of these poetic texts, both medieval and modern, and of their composition in terms of formula, theme, and story pattern (as these are used in the scholarly examination of oral epics and ballads) is in order.

The *Acallam* represents more than the infusion of Fenian tradition into the literary realm. In its agenda of reevaluating the past and in its insistence on the necessity for Irish Christian learned culture to take on the responsibility of recording that past, the text (especially with its "gimmick" of the saint interviewing pre-Christian heroes) adumbrates a period of transition and retrenchment. In the period between the eleventh and thirteenth centuries, many forms of literary production, and many of the families devoted to literary pursuits that had developed in the monastic milieu of early-medieval Ireland, moved, or were moved, out of the ecclesiastical establishment under pressure from reforms within the Irish Church. Literature and its preservation became primarily secular affairs under the patronage of nobles, although the writing of religious literature, and literary activity within the religious milieu, continued as well. In the wake of this cultural shift from church to court, and also in the wake of the twelfth-century Anglo-Norman incursion into Ireland (a presence that was to have profound implications for Irish history), Irish literature became more open to a wider array of external influences, including the chivalric literature of France and England. (The Anglo-Norman invasion also brought with it Gerald of Wales, whose writings on Ireland and the Irish in the twelfth century provide us with an outsider's view of a wide range of native customs and beliefs.) The so-called romantic tale, one of the literary forms that developed during the Early and Classic Modern Irish period (1200–1700), reflects the impact of the Arthurian story and other streams of Continental courtly literature on the Irish storyteller and his scribal counterpart, although these romantic tales (which often feature Fenian heroes or other figures from the Irish narrative repertoire) also repackage existing native story elements and plots. Alan Bruford has argued that the virtuosically performed hero tale of modern Irish and Scottish Gaelic storytelling tradition is in most cases a direct descendant from the literary romantic tale or from other literary sources, but this argument has not been universally accepted. On the basis of the evidence, it is equally if not more reasonable to view the relationship between Gaelic oral and literary stories as in general the same as that between the chicken and the egg. Kevin O'Nolan's work, comparing the formulaic language and style of romantic tales and other late-medieval literary compositions with those of modern Irish storytellers, demonstrates just how complex the relationship between "written" and "spoken" forms of narrative performance continued to be throughout the medieval period and down to modern times.

See also: Beltane; Brigid, Saint; Celtic Mythology; Patrick, Saint; Samhain; Scottish Tradition; Ulster Cycle; Welsh Tradition

—Joseph Falaky Nagy

Italian Tradition. The folkloric culture of the Italian peninsula, Sicily, and Sardinia.

Medieval Italian traditions are complex because they reflect the historical developments of peoples with diverse backgrounds. The Italian peninsula, Sicily, and Sardinia were densely populated even before the foundation of Rome in 753 B.C.E. and the almost contemporaneous beginnings of Greek colonization of southern Italy in the eighth century. (This area of Greek colonization came to be called *Magna Grecia*, "Greater Greece.") Both the Romans and the Greeks faced obstacles and challenges to their future hegemonies posed by these prior inhabitants as they contended with them for land, trading outposts, and control of the seas. Some of these peoples left their names upon the lands wherein they dwelled (e.g., the Etruscans [Tuscany], the Bruzi [Abruzzi], the Veneti, the Italici). Groups such as the Ligurians and the Sabines, who have had their names recorded by Cicero and Virgil, are remembered for their fierceness and for their conflicts with the Romans. Contention sometimes led to outright war with these prior inhabitants: the Etruscans were admired and emulated by the Romans. Etr-

uscan expansion toward the coast, however, provoked a war with the Cumans (Greeks), even
though the Greeks at Pitekoussai, on the island of
Ischia, had originally maintained peaceful trading
contacts with Etruscan centers and regions with
metal ores. During the course of their descent into
the peninsula the Celts pushed back the Ligurians
and the Etruscans. The Phoenicians, predecessors
of the Greeks in Sicily and of the Romans in Sardinia, were linked to the adversaries of the Romans in the Punic Wars.

Not only bellicose divisions but also cultural
ties emerged from contacts among the peoples of
the peninsula, Sicily, and Sardinia. The Archaeological Museum of Palermo recently offered an
exhibit of Punic (Phoenician) Palermo, the fruit
of an ongoing excavation. Sardinia was colonized
by the Carthaginians (Phoenicians) prior to the
arrival of the Romans, during the Second Punic
War (219–201 B.C.E.). A Punic inscription at
Bithyia is dated as late as the third century C.E.
The word *zippiril*, Sardinian for *rosmarino* (rose-
mary), is an example of such influence. Sardinia
is unique, for it was under the cultural influence
of peoples such as the Greeks and the Berbers.

Other groups also left traces of their culture in
Italian tradition. Consider a story from Boccaccio's *Decameron* (7,1) that mentions the custom
of placing a donkey's head in the vineyard or field
for fertility purposes and for warding off evil; this
practice derives from Etruscan funeral rites and
rituals, which have left a profound mark. In
Magna Grecia, Neapolis (present-day Naples),
originally founded by the Greeks, retained its
Greek traditions despite its later conquest by
Rome and thus provided the Romans with a
nearby place in which to learn Greek philosophy,
art, literature, and religion.

Medieval popular traditions are dominated by
Christianity and by an element of popular religion that includes both regional and national
customs. Children in Sicily, the Veneto, and certain other regions of Italy receive gifts on St.
Lucy's Day, December 13; another such occasion
is the night of November 1. St. Lucy's feast comes
during the same time as the winter solstice, and
St. Lucy is thus associated in popular tradition
with (spiritual) light. In the Middle Ages her cult
became so popular that she became the distribu-
tor of gifts to children, along with Baby Jesus, St.
Nicholas, and the Befana (the good Epiphany
witch). It is quite plausible that Lucy was, therefore, the Christian version of the goddess Aurora.

Also because of her association with light, St.
Lucy became the patron saint of eyesight and eye
diseases. Even Dante Alighieri adopted her as his
protector because he suffered from bad eyesight,
and he made her a symbol of illuminating grace
(*Inferno* 2:100). St. Lucy's remains were transported from Syracuse, the city of her martyrdom,
to Constantinople by the Byzantine general Ma-
niace (1038–1042) as a symbol of his victory over
the Sicilians. They are presently in the Church of

San Geremia (St. Jeremiah) in Venice. Present-
day formulas and invocations to St. Lucy for
cures for eye diseases and for finding lost objects
go back to the Middle Ages.

Only under the rule of Odoacer (beginning in
476 C.E.) could one begin to speak of the Italian
peninsula as "Italia"—a name that originally pertained only to the region now known as Calabria.
The name was given to the whole peninsula
under Romulus Augustulus, whom Odoacer de-
posed. With this event the Western Roman Empire ceased to exist, and thus began the Middle
Ages. Odoacer was defeated by the Ostrogoth
Theodoric, who ruled from 493 until 526 and
brought with him a vast number of immigrants.
Justinian I, emperor of the Eastern Empire in
Constantinople (Justinian the Great, whose
greatest achievement was his *Codex*, a collection
of all ancient laws and the commentaries of great
jurists), sent two of his generals, Belisarius and
Narses, to reconquer the Italian province (553
C.E.).

An important factor during this period is the
emergence and independence of the Western
Church, aided by the foundation of Western
monasticism, although politically Italy was still
under the influence of the Eastern Empire. This
process of Westernization continued with the
domination of the Lombards, a people who had
settled in Hungary and then moved rapidly into
the Italian peninsula. Their king, Alboin, entered Pavia *nulli lesionem ferens* (without causing
any injury), as a savior, to the relief and acclaim
of the local population. Pavia became the capital
of the new kingdom (572 C.E.). Pope Gregory the
Great succeeded in converting the Lombards
(680 C.E.). This domination lasted until 774 C.E.,
but it had little influence on culture or customs,
for the Lombards absorbed the Roman influence
of the conquered people, especially under the
rule of Theodolinda and Alboin.

On the other hand, the Lombards brought
some technical and agricultural innovations, a
small patrimony of influences on laws and family
life, and a number of legends and proverbs
formed around the figures of their leaders—particularly around Alboin and his wife Rosamund.
The latter avenged her father's death by killing
Alboin, who had given her wine to drink from a
cup made of her father's cranium. A variation of
this motif inspired Boccaccio's tale of Ghismunda
and Tancredi (*Decameron* 4, 1). The linguistic influence of the Lombards was mainly felt on words
related to war and the military: *castaldo* (king's
steward), *sperone* (spur), *guerra* (war), but many
localities besides Lombardy bear names of Lombard origin. There is no Lombard literature, but
Paulus Diaconus is their major historian. His *Historia Langobardorum* (History of the Lombards)
describes the migrations, deeds, legends, and adventures of this people.

One of the glories of the Lombards is the
monastery of St. Colombanus at Bobbio, which

was built with the support and assistance of this Germanic people. It became a center of learning and piety. An account of the Lombards is also found in *The Golden Legend* of Jacobus de Voragine in the story of the pope St. Pelagius. And in *Origo gentis Langobardorum* (Origin of the Lombards), by a certain Theodaldus, one also finds an account of the origin and the legends of this people.

The Lombards occupied most of the North, but cities such as Venice and Ravenna were never under their control. They were engaged mostly in warfare and agriculture, but only landowners could be in the army. They left their mark on the physiognomic traits of the population: they were physically a strong, tall, and fair people. In the Genoese dialect, the word *lambardan* means a tall, strong, graceless person. The word *langubardu* is an astacus—a type of crustacean with scissor-like claws—a creature with which the Genoese chose to associate the Lombards. The word *fara*, which means ownership by a collective group or lineage of a group, was the Lombard name for the partition of occupied land. There are several towns in Abruzzi bearing this toponym: for example, Fara San Martino, Fara Filiorum Petri. Collective kin groups known as *consortes* were part of this system, a tradition that resulted in the clan known in Dante's time as *consorteria* (cabal).

The Lombards did not succeed in expelling the Byzantines from the southern part of the peninsula. In this they were opposed by the pope, who received in recompense the territory of Sutri (728), which made the Church a temporal power. The Lombard kings' attempt to conquer all of Italy caused the ruin of their monarchy, which was soon replaced by the Frank invaders under Pepin (754).

The well-developed and highly organized society of the Franks bears no comparison to that of the previous Barbarian invaders. Charlemagne established the *Regnum Italicum* (Kingdom of Italy) in 781 C.E. and became Holy Roman emperor in the year 800. The Frankish reign lasted until 963, when Otto the Great, emperor and king of Germany, came to Italy to depose the last Frankish king, Berengar II. During this time Venice was allowed to become more independent, and the Duchy of Benevento remained autonomous with a large territory.

Under Frankish rule the form of government remained largely unchanged. Dukes were replaced by counts and marquis. The principle of *faidus* (feuds) prevailed over the private vendetta, which, however, was legal in cases of homicide, rape, abduction, or adultery. Among the elite there was a notable increase in literacy. There was no development of vernacular literature. Two figures, however, stand out: Paulus Diaconus, the author of the above-mentioned *Historia Langobardorum*, and Peter the Grammarian—eminent intellectuals of the Carolingian Renaissance. In Italy, commerce, including the importation of goods and slaves, increased by way of seaports such as Genoa and Venice. Under the Franks, military subscription was obligatory. Service was based on the amount of land owned. Beginning with Otto the Great, the Kingdom of Italy was ruled by the German emperor, who was also king of Italy. From Charlemagne's time Italy was divided in three parts: the Kingdom of Italy, comprising all of the northern and central part; the papal state, consisting mostly of Latium; and the Duchy of Benevento, including Abruzzi, Campania, and the rest of southern Italy.

One historical event that left its mark on the culture and civilization of southern Italy was the Arab invasion of Sicily, which culminated in the capture of Palermo in 831. The first Arab invasion took place in 652, followed by others in 669, when the Arabs entered Syracuse, and they soon afterward seized the island of Pantelleria, which they used as a base from which to raid the entire southern Italian coast. In 740 Habib ibn Ubaidah laid siege to Syracuse. From this date onward Arab incursions continued periodically until 827, when, at the instigation of a Byzantine governor, the Arabs moved decisively to conquer Sicily and established Palermo as their capital.

The Arabs remained in Sicily for almost two centuries, during which time they created an Arab Sicily with a distinct culture and civilization. They did not stop there; they seized Brindisi, Taranto (837–838), and Bari (841) and even threatened Rome (846). Indeed, all of Italy was threatened by an invasion. Arab influence penetrated every aspect of life, especially in Sicily, because of the length of their rule. Arab influence can be found in popular songs and musical rhythms, in poetry, in folktales, and in legends. A character well known in Sicilian folktales, Giuffa, is of Arab origin. He is the typical wise fool. An Arabic Andalusian traveler of the twelfth century, Ibn Jubayr, gave a colorful account of Arab Sicily.

The Arab domination of Sicily and parts of southern Italy lasted well into the eleventh century—Palermo fell to Robert Guiscard in 1072—and transformed the island culturally and economically. The local Arab-Sicilian dynasty, called the Kalbite—made up of wise administrators, artists, and poets—began to disintegrate around 1060, and various cities such as Palermo, Syracuse, Trapani, and Noto were under the rule of local emirs. Rivalries eventually led some of these local rulers to invite the Normans to intervene. Messina fell to the Normans in 1061; Castrogiovanni in 1064; Palermo in 1072. Ibn al Ward, the emir of Syracuse, briefly reoccupied some cities until 1091, when Roger of Hauteville became great count of Sicily and Calabria, thus setting down the foundation for a kingdom that would last until the nineteenth century, through different dynasties and royal houses. As a result, it created the great divide between north and south that is still a threat to the unity of Italy today. The Normans absorbed and adopted the Byzantine-Arab civilizations. They created a modern state that was unified and culturally diverse. They perfected methods of administration, such as the Arab *dohuana*, from which the term *dogana* (customs) derives. The Norman period was a splendid time for the cultural and economic development of Sicily—diverse in languages, cultures, architectural styles, and traditions. A city such as Palermo, where Latin, Arabic, Italian, Greek, French, and English were spoken, represented an image of enlightenment and cultural splendor that was later to be maintained by the Houenstaufen dynasty, in the person of Frederick II.

The cultural force of the Arab presence in Sicily and southern Italian territories, such as the Emirate of Bari, must not be underestimated. The oral transmission of legends, myths, tales, music, and poetry was to become enormously important. Equally important were stories from the East such as the *Thousand and One Nights*, the *Disciplina clericalis* of Petrus Alfonsi, *The Seven Sages*, and *The Book of Kalila and Dimna*. These stories were being transmitted in written and oral form and they filtered through to the earliest collection of Italian tales, *Novellino* (end of the thirteenth century), and to Boccaccio's *Decameron* (c. 1349–1351). Holy Roman Emperor Frederick II (d. 1250) would later become a major cultivator of Arab culture and learning; his own treatise on falconry owed much to Arab texts. The poetry developed at his court in Palermo, the *Scuola Siciliana* (Sicilian School of Poetry), was undoubtedly influenced by the songs and poetry of the Arabs. The art of the Sicilian School, which was to become the first Italian school of poetry, was exported to Tuscany and the rest of Italy and transformed by poets such as Guittone d'Arezzo (d. 1294) of the Tuscan-Sicilian School, Guido Guinizelli (d. 1276), Dante Alighieri (d. 1321), and Guido Cavalcanti (d. 1300) of the *Dolce Stil Nuovo* (Sweet New Style), in which courtly love and Averroistic elements can be traced and in which the image of woman was elevated almost to the level of divinity.

Figures such as Leonardo Fibonacci (the inventor of the *liber abaci*) and Michael Scot lived at Frederick's court, directly absorbing the Arab influence. Scot was a famous astronomer and alchemist (see Dante's *Inferno* 20:115–117) to whom many prophecies were attributed, including one, related by the chronicler Salimbene of Parma, about the future of some Italian cities. During the period of Arab domination, poetry was a major cultural endeavor, especially under the Kalbite dynasty; the best-known Arab-Sicilian poet is Ibn-Hamdis (d. 1132). In contrast to the three centuries of Byzantine domination, the two and a half centuries of Arab political rule created a resurgence of both the countryside and the cities from earlier squalor and misery. Agriculture, for instance, underwent a significant development. The Arab rulers were tolerant toward Christians and Jews, and so the cultures and the customs of the people became enriched and diverse. This influence is to be found in every aspect of life: personal and place names, customs and usages, popular beliefs, sayings, linguistic expressions, urban structures of old quarters, markets, squares, food, and clothing. The Palatine Chapel in the Royal Palace of Palermo (constructed 1132–1140) is an example of Arabic and Byzantine art coexisting at the time of Roger II (c. 1130).

Arab civilization enriched the entire peninsula through the powerful political force of the Kingdom of Sicily. In the early part of the thirteenth century Italian cities underwent rapid economic development, as the power of the communes offset the central hegemony of the emperor. Economic progress brought about cultural enrichment and a definite imprint on folk culture in every aspect of life. The creation of guilds and corporations, architectural activity, the rise of the cities—all had a great effect on all aspects of daily life: clothing, festivals, saints, feasts, popular literature, music, dance, the calendar as a whole. We might consider specific items such as births, weddings, funerals, and feasts. In his *Antiquitates*, Ludovico Antonio Muratori attempted to reconstruct these popular traditions by recording fashions in dress, nuptials, spectacles, and games and by studying such sources as chronicles and legislation from the period of the Barbarian invasions. In speaking of Odoacer, whom he praises, Muratori states that there have been Barbarians much more prudent and clean than the Romans and the Greeks. He considered mimes and historians popular poets.

Life-Cycle Traditions

Rites of passage attended major transitions in the life cycle. Birth, an event accompanied by a great many rituals, was centered around the infant's baptism. It was a sin to kiss an infant before he or she was baptized. The midwife carried male infants to church on her right arm, females on her left arm. Upon returning home, she would recite the formula "You gave me a pagan; I bring back a Christian." The godfather threw confetti—a symbol of plenitude whose origin probably goes back to the Roman practice of giving *sacra natalicia* (holy birthday) gifts. This was followed by a banquet or refreshments to celebrate the presence of a new member of the community.

There was also a rite of purification for the mother, derived from the Hebrew tradition, especially from the story of Mary's Purification, celebrated on the day of Candelora, so called because of the custom of distributing candles, which, according to popular piety, offer protection against such calamities as bad weather (Candlemas, February 2). This feast day coincided with the Roman rite of the Lupercalia (during the course of which nearly naked priests struck women, attempting to render them fertile) and the days of purification called Iunio Februata.

The custom of singing *ninne-nanne* (lullabies) to infants is of Roman origin. In the Middle Ages such poems were thought to have been sung to the Infant Jesus by the Virgin Mary. Dante records a lullaby in a verse, *"colui che mo' si consola con nanna"* (*Purgatory* 23:111), as a custom to placate children. First Communion and Confirmation are connected to rites of passage in primitive and ancient religions. The colors used for the vestiary were also significant: Arnold van Gennep indicates that in France pink and red were for males, and white and light blue were for females, these being the colors of the Madonna. These colors were later inverted in Italy. In Dante's time baptisms were registered in a parish with little balls or fava beans: black for males, white for females. The same colors were later used for balloting during the Councils of the Republic: black, yes; white, no.

Various wedding rites and customs derived from Eastern (Indian) and Roman rites, such as the groom crossing the threshold without touching it with his feet. The bride's veil and apron were red, according to Roman customs. The banquets—their duration and the foods served—were also traditional. In Florence the first banquet lasted three days; the second was held eight days later at the bride's house. The dance was both a sacred ritual and a symbol of fecundity.

Death and funeral rites often followed ancient customs. For example, the custom of placing a rock or stone under the deceased's pillow goes back to the Romans and their veneration of the god Terminus; it meant that the person may have violated the boundaries of the land marked in stone. The *corrotto*, the mourning and lamentations held by relatives, friends, or even professionals, is derived from funeral customs of ancient origin, as depicted in Homer or on Egyptian or Etruscan tombs. Among the Romans, professional mourners were called *prefiche*. Though Christianity sought to eliminate this custom, it endured, especially in the southern regions and on the islands. Similarly, the custom of placing a coin in the mouth of the deceased is also of very ancient origin, the idea being that the deceased would pay for his or her journey with this coin. In certain regions of Italy a friend or a neighbor, the *consolo*, would arrange the banquet after the funeral rites. This Roman custom survives to this day. On the Day of the Dead, All Souls' Day, it was customary to eat chickpea soup—an ancient funeral dish derived from the Romans and Greeks.

Feasts and Festivals

In medieval Italy special attention was given to expressions of popular piety for particular favors received by patron saints. Several saints were especially popular for the protection they could af-

ford: St. Lucy (eyes), St. Agatha (breasts), St. Blaise (throat), St. Anthony (animal protection), St. Julian (hostels, hospitaliers), St. Christopher (travelers), St. Joseph (carpenters), St. Amedeus (hair stylists), St. John (printers), St. Eligius (blacksmiths), St. James (hatmakers), and many others. Many saints and their feasts are associated with pagan deities. Others are tied to rural life, such as St. John the Baptist (flowers and fruits, June 24), the feast of Mary's Assumption (harvest, August 15), St. Bartholomew (eggs, butter, cheese, August 25; also a feast of eating and drinking), and St. Nicholas (water, bread, gifts, December 6).

Every guild or *compagnia* had a pageant, a theatrical representation, or a procession. Pilgrimages to Rome, Jerusalem, Santiago de Compostela, and San Michele in the Gargano (Apulia, modern Puglia) were popular and were a source of many legends, traditions, folksongs, special clothing, and income. The Via Francigena connected Apulia to Rome and to Lucca and then split—toward Liguria, to southern France, on to Galicia (to the shrine of St. James)—or toward the northeast via Bologna, Piacenza, and the northern countries.

The Milky Way, in popular culture, was called Il Cammino di San Giacomo (St. James's Way). In Sicilian and Calabrian folklore St. James's Way was the conduit through which the dead continued to communicate with the living. Medieval alchemists used the word *compostela* in the phrase *campus stellae* (field of stars) as the primary matter joined with the stars. St. James was thus the patron saint of alchemists.

The number of local pilgrimage shrines was stunning, and each one had its own color, customs, and rites, such as St. Paul of Galatina, in the Salento region of Apulia, sacred to people who have been bitten by tarantulas, snakes, and spiders. The *tarantolati* (the victims of tarantulas) executed a ritual dance that would free them from the tarantula bite (June 29). The belief in the efficacy of relics of saints (as in Boccaccio's *Decameron* 1:10 and 6:10) was common in such practices.

Among the popular feasts, special notice must be given to the Carnevale (Carnival). A burlesque character personifying Carnevale was playfully "put to death" in public after a period of pleasures and dissipation. At his side was Old Lady Quaresima (Lent). Carnevale season usually began on January 17 (St. Anthony's feast day) or on February 2 (Candelora or Candlemas). The departure of the Carnevale character could be enacted in various ways: via a parody of a funeral, for example, or through the burning of a straw man. The contrast between Carnevale and Quaresima became part of the early literary tradition, as in Guido Faba's epistle, *De Quadragesima ad Carnisprivium* (thirteenth century). Lorenzo de Medici's "Trionfo di Arianna" is one of the most celebrated *Canti Carnascialeschi*

(Carnivalesque Songs). Carnival was celebrated with masks and pageants, accompanied by popular dances. Most famous were those held in Florence, Venice, and Rome. In Bologna there was a battle between Carnival, on a big horse, and Lent, on a small one. A summer carnival took place in some regions of Italy: in the Tuscan town of Barga, near Lucca, there remains a summer carnival in which the *maschere* (costumed characters) satirically poke fun at the establishment. Summer carnivals also took place on the feasts of Corpus Christi (June 8) and of St. John the Baptist (June 24).

In Verona and Ivrea (Piedmont region) there were two of the oldest forms of the Carnival. In the version at Ivrea people wearing red berets would rush to watch a *belle muliera* (beautiful woman) who would free the population from the abuses of the feudal lord. In Sicily the names *lu nannu* and *la nanna* stood for the Old Man and his Wife who were sacrificed because they represented fun and joy being taken away. This departure provoked the funeral lament called *ruculiamentu* in Sicily and *corrotto, repito*, and *vocero* in other regions. This lament is a parody of the funeral lament of the *prefiche* present in Sardinia, Corsica, Abruzzi, and Campania.

Feasts, festivals, games, and pageants all served the human need for cleansing rituals in response to the miseries of war and plagues on Italian soil. Of course, carnivals incurred the wrath of clergymen, such as St. Bernardino of Siena (d. 1444) and Girolamo Savonarola (d. 1498), and even of Erasmus during a visit to Siena in 1509. Calendimarzo and Calendimaggio (the Kalends of March and May—that is, March 1 and May 1) are especially famous for the many rituals, rites, dances, bonfires, and country feasts that preceded and followed labor in the fields. There was a custom called *incantate*, in which the peasants harvesting wheat would yell insults at people. Every religious feast of major importance in the liturgical calendar provided a special ritual or representation for the popular imagination, through sacred drama, songs, popular tableaus, or elaborate dramatic processions of the Passion of Christ. Magical practices, amulets, rituals, and formulas were very common.

The popular religion easily replaced ancient gods with the saints venerated by Christendom. Symbols such as the cross, liturgical expressions, and ejaculations (very short prayers, often only phrases) became amulets, magical formulas, and talismans. The cruciform sign present in many cultures became the amulet of Christians, who transferred to it the power and protection needed against the maleficent practices and incantations of magicians, witches, and devils.

Dances and Games

Very popular dances included the *ballo a tondo* (a type of round dance), also called *ridda* or *ruota* (wheel), and the *tresca* mentioned in Dante's *Inferno* (7:24; 14:40–42; 16:19–27). In *Paradiso*, however, the dances are the slow, calm type of religious dances sanctioned by the Church. Both Dante and Boccaccio list a number of musical instruments common in their times: harp, pipe, cither, guitar, horn, gig, lyre, lute, tuba, and instruments *ad archetto* (bowed), such as the crotta, rebeck, and viella. Collections of tales such as *Ii Piovano Arlotto* (a type of country cleric and merry priest), Sercambi's *Novelle*, and the works of other *novellieri* (short-story writers) such as Sacchetti, Bandello, Masuccio Salernitano, and others are a rich source of folklore. In Boccaccio's *Decameron* (8,2) a peasant character named Monna Belcolore (Lady Beautiful Color) displays knowledge of songs, dances, and instruments. She is described as being able to play the tambourine, dance a reel or a jig, and sing notoriously spicy songs. Indeed, songs and dances are scheduled at the end of every day of the *Decameron*. The rich folkloric tradition in Italy during the Middle Ages is intrinsically tied to other European countries bordering the Mediterranean. As neighbors, they form a shared world of beliefs and ways of life—a treasure still affecting today's world.

See also: Arabic-Islamic Tradition; Carnival; Dante Alighieri; *Decameron*; Saints, Cults of the

—Giuseppe C. Di Scipio

J

ames the Elder, Saint (first century C.E.) [Latin *Jacobus,* Spanish *Santiago*]. One of the 12 Apostles of Jesus Christ.

From the New Testament we know that James was a fisherman and was nicknamed Boanerges (Son of Thunder). He was the first of the apostles to be martyred, by Herod Agrippa I, in the year 44 C.E. Any details about his activities after Christ's death and before his own and his subsequent miraculous works are speculative. Yet around this figure wound an intricate story that became codified in about the twelfth century. Its development incorporated elements from folk traditions that include boat burials, stone cults, and Celtic religious rites. The legend of James became intertwined with Christian explication, commingling ecclesiastical motives and historical circumstance.

The saint's biography is in some respects a series of tenuously connected tales, several of which exist in multiple versions. His legend can be loosely divided into three parts: activities before his death; burial, the tomb's later discovery, and resultant pilgrimage to the site; and the saint as Matamoros.

The standard *vita* begins after Pentecost and places James on the Iberian Peninsula to preach and convert. He gained only a handful of disciples in the northwest region of Spain called Galicia. Returning to the Holy Land, he passed through Zaragoza. There, in her only miraculous appearance while she was still alive, the Virgin Mary commanded him to build a church to commemorate her son. As proof of her identity she brought with her the pillar on which Christ had been flagellated (hence the origin of a common Spanish name for a woman, Pilar). A later tale relates that, further on his journey, the saint stepped on a thorn and was unable to remove it. The Virgin sent angels to help. A chapel near Lérida commemorated this event.

After his beheading St. James's body was placed in a boat, which miraculously landed at Iria Flavia (modern Padrón) on the northwest coast of the peninsula. James's few converts pulled his body ashore, but having no tomb ready, they laid it on a stone, which miraculously conformed to hold the saint's body. The saint's disciples asked the area's pagan Queen Lupa for permission to bury him. She was adamantly opposed, giving the disciples impossible tasks to perform in exchange for her permission. The best known of these was to yoke two wild oxen to their cart. When the oxen saw the saint's body, they immediately walked tamely to the cart to be yoked. The saint was buried.

Nothing is said about the next seven centuries. The tomb was not discovered until about 814. One version of its discovery relates that shepherds guarding their flocks saw a particularly bright star, which they followed to a hidden burial place. Bishop Teodomiro was consulted, the tomb was opened, and the body of St. James was recognized. A small church was erected there, followed by another, larger shrine. The area around the chapel had probably been inhabited in the pre-Roman and Roman eras, but its development is inextricably linked to the saint's cult. Its name, Santiago de Compostela, attests to this close relationship. Yet even the etymology of *Compostela* has been variously interpreted as *campo stela,* "field of stars" or "pretty site."

This biography was made even more complex when Santiago took on a militaristic role in Spanish history. In the year 711, the *musulmanes* (Spanish *moros*) from Africa invaded and conquered nearly all of the Iberian Peninsula. In time, the few Christian holdouts in the northern mountains began skirmishes to push south, initiating the famous Spanish Reconquest (completed in 1492). At a place called Clavijo in about 850, in a battle designed to end an onerous yearly tribute of 10 or 100 or 1,000 (depending on the version) virgins, from the sky descended a knight on a white horse wielding a sword against the Moors: Santiago, now named Santiago Matamoros (Moor-slayer).

People were already visiting the shrine of the saint's burial place for cures, devotion, and prayer. But now political and devotional motives merged. When Santiago aided the Christians in their fight against the Moors, the political rulers acknowledged their debt by increasing donations, both monetary and territorial. Pilgrimage to Compostela became popular, reaching its high point in the twelfth century.

Pilgrims to Santiago's tomb in Compostela returned home with a scallop shell as symbol of having journeyed there, perhaps because St. James returned to the peninsula from the sea or perhaps because in an early miracle attributed to him he saves a man from drowning in the sea. Confraternities (religious groups of lay people) dedicated to St. James were common in communities throughout Western Europe. They aided pilgrims and often held local festivals on the saint's day.

Localized belief in the saint's powers is evidenced by numerous shrines and chapels named in his honor throughout Europe. The saint is represented throughout most of northern Europe as a pilgrim, with the wayfarer's attributes of staff, satchel, hat, and long cloak and a scallop shell as his identifying mark. Within the Iberian Peninsula he is widely represented as Matamoros as well, generally in a white tunic, astride a white horse, wielding a sword and crushing Moors beneath the horse's hooves.

The *vita,* now long and multifaceted, apparently evolved slowly during its first few centuries. The earliest records linking St. James the Apostle to the Iberian Peninsula began appearing in the seventh century, but they may be later interpolations. The English monk Aldhelm of Malmesbury (d. 709) wrote a clear reference to St. James's having preached in Spain, and several other authors did likewise in that and subsequent centuries. The twelfth-century *Liber Sancti Jacobi* (Book of Saint James) codified his legend for Christianity and made evident the importance of making a pilgrimage to his tomb. The mixture of ecclesiastical and popular beliefs was generally accepted as true throughout the Middle Ages, although the history was not made official Church doctrine until 1884. For the most part, it was not until the Reformation and the Protestant movement that skepticism was heard or broadly written. Even the nucleus of his identity as Matamoros is questioned, since both the tribute and the battle are now debated by historians, but it was an aspect of the saint's legend that was not contested until recently.

See also: Hispanic Tradition; Pilgrimage; Saints, Cults of the

—Linda Davidson and Maryjane Dunn

Jesus Christ. Believed by Christians to be the Son of God and the second person of the divine Trinity.

New Testament accounts of Jesus' career are well known. The canonical Gospels (Matthew, Mark, Luke, and John) should not be classified as biographies as the term is conventionally understood: they are, rather, works of theology, even though they are based on the life, work, and death of Jesus of Nazareth. Nonetheless, all but the most die-hard modern skeptical scholar would concede that the narratives are based on historical events.

Historically based though they may be, these Gospels only relate disparate events; none of these narratives provides a complete picture of Jesus' life. The Gospels describe his birth; then, they relate an incident that occurred when he was 12. After another gap, he is encountered being baptized by John the Baptist before embarking on a ministry of possibly three years' duration, during which he is reported to have taught many people, to have traveled around Palestine accompanied by a core of 12 disciples, to have performed many miracles, and then to have been arrested in Jerusalem, ultimately tried by the Romans and crucified. The Gospels end with reports that Jesus was raised from the dead and with accounts of his post-Easter appearances.

After his death and Resurrection, the one who in the Gospels is the proclaimer becomes the one who is proclaimed by his followers. The rest of the New Testament outside the Gospels is concerned with the founding and growth of the Church. Groups who were converted and followed Christ's teaching encountered many social, administrative, and theological troubles because the new religion was breaking away from its Jewish roots and heritage. The Acts of the Apostles and the Epistles, principally those written by or in the name of Paul, enable us to plot the growth of Christianity and its problems in the first century.

Normative Christianity thereafter used the New Testament writings as its foundation documents, and by the fourth century, the Church, East and West, had agreed on the canon of Christian scripture. Events in Jesus' life were made the centerpieces of Christian celebration and worship as the liturgy developed and as ecclesiastically approved lectionaries were adopted. Jesus' teaching was meditated upon and preached about by influential patristic writers. Church councils deliberated about his person, and especially about his relationship to God. Popular piety accepted at face value the events and teachings attributed to Jesus by the Evangelists.

Other writings, particularly those of the second century, attempted to build on the New Testament Gospels and to plug perceived gaps in the biographical details about Jesus as seen within the Gospels of Matthew, Mark, Luke, and John. The so-called apocryphal Gospels are full of imaginative details about Jesus, particularly concerning his formative years; very few details in them are likely to be historical. Some Gospels, such as the influential second-century Protevangelium of James, relate stories about Jesus' ancestry. Others tell stories of his boyhood. The Arabic Infancy Gospel has a cycle of stories in which Jesus performs many miracles during the Holy Family's sojourn in Egypt.

Another of these early apocryphal writings, the Infancy Gospel of Thomas, has various episodes set in Jesus' childhood: he works in his father's carpentry shop, runs errands for his mother, and astounds his schoolmasters. In addition to such stories, the Infancy Gospel of Thomas relates several miracles in which Jesus, almost an enfant terrible, performs various destructive acts on those who vex him. Bizarre as some of those stories are, they nevertheless reflect an orthodox tendency in early Christianity to emphasize Jesus as a real flesh-and-blood human born of a woman and brought up as a normal child, albeit one with divine power over life and death.

That emphasis conflicts with several "heretical" interpretations, especially Gnostic and Docetic. Those interpretations of Jesus gained in popularity in the second century and threatened the traditional, orthodox view by denying him an actual physical existence during his ministry and by stressing only his supernatural nature. Believers who were determined to defend orthodox teaching had to counter such heretical interpretations. The apocryphal tradition—superstitious, uncritical, and magical though it may appear to sophisticated modern minds and castigated as it was by ecclesiastical authorities determined to concentrate attention on only the New Testament writings—nonetheless had an enormous influence on subsequent writings, art, and devotion and assisted in preserving the teaching about the physical ministry of Jesus of Nazareth.

However, in one influential apocryphal text, the second-century Acts of John, part of the narrative (especially the chapters normally numbered 87–105, known from only one manuscript) seems to have been contaminated by Gnostic ideas. Jesus' earthly body is described there in mystic terms. It is not unchanging but, rather, capable of adopting varying guises—an old man or a youth; bearded or clean-shaven; short or towering. His body is sometimes solid, sometimes immaterial and incapable of leaving even a footprint on the earth (Acts John 89, 93). Here, Jesus himself describes his Crucifixion as being that of only a phantom body, the "real" Jesus being distanced from these events (Acts John 97, 101).

What therefore ultimately emerged in writings about Jesus were two often diametrically opposed pictures: one, the Incarnate Messiah; the other, the divine Son of God. Both pictures, of course, may be found even within the New Testament writings themselves, but distortions of both are to be seen throughout Christianity and Christian writing. Christian theological thinking has had to try to explain, resolve, or reconcile many such contradictions. Christian art likewise is divided between pictures of Jesus as Pantocrator (Ruler of All) or with a nimbus and those that locate him in naturalistic scenes as a man among mankind. Popular belief in general has tended to focus on his well-known miracles—healings, exorcisms, and especially such nature miracles as the feeding of the 5,000 or the walking on the water—but Christian devotion also emphasizes his role as eternal and risen, at one with God, and as the eventual inaugurator of the End Time, when he is to reappear in glory.

Inevitably, it was the biblical accounts of Jesus' deeds and preaching that motivated orthodox Christian devotion, practice, and teaching throughout subsequent centuries. Until the radical Lives of Jesus in the nineteenth century and recent publications of liberal scholarship, uncritical readers of the Bible accepted the New Testament's portrayal of Jesus as teacher, healer, and Savior. The additional, apocryphal, stories of his infancy and boyhood had a limited impact.

There is, however, one popular nonbiblical story about Jesus that was used in medieval folklore; namely, Jesus' descent to the underworld. The belief that Jesus preached to the departed in the period between his death on Good Friday and his Resurrection on Easter Day and led the faithful out of Hades and into Paradise may have been based on a particular interpretation in 1 Peter 3:19; however, in its developed form it is found in the second half of the Gospel of Nicodemus, probably composed in the fifth to sixth centuries. The scene, known as the Harrowing of Hell, was performed by the saddlers in the York cycle of medieval mystery plays. The Christian credal statement, "He descended into hell" is evidence of the influence of this tradition.

See also: Christmas; Grain Miracle; Harrowing of Hell; Joseph, Saint; Mary Magdalen, Saint; Virgin Mary

—J. K. Elliott

Jewish Tradition.

Jewish Tradition. The beliefs, customs, verbal traditions, folk arts, and folklife shared by communities belonging to the Jewish faith.

One of the most pervasive concepts shaping the lives and culture of medieval Jews was that of *galut* (diaspora), the sense that Gentile hatred and Jewish sins had robbed the Jewish people of their glorious past and precipitated the disaster of their dispersion and degradation. Jewish communities of the Middle Ages thus shared a lack of sovereign territory and a powerful yearning for an irretrievable time.

Medieval Jews were divided into two main groups: those communities living under the peoples of Islam, from Yemen in the East to Spain and Morocco in the West, and those Jews living in Christian realms, from the Byzantine Empire to England. There had been Jewish communities in Egypt and Babylonia since biblical times, and in Europe Jewish settlements antedated the Roman Empire. Jewish collective memory, however, identified the dispersion with the two great destructions of Jerusalem: that of the first temple, in biblical times, and that of the second temple, carried out by the Romans in 69 C.E. Though the destruction of the second temple was accompanied by the destruction of the remnants of Jewish political existence in Palestine, paradoxically, this violent and futile act created the conditions for the flowering of European Jewish culture. Historians agree that the Jewish Middle Ages began with the invasion of Palestine by Muslim armies and the establishment of the Muslim states in the mid-seventh century. These events separated the Jewish communities of the newly emerged Muslim world from those of the Christian realms and laid the foundations of medieval Jewish social, religious, and cultural life.

Although separated geographically, the Jewish communities maintained a close relationship across the cultural divide between East and West. This made both the communities and their folklore ideal mediators between Arab and Christian cultures. Books were translated from Arabic into Hebrew and thus entered Europe via Jewish culture; Jewish travelers, emigrants, and wandering scholars spread customs and narrative traditions from Europe to the East and back.

Hebrew and Jewish Concepts of Tradition

A core question in any study of medieval Jewish folklore concerns language. Hebrew was the sacred tongue, the main language of the ancient sources, yet during this period it was not a "living" language, as it was not used for ordinary communication. Jews communicated among themselves and with their neighbors in Arabic or in the European vernaculars. By the central Middle Ages Jews had developed their own vernaculars: Judeo-Arabic, Judeo-German (Yiddish), and Judeo-Spanish (Judizmo, Ladino). These initially modest means of oral communication developed into full literary languages. Further complicating this situation is the fact that though Hebrew was not a "living" language, neither was it "dead." For Jews, one consequence of the East-West divide was the necessity of arriving at a means of communication. Ancient customs and traditions (the daily prayers and yearly rituals conducted in Hebrew) provided the only common tongue.

The availability of Hebrew enabled local communities to host students who journeyed to Iraq to study in Torah academies, helped merchants trading in the East, and allowed emissaries traveling in Europe to raise money for the poor of the Holy Land. If an author wished his book to be read by Jews everywhere, he had no choice but to write in Hebrew. This state of affairs puts Jewish folklore of the time in an awkward perspective: the language of everyday Jewish life was the local vernacular; their folklore was undoubtedly created and transmitted in the vernacular as well. Yet almost all Jewish folklore of the Middle Ages was set down in documents written in Hebrew. Tales of all genres, magic formulas, descriptions of rites and customs, and travelers' accounts all appear in Hebrew. This aspect of the preservation of Jewish traditions bears comparison to the complex relations between Latin and the vernacular dialects in medieval Europe.

But the similarity ends when the different social status of the two languages is considered. Latin was the preserve of the learned elite; teaching it to only a few safeguarded the authority of the Church. While most Europeans of the period were illiterate, literacy in Hebrew was a religious imperative for Jews. Every male Jewish child between the ages of three and five attended school, where he learned to read and write Hebrew and acquired a basic understanding of the Bible and the Mishnah (Oral Law). This primary education enabled Jewish males to read prayers during synagogue services and to understand the reading of the Bible. The practice of educating children "democratically" was the reason that the balance of oral and written traditions in Judaism was different from the balance between those traditions in the surrounding culture. Folkloric documents—including collections of tales, lists of folk cures, and magic practices—were written to be read by a literate audience, not to be recited orally or read aloud by storytellers or preachers. This gave the Hebrew folkloric document a different character from that of its counterparts in other medieval cultures. The written document was not only a means of preserving folklore but a folkloric item in itself.

A basic concept of medieval Judaism was *shalhelet ha-kabbalah* (the chain of tradition); that is,

each generation is one link in a long chain starting with the giving of God's word to Moses, who transmitted it to Joshua, and Joshua to the Elders, and the Elders to the Prophets (Mishnah Avot 1:1), and on and on to the learned rabbis of the Middle Ages. This ultraconservative model of tradition presented every cultural asset as having originated fully formed in the ancient past, and it impeded the emergence of new cultural creations and patterns of life. Yet medieval Jewish culture did produce new texts, customs, and traditions, circumventing this formal barrier with the aid of another basic concept: *minhag* (local custom). When ancient, formal law clashed with the needs of medieval life or thought, local custom—the folkloric practice common in the local community—was permitted and became part of the official law. *Minhag*, as the vehicle for the renewal of traditions, was a powerful tool; it was the chief instrument of change in the social and economic life of medieval Jews, in the development of new liturgical and ritual forms, and in the creation of new narratives. From the folkloric perspective, *minhag* bridged the gap between the learned, official religion and folk culture. It also opened a door between distinct Jewish folk cultures, allowing customs and beliefs to pass through, to gain currency in other communities, and ultimately to be recorded in legal documents.

Absorption of Foreign Traditions
Official Jewish culture eventually absorbed many newly created or originally foreign folk customs pertaining to life and year cycles. One example is the custom of the "night watch," wherein a week-old male infant is guarded the night before his circumcision to forestall any demonic kidnapping attempts. Another is the breaking of the glass beneath the bridal canopy, originally a typical deterrent against demons who might otherwise endanger the marriage. The official religion, after banning this practice as part of idolatrous, pagan cults, transformed it into a symbolic ritual recalling the grief over Jerusalem's destruction. In performing *kapparot* (expiation), one symbolically transfers all of one's sins to a fowl and then sacrifices it on the eve of Yom Kippur (Day of Atonement). Also belonging to this category are certain dances performed by men and women during marriage festivals, and many death customs, such as placing a rock on a grave, tossing grass behind one's back before leaving the cemetery, or the family of the deceased taking a different route home so as not to be followed by the dead man's soul.

Medieval rabbis deliberated over these customs and dozens more and, acknowledging their folkloric or non-Jewish origin, rejected them as *darkei akum* (idolatrous) or immoral. Ultimately, however, common practice prevailed, and rabbinic authority had to accept local customs through the agency of *minhag*. Talmudic literature, central to the cultural activity of the preceding period and to a great extent of the Middle Ages as well, is an all-encompassing creation. It incorporates most of the period's cultural components: scriptural commentary and medicine, law and astronomy, linguistics and historiography, liturgical poetry and geography—all in the course of a single, unbroken, and largely undifferentiated discussion.

By the height of the Geonic period (Iraq-Babylonia, eighth and ninth centuries), a tendency had evolved to create special works on law, Hebrew grammar, Jewish philosophy, liturgical poetry, and historiography. This significant cultural phenomenon, known as the separation of disciplines, was connected to a parallel development in Arabic culture during the first centuries of Islam. The first Hebrew anthologies of folk narratives—which preserve information on the creation and spread of the rich folk traditions among Jewish communities—belong to that time, place, and cultural milieu. Although the collections of medieval Hebrew folktales were, with few exceptions, anonymously composed, research has established that two of the earliest, namely the *Midrash of the Ten Commandments* and the *Alphabet of Ben Sira*, were created in the eighth to ninth centuries and originated in the region of Iraq-Persia.

Talmudic and midrashic activity (that is, the creation of commentaries on the Scriptures), so dominant in late antiquity, continued unchecked by the development of folkloric anthologies in the Middle Ages. Midrashic works such as *Midrash Genesis Rabbati* (Provence, eleventh century), *Yalkut Shimoni* (Germany, thirteenth century), *Midrash ha-Gadol* (Yemen, thirteenth century), and *Yalkut ha-Makhiri* (Provence, fourteenth century) continued to zealously preserve the literary frameworks of the past. These midrashic anthologies belong to the first type of medieval Jewish folkloric traditions, those based in antiquity that lived on into the Middle Ages. These archaic midrashic works are folklorically less interesting, however, than the medieval folk-narrative anthologies, much of whose content (about one-third) originated in talmudic-midrashic literature. Though drawn from the writings of the past, many of these tales reappear in the later works not as verbatim variants but in new versions. This is another indication that the midrashic folktales were told orally in the Middle Ages and refashioned, as are all folkloric works, in order to express not only the old norms but also, and more important, the contemporary concerns of the narrating society.

The second type of medieval Jewish folkloric tradition involved borrowing from neighboring cultures. Here the experience of the diaspora—the essence of Jewish life in the Middle Ages—left its deepest marks. Every Jewish community of the period, from England to Yemen (and perhaps even further east), was a cultural minority among Christians or Muslims. The demands of daily life, economics, politics, and cultural debates necessitated close ties between Jews and their neighbors, and naturally the greater cultural influence was exerted upon the minority. Jewish religious restrictions nevertheless kept Gentile customs and traditions from encroaching too deeply, and Jewish life remained separate and "other."

The omnipresent confrontation between ancient, sacred traditions and local, non-Jewish folklore was an unavoidable feature of daily life and the major shaping influence on medieval Jewish folklore. The folklore anthologies of the period exhibit this conflict by presenting narratives originating in sacred talmudic literature alongside non-Jewish erotic *novelle* or demonological tales. The folk *novella* "Crescentia" (AT 712), the demonological tale about the marriage to a she-demon (motif F302), both originating in Christian or Arabic folklore, appear in the Oxford manuscript collection of tales of the twelfth century alongside the midrashic tales of Rabbi Akiva, Hillel the Elder, and the destruction of Jerusalem. Another important feature of the borrowing process is the translation of folkloric compositions into Hebrew (and later in the Middle Ages into Yiddish and Judeo-Arabic). The principal medieval frame tales and romances—including *Kalila wa-Dimna*, *Tales of Sendebar*, *Thousand and One Nights*, *Romance of Alexander*, *King Arthur and the Round Table*, *The Romance of Antar*, *The Prince and the Hermit (Barlaam and Josaphat)*, and the knightly romance *Amadis de Gaula*—were translated into Jewish dialects and became a part of the Jewish culture of the period. The Judeo-Spanish ballad was one of the most important literary-folkloric creations of the period. Spanish Jews adopted oral poetic narratives (*romanceros*), recited them in their own Judeo-Spanish dialect, and made them part of Jewish culture. After the expulsion from Spain (1492), Jews scattered in the Balkans, Turkey, Morocco, the Netherlands, and Palestine continued to see these ballads as part of the cultural heritage and collective memory from their beloved *Sefarad* (Spain). They continue to perform them to this very day.

Both the borrowing of non-Jewish folk traditions and the translation of folkloric compositions are more culturally complex than the revision of older Jewish traditions because the newer materials had to undergo a process of Judaization. The inclusion of international folk narratives in the collections of folktales or the translation of whole compositions into Hebrew was never merely technical; rather, it transformed the borrowed traditions in ways that were sometimes superficial, at other times profound. Some changes were linguistic, and others involved the inclusion of Jewish customs and rituals or the rejection of non-Jewish ones. Scripture and Talmud were quoted, references were made to events from Jewish history, and sometimes the whole structure of a tale was altered to make it correspond to Jewish moral and religious norms.

In his introduction, the translator of the *Romance of King Arthur* (1279) explains why he, a pious Jew, occupied himself with such trifles as Gentile romances:

> I attempted the translation of these conversations for two important reasons: The first was the preservation of my physical well-being.... The second and most important reason for my translation was that sinners will learn the paths of repentance and bear in mind their end and will return to God, as you will see in the conclusion [of the story].

He went beyond translating to reconstruct the romance so that this "sin and punishment" pattern, so important to him as a medieval Jew, would become the narrative focus of the Hebrew version. The synthesis between non-Jewish narrative structures and Jewish cultural norms was not without consequences. In most stories belonging to this type, there is a sharp tension between the pagan, Christian, or Muslim narrative models and Jewish religious and social norms. This tension, inseparable as it was from the mentality of medieval Jews, is one of the most important characteristics of Jewish folklore of the time.

The main folk narrative genres of late antiquity lingered in the Middle Ages, but with diminished popularity. For example, the main narrative genre in the talmudic-midrashic literature was the rewritten biblical story, in which the original tale was expanded and reworked to suit the new generation's cultural and political interests and literary tastes. These creations of the preceding age were the main building blocks of the medieval midrashim (plural of midrash). Medieval Jews, however, preferred those rewritten biblical narratives that embodied the literary and cultural values peculiar to their own day. *Divrei ha-Yamim Shel Moshe* (The Chronicles of Moses; tenth–eleventh centuries) is one such narrative. The story is constructed as a heroic epic, narrating the life of Moses from birth to death as a sequence of heroic deeds, in the best literary tradition of the Middle Ages. Even so, all the narrative blocks upon which this epic tale is built are taken from talmudic literature, thus strengthening the tendency to synthesize traditional material with the new form. Another interesting narrative of the same period is *Midrash va-Yissa'u* or *Milhamot Bnei Ya'akov* (The Wars of the Sons of Jacob), which recounts the wars waged by the tribes, the sons of Jacob, against the Canaanite peoples, after the rape of their sister Dina. The wars are typical knightly fights, using the same norms, strategies, feudal mores, and weapons as those of the chivalric romances. Yet here, too, most of the narrative materials are taken from the apocryphal *Testaments of the Twelve Tribes*, written during the second temple period. Another type of medieval rewritten biblical story is *Sefer ha-Yashar* (The Book of Right Deeds). It retells

biblical stories from the Creation to Joshua's conquest of the Land of Canaan. The stories are expanded and written in elevated Hebrew style, with much emphasis on dialogue, dramatic situations, and pathos. The short, condensed biblical tales are transformed into expanded *novelle*, in the best literary style of the late Middle Ages.

The dominant narrative genre in medieval Jewish traditions, as in those of Christian culture, was the exemplum. This genre also possessed roots in ancient Jewish traditions, as evidenced both in talmudic literature and the Christian New Testament. The first Hebrew tale collection of the Middle Ages, the aforementioned *Midrash of the Ten Commandments*, was constructed as a series of exempla, in which folktales illustrate the importance of observing each biblical commandment, the punishments for transgressions, and rewards for obedience. Another important medieval collection of exempla is the *Hibbur Yafeh min-ha-Yeshu'ah* (An Elegant Composition Concerning Relief after Adversity), written in the eleventh century by Rabbi Nissim ibn Shahin of Kairouan of Tunisia (it is one of the few Hebrew narrative works of known authorship). That Rabbi Nissim, a leading religious authority of the day, should have published this work in the contemporary Jewish-Arabic dialect and busied himself with folkloric material is one of the clearest indications that the dichotomy between "learned" and "folk" culture in the Middle Ages was indistinct. The tales are set in a rhetorical context. Each chapter focuses on a central norm, and in each of them the teacher explains its importance and offers the story as validation. Most of the tales had roots in Arab culture and were adapted to suit Jewish norms and lifestyles, giving rise to that characteristic tension discussed above. One of the earliest Christian exempla collections, the eleventh-century *Disciplina Clericalis* (Clerical Discipline), by Petrus Alfonsi, should be considered part of the same Jewish tradition. Petrus Alfonsi (known as Mose Sefardi before his conversion from Judaism) was familiar with Judeo-Arabic folk traditions and used them to express his Christian values and ideas, thus becoming one of the first Christian writers to use folktales as exempla. The influence of Jewish narrative traditions upon one of the central cultural creations of medieval Europe is clear and evident here.

The most important collection of Jewish exempla is *Sefer Hasidim* (Book of the Pious) by Rabbi Judah ben Samuel he-Hasid (the Pious) of Regensburg (twelfth or thirteenth century). *Sefer Hasidim* is a collection of pietistic norms directed toward the "good people" of the Jewish communities—those few Hasidim willing to accept Rabbi Judah's extreme religious standards. Some 400 short stories are scattered throughout this voluminous code of rules. Most are presented as personal experiences of either Rabbi Judah himself or of reliable authorities, and each of them illustrates or reinforces one of Rabbi Judah's rulings. The didactic function of these short stories is stressed: "That is why *Sefer Hasidim* was written: so that its readers would know what to do, and what ought to be refrained from." Thus, each tale emphasizes a lesson in the terrible punishments suffered by sinners and the great rewards enjoyed by the righteous.

The stories abound with vampires, *strigae* (witch-like beings that sucked the blood of children), seducing demons, witches assuming the shape of cats, and the evil powers of the underworld. The appearance of these medieval German folkloric figures in *Sefer Hasidim* is evidence of close relations between Jews and their non-Jewish neighbors on the folk-cultural level. It is also noteworthy that a leading social figure, Rabbi Judah, the founder of a new religious movement, intensively utilized non-Jewish folkloric traditions to advance his political and moral goals. His use of exempla is similar to that of his Christian contemporaries.

In addition to being a narrator of folktales and the creator of a collection of exempla, Rabbi Judah he-Hasid was also the hero of a hagiographic cycle. Like the rewritten biblical tales and the exempla, legends of the rabbinic sages were a part of ancient traditions. Indeed, legends of Jesus had belonged to this genre of Jewish folklore and initiated Christian folklore's hagiographic tradition. The chief distinction between Jewish and Christian medieval hagiography is that Judaism never envisioned sainthood as an established norm. Medieval Jewish saints were those leading Jewish sages (writers, biblical commentators, philosophers, moralists, poets, mystics) whose deeds the people found worthy of retelling—in realistic or miraculous mode. These saints fulfilled community expectations in safeguarding them from their cruel and dangerous neighbors. Saints' legends appear often in the Jewish literature of the period: in biblical commentaries and legal tracts, moral treatises, and mystical writings. Yet purely hagiographic collections are few. The eleventh-century *Megilat Ahima'az* (The Scroll of Ahima'az) is the first known to us. A rhymed family history from southern Italy, it recounts 200 years of deeds by the leading family members. The patriarchs of the family constantly confront non-Jews, especially kings and religious leaders, and perform various miracles to protect their family and community from evil.

It is only in the late Middle Ages, however, that we find the full-fledged hagiographic collections concerning the most renowned Jewish luminaries, Rabbi Shelomoh ben Itzhak (Rashi), Maimonides, Rabbi Abraham ibn Ezra, and Nahmanides among them. The main collection is in the form of a historiographic work: the mid-sixteenth-century *Sha'shelet ha-Kabbalah* (The Chain of Tradition), by Gedaliah ibn Y'hya. The links of his "chain" are the sages from ancient times to the sixteenth century. He relies heavily on oral folk traditions ("as told to me by the elders of that community") and on other ancient collections of tales. It is clear that such folk traditions were the basic data for the construction of the legendary biographies of many of the Jewish saints of the Middle Ages. The same century gave rise to the collections of another hagiographic cycle—that of Rabbi Judah he-Hasid and his father Rabbi Samuel he-Hasid—in Hebrew and Yiddish traditions. The legends collected in this cycle, like those collected by Gedaliah ibn Yahya, were undoubtedly a product of medieval rather than sixteenth-century notions. They had been transmitted orally and recorded by folk writers either in the original dialects (Yiddish, Judizmo) or in Hebrew. This cycle had an important impact on all later Jewish hagiography, as it laid the model for the European *Hasid* (i.e., the charismatic, religious, wandering miracle worker) who appears mysteriously wherever he is needed to guard a Jewish community in distress. The narrative models established by these late-medieval legends of saints formed the basis of Jewish folklore in the sixteenth and seventeenth centuries, and they indicate the importance of medieval Jewish traditions for all later Jewish culture.

See also: Arabic-Islamic Tradition; Golem; Hispanic Tradition; Judah the Pious; Judith; Lilith; Passover Haggadah; Purim

—Eli Yassif

Jews, Stereotypes of. The medieval Jew as popularly imagined—following the New Oxford English Dictionary's definition of "stereotype" as "a preconceived, standardized, and oversimplified impression of the characteristics which typify a person" or group, emphasizing here such popular conceptions rather than the various accusations that were made about alleged Jewish actions.

From the early Middle Ages Jews were clearly linked with the twin realms of Satan and sorcery. Their link with the former, evident already in the Gospel of John (8:44) and Revelation (2:9, 3:9), was greatly emphasized by John Chrysostom of Antioch, who late in the fourth century asserted that "the souls of the Jews and the places where they congregate are inhabited by demons" and that "the Jews do not worship God but devils." During the course of time, as Robert Bonfil has noted, "the tendency to connect the Jews with the devil became a fundamental and persistent aspect of Christian attitudes toward Jews and Judaism."

In the twelfth century Peter of Blois, who was born in minor French nobility but served as deputy to the archbishops of Canterbury for two decades, linked the Jew's demonic character with a host of other "annoying" traits: "For the Jew is always inconstant and shifty," he wrote in his *Contra perfidiam Judaeorum* (Against the Treachery of the Jews). "At times he affirms, at times he negates, he quibbles about the literal meaning, or he refers all matters to the times of his own messiah, that is, of the Antichrist. After the manner of the devil his father, he often changes into monstrous shapes." In thirteenth-century Spain the Dominican priest Raymond Martini, who was an accomplished student of rabbinic literature, asserted in his *Pugio fidei* (Dagger of Faith) that it was the devil who had blinded the Jews to the true (allegorical) meaning of the Mosaic commandments. Martini also argued in his widely circulated polemical work that it was Satan who returned them, "by some demonic miracle" to observing those commandments (such as circumcision and the Sabbath) that God himself had clearly intended to nullify through Roman persecutions.

The association between the Jewish messiah and anti-Christ mentioned by Peter of Blois had been made as early as the ninth century by Rabanus Maurus, archbishop of Mainz. In the central Middle Ages such leading scholastics as Thomas Aquinas and Albertus Magnus subscribed to the view that anti-Christ would be born in Babylon to the tribe of Dan, that he would proceed to Jerusalem where he would be circumcised, and that after persuading the Jews that he was their mssiah he would rebuild the Temple and organize a vast army of conquest. Paradoxically, another notion developing during the same period in European Christendom was that Jews were cowardly and effeminate, so effeminate, in fact, that Jewish men as well as women menstruated monthly.

The popular legend of Theophilus, the oldest Latin version of which dates from the ninth century, but which probably originated in sixth-century Anatolia and later served as the basis for the story of Faust, explicitly linked the Jews, the devil, and the magical arts. Theophilus, who "sought not for divine but human glory," made contact with a Jewish sorcerer, who in turn took him to the devil. Similarly, several medieval versions of the Passion play presented the Jews of Jerusalem, instigated by Satan, as working their most potent charms against Jesus. At the Church's Council of Béziers in 1255, attended by King Louis IX, it was decreed that "Jews should desist from usuries, blasphemies and sorceries." And in Matthew Paris's account of the ritual murder of "little Hugh of Lincoln," whose body was found in the same year, 1255, we read that the Jews had "disemboweled the corpse, for what end is unknown; but it was said to practice magical arts."

During the later Middle Ages, with the popularization of the ritual murder accusation across Europe, different theories emerged as to why Jews needed Christian children or their blood, some of which were reflected in the "confessions" attributed to the Jews themselves. In the spring of 1475, after the dead body of a 2-year-old boy named Simon was found in Trent, a 25-year- old local Jew

"explained" under torture that his coreligionists needed Christian blood since "if they don't use blood they'll stink." This, of course, was an allusion to the old myth of the *foetor judaicus*, which allegedly disappeared automatically on the administration of the waters of baptism. Scholars have pointed to a late-sixth-century poem by Venantius Fortunatus, composed after the Jews of Clermont were forcefully converted in 576 after attacking a former coreligionist who was baptized on Easter/Passover of that year, as the earliest source alluding to the alleged sweetening of the Jewish stench through baptism.

A number of later medieval legends repeat this stereotype. One, reported early in the thirteenth century by Caesarius of Heisterbach, told of a Jew of Louvain whose daughter, after her baptism, suddenly became aware of a foul stench emanating from his body when he came to rescue her from the Cistercian convent into which she had been placed. In 1401 the city council of Freiburg petitioned Duke Leopold to expel the Jews, who were believed to constitute a danger since "every seven years all Jews must obtain Christian blood," which they either ingest or smear upon themselves. This was done, it was claimed, "for the prolongation of their lives, and particularly from a desire not to stink, for when they lack this blood they stink so foully that no one can remain near them." Yet there were, in time, also some learned Christian skeptics. Martin Luther, in his 1523 essay "That Jesus Christ Was Born a Jew," advised that Jews be dealt with kindly and instructed through Scripture concerning the truths of Christianity. "If, however, we use brute force and slander them," he asked, "saying that they need the blood of Christians to get rid of their stench and I know not what other nonsense of that kind ... what good can we expect of them?"

There were indeed various kinds of "nonsense" circulating in German-speaking lands during the late fifteenth century about the Jewish "need" for Christian blood. In 1476 a Jew "confessed" in Regensburg that his coreligionists drank Christian blood and smeared it on their unleavened bread as a prophylactic against leprosy, and in Baden, in the very same year, another Jew "admitted" that they used Christian blood in order to alleviate the wound of circumcision—a confession first heard in Endingen some seven years earlier. This explanation was later recorded during a 1494 investigation of an alleged ritual murder in Tyrnau (now in the Czech Republic), whose Jews also allegedly explained that both Jewish men and women had found Christian blood an effective means of alleviating their menstrual cramps!

The myth of male Jewish menstruation, as I. M. Resnick has recently shown, goes back as far as the thirteenth century, to Jacques de Vitry, bishop of Acre (in Palestine), who wrote in his *History of Jerusalem* that as a divine punishment for having killed Jesus, the Jews had become "weak and unwarlike, even as women." Moreover, he added, "it is said that they have a flux of blood every month," God having "smitten them in the hinder parts and put them to perpetual shame." A similar assertion was made around the same time by Caesarius of Heisterbach, who included in his *Exempla* a number of stories concerning Jewish girls who were attracted to Christian men. In one of these the girl explained to her prospective "date," a nephew of the bishop of London, that her father watched her so carefully that they could meet only "on the night of the Friday before your Easter." Caesarius provided an interesting explanation: "For then the Jews are said to labor under a sickness called the bloody flux, with which they are so much occupied, that they can scarcely pay attention to anything else at that time."

This theme reappeared later in the thirteenth century in the writings of the Dominican Thomas of Cantimpré, who also claimed that Jews, both male and female, suffered from a bloody flux, which, as in the case of Caesarius, may have referred to hemorrhoids rather than menstruation. Thomas's special contribution, however, was to claim that Jews believed this "flux" to be curable only with Christian blood. "It is hence quite evident," he added, "that according to custom, Jews shed Christian blood in every province they inhabit. It has certainly been established that every year they cast lots in each province as to which community or city should produce Christian blood for the other communities."

In 1943 the American rabbi and scholar Joshua Trachtenberg wrote that "the only Jew whom the medieval Christian recognized was a figment of the imagination." These bold words contain no small measure of truth, although they are perhaps less persuasive today than when they were first published—precisely a decade after Hitler's rise to power. The rise of Nazism in Germany and its catastrophic consequences led to much scholarly inquiry into the dark history of what today would be called Europe's "construction of the Jew." Trachtenberg's *The Devil and the Jews*, which carried the telling subtitle *The Medieval Conception of the Jew and Its Relation to Modern Anti-Semitism*, was preceded during the 1930s by important discussions of these issues by the British scholars James Parkes and Cecil Roth.

The latter, whose 1938 essay "The Medieval Conception of the Jew" was clearly echoed in the subtitle of Trachtenberg's book (and later, in one of the chapter titles of Guido Kisch's *The Jews in Medieval Germany*), advanced the thesis that Jews were seen by medieval Christians as being fundamentally different, in both body and mind, from other human beings: "There were numerous natural signs," he wrote, "which clearly indicated to the popular mind that the Jews were a race apart, cursed for all eternity." Similarly, Trachten-

berg asserted that for medieval Christians the Jew was not quite human, but rather "a creature of an altogether different nature, of whom normal reactions could not be expected."

By contrast, Guido Kisch, himself a refugee from Nazi Germany, was sharply critical of historians, both Jewish and Gentile, who sought, anachronistically in his view, to present the medieval perception of the Jew in racial terms. "Race," he stated unequivocally in 1949, "was no factor in the medieval attitude toward, and legal treatment of, the Jews." Kisch's position, however, was not widely adopted. In 1978, four decades after the appearance of Roth's influential article, Lester Little was able to state confidently that during the eleventh to thirteenth centuries European Christians regarded Jews "as inferiors, as some class of sub-human beings. They wrote tracts to prove the point, extended the argument with pictorial and plastic representations, and fixed the point by law."

It is perhaps appropriate to quote, in conclusion, the ringing words with which Roth concluded his twice-reprinted 1938 essay: "It is possible to acquit the ordinary man of the Middle Ages of unreasoning cruelty in his relations with a people whom he was encouraged to consider in so distorted a light; but not our own contemporaries, who revived an equally preposterous conception in this ostensibly enlightened age."

See also: Blasons Populaires; Blood; Magic

—Elliott Horowitz

Joan of Arc, Saint (1412?–1431). French war heroine and popular religious figure, canonized in 1920.

Joan's triumphs—the liberation of Orléans (May 8, 1429) from the English and the crowning and anointing of the Dauphin Charles VII in Rheims (July 17, 1429)—and her pathetic trial and death at the stake made her a legend in her own time.

Coming from a 17-year-old "maid" (she liked to call herself *La Pucelle*), her deeds seemed supernatural. She was worshipped and feared, and was finally condemned as a heretic in Rouen on May 28, 1431. Her judges could not forgive her for her loyalty to the saints—Michael, Margaret, and Catherine—who had appeared to her and instructed her since she was 13. Led by the archbishop of Beauvais, Pierre Cauchon, clerics from the University of Paris could only consider such a denial of Church authority with suspicion. One consequence of their mistrust was their determination to demonize her; in this way they were also opportunely undermining Charles VII's legitimacy.

The customs that Joan shared with the other youngsters in her village of Domrémy—the dances, the picnics around the Fairy Tree on the second Sunday of Lent, the stations of the cross at the healing fountain—offer us intimate views of late-medieval village ritual. Testifying at her trial, Joan described the Fairy Tree:

> There is a tree called the Ladies' Tree, and others call it the Fairies' Tree, near which there is a spring of water; and I have heard tell that those who are sick and have the fever drink the water of this spring, and ask for its waters to recover their health.... It is a big tree called beech from which fine Maypoles are made.... Sometimes I went out with the other girls and by the tree made garlands ... for the image of Our Lady of Domremy; I have seen the girls put such garlands on the tree's branches and sometimes I myself put some on.

At Joan's rehabilitation hearing in 1450 many of her fellow villagers added their testimony to enrich this portrait of festive life. Yet at her trial in 1431 such information had been used by her accusers exclusively as evidence of diabolical idolatry.

Even Joan's most sacred and religious actions could be interpreted as magic: for example, her frequent reception of communion, which was seen as a misuse of the Eucharist, or the power emanating from her virginal body. The questions she was asked at her trial demonstrate her judges' concern about her healing powers, her alleged use of a mandrake, and the nature of the sign that allowed her to recognize the dauphin in a crowd of nobles when she met him for the first time. Other controversial points were her miraculous discovery, at the chapel of Saint Catherine de Fierbois, of the sword she bore in battle; her banner with the representation of God holding the world and of her two female saints displayed on it; and her ring, engraved with the words "Jesus Maria."

Joan could not completely deny that a cult had developed around her, for people had tried to touch her ring or her hand, venerated images of her, and celebrated masses in her honor. She was recognized as the miraculous female savior who had come from an oak wood in Lorraine, an extraordinary apparition that had been announced by a prophecy widely attributed to Merlin.

In spite of the solitary nature of her visionary experience and the publicity of her condemnation, Joan of Arc was a figure of her time. She takes her place in a line of female prophets, among them Catherine de La Rochelle, who tried to compete with her. And around 1440 another similar figure, Claude des Armoises, was sponsored by Joan's brothers. They exhibited Claude as Joan, dressed as a man, and fighting as a warrior as she had done.

Joan's male attire is all the more important inasmuch as the accusation of apostasy against her was based on her dress. Joan's clothing crystallized her transgression of the accepted canons of womanly behavior and gave rise to the more general discomfort generated by the blurring of fundamental categories.

See also: French Tradition; Saints, Cults of the; Woman Warrior

—Madeleine Jeay

Joseph, Saint. Husband of the Virgin Mary and putative father of Jesus.

Although the two genealogies of Jesus found at the beginning of the Gospels of Matthew and Luke were originally traced through the carpenter Joseph, the betrothed of his mother Mary, it is quite clear from the New Testament's birth narratives that Joseph is only the putative father of Jesus, Mary's conception of Jesus having been achieved through divine intervention. Modern critical biblical scholarship has invested much energy into discussing the historicity of the accounts of Jesus' birth, the alleged typology (the idea that Old Testament characters foreshadow those of the New Testament) with Joseph's patriarchal namesake in the Old Testament, and the apologetic motives behind the Gospels as a whole. Christian theology meanwhile continues to debate the significance of the virginal conception of Jesus and in effect to ignore Joseph.

The biblical accounts of Jesus' birth and the postbiblical elaborations of them, notably in the second-century apocryphal Gospel, the Protevangelium of James, portray Joseph as a loyal husband, accepted publicly as the actual father of Jesus. But in the apocryphal tradition Joseph is given an increasingly important role. He makes the Holy Family a complete and recognizable unit: a number of legends, notably in the Arabic Infancy Gospel, have Joseph prominent in several stories concerning the flight to and sojourn in Egypt. In the Infancy Gospel of Thomas he acts as a normal father, overseeing Jesus' education, working with him in the carpenter's shop, and even reprimanding him. Some medieval art was inspired by these domestic scenes.

In the Protevangelium Joseph is given an important monologue (PJ 18), in which he describes how all of nature was put into a deep sleep at the moment of Jesus' birth. The Joseph of the Protevangelium is no mere village carpenter but a building contractor, whose work takes him away from home for months at a time. More significantly, he is portrayed as an elderly widower with grown-up children from an earlier marriage. As a consequence of this, we see the development of portrayals of Joseph as a buffoon in later medieval mystery plays, where he is an old man with a young wife, almost a caricature cuckold, and thus a comic character.

The details about Joseph's previous marriage, found in the Protevangelium and in later legends dependent on it, served to satisfy those Christians who were perplexed by the references in the New Testament to Jesus' siblings alongside the teaching about Mary's virginity. Describing these siblings as Jesus' half brothers and half sisters helped preserve the developing doctrines that Mary was a perpetual virgin.

In contrast to stories elsewhere, including the traditions within the New Testament itself, in which Joseph appears as a relatively inconsequential character, we find in the fifth- to sixth-century *History of Joseph the Carpenter* a lengthy narrative, mostly put onto Jesus' lips, telling of the death of Joseph at a great age. Such a narrative, which enjoyed great popularity, especially in the East, acted as a counterpart to the many apocryphal legends about Mary and her death. The stories about Joseph served to enhance his reputation and ensure subsequent devotion to him, leading to his canonization. As St. Joseph he came to be revered as the patron saint of workers and of a good death. Christian tradition thus eventually made him more than merely the foster parent of Jesus or the husband of the Virgin Mary.

See also: Christmas; Jesus Christ; Saints, Cults of the; Virgin Mary

—J. K. Elliott

Judah the Pious (c. 1150–1217) **[Judah ben Samuel he-Hasid].** German Jewish religious leader, mystic, and storyteller, generally considered the founder of the *Hasidei Ashkenaz* (German Pietists) movement, and the main author of its founding composition, *Sefer Hasidim* (Book of the Pious).

Judah he-Hasid is the author of many books on Jewish philosophy and mysticism, commentaries on the Hebrew Bible, and books on Jewish prayers and religious morals and education. Like many of his contemporary European Christian authors, Judah he-Hasid can be considered an amateur ethnographer. He had immense interest in storytelling, in supernatural beings and events, and in out-of-the-ordinary beliefs and customs—and an interest in recording them in writing. As in the case of his Christian contemporaries, the main drive behind his ethnographic work was undoubtedly primarily religious. His immensely interesting work, *The Tractate "He Has Made His Wonderful Works Be Remembered,"* recently discovered, sheds much light upon his motives for these activities. The title of this work is taken from a verse in Psalms (111:4). In his special interpretation, it expresses the idea that God's power is revealed in this world through unusual and unnatural phenomena. In this tractate, Judah the Pious describes dozens of phenomena that have no rational explanation, attesting to his great interest and constituting a great contribution to the understanding of medieval folklore. In his opinion, all these phenomena are the ultimate proof of the existence of God and of his control of this world. In his many writings, most of which are still only in manuscript form, he describes *strigae* (witch-like beings that sucked the blood of children), monsters, vampires, revela-

tions of heavenly voices, the dead coming back to this world, supernatural healing, outstanding dreams, magic practices, various demons, and many more. All these he ties to one, all-inclusive theological system, but they should be considered also a major contribution to the study of medieval European folklore.

The most interesting contribution of Judah he-Hasid to Jewish folklore is in the field of folk narrative. In his theological, mystical, and interpretive works, he included dozens of stories as integral parts of his theoretical discussion. Judah the Pious's extreme moral values did not allow him in any way to invent stories and treat them as "fictions." He heard all these stories and recorded them from "reliable folk," and so they constitute important evidences of folk and oral traditions in the Jewish communities of medieval central Europe.

The founding text of the German Pietist movement that Judah established (or rather, hoped to establish, without great success) was *Sefer Hasidim*. In this large composition, Judah the Pious reveals his religious, moral, and social convictions, which he considers the foundation of a new and revolutionary trend within traditional Judaism. This trend is outstanding for the extremity of its religious and moral values, which verge on asceticism (which is prohibited in Judaism)—hence pietism. Judah attempted to promote these new ideas and insights by way of tales. Thus, *Sefer Hasidim* includes hundreds of stories of many types and themes. Since all these tales function as vehicles for promoting religious and moral values, they all should be considered as exempla—actually one of the major contributions to the creation of European exempla in the peak of the period of its creation—which has not yet been acknowledged by the students of this genre.

Among the exempla included in *Sefer Hasidim*, there is one remarkable group of stories—about a quarter of the more than 400 tales—that are outstanding and innovative, even in comparison with the rich body of Christian exempla. These are short, condensed narratives in which the main *dramatis persona* is the *Hakham* (wise man)—the leader of the religious community—to whom people come for advice in intimate matters, personal, social, or economic; the stories thus reveal very important and telling details about daily life in Judah's time. There was no way that Judah the Pious could know about such intimate matters unless he himself was the *Hakham*, unless he himself recorded these hundreds of cases brought before him as religious leader. These exempla, in which the saint himself is the narrator of the tales as well as their main hero, are of great importance for the study of medieval exempla.

In the fifteenth and sixteenth centuries hagiographic tales about Judah the Pious started to appear in manuscripts and early books in Hebrew and in Yiddish cycles. The cycles began with the exceptional figure of Judah's father, Rabbi Samuel, whose pietism and deeds presaged the miraculous birth of the real hero, Judah the Pious. In these tales Judah is depicted as the backbone of the Jewish community, as its guard against its Christian enemies, as the ultimate Jewish sage, fluent in all the branches of religious and secular science, a master of magical knowledge and practice. The main sources of these saint's legends attest to their origin and spread in the Yiddish language—the spoken vernacular of the Jewish communities of central Europe, northern Italy, and, later, Eastern Europe. This proves that Judah the Pious became one of the central heroes of Jewish folklore at the close of the Middle Ages and the dawn of early modern times.

See also: Exemplum; Golem; Jewish Tradition

—Eli Yassif

Judith [Hebrew *Yehudite*, Latin *Iudith*]. First depicted in the Greek Apocrypha as the pious Jewish widow who seduces and cuts off the head of the Assyrian general Holofernes with his own sword and returns triumphant to Bethulia.

Central to the tale of Judith is God's use of a faithful woman to intervene in history. Judith's great beauty and felicity, as well as her prayers and purity, all contribute to this triumph. While many scholars agree that the apocryphal text appears to allude to the revolts of Judas Maccabaeus in 164–161 B.C.E., the range of speculations as to its date of composition extends from as early as the period of the Jews' return from Babylonian exile in 538 B.C.E. to as late as the Roman rule of Herod Agrippa I in 40 C.E. The book contains many historical inaccuracies and anachronisms, and it is believed by most scholars to have been a popular legend or parable composed to maintain the nationalistic spirit of the Jews. The text was not included in the Hebrew Bible, but the Jewish community maintained the Judith legend in its oral tradition until it was recorded in the Middle Ages in the form of midrash.

Midrashim, or homilies, dating from the tenth or eleventh century recalling and elaborating on Judith's heroism, were read in the synagogue during Hanukkah, the Feast of Dedication. *Yehudite*, the Hebrew for Judith, translates as the "Jewess," and the midrashim are often themselves compilations of narratives recounting the heroism of Jewish women. One midrash gives to the high priest Yohanan's daughter, an unnamed young woman newly married and thus obligated to have intercourse with Jerusalem's Greek viceroy, the role of leading Judah's men in a revolt in which the viceroy is decapitated. This act inspires the widow Judith to decapitate the Greek king. Thus, young bride and widow act in conjunction to preserve the Israelite women from rape and to save the city from invasion. In another midrash we are presented with Judith, a virgin (*betulah* in Hebrew)

who slays Seleukos, a conquering Gentile king of Jerusalem. In this version Judith states that she is "impure," or menstruating, and she is granted permission to perform a ritual immersion and to move freely about the camp. It is under this cover that she first escapes the king's advances and later is able sneak past the guards with his head.

In the tenth-century Anglo-Saxon poem *Judith* the poet constructs a Judith figure who is a conflation of a saint and an Anglo-Saxon heroine. It is generally believed that the poem was sung at banquets given by kings and nobility. Of interest to scholars are the radical changes the poet makes to the apocryphal biblical account. Judith's sexuality and seductive powers are written out of the narrative. Judith's faith endows her with the strength to slay Holofernes; however, the fact that a woman has slain Holofernes is not emphasized. Both Christian and pagan elements are added to the poem: a prayer in which Judith invokes the Trinity is included, as is a battle in which the Hebrew warriors triumph over the Assyrians. It is only after the army triumphs that Judith is celebrated by her people. The tale has been compared to medieval hagiography because Holofernes' lust and malice turn to folly, and Judith's chastity and faith are instrumental in sending Holofernes to a Christian hell.

Popular ballads preserved and retold the apocryphal account of Judith's adept manipulation of Holofernes' desire. According to Edna Purdie, the Early Middle High German *Judith* (or *ältere Judith*), dating from about the eleventh century, was probably sung by a *Spielmann*, a type of wandering balladeer. The action of the poem is located in Bathania, which resembles a medieval German town. Central to the drama is Holofernes' immediate and overwhelming desire for Judith and Judith's active manipulation of this desire. It is Judith and not Holofernes who suggests a *Brutlouf*, a kind of feast that often signals the enemy's impending defeat in Germanic tales. After Judith steals Holofernes' sword, she prays on behalf of the town. It is the intervention and direction of an angel that is emphasized at the conclusion of the ballad rather than Judith's faith or action.

In late-medieval literature Judith comes to represent a certain ambivalence toward women assuming political power. She also represents the potential of love and desire to bring down men of might. Christine de Pizan extols Judith's power and wisdom in *The City of Ladies* and argues that Judith's story supports the inclusion of women in the political sphere. In "The Tale of Melibeus" Chaucer uses Judith to portray Good Counsel, while in "The Monk's Tale" he depicts Holofernes as a great man seduced by a clever woman. In an effort to warn men against the power of love, Petrarch portrays Holofernes alongside Samson in his poem "Triumph of Love."

See also: Jewish Tradition

—Sandra H. Tarlin

Knight

K **night.** A member of a social class with roots in the eleventh century; a heroic figure in romance and chronicle.

The English word *knight* comes from the Old English *cniht*, meaning "young man" or "warrior." In Anglo-Saxon England to be a young man was almost by definition to be a warrior. In Germany at that period the situation was much the same, and the German *knecht* applied to the same broad category. Before the twelfth century these terms applied to farming men as much as to the nobility.

Knighthood in the form we now recognize it began in France in the ninth century and flourished throughout Europe in the twelfth and thirteenth centuries. The French word for knight is *chevalier*, which (like the Spanish *caballero* and the Italian *cavaliere*) literally signifies one who fights *à cheval* (on horseback). The designation of a "horseback" warrior indicates the formation of a noble warrior class, distinct from the farmer foot soldiers who, now defined by their work instead of their role in warfare, came to be known as peasants.

In the chaos that followed the collapse of the Carolingian Empire, mounted warriors were among the few authorities in France, and though they would defend the peasants against outside attacks, they were oppressive rulers. They ruled by force of arms and got most of what they wanted through violence—robbery, assault, torture, or rape. They fought one another constantly, struggling for wealth and power and pursuing personal vendettas. They did not become a well-defined class with a code of courtesy until two centuries later.

In the eleventh century, with what is often called the medieval peace movement, these brave but ruthless warriors began to be defined as upholders of the law and protectors of the weak. Many were beginning to tire of living in a state of continual war and to wish for the security that a measure of peace might bring. The Church, whose unarmed officers were often victims of their violent attacks, brokered the first agreements to limit personal war and reduce the targets of violence. The Peace of God, arranged by various French Church councils in the late tenth and early eleventh centuries and achieved with immense difficulty, outlawed attacks on unarmed peasants, clerics, and other helpless victims. Once the warrior chiefs agreed to this measure, they found themselves in the position of working together to enforce it. Since few others had either the might or the authority to do so, warriors had to police one another and to control the unregenerate robber barons among them. Thus, the ideal of a brotherhood of warriors, united to enforce justice, came into being. The Truce of God (beginning c. 1040), which limited personal war to certain days of the week, enjoyed less success because most warriors were not yet ready to obey it. What helped solve that problem was the crusading movement, which, beginning in the late eleventh century, effectively redirected the chevaliers' blood lust away from one another and toward the Muslims in the Holy Land.

Around this time an elite, somewhat unified class of mounted warriors began to call themselves knights. The original purpose of the High Order of Knighthood, as it developed through the Peace of God and the Crusades, was best articulated by the English cleric John of Salisbury in 1159:

> What purpose does ordained knighthood serve? To protect the church, to battle against disloyalty, to honour the office of the priesthood, to put an end to injustice towards the poor, to bring peace to the land, to let his own blood be spilled for his brothers, and, if necessary, to give up his own life.

When a young man who qualified for knighthood came of age, he went through an increasingly elaborate ceremony, whose most important feature was the transfer of arms, especially the sword, usually from an older knight to the young initiate. When the young man received the sword, he vowed to use it for appropriate purposes, as defined by his role as *justicier*, including the defense of Holy Church, as well as the weak and helpless, including widows, orphans, and the poor. In the early days, after presenting the sword the older knight would strike the candidate across the face. In the later Middle Ages this blow—known as "dubbing"—developed into a light, symbolic touch on the shoulder with the flat of the sword. Originally, however, it was a hard slap or even a box to the ear, which the young man had to take without flinching or retaliating.

As the dubbing ceremony developed, and with the Peace of God and the Crusades, the making of a knight began to acquire the character of a religious ritual. During the eleventh century medieval writers began to speak of "ordaining" instead of simply "making" a knight. By the twelfth century the blessing of the sword had become an essential part of the ceremony, and newly ordained knights were receiving their arms directly from the hand of a cleric. In the late Middle Ages the religious component increased. Candidates began to hold vigils the night before their dubbing and to pray over their armor in preparation for their knighting.

From this creative fusion of Christian and warrior ethos came the code of conduct that we know as chivalry. At the height of its influence, from the mid-twelfth to the late thirteenth centuries, the chivalric ideal had manifested itself in three distinct types. All are distinguished by firm loyalty, but they differ in the objects of their loyalty. The oldest type is the *miles Christi* (soldier of

Christ). Born of the crusading movement and represented in literature by Galahad (among others), the *miles Christi* was defined by his devotion to God and the Church. This was the ideal that John of Salisbury described. It also inspired the founding of the military religious orders, such as the Templars and Hospitallers, and it gained influence as the importance of these orders increased. The second type, which developed somewhat later, exemplified ideal knighthood as a feudal institution: the "warrior knight" is always ready for battle, not for God but for his lord or king. In literature, the knights of the Round Table, who never refuse a challenge and undertake quests for the glory of King Arthur, are warrior knights. The third type, with whom most modern readers are familiar, is the lady's knight, sometimes called the gallant knight. The lady's knight, represented by Chrétien de Troyes's Lancelot, Erec, and Yvain, among others, incorporates another ideal, that of idealized, "courtly" love, in which the lover stands in quasi-feudal or even quasi-religious subjection to the lady. In this respect the gallant knight mimics the other two types. All his brave deeds, which the lady inspires, are for her glory rather than the glory of God or king. The extent to which this noble (courtly) ideal influenced the real conduct of knights toward women is, of course, a matter of some debate. While no one claims that knights consistently treated women with the reverence depicted in courtly literature, it would be equally absurd to assume that the gallant ideal had no influence at all. Noble women particularly, who were part of knightly society, exerted considerable power and were entitled to the respect of their husbands' retainers.

Social Context

The word *miles*, usually employed in medieval Latin to signify a knight, originally had no class implications. However, as already mentioned, from the ninth century forward warfare was dominated by trained mounted warriors, who furthermore assumed the cost of arming themselves as well as breeding and training their horses. Because of the time and expense involved, only those with considerable landed wealth could fight on horseback. By the eleventh century knighthood became synonymous with landed nobility, and *miles* therefore came to signify a member of the ruling class.

Because the idea of knighthood developed before the nobility had been defined as a legal class, the qualifications for it underwent some evolution. When the dubbing ritual began, any knight could perform it and thereby "make" another knight. However, in the twelfth century the French "knightly class" (knights and descendants of knights) became concerned about an increasingly wealthy group of urban tradesmen who might acquire the means to become chevaliers and therefore the social equals of the old nobility.

Knighthood had become an important part of what separated them from the rest of society, and those who wished to keep it an exclusive club changed the law to the effect that only a man whose father or grandfather had been a knight could become one himself. *Miles* by this time had strong class connotations and had come to replace *nobilis* as the preferred term for what was now a ruling warrior class. By the later Middle Ages nobility throughout Continental Europe meant the hereditary right to be knighted, whether or not one exercised that right.

In England, however, the legal definition of knighthood developed differently. Because of the small number of knights in Norman England and the imperial ambitions of the Plantagenet kings who succeeded the Normans in 1154, as many military captains as possible were needed. Therefore, the royal government began "distraint of knighthood" (i.e., requiring anyone whose land yielded a certain income to formally accept knighthood and the military obligations it entailed). Thus, knighthood in England came to be defined by income, rather than birth, as it was in the older Continental systems.

The everyday life of knights is difficult to reconstruct, since literature tends to focus on the important events rather than the daily routines. Chivalric romances create the impression that a typical knight's life consisted of a string of adventures, courtly festivals, and amorous intrigues. Given the responsibilities that we know knights had—to be available to serve their lords and administer their own estates—this image cannot be accurate. Nevertheless, some of the common features of romances—the young knight leaving the court to seek adventure, the quest for spiritual salvation, and sublimated, idealized, "courtly" love—may have had a basis in the realities of knightly life.

Only one son could inherit the father's land and castle, and even before the establishment of strict primogeniture that son was normally the eldest. Younger sons were often not permitted to marry because the establishment of several sons as heads of households would mean dividing the estate. The sons who did not inherit the castle frequently went to live in the lord's castle, where they lived in dormitory-like arrangements with other knights in the lord's service. With a large number of restless, competitive, hot-headed young warriors living in close proximity, tensions were inevitable, and many of the journeys, hunts, and formal displays of prowess, such as jousts, in which knights participated may have been designed to manage this tension. In addition, newly made knights were often sent on tours for as long as two years, probably for the purpose of spending some of their youthful enthusiasm before they entered the lord's service. When romances refer to a young knight leaving the court to seek adventure and prove his manhood, they may be referring to this practice.

The quest for the Holy Grail has a real-life analog in the Crusades. Prior to the crusading movement, a layperson generally sought salvation indirectly by donating to a religious community, in exchange for which the monks would pray for his soul. The new definition of *miles Christi* that emerged during the Crusades gave warriors a way to obtain salvation for themselves while practicing their own profession. The great Cistercian promoter of the Crusades, Bernard of Clairvaux, wrote with pride of the many criminals and potential criminals who, through the crusading movement, had become soldiers of Christ. It is surely no coincidence that the most famous of the French prose Grail romances, *La queste del saint Graal,* was written by a Cistercian monk at the height of the crusading movement.

Finally, the much-debated phenomenon of courtly love may be explicable in the context of numerous rival warriors living in the same castle. A modern reader may have difficulty seeing why it might actually be in the interest of the lord of the castle to have the knights who resided there desire his wife. However, the lady in courtly literature is often unattainable, and this fact does not prevent the knight from loving her. On the contrary, it increases his passion and allows his idealized image of her to remain intact. More important from the lord's point of view, it had the potential to inspire young men to great feats of arms—for the glory of the lady, but certainly also to the advantage of the lord. The lady of the castle was a natural object for the admiration and even devotion of the many unmarried young men who benefited from her munificence. Because the rules of courtly love demanded irreproachable knightly conduct in the lover, it could also limit the violence resulting from rivalries off the battlefield. Knights did occasionally succeed in absconding with the wives of their lords, but this was uncommon, and the benefits to the lord of inspired but well-behaved soldiers may have been worth the risks.

The Role of Chivalric Ideals in the Life of the Nobility

The extent to which the chivalric code governed the conduct of actual knights has been the subject of much controversy. No one, of course, would claim that knights consistently lived up to their vows. Perfect knights are almost as rare in literature as they must have been in life, and numerous antichivalric texts attest to the failure of knights to live up to their own code of conduct. The question is whether this code ever had an application to real life and when, if ever, it ceased to have one. In other words, was the knightly code ever a practical guide to handling real situations, or was it entirely the stuff of romances, festivals, and courtly displays? Lee Patterson has outlined the three major positions that scholars have taken on this subject, and they follow a rather unusual pattern: instead of becoming more

skeptical over time about the usefulness of chivalry, they become less so. First, Johan Huizinga argued that chivalry was always an act and only got its practitioners into trouble when they tried seriously to live by it. For Huizinga the only difference between the chivalry of the fifteenth century and chivalry at its "height" (in the twelfth and thirteenth centuries) is that in the later period the nobility could no longer pretend to take it seriously. Thus, chivalric displays became more elaborate and stylized—more obviously playacting. Later, Arthur Ferguson softened this position by claiming that chivalry did at one time have a practical purpose, but that it ceased to have one in the later Middle Ages because of political and social changes that were in the process of transforming medieval Europe into Renaissance Europe. Finally, Malcolm Vale argued that the chivalric code continued to be of practical use through the end of the Middle Ages. He cited the importance that heavy cavalry continued to have in warfare and the influence of chivalric values on later codes of conduct. Most scholars agree that the knightly code continued to affect the values, if not the conduct, of the aristocracy in Europe long after the end of feudalism and that even in modern times it retains its power as an ideal.

See also: Chrétien de Troyes; Courtly Love; Knights Templar; Romance; Tournament

—Leigh Smith

Knights Templar. An order of religious knights similar in origin to such other groups as the Knights of Saint John (Hospitallers) and the Teutonic Knights.

The Knights Templar were one of several organizations, or orders, of religious knights that developed in the Holy Land during the era of the Crusades. However, the Templars became the best known through their spectacular successes—and also through the even more spectacular nature of their demise. In the last years of the eleventh century Western Europeans under the leadership of Godfrey of Bouillon had waged the First Crusade, which culminated in the recapture of Jerusalem, in 1099. By the second decade of the twelfth century the Knights Templar had developed informally into a group of French knights dedicated to protecting pilgrims traveling on the dangerous highway between the port of Jaffa and Jerusalem. Under their leader, Hugues de Payens, the Knights received the patronage of King Baldwin II of Jerusalem and were granted quarters near the site of Solomon's Temple. The Knights professed chastity and obedience to the Patriarch of Jerusalem; they would eventually, with papal permission, assume a white garment emblazoned with a red cross.

At the Council of Troyes in 1128 the Templars received official Church recognition and the attention of Bernard of Clairvaux. In *De laude novae militiae* (In Praise of the New Military

Order) Bernard devised a rule for the Templars. *De laude* answered the thorny question of how a religious order, traditionally barred from shedding blood, could bear the sword. Bernard argued that the religious knight "is the instrument of God, for the punishment of malefactors, and for the defence of the just. Indeed, when he kills a malefactor, this is not homicide but malicide—the destruction of evil. Consequently, by carrying out such an act, the knight is accounted Christ's legal executioner against evildoers."

A bull published by Pope Innocent II in 1139 made the Templars solely answerable to the Holy See. The order grew in numbers and was organized into ten provinces stretching from Jerusalem to Hungary to Portugal.

Over the course of the next two centuries the Templars became involved in crusader conflicts with the Muslim kingdoms surrounding Jerusalem. The Templars' aid to King Louis VII of France during the Second Crusade in 1147 exemplifies the nature of such entanglements. Templar fortresses and manors were built not only in the Middle East and in Saracen-threatened Spain but also in Cyprus and in many parts of Europe. In 1291 the Templars formed part of the Christian forces defeated at Acre, the last major Christian stronghold. After the fall of Acre the order moved its headquarters to Cyprus.

Though individual members committed themselves to poverty, the wealth of the Templars grew through donations by benefactors. With their increasing wealth, Templars became personal bankers to various rulers. Henry II of England entrusted the Templars with the money paid in recompense for Archbishop Thomas Becket's murder. The Templars lent funds to Louis VII for the Second Crusade, and eventually the Templar headquarters in Paris became the de facto royal treasury of France.

Inevitably stories of Templar arrogance in the face of their visible wealth tainted the reputation of the order. William of Tyre instigated clerical opposition to the Templars at the Third Lateran Council in 1179. William claimed that the Templars had sold an Egyptian convert to Christianity to the Egyptian authorities for a huge sum of money. It was also alleged that the political terrorists known as the Assassins had been on the verge of converting to Christianity, but the Templars had intervened, lest they lose tribute money from the Assassins. Pope Innocent III cited the order for pride and for abuse of papal exemption in 1207. In 1265 Pope Clement IV echoed the accusations of pride. Similar complaints were lodged against the Hospitallers. Despite an uncooperative rivalry that emerged at times between the Templars and the Hospitallers, prominent knights such as Ramon Lull of Catalonia called for a union between the two military orders for the purpose of advancing the faith against Islam more effectively.

The long-standing relationship between France and the Templars was strained by King Philip IV's increasing opposition to papal influence within his realm. While many Templars (including the grand master, Jacques de Molay) were French, and the order provided crucial financial services to the French crown, the Knights owed their final allegiance to the pope. The king desired greater control over the appointment of bishops and control of Church property, and he had also put pressure on Clement V to establish a residence in Avignon, which was not actually part of the kingdom of France but was closer to Philip's sphere of influence than to Rome.

It is not completely clear which of the king's inclinations toward the Templars played the larger part in motivating his final drastic action against them: whether he was moved by the piety he professed as befitting the most Christian king of France or driven by his desire for a possible transfer of Templar properties to France's guardianship and enrichment. Irrespective of his motives, however, on the morning of October 13, 1307, the king's officers arrested members of the Templars throughout France.

The "supremely abominable crimes" of which they were accused included denial of Christ, obscene ritual kisses, homosexual acts, and idolatry. By the following year these charges had been formalized and expanded into 127 articles, including among them new charges alleging their disbelief in the sacraments, the practice of lay absolution, the existence of sinister secrets, and rampant greed. Surviving depositions show the Templars admitting to such behaviors as spitting and urinating on the cross and kissing their brethren not only on the mouth (a standard part of the Templar reception ceremony) but also on the lower back and anus.

It was further alleged that they were being encouraged to commit sodomy (one knight claimed three encounters with Jacques de Molay himself in a single night), to worship and adore cats and a certain other idol, and to desecrate the host at mass. Though it was never discovered, this other idol was said by some to have been a head—perhaps that of Hugues de Payens himself. Accusations of witchcraft, sodomy, and heresy were linked in the popular imagination at this time; Catharist heretics and Jews were victims of denunciations broadly similar to those leveled at the Templars.

Pope Clement V was skeptical of the charges; however, he eventually commissioned papal inquiries to hear confessions. The zealous Philip IV urged other kings to arrest and interrogate the Templars in their jurisdictions, but such monarchs as Edward I of England and Juan I of Aragon displayed even more skepticism and delay than did the pope. Torture was not permitted under English or Aragonese law, and it took the intervention of the pope to implement it. Most of the confessions on record were probably made under torture or the threat of it, for in places where torture was slow in coming or non-existent, few confessions were extracted. Although defenders came forward among the Templars in France, in 1310, 54 Templars were burned at the stake for their alleged crimes. At the Council of Vienne in 1312–1313 the pope finally suppressed the order. Jacques de Molay and other Templar leaders were executed by burning in 1314, even though they persisted in adhering to their retractions of their original confessions of guilt. Their property was to be dispersed to the Hospitallers (except in the Iberian kingdoms), but what transfers took place were diminished by delay and by the expenses demanded by the French crown and others.

A sometimes outlandish interest in the Templars began to develop in the eighteenth century, particularly in France and Germany. In these countries the Templars were connected with the developing legends of Freemasonry, and they were seen as champions of a secret and benevolent wisdom in the face of ecclesiastical corruption. Complex nineteenth- and twentieth-century conspiracy theories (such as that of the Abbé Barruel) have placed the Templars in a conspiratorial chain of esoteric knowledge stretching from the Manichaeans to the Jacobin-led Freemasons of the French Revolution. The legends of the Templars have far outgrown their relatively brief historical involvement in the faith and politics of Western Europe.

See also: Homosexuality (male); Knight; Witchcraft

—Graham N. Drake

*L*ear, King. Central figure of one of Shakespeare's greatest tragedies, a story deriving from Geoffrey of Monmouth's *Historia regum Britanniae* (History of the Kings of Britain), and also popular in many postmedieval folktales.

In Geoffrey's *Historia* (c. 1138) the aging King Lear, with three daughters but no sons to inherit his kingdom, declares that he will give his kingdom to the daughter who loves him most. The two oldest daughters declare infinite love for him, but Cordelia, the youngest, simply insists that she loves him as a daughter loves a father. Lear divides the kingdom between Goneril and Regan and exiles Cordelia. Soon the two older daughters begin treating him shamefully. Lear seeks out Cordelia, who has married the king of France, and Cordelia's husband helps him regain the crown of Britain. Cordelia and her husband inherit the throne.

Shakespeare's version—which came to him through an intermediary source, probably *Holinshed's Chronicles*—follows Geoffrey's fairly closely but lacks the happy ending; instead, Cordelia is killed through treachery as Lear attempts to regain his kingdom. Lear then dies of grief.

In the postmedieval folktale "Love Like Salt" (AT 923), the action parallels Geoffrey of Monmouth more closely than Shakespeare. A father drives his daughter from his home because she says she loves him like salt. The heroine undergoes many trials and adventures—which often follow the plot of the famous tale of "Cinderella" (AT 510). Finally returning home, she serves her father unsalted meat to demonstrate that love like salt is something special, and the two are happily reconciled.

Geoffrey's story is sometimes held to be a Welsh traditional tale associated with the hero Llyr, whose name has been seen as underlying Lear. In the Four Branches of the Mabinogi, Llyr is the father of Bran, Branwen, and Manawydan, and though his own genealogy and family relationships can be deduced from some other references, there are no narratives extant about him. He may, however, be the same as the Llyr Llediaith, called in the Triads "one of the three exalted prisoners of the Island of Britain" on account of his imprisonment by Euroswydd. *Llyr* occurs as a common noun, "sea," and the Welsh hero is probably the counterpart of the Irish Lér, the seagod and father of Manannán. Geoffrey of Monmouth refers to Leir as the eponymous founder of Leicester (Legrecestra, Lerechestria). The Welsh name of the city is Caerlyr and it was natural, therefore, for the Welsh translators of the *Historia* to use the familiar form Llyr for the Latin Leir, but they do not add any material relating to the native Llyr to their translations. The story may have a traditional basis, but there seems to be no reason for claiming this version or the name Lear as one of Geoffrey's putative Welsh sources.

See also: Geoffrey of Monmouth; Triads of the Island of Britain

—Brynley F. Roberts

Legend. A historicized and localized traditional oral prose narrative presented as a true account, often centering on a supernatural or other extraordinary occurrence.

Legends express the collective values and beliefs of the group to whose tradition they belong. Medieval authors frequently used legends, incorporating them into the framework of larger works and occasionally changing them from prose to versified accounts. Legends from the medieval oral traditions are represented primarily in texts, although material enactments of legends in diverse forms such as paintings, manuscript illuminations, pictorial monuments, and tapestries are commonplace.

The English term *legend* is a source of potential confusion for international scholars, since it can be easily mistaken for the Latin term *legenda*. The German word for legend, *Sage*, and its Scandinavian cognates—for example, Danish *sagn*—are all related to the Old English *secgan*, "to say," and thus maintain the sense of orality that is a primary feature of the genre. In contrast, *legenda* (meaning "that which should be read") refers to literary compositions—saints' lives and other hagiographic writings. These literary works, which relate the biographies of religious figures and focus on miraculous episodes, were intended to be read during the religious offices on a specific saint's day. Because of the focus on supranormal events, authors of *legendae* made frequent use of legends in their compositions. Thus, it is not uncommon for similar events to be attributed to different figures in the saints' lives.

The Grimm brothers were among the first folklorists to define the legend, suggesting in the introduction to *Deutsche Sagen*, their 1816 collection of German legends, that "the märchen [fictional folktale] is more poetic, the legend is more historical." The view of legends as being historically true has informed a great deal of the scholarship on the genre. Most early studies of legend sought to isolate the historical kernel of the accounts. Consequently, individual episodes about named people in medieval texts often came under close scrutiny in an attempt to discover the "true" events embedded within the texts. However, Jan Vansina and other scholars have suggested that legends often do not represent accurate recordings of historical events. Rather, the value of the legends as historical documents may lie in their ability to reflect the social and cultural environment of the tellers. Thus, legends provide useful ethnographic information. Since legends have also been inscribed in the archival record by a medieval author, the study of which legends are chosen to be recorded and how they are used may also reveal aspects of the social and cultural conditions surrounding the literary composition of the work.

Axel Olrik attempted to build a closed generic system describing the forms of the legend, all of which were governed by his "epic laws" in folklore composition. By examining nineteenth-century folklore collections and medieval source materials he developed the categories "lay," "saga," and "legend," among others. Olrik placed two major forms within the saga category: the heroic saga, which was a presumably historical account (such as the Icelandic sagas), and the folktale, which was a fictional account. He reserved the term *legend* for short, mono-episodic accounts that were performed conversationally. He divided legend, in turn, into two main categories: origin legends and anecdotes. Olrik's system reveals the numerous genres of folklore that often were incorporated into medieval texts. Later modifications of the system by scholars such as Carl Wilhelm von Sydow reveal the interplay between genres in oral tradition.

Legend is typically a highly localized narrative and has been characterized as highly oikotypified—that is, highly reflective of local conditions. Von Sydow introduced the concept of oikotypes (ecotypes) to explain differences between similar folk expressions collected from disparate tradition groups. Tale tellers change a narrative to fit their social and geographic environments. Authors of medieval texts also changed the narratives to fit their needs whether they received the story from oral sources, written sources, or a combination of the two. These two processes of variation—variation in the oral tradition and variation within the written record—account in part for some of the interesting disjunctures between individual episodes in different medieval versions of the same story. One can find examples of this type of variation in the Tristan romances by Béroul, Thomas of Britain, and Gottfried von Strassburg, as well as in the Old Norse–Icelandic *Tristrams saga ok Isöndar*.

The events narrated in legends are related to particular places. The extreme localization of the account in turn adds to the believability of the account. According to Robert A. Kaske, *Sir Gawain and the Green Knight* includes a noteworthy example of such extreme localization in the detailed description of the Green Chapel where Sir Gawain and his adversary are to meet. In this case, the medieval author has apparently localized the traditional account to an area well known to the local audience.

Just as events in legends are linked to specific places, they are also frequently linked to specific people. The inclusion of known individuals in the legend contributed in large part to the view that it represented a truthful recording of a historical event. However, identical stories with different named *dramatis personae* appear time and again throughout the medieval corpus. Thus, the murder of King Aethelberht (d. 794) in the hagiographic texts concerning Mildrith is part of a tradition of stories concerning murdered royal saints. The medieval legend teller and the medieval author in turn not only alter place names and topographic features to fit the geographic (synchronic) needs of the work but also adapt the personages in the legends or legend texts to fit the historical (diachronic) needs of the work.

In an interesting study of medieval legends and their contemporary analogs, Shirley Marchalonis shows how legends from medieval texts are "updated" to fit the demands of modern culture in contemporary tradition. This process of variation can be referred to as "historicization," and it requires a modification of the Grimms' original characterization of legend. Legend is not a historical narrative but, rather, a historicized narrative.

An important characteristic of legend is its narrative form: a legend tells a story. The minimal requirement for a narrative is that it must include a temporal sequence: X then Y. This distinction helps separate legend from many other oral traditions prevalent during the medieval period, including genealogies, charms, proverbs, descriptions of local phenomena, and other non-narrative genres of folklore that also were frequently included in medieval texts. Medieval authors, however, did not always record entire legend texts. Instead, they could refer to legend tradition. While a genealogy, such as the one from the opening of *Egil's Saga*, may or may not have been part of an oral tradition, the mention of Kveld-Ulf's great strength, sagacity, and ability to change shape certainly reference various legend accounts: "There was a man called Ulf the Dauntless. Ulf was such a big and strong man that he had no equals.... He could give good advice in all matters for he was very wise.... He was sleepy in the evening, and it was rumored that he must be a great shape-changer."

Medieval scholars refer to "legend cycles." Perhaps one of the best is the Sigurd cycle, the basis for the *Nibelungenlied*, *Völsunga Saga*, and numerous Eddic poems. Often these groups of legends are referred to as if they were a single legend with locutions such as "the legend of Sigurd." Legend does not typically include multiple episodes; rather, it relates to a single event. Therefore, it may be more accurate to speak of "the legends about Sigurd." Medieval compositions frequently include several legends that have been written so as to refer to the same individual, thereby constructing a multi-episodic account of an individual or individuals that may or may not have been extant in oral tradition.

Despite the brevity of the mono-episodic legend account, its form is extremely elastic. Legend can be contracted or expanded in the medieval text depending on the requirements of the composition. Such expansion and contraction mirrors the form of legend in oral circulation, often serving rhetorical purposes. While medieval scholars interested in developing stemmata (genealogies of manuscripts) engage in the comparison of episodes from the various redactions, the mutability of legend makes such studies problematic, since one cannot necessarily determine the relative compositional age of episodes through the examination of the episode's complexity. The medieval text is not immutable, and it was under narrative pressure from both the written tradition and the oral tradition.

One of the most frequent uses of legends in medieval representations is to explain empirically observable phenomena, such as why a certain geographical feature is the way it is or why a church is built where it is. Legends were also used to "teach," as evidenced by their frequent use in exempla. Thus, the story known to early-twenty-first-century scholars as "The Spider in the Hairdo" appears in a late-thirteenth-century collection of English exempla:

> There is a sermon story of a certain lady of Eynesham ... who took so long over the adornment of her hair that she used to arrive at church barely before the end of Mass. One day, "the devil descended upon her head in the form of a spider, gripping with its legs," until she well-nigh died of fright. Nothing would remove the offending insect ... until the local abbot displayed the holy sacrament before it. (G.R. Owst, *Preaching in Medieval England* [1926], p. 170)

Certain events were so traumatic in medieval society that they spawned numerous tales. Perhaps the greatest ecological crisis of late-medieval Europe was the Black Death, which ravaged most of Europe in the mid-fourteenth century. Legends of the plague—how it arrived, and the aftermath of its indiscriminate killing—proliferated, as evidenced by contemporaneous accounts of the plague. Five hundred years later one could still collect legends about the plague throughout Europe. For example, the nineteenth-century Danish folklorist Evald Tang Kristensen collected numerous plague legends from the rural Danish population, including:

> After the Black Death, all of the people in two towns had died out. Then there was a dog which ran from the one town to the other every day, and when it was investigated, it turned out that it was nursing and taking care of a child which was still alive in the other town.

Repeated epidemics reinforced the need for these stories and guaranteed their longevity in tradition.

Legend was not only recorded in texts by medieval authors but was also reenacted in art and other material forms. One of the best-known works of art from medieval France, the Bayeux Tapestry, enacts pictorially, with occasional captions, the story of William of Normandy's quest for the throne of England. In scene 17 of the tapestry Duke Harold pulls men from the quicksand near Mont-Saint-Michel. The scene is accompanied by the short title "Hic Harold Dux trahebat eos de arena" [Here Duke Harold pulled them from the sand]. Here a legend about a supernatural feat of strength is enacted pictorially. In the composition, the tapestry weaver relied on a believable, mono-episodic, highly localized, and historicized oral account—a legend—of Duke Harold's remarkable feat. In turn, the episode is incorporated into the larger work narrating William's quest for the throne.

Many medieval authors and artists can be considered among the earliest collectors of folklore. Medieval legend exists only in their works as written or pictorial representations, offering us a snapshot of what was apparently a rich and vibrant oral tradition. Legends collected after the Middle Ages often resonate well with records from the medieval materials, but they exhibit key characteristics of legend—localization, historicization, and an expression of the values and beliefs of the tradition participants—that make them expressions of the people from whom they were collected. Although one finds a strong continuity between medieval legends and more contemporary expressions, it is not fruitful to speak of "survivals." Rather, one can look at how the legends are used in the different periods to understand the values and beliefs of the tradition participants contemporaneous to the legend recordings.

Legend as Debate

Legends tend to circulate in variants that represent different individuals' and communities' views on the truth and specifics of the story. Because contrasting views are typical of the genre, the legend often unfolds as a debate or incorporates aspects of debate as participants taking different stands present their varied opinions and evidence. In his preface to the first printed edition of Thomas Malory's *Le Morte Darthur* (1485), William Caxton presents an account of just such a legend debate. He states that he considered the story of Arthur false and unworthy of being published until various of his friends came forward with arguments and evidence persuading him that Arthur had actually lived. To those who wanted him to publish Arthur's deeds, says Caxton,

> I answered that diverse men hold opinion that there was no such Arthur.... Whereto they answered, and one in special said, that there were many evidences of the contrary. First, you may see his [tomb] in the monastery of Glastonbury.... And in diverse

places of England many remembrances ... of him ...; in the castle of Dover you may see Gawain's skull and Cradok's mantel; at Winchester, the Round Table; in other places Lancelot's sword and many other things. Then, all these things considered, there can no man reasonably gainsay but there was a king of this land named Arthur.

Similarly, near the end of his tale of Arthur, Malory refers to the debate over Arthur's final fate:

Yet some men say in many parts of England that King Arthur is not dead, but [was taken] by the will of our Lord Jesus into another place; and men say that he shall come again and win the Holy Cross. Yet I will not say that it shall be so, but rather I would say: here in this world he changed his life. (Both selections from Sir Thomas Malory, *Works*, ed. E. Vinaver, 2nd ed. [1967], with spelling modernized)

Such debates are signs of the power and vitality of legends, as well as indicators of how dramatically they may change in perspective and content from telling to telling.

Because legends often test the limits of belief, their subject matter is very nearly limitless and will vary in accordance with the beliefs of each teller and community. Tales flatly labeled fantasies by most modern readers were told as belief tales in certain medieval contexts. For example, the twelfth-century Welshman Gerald of Wales tells of a 12-year-old boy who, one day in the woods, encountered "two tiny men ... no bigger than pygmies," who led him through a tunnel in the earth into a rich and beautiful but dark country, without sun or stars. He made friends with the tiny inhabitants and frequently came and went. He told his mother about this otherworld, and she told him to steal some of the gold that "was extremely common in that country." The boy ran home with a golden ball, but the tiny men caught up with him and took it back and disappeared with it. From that day forward, the boy could never again find the entrance to that magic land (Gerald of Wales, *The Journey through Wales*, trans. L. Thorpe [1978], pp. 133-36).

Many twentieth-century scholars have labeled his story a märchen, a fictional folk narrative filled with magical elements. But as told by Gerald, the tale clearly shades into legend. Gerald introduces it by suggesting that he can identify the approximate time and place and perhaps the exact person involved: "Somewhat before our time, an odd thing happened in these parts. The priest Elidyr always maintained that he was the person concerned." At the end of the tale Gerald debates with himself over its truthfulness: "If I reject [the account], I place a limit on God's power, and that I will never do. If I say that I believe it, I

have the audacity to move beyond the bounds of credibility, and that I will not do either." Others believe this tale, and even though Gerald refuses to commit himself, he participates in the transmission and continuing life of a legend by retelling it and pondering its believability.

See also: Black Death; Exemplum; Folktale; Saints, Cults of the

—Timothy R. Tangherlini

Lesbians. Women who elected other women as affectional or sexual partners.

Women who had partners of the same sex in the Middle Ages have been studied very little in comparison to men, and not until recently. While medieval folklore per se does not appear to be a major source for understanding dissident sexuality among women, some key texts that concern their history contain folkloric motifs or pertain to folklife broadly conceived. Among the latter one might include historical documents (letters of pardon, chronicles, trial accounts) depicting same-sex relations among women from the peasantry or the artisan classes; however, these cases say little about folk tradition itself. Among the former one finds Etienne de Fougères' didactic treatise on women, the *Livre des manières,* which evokes women who have sex with other women. The learned and influential bishop's crude language belongs to a long-standing discourse on sexuality by French clerical writers who used the vernacular rather freely, interspersed with sexual punning and innuendo, a tradition that stretches from Guiot de Provins's *Bible moralisée* to Jean Molinet at the turn of the sixteenth century. Etienne de Fougères' tract derides women engaging in same-sex love, strikingly rendered in the motif of the hen who acts like a rooster, a motif echoed in the incompetent rooster who does not sing and does not chase the hens, setting itself for immediate slaughter (a story featured in the *Heptameron,* for instance).

Furthermore, the corpus of the French fabliaux includes many situations where gender-inappropriate behavior calls in question normative order, but same-sex acts are not mentioned. Several late-thirteenth- and fourteenth-century romances, such as *Yde et Olive, Roman de Silence,* and *Tristan de Nanteuil,* deal with same-sex desire among women only indirectly, although some have suggested a lesbian presence in them, while the figure of the man-woman who weds another woman stands out. There are many elements of folklore in these texts, and for *Tristan de Nanteuil* at least, a strong folkloric structure has been suggested.

The possibility that women could function sexually without men was a topic carefully eschewed by religious and secular authorities. When such acts were alluded to, they were likely to fall under the general rubric of *sodomy,* a term used in a variety of senses, from the narrow technical meaning (designating all anal sex, heterosexual or not), to a wider range of same-sex practices that did not involve anal contact. The construction of the category of sodomy goes beyond the scope of this entry, but it constitutes an important historical and theological background for understanding the very linguistic silences surrounding the lives of women who did not comply with heteronormativity. Culturally frightening possibilities that women might deviate from the established sexual and gender order cannot be separated from medieval medical doctrine, together with the enormous authority of the Aristotelian model, according to which women are physiologically and emotionally imperfect, incomplete, and approximate, albeit sexually brazen. The most important is that women's bodies contain the trappings of the male organs, but in a state of inadequacy or inversion (the internal spermatic sacs, inverted inside the body instead of being apparent on the outside), leading some, like Thomas Laqueur, to propose a "one-sex" model for the construction of sexuality before 1700.

The presence of "lesbians" and "lesbian" acts in the Middle Ages is still barely being decoded and unraveled from uncooperative bits of evidence. Moreover, the very project of speaking of "lesbianism" during the medieval period may be not only a terminological anachronism; it may also reflect the inability to transcend binary oppositions. Gender transgression and transference of same-sex eroticism to iconographic and literary motifs and to social and religious interactions might be more fruitful areas of inquiry. In this vein Karma Lochrie, for instance, has argued for a reading of a common late-medieval image, the wound of Christ, as a same-sex eroticized icon in the experience of female mysticism. Kathy Lavezzo has fruitfully applied the concept of homoeroticism to a deconstruction of the feminine in the life of the mystic Margery Kempe. Same-sex love between medieval women is presently the object of more research, as indicated by the essays edited by Francesca Canadé Sautman and Pamela Sheingorn.

See also: Homosexuality (male)

—Francesca Canadé Sautman

Lilith. A female demon, focus of numerous medieval folk narratives and folk beliefs.

Variations on the name *Lilith* appear as early as the second millennium B.C.E. in Sumerian and Babylonian magic texts, where Lilith is portrayed as a she-demon (or group of demons) with long hair and wings. The dual function of these demons—to seduce men in their sleep (thus being the cause of nocturnal emissions) and to kill newborn babies—persisted in all future appearances of this figure. In ancient Jewish literature, the Hebrew Bible, and rabbinic commentaries, there are clear evidences of the persistence of belief in Lilith. In the Hebrew Bible, there is one enigmatic passage (Isa. 34:14) in which the word *lilith* appears. However, it is difficult to know if it refers to a night owl or to a demon. In several instances in the Babylonian Talmud (fifth century C.E.), Lilith is mentioned as a winged demon with woman's face and long hair—a description that connects her to the ancient demonology of Mesopotamia.

In the Middle Ages a great intensification of the appearances and function of Lilith occurred. The most important and influential source was the Hebrew *Alphabet of Ben Sira*. This is an early collection of tales (ninth to tenth centuries) composed in the Jewish communities of Iraq and Iran. The story of Lilith here starts with the description of an amulet on which three mysterious winged figures are drawn and called by their names: Snwy, Snsnwy, Smnglf. The amulet was inscribed by the main hero of this composition—the child prodigy Ben Sira—and was to be used for saving the newborn son of the king of Babylon. When the king demands an explanation of these signs, Ben Sira tells him the story of Lilith: When God first created humans, he created them male and female, both from dust. The man was called Adam, the female Lilith. When they were about to perform the first sexual act, they started to quarrel about who would take the upper and the lower positions. When Lilith saw that the dispute could not be settled, she pronounced the great name of God and flew away, leaving Adam alone. He turned to God complaining about being alone, and God sent three angels—Snwy, Snsnwy, and Smnglf—to bring her back. They met her in the middle of the Red Sea, but she did not consent to return to Adam, as she knew she was created to harm human babies and to become the mother of the whole demonic race by becoming the devil's mate. The three angels forced Lilith to vow that she would not enter a room of a woman with a baby if she saw there an amulet with the form and names of these three angels.

It is clear from the form and style of this tale that it is an etiological myth that explains a very popular belief or custom, which is documented by archaeological findings in Iraq (e.g., in the late-antiquity and early-medieval Jewish settlement of Nippur). Hundreds of so-called magic bowls, complete or in fragments, were discovered in many locations. These round, terra-cotta plates were inscribed with magic formulas in Aramaic, the Jewish vernacular of the time. These artifacts were used as amulets, as protective artifacts for preventing malevolent demons from entering the house. One of the most popular names found there was that of Lilith, as well as variations of the names of the three angels. On some of these bowls, as part of the magic formula, was found a short narrative *(historiola)* about a woman who gave birth to 6 or 12 children. A male vampire-demon called Sideros (Greek: iron) or Gyllou (the Arabic *Ghūl*) devoured each one of them immediately after birth. When the woman was about to give birth to another child, she fled to a room or tower secured by iron gates that the demon could not penetrate. When the woman's three brothers (or saints)—Snwy, Snsnwy, and Smnglf—entered, attempting to help her, the demon entered with them in disguise and devoured the baby. The three brothers caught the demon in the middle of the sea and made her vomit up the babies and swear that she would not enter any place that was protected by their names.

This is one of the most widespread magical narratives in medieval Christian Europe (where the helpers are three saints), in Judaism (where the helper is Elijah the Prophet), and in Islam. We see here a perfect example of the close connections between belief, custom, material culture (form and meaning of amulets), and folk narrative.

The influence of the demonic figure of Lilith on medieval folklore was rich and varied. Some of the most popular amulets in medieval and early modern Jewish culture were those with the inscription, "Adam and Eve: Lilith Out!" accompanied by various drawings of three mysterious figures. Such amulets can be seen today in almost every Jewish ethnographic museum in the world.

In some narrative traditions Lilith was identified with another important figure of Jewish and Arabic folklore, the Queen of Sheba. From her earliest appearance in folk traditions, the queen has been described as semidemonic, but only her identification with Lilith labeled her as a temptress demon whose function is to attack men sexually. The Queen of Sheba's pilgrimage to Jerusalem to meet with King Solomon (1 Kings 10) becomes an attempt to seduce the strongest and wisest human being of the time, to kill him and so harm the whole human race. In the medieval Jewish mystical tradition of the Kabbalah, Lilith has an important role as the wife of Asmodai—the king of demons—one of the two most powerful beings of the realm of evil, and as the mother and ruler of the demonic kingdom. In some astrological expressions of the Kabbalah, Lilith is related to the planet Saturn, and all people with a melancholy disposition (the "black humor") are her descendants.

In world folklore Lilith appears under different names: in Arabic folklore she is known as the Karina al-Tab'ia, and in European folklore as the Lamia or Striga. In the famous legend about the female Pope Jutta or Johanna, accused of being a demon, the pope's grandmother is named Lilith.

Lilith has been interpreted in various ways. The dangers of birth, and the high percentage of death in the process, offer one explanation of the origin and popularity of these beliefs and narratives. Lilith may also be considered a psychological projection of the fears surrounding the dangers of childbirth, and the amulets may be seen as expressions of the need for emotional support. Another interpretation is connected to the sexual character of Lilith. She is the "other" woman—the dream girl that will never be realized; this is why, in most narratives and beliefs, Lilith appears to men in their sleep, as night fantasies. However, the feeling of guilt from these forbidden fantasy meetings enhances fears of dangerous consequences. One direct consequence is harm to babies, the legal offspring of the official ties with the legal, real wife; according to such interpretations, the psychological meaning of the female demon's devouring women's babies is rooted in envy. Another interpretation is the Jungian one, which connects Lilith with the dark, nocturnal side of the feminine existence (the Hebrew meaning of the word *lilith* is "the nocturnal one") and with other related archetypes.

See also: Childbirth; Vampire

—Eli Yassif

Loathly Lady. A monstrously ugly woman under enchantment (motif D732), who figures in medieval Irish, French, and English stories as well as in oral folktales of the twentieth century.

The plot shared by medieval and modern tales is classified AT 406A, "The Defeated King Regains the Throne." Although the oral tales (known principally in Poland) contain an episode, not found in medieval versions, in which a defeated king regains his kingdom with the help of the loathly lady, medieval and modern versions both contain these episodes: (1) An old woman appears suddenly in the woods at a moment of great discomfiture for the hero; (2) the hero makes a rash promise to the lady in return for her supernatural help; (3) the hero shows reluctance when he learns he must marry the hag; (4) the old woman changes into a young girl after being accepted by the hero in marriage. The transformation of the lady is closely associated with the motif of sovereignty, whether over a kingdom or in marriage. The youthful hero is tested by his willingness to accept the lady in all her loathsomeness. In return, she becomes young and fair and may also confer kingship of the realm upon him.

The medieval loathly lady tales are especially well known in their Irish and English variants, which form two distinct groups. In the Irish historical legends, including "The Adventures of the Sons of King Daire" (in the *Cóir Anmann* and *Metrical Dindshenchas*) and "The Adventures of the Sons of Eochaid Muigmedón," the loathly lady is Ériu, the Sovereignty of Ireland personified (motif Z116). She is of monstrous size and hideous demeanor, with rugged features suggesting the untamed land. The hero must prove his fitness as a ruler of Ireland by loving the hag in her ugliness, a task said to be difficult at first but goodly in the attainment, symbolized by the lady's transformation to a radiantly beautiful young woman.

In the Middle English romances, including Geoffrey Chaucer's "Wife of Bath's Tale" (c. 1390), sovereignty is associated with love and marriage. Only after the young husband grants mastery to his wife does she retain her fairer form. This reinterpretation of the sovereignty motif reflects the riddle found in the English tales: "What do women most desire?" The hero's marriage to the hag is the price for her correct answer to this riddle. Except for John Gower's "Tale of Florent" (c. 1390), the English poems are all set in Arthur's court. The tail-rhyme romance *The Wedding of Sir Gawain and Dame Ragnell* (c. 1450) and the related ballad "The Marriage of Sir Gawain" (ballad 31 in F. J. Child, *The English and Scottish Popular Ballads*) seem likely to have been presented in popular oral performances.

In all the English versions except Chaucer's, the loathly lady is described at great length. In *The Wedding of Sir Gawain*, for example, she looks "like a barrel": her cheeks are as wide as a woman's hips, her shoulders a yard broad, her pendulous breasts large enough to be a load for a horse.

Once the loathly lady has told the hero what women most desire, he must marry her. On their wedding night, she tells him that she has been under enchantment, but now married, she has regained the power to be fair by day and foul by night, or vice versa, and she asks the hero which way he would have her. The hero, then, must choose between the public esteem of a beautiful wife and his private enjoyment of her, a choice between love and honor. The knight cannot make up his mind and asks the lady to decide. Once she has been granted the sovereignty of choice, the spell is completely broken and she is beautiful both day and night.

Only "The Wife of Bath's Tale" varies the ending significantly. Here, the loathly lady asks the knight if he would have her beautiful and faithless or ugly and faithful, two conditions that mirror the life story of the fictional Wife of Bath herself as presented in Chaucer's *Canterbury Tales*. Just before telling her tale, the Wife has revealed that she has been married five times: as a beautiful young woman she had been faithless to her early husbands, but as an aging woman she was hopelessly attracted to her last. When the knight asks the lady to decide, she becomes both beautiful and faithful, creating a happy ending for the story as well as a fantasy solution for her own condition as an aging woman. In changing the question traditionally posed at the tale's end, Chaucer echoes the styles of oral artists who alter received plots to fit their personal purposes.

In 1299, nearly a century before the first surviving English loathly lady romance was written, a loathly lady appeared among the characters in an interlude performed at the court of Edward I. The costumed figure—decked out with donkey ears and an enormous nose—rode up to Edward's knights and demanded their help.

Efforts to trace the path of the loathly lady from Ireland to England have produced much speculation involving Norse, Scottish, Welsh, and French analogs. A plausible theory is that the tale was carried by Breton *conteurs* to France, possibly via Wales, along with the other Celtic tales that later became the Arthurian romances. Although loathly ladies appear in several Perceval romances, no clear parallels to the Irish and English traditions exist in French romance. A highland Scottish *märchen*, "The Daughter of King Underwaves," and a lowland Scottish ballad, "King Henry" (Child 32), illustrate the continuation of the tale within Celtic and English oral traditions. The loathly lady who visits King Helgi in *Hrolfs Saga kraka* provides a Norse parallel, while the German *Wolfdietrich* contains a similar episode.

See also: Arthurian Lore; Gawain; *Sir Gawain and the Green Knight*

—Cathalin B. Folks and Carl Lindahl

Lugnasa [Lughnasa]. August festival named after the Celtic god Lug (Lugh), whose cult was widespread in the Celtic lands of Europe.

Lug appears to have been the focus of a harvest cult in Gaul, as classical writers attest to a great festival at Lyon (Celtic *Lugudunon*; Latin *Lugudunum*, "fortress of Lugus") on the first of August. A festival called in the Irish language *Lughnasa* (earlier *Lughnasadh*), marking the beginning of autumn and the ripening of the crops, has been celebrated in Ireland since ancient times. This festival occurred on August 1 in the Julian calendar, dividing the summer half of the year into the summer and autumn seasons, and also gave its name to the first month of the autumn season (*Lúnasa*, August).

In ancient Ireland the festival of Lugnasa was reputed to be a time of assembly and of celebration. A measure of the festival's outstanding importance is that two great assemblies are said to have been held on it, Oénach Carmain and Oénach Tailten. The site of the Carmain assembly is not definitely known and Tailtiu is modern Teltown in county Meath, about eight kilometers northwest of the town of Navan. A series of ponds and enclosures in the present-day Teltown complex, including a large circular enclosure known as Rath Dubh, are thought to be the archaeological remnants of this notable assembly site.

In medieval times, the *Oénach*, or fair-assembly, was an event at which great crowds gathered, and apart from its political or religious significance it also appears to have been a notable occasion for trading and popular entertainment. The assembly of Carman is the subject of a dramatic poem composed in the eleventh century and occurring in a collection of onomastic verse-texts, the *Metrical Dindshenchas* (4:2–5), while a less elaborate account of the gathering and its significance occurs in the somewhat later *Prose Dindshenchas*. This assembly seems to have died out in the Middle Ages.

The Lugnasa assembly held at Tailtiu is also

featured in a long poem in the *Metrical Dindshenchas* (4:147–163). An entry in the *Annals of the Four Masters* for the year 1168 records that the crowds attending Oénach Tailten were so great that "their horses and cavalry" extended for a distance of six and a half miles. Small local gatherings are said to have continued at Teltown until the eighteenth century.

While August 1/Lugnasa is still technically regarded as the first day of autumn in Ireland, it seems that even in the Middle Ages the outdoor gatherings and festivities were transferred to a nearby Sunday, either the last Sunday in July or the first Sunday in August, for convenience. The major reason for this change was probably to enable different communities to congregate for celebration and recreation on a day of leisure rather than on an ordinary working day at this time of the agricultural year.

One effect of this change was that the eve and first of August, as particular points of the year, faded into relative unimportance in the folk consciousness, unlike the festivals of Beltane (Bealtaine) and Samhain, which remained significant calendar landmarks. Magical occurrences, so characteristic of the festivals of Samhain and Beltane, are also barely perceptible in the surviving beliefs and customs about Lugnasa.

Another result is that the old name of the festival went largely into decline and was replaced by a variety of names in many localities. Some of these, such as *Domhnach Deireannach (an tSamhraidh)* (Last Sunday [of Summer]), specify that the celebration of the festival took place on the last Sunday of July, while other appellations, such as First Sunday of Harvest or First Sunday of August, clearly indicate that the festival was held on the first Sunday in August.

Designations such as Mountain Sunday, *Domhnach na bhFraochóg* (Fraughan Sunday, Bilberry Sunday), and Garland Sunday reflect the fact that festive gatherings were held on heights and that activities such as picking wild berries and making garlands of wildflowers were practiced. The name Lough Sunday demonstrates

that another favorite gathering place at Lugnasa was beside a lake or a river, and it seems that in addition to recreational pursuits the ritual swimming of horses and cattle was also widely practiced at this time. Names such as *Domhnach an Phatrúin* (Patron Sunday) and *Domhnach an Tobair* (Well Sunday) indicate that there were many well-assemblies (i.e., visits to holy wells) held at this time, too, though the connection with the ancient festival of Lugnasa seems tenuous for some of these.

That some hilltop Lugnasa gatherings took on a religious character in the course of time and became pilgrimage sites is shown, for example, by the designation *Domhnach na Cruaiche* (Reek Sunday), referring specifically to the pilgrimage to the summit of Croagh Patrick (*Cruach Phádraig*) in county Mayo, a peak some 2,500 feet high. In 1453 a relaxation of canonical penances was granted by papal letter to those who made the pilgrimage to the top of Croagh Patrick on the last Sunday in July and gave alms toward the upkeep of the chapel on its summit.

Another name, *Domhnach Chrom Dubh* (Sunday of Crom Dubh), commonplace in medieval times, remained prominent in the folk traditions of the eastern part of Ireland from county Down in the north to county Wexford in the south, and in the Gaeltacht, or Irish-speaking areas, from Donegal Bay in the northwest to the Dingle peninsula in the southwest. Tradition represents Crom Dubh as an archetypal pagan and as an opponent of St. Patrick, who nevertheless succeeded in converting him. In the myth of Lug, the central topos is Lug's struggle with and slaying of Balar of the Baleful Eye, but as there is no explicit mention of this theme in the folk traditions of the Lugnasa festival, it is likely that in the surviving Lugnasa legends the contesting pair, St. Patrick and Crom Dubh, have taken the place of Lug and Balar of the earlier myth.

See also: Beltane; Celtic Mythology; Irish Tradition; Samhain

—Patricia Lysaght

$\mathcal{M}$*abinogi* [The Four Branches of the Mabinogi; Pedair Cainc y Mabinogi]. A cycle of four Middle Welsh prose tales.

The work takes its name from colophons at the ends of all four branches, each saying in effect, "and thus ends this branch of the *Mabinogi*." But it is far from clear what, beyond "tale" itself, the word *mabinogi* actually means. Of the various suggestions that have been made—for example, that a *mabinog* was an apprentice bard and the tales are essentially exercises or practice pieces, or that the word derives from the Welsh noun *mab* (son, boy) and refers to stories about the youthful exploits of a hero, or that it refers to material concerning the British god Mabon—none seems to apply to the work we have.

The colophon at the end of the First Branch has the form *mabinogion*, which is probably a scribal error. It has become a familiar and established form in the modern period, however, because of Lady Charlotte Guest's widely influential edition and translation of 12 heterogeneous medieval Welsh narratives—including the Four Branches—all gathered under the title *The Mabinogion* (1838–1849). The more accurate term *Mabinogi* applies only to the narratives of the Four Branches.

Those narratives are (1) *Pwyll, Prince of Dyfed*, (2) *Branwen, Daughter of Llyr*, (3) *Manawydan, Son of Llyr*, and (4) *Math, Son of Mathonwy*. They appear to be the work of one author, writing probably at the end of the eleventh century and perhaps in southwest Wales. Nothing is known of him (or, less likely, her) or of the audience for which he wrote. He was undoubtedly a Christian, perhaps even a cleric, but almost no Christian references are visible in the tales he tells. What the stories do reveal is a familiarity with court behavior, a knowledge of the procedures and language of the Welsh Laws, and a mind possessed of a large store of traditional lore.

Nothing else quite like the Four Branches of the Mabinogi survives in medieval Welsh literature. In a comparative perspective, the narratives strongly suggest the world of the European-Asiatic märchen, but they also suggest saga and romance. Like epic and saga they are concerned with war and lineage, with the demands of honor and vengeance, and with human society and the hero's duty therein. Like romance they are concerned with stories of love, courtship, and betrayal; with tests of a hero's prowess and the maturing of his understanding; and with otherworld regions where the transformations of understanding take place. But folktales and a concern with the triumphs of cleverness, of magic, and of adventure itself appear to supply the fundamental narrative material.

Tales and narrative motifs known elsewhere appear in abundance in the Four Branches. In the First Branch there is a Fairy Mistress tale, a form of story well known in the oral legends of most of the world (motif F302); a Calumniated Wife tale (K2110.1), one of the favorite stories of the Middle Ages; and episodes echoing the widespread folktale "The Twins or Blood-Brothers" (AT 303). The Second Branch, a story of the failure to unite the two realms of Britain and Ireland through a dynastic marriage, has a magic cauldron that revives slain warriors (motifs D1171.2, E607.5), an iron house disguised as a banqueting hall in order to trap and roast hostile guests (K811.4), magnetic stones in the river Shannon that pull the nails out of boats (F806; cf. F754), warriors concealed in flour bags, and a Vital Head (E783) that remains alive and talkative after being cut off a slain king. The Third Branch is a story of enchantment and disenchantment similar in plot to many märchen: a magic mist descends and empties the land of people and domestic animals; a white boar is a Guiding Beast (N774) that lures the protagonist into a phantom castle that disappears at nightfall, taking him with it helplessly stuck to a magic fountain (D1641.1); fairies transformed to mice lay waste to three wheat fields, until one is captured and becomes the means for disenchanting the land. The Fourth Branch is, among other things, a story of transformations (D1–D699): mushrooms turned into horses and dogs, seaweed into fine leather shoes, empty air into illusory fleets and armies, men transformed to animals of both sexes, a child transformed to a creature of the sea, and flowers changed into a woman, then into an owl. Such traditional elements furnish the narratives of the Four Branches and also of many other medieval tales, of stories in the *Thousand and One Nights* and the Grimms' *Kinder- und Hausmärchen* (Children's and Household Tales), and of oral folktales the world over.

The four complex and sometimes enigmatic stories the Welsh author fashioned from that material are all complete and coherent narratives, though with some gaps and loose ends attributable to the vagaries of manuscript transmission. The relation of each branch to the others, however, and to a unified whole (if there is one), has been perplexing. Various scholars have suggested that the Four Branches are the incomplete or fragmented remnant of some earlier, more unified narrative—a developed body of mythology or a complete saga recounting the birth, exploits, and death of a hero. Whether or not earlier forms of the Four Branches of the Mabinogi ever existed, such reconstructions remain hypothetical, and the work we have remains the imperfectly understood masterpiece of medieval Welsh prose narrative.

See also: Accused Queen; Celtic Mythology; Folktale

—Andrew Welsh

Maelgwn Gwynedd (d. 547) [Maglocunus, Malgo]. King of Gwynedd and one of the foremost British kings in historical writings, saints' lives, and legend.

Gildas, his contemporary, describes him as *insularis draco* (dragon of the island, probably Anglesey, the traditional seat of the kings of Gwynedd) and condemns him for quitting the monastic life after once having taken it up, for violently deposing his uncle the king, for killing his wife and nephew in order to marry the nephew's wife, and for listening too much to the praises of poets. Gildas also comments on Maelgwn's great height, an element apparently retained by medieval poets, who frequently refer to him as Maelgwn *hir* (the tall). With what may be an origin legend for Gwynedd, a legend that strengthened Maelgwn's power by ascribing to him founding ancestors, the ninth-century *Historia Brittonum* (History of the Britons) records that Maelgwn's great-great-great-grandfather Cunedda, along with his eight sons, had come from Manaw Gododdin (present-day eastern lowland Scotland) to Gwynedd, whence they expelled the Irish. Maelgwn in turn figures as a favored progenitor, the proof of power, in the genealogies.

The tenth-century *Annales Cambriae* (Annals of Wales) records that Maelgwn died from the Yellow Plague in 547 and then adds a proverb, "The long sleep of Maelgwn in the court of Rhos." Maelgwn's "long sleep" and his death from plague become one of his most persistent traditions. The twelfth-century *Life of St. Teilo* describes the Yellow Plague as a column of watery cloud that seized Maelgwn and destroyed his country. The proverb was referred to by the fourteenth- and fifteenth-century poets Dafydd ap Gwilym, Tudur Aled, and Huw Cae Llwyd, and was eventually recorded in 1632 in John Davies's Latin-Welsh dictionary. The story behind the proverb apparently existed alongside it. The thirteenth-century writer of *Brut Dingestow*, a translation of *Historia regum Britanniae* (History of the Kings of Britain), repeats Geoffrey of Monmouth's statements about Maelgwn's handsomeness, bravery, generosity, sin of sodomy, and vicious conquering of six neighboring islands, but then, in an indication of a tradition too well known to be omitted, adds the report that Maelgwn went into the church near his own castle in Degannwy and there died. Although the fuller narrative must have been known, our earliest record of it comes from an eighteenth-century scholar's copy of the Triads, wherein he notes that Maelgwn had locked himself away in isolation in Rhos church in order to avoid the plague but that one day as he peeked through a chink in the door he was infected and died. When his men came to him they thought he was asleep, and only after a long wait did they realize he was dead. Thus, the proverb is used to describe one who sleeps too long or has died.

Maelgwn Gwynedd, like Arthur, plays an important role in the saints' lives, where, as an aggressive troublemaker, he provides the foil against which the saint can prove the superiority of his sanctified power over the secular power of even the mightiest kings. He comes into conflict with Cybi over hunting a goat that seeks sanctuary with the saint, with Brynach by demanding food and then stealing a cow that proves to be uncookable, with Curig by stealing panniers full of food, and with Cadog over a kidnapped maiden. Apparently irked by saintliness, he tries to trap Padarn by leaving in his safekeeping "treasure" bags filled with moss and gravel and then, upon retrieving the bags, claiming that the treasure had been stolen. He attacks Tydecho with even greater determination. According to a fifteenth-century *cywydd* (and an oral collection in the twentieth century), he leaves horses with Tydecho to be fed on a frozen hillside by the saint's prayers. When the horses are returned fat and healthy, he steals the saint's plowing oxen, and then sets his dogs on the wild animals that come to replace the oxen. The saint finally stops Maelgwn by making him stick to the rock on which he sits until he agrees to the saint's terms.

Maelgwn's traditional role as a king (not simply a warrior) places him at the center of a number of nonhagiographical narratives as well. An early-fourteenth-century poem tells of the king who, while traveling with his court, commanded his bards and musicians to swim across a river. When they reached the other side, the harpists were unable to perform with their sodden instruments, but the bards were able to compose as well as ever, thus showing their superiority. One late-fourteenth-century law text tells how, through the use of a specially constructed chair with waxed wings, Maelgwn won the right to be king by floating on the incoming tide at Aberdovey while his competitors were forced to flee. A sixteenth-century folktale (believed to have ninth-century antecedents) shows Maelgwn as the great king in whose court at Degannwy the poet Taliesin proves himself as a young man. Taliesin's foster father Elphin boasts that his wife is as chaste as Maelgwn's and his poet more skilled than Maelgwn's and is accordingly thrown into prison until he can prove his words. Taliesin, using his foresight, substitutes a servant for his foster mother when Maelgwn's son Rhun comes to test her and then, using magic skills, causes Maelgwn's 24 attendant bards to utter nonsense syllables when he goes to court to compete with them. Another sixteenth-century text records a variant of the tale of the lost ring found in a fish (AT 736A; motif N211.1), in which Maelgwn's wife loses a valuable ring while walking by the sea and proves to her jealous husband her essential innocence (through the intercession of her brother, Bishop Asaph) only when the ring is found inside a fish served to the king.

The diversity of narratives connected with Maelgwn, the references in medieval poetry to these and various other events in Maelgwn's life, and hints such as one found in a triad that lists Maelgwn's cow Brech (i.e., Speckled—probably a cow of plenty) as one of the three foremost cows of Britain suggest that Maelgwn was a far more important character in medieval Welsh legendry than is made evident in the scattered, extant records. Whether in the cryptic allusions in poetry (which indicate an underlying depth and range of traditional knowledge about him) or in his placement along with Arthur as the great tyrant of hagiography (which indicates he was traditionally recognized as a figure of great secular power), we find traces of what must have been a particularly rich, diverse, and strong tradition.

See also: Geoffrey of Monmouth; Triads of the Island of Britain

—Elissa R. Henken

Magic. An alternate mode of rationality, frequently portrayed as deviant because of its divergence from the religious and scientific rationalities; a cluster of practices (ranging from astrology and alchemy, to the use of charms and amulets, to sorcery and necromancy) that all operate on the principle that the natural world contains hidden powers that human beings can possess or tap for practical purposes, both good and evil.

Medieval notions of magic must be seen in the context of the systems of thought and organization that produced the concept and in the context of the intellectual, religious, and social changes from late antiquity to the Renaissance. Because magic is an evolving concept, a wide variety of things believed and practiced between 500 and 1500 could have fallen into this category at one time or another from someone's perspective. In particular, the so-called Twelfth-Century Renaissance altered the intellectual paradigms for understanding knowledge and nature such that magic was defined in new ways, and this created a widening gap between intellectual modes of rationality and popular, or folk, understandings of the natural world.

Cultural Influences

Concepts of magic current in the Middle Ages are rooted in the diverse origins of medieval culture: the classical inheritance, the native (Celtic, Germanic, Slavic, and so on), and the Christian. The interactions among these three involved both opposition and overlap, both conflict and assimilation. These intertwining roots, in turn, contributed to complex relationships in the medieval period between magic and religion, magic and science, and magic and folklore.

The negative overtones to the idea of magic begin in the classical origins of the word itself: the Latin *magus* ultimately derives from an Old Persian word for a learned man, especially one who practiced various arts such as astrology and perhaps some forms of wizardry. They were ambivalent figures in classical society, like the Three

Magi, educated pagan foreigners (probably from Persia) whose practice of astrology led them to the site of Christ's birth. The Greco-Roman magus was thus typically a "foreigner" in some sense—either literally or figuratively, as one who lived beyond the borders of normal society—and who had mastery of the secret knowledge to do such things as divining from the entrails of animals, speaking curses, interpreting oracles, or providing amulets of magic stones or animal parts to ward off evil. The respect for and yet fear of occult knowledge and occult power, expressed in classical literature by Pliny (23–79 C.E.) in his *Natural History* (Books 28–37), was passed on to the Middle Ages through Christianity.

A second, separate strand in the medieval view emerges from the heritages of the Germanic peoples who settled in Europe in the fourth through seventh centuries and of their Celtic predecessors. The few remnants of their practice survive mostly in the works of Christian writers, though evidence from oral tradition suggests a much earlier origin—for example, the Old Irish epic *Táin Bó Cúailnge* (Cattle Raid of Cooley), the Welsh *Mabinogi*, and the Icelandic *Prose Edda* of Snorri Sturluson, which, though composed in the thirteenth century, is based on ancient tradition. From these gleanings, certain generalizations can be made about their animistic and polytheistic beliefs and practices, including propitiating spiritual entities in the natural world when using nature's resources; speaking incantations to cause, prevent, or cure ill effects; carrying amulets to ward off unseen spiritual entities; the use of runes to effect material change; and worshipping at sacred sites such as wells or trees. Possessors of the secret knowledge (priests, druids, cunning men or women) were respected as necessary to society and feared as a power with which to be reckoned. These practices would later be classified as magic by Christian authors, but in their own context they were part of the natural medicine and religious worship of the Celtic and Germanic peoples.

The third strand, then, that weaves into these other two and brings them together is Christianity—a monotheistic religion that has an inherent bias against practices that detract from the idea of the sovereignty of the one God. The biblical story according to which Simon Magus tries to buy power from the apostles epitomizes Christianity's antipathy to the coercion of supernatural forces, identified with demonic forces working through illusion or tricks. The view of the most influential late-antique theologian, St. Augustine of Hippo (354–430), became dominant in the medieval West: he condemned magic utterly, but he also believed that the created world contained virtues, or powers, that could be legitimately tapped for good purposes (see his *City of God*, Books 8–10).

The obvious initial reaction of the contact (500–800 C.E.) between classical-Christian culture and native cultures is confrontation. Germanic religions and beliefs were classified as being magic and of the devil; the sites of worship were literally uprooted by the monastic missionaries; and the spells were countered by more powerful prayers to the only true God. Bede, in his *Ecclesiastical History of the English People* (731), relates that the pagan king Aethelberht would only meet with the Christian missionaries outdoors, lest they use some power of dark sorcery (*maleficae artis*) to deceive him; but he soon learns that they come "armed not with diabolical, but with divine power," carrying a cross as a sign of that power. After their conversion to Christianity, the cross becomes a powerful talisman against diabolical magic.

The Latin term *magic* was employed by Christian authors to describe a whole range of practices for which there was no single equivalent in the vernacular languages. Witchcraft, sorcery, charms, necromancy, and divination were lumped together with things pagan and demonic as excluded from a Christian worldview. But the belief in hidden virtues, or powers, in the natural world survived—a belief held in common by the classical world, the Christian Church, and the Celtic and Germanic peoples, allowing for certain kinds of assimilation of older within newer beliefs and practices. Thus, the combination of these three heritages left some overlapping and accommodations that have, on various grounds, been classified as magic. These gray areas in medieval views can best be seen at the boundaries: between magic and religion, magic and science, and magic and folklore.

At the crossroads of magic and religion there is the belief in the power of words to effect change in natural objects. This power can be seen in the Christianized Germanic practice of charms, incantations that bring out the effective virtues of an herb, as well as in the Christian liturgy (the Eucharist and exorcisms, for example). The most prominent evidence of this belief in the overlap between supernatural power and material things is found in the use of saints' relics (such as their bones, or even moss from holy footsteps) to accomplish miraculous cures—stories popularized at the pilgrimage sites that now dotted the landscape, superimposing themselves upon or displacing the ancient religious sites of wells and trees.

Magic, Science, and Religion

In the medieval worldview the ambivalent relationship between magic and science is linked to the radical intellectual changes that began in the twelfth century in the universities of Europe, where scientific knowledge produced by human reason was seen as distinct from religious or revelatory knowledge. Various forms of magic were caught in the middle, seen not as religion but as questionable science. Some forms of magic were condemned as demonic, while others were defended as intellectually viable science (natural

magic), consistent with the created order. This natural magic, or occult science, of the scholars relied on a model in which occult virtues were at work invisibly: microcosm and macrocosm were interlocked, influencing one another, and material objects corresponded to various body parts, so that certain gemstones, for example, were believed to have hidden virtues to cure ailments or ward off ills. Thus, astrology, divination, and alchemy developed alongside mechanical technology and astronomy. This intellectual flirtation with forms of magic, influenced by Arabic science and Hebrew mysticism (especially the Kabbalah), is evident in the debates over natural versus demonic magic from the central Middle Ages through the Renaissance in such prominent thinkers as John of Salisbury, Nicole d'Oresme, Roger Bacon, Albertus Magnus, Johannes Trithemius, and Marsilio Ficino.

This increasingly complex understanding of the natural world through human sense observation and reason in the twelfth through the fifteenth centuries also led to a widening gap between the view of nature held by those who regarded themselves as an intellectual elite and the far more popular view that was still immersed in an animistic view of nature. Consequently, many popular practices, such as medicinal charms, amulets, divinations, and adjurations, were rejected by the learned as "low magic." Such folk magic was condemned on religious grounds as well: the perceived heterodoxy of folk belief and practice, its apparent roots in pagan beliefs, and its increasing distance from the intellectual theologies and cosmologies governing the emergent sciences contributed to their condemnation as magic of the devil. The *Malleus maleficarum* (Hammer of Witches), a product of fifteenth-century Inquisitors, is a compendium of all kinds of practices that were condemned on various grounds but were lumped together as superstitious and demonic. Hence, magic became part of a growing "underworld" of unorthodox practices, such as necromancy, witchcraft, and heresy—all forms of deviance from a norm now asserting itself in greater clarity than ever before.

Nonetheless, magic survives under a guise of respectability in literature and in the ambivalent person of the magus, half-scientist, half-magician, a person who had within himself and could use the knowledge of powerful words and forces. Nowhere is this ambivalence clearer than in the Arthurian literary tradition, with its semipagan Merlin and Christian King Arthur, its magic swords and Holy Grail, its fairy worlds and hermit forests, its quests and pilgrimages. This literary realm mirrors the tensions in the real-life practice of magic between diversity and orthodoxy, regional folk practice and the intellectual centers of debate.

The most recent and broadest interpretations conceive of magic as a culture-specific concept, rooted in the evolution of European values and systems of thought. This has two consequences: (1) When the concept is applied to cultures outside of Europe, it carries with it all the baggage of Eurocentric worldviews. (2) Within European history the parameters of the concept have changed over time. Scholars of various eras, from the twelfth to the twentieth centuries, have thus defined magic as unacceptable, but for different reasons. In many ways these definitions illuminate the worldview of their makers more than they do the field of magic. To control this wide-ranging diversity in the use of the concept of magic, the texts and perspectives of the people living in Europe 500–1500 should be used to define the term; employing later conceptions of magic, applying them anachronistically, only confuses the matter. That has, nevertheless, been the predominant scholarly approach until quite recently.

In general, medieval Europe perceived magic as an unnatural use of material reality and therefore defined it in opposition to religion. From biblical times onward magic has been defined in opposition to religion, and religion could claim to be true to the extent that it opposed or, better yet, defeated the powers of magicians. Thus, in Exodus Moses and Aaron surpass the magicians of Egypt. Much later, in the Acts of the Apostles, Simon of Samaria astounds and misleads the local people with his wizardry (*magiis*) until he is outshone by the preaching and miracle working of St. Philip. In the fifth century, when St. Patrick seeks to carry out his conversion of Ireland, he bests a druid in a wonder-working contest that ends when the saint causes the druid to be raised high in the air and then dropped, causing his dramatic death. Still later, in the thirteenth-century *Golden Legend* of Jacobus de Voragine, perhaps the most widely influential medieval collection of saints' lives, St. Peter defeats Simon Magus before the emperor's court by ordering Simon's devils to cease holding the magician up while he seems to be flying, thus making him fall to his death. This list could be much extended, as it became commonplace for Christian heroes to prove their power by defeating magicians and thereby revealing magic to be either illusory or diabolical.

The other view that dominated medieval thinking was that magic is the opposite of science—a view that developed from the twelfth century on and gradually came to supersede the religious objections in prominence. Both oppositions were still in operation in the nineteenth and twentieth centuries, when much of the foundational scholarship on magic was written. In the first opposition, that of magic versus religion, modern scholars argued that magic was manipulative in its use of nature and power rather than supplicative, like religious prayers. In the medieval period, however, this religious comparison posited magic as the opposite of miracle: magic was an illusion of the devil, in contrast to the miracle, which was a divine intervention in the natural world. Appeals to hidden powers other than God, even to effect a good end, were suspect. Those powers, if not from God, must be demonic, and the person invoking such power, if he were not a priest, was then in competition with Church authority. Anyone with the skill to use that kind of power, even for good, could potentially use the same power for evil and hence was feared. Overlaps between magic and religion appear more readily to the modern or post-Reformation eye than to the medieval eye and have led to the designation "Christian magic," an oxymoron anachronistically applied to the medieval Church but that nonetheless highlights certain basic similarities in view between magical and religious practices, particularly in the early-medieval period (800–1100).

In opposition to science, magic has been portrayed as irrational. In the expanding intellectual environment of the twelfth century, the increased distinction between human reason and divine revelation and between the natural and the supernatural led to the medieval view of magic as a use of nature relying on supernatural or occult powers for practical purposes. Again, this occult power was two-edged: if it existed, then the possessor of such knowledge could use it for good or ill. From a modern definition of science, such magic is irrational on the grounds that its assumptions about nature cannot be verified and its methods are not empirical.

Unlike the modern scientific view, which assumes only one legitimate mode of rationality, medieval views accepted the existence of rationalities other than human reason or science (such as faith in divine revelation). The postmodern move away from science as the only way of knowing recognizes the diversity of many modes of rationality that operate logically within their own frames of reference. Magic need not be classified as an irrational set of beliefs without any coherence. Rather, it can be seen as a logical system of belief and practice operating on different principles than science or religion.

Within any of these frames of reference, religion or science, medieval or modern, the boundaries between one category and another are fluid; one person's science or religion is another person's magic. A history of the concept of magic is therefore not peripheral to medieval culture but central to it—an important crossroads, as Richard Kieckhefer has argued, between the various aspects of medieval culture. Most of all, the study of the concept of magic and its interactions with the intellectual paradigms of the scientific and religious realms illuminates the role of folklore and popular culture as a dynamic element in the formation of European thought.

See also: Amulet and Talisman; Magic Manuals; Witchcraft

—Karen Louise Jolly

Magic Manuals. Medieval literature specifically devoted to explicitly magical formulas, commonly found in the form of works on astral magic (of which *Picatrix*, the thirteenth-century Latin translation of an Arabic compilation, is the most famous example), writings on the related practice of necromancy, and collections of experiments for magical tricks.

Magical formulas also occur in other, widely differing types of medieval manuscripts: magical experiments are sometimes found in miscellanies and books of household management; medical compilations may contain charms and receipts for magical healing alongside nonmagical material; treatises on herbs (herbals), stones (lapidaries), and animals (bestiaries), or sometimes on specific plants (such as the oak), or beasts (such as the vulture) may describe the magical "virtues" as well as other qualities of their subject matter.

Occasionally one finds manuscripts that give a variety of magical material, representing both natural and expressly demonic magic. One good example is a fifteenth-century Middle Netherlandish manuscript, MS 517 of the Wellcome Historical Medical Library in London, edited by Willy Braeckman. This manuscript contains 24 sections. A small number of them pertain to divination, telling how to detect a thief, for example, or how to learn the truth about the past and future. There are formulas for arousing love, a formula designed to induce orgasm, and another to prevent a wife from committing adultery. The bulk of the material in the manuscript, however, falls into the general category of magical tricks: there are formulas for becoming invisible and for making people become dirty in their bathwater, making peacocks white, making a dog dance, and making a horse stand still or fall down as if dead. The manuscript has in addition a fragmentary moon-book (book of lunar astrology) and a puzzling experiment ascribed to Solomon.

The types of procedures recommended are various. A few of the formulas include an explicit invocation of demons, whether elaborate or simple; to prevent adultery, a man is told he should draw a circle around his wife's genitals with the tail of a lizard while invoking four devils. The magical tricks are for the most part simple: a woman can be made to leap naked from her bath if eggs are tossed into it, while a brooding peahen will give birth to white peacocks if she is made to look constantly at a white cloth. Magic characters inscribed on metal are recommended for the extermination of mice and flies. And to travel quickly wherever one wishes to go, one should concoct an ointment with seven herbs, the fat of a goat, and the blood of a bat and smear it on one's face, hands, and chest while reciting a brief formula.

See also: Amulet and Talisman; Magic; Witchcraft

—Richard Kieckhefer

Mandeville's Travels [The Travels of Sir John Mandeville]. A fourteenth-century travel narrative, originally written in French (or perhaps Anglo-Norman), purportedly a first-person account of an English knight's travels to the Holy Land and points beyond.

Versions of *Mandeville's Travels* are extant in about 300 manuscripts and early printed texts. The work includes geographical and astronomical data, pilgrimage routes, discussions of relics and holy sites, legends, folk beliefs and customs, and personal experience narratives about adventures. It contains an encyclopedia of information regarding beliefs, practices, customs, and perceptions held in medieval Europe. It also contains information and descriptions of beliefs, practices, and customs of peoples living in lands unfamiliar to most Europeans of that time.

Despite the author's apparent knowledge and experiences, critics have been unable to come to a consensus about whether the author, whose true identity is unknown, gained his information through firsthand experience or from reading other travelers' writings. Nevertheless, the *Travels* can be read as a memoir, for the author "recreates" adventures, developing an engaging narrative persona who explains unfamiliar or bizarre items in terms familiar to his audience, often creating parallels between pagan and Christian practices—for example, cannibalism is compared with receiving the Eucharist. Whether the work should be considered nonfiction or fiction remains a subject of debate.

Numerous genres and subgenres of folklore are presented within cultural contexts: proverbial sayings ("old sayings"), folk beliefs (religious and secular), legends (religious, place name), religious and secular customs (revolving around birth, death, and marriage), rituals, charms, cures (some with miracle narratives), personal-experience narratives, and weather lore. The narrator also discusses the functions of the folklore. His attention to Europeans' perceptions of foreign beliefs and practices allows readers to see folklore in double focus: both in terms of the practices of the cultures being described and in terms of the folkloric attitudes and stereotypes of the writer and his culture.

In the first half of the book (travels to Palestine), much of the folklore centers on folk beliefs, cures, saints' relics, and references to well-known religious legends. However, exotic secular or non-Christian legends are generally well developed. Discussions about the beliefs and practices of Christian sects and heretics are less developed. Holy sites are merely listed, unless there are exotic legends attached to them. At times the narrator uses legends to validate his experiences and beliefs.

The second half of the work (travels to East Asia) contains fully developed exotic legends and heroic personal-experience narratives. These "edge-of-the-world" experiences are placed in cultural contexts that make them more familiar. His personal-experience narratives validate medieval legends, beliefs, and other stories about Prester John, the Great Khan, and the existence of an earthly paradise.

The two predominant genres of folklore used in *Mandeville's Travels* are legends and personal-experience narratives. Within these the author has woven examples of other genres, thus creating a believable portrait of living cultures.

See also: Foreign Races; Travel Literature

—Elizabeth MacDaniel

Manuscript Marginalia. Little drawings accompanying written texts from the mid-thirteenth century forward, often merely "emptily" grotesque (though some may have served a mnemonic or "bookmark" function, enabling readers both to recall and quickly relocate key passages), but some clearly serving as commentary and alluding to the text in some (often irreverent) way.

One example of irreverent commentary is a drawing of a naked woman in the *bas-de-page* (bottom margin) of a fourteenth-century French Psalter. This drawing appears on a folio in which the word *Quoniam* (here meaning "because," but commonly used among European literati to mean "vagina") is twice highlighted. Other marginalia bear no obvious relation to the texts they border—such are the highly important series of scenes (some 600 illustrations in all) in the lower margins of a manuscript of canon law known as the Smithfield Decretals, written in Italy but illuminated in England probably in the 1300s. The exempla, fabliaux, and folktales illustrated include the romances of Guy of Warwick (whose story, together with that of Beves of Hampton, is also illustrated in the Taymouth *Hours*) and *Florent and Octavian*, and a tale related to Chrétien's *Yvain*. The *Miracles of the Virgin* in this manuscript include the famous pact of Theophilus with the devil (H1273.1), the sacristan and the knight's lady, the lost foot restored (V411.3), the Jew of Bourges, and the painter and the devil (P482.1), and they are supplemented by many similar stories from saints' lives. The world-turned-upside-down motif is exemplified in the scenes of the hound captured and executed by the hares—one hare thumbs his nose at the hanging dog, an early attestation of this gesture in European art—and the fox-bishop preaching to a congregation of birds who eventually hang him for his assaults on the flock. The fabliau of the mischievous boy who leads the blind man is illustrated, as is the popular tale (for which, paradoxically, no written source has ever been found) of the apes who rob the peddler's pack. Similarly difficult to "fix" textually is another popular scene, the abduction of a human female by a Wild Man (in the Taymouth *Hours* sequence the elderly knight who kills the *wodehouse* and rescues the damsel is clearly identified as Enyeas); other sequences include the clever daughter, the hermit who got drunk, part of the tale of the

wright's chaste wife, and the narrative of the *Legend of the Three Living and the Three Dead*.

Another French manuscript of the Decretals illustrates one of the *causae* dealing with legitimate marriage with an illustration of a cuckolded husband from whose head a superb pair of antlers rises—an allusion to the cuckold's horns (c. 1300), by far the earliest visual depiction of cuckoldry known; another contemporary French copy discusses and illustrates a woman holding a changeling.

Careful scrutiny of marginal paintings can also reveal details of folk custom and practices; for example, the celebrated Luttrell Psalter (East Anglia, c. 1340) depicts a corn dolly in its reaping scene, men breaking up clods of earth with a mallet (cf. the surname of Robert Clodhamer, attested in Essex in 1260), and a sheep that has a bell suspended between its horns and is therefore identified as the bellwether, the origin of our metaphorical sense, "leader."

L. Randall's *Iconographical Index* will disclose many depictions of folktale motifs, such as that of shooting at the father's corpse to determine the rightful heir, in which the man who cannot bring himself to shoot is declared the true son (H486.2). Also common are the various constituent motifs of the world turned upside down, representations of proverbs (especially in Flemish manuscripts—a tradition that was to reach its climax in the work of Pieter Brueghel the Elder), and even the occasional riddle depiction (that of the incompatible animals who must be rowed across the stream in the correct combinations). The Metz *Pontifical* includes a series in which a tailor is terrified by a hare, an allusion to the popular opinion of the proverbially unmanly nature of that particular occupation. Allusions to numskull tales of the Wise Men of Gotham type include at least three examples of the hare with a purse tied round its neck, dispatched by the idiot villagers as the speediest way of getting their overdue rent to their landlord.

Other marginal illustrations attest to medieval anti-Semitism and xenophobia: caricatures of grotesquely hook-nosed Jews are to be found in the borders of official documents, for example, and one French manuscript, in what has an excellent claim to be considered the earliest political cartoon, depicts the English king Edward I naked, except for the gauntlet on which his falcon perches, and with a very long tail—an allusion to the popular *Angli caudati* (tailed English) gibe.

See also: Iconography; World Turned Upside Down

—Malcolm Jones

Map, Walter (c. 1130–1209/1210). Secular clerk and Latin writer whose work sheds considerable light on Welsh legendry.

Map was a native of the Welsh Marches and possibly was of Welsh descent, though it is unclear whether he considered himself Welsh. Educated in England and Paris, he served first Gilbert Foliot, bishop of London and Hereford (Map was himself a canon of that cathedral) and then Henry II. In 1197 he became archdeacon of Oxford. The Old French prose *Lancelot* and some Latin verse have been attributed to Map; however, these works are no longer assumed to be his, and he is most noted as the author of *De nugis curialium* (Courtiers' Trifles), which has been preserved in one fourteenth-century manuscript (Bodley MS 851).

The text is a series of narratives, some fragmentary or in note form, including histories, romances, legends, anecdotes, and gossip, with special emphasis (and well spiced with vitriol) on the courts of England, France, and Wales and on the religious orders. Map, like his friend Gerald of Wales, was a sardonic, witty observer of contemporary court life, and like his fellow archdeacon he collected traditional narratives and beliefs as well as current gossip. His reminiscences and comments on contemporary figures are useful, though not unbiased, historical evidence, and though editors judge that he purposely rewrote, contorted, and even invented many narratives for satiric and other idiosyncratic purposes, Map nonetheless provides good examples of traditional legends and anecdotes. He relates several instances of a fairy bride taken from a lake or a midnight dance and remaining only until a taboo is broken. He also tells of a dead wife saved by her husband when he pulled her out of a fairy dance and gives several accounts of the unquiet dead. Another internationally recognized motif appears in a story he tells of a Welsh king who is forced to accept the reflection of money as recompense for a crime committed only in the wrongdoer's dream (motif J1551.1). He also recounts the origins of King Herla's ghostly or Wild Hunt (E501) in the problems created by the supernatural passage of time spent at an otherworld wedding feast. He provides one hagiographic legend in which all those who eat bread improperly demanded of Cadog are swallowed by the earth. Map's narratives are clearly localized, even to the point of his identifying the children left behind by a fairy bride. Whether he heard them that way or changed them, they indicate his familiarity with oral tradition and give us a glimpse of the narratives current in twelfth-century Western Europe.

See also: Fairies; Fairy Lover; Gerald of Wales; Welsh Tradition; Wild Hunt

—Elissa R. Henken and Brynley F. Roberts

Marie de France (fl. late twelfth century). The most celebrated female poet of the Middle Ages, translator of an otherworldly vision, creator of a collection of fables, and known primarily as the author of 12 short romances, the *lais*, courtly French adaptations of tales from Breton and Welsh traditions.

We know little more about Marie than her name and her distinctive voice. At the opening of her *Fables* she declares, "I am Marie, and I come from France"—that is, from Île-de-France, the region of Paris. This one line provided modern scholars with their sole justification for calling her Marie de France, a name she did not call herself. Elsewhere in her poetry she simply says she is Marie, a name so common in her time and place that her historical identity will probably never be discovered. But her *lais* suggest that she spent time in England or Normandy (or, more probably, both) living in close proximity to the Celtic Bretons and Welsh, from whom she claims to have gotten her stories. Introducing one of the *lais*, she says "*Laüstic* is its name, I believe, and that is what they [*li Breton*, "the Britons," i.e., the Bretons or the Welsh] call it in their land. In French it is *Rossignol*, and *Nihtegale* [Nightingale] in proper English"—suggesting her familiarity with the French/English/Celtic borderlands and the possibility that she was trilingual. Marie's poetry also demonstrates an accurate knowledge of Breton, Welsh, English, and Norman towns and regions; it is reasonable to assume that she spent time on both sides of the English Channel, probably with the court of Henry II (r. 1154–1189), who ruled Normandy as well as England.

Marie presents herself as a forceful, innovative, hardworking, and controversial personality. In the Prolog to her *lais*, which was dedicated to a "noble king" (again, probably Henry II), she states that anyone gifted with "knowledge and truly eloquent speech has a duty not to remain silent." She then boldly announces that in searching for a theme for her writing she decided to discard tales based on classical models and to do something never done before, to take "lays which I have heard" and render them in verse—suggesting here, as in many other passages in the *lais*, that she received them directly, or at relatively close remove, from British oral traditions.

Beginning her first *lai*, *Guigemar*, Marie speaks pointedly of her critics: people who act "like a vicious, cowardly dog which will bite others out of malice." There is only one contemporary reference to Marie, but it is very illuminating because it seems to come from one of those detractors to whom she refers; Denis Pyramus, writing in England circa 1180, speaks of a "Dame Marie" who composes poems "that are not at all true." He adds that nobles enjoy her poetry and, more especially, that her poems "please the ladies; they listen to them joyfully and willingly, for they are just what they desire." Pyramus suggests here that Marie was writing, above all, for a female audience; her popularity with women may have contributed to the controversy that she provoked.

Marie's *lais* are as distinctively woman-oriented as they are Celtic in atmosphere. A good example is *Yonec*, a work of particular interest to folklorists because it is the earliest version of a tale type (AT 432, "The Prince as Bird") still current in oral tradition in the twenty-first century.

A rich old man marries a young woman and jealously locks her in a tower, where his aged widowed sister watches her every move. After seven years of imprisonment the wife prays that a young knight might secretly come to visit her, and instantly she sees the shadow of a hawk in her tower window. The hawk transforms into a handsome man, who becomes her lover, visiting her whenever she wishes, until the old woman discovers them and reports back to the husband, who has a row of razor-sharp spikes set on the window. The next time the hawk-prince alights to visit his lover he is mortally wounded. He tells his love that she is pregnant and will bear a son, Yonec, who will avenge them. The knight leaves, and his lady jumps from the window in pursuit, following the trail of blood through a cleft in a hill until she finds her prince. As he lies dying, he gives her a sword, to be presented to her son. She returns home and bears her son. Years later, while traveling with her son and aged husband, she comes upon the tomb of the hawk-prince. Just before dying of grief, she presents the sword to her son, who kills the old man and then becomes the ruler of his hawk-father's realm.

Marie's tale differs in substantial ways from other versions of "The Prince as Bird." For one thing, Yonec concerns a tragic love, while the folktales overwhelmingly end happily, with the woman healing the bird-prince and then marrying him. The death of Marie's prince may be her comment on the rarity of reciprocal married love in her own courtly circles. Also, in other written and oral versions told from the end of the Middle Ages to recent times, the bird-lover is betrayed by the young woman's cruel stepmother or jealous sister. Marie is exceptional in giving the woman a husband and making him the cause of the lover's death. The cruel husband who locks up his wife is a major figure in others of Marie's lais (e.g., Guigemar and Laüstic). Through this figure, Marie seems to be criticizing the loveless husbands of her own time—perhaps even Henry II, who imprisoned his own wife, Eleanor of Aquitaine.

As much as they are protests of loveless marriages, Yonec and the other lais are celebrations of true love. In Laüstic, Chatival, and other lais, adultery is preferable to loveless marriage, but in Bisclavret and Equitan, adulterers are punished. Marriage for true love seems to be Marie's highest, if seldom attainable, good, as in Eliduc, where a married hero embarks on an affair. His lover dies upon finding out that the hero is married. The man's wife visits the tomb and through a miraculous cure brings the lover back to life, reunites her grieving husband with his beloved, blesses their union, and retires to a convent so that her husband can marry his new love.

Eliduc, like Yonec, possesses extensive analogs in modern oral tradition. The postmedieval folktale known as "The Three Snake Leaves" (AT 612) concerns a grieving husband who, while visiting his wife's tomb, sees a snake or other animal (in Eliduc, a ferret or weasel) resuscitate its dead mate with a plant. Imitating the snake, the man administers the plant to his wife and brings her back to life. Eliduc differs from this traditional pattern (just as Yonec differs from its analogs) in making the true lovers adulterers—a theme that must have appealed to many in Marie's audience and perhaps outraged others. But Eliduc ends with a happy marriage. Of the four of Marie's lais that do end happily (Eliduc, Guigemar, Milun, Fresne), three begin with adultery, but all four end in loving marriages.

Scholars tend to assume that the lais are Marie's earliest surviving works and that her Fables—103 short, moralized poems, most of which have at least one animal character—came next. If the Fables do indeed constitute the later work, they could be—and sometimes are—dismissed as mere translations from Latin. Yet in several senses the Fables are as boldly new as the lais. First, although the first 40 poems seem to be translations that closely follow the famous Latin fable collection known as the Romulus (which circulated throughout medieval Europe for eight centuries before Marie), the remaining 63 exist in no surviving earlier version.

Second, these last 63 fables seem to come from both written and oral sources; in using them, Marie blends popular and learned traditions much as she does in the lais.

Third, Marie's fables stand out from contemporary collections in how they treat female characters. In Marie's fable 70, a fox propositions a bear. When the bear refuses, the fox says, "I'll make you want it." The bear, driven into a rage by the fox's sexual grossness, pursues him. To trap the bear, the fox runs into a thorn bush. The bear follows and gets caught in the thorns; the fox takes advantage of the bear's helplessness by raping her. Harriet Spiegel points out that the contemporary male authors of Ysengrimus and Roman de Renart tell a tale with a similar plot, but in Ysengrimus the female victim eventually enjoys the sexual assault, and in Renart she invites it. Marie, however, marshals our sympathies for the bear as a deceived and violated female.

The work by Marie that comes closest to being a direct translation of a Latin source is Espurgatoire Seint Patrice (St. Patrick's Purgatory), probably her last surviving poem. First written in Latin in the 1180s by the English monk Henry of Saltry, the tale was one of the most popular of its time. It was translated independently by at least four French authors and, later, many times into English and other languages. Espurgatoire Seint Patrice, which combines Christian doctrine with the theme of knightly bravery, describes a terrifying otherworld journey undertaken in the mid-twelfth century by an Irish knight named Owen. The knight, burdened by sins, descends into a pit. Surrounded by demons, he journeys through landscapes of tortured souls—pierced by burning nails, eaten alive by serpents and dragons, hanging from hooks that pierce their eyes, throats, breasts, and genitals—and finally sees the gates of hell and heaven before returning to earth, cleansed of sin. The story is attached to Lough Derg in county Donegal, Ireland, site of an actual underground pilgrimage site still visited today, where pilgrims subject themselves to ascetic ordeals and experience visions.

Marie's *Espurgatoire* may depart only slightly from its Latin source, but her changes are of great significance, as M. J. Curley has pointed out. Whereas the earlier work was written for a church audience, Marie writes for *la simple gent*, "simple folk," a lay audience. Marie also values the bravery of Owen and she exalts him above the monks, saying that Owen's trials compare to the monks' trials as an eagle compares to a finch. Finally, though Marie's source comments on the "beastly," barbaric nature of Irish people, Marie refuses to repeat any such ethnic slurs in her poem.

Indeed, all of Marie's surviving works are infused with a sense of compassion rare for her time, a compassion that extends even beyond her sympathy for the plight of women. The peasants whom she portrays in her *Fables* frequently show humanity and intelligence—unlike the peasants that appear in the works of such contemporaries as Chrétien de Troyes. In her *lai* of *Lanval*, Marie depicts the virtues of a poor knight and praises him for freeing prisoners and feeding the poor. Marie's immediate circle was doubtless aristocratic, but she seems to have spoken directly to the less powerful people both inside and outside that circle. It should not be surprising that so many of her tales possess close analogs in the oral traditions of lower-class Europeans of later centuries, and it is altogether possible that Marie first heard some of her tales performed by the disenfranchised people of her own day.

See also: Fable; Fairy Lover; Folktale; French Tradition; Purgatory

—Pack Carnes and Carl Lindahl

Marriage Traditions. Lore surrounding the most important social rite in medieval Europe, a rite all the richer because, in the absence of formal rites of initiation, this institution marked the transition from adolescence to adulthood.

Marriage traditions may be understood as the sequence of events taking place from courtship and betrothal to the performances required from the newlyweds in seasonal rites involving the youth of the community—for example, on the first Sunday of Lent or on the Feast of St. John (June 24). An extended conception of marriage would also include the rituals practiced by girls in order to divine the identity of their future husbands. We should even take into account the whole training of the young within their family and their community. Perhaps more effectively than from the Church's pedagogy, youngsters learned from such courtship customs as the May

festival custom of fixing branches of certain trees on girls' doors: a branch of hornbeam could be a sign of appreciation; a branch of eldertree or a cabbage, a sign of depreciation. They also learned from such matchmaking rituals as the *daillements* in Champagne and Lorraine, where newlywed couples paired off boys and girls. In addition, children took part in a family discourse involving matrimonial memories and the narration of alliances and genealogies, so they normally chose partners who fit their family's strategies. Those discourses might take place during evening get-togethers known as *veillées*, which along with fairs, pilgrimages, and such festivals as Carnival and May Day constituted the main settings for meeting and courting. In such festive settings there was a great difference between the behaviors of already-constituted couples, who were discreet and quiet, and unattached youngsters, who played unequivocal sexual games. Folklorists have observed different customs allowing a certain amount of sexual freedom during the courting period, especially in popular milieus: *kiltgand* in Germany, Switzerland, and eastern France, and *maraîchinage* in Charentes and Poitou.

The betrothal was usually made official by an intermediary from the groom's family—a kinsman, a godfather, or a matchmaker—in charge of the proposal, the promise being granted by the girl's father. As a third person, this intermediary could feel free to discuss the material aspects of the agreement, namely, the dowry. He also acted to temper feelings of frustration if the proposal was refused. The betrothal constituted the first real act of marriage, accompanied by rites similar to those of the actual wedding, the main aspect being its public nature. The exchange of gifts symbolizing the agreement began at that stage with a special present from the groom to the bride (a scarf or an apron) and some form of compensation to his fellow bachelors (food, wine, money). The Church usually controlled the betrothal ceremony: impediments and freedom of consent were verified, a benediction by the priest was added to the words of promise and the joining of right hands, the most ancient rite. As a consequence, sexual union was implicitly allowed during the critical period between betrothal and marriage, and a breach of contract, though possible, was a serious affair.

Over time, the priest took on increasing importance in the marriage ritual itself, with the progressive substitution of the priest for the bride's father. Traditionally, father and groom had been prominent figures—they exchanged a woman—and the two main components had been the transfer of authority to the husband and the sexual union. But by the fourteenth century in France the Church asserted its role in the marriage, and it was the priest who gave the bride to the groom. The evolution underwent another shift after the twelfth century, as the rite of acceptance by the groom became a rite of mutual acceptance. By the fourteenth century the focus was on the spouses: they pronounced the mutual vows previously uttered by the priest.

The marriage ceremony itself can actually be considered as a rite of passage. The sequence of events, though not strictly fixed, followed the three-step pattern of a rite of passage: the separation taking place at the father's home with tears, paternal benediction, and signs of grief; the transitional moment of the procession; and finally, after the ceremony, the integration into the new household and life. The procession represents this passage, with its two moments leading from the bride's household to the church and from the church to the groom's household. The procession's motion through both space and time, dividing the event into successive stages, shaped the ritual. Other markers of ritualization were the costumes and ribbons that the groom gave the guests to wear and the music and songs performed during the procession.

Before the eleventh century the family ritual was usually performed in the household, moving then to the front steps of the church and finally into the church. The central gesture of the ceremony was always the joining of the couple's right hands as a symbol of the bride's transfer and later of their mutual agreement. The other physical sign of their union, the kiss, peculiar to the betrothal, marked the conclusion of the wedding ritual. Other symbols of union included the nuptial cord that bound the spouses and the veil placed above their heads during the benediction. The ring has remained, through the ages, the very symbol of the union in its many aspects. Given by the groom—no ring was bestowed by the bride before the sixteenth century—the ring represents the sexual union as well as the social and economic exchange, also symbolized by jewels or coins given to the bride and consecrated.

In thirteenth-century German villages the families of the bride and groom created a literal ring around the couple, standing in a circle as the bride's father or a village elder asked the man and woman to make their mutual vows. Once the vows were declared the groom took possession of his wife by stepping on her foot, the same gesture used in Germany to seal business deals.

Having taken control of the marriage ceremony by presiding over the benediction inside the church, the priest extended his influence into the nuptial bed. In some customs, for example in Brittany, after the mass he prescribed a period of abstinence for a few days (called the Tobias nights). His intervention in the nuptial chamber reflected an interesting manifestation of syncretism. In addition to the priest's aspersing with holy water and his prayers to keep evil spells from endangering fecundity, unofficial magical practices might be performed: the cleansing sprinkling of salt, practices to ward off impotence, or acts involving the umbilical cord or menstrual blood of the bride to secure fecundity. The public

character of this bedside event, involving the participation of the community, was maintained throughout the wedding night. Between the rite of undressing the bride (performed by her female relatives, friends, and neighbors) and the wedding soup joyfully offered by the youngsters, intercourse could only enjoy a quasi-intimacy, the sexual consummation being a concern for the whole community.

The exchange of gifts constituted a fundamental aspect of the ritual, taking place first at the betrothal and renewed at the marriage. The groom and the bride gave presents to each other and to the relatives and the young bachelors. The groom presented a ritual gift of the wedding shoes to his bride, and she presented him the wedding shirt she had sewn. During the feast the groom had to compensate his mates for their loss of a potential wife with money or, more often, wine and food. (In England the groom hosted tavern parties known as "bride's ales.") Such tributes, especially important if the groom was an outsider to the community, began as early as the betrothal, to be repeated on the eve and night of the wedding. The bride might have to show her solidarity with poor girls by giving them fabric for their trousseaus. Fashioning the trousseau—this display of her wealth and industriousness—was a major occupation for betrothed girls. The trousseau was the bride's part in the exchanges between families, the groom's part being the wedding garments given to the relatives and the expenses of the feast. The wedding feast was a synthesis of the essential meanings of the ritual of marriage itself. Drinking and eating together symbolizes the union, while the festive aspects of the gathering, abundance and freedom of speech, songs and gestures (for example, the rite of exchanging punches, described by Rabelais in the sixteenth century) evoke Carnival and its implications.

The multiple meanings implied by marriage traditions are characteristic of any ritual: their rich symbolism is always open to new decipherings and developments in spite of their permanence. The objects and gestures of marriage rites function like a language and support many connotations. Take the example of the distaff, an erotic emblem, an image of fecundity but also of the domestic chores of women. The distaff may be used to signal the bride's acceptance of a proposed fiancé or as test of her ability to respond to what is expected from a wife (fecundity and industriousness) when she is required to spin before entering her new household. As shown by the distaff, ambiguity is another characteristic of marriage rites, at least when women are concerned. Are the rituals meant to test her abilities? To recognize her central importance in the household? Or to convey the feminine threat she inspires? Meanings overlap: the ring evokes possession by the husband, in all senses of the term, as well as the union and its fruits, which are also manifest in the drinking and eating together. This exchange of food and gifts and the public character of the event epitomized in the procession work together to accomplish the transfer of a biological reality into a social one.

See also: Charivari; Festivals and Celebrations; Rites of Passage

—Madeleine Jeay

Martinmas [November 11].

A major Church festival, marking the burial of St. Martin, Bishop of Tours, already legendary at the time of his death in 397 C.E.; a popular celebration marked by intense feasting, drinking, and play.

The penitential season of Advent, largely a Gallic invention, began to be reckoned from St. Martin's feast and became known as *Quadragesima Sancti Martini* (St. Martin's Lent). Something of a Carnival to this lesser Lent also developed, for we have specific prohibitions in the Council of Auxerre (573 C.E.) against all-night vigils before Martin's feast. The day's close proximity to both the Celtic and Germanic celebrations of the new year contributed, no doubt, to the secular side of its celebration.

Martinmas became a kind of threshold holiday, both the last harvest festival and the first winter revel. It marked the end of the slaughtering of the livestock (beef, pigs, geese, and so on) that was not being kept over the winter and thus provided the occasion for a great carnivorous feast. November was the Anglo-Saxon Blotmonath, "slaughter month," also a common designation in other Germanic languages. Blessing with Martinmas blood is an ancient tradition in Ireland, and Patrick himself supposedly instituted a pig sacrifice. Often the Martinmas slaughter was accompanied by blood sports such as the bull-running in Stamford, Lincolnshire, which goes back at least to the fourteenth century, or the wild boar combats staged in sixteenth-century Würzburg.

Martinmas was also the period when the murky new wine was first broached. Thus, we have all the ingredients for serious festivity, and the rise of such early proverbial expressions as *faire la St. Martin* (to live on Easy Street) or terms for drunkenness like *mal de St. Martin* (St. Martin's illness) or the Spanish *del blago de sant Martin tannido* (touched with St. Martin's staff) from Gonzalo de Berceo's *Milagros de Nuestra Senora* (c. 1240). In his *Life of Charlemagne* (c. 885) Notker the Stammerer records a newly appointed bishop's unfortunate Martinmas carouse, and *The Saga of Olaf Tryggvason* relates how, in 996, the ferocious missionary king substituted toasts to St. Martin in place of those to Thor and Odin. German crusaders lost the city of Jaffa in 1198 because of their overindulgence on St. Martin's Eve, and as late as 1563 William the Silent, prince of Orange, and his cronies were getting dangerously inebriated on Martinmas.

Early November was also the turnover period

for many agricultural laborers, who, it may be assumed, empathized with the beggar half of the famous icon of the "Charity of St. Martin" (in which St. Martin, as a young soldier, cuts his cloak with a sword to share it with the shivering mendicant). The coincidence of this image with Martinmas as the first winter feast threw into high relief the needs of the destitute at the onset of bad weather and the obligations of the privileged to share harvest largesse. This contributed to a creative tension between societal strata throughout Martinmas festival expression and added an almost Saturnalian quality to the profane celebration of the day.

The goliardic poets (often wandering students who, in the central Middle Ages, composed and performed satirical songs) Hugh Primas (fl. 1130–1140) and the Archpoet of Cologne (fl. 1160) frequently assumed the persona of the Martin beggar and invoked Martin's generosity against more penny-pinching ecclesiastics. The *Minnesänger* (love poet) Walter von der Vogelweide was more fortunate, having received a furlined cloak from Bishop Wolfger of Passau as a Martinmas gift in 1203. Secular and evidently raucous songs for the Martinmas feast also developed early on. In 1216 Thomas of Cantimpré fulminated against a *"cantus de Martino turpissimus"* [most foul song about Martin], popular through France and Germany, that the cleric claimed was composed by the devil himself. The Martinmas song tradition was particularly strong in the German language. The fourteenth-century Monk of Salzburg composed several *Martinslieder* (Martin songs) praising the *"liebe, czartter, trawter heer mein"* [the beloved, tender, true lord (of the feast)] and emphasizing its democratic character: *"Dy grossen / dye klainen / gemainen"* [The great / the lowly / together]. The tradition remained strong through Oswald von Wolkenstein; court composers such as Ludwig Senfl, Thomas Stoltzer, and Orlando di Lasso; Renaissance collectors of native song such as Georg Foster and Melchior Francken; and on into contemporary folklore in an unbroken tradition.

Although Martinmas did not develop into a locus for intense dramatic activity, as did Christmas and Carnival, performances did nevertheless arise from the feast. The fifteenth-century French *sermons joyeux* (parody sermons) *de saint Raisin* (on the Holy Grape) and *de Bien Boie* (on Good Drink) belong to Martinmas rather than to the Carnival season, and the *Sermon de la Choppinerie* (Sermon on Drinking) depends on the rivalry between St. Nicholas Day and Martinmas as occasions for organized boozing. The late-fourteenth-century Swiss play *Ein Streit zwischen Herbst und Mai* (A Fight between Autumn and Spring) also belongs to the orbit of Martinmas and features comical personifications like those commonly found in the Combats between Carnival and Lent. The delights of Martinmas are frequently drawn upon in other German winter versus summer debates, for example, the calendar poems of Hans Sachs, and can be found as well in the English *Debate and stryfe betwene Somer and Wynter* (c. 1530): "Somer, men make greate Joy what tyme I com in / For companyes gadareth togyther on eue of / seynt martyn." As late as the eighteenth century an "impious" and "dissolute" *Martinsspiel* (Martin play), whether an actual drama or some sort of drinking ritual, was reported for Tartu (Dorpat) in Estonia. Martinmas also marked one of the earliest occasions for rural winter masquerades in more recent folk populations: straw-suited guisers in Orkney and Shetland, the *Pelzmartl* (Furry Marty) monster in Swabia, and the Wolf of the *Wolfauslassen* in Bavaria. Wolf-pelted Martinmas masqueraders are recorded in Braunschweig as early as 1446.

Martinmas was also a favorite setting for comic tales. The saint appears as a Trickster figure in the French fabliaux *Les iiii souhais Saint Martin* (The Four Wishes of St. Martin) and *Des sohaiz que Sainz Martins dona Anvieus et Covietos* (The Wishes That St. Martin Granted Envious and Covetous). The early-thirteenth-century German poet known as Der Stricker composed a comic tale, *Die Martinsnacht*, in which a rich Austrian farmer, celebrating St. Martin's Eve with his people, hears a commotion in his cow barn and rouses himself to trap the thief. The cattle rustler, as a ruse, strips himself naked and is found blessing the animals in their stalls. He informs the befuddled peasant that he is St. Martin himself, newly arrived from heaven (*Martinisegen*, invocations of Martin's protection for domestic animals, go back to the ninth century in the Alpine regions). The naked "saint" then instructs the peasant to rejoin his household and joyfully carouse with the new wine that is Martin's special gift. The farmer ecstatically returns to the house to inspire an orgy of celebration, during which the thief makes off with the entire herd.

Paralleling the *Martinslieder*, Martinmas comic tales are also continuous in the German tradition through the centuries. Four tales in Georg Wickram's collection *Das Rollwagenbüchlin* (1555), and others in Johannes Pauli's *Schimpf und Ernst* (1522) and Hans Wilhelm Kirchhof's *Wendemuth* (1563), have Martinmas settings and involve itinerant musicians and singers, scatological play with the "sweet Martin's milk," and a priest's defense of a Martinmas sausage slung in his belt while he celebrates Mass. Hans Sachs wrote a dream vision of the suffering goose population on Martinmas, *Der faisten gens sorgfeltig clag / Auf den kunfting sant Mertens-tag* (The Fat Goose Cries Sorrowfully / at the Coming of St. Martin's Day; 1569), and Martinmas is also the context for the 4,000-verse satire *Gans König* (Goose King; 1607) by the Protestant pastor Wolfhart Spangenberg. The Martinmas festival as comic occasion was not confined to the German tradition, however; witness the opening of the well-known Scots ballad "Get Up and Bar the Door":

It fell about the Martinmas time
And a gay time it was then,
When our goodwife got puddings to make,
And she's boiled them in the pan.

The ballad not only presumes Martinmas hospitality based on the abundance of sausage materials from the slaughter, but it also constellates many distinctly carnivalesque elements: night wanderers gorging themselves on puddings "white and black," threats of befouling (shaving the silent goodman with pudding broth) and of cuckolding (kissing the goodwife), leading to the ultimate triumph of Woman over Man (the goodman is first to break the bargain of keeping silent and must therefore get up and bar the door).

Thus, Martinmas served as a kind of shadow Carnival, ushering in as opposed to ushering out the winter reveling season over several European cultures. It is ironic that the fourth-century ascetic and destroyer of pagan cult sites should become the patron of such a secular festivity and be associated with such profane heroes as Gargantua (Rabelais, 1.36) and Falstaff (2 Henry IV, 2.2).

See also: Advent; Carnival; Festivals and Celebrations; Harvest Festivals and Rituals

—Martin W. Walsh

Mary Magdalen, Saint (fl. first century C.E.) [Greek, Maria Magdalini; also Mary of Magdala, Mary Magdalene]. The leading female disciple of Jesus Christ.

In the New Testament Mary Magdalen is described as one of the women followers who supported Christ with their own means (Luke), and she was therefore probably wealthy. She was present at the crucifixion (Mark, Matthew, Luke, and John) and saw where Christ's body was placed before burial.

According to the Gospels she was one of the two or three Marys who went to the tomb, taking spices to anoint Christ's body; they found the empty tomb and either one or two angels who told them of the resurrection. According to John she went alone to the tomb and met the risen Christ, who told her to tell the disciples of his resurrection. In Luke and Mark she is also described as having had seven devils driven from her.

By the twelfth century she had an entire *vita*—a past history and a post-Ascension apostolic and eremitical career, incorporating such typical hagiographical themes as crossing the sea, preaching and converting, and repenting in the desert. Elements such as monastic rivalry, the classic *furtum sacrum* (holy theft—i.e., of sacred relics), and the "invention," or discovery, of her relics enrich her story. She also had a new character, that of the repentant whore, a model of repentance for all sinners (particularly prostitutes), embodying ecclesiastical propaganda and popular piety. This was the result of the conflation of her New Testament character with those of two other biblical women: Mary of Bethany, and the woman described as a "sinner" in Luke, chapter 7—a story that was confirmed by Pope Gregory the Great in about 591. Added to these characters there was the accretion to her of the legend of St. Mary of Egypt, a repentant prostitute who crossed the sea to Palestine, spending 37 years in the desert, naked except for her hair, repenting for her sins and dying.

The standard *vita* of Mary Magdalen begins before her meeting with Christ: Jacobus de Voragine's thirteenth-century *Golden Legend* relates that she was the beautiful daughter of a rich nobleman. Her conflation with Mary of Bethany endows her with siblings Martha and Lazarus and the New Testament narratives concerning them. She inherits the castle or town of Magdala. To some writers she is a harlot; to others, her licentious life is merely a natural adjunct to her beauty and wealth. In the thirteenth-century Benediktbeuern Passion play, she is a vanity figure, putting on makeup to seduce lovers; her only desire is to live in libidinous luxury. Scenes of her worldly life—including dancing, playing ball, and riding—appear in medieval manuscripts and fresco cycles, where Martha and Lazarus reprimand her while she stands with her lover's hand placed on her hip. Brought to her senses either by Martha and Lazarus—or by seeing Christ himself—she repents and in the character of Luke's sinner goes to the house of the Pharisee, weeps on Christ's feet, dries them with her hair, and anoints them.

Another reason for Mary Magdalen's profligate past is given in the story—possibly known as early as Bede (d. 735) and much debated in the Middle Ages—of her marriage at Cana to St. John the Evangelist, who leaves his bride at the feast to obey the call of his Lord. The jilted Magdalen decides to become a prostitute, and the seven devils enter her.

On her conversion Mary Magdalen becomes one of the inner sanctum of Christ's followers: she is described as "the sweet lover of Christ." Through her conflation with Mary of Bethany she is portrayed as present at the raising of Lazarus. She appears in scenes of Christ's Passion. Her meeting with the risen Christ, in the scene called the *Noli me tangere* (Do Not Touch Me), is one of the most touching images of her in the Middle Ages. The scene of her announcing the resurrection to the disciples, as the "Apostle to the Apostles," although very rare, was particularly important to medieval women. Some medieval writers even maintained that she was present at the Last Supper. She is always identifiable by her long golden hair, red cloak—red symbolizing her love and fidelity to Christ—and her ointment jar. In northern European art she also usually appears in dark green, often elegantly dressed and coifed, and with her jar.

After the Ascension Mary Magdalen retired to a cave in the wilderness to mourn Christ's death; she fasted and prayed, and angels carried her to heaven for divine sustenance; she was found by a priest who gave her the last sacraments and buried her. Miracles abounded from her tomb. This ninth-century addition to Mary Magdalen's story derived from the *vita* of St. Mary of Egypt. In a later version Mary Magdalen, now naked and repentant, with only her long golden hair as a mantle, told the priest of her sinful past before expiring. A confusing variety of tales ensues. In the twelfth century Mary Magdalen's cave was said to be in Provence. Persecuted by pagans or Jews and accompanied by Martha and Lazarus, the three Marys, servants, and others (including, according to some, St. Maximinus), she had been put to sea from Palestine in a rudderless boat that was guided by the hand of the Lord and that brought them to Gaul, where Lazarus became bishop of Aix, Martha tamed the dragon in Tarascon, and Mary Magdalen preached to and converted the pagan prince of Marseilles and his wife. After 30 years in eremitical retreat, she was taken to Bishop Maximinus's church in Aix for her last confession and communion; there she died and was buried.

The first known cult of Mary Magdalen dates from sixth-century Ephesus. In the West the earliest references are in the late tenth century. In 1050 the abbey of Vézelay in Burgundy listed Mary Magdalen as one of its patrons, claiming to possess the remains of the illustrious saint and close familiar of Christ, brought thither in a "holy theft" from Aix. As a result Vézelay became the most important pilgrimage center in France, en route for Compostela. It was unrivaled until the end of the twelfth century, and engendered the tales of her apostolic career to ensure its fame. In 1256, on the arrival of a papal envoy sent to look into the abbey's decline, some bones and a quantity of female hair were "discovered." In 1279, however, the discovery of Mary Magdalen's "true" body by monks at St. Maximin in Provence eclipsed Vézelay's claims.

In the Middle Ages Mary Magdalen was the favorite female saint after the Virgin Mary. She was listed in the litany of saints before all the virgin saints except the Virgin Mary. From the thirteenth century to the fifteenth, her feast day, July 22, first known in Ephesus, was one of the most important Church festivals, a *double* (i.e., a feast so important that parts of the divine service were sung twice). Because of her role as Apostle to the Apostles, the Creed was recited in the mass for that day, an honor reserved for particularly important feasts. The feast of her conversion was noted in Merovingian calendars and in the Old Irish Martyrology of Oengus as March 28 and in Germanic countries between the thirteenth and fifteenth centuries as April 1.

Patron saint for all sinners, she was particularly so for repentant prostitutes, for whom a special Order of the Penitents of St. Mary Magdalen was set up for their recuperation in 1227. She was especially popular with the Mendicant orders from the thirteenth century to the fifteenth. She was also patron saint of, among others, hospitals, leper houses, scent makers, flagellant confraternities, and colleges at the universities of Oxford and Cambridge. Her arrival in France is still celebrated annually in St. Maximin on July 22, when a blackened skull, said to be hers, is carried in procession by villagers.

Despite ecclesiastical furor in 1518 caused first by the humanist Jacques Lefèvre d'Étaples's refutation of the composite Mary Magdalen (a gesture that led to his being accused of heresy) and later by skepticism from the Protestant churches, the Church of Rome continued to adhere to and use this composite figure—particularly during the Counter-Reformation—until 1969.

See also: James the Elder, Saint; Jesus Christ; Virgin Mary

—Susan Haskins

Masking. Disguising in formulary ways, whether for social or religious, serious or playful reasons.

Masking to suggest human transformation into sub- or superhuman forms was denounced by the Christian church from Maximus of Turin's time (fl. 450) to that of Jean Savaron (fl. 1610) because it suggested communion with, if not absorption into, demonic forms: Maximus wrote, "Is there anything in the world as false and unclean as those men, formed by God, who transform themselves into cattle, wild beasts, or monsters [portenta]?" And "Le diable est l'auteur des masques" [the devil is the author of masks], wrote Jean Savaron (Traité contre les masques, Paris, 1608).

Man, made in God's image, is not simply superior to but alien from the natural world. Man, but not woman, is nature's lord. To assume the masks of nature misuses man's God-given power to command nature rather than imitate it. Commanding nature means commanding women, due to their involvement with reproduction, and hence masking as women was for medieval Christian clerics as disgusting as the imitation of animals, as Caesarius of Arles thundered in his sermon 192, "On the Kalends of January" (c. 530): "Others wear the heads of beasts so they do not seem to be men.... And what sort of thing is it, indeed—how shameful it is—for those born as men to be dressed in women's vestments!" To non-Christians and demi-Christians—the majority of medieval people—this entirely negative opinion of vegetal, animal, atmospheric, and human reproductive powers was not convincing. The socially elite as well as the nonelite peasants, pastoralists, and hunters, and all manner of men thinking about female generative powers, practiced a variety of propitiatory, exorcist, apotropaic, and healing practices that demanded conciliation and sometimes masked imitation of the force of natural things, however much they may have differed in their judgment of the meaning of nature.

Medieval Christian believers and less-than-believers did agree on one point, which worked as strongly as the doctrine of superiority to nature in condemning the masking practices common to Roman and non-Roman inhabitants of Europe after 315: spirit is more powerful than matter. In Western tradition spirit has normally been figured as nearly invisible matter, as a kind of wind or breath. Its superiority to more visible matter meant that when maskers pretended to be fluttering ghosts, fairies, or other such twinkling terrors, they were not merely imitating but had channeled into themselves spiritual powers less than God's but more than man's: they possessed or were possessed by "demonic" powers, which for all Christians—with the exception of a few mystics—were equivalent to the powers of devils. Theologically schooled medieval Christians might be able to view maskers imitating horses, bears, oxen, goats, stags, or women simply as ignorant of man's God-given sovereignty over nature, but they could not dismiss ghostly games as stupidity. Ghosts were bearers of spiritual power. They conveyed messages from other worlds, and the doors to these worlds—to those of the saintly and the sinful dead, to the fecund underworld and the star-filled overworld—were not securely fastened and could not be, for liturgical, sacramental, and theological reasons. The worlds represented by maskers who donned ghostly shapes were, as philosophers maintained, more real than the everyday visible world. Those who masked in such ways represented forms that could neither be trusted nor eliminated from medieval understanding. Authorities therefore tried to push them to ideological and performative margins.

Dangerous yet ineluctable as it was for Christian monotheism, the masking world even on the margins was allowed little ritual elaboration, and so it took playful forms. Playful rather than seriously ceremonialized masking was an easy direction to develop, for all performance, since it is theatrical, is ambivalent. Performing encourages believing, especially if what is performed is ideologically and institutionally supported in massive sociopolitical ways. But preparing to perform requires practicing techniques—that is, those of making masks and acting in them—and so it fosters distantiation from belief. The more that performance takes place on institutional and ideological margins, the more rapidly distantiation occurs, as masking becomes a theatrical game. Moreover, masking performance is stylized performance; masking more than other forms of theatrical technique requires its practitioners to develop generalized, stereotypical mimicry that, subtracted from ideological and ritual supports, verges toward the playful, ironic, and ridiculous rather than the dreadful.

Students of medieval masquerade have four main kinds of sources at their disposal. First and most numerous until the thirteenth century were the Church's prohibitory statements in sermons, Church council edicts, penitentials, and local monastic and cathedral chronicles. These materials were ordered and analyzed between 1880 and 1928 by a series of scholars (Edmund K. Chambers and Wilhelm Boudriot most eminently) whose work has been recently restated with few additional materials by Dieter Harmening. The second most numerous group of sources emanates from town records, which with few exceptions began only in the thirteenth century. Masking references here are to regulation, repression, or the consequence of crimes committed during masking festivities. They have been most thoroughly investigated by historians of festivity like Hans Moser, Julio Caro Baroja, and Roger Vaultier. Third come aristocratic and feudal records of festivities. The literary and iconographic materials prepared for the pleasure of nobles and courtiers sometimes give clues to masking practices otherwise unrecorded: a famous case is Jean Froissart's account of the Bal des Ardents, the Wild Man dance at Christmas 1393 in Paris, when King Charles VI was nearly killed by accident. The fourth and chronologically latest kinds of sources are the proto-anthropological accounts of humanists such as Joannes Boemus, who included an extraordinary list of festive maskers in his *Customs, Laws, and Rites of all Peoples* (1520).

The less than two dozen documents dating between 300 and 1000 are, as reports of masking practice, even fewer than they appear to be because of the tendency of medieval churchmen to copy their predecessors rather than to look out the window. Sermons 192 and especially 193 by Caesarius of Arles, the latter mentioning maskers imitating horses and stags, were copied a half dozen times and more by Church councils (e. g., Auxerre, 573), compilers like Isidore of Seville (*De ecclesiasticis officiis*, I, 41), writers of confessional handbooks (the penitentials, especially those from Frankish Gaul, 700–850), and energetic sermonizers like Abbot Pirmin and Regino von Prüm. Of course, extant sources represent only an incalculable fraction of the actual denunciations of masking practices. No way has yet been invented to estimate either the extent and variety of unorthodox naturalistic and spiritualistic masking practices or the extent of ecclesiastical concern about them. From the ninth century some Germanic and Slavic modes of masking are documented, supplementing the earlier Celtic and Roman kinds. Wild Men maskers performed at the Byzantine court in the early tenth century, and the famed Germanic Wild Woman figure Perhta/Berta is indirectly documented near Salzburg in the same century.

Nonecclesiastical sources in Western Europe emerge in the thirteenth century. The Church's own marginal figures are the best documented maskers between 1000 and 1300: the Feast of Fools and the Feast of the Boy Bishop festivities during the Twelve Days are known from Joannes Belethus onward (fl. 1160–1190, Paris). Next in importance come the translations of Romance literature after 1100 into costumed performances. In addition to King Arthur and his knights there are the mock siege of a castle of love at Treviso in 1214, the joust of the green knight at Friesach in 1227, and Ulrich von Liechtenstein's month-long jousting tour, garbed as Frau Venus, which proceeded from Venice to Bohemia in 1238. A variety of urban sources for the thirteenth century mention Wild Men and giants; should we also suppose that the goliardic poets (often wandering students who, in the central Middle Ages, composed and performed satirical songs), as disciples of Goliath, sometimes masked as giants? At Huy in 1250 and at Magdeburg in 1285 youthful merchants' sons rivaled the nobility in lavish transvestite and Wild Man costuming.

As European courts and cities distanced themselves socioculturally from the rural areas on which they still depended for food and taxes, they also distanced themselves from Church prohibitions. After 1300 the Church itself seems to have tacitly adopted a policy of accommodation. Denunciations practically cease. The two favorite masquerades between 1300 and 1550 were those of Wild People, male or female, and fools, mostly male. These two masking types are found everywhere, on town and noble coats of arms as well as in street processions, in rural Switzerland and Savoy as well as in urbane Venice and Nuremberg, in comic literature (Rabelais) as in humanist tracts (Erasmus's *Praise of Folly*; c. 1511).

Christian doctrine lost—and won. The goat-bird-devil who paraded in Schembart Carnival at Nuremberg in the early sixteenth century did not seek to become the natural forces represented in his costume, nor did he encourage those watching him to imagine his effective possession by some such overpowering mystery. In a basket on his back an old woman gesticulates excitedly in conversation with a miniature replica of the masker. The woman is a witch, or a would-be one. The masker offers spectators a human drama, a diabolical thing that some people do. In Carnival time, in miniature, this bad thing became funny. It did not lose the Christian coordinates of its meaning, but in the long run using such images in Carnival could only diminish superstitious fear of the devil and loosen the grip of witchcraft on people's minds. It did so by enlarging people's sense of control over their representations of the world.

Masking like this unmasks. The world's vast evil is reduced to the dimension of puppets in a basket. Christianized humanism joined with peasants' and townspeople's desires for the prosperity of their animals and crops to allow people to think beyond the alternatives of sacral use or misuse of the world's powers. A rationalizing religious sense might deal with drought and famine straightforwardly by supporting schemes for grain storage and distribution to the poor, and not only by urging parades of saving reliquaries. Such a religious sense tolerated mask-filled holidays, and even found an ironical wisdom in them.

In Carnival time, wrote a fifteenth-century German humanist in a jovial dialogue, "the genius expands." Dietrich Gresemund uses the word *genius* to refer not to special talent but to the old Roman sense of a guiding spirit, innate in people, that inclines them to sociability. This time, Gresemund continues, should not be called the time of "giving up meat" (*carnelevare*, the Latin word from which *carnival* is derived, refers to the end of meat eating at midnight on Fat Tuesday before Ash Wednesday and Lent). One should refer to it "with the higher Latin name of *geniale tempus* (genial time)." But if I behave as you suggest, expostulates Gresemund's interlocutor in the dialogue, "people will call me an ass." "Indeed you are, since you are a man," responds Gresemund. In the optimistic atmosphere of Christian Renaissance humanism, animal masks reminded Carnival players of their links to nature without subjecting them to it. In this atmosphere Hellekin, the monstrous ghost of medieval superstition, could become Harlequin, the commedia dell'arte figure of farce, whose black, dog-like face stimulates scatological clowning, not fear. Masking had become masquerade, gutted of its shared ideological substance; masking turned toward the subjectively inspired seductions of modern times.

See also: Bal des Ardents; Carnival; Charivari; Drama; Festivals and Celebrations; Fool; Fools, Feast of; Martinmas; Wild Man; Wild Woman

—Samuel Kinser

Maxen Wledig [Maxen the Emperor]. In Welsh historical legend, the Roman emperor who searched for and discovered the British princess whom he had seen in his recurrent dream.

By his marriage to her at Caernarfon in north Wales, he obtained the kingdom of Britain and was the ancestor of a number of the dynasties of Dark Age Britain. Rebellion and betrayal at Rome caused him to return there to reclaim his throne. His campaign was assisted by troops from Britain, some of whom were rewarded with lands and settled, under their leader Cynan, in Armorica, which became "Little Britain," Brittany.

The story of the dream maiden (motifs H1381.3.1.2.2, T11.3, D1976.2) is related in *The Dream of Maxen Wledig,* the earliest text of which is found in the mid-thirteenth-century Peniarth Manuscript 16. The underlying motivation for the legend appears to be the need for a version of the Roman conquest of Britain that would not offend the sensitivities of the Welsh and that would at the same time reinforce a sense of pride in seeing themselves as the heirs of the empire, a theme in medieval Welsh historiography that can be recognized in Gildas, in the learned legend of Brutus, and in the Dark Age genealogies.

The historical Maxen is Magnus Maximus, a Roman general in Britain who was raised to the purple in 383. Though his brief rule ended in 388, when he was killed by his rival Theodosius at Aquileia, the exodus from Britain to win the emperor's throne and the subsequent founding of Brittany impressed itself on Welsh and Breton historiography and is found in Gildas and in *Historia Brittonum* (History of the Britons), attributed to Nennius. Geoffrey of Monmouth used the same nexus of tradition in the *Historia regum Britanniae* (History of the Kings of Britain), but he calls the emperor Maximianus. Maxen appears to be the result of a confusion of names with Maxentius: the Welsh genealogies have Maxim, closer to the historical Maximus. The number of allusions both to the dream tale and to the historical traditions themselves in other sources indicate a widespread knowledge of Maxen, his Roman context, and the foundation of Brittany.

See also: Brutus; Geoffrey of Monmouth; Gildas; Nennius

—Brynley F. Roberts

Medicine. The diagnosis, treatment, prognosis, and prevention of disease; surgical operations; and the care of wounds.

In medieval medicine, beliefs and processes deriving from folklore appear in theories of the origins of diseases, the substances (plants, animals, and minerals) used to cure them, and the ritual practices used for prophylactic, curative, or prognosticatory purposes. During the millennium between 500 and 1500 one of the most common forms of treatment was the herbal remedy. Pharmaceutical recipes for medicines made from plants (and other natural ingredients) were copied continuously in a manuscript tradition extending back to the *De materia medica* of Dioscorides, the Greek writer from Anazarbus (in modern Turkey), and the *Historia naturalis* of the Roman encyclopedist Pliny the Elder, both of whom lived in the first century C.E. Because much essential information about plants, their location, the most useful parts, and methods of collection and application is omitted from the medical recipe books, such information would have been acquired by word of mouth, personal observation, and practice. In the long textual tradition, herbal recipes based on current and local practices are difficult to distinguish from ones ultimately deriving from ancient and early-medieval written sources. If, however, the recipes were made from the directions in the books, as the evidence suggests they were, then many ancient recipes were continually being brought into existence within new communities under new circumstances.

Early Vernacular Medical Books

The earliest vernacular medical writings of the European medieval period are those of the Anglo-Saxons; in many ways they are representative of medical practices elsewhere in Europe. Folklore and remnants of Greek and Roman medical theory combine freely in the Anglo-Saxon medical books (Bald's *Leechbook*, *Leechbook III*, the *Herbarium* with its associated texts, *Lacnunga*, and *Peri didaxion*). Folk beliefs about the origins of diseases are suggested by the names of ailments. For example, a man or a horse may suffer "elfshot." Other causes of ailments include flying poisons, elf adle (fever) and water-elf adle, elf trick, dwarfs, demons, temptation by a fiend, devil sickness, mares that ride men at night, and a variety of "worms." Evidence that healing practices were passed from one healer (Anglo-Saxon *læce*, later *leech*) to another appears in Bald's *Leechbook*, where two healers, Oxa (1, 47) and Dun (2, 65), are credited with having taught specific remedies. Phrases such as "leeches teach" (2, 20), "leeches who were wisest taught" (1, 72), and "unwise leeches say" (2, 59) offer some evidence of a healing tradition, either oral or textual. Curatives were often dispensed as prescriptions for patients to perform on their own. For example, in the *Lacnunga* (fol. 185) instructions are given for a woman who is unable to carry a child to term: she is to go out and step over a man's grave three times while repeating a charm to prevent miscarriage. Later, when pregnant, she is supplied with a charm to recite as she steps over her husband in bed; and finally, when she feels the child quicken, she must go to the church altar and declare it in a formula.

The folk medical practices (Germanic, Irish, and Romano-Gallic) recorded by the Anglo-Saxons include spoken and written charms, amulets, writing on objects to be ingested, and rituals, such as for gathering and preparing herbs, for relieving medical conditions, and for determining the sex of a child. Recipes typically combine more than one of these practices and some can be lengthy. In Bald's *Leechbook I* (39), a simple ritual for treating a felon (an infection of the end of the finger or toe, most commonly caused by splinters or needle pricks) calls for carving the name of the patient on hazel or elder wood or a spoon, then filling the letters with blood and throwing it over the shoulder or between the thighs into running water, all to be done silently. Implicit in this remedy is incising and draining the infection, which remains the treatment of choice today. In chapter 63, a thoroughly Christian healing ritual for a "fiend-sick" man (one mentally disturbed) recommends that the patient drink from a church bell (demons flee the sounds of church bells) ale mixed with herbs and lichen. These should first be collected from a church and a cross, respectively, and then sacralized by having seven masses sung over them.

Learned Physicians and Folk Practices

Medicine in Europe changed greatly between 1050 and 1400 because of (1) the rediscovery of the works of Galen and the Hippocratic writers

via translations from Arabic and Greek, in successive waves from about 1050 to 1150 and 1250 to 1325 (when new Galenic materials were introduced); (2) the rise of universities and medical scholasticism (Aristotelian logic and expository methods theorizing medical discourse); and (3) corporations and licensing (by which midwives, "empirics," and other traditional healers were generally declared unqualified). Yet at the practical end, despite the influence of academic Galenic medicine and religious reform aimed at eradicating "superstitious" practices, herbal and recipe books survived and proved adaptable and conservative of folkloric elements validated by experience as much as authority. Traditional healing rituals had long been flexible enough to incorporate Christian motifs not condemned until the Counter-Reformation. Learned, university-trained physicians and also surgeons relied less frequently on traditional therapies such as amulets, rituals, and charms than did nonacademic medical practitioners and local healers. Although Gilbert the Englishman's thirteenth-century Latin book of medicines contains few charms and rituals, as one might expect from one that follows the Galenic tradition closely, he does include certain trusted "empirica" (traditional practices), such as directions for gathering the plants comfrey and daisy on the day of the vigil of St. John the Baptist "at the third hour" while reciting the Lord's Prayer three times. During the process, the collector should speak to no one. He or she must use the juice of the plants to write on a bit of parchment, "The Lord said, Increase + utbiboth + and multiply + thabechay + and fill the earth + amath." These words tied around the neck of a man during sex will promote conception of a male child; around the neck of the woman, a female (7, 287).

Fifteenth Century

For what diseases and complaints do we find folk cures in late-medieval books of medicines? Cambridge University Library MS Additional 9308, which was written about 1400, is a typical late-medieval doctor's handbook. It lists about 256 medicines, consisting of herbal teas, pills, plasters, ointments and salves, powders, oils, charms, and short healing rituals. These medicines are arranged in the conventional order starting with the head (headache) and moving down the body to aching and swelling in the legs or feet. In this work (and elsewhere) charms are prescribed, in the same manner as herbal preparations, for a "hawe in the eye," toothache, a " bloody flux," wounds, shooting pain in the sinews, worms in the ear, and trouble from a wicked spirit. A widespread charm against thieves, beginning "In Bethlehem was Christ born," often occurs in medicine collections. It implies the need for protection from the muggings often suffered along with loss of property by people traveling the roads. To prevent the robbery was to prevent the danger to life and limb. Besides spoken incantations, this Cambridge manuscript prescribes several overtly religious rituals for fevers, such as one on folio 14v. In this "medicine" the patient is instructed to consume, over three days, communion wafers on which have been written (probably symbolically or by pricking) devotional words to the Trinity in Latin. Each day before taking the prescribed host with its special words, the patient repeats the Our Father, the Ave Maria, and the Creed, once on the first day, twice on the second, and finally three times on the third.

All the incantations in this manuscript are Christian, but the use of Christian formulas in this manner was at times condemned by both university-trained physicians and the Church. Nevertheless, it is clear from the number that have been recovered and preserved in museums that wax and gold images of the Agnus Dei (Lamb of God), pilgrim badges, and saints' relics worn on the body or displayed in tiny reliquaries were popular means of warding off illnesses of body and soul. Brooches, pendants, and rings like the Coventry Ring in the British Museum, bearing the symbols of the wounds and Passion of Christ accompanied by words including, "The five wounds of God are my medicines," were worn as a protection against various spiritual and physical threats to the body and soul. Particularly widely used in England were so-called cramp rings, which kept away not only epilepsy but convulsions, rheumatism, and sudden stiffenings of the muscles. The sacralization of the rings through the process of forging them from the offerings of Good Friday and through their distribution by the monarch, whose power extended to miraculous healing, combined to endow them with strong powers (virtues) for warding off sudden muscular rigidity or pain and consequent falls. Another object made for medicinal purposes was a roll of stretches of parchment sewn together end to end on which drawings of the implements of the Passion or seals containing signs and words were depicted. Sometimes a roll of this kind was bound around a woman in labor to convey the power to deliver a child.

Some English medical and surgical practitioners in the fourteenth and fifteenth centuries, such as John Gaddesden, John Mirfield, John Arderne, and Thomas Fayreford, include charms, amulets, and curative or preventative rituals among their treatments. Gaddesden, for example, in his compendium *Rosa Anglica* (c. 1314), gives directions for properly collecting the herb sanguinaria with prayers and then for hanging it around the neck of a patient to stop bleeding. In another treatment to stop bleeding, the practitioner must write St. Veronica's name, Beronixus for a male or Beronixa for a female, on the forehead of the patient. Gaddesden provides several narrative charms to stop bleeding as well. The narrative charms employ motifs based on traditional legends: Zacharius, who was killed at the altar,

Longinus or Longeus, who pierced Christ's side as he hung on the cross, three good brothers who met Christ on Mount Olivet while seeking herbs to cure wounds. An ointment to make hair grow depends on an analogy between the desired long thick hair and the ingredients of the cure, "withy" (willow) and "maydenhair." The use of sanguinaria, the narrative charms, and the components of the ointment for baldness are built in part upon analogical associations between two words (*sanguinaria*, the herb, and *sanguis*, the blood), image and object (hair and the willow), and a divine (if apocryphal) scene and the immediate circumstance (the pierced Christ and the wounded, bleeding patient). In the past, since the time of James G. Frazer, it has been the practice of anthropologists and historians of medicine simply to categorize these kinds of associations as acting according to naive beliefs that "like cures like" (*similia similibus curantur*) or in "mimetic" or "contagious magic." The assumption was that any practitioner who used such methods was simply subject to "irrational" and "primitive" beliefs. Recently, however, the work of the anthropologist Stanley Jeyaraja Tambiah has suggested that more complex uses of metaphoric language and pragmatics are at work in these kinds of ritual cures.

Other Theories

The argument has been made by M. L. Cameron and others that charms were employed only in hopeless or difficult cases, but that argument does not take sufficient account of the prophylactic purpose of the many charms meant to ward off toothache, fever, eye trouble, skin infections, or sudden pain. It does not account for the beneficial psychological effects of charms like the "Seven Sleeper Charm" to relieve insomnia. Nor does it take into account the calm and confidence that the narrative charm of the three brothers (monks whom Christ instructed how to cure wounds) might convey to someone being carefully tended (with lanolin and wool) for a bleeding wound. Charms and their accompanying rituals work within the specific social context of the patient's suffering or anxiety. Through associated words, actions, and images, they reinstate or reinforce mental and social conditions of good health. Charms containing only Christian themes may be indistinguishable from some forms of prayer.

Other authorities on medieval folk or popular medicine, such as Tony Hunt, distinguish folk medicine as a received tradition of herbal lore from magical or superstitious medicine, which includes incantations and other practices thought to have no rational or experimental basis.

In this article, however, I have not focused on the issue of "rational" versus "irrational" medicine, since the line between the two has not remained stable in our era any more than in the Middle Ages. For example, on the one hand, herbal remedies once labeled irrational and magical have been proved to work through verifiable chemical pathways, and, on the other hand, the relevance of the placebo effect has yet to be fully explored experimentally. As indicated above, during the Middle Ages itself, what rejection there was of traditional folk medical practices derived from three sources: the influence of classical Hippocratic and Galenic attitudes toward the practice of medicine; the establishment of credentials and guilds of physicians, surgeons, and apothecaries, which devalued nontheoretical healers; and the Christian Church, which periodically issued warnings against healing practices like the use of amulets that seemed to rely on powers other than those of the Trinity, Mary, and the saints. However, medieval Europeans were as resourceful as moderns, so when professional medicine was inaccessible, as it was in the countryside or among the urban poor, traditional practices and unofficial healers offered help for some conditions. The lady of the manor, some moderately literate villager, a priest, or an herbalist could be asked for something: a charm, a salve, or what to "do" that would help cure or keep away some ailment.

See also: Amulet and Talisman; English Tradition: Anglo-Saxon Period; Magic; Magic Manuals; Orality and Literacy

—Lea Olsan

Memento Mori [Latin "Remember you must die."]. Generic term used to describe objects or writings serving as reminders of human mortality, especially popular in northern Europe from the late thirteenth century.

Closely related to imagery of the macabre—that is to say, grisly representations of the human body in the process of decomposition—the main emblem of the *memento mori* is the figure of Death, personified as a skull, skeleton, or decaying corpse. While the medieval tradition has numerous classical precedents, such as the popular pagan motifs of *carpe diem* (seize the day) and *ubi sunt* (where are they now?), ancient *memento mori* warnings were as much concerned with the need to enjoy life while there is still time as with the injunction to contemplate death. In contrast, the medieval version illustrated the futility of earthly life, alluding to the biblical warning in *Ecclesiastes* 1:2 that "all is vanity" and stressing the need to repent.

Although there was not an extensive tradition of *memento mori* in the early Middle Ages, the Old Testament contains several passages alluding to the macabre sentiment (e.g., Job 7:5, "My flesh is clothed with worms and clods of dust"). Indeed, some of the earliest visual depictions of the theme in Christian contexts are found at the foot of crucifixion scenes, where Adam's skull and bones symbolize the notion that corporeal decay is the prelude to resurrection. However, it was not until the eleventh century that Christian literature began to meditate at length on the moral consequences of earthly vanity and the impermanence of material things. The attitude of *contemptus mundi* (contempt of the world) was especially prevalent in monastic contexts, where monks were lectured on the follies of worldly power, wealth, and beauty. Around this time religious discourse increasingly adopted the putrefied corpse as a symbol of the ephemeral nature of earthly existence. The twelfth-century "Poema Morale" describes bodily decay as a kind of living death:

Mi bodi that sumtyme was so gay,
Now lieth and rotith in the grounde.
Mi fairhed [fair appearance] is al now goon awai,
And I stynke foulere than an hounde.

It was only in the thirteenth century that reflective literature on death became popular in more secular contexts. Poems such as the *Legend of the Three Living and the Three Dead* were particularly well known in France and functioned as grim warnings to the living to amend their lives in order to save their souls (see illustration). Three wealthy young men, out hunting and parading their finery, come across three cadavers in various states of decay. The latter admonish the men to change their worldly ways before it is too late, declaring that "you will be what we are; we are what you will be." Their sobering motto has the desired effect on the living, one of whom, in a vernacular French version of the poem, announces: "I desire, friend, to amend my life."

Although the three living are invariably rich powerful men—or in certain cases, noble women—the popularity of the *Legend* across all sections of society is indicated by its frequent portrayal in medieval England in parochial contexts. At least 50 English parish churches contained wall paintings of the subject, including Charlwood Church, Surrey (fourteenth century) and Widford Church, Oxfordshire (c. 1325). The nave, where such paintings were commonly executed, was an important forum for medieval preaching, and it is not surprising that the themes of the *Legend* also appear in sermon texts. One twelfth-century homily announces: "Before I was such a one as thou art now. Look on my bones and my dust, and leave thy evil desires!"

The *Legend* was also popular in manuscript illuminations. An especially colorful rendition appears in the Psalter of Robert de Lisle (c. 1310), where three lavishly dressed kings stumble upon their ghastly, worm-ridden doubles.

While images like the latter were intended to instill fear in the viewers and so cause them to mend their ways, poems pondering the theme of *vado mori* (I go to die) contained no element of choice: death is immediate and inevitable. This emphasis on fear of sudden death also pervades genres such as the Dance of Death, perhaps the most sophisticated and refined category of late-medieval *memento mori*. What characterizes all such images and texts is a notion of the mirror image. Like the iconography of the Dance of Death, which portrays each degree of society alongside a skeletal counterpart, and like images of the *Legend*, which bring the living face-to-face with their doubled selves, funerary monuments occasionally depict the buried individual as a naked cadaver—mirroring the "infected" state of their sinful soul. The notorious *transi* tombs of the fifteenth century, though mainly the province of wealthy bishops, testify to the significance of doubling in the *memento mori* tradition. Containing two effigies—one a rotten corpse, the other an idealized figure lying in state—such monuments were sometimes constructed before the death as harsh reminders to their future inhabitants to spurn worldly pleasures. Late-fifteenth-century skeleton brasses in English parish churches attest to the theme's wider diffusion.

In Netherlandish art of the late fifteenth century, the mirror motif is expressed in even more literal terms. One engraving, now in Trinity College, Dublin, represents a skull in a round frame surrounded by the motto: "In this mirror, so may I learn, how from sin, I ought to turn." Here the mirror directly faces the viewers, who are forced to see themselves as already dead—a bleak exercise in penitential self-reflection.

The chief mental image in all instances of *memento mori* is, of course, the transitory nature of things. By the fifteenth century, images of Death as a lone figure appear in visual contexts, wielding a great scythe or an arrow or carrying an hourglass. Death becomes the triumphant leveler, effacing social distinction with one stroke of the scythe of time. Tarot card designs from the fifteenth century often represented Death in such a pose.

Many scholars have related the increased prevalence of macabre imagery in the later Middle Ages to the impact of the Black Death in 1348 and the subsequent ravages of plague, which supposedly contributed to an atmosphere of cultural anxiety and an obsession with death. However, such views have increasingly come under attack from scholars who wish to criticize such a monocausal explanation; they suggest that the plague's influence was at most a catalyst rather than an initiator of change. Another hotly debated question centers on the mental attitudes that *memento mori* convey. Though according to Johan Huizinga the macabre arose from "deep psychological strata of fear," for Philippe Ariès it exhibited a hedonistic "love of life," operating as a "strategy for the afterlife" that simultaneously celebrated people's passionate attachment to things.

See also: Dance of Death; Funeral Customs and
   Burial Rites; Iconography

—Robert Mills

Merlin. Legendary seer, magician, and counselor to King Arthur; a literary figure derived from the Welsh Myrddin tradition and the wonder child Ambrosius in the *Historia Brittonum* (History of the Britons) attributed to Nennius.

The figure of Merlin developed in medieval Britain and France from a combination of local legends and folk motifs to become the pan-European paradigm of all-encompassing wizardly powers in Arthurian romance. He was popularized as Merlinus and first associated with King Arthur in three works by Geoffrey of Monmouth: the *Prophetiae Merlini* (Prophecies of Merlin, c. 1134–1135), the *Historia regum Britanniae* (History of the Kings of Britain, c. 1138), and the *Vita Merlini* (Life of Merlin, c. 1150). The *Prophecies of Merlin*, a lengthy series of obscure predictions made by the fatherless boy Ambrosius Merlin before King Vortigern, was incorporated at the midpoint of the *History of the Kings of Britain*, where it serves to introduce the history of King Arthur. Geoffrey's other major additions to the legend of Merlin are the seer's miraculous birth (sired by an incubus, or invisible spirit), his prediction of Vortigern's death and subsequent role of adviser to the kings Ambrosius and Uther, his construction of Stonehenge, and his disguising of Uther, himself, and another as Duke Gorlois and his retainers so that Uther may satisfy his lust for Gorlois's wife Ygerna and engender Arthur. However, Merlin disappears from the narrative before Arthur comes on the scene; Geoffrey only presents him as knowing Arthur in the *Life of Merlin*, where he summarizes events from the *History*, and the bard Taliesin implies that he and Merlin had conveyed Arthur to Avalon after the battle of Camlan.

Subsequent writers embroidered considerably upon the elements popularized by Geoffrey, separating the figure of Merlin from Welsh tradition and incorporating him into chronicles and romances about King Arthur and his knights. Although Chrétien de Troyes, the finest early romance writer, does not employ Merlin as a character in his writings, other French romance writers developed his role into one equaling Arthur's. The Burgundian poet Robert de Boron (late twelfth–early thirteenth century) wrote *Merlin* (c. 1200), of which only the opening fragment remains, which develops the incubus tradition of Merlin's birth into a full-blown scheme of the devils in hell to engender an anti-Christ who will lead humanity to destruction. One of the devils ruins a wealthy man and corrupts two of his three daughters before impregnating the third in her sleep. Her repentance and her confessor Blaise's immediate baptism of the child at its birth redeem Merlin to become God's instrument in salvation history. Even though he is half devil—with his father's hairy body, dark visage, and knowledge of past and current events—the child is also blessed with divine foreknowledge. His amazing precocity and preternatural awareness allow him to save his mother from being executed for bearing an illegitimate child by demonstrating that her judge does not know he himself is an illegitimate son of the parish priest. Many other episodes in which Merlin demonstrates his powers of perception are included in the two prose revisions and continuations of Robert's romance—the *Merlin* that is part of the lengthy Vulgate cycle (c. 1215) and the *Suite du Merlin* (c. 1230)—and the English adaptations of them, from *Of Arthour and of Merlin* (c. 1250) through Thomas Malory's *Le Morte Darthur* (1470).

In these treatments the implications of Merlin's insightful powers are explored in many other ways not included in early Welsh poetry or in Geoffrey of Monmouth's works. Taking Blaise as both tutor and scribe, Merlin narrates the history of the Holy Grail and all events through Arthur's early years. He advises that the Round Table (first mentioned by the Anglo-Norman poet Wace) be built as a replica of the table of the Last Supper and Joseph of Arimathea's Grail table. He arranges for Arthur's fostering and for the Sword in the Stone tests that prove Arthur's right to become king and Galahad's destiny as Grail achiever, creates the Siege Perilous in which only Galahad (and Perceval in some romances) may sit, and advises kings and nobles of events elsewhere and in the future that will affect them: Guinevere's adultery with Lancelot, Arthur's demise, and even his own death. He serves as war strategist and general. He also controls natural phenomena, calling up darkness, storms, and winds to aid his friends in battle. He frequently takes on the shape of a young boy, squire, rustic peasant, Wild Man, mature man or ancient, and even male deer in order to further a plan, teach a lesson, or simply have a joke. He saves Arthur's life in battle with King Pellinor, and after Arthur has lost his sword conducts him to the Lady of the Lake's gift of Excalibur. Finally, he creates monuments and inscriptions to memorialize and foretell significant events and combats. Through all of these functions he serves as central organizer and explicator (though often a cryptic one) of God's plan for the earthly successes of chivalric society and the spiritual challenges of the quest for the Holy Grail.

Robert and his continuators also expand upon hints—in the Welsh poem *Yr Afallennau* (The Apple Tree) and the *Life of Merlin*—that Merlin has had a lover or wife. The French and English works provide Merlin with a mistress named Viviane or Niviane, who eventually imprisons him in an invisible tower (the Vulgate *Merlin*), hawthorn bush (the Middle English *Prose Merlin*), a stone tomb within a cliff in Brittany (*Suite du Merlin*), or a rock on the Cornish coast (Malory). The pedigree of Merlin's mistress as the daughter of a landholder favored by the divine huntress Diana (who is not as chaste in medieval legend as in classical myth) or as an adherent of the Lady of the Lake crowns Merlin's folkloric roots as Wild Man and forest dweller. His final cry when he succumbs to his fate also counterpoints the significant laugh he utters as madman or young boy on occasions when he divines the truth of events ignored by others in his company. An important element distinguishing the Vulgate *Merlin* from the *Suite du Merlin* and the works of Malory is the darker character of Merlin in the latter, where he is portrayed not as courtly lover solicitous of his lady but as a lustful old man. However, in the *Didot-Perceval* (c. 1220–1230), as in the *Life of Merlin*, Merlin survives Arthur's reign and retires to the woods to build a hermitage he calls his *esplumoir* (technically, a cage for molting hawks).

As the Arthurian tradition incorporating Merlin develops, he is increasingly attributed with magical powers. For example, Geoffrey of Monmouth states that Merlin uses drugs to disguise Uther, Ulfin, and himself, and mechanical tackle or contrivances to move Stonehenge; the French romance writers and later chroniclers explain such marvelous elements as magic and even necromancy as the supernatural Grail theme is introduced and Arthurian legend becomes more fantastic. By the end of the Middle Ages Malory accepts the magic but reduces these elements and Merlin's role significantly, concentrating less on marvel and more on the practical social and political themes revolving around kingship and the courtly lifestyle.

Merlin's major role of prophecy persists throughout the medieval period. From Geoffrey onward Merlin practices two styles of prophecy: as an oracular seer like the Delphic Oracle or Cumaean Sibyl, whose predictions cannot be comprehended until after they come true, and as a plain-speaking and all-knowing adviser. This role is often linked with other folkloric elements. The threefold death motif (M341.2.4), which appears in traditions surrounding the shadowy figure of Lailoken, is repeated by Robert de Boron and his redactors; when Merlin is asked to establish credibility by demonstrating his power, he foretells three different deaths for the same person, who has donned disguises to fool the seer yet subsequently confounds expectation by dying as predicted. Lailoken's significant laugh generates another motif associated with this preternatural insight. On his way to King Vortigern, the boy Merlin's laughter signifies the imminent death of a man buying new shoes and the singing of a priest ignorant that the child whose funeral procession he is leading is his own. On another occasion, when Merlin is disguised as a Wild Man being taken to the Roman emperor, his laughter signals his awareness that the man who has captured him is a woman in disguise, that a group of beggars is sitting over buried treasure, and that three involuntary blows given by a squire to his master at mass are symbolic rebukes for human covetousness of worldly riches. As in the Lailoken story, Merlin also reveals that the emperor's wife is unfaithful to him. Other recurring folkloric motifs associated with Merlin in medieval literature include his physical resemblance to his father (though he lacks horns, cloven feet, and tail), his portrayal as a lover with a fairy mistress, as a *senex amans* (aged lover), as a wise man outwitted by a woman, and—like King Arthur—as a man whose end is debatable and who may return at future need.

Merlin's character is less pervasive in medieval European literatures other than English and French, but he appears in all of them, especially in translations or works based upon Geoffrey of Monmouth and the French Vulgate (or Lancelot-Grail) cycle. In contrast to the romances, medieval chronicles (since they are reputedly documenting actual history) deemphasize Merlin's lesser magics and romantic entanglements, concentrating, rather, upon his demonic inheritance, prophetic powers, and furtherance of Arthur's rule. For example, Ranulf Higden (d. 1364) is skeptical of Merlin's powers, although his translator and commentator John Trevisa (c. 1342–1402) is more accepting. In general, Merlin in medieval literature acts as a mediator of both supernatural and natural knowledge whose developing character as Wild Man, half human, poetic bard and prophet, magician, strategist and counselor, and even would-be lover incorporates crucial ambivalences operating within the medieval human psyche and society. These ambivalences—such as between good and evil, rationality and irrationality, nonhuman and human, and insight and blindness—were strengthened by the gradual accretion of Christian religious doctrines, new technologies, and developing literacies (of which he is always reputed to be a master) to the Merlin figure's pre-Christian shamanistic origins. In these ways his figure became central to Arthurian visions of the ideal society and its discontents, visions in which he is portrayed as a predominantly good but flawed master of all wisdom.

See also: Arthurian Lore; Geoffrey of Monmouth; Gerald of Wales; Myrddin; Nennius; Taliesin; Triads of the Island of Britain; Wild Man

—Peter Goodrich

Mermaid. A "fabulous beast," also known as the siren.

The mermaid's image and moral signification developed in religious contexts—bestiaries and church carvings—depicting her as a woman above the hips and a fish below. The mermaid's allegorical role was based on the sirens of antiquity, whose irresistible voices were said to lure seafarers to their deaths. As interpreted by Church authors, the siren lulled the soul to sleep with her song and then destroyed it. Yet the two narrative mermaids of medieval origin have little in common with the mermaid-siren of the bestiaries. Both Melusine of France and Liban of Ireland appear to be local traditions to which the mermaid icon became affixed. Melusine was the fairy bride in a fruitful but tabooed marriage; Liban sacrificed elemental longevity for a Christian soul. Both manifestations suggest that the figure of the mermaid possessed associations ranging far beyond the allegory.

The polyvalence of the mermaid icon was in part a reflection of earlier interpretations of the siren's song. Clement of Alexandria (c. 160–c. 215) had likened it to the lure of Greek wisdom, while St. Ambrose (c. 339–397) and St. Jerome (c. 340–c. 420) associated it with worldly pleasures, particularly secular music. For Isidore of Seville (c. 560–636) the siren was a treacherous prostitute, an account that accords with an oral tradition unearthed by Boccaccio (1313–1375) and recorded in his *Genealogy*. Thus, the mermaid would become emblematic of heresy, worldly pleasures, and lust. Indeed, Siegfried de Rachewitz claims that heresy was the icon's primary signification.

The early Latin bestiaries followed classical tradition in showing the siren as a bird-woman, but the British *Liber monstrorum* (tenth century) gives her the tail of a fish. This metamorphosis was popularized by the Anglo-Norman Bestiary of Philippe de Thaon (Cumberland, early twelfth century), which shows a siren with the feet of a falcon and the tail of a fish. The author also alters the allegory somewhat by comparing the siren to the world's riches; just as she sings in the tempest and cries in fair weather, so wealth perverts a man's soul. The metaphor suggests an intrusion, for both wealth and weather were associated with maritime spirits. The English Bestiary (Northumberland, thirteenth century) also depicts a fish-tailed siren, but it gives her a new name. She is called a "mereman" whose upper body is "a meiden ilike" [like a maiden's], a gender anomaly that may reflect the influence of the male Germanic water spirit known as the nix.

But even as the Church was shaping its didactic mermaid, a secular version emerged in the British Isles. In the *History of the Kings of Britain* (c. 1138), Geoffrey of Monmouth tells how the ships of Brutus and his Trojans were surrounded and almost overturned by "sea-monsters called Syrens" when they entered British waters. A century later, Gervase of Tilbury recounted much the same story in *Otia imperialia* (Imperial Pastimes, c. 1211), adding that even in his own day mermaids and mermen continued to inhabit the British ocean in considerable numbers.

The specifics of the siren's transformation from bird-woman to fish-woman are obscure, but existing manuscripts suggest a Western matrix with localized intrusions. Such an impression is supported by the distribution of mermaid art, for the earliest examples lie west of the Rhone, including one in the crypt of the new Norman castle at Durham. These mermaids are varied and naturalistic; often they are shown holding a fish.

Only in the twelfth century did mermaids begin to appear east of the Rhone, and many of these introduced a distinctive new icon: the girdled, twin-tailed mermaid (see illustration). With an uplifted tail in each hand, she assumes a spread-eagle pose some have interpreted as sexual display. Although these mermaids may appear to continue the tradition of the siren as prostitute, they are apparently derived from images like that preserved in a Roman painting entitled *Serena* (Fair Weather), not *Syren*. Serena's gesture may well have contributed to the mermaid's reputation as a sexual predator. Indeed, the mirror and comb—a fundamental component of depictions of the Whore of Babylon—did not become a standard feature of mermaid iconography until the fourteenth century.

Although the linguistic trick that produced the twin-tailed mermaid is transparent, it was probably secondary. A simpler fish-tailed siren had already evolved. And while sea fairies, lake ladies, and seal maidens would be drawn into the icon, the ecclesiastical model is more likely to have been the Greek nereid. Her existence had been affirmed by Pliny (23–79 C.E.) in his *Natural History*, a work that remained a pillar of secular knowledge. And while Pliny's nereids were simple merwomen whose "piteous cries" suggest seal sightings, they provided the medieval world with an iconographic template for its projections.

In the late Middle Ages the mermaid became the focus of full-scale narratives. The legendary Melusine of France appears to be the first in a long line of mermaid wives who abandon home and family when an imprudent husband violates a certain taboo. Indeed, Melusine is the apocryphal ancestress of the house of Lusignan, once masters of the Poitou region of France. Sabine Baring-Gould calls her "the first mermaid," and he may be right in that she is the first to have a surviving story of her own. The most famous version is recounted in the late-fourteenth-century romance *La noble histoire de Lusignan* (Noble History of the Lusignan Family), by Jean d'Arras, which tells how Melusine endowed her husband Raymond with castles and progeny until he broke the promise he had made as a condition of their marriage: he had agreed never to observe his wife when she retired to her bath on the Sabbath. At that time, Melusine assumed her half-animal form, and when Raymond eventually broke the taboo, he saw that his wife's lower body was a giant fish tail.

But Melusine's fish tail was actually an intrusion; earlier traditions give the ambiguous fairy wife the identity of a dragon and the tail of a serpent. Whether this iconographic change was initiated by Jean d'Arras or reflects a broader, orally transmitted variation, it suggests a reference to the mermaid-siren, who by the fourteenth century had acquired an identity of her own.

At the other end of the moral spectrum is the Irish mermaid Liban. The first phase of her story is told in the eleventh-century *Book of the Dun Cow*, which makes her the daughter of Eochaid McMaireda. When the spring under Eochaid's house overflows to form Lough Neagh, Liban is the only one of her people to survive. She and her dog live trapped beneath the lake for many years until she is finally given the tail of a salmon and her dog is turned into an otter. The story is picked up by the seventeenth-century *Annals of the Kingdom of Ireland,* a chronicle based on older manuscripts and traditions. The entry for the year 558 notes simply that "the mermaid, i.e., Liban, the daughter of Eochaidh, son of Muireadh," was taken by the fisherman of Comgall of Bangor. Longer versions of her story, such as the one in Patrick W. Joyce's *Old Celtic Romances* (1879), tell how Liban encountered an envoy of Comgall on his way to Rome and begged him to take her out of the waters and into his nets. He agreed, returning in a year's time with a company of holy men who hauled Liban ashore and baptized her Muirgen (Sea-Born). The mermaid declined a life on earth, however, and died, becoming one of Ireland's holy saints.

The notion of a Christian mermaid not only endured at Bangor but spread across the Irish Sea to Iona, where Scottish tradition remembers a mermaid who loved a monk during the time of St. Columba. She begged the unnamed monk for a soul, but he rejected her passion, inviting her to accept the love of Christ instead. This mermaid could not give up the sea, however, and she swam away; her tears became the pebbles on Iona's shore. A fourteenth-century cross on a nearby Argyllshire coast seems to commemorate Liban and her Scottish counterpart, for it is crowned with a mermaid whose ears resemble those of a dog.

As mermaids, Melusine and Liban have little in common, but together they illustrate how historical context can create enduring narrative traditions from unlikely icons.

See also: Bestiary; Fairies; Fairy Lover

—Judith Gilbert

Midsummer [June 24]. Also known as St. John's Day, noted for its "somergames," celebrated with dancing, sports, folk drama, and other entertainments.

Somergames may have originated as celebrations of the summer solstice around pagan temples. The clergy seems to have tolerated these customs until the early thirteenth century, when there was increased concern to educate the laity in the elements of the faith (as, for example, at the Fourth Lateran Council in 1215) and to control the expression of piety. Some reformist clergy were offended by the Midsummer festivals and other activities that were held in the churchyards and cemeteries. They thought drinking and feasting constituted the sin of gluttony and encouraged that of lechery. Similarly, dancing or caroling (ring dancing) enticed the senses. Other games, wrestling and tilting at the quintain, were thought inappropriate because they were games of chance. The basic concern, however, seems to have been that these activities polluted sacred precincts. In the campaign against somergames, John of Bromyard and others often cast them as pagan survivals or inventions of the devil, the latter point being that the parishioners were participating in imitations of the sacred mass and the feast of Christ's body that *were held within the church proper*. Despite the reformist effort, parish festivities, often called Scotales, continued well into the sixteenth century in England.

There are elusive references to one kind of game in which young clerics or laypeople dressed as torturers and devils in order to torment persons representing Christ and the saints. These apparently are not scripted dramas but improvisations. Our best description comes from a sermon exemplum in which the preacher cites the predicament of a person who agreed to be Christ in a somergame. He says that he looked to his left and to his right, where he saw Peter and Andrew crucified with him, and he saw how much the three of them suffered from lack of food and torment in contrast to the torturers and demons below. The preacher's description of these activities suggests that the spectators urged the torturers and demons on and rewarded them with food and drink, according to how well they performed their tasks. When the person who represented Christ was asked if he would play the same role the next year—because he had done it so well—he said that the following year he wanted to be a devil or torturer.

It is difficult to know how such a game may have arisen or what it might represent. It is possible that local populaces partially Christianized some pagan game in which members of the village acted as surrogates or scapegoats in order to coerce the gods into renewing their allegiance to the community. The only rationale we have from the late Middle Ages is the secondhand report of the author of the *Tretise of Miraclis Pleyinge*, who claimed that the participants defended their actions on the grounds that they brought the spectators to a penitential frame of mind at the sight of the torment that Christ and the saints underwent, and that it induced moral behavior when they saw the fate of the devils who did the tormenting. He rejected both arguments on the grounds that such jesting with the sacred was unseemly and conducive to gluttony and lechery, since the spectators were drinking and feasting during the game.

See also: Drama; Festivals and Celebrations
—Lawrence M. Clopper

Minstrel. A professional entertainer with instrumental skills; an omnipresent and popular figure at every level of medieval society.

Originally, the term (from Old French *menestrel*, meaning "little servant") specified a retainer to a king or other great person. Though later used more loosely of performers in general, it continued to carry an implication of dependent status. Other defining characteristics of the minstrels were professionalism (they were paid for their services in money or gifts) and versatility. Though the great majority were able to play a musical instrument, this was but one of many performance skills they might have at their command. Those accounted minstrels in contemporary records also included storytellers in song or verse, actors, jesters, dancers and acrobats, jugglers and conjurers, and exhibitors of performing animals. Though royal minstrels were nearly always male, others could be of either sex.

From the early Middle Ages onward entertainers were usually referred to in Latin documents as *mimi et histriones* (literally "actors") or *joculatores* (literally "jokers"). Traveling widely in family-based groups, they are pictured in some fourteenth-century manuscripts as wearing masks and animal costumes as they dance and play their instruments. Their usual venue in both town and country was the marketplace or churchyard. Though popular among all classes of the laity, they were condemned by clerical authors for their typical obscenity and the sometimes sacrilegious nature of their performances. They were regarded by the Church as a corrupting, potentially anarchic element on the fringes of society.

However, in England and in other countries of northern Europe the effect of the Church's condemnation of the *mimi* was mitigated by the influence of other, equally ancient performance traditions, those of the harper-poets: Germanic or Scandinavian *scop*, Anglo-Saxon *gleoman*, and Celtic *bard*. In contrast to the *mimi*, with their unattached status and satiric bent, the harper-poets were employed by tribal lords to celebrate in story and song their heroic deeds and those of their ancestors and thus to remember and recount those links with the past that were essential to the identity and coherence of the group. They were accorded an honored place at the lord's table and among his retinue of noble warriors.

The term *minstrel* was first used by the twelfth-century French poet Chrétien de Troyes to denote performers at a royal wedding and may represent an amalgamation of the two traditions. Chrétien's minstrels are described as leaping and tumbling, singing and telling tales, as well as playing instruments. In the fashionable, chivalric language of the time, their function was to make *joie* and thus to confer honor on the givers of the feast. The more minstrels who were present on such occasions, the greater the *joie* and the greater the honor.

In spite of continuing ambivalence in the Church's attitude toward them, minstrels rose in number, popularity, and status during the twelfth and thirteenth centuries under the stimulus of royal and magnate patronage. Their humbler colleagues, touring village fairs and town markets, provided a pool of talent and varied skills on which the aristocratic patrons could draw as required. In England 426 minstrels were present at the wedding of one of Edward I's daughters in 1290. Among the performers recorded at another royal marriage in 1296–1297, an unattached acrobatic dancer named Matilda Makejoy was rewarded with two shillings (the smallest fee) and later recruited to entertain the royal children at Windsor.

In France the characteristic minstrel instrument was the *vielle* or viol, a forerunner of the fiddle; in England the small, 12-stringed harp remained dominant until early in the fourteenth century, when it was overtaken by the *vielle* and other more exotic instruments such as the nakers (tunable drums, originating in the Middle East) and lute. Both harp and *vielle* were used to accompany storytelling in the form of improvised and memorized verse. In France the harper-poets were known as *trouvères* or *troubadours;* though some of these were accounted minstrels *(jongleurs)*, others were of greatly superior status. In England, as elsewhere, the harper-poets were the cream of the minstrel profession, and at the great Pentecost feast of 1306 (when the future Edward II was knighted by his father), 26 of the 119 minstrels whose specialty was noted were accorded the title Master along with the squires and university graduates, provided with a horse to ride and a servant to attend them at the king's expense, and given a daily wage and additional rewards on the occasion of feasts so that they were able to maintain permanent households in London or elsewhere and become substantial citizens of the rising merchant class. Favorite performers were exempted by the king from payment of taxes, and some are known to have been literate—probably in several languages. The groups of minstrels permanently retained by the king (numbering about 30 in the reign of Edward I) were replicated in smaller numbers at each descending level of the armorial class. By the beginning of the fourteenth century there was hardly a country knight who did not keep at least a harper among his permanent household. Such men were also employed by bishops and abbots in their capacity as secular magnates.

In the Plantagenet court, minstrels were of two kinds: those who were in regular attendance on the king (who commonly combined their activity as entertainers with other, more utilitarian duties as messengers, watchmen, and so on) and those who "came and went," dividing their time between performing for the king, especially on the major feasts, weddings, and other occasions, and touring on their own behalf as the "king's harper" or "king's piper" or in small ensembles of brass or string instruments—a pattern of employment that persisted to as late as the Tudor era. In peacetime the travels of leading minstrels of all nations were Continental in extent, and they

might then be entrusted with messages and gifts to foreign rulers and magnates, fulfilling (along with the heralds) a semi-diplomatic function.

During the fourteenth and early fifteenth centuries assemblies *(escoles)* of minstrels were held in the Low Countries and in Beauvais. They were attended by performers from all over Europe, including some from England.

Royal and baronial minstrels also had an important function in medieval warfare, when the king's household might become (as in England in the reigns of Edward I and III and Henry V) the headquarters battalion of the royal army, and minstrels were then expected to contribute, along with other court officials and servants, to its effectiveness as a fighting unit. Harpers were present on the thirteenth-century field of combat to observe the individual acts of knightly valor and prowess to which chivalry attached such significance; these were to be memorialized later in the form of *sirventois*, or "duty" songs. Some few of these have survived in written form, illustrated by blazons (coats of arms) of the participant knights. Trumpeters took on the duty of signalers—the only immediate communication in battle available to the medieval commander—and drummers and cornet players contributed to a cacophony of sound that was designed to stiffen the resolve of one's own side and strike terror into the enemy as opposing armies advanced toward each other. Henry V took minstrels with him to France in 1415 under the leadership of their marshal, John Cliff. In addition to their military duties, they were required to serenade the king's new French bride, Catherine of Valois, for an hour at daybreak and again at sunset.

From the fourteenth century onward efforts were made by unattached performers resident in towns to secure for themselves a recognized status in society—and thus a degree of protection—commensurate to that already enjoyed by royal and other "liveried" minstrels. Some came together to form associations with regulated entry under the nominal patronage of local lords (the "minstrel courts"); others forged links with craft and other religious guilds, to which they might be admitted as waged retainers to town boroughs, combining the functions of a nocturnal musical watch with that of a civic band. In England these latter were known as "waits," and in Germany, as *stadtpfeifer*. As musicians, the waits outlasted all other types of minstrels, surviving in some English towns to as late as the nineteenth century.

The general decline in minstrelsy at the end of the late Middle Ages was due to the cumulative effects of connected social changes: a breaking down of the originally undifferentiated functions of court officers and servants under pressures of reform; the introduction of a new concept of monarchy whereby the king (and his subservient lords in imitation) withdrew from the public arena in which they had formerly moved to the privacy of the inner chamber; increasing specialization of performance skills in response to new challenges and demands such as those that gave rise early in the fifteenth century to the emergence of the players (originally "interluders"); and the enactment of increasingly repressive vagrancy laws. Most profound and significant in its effects—because it struck directly at what had everywhere been regarded as the highest reaches of the art—was the increase in literacy among the minstrels' patrons, along with a greater availability to them of books and notated music, first in manuscripts and later in printed form. This rendered the functions of the oral poets and improvisatory instrumentalists progressively redundant. Though there was obvious gain in these developments, there was also loss, not only in terms of a seepage of extemporaneous performance skills, which could never be recaptured, but also in social cohesion. For the minstrel audience—seen most typically in the great hall of some country lord, seated at table with all his dependents—was then dispersed.

State records from the reign of Henry VIII reveal the gradual displacement of minstrels in personal attendance on the king by graduate and church-trained virtuosi and composers from the royal chapels and abroad. By the reign of Elizabeth the "auncient minstrell" (a harper) described by Robert Laneham as present on the occasion of the queen's visit to Kenilworth in 1575 had become a figure of fun and an object of merely antiquarian interest. Those who had formerly been known as minstrels did not disappear from the scene, but they became increasingly specialized, performing as professional musicians, players, tumblers, or "jugglers" (conjurers in the modern sense). The harpers—their skill as versifiers taken over by clerkly poets such as Chaucer—were reduced in status to street musicians, begging for pennies. Only at the lowest social level of market and fair were minstrels able (against considerable odds) to maintain to some extent the old versatility and peripatetic ways of their predecessors—to emerge in later centuries as circus, fairground, and music hall (burlesque) performers.

The quality and diversity of the contribution that minstrels made to medieval culture at all levels has yet to be adequately assessed and acknowledged. In the countryside they added gaiety to traditional ceremony and festal drama. In towns and cities the participation of the waits and other minstrels in guild feasts and street processions gave to the developing Corpus Christi drama that element of "play" that lay at the heart of medieval entertainment and was the air that minstrels and players breathed in common. While the authorship of the later Middle English romances—including such masterpieces as *Sir Orfeo* and *Sir Gawain and the Green Knight*—remains unknown and controversial, there can be no doubt of the principal part that minstrels played in the evolution of the genre. The flowering of secular music and drama in the Renaissance would not have been possible if the sophisticated skills on which both the new music and plays depended for their performance had not been pioneered and developed by minstrels. The shift of emphasis from the spoken word and improvised music of the minstrels to the written word and notated music of poets and composers in the later Middle Ages and Renaissance marks a sea change in the cultural climate, a change whose consequences can hardly be exaggerated.

See also: Drama; Harp

—John Southworth

Misericords. Carved ledges beneath the seats of many late-medieval choir stalls (especially in larger parish churches and cathedrals) throughout Europe, believed to have originated as a concession to the infirmity of aged monks (Latin *misericordia*, "pity"), who might rest on the ledge of the tipped-up seat yet still appear to be standing.

The great majority of British misericords—unlike other European seats—are distinguished by subsidiary carvings, called supporters, that flank the central ledge and may complement or otherwise comment on it. Similar carvings are also found on the armrests, or stall-elbows, of English and Continental church seats. Misericords are a still undervalued source of folkloric iconography (the bulk of them are unrecorded in published works and earlier descriptions of their subjects are often inaccurate), but they are a source that needs to be used with care. (See illustrations.)

A surprisingly small proportion of misericords (certainly fewer than 10 percent in Britain, for example) are carved with overtly religious motifs, and there is evidence from surviving (Flemish) contracts that the carvers were in fact given carte blanche on the choice of subjects, which would, after all, have been out of sight most of the time.

Many folkloric inversions are given visual representation in the misericord corpus: the world-turned-upside-down motif of the mice hanging the cat, for example, appears at Great Malvern (c. 1480), while Beverley Minster's famous cart-before-the-horse (c. 1520) is flanked by a representation of the impossible feat of milking the bull (motif H1024.1).

Proverbs and especially proverbial follies are well represented in misericords: At Bristol (c. 1520) a man attempts to drive a slug by whipping it with a flail and incidentally attests to a variant of a contemporary nonsense couplet found in Skelton. At Windsor (c. 1480) the small birds with sacks across their backs flying toward a post-mill illustrate another impossible motif given a misogynist application in a Middle English nonsense carol:

> Whn wrenys cary sekkes onto ... the myll
> Than put women in trust and confydens.

Religious folklore is illustrated primarily by those few misericords that depict key episodes from saints' lives—for example, the proverbial folly, successfully accomplished by St. Werburg, of penning wild geese in an open enclosure carved on a stall in Chester Cathedral (c. 1390). A complete *danse macabre* cycle in Coventry Cathedral was destroyed in World War II.

Antifeminist themes are commonplace, especially the depiction of viragoes who beat or otherwise humiliate their husbands, as in the battle for the breeches (e.g., at Hoogstraeten, Netherlands, 1532–1546) or the old maid who must lead apes into hell at Bristol. At Champeaux a woman lying on an anvil is being reforged so that her husband may enjoy a younger wife. The fifteenth-century bridled scold at Stratford-on-Avon—perhaps a reference to the traditional tale "The Taming of the Shrew" (AT 901), later to be the subject of Shakespeare's famous play—is perhaps related to the locked-lips motif of the woman at Ponts-de-Cé (early sixteenth century), a constituent of the Ideal Woman topos. At Estavoyer-le-Lac in 1524, where a male head similarly appears with padlocked lips, it is transformed into an Ideal Servant.

Heroes of popular story depicted include several English examples of Marcolf as a goat rider, a possible giant from a "Jack and the Beanstalk"-type tale (AT 328; New College, Oxford, late fourteenth century), and Aesopic fables (especially in Spain). Popular episodes from Arthurian stories are also found: an illustration of the portcullis dropping on Yvain's horse (Enville Church), the famous image of King Mark looking down from the tree beneath which Tristan and Isolde are holding their tryst (e.g., in Chester), and a representation of the Swan Knight (in Exeter). Allusions to the tale of the peddler whose pack is rifled by apes appear at Manchester and Beverley. The motif of the swaddled infant carried off by an eagle (Lathom Legend, motif R13.3.2) appears at Manchester as the Stanley family's badge. The irrepressible Reynard appears on several English misericords, but the only certain instances drawn from the beast-epic proper are at Bristol.

There are also many fascinating illustrations of popular custom (not to mention agricultural practice), including an egg dance at Aarschot (c. 1515), a possible hobbyhorse at Sherborne, and folk punishments such as the backwards ride (e.g., Hereford, c. 1350). Valuable records of gesture are also recorded: the thumbed nose at Beverley, for example, and the insulting anal presentation on several French misericords. A robust attitude toward scatology is evidenced throughout the misericord corpus: men defecating are depicted on Spanish stalls, as is a humorous *Geldscheisser* (shown depositing a tidy heap of coins) at Amsterdam. Less humorously, contemporary prejudices are also attested, as in the anti-

Semitic images to be found on certain Flemish misericords.

See also: Iconography; Punishments; World Turned Upside Down

—Malcolm Jones

Monks. Men who have withdrawn from the world to devote themselves to a religious life, either as hermits or in communities.

History

Although its origins appear to have been quite ancient, the ascetic way of life that eventually developed into monasticism began to emerge in its most famous and influential form in the Egyptian desert during the late third and early fourth centuries of our era. The earliest Desert Fathers to attract attention were St. Anthony of Egypt (d. 356), whose biography by Athanasius was translated into Latin by Evagrius and became widely popular throughout Western Europe, and St. Paul the Hermit (d. around 345), whose life inspired many later saints' lives through the account of the great scholar and biblical translator St. Jerome. The spirituality of the desert was fundamentally ascetic, that is, a form of living characterized by withdrawal from the world to remote places and by a discipline of austerity and prayer. The first Desert Fathers were hermits, or anchorites, living alone with only occasional visitors from the outside, but they soon attracted others so that loose communities of these ascetics came to share some common religious exercises, together with such basic necessities as food and clothing and eventually a common discipline or rule. As these ascetic practices spread to the West, they quickly became established in Italy, Gaul, and Spain, perhaps in part out of a desire to find in the life of the spirit a more stable foundation than appeared possible in the material world of the rapidly disintegrating Roman Empire.

By the fifth century monastic communities were forming even in far-off Ireland, where some of those inspired by desert spirituality sought refuge in the remoteness of offshore islands and others developed "families" based on the model of the traditional Celtic clan—often in direct relation to a local clan. These new monastic "clans" were thus not separate from the society around them, since especially in their early stages they were filled with St. Patrick's missionary zeal to convert the world rather than simply withdraw from it. Such conversion, in Ireland and elsewhere in northern Europe, never eliminated or even totally replaced folk religious beliefs and practices. But once the Irish had become at least officially Christian their monks turned to more scholarly and literary tasks. Irish monastic foundations became great centers of learning that carried their learning to Anglo-Saxon England and then to the Continent after the fall of most Roman cultural institutions during the fifth and sixth centuries—thereby influencing the gradual rebuilding of learned institutions that laid the foundation for the Carolingian cultural revival of the eighth century. In the meantime, monastic culture with more direct continuity with Roman traditions developed in Italy and westward along the Mediterranean rim, with the most famous monastery being Monte Cassino founded by St. Benedict of Nursia around 529. St. Benedict produced the famous Benedictine Rule that eventually was to become the standard on which monastic discipline throughout the West would be based. As had others before it, this rule sought to regulate everyday life in the monastery, dividing the day into "hours" for different kinds of prayer, study, or work at times scheduled from 2 A.M. until 8 or 8:30 P.M. and specifying the responsibilities for different assignments within the community, from the abbot through the brew-master and the guest-master (who supervised the hospice).

Thus, monasticism as a great religious movement was also a great social and cultural movement, blending Eastern traditions inspired by the desert with the Western traditions from Ireland and Italy. Yet its subsequent history was largely dominated by Roman authority. During Charlemagne's reign, the Benedictine Rule became obligatory for all monks and nuns throughout Frankish lands. By 910, however, the foundation of the abbey at Cluny signaled major monastic reforms, especially curtailing the activities of monks outside the monasteries, but Benedictines continued to serve as bishops and even popes from the tenth to the twelfth centuries. Concern over such "worldliness" led to further reforms, with perhaps the most radical return to the ideals and practices of the early tradition occurring in 1084 when Bruno of Cologne established the first Carthusian hermitage at La Grande Chartreuse. By the fifteenth century there would be more than 190 Carthusian charter houses spread throughout Europe, governed by strict discipline requiring the monks to live for the most part in quarters sealed off from one another, almost as "hermits" within a community of hermits. Only slightly less radical, and certainly more famous, was the Cistercian reform founded by Robert of Molesmes and Stephen Harding in the twelfth century as a rival to Cluny, insisting on the contemplative and ascetic practices of poverty, manual labor, and, as is well known, even silence. Despite these reforms there was a general decline in monastic influence on the culture as a whole during the later Middle Ages, as the most brilliant leaders of ecclesiastical culture tended more often to be the Dominican and Franciscan friars who dominated the faculties of the newly formed universities.

Monasticism and Folklore

Although monastic leaders in the Middle Ages claimed that the distinctiveness of their life and culture derived from withdrawal from the world in one form or another, throughout the period there were complex interactions between the monastic communities and the larger societies in which they continued to play important roles in various ways. Though there is a sense in which the monasteries developed as communities with their own culture and their own lore, they also were part of a larger cultural network through which folklore not only circulated "outside" but also within the monasteries themselves. In fact, the only written records we have for much folklore, especially in the early centuries, are to be found in works produced by monastic writers and reproduced by monastic scribes. Nevertheless, there is no reason to believe that all medieval folklore was preserved in this way, since living traditions of oral storytelling and singing flourished throughout the period and continued into modern times in some forms. Moreover, not all folk culture took verbal forms requiring transmission through either literate or oral media: there is much evidence of material culture as well, from traditional methods of weaving to wood carving. In techniques of production, at least, there are close similarities between material culture within and without the monasteries. Yet when monastic writers did reproduce folkloric materials, they usually did not just transcribe the folklore they heard from oral tellers; they generally reshaped such oral lore to suit their own purposes. Likewise, lore cultivated in the monastery could assume quite different forms and emphases when it spread among the surrounding folk. These back-and-forth relations between monastic folklore and folklore "outside" were often so complex that it may clarify matters to set these relations within the social context that produced them.

First, there was the lore of the monastic communities themselves, circulating in both oral and written forms within a given monastery as well as from one monastery to another (though sometimes by circuitous routes). Such lore served the vital function of defining these communities, both in themselves and in opposition to others "outside," usually the lay society though sometimes ecclesiastical competitors. In addition to the vast, well-known body of formal learning presenting the official view of monastic, or more generally, of Christian culture, there was also a kind of folklore of the monasteries providing *informal* education, legitimacy, justification, and motivation for their mode of living. This informal lore promoted their beliefs and practices as traditional communities, thus providing them with identities as more or less exclusive communities. While there was usually no effort to conceal this "insider" lore from the populace at large, it is clear that many of the stories in Gregory the Great's famous *Dialogues*, for example, not only recount events orally circulating among the monastic communities but also express the informal codes that did not get written down in such a formal way as in the Benedictine Rule.

Gregory presented several tales about the envy of some monks toward the saintliness of one of their brothers, along with the disastrous consequences of such envy for themselves and the community. There were also fellow churchmen outside whose envy of the monks inside could present terrible dangers. For example, Gregory relates that in the district of St. Benedict's monastery there lived a local priest named Florentius who became so furious at the public veneration of the saint among the populace that he gave poisoned bread to the holy man "as though it were a sign of Christian fellowship." When the saint commanded a raven to dispose of the poisoned bread, the enraged Florentius sent seven "depraved women" to dance in the garden of the monastery and corrupt the younger brothers. While St. Benedict was leading his fellow monks to safety, word reached him that God had caused Florentius's house to collapse and crush him horribly (*Dialogues* 2.8).

The main events of this legend would have been accessible to the people of the district, but the story would have had special meaning within the communal context of the monastery. For this insider audience the story relates the dangerous antagonism of an outside clerical competitor for the people's approval and perhaps gifts. The saintly legislator for Western monasticism could even make the raven do his bidding, and he not only protected himself from physical harm, but—perhaps more important—he protected his younger brothers from the ever-present spiritual danger of sexual sin. Such danger had become a commonplace in monastic lore from the lives of St. Anthony of Egypt, St. Paul the Hermit, and St. Hilarion onward, and Gregory had earlier depicted St. Benedict's own heroic resistance to the mere memory of a woman's beauty, throwing off his garment and rolling naked in a patch of thorn bushes and nettles until he was covered in blood. This measure was so successful that he told his followers he was never again tempted by the flesh (*Dialogues* 2,2). Even so, St. Benedict did not require such severity of the young brothers tempted by Florentius's "depraved women," choosing the more customary monastic strategy of withdrawal from the temptations of the world. Finally, even though God's justice is displayed in Florentius's horrible death, when St. Benedict heard of it he wept, not only because the priest had died but also because one of his own monks had rejoiced over it and the saint had to punish this vengeful brother as well. Thus, the story is more than the celebration of marvelous events in the life of a great saint; within the monastic context where it circulated orally before Gregory wrote it down, the story informally expressed elements of a code vital to members of that community.

Second, folklore entering the monastery from a nonmonastic folk group outside was generally represented as what Bede calls *fama vulgante* (popular rumor) or as what the penitential manuals often saw as folk practices to be censured. Lay figures could be venerated as saints, of course, and the stories of their deeds, along with stories of miracles associated with their relics after death, could gain authority, at least initially, from becoming widespread among the people. It appears that just such stories circulated about the Anglo-Saxon St. Oswald and St. Edmund, who were both kings whose deaths conveyed not only religious but also patriotic virtues, since they both died defending a Christian people against their "heathen" enemies. Their legends were eventually recorded by monastic writers, but not before they had wide oral circulation in England and abroad. Indeed, a holy man told Bede that the legends of St. Oswald had spread even to the peoples of Ireland and Germany.

Third, folklore could be taken over by monks to serve some ecclesiastical function, as in the numerous folkloric elements whose meaning and function will have shifted in tales redesigned according to the aims of the clergy. In such cases folkloric elements in the stories are no longer represented as they would be in versions circulating outside. For example, Odo of Cerinton, an English Cistercian of the twelfth century, related the familiar folktale in which the mice debate which of them shall bell the cat, but he gave the tale a special ecclesiastical meaning by claiming that it was about monks and other clerics and subjects of an unpopular prelate; though all wanted him removed, none dared to take direct action.

Fourth, terms such as *accommodation* or *appropriation* do not adequately represent the dynamic, often dialectical interactions between monastic and folk cultures, and such terms may in some cases distort the meaning and function of these interactions. In general, monastic culture was not so insulated from the surrounding social context as monastic rhetoric might lead us to believe. With the exception of abbots, abbesses, and monk bishops, who were typically appointed from the aristocratic class, many monks came from the farms and hamlets around their monastery, and monastic holdings generally included lands cultivated by a lay population that was loosely associated with the monastic *familia*. Moreover, the case of St. Cuthbert preaching in the wilds of northern Britain indicates that at least in the earlier centuries monks carried out many of the functions among the people that later were fulfilled by parish priests. Except for such strictly cloistered orders as Cistercians and Carthusians, most monastic communities developed a social and economic basis for interacting with at least the populace of their own locale. Under such conditions it was easy for folkloric materials, including legends, proverbs, or cures—such as the use of scrapings from an Irish book as an antidote for snakebite—to circulate between the worlds inside and outside. In the process these legends may have changed somewhat in both meaning and function, with the direction of change depending on the direction of flow: from the folk community to the monastery or, as often happened, from the monastery to the surrounding folk community (or *back* to the folk community if that is where the folklore had originated).

Meaning and Function

A revealing case of these movements and transformations is hagiography, the vast and popular literature of saints' lives. These lives often resemble the märchen and legends studied by folklore scholars. But within the social and performative context of the monastery the familiar folkloric elements in saints' lives take on new, often totally transformed meanings and functions. Bede's story of Cædmon begins with an account of informal singing among a group at or attached to Whitby Abbey. At first this seems merely to describe a commonplace folk entertainment in which the harp passes from hand to hand and each person takes a turn at singing. But the story takes on new meaning when Cædmon miraculously receives a poetic gift and begins to compose religious songs based on biblical themes taught to him by the monks.

In many cases there was an effort to impose an "official" meaning and function on the narrative rather than leave it open to the rich (and dangerous) variability it could have in live performance in traditional folk group settings. For example, numerous widespread stories relate the magical powers of animals or of the friends or foes of animals. But in saints' lives the stories of bears, birds, lions, serpents, fish, and the like are told to exemplify the power of God working through his saints. Thus, it would be misleading to treat these elements in saints' lives as if they were simply "variants" of similar folkloric narratives. For, as in all folklore, the meanings and functions of such elements are specific to the particular communal process in the social context within which they are related, and so a shift from one such context to another will produce a corresponding shift in meanings and functions. For example, though folklore is filled with numerous tales of humans befriending normally dangerous animals, Gregory endows one such tale with special significance for a monastic community: It seems that a certain monk was left by himself to tend an otherwise abandoned foundation and prayed for consolation in his solitude. Rising from his prayer, he discovered at his door a bear that bowed its head to the ground to show its servitude to the monk. "Brother Bear" became shepherd to the monk's small flock of sheep until some envious monks from a nearby monastery killed the bear out of spite. In his anger at the killers, the holy monk pronounced a curse on them, whereupon they contracted leprosy and died terribly. Realizing the guilty consequences of his malediction, the monk did penance for his action for the rest of his life. As Gregory concludes, this story functions to admonish all men of God against using "the weapons of malediction in anger," however righteous that anger might be (*Dialogues* 3,15).

A similar process takes place in stories about miracles. While miracles at first glance seem reminiscent of, or even overlap, the marvels that fill märchen and folk legends, they are often reshaped by monastic tellers of saints' lives. Just so, the popular monastic legends of the Irish St. Brigid recall supernatural powers over nature and the products of nature, perhaps associated with a pre-Christian Celtic divinity of the same name. Brigid could miraculously increase supplies of butter or milk, and she could even change bath water into beer for thirsty visitors. Her feast day was assigned to February 1, the beginning of the Celtic spring and the date of the ancient festival of Imbolc. Gerald of Wales (d. 1223) described a fire tended for hundreds of years by nuns at her shrine, which was surrounded by a circle of bushes that men were forbidden to enter. Thus, legends of St. Brigid as "the Mary of Ireland" promoted a female monastic founder (she was said to have established the foundation at Kildare, from *Cill Dara*—literally "church of the oak tree") whose prestige was perhaps second only to that of St. Patrick himself. In addition, her legends, which were spread largely by male monastics, added greatly to the power of the Kildare monastery in the ecclesiastical politics of the Middle Ages.

The events in the saints' lives exemplify the virtues promoted (or the vices condemned) by the Church through its monastic literature, though these lives came to be related in contexts outside the monasteries as well. The lives and the miracles they recount were seen as revelations of divine power, and according to Gregory the Great (*Dialogues* 4.38), the vividly memorable descriptions of the saints' miracles functioned to impress their meanings on the minds of their audience. The saints struggle toward an ideal asceticism in this life in order to pass over the border to eternal life. Monastic saints are therefore often represented as figures who live in a kind of borderland. The Anglo-Saxon St. Guthlac retreated beyond the edge of civilization to Crowland, and St. Cuthbert left the community at Lindisfarne for the solitude of a remote island far out in the sea.

Saints as borderline figures are thus divinely endowed with special power—ultimately to produce miracles on this side of eternity after dying and passing to the other side. Signs of their sainthood appear in the *presence* of their tombs, in accounts of their uncorrupted flesh and odor of sanctity after burial, and of course in the numerous miracles produced by their relics. Bede's *Ecclesiastical History of the English People* (731) is filled with such accounts, most of which take place through monastic saints whose relics, like those of St. Cuthbert, reside in churches tended by monks. Saintly monks may also return in visions or as helpers to those still on this side of the eternal border, as in stories about St. Martin of Tours (c. 316–397). Indeed, the very paradox of the saints' presence-in-absence is embodied in relics, which are seen to be media through which God extends grace and mercy. As such, relics are sharply distinguished from the officially condemned use of magical talismans that many believed to have power in their own right.

A rather different kind of border is depicted in the case of women who cross gender lines, dressing as men in order to become monks. Jacobus de Voragine's enormously popular *The Golden Legend* (c. 1260) relates the story of a certain St. Margaret who is forced into marriage despite her wish to remain a holy virgin. On her wedding night she abstains from sexual relations with her husband, cuts her hair, dresses in men's clothes, steals away, and eventually arrives at a monastery, which she joins as Brother Pelagius. After several years as a monk, and against her will, she is made director of a community of nuns. One of the nuns is seduced by a devil, commits adultery outside the monastery, becomes pregnant, and accuses Brother Pelagius of being the father. Confined for some time to a cave as punishment, Brother Pelagius, realizing that death is near, writes to the monastic community revealing that "he" is actually a woman. When the monks and nuns arrive, they find St. Margaret dead, confirm her womanhood, and bury her with honor.

In another legend, St. Theodora, a married woman, is tricked by a witch and commits adultery. Realizing that she has sinned, "she cut her hair, put on men's clothes, and hurried to a monastery," leaving her husband to wonder what has become of her. Now as Brother Theodore, the new monk earns a reputation for piety and even performs miracles. Eventually, however, a pregnant woman accuses Brother Theodore of fathering her child, and the abbot banishes the monk from the monastery. St. Theodora raises the illegitimate boy, feeding him with milk from the herd she tends. When the abbot finally allows her to return as Brother Theodore, the child enters the monastery as well. When she dies, she is recognized as a woman after all and buried with honor. Her husband lives out his life in her monastic cell, and eventually her foster son is elected abbot of the community on account of his great virtue.

Not all monastic legends present monks in saintly roles, of course, and there were notable satirical attacks on monks in the Middle Ages. In the famous eleventh-century fables about Ysengrimus, a wolf given to eating sheep escapes by taking a monastic habit and tonsure and continues its savagery in this new guise. When questioned about this, the wolf replies, "Sometimes I am a monk, sometimes a canon." Around the same time, Ælfric Bata, a Benedictine schoolmaster in England, wrote colloquies—model conversations—in Latin for his students learning the language. In the exchanges between the master and his students, there are several references to monks' drinking, even drinking to such excess that on one occasion the monks forget to sing the compline hymns, calling instead for "more mead, wine, or good beer." In another case, Ælfric Bata hints at a homosexual relationship between a young monk and an older monk, and in still another he presents a scatological exchange of insults: when a student says he wants the master smeared with dung, the master replies that the student is himself various kinds of dung—goat, sheep, horse, cow, and pig dung. Later, in the thirteenth-century *Land of Cokaigne*, young monks come upon a group of nuns swimming nude and carry them off to the abbey, where they teach the nuns a form of prayer "with raised legs, up and down." Such stories circulated widely in popular lore and during the Reformation were used to justify the dissolution of the monasteries in England under Henry VIII.

Nevertheless, in its own lore, perhaps even more than through official pronouncements, monastic culture presented itself as the visible incarnation of the highest forms of Christian spirituality. Even when monks related legends about brothers who failed this ideal, they typically still represented the monastery as an ideal community. For example, Bede recounts the story of a blacksmith brother who lived a "drunken and dissolute life" even within the monastery. As his death approached, this smith foresaw the terrors of his own coming damnation in the most vivid terms and related them to the other brothers shortly before his death. Bede goes on to say of this legend that "it happened recently in the Province of Bernicia [in northern England], and was talked of far and wide, rousing many people to do penance for their sins without delay. And may the reading of this account have the same effect." As such, the legend provides a good example of monastic lore circulating "far and wide" beyond the monastery itself, both in oral and written performances, leading people of all social groups to embrace the holy life whose value was expressed so movingly in the legend—perhaps more movingly than in the official documents that many modern scholars analyze as authoritative sources of medieval religious life.

See also: Bede the Venerable; Nuns; Relics; Saints, Cults of the

—John McNamara

Morgan le Fay. King Arthur's half sister—a mysterious, powerful, yet peripheral character in medieval romance.

Because her name and sometime her traits resemble those of many supernatural women in Welsh and Irish tradition, many assume that Morgan is a remnant of a pagan Celtic goddess or spirit. Morgan's Celtic genealogy may include war goddesses (Irish Morrigan and Macha) as well as waterfolk (Irish Muirgen, Welsh Modron, and Breton Morganes)—though none of these figures can be positively identified as her ancestor.

About 1216 Gerald of Wales wrote that in the "*fabulosi Britones*" [tales of the Britons] an imaginary goddess named Morganis transported Arthur to Avalon to heal him. This is one of our few documented links between the Celtic oral tradition and the figure that would emerge in romance as Morgan le Fay.

Morgan developed a split personality during several centuries of medieval romance. In twelfth-century Arthurian tradition, beginning with Geoffrey of Monmouth's *Vita Merlini* (Life of Merlin), she is the noble and beneficent queen of the Isle of Avalon and healer of the mortally wounded Arthur. Chrétien de Troyes also alludes to Morgan's medicinal wisdom. However, her knowledge of magic acquires darker associations in later romance traditions.

In thirteenth-century French works, particularly the prose romances of the Vulgate and Post-Vulgate cycles, Morgan's exploits as an enchantress, as well as her physical appearance, grow increasingly ugly. In the Vulgate *Lancelot*, Guinevere earns Morgan's everlasting enmity by interfering with one of her amours. Morgan's reprisals include the repeated imprisonment of Lancelot, whom she tries to woo away from Guinevere by force or seduction. Morgan also tries to reveal the couple's adultery to King Arthur. Her wickedness is even more apparent in the *Prose Tristan*, where her machinations against Tristan parallel her plotting against Lancelot.

Arthur becomes entangled in the web of Morgan's treachery in the Post-Vulgate *Roman du Graal* (Romance of the Grail). Her schemes center on repeated thefts of Excalibur's life-preserving scabbard. Although thwarted in attempts to give the scabbard to various of her lovers, she ensures Arthur's ensuing vulnerability by casting it into a deep lake.

The ultimate degradation of Morgan's character occurs in the late-thirteenth-century French *Prophecies of Merlin* during a sorcerous duel between the now aged enchantress and the beautiful Dame d'Avalon. Not only does the dame bewitch Morgan into removing her clothing, revealing to all the fraudulence of her youthful appearance, but the naked Morgan must also suffer the final humiliation of seeing the clothes burned before her eyes after a devil whisks them to the top of a high tower.

Morgan's reputation fares little better in fourteenth- and fifteenth-century English romance. In *Sir Gawain and the Green Knight* she is the crone whose age and ugliness are contrasted with the beauty of Sir Bercilak's young wife. After Gawain completes his adventure, he learns from the Green Knight/Bercilak that the old lady is his aunt, Morgan le Fay; furthermore, she was the instigator of Bercilak's challenge and the ensuing quest. To one familiar with Morgan's history in previous romances, the motive for sending the Green Knight to Camelot should come as no surprise: she intended frightening Guinevere to death.

Although Morgan plays her usual role as antagonist to the Round Table in Thomas Malory's romances, she is perhaps best remembered there for the ambiguities surrounding Arthur's death. As she fetches the dying Arthur to Avalon on her barge, she is once again the benevolent queen, full of tender concern for the brother whose head she cradles in her lap; her ministrations offer the only hope for Malory's *Quondam rexque futurus*, the Once and Future King.

See also: Arthurian Lore; Celtic Mythology

—Cathalin B. Folks

Motif. A narrative trait, character, or action, "the smallest element in a tale having the power to persist in tradition" (Stith Thompson).

Motifs provide many of the details and building blocks that make a narrative meaningful and memorable for listeners and that allow narrators to reconstruct a tale at each telling. Stith Thompson designed the second edition of his six-volume *Motif-Index of Folk-Literature* (1955–1958) as a catalog of worldwide traditions, including cultures and genres as diverse as Polynesian myth and Native American jokes. However, because Thompson was himself by training a specialist in medieval and European traditions, the index is more thorough in covering medieval European folklore than the lore of other times and places. Various medievalists, working with Thompson or with his encouragement, wrote specialized motif indexes applying and expanding his system to explore specific medieval traditions. Among the most important are Gerald Bordman's *Motif-Index of the English Metrical Romances* (1963), Inger Boberg's *Motif-Index of Early Icelandic Literature* (1966), Tom Peete Cross's *Motif-Index of Early Irish Literature* (1969), and D. P. Rotunda's *Motif-Index of the Italian Novella* (1942).

According to Thompson, a motif has to have something "unusual and striking about it" in order to maintain its power to persist in storytelling tradition. Thus, Thompson provides a motif for cruel stepmother (S31), but not simply for mother; a motif for magic throne (D1156), but not simply for throne; a motif for speaking buttocks (D1610.6.3), but not simply for buttocks.

Thompson divided motifs into three major categories. First, a motif may be a character in a tale—for example, a witch (G200), dragon (B11), faithful animal (B301), or unpromising hero (L101). A second category of motifs comprises "certain items in the background of the action," such as magic objects (e.g., D1171.6, Holy Grail), unusual customs (e.g., S263, human sacrifice to appease god), and strange beliefs (for example, that multiple birth is a sign that a mother has slept with more than one man, T587.1). Third, a motif can be "a single incident," an action that by itself constitutes a brief tale, such as the motif of putting the devil into hell (K1363.1), which appears in medieval Italian tales as well as in modern oral folktales: in order to have sex with a woman a man explains that his penis is the devil and her vagina is hell, and that the Christian thing to do is to put the devil in his place.

Thompson arranged his index by content and theme under 23 categories, giving each an alphabetical heading (and omitting the letters I, O, and Y): A contains Mythological Motifs (e.g., A671.2.2.3, rivers of fire in hell); B, Animals (e.g., B524.1.4, wolf defends master's child against serpent); D, Magic (e.g., D1338.4, bath in magic milk rejuvenates); F, Marvels (e.g., F991.1, bleeding lance); T, Sex (e.g., T11.2.1, lovers meet in their dreams); V, Religion (e.g., V1.8.3, dog worship), and so on.

Folklorists use motifs in the comparative study of folktales, seeking to find, for example, how a given story might have changed over time or how tales differ and spread from culture to culture. For example, some motifs, such as the magnetic mountain, which pulls nails out of passing ships (F754), are common in medieval Islamic tales but do not occur in Europe until substantially later, an indication (if not proof) that Islamic tales and storytelling styles began influencing European narrators in the late Middle Ages.

By comparing the treatments of certain motifs or clusters of motifs researchers can learn something about comparative cultural aesthetics and values. For example, beginning in the second half of the twelfth century French authors wrote many Arthurian romances that borrowed Celtic narrative traditions from the Welsh and Bretons, adapting the details to reflect French cultural traditions and values. Romance writers seized upon such characters as the fairy lover (F301), particularly the fairy mistress (F302), who requires of her mortal lover that their love be kept a secret (C999.1.1.4). Such story elements were well suited to late-twelfth-century literary tastes and courtly games, in which depictions of a male's secret love for a divinely beautiful woman became a sort of literary obsession.

Yet the French authors borrowed very selectively from their Celtic sources. In Welsh and Irish narrative traditions the fairy otherworld could be visited by traveling underground, especially into a burial mound (F211), underwater (F212), or simply on the surface of the earth—for example, through the unknown depths of a forest. In contrast, in the French romances of Chrétien de Troyes and his followers the otherworld is almost always found only by taking the third type of route, overland. The French writers chose the one path that would make the fairy realm seem most familiar to their listeners, the route that knights typically followed when they set out on adventures in earlier French heroic literature or in real life. Thus, a close examination of the various motifs of related narratives can help researchers discover the cultural boundaries, cross-cultural continuities, and the worldviews of medieval communities.

For all its potential usefulness, the study of motifs has suffered extensively from misconceptions and misapplications. Most common is the belief that any item found in Thompson's index is necessarily, by virtue of that fact, part of an oral folk tradition. Such is simply not the case. Thompson deliberately titles his work an index of *Folk-Literature*, and in his subtitle he mentions that romances, fabliaux, and jestbooks were among his most important sources. A reader of the Middle English romance *King Alexander*, impressed by the author's description of giant trees that cast two-mile-long shadows, may turn to a motif index to see if this motif exists in folk tradition. Bordman's *Motif-Index of the English Metrical Romances* indeed lists a motif for two-mile-long tree shadows (*F811.14.2), which may lead one to think that it is a staple in folk tradition—though in fact the motif has been found only in *King Alexander* and may be the author's unique invention.

A second misconception is that if the same motif appears in two tales, the tales must be closely related. To the contrary, many motifs are so simple that they could easily have been independently invented: For example, the figure of the cruel stepmother (S31), such a widespread fixture in medieval romance and modern European folktales, is even more widespread throughout the world. To claim that two different tales about cruel stepmothers have a close historical relationship simply goes beyond the intent and the capabilities of the *Motif-Index*. Folklorists generally argue that only lengthy and complex tales are likely to be related through direct chains of oral transmission.

Another difficulty with Thompson's index is his insistence on defining motifs as "strange" and "unusual"; in so doing, he tends to make folk tradition itself seem more strange and unusual, more set apart from elite culture, than it actually is. Furthermore, Thompson almost invariably judges the "strange" and "unusual" in terms of twentieth-century expectations rather than in terms of the values of the communities from which the stories come. For example, the humiliation of corpses (Q491) is an action that current mainstream Western culture finds abhorrent, but it was a reality in late-medieval life; in London, for instance, the heads of executed criminals were daily displayed.

Finally, the classification system of the index is imperfect, as is perhaps inevitable in any attempt to catalog the narrative traditions of the entire world. For example, the letter B is devoted to animals, yet we find animal worship under V (Religion), animals help man perform task under H (Tests), lions abducting children under R (Captives and Fugitives), and child taught to steal lion whelps under T (Sex). In spite of the fact that Thompson provides a detailed index of the nouns found in the motif titles, researchers need to spend significant time with the index, learning its quirks, before they can use it effectively.

See also: Folktale

—Carl Lindahl

Myrddin. Legendary Welsh seer.

Myrddin appears as "Merlinus" in Geoffrey of Monmouth's *Historia regum Britanniae* (History of the Kings of Britain, c. 1138). The British king Vortigern is advised to sprinkle the foundations of the citadel he is attempting to build with the blood of "a fatherless boy" to prevent their mysterious disappearance each night. The boy Merlinus, the offspring of a nun and an incubus, is discovered at Caerfyrddin (present-day Carmarthen), but he confounds Vortigern's sages by revealing the true reason for the disappearing foundations. Beneath the citadel is a pool, and at the bottom of the pool are two hollow stones in which two dragons are sleeping. They awake and begin to fight. Merlinus explains that these are the red dragon of the British and the white of the Saxons, and he proceeds to prophesy the future history of Britain, in increasingly ambiguous language, in what is now Book 7 of the *Historia*.

Merlinus reappears when Aurelius Ambrosius seeks his help in devising a fitting memorial for the Britons massacred by the Saxons at "the treachery of the long knives," and he subsequently succeeds in transporting a group of standing stones called the "Giants' Dance" from Ireland to Stonehenge; thus, Geoffrey credits Merlin with establishing that famous stone circle. Later Merlin explains the portent of a meteor to King Uther Pendragon as the king prepares to regain his crown. Merlin's final role is to give Uther the form of Duke Gorlois so that he can sleep with the latter's wife Ygerna, as a result of which Arthur is conceived.

Geoffrey of Monmouth's account of the wondrous boy Merlinus, "who is also called Ambrosius," is taken from the *Historia Brittonum* (History of the Britons), where it forms part of the tale of Ambrosius at Dinas Emrys (Stronghold of Ambrosius), but the sources of the other episodes in Geoffrey are not known. The discovery of the boy at Caerfyrddin suggests that the name *Merlinus* is Geoffrey's latinization of the Welsh *Myrddin*, often spelled *Merdin* in Middle Welsh. If the name *Merdin* were pronounced in Latin or French fashion, it would have unfortunate connotations (Latin *merda*, French *merde*, "excrement").

Myrddin (pronounced *merthin*), the prophet par excellence of Welsh tradition, had a well-formulated legend associated with his name prior to Geoffrey of Monmouth. As far as can be re-created from numerous sources—including five series of early (pre-Geoffrey) Welsh poems, Geoffrey of Monmouth's *Vita Merlini* (Life of Merlin), the work of Gerald of Wales, and allusions in the

Triads of the Island of Britain—Myrddin, together with his lord Gwenddolau, fought at the battle of Arfderydd in modern Cumbria. The *Annales Cambriae* (Annals of Wales) record a battle fought in the year 573 in which Gwenddolau was killed "*et Merlinus insanus effectus est*" [Merlin went mad], and the Triads confirm that there was a saga about this conflict between rival north-British kings. Myrddin lost his reason—from remorse at the death of his lord (for which he held himself responsible), from the trauma of battle, or as the result of a terrifying vision—and fled to the Caledonian Forest, in what is now Scotland, where he lived the life of a Wild Man, deranged but possessing prophetic powers, in terror of King Rhydderch of Strathclyde and rejected by his sister (or lover), Gwenddydd. He seems finally to have been reconciled and to have returned to court healed.

In one of the Welsh poems Merlin is called Llallogan. This may be a form of the name *Lailoken*, a figure whose legend (motif M341.2.4), essentially the same as that of Myrddin, has been preserved in fragmentary form in the life of St. Kentigern of Glasgow by Jocelin of Furness (c. 1180) and that is analogous to the Irish story of Suibhne Geilt (Suibhne the Wild Man). The Welsh legend may therefore have been told originally of Llallogan and may have been relocalized in Wales when the name *Myrddin* was created from the place name *Caerfyrddin* (the town where Merlinus was discovered, according to Geoffrey's *Historia*). Whether Myrddin is a secondary development from the Llallogan legend or analogous to it, he was already established as a major prophet by the tenth century, when he appears in the poem *Armes Prydein*, foretelling the victory of a British-led confederation against England's King Aethelstan (c. 930). The prophecies are introduced by such phrases as "wise men foretell" and "the Muse foretells," which suggests that Myrddin's powers were regarded as being those of poetic inspiration, and it may be significant that a line in the *Gododdin* refers to the "fair poetry of Myrddin." In later medieval Welsh poetry there are frequent allusions to Myrddin as an exemplary poet. It may be that Myrddin, like the celebrated Taliesin (also the subject of legends), was a historical north-British poet. If so, however, none of his verse survives under his name—in which case the transformation of the bard as seer into a mythic character would be complete, but at the cost of losing the historical persona.

Geoffrey of Monmouth appears only to have known Myrddin's name and reputation as a prophet when he wrote the *Historia* (c. 1138), but a few years later (c. 1150) he had learned of the genuine tradition, which he used in his *Vita Merlini*. Though he attempted to identify this figure with the prophet of the *Historia*, the differences could not be reconciled, and Gerald of Wales in his *Itinerarium Cambriae* (Journey through Wales) proposed two Merlins: "Merlinus Ambrosius who had prophesied before Vortigern," and Merlinus Silvestris (Caledonis), the prophetic Wild Man of the woods (2, 8).

Clas Merddin (Myrddin's Precinct) was said to have been the first name of the island of Britain, perhaps a trace of a Welsh origin legend. Fragments of other Myrddin legends have been preserved in Welsh verse of the fifteenth and sixteenth centuries—for example, his death on a pole in a weir, his role as lover, his imprisonment in the glass house, and his burial place on Bardsey Island off the Lleyn Peninsula, Caernarfonshire.

See also: Arthurian Lore; Geoffrey of Monmouth; Gerald of Wales; *Gododdin, Y*; Nennius; Taliesin; Triads of the Island of Britain; Wild Man

—Brynley F. Roberts

Myth. A sacred narrative, featuring divine beings, normally unfolding in the timeless past, sometimes accompanied by ritual, and often functioning to explain the workings of nature or the structure of society.

At least, that is one definition—but the term *myth* has been applied and misapplied in so many ways that it has become nearly meaningless. When Sabine Baring-Gould wrote his highly influential *Curious Myths of the Middle Ages* (1866), he filled his book not with myths but with legends about such figures as Prester John, Pope Joan, and Tannhäuser, and what he meant by *myth* was essentially "a story that is not true but that unenlightened people believe." Baring-Gould's use of the term is still reflected in daily usage in English, when people label any false report a myth. When Norma Laura Goodrich compiled her popularizing collection *The Medieval Myths* (1961), she used the term in a different sense, as a label for such works as the Old English *Beowulf* (properly speaking, an epic or heroic legendary poem) and the Middle Welsh *Peredur, Son of Efrawg* (more appropriately labeled a romance or a tale), neither of which would be considered a myth by folklorists.

Perhaps the most common understanding attached to the word *myth* is "the other group's narrative religion." Jews, Christians, and Muslims rarely identify the sacred stories of their own, overlapping religious traditions as myths, but they may readily apply the term to the sacred stories of Hinduism or Buddhism or, even more commonly, to the creation stories of Greek and Roman religions, of the tribal religions of the early-medieval Celts and Scandinavians, or of present-day Africans, Melanesians, Native Americans, Polynesians, and Sámi (Lapps). Today's folklorists tend to work, explicitly or implicitly, with this definition, although many have taken exception to such an ethnocentric concept of myth. If the tales of the medieval Scandinavian believers in Odin and Thor fulfilled much the same needs and purposes for non-Christian Scandinavians that biblical tales fulfilled for medieval Christians—to explain the origin of the world, the relationship between humanity and the divine, and the fate of the dead in the afterlife—then the tales of the two religions should be given the same name and should be considered equally.

Separate articles in this encyclopedia treat the relatively well documented Celtic and Scandinavian mythological traditions, and the entries on Baltic Tradition, Finno-Ugric Tradition, Hungarian Tradition, and Slavic Tradition, East, discuss the less well known mythologies of the peoples of Eastern and northeastern Europe. Here there is only space to discuss some of the ways in which it may be useful to think about myth in the context of the highly Christianized traditions of Western Europe in the later Middle Ages.

Etiological Narratives as Myth
As folklore focuses on the unofficial side of organized religion, the primary folkloric interest in myth is in the ways that people reapply sacred narratives and concepts in their daily lives to express community beliefs, values, and aesthetics. One way in which they did so was through *etiological narratives*, that is, stories that explain the origin of natural phenomena, rituals, and social groups. In Anglo-Saxon England, significantly after Christianity had become the official religion, the kings of Wessex continued to trace their ancestry back to Woden (Odin), the chief god of their pre-Christian religion. In thirteenth-century Iceland Snorri Sturluson wrote of Odin as a great and powerful king who had settled Scandinavia. In such traditions Odin has been euhemerized, or explained as a deity derived from a larger-than-life mortal. Yet he remains the subject of a story that explains the origins of the Scandinavian people, allowing thirteenth-century Icelanders to account for their origins both through the Christian narrative of God's creation of the universe as well as through an altered version of older accounts in which Odin was an agent in their creation.

The brothers Jacob and Wilhelm Grimm, who initiated the scholarly study of folktales, also developed a theory that the märchen they assembled in the famous *Kinder- und Hausmärchen* (Children's and Household Tales, popularly known as *Grimms' Fairy Tales*) were descended from ancient Germanic myths. Jacob, the older brother, developed this thesis at great length in his magisterial *Deutsche Mythologie* (Teutonic Mythology, 1835). Yet whatever the source of such tales, a more relevant question for medievalist folklorists is whether such tales functioned mythically in the Middle Ages, by explaining the origins, conditions, and fates of human beings. Apparently a few narratives related to modern oral folktales did indeed function as such, at least on a limited scale. There is a series of narratives, surviving at least from the twelfth century, that explain the origins of some of the most powerful French noble families. In the founding story of the house of Bouillon, surviving from the late twelfth century in several chansons de geste, the celebrated crusader knight Godfrey of Bouillon is descended from a supernatural incident in which the countess of Bouillon gives birth to seven children, each with a silver chain around its neck. When the chains are removed from six of the children, they are transformed into swans; the one child left in human form, later to be known as the Swan Knight, is able to restore five of his siblings to their original shape, but the seventh remains a swan and accompanies the Swan Knight on his adventures. The Swan Knight becomes the ancestor of Godfrey. This medieval tale, appearing in the chansons de geste *Elioxe*, *Beatrix*, and *Le geste du chevalier au cygne*, bears a strong resemblance in plot to the Grimms' tales "The Twelve Brothers" and "The Six Swans" (AT 451) and several other modern oral märchen. Some versions of the medieval tales begin with the birth of the swan children and then carry the story of the Bouillon family forward to its climax, Godfrey's conquest of Jerusalem (1099), thus linking the supernatural account in a direct chain to one of the most celebrated moments in medieval Christian history. Similar etiological narratives were told of the Lusignan family, descended from the mermaid (or serpent-woman) Melusine, and the Plantagenets (who became the ruling family of England, 1154–1399), descended from a demon queen who finally disappeared, shrieking as she flew into the air, when her husband sprinkled her with holy water.

In the oral tales of the lower classes, humbler but equally imaginative narratives explained the origins of certain unofficial rituals. In the thirteenth century in southern France a Church Inquisitor discovered the existence of a popular cult that practiced rituals at night at the grave of a dog that they called "Saint" Guinefort. The rituals were to protect sickly children. The people used an etiological myth to explain Guinefort's special powers: The dog had indeed died a martyr, protecting an infant from a snake. But when the dog emerged from the baby's room with its mouth smeared with blood, members of the household assumed it had injured the child and killed the dog before discovering the truth. This basic plot of the Guinefort story, known as "Llewellyn and His Dog" (motif B331.2), occurs widely in medieval and postmedieval Europe, but only here does it function as an etiological myth.

The figures of Christian devotion often attracted myth-like narratives in the Middle Ages. One such tale, studied by Pamela Berger, is the legend of the grain miracle, an account of how the Virgin Mary miraculously caused a field of grain to grow to ripeness in one day: Pursued by Herod's soldiers, who seek to kill the infant Jesus, she passes a man sowing his field. She tells the man that if anyone asks him if he has seen her, he should reply that he has not seen her since he sowed his field. She then causes the grain to grow, and when the soldiers come looking for

Mary, the farmer informs them that she has not passed by since the field was sown. The soldiers give up the search.

Berger suggests, soundly, that the tale of the grain miracle served to explain Mary's relationship to the fertility of the fields and hence retained a mythic function, underlining the importance of invoking the Virgin to make the crops grow.

Myth and Ritual

The cult of Guinefort and the grain miracle narrative illustrate the close relationship between myth and ritual. Some myths function to explain rituals; some rituals effectively "act out" myths. Studying the various magico-religious fertility practices of nineteenth-century European peasants, such scholars as Wilhelm Mannhardt, in *Antike Wald- und Feldkulte* (Ancient Forest and Field Cults, 1877), and James George Frazer, in *The Golden Bough* (first edition, 1890), concluded that such religious acts were timelessly old and that many ancient myths and their medieval analogs were derived from these rituals. Jessie Weston, in particular, saw the Grail romances as being descended from such rituals. In her view, such works as the *Perceval* of Chrétien de Troyes (c. 1190) and the *Parzifal* of Wolfram von Eschenbach (c. 1205–1210) were therefore essentially myths, or the memories of myths, in which the fate of the land was essentially tied to the king: if the king's health failed, the land became waste. Weston's book, *From Ritual to Romance* (1920), influenced medievalists for decades. While there are surviving Irish mythological texts that strongly assert the relationship, even the marriage, between the king and the land, there is no evidence to support the notion that Wolfram's and Chrétien's listeners would have experienced the Grail romances as the mythic expressions of surviving fertility cults. Rather, both Chrétien and Wolfram presented the Grail not as an agent of earthly fertility but as a vessel of Christian salvation. If the Grail romances are mythic in any sense, it is as Christian myths, narratives expressing a relationship between human beings and sacred objects related to the Passion of Christ.

Classical Myth in Medieval Contexts

Greek and Roman mythology provoked varied responses from Christian intellectuals. Some considered these stories of pagan gods abhorrent to Christian doctrine, but others retold them with relish, and many reinterpreted the tales in a religious light, to the point that the popes retained "mythographers," scholars who explained the stories of the gods in terms of Christian doctrine. These stories may be said to have functioned, at least to a limited extent, as myths because the Vatican interpreters read the tales of the ancient pagan deities as part of the plan of the Christian God to explain moral and spiritual truths to humanity in coded terms.

The narratives of classical mythology remained popular in story collections. Ovid's *Metamorphoses* was particularly well received, and it was rendered into the vernacular languages in rhymed form, with the myths now given Christian morals. The story of Orpheus was particularly popular. Told in Old English as early as the ninth century, it also became the inspiration for a medieval romance, *Sir Orfeo* (or *King Orfew*), in which Orpheus was now identified not as a classical hero but as a medieval king. In the romance Orpheus is descended from King Jupiter and King Juno (who is a female, Jupiter's wife, in Roman mythology). In the Roman version, the wife of Orpheus travels to the underworld to bring her back. In the medieval romance, it is the King of Fairy who spirits the woman away. In both versions the hero wins his wife back by playing the harp masterfully and winning a favor from his otherworldly host (Pluto in Ovid, the fairy king in the romance). However, in the myth Orpheus looks back upon his wife before she has left the otherworld, and she is condemned to return to the land of the dead, while in the romance she is happily restored to the kingdom.

Sir Orfeo and the many other retellings of classical myths were highly popular among all classes of people in the late Middle Ages, but they functioned principally for entertainment and very seldom if ever for sacred purposes. The *Complaynt of Scotlande* (1547) presents a list of stories told by Scottish shepherds. The shepherds related heroic narratives about Sir Gawain and King Arthur and folktales about three-headed giants and three-legged dogs—but even in their isolated work, they also retold the tales of Jupiter and Io, Perseus, and Hercules, once-sacred narratives that had become staples of medieval written and oral storytelling, tales told for entertainment, which they remain to the present day.

See also: Celtic Mythology; Fairy Lover; Grain Miracle; Guinefort, Saint; Mythography; Richard the Lion-Heart; Scandinavian Mythology; Swan Knight; Trickster

—Carl Lindahl

N

ames, Personal. Human names, and names given to domestic and working animals, rarely studied for their folkloric implications but of significant cultural value.

Certain names were used generically—for example, Middle English *Malkin* for a woman of doubtful sexual reputation—but it is nicknames, recorded in such sources as tax rolls and other official lists, that have much to tell us.

The interpretation of compound names is a field in which caution should be exercised. A comparative corpus of such names is an essential prerequisite for any reliable conclusions, and a knowledge of name formation is necessary before sound etymologies can be advanced.

A thirteenth- and fourteenth-century Arras source lists one "Car de Lion," more familiar as the sobriquet of England's King Richard I, the "Lion-Heart," but what are we to make of Carde-vake (Cow-Heart, attested 1223–1246) and Car de Veel (Calf-Heart, 1255)? The implication is surely the opposite of "Lion-Heart," for these nicknames imply cowardice, as presumably does the colorful East Anglian Godlef Crepunder Hwitel (Creep-under-the-Coat/Blanket).

Medieval nicknames are potential sources for all kinds of popular attitudes to physical appearance and personal habits. Sexual nicknames are particularly striking and informative. Big-breasted women are not favored in such names, as attested by the thirteenth-century French Alice Pis de Vache (Cow's Udder), the twelfth-century Bavarian Zitzel-ziege (Titty Goat), and the character in several fifteenth-century German Carnival plays named Seututt (Sow Tits). The perennial concern with penis length seems implicit in such nicknames as Urbanus and Zacher Langzers (Long Penis) and Alan Coltepyntel (Colt Penis), and also the related Joh[annes] Tupballock (Ram's Testicle, 1338), but it is difficult to know whether the sobriquet of Bele Wydecunthe (Wide Cunt, 1328) was a token of approval or not. Richard Luffecunt (1276) is, at least, straightforward, but the extraordinary Simon Sitbithecunte (Norfolk, 1167) perhaps deliberately suggests the image of a cat waiting by a mouse hole. In the name John Cruskunt (Crush Cunt; Cumberland, 1338), however, there is probably more than a hint of masculine approval; consider the *con crossue* (cracked cunt) of the *Roman de la rose*, in which the nut-cracking imagery suggests that the several men nicknamed Notehake (Nuthatch, 1220–1379) are unlikely to have been named after the bird. The nickname given to Perette du Trou-Punais (Of-the-Stinking-Hole), one of the women in the *Evangiles de quenouilles* (Gospel of the Distaffs, c. 1475), seems to convey male disgust with female sexuality.

The presumably proverbially celibate Maci Qui-ne-fout (Who-Does-Not-Fuck; Paris, 1292) is to be contrasted with "*Michault qui fut nomme le Bon Fouterrre*" [who was named the Good Fucker] of François Villon's *Testament* (Paris, 1461) and John le Fucker (1278), the latter the earliest attestation of this taboo word in English. The colorful names borne by or given to prostitutes are also of interest in this connection: from fourteenth-century London, Clarice la Claterbal-lock (Clatter-Ball, 1340; cf. *Pantagruel* 27: "*Ii n'est ... clicquetys que de cuilions*" [There is no clattering like ballocks]) and Alice Tredewedowe (Tread-widow), and from the same city a century and a half later, Pusse le Cat; Bouncing Bess; Katherine Sawnders, alias Flying Kate; and Joan Havyer, alias Puppy.

Scatology is also well represented, with some names presumably referring to personal habits. In Bruges in 1383 we hear of Jan, the son of Jan Elux, called Schijt in de Zee (Shit in the Sea), who was perhaps no more than eccentric in this regard, but the fourteenth-century German Er-hart Schisingarten (Shit in the Garden) was clearly notorious for having fouled his own, or worse, someone else's, nest—cf. the peasant woman named Jutzin Scheissindpluomen (Shit in the Flowers) in Heinrich Wittenweiler's *Ring* (German, c. 1400), and the thirteenth-century Johannes Caca in Basilica (basilica, or perhaps cathedral). Jehan Pet d'Asne (Donkey Fart; Oudenarde, 1275) was presumably given to noisy farting, but Roland le Fartere (c. 1250) held land in Suffolk by serjeanty of appearing before the king each Christmas day to perform "*unum saltum et unum siffletum et unum bumbulum*" [a jump, a whistle, and a fart]!

Xenophobia and racism must also be expected in nicknames: in 1354 Jean le Bon received the gift of a handsome black man from Peter of Aragon; the man's name was Charles Blanc. Similarly, a black trumpeter in Henry VII's employ in 1507 was known as John Blank.

Proverbial stupidity was perhaps implied by such names as Milkegos (Milk-Goose, alluding to the folly of trying to milk nonmammals; Norwich, 1288), Pendecrowe (Pen-Crow), and Betewater, and also from an English document, the French equivalent, Froisselewe. Certain bird and animal nicknames must also have been used to imply stupidity: John Goose, "my Lord of Yorkes foole."

Character traits such as miserliness are conveyed by such names as Jehan Clo Bourse (Closed Purse; Oudenarde, c. 1275) and by such colorful metaphors as Escorcherainne (Skin-the-Toad; Paris, 1292) and the late-twelfth-century Englishman nicknamed Pilemus (Skin-the-Mouse? cf. the English "skinflint"). At least, it is difficult to believe such names were truly occupational. The name Ricardus Pilecat (Skin-the-Cat, 1165), on the other hand, clearly refers to actual cat skinning, a practice resorted to by only the poorest peddlers. Compare the boast of a superior fifteenth-century chapman: "We ben chapmen ... We bern abowtyn non cattes skynnes" and the fact that *katzenschinder* (cat skinner) was a term of abuse in late-medieval Germany.

Humor abounds in nicknames—many must have been applied ironically, but only rarely are we in a position to share the joke, as in the case of the name Drinke Water, which must sometimes have been applied to a drunkard and was applied to at least two fourteenth-century innkeepers: the Londoner Margery Drynkewater was the wife of Philip le Tavener (1324), and four years later a Thomas Drinkewater is recorded as landlord of Drinkwaterestaverne. Estienne iiij Gueles (Four Throats; Paris, 1292) was also, presumably, a big drinker.

The names of folk heroes were also sometimes given to those thought to display similar traits. Robert le Deable (Paris, 1292) may have gotten his name from the popular romance *Robert le Diable*, and a member of a Berkshire outlaw gang, William son of Robert le Fevere, bears the nickname William Robehod, which attests to knowledge of the folk hero Robin Hood as early as 1261–1262.

In Brunswick in 1526 we hear of a horse named Ulenspeygel, interesting evidence for the popularity of the Trickster in what was after all the hometown of Hermann Bote, who made the earliest codification of Eulenspiegel stories (1510). A list of dogs' names from Zurich in 1504 includes *"Nieman* [Nobody] *und was bob gschicht hat er than"* [and whatever bad thing happens he did it]. Other names relate to their masters' occupations: Stosel (Pestle) the apothecary's dog, Hemmerli (Little Hammer) the locksmith's dog, and Speichli (Little Spoke) the wagoner's dog.

See also: Eulenspiegel; Iconography; Names, Place
—Malcolm Jones

Names, Place. Titles bestowed on natural and human-made features of the environment, often the subjects of legend, and reflecting in many other ways the traditional values and beliefs of those who coin and employ them.

The role of place names in medieval folklore is difficult to assess, but it is clear that many peoples have attached great importance to naming mountains, rivers, fords, valleys, farmsteads, towns, and so forth; and as different peoples occupy or conquer a territory, they often adapt these older names to their own language or change them entirely. Some place names have mythic or religious significance, while others appear to be related to a people's sense of their familial, communal, or ethnic identity and traditions.

Even a superficial glance at place name dictionaries of countries for which reliable compendia exist reveals the astonishing extent to which practically all major places, as well as many not-so-important ones, had already been given individual identities through their names by 1500; in fact, a considerable number of them had already enjoyed a long named existence in premedieval times, having passed through two or three different languages in the process. For most or all of these names, their original lexical meaning had ceased to have any significance by the end of the Middle Ages. What now mattered was the names' acquired referential function. They had created not only an interdependent regional, national, and even international identification but had also shaped wilderness into knowable structured landscapes and familiar habitats. Whether names originally identified farmsteads, designated natural features associated with the place, or referred to visual distinguishing characteristics (such as shape, color, and size), their medieval content was usually no longer identical with what it had been when they were first applied, nor was it the same as in modern usage. Whatever associations or reactions may have been evoked in the medieval folk at the mention of certain place names, these folk lived in rural and urban landscapes structured, though by no means saturated, by cumulative namings.

Similarly, the degree of importance that individuals or communities attributed to place names varied considerably. In times when travel was limited in distance for the majority of the population, though by no means restricted otherwise, it must have been difficult to distinguish names of places in faraway lands from those altogether imaginary, such as Anostus, which Claudius Aelian (second–third century C.E.) located beyond the entrance to the Mediterranean; the Ape Kingdom of the *Thousand and One Nights*; or Avalon (and, of course, Camelot) of the Arthurian cycle. On a disc-shaped earth, such places would lie, on the whole, beyond the horizons bounding individual human experience, and it is not surprising that beyond the horizon of horizons lay the Gaelic Tir na nog, "the land of the ever young from where no mortal has ever returned." In such a world, the reality of fictions and the fiction of reality were hard to distinguish, should somebody want to make such a distinction. In any case, medieval folk culture, together with other cultural registers, had available to it a toponymic inventory that ranged from personally known named localities in the vicinity of where one had one's everyday being to unvisited, yet to be explored, and often imaginary named places that existed essentially only on the maps of the mind.

Researchers can look in folk narrative genres for the folk cultural use of place names, but such an approach is sometimes hampered by the difficulty we have in declaring such stories to be positively medieval. From critical examination of more recent folk narratives, whether with medieval antecedents or not, we know the narrating of the past as place, as well as time, requires very different techniques in the employment of place names in different genres. Whereas some märchen are unspecific about the location of their events, expressed in general phrases such as "beyond the beyond," "on the edge of a large forest," "in a certain part of the wide world," "in a wild part of the country where strangers seldom came," legends rely heavily in their claims to truthfulness or at least believability on naming specific locations for their stories. In the Grimms' *Deutsche Sagen* (German Legends), for example, nine of the first ten legends are associated with specific locales: respectively, with Bohemia (1), the Graubünden Alps (2), the Harz Mountains (3), the Meissen Mountains of Hesse (4 and 6), Horsel Mountain (5), the village of Schwarza in Thuringia (7), various Waldenfels elsewhere, Köter Mountain (9), and Boyne Castle (10); the remaining 575 legends amply support such strong links of stories to place names.

Even more than being anchored to specific locations with the help of named places, legends are closely linked to place names when their express purpose is to explain the origin of a name. Such is the case in Grimm legend 457, in which both the place names Odenwald and Seligenstadt are derived from exclamatory phrases said to have been uttered by Imma, Emperor Charlemagne's daughter, and by Charlemagne himself. The German names Altona and Einbeck have similar legendary explanations, while names such as Aroleid in Switzerland, Boxberg in Germany, and Rottenmann in Austria are said to have originated in memorable events. In England, origin legends are attached to such place names as Bulstrode, Crawls, Godshill, Kilgrim Bridge, Osmotherly, and Winwick, and in medieval Irish Gaelic tradition a separate narrative genre, the so-called *Dindshenchas*, was devoted exclusively to the explanation of place name origins. It is noteworthy that two stimuli that—according to the best scholarly opinion—rarely, if ever, figure in the *creation* of place names are said to have been responsible for practically all these folk-cultural (re)interpretations of names: the incident and someone's curious or memorable utterance. Without claiming that (apart from the *Dindshenchas*) any of these tales and legends have any definite medieval roots, although some of them do indeed have such, it is probably safe to assume that the situation in the Middle Ages did not differ much from that encountered in the last few centuries. Reflexes of folk narratives found in literary works such as Boccaccio's *Decameron* or Chaucer's *Canterbury Tales* tend to support such an assumption, as do early variants of the tale types such as those assiduously collected by Walter Anderson for his study of "The King and the Abbot" (AT 922), one of the best-attested late-medieval humorous tales.

It can also be argued without much fear of contradiction that in the area of folk speech—or more precisely, folk onomastics—unofficial, vernacular names complemented their official counterparts, whether as nicknames or as dialectal variants. Indeed, in the absence of regulated official spellings and standard pronunciations, the unofficial names are likely to have been even more common in oral tradition than they are now. In many countries, particularly in central Europe, the fourteenth and fifteenth centuries also witnessed the beginning of the transformation of place names into surnames: individuals came to be identified as being associated with estates or farms they owned or occupied, or in the case of in-comers to a community, a place name surname indicated the place from which they had come, thus reemphasizing in the local context their status as strangers and outsiders.

From the point of view of modern scholarship, medieval place names are useful in the investigation of settlement history. In particular, the spatial distribution of certain names has been interpreted historically in many countries (e.g., Denmark, England, Germany, Scotland, Sweden) in the search for chronological stratification in the languages spoken in the countries concerned. It is, however, necessary to bear in mind that the treatment of maps of space as maps of time is less straightforward than it may seem, since spatial distribution is often open to a variety of temporal interpretations.

See also: Names, Personal

—W. F. H. Nicolaisen

Nennius (fl. c. 800) [Nemnivus]. Historian and cleric, possibly monk, usually credited as the author of the *Historia Brittonum* (History of the Britons). He may have come from southeast Wales (he shows familiarity with some of the traditions of Ergyng and the Severn valley), though he calls himself a pupil of Elfoddw (a bishop of north Wales of that name died in 809).

Later (eleventh-century) manuscripts of *Historia Brittonum* ascribe the composition to "Nennius." A chronology in the text sets the date as 829–830. Another manuscript, dated 820, ascribes the composition of a rune-type alphabet (in response to an Englishman's taunt that the British had no alphabet) to "Nemnivus." These are probably references to the same person, motivated in each case by personal national sensitivities. Authorship of the *Historia Brittonum* is now accepted as not known; other extant earlier texts represent earlier versions of the compilation. Nevertheless, whoever he was, the historian who for centuries has been known by the name Nennius composed a valuable record of history and folklore taken, he claims, from Roman, Irish, English, and Church writings and from the "tradition of our [British] elders."

Providing a history for the British as Bede had done for the English, Nennius lays out the ages of the world and traces British origins to both Adam and the Roman Brutus before going on to the Roman period and the Saxon invasions. Although the preface modestly claims that the author made a compilation of materials, scholars agree that the *Historia Brittonum* has a well-defined structure and attempts to trace the national origins and development of the British/Welsh. The text is notable, too, for its attempts at comparative chronology (i.e., dating one event by another, though these connections appear more authoritative than the evidence warrants). As such, it is in the medieval tradition of historical writing that Nennius played a role in shaping Welsh perceptions of their own history. Although he, like earlier commentators, considered the Saxon conquest to be God's will, he shifted its interpretation from being a punishment for British sinfulness (as Gildas had claimed) to being a result of naive thoughtlessness in welcoming the foreigners.

Moreover, Nennius also relates a great deal of traditional information, sometimes providing the first or even only record of it. He tells of the British who had followed Maximus to conquer Rome settling in Brittany on their return, slaughtering the male inhabitants, marrying the women, and cutting out the women's tongues so that they would not sully the language. The Welsh term *lled-taw* ("semi-silent"), applied to this population, is thus credited with giving its name to the region, *Llydaw* (Brittany). The story is repeated in *Breuddwyd Maxen Wledig* (The Dream of Emperor Maxen) and referred to in the Triads of the Island of Britain. He reports the dealings of the British ruler Vortigern with the Saxon Hengist, setting off the Saxon invasions. He records the tale of Emrys (Latin Ambrosius, the "fatherless boy" whose blood is sought to prevent the disappearance of the building materials for Vortigern's tower, who reveals that the cause of the disappearances is red and white worms or dragons hidden in an underground lake, and who prophesies the eventual victory of the British in driving the Saxons out of the land); the treachery of the long knives by which the Saxons slaughtered the British at a peace conference; stories from the lives of Saints Patrick and Germanus (e.g., a poor man who feeds the saint his only calf finds it whole and unharmed the next day); and a series of wonders from the islands of Britain (e.g., a river that rises like a mountain, the Baths of Badon in which the water is always whatever temperature the bather desires), Anglesey (e.g., a hill that turns itself around, a self-propelling stone), and Ireland (e.g., a lake full of pearls and surrounded by concentric circles of tin, lead, iron, and copper).

Historia Brittonum has been held to have particular importance for the study of Arthurian legend. It is the first reference to Arthur in a historical context, listing the 12 battles this *dux bellorum* (war leader, but not a king) fought against the English (and mentioning also the tradition that he carried Mary's image on his shield). The battle list may derive from a literary source, and most of the sites cannot be securely located, making the value of this chapter (56) as historical evidence difficult to assess. The *mirabilia* section has two Arthurian wonders—the footprint made in stone by Arthur's dog when they were hunting the great boar Porcum Troit (an episode found later in *Culhwch and Olwen*) and Arthur's son's tomb, which changes its length to match anyone lying next to it—that are evidence for topographical legends associated with Arthur in southeast Wales in the ninth century.

Nennius's noting of variant traditions and his personalized reports indicate clearly that he drew directly from oral tradition. For example, after reporting that Vortigern was killed when a fire from heaven destroyed his tower, he states, "This is the end of Vortigern, as I found it in the book of Blessed Germanus; but others have different versions," and then he reports two variants: that Vortigern died of a broken heart after long, lonely wanderings, and that "others say" the earth swallowed him on the night his fortress was destroyed. In recording the wonders of Britain, he admits having tested a plank that supports men in the middle of a spring and the tomb that cannot be measured the same twice.

See also: Arthurian Lore; Maxen Wledig; Myrddin

—Elissa R. Henken and Brynley F. Roberts

New Year's. A celebration marking the passing of time and the repetition and constancy of the seasons on the day believed to end one year and begin another.

From very early times, late March seemed a natural choice for celebrating the beginning of a new year, since spring began around that time and new crops were planted. The ancient Babylonians invented one of the first calendars and established March 25 as the beginning of the new year. For the ancient Celts, the new year began at Samhain, a holiday normally celebrated on November 1. The pagan Romans celebrated their New Year's feast of *Kalendae* (the first of the year) from January 1 to January 3. In 46 B.C.E. Julius Caesar set up what became known as the Julian calendar, in which the year was divided into 12 months of 30 or 31 days, with an extra day in February every four years. The Julian calendar also changed New Year's Day from March 25 to January 1. Both dates were maintained as New Year's Day in Europe throughout the Middle Ages; for example, in England March 25 was the beginning of the year for governmental record keeping, but January 1 was the date for New Year's celebration. Moving the celebration of New Year's Day to January 1 placed it in the season evoking the ancient respect and fear associated with the shortest and darkest day of the year, which in pagan Rome was the time of Saturnalia rituals and which was transformed into the Christmas celebration of the Christian religion. Another important function of this shift was to make way for the medieval celebration of the Twelve Days, from Christmas Day (December 25) to Epiphany (January 6).

The Twelve Days became the focus of intense merrymaking and role reversal during the late Middle Ages. As is the case with the Feast of Fools, the Boy Bishop, and the Subdeacons in the Church, the secular focus on mumming and the wassail tradition have their roots in pre-Christian folk customs. Strategically situated between Christmas and Epiphany, January 1 not only was the Feast of the Circumcision but also served as the natural place within the Twelve Days' celebration to reenergize and renew the festivities. In England trumpets heralded the commencement of New Year's Day at the moment when the king put on his shoes. Both king and queen exchanged and received presents from other government dignitaries. Monetary gifts were usually given to officers of the households and religious leaders. Surviving household accounts record that the earls of Northumberland and Rutland enacted similar scenes at their residences. It is possible that these New Year's gifts were the forerunners of modern Christmas presents, although whether this custom was followed by commoners has not been documented. At the end of the day, a huge banquet was normally held.

Scenes in the fourteenth-century *Sir Gawain and the Green Knight* vividly portray many noble holiday customs during the Twelve Days, including lords and ladies attending mass and exchanging handsels (hand gifts) as holiday presents. The giving of handsels was thought to ensure good fortune for the coming year. In his poem *Handlyng Synne* (1303), Robert Mannyng refers to handseling and condemns it as a superstitious practice.

See also: Boy Bishop, Feast of the; Christmas; Festivals and Celebrations; Fools, Feast of; Games and Play

—Bradford Lee Eden

Nibelungenlied [*Song of the Nibelungs*].

Anonymous Middle High German poem, composed about 1200 C.E., that depicts the tragic history of the Burgundian royal family.

Many different early-medieval legends and tales seem to have contributed to the creation of this text, and the major manuscripts (labeled by scholars A, B, and C) still reveal the discrepancies between the individual parts of the epic. Nevertheless, we can safely assume that the work was put together by one or more authors working in the vicinity of Passau, Bavaria, where Wolfger von Erla served as bishop; the bishop may even have commissioned the author(s) to translate the oral traditions into a written text. As the narrator indicates in the first stanza, the epic or its parts had once been performed orally, though in its present form the *Nibelungenlied* also represents the workings of a written culture.

The narrative first treats the life of the hero Siegfried, who resembles an ancient Germanic god in his invincibility: As a result of bathing in dragon's blood, Siegfried has acquired impenetrable skin (except for a vulnerable spot between his shoulder blades). Siegfried woos the Burgundian princess Kriemhild in Worms but is not allowed to marry her until he has helped her brother, King Gunther, woo and marry the Icelandic queen Brünhild, a fierce "maiden king" who will marry only the man who can defeat her in three feats of strength so taxing that they could prove fatal to the suitor. Gunther relies on Siegfried to win his bride. By means of a magic cloak, which makes him invisible and provides him with additional strength, Siegfried outperforms the powerful Brünhild while Gunther goes through the motions, thus deceiving Brünhild into believing that he is her rightful vanquisher and husband. Once back at Worms, Siegfried marries Kriemhild and Gunther marries Brünhild on the same day. But Gunther must solicit Siegfried's aid once again when Brünhild, doubting that Gunther is strong enough to have won her, rejects him on their wedding night and hangs him on a nail until daybreak. Using his magic cloak and desperately rallying all his strength, Siegfried takes Gunther's place in bed and overpowers her, allowing Gunther to consummate the marriage. But Siegfried takes her belt and ring, thus symbolically raping her; he gives these two trophies to Kriemhild.

The two women later begin to quarrel over their social rank, and an angry Kriemhild reveals that Siegfried was the man who overpowered Brünhild in her bridal bed. Enraged, Brünhild demands vengeance, and Gunther's vassal Hagen, who bitterly dislikes Siegfried, now plots to murder him, both to avenge his queen and to eliminate his superhuman enemy. Hagen, who has wrested the secret of Siegfried's vulnerable spot from the naive Kriemhild, goes hunting with Siegfried and kills the hero by spearing him from behind as he is drinking from a spring.

The rest of the tale focuses on Kriemhild. She mourns her husband's death for 13 years until she is wooed by the Hunnish King Etzel (Attila). She eventually accepts his offer despite the strong love she still feels for her deceased husband and despite religious objections (Etzel is a pagan) because she hopes to use him to exact revenge for her husband's death. When she has established herself as the Hunnish queen and gained even more power than Etzel's former wife Helche, Kriemhild invites her brothers and their men for a visit and incites a battle at her court. The battle soon leads to an Armageddon, a devastating battle in which, one by one, the principal actors in the poem, most of the Huns, and all the Burgundians are killed. A Germanic hero, Dietrich, serving at Etzel's court, deeply regretting the horrendous slaughter, eventually captures and fetters Hagen and Gunther and hands them over to Kriemhild. Now her time has come: she first orders Gunther killed and then decapitates Hagen herself. Dietrich's liegeman, Hildebrand, however, out of grief over Hagen's death and out of hatred against women taking up weapons, slays Kriemhild as well.

The *Nibelungenlied* concludes here, but a later epic poem, *Die Klage* (The Lament), resumes the narrative, focusing entirely on the aspect of mourning. The corpses are brought together and buried, and then the sad news is communicated to the Burgundians as heart-rending grief grips all relatives and family members. In this poem, Etzel disappears, as far as the narrator is able to tell, devastated by the enormous grief.

The epic seems to have enjoyed extensive popularity, as we can tell on the basis of a large body of manuscript copies created from the thirteenth through the sixteenth centuries (11 complete and 24 fragmentary copies have survived).

The legendary traditions of the *Nibelungenlied* also surfaced in the literature of thirteenth-century Scandinavia. *Thidrek's Saga*, a prose work probably from the first half of the thirteenth century and perhaps the work of a Norwegian, closely parallels some parts of the *Nibelungenlied*, seems to be based on the same sources used by the German poet, and may in fact be a translation of a Low German book. In Iceland Snorri Sturluson's *Edda* (c. 1220–1230) and most of the poems of the second half of the *Poetic Edda* (c. 1250) feature many of the same characters as appear in the *Nibelungenlied*, but they tell a story based on traditions significantly different from those that inform the German poem. The main narrative of the prose *Völsunga Saga* (mid-thirteenth century) comprises a prose retelling of the *Poetic Edda*.

The *Nibelungenlied* incorporates legendary traditions concerning individuals who lived and events that unfolded more than seven centuries before it was written: for example, the final scene, in which Etzel's (i.e., Attila's) men kill all of Gunther's men, ultimately derives from a Hunnish slaughter of the Burgundians in the year 437. The *Nibelungenlied* is too far removed from these events to offer a blow-by-blow account of early-medieval Germanic tribal history; rather, it embodies a strong sense of heroic ancestry that kept the poem's principal characters alive in legend many centuries after they—and even their tribal cultures—had disappeared. Although a number of allusions to Christianity point out the religious framework prevalent around 1200, the epic was not based on any particular religious concepts; rather, its primary focus is on heroism, revenge, and furious battles. In many respects, the *Nibelungenlied* also reflects the gender conflicts of the central Middle Ages and additionally thematizes the struggle of a society that tries to survive the challenge of such dangerous outsiders as Siegfried and Brünhild. These two, we may surmise, were originally destined for each other but were drawn into the courtly world of Worms. This culture clash in turn brought about hatred, jealousy, envy, and fear that led to the bloody end.

Of the three major versions of the *Nibelungen-lied*, manuscript C is the least reflective of old-fashioned tribal heroics and most courtly in character. In comparison to the other two versions, the C version makes Hagen more villainous and extends more attention and sympathy to Kriemhild.

At the end of the Middle Ages the original *Nibelungenlied* seems to have been forgotten, but alternative versions, such as the *Lied vom hürnen Seyfrid*, first printed in 1530, addressed more-popular tastes and sold on the early modern book markets until the end of the seventeenth century.

When the original *Nibelungenlied* was rediscovered by the Lindau physician Jakob Hermann Obereit in 1755, it was soon transformed into a national poem of canonical quality, even though initially Prussia's King Frederick II ridiculed it as rubbish unworthy of a place in his library. The Swiss philologist Johann Jakob Bodmer was the first to print a selection of the text in 1757, and in 1782 Christoph Heinrich Myller published the first full edition. The romantic philosopher and philologist August Wilhelm von Schlegel offered the first critical reading of the epic in one of his Berlin university lectures in 1802/1803. Since the early nineteenth century, many critics have considered the *Nibelungenlied* the German equivalent of Homer's *Iliad*: a national epic representing Germanic virtues and values through its emphasis on heroic events and figures.

The famous German philologist Karl Lachmann postulated in 1816 that the *Nibelungenlied* represented a conglomerate of individual heroic lays merged together by some scribe. In 1921 Andreas Heusler suggested that the epic consisted of two separate pieces that had been combined only later, but Joachim Bumke's research leads us now to assume that the *Nibelungenlied* was probably composed and written down in a writer's workshop, the *Nibelungenlied-Werkstatt*.

The number of translations, narrative re-creations, dramatizations, musical treatments, radio plays, poems, movie scripts, parodies, and satires that have emerged since the early nineteenth century is legion. One of the most influential versions proved to be the opera *Götterdämmerung* (Twilight of the Gods), by Richard Wagner (1813–1883), whose treatment draws heavily not only upon the *Nibelungenlied* but also on its Scandinavian analogs and his own imagination. Both scholarly and popular interest in the epic has remained strong over the centuries, as we can tell from the many modern critical studies and the large number of literary adaptations and translations.

See also: Burgundian Cycle

—Albrecht Classen

Nightmare [Old Norse *Mara*]. One of many names for beings related to witchcraft (or magic) in Old Norse and later medieval Scandinavian literature.

The conceptions of the mara correspond with

beliefs in night-hags and assaulting demons known from all over the world. It is questionable, however, whether it is possible to distinguish between the mara and other shapeshifters. The mara in Scandinavian tradition was ambiguous and terrifying; she changed her guise, assaulted men and cattle, and caused agony and economic disaster. The mara was principally a female figure, who attacked men and livestock at night. When the cattle were found weak and exhausted in the morning it was said to be due to the mara. Her assaults were always connected with a feeling of anxiety and suffocation. The mara was believed to oppress and weigh her victim down when tormenting and riding it. There is also an undercurrent of latent sexuality more or less manifest in the mara traditions.

The ability to change shape and to act outside of the ordinary body in a temporal guise were vital characteristics in many different Norse myths and conceptions. The materialized will, power, or lust was a theme common to many texts. Etymologically, the term *mara* is related to the Indo-European root *mr*, "to crush," which is most interesting considering the actions ascribed to the mara in Norse texts.

The first time the term *mara* appears is in *Ynglingatal*, in the story of the death of King Vanlandi. This account was later enlarged by Snorri Sturluson in his *Ynglinga Saga*: When deceived by the king, his wife Drifa sends the mara on him with the help of a woman well versed in witchcraft, a *seidkona*. The mara crushes the deceitful king's legs and finally stifles him to death. The most detailed description of the deeds of a mara can be found in *Eyrbyggja Saga*, chapters 15 and 16, where two women, Katla and Geirrid, both skilled at magic, struggle for a young man's favor. As in most Norse stories of witchcraft, the erotic theme is apparent. The two women, however, have different ways of using their wisdom.

Katla's allurements are repeatedly rejected by the young man, who favors the company of Geirrid. One night Geirrid can see that Katla is up to some gruesome revenge and warns the young man, who rejects her advice. He is then found by his family severely hurt by the attack of the mara. Geirrid is falsely accused of being a mara and is taken to court, but on the basis of the oaths of relatives she is released. The episode has been called Scandinavia's first witchcraft trial, and the charge is being a mara. The conflict comes to an end in chapter 20, where the guilty woman is stoned to death. This episode could be analyzed in relation to some early Christian laws from Norway, where the act of riding other persons or their cattle is punishable by fine.

Witchcraft always has an originator, striving for specific ends. It has a cause and an effect, a purpose and tangible consequences. Snorri tells in *Ynglinga Saga* (chapter 7) how Odin lay as though dead or asleep while his soul (*hugr*) was accomplishing various deeds for himself or others in the shape of a bird, an animal, a fish, or a serpent. His physical body was left behind; only his soul assumed different temporary guises.

In the lays of the *Poetic Edda* no maras are mentioned, but other names for beings of a similar nature occur. In *Havamal* 155, Odin's supreme magical power is commended when he hinders the souls of some night-hags (*tunridor*) from returning to their physical bodies. Obviously, they are acting like maras, as are the *myrkridor* (dark riders) in *Harbardsljad* (The Lay of Harbard, stanza 20). The *myrkridor* are mostly interpreted as "witches" in translations of the text. The term *kveldridor* (night or evening riders) is used in both poetry and prose for characters of a similar kind. None of these texts gives any comprehensive description of the transformation itself.

Christian authors often mention the mara in late-medieval religious tracts as a translation of "incubus" and "succubus" (male and female shapeshifting demons who could seduce humans at night). After the Reformation, the Church also continued to warn against the capabilities of the devil, who made shapeshifting possible.

The mara is one of the most common creatures of folklore recordings of the nineteenth and twentieth centuries, and the structure of the legends corresponds in all important details with the medieval texts: an envious or evil person, often a woman, uses the power of transformation to gain advantages in a temporal guise. Most mara texts deal not with the act of shapeshifting but with the apotropaic rituals of how to ward off, reveal, and punish the person in the vicinity who is causing this suffering.

See also: Scandinavian Tradition

—Catharina Raudvere

Nine Worthies [French *Les neuf preux*].

A set of famous heroes who constitute an important topos in late-medieval art and literature by embodying the chivalric ideal for both the aristocratic and merchant classes.

With a numerical configuration drawing upon the mysteries of the number three and its square, the Nine Worthies consisted of three pagans (Alexander, Hector, and Julius Caesar), three Jews (Joshua, David, and Judas Maccabaeus), and three Christians (Arthur, Charlemagne, and Godfrey de Bouillon). It is only in England that the phrase *Nine Worthies* is used, as for example in the fifteenth-century poem *The Floure and the Leafe*: "Tho nine crowned be very exemplaire / Of all honour longing to chivalry, / And those, certaine, be called the Nine Worthy" (502–504). The first known occurrence of *les neuf preux*, as they were called in medieval France, is in the French courtly romance *Voeux du paon* (Vows of the Peacock), written by Jacques de Longuyon around 1312, his addition to an older *Romance of Alexander*. Jacques' hero, Porus, is praised for having fought more bravely than even the nine great heroes of the past. Perhaps Jacques derived his idea from Old French historiography, in which lists of names of great historical figures were sometimes included to denote valor and excellence; however, the specific choice, number, and arrangement of heroes seems to be original with him.

It has been suggested that the choice of numerical configuration is owing to the tradition of the Welsh triads—a form of medieval Welsh verse in which heroes were grouped together in trios because of some distinguishing characteristic each of the three held in common. In any case, the concept of the Nine Worthies quickly gained popularity and became a literary motif for other French poets, including Guillaume de Machaut and Eustache Deschamps. It quickly found its way into texts written in Latin, German, Middle English, and Middle Scots. Moreover, the pattern was imitated in the creation of a set of Nine Female Worthies; this apparently was Deschamps's invention. There was on occasion the addition of a tenth worthy, a concession by later writers to national or local tradition, such as Robert the Bruce in Scotland or Bertrand du Guesclin, defender of the French crown in the Hundred Years' War. The topos quickly found its way into dramatic productions as well. There was a pageant of the Nine Heroes in Arras as early as 1336, and the idea remained popular for more than a century. The Coventry Leet Book, for example, records entertainment provided for Queen Margaret in 1455 and indicates that the Nine Worthies were an important part of the spectacles, each hero providing a speech of welcome.

The most extensive literary treatments of the topos in English literature are found in the alliterative *Morte Arthure* (c. 1360), lines 3406–3445, and in the fifteenth-century *The Parlement of the Thre Ages*, lines 297–583. The former is one of the most artistic depictions of the Nine Worthies, for in it each hero is uniquely introduced, and together they further the plot of the poem by aiding in the interpretation of Arthur's dream. The anonymous author of *The Parlement* also displays some originality by combining the Worthies topos with the *ubi sunt* (where are they now?) topos, a convention in classical and medieval literature involving melancholy reflection on the passing of former glories and the transitoriness of life in general. Thus, in *The Parlement* a personified Old Age recalls the Nine Worthies and their deeds to strengthen his argument that all worldly joys are vanity since death eventually triumphs.

Further testimony to the immediate popularity of the Nine Worthies in the fourteenth century is their representation in the visual arts of the period. The Nine Heroes were sculpted on the panel piece at the chateau of Coucy before 1387 (and here Bertrand du Guesclin makes a tenth) and also at the Hansa Saal in Cologne and the fourteenth-century Schöne Brunnen at Nuremberg. Frescoes dating from about 1390 adorn the walls of Castle Ruckelstein outside Bolzano, Italy. The Nine Worthies have been found depicted on enameled cups, playing cards, manuscripts, and stained glass windows. But among the most impressive representations are those woven into tapestries. Several of the great fourteenth-century nobles are known to have owned tapestries depicting the Nine Worthies, including Charles V, Louis of Anjou, Philip of Burgundy, Charles VI, the count of Hainaut, and Jean, duke of Berry, who also had statues of the nine on his fireplace at Bourges and on his castle keep, called Maubergeon, at Poitiers. The duke of Berry's impressive set of what were once three tapestries, probably woven in about 1385, was acquired in mutilated fragments by the Metropolitan Museum of New York in the second quarter of the twentieth century; they have been repaired as far as possible and are currently displayed at the Cloisters in New York City.

See also: Arthur; Charlemagne; Swan Knight; Triads of the Island of Britain

—Deanna Delmar Evans

Novella. A term with at least three meanings relevant to medieval folklore: (1) for students of folk narrative, a long fictional narrative, largely realistic in its presentation, as opposed to the magic tale (märchen or *Zaubermärchen*), which embeds supernatural beings and occurrences; (2) in medieval literary history, a later medieval prose tale (French *nouvelle*), generally fictional and widely circulating in collections and focusing more on entertainment than most earlier medieval collections written expressly to edify (no matter how entertaining their authors thought them); and (3) the Italian *novella*, a medieval short story, incorporating a vast number of genres.

The *novella* originates from popular and oral sources; thus, folk traditions are embedded in the form and serve as an important vehicle for its development. The role of oral transmission as a source for the *novella* is pivotal and continues to be the subject of lively discussion. As late as the appearance of Boccaccio's *Decameron* (c. 1349–1351) one finds the markers suggestive of oral narration and transmission, as in the Proem to Day 4, in which the author defends himself against the envious accusations of his detractors by telling the story of Filippo Balducci, who attempts to shelter his son from women. When the son, as a young man, sees his first woman, the father says they are devils and goslings; the boy asks if he can take one home and learn to feed it. This tale (AT 1678, "The Boy Who Had Never Seen a Woman") has been reported throughout Europe in both medieval manuscripts and postmedieval oral performances. Though Boccaccio's possible sources range from the exempla of Jacques de Vitry to the fables of Odo of Cheriton (e.g., "De eremita juveni" [On the Young Hermit]), the *Speculum vitae* (The Mirror of Life) of Vincent of Beauvais, and the *Novellino* (the very first collection of Italian tales, late thirteenth century), all of them originate from oral sources, mostly from the East. Boccaccio makes the tale his own by tailoring it to address the women in his audience.

Boccaccio employs the well-known device of inscribing a story within a story to incorporate his belief that the *fabula* (fiction) is something useful, not harmful, and that both *fabula* and *parabula* (parable) are poetic terms based on truth and with historical meaning—what the theologians would call *figura* (in his *Genealogia deorum gentilium*, 14, 9). Oral tradition is at the heart of the art of the *novellieri* (writers of *novelle*) because they describe characters that crowded the streets of Florence and other Italian or European cities and because the *novella* is by nature written in the humble or "low" style of writing, as Boccaccio himself states. In his well-known *novella* of Federigo degli Alberighi (*Decameron* 5, 9), who sacrifices his sole possession, a falcon, for the love of Madonna Giovanna, Boccaccio states that this tale was one of those oral tales belonging to the repertoire of Coppo di Borghese Domenichi, an illustrious Florentine who excelled in storytelling and spoke with great eloquence.

From oral transmission there develops the interesting phenomenon of the popularization of such legendary classical figures as Virgil, Aristotle, and Socrates and, later, Dante, Cavalcanti, and Giotto, who easily became the subject of tales or anecdotes by Boccaccio, Sacchetti, Sercambi, Poggio Bracciolini, and others. At times such narratives are found in chronicles, as in the case of a sixteenth-century Venetian chronicle that recounts how Dante, having been served a small fish at the table of the Doge, obtained a larger one through a ruse.

Oral transmission is undoubtedly a major force in the Italian *novelle* of the thirteenth and fourteenth centuries: witness the anonymous *Novellino* (c. 1300), the earliest collection of Italian tales, whose introduction places major emphasis on the spoken word, *fiori di parlare* (flowers of speech), and on the process of oral transmission. In its aesthetics it projects a strong interest in the art of storytelling, as Boccaccio would later profess and demonstrate. *Novellino* is indeed the summa of oral tradition, transformed into a written text containing a melange of exempla, anecdotes, and short tales whose sources are varied and span a vast amount of time, encompassing ancient myths, Arthurian legend, contemporary history or chronicles, and biblical and mythological characters, including Alexander the Great, a Greek sage, the sultan, the Slave of Bari, and so on. It is significant that this collection begins with a narrative concerning an embassy sent to Frederick II by Prester John (to whom was attributed an apocryphal letter to Frederick II) and ends with the same Frederick visiting the Old Man of the Mountain, "il Veglio." Prester John's letter to Frederick II and the Old Man of the Mountain had been the subjects of widespread legendry throughout Europe for a century before

the *Novellino* appeared, and by bringing Frederick II in personal contact with these two mysterious figures, the anonymous author demonstrates that Frederick, too, has reached legendary status (see *Novellino* 100).

Novelle adopt popular styles by inserting such oral formulas as "*ed era di notte*" [it was at night], "*ed era molto di notte*" [it was deep into the night], and similar variations, reflecting the tradition of the *veglia* (literally, vigil), during which oral stories were exchanged throughout the night. Such devices set the stage in nocturnal ambiance, creating the color, surprise, tension, adventure, and suspense typical of oral narratives.

As Stith Thompson has stated, while the form may change, the "plot structure of the tale is much more stable and more persistent than its form." The melange of sources—written and oral, learned and popular—may have provided a logical justification for the storytellers to innovate, constantly changing their classical or oral sources to reflect changing sociopolitical conditions and aesthetics. Thus, the fluidity of the written *novella* tradition closely parallels that of skilled oral artists, who recraft their tales for varied audiences.

Many fourteenth-century *novellieri* preceded Giovanni Boccaccio's *Decameron*. Francesco da Barberino (1264–1348) wrote *Del reggimento e costumi di donna*, a book of etiquette for women of various social statuses, with suggestions on toiletries, ornaments, and deportment, which also contains tales. Domenico Cavalca (1270–1343) of Vicopisano, a preacher who founded the convent of Santa Marta for converted prostitutes, was known for his work with the sick and the poor. He is the author of *Lo specchio di croce* (Mirror of the Cross) and other works in which he utilized exempla, anecdotes, miracles, and proverbs—all in a vernacular meant to be understood by the unlearned and the "idiots" ignorant of "grammar." Jacopo della Lana (1290–1352) authored a commentary on Dante's *Divine Comedy* in which he often injected contemporary and ancient fables or excerpts from chronicles. Iacopo Passavanti (1300–1375), a Dominican friar, wrote *Specchio della vera penitenza* (The Mirror of True Penitence), an anthology of exempla derived from the Bible, Bede, Jacques de Vitry, the *Alphabetum narrationis* (Alphabet of Stories), and other sources, which he personalized and elaborated with his unique style.

Among the *novelle* written after the *Decameron* is *Il pecorone* (The Big Sheep) by Ser Giovanni Fiorentino, begun in 1378. Told by the monk Oretto and the nun Saturnina over a period of 25 days, *Il pecorone* includes both fabulous tales and anecdotes from chronicles. The tale of Giannetto and the Belmonte woman (4,1), retold later by Gianfrancesco Straparola in his *Piacevoli notti* (Facetious Nights), reappears in Shakespeare's *Merchant of Venice* (AT 890, "A Pound of Flesh"). Of notable importance for his representation of Italian fourteenth-century customs and society is Franco Sacchetti (1332–1400), author of the *Trecento novelle* (Three Hundred Novellas). Actually he wrote only 228, organized according to themes or characters, with a brief introduction for each tale and a commentary at its end. Sacchetti, who had a very rich political and social life, was an acute observer of the traditions and lifestyles of everyday people, including shopkeepers, merchants, maids, peasants, and servants. Sacchetti's subject matter, characters, and language all embed popular traditions.

Great credit must be given to the Lucchese *novelliere* Giovanni Sercambi (1348–1424), who wrote the *Novelliere* (short-story collection, late fourteenth century) or *Novelle*, whose themes and sources derive from the most varied traditions, many of them oral. Sercambi may be an inelegant writer when compared to Boccaccio (24 of his tales derive from the *Decameron*), but he is important for both his use of popular traditions and his written sources. He was the first in Europe to utilize the frame tale of the *Thousand and One Nights*, a century before Ludovico Ariosto drew upon this famed Arabic collection in canto 18 of *Orlando furioso*. Sercambi, who had an apothecary shop in Lucca, traded widely in spices and herbs as well as manuscripts. His sources range from oral contemporary accounts to the pious *Disciplina clericalis*, the story of Amicus and Amelius, the fabliaux, *The Seven Sages*, the *Favolello del geloso*, the *Exempla* of Jacques de Vitry, the *Gesta Romanorum*, and the Italian *Cantari* tradition.

Another relevant collection is *Facezie, motti e burle*, by Piovano Arlotto, 1396–1484, a country priest who lived among peasants and who retells stories witnessing both curious local occurrences and national events. Oral traditions of the lower classes also appear in *Esopo Toscano* (fourteenth century), which retells animal tales in imitation of Aesop. The anonymous author, rather than simply translating, amplifies, integrates, and popularizes the language and textures of his *novelle*. This earthy style developed during the merchant era of the thirteenth and fourteenth centuries, through people such as Paolo of Certaldo and Giovanni Morelli, who strove to express the truth at the popular level and in vernacular language.

One important nonanthologized *novella* is *Il grasso legnaiuolo* (The Fat Wood Carver), deriving from oral traditions and the street life of Florence. Its subject is a *beffa*, a practical joke played by the famous architect Filippo Brunelleschi and his friends upon one Manetto Ammannini, carpenter and inlayer. Filippo is the master magician whose genius, imagination, power of persuasion, and magical incantations succeed in convincing Manetto that he is someone else named Matteo. From an oral source we have three written versions, the first attributed to Antonio Manetti (1423–1497), author of a *Life of Brunelleschi* and a Dante scholar. But the ultimate source is Brunelleschi, who created the incident and passed on the story orally.

Boccaccio exerted great influence on many later *novellieri*, including Masuccio Salernitano (1415–1475) and Anton Francesco Grazzini, alias Il Lasca (1503–1584). The tales of Straparola's *Piacevoli notti* (Facetious Nights, 1550–1553) and Giambattista Basile's (1575–1632) *Pentamerone* continue the development of the medieval traditions represented in the *Novellino* and the *Decameron*. Indeed, as Stith Thompson points out, many postmedieval oral folktales probably came from Italy, and it is impossible to determine whether the *novella* authors derived them from contemporary oral tradition or invented them. Some current folktales—including "The Wager on the Wife's Chastity" (AT 882) and "The Luck-Bringing Shirt" (AT 844)—probably owe their current forms to medieval *novella* writers.

See also: *Decameron*; Folktale; Frame Tale; *Thousand and One Nights*

—Giuseppe C. Di Scipio

Nuns. Women in religious life who either have withdrawn from the world to devote themselves to cultivating their spirituality or, in some orders, have devoted themselves to a specific mission in the world, such as teaching or caring for the sick.

Ancient Beginnings

As the apostolic movement began in an organized way after Pentecost, women as well as men followers of Jesus moved into the cities and countryside to preach the messages of their messianic leader. One of the basic tenets of his teaching, and possibly the most socially radical, was "In Christ there is neither bond nor free, Jew nor Greek, male nor female." From this revolutionary ideal came the formation of groups of women and men living together in chaste conditions as they preached, offered hospitality to travelers, and tended the sick and poor. They lived and worked together in a syneisactic community—that is, one in which they created the concept of what can be seen as a third gender, an androgynous gender, or even better, the concept of transcending gender altogether in order to form a new kind of identity. The dedication to chastity and celibacy, which allowed this syneisactism, has persisted in some forms throughout the years, despite society's attempts in the form of the papacy, the male monastics, and the monarchy to undermine what they saw as a threat to the patriarchal ordering of life.

In the Roman period the women who participated in this revolutionary movement were from all classes of society. There are few accounts left to us of what the average woman experienced in such circumstances. The most sensational narratives are those of the heroic desert mothers living as hermits in the wilderness and of the women murdered in the game arenas of Rome during the persecutions. These were formidable, even super-human women, who seem to assume an almost mythic stature with Mary of Bethany as the hermit and her sister Martha the dragon-slayer. In the legends they take on the masculine attributes of the warrior woman. In the realities of the city of the early apostolic movement, house churches sprang up. These domestic communities, extending into the third century, were communal households of Christians, households where they could worship, study, and provide a safe house for the wandering preachers. The need, both economic and spiritual, for a sheltered place set the precedent for the later communities of kindred souls who felt that they could only conduct their quest for holiness and their conversional mission within a relatively closed circle of like people. It suggests not only the need for a sanctuary or refuge that would provide physical safety but also a need for a space, enclosed and shut away from the corruption of the world, where in silence they could meditate, pray, sing, chant, and exert excruciating discipline over body and mind.

Early Middle Ages

By the fifth and sixth centuries, as the Germanic peoples conquered the Continent by the sword and were themselves conquered by the cross, groups of nuns and chaste couples from all layers of society began retreating to the cloistered walls of the monasteries within the city. Women from the conquered and conquering groups began seeking a life that was safe from the violence of the warring society and the earthly husbands their families sold them to. Widows and virgin women, often from the elite classes, old and destitute women, and even prostitutes vowed their lives to chastity and celibacy as they entered what they saw as the safe haven of the monastery. Small house monasteries were established, supported, and led by such women as Genevieve of Paris and Queen Radegunda, who established Sainte-Croix of Poitiers in 550. Radegunda, herself a prize of war won by her husband Chlotar, escaped her marriage with the help of a bishop and formed a monastery that set the trend for the regular life with the adoption of the *Rule for Nuns* of Caesarius of Arles.

Narratives abound of desperate measures taken by women, with the considerable help of divine intervention, to escape the horrors of rapacious men and imposed marriage and childbearing. St. Brigid's mutilated body and St. Angadrisma's leprous body save them from such fates, but their bodies are restored to health after their consecrations as nuns. Throughout the following centuries the great dynasties of abbesses exert considerable control over monasticism, often ruling over double monasteries for men as well as women, especially in the North. In such foundations, women and men monastics helped each other with spiritual advice and with the daily

running of the monasteries. Hilda of Whitby and Aidan, Cuthbert and Ebba, Patrick and Brigid work together to sustain the missionary effort and their own frequently self-absorbed dedication to the spiritual ideals of chastity and celibacy. Many had great libraries, taught and reared children given over to them by parents with differing agenda, and provided refuge for travelers and charity to the poor. The women's writings have seldom been preserved, never having been privileged by a society often dedicated to the subordination of women, but in *Bede's Ecclesiastical History of the English People* (731) and similar sources we do have the reports of women's oral tradition, which circulated news, stories, miracles, and other happenings among the inhabitants of the monasteries.

According to Jo Ann McNamara, threats to these syneisactic formations that so closely resemble the concept of equality in earlier Christianity were always present. With gynophobia frequently running rampant, the earthly institutional powers were obsessed with the notion that any man, but especially the male monastic, was unable by nature to control his lust in the presence of women. This attitude changed its focus as the woman, seen as the reincarnation of Eve, became the culprit. What frequently underlay these waves of fear, confirmed by stories of women tempters egged on by Satan and his demons and by scandals alleging unspeakable goings-on within the double monasteries, was a political agenda that demanded that powerful women, threatening the patriarchal rule of society, be rendered invisible. One method of exerting control was to introduce the concept of nuns as Brides of Christ. Placing women religious in the position of wife, albeit a wife of the highest stature, largely undercut the concept of third gender or nongender. The image of the nun as a devoted wife of this spiritual union developed with the cult of Mary, the Blessed Mother, and in another odd juxtaposition, with the cult of Mary Magdalen, who was believed by many in the Middle Ages to be a repentant harlot and therefore the saint of prostitutes. Perhaps this parallel is not so odd if one considers that nuns and prostitutes are the two categories of women who put themselves on the margins of society. They are both outside a norm that for centuries has insisted that the proper place for women is in the home, being wives to earthly husbands and bearing children. The newly found image of nuns as Brides of Christ certainly must have changed these women's concept of themselves. In a sense this strategy backfired, as the "brides" reappropriated the warrior concept and wedded it to an all-powerful concept of the nun as the heavenly queen and helpmate of the spiritual husband and father.

Not surprisingly, not every woman who fled a dangerous outside world to find refuge in the monastery wanted to stay. Some were forced into the convent by family members who saw the life as safer than that of the outside world or by family members who wanted to rid themselves of the burden of wife, aged mother, or daughter. Claustration, that is, living exclusively in a cloister, cannot have been for everybody. The collections of exempla reveal this situation in their warnings of what happens to those who renege on their vows, although it is possible that not all of the women had even made vows of consecration. One such warning came from a narrative of Faremoutiers by a certain Jonas of Bobbio, in his *Life of Abbot Columban*. Several of the women inhabitants tried to escape the monastery, lowering themselves on ropes, but they were captured before they could escape to freedom. Some repented. The ones who did not died of a terrible fever. As their sisters surrounded their beds, the unrepentant suffered the most terrible delusions of attacking Ethiopians who visited upon them such unspeakable acts that they begged to be released. After they died and were buried, their remains were dug up, but nothing was left of them but ashes. Tales of this type may have come from the subconscious of the women themselves, whose own bodies and sexuality were always used against them, or such tales may have originated with fantasizing males.

The eighth century brought important transformations to monastic life. The invading Muslims caused a fleeing and reassembling of communities in Spain, Italy, and Frankland. The power of an institutional episcopate, dominated by men, attempted to force more standard rules on monastics of both sexes. Women religious could never administer the sacerdotal offices, but they had participated in peripheral service to the altars, processionals, ringing of bells, and lighting of candles. Nuns had always shared equally in the power of prayer with their male colleagues, prayer being one of the primary sources of their ability to attract patronage. With the attempts to enforce reforms, the nuns were officially prohibited from participating even in peripheral rituals, and the long-term effect of these reforms was to seriously mitigate their powers. Whereas in earlier centuries communities could choose among various rules, especially in the North, now the religious came under either the Benedictine or Augustinian Rules. The attack on the double monasteries gained strength, and nuns were threatened with death if they did not concede to the reforms. But in the outlying areas there were small communities that maintained hospices for poor women and widows. In these now largely forgotten and never officially recorded communities, nuns appear to have carried on a quasi-priestly role from necessity. Many were canonesses, who, though they lived chastely, had not taken permanent vows. They could retain their property and leave to marry. Others were Beguines who had the right to earn money. Both groups could keep servants.

Monasticism had always had a lay component

with a strong dedication to performing works of charity, and many of these communities still maintained that structure. One example is Liutberga's cell at Wendhausen. A nun working as a business manager for an aristocratic house, Liutberga built up a hermitage with her knowledge of cloth making and dyeing. Besides educating girls, she also introduced liturgical innovations, instituting the *horarium*, the offices that mark the hours of a monastic day. Another example of relative openness to the world was convent drama. Though these dramas were mainly popular later in the Middle Ages, they may have been common in the royal abbey of Gandersheim. The educated and talented nun of Gandersheim, Hrosvitha (d. c. 1000), wrote plays, poetry, and histories in Latin, valorizing the Desert Mothers and other narratives from the apocryphal Gospels. Much of their content demonstrated the virtue of women, probably to counteract the popular ancient farces depicting both women's frailty and weakness and the power of their seductive wiles to ensnare men and so bring them to ruin. Most likely the plays of this feminist nun were acted out in the abbey to audiences of the nuns and royal visitors and patrons. Later on convent dramatizations were criticized, with the prohibition of Aachen forbidding nuns from dressing in men's costumes in order—or so it was claimed—to act the part of sexually uncontrolled men chasing innocent women.

With the Mass becoming more and more a part of the male monastic life, the nuns, forbidden to carry out any duties having to do with the administration of the sacraments, lost much of their patronage. Benedictine Rule had spread throughout Europe by the eleventh century and thus drove nuns further into claustration within the confines of the convent. Adaptation to the communal life and the "communal table" became more and more a project of the nunneries. Although monasteries enjoyed royal support, the increasingly strengthened episcopate was steadily gaining more control over the monastics during the central Middle Ages. Bishops attempted to foist care of the nuns onto the male orders, but the monks were fighting their own institutional battles for autonomy, and the financial support of nunneries was a burden. This dependency on others now being forced upon the nuns must have crept into the psyche of many of these women.

With the privileging of the discipline of self-control by monks came the substantial creation of the entity over which they must demonstrate this control, women. Just as the earlier usurpation of the power of women religious created nuns as Brides of Christ, so the eleventh-century created the cult of Mary, the Mother, the Blessed Virgin, with a relatively new image of her as submissive and silent. Mary became the spiritual abbess for her children in the nunneries. They, in imitation of her, had to be inaccessible, hidden, silent.

Resurgence in the Central Middle Ages

There was, however, a counteraction: a revival of the apostolic life, carried on primarily within the cities teeming with people of all classes and a growing materialism that made obvious the contrast between the thriving and the destitute. Women and men, as of old, worked together in this revival to try to eradicate the injustices of a greedy, grasping society. Some historians speculate that this resurgence might have been a woman's movement. Some even speculate that the movement began in the early Middle Ages and was only brought to light because of the reform movement. Poverty and charity became privileging characteristics of the movement, as its participants wished to tread in the steps of Christ. The cities became their desert. Women and men religious again formed partnerships: Marie d'Oignies worked with Cistercians in the area of Nivelles; Hildegard von Bingen worked with monks of Trier; Disibodenberg carried on a correspondence with Bernard of Clairvaux; Clare of Assisi and Francis of Assisi established the Franciscan Way; Diana d'Andalo followed Dominic of Spain as he founded the Dominican Way. These women activists were often mystics or anchoresses. Besides transforming their mystical experiences into liturgy, they established infirmaries and founded hospitals, and they even preached. They became the conjunction of Mary of Bethany, the recluse, and her sister Martha, associated with charity, hospitality, and dragonslaying.

The power of these women mystics was considerable, and their mystical experiences revealed striking meanings and interpretations of the Gospels. Douceline de Digne, a Beguine, shared her understanding of the Trinity, which she learned through her visions. In a rather amazing reversal, Hildegard von Bingen used the power of woman's fertility by combining Eve and Mary: the sin of Eve is redeemed by Mary's birthing of the Christ child, while the symbol of the fruit of the first sin is transformed by the fruit of Mary's womb. An angel told Elisabeth of Schonau that her vision of a weeping woman of light was Jesus, who took on the female form in order to incorporate his mother Mary into the image. Some years before Francis of Assisi received his famous stigmata, Marie d'Oignies reported suffering intense pain in the same places on her body as Christ's wounds in the Crucifixion. The mystery of the Sacred Heart was revealed to Gertrude by John the Evangelist in a vision. Catherine of Siena, after being refused the Eucharist by priests, was on two occasions given the Eucharist by Christ himself. Elisabeth of Schonau was given to falling into trances of ecstasy as the chalice was raised, though she could not literally see it, since she was not allowed within the sacred space. What she did see was the crucified Christ pouring blood into a chalice.

Having witnessed demonstrations of the divine on these holy women, the more ordinary nuns in their communities often had their own less dramatic visions and trances, obtained through self-mortification. These inspirational experiences were written in nunbooks to share with their sisters. Unfortunately, many of the nunbooks were later confiscated and presumably destroyed.

Late-Medieval Repressions

The mystical sisters were not silent in their disdain of the clergy. Not only were they openly critical, but their appropriation of the sacraments through visionary experiences and their accounts of the crimes and abuses of the impure clergy attained through visions were particularly threatening to the hierarchy and were declared heretical. Repression began, with gynophobia as its catalyst. The end of the Middle Ages saw an influx of accounts of scandals committed by the religious. Bawdy stories abounded, especially depicting the exploits of cloistered nuns and monks. The attacks on the women religious were particularly violent. Nunneries were broken into; there are accounts of the rape of nuns and the destruction of nunneries and their relics. There are also heroic stories of nuns who attempted and sometimes succeeded in protecting themselves and their nunneries. The Beguines and Tertiaries were outside the Church and were thus particularly vulnerable. Many were persecuted, and some were burned at the stake as heretics. No doubt some of the stories of scandal were true. What is also true is that medieval nuns performed overwhelming acts of charity—embodied in their hospitals, educational institutions, homes for the aged and the orphaned—throughout their history as a sisterhood.

See also: Monks; Saints, Cults of the

—Cynthia Marshall McNamara

Olaf, Saint (995?–1030). Norwegian saint and king of the eleventh century.

Honored as one of the country's three patron saints (along with Sunniva and Hallvard), Olaf inspired a body of religious and popular lore unrivaled in Norwegian tradition. Olaf Haraldsson was declared a saint only one year and five days after his death at the battle of Stiklestad on July 29, 1030; his rule (reigned 1016–1028) had marked a turning point in Norwegian history, concluding the country's official Christian conversion and accomplishing the kingdom's final unification.

Although St. Olaf's predecessor, Olaf Tryggvason (reigned 995–1000), had significantly contributed to these ends, the figure of St. Olaf receives single-handed credit and combines the exploits of both Viking kings. The cult of St. Olaf spread with phenomenal speed throughout Scandinavia and beyond to the Baltic states, the British Isles, northern Germany, and France, as attested by the skaldic poets Sighvat Thordarson and Thorarin loftunga (c. 1030–1040), a British liturgy for St. Olaf's Day (July 29) from about 1050, and Adam of Bremen's history (c. 1070). Veneration of Olaf attained greatest potency in Nidaros (Trondheim), where Christ Church (subsequently Nidaros Cathedral) housed Olaf's body, the goal of international pilgrimages especially during the days surrounding St. Olaf's Day, which the *primstav* (medieval calendar stick) denoted with Olaf's attribute, the axe.

Downplaying the historical Olaf's warrior ways and political ambitions, ecclesiastical tradition portrays him as a Christian martyr. Abundant sculptures, paintings, and reliefs (produced 1100–1500; see illustration) depict the saint in this role, peacefully holding his axe, and often trampling a dragon bearing a face that resembles his own—an image alternatively interpreted as his former pagan self or his half brother Harold (Hardraada, king of Norway, 1045–1066), whom a widespread folk ballad cast as the pious Olaf's heathen rival. Such a mixture of official and folk religion characterizes much of the tradition surrounding St. Olaf, particularly his role as originator of countless curative springs, whose properties (and, frequently, veneration) predate Christianity but are ascribed by legend to a combination of the saint's prayers and his supernatural physical strength.

Folklore most persistently portrays Olaf building churches, against the protests of mighty Christian-hating trolls whom he transforms into distinctive stone formations in Norway's mountainous terrain. This is an activity that the Swedish cleric Olaus Magnus's *Historia de gentibus septentrionalibus* (History of the Nordic Peoples, 1555) also attributes to the saint. Olaf's tradition appropriates the Old Norse god Frey's power over fertility to such an extent that the farmers, fisherman, and sailors as well as the merchants of the Hanseatic League, all of whom adopted Olaf as their patron saint, appealed to him for good yields and protection.

Olaf also inherits the quick temper, enormous strength, and giant-slaying function of the god Thor. Although Olaf is initially depicted as being clean-shaven, folk portrayals after 1200 show him with a red beard, which may also be borrowed from Thor. Images of a more purely ecclesiastic origin were more probably inspired by the visage of Christ, whose serenely regal demeanor Olaf also assumes.

The mixture of the religious and the popular marks even the official ecclesiastical record of Olaf's miracles, the *Passio et miracula beati Olaui* (Passion and Miracles of Blessed Olaf). Assembled about 1175 by Archbishop Eystein Erlendsson, this record includes, in addition to the familiar hagiography, an episode depicting Olaf helping a man escape from the *huldrefolk* (hidden people) of Norwegian folk belief. Twelfth- and thirteenth-century Icelandic sagas, perhaps based on now lost accounts of Saemund Sigfusson (1056–1133) and Ari Thorgilsson (1068–1148), further chronicle both the folk and ecclesiastic elements of Olaf's tradition; however, during the fifteenth century the plethora of saints competing for worship caused the ecclesiastical Olaf to lose his individuality. After the Reformation (1537) his cult rapidly disappeared, but local folk legends of his prodigious strength and its indelible impact on Norway's landscape lived on for centuries, surviving in some places to this very day.

See also: Saints, Cults of the; Scandinavian Mythology; Thor

—Kathleen Stokker

Orality and Literacy. The production or experience of texts without the use of writing (orality) or with the use of writing (literacy).

The term *orality and literacy* is a shorthand way of referring to a theory or set of theories about the implications of these two conditions. Do different cultural and mental habits go with the different ways of making and experiencing texts? Do authors compose differently when they expect their work will be heard by a group rather than read by one person alone? And how does literacy, once it arrives, interact with orality?

Orality-Literacy Theory

Unlike oral-formulaic theory, which focuses on texts composed and performed without any use of writing, orality-literacy theory is most interested in the transition from or the interaction between "ear" texts and "eye" texts.

The transition view is characteristic of the scholars who first developed orality-literacy theory in the 1960s. These theorists identified orality with nonliteracy and a communal (folk)

mentality, and literacy with a critical, analytical mentality. They assumed that members of a non-literate culture would naturally begin reading privately (and developing the associated intellectual skills) as soon as they had the literacy and the books to do so. The Middle Ages are particularly prominent in this theorizing, because that was the period in Western tradition when literacy (in the sense of ability to read) took hold and the technologies of book production improved. Most scholars who follow this thinking see a quick transition from the period when minstrels performed from memory for groups of listeners, to the period when authors sat alone writing their books for readers who would sit alone to read them.

In the 1970s and 1980s, however, social scientists began dismantling the transition view, which anthropologist Ruth Finnegan labeled the Great Divide model. To say that literacy was the only source of analytical thinking, they pointed out, implied that nonliterate people could not think logically. It was easy for anthropologists to provide many examples of nonliterate groups who could indeed organize and analyze phenomena and of oral authors who produced the kind of ironic or self-conscious texts that supposedly were only possible within literate cultures. The social scientists also argued against the evolutionary assumption that literacy replaces orality the way that mammals replaced dinosaurs. Rather, they showed that orality and literacy can and do coexist long-term in many cultures, including that of the modern West (think, for example, of the popularity of audio books).

Recently these arguments have been finding their way into discussions of medieval literature, where scholars are beginning to emphasize the interaction between "oral" and "literate" habits. Carl Lindahl argues for Chaucer's close relationship to oral genres and modes of behavior, while D. H. Green and Joyce Coleman have assembled literary and historical evidence to show that in Germany, Britain, and France written texts continued to be read aloud long after literacy rates rose, and even after the invention of printing. This view gives prominence to the mixed oral-literate mode usually called aurality, in which a reader (or "prelector") reads a written text aloud to one person or to a group of people. In the Middle Ages the members of such groups were often literate, book-owning people, who often chose to experience literature in a social setting.

Oralities and Literacies

The effort to break down the polarized, Great Divide view has led theorists recently to formulate the idea that there are many different oralities and literacies rather than one, universal form of each. While some scholars continue to work with the older categories, others are developing the idea that each particular situation must be closely observed and described. Generalizations about orality and literacy, and about their interaction, may become possible once enough of these "ethnographies" have been accumulated.

There is evidence to show, for example, that while audiences in late-medieval Britain and France liked to have books read to them, the experiences took very different shapes in the two cultural areas. A description of the court of the English king Edward IV in about 1471 notes that the king's esquires were

> accustomed from of old, winter and summer, in afternoons and in evenings, to withdraw to lords' chambers within court, there to keep honest company after their cunning, in talking of chronicles of kings and other policies [books about government], or in piping, or harping, singing, and other pleasant activities, to help entertain the court and amuse visitors.

The phrase "talking of chronicles" suggests a public reading that quickly turned into group discussion. In this relaxed, almost festive atmosphere, reading and discussion take their place among other entertaining activities, such as piping and singing. Similarly, the esquires mix easily with the lords and "visitors," without much emphasis on status differences.

In France and in Flanders (ruled in the late Middle Ages by the dukes of Burgundy), chronicles and works of instruction were read aloud in a much more formal, hierarchical atmosphere. A particularly vivid example comes from 1407, during a shaky period in French politics, when the old Duke Louis of Bourbon invited the king's courtiers to dinner. According to his biographer, Louis sat alone at the high table, with his guests ranged below him; everyone ate silently while the duke "had read continually at his dinner the gestes [deeds] of the most famous princes, the former kings of France, and of other men worthy of honor." This account suggests (and many other accounts confirm) that Franco-Burgundian readings were intended more to indoctrinate listeners than to stimulate them to discussion and debate.

Aural Dynamics

Across cultural areas, the dynamics of medieval aurality meant that authors, including Chaucer, were experienced in an environment that was subject to many of the folkloric processes characteristic of face-to-face interaction. References to people crying and applauding as they listened to heroic romances read aloud evoke the bonding and intensification of experience typical of folkloric narration. This was as true for Latin texts as it was for vernacular ones: the foundation statutes of many Oxford and Cambridge colleges, for example, include arrangements for students to relax occasionally by reading Latin poems to each other for fun.

The aural text was also often "emergent" in the folkloric sense—that is, the same text could come out different every time, depending on who was there, what section of the text they wanted to listen to, and what they did and said while the reading was going on. Edward IV's esquires, for example, presumably negotiated which portion of what text they wanted to hear on any given day, and their discussions would no doubt relate what they heard to their own particular ideas and situation. The way in which Chaucer's pilgrims interrupt one another's stories, sometimes even demanding that the teller abandon the story if it bores them, is further evidence that medieval listeners interacted freely at every stage of the reading session.

The variability of the text as performed was abetted by the *mouvance* (variation) to which scribal texts were always subject. Scribes commissioned to make a new manuscript copy of a given text often edited the copy to favor the interests of their patron. Many of the people who made copies of *The Canterbury Tales*, for instance, simply picked out their favorite stories and left the others behind; often, too, they would fiddle with the poetry a bit or add marginal glosses commenting on the text. Copyists would also "translate" the text into their own dialect or language. The result is that for many works one can say, as Phillips Barry did of the ballad, that there are "texts but no text." Medievalists used to ignore these "bad texts" in their attempts to reconstruct the author's original version, just as folklorists used to try to reconstruct the urform, or presumed original version, of a given tale. More recently, however, medievalists are beginning to be interested in what these manuscripts say about how particular audiences related to the texts.

The interplay between oral and literate environments, at all social levels, made it easy for folklore (or folklorically reworked material) to pass into and out of written form—a process that can be traced in the short, entertaining, or didactic narratives that fill much of late-medieval literature. In 1353, for example, the Chevalier de la Tour Landry made his household priests read him the Bible, chansons de geste (heroic romances), chronicles, and other works; he then turned around and dictated his own version of the stories he liked, adding his own *memorates* (personal-experience narratives) and commentary, to make a book of advice for his daughters.

Performance is also an important factor linking both orality and aurality to folklore. Performers could act with their voices, and they could use gestures and even acrobatics (for those unencumbered by instruments or books) to bring the text to life. In the later fourteenth century, Gilles Malet—the favorite reader of King Charles V of France—was noted for his ability to read intelligently, underlining the key points of the discourse (Charles followed the French prelection model in favoring such light reading as Aristotle's

Politics and Augustine's *City of God*). Other listeners had less austere criteria: the author of a lyric called "The Fair Maid of Ribblesdale" (c. 1314–1325), for example, is simply happy that his love has

> a merry mouth to speak with,
> with lovely faithful lips of red,
> romance for to read.

The primary texts make it clear that medieval people listened to texts because they liked to—whether the listeners were literate or illiterate, whatever the kind of text, and whatever language it was in. Apart from the basic pleasure of sharing time with family and friends, medieval listeners enjoyed the social bonding, the intensification of experience, and the many components of performance that heightened their understanding and appreciation of the text.

—Joyce Coleman

Ordeal. A trial in which the accused submits to a torturous physical test whose outcome is presumed to be determined by God.

To modern sensibilities, trial by ordeal is an enigma: inscrutable, unreasonable, and quintessentially medieval. In its application, however, the ordeal was not the first recourse in a medieval legal proceeding; rather, it served as a last resort in particularly difficult cases when determining the truth required divine intervention—for example, when witnesses were either unreliable or too few in number. Employing either fire or cold water to render a judgment in a case when the truth could be discerned through no other means, ecclesiastical officials would oversee the proceedings. The most common required the accused either to withdraw a hot iron from a boiling cauldron or to walk over hot plowshares, after which the severity of the burns would determine guilt or innocence. In the ordeal of cold water the accused would be tested for buoyancy; floating indicated guilt. Other, less painful forms of the ordeal also existed, particularly for ecclesiastical cases. One notable example, the Carolingian "ordeal of the cross," required a participant, standing with his arms raised before a cross, to endure longer than his competition. Typically Church officials were exempt from the ordeal, as were Jews, and certain towns were able to gain exemptions from application of the ordeal as well. A deep and abiding skepticism concerning the ordeal, centuries of debate in intellectual circles, and criticism by writers of romances and sagas eventually led to a ban on ecclesiastical participation in the procedure by Pope Innocent III in 1215 C.E.

Possibly Frankish in origin, the ordeal throve in Europe at least from the time of its first reference in written legal codes in the fifth century C.E., and it remained in use in certain areas even after the ban imposed by Innocent III. The ordeal spread throughout Europe, particularly to Scandinavia, along with the spread of Christianity, and it was typically administered by local Church officials, who held exclusive rights over particular areas and whose hold on this power over the laity was rendered all the more attractive by the legal fees paid both to the Church and to assorted officials who helped to administer the procedure. Since the practice was both entrenched and profitable, and since it could also be manipulated for political reasons, it lingered, particularly in Hungary and southeastern Europe, through the thirteenth and fourteenth centuries. The ordeal of cold water used to test the charge of witchcraft—the "swimming of witches"—is the most remarkable example of the survival of the ordeal; it is documented in America and in Europe in the eighteenth century and in Hungary in the nineteenth. By banning ecclesiastical participation, Innocent III essentially forced the death of a practice that was of questionable civility and reason to its critics, medieval intellectuals who were concerned by the lack of scriptural authority on the matter and by the presumptuousness of requesting miracles from God on demand. As Robert Bartlett observes, the late-medieval legal system would adapt in two significant ways: in countries like England and Denmark it would hasten the creation of the jury system, and, less fortuitously for contemporaries, it would also encourage a rise in institutionalized torture and inquisition.

Though the ordeal was used in reality to judge a wide range of crimes, one of the most prominent themes appearing in medieval literature is of the ordeal used to judge unfaithful wives (motifs H400–H459). In the poem *Gudrunarkvida III* in the thirteenth-century *Poetic Edda*, for example, Queen Kudrun is accused of adultery by her serving woman, Herkja, and proven faithful by the ordeal of hot water. Peter the Chanter tells of how the wife of St. Gandulphus was forced to submit to the ordeal by hot water in a spring summoned by the saint himself, only to be proven guilty by her excessive scalding. The best-known example of the ordeal's being used against an adulterous wife is also one of the most popular of the Middle Ages, the tale of Tristan and Iseut, in which Queen Iseut must submit to the ordeal of hot water as a result of her adulterous affair with her husband's best knight. The tale of Tristan essentially combines the most prominent motifs that concern the ordeal: the unfaithful wife (motifs T230, T481) and the equivocal oath (M105).

Tales that involve the ordeal sometimes imply a faith in its straightforward ability to determine the truth, particularly in hagiographic works. In the *Life of St. Aethelwold*, a cook's faithfulness to his abbot is proven through the ordeal of hot water. Ponce, abbot of Andaone, uses the ordeal to settle a quarrel over ownership of a plowshare, and St. Liobam, abbess of Bischoffsheim, successfully endured the ordeal of the cross as a representative of her convent to prove its collective pu-

rity when a drowned newborn was found nearby. Despite these and other examples of the reliability of the ordeal, however, more common is its presentation as being easily manipulated. In the *Decameron* (8, 6) Boccaccio tells the story of two men, Bruno and Buffalmacco, who are accused of stealing the boar of a simpleton named Calandrino. They manipulate a variant of the ordeal of bread and cheese, in which one's ability to swallow blessed food—in Boccaccio, ginger pills and wine—determines one's guilt or innocence. Bruno and Buffalmacco slip Calandrino a pill that causes him to cough, thereby "proving" that he has stolen from himself. Other literary characters are more cunning: in the thirteenth-century *Saga of St. Olaf,* Sigurd Thorlaksson flees rather than submit to an ordeal that he knows King Olaf will manipulate for political reasons. The *Ljosvetninga Saga* tells the story of a paternity suit in which attempts to settle the matter by the ordeal of hot water result in an uncertain verdict as the parties quibble over the presiding priest's allegiance and disagree over his judgment of the accused woman's burns.

The motif of the tricked ordeal finds its most rich and prominent expression in the Tristan and Iseut story. One of the prominent episodes in the tale hinges upon the queen's ability to manipulate the oath in her favor by deceiving onlookers while still telling the literal truth (motif K1513); this episode recurs commonly in postmedieval folklore as an independent tale (AT 1418, "The Equivocal Oath"). Versions vary; in Béroul's romance, for example, Tristan, dressed as a leper, ferries the queen across a river on his shoulders in sight of all, so that later she can swear that she has had no man between her legs except the leper. In Gottfried von Strassburg's version, Tristan pretends to be a poor pilgrim who carries Iseut ashore and then promptly falls, as if accidentally, in her lap, so that she can swear later that no one has been in her arms except the beggar. Of all the versions of this tale disseminated throughout Europe, from England to Iceland, none is more memorably critical of the ordeal itself than Gottfried's. He writes with characteristic wryness:

Thus it was made manifest and confirmed to all the world that Christ in His great virtue is pliant as a windblown sleeve. He falls into place and clings, whichever way you try Him, closely and smoothly, as He is bound to do. He is at the beck of every heart for honest deeds or fraud. (*Tristan*, trans. A.T. Hatto [1967], p. 248)

The debate over the efficacy of the ordeal, then, is mirrored in the literature of the Middle Ages. While the ordeal is often used to demonstrate the miraculous abilities of certain saints, its susceptibility to manipulation and fraud, and the presumptuousness of demanding God's intervention at its every application, are criticisms developed with insight by medieval storytellers. The great universities of Paris and Bologna and the Fourth Lateran Council (1215) were not the only places where the ordeal was debated, and the distrust eloquently expressed in sagas and romances undoubtedly characterizes the same deep and abiding doubts that led to the ban imposed by Innocent III. The official abandonment of the ordeal early in the thirteenth century rather than later in the period should dispel the stereotype that superstition perpetually dominated reason in the Middle Ages, and the doubts expressed by medieval poets and storytellers, skeptical laymen in an age of faith, should corroborate this notion. It had its defenders, to be sure, but even when used only as a judicial last resort in difficult cases, the ordeal engendered such debate that the greatest churchmen of the time and some of the period's greatest literary figures would ultimately agree on its ineffectual and questionable nature.

See also: Punishments; Trickster; Tristan and Iseut
—Jeff Sypeck

Otherworldly Journey. A major motif (Fo–F199) in the belief tales and fictions of medieval Europeans.

Otherworldly journeys occur frequently both in traditions of pre-Christian times and in the works of Christian poets and storytellers. Some take place within the otherworld itself; others, between this world and other realms. There are many accounts of journeys to the land of the dead and to the regions of heaven and hell in Christian vision literature.

The journey from the familiar world may begin when a door opens in a fairy mound or when the traveler descends under a lake or the sea, steps into a boat, or is carried away through the air by a supernatural guide. There is two-way traffic between the worlds; mortals may visit the otherworld for brief or extended periods of time, and supernatural beings, both beneficent and evil, may journey to earth and have dealings with men. Many traditional märchen of postmedieval times are concerned with the supernatural journey of a youthful hero or heroine, so the subject is one familiar from childhood.

Old Norse Traditions

In Old Norse literature we find frequent examples of journeys within the supernatural world, based in medieval times on memories of the adventures of the old gods. The god Odin, known as "Roadwise" and "Wanderer," journeyed continually around the earth, stirring up mischief and imposing his will on kings, and he also visited the Land of the Dead or the realms of ancient giants to seek hidden knowledge.

In the cosmology of the northern myths, the world of humankind was one of a series of nine worlds around Yggdrasil, the World Tree, and gods, giants, and heroes might pass from one world to the other. The regions are represented as lying far apart, with vast distances between them, so that the journeys were long and dangerous. The emphasis on difficult roads through mountains and forests in the cold and dark may have been partly inspired by the Viking Age exploits of warriors and merchant adventurers making extensive journeys in the north and east of Europe. It has also been suggested that Odin's journeys to the realm of death may owe something to shamanic traditions among the peoples of the far north.

Another powerful god of the Viking Age, Thor, made frequent visits to Jötunheim, the land of the giants, to strike down enemies of the gods of Asgard, and accounts of such journeys are found in some of the earliest skaldic poetry preserved in Iceland. One of the most famous of Thor's journeys was that to the realm of a deceiving giant, Utgarda-Loki, a world beyond the gods' kingdom of Asgard. The way there led through a deep forest. When Thor and his companions arrived at the giant's stronghold, they were apparently humiliated in a series of contests, but in fact Thor's mighty strength had brought terror to the giant ruler, who deceived Thor by his magic. Here we have a sophisticated account of a supernatural journey, told with sardonic humor by Snorri Sturluson in the thirteenth century; we do not know his source.

In another tale, again from an unknown source, Snorri records that when the much-loved Baldr was slain, his mother, Frigg, sent the messenger Hermod to the realm of death to see if the goddess Hel, who ruled there, could be persuaded to let him return to Asgard. Hermod travels across a vast gloomy waste, crossing mountains and rivers. This is the route the dead are said to take, and at one bridge a giantess challenges those who enter the realm of death. Sometimes the gods take on bird form to travel between the distant worlds, as when Loki, borrowing a "feather form" from the goddess Freyja, goes to search for Thor's stolen hammer, or to recover Idun and her golden apples from the giants. Another poem that describes a perilous journey to the otherworld is *Svipadagsmál.* In this work, Svipdag is given directions by his dead mother, from her grave mound, to pass over high mountains and mighty rivers, in a region of intense cold, in order to confront a terrible giant and win Menglöd as his bride. Svipdag is an unidentified hero, but his journey resembles that of Skirnir, the messenger of the god Frey in the Eddic poem *Skirnismal;* he, too, passes through a dangerous underworld realm to encounter a giant and win the giant's daughter Gerd as Frey's bride.

Writing about the same time as Snorri, the Danish historian Saxo Grammaticus knew other tales of journeys to the supernatural world. In Book 1 of his *History of the Danes,* an old man who appears to be Odin wraps the hero Hading in his cloak and takes him on his horse to his own realm. On another occasion, a giantess takes him to a land where fresh herbs grow in winter and tells him that this is where he will come after death.

English and Celtic Traditions

The journeys of human heroes to the otherworld take many different forms. In the Anglo-Saxon heroic poem *Beowulf*, after the mother of the monster Grendel has come to avenge her son on the Danes, the hero tracks her back to the dark lake beneath which she dwells. Once he dives into the water he has entered a supernatural world, where the fierce conflict between them takes place.

Another medieval hero who first traverses the familiar countryside at the commencement of a supernatural journey is found in the fourteenth-century alliterative poem from northern England, *Sir Gawain and the Green Knight*. Gawain travels in the belief that his death awaits him, and his mood is reflected in the country through which he journeys, bound fast in bitter cold. When he reaches the Green Chapel he at last confronts his supernatural adversary, whose head he had cut off a year earlier, issuing out of a cave or mound, and now Gawain must submit to a blow from his great axe. The unknown poet gives deep human significance to this fateful journey, stated rather vaguely to have been brought about by the machinations of the supernatural being Morgan le Fay.

The journey through the Waste Land also appears in the romances of the Grail, when knights from Arthur's court, Perceval and Gawain in particular, reach the castle of the Fisher King, see the broken sword, the bleeding lance, and the Grail, and are given an opportunity to heal the king and restore the land that has been laid waste. Many other quests undertaken by Arthur's knights involve meetings with characters from the otherworld and may be regarded as supernatural journeys. In the Welsh *Mabinogi*, Pwyll, the prince of Dyfed, journeys to Annwfn, the otherworld, later identified with hell, to take the place of its ruler, and the poem "The Spoils of Annwfn" makes a reference to the journey of Arthur himself into this land, a journey on which many of his men were lost.

A group of strange tales of supernatural journeys in Irish literature are those known as the *Immrama*, accounts of voyages to strange and fantastic islands that became very popular in medieval times. Some are clearly influenced by Christian teaching and antiquarian speculation, and it was easy to fit ingenious fantasies and marvels into the voyage framework. The best-known tale, "The Voyage of Bran," goes back at least to the tenth century and may be considerably older. In it Bran is visited by a woman with a silver branch in her hand who tells him of wonderful islands. On the way to the islands he and his followers meet Manannán in his chariot and hear of the marvels of Mag Mell, his kingdom beneath the waves. There are clearly links between these tales and the traditions of the bright otherworld outside time visited by Irish heroes in the tales known as the *Echtrai*. The heroes of the *Echtrai* are led away by supernatural maidens who entice them into an otherworldly mound or lure them across the sea. After what seems only a brief stay, they may return to their own land to find that hundreds of years have slipped away, and when they set foot on the earth they crumble into dust. This bright country, free from corruption or sorrow, with rich orchards, feasting, and fair women to welcome the visitors, has many names, such as "Land of the Living," "Land of Women," or "Plain of Delight." Some of the poems included in the accounts of journeys may go back to the seventh century.

It seems possible that these Irish traditions may have influenced a series of strange tales in Old Norse literature about visits to the kingdom of a mysterious ruler called Gudmund of Glasisvellir. These are found in some of the late legendary sagas whose setting is Norway rather than Iceland and that contain many tales of journeys to strange lands of enchantment. The realm of Gudmund is known as the Field of the Not-Dead, and also as *Glasisvellir* (Glittering or Glassy Plains). Here there was no sickness or death, and those who visited Gudmund's kingdom were welcomed by his fair daughters. Saxo Grammaticus was also familiar with these traditions; he brings them into his account of the voyage of Gorm to the land of the giant Geirruth in Book 8; he places a dark land of death beside Gudmund's bright kingdom.

Christian Traditions

In the medieval period there is a vast Christian vision literature in which the visionary journeys to heaven or hell and then returns to describe what he or she has seen. An early example is the chilling narrative related by the eighth-century Anglo-Saxon historian Bede the Venerable. Bede recounts the story of a Northumbrian man who regained consciousness after his apparent death, and was conducted by an angel to behold the horrors of the purgatorial realm on the borders of hell. In this region sinners are tormented both by devils while they suffer also from extreme heat and freezing cold. He was then led to the borders of heaven, although he was not permitted to penetrate further. He became a monk after his recovery, and Bede seems to have learned much about him from an old monk in Ireland who had known him well.

The vision of the monk of Wenlock, from about the same period, describes how angels took him above the earth; from there he could see it surrounded by fire, the torments of sinners who appeared like black birds, and a narrow bridge over which virtuous souls might pass to the heavenly Jerusalem.

This testing bridge is a frequent image in such supernatural journeys. It is found again in the Norwegian *Draumkvæde* (Dream Poem) of the thirteenth century, which describes Olav Asteson's dream of a visit to the otherworld as he slept from Christmas to Epiphany. He had to pass over Gjallar bridge, high in the air, fitted with sharp hooks and guarded by savage animals, and also through thorns and a horrible stinking marsh. A more unusual treatment of a journey to discover the fate of the dead is the Norwegian *Solarljod* (Lay of the Sun); although it has survived only in late manuscripts, it appears to contain some imagery from earlier pre-Christian beliefs.

The idea of rewards and punishments revealed in a journey persisted in popular tradition in northern England until the seventeenth century in the form of the Lykewake Dirge, said by the antiquarian John Aubrey to have been sung by women at funerals. In this song, only those who have helped others on earth survive the thorns of Whinny Moor and pass over the "Brig o' Dread" in safety. Another example of the popular treatment of this widespread theme is the Irish tradition of St. Patrick's Purgatory, said to have been visited by a knight named Owen in 1153, when he entered the cave at Lough Derg in county Donegal. Many of these visions are repetitive and tedious, but the possibilities of the development of the theme in the hands of a master poet are revealed in Dante's *Divine Comedy* of the early fourteenth century.

See also: Annwfn; Arthurian Lore; *Beowulf*; Dante Alighieri; Irish Tradition; *Mabinogi*; Morgan le Fay; Scandinavian Mythology; *Sir Gawain and the Green Knight*; Snorri Sturluson's *Edda*; Valkyries

—Hilda Ellis Davidson

Outlaw. A person placed beyond society's protection, and often said to bear a "wolf's head"; that is, the value of his life was equivalent to a wolf's, so it was considered a benefit to society to kill him.

In the early Middle Ages a sentence of outlawry often expressed a society's inability to enforce its legal codes; it was invoked when an accused lawbreaker fled justice. Because the sentence of outlawry placed a person beyond the protection of the law, it was in effect a death sentence. Later, as the systems of law enforcement grew more effective, the punishment of outlaws became less severe, and a sentence of outlawry often resulted in exile rather than death. As power became centralized in the hands of kings, outlawry increasingly became a political weapon with which to threaten or remove dangerous opponents, and outlaw tales and songs rapidly became expressions of social discontent.

Our fullest outlaw narratives—for instance, those of Hereward, an eleventh-century English outlaw; Fulk Fitzwarin, a thirteenth-century Norman baron; and Eustace the Monk, a thirteenth-century French adventurer and cleric—empha-

size political grievances. By the time of Robin Hood at the end of the Middle Ages the outlaw narratives, now most commonly found in ballad form and featuring nonaristocratic heroes, had moved away from specific political events but nevertheless retained their flavor of social protest.

Our understanding of outlawry today differs greatly from the practices of the Middle Ages. Outlawry originated as an institutional method for dealing with individuals in a society whose laws were designed to deal with groups. The laws served mainly to regulate intergroup conflicts in kingdoms made up of smaller kinship or tribal groupings. These groups were responsible for the behavior of their individual members, and a person claimed by no group had no legal standing in the larger society and thus could be officially declared outside the law. A legal declaration of outlawry only recognized what was already the case: that such an individual had no one to take his side if he were injured or slain, and he could be killed with impunity. As power became more centralized and the role of kinship groups and the power of tribal chieftains lessened, outlawry came to be a prerogative of the crown and was often used as a political weapon to remove enemies or powerful rivals of royal authority by exiling them. Thus, the *Anglo-Saxon Chronicle* relates that in 1051 King Edward the Confessor outlawed Earl Godwin and his son Earl Swein as a result of a power struggle among the most powerful Anglo-Saxon families.

Outlawry as often indicated political disfavor as it did criminal behavior, though there are still brief reports in charters, wills, and other documents that indicate that outlawry remained a common punishment for lawbreakers, particularly for those who committed crimes against society rather than against an individual. Outlawry, then, was a complicated, changing social and political phenomenon that underscored the often antagonistic relationships between centralized power and local authorities. It flourished especially in times of social unrest and change, when court cases often might be decided on the basis of political expediency rather than legal evidence. In such times, those lacking political influence frequently fled to the woods rather than face the court. Such men probably formed the outlaw bands led by more aristocratic leaders, such as Fulk Fitzwarin.

About the outlaws themselves we know relatively little, aside from the few narratives that have survived. Several outlaw stories survive from the troubled reign of King John in the early thirteenth century. The most famous are about the Anglo-Norman baron Fulk Fitzwarin and the Boulonnais monk, pirate, and outlaw Eustace the Monk. Both were aristocratic adventurers rebelling against their lords for political reasons. Eustace, active in both France and England, left a lasting impression upon the imaginations of people on both sides of the channel. A hundred years after his death he was still appearing in English stories as a foreign tyrant who had laid waste distant lands and then turned upon England.

The earliest outlaw for whom popular narratives survive in England is Hereward. He was outlawed during the reign of Edward the Confessor at the instigation of his family, who apparently could not control him. He left the kingdom but returned after William the Conqueror became king, and he carried on as a political outlaw, leading armed troops in rebellion against William. Stories about Hereward continued to be told for centuries after his death, although most are attested only by references to them in chronicles, genealogies, and other historical sources.

In the stories about this early English outlaw we can already see motifs that will reappear in later stories of medieval outlaws right up to Robin Hood. One such motif is that of the outlaw disguising himself as a potter and spying upon his enemies, which occurs in twelfth-century tales of Hereward, thirteenth-century tales of Eustace, and a fifteenth-century ballad of Robin Hood, with enough similarity to indicate that it is a stock set piece for the outlaw hero narrative. It is only one of many shared incidents in these surviving outlaw narratives. Many similar features are also found in the Icelandic sagas of the outlaws Gisli and Grettir.

The sagas of Iceland generally deal with conflicts, often involving one or more killings, that lead to feuds, followed by efforts to resolve the conflicts through law, and when legal settlements fail, by judgments of outlawry. The Icelanders saw themselves as a people defined by law, as in Njal's famous statement: "With laws shall our land be built up but with lawlessness laid waste." The first part of *Njal's Saga* portrays ideal examples of feud resolution through legal settlement and compensation for persons slain. But ultimately Gunnar is declared an outlaw, and when his wife Hallgerd refuses to help him in his last battle, he is killed by his enemies.

Still more famous as an outlaw is Gisli, who, through several clever and daring escapes, spends many years evading those who would kill him, until his final stand when, aided by his loyal wife, he fights valiantly until felled by overwhelming odds. Gisli thus becomes an outlaw hero, as does another famous saga hero, Grettir the Strong. Unlike the resourceful Gisli, Grettir relies mainly on his massive strength to kill human foes, a huge bear, the revenant Glam, a berserk, and a female and a male troll (in scenes reminiscent of *Beowulf*). He is an outlaw even longer than Gisli, and his doom is just as certain: "For great strength and good luck do not always meet in the same man." The mother of one of his enemies carves runes in a tree root, and when Grettir tries to cut the charmed wood he wounds himself severely. In his weakened state he is overcome by attackers and dies an outlaw hero.

In Ireland outlaws could be equally heroic, though outlawry itself took a different form, at least in the sagas. In the Fenian cycle of tales associated with Finn (Fionn), there is a society of young men warriors that exists outside regular society—and outside its law. In numerous adventures, Finn and other heroes thus stand in an ambiguous relation to regular society, and they are capable of providing benefit as well as harm. They could, however, be incorporated within the normative social structure, generally through entering into sexual relationships with women.

Even the Church adopted some of the forms of outlawry. During the age of the persecutions Christians were declared outlaws by the Roman government for their refusal to sacrifice to the old gods, which under Roman law made them traitors against the state and therefore subject to capital punishment. But the early Church turned the martyrs into outlaw heroes, claiming that in following a higher law than that of the state they were willing to sacrifice their freedom and even, in some sensational cases, their lives. Later, after the Church became a powerful institution in its own right, it could enforce its own form of "spiritual outlawry" against those judged to be heretics or against those who otherwise defied ecclesiastical law and authority, and it could exercise the ultimate banishment of excommunication. Unless proper atonement were made, this was considered a "spiritual death sentence" on the principle of *extra ecclesiam nulla salus* (outside the Church there is no salvation), exiling the outlaw to eternal damnation in hell.

All of this indicates that there was a long-standing tradition of outlaw narrative, with its own sets of motifs, that predated the few surviving narratives we have. Reconstituting this tradition is difficult, since so few actual narratives survive, and much work remains to be done in assembling and evaluating the scattered fragmentary references to outlaws and outlaw stories of the Middle Ages.

See also: English Tradition: Anglo-Saxon Period; English Tradition: Middle English Period; Folklore; Owain Glyndwr; Robin Hood; Sagas of Icelanders

—Timothy J. Lundgren and John McNamara

Owain (sixth century) [Owein, Owain ab Urien].

Historical figure, ruler of Rheged (part of present-day lowland Scotland and northern England), and legendary associate of Arthur.

Many Welsh princes and heroes are named Owain, making it often difficult to determine which Owain is meant in any particular reference. In some cases, such as in vaticinatory (prophetic) poetry, Owain is almost a generic name for the deliverer. The Owain discussed here is the one identified as the son of Urien.

The sixth-century poet Taliesin portrays him as a peerless warrior defending his kingdom from Saxon invasion. As people migrated from the

North (Rheged and neighboring kingdoms) to Wales, traditions about Owain and other figures of the North moved with them. Thus, he appears as one of the northern heroes in the ninth-century poetic cycle *Canu Llywarch Hen* set in north and central Wales, and the ninth- or tenth-century *Englynion y Beddau*, a series of verses on the graves of heroes, places his grave in Wales rather than in the North. Both of these examples also indicate his development into a traditionally accepted hero.

By the twelfth century his heroic role had expanded beyond simply that of a great warrior. The *Fragmentary Life of St. Kentigern*, naming Owain as the saint's father, explains that he went to the mother in the guise of a woman (the only way he could get near her), which left the innocent young woman with the impression that she remained a virgin. The saint's descent from Owain entered Welsh tradition, where it is recorded in the genealogical tracts *Bonedd y Saint*. Further indication of the expansion of Owain's legendry comes in the Triads: he is listed as one of the Three Fair Womb-Burdens (along with his sister Morfudd) and as one of the Three Fair Princes of the Island of Britain, his wife is noted as one of the Three Faithless Wives, and his horse (one of the Three Plundered Horses) and bard (one of the Three Red-Speared Bards) are named. The Triad on his birth names his mother as Modron (the Mother goddess or possibly a namesake), daughter of Avallach (a mythical ancestor in the genealogies). However, in a folktale preserved in the sixteenth-century manuscript Peniarth 147 (at the National Library of Wales, Aberystwyth), she declares herself daughter of the king of Annwfn (the Welsh otherworld). According to the tale, barking dogs prevented anyone from approaching a certain ford until Urien of Rheged dared, whereupon he found a woman washing in the ford. He forced himself upon her, for which she thanked him because she had been fated to wash there until she conceived a son by a Christian. She told him to return in a year for his children, Owain and Morfudd. More information on the story of Owain's faithless wife may be provided in a sixteenth-century source suggesting that Owain's wife was taken by his nephew, whom, out of mercy, Owain forbore to kill. Each of these Triads hints tantalizingly at far richer narrative tradition.

Nonetheless, the most notable development of Owain's tradition draws him into the Arthurian cycle. Serving as a knight in Arthur's court, he is the hero of a Welsh Arthurian romance, the thirteenth-century *Owain*, or *Iarlles y Ffynnawn* (The Lady of the Fountain), which corresponds to the French romance *Yvain* by Chrétien de Troyes. Owain fights the Knight of the Fountain, wins the Lady of the Fountain, and becomes the guardian of the Fountain. The tale concludes with a reference to Owain's *teulu* (war band), apparently a flock of ever-victorious ravens. The war band appears again when Owain takes a central role in the twelfth- or thirteenth-century Welsh narrative *Breuddwyd Rhonabwy* (Rhonabwy's Dream), in which he and Arthur play the board game *gwyddbwyll* while Arthur's men and Owain's ravens fight each other. An earlier (twelfth-century) reference to Owain's ravens in battle as well as later poetic references indicate the existence of a more extensive but now lost tradition.

The development of the historical Owain ab Urien into a member of Arthur's court might be explained simply as the effect Arthur commonly had of drawing others into his orbit, but the references in the Triads and the specific narratives involving his birth, the Lady of the Fountain, the ravens, and Kentigern suggest that Owain was in his own right the subject of a full, diverse range of legendry.

See also: Arthurian Lore; Chrétien de Troyes; Welsh Tradition

—Elissa R. Henken

Owain Glyndwr (c. 1354–c. 1416) [Owain ap Gruffydd Fychan, Owen Glendower].

Last Welsh-recognized Prince of Wales.

At the beginning of the fifteenth century Glyndwr led the last armed rebellion of the Welsh against the English. He was seen in his own time as a national redeemer and has retained that image, becoming a primary symbol of modern Welsh nationalism. Glyndwr arose during a period of great social and economic unrest, which had been growing since the death in 1282 of Llywelyn II and the subsequent conquest of Wales by England's Edward I. The Welsh chafed under English rule, which denied rights for the Welsh and imposed heavy taxes. A change of economic system and the plague added to their hardship. Glyndwr's rebellion began as a land dispute with his neighbor Reginald Grey, lord of Ruthin, that escalated into full revolt when Parliament and Henry IV rebuffed petitions for redress. Supporters declared Glyndwr Prince of Wales, and on September 20, 1400, Glyndwr started the war with an attack on Ruthin. He was declared an outlaw and his lands were made forfeit, but most of the Welsh, including students and farmworkers returned from England, supported him in what was primarily a guerrilla war. By 1405 Glyndwr controlled Wales, had pushed into England, and formed an alliance (the Tripartite Indenture) with Edmund Mortimer and the Percys of Northumberland. Glyndwr's tripartite plan for an independent state—a parliament (which first met in Machynlleth in 1404), an independent Welsh church, and a university system—seemed the realization of a new golden age. But in 1406 the balance changed, and by 1416 the war was lost.

Glyndwr was recognized in his own time as a national redeemer—the hero whose coming (from afar or from a long sleep) is awaited so that he might restore the nation to its former glories. The pattern of expectation was well established in Wales through a long line of heroes (including Cynan, Cadwaladr, and Arthur) who, it was prophesied, would rid the land of alien intruders and after a period of great chaos establish a time of peace, bounty, and justice. Glyndwr himself pointed to the prophecies, for example, in letters written to the king of Scotland and the lords of Ireland reminding them that the prophecies promised not only his success as a deliverer but also their help in accomplishing it. After the rebellion's defeat, the redeemer role became even clearer, with expectations of Glyndwr's eventual return to finish his work. An early history, compiled shortly after 1422, reports Glyndwr's disappearance in 1415 and notes that while "very many say that he died, the seers maintain he did not." Later legendry shows him asleep in the hills, awaiting the proper time for his return (motif D1960.2). One legend, reported repeatedly since its first record in 1548, relates that Glyndwr, while walking on Y Berwyn, meets an abbot who tells him he has risen too early. By the nineteenth century, a legend attached to many areas records a drover or shepherd discovering a cave with treasure, sleeping warriors, and an especially splendid, central warrior (told also of Arthur and Owain Lawgoch, depending on location). The early-fifteenth-century history contains several other items that also exemplify facets of Glyndwr that were developed in later legendry. Escaping from his enemies' grasp into the woods and retaking Aberystwyth Castle through a verbal ruse (variants are recorded for both of these in each succeeding century) are early examples of legendry depicting Glyndwr as a trickster who through cunning, disguises, and prowess moves freely among his enemies and escapes their traps. His role as a master of escape is also demonstrated by the battle at Mynydd Hyddgant, where Glyndwr's small band (120 men) routed the massed troops surrounding them, and by his escape into hiding at the end of the war. The burning of Cardiff and Abergavenny is an early sign of Glyndwr's destructiveness, first noted in a pre-1400 cywydd (poem, pl. cywyddau) in which the poet Iolo Goch declares, "Neither grass nor dock grew or even corn in his path." The tradition of Glyndwr's destructiveness became so strong that almost any burned ruin may be attributed to him. The continuity of tradition for the few legends found in medieval sources indicates that material found only later may in fact have existed earlier. Glyndwr left his mark all over the Welsh countryside, though mainly in the North and in his home area of Corwen, with a variety of fields, mounds, foot- and hoofprints, and sword cuts all assigned to him. Caves, in particular, figure prominently in Glyndwr's legendry, serving sometimes as bases for his guerrilla operations and sometimes as hiding places after his narrow escapes.

The English view of Glyndwr is quite different from the Welsh view. English histories portray him as treacherous (turning on his king and failing to support his cohort Percy at the 1403 battle of Shrewsbury), inordinately cruel, and a wizard controlling the weather. Some of these elements were later depicted by Shakespeare in *Henry IV, Part I*.

See also: Arthurian Lore; Sleeping King

—Elissa R. Henken

*P*assover Haggadah. One of the most popular Hebrew texts even among nonreligious Jews, a compilation of thanksgivings, prayers, midrashic commentary, and psalms recited and acted out at the Seder (Hebrew for "order") around the ritual feast partaken on the eve of the Passover festival.

The present version of the Haggadah (Hebrew for "telling"), with modifications according to various Sephardic, Ashkenazi, and other Jewish community traditions, received its form between the thirteenth and fifteenth centuries. The Haggadah text invites completion and elaboration by the Seder participants on the theme of "from slavery to freedom," as the Seder banquet incorporates a series of ritual words and acts (indicated by "stage directions") celebrated by the Jewish family at home in order to relive the Redemption of the Israelites from Egyptian bondage. The Haggadah has not been assembled by any one particular author.

The collage-like text is composed of excerpts from the Old Testament, the Mishnah and the Midrashim, following the commandment to celebrate Passover and commemorate salvation for the younger generations, according to "Thou shalt tell thy son" (Exod. 13:8).

From the thirteenth to fifteenth centuries, and also in its regard to the destruction of the second temple in 69 C.E. and the exile of the Jews to various diasporae, the Passover ritual and its central element, the reciting of the Haggadah, have been interpreted as a major expression of Jewish yearnings for national as well as ultimate mystical redemption. The main motif is the Exodus from Egypt, conceived as both historical and metaphoric; the main modality is that of speech as a ritualistic religious act. One of the main functions of the Haggadah is the commemorative-memorial aspect, in which the performative speech act of reciting the text unites the participants with Jewish faith, myth, and history.

The Haggadah Structure

1. The blessing, *Kiddush*, is prescribed for all festivals, and not specific to the Seder service.

2. In the performative "*Ha lahma anya*" [This is the bread of affliction], the leader of the Seder declares the matzah (unleavened bread) to be the same as the matzah eaten by our forefathers in Egypt. It is not dissimilar in its religious performative function to the essential Christian "Hoc est Corpus Christi." This earlier Jewish esoteric version can be regarded as an act of transtemporalization rather than an act

of transubstantiation. Both modes implicitly demand the active participation of the believer. This typically self-referential, self-supporting statement in the Haggadah is followed by an invitation to anyone hungry to join the meal, then by a wish: "This year we are here; next year, Jerusalem. This year—slaves; next year—free people." Whereas the *Encyclopedia Judaica* sees no clear connection between the parts, it may be suggested that all three are variants of a basically mystical speech act that does not describe a situation but constitutes it, as befits a ceremony of this kind.

3. "*Mah Nishtana*" [Why is this night different from all other nights?] is a series of four questions, again regarding these same festivities in a self-referential mode: why the matzah; why the bitter herbs; why the twice dipping of the bitter matzah; why the comfortable reclining (rather than sitting) at the banquet table? This section is traditionally declaimed or sung by the youngest member of the family, thus creating an educationally important and live generational dialogue.

4. "*Avadim Hayinu*" [We were slaves] is the compact introduction to the Passover story and the beginning of the "explanation" or actual "telling" of the Redemption story. The section ends with "whoever dwells on telling about the exodus from Egypt is praiseworthy."

5. "*Ma' aseh be-Rabbi Eliezar,...*" is a story about four leading Mishnaic scholars who convened at the Seder and were so carried away with telling the Passover story that their students had to remind them that it was time for the regular morning prayer. It is a story within a story, a play within the role playing of the Passover story. This meta-ritual mode is sustained in the next section, too.

6. The narrative of the four sons (also found in Mekh. Pisha 18) treats four types of potential attitudes to the Passover ritual itself: the wise, the wicked, the simple, and even "the one who does not know how to ask." This multicategorical classification has traditionally been regarded as problematic, but it can be explained as an attempt to create a live dialogue throughout the Seder, be it even with objecting, simple, or disinterested participants. Each son receives an answer commensurate with both his question and the way he poses it, or does not.

7. "*Yachol me' Rosh Hodesh*" [One can at the New Moon] is an exegetical approach to the particular moon calendar and precise time allotted to the Eve of Passover.

8. "*Mi-Tehila Ovdei Avodah Zarah ...*" intro-

duces the Passover story, starting with the times in which the Israelites worshipped idols. An interesting link is established here between spiritual and geographic proximity: the Land of Canaan—as a divine promise and the worship of the One God.

9. "*Arami Oved Avi*" [literally, A wandering (or lost) Aramean was my father] is a midrashic elaboration on biblical sources, emphasizing the obligation to expound on the redemption story. An important idiom here is "*Anus al pi ha-dibbur*" [compelled by speech], in which the midrash links the performative function of the divine promise with the individual's duty to use speech during the Seder.

10. Commentaries on the ten plagues and on the crossing of the Red Sea (Exod. 14), emphasizing that it was God himself who performed all the miracles. It is a tradition at the Seder to follow the recital by spilling a drop of wine for each of the plagues.

11. "*Kammah Ma' alot ...*" is a praise poem to God's wonders, preserved in the desert, the Sabbath, and the Torah, the Promised Land, and the erection of the Temple, which are described as divine gifts.

12. *Passover, matzah,* and bitter herbs are an intratextual verbal summary of the entire Haggadah, according to Rabban Gamliel, and a minimum requirement for those who are unable to participate in the whole ritual.

13. "*In every generation, one must regard oneself as if he or she had gone out of Egypt.*" This Mishnaic passage explains the importance of using the first-person (singular and plural) form, in which the observant Jew accepts both individual and social responsibility for being redeemed by God. Again, this is an act of transtemporalization joining the generations from early times to the present.

14. *Hallel* is a praise prayer in two parts.

15. The text of the blessing "*Gaal*" [He who redeemed us] again mentions the commandment to eat matzah and bitter herbs. At this point in the Seder it is customary to have the meal. After the festival meal (and grace), the second part of the Seder begins.

16. The second part of the Seder begins with "*Pour Thy Wrath*" on the nations who have oppressed the Israelites.

17. Next comes the last part of the praise prayer "*Hallel*" [Praise].

18. Another benediction—"*Yehallelukha*" [All thy works shall praise Thee]—is recited and sung, mostly by the Ashkenazi Jewish tradition.

19. The great *Hallel* (Psalm 136), with the refrain "For his loving kindness endureth forever," is presented.

20. "*Nishmat Kol Hai*" [The breath (or soul) of every living thing shall praise Thy Name] is recited.

Textual Elaborations

The Seder ends with the words "The order of Passover is accomplished ... Next year in Jerusalem." However, it is an old tradition, dating to medieval times, to continue the event with songs, poems, and other textual elaborations on the theme of Redemption, which are included in many versions of the printed Haggadah, such as "And It Came to Pass at Midnight," "To Him Praise Is Becoming" (based on the alphabet), "Who Knows One?" and "Only One Kid." Some of these poems are meant to entertain the children. Since the Haggadah's text indeed invites active participation, many communities and families nowadays may add to the prescribed text personal stories of redemption, related to historical events such as World War II, the Holocaust, the establishment of the State of Israel, or they may tell tales of immigration. Of special interest, and indicating the vitality of the medieval Haggadah text, are the Haggadah versions read in the Kibbutzim, which emphasize agricultural, natural, and seasonal themes while omitting the more traditional religious ones.

The Haggadah is replete with prescribed ritual acts that also function as structural units, such as washing of the hands (purification), karpas (dipping herbs and eating them), afikoman (the middle of three matzot [pl. of matzah] displayed on the Seder table). The top matzah is symbolic of the Kohanim, the middle matzah represents the Levi'im, and the bottom matzah is understood as the Yisrael, or the nonpriestly Jewish population. Furthermore, different communities have their own traditions of more fully enacting the exodus by dressing up like the ancient Israelites, in white sheets, stick in hand, and sack on shoulders. The Passover table is set with a special cup reserved for the prophet Elijah, who is the herald of the Messiah. In some communities there may also be an empty chair at the table reserved for the prophet. The Seder is habitually held with the father of the family at the head of the table, leading the assembled large family in the ceremony. Often, "parts" are given to members of the family to read, recite, or sing. Some parts are sung by all participants. Since the text is a ritual, the sensual elements are highly significant. For example, the matzot are covered, then partly revealed, then covered again. The wine glasses are lifted with the right hand, while the left hand is raised. Other kinds of ritual and symbolic foods are also alternately covered and uncovered. As in many other rituals, the "correct" performing of the Haggadah, too, demands total commitment, while the text and the nonverbal performative acts in it educate the participants toward that commitment itself.

The reading aloud of the Haggadah is not the simple reciting of a text; rather, it is a multisensual experience, appealing to sight and sound, touch, smell, and taste. In theatrical terms, the Haggadah is a complex and sophisticated "play," composed of dialogue text and "stage instructions" that relate to light and movement, time and space, intergenerational relationships—encouraging free individual expression through the prescribed religious, social, and national text. As an opening into an explicit hermeneutic circle, the Haggadah can be regarded as an invitation to a dialogue, in which the ancient tradition interprets itself through the participants and—vice versa—in which the participants understand their personal and Jewish identities through the Haggadah.

Haggadah Commentaries

Despite a great number of unifying elements—such as the theme of Redemption, typically ritualistic self-referential structures, formulas of three and four, and an intensive reliance on the ascribed sanctity of earlier textual materials—the Haggadah still poses many textual problems. One important commentary had already been composed in the fourteenth century (*Orot Hayyim* by Aaron Ben Jacob Ha-Cohen), and another by Abudarham dates to 1566. Other commentaries added their own elaborations, according to the historical and theological conditions; such as Abrabanel in *Zevah Pessah* (1545), who poses 100 questions and answers them in direct relation to the meaning of the Haggadah in his own days. The Haggadah has received mystical interpretations (by R. Moshe Alshekh or R. Judah Löw of Prague, 1582), Halachic explanations, and various homiletic compositions. In the nineteenth century a more critical approach was used in an attempt to analyze the sources and determine linguistic and historical origins.

Manuscripts

The Haggadah is probably the most popular text in Jewish religious literature. Differing recensions have been preserved in manuscripts, from the thirteenth to the fifteenth centuries, from all countries in which Jews have lived, and also in fragments from the Cairo *Genizah*. The oldest versions appear to be those in Saadia Gaon's prayer book (tenth century? eighth century?), in the Vitry prayer book (eleventh century), and in Maimonides Mishne Torah (twelfth century). Since the fifteenth century there have existed more than 2,700 editions of the Haggadah, and it has been translated into most Jewish languages (such as Ladino, Yiddish, or Judeo-Arabic).

See also: Jewish Tradition

—Shimon Levy

Patrick, Saint (d. probably 493). Celebrated as the patron saint of Ireland and the apostle to the Irish whose mission in the fifth century furthered the establishment of the Christian Church in Ireland.

Saint Patrick's stature as a national figure has made his feast day, March 17, an international celebration of Irish culture and history. The historical Patrick is known through two documents generally considered to be the authentic works of Patrick himself, the *Confession*, in which he relates much of his life story, and the *Letter to Coroticus*, a tract in which he castigates a British ruler named Coroticus whose soldiers had raided the Irish coast, killing and capturing several recently baptized Christians.

The legendary Patrick begins to emerge later, in the seventh century, with the appearance of a Latin *vita*, composed by one Muirchú, a member of the Patrician church of Armagh, Patrick's major foundation, and a series of *acta* (acts) composed by one Tírechán, a bishop. Muirchú bases some of his *Life of Saint Patrick* on Patrick's own *Confession*, some of it on other (lost) sources; apart from the sketchy biographical material he uses, he relates miracles performed by the saint. Tírechán's memoir is a collection of local traditions; its main purpose is to catalog Patrick's churches and disciples, yet it also adds a few miraculous events. Other *Lives* from the eighth and ninth centuries further embellish the Patrician legend, which reaches its apogee with the anonymous composition known as the *Tripartite Life*, written mostly in Irish, around the tenth or eleventh century. In the second and third sections, the text relates a string of miracles and prophecies performed by St. Patrick; the first section contains an almost entirely legendary biographical account that relates miracles at his birth and during his youth and records his death at age 122. A homily in Middle Irish on the life of Patrick also appears in the late-fifteenth-century collection contained in the *Book of the Dean of Lismore* and contains much of the material of the earlier texts.

Patrick was born in Britain into a Christian Romano-Celtic family: his father, Calpornius, was a deacon and his grandfather, Potitus, a presbyter. Muirchú gives his original name as Sochet, and the name of his mother as Concessa. The exact dates of his lifetime have been and are still a matter of debate; R. Hanson argued the popular notion that Patrick was born around 390 C.E., went to Ireland some time between 425 and 435, and died around 460. However, recent investigations by David Dumville and others point to 493 as the more likely year of his death, thereby placing his mission in the latter half of the fifth century. Patrick names his home as the town of Bannaventa Berniae. The site has not been successfully identified; however, it is assumed to have been on the west coast of Britain.

According to his own account, Patrick was captured by raiders when he was 16 and sold as a slave in Ireland, where he was made a herdsman (Slemish, in County Antrim, is traditionally held to be the site of his captivity). After six years in slavery he heard a voice in a dream telling him a ship was ready for him, although it was 200 miles away. Patrick escaped, found the ship, and persuaded the pagan sailors to take him aboard. He eventually returned to his family in Britain. There he received a vision of a man whom he names Victoricius; this man handed him a letter from the "Voice of the Irish," urging him to return to Ireland to preach. Patrick then trained as a priest (under St. Germanus of Auxerre, according to Muirchú), was ordained as a bishop, and was sent to Ireland.

The rest of his *Confession* is aimed against criticisms by British bishops of his unsuitability, misappropriation of funds, and improprieties involving the acceptance of gifts from female converts. Although Patrick humbly acknowledges a lack of sophistication in writing and learning, he denies the accusations of misconduct and justifies his actions. There is no evidence that these charges were ever proven against Patrick, and despite the efforts to discredit him his mission was successful.

The legends of St. Patrick begin with the prophetic dreams and visions recounted in his own *Confession*; his prophetic ability is elaborated in his later *Lives* and in the *Lives* of other Irish saints (whose birth or arrival he prophesies). Patrick becomes a miracle worker of note; consistent in his legends are his frequent conflicts with the druids of the high king of Tara, Loegaire (although the office of high king was a later invention of the Uí Neill clan). The king's druids had prophesied that an "Adze-head" (perhaps a reference to the monks' tonsure) would come to their shores and that their religion would subsequently be destroyed.

At Easter, contrary to native custom, Patrick lit a fire on the hill of Tara. This unorthodox gesture led to a confrontation with the king and his druids. One druid was cast into the air, and his head was smashed against a stone; before Patrick could be seized an earthquake caused the king's horses to bolt with their chariots. Another druid then tried to poison Patrick; however, Patrick blessed the cup and caused the poison to fall out. Patrick and his followers escaped capture by the king through Patrick's blessing, which made them appear to be deer as they made their way safely into the wilds. (This episode became the frame tale in the *Tripartite Life* for the hymn known as "The Deer's Cry" or "Saint Patrick's Breastplate," which is attributed to the saint.) The king then arranged a trial by fire between Patrick's disciple, Benignus, and the king's remaining druid. During the course of this ordeal, the druid was burned alive; however, Patrick's disciple was unharmed.

Patrick was not the first Christian missionary to Ireland; some texts mention an "Old Patrick," who was almost certainly Bishop Palladius, sent to Ireland by Germanus. Bishop Palladius died before Patrick was appointed. Patrick became associated in legend with St. Brigid, but their connection is more reflective of the rivalry between the churches of Armagh and Kildare than of any real relationship. St. Patrick's emblems are snakes and shamrocks; the legend that he banished all snakes from Ireland is a fairly modern one, and it should be taken as a metaphor for his Christian mission against paganism, since Ireland has never had indigenous snakes. The traditional site of Patrick's burial is at Downpatrick, in County Down.

See also: Brigid, Saint; Saints, Cults of the

—Dorothy Ann Bray

Peasants. Medieval agricultural workers, who comprised the vast majority of people, and whose work fed virtually everyone, in Western Europe.

Peasants changed the face of the Continent, transforming forests into vast expanses of farm fields, creating the economic base for the complex cultures and growing urban centers of the central and later Middle Ages; moreover, they created a village culture that greatly influenced folk traditions at all levels of society.

Peasants, who stood between landowners and slaves on the social ladder, worked the lands of the nobles and clergy. A peasant did not own a plot of land but, rather, belonged to it, legally bound to obey the will of the landowner. In many areas (as in England after 1100) peasants who paid rents for the right to occupy the land were considered "free" and those who instead exchanged labor for land use were called "unfree"— or *villeins* (literally, "villagers"). This distinction can be misleading, however, because the conditions under which free peasants lived were sometimes as difficult as those of villeins, and some villeins possessed considerable prosperity and social power. Furthermore, a significant proportion of the medieval peasantry discharged their obligations to their lords through both rents and labor. These obligations were sometimes nominal, but at least as often they were staggering. A given agricultural household might owe its lord as much as 100 percent of its income and as much as 250 days of manual labor per year by all able-bodied workers.

The peasantry emerged as a distinctive class only in the eleventh century after a long process of social and technological change. In much of early-medieval Europe, most of the land was cultivated by free families who not only performed agricultural work but also frequently contributed military service to their lords. The number of free farmworkers declined sharply after the eighth century as the manorial system gained greater and greater prominence.

The manorial system had its roots in early-medieval Europe. After the fall of the Roman Empire, the Church and the Germanic aristocracy became the major landholders, and they typically divided each of their estates into one large *desmesne* farm and many small tenant holdings. The lord managed the cultivation of the desmesne farm, while his tenants, given *dominium utile* (rights of usage), managed the holdings to which they were assigned. But in return for the right to inhabit and work their holdings, tenants were also required to work the desmesne farm alongside the lord's slaves. The rudiments of this system developed early in the Middle Ages and began to exert a transforming influence on European culture in the seventh and eighth centuries as massive desmesnes sprang up in the rich, productive soil of northern France and spread into neighboring regions.

As the manorial system grew, estates became larger and larger. This efficiently centralized system of food production helped support the similarly centralized Carolingian Empire in the ninth century, and the empire in turn helped foster the spread of the manorial system. In the ninth through eleventh centuries the number of slaves dwindled, and slavery disappeared from many regions, but the peasant population exploded. Giant estates progressively absorbed formerly free farmers and turned them into tenants through various means: for purposes of protection or in hopes of greater prosperity, free farmers would voluntarily put themselves into bondage to the desmesne lord; or through acts or threats of violence, the lord would force free farmers to become his tenants; or the lord would oversee the clearance of forest land, assigning families to this land once it had been converted into fields. The eleventh through thirteenth centuries were also an age of massive rural growth, as this huge conscripted workforce was set to clearing forests, creating new farmlands, and establishing new villages.

Hand in hand with the manorial system, certain developments in land use and technology worked against the small family farms and catalyzed the formation of large peasant communities. Because medieval fields were insufficiently fertilized, the soil grew poor quickly unless crops were rotated. The three-field system of crop rotation, employed at least as early as the eighth century by monastic desmesnes, greatly enhanced crop yields: each year one field was planted in winter grain, a second lay fallow to be fertilized by animals, and a third was planted in summer grain. During a three-year period each field would go through all three stages of cultivation. It would be planted first with wheat, rye, or barley, the winter grains sown in the fall and harvested early the next summer, then it would be left fallow until the next spring, when it would be sown with such summer grains as oats or barley (again) or with legumes, such as peas, that would replenish the soil. When these were harvested in late summer the field would lie fallow again.

Such planting required concerted planning efforts and cooperative work.

Similarly, the increasing use of the heavy wheeled plow favored large-scale farming. Earlier plows simply broke the earth, but the wheeled plow turned and enriched the soil and plowed under the weeds. The new machines required four or more oxen to pull them, and most families could not afford either to maintain the heavy machinery or to sustain such a large number of oxen. Communal work, pooling the resources of many families, generally proved more profitable as a whole. At the same time that agricultural workers were forced into greater dependence on their lords, the nature of their work forced them to become more dependent upon each other.

With such an increasingly productive and broad-based system of agriculture, northern and central Europe were able to support large urban populations, and cities such as Paris grew dramatically. In this complex society work grew more specialized. Peasants, once both farmers and warriors, were now full-time farmers, and the aristocracy developed its own exclusive warrior class, the knights. Knights and peasants progressively defined themselves as distinct classes in contrast with each other.

The writings of medieval clerics reflected these social divisions. From the eleventh century forward, social theory divided the human population into three estates, or classes: The knights (*miles*) were fighters (*bellatores*), charged with protecting the other classes; the clergy (*clerus*) were prayers (*oratores*), who prayed for the other classes; and the peasants and serfs (*cultori*) were the workers (*labores*), whose industry sustained the other two classes by providing them food and labor. The first two estates were effectively the owners of the third, who comprised the great majority of the medieval population. In England in the fourteenth century, peasants and serfs numbered at least 60 percent of the population; in France during the same period, 80 percent; in Germany and Eastern Europe, 90 percent.

Although few among the *miles* ever admitted kinship with the peasantry, various individuals and groups from among the *clerus* saw their work as more continuous with that of the *cultori*. The sixth-century Rule of St. Benedict, outlining the proper behavior of monks, insisted that they partake in labor typically considered peasant work. But just as the knights increasingly distanced themselves from the peasants, so too did most of the clergy, and most well-off clerics considered farm work beneath their dignity. In the late fourteenth century, when the French monastery of La Trappe fell upon hard times, the monks plowed and harvested their own lands, but the bishop judged such work inappropriate and successfully petitioned the pope for economic relief.

Class distinctions between peasants and the other estates were reinforced by a number of customs and pronouncements from the clergy and nobles. Even the daily bread of the Middle Ages was apportioned along class lines. White wheat bread was reserved for the upper classes, while the peasants ate brown rye bread; in times of famine, when aristocrats might have to eat rye bread, peasants and their livestock were to eat oats.

Regulations further divided peasants from the other estates. The twelfth-century Frankish *Imperial Chronicle* regulated peasant clothing, stating, "Peasants are not allowed to wear any colors other than black or gray." Although their ancestors had been warriors and they customarily carried weapons, peasants were now required to finance wars with taxes rather than to fight; some laws forbade them to bear any arms within the village and allowed them no more than a sword when traveling on the dangerous roads. The *Imperial Chronicle* goes even farther: "Should a peasant be found in possession of a sword he shall be bound and led to the church fence, where he should be detained and thoroughly beaten. If he has to defend himself against an enemy, let him use a staff."

In fourteenth-century France, as in most of Europe before that date, a lord possessed massive legal control over his villeins, pronouncing judgments on any crimes committed by the workers. Even the most intimate choices of peasant life fell under the sway of the lord, who often prohibited peasants from marrying anyone outside his desmesne.

Many proverbs, stereotypes, and legends developed to explain the relations of the classes to each other and to assert the essential differences between classes. In order to justify their sense of superiority to peasants, aristocratic clergy narrated etiological legends accounting for how the peasantry came into being. They embroidered upon the Bible, claiming, for example, that Cain was the first bondsman and that peasants, as descendants of Cain, deserved their servitude as a hereditary punishment. Similar stories asserted that peasants were descended from Ham, the son of Noah cursed by God for laughing at his father's nakedness. Such legends were adapted in urban mystery plays of the fifteenth century—for example, the Towneley *Mactatio Abel* (Murder of Abel) and the York *Cayme and Abel* depict Cain as a peasant. Ironically, the class whose labor had made European cities so large and prosperous became the subject of mockery in its public dramas.

In art and literature the peasant took on animal characteristics, appearing effectively as a different species from the people of more-privileged classes. Fourteenth-century English paintings and writings depicted nobles with delicate, narrow noses but rendered peasants—such as the Miller, in Chaucer's *Canterbury Tales*—with "camus" (squashed, pug) noses and a generally beastly appearance. The thirteenth-century French romance *Aucassin et Nicolette* presents a typically grotesque description of a peasant: "His head was big and blacker than smoked meat; the palm of your hand could easily have gone between his two eyes; he had very large cheeks and a monstrous flat nose with yellow nostrils; lips redder than uncooked flesh; teeth yellow and foul."

The peasants too had their origin stories, and predictably these diverged sharply from those promoted by the aristocracy. Peasants were convinced that it was not God but human beings who had created their servile conditions and that therefore, according to God's law, peasants and nobles were equal and should be treated as such. Even if the aristocracy despised the peasants, they were aware of this opposing view. Jean Froissart, a chronicler and servant of kings, summed up the position of the peasant leaders on the eve of the English Peasants' Revolt (1381):

> These unhappy people ... said that they were kept in great servage, and in the beginning of the world, they said, there were no bondmen, wherefore they maintained that none ought to be bond without he did treason to his lord, as Lucifer did to God; but they said that they could have no such battle for they were neither angels nor spirits, but men formed to the similitude of their lords, saying why should they then be kept so under like beasts. (Trans. Lord Berners, in L. Patterson, *Chaucer and the Subject of History* [1991], p. 264)

There was also a significant literature, based on folktales, that depicted peasants as cagey subversives, able to overcome their disadvantages through superior intelligence and trickery. *Unibos*, an eleventh-century Latin poem written in Germany, portrays a poor peasant who hoodwinks his greedy and powerful neighbors, tricking them out of their goods and ultimately inducing them to kill their wives and themselves; this plot survived the Middle Ages and persists to the present day as "The Rich and the Poor Peasant" (AT 1535). One enormously popular folktale theme was the contest of wits between a wily peasant and an overbearing king. The most popular plot involves a king who threatens the abbot of a monastery with punishment or death if he cannot correctly answer a series of riddles. A peasant or shepherd substitutes for the abbot and defeats the king (AT 922, "The King and the Abbot"). The Trickster assumed various guises in various tellings. Sometimes the king was the legendarily wise Solomon of biblical tradition and the Trickster a peasant named Marcolf, notorious in late-medieval literature for his antiauthoritarian acts. Such tales no doubt served as a kind of compensation fantasy for a social class unlikely to win contests of social or political power but clearly interested in "winning with words." The violence of these tales is noteworthy: they typically focus not merely on a contest but on a life-and-death struggle between rich and poor.

Daily Life and Work

Throughout Europe the most common unit of peasant community was the village. The size of the village was determined by natural and political factors. Ideally, the village would be no larger than could be supported by the bounty of the surrounding land that the peasants worked; most villages contained from 20 to 100 households. In areas where warfare was common, peasants clustered in larger numbers for mutual safety, at the risk of starvation in years when their crop yields could not easily support them. Both to preserve the best lands for farming and to protect themselves from invaders, peasants in many areas tended to erect their villages on hilltops and to clear their fields in the lowlands at the base of the village.

This interdependent living situation, accompanied by continual communal work, has led many people to see peasant society as perfectly egalitarian and communal. In reality, however, there was great variation in wealth and status among the peasantry. Rodney H. Hilton has classified thirteenth-century English peasants into three groups. The free tenants were not necessarily more prosperous than the villeins, but they possessed such legal privileges as relatively low rents, token work services, and occasionally the right to transfer land. The villeins owed substantial and often degrading work services to their lords. The third group, the cottagers, comprising both free and villein families, were land-poor villagers whose holdings, generally no more than two acres, were insufficient to feed them so that they were forced to ply other trades and take on all sorts of extra labor in order to survive. Such uneven distribution of resources inevitably produced hierarchies; Frances Gies and Joseph Gies, in their study of the south English village of Elton, found a population divided much according to Hilton's model and further found clear status differentiation among the villagers—eight families, accounting for less than 4 percent of the village households, occupied more than 50 percent of its most important leadership positions, such as reeve or beadle (titles given to those who managed work on the manor), juror or ale-taster.

Peasant work was extremely grueling—and never-ending. The peasant's cycle of agricultural work began with plowing. In Europe north of the Alps there were two major plowing seasons; where the wheel plow was used, each field was plowed twice in the same season: once to allow the manure and stubble to decompose and again perhaps a month later to aerate the soil. After the second plowing peasants sowed the grain by hand. Following the sowers was a horse-drawn harrow, which had rake-like teeth that buried the seed beneath the topsoil before the birds could eat it. While the grain was growing, peasants would be weeding the fields. At harvest time the grain was cut, stacked or sheaved, and taken from the fields. In the barn peasants threshed the grain with flails to separate the heads of grain from the stalk and then winnowed it, using a winnowing fan or another device to fling the grain heads into the air, separating the fruit from the chaff. Because there were two plowing seasons, there were two seasons for most of the other activities, so that a peasant's work calendar in south England would look something like this:

January	first plowing for summer crops
February	second plowing for summer crops
March	sowing, harrowing summer crops
April	weeding fields
May	sheepshearing, weeding fields
June	weeding fields, harvesting winter crops
July	weeding fields, harvesting hay, harvesting winter crops, threshing, winnowing
August	harvesting summer crops
September	harvesting summer crops
October	plowing winter fields, sowing winter crops
November	sowing and harrowing winter crops, slaughtering the beasts
December	threshing, winnowing

Many peasants performed all this work both on their own customary holdings and on their lord's.

But this was hardly the extent of the peasants' labor because they also planted, tended, and harvested their own vegetable gardens; raised, fed, milked, herded, and slaughtered their own livestock; tended their poultry; made butter and cheese; raised and treated the flax from which they wove, spun, and sewed their own garments; thatched their own roofs; and built their own houses periodically (a typical peasant house stood no longer than 30 years), often when commanded to do so by their lords.

This staggering workload was distributed among men, women, and children. Peasant children became engaged in work at such an early age that one historian has remarked that their socialization consisted almost entirely of learning their parents' work. From a very early age boys would follow their fathers into the fields to assist with the crops, while girls stayed with their mothers and aided them in the work of barn, house, and garden.

Women carried a particularly burdensome workload. During the seasons of the most-intensive farm labor, women worked alongside men in the fields, often guiding the plow teams and sewing the seed; during harvest, when the entire family passed the days in the fields, women bearing sickles cut the grain and gathered the sheaves—and, judging from surviving illustrations, they did so at least as often as men.

In addition to their huge share of fieldwork, women did nearly all the housework: caring for domestic animals, milking, shearing, cooking, making soap. They also engaged in many cottage industries, through which—if they were sufficiently prosperous to produce a surplus—they provided not only for their own families but also for other villagers. Two of these professions, cloth making and brewing, were conducted primarily by women. Medieval writings depicted spinning and weaving as the archetypal work of women and made the alewife a major stereotype in portrayals of village life.

There was a positive side to this extraordinary workload. By sharing so extensively in the daily business of staying alive, women reached equality or near equality with men in several social arenas. Rodney Hilton has argued that peasant women had more freedom and "a better situation in their own class than was enjoyed by women of the aristocracy or the bourgeoisie, a better situation perhaps than that of the women of early modern capitalist England." In late-medieval England peasant women were much more likely than were upper-class women to inherit land, to retain their lands and rights as widows, or, if they remarried, to pass on lands to the children of their first marriage rather than to their husbands. They often engaged in the management of family lands and in market activities such as moneylending, and in some places they even served as elected officials, as well as leaders in peasant rebellions.

In most of late-medieval Europe the average peasant family had three or four children. The importance of children as workers may have led peasants to desire more offspring, but family farmholdings were generally so small that a large family could be a virtual guarantee of poverty for the next generation. In most places, only the oldest son would inherit rights to the use of the house and land, and the others would be at a great disadvantage. The success of daughters depended largely on the dowries that their parents could provide them: the more daughters, the smaller the dowry for each.

Peasant houses offered a dramatic picture of the intense communality of peasant lives and their dependence on nature. In the smaller dwellings, often no larger than 10 by 20 feet, all family members slept in the same room. Larger dwellings might offer more privacy for some members of the family, but if peasants occupied a longhouse—a house type found throughout England and in much of northern Europe, measuring perhaps 15 by 50 feet—they would share their quarters with their livestock, which occupied stalls at one end of the house while the peasants slept at the other. Thus, even in their sleep, as daily in the garden and field, peasants were surrounded by the living things that sustained their own lives.

The body heat of the animals helped warm the peasant house, but the major source of heat was the central hearth—an open fire, built on flat stones near the center of the dwelling. The hearth also served to provide cooking heat: round-bottomed pots were laid in the fire or, less often, set or suspended above the coals by tripods or hooks. Bread was baked on the stones in the midst of the fire. Typically there was no chimney or hole in the roof, so the smoke lingered in the house. On winter nights peasants kept warm by sitting or lying on their sides near the fire, thus avoiding the smoke that filled the upper portions of the house; the hearth was the center for family socializing and storytelling.

Festive and Ritual Folklife

According to clerical opinion, peasants persisted in pagan practices long after the nobility had adopted a more or less orthodox Christianity. Indeed, the word *pagan* meant "people of the village or countryside," and clerics long assumed that such people were untouched by Christianity.

The reality seems to be more complex, suggesting that the peasantry, like the official Church itself, blended many of its earlier non-Christian customs with the new religion and did not distinguish the components of its festivals as "pagan" and "Christian," as we often do today, but experienced them as part of one continuous whole.

The Church fixed its major feasts on dates that had earlier marked pagan celebrations: for example, the Persian-Roman celebration of *Sol invictus* (Unconquered Sun) became Christmas, and the Celtic New Year's, Samhain (November 1), later became All Saints' Day. These festivals were retained because they possessed important social functions, marking major turning points in the agricultural calendar, breaks in the rhythm of seasonal work, times when peasants could socialize—not only relax but also conduct communal meals, go courting, and engage in other activities reinforcing the social ties that bound them to their fellow villagers.

Such rites remained as vital to country life in Christian times as they had been before, and the Church could not afford to neglect their importance. Thus, as early as 601 Pope Gregory the Great wrote instructions to his missionary Mellitus on how to re-adapt such traditions in converting the pagan Anglo-Saxons: "Because they have been used to slaughter many oxen in the sacrifices to devils, some solemnity must be exchanged for them on this account ... [so that they may] no longer offer beasts to the Devil, but kill cattle to the praise of God in their eating." Thus, November, known to the Anglo-Saxons as Blotmonath (the month of sacrifices), became the season for celebrating All Saints' Day (November 1), All Souls' Day (November 2), and especially, the feast of St. Martin (November 11), held at a transitional point in the year, marking the end of the work in the fields. At this time peasants slaughtered the animals that their limited stores of grain could not support through the winter. The break in the work cycle and the sudden abundance of food made early November a perfect time for feasting, as religious activities were combined with revelry and courtship.

Most of the holidays possessed religious and magical dimensions related to the all-consuming concern of staying alive, so that certain ritual activities for promoting vegetable, animal, and human fertility played major roles in the celebrations. In springtime in tenth-century Germany, as well as in many other parts of Europe before and since, peasants took to the fields with ritual activities aimed at ensuring good harvests. In 939 the abbess of Schildesche issued an order that "instead of parading like pagans through the fields," the parishioners should carry the image of the patron saint and then spend the night in the monastery courtyard "keeping solemn vigil over the holy relics"—before, they had very likely spent the night courting in the fields.

Thus, even the most official and sacred rituals of medieval Christian Europe were structured to incorporate the festive patterns of country life and to accommodate the peasants' considerable social needs, which were in turn dependent on the cycle of seasonal work and the workings of nature. Most village festivals possessed at least two dimensions: an official religious side and a festive social side, which sometimes stood in opposition to each other but which overlapped substantially. At Eastertide, for example, the solemn celebrations of Holy Week, climaxing at Easter Sunday, were followed in English villages by Hocktide, the following Monday and Tuesday, an important village festival during which young men and women probably participated in courting games. Similarly, the solemn late-spring processions of Corpus Christi (the Body of Christ)— in which the local priest, holding aloft the Eucharist (the communion bread symbolic of Christ's body), was led by the peasants in a circle around their village—possessed a secular counterpart: the beating of the bounds, a vitally important community observance. Three weeks before Corpus Christi, during the Rogation Days, the village men and boys made their own procession to all of the boundary markers on the outskirts of their village. Stopping at each of the markers—trees, ridges, rivers—and feasting and drinking at each, the men would throw boys up against the trees or toss them into the streams, marking precisely the territory of their shared interests and playfully initiating boys into their grown-up role of defending that territory and making it prosper.

No medieval festive season was more important than Christmas, not only because of its great religious significance but, especially for the peasants, because it marked the longest break in the entire work year, during which natural conditions guaranteed that there would be little work in the fields, thus granting time for nearly two weeks of continuous celebration: the Twelve Days of Christmas. The official Church celebrations— Christmas, New Year's, and Epiphany, falling at the beginning, middle, and end of the Twelve Days—provided a rich Christian context for the festivities. But there was an extensive secular side as well. Peasants were brought together with their lords in lavish feasts at the castle or the abbey, in which the two estates shared their festive folklife. To be sure, even in these festivities the lords exercised a demeaning dominance over the peasants. The villagers had to pay extra rent—by brewing ale and providing bread, chickens, and other foodstuffs for the feast. They were also treated unequally, according to their means: For example, at a Christmas banquet at Wells Cathedral, John de Cnappe, a well-off peasant, and his partner and tenants were provided with two loaves of white bread, beef, bacon, hen stew, cheese, and "as much beer as they will drink in the day." On the same day, Roger Bat, a poor peasant, had to provide "his own cloth, cup and trencher," but he could "take away all that is left on his cloth and shall have for himself and his neighbors one [loaf of white bread] cut in three for the ancient Christmas game"—probably a game similar to "King of the Bean," in which a single bean is concealed in a cake that is shared by many, and the person whose piece contains the bean becomes "king" for a day.

Yet even as they were set apart from the nobles, peasants would note the influence of their own lifestyles on the folklife of the nobles, as lords and ladies engaged in caroling, that is, circle dances accompanied by song, a dance form they had adopted from the peasantry. If during Christmas, as at every other time, the peasants gave more to their culture than they received, they were conspicuously present as the social force upon which late-medieval society was based.

See also: Christmas; Festivals and Celebrations; Harvest Festivals and Rituals; Knight; Martinmas; Peasants' Revolts; Plow and Plowing; Spinning and Weaving; Trickster; *Unibos*

—Carl Lindahl

Peasants' Revolts. Violent mass insurgences, mounted throughout the Middle Ages, through which various groups among the European underclass sought to enhance their socioeconomic status.

Though these were often labeled peasants' rebellions, urban workers—artisans, wage laborers, small traders, and others—were commonly involved, for such actions pitted the lower classes against the upper. Rooted in part in subversive folklore stressing egalitarianism as the fundamental fact of nature, uprisings against secular and ecclesiastical targets occurred sporadically as loosely organized groups of peasants, or their urban counterparts, vented their frustration at their oppression and deprivation. While none of these movements succeeded fully in redefining the role of the underclass, they collectively contributed to a gradual evolution of democratic ideals.

In the early Middle Ages such insurgences were limited mostly to local conflicts; however, from the fourteenth through the early sixteenth centuries European society witnessed many outbreaks of widespread protest among the lower classes, who took their grievances to the streets of major cities. The largest of such rebellions in England was the Peasants' Revolt of 1381, sometimes referred to as Wat Tyler's Rebellion; preceding it was the most infamous period of peasant unrest in France, the Parisian Jacquerie of the 1350s, as well as the 1378 Florentine uprising of artisan classes known as the Tumult of the Ciompi. Many years of underclass discontent reached their climax in Germany in an episode known today as the Peasant War of 1525.

Earlier in the medieval era smaller groups of peasants or urban poor rebelled against antagonists they deemed responsible for their impoverished conditions and limited freedoms. Thus, in 643 the Lombard king Rothari issued an edict condemning serfs who attacked landlords' property. In the ninth century, French and Italian estate owners established legal orders, such as the Edict of Pitres of 864, against peasants attempting to evade service or protesting rent increases beyond what their ancestors had customarily paid. The denial of traditional obligations of servitude led to a localized peasants' war in Normandy in 996, a brief revolt in Brittany in 1008, and uprisings in the Low Countries in 1095. The emergence of certain democratic heresies, such as the Alleluia enthusiasm in Italy in 1233, further fueled the flames of revolt by religious sects, including the Pastoureaux in France in 1251 (and again in 1320)—as well as those later inspired by Lollardism in fourteenth-century England. Other peasants simply disputed demands that they render tallage, and numerous such protesters were imprisoned in Orly in 1252 and in Bagneux in 1264.

Another key motive for mass protest was the collective desire for unrestricted access to nature's bounty, specifically the freedom to hunt, fish, and take wood from forests. Feeling certain of its rights to harvest flora and fauna, the peasantry first launched localized insurgences against landlords who attempted to disallow such practices, hence denying the people the building materials, fuel, and meat that their ancestors had procured freely.

Later, food shortages prompted larger protests, such as the rioting in Spain and Portugal (1333–1334) following consecutive bad harvests. The demand for access to natural resources remained a popular issue throughout the later Middle Ages. Folkloric outlaw ballads—such as the fifteenth-century "Rhymes of Robin Hood"—celebrated the adventures of common men who dared to live beyond legal authority, enjoying a utopian fellowship while partaking freely of forbidden bounty in the wilds.

Inadequate resources ultimately prompted peasants to seek other ways of procuring life-sustaining necessities. Many accepted work as artisans or day laborers for wages, thus leading to the manifestation of a rural proletariat throughout Europe. In the later Middle Ages most peasant rebellions took place in response to disappointments among people who first had experienced some measure of improved economic prospects only to be denied further hopes of progress. In the 1320s peasant uprisings flared up in Ypres, Bruges, and elsewhere in Flanders. The 1330s to the 1350s saw popular revolts emerge in Ghent, as well as the Cola di Rienzo rebellions in Rome. Demographic changes caused by the Black Death of the mid-fourteenth century, along with increasing taxation by governments embroiled in wars, created economic tensions and dislocation that erupted in violent protest. In many cases insurgent action was triggered by the articulation of themes of social equality as a natural ideal wrongly forsaken by cultural deviations. Such attempts at revolt ultimately provided the underclass with legendary heroes who dared to defy the authority of the establishment and sought to assert the natural rights of common people.

The English Peasants' Revolt of 1381 yielded three of the most notorious prototypes of the rebellious peasant leader. Following the oppressive Statute of Labourers of 1351 and a series of unjust poll taxes, the rebel priest John Ball first emerged as a popular hero proclaiming fundamental egalitarianism, exemplified in a famous couplet traditionally associated with him: "When Adam delved and Eve span, / Who was then the gentleman?" Ball, along with an ambiguous figure known as Jack Straw (probably a code name) and the dominant rebel spokesman Wat Tyler (who while in conference with the king was murdered by royal attendants, thus effectively terminating the revolt), all figure prominently in official records and popular recollections of this momentarily cataclysmic event. Following several days of violent symbolic action and demands (temporarily conceded by Richard II) for the end of serfdom, Wat Tyler was murdered by a royal partisan during a conference with the king, thus effectively terminating the revolt, and the other leaders were soon executed. The kings' men then displayed these rebels' heads upon London Bridge as a warning against further peasant aggression.

The 1381 uprising offers representative examples of the symbolic logic often employed by rebels in choosing targets of destruction. For instance, in St. Albans in 1381, following years of dispute over the abbot's mandate that hand-operated flour mills be outlawed and that the top half of every millstone be seized (thus forcing people to pay to use the abbey's horse-powered mill), the peasants broke into the abbey parlor, where the illegal millstones had been used to pave the floor. After removing the stones the people congregated and broke them into pieces, which were distributed in a ritual that mocked the breaking of bread in communion services. In London this sense of orchestrated carnivalesque spectacle included an attack on the Savoy Palace, which belonged to the hated aristocrat John of Gaunt. Rebels prohibited each other from pillaging the treasures; instead, they broke them and threw them into the Thames or the sewers. They set fire to the structure and used the nobleman's precious vestments to form an effigy, which they pierced with arrows and swords. Likewise, they sacked and burned Lambeth Palace, which belonged to the equally despised chancellor and archbishop, Simon Sudbury. While tossing his possessions into the flames, the people are said to have shouted, "A revel! A revel!" Hence, rather than randomly rioting, the insurgents often focused on signifiers of abusive authority, which they destroyed in a spirit of celebration.

Several prominent European peasant uprisings survive in popular imagination in the form of folkloric nicknames. The series of ultimately violent revolts in France in the 1350s, known as the Jacquerie, derived their name both from Jacques Bonhomme, a nickname traditionally applied to villains, and from *jacque* (a predecessor of the English word "jacket"), the name of the short blouse commonly worn by peasants. In central France from the 1360s through the end of the century, a localized series of outlaw actions by peasants (who abandoned their work and lived by pillaging) became known as the Tuchin movement, inspired by the word *touche* (woodland, moor) or *maquis*, the latter term eventually yielding the word *maquisards*, referring to underground resistance forces. In Flanders in 1379 a rising of the menial workers came to be known as the revolt of the Blue Thumbs (or Blue Nails), so-called because some of the protesters worked as dyers in the burgeoning textile industry. During a brief rebellion in Paris in 1382, a mob of urban poor raided an arms depot and stole thousands of lead mallets; the episode was thus remembered as the rising of the Maillotins. In Germany a series of sporadic revolts, from 1493 through 1517, were dubbed the Bundschuh after a type of footwear common among peasants. Such events thus live on in folk consciousness via the memorable images conceived to identify them.

As the peasantry gradually lost much of its sense of a hereditary claim to the land, it developed a keener, urban-based class consciousness, inspired in large part by mass insurgences of the people. Though the immediate social gains of most medieval peasant revolts were minimal and the establishment response was typically harsh, such actions ultimately signaled to European society the emergence of democratic egalitarianism.

See also: Peasants

—Roger Wood

Phallic Imagery. Male exhibitionist figures, especially those carved in stone, found throughout the Middle Ages, but especially predominant in the Romanesque period in Britain and France, with a distinct subtype, the so-called *spinario*, that derives from a classical statue in which the figure is portrayed with one leg drawn up across the other, ostensibly in order to remove a thorn from his foot, a pose that allows "accidental" exposure of the genitals.

In Spain a number of "megaphallic" corbel figures have recently been identified as the peasant upstart Marcolf, a trickster figure famed in medieval tales. Isolated images of the phallus are also found on the exterior corbel tables of French and Spanish Romanesque churches (and even in choir stall woodwork, as at Ciudad Rodrigo).

On a completely different scale, but also from the late Middle Ages, an increasing number of phallic images are coming to light from riverine deposits throughout Europe (but especially from the drowned villages of the Schelde estuary) in the form of small lead badges with pins for attachment to the clothing. These badges (which also depict the female sexual organs) constitute a genre of popular imagery of disproportionate and hitherto unrecognized importance. The sudden emergence of this sexual iconography in the fifteenth century is probably to be attributed to the rediscovery of caches of small late-Roman bronzes, among which phallic *tintinnabula* (bells; the origin of the bells tied round the "necks" of several phallus badges and French tokens) and phallic pendants are common. It is uncertain whether these badges functioned apotropaically (i.e., to ward off evil); to modern eyes, at least, they must often seem humorous, though laughter, of course, was also a medieval specific against the evil eye. The many daily activities in which the badge phalli are engaged include crewing ships, carrying a phallus-crowned vulva on a litter (in parody of a Marian procession?), pushing a wheelbarrow full of phalli, or acting as a mount for a fiddler or as "hawk" for a vulva on horseback, while still other phallus-raptors perch on the stylized vulvas on which they prey. The concept of independent, ambulant sexual parts is reminiscent of the similarly dismembered organs found in late-medieval French riddles and such fabliaux as "The Knight Who Made Cunts and Assholes Speak."

Another such badge depicts a hood, from the face of which protrudes a thick phallus, visual confirmation of the piece of sexual lore that the character of the nose reveals that of the penis (attested in medieval times, in a Latin tag from the medical school at Salerno). A particularly grisly instance of this equation occurred on the death of Simon de Montfort at the battle of Evesham in 1265, when his body was mutilated, his genitals cut off, and the testicles hung on either side of his nose.

Although much rarer, winged phalli are also found among the marginal illustrations of illuminated manuscripts. Another phallus-bird adorns a fourteenth-century wooden casket, where, in a notable pun, its glans (pecked at by a real bird) is positioned so as to pun visually on the acorn (*glans*) that hangs from the adjacent oak tree. One *Roman de la rose* (Romance of the Rose) manuscript even depicts nuns plucking phalli from a tree growing in its margin, and another tree bearing similar fruit is depicted on an early-fifteenth-century German casket. A monstrous, outsize phallus-bird, which appears to watch a couple as they copulate, is also the subject of a unique late-fifteenth-century Italian engraving; such rare survivors remind us that this category of imagery is peculiarly prone to deliberate destruction. As recently as the 1970s, for example, a small wooden fifteenth-century figure of a man masturbating was broken off the underside of the chancel stall canopy in Ripon Minster, England (another contemporary example of this subject survives in the stallwork of Oviedo Cathedral, Spain). Safe from the depredations of prudes and iconoclasts, several phallic figures survive on English cathedral roof bosses.

Ithyphallic figures (i.e., depicting erect penises) are to be found applied to vessels such as earthenware jugs (especially the so-called knight-jugs in thirteenth-century Scarborough ware) and bronze *aquamanili* (water vessels); there are even late-fifteenth-century German glass phalliform drinking vessels extant, and a unique unnoticed representation of a woman drinking from one is depicted on one of the supporters to a Bristol misericord (c. 1520). The series of late-medieval bronze ithyphallic figures earlier identified as *ae-olipiles* (fire blowers) are now thought to derive from ornamental garden fountains, forerunners of the celebrated Brussels "pissing mannekin"—a Renaissance statuette in the form of a small boy urinating, cast in 1619, which has spawned numerous imitations.

The case of the priest of Inverkeithing, Scotland, who in Easter week 1282 compelled young girls to take part in a dance that he led, carrying a phallus-topped pole, "in honor of Priapus," seems to have been part of some genuinely phallic (fertility?) ritual, but it serves to remind us that performance is also an aspect of iconography. Some time before 1327 at Pamiers near Toulouse, a festival known as the Cent Drutz (Hundred Lovers) included a procession in which members of the clergy were satirized by banners depicting male and female genitalia. The use of sex organs as satirical weapons is similarly attested in Zurich in 1455, when an apprentice hired a painter to depict four coats of arms featuring male and female genitals. The inevitable French pun on *vit* (penis) and *vie* (life), besides appearing in riddles and visually in an extant *rébus de Picardie* (c. 1500), was even the subject of a daring burlesque political procession or charivari in the opening years of the sixteenth century entitled *Le vit de François Premier* (The Penis [Life] of Francis the First), in which a gigantic phallus in a pageant car was pulled through the streets of Paris and on-lookers were invited to come and flagellate the royal member.

Superficially similar, but only distantly related, are images of the phallus in wax and dough. It is well known that images of the organs of both sexes were baked in bread in antiquity, and there is evidence in works of the later Middle Ages for the continued production of both: in the eleventh-century German-Latin poem *Ruodlieb* there is reference to both *coronellas* (ring-shaped rolls) and *menclas* (i.e., *mentulas*, penis-shaped rolls). Also from the threshold of the early modern period is a passage from Sir Thomas More's *Dialogue Concerning Heresies* (1528): a newly married English couple visit the church of St. Valéry in Picardy, where they find, to their astonishment, that the local infallible preventative against the stone (i.e., gall- and bladder stones) involves measuring the sexual organ (*gere*) in question so that a votive model of it could be made: "for lyke as in other pylgrymages ye se hanged vp legges of waxe or armes or suche other partes so was in that chapell all theyr offrynges yt honge aboute the walles none other thynge but mennes gere & womens gere made in waxe." An actual example of just such a wax phallus (though evidently used here as a lucky charm) may be seen hanging from the drone of a bagpipe (itself a medieval phallic symbol) depicted in an engraving issued circa 1470–1480 in Ferrara. In this Italian context, there is a most suggestive letter written by the poet Pietro Aretino, ten years after the scandal caused by the publication of his *16 sonetti lussuriosi* (16 Lascivious Sonnets), also entitled *I modi* (The [Sexual] Positions), and illustrated by the engravings of Marcantonio Raimondi, from original designs by Giulio Romano in Venice in 1527: "It would seem to me that the thing which is given to us by nature to preserve the race, should be worn around the neck as a pendant, or pinned onto the cap like a badge." We must note, however, that Aretino specifically does not say that such is in fact the fashion, but it seems not unreasonable to suspect that this was indeed the practice, in the light of the Dutch badges, the Ferrarese bagpiper, and the ancient custom of wearing phallus-shaped amulets, which survives to the present day.

Reformers frequently inveighed against the phallic rites that they had discovered: practices to promote fertility or overcome barrenness, which we may safely assume reached back well into the Middle Ages. When Protestants took the Alpine village of Embrun in 1585, for example, they were horrified to discover the phallus of St. Foutin (the saint's original name, Photinus, had been folk-etymologized as if it derived from French *foutre*, "fuck"), its glans stained red with libations of wine, called *saint vinaigre* (holy vinegar), which was then collected and used by women in "a rather strange custom."

There are many unequivocally phallic symbols apparent in late-medieval art. Knives and all types of thrusting weapons are obvious examples; consider the late-medieval dagger known as a ballok-knyf (featuring a plain upright haft flanked at its base by two testicular protuberances). "I am the sheath; you are the sword," says a girl to her lover in a fifteenth-century German Carnival drama. The pilgrim's staff is another example: the climactic moment illustrated in some *Roman de la rose* manuscripts depicts the pilgrim-lover thrusting his staff through the aperture in the base of the statue of Venus, and several Dutch badges depict a frontally presented vulva on pilgrimage with rosary, pilgrim's hat, and phallus-tipped staff.

Phalluses and phallic images invade the iconography of the dream world: in the Middle English *Partenope of Blois* a husband who believes he is being cuckolded dreams that "he thogte he sawe hys neygbore drawe oute hys swerde, / And fulle hys scawbarte [scabbard] he thogte that he pyssed." Whatever the psychological implications, the English mystic Margery Kempe (c. 1373–c. 1440) was assailed by "horybyl sychtys [sights] & abhominabyl," with all sorts of men "schewing her [their] bar membrys vn-to hir."

It is probably no coincidence that the popular dream manual *Somnium Danielis* (Dream of Daniel) does not feature the dream of losing one's penis before about 1475, when a manual in Rome appeared that interpreted dreaming of loss of the penis to mean failing in an endeavor, but such loss due to witchcraft had become a very real fear at precisely this time. The *Malleus maleficarum* (Hammer of Witches, c. 1485) refers to the belief that witches assembled collections of up to 30 penises and put them into birds' nests or shut them up in boxes. Both species of prison are depicted in contemporary art, the former on a Dutch badge of a tree in which several such "birds" perch, the latter as part of a woodcut illustrating superstitions in the 1486 Augsburg edition of Hans Vintler's *Blumen der Tugend* (Flowers of Chastity).

See also: Bestiality; Iconography; Scatology; Sheela-na-Gig

—Malcolm Jones

Pilgrimage [From Latin *per agere*, "through the field"]. A journey to a religious shrine in order to pay homage to a recognized intercessor, and through that activity to pay homage or request a special favor from God.

Pilgrimage has served a variety of functions in virtually every religion and civilization. It reached its zenith in Western European Christendom during the eleventh–thirteenth centuries, with thousands of pilgrims visiting more than 10,000 pilgrimage sanctuaries yearly in Europe alone. Underlying goals for pilgrims were legion: seeing and reverencing a holy site or relic, gaining pardon for a specific sin, obtaining a specific type of indulgence, fulfilling vows, or paying penalties, as prescribed by canon or civil law. Some adventurous persons made pilgrimages

purely for pleasure or out of curiosity about new lands. The majority of pilgrims probably traveled for a combination of these reasons.

Medieval pilgrimage sanctuaries can be divided into three basic ranks: (1) places connected directly with Jesus, the Virgin Mary, the Apostles, or a few early Christians; (2) shrines linked with important, well-known saints and martyrs, their relics, or their miracles—often promoted by powerful religious communities; (3) local sanctuaries devoted to lesser-known saints (sometimes not officially recognized by the Church) or places that commemorated popular beliefs about miraculous occurrences. The three most important pilgrimage destinations were Jerusalem, Rome, and Santiago de Compostela—all of which have long, distinguished ecclesiastical histories. The next most important sites include such shrines as Canterbury, England (site of the martyrdom and sepulcher of St. Thomas Becket); Cologne, Germany (tomb of the Three Magi); Assisi, Italy (sepulcher of St. Francis); Bari, Italy (relics of St. Nicholas); Mont-Saint-Michel, France (appearance of the Archangel Michael).

The least renowned today but the most "popular" in their development (in terms of having been most, and most directly, influenced by folk culture) were the myriad of smaller shrines visited by pilgrims from nearby towns and regions. These shrines became localized pilgrimage centers for a variety of reasons. Some were founded to commemorate a miraculous act that had occurred at the site (e.g., the sudden appearance in Loreto, Italy, of the Virgin Mary's childhood home, brought to the site by angels); others were devoted to local saints (e.g., Winifred of Wales, whose relics were translated to the monastery of Shrewsbury, England, in 1138). Still others were created to celebrate a supernatural event (the Holy House of Walsingham was built after the widow Richeldis witnessed an out-of-season snowfall outlining the dimensions the shrine was to have). Many shrines had healing properties, some for specific afflictions (San Juan de Ortega, Spain, was visited by Queen Isabella I of Spain in her search for a cure for her infertility). Other holy sites were visited in pilgrimage by individuals or groups seeking help in curing plagues or changing weather patterns (rain to drought or vice versa). In some instances, pilgrims' petitions had been answered at home, but gratitude caused them to go on a pilgrimage to thank the appropriate saint or fulfill a vow.

One could make a pilgrimage alone, but there was safety in numbers. Wealthier pilgrims would travel with their retinues, and occasionally towns or guilds would send a communal delegation. Most pilgrims walked, but the more fortunate traveled on horseback or used pack animals. Pilgrimage to distant areas (such as Jerusalem or Compostela) could take more than a year to complete; a pilgrim's properties were protected by law during his or her absence. Because long-distance pilgrimages consumed both time and money, shorter pilgrimages to closer, local shrines gained in popularity.

Sometimes created to promote a pilgrimage site, sometimes in response to the arrival of pilgrims, many miracle tale collections exist for both well-known and more obscure saints. Some collections are specific to a shrine or relic and serve as a who's who of the devout who were cured there (e.g., the 28 miracles effected by the relic of the hand of St. James in Reading Abbey, England, from 1127 to 1189). Others are collections about miracles wrought in a variety of locales by a single saint (such as those narrated in the *Cantigas de Santa María*). Many of the collections describe a "slice of life," treating all—upper and lower classes, saints and sinners—in the same fashion. To a greater or lesser degree, all miracle collections describe archetypal patterns of wondrous acts: touching a rod to the ground to create a spring; curing blindness by touching the afflicted eyes with holy water, an amulet, or some other holy, pertinent object; rescuing a victim from demons; the strange breaking of captives' chains, usually so that Christians might escape from the clutches of the infidel.

Dante, in his letter to Can Grande, uses three words to denote pilgrims: *palmieri, romei, peregrini* (palmers, romers, pilgrims). Each of these terms designates the pilgrims' destination to one of the three most important shrines and also signals the importance of the symbols and the dress of pilgrims. Jerusalem pilgrims (*palmieri*) were often depicted carrying palm branches as souvenirs of their trip to the Holy Land. Pilgrims to Rome (*romei*) could purchase small badges made like the keys of St. Peter to sew to their garments. Pilgrims to Santiago de Compostela (*peregrini*) became the most popular in their form of dress and insignias. The broad-brimmed hat—brim turned up and held in place with a scallop shell—gave the pilgrim practical relief from the burning sun or the driving rain. The long cape, with a shorter shoulder cape, served as both coat and bedroll. The staff and purse, however, developed their own history—not only for practicality but also as representative items. The staff represented the "third leg" of the Trinity and helped to fight off the hounds of the devil (and other wild beasts encountered en route), while the purse was open at the top, signaling the ideals of charity and openness. This symbolism was popular; it occurred in sermons as early as the twelfth century and persisted as popular metaphoric imagery in literature through the fifteenth century.

Pilgrimage was fraught with dangers, but it tempted those contemplating it with rich rewards of freedom from the mundane, protection of one's land, and escape from military service, as well as the opportunity to see new, exotic lands. Pilgrimage could also serve as a link between this world and the next. Belief in the otherworld was evidenced in Ireland, for example, where in the Middle Ages people believed that St. Patrick had descended into a cave and passed through it into a vision of life after death. Some persons, disapproving of pilgrimage, warned of the danger to one's soul. Proverbs such as the Spanish "Ir romera, volver ramera" [Leave as a (female) pilgrim, return as a prostitute] speak to the negative connotations of pilgrimage, which suggests that it is a threat to the soul and to social stability.

As early as the fourth century, St. Cyril of Jerusalem complained that slivers of the True Cross were being "distributed piecemeal to all the world." By the fourteenth century skepticism and blatant disbelief were already attested in literature: Chaucer's Pardoner in *The Canterbury Tales* is said to have sold pigs' bones as relics while on a pilgrimage to the tomb of St. Thomas Becket. The Reformation ended the widespread belief in the efficacy of pilgrimage. The Protestant John Calvin (1509–1564) signaled the foolhardiness of the people's belief by publishing an account of the multiple instances of relics worshiped in Europe at that time: for example, the numerous heads of John the Baptist and vials of breath of the Virgin.

In spite of a severe decline in the numbers of pilgrimages, popular pilgrimage did not die out completely, either during or after the Reformation, and many shrines are seeing a resurgence in the numbers of pilgrims who visit them. Pilgrimage was also brought to the New World, where it became integrated into the local customs of many of its populations.

See also: Becket, Saint Thomas; James the Elder, Saint; Relics; Saints, Cults of the

—Linda Davidson and Maryjane Dunn

Plow and Plowing. The farm implement and work most crucial for sustaining large populations, instrumental in the development of medieval Europe's urban centers.

Evidence of a field system of agriculture from the Iron Age (c. sixth–first centuries B.C.E.) forward attests to the repeated use of some form of implement to prepare soil for planting in Western Europe. At first little more than a sturdy, conveniently shaped bough with a pointed end, the early plow was used to scratch the surface of the soil. Some of the simpler plows could be used even without a draft animal to pull them; such implements as the Scottish *cashrom* (foot plow, operated by one man, and in use into the twentieth century) could serve small populations in hilly regions. The symmetrical hook-plow, more common in more-populous areas from ancient times, permitted adjacent furrows, grooves in the ground made by the coulter (a long, pointed shaft designed to penetrate the soil), followed by the share (a wedge-shaped blade to widen the furrow). Hook-plows worked well in the lighter soils of Mediterranean Europe, where they remained the preferred plow type throughout the Middle Ages. However, they could not turn the soil, and they were very inefficient in the thick soils of northern Europe.

Northern European agriculture was greatly aided by the introduction of the wheeled plow, developed first, but little used, by the Romans. The wheeled plow possessed a moldboard, which turned the soil to the side. This heavier equipment required a larger plowing team. The Domesday Book (1086) specifies eight draft animals, but no surviving medieval illustration pictures more than four. In his twelfth-century *Description of Wales* Gerald of Wales comments that the Welsh used oxen as plow beasts, sometimes in pairs but more often four at a time. He also comments that the typical Welsh plowman walked backward, leading the animals dragging the plow and encouraging the beasts forward with words, song, or whistling. This practice has been explained as an effort to forestall damage to the plow by spotting rocks close to the soil's surface and reflects another concession made to the influence of terrain on plowing practices.

Since maneuvering the cumbersome equipment and multiple-animal teams posed problems even for the most adroit plowmen, the wheeled plow favored working fields in long strips—a furrow-long, or furlong—over the square plots achieved with both ard and hook-plow. *Piers Plowman* suggests that a half acre could be plowed in a long morning's work. Ultimately, however, the particular conditions of the soil dictated the predominant pattern of plowing, and the climate determined its exact timing.

The wheeled plow was used as early as the sixth century in south-central Europe, but the technology spread slowly, and it was the eleventh century before most of northern Europe had adopted it. The greatly improved grain yields made possible by the new tool contributed to a population explosion and the establishment of major urban centers in the North.

Just as important as the wheeled plow for increasing the productivity of the land was the three-field system of land use. In the early Middle Ages large-scale plowing and planting generally involved two fields, one lying fallow and the second divided between autumn and spring plantings. The more complex three-field system existed as early as the ninth century but did not come into general use until the twelfth. As one field lay fallow, a second and third were devoted to fall and spring crops, respectively. Routinely rotated to ensure the continued fertility of the land, these fields were divided into strips—each strip approximately 24 furrows wide—and these strips were assigned to all families involved in cultivation.

Peasants might own sufficient land to feed their families, but they needed access to a plow and plow animals if they were to work that much land, and both plow and animals factored into the relative wealth of a family. Peasants who did not have the means for independent subsistence, though, might hire themselves out to labor for others or borrow a neighbor's plow and animals to work their holdings.

More than just an important item of preindustrial material culture, the plow not only provided an efficient way to order the natural environment, it also shaped the conventions of parceling land itself: the vocabulary by which individual holdings of Anglo-Saxon England were established generally relates to the act of plowing. In Kent householders measured their holdings in *sulung*, a term directly related to the Old English *sulh*, "plow," and cognate with the Latin *sulcus*, "furrow." Moreover, after repeated Danish incursions in the Northeast, specifically the area north of the Welland, the unit of land was the *plogesland*, an obvious cognate to plow.

It is not surprising that the plow, so instrumental in shaping the land, would also be seen as shaping the sky. In medieval England the constellation Ursa Major, now commonly known as the Big Dipper, was called "Arthur's Plow," after the legendary king, and the neighboring constellation Boötes, identified as "the Herdsman" in other eras, was known as "the Plowman," as its brightest star, Arcturus, was called the "Plow Star."

The plowing practices of England intersect the customary cycles of seasonal and Christian ritual with the observance of Plow Monday, the holiday falling on the Monday after Epiphany and concluding the 12-day celebration of Christmas. Also known as Rock Monday, or St. Distaff's Day in some places, Plow Monday signaled a return to work: women resumed their hearth-side spinning, and men anticipated a return to the fields for the year's first plowing, which occurred between Plow Monday (about January 7) and Candlemas (February 2) to allow time for the manure and stubble to decompose before planting began. A fifteenth-century record mentions a custom to ensure "good beginninge of the yere" and good fortune throughout the year: men would lead a plow "about the fire," in one symbolic act joining the instrument with which they earned their bread to the hearth, the center of domestic life.

In postmedieval celebrations of Plow Monday, young plowmen of a village assembled to drag and display a plow—often referred to as the fool plow or white plow, which suggests its decoration—from house to house. The procession, led by a man dressed up as an old woman and accompanied by a fool carrying a stick or whip, collected pennies from each household.

See also: Festivals and Celebrations; Peasants

—Michelle Miller

Prester John. Legendary Christian priest-king of India.

The first documented account of Prester John can be traced to *Historia de duabus civitatibus* (History of the Two Cities), the twelfth-century chronicle by the German ecclesiastic Otto,

Bishop of Freising. Bishop Hugh of Jabala, whom Otto met in Viterbo in 1145, told him about a certain Nestorian Christian king and priest, Presbyter Iohannes, who lived far to the east (in what is now south Asia) and had fought the kings of the Persians and Medes. Bishop Hugh's story possibly alluded to the attack and defeat of the Seljuk sultan Sanjar by the Qara-Khitai, or Black Cathayans, a people subject to the Chinese empire, on the steppes near Samarkand in September 1141. Prester John is said to have descended from the lineage of the Magi and to have possessed great wealth, including a scepter made from a single emerald.

Stories about Prester John, however, were widespread in Western Europe even earlier and were linked to the Christians and the legend of the shrine of the apostle Thomas in southern India. According to an anonymous tract written in the year 1122, John, patriarch of the Indians, came to Rome to visit Pope Calixtus II in the company of papal envoys returning from Constantinople. He spoke of his capital city as Hulna, through which flowed the Physon, one of the rivers of Paradise, whose waters were full of gold and precious stones. He gave a detailed description of the shrine in which lay the uncorrupted body of St. Thomas. On the saint's feast day the dead apostle administered the wafer to all, but he refused it to sinners, who then repented or died. This incident was corroborated in a letter by Odo of Rheims, abbot of Saint-Rémy, who says that he was present at the papal court during the visit of an Indian archbishop whom he does not name. More restrained than the anonymous account, Odo explains that the archbishop, through an interpreter, told the story of how he and his people had been converted to Christianity by St. Thomas, whose body was preserved in the cathedral. According to Odo, however, St. Thomas did not distribute the wafer but received gifts from the parishioners instead. The scholars Charles F. Beckingham and Vsevolod Slessarev agree that archbishop John could not have come from India, mainly because of the confusion about India's location. Slessarev believes that he came from Edessa in Syria, a place that was also associated with St. Thomas.

Twenty years after Otto of Freising's account there appeared a letter supposedly written by Prester John and addressed to the Byzantine emperor Manuel Comnenus. A copy was forwarded to Holy Roman Emperor Frederick I, Barbarossa. The exact date of the letter is not known, but according to the chronicler Alberic de Trois Fontaines (1232–1252), it was written in 1165. Some consider Pope Alexander III's letter to the "King of India," dated September 27, 1177, to be a reply to Prester John. In his letter Prester John claimed to be the Christian ruler of the great expanse of the Three Indias. His kingdom was filled with enormous wealth and exotic flora and fauna, and his subjects were free from vice. There are more than 100 manuscripts of the letter's Latin version, and Friedrich Zarncke, who produced the standard edition, established that there were five later versions, each with additions. Most scholars agree that the letter was written in Latin, although Alexander Vasiliev claims that it was written in Greek. Slessarev shows that the Greek words in the letter were loanwords of official titles familiar in the West. There is also consensus among scholars that it was written in Western Europe, since the author mentions the small quantity and poor quality of horses in India, a well-known fact among Western merchants trading in the crusader states. The letter was translated into a number of European languages and Hebrew, and it became widely popular. Songs purporting to contain parts of the letter were sung by minstrels throughout Europe.

Through the centuries Prester John has been placed in different parts of the world. In the late twelfth century he was confused with Genghis, the great khan of the Mongols. Yet travelers to central and East Asia could not find him there. In the thirteenth century Marco Polo asserted that Prester John was the Nestorian ruler of the Turkish Kerait clan named Togrul, whose title, *Unc* or *Ung Khan* (*Wang Khan* to the Chinese), could have been confused with "King John." In his letter Prester John claimed to rule the Three Indias. When he was not found in the first two (i.e., north and south India), it was assumed that he was in the third India, identified by medieval geographers as the Horn of Mrica, or Ethiopia. The confusion between India and Ethiopia was an old one. Moreover, Ethiopia was practically inaccessible to the Western world, and the shift of Prester John's kingdom from Asia to Mrica was related to the visit of the Ethiopian embassy to the West in the fourteenth century. Prester John therefore came to be associated with the Christian emperor of Ethiopia. It was only after Mrica had been circumnavigated by the Portuguese that an accurate account of Prester John's kingdom was gleaned from the writings of Father Francisco Alvarez.

Although the location of Prester John's empire was supposedly established, his legend remained alive. The Jews took an interest in Prester John and translated the letter into Hebrew after hearing the story of Eldad ha-Dani, who claimed to be a member of the Ten Lost Tribes of Israel, among the inhabitants of Prester John's empire. Vasiliev mentions medieval Russian interest in India's riches and marvels. Modern scholars have suggested that Prester John's letter was a Western forgery, used as a piece of propaganda to help Emperor Frederick Barbarossa in his struggle against Alexander III. In an essay in *Prester John, the Mongols, and the Ten Lost Tribes*, Bernard Hamilton states that Prester John was a creation of the world of the Crusades. Crusaders were glad to learn of the presence of Christians in the East, potential allies in their fight against Islam. The

Prester John legend remained alive for four centuries. Yet even when he was no longer needed and his importance faded, Prester John lived on in the literary and historical imagination of the West.

See also: Crusades; Travel Literature

—Binita Mehta

Proverbs. Concise, traditional statements of communally accepted truths, expressed as metaphors in fixed, easily memorized form, passed on orally from generation to generation, and used to convey wisdom, morality, and group values.

Popularity and Provenience of Medieval Proverbs
Proverbs permeate medieval literature, and they were also in frequent use at all levels of oral communication, from didactic sermons to everyday discourse. Latin served as the lingua franca among the learned population of medieval Europe, so it should not be surprising that classical Greek and Latin proverbs remained in circulation. Biblical proverbs and wisdom literature in general were also in wide circulation and were employed freely as formulaic rules of behavior and social interaction. Some of these sayings from the wisdom literature might best be described as *sententiae*, or sententious remarks, for not all of them did in fact possess true proverbial currency among the general population. Just as there was a degree of separation in the Middle Ages between the religious and secular spheres and between the learned and popular spheres, there also existed a split between Latin *sententiae* and vernacular folk proverbs. These two genres were, however, usually treated identically by medieval authors, and it is often impossible to make clear delineations between them.

There are three reasons for the predominance of proverbial language in the Middle Ages: First, there was a deep-rooted interest in communally expressed wisdom, which is easier to remember than philosophical treatises. Second, proverbs were useful educational tools for teaching proper social conduct and were also well suited to language instruction, where they were employed in translation exercises: students translated Latin proverbs into their native vernaculars and vice versa. Third, together with biblical passages, proverbs served didactic purposes for preachers, especially when they delivered sermons in the vernacular. Moreover, it is important to remember that the great majority of medieval people lived in an oral society in which, of necessity, they communicated rules, regulations, insights, advice, and the like in a linguistic form that could easily be remembered and handed on. The short proverb, with its formulaic structure and such poetic devices as alliteration, rhyme, and parallelism, was a perfect linguistic device for achieving this goal.

There are basically three groups of medieval proverbs, which makes their study so interesting and yet, at the same time, so challenging. There are, first of all, the classical and biblical proverbs that circulated initially in Latin and then in translation in the various vernacular languages. The proverb "Big fish eat little fish" is an example of the classical proverbs, while "Pride goes before a fall" (Prov. 16:18) is one of many common biblical proverbs. The fact that such proverbs were translated verbatim from Latin into the various vernacular languages explains why even today they are identical in the modern European languages. The second group, and an amazingly large one, comprises those *sententiae* and proverbs in Latin that originated during the Middle Ages. Many proverbs, for example, "New brooms sweep clean" originated in medieval Latin and were subsequently translated into the other European languages. Hans Walther has assembled nine massive volumes of *Proverbia sententiaeque latinitatis medii aevi* (Medieval Latin Proverbs and Sententious Sayings) listing 44,468 Latin proverbs, with hundreds of variants, from Latin collections, both major and obscure, as well as other written sources. The third group consists of sayings indigenous to a particular vernacular language, such as, for example, the English "Young saint, old devil" or "When Adam delved and Eve span, who was then the gentleman?" However, it must be remembered that teachers in the schools used vernacular proverbs as well as classical ones as translation exercises, so that these very proverbs often appear in Latin as well. In addition to the educational force that helped spread many of these proverbs throughout Europe, there was also plenty of social, economic, and political intercourse that caused vernacular proverbs to be borrowed and translated.

Major Collections
The most comprehensive comparative study of medieval proverbs and proverb collections of the Germanic and Romance languages is Samuel Singer's *Sprichwörter des Mittelalters* (Medieval Proverbs). Singer studies the oldest Germanic proverbs, found in such texts as the Old High German heroic song *Hildebrandslied* (Lay of Hildebrand, c. 810) and the Old Icelandic *Eddas* (thirteenth century). He presents the proverbs contained in the *Dialogue of Salomon and Marcolf* (c. 1180–1190) and analyzes those presented in the work of the ninth-century monk Notker of St. Gall. In addition to Singer's work, there are also richly annotated editions of such major individual proverb collections as the *Fecunda ratis* (The Richly Laden Ship, 1023) by Egbert von Liège, the Latin *Proverbia rusticorum* (Proverbs of the Peasants, thirteenth century), the French *Proverbes au vilain* (Peasant Proverbs, thirteenth century), and *Bescheidenheit* (Discretion, c. 1215–1230) by the German poet Freidank. The last was critically edited in 1834 by Wilhelm Grimm, who also assembled a small collection of

Middle High German proverbs that he had found in German literary works. Singer's exemplary work is still being continued today by a paremiographical (that is, concerned with collecting proverbs) research team compiling a *Thesaurus proverbiorum medii aevi* (Thesaurus of Medieval Proverbs) in Bern, Switzerland. The first volume appeared in 1995. The thesaurus will ultimately contain about 80,000 medieval proverbs from the Germanic and Romance languages that have been located in European literary works from between 500 and 1500.

The study of medieval proverbs is best divided into paremiographical and paremiological (study of proverbs) aspects. It should not be surprising that there exist large numbers of Latin and vernacular proverb collections. The most influential collection of classical Latin proverbs is without doubt the *Disticha Catonis* (Cato's Distichs, third century C.E.), which became very popular in the Middle Ages. Teachers used it for instructional purposes in schools, and there were many vernacular translations that played a major role in popularizing classical proverbial wisdom in medieval times.

Other major European collections usually present vernacular proverbs in Latin translation, offer both vernacular and Latin versions of the same proverbs, or assemble only vernacular texts. Noteworthy among these regional collections are, in Dutch, *Proverbia communia sive seriosa* (Common and Serious Proverbs, ten editions between 1480 and 1497); in English, *Durham Proverbs* (a manuscript of Anglo-Saxon proverbs from the eleventh century), *The Proverbs of Alfred* (thirteenth century), and *Proverbs of Hendyng* (fourteenth century); in French, *Proverbes au vilain* (thirteenth century) and *Les proverbes Seneke* (Proverbs of Seneca, thirteenth century); in German, *Proverbia Henrici* (Proverbs of Henry, thirteenth century), Freidank's *Bescheidenheit* (c. 1215–1230), and a Latin version, *Proverbia Fridanci* (Freidank's Proverbs, fifteenth century); in Spanish, *Libro de los buenos proverbios* (Book of Good Proverbs, fourteenth century) and Santob de Carrín's *Proverbios Morales* (Moral Sayings, fourteenth century). These and other early collections are of great significance for historical studies of individual proverbs, since they help to establish the earliest variants of proverbs that are often still current today. Most of them have now been incorporated into superb historical proverb dictionaries that also include the vernacular proverbs found in the literary works of the various languages. Of particular value are the reference volumes by Bartlett Jere Whiting, *Proverbs, Sentences, and Proverbial Phrases from English Writings Mainly before 1500*; James W. Hassell, *Middle French Proverbs, Sentences, and Proverbial Phrases*; and Giuseppe Di Stefano, *Dictionnaire des locutions en moyen français* (Dictionary of Middle French Phrases).

Proverbs in Literary Context

Paremiologists, folklorists, and literary historians have also turned to the use and function of proverbs in medieval poems, dramas, epics, and various prose works. Earlier literary investigations merely identified and listed proverbial texts, without any contextual information. Nevertheless, such collections of proverbs from literary works became important textual materials for the above-mentioned historical dictionaries. Today scholars usually combine the identification of proverbs in a particular medieval work with an interpretation of its use, function, and meaning. There is hardly a major author or literary genre that has not been investigated for its proverbs, from medieval exempla and fabliaux to vernacular sermons, from folksongs to the "Ballade des proverbes" (fifteenth century) by François Villon, from *Beowulf* to the *Eddas*, from German heroic epics to the French chansons de geste to the internationally disseminated Arthurian epics. Even such medieval Latin beast epics as the *Ysengrimus* (1148–1150) or the tenth-century Latin plays of the German nun Hrosvitha of Gandersheim have been studied. Major studies exist on the proverbial speech included in the works of Geoffrey Chaucer, John Gower, John Lydgate, Chrétien de Troyes, Eustache Deschamps, François Villon, Hugo von Trimberg, Oswald von Wolkenstein, and Johannes von Tepl. Two investigations stand out for their methodological and interpretive value. Elisabeth Schulze-Busacker's comprehensive study of medieval French epics includes both a collection of 2,500 proverbs in their literary context and detailed interpretive comments on medieval French proverbs in general and on their literary and cultural significance in the literary works of Chrétien de Troyes, Gautier d'Arras, Hue de Rotelande, and others. And Wernfried Hofmeister speaks of "proverbial microtexts" and establishes useful criteria (e.g., form, structure, metaphor) for discovering little-known, or perhaps yet unknown, proverbs in medieval literature.

Hofmeister's methodology will be particularly helpful when scholars look in more detail at such major German *Minnesänger* (love poets) as Reinmar von Hagenau or Walther von der Vogelweide or at the lyric poetry of the troubadours. While a few shorter articles do exist on proverbs in poems, a much more inclusive study is needed, as it is also for some of the lesser-known epics. There have been several studies of the *Nibelungenlied* (Song of the Nibelungs, c. 1200) and the *Roman de la rose* (Romance of the Rose, c. 1275–1280), but the German *Kudrunlied* (Lay of Kudrun, c. 1230) still awaits examination, and scholars are just beginning to express interest in such epics as the *Canso de la Crosada* (Song of the Crusade, twelfth–thirteenth centuries) describing the Albigensian Crusade. It would, of course, also be of considerable value if scholars were to look at nonliterary texts, such as letters, reports, chronicles, and legal documents. In this vein, the Paston Letters (fifteenth century) that were exchanged by a noble family in the East Anglian region of England show that the letter writers used proverbs in giving counsel, as supporting arguments, and to enhance style. And for legal documents, there is also Brigitte Janz's unique analysis of 105 proverbs found in the medieval German law book *Sachsenspiegel* (1221–1224) by Eike von Repgow.

The Iconography of Proverbs

There is one final fascinating aspect to the study of proverbs in the Middle Ages: their iconographic representation. The finest example of this is a fifteenth-century French manuscript of 182 eight-line proverb stanzas, edited by Grace Frank and Dorothy Miner. Individual woodcuts depict such common proverbs as "Strike while the iron is hot" and "Don't let the cat out of the bag." A fifteenth-century Flemish proverb tapestry, now housed in the Isabella Stewart Gardner Museum in Boston, illustrates 11 proverbs; it must be seen as a definite precursor to Pieter Brueghel the Elder's famous oil painting *Netherlandish Proverbs* (1559). But there are also woodcuts, prints, engravings, and misericords that illustrate proverbs, and in particular the proverbial theme of the world turned upside down. Art historians have dealt with some of these, and Lutz Röhrich has illustrated his lexicon of proverbial expressions with dozens of them, in addition to citing the medieval proverbs as early historical references. As Röhrich so convincingly shows, illustrated proverbs are of major help in explaining obscure verbal references to such items as torture devices or agricultural implements. Röhrich also cites numerous examples that illustrate the relationship between proverbs and folk narratives and fables during the Middle Ages: the proverbs are either cited directly in the narratives or else they follow and concisely summarize the longer tales. There are, of course, also etiological tales—that is, tales that explain the origin of proverbs. Such is the case of the fable of "The Fox and the Grapes," used to explain the proverbial expression "sour grapes": a fox, unable to reach a cluster of grapes, gives up, claiming that he didn't really want them, as "they were sour anyway."

The rich field of medieval proverbs is not yet completely tilled, and much still remains to be done by art historians, folklorists, linguists, literary historians, paremiologists, and others. While studies concerning the proverbs of a particular language are important, it is also necessary to strengthen the comparative work on proverbs. Though the Middle Ages are generally characterized as a period of cultural isolation, they had in fact a rather international culture, which is evident from the large number of Latin and vernacular proverbs reflecting the sociopolitical and cultural life of the Middle Ages.

See also: Blasons Populaires; Iconography; Misericords; World Turned Upside Down

—Wolfgang Mieder

Punishments. Acts of retribution practiced upon the bodies, material possessions, reputations, and psyches of individuals judged to have violated codes of behavior, here specifically referring to acts of a primarily symbolic nature taken against or required of a person believed to be guilty of misconduct; sometimes—but certainly not always—preceding, coinciding with, or following corporal punishments such as hanging and beheading.

Common medieval symbolic retributions included posting or distributing paintings or drawings of the miscreant in demeaning bodily positions and clothing; advertising the misdeeds of the accused in poetry, song, and chronicle; abusing or insulting the offender in effigy; confiscating and destroying or defacing a significant item of personal property such as a seal, sword, or armor; forcing the malefactor to appear in public wearing defamatory headgear or an object such as a whetstone around the neck; parading the criminal through the streets in a barrow or seated (often backward) on the back of an ignominious animal such as an ass.

Punishments—attested by images, literary works, and chronicles, both in visual representations and in descriptions of imaginary or actual events—were performed in the open, in the sight of all classes of people. Pictorial and written representations of medieval punishments offered an iconography of symbols of crimes and punishments that all could read and interpret. A mesmerizing quality inherent in irresistibly horrible or delightfully ludicrous punishments made them memorable, and because of the high degree of visual interest in these punishments, there was apparently a high degree of communicability between literary descriptions and visual images of punishment and the actual sight of punishments meted out in the streets, combined with the fear, the shame, and the often acutely perceptible discomfort and pain that they involved.

Punishments and Pictures

Use of a defamatory or shaming picture—a painting or drawing of the offender—began in Italy in the late thirteenth century and had spread to northern Europe by the early fifteenth; it seems to have been in France, during the Hundred Years' War, that the English first became aware of the practice. One manuscript of the English historical chronicle known as the *Brut* records that during the duke of Burgundy's siege of English-held Calais in 1436, individuals in Bruges sold paintings on cloth of Englishmen being hanged by their heels and presented interludes and plays in mockery of the cardinal of Winchester and other Englishmen. Two years later the *Bourgeois de Paris* chronicles how three English lords, the earl of Suffolk, Lord Willoughby, and Sir Thomas Blount, were also depicted on painted cloths, hung at each of the four gates of Paris. Similarly, when Jean Dunois besieged the castle of Harcourt in 1449, he had its captain, Richard Frognall, "hanged by the feet in painting at the door" because he had broken his oath by taking up arms against the French. By 1453 the English had adopted the practice themselves, and at the battle of Castillon in that year the English leader John Talbot carried several mock standards bearing inscriptions and devices intended to be insulting and disdainful to the French.

The *Schandbilder* (German for "shaming pictures") of fifteenth- and sixteenth-century Germany provided a special pictorial form of medieval punishments. These images, painted and drawn on large sheets of paper, were accompanied by *Scheltbriefe* (threatening and insulting letters) and displayed somewhat like Wanted posters in public places, to the great shame of the persons complained of; indeed, sometimes the mere threat of posting such an image was enough to cause the malefactor (often a debtor) to make reparation. The humiliation and scorn that these images communicated apparently even mortified the artists who created them. In Italy, for instance, production of these images was considered a particularly demeaning commission. At the outset of his career in 1440, Andrea del Castagno was ridiculed for painting the Albizzi conspirators, and Andrea del Sarto went to great lengths to create similar paintings in 1530 while screened from public view. It is hardly surprising that, as Ortalli notes, of the 112 such paintings of criminals made between 1274 and 1303, just over half were done by painters themselves accused of murder. There is no doubt, either, of the extreme shame such a painting visited on miscreants and their family: at least one man preferred to be hanged in reality rather than in image to avoid having his reputation so publicly and enduringly sullied in paint.

Another form of punishment was the practice of humiliating the miscreant in poems and songs. The Scottish Sir Simon Fraser, captured by Edward II's troops at the battle of Kirkencliff in 1306 and executed in London shortly thereafter, received a grisly memorial: a contemporary English poem recounted in sadistic detail the horrors to which Sir Simon was subjected, describing how, dressed in sackcloth, hands and feet manacled, and with a "garland" of periwinkle on his head, he was drawn on a bullock-hide from the Tower of London through Cheapside to the gallows, where he was hanged, beheaded, and disemboweled, after which his head was impaled on London Bridge and the rest of his body hung in a gibbet.

As in the case of the *Scheltbriefe* and the *Schandbilder,* written descriptions of misdeeds were often accompanied by pictures, making it possible for the nonliterate public to know what was going on as the spectacle of punishment was brought before their eyes. In fifteenth-century Île-de-France a dishonest chicken farmer was led to his punishment wearing a miter with chickens and other fowl painted on it and with "an abundance of writing"; in 1511 a lax forest ranger was paraded around in a paper miter decorated with standing and fallen trees; in both cases, the images, rather than the writing, narrated the story to the majority of people.

Symbols Employed in Punishments

A number of symbols and punishments—notably, the pillory and whetstone—were tied to lying. In 1364 John de Hakford was found guilty of making a false charge of conspiracy against the chief men of London. He was given a year's prison sentence and in addition was obliged once a quarter to stand in the pillory without hood or girdle, barefoot, with a whetstone hung by a chain from his neck. The whetstone was a folk symbol implying that though the liar's tongue had been made so sharp already, it might still be further whetted for even more outrageous lies! A more drastic punishment for lying was to have one's tongue bored through; a woodcut in Wynkin de Worde's edition of Stephen Hawe's *Passetyme of Pleasure* (1509) shows a man with his feet in the stocks and a woman performing a very business-like operation on his tongue with a hand drill.

As a legal maxim published by the medieval Scottish Parliament put it, "There are two things that everyone ought to guard carefully, and that is, his tongue and his seal." The seal was closely identified with its owner, and royal seal matrices might be destroyed ceremoniously in an obvious act of symbolism. In 1292, for instance, the seal of the guardians of the Scottish kingdom was broken up in recognition of Edward I's overlordship, while eight years earlier, after his defeat of the Welsh prince Llywellyn's wife and brother, Edward had their seals melted down and made into a chalice. There were other punishments involving the malefactor's own possessions: the major tools of a trade, class, or profession were confiscated and then debased or destroyed. The ritual breaking of his sword appears to have been one of the actions performed in disgracing a knight, a symbolic echo of the ennobling dubbing ritual. Edward Hall's chronicle (completed c. 1532), referring to the events of 1462/1463, relates that before Sir Raufe Gray was beheaded, his gilt spurs were cut off, his coat of arms defaced, and his sword broken over his head.

Tradespeople also suffered punishment that linked them to the tools of their trade: dishonest traders were paraded through town to the pillory together with their fraudulent wares. G. R. Owst quotes an example wherein one John Watte, a spurious pardoner, was sentenced to ride through Cheapside seated backward on his horse, the forged indulgences dangling round his neck. According to medieval satires, bakers and alewives were among the most notoriously dishonest tradespeople; the early-fourteenth-century *Holkham Bible Picture Book* pictures a baker with peel and scales and an alewife with short-measure tankard on her head, carried on the shoulders of devils toward the hell-mouth. A quack named Roger Clerk—whose medical practice consisted almost entirely of urinalysis—was subjected to a charivari in London in 1382; he was paraded through the city seated backward on a horse, holding the tail as reins and with two urinals tied around his neck, together with a whetstone, the latter being the proverbial prize for a mighty liar.

Even upper-class offenders were subjected to being paraded through the streets decked in symbols of infamy. Captured for acts of rebellion against Henry III, Hugh Despenser the Younger was mounted on "the smallest, skinniest, and most wretched horse," forced to wear a tabard with his arms reversed and a crown of nettles on his head, and paraded behind the royal train to the sound of trumpets. Hugh was greeted by insults, yells, and the blowing of horns—all of which sounds very like the "rough music" of a charivari. Finally, the wretched man was condemned and executed.

Punishments Involving Processions

Some punishments invoked class associations, for instance, forcing nobles to perform menial and stigmatized tasks. For example, a late-fifteenth-century German picture represents a noble named Heinrich von Veltheim skinning a dead horse, a dishonorable occupation. Some punishments, however, seem to have spanned all the classes. Riding backward, for example, was a particularly popular punishment, attested in a wide variety of contexts and applied to many different types of crimes committed by members of different social classes. The culprit is seated on a horse or—preferably—a donkey so as to face the animal's tail, which he or she is sometimes made to hold in the hands in place of reins. In fourteenth-century France this penalty was applied to cowards. Clerics were not immune from this type of punishment; a *Schandbild* of circa 1540 depicts an ass on which an abbot is mounted backward, one hand grasping the animal's tail and the other his crosier. In 1444 in present-day Croatia an elderly woman was accused of witchcraft, of using spells to lure rich lovers to her daughter. An ecclesiastical court condemned her "to be led through the town by her daughter, seated on a donkey but turned backward to face its tail and smeared with excrement." After the penalty of backward ridings had been abandoned by official courts, it still appeared as an element in traditional acts of popular justice.

Humiliating headgear is another common element in many punishments, representing an ancient tradition that perhaps ultimately even underlies the old-fashioned dunce's cap of the schoolroom. In the German Middle Ages, however, the incompetent student was literally made an ass, not only by being called *asinus* but more drastically by being made to wear an ass's head, as depicted in Rodericus Zamorensis's *Spiegel des*

menschlichen Lebens (Mirror of Human Life) issued in Augsburg in the 1470s. The miter was also frequently used in penances and punishments, both as a humiliating device and as an emblem of sinfulness. Those thought to have regal ambitions might be humbled by mock trappings of royalty; the most famous example, of course, is the crown of thorns, purple robe, reed scepter, and mocking inscription "King of the Jews" that were forced on Christ.

Being wheeled in a barrow was regarded as a particularly ignominious punishment, perhaps popular rather than official. Johan Huizinga cites "a theatrical display of hyperbolic humility" witnessed by Olivier de la Marche in about 1440, when the titular king of Naples, who had renounced the world because of the exhortations of St. Colette, entered a town carried in a sort of wheelbarrow "not differing from the barrows in which dung and ordure are usually carried." Similarly, an illumination in the Taymouth *Hours* (c. 1325) features a fearsome devil who trundles seven naked souls in a barrow toward the gaping hell-mouth.

Various popular festive practices—including carnivals and charivaris—comically mimicked medieval punishments. In certain enactments of the Feast of Fools, for example, the ruling fool, named Bishop for a day, rode backward on an ass in procession to the church, just as Hugh Despenser rode to his trial.

Gender, Class, and Punishment

Some types of punishments crossed gender boundaries, attempting to feminize men and chastise women who seemed to violate acceptable behavior for their sex. So strong were the female associations of the distaff that they were exploited as the basis for one of the characteristic medieval punishments by humiliation: in thirteenth-century England men convicted of slander—considered a peculiarly female crime—were paraded in public carrying a distaff. Complementary punishments assigned male attributes to women. The woman who "failed" to marry was the subject of special scorn (unless, of course, her celibacy was sanctified by religious vows). An apparently historical practice was the German custom of obliging unmarried women to pull a plow, illustrated about 1530 by Erhard Schoen for a poem by Hans Sachs, and it seems to have been particularly at Carnival time that unmarried women were most in danger from such communal disapproval and ridicule.

There were also posthumous punishments awaiting spinsters: for example, to "lead apes in hell," as Kate fears she will have to do in Shakespeare's *Taming of the Shrew*. The earliest written reference to this motif dates from about 1560, but this is one of several interesting cases in which a representation of the speech idiom in art antedates its earliest literary attestation, for one of the Bristol misericords carved in 1520 depicts a devil in the jaws of hell receiving a naked woman leading four apes on a leash. Among other punishments for women, several were assigned to scolds: a mortar placed around the neck, a watery plunge in a ducking stool, and a tongue bridle. Prostitutes were often ridden through the streets in a barrow. Kunzle notes that in Rome in 1525, in a variation on this type of punishment, the poet Maestro Andrea constructed a sort of mobile exhibition in the form of a barrow containing papier-mâché effigies of all the older Roman courtesans, each inscribed with the woman's name; disguised as a crippled beggar he wheeled it through the streets and emptied the barrow into the Tiber in front of the pope as his finale. It is satisfying to be able to report that he was later beaten through the city by the vengeful courtesans he had thus ridiculed.

In a society structured into strict gender- and class-based hierarchies, and where the sense of status and honor was so powerful, any reversal of the "natural" and the "seemly" assumed explosive force. In some cases, as in the motifs of "folly" and "topsy-turvydom" discussed elsewhere, the reversals were merely humorous; in others, such as the alleged unruliness and violence of "scolds" and "viragoes," they were perceived as simultaneously ludicrous and threatening. As we pursue the interpretation of these varied but related iconographic motifs, we find the themes of reversal and ridicule, of folly and sin, of Carnival and punishment, echoing one another, even blending together. In the many punishments by ridicule and humiliation, the aim was to exploit reversal in order to degrade the offenders and by implication to reassert right order in the community that assembled to mock them. The little images in manuscript margins and the carvings inconspicuously tucked away under misericords lead unexpectedly deep into the psychology and social attitudes of the Middle Ages.

See also: Charivari; Fools, Feast of; Ordeal

—Malcolm Jones and Myra Corinne Williams

Puppets and Puppet Plays. Figurative, mainly three-dimensional representations of gods, humans, and other real or fantastic beings, and the various kinds of spectacles in which they are employed, manipulated by human agency.

There are many kinds of puppets, classified by the technique of manipulation. The word *puppet* originated from the Latin *pupa*, which became "poppet" in the earliest English reference to such figures. The puppet belongs to an extensive family of simulacra, with androids and automata being close space-age cousins. Puppets were known in the ancient cultures of India, China, Greece, Rome, and Byzantium.

Early Evidence

Western Christianity had an aversion to all forms of pagan art and its carnality; nevertheless, wandering comedians, or mimes, were able to integrate puppetry into the folk culture of the medieval period. Sometimes the mimes or puppeteers were present among court performers, as is proven by a list of players received in 1273 by Alfonso the Wise of Castille, which mentions *cazurros*, entertainers who neither spoke nor sang but who trained monkeys, goats, and dogs—and who handled puppets. Thus, puppets were often combined in performances with trained monkeys, past masters at imitating and mocking the human condition.

Evidence of puppets in the Middle Ages is found even earlier—in the second part of the twelfth century—in a miniature from the codex *Hortus deliciarum* (Garden of Delights), written between 1175 and 1185 by the German prioress Herrad of Landsberg. (See illustration.) The miniature shows two puppet knights hung on strings stretched horizontally over a table surface, the place of combat for the potential antagonists. The manipulators of the strings are visible, stationed on opposite sides of the table, in costumes suggesting some affiliation to the order of knighthood. The knight puppets bear shields and swords, which they hold aloft as if in combat. French puppeteers called this kind of puppet *marionnette à la planchette* (table, or board, puppets). Other historical names were *bavastel* (Spanish) or *Taterman* (German), but these terms did not survive to the present time.

The miniature mentioned above is complemented by the inscription "In ludo monstrorum designatur vanitas vanitatum" [In the game of the demonstrators is signified the vanity of vanities]. There is also a side text, which gives what amounts to a comment on the human existential and moral situation according to Christian teaching. It may be that this marginal text was recited during the puppet show. Such narrative forms of performance were common, especially among people who wanted to convey religious precepts along with entertainment.

Some medievalists interpret the picture in the *Hortus deliciarum* as an example of the pious prioress's moral teaching, an opinion based on the written comments beside the picture referring to the ephemerality of human existence. Puppet historians, on the other hand, take the picture as a representation of an aspect of medieval life, providing concrete documentation of a puppet entertainment. Hans Purschke was convinced that puppets were brought to England and other European countries by crusaders returning from Palestine. Initially, the knightly veterans of the holy wars staged their own puppet shows in their homes—and in Purschke's opinion, Herrade's miniature depicts such a scene. Later, conjurers took up puppetry for popular entertainment.

French literature of the fourteenth century is full of evidence of these puppets, which were sometimes named *balestiaux, béteaux*, or *basteaux*.

The minstrels who showed them appeared often before kings and courtiers. The same kind of puppets, called *bavastels*, were known in Spain. In 1211 a certain Fadet, probably a minstrel or traveling performer, was advised to visit the court of Pedro II and to show his "*bavastels* in their assault on the castle." The sixteenth-century researcher Jaume Roig claimed that *bavastels* were the entertainment most beloved of the Catalan court on rainy days.

The Spanish *bavastels*, it seems, were not restricted to two combatants; they might consist of a battalion of fighting knights so manipulated that they seemed to attack a small-scale castle. Jeronimo de Blancas attests to this, giving a description of a show that was part of the coronation ceremony of Fernando I in Zaragoza in 1414. The show was arranged on a large, wheeled platform with the numerous manipulators hidden in the scenery, that is, in the scaled-down town and *castillos*. Effective concealment within an artificial tower or "little castle" may well have inspired some players to name the first independent puppet stages *castillos*. This supposition is confirmed by the fact that most portable stages in Western Europe were called "little castle" (*castillo* in Spain, *castelli* in Italy, *castelet* in France and Belgium) and bear the name to this day.

The tower-like castle stage has its earliest appearance in two miniatures from the Flemish manuscript *Li romans du bon roi Alexandre* (The Romance of the Good King Alexander) by Jehan de Grise, dated 1344. Both miniatures show a roughly castle-shaped puppet booth, with a tower on each end and between them a playboard without a proscenium. A rainbow arch connects the towers. The first miniature shows two fighting knights, centrally placed, so that the two squires in the towers on either side of them, armed with clubs, look down on the combat. In the second miniature, an armed puppet squire is talking to a lady, and next to the booth a group of women is watching the show. Of course, the puppets in these miniatures are not *marionnettes à la planchette*. By the mid-fourteenth century hand puppets or simple rod figures—usually held over the heads of the players—had replaced figures manipulated by strings.

The earliest mention of hand puppets is probably in the German didactic poem *Der Renner* (The Winner), written between 1290 and 1300 by Hugo von Trimberg. The author speaks of a new technique of performance (*ander goukel spil*) that involved making kobolds (gremlins, or spirits of the hearth) appear from under the player's cloak to entertain audiences.

In Germany there were puppets known as *Goltpurgen*, which Purschke associated with Goltburgh (Gold Castle), concluding that this nomenclature was another reference to the booth shaped like a castle. The name survived in Germany until the end of the sixteenth century, with the hand puppets continuing to perform plays with chivalric themes, acting out heroic stories that were often set to music, such as the song about the conflict between Hildebrand and his son Hadubrand.

At about the same time, a new theme emerged, the story of *Meister Hämmerlein* (Master Little Hammer), a character belonging to the tradition of the morality play. Hämmerlein was a grotesquely ugly instrument of rough justice, which he delivered to all his adversaries by means of "hammer blows." He was not actually the devil but, rather, more similar to the allegorical character of Vice common in medieval drama.

While it seems likely that performers using hand puppets were beginning to develop dialogue in their shows, there is other evidence that puppet demonstrations continued to be accompanied by recited songs. The fifteenth-century German version of the old French romance of chivalry *Histoire de Maugis d'Aygremont* (in German, "Malagis") tells the story of Oriadne, the fairy from Roselfeur, who is parted from her beloved student Malagis and undertakes a long journey disguised as a *jongleur*. She finally finds him in the castle of Aigremont among the guests celebrating a marriage. Oriadne offers to entertain the wedding party. She requests a table on which to arrange her stage and presents two beautiful puppets, one of a student magician and the other of a fairy. At the same time she recites the story of their love, thus allowing Malagis to recognize her. Considering Oriadne's situation as a lone traveler, her staging could only have been improvised and the puppets simple; they were probably hand puppets or even small rod figures.

Puppetry in Church Contexts
After 1310, when the Synod of Trier encouraged the use of pictorial presentations for evangelizing and the propagation of religious knowledge, churches gradually filled with sculptures, bas-reliefs, and paintings. Christian doctrine had changed dramatically. What had been considered idolatry returned in triumph to reinforce faith. In some churches worshippers were fascinated by life-sized, movable figures of Jesus Christ that served to illustrate liturgical events. Particularly noteworthy is the *mitouries*, a mechanical presentation of the Assumption of the Virgin Mary, performed in Dieppe, France, in the fifteenth century.

The first germs of liturgical theater sprang from the most important events of the Christian Gospels, commemorated as the main holidays of the Christian calendar: Easter, celebrating the Passion and Resurrection of Christ, and Christmas, the festival of the Nativity. Performers using puppets almost certainly assisted at the creation of mystery plays, although little documentation is now to be found. We know most about the exhibition of small crib figures in Nativity worship, a custom started by St. Francis in 1223 that spread quickly all over Europe. Such exhibitions were a strong attraction for church visitors, and for some clerics the animation of the figures was a natural progression. In fifteenth-century Poland, for example, Bishop Grzegorz (Gregory) of Sanok suggested introducing an element of movement into the crèche display.

The first evidence of puppets acting in performances of the Passion or Nativity comes from the sixteenth century, and such performances continue to persist in many countries as typical folk entertainments. In sixteenth-century England in the church of Whitney, comic elements were introduced in the puppet of Jack Snaker, according to Lambarde, a collector of antique curiosities.

In France and Spain Nativity performances were mounted in a special stage called the *retablo*—a church implement, a movable or fixed altar in the form of a cabinet, enclosing decorated panels. It is similar to the simultaneous or composite stage that in Gothic art included a number of sections, or so-called areas, for the presentation of a subject. A simultaneous puppet stage was probably used in Krakow in 1506. There is a register of expenses of the Polish court in which one may read that three florins were given as a fee for the presentation of a comedy: "Magistro de Omnibus Sanctis, qui comediam in praesencia [domini] principis recitavit faciendo tabernacula cum personis" [To the Master of All Saints, who recited a comedy in the presence of the crown prince, making enclosures with characters].The meaning of this note is somewhat obscure; nevertheless, my interpretation is that the Master from the All Saints school in Krakow used enclosures with figures (characters) to illustrate his own recitation.

It is striking that many puppet theaters retained the names of church implements such as *retablo* or *tabernaculum*. In fifteenth-century Germany the popular name for these puppet spectacles was *Himmelreich* (Kingdom of Heaven). The origin of the name is not known, but we may guess that it might be another example of the retablo. The retablo type of theater was also employed for secular themes, first evidenced in Germany in 1512, in Thomas Murner's poem *Narrenbeschwörung* (Fools' Spells). The narrator in the poem is one of the wandering players with their *Himmelreich* cabinet, here including at least five separate scenes—some of an anticlerical nature—probably each in a separate compartment.

In Spain the retablo was used in other forms of medieval entertainment, in particular in dramatizing the chansons de geste and songs about Charlemagne and his knights in the form of *El retablo de Maese Pedro*, as described by Miguel de Cervantes in his monumental *Don Quixote*. Since the book was published before the beginning of the seventeenth century, its realistic detail documents the process of transforming sacred objects into profane implements—especially in that Cervantes presents the player, Master Pedro, as an outlaw sentenced for indefinite punishment in the galleys.

The Skomorokhi

Just as the Roman Church fought all ancient popular customs surviving among the common folk, so did the Orthodox church within its dominions. The main enemies were the *skomorokhi*, or wandering players. First observed in Bulgaria, they had preserved many folk customs and rituals reflecting both their own culture and their Greek inheritance. From the ninth century onward such players were termed *skomrakhi* in Serbia and Bulgaria, and *skomorokhi* in Ukraine, Russia, and Poland. Their name may have originated in the Greek *skommarchos*, which referred to mimes, dancers, acrobats, and musicians. There is another possible origin in the Middle-Latin word *scamara*, meaning "robber." The *skomorokhi* were dedicated to a carefree existence, as far as possible from the impositions of authority. Pictures of the musicians have been beautifully preserved in the eleventh-century frescoes of the Orthodox church of St. Sofia in Kiev. *Skomorokhi*, according to references in Polish literature, included folk choral singers and puppet players. There is evidence that at the end of the sixteenth century they were liable for a special taxation, which means that some had settled and were by then recognized as citizens.

Skomorokhi tradition endured about seven centuries in the Slavonic countries. The last information available about the presence of this puppeteer tradition comes from Russia. Adam Olearius, traveling in 1634 from Holstein to Persia, reported his experiences in his journal and included a description of a performance by a group of *skomorokhi* along with a drawing of the show. The picture represents an open area, perhaps for public recreation. In the foreground there is a puppet player hidden within his portable booth, which looks like an all-enveloping sack worn by the puppeteer, tied at the waist and covering the body, head, and hands, while the lower legs remain visible. The play board, above the player's head, is circular, and his hand (or rod) puppets, including a horse and some human figures, are visible.

Olearius left a comment on the drawing pointing out that the puppet play displayed the sodomite customs of the Russian population. This evidence is of great cultural value: the show he witnessed evokes the erotic performances of ancient Greek and Byzantine mimes and also emphasizes that the biological and corporal current was still flowing in the popular theater of the seventeenth century, in opposition to the asceticism imposed on folk throughout many centuries by the official Church.

Puppetry in the Middle Ages, as in many other eras, belonged to folk culture. Wandering comedians brought puppet shows from village to village and from fair to fair. As a curiosity puppets were also presented in the courts or castles. The social status of the tradition changed when puppets and other figures were used for propagation of religious ideas, and performances were organized by priests and executed by church servants. However, when the ecclesiastic authorities banned theater and puppetry from churches, puppets returned to the hands of folk comedians. As medieval folklore preserved some elements of ancient entertainments, so some forms of medieval art have been preserved in folk art of later times. The Nativity, a puppet play born in Middle Ages, is still performed in such countries as Spain, Belgium, Poland, and Ukraine.

See also: Drama; Games and Play; Minstrel

—Henryk Jurkowski

Purgatory. In Catholic tradition, a place of temporary punishment in the afterlife for those whose souls need to be purged before they can enter heaven.

The concept of purgatory evolved slowly. The folk religiosity of the Jews and the early Christians was already predicated on the possibility of the cleansing of sin in the hereafter (cf. 2 Macc. 12:39ff.). The prayers for the dead, which can be found in the official liturgy since the early days of Christianity, also demonstrate that one expected to be able to help the dead out of a state of torment and into heaven. In the early Middle Ages many monastic visions of the hereafter depict a purgatory, even though the term itself first appears only in the twelfth century. At the Council of Lyon in 1274, purgatory became part of the official dogma as a third place between heaven and hell. It appears that regular Church collections for "poor souls" (i.e., the tormented spirits of the dead) were a special invention of the clergy in fourteenth-century southern France, where they were still struggling against the remaining Cathari who did not believe in purgatory. The increase in the fifteenth century in devotions for poor souls is, however, clearly a pan-European phenomenon; it would still be significant in the Baroque period, as is attested by the numerous altars for poor souls, with their burning flames and imploring figures, that have been preserved from the eighteenth and nineteenth centuries (primarily in rural churches in southern Germany and Austria). At the end of the Middle Ages the clergy sold innumerable indulgences in order to shorten the time that souls of dead loved ones, or one's own soul, would spend in the underworld. Their own specialists, *Sacerdotes purgatorii,* in Middle French *purgatoriens,* purgatory priests, collected donations at burials and other services. The extreme pressure of unconditionally needing such expensive priestly masses and indulgences to

be cleansed of sin finally led to the questioning and the renunciation of the teachings about purgatory during the Reformation. In the thirteenth century Berthold von Regensburg had already calculated the value of a mass: ten years of torment would, through one mass, be reduced to six weeks.

Medieval Christians imagined two means by which one could be purified of one's sins after death. One of these was on earth itself. In the legend of the Irish St. Brendan, for example, the saint reaches a purgatory-like mountain island in the course of his adventurous sea voyage. There souls in the form of, among other things, fiery birds—the most common animal representation of the soul in the folk tradition—are tortured with fire, wind, ocean waves, and icy coldness in order to be cleansed of their sins. The entire complex of the "raging army" (also called raging hunter, Wild Hunt, retinue of Satan, *Wilde Jagd, mesnie Hellequin,* etc.) also belongs in this category. The Germanic and Celtic idea of the dead flying through the air became in Christian interpretation a flock of repenting sinners moving on together in a storm. The most interesting example of a poor soul appearing on earth is probably the one offered by Arnt Buschmann's miracle (circulated in German, Latin, and Danish): Buschmann was a well-to-do farmer in the vicinity of Duisburg who in 1437–1438 received a series of apparitions of his grandfather. The grandfather, first appearing in the form of a dog, asked him for salvation from the punishments of purgatory that he, as a ghost, had to suffer on earth from the torments of a devil. This ghost had a lot to say about the otherworld and its customs, and in so doing he praises the ways in which the people, as members of Holy Mother Church, can provide mercy, including punctually paying their tithes. He also provides a view into the rural hierarchy of values of his time, something that no other source offers.

The other place for the purification of one's sins was in a purgatory located below the earth. Medieval people possessed detailed knowledge of this underground purgatory. And they believed themselves to have solid proof of its existence, as the twelfth-century texts on the Purgatory of St. Patrick circulated through all of Europe, describing a fairly authentic entrance into the underworld on an island in Lough Derg in county Donegal in Ireland (a site of pilgrimage visited yearly, even today, by tens of thousands of Irish). The author of the oldest tract tells (anachronistically!) how the purgatory sermon of St. Patrick was met with so much disbelief by the Irish that God had to perform a miracle, namely, the opening of a direct entry to places of torture for the living. Then he renders an oral account of a knight named Owen, who, around 1150, spent three days in this underworld. Owen had to experience all the tortures himself: the wheel of fire, the river of ice, the fire of brimstone, the narrow bridge to Paradise, and so on. The approximately 150 extant Latin manuscripts and just as many or more translations in the vernacular testify to the popularity of this earthly subterranean pilgrim's account. The legend of Owen was also known in modern times, as put into dramatic form by Lope de Vega and Pedro Calderón de la Barca and reworked into a Breton mystery play. The Irish purgatory-cavern was a sought-after destination of knightly pilgrims from all over Europe, many of whom passed on to posterity their experiences (which more or less resembled Owen's). Those whose authorship can be traced to the Hungarian magnate Georg Grissaphan from the year 1353 are particularly informative.

Apparently more widely known was the *Visio Tundali*, which was written down in 1149 in Regensburg by the Scottish monk Marcus. Tundal's journey to the hereafter was translated into all of the vernacular languages (including Old Norse and Old Russian), and it was also put into print early on. Luther still quoted from it, and the Jesuits had it performed on the stage. First, the soul of the Irish knight Tundal has to walk through the regions of punishment in purgatory under the guidance of his guardian angel. For example, he must cross a bridge of nails, the width of a hand, under which towering, fire-spewing monsters lie in wait for their victims; he has to get past a winged beast who digests the souls of monks and nuns into a sea of ice, where they become pregnant with snakes that tear them to pieces from inside; he has to come before the prince of hell who is shackled to a grill; and so on. The souls in this "upper hell" know about their future salvation, and so we know it is about purgatory, even though the term itself does not occur.

Of the many visions of purgatory from the central Middle Ages, the one of 1189 from the Schleswig-Holstein peasant Gottschalk should also be cited—another text wherein speaks a member of a class generally thought to be voiceless during the Middle Ages. The first station here is composed of a large plain full of bushes with sharp, dense thorns that cannot be dulled. At the edge of this horrible place of trial, angels will give the souls a pair of shoes from a giant linden tree—but only if during their earthly life they themselves have at one time given shoes to the poor. These shoes for the souls find their closest analogy in the pre-Christian religion of the northern Germanic people. They had a custom in which "Hel-shoes" were put on the dead, to be worn as they traversed the path to Hel (as the goddess of the underworld was named) or to Valhalla. There is also a series of later sources from this same area that depict this belief, such as the Norwegian *Draumkvæde* (a visionary folk ballad that goes back to the Middle Ages) and the English Lykewake Dirge. The stream full of sharp objects, which follows in Gottschalk's vision, is also clearly reminiscent of similar rivers in Old Norse

sources. This portrayal demonstrates well the mixture of religions in a region that had only recently become Christianized.

In the late Middle Ages the depictions of purgatory, namely, in the writings of mystics, often become less pronounced; there are, however, exceptions, such as the sadistic descriptions of St. Frances of Rome (d. 1440) or of an anonymous English female contemporary. In addition, the older texts circulated now in vernacular translations and were used in sermons. The belief in purgatory that was nurtured by such fantasies became at that time the greatest impetus for pious deeds. It was therefore to the advantage of countless needy people, who, in place of the poor souls, were given alms and baths free of charge (so-called baths for the souls) and provided with nursing care.

In the plastic and graphic arts purgatory was represented far less frequently and much later than heaven and hell. In general these portrayals of purgatory's places of torture are hardly distinguishable from those of hell in terms of landscape and punishments. What enables one to make a distinction is that they show, on the one hand, the angels descending into purgatory in order to liberate souls and, on the other hand, the souls themselves making imploring gestures, which would no longer have had meaning in hell. A number of pertinent illuminations can be found, primarily in Gothic books of hours. As a rule they appear in the section devoted to the memory of the dead and were intended to arouse sympathy for the poor souls. One also finds pictures of purgatory on retables with movable wings, with which the altars of the brotherhoods of the poor souls were usually decorated. The predella of such a reredos (c. 1500) in the Landesmuseum in Linz, for example, shows a part of the scene so often described in visions of the hereafter: the boiling cauldron, the fire pit, but also the realm for cooling the already risen souls (*refrigerium*). Angels bring these souls bread and wine, among other things, and carry the purified ones to a pleasing place.

The greatest concentration of paintings with this theme seems to be in southwest and central France, for one finds preserved there far more frescoes with depictions of purgatory from the fifteenth and sixteenth centuries than in any other region of Europe. The pictures were also supposed to convince those in southern France, who still secretly believed in Catharism, of the reality of purgatory. In Montaillou, however, it was still believed in the early fourteenth century that the dead (who are portrayed as very much alive) would not atone for their sins in one place during their time of purification but, rather, would have to run hurriedly from church to church until they were allowed to enter the place of rest. Purgatory is almost nonexistent in the very detailed documents of the Inquisition about the Cathari! In the plastic and graphic arts, there are also regionally specific traditions. So, for example, the pictures of purgatory spanned over by a bridge of trial in the shape of a saw seem to be limited to Mallorca, where evidence of them can be found in paintings and woodcuts as of the sixteenth century.

See also: Dante Alighieri; Harrowing of Hell; Hell; Marie de France

—Peter Dinzelbacher

Purim. Jewish holiday, observed since biblical times on the fourteenth, fifteenth, or both of Adar (generally falling during late February or early March) and commemorating the deliverance of the Jews during the reign of the Persian King Ahasuelrus from Haman's plot to exterminate them, as described in the Book of Esther.

Since Haman was described in Esther as an "Agagite," that is, a descendant of Agag, king of the Amalekites, Purim also served through the ages as a reminder to Jews of their ongoing war with their archenemy Amalek, who had been the first to attack the Israelites after their exodus from Egypt and whose memory they had afterward been commanded to destroy. The biblical verses (Deut. 25:17–19) containing that divine command were customarily read on the Sabbath before Purim, which came to be known as Shabbat Zakhor. And since according to biblical genealogy Amalek was a grandson of Esau, whom medieval Jews saw as a symbol of Christianity, the period between Shabbat Zakhor and the holiday of Purim provided ample opportunities for Jews to express, directly or indirectly, their hostility toward Christians and their religion—whose founder, moreover, had met his death in a manner strikingly similar to Haman's.

In fact, Sir James Frazer, in the second edition of his *Golden Bough* (1900), went so far as to suggest that Jesus may indeed have been killed by his former coreligionists as part of their violently carnivalesque Purim celebrations, a suggestion that he preceded with the following explanation:

Now, when we consider the close correspondence in character between the Jewish Purim and the Christian Carnival, and remember further that the effigy of Carnival ... had probably its prototype in a living man who was put to a violent death in the character of Saturn at the Saturnalia, analogy ... would suggest that in former times the Jews ... may at one time have burned, hanged, or crucified a real man in the character of Haman. There are some positive grounds for thinking that this was so.

Not surprisingly, Frazer's radical suggestion connecting the Passion of Jesus with Jewish festive violence on Purim was rejected by most scholars, and the author himself cautiously relegated it to an appendix in the third edition of the *Golden Bough*. But even scholars who explicitly rejected Frazer's thesis, such as the historian and folklorist Joseph Jacobs, acknowledged that Jewish celebrations of Purim had since late antiquity frequently reflected an anti-Christian animus. In his entry on Purim for the legendary eleventh edition of the *Encyclopedia Britannica* Jacobs mentioned, for example, the "Purim law" of 408 promulgated by Emperor Theodosius II—which prohibited Jews from "setting fire to Haman and from burning with sacrilegious intent a form made to resemble the holy cross, in contempt of the Christian faith"—and an incident of circa 415 in the Syrian town of Inmestar in which some drunken Jews had, as Jacobs wrote, "illtreated a Christian child during some Purim pranks and caused his death." The Inmestar incident was reported by Socrates Scholasticus in his *Ecclesiastical History*, but Jacobs neglected to mention that according to Socrates the child had been hung on a cross.

The anti-Christian aspects of Purim celebration continued during the central Middle Ages, spreading from Byzantium to Western Europe. During the eighth to eleventh centuries Jewish converts to Christianity in the Byzantine Empire were required, in addition to renouncing "every Hebrew law, custom, and ceremony," to specifically "anathematize those who celebrate the festival of Mordecai [i.e., Purim]—and those who nail Haman to a piece of wood, and joining it to the sign of the cross, burn them together while hurling various curses and anathemas against the Christians." In late-twelfth-century northern France, as we learn from both Jewish and Christian sources, a Jew in the town of Bray (or perhaps Brie) was murdered by a Christian who happened to have close ties with King Philip Augustus. The Jew's relatives bribed the local countess to have the assassin put to death, and, in the ambiguous words of the Hebrew chronicler Ephraim of Bonn, "They hung him on Purim." As a consequence of these events the king had 80–100 of the town's Jews burned. The Latin chronicler Rigord, unlike his Jewish counterpart, did not give the date upon which the Christian's execution took place, but he left no doubt that the Jews themselves had performed it, asserting that in the process they had reenacted certain aspects of Christ's Passion. Combining both accounts, we are presented with a brazen act of ritualized aggression directed both against a Christian murderer and the Christian religion. Such a daring act would probably not have been performed by the Jews of Bray/Brie, however, without the boost offered by the carnivalesque atmosphere of Purim and without the sense on the part of its perpetrators that such brazen behavior was appropriate to their annual festival of reversal.

The theme of reversal, it should be noted, appears quite explicitly in the Book of Esther, which was read by Jews from a scroll twice, first at night and then in the morning, during the holiday of Purim. The month of Adar is described therein as "the month that had been turned for them from sorrow into gladness and from mourning into a holiday" (9:22), and Purim itself is described as "the very day when the enemies of the Jews hoped to get mastery over them, but which had been changed to a day when the Jews should get mastery over their foes" (9:1). The rabbis of the Talmud, in that spirit of reversal, had asserted that a Jew must become so drunk on Purim that "he knows not the difference between 'Cursed be Haman' and 'Blessed be Mordecai'" (Megillah 7b), and various other rites of reversal, such as cross-dressing and masquerade, came to characterize the holiday's observance in medieval Europe.

Although many encyclopedias and reference works report that the custom of masquerading on Purim began among the Jews of sixteenth-century Italy under the influence of the local Carnival, it is clear that this custom, even in its radical form of cross-dressing, existed among the Jews of Provence as early as the fourteenth century. In the fifteenth, cross-dressing on Purim was practiced even among the relatively conservative Jews of Germany, as Rabbi Judah Minz, who later moved to Padua, candidly testified. Although the custom may have spread northeast from Provence, it is no less likely that the Jews of Germany had been influenced in a number of ways by the pre-Lenten *Fastnacht* (Carnival) festivities of their Christian neighbors. In 1458, for example, the raucous *Schembart* procession spilled into the Jewish quarter of Nuremberg, and although the town's Jews were expelled in 1499, it is likely that before their departure they were exposed to some of its famous *Fastnachtspiele* (Carnival plays). The Nuremberg native Hans Sachs authored no fewer than 85 plays of this type between 1517 and 1560, one of which was based on the Book of Esther and referred to Purim as a Jewish *Fastnacht*—perhaps for the first time. Scholars have suggested that the popular Yiddish dramatic form of the *Purimspiel*, which first emerged among Ashkenazic Jewry in sixteenth-century Italy, drew heavily upon the frequently raucous *Fastnacht* plays that these Jews had first encountered before crossing the Alps.

See also: Carnival; Festivals and Celebrations; Masking; Midsummer; Passover Haggadah

—Elliott Horowitz

Relics. Physical objects accorded spiritual significance by Christians because of their association with the saints.

The veneration given to relics was one of the cornerstones of the practice of Christianity in the medieval West. It was through relics that living Christians could seek the patronage and the help of the saintly dead now resident in heaven. While relics were also important in the medieval Christian East, the veneration of icons, or holy pictures of the saints, was equally or perhaps even more important in Byzantine lands. The most significant relics are bones and other vestiges of the saints' own bodies. Relics, however, also include items that belonged to or were used by a saint, such as clothing or books. Similarly, objects such as pieces of cloth or vials of water that come into contact with saintly bones take on the status of relics. The Roman Catholic Church distinguishes these three categories as first-, second-, and third-class relics.

The public veneration of the saints through their relics took many forms. Shrine churches were erected over the tombs of many saints, such as Agnes or Peter outside the walls of Rome, Martin at Tours, or Francis at Assisi. These shrines attracted pilgrims, often from long distances. More fragmentary relics were set inside elaborate containers, or reliquaries, made from precious metals and jewels. Canon law also required that fragmentary relics be placed inside altars as part of the ritual of consecration. And since the body of a saint would be called gloriously forth from the tomb at the Last Judgment, burial near saintly tombs (*adsanctos*) was greatly valued by those who wished to share in the saintly resurrection. Veneration of relics, however, was only one part of the cult of saints. Liturgical and other forms of prayer directed toward the saints—most particularly on the feast days dedicated to the honor of individual saints—were practiced throughout the Christian Church and did not require the physical presence of remains of the saint in question.

In order to understand the religious practices that coalesced specifically around relics in medieval Christianity, it is essential to view relics in an eschatological perspective. A saint was above all else a person whose soul currently resided in the heavenly court. On the day of the Last Judgment, every human being's body was to be reassembled from the pieces that had once constituted it. Thus, the corporal, anatomical relics of the saint were objects that not only had been part of the saint but continued to be an essential part of the saint's person on earth, and they would be part of the saint's glorified body following the Last Judgment. Seen from this perspective, a tomb or reliquary did not simply contain dead bones. To pray before a relic was to address a living member of the divine court who could bear one's petitions directly to God. Relics were not merely a symbol of the saint; they also denoted the saint's continued physical presence in this world. As a fifth-century inscription at the tomb of Martin of Tours (d. 397) read, "Here lies Bishop Martin of holy memory, whose soul is in the hand of God, but who is completely present here, manifesting through the power of miracles his every grace." Relics thus provided, in the evocative phrase of Peter Brown, "joinings of Heaven and earth."

Relics served to objectify and transmit the power (Latin *virtus*) of the saints. As such, they were utterly essential to the practice of Christianity in the Middle Ages. They provided a focus for beliefs about the saints, their patronage, and their supernatural power. It is important to remember, however, that at least according to orthodox theology this power came directly from God. It must also be kept in mind that the honor shown to the saints was considered to be an intermediate means to the final end of worshipping God. Augustine of Hippo (d. 430) remarked, "When we make our offerings at shrines, it is to God. The martyrs have their place of honor ... but they are not adored in the place of Christ." Specifically, theologians distinguished between the veneration due to saints and their relics, on the one hand, and the worship or adoration that was reserved only to the Godhead, on the other.

The public veneration of relics grew in importance and geographic scope during the last decades of the fourth, and first decades of the fifth, centuries, particularly under the impetus provided by Ambrose of Milan (d. 397). There was some significant opposition on the part of learned clerics, such as Jerome's opponent Vigilantius; Augustine himself was not fully convinced of the propriety of relic cults until the final years of his life, at which time he took up the cause of the cults of St. Stephen and others with gusto.

From at least that time, the clerical hierarchy exerted significant efforts directed both toward promoting and controlling the veneration of relics among the laity. They were concerned both with the authenticity of relics themselves and with the orthodoxy of the practice of veneration. Much ecclesiastical legislation controlled the transfer or sale of relics, as well as the beginning of the cults of new relics or saints. In the *Admonitio generalis* of 789, Charlemagne ordered that "the false names of martyrs and the uncertain memorials of saints should not be venerated." Thus was inaugurated a custom by which bishops controlled the practice of relic veneration within their dioceses. In the later Middle Ages the papacy slowly usurped some of this authority, in particular through the practice of canonizing new saints through the issuance of a papal bull. As with the Mass, the veneration of relics usually took place within a church or other sacred space and under the eye of supervising clerics or monks.

Thus, the veneration of relics provided an important link between the worlds of the clergy and the laity. Nonetheless, some relics did come into lay hands, and some practices of relic veneration did not win clerical approval, and so there are certain aspects of the cult of relics that properly belong to the realm of folklore. In the mid-ninth century, for example, Bishop Amulo of Lyon criticized a new relic cult, primarily involving women, that had begun in Dijon. He declared: "Some miracles have begun to occur in the church." These miracles were not, however, cures and healings, by which some indication of divine compassion and approval would be shown, but rather "blows and pressures, from which in this house of prayer pitiable little women suddenly fall down, thrash about, and are seen to shake violently." These were thought to fall outside acceptable bounds. Another example is provided by a cult that developed near the village of Sandrans in the mountainous Dombes region of France. This shrine was used by the local laity in particular for the curing of sick infants, and it centered on the bones of a greyhound named Guinefort, who was believed to have once saved the life of his master's son and heir, only to be killed in a canine version of martyrdom. Eager laypeople also frequently obtained dubious or fraudulent relics, as the mention of the "pygges's bones" that belonged to Chaucer's Pardoner has famously made clear. Aside from the writings of a very few intellectual iconoclasts, such as Claudius of Turin (d. 827), most clerical critics of relic veneration did not focus on the practices employed by the laity; instead, they regretted the lack of clerical supervision or of proper guarantees of the relics that were venerated. Perhaps the most famous medieval diatribe against the cult of relics is to be found in the first book of Abbot Guibert de Nogent's *De pignoribus sanctorum* (On the Relics of the Saints). Guibert (c. 1064–c. 1125), however, was personally devoted to the veneration of relics; on close examination, his work is clearly a plea for closer clerical control over lay religious expression rather than the protorationalist critique of superstition that some have tried to make it. The Abbot of Nogent particularly cherished the importance of hagiographic traditions in guaranteeing the authenticity of relics:

> [Relics] are things worthy of our reverence and honor in exchange for their example and protection. In these matters the only method for calling a person a saint which should be considered authentic is one which relies not on opinion, but on time-worn tradition or the evidence of trustworthy writers. (*De pignoribus sanctorum* 1,1)

One of the most striking aspects of the cult of relics in medieval Christendom was the success

that the clerical hierarchy, urged on by men like Guibert, had in imposing norms of practice on the laity.

See also: Becket, Saint Thomas; Cross; Guinefort, Saint; Saints, Cults of the

—Thomas Head

Richard the Lion-Heart (1157–1199) [*Coeur de Lion*].

Richard I, crusader king of England (1189–1199), subject of many dramatic legends and romances, some of which have dominated perceptions of him down to the present day.

Son of King Henry II and Eleanor of Acquitaine, both figures of legendary stature in their own right, Richard committed his first legendary act in 1173 (when he was 16), when he participated in a rebellion against his father. At this time Henry had four sons, and each considered the provision Henry had made for him inadequate. Richard and his brothers found eager allies in King Louis VII of France, their father's longtime enemy, and their mother, Eleanor, who had also become estranged from Henry. The rebellion was unsuccessful but led to other conflicts, and Richard's relationship with his father was still bitter at the time of Henry's death in 1189.

Nevertheless, when Henry died Richard became king of England. He was widely admired in the Middle Ages, but he has recently been criticized for his lack of interest in English affairs. Indeed, during his ten years as king, he spent less than six months on English soil. After inheriting the throne he remained in the country only long enough to raise the large sum necessary to begin the Third Crusade. In 1190 he departed for the Holy Land, along with King Philip Augustus of France.

In the summer of 1191 the crusaders reached Acre, a Muslim-held port city near Jerusalem. Guy de Lusignan, the former king of Jerusalem, was besieging Acre, but the Muslims, led by Saladin, sultan of Egypt and Syria, had trapped Guy's army between themselves and the town. Richard came to Guy's aid just in time, and they managed to continue the siege until the officials of the starved city sent a message to Saladin that they would have to turn it over to the Christians. Saladin, whom many legends treat as Richard's Muslim equivalent, honored the agreement, and the Christians took control of Acre. They were setting their sights on Jerusalem when Philip announced that he had pressing business in France and was taking his troops home. This sudden departure made Richard suspicious, despite Philip's promise that he would not invade Richard's territory in his absence. Furthermore, Richard lacked the manpower and resources to hold Jerusalem, even if he were able to take it. For these reasons, much to the consternation of his army, Richard decided not to attack Jerusalem. Instead, he made an agreement with Saladin whereby the Muslims would retain control of the city but the Christians would be permitted to enter and visit the holy places in safety.

Richard's crusading exploits were so admired that even his enemies praised him. Not only English but also French and even Arabic chroniclers expressed their admiration. As Richard's legends passed into romance, however, the angelic and the diabolic existed side by side. In the Middle English romance *Richard Coeur de Lion* an angel appears to him three times to direct him into battle and warn him of defeats, signifying his godliness, but Richard also expresses a grimmer nature when he has the heads of Saracens roasted and served to Saracen ambassadors.

On his journey home Richard was captured by Leopold of Austria, essentially sold to Emperor Henry VI, and held for ransom. Despite the efforts of Philip, who had broken his promise and attacked Richard's French holdings with the collusion of Prince John, Richard was released in 1193 after payment of his ransom. He spent the next several years regaining the territory that Philip had taken. He died in a siege of the Castle of Chalus, in Aquitaine, in 1199. He had apparently lowered his shield to applaud a crossbowman who was standing alone on the castle wall, fending off arrows with a frying pan. When Richard lowered his shield, the archer fired and hit him in the shoulder. He died when the wound became infected, but not, the chronicles assure us, before making a sincere confession and forgiving his assailant.

Richard participated in the making of his own legend. In 1174 at the court of Poitiers, shortly after his revolt against his father, he told the tale of his descent from a demon queen who married his ancestor, Black Fulk of Anjou. According to Gerald of Wales, "King Richard often used to mention this ancestry, saying that it was not remarkable that sons of such a stock should plague their parents and brothers one after the other. For he said that they all came from the devil and would return to the devil."

The story was retold often, eventually in a form that made Richard the son of the demon queen. In the Middle English romance *Richard Coeur de Lion*, Henry II marries a beautiful maiden named Cassodorien. She is a model wife, and the marriage is happy. However, her habit of leaving church before the sacraments are given bothers Henry and his ministers. One day they agree to restrain her and force her to stay for communion. As soon as the sacrament begins she clutches her daughter and one of her sons (John) and flies out the window. She drops John on the ground but vanishes forever with her daughter. This legend of the demon queen (motifs A511, F302) was retold in many forms, often about members of Richard's family and often about other nobles.

Another legend explains how Richard came to be known as the "Lion-Heart": During his captivity, Emperor Henry's daughter falls in love with him. She orders a trusty servant to have him taken to her room in the evening, and they spend many pleasant nights together before her father finds out. The emperor is furious at his daughter's disgrace and wishes to kill Richard on the spot, but his counselors warn him that murdering his royal prisoner would be hard to excuse. He decides instead to release a hungry lion in his cell, so that the lion, not Henry, will kill Richard. However, Henry's daughter hears of the plot and warns her lover, who asks her for 40 scarves to wrap around his arm. When the lion roars, Richard reaches his wrapped arm down the lion's throat and pulls out his heart. Of course, the beast immediately dies, and Richard marches into Henry's court. He eats the heart in front of the emperor and his counselors, who hastily make arrangements to accept the ransom and send this dangerous man back to England.

Perhaps the most famous legend also concerns his captivity by Emperor Henry. Since no one knows where the English king is being held, Blondel, a minstrel, sets out to find him. Blondel walks from castle to castle, singing songs the two composed together. Eventually he reaches a certain castle in Germany, and when he sings the first line Richard answers with the second. Thus, the king is found and ransomed. This is the legend that Sir Walter Scott adapted, substituting his Ivanhoe for the minstrel who finally locates the king.

See also: Crusades; Legend; Romance

—Leigh Smith

Riddle. A fundamental and extremely widespread form in both oral folklore and written literature, which can be generally characterized as a verbal game consisting of a question and answer.

Riddles appear in the oral traditions of nearly all human societies and are found among the oldest written records. The riddle question describes something in confusing or contradictory terms and asks "What is it?" or "What is its name?" The confusion or contradiction may be implicit in the description itself or explicitly expressed in a "block element." A general distinction can be made between folk riddles (or popular riddles) and literary riddles (or art riddles, learned riddles). Medieval riddles are for the most part literary.

The processes of description and blocking display endless variation in riddles. A folk riddle from Togo, in West Africa, "A man walks with you and you cannot catch him," appears to describe an ordinary walking companion but then precludes that answer by saying that it is a walking companion whom you can never catch or catch up with. The answer, "shadow," resolves the puzzle by shifting the sense of "man" from the literal to the metaphorical level. Instead of seeing one's shadow as a walking companion, the fairly vague "man," a Portuguese-language folk riddle from the Cape Verde Islands allows the speaker to present the shadow as his or her child: "I have a child. No matter how far I run, I cannot catch him. When I sit down, I catch him." Here the block element is a more complicated notion, that one cannot catch the child by running after him but can catch him by sitting down. This is a result that seems to contradict experience but that just might not (given the perversity of active children). A Turkish folk riddle changes the terms of the description by focusing on the darkness of the shadow, now seen as a raven pursued by a hunter, but the block element remains essentially the same: "I cannot catch up to a certain raven; if I catch up to it, I cannot capture it." All three "shadow" riddles present the puzzle of a living being (man, child, raven) who cannot be caught; all are ultimately metaphors with one term concealed; that term (shadow) appears in the answer.

Another form of riddle is based more on lexical or grammatical ambiguity, that is to say, on punning. At times such wordplay will limit a riddle to a particular language, but some puns easily cross linguistic borders. A medieval riddle known in both Latin and Old English versions describes the rueful paradox of the book moth, who "devours" letters ("letters," "words," "the Muses," "the speech of man") but is never the wiser for it. Yet another form of riddle depends on problems or contradictions in our ways of understanding things. Another riddle found in both Latin and Old English is "fish in the river." The Old English version alone describes the fish as a dweller who remains still while his dwelling moves on, yet who does not, and cannot, leave his dwelling as long as he lives. These primary forms of riddles (sometimes called true riddles) are all related—a pun can be thought of as a metaphor—and are usually distinguished from a host of other kinds of puzzling questions associated with them both in medieval manuscripts and in modern riddle sessions: dialogue riddles (the answer identifies the speakers of a fanciful dialogue), biblical riddles (the answer is a character in the Bible), wisdom questions (the answer must be known already, as in a catechism), conundrums (the answer is a pun), catch riddles (the apparent answer is a trick to embarrass the one answering the riddle), charades (the answer is a word or phrase described syllable by syllable), arithmetical puzzles, acrostics, rebuses, and the like.

Oral and Literary Medieval Traditions

There can be no doubt that an oral tradition of folk riddling flourished throughout the Middle Ages; nevertheless, the medieval riddles we know largely represent a sophisticated and self-conscious genre of writing. Although all verbal folklore from the medieval period is "literary," in the sense that it all has reached us in some written form, the riddles are literary to an even greater degree, since they are productions of a learned class of churchmen, scholars, and scribes who developed the folk riddle into sophisticated

poetry that became increasingly more elaborate in form, more polished stylistically, often more complex in theme, and also more abstract with regard to subject matter. Even when medieval riddles feature the same subjects as folk riddles— and this happens frequently—the literary treatment sets them apart and calls up a context typified more by the ink horn than by the drinking horn (though both objects become the subjects of medieval riddles). For that reason, medieval riddles are generally placed under the larger rubric of "wisdom literature," which includes along with riddles versified collections of maxims and other sayings; poems cataloging calendrical, geographical, and bestiary lore; instructional poems setting forth lists of ethical precepts; sets of metrical charms for use in magical practice (for protection, healing, or fertility); and other forms that order and give authority to the conventional lore of society. The folklore of oral, pre-Christian culture is at times heard in the background of medieval wisdom literature, particularly in the metrical charms, but the genre reaches back far more directly to written traditions, to classical literature and especially to the wisdom books of the Old Testament (Proverbs, Job, and Ecclesiastes). Medieval riddles, then, are at once the learned entertainment of a particular class, an established (if minor) form of poetry, and a repository of conventional knowledge.

An influential collection of 100 riddles by Symphosius, a late-classical writer of whom nothing else is known, can be considered to be the fountainhead of the tradition of literary riddling in medieval Europe. Writing perhaps sometime in the fifth century in good Latin, Symphosius composed a "shadow" riddle that like the folk riddles uses the fundamental idea of a being whose nature appears to contradict itself, a being who can be seen but not caught. But a number of literary flourishes adorn and perhaps nearly obscure the central metaphor:

Umbra

Insidias nullas vereor de fraude latenti;
Nam deus attribuit nobis haec munera
formae,
Quod me nemo movet, nisi qui prius ipse
movetur.

[Shadow
No snares I fear from lurking fraud;
For a god has bestowed upon me this gift of
form,
That no one moves me, unless he himself
first be moved.]

The riddle first of all draws on classical rhetoric by making the subject itself the speaker, employing the figure of prosopopoeia. The first line then expands the folk idea of the pursued shadow into a view of the world as a place of snares and fraud. Only the speaker, because of his unique nature, can move confidently and safely through that threatening world—the second line adding the classical literary touch that this is the gift of a god. In the final line the picture of the shadow and the world it inhabits is given a complex moral dimension in the paradoxes of the mover moved and the betrayer betrayed: the enemy who, moved by his own hostile intentions, inevitably gives away his position of "lurking fraud" by moving first himself. All that is cast by Symphosius into a poem of three hexameter lines, as all his riddles are, and given a title that reveals the answer.

Early-Medieval Collections
The early Middle Ages saw a number of collections of Latin literary riddles that followed Symphosius's model. Sometime around the seventh century, perhaps in Italy, an unknown author composed a group of 63 riddles, as we have it, now known as the Berne riddles after the oldest manuscript containing them. Late in the seventh century the English bishop and scholar Aldhelm (d. 709) composed 100 riddles, clearly in imitation of the "century" of riddles by Symphosius, though Aldhelm's riddles are generally longer. English churchmen of the time seem particularly to have been drawn to the form: early in the eighth century Tatwine (d. 734), another English bishop, composed a set of 40 riddles, which was then completed with 60 riddles by "Eusebius"—who may have been Hwætberht (d. 747), abbot of Wearmouth—to make another collection of 100. The missionary bishop Boniface (d. 754) wrote a collection of 20 riddles on the Virtues and the Vices, the culmination of a tendency toward more abstract subjects in Latin riddle tradition. Throughout that tradition the riddles display, and usually amplify, the literary characteristics of Symphosius's riddles. In all of Aldhelm's riddles, for example, the subject speaks the riddle itself ("Cernere me nulli possunt nec prendere palmis" [None can espy me, none lay hands on me], begins his riddle for "wind"); there are frequent allusions to learned tradition, both classical and biblical; the solution for each riddle appears in its title, a sign that any folk context of a game or contest has been abandoned in favor of some other purpose. That purpose clearly was entertainment and learned display, but the riddles also form part of Aldhelm's *Epistola ad Acircium de metris* (Letter to Acircius Concerning Poetry)—a work on Latin prosody—and were perhaps intended to serve as examples of hexameter versification as well.

Beyond the domain of Latin culture, there were, from the tenth century onward, flourishing traditions of literary riddling in Persian, Arabic, and Turkish, and long-established traditions in Greek and Hebrew had continued into the Middle Ages. In Western Europe riddles in the vernacular languages appeared relatively late in the medieval period. An important exception is a

body of Old English riddles (from 91 to 96, depending on how they are edited) contained in the tenth-century manuscript known as *The Exeter Book*. The riddles were composed, apparently by various authors, between the eighth and the tenth centuries. The vigorous Latin tradition of riddles in England in the eighth century suggests that an early date is likely.

Old English Riddles
The Old English riddles bear some relation to that tradition, both in general and in specific instances: three of the riddles derive directly from Symphosius, two more are adapted from Aldhelm, and a number of others take up the same subjects as Latin riddles. But with the exception of one riddle in Latin, the riddles of *The Exeter Book* are Old English poems, composed in the accentual meters of classical Old English prosody. Unlike the Latin riddles, they do not give away the answers, and they avoid taking abstractions as subjects (though "Creation" does appear, adapted from Aldhelm). Their subjects are, instead, the tangible things of the visible world—farm tools, battlefield weapons, kitchen implements, domestic animals, and wild birds—all seen in an oblique new light through the lens of the riddle.

One of the best examples from *The Exeter Book*, both as riddle and as poem, turns on the concept of light itself—specifically, the light of the moon and sun. (This, at least, is the generally accepted solution.) The daily and monthly cycles of moon and sun are figured in the riddle's metaphorical narrative of a raid, a plundered treasure, and the rescue of the treasure by its rightful owner—imagery reflecting a recurring reality in Anglo-Saxon life. First, the raid:

Ic wiht geseah   wundorlice
hornum bitweonum   huþe lædan,
lyftfæt leohtlic   listum gegierwed,
huþe to þam ham   of þam heresiþe.
Walde hyre on þære byrig   bur atimbran,
searwum asettan,   gif hit swa meahte.

[I saw a wonderful creature,
carrying plunder between her horns,
a shining vessel of the air elegantly
     adorned,
plunder to her home from the raid.
In that fortified town she wished to build
     for herself,
skillfully to set up, if it might be so, a
     bower.]

The crescent moon is a warrior in a horned helmet, carrying away light she has plundered. With precise observation and accurate knowledge, the riddle describes a time shortly before dawn, in the last stages of the lunar cycle—and perhaps describes as well "the old moon in the new moon's arms," the earth-lit orb faintly glowing within the bright sunlit crescent. The medieval riddle master knew that the light of the moon is taken from the sun, and in the next section of the riddle he describes the recovery of that treasure. The sun rises over the horizon and the moon is put to flight, losing its light to a stronger warrior:

Ða cwom wundorlicu wiht   ofer wealles
     hrof
seo is eallum cuð   eorðbuendum;
ahredde þa þa huþe,   ond to ham bedraf
wreccan ofer willan—   gewat hyre west
     þonan
fæhþum feran,   forð onette.

[Then came a wonderful creature over the
     top of the wall
who is known to all earth-dwellers,
who recaptured that plunder and drove
     homeward
that wanderer against her will—she went
     west from there
grudgingly traveling, she hastened forth.]

There the riddle could end. But the poet added three final lines of quiet mystery, describing the dawn into which the moon has disappeared, bereft of light:

Dust stonc to heofonum;   deaw feol on
     eorþan;
niht forð gewat.   Nænig siþþan
wera gewiste   þære wihte sið.

[Dust rose to the sky; dew fell on earth;
night went forth. No one afterwards knew
the fate of that creature.]

Riddles within Narratives

Medieval riddles are also found embedded in many forms of narrative, where they function as plot elements. The Middle Ages knew the story of Samson and its special form of riddle that appears only in narrative contexts. Now called a neck-riddle, it takes its name from the story of a condemned man who saves his life by proposing a riddle his executioners cannot answer. A neck-riddle is based on some personal experience of the riddler, as Samson's riddle is (Judg. 14), and it cannot be solved without that private knowledge. The Bible also mentions that the Queen of Sheba came to test the wisdom of Solomon with riddles (1 Kings 10). The Old English dialogue poem known as "Solomon and Saturn II" is cast in the form of such a verbal contention, a contest of wisdom questions between pagan (Saturn) and Christian (Solomon). The Latin romance *Apollonius of Tyre*, of which many versions circulated in the Middle Ages (and into the Renaissance, in Shakespeare's *Pericles*), begins with an incest riddle, based on confusion in kinship structures, which functions in the story as a suitor task. After many adventures the hero is reunited with his

long-lost daughter through the use of ten riddles from Symphosius that serve as part of the story's recognition scene.

In the Middle Welsh Four Branches of the Mabinogi the traditional narrative motif of a wife betraying the secret of how her husband may be killed (motif K2213.4.1) is based on a complex set of paradoxical tasks (H1050ff.) that are well known in riddle form in traditional folktales such as "The Clever Peasant Girl" (AT 875). The fourteenth-century Spanish *Libro de buen amor*, a frame tale collection, includes an elaborate allegory based on the widespread year riddle (H721), which there takes the form of 12 men (the months of the year) in the glowing pavilion of Sir Love.

Finally, riddle ballads such as "Riddles Wisely Expounded" (ballad 1 in Child's *The English and Scottish Popular Ballads*), "The Elfin Knight" (Child 2), "King John and the Bishop" (Child 45), "Captain Wedderburn's Courtship" (Child 46), and "Proud Lady Margaret" (Child 47)—which are again contests in wisdom questions—have their roots in the late Middle Ages.

Wisdom questions in the narrative frame of a contention are also found among the many examples of gnomic lore in the Old Norse *Poetic Edda*. By contrast with true riddles, wisdom questions test old ways rather than new ways of knowing things: they would deal with the traditional mythology of the sun and the moon, for example, or with the names for "sun" and "moon" in poetic diction, but they would not include the riddle of a plundered treasure of light.

In *Vafthrúdnismál* (The Lay of Vafthrudnir) Odin and the giant Vafthrudnir engage in a contest based on mythological lore. When the giant asks for the names of the horse that draws day into the heavens and the horse that brings night into the eastern sky, Odin correctly answers that the first horse is Skinfaxi (Shining Mane) and the other is Hrimfaxi (Frost Mane): "Drops of foam fall from his bit, and from that comes the dew in the valleys." In *Alvissmal* (The Lay of Alvis) Thor detains the dwarf Alvis (All-Knowing), who is eager to carry away Thor's daughter for his bride, with questions concerning the lore of names. "What is the moon called?" Thor asks. Alvis replies:

Máni heitir með mönnom,   enn mylinn
     með goðom,
     kalla hverfanda hvél helio í,
scyndi iötnar,   enn scin dvergar,
     kalla álfar ártala.

[Men say the Moon, but gods, False Sun; in Hel it's Whirling Wheel; for giants Speeder; for dwarfs it's Shining One; elves call it Counter of Years.]

Such questions are not "solved" but simply answered: the contradictory description of the riddle is not part of their challenge. But the answers to the questions—the names—are themselves often riddles in miniature, the fixed epithets and frozen metaphors of a traditional poetic diction.

Late-Medieval Riddle Collections

At the end of the Middle Ages collections of riddles and other forms of questions began to appear in printed books. The French *Adevineaux amoureux* (Amorous Riddles), a large collection made in Belgium or northern France, was printed by Colard Mansion of Bruges around 1479. This important miscellany contains courtly questions of love (*demaundes amoureuses*), a large number of true riddles from both oral and literary traditions, and such other forms as wisdom questions, biblical riddles, joking riddles, obscene riddles, and arithmetical puzzles. A "sun and moon" riddle, which has many analogs in oral tradition, exemplifies the popular component of the collection:

> *Demande.*: Qu'est ce qui tout le jour va dessus roinsses et espines et ja n'y deschirra chappron ne cottes simples?
>
> *Response.*: Ce est dit pour le soleil et pour la lune.

> [*Question.*: What goes the whole day over brambles and thorns and will never tear its hood or petticoat?
>
> *Answer.*: This is said for the sun and for the moon.]

Another French collection of the late fifteenth century, *Demandes joyeuses en maniere de quolibets* (Amusing Riddles in the Form of Quodlibets), became the basis for the first English riddle book, *Demaundes Joyous* (Amusing Riddles), printed in London by Wynkyn de Worde in 1511. The questions range from the biblical to the bawdy—from "What was he that slew the fourth part of the world?" ("Cain when he slew his brother Abel, in the which time was but four persons in the world") to "Which is the most cleanliest leaf among all other leaves?" ("It is holly leaves; for nobody will not wipe his arse with them")—and show the riddle leaving the world of medieval wisdom to enter that of Renaissance wit.

A touchstone of medieval thought was St. Paul's phrase "Videmus nunc per speculum in aenigmate, tunc autem facie ad faciem." For a modern reader, the traditional translation—"For now we see through a glass darkly, but then face to face"—has become somewhat misleading. The "glass" is not a window but a looking glass, a mirror (*speculum*), and the adverbial "darkly" is literally "riddlingly," or "in riddles" (*in aenigmate*).

For medieval readers, Paul's words must have resonated profoundly and may in part explain the delight some of those readers took in riddles. They were used to thinking of the world as a mirror in which all creation spoke of itself as something more than meets the eye. Perhaps the "wonderful creatures" of the riddles continually re-created that sense of the world for them, and the riddle form itself allowed them to experience in small the notion expressed in part in Paul's eschatological promise that what is concealed will be revealed.

See also: English Tradition: Anglo-Saxon Period

—Andrew Welsh

Rites of Passage. A term coined by Arnold van Gennep to describe ceremonies accompanying major transitions in an individual's life.

Rites of passage possess three major phases: separation from a previous world, transition, and incorporation into a new situation. Reflecting the importance given by van Gennep to the transitional phase—the threshold, or *limen*—he calls the rites of separation, preliminal rites; those executed during the transition, liminal rites; and the ceremonies of incorporation, postliminal rites. Even when these stages are not equally articulated in a given ritual, they occur in sequence in ceremonies surrounding the three major stages of life: birth, marriage, and death.

Rites concerning the pregnant woman are in close relation to those centered on the newborn child. During her pregnancy and after the birth of her child, the mother is in a stage of transition (most often for a period of 40 days, in imitation of the biblical custom) until the ceremony of *churching*, when she is reincorporated into the Christian community. Churching functions both to purify her from the polluted character of the conception (also conceived in terms of original sin) and to reinsert her into normal activities. As a symbol of her new status and life, she wears a new dress. Once the churching has taken place, she is then allowed to go to church again and to resume her conjugal life with her husband (provided she does not breast-feed her baby, for a taboo forbids sexual intercourse during nursing). Like all transitional stages, pregnancy is characterized by vulnerability and danger. It is a time when the pregnant woman is driven by extravagant desires, which are to be satisfied at any cost. To protect the infant from birthmarks and malformations, she must respect prohibitions: on sexuality, on food (ingestion of hare's head), and on some contacts, for example, with red fruit. After birth the transition is marked by the disorder characterizing all liminal situations, with visits to the mother's special confinement bed. Here we find the midwife and the women from the neighborhood and family sharing food, drink, and gossip.

For the newborn child the transition ends with baptism. During this period the infant is vulnerable to evil spirits and witches. The ritual of baptism emphasizes both the stage of separation, to "exorcise" original sin and the devil's influence through purifying acts (the priest applies his hand, salt, and saliva, and makes the sign of the cross), and also the stage of incorporation, bringing the child into the community of Christians. Children who die before baptism remain in a liminal situation, condemned to return to earth as ghosts and bad spirits. A series of authorized practices was devised to ensure baptism for the newborn. In emergencies, even women, usually midwives, could conduct these rituals. Even though the fetus cannot be baptized when still in the mother's womb, baptism is allowed if the mother is dead and the fetus is extracted by cesarean section, or as soon as a part of the body emerges. Some saints' sanctuaries were the sites of rituals to reanimate dead or stillborn infants so that baptism could be performed on them.

Marriage rituals act as a bridge connecting a natural given of life, sexuality, to such forms of social organization as the family, the community, and the Church. The wedding procession articulates the pattern of the rite of passage by inscribing its three stages in space, beginning at the father's house, where the separation takes place, moving to the site of the ceremony itself, and ending at the threshold of the new home, where customs of incorporation occur: grain is sprinkled, or tests are imposed on the bride, such as spinning with her distaff.

As a symbol of passage, the procession is also a fundamental component of baptisms and funerals. Similarly, the sharing of food and drink after these ceremonies serves as a rite of incorporation and communion. Thus, feasting and drinking also mark the conclusion of funerals. In each case, also, postliminal rites are performed in order to reconfirm the new situation. Special activities are reserved for newlyweds, such as lighting the ritual fires on St. John's Day (June 24). For marriage the period of transition can be said to extend to the birth of the first child.

For death, even if the sequence of rites ends after the prescribed mourning period, commemorative services are performed to aid the incorporation of the dead person's soul into the otherworld. After the funeral mass novenas are offered, and the first anniversary of the death is observed with a banquet. Theoretically, there is no end to this collaboration of the living in the deceased's salvation, as illustrated by the custom of perpetual weekly masses. Uncertainty about the deceased's incorporation into the body of the Saved in Paradise gives rise to two concurrent images of transitional status: the wandering of the souls of the wicked and their sojourn in Purgatory, a place of purification. The final reconciliation, or its prospect, are as important for the living as for the dead because of the threat posed by the dead, in the form of incubi and succubi, or by the troupe of haunting ghosts called the *mesnie Hellequin* (motif E501).

For all these reasons, sudden death is considered a curse. It does not allow time to accomplish the passage properly. The ritual complex begins before death with rites of separation and purification accompanying the agony: anointing, prayers,

blessing, preparation for death (confession, absolution, reconciliation), and the *viaticum*, the last communion, by which the soul will join the community of saints at the final resurrection. An important act, well documented for the fifteenth century, is the will, the last public transaction with the community of the living—family and parish. The procession, an important component of funeral ceremonies, illustrates the social status of the deceased. Rites of separation are prominent, with the double stage of putting the corpse in the coffin and then in the grave. The liminal period sets apart the mourning group, which dresses in different clothing and suspends its social life. Repeated commemorative ceremonies on behalf of the dead, for example, at All Souls' Day (November 2), show that their definitive separation from the living is impossible and that they constitute an age group, the final one. Cemeteries are near the abodes of the living, their space being used as the equivalent of a public square for a diversity of social events from fairs to dances.

There are no specific European initiation rituals, but a set of traditions exist that are meant to separate the young from an asexual world and to incorporate them into the world of sexuality. Rites of courtship and marriage play such a role. Initiation occurs also through other social promotions, such as accession to knighthood or a guild. By the thirteenth century the dubbing ceremony had acquired the prestige of a quasi sacrament. After the separation from the Old World through confession and fasting the day before, and the transition of a night of solitary vigil, the candidate performs a double integration, religious and secular. He hears mass and takes the oath to uphold the honor of chivalry; he is girded with his sword, kissed, and given the palm by his sponsor.

Another quasi-liturgical rite of medieval society, the coronation of kings, also follows the pattern of rites of passage. Royal consecration implies an increase of status, an access to sacred power, as exemplified by the gift to cure the king's evil (scrofula). Here again, processions from place to place inscribe in space the moments of the rite. At the coronation of the king of France taking place in Rheims, the cortege leaves the bishop's palace after the ritual awakening and rising of the king (as signs of separation from the profane and awakening to a new life) and returns to it after the ceremony. The movement in the cathedral also represents this progression toward the sacred. After a pause on the threshold, there is a procession to the altar. There, after he has taken off his old outer garments as a last gesture of separation, the king's incorporation begins: knighting, unction with holy oil, conferring of the insignia (tunic, ring, scepter, crown), and mass.

The coronation ceremony parallels the ecclesiastical ordination, both presenting analogies with marriage rituals. In ordinations the principal rite is tonsure, the shaving of the top of the head, as a sign of both separation from secular life and incorporation in the religious community. In some traditions feasting and dancing marked a priest's first mass, while in the Tyrol his mock marriage is performed.

The system of rites of passage can also be applied to seasonal rites celebrating the changes associated with natural cycles. Rites of spring dramatize the idea of death, expectation, and rebirth, and the main Christian celebrations, Christmas and Easter, follow the same pattern. Youth groups and their "fool societies" were responsible for the calendar festivities, from the Feast of Fools of Christmastime to Carnival and the Midsummer fires. Young men also exerted power in charivaris, which ritually mocked second marriages. Relative tolerance of misrule surrounded these activities, as is typical of transitional periods. Youths express the state of *liminality* proper to their age group and the spirit of *communitas* (community) manifest in such festivities.

Liminality and *communitas* are two notions Victor Turner developed, in his adaptation of van Gennep's model, to stress the autonomy acquired by transitional periods. Turner emphasizes this interstitial phase between two statuses and extends it to any condition on the margins of everyday life. During liminal phases the breach of norms governing social relations gives rise to *communitas*, an unstructured and relatively undifferentiated community of equals—for example, in pilgrimages, where social boundaries are relaxed and the journey's end is celebrated by the usual custom of reintegration, the sharing of food with the community.

See also: Childbirth; Festivals and Celebrations; Funeral Customs and Burial Rites; Marriage Traditions

—Madeleine Jeay

Robert of Sicily. A popular Middle English poem that shares a plot with ancient Asian tales and twentieth-century folktales, a plot that folklorists classify as AT 757, "The King's Haughtiness Punished."

Robert of Sicily is the story of a king who hears the Magnificat (My Soul Gives Praise to the Lord—the first words of Mary's response to the angel of the Annunciation) sung in church. Robert hears the line "He has put down the mighty from their seats" and rebels against God and assumes that no one can remove him from his high position. In punishment, God sends an angel to take Robert's place as king while Robert is made the court fool. Robert's hair is cut short, as a sign of his humiliation and subservience, and he is given an ape for a companion. Robert eventually repents and is restored to his royal honors by the angel. He is a better and wiser king for the duration of his reign.

The poem is often classified as a romance, and it does possess certain traits normally associated with the genre. For example, Robert is called "of chiualrie flour," that is, a flower of chivalry, a typical romance epithet. Yet *Robert of Sicily* also contains and synthesizes folk tradition, biblical exegesis, and history. (Robert seems to be a conflation of the eleventh-century Norman Robert Guiscard and his nephew, Roger the Great, king of Sicily.) The poem does an excellent job of teaching its lesson: pride goes before a fall. The Magnificat scene underscores the motif of arrogance humiliated and punished.

The story of *Robert of Sicily* was popular during the Middle Ages and Renaissance. There are ten versions in Middle English (dating from c. 1375 to c. 1500) and references to three dramatizations in the fifteenth through the seventeenth centuries. It has many analogs that lack the Magnificat scene. In the fourteenth-century story collection *Gesta Romanorum* (Deeds of the Romans), for example, the character analogous to Robert is the Emperor Jovinian, and the story necessarily lacks the Christian reference. In the Latin, French, German, and Italian versions the proud ruler is taking a bath when the angel takes his place, and thus he must face the world not only without his throne but naked as well.

Robert of Sicily uses several folkloric motifs and themes. Most prominent is the motif of the proud king displaced by an angel (L411). Other themes are shapeshifting (the taking of another's likeness) and pride punished, especially by the cutting off of hair. Some of the motifs combine the exegetical and folk traditions. To humiliate Robert as much as possible, the angel-king has him garbed like an ape and given an ape as a companion. In Christian tradition the ape was a symbol of a sinner or of a repentant sinner turning to God. In medieval folk tradition the ape was also often a symbol of a fool. The exegetical and folklore traditions come together when Robert finally prays, "Lord, on thi fool thow haue pité."

The history of *Robert of Sicily* is one of many versions both medieval and modern, but there is a dearth of scholarship on this work, and the scholarly work that exists is usually brief. It seems probable that profitable studies of *Robert of Sicily* can derive from awareness of its folkloric dimensions, especially as it takes its narrative power from the theme of the return of the king, which Robert reenacts. Comparison of the extant manuscript versions helps us to assess the poem's debt to traditional oral poetic composition, even though it is of the highly literary genre of romance. We need to be aware of the conventions of oral rhetoric in order truly to appreciate the poem's artistry.

See also: English Tradition: Middle English Period; Fool

—Alexandra H. Olsen

Robin Hood. English folk hero, celebrated in ballads, plays, and games in the late Middle Ages. According to legend, transmitted primarily through the ballads, Robin Hood was the leader of an outlaw band that included Little John, Will Scarlett, and Much the miller's son. They robbed passersby from the shelter of Barnesdale or Sherwood Forests, and Robin Hood was renowned for his skill at archery. No firm evidence of his real existence has ever been confirmed despite unremitting efforts to find historical proof linking him to a particular era. The earliest reference to Robin Hood occurs in a scribal interpolation in the legal records of the thirteenth century, but it is not until the fourteenth that references to Robin Hood become plentiful.

It is the ballads that have primarily carried the Robin Hood stories down to modern times, and there are only three that can firmly be attributed to the medieval period: the "Gest of Robin Hood," "Robin Hood and the Monk," and "Robin Hood and the Potter." Additionally, the ballads "Robin Hood and Guy of Gisborne" and "Robin Hood's Death" are often thought to have a late-medieval origin. Of the medieval Robin Hood ballads, the "Gest of Robin Hood," a unique and skillful combination of earlier ballads into a much longer work (c. 450 stanzas), had the greatest influence on the later development of the Robin Hood tradition. The tradition that developed after the Middle Ages considerably changed the medieval outlaw, and many elements of the current Robin Hood legend have little or no basis in the medieval tellings, including his being part of the Saxon resistance to the Norman Conquest, his habit of robbing from the rich to give to the poor, his aristocratic descent, and such companions as Friar Tuck and Maid Marian.

One of the unique aspects of the medieval Robin Hood narratives is their insistence upon the yeoman status of their hero. Robin and his followers are neither peasants nor nobles but, rather, represent a class of free, untitled commoners. In such works as the "Gest of Robin Hood" the hero outwits richer and more powerful people, such as corrupt clergymen. It has been suggested that the Robin Hood ballads may represent the assertion of a yeoman ethic that idealizes the vigor and morality of the yeoman class, in a push for greater social and political privilege. This interpretation would view the Robin Hood of the ballads as a moral standard and a tester figure for the other yeomen and the authorities who come into contact with him.

See also: Folklore; Outlaw

—Timothy J. Lundgren

Romance. A narrative genre of widespread influence in Western Europe between the twelfth and fifteenth centuries.

The Old French word *romanz* was first used in a literary sense to distinguish works written in vernacular French (*romanz*) from those in Latin, as when Robert Wace opposes his *Brut* to its Latin model: "Del livre oez la verité / Qui en romanze est translaté" [Hear the truth of the book, which is translated into Romanz; 7–8]. Similarly, the earliest English sense of the word seems to have been "a work in French." The version of the English romance *Beves of Hampton* found in the Auchinleck Manuscript (c. 1330) refers to its model alternately as "the Frensch" and "the romance" (1782, 1537). In both languages, the term came to designate a type of narrative notoriously difficult to define but frequently characterized by such features as a central hero, a chivalric code of conduct, an episodic structure involving adventures in love and in war, an interest in marvels, a characteristic remaking of ancient or foreign cultures in the image of contemporary Christian feudal culture, and frequently a happy ending involving the successful outcome of the hero's adventures and his marriage. Contemporary catalogs of romances list them by their central characters, suggesting that the presence of a certain kind of hero was a defining characteristic of romance for medieval audiences.

Composed in nearly all the European vernaculars, cyclical romances shared a set of characters and a common background, the major cycles being devoted to Alexander, Charlemagne, Arthur, and the siege of Troy. A large number of romances, however, have no close connection, or no connection at all, to the great cycles. At the end of the twelfth century, Jean Bodel divided the French romances into the "Matters" of France, Rome, and Britain, a mode of classification that has remained influential and to which modern scholars have added the "Matters" of England and of "Araby," or the Orient.

Overview of the Genre

Although romances were composed, performed, and enjoyed throughout Europe, many of the most innovative and characteristic examples of the genre originated in France. The *Perceval* and *Lancelot* of Chrétien de Troyes were among the most influential of medieval romances, inspiring continuations and retellings in most European vernaculars. A brief look at one of Chrétien's romances is perhaps the best way to communicate the nature and the major preoccupations of the form as it flourished in twelfth-century France. *Yvain* (c. 1177) opens with a discussion of the practice of love and courtship, contrasting the brilliant lovers at King Arthur's court with the sorry state of wooing in the narrator's own day, in which, he laments, it has been reduced entirely to lies and vanity. These prefatory remarks alert Chrétien's audience to his love of irony and play. As the story begins, we quickly discover that even in the idealized long-ago world of Arthur's court, knights and lovers already had their shortcomings. *Yvain*'s opening also illustrates the aristocratic milieu in which French romances were set, with its characteristic interest in "courtesy"—meaning at once the quality of a knight's or lady's personal conduct and the appropriateness of that conduct to the specialized and challenging world of the court. The tale's central action involves a particularly serious violation of courtesy: the breach of a promise. After his marriage to the beautiful and highborn Laudine, Yvain is lured away by another knight, Gawain, to undertake a series of challenging adventures. Although he promises Laudine that he will return at the end of a year and protests strongly that he could scarcely leave her even for so long, he forgets his promise. Laudine is deeply affronted, and Yvain must win his way back into her esteem. Thus, the tale's emphasis is not so much on the various deeds that Yvain successfully performs as on the problem of how love can stand up to outside pressures, especially the pressure to uphold one's reputation for valor. Chrétien's *Erec et Enide* presents a similar conflict, and all of his romances share this impulse to subject chivalric ideals to severe tests.

While *Yvain* demonstrates the courtly affiliations of Chrétien's work, it also contains shadowy but intriguing traces of the older tales to which he gave his distinctive treatment. For example, Yvain's beloved lady, Laudine, defends a magic fountain, essential to her well-being, and she confers upon Yvain a ring that will make him invulnerable. Although Chrétien gives no indication that his heroine is a supernatural being, most scholars would agree that at some earlier stage of the tale's development she would have been a fairy. Her attendant, Lunette, also shares traits with the supernatural helpers of legend and folktale: at a crucial moment, for example, she provides the hero with a ring that makes him invisible. Yvain in some important ways resembles the mortal held captive by a fairy so that he will protect her kingdom, a role widespread in Celtic folklore. In a near-contemporary and related Arthurian tale, Marie de France's *Lanval*, the role of the supernatural is more overt and the hero's lady is indeed a fairy, invisible or visible as she chooses, who carries him off to her otherworld realm at the end of the *lai*.

French romance exerted a powerful influence in Germany, where Chrétien's works were imitated and continued, most notably by Wolfram von Eschenbach in his *Parzival* (c. 1210). Another important German work, Gottfried von Strassburg's *Tristan*, was composed at about the same time and was modeled on the Anglo-French romance by a poet called Thomas of Britain (c. 1180). Both German poets seem to have been attracted to the religious and mystical elements present in French romance. Although in Chrétien these elements were often subordinated to his interest in the tensions between individual actions or desires and a collective courtly code, in these two great German works the emphasis is on spiritual enlightenment rather than on the achievement of love and marriage.

Verse romances in English began to appear in the thirteenth century and proliferated in the fourteenth. By the fifteenth century many tales were recast in prose. Metrical romances based on English legend include *King Horn*, *Havelok the Dane*, *Beves of Hampton*, and *Guy of Warwick*. These works show less interest in erotic passion and the intricacies of courtly behavior than do the majority of French romances; they address broader human issues, such as the establishment of one's adult identity and rightful place in the world. The well-known English Arthurian romance *Sir Gawain and the Green Knight* differs from Continental romance not just in its narrative manner but also in its use of an ultimately Germanic verse form, the alliterative long line. *Gawain* was composed by an anonymous poet of the English West Midlands in the last quarter of the fourteenth century. Often judged by modern audiences as the most brilliant and compelling of English romances, the poem presents a hero enmeshed in an interlocking web of very serious games, which are, as it turns out, tests. Most prominent among these are an exchange of blows and a sexual temptation. A green man challenges the hero to deliver a blow with his fearsome axe and to accept a return blow one year later. The test is of Gawain's fidelity to his pledged word, a major chivalric value, but also of his physical courage. On his way to keep his obligation, Gawain accepts the hospitality of a host who also tests him, sending his alluring wife to try Gawain's chastity, his loyalty to his host, and his fidelity to another promise, that he will exchange his winnings with his host. The exchange of winnings is another folkloric element, as is the testing host. Part of the poem's great attraction for modern readers is the way in which the poet makes original and arresting use of deeply resonant traditional materials.

Roughly contemporary to *Gawain* but in a very different style are the romances of Geoffrey Chaucer's *Canterbury Tales*. The *Canterbury Tales* is a great collection of Middle English narrative genres, and it is a mark of the genre's importance that "The Knight's Tale," "The Squire's Tale," "The Wife of Bath's Tale," and "The Franklin's Tale" are all romances. "The Man of Law's Tale" and "The Clerk's Tale" are also sometimes classed as romances, and at any rate they clearly share important romance traits. Finally, "The Tale of Sir Thopas" is variously held to parody the romance genre, to ridicule bad romance, or, perhaps, since the tale is represented as the pilgrim Chaucer's own, to caricature those aspects of Chaucer's own style that derive from English metrical romance. Another English Arthurian work, Thomas Malory's *Morte Darthur* (1469–1470) derives from a large, multiform body of thirteenth-century French legends. Malory reshaped the legends he inherited into a consistent literary whole in prose, a synthesis that strongly influenced later representations of Arthurian legend in English poetry and prose.

Literary and Folkloric Ancestry

The various theories of medieval romance's development are sometimes presented as mutually exclusive, but in fact we should expect to find numerous lines of descent and influence informing so large and diverse a collection of narratives. Most venerable is the argument that medieval romance derives from earlier heroic narratives, including the chansons de geste in France and the national epics of Germany and Spain. According to this view, the older narratives were transformed in response to important cultural changes in the twelfth and subsequent centuries. Most notable among these changes is a deeper interest in the literary representation of interior states. This development is associated with the rise of a more personal and confession-oriented form of Christian religious practice and with the increasing importance of writing and private reading. A striking example of the shift from public obligations to personal motivation is the Anglo-Norman *Eneas* (c. 1155), which retells Virgil's *Aeneid* for medieval audiences, amplifying the attenuated relationship between Aeneas and Lavinia into a full-blown Ovidian love story. The continuity between the chansons de geste and the French and English Charlemagne romances also illustrates a direct line of descent from epic to romance. The Charlemagne romances use the same characters and at times even the same plot elements as the chansons de geste, yet they give them the particular literary treatment that we associate with romance.

The "transformed epic" theory of romance development can by no means account for the entire genre, however. A second line of descent links medieval romance to the long prose narratives of late antiquity, including the so-called Greek romances and, more important, the late-Latin versions of the Troy story. The Troy narratives attributed to Dares Phrygius and Dictys Cretensis are sparse and somber epitomes that had already come a long distance from what could meaningfully be called "epics." Among the earliest extant medieval romances is the mid-twelfth-century *Roman de Troie* of Benoît de Ste.-Maure, a medievalized account of the fall of Troy that owes more to the late prose epitomes than to the epics of classical antiquity. Another narrative genre, the saint's life or legend, developed alongside romance in a relationship of mutual influence. Saints' lives in Latin began to appear between the fifth and ninth centuries, and the genre flourished in the European vernaculars from the eleventh to the fifteenth centuries. Like many romances, saints' lives frequently follow an individual on a solitary quest and trace his or her inner growth. The two genres are very different—one celebrating worldly reputation and erotic joy, the other humility and self-denial—

yet they clearly influenced one another in important ways, to the extent that scholars have frequently included under the wide umbrella of romance a subgenre such as "exemplary romance" or "hagiographic romance."

Finally, and of particular interest to past folklorists, is the hypothesis, most often raised in connection with Arthurian romance, that identifies folklore genres as forerunners of medieval romance. Roger S. Loomis's argument that the twelfth-century Arthurian tales of Chrétien de Troyes borrow heavily from older legends in Welsh has been hotly contested since the 1960s, but it has never been disproved. A similar controversy surrounds the *lais* of Marie de France, who claimed to have recorded in writing the orally circulating narrative songs of the Bretons. Eugène Vinaver held that the "matter" of medieval romance descended from folkloric sources but that, in their narrative treatment of these inherited tales, early romance writers such as Benoît were influenced by the medieval tradition of marginal and interlinear glossing. Accustomed by education to explicating a given text's rhetorical figures, learned allusions, and underlying religious and moral teachings, the early authors of romance incorporated these glosses into their narratives as authorial commentary, producing a new kind of self-explicating storytelling. A problem with verifying hypotheses about folkloric ancestors is that most surviving folkloric analogs to medieval romance were collected in recent centuries. Often the investigator is unable to distinguish between a possible parent form for a medieval romance and that romance's own offspring, subsequently reintegrated into oral tradition. Thus, as early as 1964 Francis Utley encouraged folklorists to investigate a tale's cultural transformations and its passage in and out of literary circulation. Attention to "the oral process," he urged, is "vastly more important than origins," a position shared by most folklorists today.

Audience and Social Context

During its formative period in twelfth-century France, romance was profoundly affected by aristocratic patronage. Chrétien de Troyes composed his works at the court of Marie, Countess of Champagne, daughter of Louis VII of France and Eleanor of Aquitaine. His *Lancelot* identifies Marie as his patroness, and his *Perceval* is dedicated to Philip of Flanders. As we have seen, Chrétien's works show a deep preoccupation with the concerns of the chivalric elite, including dynastic marriage, the disposition of property, subtle questions of conduct and self-presentation, and the social and emotional complexities surrounding the aristocratic code of courtesy or courtliness. Although the social distribution of the audience for romance grew much wider over the succeeding centuries, the great and continued influence of twelfth-century French romance ensured that courtesy, even in transformations that Chrétien would scarcely have recognized, remained a central focus throughout the history of the form.

Medieval romance frequently expresses a deeply felt tension between vassal and overlord that indicates a genuine historical connection to the problems of late feudalism as they appeared to medieval aristocracies. Both the antagonism between King Mark and Tristran in the versions of the romance of Tristan and Iseut and the strain on the relationship between Arthur and Lancelot in Chrétien's work demonstrate the culture's interest in what kind of loyalty a vassal owes to a limited or flawed but legitimate sovereign. This central issue persists into the prose romances of the fifteenth century and plays a role in the tragic ending of Malory's *Morte Darthur*. The strain imposed by Continental inheritance practices also left its mark on romance. Georges Duby has argued that much Old French literature, romances included, articulates the concerns of the many highborn men who were cut off from wielding any real power by inheritance laws that conferred wealth and titles only on the oldest of male siblings. In England during the period of romance's flourishing, these sources of strain were less severe: inheritance laws were less likely to cut off aristocratic sons from wealth and power, social mobility was more possible, and royal power was more secure. Thus, in English romance prior to Malory we find less evidence of bitter and insoluble tension between retainer and overlord. Rather, as Susan Crane has argued, "insular romances" (i.e., those written in Britain) attempt to resolve the tensions by accepting royal power but implying that it is also in the interest of royalty and commoners alike for England's landed barons to flourish.

Particularly in England, the evidence of the texts themselves suggests that romance circulated widely, well beyond the highest educational and social circles. Within the large corpus of Middle English narratives designated as romance we find a broad spectrum of works. At one extreme are tales like *Gamelyn*, *Havelok*, or the *Tale of Rauf Coilyear*, skillful but easily accessible stories that show considerable interest in the problems, pursuits, and interests of ordinary people. At the other are the romances of Chaucer, John Gower, and the anonymous *Gawain* poet, works of considerable learning and stylistic complexity, often with highly ambitious narrative strategies. The audience even for a single tale can range widely over the social scale, as was apparently the case with the early-fourteenth-century *Seege or Batayle of Troye*. Whether read aloud, recited from memory, or read privately, this tale is sufficiently entertaining and self-explanatory to reach an audience with a minimum of prior literary experience and little or no acquaintance with the Troy story. Its author carefully introduces even the most prominent Greek and Trojan heroes and identifies them by nationality throughout the poem. Yet it would be a mistake to relegate the *Seege* only to the lower ranks of society. In the mid-fourteenth-century manuscript Arundel 22 it keeps company with a prose history of the British monarchy, translated into English first from Geoffrey of Monmouth's *Historia regum Britanniae* (History of the Kings of Britain) and then from Wace's *Brut*. The book is an expensively executed compilation made for a reader of means, and the presence of the *Seege* in such a setting argues for a wider audience than the frequently applied designation "popular" might suggest. The large and well-known romance collection called the Auchinleck Manuscript (National Library of Scotland MS Advocates 19.3.1) contains some of the best known English romances (including *Guy of Warwick*, *Beves of Hampton*, and *Sir Orfeo*) in combination with English legends, macaronic poems, and moral treatises, as well as carols and recipes in Latin. The Lincoln Thornton Manuscript (Lincoln Cathedral Library MS 91) contains nine English romances as well as Latin prayers, antiphonies, collects, and psalms. Like all attempts to sort out piles of medieval texts and assign them exclusively to the lower classes, the relegating of English romance to "popular" or little-educated audiences conflicts with the surviving evidence.

Romance Texts as Bearers of Medieval Folklore
Many of the most memorable medieval romances handle highly traditional materials in a fresh and arresting way. In the opening lines of his *Erec et Enide*, Chrétien describes himself as giving beautiful artistic form (*"une molt bele conjointure"*) to a tale of adventure (*"un conte d'aventure"*) that already exists. While Chrétien's romances clearly reflect the values of the highborn patrons to whom they were dedicated, the received tales or legends on which they are based would have circulated among a much broader range of people. The dynamic and integral relationship between *conte* and *conjointure* has long been a central issue of Chrétien studies, and the dominant view holds that as a man of learning, probably a cleric, Chrétien used his rhetorical skills to transform folktales and other popular narratives into a form both more stylistically elaborate and more directly reflective of aristocratic values. In an article of interest to folklorists, E. B. Vitz has challenged the established view of Chrétien as a cleric and man of letters. Rather, she argues that despite his protestations of superiority to oral performers of traditional narratives, Chrétien was in fact likely to have been himself a particularly skilled *menestrel*, or popular entertainer who recited his works from memory.

The relationship between literary romance and oral storytelling remains a subject for debate, but the surviving texts reveal a kind of performativity or residual orality that distinguishes them from genres more fully assimilated to written modes of thought and expression. The narrator of Wolfram von Eschenbach's *Parzival* famously insists that he is entirely illiterate and that his work has no connection with books, and the narrator of Geoffrey Chaucer's *Troilus and Criseyde* (c. 1387) makes numerous allusions to his presence before a listening audience as well as to the composition of his text in writing. Romance's ambivalent attempts to preserve orality in textuality support Brian Stock's argument that medieval orality and textuality are best investigated as coexisting aspects of the surviving texts rather than as binary oppositions.

What use the folklorist can legitimately make of the traditional materials embedded in medieval romance remains a crucial and contested issue. The surviving romances circulated in writing, and thus those who insist on oral transmission as an essential criterion for identifying folklore will not consider the romances, or any other medieval texts, as viable sources. However, much new thought in the field of medieval folklore consists of creative responses to this apparent impasse. Aron Gurevich and Brian Stock have both argued powerfully that we must acknowledge and learn to work with the oral in the written, the fragments of oral beliefs and genres, both popular and elite, that survive in medieval texts. The task of developing a sound methodology for doing so is under way. Medieval romance is at best a highly problematic source for recovering orally circulating tales or the lore of the least-powerful members of medieval society, but its wide dissemination—geographically, demographically, and temporally—makes it a richly promising medium through which to study processes of social accommodation and transformation.

See also: Chaucer, Geoffrey; Chrétien de Troyes; Folktale; Guy of Warwick; Marie de France; *Sir Gawain and the Green Knight*

—Nancy Mason Bradbury

Runes and Runic Inscriptions.

The letters of the native Germanic alphabet, called the *futhark* after the first six signs (runes), and messages created by the carving of runes into such surfaces as bone, stone, or wood.

Runic was probably invented around the beginning of the first century C.E., inspired by one or more Mediterranean alphabets. Each rune had a meaningful name beginning with the sound it represented (e.g., "f"—Proto-German **fehu*, Old English *feoh*, Old Norse *fé*: "cattle, wealth"). As the branches of Germanic became differentiated, the Anglo-Saxons and Frisians expanded the original 24-rune *futhark* (Older Runes) to 26 to 31 signs (Anglo-Frisian Runes), while the Scandinavians streamlined it to 16 (Younger Runes). Runes were supplanted by the Latin letters (Anglo-Frisian, c. 1000; Scandinavian, c. 1500), eventually becoming another occult alphabet in *The Book of Ballymote* and numerous *Cypriani*.

Runic is an epigraphic (carved or engraved) writing system. Inscriptions survive on stones both cut and natural, weapons, jewelry, coins, wooden sticks, and the walls of buildings, some of these types being more common in certain periods than others. Stereotyped memorial inscriptions on stone, maker's inscriptions, and *futhark* inscriptions appear in all periods, as do indecipherable (or at least, undeciphered) texts. How representative the surviving corpus is for any period and place is debated.

Inscriptions in the Older Runes (c. 150–700) are the most problematic to interpret and have attracted many magical and cultic explanations. A few decipherable inscriptions on thin gold plate (e.g., *alu*, "beer"?) may have functioned as amulets. The Anglo-Frisian inscriptions (c. 400–900) are more difficult in the pagan period, but after about 650 they appear in Christian burial contexts, including on St. Cuthbert's coffin. Unique but important is the Ruthwell Cross inscription (eighth century), which records an earlier version of the Anglo-Saxon poem *The Dream of the Rood* than that in the *Vercelli Book*. Viking Age inscriptions (c. 750–1050, Younger Runes) are best known for appearing on monumental memorial stones, especially in Uppland, Sweden, in very stereotyped formulas. These runes were also carved by Scandinavians abroad in Greenland, the British Isles, Russia, and Turkey. The corpus of medieval runic inscriptions (c. 1050–1500, Younger Runes with medieval refinements) is unique for its sizable number of inscriptions on wood, many from towns and church buildings. This is the least-stereotyped group of inscriptions; it includes love letters, price tags, curses, and poetry in Scandinavian and Latin.

Treating runes as inherently magical signs has fallen out of scholarly favor since A. Bæksted (1952), though the idea that magic residing in the rune names could be accessed through the individual runes continues to appear (e.g., in the work of S. Flowers). The magical character of runes has typically been linked to the circumstances of their invention, which removes much of the debate from the medieval period. However, J. Knirk has recently turned attention to interpreting nonsemantically resolvable inscriptions (including medieval ones) without the framework of a priori magical runes. The medieval town finds have also increased the number of known inscriptions with clearly magical content.

Five alliterative Rune Poems that riddle on the names of the runes survive in Old English, Danish, Icelandic, Norwegian, and Swedish. They, along with the nonriddling, Continental *Abecedarium Nordmannicum*, have been used in reconstructions of the original rune names. There has also been some investigation of the possibility of an ur–Rune Poem or a broader Germanic tradition of runic riddling, as in J. Louis-Jensen's research.

Ruthwell Cross–like cases of poetic preservation are extremely rare, but a number of inscriptions preserve poetic meters, subjects, and motifs from heroic legend and myth otherwise known only from significantly later manuscript sources. Runes are mentioned with some frequency in Old Norse literature. The Eddic poems describe a supernatural origin for runic knowledge, whether acquired initially by Odin or passed on to humans (*Havamal* 80, 139; *Rigsthula* 46); they suggest the use of runes in beneficial and hostile magic (*Sigrdrifumal* 7–14; *Skirnismal* 36); and they depict the use of runes in sending secret messages (*Atlakvida* 4). Legendary sagas and the Sagas of Icelanders show runes used in magic both helpful and harmful (*Egil's Saga* 72; *Grettir's Saga* 81), often by characters with traits like Odin's. There is no consensus at this time as to how to understand the thirteenth-century literary portrayal of runes in relation to any historical reality, but the overall trend since the 1960s has been toward conservatism.

See also: English Tradition: Anglo-Saxon Period; Scandinavian Tradition

—Merrill Kaplan

*S*agas of Icelanders [Íslendin-gasögur, also known as the Icelandic Family Sagas].

Anonymous prose narratives recorded during the thirteenth century (c. 1220–1300 C.E.) that purport to be objective accounts of the Viking or Saga Age (c. 870–1050 C.E.) when Norwegian chieftains—ostensibly as a way of escaping the encroaching power of the monarchy—migrated to Iceland.

There they established a commonwealth that lasted until 1262–1264, when they submitted to the rule of the Norwegian king. Iceland converted to Christianity relatively late (1000 C.E.), making the 35–40 Sagas of Icelanders that have survived valued—but much debated—sources of information about pre-Christian or pagan society and social practices: laws and customs, dreams and omens, rituals and ceremonies, superstitions and supernatural beings, and games and proverbs. Although the origins of the Sagas of Icelanders are elusive, their plain and sparing language, their anonymous narrators, their attention to everyday matters, and their use of dialogue to create lively and memorable scenes suggest that their roots lie in oral tradition, hence their affinity with folktale narrative. The word *saga* (plural *sögur*) itself suggests these oral roots: it is related to the verb *segja*, to "say" or "tell." There are many types of sagas recorded in Iceland in addition to those that we today call Sagas of Icelanders: sagas of kings, saints, bishops; legendary (or heroic) sagas of ancient times; chivalric romances; and contemporary sagas about the turbulent events of Iceland during the thirteenth century, when the Sagas of Icelanders were being recorded.

Had a thirteenth-century Icelander left a description of how sagas were composed or recorded, it would have spared later scholars much effort and ink. During the sixteenth and early seventeenth centuries Scandinavian historians, eager to document the early histories of their kingdoms, took the sagas at face value and relied on them as faithful transcriptions of local traditions that had been preserved orally until they were finally written down. The Latin alphabet was introduced and adapted for writing in the vernacular after the conversion to Christianity. The native runic alphabet used previously was suited only for shorter inscriptions. Longer texts or verses would have had to have been memorized and performed orally. Although the early view that the Sagas of Icelanders are reliable historical accounts has been overturned, there is still debate on the role that oral tradition played in saga composition.

Some scholars, proponents of the so-called bookprose view, downplay that role. They consider oral tradition as only one of many sources and claim that the sagas were literary products of medieval authors who merely used disconnected oral traditions as a way of lending an impression of authenticity to their mostly imaginative evocations of the past. These scholars emphasize the influence of other written sources available in Iceland during the thirteenth century: histories, genealogies, law codes, and other sagas, as well as foreign secular and sacred works that were imported to Iceland. On the other hand are scholars, adherents of the so-called freeprose view, who propose that longer prose narratives might have taken shape around the verses and local legends that had been preserved orally during the 250 years between the time the events took place and when the sagas were recorded.

Manuscripts

The most concrete evidence in this debate would seem to be manuscripts written on vellum (treated animal skin, sheepskin in Iceland). However, none of the original vellums of the Sagas of Icelanders have survived. A few fragments of vellum contain sagas dated to the latter half of the thirteenth century, but most of the surviving manuscripts are copies of earlier manuscripts made during the fourteenth, fifteenth, and even sixteenth centuries. Dating the texts is therefore problematic. *Egil's Saga*, one of the more biographical sagas, is organized around the life of an obstreperous poet (or *skald*) who feuds with the king and queen of Norway. This saga is thought to have been recorded circa 1220–1240, that is, before the commonwealth collapsed. Some scholars believe that the great Icelandic historian and chieftain Snorri Sturluson (1179–1241), who wrote the *Heimskringla* (History of Norwegian Kings) and a treatise on poetic verse and Norse mythology (*Prose Edda*, or *Snorra Edda*), also wrote *Egil's Saga*, but this remains a conjecture.

Verses

Sagas of Icelanders, like the kings' sagas, contain verses said to have been composed at the time of the events. They are often situated in a historical context, and the name of the poet is preserved as well. In his prologue to *Heimskringla* Snorri claims that these poems were memorized and transmitted orally. But the dating of the skaldic verses recorded in the sagas is controversial. Some scholars have questioned the authenticity of the verses spoken and composed by saga characters and have suggested instead that the medieval author composed the verses. They point out that the archaic style and poetic diction could have been imitated by the authors, who composed the verses themselves to suit their prose narrative. Snorri Sturluson's *Edda* (c. 1220) was probably written as a textbook instructing younger poets in the old pagan techniques and myths that were losing popularity and being replaced with newer forms. On the other hand, there are scholars who distinguish between "authentic tradition" and "oral tradition," noting that the verses may not all have been composed in the tenth century by the people in the sagas but, rather, could have been composed orally after the events and become part of oral traditions about these historical people and events before the sagas were finally recorded. In support of oral tradition, these scholars find occasional conflicts between the verses and the prose in the sagas, conflicts that an author, if not bound by tradition, would have reworked. Even Snorri himself, they point out, at times did not necessarily understand the poetry he quotes.

Other Evidence

Although there is no concrete proof of the existence of oral sagas, other evidence is commonly offered in support of the freeprose view: (1) allusions in the sagas to saga telling and the naming of oral sources; (2) the availability and assumed common knowledge of saga tradition when Sturla Thordarson (1214–1284) revised the *Landnamabok* (Book of Settlements); (3) allusions to other, divergent oral traditions that undermine the notion of an author in complete control of his sources; (4) the recurrence of several notable Saga Age personalities in unrelated contexts; and (5) the parallel tradition of the oral, legendary (heroic) saga—translated, probably revised, and recorded in Latin around 1200 by the Danish historian Saxo Grammaticus, who credits Icelanders as his sources of pagan Scandinavian history.

According to those who hold to the bookprose view, such evidence might be nothing more than the "authenticating" devices used by medieval authors with access to written sources and mere fragments of oral traditions. Scholars have mainly agreed that the most productive questions are those that ask what in the saga can be attributed to written sources and what to native tradition. Working saga by saga, scholars in the bookprose tradition have contributed much to our knowledge of the correspondences between sagas and the written sources available in the monastic institutions, the episcopal seats, and the Church farms of great families. Those who hold more to the freeprose view have used a structuralist approach to identify the building blocks of saga narrative. A six-part paradigm has been a popular and useful way of organizing the feud structure of many of the sagas. The events of the saga, according to Theodore M. Andersson, can be arranged in segments: an introduction, a series of conflicts, which lead to a climax, followed by revenge, a reconciliation, and finally an aftermath. This paradigm may have played a role not only in the way feuds were conducted during the Saga Age but also in organizing the events of the

oral sagas, thus allowing them to be recalled and transmitted orally. Using a both-and approach, Carol J. Clover has ascribed the overall organization of the sagas—their convoluted way of weaving together various subplots—to a Continental, literary aesthetic similar to the one found in French romances. The individual scenes making up the subplots are credited to native storytelling tradition.

Given the lack of more concrete evidence, the debate will perhaps never be resolved. In my view, the most persuasive theory of how this unique blend of learned and popular material could appear as fully fledged sagas, with such a consistency of style, structure, and worldview, must include the presence of a flourishing oral narrative tradition prior to the recording of the sagas.

Social Context

Egil's Saga is decidedly antiroyalist; it favors the independent farmer-chieftains who refuse to be intimidated by the Norwegian king, although they may be, like Egil, flawed heroes. The masterful *Njal's Saga* has a tragic tone; it leads the reader to lament the loss of the most-valued members of society when their lives get caught up in the tension between the old heroic values of honor and vengeance (associated with a decentralized, traditional system) and the new social ideals. These new ideals, emphasizing moderate and socially responsible citizens loyal to a centralized power figure, were ushered in along with the conversion to Christianity. These two sagas demonstrate why the thirteenth-century Icelanders thought these traditions important enough to record: amid the turbulent events of the thirteenth century (called the Sturlung Age after one of the most powerful Icelandic dynasties, the one to which Snorri Sturluson belonged), chieftains fought bloody battles to consolidate the power that was once distributed among 39 chieftains into the hands of just a few. The Norwegian king and archbishop also entered the fray, and the chieftains struggled not only to win dominance among their peers but also to maintain local control against the centralizing power of both the Norwegian monarchy and the universal Church. The Norwegian archbishop's goal was to separate Church affairs from those of the state and bring the Icelandic Church in line with the laws and customs dictated from Rome. Prior to this separation, Icelandic chieftains had their sons ordained as priests and supported a native church that was integrated with the Icelandic power structures. The conflict came to a head in 1238 when Norwegian bishops replaced the Icelandic ones. Deprived of their control over the Icelandic Church, the strife between the chieftains grew so violent that some Icelanders thought, no doubt, that the best way to end the bloodshed and restore the peace would be to be ruled by a king. In 1262–1264 the chieftains surrendered to the Norwegian king. Thus, the saga makers, witnessing the end of the commonwealth period and of the rule of the chieftains—who embodied this unique and local blend of sacred and secular power—would record what they knew of a vanishing era, one that began with the settlement of Iceland by their ancestors. Given the social context of the thirteenth-century audience (it is generally assumed that the sagas were read aloud from manuscripts to a socially mixed audience), one can see how some sagas might have been made to encourage an audience to resist the centralizing forces, while others were intended to offer solace to an audience as they watched an era come to its inevitable end.

Recent Scholarship

Prompted by studies of orality and literacy and how they overlap and interact within societies, Vésteinn Ólason and other scholars have recently viewed the Icelandic Family Sagas as a dialogue between the thirteenth century and the Saga Age. Taking into account this thirteenth-century context, sagas are read today as part literature, part social history. Influenced by the structuralist model that foregrounds the feud paradigm, saga scholarship in this century has emphasized feuding, honor and shame, law, and gender relations. Not surprisingly, the sagas that deviate most from the feud structure, *Vatnsdæla saga* (The Saga of the People of Vatnsdal) and *Eyrbiggja saga* (The Saga of the People of Eyri), have attracted the most attention among folklorists and anthropologists. These sagas are more collections of local traditions than literary products shaped by an author. This research has drawn attention to the mythic patterns, both pagan and Christian, that inform these narratives and pays particular attention to how societies deliver, control, organize, and store knowledge of the past for audiences in the present and future. These scholars note that whereas history functions as a "myth" for literate societies (we tend to believe what we have read), myths function as "history" for oral cultures, and they thus study sagas as cultural artifacts. Putting history and fiction under one roof, they try to reconstruct the mental landscape of the medieval Icelanders by studying how they compiled and classified sagas and other texts, as well as how they conceptualized interactions between the natural and supernatural realms and human and mythic beings. Crossing modern genre boundaries, they compare historical and mythic narratives or legendary sagas and classical sagas to determine whether they share similar structural patterns and concepts and seek to identify the operative social and ethical norms during the times these narratives evolved or were received.

Saga scholarship has thus come full circle, but with a reverse: When serious study and collection of sagas began in the late sixteenth and early seventeenth centuries, even the most mythical sagas were scrutinized for whatever insight they might give on the early history of the Scandinavian nations. Now scholars are subjecting the most historical texts to a similar process with hopes of revealing the underlying myths of those same cultures.

See also: Scandinavian Tradition

—Zoe Borovsky

Saints, Cults of the. Constituted by a faith community paying homage to a deceased member whose life and death have earned eternal reward according to popular tradition, though from the twelfth century onward procedures for recognizing saints were formalized as papal canonization.

The earliest saints' cults were devoted to the Christian martyrs; however, with the conversion of Constantine in the fourth century and the end of the persecution of Christians, fewer martyrdoms occurred, and other deceased Christians renowned for their piety and virtues began to be venerated by their communities. By the Middle Ages the classes of saints included not only martyrs but also virgins, bishops, confessors, and other categories of holy persons. As Christianity spread to pagan lands, individual saints became associated with particular localities. These "patron saints" often lent their names to the towns and cities of the newly converted country, and popular devotion to them by the local people grew into cults.

There are two broad divisions of saints: the first group is composed of those men and women, from the earliest Christian era to the present, for whose biographies reliable historical evidence is claimed, usually by naming reliable witnesses; the second group is made up of those figures whose stories circulated so widely in popular tradition that that tradition itself is used as a warrant for their truthfulness. The information about members of both groups consists largely of legendary narratives, and in both there may also be figures whose significance is largely symbolic—people whose *Lives* represent metaphors for various religious virtues. Throughout the literature and traditions of the *Lives*, we find recurring stylized themes: some wonder surrounds a particular saint's birth and youth; the saint preaches, or cures, or performs miracles in adult life; martyrs are persecuted, tortured, and executed; and whether the saint is martyred or not, miracles follow her or his death as proof of sainthood. By imitating their patron saints and other holy persons, medieval people practiced the *imitatio Christi* (the imitation of Christ) enjoined upon all Christians, since they emulated the lives and virtues of those whose imitation of Christ had already been successful and was now authorized.

In the early centuries of the Church and through the early Middle Ages there were thousands of saints' lives circulating in oral tradition, from the Egyptian desert to northern Europe. Many of these were sooner or later written down, in Greek in the East and in Latin in the West, though there was a strong vernacular tradition in places such as Ireland and England, where the people spoke nonromance languages with little connection to Latin. Saints' legends became the focal points for the cults of the saints they celebrated, whether these remained purely local cults, as was generally true in Cornwall, or spread far and wide, as in the cases of St. Anthony of Egypt, St. Martin of Tours, St. Patrick of Ireland, and St. Cuthbert of England. Saints' legends often included postmortem miracles at the sites of their burials or containers of their relics, and these often attracted numerous pilgrims to the sites. By the central Middle Ages these lives were often collected in large anthologies, most notably the single most important medieval source of the biographies of the saints—the one upon which their cults increasingly depended—*The Golden Legend* of Jacobus de Voragine (c. 1230–1298), bishop of Genoa. The fact that this collection of highly imaginative hagiographic accounts was, next to the Bible, the most frequently copied and published work of the entire Middle Ages indicates the fundamental importance of the cult of the saints.

The medieval Christian understood a saint to be simply a "friend of God"—one who had been redeemed and had gained everlasting life with God through an exemplary life, a sacrificial death, or both. According to the official teaching of the Church, saints were not "worshipped"; instead, they were "venerated": the faithful owed them *dulia* (veneration); God alone merited *latria* (worship). The greatest of all saints, in a class by herself, was Mary. The Mother of God was so far above all other human beings that she was accorded a distinct and superior form of veneration called *hyperdulia*.

Specific dates, derived from the narratives about them, were also associated with individual saints—usually the date of their deaths, considered their "heavenly birthday"—and on this date each year, public celebrations would take place in the locality of the cult. Thus arose the "Calendar of Saints," which is maintained by the Church to this day. This calendar establishes which mass is to be celebrated in honor of a given saint on his or her feast day. The calendar varies somewhat from country to country, in accordance with the local character of the veneration of the saints.

Holy Patrons

Saintly patronage was not restricted to or limited by geographical location. By the later Middle Ages the practice of adopting a patron saint for each profession and type of labor was virtually universal. The identity of the saint who protected a given profession and helped it to flourish was determined by the narrative concerning the life of the saint. Carpenters, for example, would rather obviously have St. Joseph as their patron saint, and his feast day (March 19) would be the occasion for particular celebration by carpenters.

In addition to the patronage of geographical locations and social occupations, saints also lent their protection and assistance to individual Christians who took their names at baptism. Medieval men and women in France, for example, celebrated the feast of the national patron saint, St. Denis (October 9), and if they were Parisians, they celebrated the feast of St. Genevieve (January 3) as well, most notably because she was accredited with having saved the city twice from foreign invaders. If they happened to be vintners by profession, on June 9 they would also celebrate the feast of St. Medard, invoked as the protector of vines. The phenomenon of patron saints and their feast days attests the considerable influence of symbolic narrative upon social structures.

The influence of saintly folklore, by no means restricted to the realm of religion, permeated every aspect of medieval life. The people of the Middle Ages lived in daily companionship with the saints. The feast days of the saints marked the rhythm of the weeks and months and signaled the times for planting and harvesting. Frequent sermons recounted the holy biographies (hagiographies), often much embellished with time, and the visual art that surrounded the church illustrated their sagas. Their own names welded the medieval persons' identities to that of the saint whose name they bore and designated the particular virtues and accomplishments they ought to emulate.

Even the world of commerce reflected the omnipresence of the saint. For instance, in many parts of the world, from the Middle Ages to the present, anyone in sudden need of money looks for an establishment with three brass balls over the door, the sign that designates a pawnshop. The sign is derived from an anecdote in the life of St. Nicholas. Famed for his generosity, St. Nicholas saved three young women who had been deprived of dowries because of their father's bad luck. Each night, the saint threw a bag of gold through their window until all three possessed the needed dowry.

Cults

A saint's cult consists of three fundamental and interacting elements: the narrative of the saint's life, iconographic representations, and the ritual enacted to venerate the saint. Often the hagiographic narrative gave rise to the saint's iconography as illustration, depicting either a series of narrative incidents or highly abstract emblems that the whole story of the saint and its symbolic significance conjured up in the minds of the initiated. A picture of a male figure holding a gridiron was immediately recognizable to a Christian as St. Lawrence, because he was roasted to death on just such a grid. However, iconography was not always derived from narrative; in some cases, features of hagiographic iconography were the source of saintly legend. For instance, in order to indicate the manner in which some saints had met their deaths, early Christian representations pictured them holding their severed heads. This inspired later medieval legends of the so-called cephalophores (head carriers) who, when executed, picked up their heads and carried them walking, singing, and otherwise performing various miracles. The saint's written life was then eventually modified to reflect this innovation, which had been inspired by iconography.

Similarly, the ritual involving prayers, enactments, and use of relics practiced by the faithful devoted to a particular saint was usually derived from elements of his or her biography, from the iconographic tradition, or both. Again, in some cases, the ritual itself could ferment to such proportions that it so far outgrew both narrative and iconography in symbolic richness that narrative and iconography had to be newly emended so as to accommodate the ritual.

The highlight of the practice of medieval devotion to St. Blaise (February 3) was the blessing of the throats of the faithful. This blessing was performed by placing two tallow candles in the form of an x on the throat. The explanation for the saint's particular ability to cure sore throats is derived from an anecdote in his life in which the saint, on the way to his execution, removes a fish bone from the throat of a choking child. But the ritual element of the candles is accounted for in another anecdote in which the saint, on the same journey, commands a wolf who has stolen a poor woman's pig to return it to her. In gratitude, the woman later brings him food and candles in prison. Why candles? Specified as tallow candles—that is, made with animal fat—they are intended to signify the pig that was restored by the saint. In this way the ritual creates the narrative.

The iconography of St. Wilgeforte, a purely legendary saint, is thought to be the sole origin of her biography. The Western viewer created a narrative to explain an icon composed of a Byzantine cross on which the crucified figure is dressed in what appeared in the medieval West as woman's clothing. The object of a very widespread cult in the late Middle Ages, Wilgeforte, as she was known in Germany and the Netherlands, is represented visually as a crucified figure with both beard and prominent breasts. Her legend recounts a familiar hagiographic theme of parental conflict, in which the pagan king of Lusitania (Portugal) attempts to force his Christian daughter, Wilgeforte, to marry the pagan ruler of Sicily. Praying to Jesus on the eve of her wedding to assist her in preserving her virginity, Wilgeforte wakes to find herself luxuriantly bearded. While the miracle is sufficient to discourage her suitor, it provokes the anger of Wilgeforte's evil sire, who has her crucified.

In what was exclusively a woman's cult, the prayer of her devotees created the identity of the saint. In England she was known as St. Uncumber, and women plagued by vexatious husbands implored, "Uncumber me of him"; in France Ste. Debarras received the prayer "De'barrasse-moi de lui!"; her Italian followers petitioned Santa Liberata, "Liberami da lui!"

The interrelation of these three constitutive elements of the saint's cult is highly dynamic—the one constantly informing the other, and all three mutually creative of the cult itself. The saint's cult is not, therefore, something created by an elite for the passive consumption by the people—a text produced by an author for reception by an audience; rather, it is an organic reality coming to life through the mutual activity of a faith community.

The three pillars of the medieval cult of the saints were the relic, the miracle, and the pilgrimage. The original burial place of a martyr or other saint contained his or her remains, or *reliquiae*, and it was believed that as the part shares in the power of the whole, whatever remained of the body of a saint or some intimate possession of the saint contained some of the vital power of the now glorified subject. To the devout, the existence of the relic made present the whole of which it was a part, much as in modern times one might wear a locket with a curl from the head of a loved one. Though the practice was discouraged by the Eastern Church, in the medieval Western Church parts of saints' bodies were parceled out and distributed to the farthest reaches of Europe, where churches were built in honor of the saints whose relics they housed. Reports of cures and other miracles at the tombs of saints or the repositories of their relics encouraged travel to those places, where the pilgrim would pray for some intention, in proximity to the relic. Relics could thus become an important source of revenue, or even political power, for the foundations that housed them, leading in some cases to the creation of (sometimes competing) legends as to the "true" site of a saint's relics or even their theft and relocation in another site—both of which happened in the case of St. Martin of Tours.

In *The Canterbury Tales*, Chaucer identifies the most popular medieval pilgrimage sites, all frequented by the famous Wife of Bath: Jerusalem and Rome, Boulogne in France, St. James Compostela in Spain, and Cologne in Germany. His portrayal of a pilgrimage to England's most famous site, the tomb of the martyr St. Thomas Becket at Canterbury, also probably accurately depicts some of the reasons why the pilgrimage had fallen into disrepute by the fourteenth century and why the cult of the saints was condemned by the reformers of Chaucer's day and later. For despite the good motives for pilgrimage among such characters as the Knight, the Parson, and the Plowman, the satirical portraits of the Wife, the Friar, the Shipman, the Summoner, and the Pardoner hardly represent the ideals of piety expected in devotion to the saint whose relics were the object of the pilgrimage. Nevertheless, the medieval devotion to the saints is reflected in the modern veneration among Catholics and Anglicans, some of whom still trace the steps of their medieval ancestors to ancient pilgrimage sites.

See also: Monks; Nuns; Pilgrimage; Relics; *entries for specific saints*

—David Williams

Samhain. The Celtic winter festival, the *ceann féile*, or chief festival, that signals the beginning of the winter season in Ireland.

The Irish, like their Celtic forebears, divided the year into two parts: a colder period, winter, beginning at Samhain, and a warmer period, summer, commencing at Beltane (Bealtaine) or Cetshamhain. The starting point of the winter season was November 1 (Samhain) in the Julian calendar. The month of November, the first of the winter season, is also called Samhain, having taken its name from the winter festival.

A twelfth-century recension of the Gaelic prose *Tocmarc Emire* (The Wooing of Emer) makes clear reference to the division of the year into two main seasons, and the beginning and end of these seasons are also designated: "For the year was divided in two ... that is, the summer from May to November and the winter from November to May." Presumably arising from the influence of inherited tradition and in response to climatic conditions and agricultural and pastoral realities in Ireland, these two major seasons were subdivided to give four shorter seasons of three months each. There are clear references in early Irish literature to the four quarters of the year, each marked by a quarter day, and the twelfth-century text just mentioned refers to Imbolc and Lugnasa, which were identified, respectively, with February 1 (later renamed St. Brigid's Day) and August 1 in the Julian calendar, as the festival days initiating the lesser seasons of spring and autumn. The festival of Imbolc divided the winter half of the year into the winter and spring seasons.

Each of these four seasons was heralded by a significant quarter day, a *ceann féile*, or major festival, which involved celebration and feasting and the performance of a variety of customs. The festival properly began at sunset on the eve of the quarter day, indicating the Celtic tradition that reckoned sundown as the beginning of each day and, in the context of Samhain, winter as preceding summer. Thus, *Oíche Shamhna* (literally, the night of Samhain, Samhain Eve, Halloween) refers to the last day of October.

The popular confusion occasioned in England by the adoption of the Gregorian reform of the Julian calendar in the mid-seventeenth century also manifested itself in Ireland. The correction of the calendar, which necessitated dropping 11 days out of reckoning, led to a doubling of festivals, so that November 11 became known as Old Hallow Eve (*Oíche Shean Shamhain*), and November 12 as Old Samhain Day (*Lá Shean Shamhain*), designations that were still familiar in the Gaeltacht, or Irish-speaking areas, of county Donegal in the middle of the twentieth century. The most important customs and beliefs, however, transferred over time to the "new" Samhain Day, as it was important to know exactly when to celebrate the festival in order to partake of its efficacy and to avoid its perils.

The word *Samhain* means the end of summer. Samhain was an agricultural and pastoral festival marking the time when the crops were gathered in and stored for the winter season, when livestock were taken back down to the home fields from the mountain pastures, and when the milk cows were housed and hand-fed for the winter season. Some livestock were disposed of at the fairs that were held around this time, and a small number were slaughtered for household provisions. Work contracts were terminated (sometimes on Old Samhain Day, November 12), and servants and workmen who were paid off returned home.

Samhain initiated the dark season of the year and was thus especially associated with the dead and the somber otherworld in both literature and folklore. Scholars have commented on the tendency among many peoples to regard the interface between two contrasting periods of summer and winter as consisting, in some sense, of "time outside of time" or as a temporary resumption of mythic or primordial time. As a boundary festival standing between two halves of the Celtic year but belonging to neither side, Samhain features prominently in Irish mythological literature and in Irish folklore as a moment when the barriers between the natural world and the otherworld are temporarily removed. Many tales in early Irish literature deal with the supernatural experiences and sometimes the death of heroes at Samhain. Some of the tales are concerned with encounters between mortals and the people of the *sidh* (*sídh*) (most often translated as "fairies," though *sidh* actually designates otherworld beings associated with burial mounds). Thus, Finn (Fionn) mac Cumaill, one of the most famous figures in early Irish heroic tales, sometimes kills otherworld adversaries on Samhain by throwing his spear into their mounds.

In Irish folk tradition, stories of the activities of the family dead and the fairies at Samhain are also very prominent. Samhain is a time for assembly and feasting and for the commemoration of ancestors. A great fair or assembly took place at this time at Tara, an ancient ceremonial site incorporating prehistoric burial mounds. Until recent times, preparations to welcome the family dead, including providing food, leaving the household chairs in front of a fire, and retiring to bed early, were made in homes in the belief that the dead members of the family would visit their former home at Samhain or on the Church festival of All Souls on November 2.

The element of chaos and tumult inherent in

the festival of Samhain, manifested in some of the early literary tales, is still evident in the carnivalesque behavior so prominent in the folk celebration of the festival of Samhain to the present day.

See also: Beltane; Celtic Mythology; Fairies; Irish Tradition; Lugnasa

—Patricia Lysaght

Saracen Princess. Theme of a love affair leading to marriage between a Christian knight and a non-Western princess—an Arabic, Indian, or black woman, any one of whom would be generically labeled a "Saracen."

This theme represents a curious medieval commonplace, although it has little basis in historical fact. However, in his chronicle of the First Crusade, Fulcher of Chartres (1058–1127) mentions that some intermarriages did occur after the Saracen women had received baptism. Otherwise the historical documents are mostly quiet regarding such relationships. Some scholars even argue that the crusader kingdoms were characterized by a form of "apartheid" prohibiting any personal interaction with the native population. Yet the literary evidence of the chansons de geste, romances, saints' lives, and legendary histories points in another direction, even if we are dealing here with wishful projections.

Typically the literature portrays a powerful and beautiful Saracen Princess who first helps her Christian lover to escape from prison and then escapes with him, leaving her heathen father behind. The story involves a cluster of motifs, including T91.6.4.1 (Sultan's daughter in love with captured knight), R162 (Rescue by captor's daughter), and *V331.5.2 (Saracen Princess to become Christian if Christian hero will marry her). One or more of these plot elements is found in the Middle English verse romances of *Beves of Hampton, Octavian, Richard, Sir Ferumbras,* and *The Sultan of Babylon,* and French examples are similarly numerous.

This scenario is found in such other narratives as the Middle English life of St. Thomas Becket, in the thirteenth-century *South English Legendary,* as well as the Old French *Les enfances Guillaume* (The Boyhood Deeds of William). In each the Arabic woman displays considerable magical powers, deceives her Saracen family, and finally unites with the Christian hero as her predestined lover. Secular love quickly convinces the lady to abandon her old beliefs and accept baptism as a precondition for marriage with her Christian knight.

One of the most remarkable princesses is Floripas, the Sultan's daughter in the Middle English *Sultan of Babylon,* who employs extraordinary cunning and diplomacy to thwart her father and release Christian prisoners from his control; she even goes as far as killing her governess and the jailer of the Christians in order to win Guy of Burgundy as her husband.

Other examples of the Saracen Princess motif occur in the chanson de geste *Prise d'Orange,* in Ordericus Vitalis's *Chronicle of the First Crusade* (in the tale of Bohemond of Antioch and the Princess Melaz, who later marries his cousin Roger), and even in the monumental *Chanson de Roland.* Here, Bramimonde, wife of the Saracen king of Saragossa, is the first to realize that the heathen gods have failed, and it is she who, after the utter defeat of the heathen army, is taken to Charlemagne's capital at Aix-la-Chapelle to receive thorough instruction in the Christian religion and baptism, by her own choosing—*par amur* (for love.)

In his *Parzival* (c. 1205), Wolfram von Eschenbach describes how Gahmuret, Parzival's father, marries the black Queen Belakane, whom he impregnates but then abandons as he sets out on his quest for new chivalric adventures. Gahmuret pretends, in his good-bye letter to Belakane, that their religious difference stands between them, but in reality his heart simply longs for new knightly activities. More important, in Wolfram's crusade epic *Willehalm* (c. 1218–1220), based in part on the Old French epic *Aliscans,* the protagonist meets the Saracen Princess Arabel during his imprisonment in heathen lands and falls in love with her. Since her feelings for him are as strong as his, she abandons her husband, converts to Christianity, assumes the name Giburg, and marries Willehalm.

Wolfram portrays both ladies as highly admirable, as beautiful and strong personalities who deserve the audience's respect as worthy wives of the knightly protagonists. Arabel's conversion allows her integration into Christian society, but Belakane's love for Gahmuret and her virtuous behavior also make her a shining example of a noble lady acting independently, actively, and self-assuredly. Wolfram made significant and successful efforts to suppress the traditional tendency to use the Saracen Princess motif to demonstrate the superiority of the Christian belief over others. Such open-minded attitudes possess few parallels in medieval literature; nonetheless, they are important examples arguing for the existence of tolerance in the Middle Ages.

In the Middle High German verse narrative *Herzog Ernst* (1180–1220) the traveler encounters a beautiful Indian princess, whom he tries to rescue from the hands of an evil king, ruler of a crane people. Had she not been killed by the king's entourage, she would have offered him her hand and her land. And Duke Ernst would have accepted her offer despite their differences in religion and cultural background because he found her exceedingly attractive and noble in appearance. In fact, her manner of describing her home country and her family indicates that in the narrator's view there were no major differences of political and military structure between Europe and the Eastern world and that marriages between a Saracen—or, for that matter, any woman of non-Christian origin—and a Christian knight might well be a possibility, if not an ideal.

The thirteenth-century Old French *Aucassin et Nicolette* takes up the theme of the love between Aucassin, son of the Count Bougars de Valence, and the Saracen slave girl, Nicolette. A ship captain has bought Nicolette from the Saracens, baptized her, and raised her as his own daughter. He claims that she was born in Carthage, but in her physical appearance she resembles a European princess. Aucassin's family adamantly opposes the relationship. The father's opposition is based on class difference, as he wants his son to marry a king's daughter; the fact that Nicolette comes from a "strange land" is only a minor argument against this love affair. But the two young people are so deeply enamored of each other that they eventually overcome all hindrances, marry, and, after the death of Aucassin's father, assume rulership over the country. Nicolette's foreignness is quickly eliminated both through baptism and through her conformity to Western ideals of feminine beauty. In the long run, Nicolette proves her superior intelligence, even medical knowledge, endurance, and love for Aucassin, all criteria that make her a worthy marriage partner. The audience eventually learns that she is indeed the daughter of the king of Carthage. As a baptized Christian this Saracen Princess proves to be an ideal lover and wife for Aucassin.

In 1314 Johann von Würzburg composed the Middle High German courtly romance *Wilhelm von Österreich* (William of Austria), in which the protagonist falls in love with a Saracen Princess, Agly, whom he has seen in a dream. Secretly, he sets out to find her, and he eventually arrives at her father Agrant's court, where he is raised together with Agly. Soon the two young people confess their love for each other, but they are overheard by Agrant, who sends Wilhelm on a deadly errand. He survives and after many adventures returns to his beloved, who converts to Christianity out of love for him. Despite her origin, Agly thus becomes the legendary founder of the Habsburg dynasty. The religious question separating the two is raised only in passing, and the audience is expected to admire the young lady as a loyal lover. Here, as well as in Wolfram's *Parzival*, the marriage of a Christian to a former heathen (Feirefiz and Repanse de Schoye) serves as a basis for future claims of a universal kingdom, combining the European West and the Asian Middle East.

The basic concept of a happy marriage between two people from different religious backgrounds can also be found in a number of narratives wherein the male wooer is a heathen and the princess is Christian. Such is the case in the many French, German, Dutch, and English versions of *Flore and Blanchefleur* and in the thirteenth-century French prose romance *Les enfances Vivien*. In the 849th tale of the *Thousand and One Nights* we even hear of a Christian woman who is wooed by an Egyptian Muslim who rescues her from slavery. Her love for him makes her renounce her belief and convert to Islam.

All of the Saracen Princesses display highly energetic behavior and activism. These women often show themselves more admirable than the Christian knights whom they woo: they are brave and strong characters, shining examples of female intelligence, wisdom, and political skill. S. Kinoshita, however, has convincingly argued that the Saracen Princesses' voluntary embrace of the Christian religion serves as a literary vehicle to veil the obvious military violence and imperialistic aggression of the Crusades, thus providing ideological justification for the brutal subjugation of the Arabic population by the Christian knights.

See also: Becket, Saint Thomas; Crusades; Foreign Races; Richard the Lion-Heart

—Albrecht Classen

Satan [Satanas]. One name for the devil.

In the New Testament Book of Revelation, the Hebrew name *Satan* is made synonymous with the Greek *diabolos* ("he who throws everything into confusion," the source of the English word *devil*). According to the apocryphal Book of Enoch, Satan, originally an angel, was cast down into hell by the archangel Michael ("who is like God") because of the insurrection he led against God. In the Book of Job God allows Satan to tempt Job in order to test whether the latter might forsake God. In later Christianity Satan, as prince of the earthly world, becomes the embodiment of evil itself. In Isaiah 27 he is a dragon of the sea, associated with "that writhing serpent Leviathan." Another appellation for him is Prince of Death.

Devil is a popular designation for the adversary of God. He personifies the principle of evil. In most religions he is directly opposed to the principle of good, which is symbolized by the highest being. This principle appears in its purest state in the Old Persian religion. From there this doctrine infiltrated Judaism, where Satan (as adversary) became a fallen angel subservient to God, with whose permission he may tempt mankind. As fallen angel, he is an evil spirit to whom an entire army of demons is subject.

The devil of folk tradition has little in common with this theologically based Satan, the fallen angel. In folkloric expressions, the disembodied spirit-being of Christian teaching takes on concrete anthropomorphic characteristics. In his book *De praestigiis Daemonum* (On the Deceptions of Demons; German edition, 1586) Johannes Weier, physician and opponent of the belief in witches, characterizes the contemporary notion of the appearance of the devil:

Then the devil appeared suddenly to him in a terrifying shape

with fiery eyes
having a nose crooked as an ox horn
and long teeth like a wild boar
hairy about the cheeks like a cat
and otherwise in every way terrible and
horrifying to behold.

As the devil's physical appearance evolves further it takes on more and more human qualities. This does not, however, prevent the devil of popular tradition from assuming the form of almost any animal, except, of course, for the lamb and the dove, symbols representing the divine. There are almost no limits to the human forms the devil might assume, even if some shapes—the traveler, the cavalier, the hunter—are favored. But each human shape is only a mask that is unable to conceal his devilish features: horns, tail, goat's or horse's hooves.

The witchcraft trials of the Middle Ages served particularly to promote belief in devils. Thus, many motifs that had originally pertained to other demonic beings were transferred to the devil. He took on characteristics of the giant, the Wild Hunter (motif E501), the goblin, and other demons of folk tradition, attaining a dazzling variety of appearance. The devil's replacement of the giant in folk belief was made easier by the similar positions taken by the two figures: the giants as opponents of the Germanic gods, the devil as adversary of the Christian God. Thus, the dualism of God and devil became even more pronounced in folk traditions than canonical doctrine would maintain. The devil is both prince of hell and also adversary of God.

In the earliest popular graphic images the devil is represented as a bird-like creature with claws, beak, and great wings, and, later, probably through classical influences, horns and goat's feet (under the influence of the Roman forest god Pan). In the earliest Christian representations he appears as a serpent, while in the twelfth century he is described as a demonic animal/human figure, with a pig's snout, claws, hooves, horns, shaggy hair, and a second face staring from his stomach. He is made the equivalent of Satan himself, who in pure Christian symbolism is presented almost exclusively as a dragon. Since antiquity there have been satanic cults, especially among such dualistic sects of the Middle Ages as the Luciferians, Bogomils, and Paulicianists, who sought to protect themselves by worshipping Satan, whom they considered just as powerful as God. Satanic masses (black masses), involving blasphemous performances of the Catholic mass, are often associated with this worship.

Pacts with the devil are already mentioned in the Old Testament, in the Talmud, and in the Kabbalah; these are binding contracts with the evil one, which he strictly honors. The best-known example is that of Faust, which also resonates in folk literature. Various such pacts have been handed down from the Middle Ages, for example the *Legend of Theophilus* (c. 1200) and that of *Robert the Devil* (thirteenth century; chapbook, 1496). In most narratives, the human partner to the contract is eventually saved by his repentance and inner transformation.

A common figure in medieval folk narratives is the devil deceived or tricked, who also appears in postmedieval märchen and legends. Usually there is a testing of powers between the human and the devil, who always loses, being stupid enough to allow himself to be deceived. In addition, the alliances with the devil that are familiar from the comic narrative tradition (not to be confused with the pacts with the devil discussed above) proceed from the assumption that the devil, as a conscientious and fully empowered party to the contract, will always be duped by the intellectually superior and more adroit human. This representation of the "stupid devil" also underlies medieval tales and the Carnival plays (*Fastnachtspiele*) of the sixteenth century. The contract is fulfilled deceitfully by the human but remains valid from a strictly technical point of view, and the devil is taken advantage of. In the religious dramas of the Middle Ages and those of the Jesuits, Satan serves as a contrastive figure to God, underscoring the latter's power and glory.

See also: Angels; Drama; Harrowing of Hell; Hell

—Leander Petzoldt

Sauna. A type of steam bath widely used in northern Europe during the medieval period.

Steam baths or sweat lodges are common to many cultures the world over. In northern Europe, however, a particular form of bath developed that involves steam, intermittent exposure to cold water, and the striking of the body with leafy branches, often of birch. During the medieval period the sauna enjoyed tremendous popularity among the Finno-Ugric peoples, Russians, and Scandinavians. It represented an important means of cleansing, but it also held ritual and social significance. The sauna building was used for a variety of activities besides bathing; for example, as a place to give birth and a place to dry grain. Although various factors led to the abandonment of the custom among the Scandinavian peoples during the later Middle Ages, the sauna remained popular among Finno-Ugric and Slavic populations.

The term *sauna* itself is Finnish and has cognates in the other Finno-Ugric languages of northern Europe (e.g., in Estonian and Sámi). The sauna custom probably dates from at least the period of the Baltic-Finnic adoption of agriculture, sometime around the second millennium B.C.E., but it may predate this era, and it may have occurred in another culture. A widespread and ancient term for the sauna also exists in Western and Eastern Slavic languages (*lazn'*), although by the early-medieval period the term had already been replaced by other words in many Slavic languages.

In the sauna, intense heat radiated from a heap of igneous stones that had been heated by prolonged burning of wood and that were doused periodically with small quantities of water. In the most ancient conical houses of Baltic Finns, smoke from the primitive oven (Finnish *kiuas*) could exit a central smoke hole. When log construction transformed housing into rectangular forms throughout the Baltic region, smoke from the corner stove was allowed to exit through small apertures in the roof or wall. Entering the heated sauna too soon after the completion of the wood-burning phase could lead to asphyxiation and death. Once it was safe for participants to enter the sauna, however, they found places on raised benches above a floor of wood or packed earth. Water was thrown on the stones with wooden ladles, creating blasts of steam that further elevated the room's temperature and caused intense sweating. At intervals persons left the sauna to cool down, pouring cold water over themselves, swimming in a nearby stream or lake, or even rolling in the snow. A supply of birch twig bundles for striking the body was prepared in the warm months and stored for use throughout the winter. In fourteenth-century depictions of Adam and Eve in the Finnish medieval churches of Lohja and Hattula, the first man hides his nudity from God behind the leaves of a sauna whisk.

The earliest account of the sauna institution among the northernmost settlements of the Eastern Slavs comes from the *Russian Primary Chronicle* (c. 1040–1118), whose Kievan chronicler recounts a purported visit by the apostle Andrew to the city of Novgorod. On returning to Rome, the apostle explains the sauna custom in amazement:

> I noticed their wooden bathhouses (*bani dreveni*). They warm themselves to extreme heat, then undress, and after anointing themselves with tallow, take young reeds and lash their bodies. They actually lash themselves so violently that they barely escape alive. Then they drench themselves with cold water, and thus are revived. They think nothing of doing this every day, and actually inflict such voluntary torture upon themselves. They make the act not a mere washing but a veritable torment. (Trans. S.A. Zenkovsky, in *Medieval Russia's Epics, Chronicles, and Tales* [1974], pp. 47–48)

This humorous account describes the traditional Russian sauna in detail and reflects the exotic nature of the custom in the eyes of the more southerly Slavs of Kiev. Numerous subsequent references to the sauna in clerical and legal texts demonstrate its spread and popularity in subsequent centuries. In addition to the small home saunas typical of the Baltic Finns, public saunas, serving an entire village or city district, developed as well and maintained their popularity through to the end of the medieval period.

The sauna became established among medieval Scandinavians as a result of Viking Age commerce with Finno-Ugric and Great Russian populations to the east. Although the tenth-century Arabic traveler Ibn Fadlan describes Swedish hygiene in detail, he makes no mention of any steam bath custom, suggesting its rarity among Scandinavians of the day. The twelfth-century *Sverris Saga*, however, attests to the existence of the sauna (Old Norse *badstofa*) custom in Viking Norway, and Swedish law tracts from the thirteenth century indicate the spread of the custom among Swedish farmers and merchants. By the sixteenth century the sauna had become a ubiquitous and beloved aspect of Scandinavian life. Sauna was customary on Saturdays (the day of washing) and in connection with both holidays and markets. Descriptions such as that of *Eyrbyggja Saga* (ch. 28) describe the Scandinavian sauna as a small room, partly dug in the ground for insulation and often equipped with an antechamber. Water could be poured in from the outside. Saga accounts also mention special clothing worn during bathing, such as hats and robes, items absent from the Slavic and Baltic-Finnic traditions. Saga details closely match archaeological evidence from Iceland and Greenland, where medieval saunas have been excavated. By the fourteenth century, however, the decimation of the Icelandic birch forests had led to the decline of the custom on the island, where plentiful hot springs, warmed by volcanic heat, replaced the wood-burning sauna. Archaeological evidence indicates the marginal development of a sauna tradition in northern Ireland, possibly introduced or influenced by Viking settlers. The steam baths constructed there were conical stone structures in which slightly different means of heating and producing steam were used.

Among the Baltic Finns, Sámi, Russians, and Scandinavians the sauna served both practical and sacred purposes. One of the most widespread sauna customs was the bridal sauna, described in detail in Olaus Magnus's *Historia de gentibus septentrionalibus* (History of the Nordic Peoples, 1555, ch. 28). Similar wedding customs existed among the Baltic-Finnic peoples and Great Russian communities.

Especially among the Baltic Finns and Great Russians, the sauna was associated fundamentally with concepts of the sacred. People turned to the sauna at key moments in the life cycle (e.g., birth, marriage, sickness, death) and at high points in the year (e.g., Midsummer, Christmas). Healers combined the sauna's heat with forms of physical treatment, herbal cures, and magic incantations. The Finnish term for sauna steam (*löyly*) finds a cognate in the Hungarian term for soul or life force (*lelek*), implying the sacredness of ancient sauna concepts. Throughout Eastern Europe, sweat was seen as the most salient aspect of the sauna experience. The Russian chronicler Nestor records the claim of two Russian witches in 1071 that humankind was created when God, after sweating in his heavenly sauna, dried himself with a piece of straw and threw it to the earth. The devil himself made it into a man, although the soul (associated with the divine sweat) remained eternal. The sauna served as the site for the washing and final preparations of the corpse. Fourteenth- and fifteenth-century Russian Orthodox clergy fought against peasant funeral customs that included food, drink, and sauna offerings to the spirits of the dead. Similar customs also became associated with calendrical feasts during the later medieval period. In fourteenth- and fifteenth-century Denmark private saunas were occasionally opened to the poor and destitute as an act of charity rewarded by dispensation. Many wills from the period stipulate offering the poor food, ale, and sauna in memory of the deceased.

The sauna was not solely a site for sacred activities, however. Many mundane chores occurred there as well. Flax and grains were dried in the sauna, and malt for beer was prepared in the sauna's heat. In Denmark and Norway public saunas became important sites of village commerce and socializing. The thirteenth-century *Sturlunga Saga* mentions a Norwegian sauna capable of holding 50 bathers at once. By the fourteenth century Copenhagen boasted three public saunas as well as numerous private ones belonging to wealthy townsmen or institutions (e.g., churches and schools). Despite clerical disapproval, the sexes bathed together in such public saunas, leading eventually to ordinances that specified separate hours or days of sauna visitation for men and women. Saunas became the site of drinking and gaming as well. In Denmark public saunas were eventually closed in response to the outbreak of a syphilis epidemic in the early sixteenth century. Such a decline never occurred among the Baltic Finns, Sámi, or Russians, however, who continued to make use of the sauna custom long after the end of the Middle Ages.

The sauna finds counterparts in the public baths of Roman and Arabic cultures, the hot baths of the ancient Germanic peoples, and the Turkish baths of Eastern Europe. The Turkish baths developed into a widespread institution throughout central Europe. The central European steam baths, which differed from the sauna in that they had multiple rooms of varying temperature and included massage, enjoyed considerable popularity during the medieval period but came to be associated with lasciviousness and prostitution. The Turkish bath institution probably influenced the development of public saunas in Denmark and Norway.

See also: Baltic Tradition

—Thomas A. DuBois

Scandinavian Mythology. Tales about pagan gods recorded primarily in Christian medieval Iceland and thought to reflect traditions and religious beliefs from other parts of Scandinavia and the Germanic world before the conversion to Christianity, much of which may be inherited from Indo-European myth and religion.

Two books, each of them now called *Edda*, comprise the most important source material. The one with medieval authority to that title is attributed to the Icelandic chieftain and poet Snorri Sturluson (1179–1241). It consists of a prologue and three parts: *Gylfaginning* (Deluding of Gylfi), which is an account of how three pagan wizards engaged in a question-and-answer session with the prehistoric Swedish king Gylfi concerning the pagan mythology; *Skaldskaparmal* (Poetic Diction), for the most part a list of poetic synonyms and circumlocutions with a few longer narratives from the mythology explaining the origins of some of these poetic tropes; and *Hattatal* (Enumeration of Meters), a praise poem to the Norwegian king Haakon Haakonsson and his regent, Earl Skuli, exemplifying numerous variations of meter and diction. Taken as a whole, the book was obviously intended as a handbook of poetics, but it has won fame primarily for the mythological narratives in *Gylfaginning* and *Skaldskaparmal*.

Snorri was working with poetic sources, and when a collection of mythological and heroic poems was discovered in early modern times, it was regarded as another *Edda* (the meaning of the title is obscure, but the best guesses associate it with poetics), that of Saemund Sigfusson the learned, who is taken to be Iceland's first historian. Since this book is primarily in verse it has been called the *Poetic Edda*, as opposed to Snorri's *Prose Edda*, and since Saemund lived about a century before Snorri the book attributed to him was also sometimes called the *Elder Edda* and Snorri's the *Younger Edda*. The last pair of titles should be avoided, since they rest on a false assumption: Snorri probably wrote circa 1220, and the collection on which the *Poetic Edda* (c. 1280) is based probably dates from circa 1250, although there is evidence for antecedents from around the turn of the century.

The works in the *Poetic Edda*, and the few similar poems in other manuscripts, have a poetic form close to that found in Old English, Old Saxon, and Old High German, a form that is therefore probably derived from common Germanic times, although it cannot be proved that the mythological poems themselves are from that period. Like the poems in the other Germanic languages, too, Eddic poems are anonymous. Another form of poetry, usually termed "skaldic" after the noun *skald* (poet), has a form unique to Old Norse, generally has named authors, and is somewhat amenable to dating. Skaldic tradition evinces certain longer mythic narratives (usually understood as descriptions of decorations on shields, hall carvings, and so forth), and this tradition also makes extensive use of kennings, two-part metaphors such as "drink of the dwarfs" for poetry, that often build on myth and therefore constitute an important source for the study of the mythology.

Many other vernacular sources offer bits and pieces of information about Scandinavian mythology, and *Gesta Danorum*, the Danish history by Saxo Grammaticus from circa 1200, contains much mythological material reinterpreted by its learned author. All these written sources postdate the conversion to Christianity by more than two centuries, since it was the Church that brought the technology of writing. Some runic inscriptions appear to contain the names of gods and antedate the conversion, but they are few and short. The only real evidence from before the conversion, then, outside of the writings of others who came into contact with Scandinavia, is archaeological and onomastic (i.e., evidence from personal and place names), and in both cases interpretation would be all but impossible without the medieval written texts. Recovery of the pagan mythology requires accepting that the medieval texts originate in older oral tradition, and interpretation of the texts as we have them cannot ignore the context of their recording.

Scandinavian mythology was a pantheistic system in which three gods might make a claim to the highest status. Around the time of the conversion it appears that Thor was the most important god, since he seems to have been set up as the chief opponent of Christ. Thor (Old Norse *þórr*, which originally meant something like "the thunderer") is the only deity whose amulet people wore a small hammer about the neck with the handle pointing down; on the handle of the hammer there were frequently two eyes. Thor's hammer (Mjöllnir, perhaps "flasher") figures prominently in myth, where it is used to slay *jötnar* (singular *jötunn*, conventionally translated "giants" but perhaps best understood as simply the beings of chaos and the unalterable enemies of the gods). Thor's greatest opponent was the Midgard serpent, a huge snake lying deep in the ocean and encircling the earth. On one occasion Thor fished it up and struck it with his hammer. This event is depicted on rock carvings from England to Sweden and was well known to the poets and Snorri. In connection with this famous fishing expedition, Thor also acquired a massive kettle the gods could use to brew beer for their ceremonial gatherings.

Thor also killed Hrungnir, the strongest of the *jötnar*, in what Snorri describes as a formal duel. Thor threw Mjöllnir at Hrungnir, who threw a whetstone at Thor. When the two weapons met in midair Mjöllnir smashed the whetstone apart and continued on to smash the giant. A piece of the whetstone lodged in Thor's forehead and was never apparently removed.

Thor was capable of giant-slaying without his hammer. Once when it was stolen, he dressed up as Freyja, the fairest of the goddesses and the ransom demanded for the hammer, and killed Thrym, the *jötunn* who had stolen it, when Thrym produced it to hallow what he thought was his marriage to Freyja. On another occasion, he journeyed off to visit the giant Geirröd without his hammer. He killed Geirröd's threatening daughters and then the *jötunn* himself. The latter myth may provide a glimpse of the view of Thor during paganism, since two surviving skaldic fragments number many giantesses among his victims, and in another poem Thor himself boasts of his killing of female representatives of chaos.

According to Snorri's Prologue to his *Edda*, which attempts to associate the gods with ancient world history, Thor was an ancient Thracian king and the father of Odin, the king who first emigrated from the center of the world to Scandinavia. In his *Gylfaginning*, however, Odin is the All-Father and chief of the gods, and it is certainly so that more myths, of more variety, attach themselves to Odin than to any other god. His name, Old Norse *Óðinn*, originally meant something like "leader of the ecstatic ones," and this name accords well with Odin's roles as god of wisdom and god of battle. With respect to the former, wisdom was associated with poetry, which according to the mythology was the product of an intoxicating drink, the poetic mead that Odin obtained from the *jötnar* after they stole it from the dwarfs. In battle Odin could neutralize his opponents by putting "battle-fetters" upon them, apparently the paralysis of terror. But his closest connection in this context with ecstatic behavior is through the berserks, fearless warriors who howl like wolves and fail to react to wounds. Odin also rules over fallen warriors, the *einherjar*, "peerless soldiers," who inhabit Valhalla ("carrion hall," perhaps from an earlier "rock slab of the dead," i.e., "grave"). Snorri reports that these champions pass their time battling all day and feasting all night, as they await the final battle, Ragnarök.

The third figure who might make a claim to chief god is Tyr, and he does so through his name, which is cognate with that of Zeus and Jupiter. If he ever was chief god, that was clearly before our texts were composed, for in them he plays only a small role, sacrificing his hand so that the terrible wolf Fenrir may be bound until Ragnarök.

Other important deities fall into the category of the Vanir, a separate race of gods who once waged war with the Aesir (the ordinary word for gods, in this myth under the command of Odin). These include Frey, who obtained a bride from giantland by sending his servant Skirnir there to obtain her by threats and bullying, and his father Njord, a shadowy figure associated with the sea who is, curiously, obtained as a husband by the giantess Skadi in compensation for a slaying. The conflict between two groups of gods was the first war and may account for the incorporation of different sorts of gods in a single pantheon; an older scholarly view held that it represented the overrunning of an indigenous population by the Indo-Europeans, with their war-like gods.

Although Snorri works hard to name a number of goddesses, none is very important, and most are defined by the role of wife: for example, Frigg is Odin's and Sif is Thor's. Freyja is marked off as somewhat different through her original membership in the Vanir.

Also numbered among the Aesir, according to Snorri, is Loki. Of joint god-giant parentage, Loki functions as a trickster by disrupting the order of the gods and then often helping to restore it. For example, he contributed to Thrym's theft of Thor's hammer and then traveled with Thor, disguised as "Freyja's" handmaiden, to retrieve it. He was unequivocally evil, however, in arranging for the blind Höd to kill Baldr, the handsomest of the gods; both Höd and Baldr were sons of Odin.

That the mythology as a whole ultimately concerns a struggle between gods and *jötnar* is made clear by the myths of the origin and destruction of the cosmos. According to the origin myth, Odin and his brothers killed the first giant and made the world from the parts of his body; according to the myth of Ragnarök (judgment of the gods), the gods and forces of chaos (led by Loki) will meet in a last battle. The wolf Fenrir will kill Odin, the Midgard serpent and Thor will kill one another, and Frey will die at the hands of the fire demon Surt. All the world will be consumed with flames. Thereafter, however, it will arise anew. Baldr and Höd will be reconciled, and a new generation of gods will rule, apparently without the interference of the *jötnar*.

See also: Eddic Poetry; Giants; Snorri Sturluson's *Edda*; Thor

—John Lindow

Scandinavian Tradition. The folkloric culture of the Nordic peoples.

These speakers of the North Germanic dialects lived mainly in present-day Denmark, the Faroe Islands, Iceland, Norway, and Sweden, as well as on the Baltic perimeter (e.g., limited coastal areas of Finland and Estonia) and in various additional North Atlantic outposts (e.g., Greenland and Shetland), and shared, besides basic linguistic continuity, many cultural traits and traditions.

History

By 500 C.E. Scandinavians had been commented on by foreign writers (e.g., Tacitus) and had themselves left some 125 inscriptions in stone and other impermeable materials written in runes (e.g., the fourth-century Gallehus horn). These inscriptions, especially rich beginning in the ninth century with the writing system called the Younger Runes, often display elaborate poetic principles and in addition to serving mainly memorial functions sometimes treat Scandinavian legendary and mythological traditions (e.g., Rök) and charms (e.g., Kvinneby amulet). Runes continue to provide contemporary witness to Nordic cultural life throughout the Middle Ages,

both in highly stylized monuments (e.g., Jelling) and in everyday communications, such as those discovered at Bryggen in Bergen, Norway. Early Church activity, such as Ansgar's missionary journey to Sweden in the ninth century and Adam of Bremen's eleventh-century history of the Hamburg-Bremen archbishopric, often provide corroborative testimony by outsiders about Nordic traditions.

Conversion to Christianity was everywhere a process aimed at the ruling class. The new religion was embraced nationally at a relatively early date in Denmark, in the ninth century (cf. Jelling), and in Norway, in the tenth and early eleventh centuries (cf. the sagas of Olaf Tryggvason and St. Olaf); the new religion was peaceably declared in Iceland at the time of the millennium (cf. *Njal's Saga*, ch. 105) and by the mid-twelfth century in Sweden, a date based mainly on the establishment of the Uppsala bishopric at the principal site of Swedish heathenism. In each case, missionary activity found success first among chieftains and kings, toward whom it was directed. Although declared for the country as a whole, some question remains—especially for Norway and Sweden, with their sometimes remote and isolated settlements—of how many decades passed before Christianity completely took hold throughout.

The early economies of this world were mainly based on agriculture, animal husbandry, and fishing, with long-distance trade to the east (i.e., Russia and the Byzantine Empire) and to the west (i.e., the Holy Roman Empire) in such goods as furs, slaves, walrus tusks, and soapstone products, an occupation that sometimes also included raiding and piracy. Those who engaged in such piratical activities were said to be *í víkingu* (in viking) or were simply "Vikings." Later developments led to the formation of large-scale forces, the so-called Great Armies, which harried England and northern France, in particular, and whose collective activities culminated in lands in Normandy, Northumbria, and other areas being ceded to Scandinavian settlers. Colonies were also established in the Orkneys, the Hebrides, and Ireland. Less bellicose relations in the East led to a series of Nordic (presumably the same as the so-called Rus) outposts, including Old Ladoga (near St. Petersburg) and possibly other sites, targeting strategic positions, such as portages around falls and cataracts, on the route to Constantinople. In the tenth and eleventh centuries many Scandinavians served in the Byzantine emperor's Varangian Guard. But with the exception of the virtually uninhabited North Atlantic islands, in none of these cases—east or west—was the Nordic population ever large enough to sustain itself over time, and this population was presumably absorbed into the native population. In a noteworthy example of this point, the Norman chronicler Dudo of Saint-Quentin writes that William I wanted his son, Richard I (d. 996), to be reared in Bayeux rather than in Rouen because "Danish" was principally spoken in the former city but French in the latter, and William wanted his successor to learn and use Danish daily. Through a series of westward expansions—usually recorded in literary sources as a pattern in which a ship is blown off course, and the reports of new lands are followed up first by individual exploration and then by settlement by an entire colony—the Norse hopscotched their way from the Nordic world proper to Shetland, the Faroes, Iceland, Greenland, and the New World, called by them *Vinland*, thus far confirmed only from the archaeological site of L'Anse aux Meadows in Newfoundland, Canada. This Norse adventure in the New World is first mentioned by Adam of Bremen and forms the core of the two so-called Vinland sagas, recorded centuries later in Iceland.

The Viking era is generally reckoned as ending in the late eleventh century, often in association with the death of King Harold Hardraada, "hardrule," of Norway in England in 1066. Three recognizable national kingdoms emerged in the Middle Ages: Norway, Sweden, and Denmark (which included large tracts of present-day southern Sweden). Following the ninth-century settlement of the island, the Icelanders formed a republic centered around local and national assemblies at which the chieftains and their followers passed laws and adjudicated cases. At the end of the 1200s Iceland fell under the dominion of Norway, and by 1397 the kingdoms of the Nordic region had been forged into the so-called Union of Kalmar under the leadership of Queen Margarete of Denmark. With Margarete no longer in power, however, things quickly fell apart, and the history of the fifteenth century may with little exaggeration be said to be that of Sweden (including Finland, which had been incorporated as part of thirteenth-century missionary Crusades) struggling to pull out of the union dominated by Denmark.

Pre-Christian Religion and Mythology

Relatively little is known about the practice of pre-Christian religion in the northern world; on the other hand, we know a great deal about its mythology. That this is the case has largely to do with the fact that the Scandinavian mythological traditions were intimately connected with its poetic practice through extended metaphors known as kennings, many of which could only be understood by recourse to characters and episodes drawn from the mythology. As a result, one of the principal sources for our understanding of this world, the *Prose Edda* of Snorri Sturluson (d. 1241), is a handbook of poetics intended for poets in a world in which widespread Christian belief had dangerously eroded native poetic tradition. This text narrates famous events in the history of the gods and suggestively lists ways in which various words can be paraphrased in mythological terms. The mythological tradition is also well represented in the so-called *Poetic Edda*, the main manuscript of which dates to circa 1280. These poems—roughly half of which are mythological, the other half heroic—are generally believed to be much older than the manuscript. The first books of the late-twelfth-century *Gesta Danorum* of Saxo Grammaticus also take up mythological themes, although frequently in euhemerized form, and much can be inferred from the language of the poets, or *skalds*, as well as from their occasional presentations of mythological themes (e.g., *Ragnarsdrapa*, *Haustlöng*). Additional information about the actual practice of the pagan religion is to be found in the comments of outside observers (e.g., Adam of Bremen) and in the archaeological record (e.g., funeral rites). Interpretations of Scandinavian mythology have followed the trends in the field more generally—meteorological, myth-ritual, Christian-influenced, historical, and comparative (especially in line with the views of Georges Dumézil).

The stories that have come down to us treat overwhelmingly the exploits of Odin and Thor against the *jötnar* (giants) and other representatives of the otherworld (e.g., the Midgard serpent), as well as the attempts of the *jötnar* to possess various goddesses, especially Freyja. Typically Odin's struggles involve his use of or search for wisdom, whereas Thor's adventures are resolved by recourse to his might and his hammer, Mjöllnir. Other narratives take up such tales as how Frey gets a wife; how the gods' citadel is built; how the Vanir gods come to live among the Aesir gods; how the soteriological figure of Baldr comes to be killed; or how the enigmatic Loki leads the giants against the gods at the final battle, Ragnarök (judgment of the gods).

Poetic Genres

Skaldic and Eddic poetry, of which much survives in various matrices, are exceedingly important sources of information about the Scandinavian tradition. Because of their great age, high aesthetic quality, and overwhelming significance with respect to Scandinavian mythology, they generally overshadow the younger forms of poetry that dominate the later periods: *rímur* (rhymes) in Iceland, *knittel* verse in Sweden and Denmark, and the ballad throughout most of Scandinavia. The *rímur* are narrative poems, divided into fits, each exhibiting different complicated patterns of rhyme and alliteration. A uniquely Icelandic genre, the *rímur* are first attested in the late fourteenth century. The materials for *rímur* are largely drawn from existing prose sagas, especially those dealing with knights and ancient times, as well as from the occasional folktale and exemplum. *Knittel*, or end-rhymed epic poetry, appears in the early fourteenth century in connection with Nordic court life and was used to translate foreign works of literature (e.g., the so-called *Eufemiavisor* [Eufemia's Songs]) and to create native rhymed chronicles (e.g., *Erikskrönikan* [Erik's Chronicle]). *Knittel* was particularly favored in Sweden, and only to a slightly lesser extent in Denmark, but it seems to have been unknown in Iceland. Ballads were sung throughout the Nordic world, although they are only rarely attested in medieval contexts (the first collections of them appeared after the Reformation). There are, however, many indications, including literary references and church paintings, that support the view that these "folksongs" represent a popular late-medieval genre. The Nordic ballads are strophic, end-rhymed, narrative songs, generally associated with a lyrical refrain, and are characterized by their objective style and use of so-called commonplaces. The subject matter of the ballads seems to have been limited only by the range of human imagination; it included everything from religious legends and courtly romance, on the one hand, to the supernatural and jocular, on the other. The long heroic ballads of the Faroe Islands maintained extraordinary continuity into modern times, including an association with dance.

Sagas and Other Prose Genres

It is one of the ironies of Nordic history that Iceland, with its small population and lacking any secular court life, is the medieval Scandinavian country best known to us today. Through its medieval writers Iceland gave extraordinary voice to the Nordic Middle Ages and its repository of traditions, producing hundreds of finely written sagas, an Icelandic word borrowed into many European languages to denote a prose narrative. Whereas by the thirteenth century the Nordic courts had largely adopted European fashions in literature, among the Icelanders, who were themselves no strangers to these new tastes, the traditions associated with the Viking Age and their own heroic past continued to generate narratives of very high standards throughout the Middle Ages (although the thirteenth century has come to be viewed by modern scholars as the classic era of saga writing).

The various types of sagas are generally labeled according to the callings of their principal figures—*konungasögur* (sagas of kings), *riddarasögur* (sagas of knights), *biskupasögur* (sagas of bishops), *postola sögur* (sagas of the Apostles), and *heilagra manna sögur* (sagas of saints)—or according to the saga's relation to time, *fornaldarsögur* (sagas of antiquity) and *Sturlunga Saga* (contemporary sagas, named after one of the great clans of thirteenth-century Iceland). Among the most interesting of these medieval forerunners of the novel are the *Islendingasögur* (sagas of Icelanders), texts that exhibit such seemingly modern concepts as interiority, character development, and a remarkable sense of dialogue. The sagas present a panoramic view of medieval Nordic life, and for the student of folklore they represent a unique

opportunity to comprehend both conditions in medieval Scandinavia and the attitudes of medieval writers toward the heroic past, whether heroic is understood in military, ecclesiastical, or personal terms.

Given the unrivaled skill with which the best of the sagas are written, it is hardly surprising that the various non-Icelandic medieval prose genres are generally overlooked. There are, however, many such texts in virtually all the vernaculars, encompassing translations of foreign originals, such as *Sju vise mästare* (The Seven Sages); reworkings of earlier Nordic texts, such as *Sagan om Didrik af Bern* (The Saga of Dietrich von Bern); and texts without known models, such as *Skämtan om abboten* (The Jest about the Abbot). To these specifically literary forms may be added such prolific and frequently nonnarrative areas as religious prose and other forms of didactic writing, such as lapidaries, grammatical treatises, and the *Konungs skuggsja* (King's Mirror). All these materials present remarkable opportunities to mine the medieval Nordic world for folkloric materials, in which it is exceedingly rich.

Belief

The importance of such aspects of routine Christian life as mass, prayer, and pilgrimage can hardly be exaggerated. In the latter category, for example, major Scandinavian pilgrimage sites included the shrines of St. Olaf in Norway, St. Knud in Denmark, and St. Erik and St. Birgitta in Sweden, and the significance of these sites for local economies and other aspects of the pilgrim trade, including folklore, was great. Observation of the Christian calendar is demonstrated on calendar staves, used into modern times in peasant communities; the stave has a winter and a summer side, and a variety of symbols mark both Christian holidays and ancient feast days.

Even in postconversion Scandinavia, religious life, although largely dictated by Christian practice, inherited some views about such things as healing and magic. Belief in witchcraft and magic is suggested throughout the sagas, and these topics are treated with much seriousness in the law codes and penitentials of all the Nordic countries. Actual evidence of witchcraft is relatively scarce, however, although there are noteworthy exceptions (e.g., the case of Ragnhildr Tregagas in Bergen c. 1324). The place of magic in everyday life, on the other hand, is more readily adduced from such things as charms and amulets. The late-medieval, whetstone-shaped amber amulet from Dømmestrup, Denmark, for example, gives witness to this protective function with its Latin inscription, which twice reads "*contra omnia mala*" [against all evils] and once "*contra … malorum*" [against … of evils].

Other Genres

Although there exist several medieval collections of riddles and proverbs, as well as some 30 riddles in *Hervarar Saga,* Scandinavia boasts nothing comparable to, for example, *The Exeter Book* of English tradition. Still, a reader of the sagas or of skaldic poetry will encounter a great deal of proverbial wisdom and riddle-like materials integrated into the texts.

A full accounting of resources for the study of spiritual culture in the Scandinavian Middle Ages would necessarily include, in addition to those areas already mentioned, such prose items as letters, encyclopedic literature, diplomataria, sermons, and synodal statutes, as well as church murals, carving in wood and bone, metalwork, and other aspects of material culture and art; moreover, a complete inventory would include such topics as folk dance and folk music.

See also: Eddic Poetry; Olaf, Saint; Runes and Runic Inscriptions; Sagas of Icelanders; Scandinavian Mythology; Snorri Sturluson's *Edda;* Thor
—Stephen A. Mitchell

Scatology. The study of the products of excretion and—in this article—the human butt.

Farting

"Why don't we fart to amuse ourselves? I can't think of anything better!" This somewhat surprising suggestion, coming from an adult and accepted with equally surprising alacrity by another, occurs in Adam de la Halle's late-thirteenth-century *Jeu de Robin et de Marion* (Play of Robin and Marion). At much the same time as Gautier, the peasant character in Adam's play, was making his indelicate suggestion as to how he and his companions should amuse themselves, Henry III, king of England, was witnessing a similar performance at court by one Roland, surnamed le Pettour in Anglo-Norman, le Fartere in English, who held land in Hemingstone, Suffolk, by serjeanty of appearing before the king on Christmas Day every year to perform "*unum saltum et unum siffletum et unum bumbulum*" [a jump, a whistle, and a fart]. Clearly Henry was no "Clerk of Oxenford," who, Chaucer in his "Miller's Tale" tells us, with apparent surprise, "was somewhat squeamish about farting."

It is clear from a number of sources that during the medieval period, not only was farting perceived as a source of amusement and a skill much appreciated in certain contexts, but it was also traditionally reckoned part of the inferior minstrel's repertoire; for example, Activa Vita (Active Life), an allegorical character in William Langland's poem *Piers Plowman,* although a minstrel, is careful to dissociate himself from that grade of the profession: he says that he does not know how to "Farten ne fithelen at festes" [fart or fiddle at feasts]. Even in the twelfth century John of Salisbury had complained that

illustrious persons allow buffoons to frequent their houses and perform before the eyes of all disgraceful actions with the obscene parts

of their bodies....worse still, these fellows are not ejected when in the turbulence of their hinder parts they cause the air to reek by emitting a series of loud noises which add to their deplorable conduct.

Several of the marginal illustrations in the well-known Bodleian manuscript of the *Romance of Alexander* (illuminated in Flanders, c. 1340) seem to feature some sort of anal entertainment, and similar instances are commonplace in medieval art. The grotesque in the margin of the early-fourteenth-century Ormesby Psalter, who points at his own exposed rear with the human hand with which his tail terminates, is the visual equivalent of Cain's familiar invitation, "Kiss my ass." But what are we to make of the man who blows a trumpet at the same grotesque? To *trump* does not appear as a synonym for "fart" until the end of the Middle Ages, but this and similar images suggest that the word was common earlier. The boorish trickster Marcolf—matched in a contest of wits with Solomon—uses the word in one of his typically scatological cappings of Solomon's proverbs. To the king's citation from the Gospels, "Of the habundaunce of therte [the heart] the mouth spekyst" (Matt. 12:34), he responds with "Out of a full wombe [belly] thars [the ass] trompyth"—even though, significantly, the Latin original has *triumphat* (triumphs).

In his *Gesta pontificum Anglorum* (Deeds of the Archbishops of England), William of Malmesbury records an incident that took place in his boyhood, about 1100, at the shrine of St. Aldhelm in Malmesbury. The crowd who assembled at the shrine for the saint's festival were entertained by a man who specialized in farting, which as William tells us, made the foolish laugh but the monks grieve; the man's impudence did not go unpunished, however, for he was then tormented by a devil and had to be forcibly restrained by being bound hand and foot—only after three days' and nights' intercession on the part of the monks was he healed. In an earlier instance of irreverence to a saint, however—unusual in that the punishment is made to fit the crime—a fart is the *punishment:* One Friday a Merovingian woman was told that the body of St. Gangolf worked miracles, to which she replied, "and so does my ass." Immediately a loud fart was heard, and thereafter for the rest of her life she could not say a word on a Friday but it was followed by a similar report.

Ass Kissing

Another form of scatology popular during the medieval period, perceived sometimes as amusing but more often as insulting, involved representations of kissing the bared buttocks, or in some instances actually forcing an individual to perform this demeaning act. In particular, kissing the devil's butt had significant folk connotations. For instance, in the Prologue to Chaucer's "Summoner's Tale," an angel says to Satan, "Shewe forth thyn ers [ass], and let the frere se / Where is the nest of freres in this place." In one of the fifteenth-century Wakefield Pageants, when Abel greets his brother, Cain replies with a brutal "Com kis myne ars!" The ass-kissing act itself is, of course, a staple of such medieval fabliaux as Chaucer's "Miller's Tale" as well as a Middle English poem concerning one Hogyn ("She torned owt her ars & that he kyst"). But Cain also suggests Abel should kiss the devil's ass, and this is perhaps also the implication of Nowadays's Latin invitation to Nought (in the play *Mankind*), as the devil, Titivillus, is their master. The motif of kissing the devil in this manner brings with it the implication of heresy or witchcraft, for the allegation that they practiced this rite was one of the commonest made against Cathars, Waldensians, Templars, and, indeed, heretics in general, from the time of Gregory IX's bull of 1233. The kissing of animals in this position—when not also a Satanic rite (as images of the devil in goat form)—is always insulting.

Excrement

Closely related to ass kissing in medieval art and literature is the process of evacuation and the ingestion of excrement. A misericord in the royal chapel of St. George's at Windsor Castle, carved 1478–1483, depicts a friar evacuating a devil accompanied by another friar and devil. The motif of anal evacuation from a demon can be seen in such earlier depictions of hell as the late-fourteenth-century fresco by Taddeo di Bartolo in San Gimignano Cathedral or Giotto's *Last Judgment* in the Arena Chapel at Padua. There are plenty of graphic illustrations of, debasing depictions of, or allusions to relieving the bowels or ingesting fecal matter in medieval art proper: an ape is the perpetrator on a tile made at Danbury in Essex about 1300, and in a roughly contemporary illustration of the Tree of Vices from a German manuscript of the *Speculum humanae salvationis* a devil similarly pollutes a sinner. The morality play *Mankind* of about 1470 has, by any reckoning, a pretty high scatology quotient; to take just one example, Nowadays mocks Mercy's Latinate diction with, "I pray you heartily, worshipful clerk, / To have this English made in Latin: / 'I have eaten a dishful of curds, / And I have shitten your mouth full of turds.'"

One of the best-known scatological stories of the Germanic Middle Ages, and one that seems to have been represented in art quite often, is the so-called *Veilchenschwank* (Violet trick). As a matter of fact, two late-fifteenth-century preachers complain that this motif, which they refer to as "Neidhart's Dance," is one of the secular subjects that is replacing the traditional religious mural paintings on house walls; it is a heady cocktail of courtly love ritual and peasant scatology. The aristocratic Neidhart sets out one morning to search for the first violet of spring; finding it, he marks the spot by covering the flower with his hat. Unknown to Neidhart, however, whose antagonism toward the peasantry was proverbial, he has been observed, and while he is returning to summon the duchess and her court that they may celebrate the discovery with a round dance, a spying peasant has plucked the violet and defecated on the spot. The court arrives accompanied by musicians and ready to dance, the duchess herself lifts the hat, and the assembled aristocrats receive a doubtless satisfactory shock. The episode is depicted in several still extant wall paintings, the earliest from the first quarter of the fourteenth century, sculpted on a series of late-fifteenth-century stone tablets, and figured in several contemporary woodcut illustrations of the Neidhart material.

Baring the Butt

The time-honored gesture of baring the buttocks at someone as a mark of defiance or insult is frequently depicted in art: for example, on a Swiss playing card of about 1530, in the margin of a fifteenth-century French book of hours, or an earlier Decretals manuscript where the gesture seems to have so shocked its victim that it has made his hair stand on end. The contortionist who exposes himself at us on a Stratford-upon-Avon misericord was clearly too much for some previous incumbent and has been drastically censored. Historical instances of the gesture abound and are recorded throughout the Middle Ages from sixth-century saints' lives onward. Referring to events of about 1080, the *Gesta Herewardi* (Deeds of Hereward) reported that a Fenland witch "at the end of her chatterings and incantations thrice bared her arse" at Hereward the Wake and his men. Fromuldus, one of the murderers of the twelfth-century Count of Flanders, was hung up in such a way that his bared buttocks were turned towards his castle "to the disgrace and ignominy of those traitors." His contemporary, an Italian nobleman named Alberico da Romano, was so piqued at losing a valuable falcon while out hunting that "he dropped his trousers and exposed his rear to the Lord, as a sign of abuse and reviling."

This gesture is sometimes significantly related to mirrors, as in the woodcut illustration to an anecdote told in the first German version of the original late-fourteenth-century French *Livre pour l'enseignement de ses filles* (Book for the Education of His Daughters) published in Basel in 1493: the elegant young woman who spends too much time and money adorning herself looks in her mirror, but to her horror sees reflected not her own beauty but the image of the devil's ass, mocking her pride in her appearance. (See illustration.) The use of this mirror figure is also attested historically: in 1462 the Viennese rebelled against the authority of Holy Roman Emperor Frederick III, and one craftsman even went so far as to bare his buttocks at the Empress Eleonore and her entourage, saying, "You should look in this mirror!" A final subtype, fairly common in art, depicts a man or animal "shooting the moon" at a man who is about to shoot an arrow at, or similarly attack, his exposed buttocks. A late-fifteenth-century example is carved on a stone roof boss at Sherborne Abbey.

It should be noted that medieval nicknames and place names offer evidence of various types of scatological humor. Nicknames also confirm the popular currency of the belief that willing disciples of Satan are initiated into his service and continue to ritualize their subservience by ass kissing. There is an interesting clutch of picturesque minor English place names of the Devil's Arse type: the famous cave at Castleton in England's Peak District, formerly one of the topographical *mirabilia* of Britain (now more genteelly known as the Peak Cavern) was named Peak's Arse in the Domesday Book and then the Devil's Arse; a place of this name is also attested at Lechlade in Gloucestershire from 1448. A Fiend's Arse Clough is found in Cheshire in 1407 and a Troll's Arse from 1335 in North Yorkshire: all are presumably unproductive or unprepossessing in some way; the tradition that a violent wind issues from the impressive cave at Castleton is very early and explains its sobriquet.

It is similarly only to be expected that scatological motifs should be a part of the world-turned-upside-down topos, in which those things conventionally regarded negatively are elevated or—as in an incident quoted in the *Malleus maleficarum* (c. 1486)—are listed among substances used in aphrodisiacs. Several roof bosses depict this type of imagery: a man who holds his nose—and seems to disprove thereby the Erasmian adage that everyone thinks his own fart smells sweet—is depicted in the roof of St. Mary Redcliffe in Bristol, while on one boss in the cloisters of Wells Cathedral we are treated to the sight of three men simultaneously so engaged. The naked man who points to his anus on this Bristol boss, however, is thought to represent the homosexual king, Edward II, who was, of course, famously murdered through that orifice.

There is evidence that the size of one's bottom was a concern in the Middle Ages: when the fourteenth-century French poet Eustache Deschamps wanted to insult the English enemy in a poem, he not only availed himself of the motif of the *Angli caudati* (Tailed English, the common slur that English people, like animals, had tails) but pointed out that they had bums like barrels, whereas the French (naturally) "have little butts" (*"portent petit fes"*). But, once again, it is the treasury of medieval nicknames that comes to our aid here: in the year of Hastings we hear of an Anglo-Saxon, Alestan, nicknamed Braders (Broad Arse). Three and a half centuries later (1421), we hear of Barbelken, a Brabant woman with the unenviable sobriquet, Groot eers (Great Arse), while the Paris tax roll of 1292 lists both a Richart Gros-Cul (Big Bum) and an Anes Cul-

Pesant (Heavy Bum); the late-thirteenth-century German Burchard (1276), nicknamed simply Burel (Bum), was presumably not so called on account of the smallness of his bottom. We should probably feel sorry for the Frenchmen Garinus Torcul (Twisted Bum) and Guillaume Cul-Percie (Pierced Bum, 1292), unless the latter is a homophobic sneer, but it is difficult to know quite what we should make of his townsman Drogo Cul de fer (Iron Bum). A contemporary Englishman named Cutte Brendhers (1279), that is, Burnt Ass, probably also deserves our sympathy, but the sobriquet of the Aalis residing in Arras in 1222 who was surnamed Hochecul (Wiggle Bum) probably denotes a bottom felt to be sexually attractive.

Urine

For the sake of completeness something should be said about urinary motifs. The only relevant medieval nickname I have come across is a character in a *Fastnachtspiel* named Saichindenkruog (Piss in the Jug), an act represented on a Swabian playing card (c. 1465), a late-medieval English earthenware tile, and—with the addition of a second jug behind—in a fourteenth-century Flemish marginal drawing. Compare the two Parisian streets mentioned in the 1292 tax roll, the Rue Quique-en-pot (Piss-in-the-Pot) and the Rue de Quiqu-en-tonne (Piss-in-the-Barrel). Medieval London also had its Pissynglane, attested from 1425, and thirteenth-century Gloucester, the synonymous Mihindelone. London's present Sherborne Lane, incidentally, was Shitteborwelane in the late thirteenth century, and there were lanes of the same name in contemporary Oxford and Romford, which Eilart Ekwall sees as a facetious formation based on *shitborough* as a nickname for a privy. A detail from Frans Hogenberg's *Proverbs* print, the immediate source of Pieter Brueghel the Elder's famous painting, illustrates the proverbial folly of pissing against the moon. In fact, this is a superstition that goes back to classical antiquity: in his *Adagia*, under *Adversus solem me meiito* (I piss against the sun), Erasmus cites the *Historia naturalis* of Pliny, who himself invokes the authority of Hesiod but notes that it is equally ill omened to piss against the moon.

—Malcolm Jones

Scottish Tradition. The folkloric culture of the various peoples who in the Middle Ages lived in the territory that became Scotland.

The Picts

The earliest cultural group known to poets and chroniclers in what became Scotland were the Picts. Their origins in prehistory are obscure, but they flourished until well into the early Middle Ages. Their very name is something of a mystery, deriving from the Latin word *Picti* (those who were painted or tattooed) used for them by the

Romans, though they were also described with the Celtic *Priteni* or *Pritani* (Old Irish *Cruithni*) from which the name of Britain is derived. The Picts actually comprised several peoples in the North, though Roman practice was to lump all of these under the name of the sociopolitical community that was most powerful or with which the Romans had most contact. They appear to have joined forces to oppose the Roman legions during the second and third centuries C.E., and thus they became a coherent political as well as cultural group first named Picts by the Romans in 297.

The Picts have left no body of writing, so their culture must be inferred from archaeological evidence, their few surviving epigraphic inscriptions on stone monuments, and what other peoples (often enemies) had to say about them. Archaeology has unearthed and epigraphy has deciphered depictions on stones of a number of weapons and tools indicative of considerable social and political organization to support organized warfare, mining, agriculture, and such arts as stone carving and music. In addition to weapons, such as swords and spears, they also used axes and pincers as tools, rode on horseback, drank from horns—according to later legend, a kind of ale made from heather—and played music on horns, barrel drums, harps (both large and small), and apparently cymbals. Earlier scholars often claimed that linguistic evidence from inscriptions indicated that they were a non-Indo-European people, with suggestions for their origin ranging over Etruscan, Phoenician, Basque, Finnish, and other possible candidates, thus adding a tantalizing mystery about Pictish identity. But more recently scholars have stressed the Celtic elements in their language—as in the majority of tribal, personal, and place names—and have suggested that what might appear to be non-Celtic elements are actually archaic forms that did not survive in, for example, Welsh or Irish.

Much has been made of Roman commentaries that the Picts had little regard for clothes, fought naked against their enemies, and decorated their bodies with tattoos, perhaps along with some kind of coloring. The Bridgeness slab, which features a sculpture of a Roman cavalryman riding down naked Pictish warriors around the Antonine Wall, may be lined up with the remarks of the Roman Herodian about Caledonians fighting against Septimius Severus in 208, claiming that they were "ignorant of the use of clothes" and covered their bodies with tattoos of animals and other symbols: "And this is the reason why they do not wear clothes, to avoid hiding the drawings on their bodies." This claim is corroborated by classical accounts of Celts in Gaul fighting naked, along with Old Irish and late-medieval Scottish Highland references to the same practice, which William Gillies states was "doubtless associated with 'mysteries' of the warrior class" in Celtic culture. On the other hand, the Picts' own representations show themselves clothed, both in arms and in more ordinary activities. Here, as in the case of the linguistic evidence, recent scholars agree that much more research is needed to solve these puzzles.

In addition to Roman sources, some allusions to the Picts by other peoples do survive in such works as the Irish Annals, Annals of Tigernach and Ulster (fourteenth–fifteenth centuries), both based on a lost Ulster chronicle of the eighth century, together with Bede's *Ecclesiastical History of the English People* (731). For example, Bede claims that they were such a force to be reckoned with that when the Roman Legions were withdrawn from Britain around 410, the Picts raided south of Hadrian's Wall and so terrified the British and remaining Romans that they invited the Angles, Saxons, and Jutes to help defend them against these fearful warriors from the far north. Later, when the Anglo-Saxons had themselves conquered Britain, expanding dynamically through Northumbria at the expense of the native populations, they then invaded Pictland, only to be decisively defeated at Nechtansmere in 685. The Picts were thus established as the dominant power in the borderland down to the river Forth. Bede also describes, though briefly, the work of Christian missionaries such as St. Ninian among the Picts from the fourth century onward. By far the most important influence, however, was that of St. Columba (in Gaelic, Colum Cille), who founded his great monastery at Iona in the sixth century. Around 710 King Nechtan brought the Pictish Church into conformity with Rome. After a period of dominance, in the 840s the Pictish kingship was apparently seized by (or fell to) the Gaelic king Kenneth mac Alpin (in Gaelic, Cináed mac Alpín), whose dynasty formed a new political union of Gaels and Picts that was to become the basis for the Scottish nation.

Gaelic Tradition

In the meantime, Gaels had been migrating from Ireland to the Western Isles and mainland of what is now Scotland since at least the third century, when Roman writers record them fighting Britons—and even Romans—south of the Clyde and Forth. This migration eventually produced a permanent Gaelic settlement, and sometime around 500 Fergus, king of Dalriada in the northeast of Ireland, also became the king of Dalriada in the area of present Argyll. Consequently, though many political changes would occur thereafter, for centuries the Gaels of Ireland and western Scotland formed a unified culture area. By 563 St. Columba had traveled from Ireland to found the famous monastery at Iona, which became the center of Celtic Christianity for Dalriada and eventually for the north of Britain. In 574 he consecrated Fergus's grandson Aedan king of Dalriada, including Northumbria, thereby establishing an integral connection between the

Church and the state, and as Gaelic influence expanded eastward the missionaries from their monasteries spread the prestige of their language as well. Thus, by the time Kenneth mac Alpin united the Gaels and Picts in the ninth century, Gaelic had already been firmly established in parts of Pictland, and there were even praise poems to Pictish kings composed in Gaelic—for example, the eighth-century *On Oengus, son of Fergus* and the ninth-century *On the Death of Cinaed son of Ailpín*. In the tenth and eleventh centuries Gaelic language and culture spread throughout the south of Scotland. The north and northwest, however, were now dominated by the Norse, whose raids had begun in the ninth century and whose influence would be felt for another 500 years. Even so, by the early eleventh century all of mainland Scotland was ruled by the Gaelic king Duncan (of Shakespeare's *Macbeth*).

Gaelic linguistic and cultural dominance began to shift, however, when King Malcolm III (Malcolm Canmore) married Margaret (later St. Margaret) in 1069 or 1070. Since his father Duncan had been killed by Macbeth, Malcolm had been reared largely in the court of the Anglo-Saxon king Edward the Confessor, who had himself been reared in exile in France and had introduced French language and customs to the English court long before the Norman Conquest of 1066. Queen Margaret was the granddaughter of the Anglo-Saxon king Edmund Ironside (d. 1016), and in the troubled times of the eleventh century she had been reared abroad in Hungary before returning to the English court, only to flee with her brother to Scotland after the conquest by William—to whom she was related as cousin. Thus, Malcolm and Margaret shared strong Anglo-Norman sympathies, and for more than two critical decades they promoted English (and French) language and culture in the Scottish court, encouraged closer ties for the Scottish Church with Rome than with its Celtic origins, and in general spread the prestige of a northern dialect of English that eventually developed into what some scholars call the Older Scottish Tongue. Gaelic continued to be spoken, of course, though over the next few centuries Middle Scots would come to predominate in the Lowlands, while Gaelic language and culture would become increasingly identified with the Highlands and the Western Isles.

The lore of this Gaelic culture long circulated in oral tradition, though scholars generally agree that some of it must have been written down even in the early Middle Ages. The bulk of these written texts have not survived, but the fact that the twelfth- and thirteenth-century manuscripts in which their contents appeared were in Old Irish argues that these earlier texts must have existed. For as William Gillies puts it, "People could not have written Old Irish in the 12th or 13th centuries, but they could copy it." Thus, by the early twelfth century, based on oral and written models, there developed a highly sophisticated Classical Gaelic for the composition of poetry, beginning in Ireland and spreading to Scotland. This was a supradialectal form in the sense that whereas various dialects of Gaelic spoken in Ireland and Scotland continued to develop and diversify, Classical Gaelic was constructed according to a rigid set of rules so that it would resist change and be understood as a language of poetry by all. Professional poets were trained both as apprentices and in schools to compose and perform intricate poetic forms, and they moved back and forth between Ireland and Scotland as a single culture area. Since much of their poetry survives in written form, employs complex poetics, and even occasionally makes reference to writing, many scholars have been inclined to regard Classical Gaelic tradition as dependent on literacy and writing—at least for composition, though actual performance would have been for the most part oral, and surviving accounts describe poetry being read by a reciter (*reacaire*). These same accounts describe the poet's withdrawal during creative periods, the techniques used to enhance concentration, and the final moment of composing and producing a written form for recitation. Even so, there were various kinds of poetic performances, and some appear to have involved extemporaneous oral composition, as in the case of threnody. Such poems would not have been inferior to written compositions, since much of what has been learned about oral composition and performance from other traditions (e.g., Greek, Balkan, or Anglo-Saxon) indicates that oral poetics can be highly sophisticated in its own ways.

Examples of this Classical Gaelic include some of the best poetry from medieval Scotland (and Ireland). The social and political role of the poet in this tradition was to compose praise poems for the chieftains and ruling family of a clan, often with genealogies and history, confirming their legitimacy and authority to exercise power. A prime example is *On Cathal Crobhdherg, King of Connacht*, by the Scots Gaelic poet Gille-Brighde (fl. 1200–1230), in which the success of the king is marked by his bringing fertility and fruitfulness to the land. As Gillies has pointed out, such praise poetry came to be considered "the highest expression of the professional poet's art." As such, Gaelic poets held a place of honor, often serving their patrons as advisers and diplomats, traveling with their own retinue and performing their poems as part of official ceremonies—even as a sign of the importance of such ceremonies—to the accompaniment of a harp (see, for example, the thirteenth-century *Donnchadh Cairbrech's Harp*). Poems would often contain mythological materials drawn largely from early Irish cycles, though these could be used to praise a contemporary Scottish (or Irish) chieftain—setting forth in the heroic references the conditions for praiseworthiness that the present ruler could be seen to fulfill in his own time. Poets thus functioned in such a society to spread the fame of their patrons according to a code of honor, or as one maxim holds, "No poet, no king." Conversely, poets also had the power to discredit rulers through satire, and while few such satirical poems survive, Gaelic tradition always allowed at least the threat that poets could spread ill fame if rulers abused their power. Ideally, however, the relationship between chieftain and poet was warm and trusting, and Gillies has pointed to the conventional image of their relationship depicting the patron as husband with the poet as wife. Many, if not most, poets emerged as charismatic, even shamanic, figures and were believed to have supernatural power. Perhaps inevitably, poets sometimes came into competition with one another, and this may be the basis for some dramatic Gaelic flytings, which inspired a long tradition of Scottish flytings—for example, the later-famous *Flyting of Dunbar and Kennedy.*

While praise poems may have provided patronage and played a crucial role in constructing Gaelic cultural identity, there are fine examples of other forms in Gaelic tradition. For example, the great poet Muireadhach Albanach O Dálaigh (fl. 1200–1224), an exile in Scotland after a killing in Ireland, composed the beautiful *Elegy on Mael Mhedha, His Wife,* perhaps the greatest love poem of the age. He also produced religious poetry in honor of the Blessed Virgin Mary, a special form of praise poetry for a great saint, as part of a long Gaelic tradition extending back at least to Dallán Forgaill's sixth-century *Elegy for Colum Cille.* Other poems treated more humorous themes, such as jibes directed toward bad pipers or "those who snore like them," while still others contain fascinating bits of lore—for example, divination could be performed by throwing a shoe over the house to see if the sole would land up or down (it was bad luck for the sole to land upward), as in O Maíl Chiaráin's fourteenth-century *Lament for Fearchar O Maíl Chiaráin.*

The social institution of Gaelic poets declined as the old Gaelic families themselves declined or changed course, largely under political pressure, and the patronage system no longer supported the institution. Under these changed conditions Gaelic poetry continued mainly in unofficial popular tradition. During the later Middle Ages and beyond, political power in the state and in the Church became increasingly concentrated in the Lowlands, fostering unfavorable stereotypes in Lowland lore of the Gaelic-speaking Highlander as crude, barbaric, uncivilized, and rebellious. A classic example is John of Fordun's famous comment from the late 1380s:

The manners and customs of the Scots vary with the diversity of their speech.... The people of the coast are of domestic and civilised habits, trusty, patient, and urbane, decent in their attire, affable and peaceful, devout in Divine worship. ... The Highlanders and people of the Islands, on the other hand, are a savage and untamed nation, rude and independent, given to rapine, ease-loving, of a docile and warm disposition, comely in person, but unsightly in dress, hostile to the English people and language, and owing to diversity of speech, even to their own nation, and exceedingly cruel.

This stereotype would persist in Lowland lore for many years to come and would only be transcended in modern times.

Middle Scots

In addition to the cultural and linguistic shifts begun during the time of Malcolm Canmore and Margaret, what some scholars call the Older Scottish Tongue developed out of a dialect of northern Middle English and rapidly gained ground throughout the Lowlands. By the time a literature in this tongue began to be written down around the beginning of the fourteenth century it had developed into Middle Scots. Although there are numerous references to a continuing oral tradition, the practice of writing literary works—from long verse narratives such as John Barbour's *The Bruce* or Hary's *Wallace* to shorter narratives and songs—flourished in the fourteenth and fifteenth centuries, though the books in which they survive generally came later. In their written forms these works still drew on living oral traditions, though there is in some poets a tendency to follow well-established models from written literature (e.g., Robert Henryson's *Testament of Cresseid,* which claims to be a sequel to Chaucer's *Troilus and Criseyde*). Even so, there is much legendary material following folkloric patterns in Middle Scots literature.

Some of the greatest of these narratives sought to form a Scottish national identity that would transcend local differences, especially in opposition to the English enemy to the south. Thus, John Barbour (c. 1330–1395) composed *The Bruce* (1372–1375), the first major work in Middle Scots, as a national epic celebrating not only King Robert Bruce's victories over the English but also the memorable period of the Scottish War of Independence as the culmination of a heroic age. Although he occasionally inserted self-conscious literary references to the classics in his poem, Barbour based his epic largely on oral tradition extending back some 60 years and more, and there are numerous formulas registering this orality: "as I heard tell," "men still say," "as old men remember and relate," and the like. Folklore scholars have shown that it is customary for legend tellers to go to considerable lengths in claiming the truthfulness of their stories, and so Barbour as legend bearer began his epic stoutly asserting that it was not only true but had the authority of tradition to verify it. Yet it is clear that this tradition had a stake in presenting Bruce in the best possible light.

Barbour's epic is thus an extended praise poem for King Robert and his loyal followers. The climax comes at the battle at Bannockburn (1314), where the army led by Bruce overcame a numerically superior English army in what is still remembered as one of the greatest moments in Scottish history. Barbour highlighted the scene in which Bruce saw the enemy Sir Henry de Bohun, a most worthy and powerful knight, in front of his men, rushed to meet this adversary in single combat, and dispatched him with a blow from his axe that cut through de Bohun's helmet to his brains. This type of scene is familiar in heroic legends, and it emphasizes the individual prowess of Bruce, thus explaining how his men were cheered by this victory and went on to win the battle. But before the battle began Bruce delivered his famous speech to his troops, as passed down in oral tradition, and during the battle itself his men were so dedicated to victory that even a group of 15,000 yeomen, boys, and carters appeared carrying sheets as banners to trick the English into thinking that fresh reserves had arrived, causing them to fall back.

In describing the carnage Barbour used a brutal realism, as he did in another memorable scene relating that Douglas, the Bruce's loyal lieutenant, attacked his family castle when it was occupied by the English just before they were to sit down to a great feast. After retaking the castle Douglas beheaded his prisoners and mixed their flesh and gore with the wine and food in the larder in a kind of mush "that was unsemly for to se." Thereafter, as Barbour noted, when people told and retold this legend they called it "the Douglas larder." It was just such dramatic legendry that made *The Bruce* a national epic from the fourteenth century onward, with generations of children committing to memory the speech beginning "A! fredome is a noble thing!"

About a century after *The Bruce* another great epic of Scotland's heroic age appeared, *The Actes and Deidis of the Illustre and Vallyeant Campioun Schir William Wallace* (c. 1477), by a certain Hary (1450–1493) whom later tradition has called "Blind Harry," though Victorians who thought this name insufficiently respectable renamed him Harry the Minstrel. According to early accounts, this blind poet gave live performances of his *Wallace*, and there are numerous references to oral presentation in the work, though there are also several references to its being written down. Internal evidence shows that Hary was familiar with events of Wallace's career that had been related in chronicles, but there is so much in the *Wallace* that is not in earlier works that most of the narrative appears to have developed in legends circulating for more than 160 years—and to which Hary, as traditional teller, significantly contributed himself.

The poetic narrative itself is a long praise poem about Wallace as Scotland's great national hero, though its extreme anti-English sentiment should be understood within the context not only of Wallace's time but also of Hary's own, as an attack on the pro-English policies of the Scottish King James III (reigned 1460–1488). Virtually from start to finish *Wallace* presented its charismatic hero killing countless English enemies, while generally outnumbered and bravely defending his land and people, first as an outlaw, then as a warrior chieftain, and again as an outlaw who became a national martyr through his execution.

Before Hary's poem, Wallace's fame circulated in folk tradition but was largely ignored in "official" literature and history. Barbour left Wallace out of his *Bruce* altogether, while Walter Bower in the *Scotichronicon* (c. 1440) gave little more than an outline of the facts of his life. Yet as early as the 1420s, Andrew of Wyntoun had observed that there were many "great gestes and songs" about Wallace in popular tradition. In fact, Wallace was becoming a folk hero, as seen in the hundreds of stones, hills, wells, and similar sites named for him and with which he was associated in folk memory—what Elspeth King has called "an unprecedented and populist canonization of a secular hero"—well before the legends of Wallace received epic treatment in Hary.

Some of Hary's most memorable legends include Wallace's various disguises, sometimes as a woman, while an outlaw evading capture by the English; his being literally nursed back to health by a young mother who suckled him at her breast after he nearly died in prison at Ayr; his beheading the laggard Fawdon while being pursued by the English and later, in a harrowing scene, being haunted by the headless Fawdon at night in a dark wood; his dream vision in which he is given his sword by St. Andrew, the patron saint of Scotland, and has his face crossed by the Blessed Virgin Mary with the saltire, the diagonal cross of St. Andrew that was later adopted for the Scottish flag; his numerous feats of valor in battle, the most historically important of which was at Stirling Bridge (1297); and his ascent to heaven being foretold to a holy monk by a spirit from purgatory, the grisly details of Wallace's actual execution being passed over—he was actually hanged, cut down and disemboweled while still alive, and then quartered—to foreground instead his confessing his sins and focusing his vision on the Psalter while dying.

A rather different representation of Scottish culture is that of Robert Henryson (c. 1425– c. 1505), who in his *Moral Fabillis* transformed the Latin tradition of Aesopic fables in the Middle Ages. In keeping with that tradition, he did tell many of the familiar fables, appending to them often-lengthy moral commentaries based on learned models. But Henryson was not only a scholar—apparently in charge of the famous school at Dunfermline Abbey—but he also became an important voice in Middle Scots poetry. His fables were therefore not merely demonstrations of scholastic virtuosity but deeply embedded in the lore and language of his land. One way this can be seen is in his manipulation of *registers*—the term by which linguists designate the specialized linguistic forms used within such different social groups as farmers, healers, warriors, cooks, lawyers, or mothers, signifying their common membership in particular social groups through their manner of speaking (though the same person can belong to more than one group) and perhaps marking themselves off from "outsiders." Accordingly, Henryson's fables are filled with the speech of lawyers and plowmen, of theologians and fowlers, and as such they register the lively diversity of everyday Scottish social life.

Some registers are related to a level of style associated with a particular cultural "level." When Henryson used the registers of law, logic, theology, astrology, and the like, he not only signified social groups for whom these registers were boundaries for inclusion or exclusion, but he also provided markers of cultural "levels" sufficiently "high" for the users of these registers to qualify for membership in elite rather than folk culture. Yet in many of the same fables that deploy the registers of "high" culture, we also find the registers of folklife as well. Not only in "The Cock and the Jasp" but still more strikingly in "The Two Mice," "The Lion and the Mouse," "The Fox, the Wolf, and the Husbandman," "The Wolf and the Wether," and even "The Preaching of the Swallow" we encounter something far more than the often-praised vividness in his portrayals of rural life. We enter the registers in which various folk groups live and interact: the registers of farming and farm life, of fowling, of country folk distinguishing themselves from urban culture, of folk groups whose very existence depends on their knowledge of animals, of the clever outsmarting the powerful, of the strong oppressing the weak, of the law as seen by those against whom it is often misused—all of which register folklife perspectives "from below" or "from the margins."

Here, as elsewhere, Scottish literature shows what Carl Lindahl has called "a remarkable degree of social breadth and social knowledge, often showing classes in competition, and almost always demonstrating a great deal of mutual knowledge between the classes."

While Henryson at times exploited the satirical possibilities of cultural differences, or even of clashes between social groups, some of his contemporaries took this much further. The anonymous *Rauf Collier* (c. 1480) begins as a takeoff on fashionable courtly romances from France, with its unlikely hero of the collier, or charcoal-burner, whose house was visited by no less than Charlemagne, though the king was in disguise, as in many popular tales. Rauf misunderstood the king's courtliness and proceeded to lecture him on manners and offer him a meal of fine game taken from the king's own forest. The king then invited the collier to court for a reward on Christmas Day, whereupon Rauf was knighted, showed his mettle by force of arms against his "betters," and eventually was made marshal of France. Other contemporary poems continued this social disruption, with images such as the monarch in "King Berdok" who in summer lived in a cabbage stalk and in winter sought the warmth of a cockle shell, or the explanation in "The Gyre-Calling" that the conical shape of Berwick Law hill was produced as "a turd" by a witch—clearly a reversal of the usual practice of associating hills with deeds of heroes or gods. A similar use of scatology occurs in a Lowlander's satire on the Gaelic Highlanders, "How the First Helandman, of God was Maid." While traveling through the Gaelic-speaking area of Argyll, St. Peter asked God if he could create a Highlandman from a "horss turd." When he had done so God asked the Highlandman what he was going to do next, and the new creation replied, "I will down to the Lawland, Lord, and thair steill a kow." Less crude but still lively descriptions of country festivals complete with dancing, courting, drinking, and fighting occurred in "Peblis to the Play," set at Beltane (Bealtaine) (the old Celtic festival at the beginning of summer), and "Christis Kirk," where "was never in Scotland heard nor seen / Sic dauncing nor deray." Perhaps the very anonymity of these poems suggests their role in popular tradition.

Yet some of the same notes are struck by one of the greatest poets of the later Middle Ages, William Dunbar (c. 1460–c. 1520). Though a poet and diplomat in the celebrated court of the last Gaelic-speaking king, James IV (reigned 1488–1513), Dunbar could satirize aristocratic pretensions in brilliantly carnivalesque descriptions, such as the dance in the queen's chamber where the court physician moves like a cobbled horse, the queen's almoner breaks wind "like a bullock" in the frenzy of the jig, and the poet himself cavorts like a colt until his slipper falls off. As a poet of the court, Dunbar could produce such serious poetry as "The Thistle and the Rose" celebrating James's marriage to Margaret Tudor in 1503. But he could also satirize a famed appointment of the king, as in the case of friar-alchemist John Damian, lampooned in "Ane Ballat of the Fenyeit Frier of Tungland." Damian later lost royal favor when he tried to fly off the wall of Stirling Castle, only to land in a dunghill and break his leg.

In his famous "Dance of the Sevin Deidly Synnis," Dunbar joined two favorite medieval themes—depicting the seven sins of pride, anger, envy, lechery, gluttony, avarice, and sloth as personifications in a macabre "dance of death." Among the sinners are not only harlots and drunkards but also priests and political backbiters. Yet the most striking images are the personified sins, with gluttony appearing as disgustingly corpulent, calling for drink and more drink, while the lecherous appear as a chain of sodomites each joined to the penis of the next. The hellish carnival ends only when the Highlanders arrive shouting in "Ersche" (Gaelic), so that even the devil cannot stand the noise and smothers them with smoke "in the depest pot of hell." Less dark, but equally satirical, is Dunbar's "Tretis of the Twa Mariit Wemen and the Wedo." The poem begins with three ladies in a garden discussing questions of love, thereby setting the audience up for a conventional presentation of courtly love. But they proceed to discuss their sexual desires and experiences with unusual frankness in speeches filled with the clichés of courtly love, thereby parodying the conventions of aristocratic romance. Once again, Dunbar has shown his genius for seeing the affectations of "respectable" society upside down.

Among the most remarkable achievements in Scottish tradition are flytings and ballads. The flyting was a kind of verse debate owing much to Gaelic verbal contests, in which a poet could either praise a friend or excoriate an opponent in an exchange of insults. One of the most famous of these exchanges in Scots is *The Flyting of Dunbar and Kennedy,* in which William Kennedy (c. 1460–c. 1508), a poet from the Gaelic-speaking country, defends this tongue as "the gud language of this land," while the Lowlander Dunbar insults his "trechour tung" for its "Heland" noise. The seeming animosity of the attack may only have been part of the play of the flyting, since Dunbar elsewhere, in his "Lament for the Makars," expressed affection for Kennedy. Even so, it is yet another sign of the stereotyping of Highlanders versus Lowlanders that extended well beyond the Middle Ages.

There is also evidence throughout the period of a vigorous flourishing of popular songs, and this has led many to search for survivals of a medieval Scottish ballad tradition. Unfortunately, these ballads were not collected until after the Middle Ages, and it is not clear how close the form in which they were collected corresponds to the form of their original performance—as in the famous cases of the version of "Lord Randal" printed in Sir Walter Scott's *Minstrelsy of the Scottish Border* (1802) and of "Edward," which Lord Hailes sent (and probably rewrote) for inclusion in Bishop Percy's *Reliques of Ancient English Poetry* (1765). Nevertheless, scholars generally agree that the subjects of some famous ballads come from medieval traditions, and this case can be made most strongly for ballads treating historical events. For example, Michael Chesnutt has done considerable study of "The Battle of Otterbourne," a Scottish ballad based on an encounter in 1388 between Scots and English, which is also memorialized in a very different way in the English ballad, "Chevy Chase." This pair also illustrates what many scholars regard as the defining context for the most important group, the border ballads that flourished along the borders between Scotland and England and between the Lowlands and the Highlands. Indeed, Hamish Henderson has pointed out that the "multi-ethnic origins of Scottish folk culture" have produced in Scots folksong a hybrid that is "often more resourceful and resilient than the pure-bred."

Finally, it is important to recognize the rich popular lore in saints' lives. Although these are generally preserved in Latin, except for a few praise poems, there is abundant evidence that the legends on which they were based circulated in widespread oral tradition, often for centuries, before being written down. Their first written form appears at least sometimes to have been in now lost versions in Gaelic, which the author of the twelfth-century *Life of St. Ninian,* Aelred of Rievaux, regarded as a "barbarous tongue" from which he must rescue his subject by presenting it in the "dignity" of Latin. While such lives drew on well-established themes in hagiography, they were clearly located in Scottish tradition—from the legend of St. Rule guided by an angel to bring the relics of the apostle St. Andrew to Fife, through the missionary activities in Scotland of St. Nynia (Ninian), St. Colum Cille (Columba), and St. Mungo (Kentigern), and on to the only royal saint, Queen Margaret, famous for her reforms of the Scottish Church. These saints were wonder workers who wrought numerous miracles, especially cures of such maladies as blindness and leprosy, both during their lives and after their deaths through the power of their relics. While Scottish saints' lives have not so far received the attention they deserve, they surely will repay future research into their formation, circulation, and power as legends.

See also: Andrews Day, Saint; Celtic Mythology; English Tradition: Anglo-Saxon Period; Fable; Flyting; Irish Tradition; Legend; Thomas Rhymer

—John McNamara

Seven Sages, The [*The Seven Sages of Rome*]. Title and title characters of a medieval frame tale extant in at least 40 versions and more than 200 manuscripts.

Known as the *Book of Sindibad* in its Eastern versions, *The Seven Sages* concerns a prince whose stepmother, the queen, attempts to seduce him upon his return from his education abroad. He rebuffs her, and the queen in turn goes to the king with an accusation of rape. The king regretfully condemns his son to death. Seven wise men (hence the seven sages of the Western title) each secure a stay of execution of one day for the prince by telling the king a story, usually about the evil nature of women. The queen tells stories of her own each day to reinstate the sentence. On the eighth day the prince speaks up on his own behalf, saving himself and condemning the queen. With slight variations, all versions follow this basic story line and contain a variety of tales about wicked women, devious advisers, and rash leaders.

While there is not complete agreement among scholars as to the origins of this tale, the theories fall into three major categories: Indian, Persian, and Hebrew. The Indian theory of origin was the first proffered. Since India had an early and thriving frame tale tradition, one might assume that this particular tale also originated there. The earliest extant texts, however, support a Persian theory of origin. Several Arab and Persian historians place the tale in Iran as early as the tenth century. Analogs to various elements of the frame tale have also been found in the Persian and early Hebrew traditions. Linguistic arguments, as well as similarities linking *The Seven Sages* frame tale to the biblical tale of Joseph and Potiphar's wife (Gen. 39–41), have been offered in support of the Hebrew theory as well.

Further complicating discussion of *The Seven Sages* are the theories concerning its transmission from east to west. Similarities between the frame stories of the *Book of Sindibad* and *The Seven Sages* prove that they are versions of a single tradition, but distinct differences between the Eastern and Western branches have led to speculation about the means of transmission. That the Eastern versions as a group predate the Western versions is undisputed. Theories of literate transmission center around a Byzantine-Roman, Arabic-Spanish, or Hebrew-Latin connection, but the lack of any transitional texts has led many to believe that oral transmission was more likely. Those who favor the hypothesis of oral transmission suggest the same routes of diffusion, along with the possibility of crusaders or merchants as carriers.

The Seven Sages was widely popular in the Middle Ages. As is the case of many medieval works, it appears to have been valued for both its didacticism and entertainment. The stories were amusing, and they contained lessons about honor, leadership, and the wiles of women. In medieval Europe *The Seven Sages* constituted part of the growing corpus of misogynist literature. More than anything else, however, its popularity and longevity are due to its inherent flexibility. Each culture incorporated its own tales into the frame, thus allowing the collection to be familiar to any audience. Similarly, details of setting and characters could be adjusted to suit a variety of contexts. Because of its range, *The Seven Sages* is responsible for carrying folktales across medieval linguistic, cultural, and national boundaries. Whether this transmission occurred orally or through writing, its effects are apparent in the number of its interpolated tales that appear individually and in other frame tales or anthologies.

See also: Arabic-Islamic Tradition; Folktale; Frame Tale

—Bonnie D. Irwin

Seven Sleepers of Ephesus. Seven noble youths of Ephesus (in present-day Turkey) who fled to a cave during the Roman persecutions of Christians in 250 C.E., slept for about 200 years, and awoke during the fifth century, when Christianity had become the established religion of the empire.

According to the legend, seven young Christians, named Constantine, Dionysius, Malchus, John, Maximian, Martian, and Serapion, gave their wealth away to the poor and hid in a cave on Mount Celion (Mount Pion) to escape the Emperor Decius, who had ordered all Christians to sacrifice to the pagan gods or be killed. They lived safely there for some time, sending Malchus out for food, disguised as a beggar. But the emperor, angry at the disloyalty of the young men, who had held high rank in his court, sent out a search party. The seven prayed for strength, and by the will of God fell into a deep sleep. After the parents denounced their sons, Decius walled up the entrance to the cave with large stones, thus ensuring their death.

According to the best-known version, recounted by Jacobus de Voragine in *The Golden Legend* (c. 1260), two Christian witnesses, Theodorus and Rufinus, wrote an account of the martyrdom and concealed it among the stones that walled up the cave. Some 372 years passed (other versions give 195, 230, or 309 years), and there occurred widespread doubts about the resurrection of the dead. The loss of faith greatly disturbed the emperor, Theodosius II (401–450), who took to wearing a hair shirt and mourning. To confirm faith in bodily resurrection, God awakened the seven martyrs and inspired a man to build a shelter for sheepherders on Mount Celion. As masons began to remove the stones from the mouth of the cave to build a hut, the seven youths greeted each other, thinking they had slept only one night. They resumed worrying about Decius's persecutions. Malchus went out to buy bread and was dumbfounded at the crosses now decorating the city gates and at the sight of people openly discussing Jesus: "Yesterday, no one dared utter His name, and today everybody confesses Him!"

When Malchus tried to spend the coins of Decius's reign, the townspeople believed he had discovered an ancient buried treasure. A crowd seized the dazed youth and hauled him before St. Martin, the bishop, and Antipater, the proconsul, who accused him of deception. But Malchus insisted that he really had come from the time of the Decian persecutions and led the mob to the cave to see his six companions. There the bishop found the sealed letter written by Rufinus and Theodorus among the scattered stones, and he read it to the crowd. All marveled at the miracle of the saints, whose faces shone like the sun.

Word was sent to Emperor Theodosius in Constantinople, who hurried to Ephesus. He and the seven saints embraced and glorified God. Theodosius exclaimed that seeing them was like seeing Lazarus raised from the dead; Maximian responded that God had awakened the seven to erase all doubts that the dead would live again. The companions went back in the cave, bowed their heads, and sank to the ground to sleep again until Judgment Day. The emperor ordered seven splendid gold coffins, and embellished the cave with gilded stones, that all might believe in the resurrection of the dead.

As the story of the sleeping saints spread, a Christian necropolis grew up around their resting place at the eastern foot of Mount Pion at Ephesus. The cave became a site of pilgrimage, and the Seven Sleepers were entered in the Byzantine calendar and enrolled in the Roman Martyrology; their feast day is July 27. Modern archaeological excavations have revealed a small church built over a rock-cut gallery, with numerous invocations to the saintly sleepers scratched in the walls. Another medieval version relates that their bodies were taken to Marseilles in a large stone coffin that is still displayed in the church of St. Victor of Gaul, martyred about 290 C.E.

The sleeping saints also appear in the seventh-century Islamic Koran (ch. 18). In that version a dog with a human voice, named Katmir (or Katrim), guarded them for 309 years, neither sleeping nor eating. When they awoke Katmir died and was taken up into Paradise. A very long sleep has been a widespread folklore motif from classical antiquity onward (motif D1960.1). The Christian version of the Seven Sleepers probably originated as a pious tale based on an earlier Syrian version that took on particular resonance in the fifth century, when the Church was beset by heresies denying bodily resurrection. Widespread and systematic persecutions of the Christians were pursued by the Emperor Decius (reigned 249–251): his method was to demand pagan sacrifice or death, as in the legend. The legend's circulation in the time of Theodosius was probably a popular response to the real theological controversies of the day. It has been suggested that the biblical locution for death—"They fell asleep in the Lord"—also may have influenced the tale.

See also: Sleeping King

—Adrienne Mayor

Shamanism. Web of culture traits whose nexus is the shaman, the visionary healer of tribal society.

The word *shaman* first appeared in English at the end of the seventeenth century, probably entering our language via Russian from Tungusic, an Altaic tongue spoken in eastern Siberia. *Shaman* is thus one tribe's word for the priest-like seer who manipulates spirits to practice medicine among cultures widely separated in space and time.

Popular synonyms are "medicine man" and "witch doctor," but "dream doctor" (Tlingit *natci*) more accurately describes the usual techniques of the shaman. Entranced, shamans send their mobile souls into "dreamtime" (Aranda *djugurba*), a mythic realm inhabited by gods and ancestors as well as other spirits in charge of healing and harrying. Sometimes in the shape of their animal guardian (Ojibwa *nigouimes*), shamans propitiate, threaten, or fight the spirits, who often have animal attributes as well. The shamans are thus messengers, psychic travelers, even shapeshifters, crossing the dangerous threshold between the worlds, gaining knowledge inaccessible to others. Maintaining the tremulous balance between mythic and quotidian realms, shamans continually reactivate the mythology of their people, keeping their gods and heroes quite tangibly alive. Shamans are arbiters of taboo, apprising their peers of their sins and the paths to atonement. Often they are also psychopomps, leading souls to or from the land of the dead. Widespread among indigenous tribal peoples, shamans have been observed in Fennoscandia, Asia, Australia, Africa, Oceania, and the Americas. Not all tribes have shamans, but among those that do, each has its own name for the seers, plus various names for guardian spirits. Each tribe envelops its dream doctor in its own mythos, and each doctor practices idiosyncratic as well as traditional techniques of spirit manipulation. Thus, the term *shamanism* carries potentially misleading connotations of uniformity; this complex of culture traits is most accurately defined in isolation for each tribe, or even for each doctor that manifests it.

While no two shamans are exactly alike, we can nonetheless find a general definition in traits that tend to recur among shamanic tribes. Like totemism, shamanism is a "total" social phenomenon: in it, according to Marcel Mauss, "all kinds of institutions find simultaneous expression: religious, legal, moral, and economic." Like the term *civilization*, *shamanism* can be defined only by a list of traits extrapolated from a wide study of discrete cultures; individual systems may lack some traits while manifesting others that are distinctly shamanic. For instance, just as some civilized societies lack writing, some shamanic tribes do not practice ecstasy, even though many Western scholars regard ecstasy as the sine qua non of shamanism. Shoshone doctors, for example, do not regularly fall into ecstatic states. And some shamans only feign the healing trance. Yet their rites involve other aspects of the shamanistic folkways treated below.

If there is a sine qua non of shamanism, it is animism rather than ecstasy. All shamanism presupposes an animistic worldview, one that posits spirits or spirit powers in every conceivable place. The Tongan word *mana* best expresses this concept: from the smallest seed to the tallest mountain, everything has its share of this ethereal spirit force, a reservoir of power tapped by the shaman. In such a worldview, there is essentially no such thing as an "inanimate object." Thus, shamanistic peoples are surrounded by countless busy spirits; the dream doctor's duty is to bend them from malevolence to beneficence.

The lore of medieval Europe reflects animism and other shamanistic traits in vestiges scattered through disparate sources. Viewed singly, such traces are not necessarily shamanic. But seen together, as here, they appear to reflect an archaic system that involved ecstatic spirit manipulation as well as other shamanic attributes. Preliterary Celtic, Finno-Ugric, and Germanic tribes probably practiced shamanism; the material presented here—a bare sampling of the evidence—represents the legacy of lost dream doctors, bequeathed to descendent literary traditions.

The sacred trees, springs, bogs, and stones of pre-Christian Europe imply animism, a belief in the numinous power emanating from places where offerings were deposited to propitiate autochthonous spirits. Such powers were associated with geographic features (e.g., the Celtic *síd* [mound], the Sámi *sieide* [sacred stone]). Adam of Bremen describes the sacred grove of pagan Uppsala, and the bogs of Germanic Denmark have yielded offerings that corroborate the ethnography of Tacitus. Aside from the bodies of human sacrifices, bogs have yielded deposits of weaponry that had been "killed"—smashed, burned, or broken—probably to subdue the residual spirit force of vanquished foes. Animated armament often figures in the later heroic literature (motif A524.2): swords like Excalibur, Grayflank (*Gisli's Saga*), and Tyrfing (*Hervarar Saga*) seem to have a life of their own, bestowed perhaps by mythic smiths like Weland or Ilmarinen of the Finnish *Kalevala* (D853, D921.3, F450.1.2, F451.3.4.2). Such smiths appear as shamanic initiators in Siberian traditions. Beowulf's byrnie and Waldere's sword Mimming both have preternatural strength bestowed by their maker Weland. The apotropaic boar crest on Beowulf's helmet has an uncanny power that originates with the weapon-smith; zoomorphic design may have been intended to animate Viking weapons as well. In their graphic appeal to animal spirits, these talismanic weapons suggest the techniques of the shaman, who also propitiates animal guardians. As Mircea Eliade points out, "'Smiths and shamans are from the same nest,' says a Yakut proverb."

The typical method of propitiation is ecstasy, the visionary trance used by shamans to penetrate the spirit realm. Merlin may reflect this sort of manticism. Celtic and Germanic oral poets were ecstatic seers, too: words like Welsh *gwawd* (poem), Irish *faith* (seer), and Old English *wod* (voice, poetry) are cognate with Latin *vates* (visionary poet). Other cognates—for example, Old English *wod* (mad)—connect poetic inspiration with psychic dissociation and with Woden/Odin ("Leader of the Ecstatic"). God of poetry and of prophecy, Odin is, as N. K. Chadwick points out, "the divine shaman" of the Germanic pantheon. Snorri recounts Odin's flight in eagle form (cf.

D152.2); shapeshifting is among the manifold shamanic traits of Svipall (the Transformer). The motif of soul travel dovetails with avian imagery in the Old English poems *The Wanderer* and *The Seafarer*. Along with Freyja—who owns a "feather-coat"—Odin has arcane connections with the Icelandic *seid*, the strongest reflex of shamanism preserved in medieval sources. In the *seid*, a circle of singers lulled the seeress into ecstasy; entranced, she gained hidden knowledge from unseen spirits. The *seid* represents a real ritual, albeit one fictionalized to an indeterminable degree in sources like *Erik the Red's Saga*, which contains, in chapter 3, a famous passage describing the female shaman Thorbjörg, who conducts a *seid* to predict the future (M301.2). Her food and clothing concentrate animal powers; she eats the hearts of beasts and wears their pelts, including the skin of a cat, Freyja's animal. Carrying a medicine bag and a magic staff, Thorbjörg "heals" a household by predicting the end of a famine.

Such predictions are one form of shamanic therapy, which involves healing in the broadest sense of the term: shamans work to make people healthy, wholesome, hale, holy. Their ecstatic quests reestablish the balance of good and evil forces by recovering stolen souls, by extracting magic "shots," by turning the weapons of evil spirits or hostile shamans back against their senders. Sympathetic magic often figures in shamanic therapy; for instance, the Old English charm "For a Sudden Stitch" pits the doctor's actual knife against the imaginary iron point shot into his patient by a witch, or elf. The point is animated by its sender's evil, and the leech literally orders it out of a patient said to be "elfshot." This complaint reflects a widespread shamanic weapon, disease-shooting, and its Anglo-Saxon cure applies medicine more shamanic than modern.

Dream doctors acquire their healing skills via elaborate and protracted initiation rites, which generally involve mythic scenes of disintegration and reintegration, often described as death and resurrection during the initiate's first ecstatic experience. In the Eddic lay *Havamal*, Odin hangs on Yggdrasil, the World Tree, to obtain runic wisdom. Cosmic trees recur in shamanic symbology, with their branches in the sky country, their trunks rising over middle earth, their roots leading down to the underworld. Shamans move through all three realms, recounting their ecstatic journeys with tales of ascent, lateral flight, and descent beneath earth or sea. Such tales are a probable source of such motifs as epic descent, as in Beowulf's submarine journey to quell Grendel's mother, who, along with Grendel, is called *wiht unhælo* (creature of unhealth) and may have some dim connection with the infernal spirits of disease. Typologically, by subduing *ellorgastas* (elsewhere-spirits) to "cleanse" Heorot and thus heal Hrothgar's misfortune, Beowulf performs a shaman-like task for the Danes.

Though Beowulf, the ultimate Anglo-Saxon hero, is a warrior prince and not a shaman, he still preserves powerful reflexes of dream doctor lore. Most notable is his subtle link with the bear, the strongest animal, guardian of circumpolar shamanic traditions. His preferred method of combat is the bear hug, which he executes with ursine strength against Grendel and Dæghrefn in the epic. His name, "Wolf of the Bees," is possibly a kenning, an alternate name for "bear." These ursine traits place Beowulf in a class of native Germanic bear heroes, along with Bjarki and Grettir (see motifs D113.2, G263.1.1). Further, these characters reflect the associated tradition of ecstatic bear warriors, the berserks (bear-shirts) stereotyped as frenzied villains in the sagas. The probable source of such heroes and villains is a preliterary Germanic bear cult—a *Männerbund*, or male warrior society similar to those of Native American cultures, whose members bore names and other attributes signifying their eponymous animal guardians. Especially where shapeshifting is implied, members of such cults share a shamanic bond with their guardian, for the most typical shamanic pursuit is the ecstatic quest in animal form. Odin undertakes this kind of quest, and he has various animal helpers, too: the eight-legged steed Sleipnir, the wise ravens Hugin and Munin, the hungry wolves Freki and Geri. In the Völsung cycle, Sigurd, initiated by a taste of dragon blood (see motifs B11.2.13, D1041), learns the language of the birds and acquires hidden knowledge from his avian guardians. In initiation, dream doctors often gain the gift of interspecies communication; the animal language brings them closer to their guardians and to the animistic realm where they travel ecstatically to find medicine for their tribes. Although European shamanism steadily disintegrated during the Middle Ages, it left many traces behind, scattered fragments of its rich mythos embedded in the most archaic strata of myth and epic, folktale and charm.

See also: Bear; Beowulf; Berserks; Burgundian Cycle; Medicine; Scandinavian Tradition; Totem; Wolf and Werewolf

—Stephen O. Glosecki

Sheela-na-Gig [Sheela]. Irish Gaelic term of unknown origin used to describe female exhibitionist sculptures, usually in stone, many of indeterminate date and repositioned in later buildings, but presumed to span the entire Middle Ages, especially in the British Isles.

The "classic" pose of the monumental sheela is a full frontal exhibition of the vulva, often by means of the figure's hands pulling apart the labiae; notable is the distinct lack of interest in the breasts. The ribs, however, are sometimes plainly indicated, adding a skeletal or cronelike aspect to the figure.

This pose has been traced from early Celtic artifacts (such as the Rheinheim armlet) to sculpture of the Romano-Celtic era and into the early-

Christian period in Ireland (e.g., the very worn figure carved on the eighth-century Adamnan's Cross at Tara or, exceptionally, the figure that forms the head of a perhaps equally old bone pin).The fact that some of these pillar-carved figures have been depicted seated cross-legged has led to the suggestion that they are related to Cernunnos, a Celtic horned male god, because of an image of a man with antlers seated thus on the Gundestrup cauldron. In Ireland, sheelas are oddly scarce in the Romanesque period—an era in which they flourished on the Continent, particularly in France.

On mainland Britain, sheelas of unknown origin are too readily assumed to be of "Celtic" date (no doubt, in part, on account of their crudity of execution), but while there is no doubt that the female exhibitionist figure enjoyed great popularity in the Romanesque period (especially in the corbel tables of French churches), the evidence will not support the claim made by A. Weir and J. Jerman that pre-Romanesque sheelas do not exist, a proposition that led them to conclude that all sheelas should be interpreted as "Images of Lust" (symbols of the deadly sin *luxuria*). Others argue that their usually exterior location and use in secular as well as ecclesiastical buildings (e.g., Irish tower houses and castles) suggest that they served a primarily apotropaic function as medieval representatives of an ancient tradition, warding off evil.

See also: Phallic Imagery

—Malcolm Jones

Ships. From Old English *scip*, a vessel with an inherent propulsion system designed for transporting cargo or people or for warfare.

Usually a seagoing craft, the ship is distinguished from the boat. The classic full-rigged sailing ship has three masts and a bowsprit. The two front masts, the fore and main masts, have at least two square sails (rectangular sails set perpendicular to the length of the ship), and the third mast, the mizzen, has a lateen sail (a triangular sail set in line with the length of the ship).

The medieval period is the single most intense period in the evolution of the European ship—from a myriad of small vessels that mostly met local needs and were designed for local conditions to the eventual appearance and dominance of major ship types that met the needs of nation-states and fulfilled their mission in uncharted waters. As the single most expensive capital investment of the Middle Ages, intimately tied to the growth of urban centers, the ship permeated every aspect of medieval culture. From banking to insurance, from crafts to mathematics, from city seal to church mural, from proverb to learned thesis, no aspect of medieval culture was left uninfluenced by the ship. Even the central institution of the Middle Ages, the Church, was likened to the ship.

It is reasonable to propose that the much-discussed term *Middle Ages* can be defined not only in political or cultural terms but also in maritime terms. The year of Columbus's discovery, 1492, could mark the terminus of the medieval period. Alternatively, a less cataclysmic proposal would suggest the appearance and acceptance of the caravel as the height of medieval accomplishment. The late-medieval period marks the time (1430–1530) at which this sailing ship gained ascendancy. Modern history, in this view, begins with the galleon.

The ship is a self-contained artificial universe, the first human construct not imitative of phenomena appearing in nature, designed to cover large distances in an unforgiving and challenging environment. It is a synergetic construct of four interacting systems: hull, propulsion, navigation, and logistics. A fifth element, ideology, helps determine the use of ships.

Shapes and Construction Methods
In the medieval period scores of variant types of ships made their appearance, with two basic hull shapes—the long ship and the round ship—dominating all design. The long ship was used for warfare, primarily powered by oars, with sails designed to assist the journey between points of engagement. The Venetian galleys and Viking long ships (e.g., the famous Gokstad ship) are the best-known examples. Though both kinds of ships were warships, the Viking long ship was intended for a use quite different from that of the Mediterranean galley. The Viking ship was an efficient troop transport, not meant to battle other vessels on water. Its oars, combined with its shallow draft, made the Viking ship able to land almost anywhere under almost any conditions. This ubiquitousness helps account for the terror that a Viking raid inspired. The Venetian galley, on the other hand, was designed to ram an enemy vessel and then allow a crew to board it. The need for ramming power and soldiery led to enormous crews and huge vessels.

The medieval round ship was used for commerce and the transport of goods and was powered by sail. The Viking knarr, the Venetian round ship, the hulk, the Hansa cog, and the Iberian carrack (cocha) are seminal examples of the round ship. Speed and maneuverability were not significant for commerce; capacity and cost of crewing were. A hybrid class of warship, the galleass, had the hull shape of a long ship but was propelled by sail and oar. It made only a brief appearance; its combined disadvantages (poor sailing characteristics and enormous crews) doomed it in a time when superior designs were evolving.

Just as there were two basic hull shapes, there were two basic methods of building hulls: the northwest European clinker, or lapstrake, method and the Mediterranean method of caravel construction. Clinker, or lapstrake, ships were built by the "shell-first" method, whereas caravel ships were built by the "frame-first" method. During the fifteenth through seventeenth centuries the Dutch evolved a hybrid method, known as "bottom-first" construction.

Viking ships and cogs are prime examples of the lapstrake shell-first method of construction. This method requires relatively few tools and little infrastructure support. The design is traditional, and necessary changes to hulls can be made "by eye" without need for formal mathematical calculations. Water tightness is achieved by the swelling of the overlapping ship-skin boards (strakes). Venetian galleys and carracks are probably the best-known medieval caravel ships. The caravel method requires the construction of internal framing first, and then a skin of edge-fitted planks is added. This method demands more infrastructure than the lapstrake method, but it has advantages in allowing a thinner ship skin, fewer nails, easier and cheaper repairs, greater hull integrity, and the creation of gun ports for cannon. The Dutch method of bottom-first construction has only recently been recognized in archaeological literature, and its positive characteristics have not yet been sufficiently explored. The chief advantage of this method of construction appears to be that it allowed the advantages of the caravel plank (frame-first) method to be applied to the familiar skin-first method that dominated northern European building for so long.

Propulsion and Navigation
Two chief methods of propulsion are to be found in medieval ships: wind or man power. Warships relied mainly on man power; merchant ships used wind. Speed and extreme maneuverability were not significant to commercial ships, but cargo capacity and small crews were, and wind power gave merchantmen the needed combination. Warships in the Mediterranean needed speed and soldiers but had few concerns about provisioning. The relatively small size of the Mediterranean and the ready availability of ports made resupply a simpler issue than it became in the open ocean.

Sail types in the period fall into two traditions. The Mediterranean lateen sail made it possible to effectively sail into the wind and to tack. This sail, however, was inferior in running before the wind. The northern European square sail, on the other hand, was perfect for running before the wind. Its limitation was in tacking into the wind. The Viking ship, the hulk, and the cog are exemplars of square-rigged ships, whereas the vast majority of Mediterranean ships and the early versions of Iberian ships carried lateen sails. In the late-medieval period the carrack combined the square sails of northern Europe with the lateen sail of the Mediterranean. This invention became the standard ship rig, which remained fundamentally unchanged until sail was replaced by mechanical power as the dominant system of propulsion.

During the medieval period the art of guiding

the ship from one place to another evolved from piloting to navigation. Piloting is the use of visual observations, landmarks, previous experience, and inherited traditional knowledge to guide a ship in largely known areas of operation. The Mediterranean Sea, for example, was a well-known body of water in which ships depended on pilotage to safely reach their destinations. Navigation is a set of methods and techniques that guide a ship from one point to another. Navigation is more generalized and abstract, less dependent on direct observation and local knowledge and therefore more useful in unknown waters. In navigation, an actual ship is set in an abstract universe, and as such this method is much more dependent on formal training and the use of instruments than piloting. The experienced Mediterranean pilot only needed a simple lead line and a rough sea chart, with perhaps a wind rose, to safely guide his vessel. A navigator in the time of Columbus, on the other hand, in addition to the lead line and a chart used the chip log, a traverse board, a quadrant, an astrolabe, a nocturnal, a sand clock, a sundial, and, most important, a magnetic compass with 32 points. Navigation and travel on unknown waters demanded literacy, so that at least one person on board could write a log.

The earliest known circumnavigation of Africa (609–595 B.C.E.) took three years to complete because the Egyptian galley fleet had to stop each autumn to plant, grow, and reap grain crops. The adoption of the heavy plow, the open-field system, and triennial rotation in the ninth century and the consequent agricultural changes in the tenth century helped produce surplus grain crops. Of consequence for seafaring was the high level of production of legumes, a cheap and plentiful supply of vegetable protein. When combined with fish protein developed in the herring and cod fisheries of the northern waters, the legumes provided the necessary nutritional basics to allow long-term ship journeys. The addition of hops as a preservative to the brewing of beer and ale in the eighth century (although not accepted by the British until the fourteenth century) helped provide a source of potable liquids that could be stored longer than plain water.

Europe's single most important contribution to the history of humanity, as J. H. Parry has pointed out, was the discovery of the sea. Almost every major culture explored the waters beyond its domain, to one degree or another, but it was the Europeans who circumnavigated the world and established the fact that "All the seas of the world are one." This innovation would not have been possible without the proper motivating impulse—ideology. European maritime ideology flowed from two impulses. One was the quest for a pure and saintly land; the other was the search for a sea route to the Indies. The first impulse helps explain the stories and facts of the voyages of St. Brendan, as well as the later searches for

Hy-Brasil and Norumbega. Perhaps even more important than these were the legends of the kingdom of Prester John, legends that sprang up in the twelfth century, describing a fabulously wealthy Christian ruler of a kingdom in India or elsewhere in the East, and that became the object of many searching voyages by sea and land. The second impulse was rooted in the thirteenth century with the crusaders' destruction of Constantinople and was later intensified by the trade competition between the emerging nation-states of the Iberian Peninsula, France, the Low Countries, and England.

In contrast, according to this thesis, the Chinese, whose ship technology was in many ways superior to Europe's in the fifteenth century, neglected to "find the sea" purely because of their ideology. Their most extensive series of expeditions—those of the Grand Treasure Fleets beginning in 1405 and culminating in 1433, with the most ambitious journey reaching Mecca and the east coast of Africa—ended on an emperor's whim. The Chinese ideology of the time did not seek trade, conquest, or a better land, and as a consequence they missed "finding the sea" and by that doomed the further development of their ships.

Medieval Shiplore

Meanwhile in the West, lore about ships and the sea flourished throughout the Middle Ages. According to the enormously popular ninth-century *Voyage of St. Brendan*, this Irish saint and his fellow monks had three centuries earlier successfully navigated a ship throughout much of the North Atlantic, perhaps as far west as Newfoundland. Early in the narrative we learn that for this voyage,

> Brendan and his companions made a coracle, using iron tools. The ribs and frame were of wood, as is the custom in those parts [i.e., Ireland], and the covering was tanned ox-hide stretched over oak bark. They greased all the seams on the outer surface of the skin with fat and stored away spare skins inside the coracle, together with forty days' supplies, fat for waterproofing the skins, tools and utensils. A mast, a sail, and various pieces of equipment for steering were fitted into the vessel.

On their journey they encounter many marvels, including an island where the birds chant hymns, an attack by a griffin, Judas Iscariot, and finally a great whale. The popularity of the work may be seen by the facts that it survives in 116 Latin manuscripts and was translated into Middle English, French, German, Flemish, Italian, Provençal, and Old Norse.

The Old English poem *The Seafarer* gives a harshly realistic description of life at sea in the North, and *Beowulf* contains sea voyages and a remarkable description of the ship burial of Scyld Scefing. Archaeology has confirmed how widespread ship burials were in Scandinavia, and one of the most important discoveries in modern times was the discovery of the seventh-century ship burial at Sutton Hoo in England (with artifacts now on display in the British Museum). Icelandic sagas are filled with ships and sailing, including the amazing feats described in the *Greenlanders' Saga* and *Erik the Red's Saga*, providing evidence, now confirmed by archaeology, that Icelanders reached North America centuries before Columbus. Moreover, ships also figure prominently in Scandinavian mythology, as in the case of Naglfar, a ship made from the nails of dead men, that carries Loki and a crew of giants toward Ragnarök, the last great battle that brings about the end of the world.

Finally, another interesting form of shiplore is the naming of ships. In 1338 Edward III assembled a fleet of more than 350 ships from 76 ports. His clerks recorded the names of 344 of them, and it is such official records that allow us to be able to assess ship-naming habits with some confidence, for only 14 of these vessels belonged to the king himself.

Given the frequent exposure to danger faced by medieval mariners, it is hardly surprising that they should endeavor to harness protective forces in naming their ships. The majority were thus placed under direct divine protection by the use of such names as *Trinite* (attested 14 times in the 1338 list), *Grace Dieu* (6), or *Seint Savour*, or, more frequently, under the protection of the Virgin or some saint, or even under the protection of the entire assembly of saints, as in the royal ship *Alhalhcog* (All Hallows cog). Devotion to the Holy Cross is evidenced in the name *Holirodeship* in a document of 1230. Easily the most popular names—more than 10 percent of the total—are those putting the ship under the protection of *Seintemarie*, and next in popularity are those named after various saints, including *Margaret* (23), although she had no particular nautical affiliations; *Nicholas* (19), claimed as the patron of sailors because when almost wrecked by heavy seas he famously rebuked the waves so they subsided; or one of the fisherman saints, *Peter* (10), *Andrew* (2), *James* (14), or *John* (15, though some of this total may well refer to the Baptist). Less popular saints, such as *Giles*—as in *Seinte Giles Cog* (8)—may commemorate the owner's namesaint or a local cult in the home port. Also attested are *Godbefore* (2), an elliptical form of the expression "May God go before us"; and *Dieulagarde* (French for "May God guard her").

Another type of name seems to be associated with attracting good fortune in a less overtly Christian manner: *Godale* (3)—as is apparent from a different vessel whose name is *Godhale* (1340)—means "good health or luck," while the 14 ships named *Godyer* (Good Year; compare the French *Bonan*, 1340) are probably similarly related to their master's hopes of doing prosperous trade. There are 2 ships named *Plente*, and 1 with the almost humorous *Waynpayn* (Breadwinner, from French *gagnepain*). Names connoting good luck include *Fortune*, *Welfare* (3), *Smotheweder* (9; Smooth Weather), and, from fifteenth-century Hull, the charming *Cumwelltohous* (Come Well to House). Equally delightful if, strictly speaking, inappropriate is *Lightfot* (Lightfoot).

See also: English Tradition: Anglo-Saxon Period; Prester John; Scandinavian Mythology; Scandinavian Tradition; Sutton Hoo

—Nicholas N. Burlakoff and Malcolm Jones

Sibyl. A prophetess of classical antiquity, supposed to prophesy under the inspiration of a deity, usually Apollo.

Several female oracles became legendary in the ancient world, and in the Middle Ages the sibyls were "adopted" by monks as pre-Christian prophets. Plato mentioned the Erythraean Sibyl, who was later identified with the more famous Cumaean Sibyl, described by Virgil in the *Aeneid* (first century B.C.E.). The Latin writer Martianus Capella spoke of two sibyls, Pliny of three, Aelian of four, and Varro tells us there were ten. Twelve ancient sibyls have come down to us: Amalthea of Cumae (the Cumaean Sibyl) and Albunea the Tiburtine in Italy; the Samian and the Delphian of Greece; Herophile of Erythrae, the Hellespontine, and the Phrygian, all of Anatolia; the Egyptian; the Sardian; the Babylonian or Persian; the Libyan; and the Cimmerian.

According to myth, the Cumaean Sibyl had asked Apollo for a life equal in years to a handful of grains of sand. She was fabled to have lived for 1,000 years and looked it. Extremely pale, decrepit, haggard, and melancholy, she wandered restlessly and knew the way to the underworld. In Virgil's version of a Roman myth that became popular in the Middle Ages, the Cumaean Sibyl guided Aeneas, founder of Rome, to Hades. Her sayings were written on leaves at the entrance to her cave, and petitioners gathered them before the wind scattered her words. In the sixth century B.C.E., according to the Roman historian Livy, she offered to sell her prophetic writings (the nine Sibylline Books) to Tarquin, an Italian king. He refused her high price, and she kept burning the books until he finally bought the remaining three at the original price.

The historical origin of the Sibylline Books is unknown. They were supposedly written in the seventh century B.C.E., in Homeric Greek hexameters, by a sibyl of the Hellespont. The books were later brought to Rome and kept in the Capitol. A college of priests was established to interpret the secret verses, which were consulted by the Roman Senate during calamities. The poems did not foretell the future but, rather, prescribed rituals to avert disaster or propitiate the gods. The actual sayings were never revealed to the public.

The original Sibylline Books were destroyed in the burning of the Capitol in 83 B.C.E., and a new collection was made by sending envoys to consult several Greek sibyls of the day. Other collections were privately owned. According to Plutarch, the mystical writings referred to upheavals of Greek cities, invasions by barbarians, revolutions, and assassinations. The Emperor Augustus destroyed some 2,000 of the new verses as spurious and placed the rest in the temple of Apollo. These new books were burned in 405 C.E. by Stilicho, the powerful Vandal general of the Emperor Honorius.

Scholars agree that the 12 extant volumes known as the Sibylline Oracles have no connection (except in legend) with the ancient Sibylline Books destroyed by Stilicho in the fifth century. The Sibylline Oracles are thought to have been composed on the model of the old Sibylline Books by Hellenistic Jews in Alexandria and various Christian authors between the second century B.C.E. and the fifth century C.E. They too are in Greek hexameter, but unlike the classical Sibylline Books, this mélange of "pagan" writings refers to events of interest to Jews and Christians in the late Roman Empire. The "oracles" that clearly predict the birth of Christ, the Crucifixion, the Resurrection, and Judgment Day were apparently written by early followers of Jesus to win converts to the new religion.

In the Middle Ages the sibyls and the so-called Sibylline Oracles were revered as counterparts to the Old Testament prophets. The thirteenth-century hymn "Dies Irae" (Day of Wrath) credited the sibyls with predicting the apocalypse. Medieval monks assigned a prophecy and an emblem to a dozen sibyls. As portrayed in art and literature, the Libyan Sibyl carried a lighted taper and foretold that "the day shall come when men shall see the King of all living things." The Samian's emblem was a rose: "The Rich One shall be born of a pure virgin." The Cumaean's emblem was a crown: "Jesus Christ shall come from Heaven and live and reign in poverty on earth." The Cumaean held a cradle: "God shall be born of a pure virgin and hold converse with sinners." The Erythraean flourished a horn: "Jesus Christ, Son of God, the Savior." The Persian carried a lantern and crushed a dragon under his foot: "Satan shall be overcome by a true prophet." The Tiburtine's emblem was a dove: "The Highest shall descend from Heaven, and a virgin be shown in the valleys of the deserts." The Delphic carried a crown of thorns: "The Prophet born of the virgin shall be crowned with thorns." The Phrygian carried a banner and a cross: "Our Lord shall rise again." The European carried a sword: "A virgin and her Son shall flee into Egypt." The Agrippine held a whip: "Jesus Christ shall be outraged and scourged." The Hellespontine's emblem was a cross: "Jesus Christ shall suffer shame upon the cross."

—Adrienne Mayor

Sir Gawain and the Green Knight. The most celebrated Middle English romance, a rich source of late-medieval festive custom and subject of innumerable speculations about its mythic nature.

Probably written toward the end of the fourteenth century in or near Cheshire, where England borders the northeast corner of Wales, this metrical romance has been preserved in the British Museum in a single manuscript that also contains *Pearl, Cleanness,* and *Patience,* all three of which are religious poems based on Christian themes. The four poems are written in the alliterative style popular in the west and north of England during the poet's day. Scholars generally agree that a single poet wrote all four works; if so, the author was devoutly Christian, a consideration that must be weighed by those who regard *Gawain* as a mythic pagan work. *Gawain* bears a particularly close relationship to *Pearl.* Both poems mix alliteration and rhyme, both contain 101 stanzas, and both display an appreciation for symmetry of design, expressed in similar stylistic devices—for example, each poem ends with words that closely echo its opening line.

Sir Gawain and the Green Knight is divided into four fits, or sections. The first fit opens at New Year's in Camelot; Arthur's court is celebrating the Christmas season, and the king refuses to eat until he has witnessed a marvel. As if in answer, into the hall rides a green man, "an aghlich mayster" (terrifying lord) bearing a holly branch in one hand and an axe in the other but otherwise unarmed. After a prolonged silence the stranger proposes "a Christmas game," an exchange of axe blows: he will sustain the first and return it in a year and a day, and the winner will earn his axe. When no one answers the challenge and Arthur makes to do so, Gawain humbly offers his service. Gawain decapitates the green man, and members of Arthur's court kick his head about the floor. Retrieving his head, the stranger identifies himself as the "Knight of the Green Chapel" and instructs Gawain to meet him at the chapel next New Year's to receive the return blow.

The second fit traces the passage of time between New Year's and the next All Saints' Day (November 1), when Gawain departs on his mission. Donning his armor, Gawain rides out through Logres (the Welsh name for England) and north Wales into the wilderness of Wyrale. On Christmas Eve Gawain prays to Mary for a refuge in which to perform his devotions. As soon as he has finished his prayer and signed himself with the cross, he spies a castle into which he is warmly welcomed by a lord, his wife, and a mysterious "ancient," an old crone. The lord of the castle proposes his own exchange: desirous to disport himself in hunting and concerned that his guest take his ease and recover from his journey, Gawain's host suggests they swap whatever they gain at the close of each of three successive days. Gawain agrees.

The third fit begins early the next morning, as Gawain's host rides out while Gawain remains in bed. While the lord chases a hind, the lady of the castle attempts to engage Gawain in "love talking," successfully procuring a single kiss before taking her leave. That evening, Gawain renders the lord the kiss and receives the deer, according to the bargain they now renew. The next day, as the lord again rides on his hunt, Gawain fends off the advances of his hostess. The two kisses she gives Gawain he dutifully exchanges that evening for the boar his host has killed. They renew their arrangement a third time, and the following morning finds Gawain's host chasing a wily fox while his hostess continues to pursue Gawain. She appears in his bedchamber bejeweled and with bare breasts. After offering Gawain a rich ring, which he refuses, she further entices him with a green "girdle" or belt, claiming it will preserve his life while he wears it. Fearful of the axe blow he will soon sustain, Gawain accepts the girdle, promising not to mention the gift to her husband. That evening, Gawain delivers three kisses to his host in exchange for the fox, keeping the girdle a secret.

On New Year's Day Gawain discovers the Green Chapel beside a roiling stream—little more than a smooth, grass-covered mound with a hollow underneath. Seeing the Green Knight whetting a huge Danish axe, Gawain prepares to fulfill his pledge. Gawain shrinks from the knight's first blow; then the knight feints a second; finally, the knight delivers a slight stroke that nicks Gawain's neck, drawing blood. Admiringly, the Green Knight confesses that he is the lord of the castle and the owner of the green girdle, Bercilak de Hautdesert. He further discloses that the old woman, actually Morgan le Fay, devised the entire ruse to scare Guinevere to death. The three blows aimed at Gawain's neck were responses to Gawain's behavior during his three days in the castle: the first two days Gawain comported himself with perfect grace and honesty, but on the third he deceived his host by concealing the gift of the girdle. Yet such a deception was not a great failing, for Gawain committed it not from intent to harm but because he "loved [his] life." Ashamed that he has succumbed to "cowardice and covetousness," Gawain declines to return to the castle and departs still wearing his green badge of shame. Back at Camelot, Arthur's company celebrates Gawain's triumph and, aping his green girdle, everyone sports a green baldric in his honor.

Thus, only toward the very end of the poem do Gawain and the reader realize how tightly the hero's adventures have been structured: the beheading episodes that open and close the action are interwoven with the game of exchanges played out between Gawain and his host at the Green Castle. Both tests are administered by the same man, and Gawain's performance in the castle game determines the outcome of the behead-ing game at the Green Chapel. Scholars have traditionally considered the author of *Sir Gawain and the Green Knight* to have created this intricately balanced plot from two originally independent stories—that is, the beheading game and the temptation episodes occurring in the middle. The beheading game possesses many analogs in twelfth- and thirteenth-century French romances; the earliest version is the Middle Irish *Fled Bricrend* (Bricriu's Feast). There is significant evidence, then, to indicate that the beheading bargain is an old Celtic theme, but there is no particular reason to believe that the poet did not derive his version from one or more of the French texts.

There is, however, no obvious predecessor for the temptation scenes. Roger S. Loomis suggests that the story of *Pwyll Prince of Dyfed* in the Welsh *Mabinogi* contains a viable analog: Arawn, king of the otherworld, changes shapes with the mortal prince Pwyll. Pwyll is to assume Arawn's throne for a year and sleep with Arawn's wife. Pwyll acts according to the bargain and occupies Arawn's bed but never touches the queen. The connections between *Pwyll* and *Gawain* are distant at best, and other proposed sources tend to be similarly distant.

Arguing that the temptation sequence derives from a folktale, Claude Luttrell construes this feature of the romance as a variant of the folktale titled "The Girl as Helper in the Hero's Flight" (AT 313), involving a hero assigned impossible tasks on pain of death by a mysterious stranger, whose daughter secretly assists in their accomplishment. Again, there is little surface similarity between *Gawain* and such folktales; furthermore, we have no evidence that the plot currently associated with "The Girl as Helper" was part of the oral tradition of the time and place that *Gawain* was written down.

Most folkloric approaches to *Gawain* focus on the Green Knight and his presumed relationship to Celtic mythological concepts. In 1949, in a very influential study, John Speirs interpreted the Green Knight as an *eniautos daimon* (annual seasonal spirit) and read *Gawain* as a fertility myth preserving ancient Druid traditions with the thinnest overlay of Christian values. According to Speirs the knight's green hue identifies him as a vegetation spirit, and his ability to survive his beheading shows his plant-like power of regeneration. Speirs sees the Green Knight as related to the monstrous heads sprouting foliage in cathedral carvings (despite a lack of evidence in Celtic tradition and documented antecedents in Roman sculpture) and to the Jack of the Green, a leaf-clad figure that appeared in village festivals (although the figure cannot be documented before the seventeenth century).

In 1916, long before Speirs wrote, G. L. Kittredge had already set out most of the evidence against Speirs's argument. There are no identifiable Celtic sources for most of the traits that

Speirs identifies as mythic: for example, the green color of the figure who loses and regains his head is found in no earlier version of the story. On the other hand, those traits that *Gawain* shares with early Celtic mythology are also found in fourteenth-century Welsh folklore: for example, the Green Chapel where Gawain meets his enchanted challenger closely resembles the *síd* (fairy mounds) of Irish myth, but it equally closely resembles the *gorsedd* (mound) where otherworldly occurrences take place in the Welsh *Mabinogi*—a body of traditional Welsh tales that, judging from surviving manuscripts, remained popular about the time that the *Gawain* poet wrote. Kittredge soundly declared that the sources of *Sir Gawain and the Green Knight* lie not in an ancient and continuous Celtic mythic tradition but in the folklore current in the author's fourteenth-century milieu, a context in which Welsh traditions mixed with the holiday customs and supernatural beliefs of English commoners and nobles.

The opening scenes of *Gawain*, for example, richly document late-medieval festive custom in the love games played at the Christmas court. References to the caroling—a round dance accompanied by song—occur no fewer than five times, four of them particularly in the context of courtship. Members of Arthur's court also exchange handsels, or year gifts, integral to medieval courting games, and we may even view Bercilak's green girdle as the final handsel of the poem. Believed to possess magical powers, these presents were exchanged to secure something equally, if not more, valuable in return. While medieval ecclesiastical writers condemned the giving of handsels, writers of lyrics and romances connected such gifts with both courtship and blessing, and handsels were distributed by the great lords who held land in the region where *Gawain* was written—for example, John of Gaunt distributed dozens of rich gifts to noble ladies at his palace in Staffordshire on New Year's Day 1380. These love tokens were also linked to contests for kisses, also represented in *Gawain*, in which laughing losers willingly remit their prizes to gracious winners.

Similarly, the sudden appearance of the Green Knight in Arthur's hall mirrors the medieval practice of playful visitations during the Christmas season. In dramatic pantomimes known as mummings, men costumed as Wild Men, monsters, devils, and other grotesque beings would visit royal halls and challenge their hosts to various contests, "Christmas games" much like those played out in Arthur's hall in *Sir Gawain and the Green Knight*. The Green Knight resembles the real-life mummers who frequented English courts during the holiday season.

It seems, then, that the magic of *Gawain* lies less in its presumed mythic origins than in its realistic portrayal of festive custom. The poem presented its fourteenth-century listeners with a fic-

tional holiday world much like their own, and when the Green Knight unsettles that world by revealing that he is something more than just another costumed mummer, the sudden conjunction of the everyday and the otherworldly creates a powerful effect, a fictional world in which magic becomes a reality.

See also: Burial Mounds; Christmas; Gawain; Green Man; Morgan le Fay; New Year's; Wild Man

—Michelle Miller

Skis and Skiing. A means of conveyance used in snowy areas of northern Europe throughout the medieval period.

Whereas the snowshoe allows its user to walk in deep snow, the ski allows the user to slide across the snow with speed and relative ease. As a mode of transportation and aid in hunting, the ski was indispensable to hunter-gatherer cultures of Europe's far north. Petroglyphs in Rodily and Alta (Norway) and on the Uiku River in Karelia depict skiing figures and elk and may represent ancient hunts. They date from as early as the second millennium B.C.E. Nearly 200 archaeological discoveries of ancient skis have been made in grave sites and in bogs and fields across northern Europe and attest to the widespread nature of the skill during the medieval period. Carbon dating and pollen analyses, along with careful study of ski form, reveal a historical evolution in ski types and changes in their use during the Middle Ages.

Although scholarly systems of ski classification vary, most archaeologists recognize several predominant types of medieval ski. Typologies are based on such criteria as length-to-width ratio, undersurface (e.g., possible existence of grooves), front point, ornamentation, foot space, and binding. The most widespread ski type—named Bothnian—has been associated with Sámi (Lapp) skiers and was probably used for both transportation and hunting. A ski discovered in Västerbotten, Sweden, has been carbon-dated to as early as 1500 B.C.E., while a similar ski from Norrbotten, Norway, bears an inscription dating it to the year 1541 C.E. A second ski type developed in southern and central Scandinavia during the medieval period. This later innovation differs from the Bothnian ski in form and binding and was probably used primarily for hunting. Exemplars have been recovered from Sweden, Finland, the eastern Baltic, Poland, and Russia. Finally, toward the end of the medieval period a third distinctive ski type developed and became dominant in Finland, Sweden, and Norway. The new ski type consisted of skis of unequal length, with a single long gliding ski on the left foot and a shorter, fur-covered kicking ski on the right. Olaus Magnus in 1555 stated that the fur used for such skis was soft reindeer calfskin. A skier using this type of ski is depicted in a wall painting from the fifteenth-century church of Österund, Sweden. The new ski type was particularly effective on hard snow and was used in the hunting of elk, deer, and bear. Regardless of ski type, however, all medieval skiers appear to have relied on a long staff for balance and additional thrust; pairs of short ski poles developed only after the medieval period.

Skiing plays a role in the mythology of a number of northern European peoples. The Sámi credited their ancestral deities—the Sons of the Sun—with the invention of the ski itself and recognized in the constellations an astral elk hunt conducted by the brothers on skis. The widespread distribution of this belief, evidenced in Sámi epic and legend and coupled with its partial transference into Finnish epic song as well, argues for its antiquity as a mythological concept. Skiing is evidenced in the mythology of the ancient Scandinavians through the skiing hunter god Ull and the skiing goddess Skadi, both of whom represent unique Scandinavian additions to the Indo-European pantheon. Textual and place name evidence indicate the popularity of the Ull cult and the association of the god with archery, winter, and skis. Skadi is depicted as the god Njord's foreign bride, the daughter of a mountain-dwelling giant. She, too, is associated with winter, mountains, and skis.

Although skiing was widespread in the medieval north, the skill remained particularly associated with the region's indigenous people, the Sámi. Early references to the Sámi by the Continental authors Procopius (c. 500–562) and Jordanes (fl. sixth century) use terms apparently derived from the Old Norse *skíthifinnr* (glide-Sámi), indicating a close association of the Sámi with skis. Ski terminology in Finnish points clearly to adoption of the skill from Sámi, and later medieval accounts of the Sámi by Saxo Grammaticus and Olaus Magnus both mention skiing as a prime characteristic of the indigenous culture. The sagas repeatedly depict the Sámi as skilled skiers, even when the text must digress from its plot to do so. Typical is the description of "Finn the Little" in the thirteenth-century *Heimskringla*, where the malicious Sámi character is described as fleet of foot, skilled at archery, and expert in skiing. Such images appear part of the stock repertoire of saga authors.

Sagas make frequent reference to Scandinavian skiers as well, especially when the skier's skill brings the hero fame or success. Examples include *Heimskringla*'s Einar thambarskelver and the skiing heroes of the *Saga of Hákon Hákonarson*, Thorsteinn skeivla and Skervaldr skrukka. Both among Sámi and among Scandinavians skiing was associated with hunting, sporting competitions, and warfare. Skiing proved particularly useful in reconnaissance.

As the medieval period came to a close the snowshoe overtook the ski as the footwear of choice in snowy conditions. Skiing remained a prized skill in mountainous or remote regions of Europe, however, becoming popularized as a sport in the late nineteenth and early twentieth centuries.

See also: Finno-Ugric Tradition; Giants

—Thomas A. DuBois

Slavic Tradition, East. The folkloric culture of the Russians, Belorussians, and Ukrainians.

The East Slavs comprised those tribes that migrated east and northeast from the probable homeland of Slavic peoples in east-central Europe. They share linguistic and cultural affinities with West Slavs (including Poles, Czechs, and Slovaks) and South Slavs (including Bulgarians, Serbs, Croats, Macedonians, and Slovenes). The three East Slavic peoples developed their distinct languages and national consciousness during the medieval period.

History

Slavic tribes settled in the forest zone on the upper reaches of the Dnieper River and in the watershed of the Dvina River by the fifth century C.E. They lived primarily in rural villages, engaging in slash-and-burn agriculture and, secondarily, in hunting and gathering. Palisaded settlements, often built on low hills, served as administrative, commercial, and religious centers.

The East Slavs settled among peoples of different ethnicity, and their language, handicrafts, and religion reflect foreign influences. Before migrating to their later habitations, the Slavs emerged as a people in close proximity to the Goths. In the North, Baltic peoples shared a lifestyle similar to their Slavic neighbors. From Finno-Ugric peoples to the north and east, Slavs adopted a range of religious ideas and customs, including those centered around the bathhouse. In the Southeast, Slavs developed a tributary relationship with the empires of the steppe: first the Khazars (seventh–tenth centuries), then the Pechenegs (tenth–eleventh centuries), then the Polovtsy or Cumans (eleventh–thirteenth centuries), and finally the Tatars (thirteenth–fifteenth centuries). Beginning in the mid-ninth century, Scandinavian traders came through the region on their way to Constantinople. The earliest East Slavic history, the *Primary Chronicle* of the eleventh century, credits Scandinavians, called *Rus*, with the establishment of the first state and the ruling dynasty. Some scholars accept the chronicle account; others believe Scandinavian influence was minimal. Regular commercial transactions between the East Slavs and the Byzantine Empire began in the late ninth century. The Rus traded furs, wax, honey, and slaves for Byzantine precious metals, weapons, and luxury goods.

By the late tenth century a rudimentary state had formed. It was centered around the city of Kiev on the Dnieper and had a secondary capital in Novgorod, the inland terminus for Baltic trade routes. The grand princes commanded the nominal loyalty of the princes of other East Slavic towns, although control of the countryside was tenuous. The fiscal and judicial systems of the medieval Kievan state found their roots in this period, although they were fully elaborated only centuries later.

In 988 Grand Prince Vladimir adopted Eastern Orthodox Christianity as the official religion of his state. The autocephalous metropolitanate of Kiev and all Rus regulated moral conduct and generally supported the grand prince's policies, even while decrying abuses of the poor and the sick. Orthodox Christianity decisively shaped high culture; Byzantine intellectual and aesthetic norms are evident in the first written language (Old Church Slavonic, developed for Byzantine missions to the Slavs), literary texts (especially saints' lives, didactic tales, and chronicles), iconography, and church architecture. The Christianization of the lower classes proceeded slowly and was completely accomplished only in the fourteenth century. Non-Christian and non-Slavic people composed a significant portion of the population from the inception of the state to the present day, serving as a reservoir for pagan ideas among the Christian inhabitants.

The Kievan state expanded to the northeast with the rise of the Baltic-Caspian trade route. The new cities on the upper Volga and its tributaries became the locus of political and economic power in the twelfth century. The fragile unity of the Kievan state could not be maintained, and civil wars erupted frequently. Princes sought military help against each other from allies among steppe nomads. These alliances made the principalities of Rus targets for the Mongol Empire, and they were conquered in two devastating campaigns in 1237–1240. The northeastern principalities remained under Mongol suzerainty until 1480. Meanwhile, the western territories that now comprise Ukraine and Belarus fell under Polish and Lithuanian rule. The Mongols (or Tatars) were absentee rulers who made little impact on either high culture or popular traditions. However, Mongol patterns of government and military organization strongly influenced those of the Russian state, centered in Moscow, that emerged in the fourteenth century.

Pre-Christian Paganism

Little is definitively known about East Slavic religion before their adoption of Christianity. Textual sources date from the eleventh century or later, and most were produced by churchmen; thus, the information they contain concerning pagan beliefs and practices is fleeting and usually biased. Some scholars have attempted reconstructions of pre-Christian religion on the basis of archaeological finds, ethnographic materials collected in the nineteenth and twentieth centuries, and comparisons with the mythic systems of other Indo-European peoples. There is much disagreement on methodology and conclusions. Although most scholars believe East Slavic religion

and society was patriarchal, a few feminist scholars have reconstructed a matriarchal pattern surviving from Neolithic cultures in the region.

Pre-Christian Slavic religion was polytheistic. Before adopting Christianity, Grand Prince Vladimir set up a unified pagan pantheon headed by the thunder god, Perun. The other deities were human and male, except the household goddess, Mokosh, and the winged dog, Simargl. For unknown reasons, this pantheon omitted important East Slavic deities known from other sources: Volos, the god of cattle, and Rod, the god of the clan, and his consorts, the Rozhanitsy. In addition to these gods, the pagan East Slavs believed in lesser spirits of streams and forest and venerated their ancestors and the Moist Mother Earth, the source of fertility. They personified the forces of nature (e.g., wind and disease) as sentient beings who, like the gods and spirits, were neither benign nor malevolent but, rather, willful. Slavs used rituals and sacrifices to cajole and propitiate supernatural forces. Protective amulets were common, often in the shape of single- or double-headed animals hung with bells, fantastic beasts shaped with elaborate knotwork, and "snake-head" designs. The cycle of festivals followed the solar and agricultural calendars, with communal rituals at the solstices, planting, and harvest. Much of the East Slavic terminology connected with religious practice originated in other languages, particularly the Iranian languages of the steppe and the Finno-Ugric tongues of the northern forests.

Folk Beliefs and Customs

Medieval East Slavic folklore, as recorded in contemporary sources, reflects a complex intermeshing of the pagan traditions of the Slavs and their neighbors with Eastern Orthodox Christianity, imported from Constantinople via Bulgaria and Serbia. The relationship between pagan and Christian elements, sometimes termed *dvoeverie* (dual faith), has been the subject of considerable scholarly debate. Marxist and feminist scholars tend to regard popular culture as overwhelmingly pagan and hostile to the Christian ideas imposed by Church and state. Russian Orthodox scholars argue that the folk readily embraced a Christian identity and retained pagan customs only out of ignorance.

With the gradual inculcation of Christianity, the Slavic pagan deities vanished from popular consciousness to be replaced with Christian figures. St. Vlasii took over the role of the pagan god Volos, protector of cattle; the biblical Elijah (St. Ilia) commanded summer storms; St. Paraskeva watched over women's work. Medieval Slavs particularly venerated Mary as the Mother of God, associating her with supernatural fertility and protection. St. Nicholas, St. George, and the Archangel Michael filled the roles of all-purpose helpers, along with dozens of other saints from the Byzantine tradition and of local origin.

Among the earliest new saints to gain a following were Boris and Gleb, young sons of Grand Prince Vladimir who were martyred in a civil war. The texts recounting their lives reflect Byzantine hagiographical motifs, biblical models, and native conceptions concerning the power of deceased relatives—particularly young innocents—to protect their living kin. Cults of miracle-working relics of saints, similar to those in Western Europe, developed in East Slavic lands, reaching their height in the fifteenth to nineteenth centuries. Beginning in the fifteenth century, Russians particularly favored *iurodivyi* saints (fools-in-Christ). Their lifestyle of wandering and disregard for physical comfort drew on both Christian and Finno-Ugric precedents; their apparently nonsensical pronouncements paradoxically revealed God's truth, especially to overrule secular and religious authorities.

Christian teachings altered some popular conceptions of the cosmos and reinforced others. Slavs continued to believe in water and forest spirits, vampires, and sentient natural forces, sometimes associating them in their harmful aspects with the demons of the Christian tradition. They accepted that certain laypeople (whom the clerical authors termed "sorcerers" or "witches") could invoke supernatural forces, either to help or to harm others. Lay healers occupied an anomalous position in clerical eyes: suspect for using herbal potions and charms but valued for their therapeutic abilities. The "Tale of Peter and Fevronia" (fifteenth–sixteenth centuries) presents a very positive portrait of the wise woman healer who performed godly miracles. Astrology and fortune-telling flourished despite condemnations by stricter members of the clergy, and they offered one way of understanding misfortune. In contrast, chroniclers drew on Old Testament parallels and presented the natural disasters of flood, drought, plague, famine, and war as punishment for sin. Other ecclesiastical texts attributed the troubles of individuals and the community not only to sin but also to the evil designs of demonic forces. Recovery came from displays of repentance, the invocation of the power of holy figures and objects, and adjuring malevolent forces to depart. For protection, persons of the lower classes and the elite both wore amulets in traditional zoomorphic shapes, crosses, and medals depicting angels and saints. These symbols also decorated homes, churches, and city gates.

Church holidays were characterized by intersecting popular and official celebrations. Popular carnivals accompanied ecclesiastical celebrations of Christmas and the beginning of Lent. The Nativity of John the Baptist (June 24) subsumed the earlier solstice festivals of Rusalii and Kupalo, marked by midnight rituals with bonfires and bathing. The holiday of the Nativity of the Virgin (September 8), coinciding with the beginning of the harvest, was celebrated with a "second mass" of bread, grain porridge, honey, and cheese dedicated to the Mother of God or to the Rozhanitsy.

Life-cycle celebrations showed a high level of syncretism. At the time of birth, a series of rituals conducted by priests, midwives, and family members protected mother and child. These included the delivery of the infant in the bathhouse, repurification of the mother, baptism of the child and cutting its hair, and blessing of the cradle. Marriages were usually solemnized not by the officially required Church ceremony but, rather, through ritual feasts and dancing designed to invoke fertility. The masters of ceremony at weddings were often men called *skomorokhi* (minstrels), who preserved the lore of the pagan priests. Funeral practices drew from both pagan and Christian sources. The populace gradually adopted the Christian services of last confession and commemorative prayers, and the Church accepted native mounded graves and food dedicated to the dead.

Although nearly all surviving medieval texts are ecclesiastical or governmental, they contain hints of a vibrant secular culture. The epic poem *Tale of the Host of Igor* recounts Russian princes' inauspicious quest for glory in battle against the Polovtsy. It is rich in imagery, and its allusions to pagan gods and omens speak to the mythic milieu of the twelfth-century Kievan elite. This text contains Iaroslavna's lament for her lost husband—an early literary reflex of this well-attested genre. A textually similar but inferior epic, *Zadonshchina* (Beyond the Don), tells of Grand Prince Dmitri Donskoi's victory over the Tatars in 1380. Other epics, called *byliny*, relate the exploits of warriors and adventurers from medieval Kiev, Novgorod, and Moscow. Because they survived only orally (the earliest written fragments date to the seventeenth century), it is difficult to reconstruct medieval originals.

See also: Baltic Tradition; Finno-Ugric Tradition

—Eve Levin

Sleeping King [Sleeping Hero]. A legendary figure, most often a king or emperor, sleeping (or biding) in some hidden place—a cave or island—until the appropriate time for his return (motif D1960.2).

Arthur, Frederick Barbarossa, Frederick II, Charlemagne, Holger Danske, King Wenzel of Bohemia, Finn (Fionn), William Tell, Thomas Rhymer, Harold and Wild Eadric after the Battle of Hastings, and Prince Marko of Hungary are among the many sleeping heroes reported in Europe in a variety of chronicles, romances, poems, and prophecies composed in various periods. While some heroes are simply waiting elsewhere, the most common form of the legend tells of a mortal who discovers the sleeping hero in his hidden place and is told who the hero is and when he will return to the outside world. Sometimes the mortal is allowed to carry away treasure, linking this legend to treasure tales. Legendry covers the details of how the hero came to be in secret repose: for example, he might be seeking healing from battle wounds. It also tells how long he will sleep: he might sleep until his nation most needs him or until Judgment Day. Various signs, depending on the particular legend, may indicate that he will sleep until a preset time, the arrival of a worthy petitioner, or the time of greatest need; it may be that he will not appear until his beard grows to a certain length, until a barren tree blossoms in winter, or until a sword is drawn, a horn is blown, or a bell is rung. Descriptions of his sleeping place vary, as do his condition and the circumstances of his discovery. His resting place may be filled with armed warriors, stabled horses, and vast treasures. The hero may be lying in the center or seated at a table or tended by women. His discovery may come about in one of several ways: He may be found by a mortal (generally a shepherd or groom) pursuing a lost sheep or runaway horse, or by a man buying horses for the sleeping warriors, or through the actions of a wise man. Someone may simply stumble upon or through the entrance hole, or the mortal may be invited in by the hero, who, in a pause from sleep, has been prowling the hillside.

Arthur is the most prominent and best documented of these heroes, and his role as a sleeping hero was known throughout Europe (and may have provided the model for other sleeping heroes). Though the earliest recorded legend of Arthur as a sleeper in a cave is Gervase of Tilbury's circa 1211 account of Arthur in Mt. Etna, and the earliest Welsh account does not appear until the sixteenth century, attestations to British belief in the king's survival and eventual return occur repeatedly in twelfth-century English and French texts. Nineteenth- and twentieth-century collections show that the legend became widespread (localized in many places) throughout Wales, England, and Scotland, with Craig-y-Dinas (south Wales) and Cadbury (Somerset) among the most frequently noted specific locations.

These sleeping heroes are often redeemer heroes, whether for a nation or for a religious or economic group. The legend often arises at a time when a group with a distinct sense of itself feels deeply oppressed by outsiders; the sleeping hero is looked to in order to satisfy the yearning for better times, both past and future. The cave legend may be applied to a potential redeemer whose promised hope is not yet fulfilled, as with the fourteenth- and fifteenth-century Welsh heroes Owain Lawgoch and Owain Glyndwr, whose attempts at gaining independence for Wales, though unsuccessful, have led to them sharing the cave legends in Wales with Arthur.

See also: Arthurian Lore; Charlemagne; Owain Glyndwr; Thomas Rhymer

—Elissa R. Henken

Snorri Sturluson's *Edda* [*Prose Edda*]. Important medieval Icelandic work detailing old Scandinavian myth and heroic legend.

A member of one of Iceland's most influential families, Snorri Sturluson (1179–1241) was a wealthy landowner, politician, and man of letters. He grew up the foster son of Jon Loptsson and the foster brother of the bishop Páll Jónsson, and may have acquired some book learning at Oddi, Jon's farm. Besides his *Edda*, Snorri was also apparently the author of *Heimskringla*, the most important collection of sagas about the lives of the kings of Norway, and perhaps also of *Egil's Saga*, one of the so-called Sagas of Icelanders.

Toward the end of the second decade of the thirteenth century he made a trip to Norway and visited at the court of the boy-king Haakon Haakonsson and his guardian the Earl Skuli, and thereafter he wrote the *Hattatal* (Enumeration of Meters), a praise poem to them in the traditional skaldic style, exemplifying 100 metrical and stylistic variations and equipped with a commentary. Next, according to the standard view, he wrote a treatise on the language of poetry (*Skaldskaparmal*), consisting mostly of semantically arranged lists of kennings (metaphors) and poetic vocabulary but including a few narratives presenting the bases of the kennings in myth and heroic legend. Then he composed a separate text, *Gylfaginning* (Deluding of Gylfi), which consists exclusively of myths on which kennings are based, embedded in a frame story. In the extant versions of the work, these follow a Prologue in the order *Gylfaginning*, *Skaldskaparmal*, *Hattatal*, sometimes with additional materials. The oldest manuscript, *Codex Upsaliensis* from circa 1300, calls the book *Edda* and attributes it (or its arrangement) to Snorri.

Iceland had been Christian for more than 200 years when Snorri wrote, and he faced the problem of discussing a poetic language based on pagan myth. His solution relied in the first instance on the Prologue, which is unequivocally Christian and which places the settlement of Scandinavia in the context of a migration from Anatolia. In a typical medieval etymology based only on a similarity of sounds, Snorri understood the term *aesir* (gods) as "Asians" and created a euhemerization; Odin and the Aesir/Asians were the historical beings who undertook this emigration. In *Gylfaginning* Snorri took the additional step of creating a frame story in which the prehistoric Swedish king Gylfi meets three magicians who are descendants of the original Aesir and who recount their exploits (the mythology). The "deluding," we may guess, was that Gylfi somehow took men or their ancestors for deities and thus was responsible for bringing the old belief in the Aesir to the north. Finally, Snorri or a later redactor of his work wrote in *Skaldskaparmal* that young poets were not to believe in the stories in the *Edda*.

Snorri intended his *Edda*, then, as a handbook

of poetics, and the title seems to be based on the Latin verb *edo* (compose). *Gylfaginning* and the narratives in *Skaldskaparmal*, however, represent the first attempt at a vernacular mythography in the North, and in several cases Snorri's *Edda* has the best version of a given myth. The kennings in *Skaldskaparmal* are themselves independently valuable in understanding the mythology and heroic legend.

See also: Eddic Poetry; Myth; Scandinavian Mythology; Scandinavian Tradition; Trickster
—John Lindow

Spinning and Weaving. The processes of making string and cloth.

Until the twelfth or thirteenth centuries, medieval modes of making string (thread, yarn, rope) and cloth (for both clothes and furnishings) continued technology used in Roman times. New methods (like carding) and new tools (e.g., treadle loom and spinning wheel, both based on Eastern technology) eventually began to change and speed up the slow traditional processes that consumed a high proportion of human labor hours.

Spinning and weaving were basically women's work, although men often contributed to cloth production at both ends of the process (fiber production and marketing), and as the organization of commercial textile industries increased, men also wove and tailored. Most European folklore concerning spinning and weaving, however, deals with women, to the point of treating them as synonymous: consider the term *the distaff side* or the folk rally

When Adam delved and Eve span,
Who was then the gentleman?

Divine patrons of spinners were female, too: St. Catherine, Hagia Paraskevi, Freyja, Mokosh, nixies, willies (vily), and so on.

Spinning

Linen (derived from flax stems) and wool were the most common fibers of medieval Europe. Plant-stem fibers—used for thread since 25,000 B.C.E. (Upper Paleolithic)—require a long process of retting (rotting), braking (pounding), and hackling (combing) the woody parts of the stem away from the fibers before they can be spun into thread. The golden color of much flax helped instigate tales of spinning flax into gold (motif H1021.8).

In Scandinavia and the Baltic, where it was too cold to grow flax well, hemp and nettle were processed similarly. Hemp (much used in central Europe) is coarser than flax and became the preferred fiber for ships' rope, since it resists saltwater, but Eastern Europeans also used it for clothing. The northern nettle produces a fine, silky fiber long preferred in Scandinavia for the woman's foundation garment (chemise). Making

fine cloth from stinging nettles must have seemed impossible to those not accustomed to it, for it led to several folktales about magical cloth from nettles. Remains of nettle cloth, originally assumed to be linen, were found on the Oseberg ship, a ninth-century queen's burial in Oslo Fjord.

Wool first appeared in Neolithic Mesopotamia, about 4500 B.C.E., when local strains of domestic sheep began bearing usable wool (wild sheep grew unspinnable fiber). By Roman times breeds had improved in woolliness, but the development in medieval Spain of the merino sheep with its particularly fine, long, soft fleece led to skirmishes and even wars, as foreigners (especially from Britain and Holland) tried to steal merino rams to improve their own breeds and keep up with the growing textile market. Wool had first to be shorn from the sheep; it then had to be cleaned of burrs, dirt, grease, and sweat; and its tangles had to be removed by combing or carding. It could be sorted into natural colors, and white wool could be dyed before or after spinning. Woolen yarns prior to the thirteenth century were combed; that is, the fibers lie parallel. This worsted yarn is very durable but feels harsh. The innovation of carding—using opposing boards set with many rows of nails or thorns to fluff rather than comb the wool—distressed traditionalists when it was introduced, as we learn from regulations and prohibitions of this faster method in fourteenth-century Valenciennes, Gand, Troyes, and other northern cities.

Silk, cultivated in China from the indigenous silkworm *Bombyx mori* since 2000 B.C.E., was traded into Europe by Roman times. Presently silkworms and mulberry (this species' only food) were smuggled west to start rival industries, especially in Syria. The silk industry reached Palermo with the ninth-century Arab invasion of Sicily, moving thence to Italy (Lucca, Florence) in the 1280s. Because of its high cost, silk—like metallic thread—was used mostly by and for the nobility and the Church. It was not beneath rich ladies to spin silk or embroider gold.

Although cotton was domesticated in India before 3000 B.C.E., a new plant variety suited to northerly climates became available only in medieval times, reaching Europe (Greece, Italy, Spain) via the Muslims. Spanish cultivation is first noted in the ninth century.

Modes of spinning thread depended partly on fiber length. Europeans traditionally spun linen and wool with a low-whorl drop-spindle—a stick with a small flywheel (whorl) at the bottom. It is set twirling with thumb and finger like a top, then dropped so it hangs from the thread and adds twist while more fibers are paid into the growing thread to lengthen it. (Originally, *spin/span* meant "stretch, lengthen" rather than "twirl"—as in a bridge span or spinning tales.) Flax fibers are so long (often four feet) that they must be bound loosely on a distaff (from *dis-staff*, "fiber-stick"), since a human arm is too short to hold them out far enough. Wool can be either hand held or bound to a distaff. Shapes of distaffs varied considerably within Europe, the wide flat kind used in Eastern Europe often being painted with propitious designs.

Other fibers required other methods. Silk is unwound directly from the cocoon in gossamer-thin filaments up to 1,000 yards long. By unwinding several cocoons at once and giving an occasional twist to keep the strands together, the silk reeler makes spinning unnecessary, although short silk can be spun like cotton. Cotton fibers are so short and slippery that the spindle must be supported, not dropped, to avoid breaking the thread. Gold and silver threads were cut as strips from thin metal sheets and used thus or wrapped around a spun linen or silk core. Thread of drawn wire was introduced in the ninth century, and cheaper thread of gilded membrane in the twelfth. Charlemagne reputedly had an asbestos cloth.

Spinning consumed enormous amounts of time, five or ten times what it took to plain-weave the same amount of thread. (The fineness of the thread and the type of weave affect this factor, of course.) Since spinning was the bottle-neck, women spun constantly, while doing other tasks: a miniature in the Luttrell Psalter (c. 1340) shows a woman feeding chickens with distaff and spindle tucked under her arm; a stained glass cathedral window of about 1360 in Erfurt shows a woman spinning while rocking a cradle; a wood-cut in Olaus Magnus's *Historia de gentibus septentrionalibus* (History of the Nordic Peoples, 1555) shows a Scandinavian woman spinning by the light of a burning splint held in her teeth as she pulls retted flax from bundles tucked into her headband—a hazardous arrangement necessitated by the long, dark winters.

In the thirteenth century a simple spinning wheel reached Western Europe, evidently derived from silk-winding reels of China and India. Regulations against it in Germany and France in the 1280s demonstrate its presence and perhaps a poor initial design. By 1480 it had been much improved by adding a flyer (which enabled winding the thread while continuing to spin) and eventually a treadle. Spinning wheels quadrupled the hourly output. Despite this saving, Balkan and Greek women seldom adopted the spinning wheel because they usually spun while herding sheep or traveling between villages. Women in colder climes, however, sat indoors to spin and found the wheel a great boon.

Since flax is best spun damp, Eastern European women often used the bathhouse for this task, excluding men and claiming patronage by vindictive female spirits (Mokosh/Mokusha, *vily/rusalki*). Friday (the day of Frigg, Venus, and Paraskevi) was sacred to these goddesses, who forbade spinning on that day and during their festivals (e.g., the Midwinter, Midsummer, and spring Rusalii of Eastern Europe).

Weaving

Early-medieval Europe inherited two large looms, both upright: the warp-weighted loom and the vertical two-beam loom (also known as a tapestry or rug loom). The former, developed in Neolithic Europe, was the principal loom of Greek, Roman, and other European households and persisted long in Iceland and Scandinavia (even to as recently as 25 years ago). A thirteenth-century Austrian manuscript depicts it clearly. The warp (foundation threads for the cloth) hung from a beam bound across two uprights, with the threads held taut by weights at the bottom; the weaver(s) stood before the loom, pushing upward the rows of weft (cross-threads inserted to form cloth). The two-beam vertical loom, however, was much less tiring, since the weaver sat in front of the warp (here stretched between a top and bottom beam) and beat each new row of weft downward. Both looms take little floor space, unlike Middle Eastern ground looms, and hence are more suited to rainy Europe, where weaving must occur indoors and largely during the long winter. Both looms accommodate many weaves and sizes of cloth, but the warp-weighted loom is not suited to slippery fibers like silk or to weaves requiring high tension (knotted pile, tapestry). The two-beam vertical loom apparently reached Rome from its conquests in the Middle East, where it had been known for millennia. (Two- and three-beam vertical looms were probably also known in prehistoric northern Europe.) Soon it became the primary loom, as depicted in the ninth-century Utrecht Psalter and an eleventh-century manuscript, *De universo*.

Around 1200 a new and more efficient loom appeared, again using Eastern ideas: the horizontal treadle loom. In earlier looms, one had to separate the warp threads into sheds (openings to insert the weft) by pulling a bar with the hands. The new loom used the feet for this: twin bars were counterbalanced on pulleys above the warp (now running horizontally between two beams) and attached by ropes to treadles under the warp. The weaver sat before the loom and changed the shed by depressing alternate treadles.

Since this mechanism made a wider shed, the freed hands could manipulate another key improvement: the true shuttle. Instead of shoving a bobbin slowly through the warp, the weaver could now shoot it across the entire warp with a single flick of the hand—provided the bobbin lay inside a boat-shaped carrier designed to skim on the lower half of the now horizontal warp. The earliest European image of a horizontal treadle loom, in an early-thirteenth-century English manuscript, already shows the boat shuttle. By the fourteenth century this efficient loom-and-shuttle was used all over Western and central Europe, continuing today as the most popular hand loom.

Small portable devices for making narrow bands also existed. To form sheds, some used a rigid heddle (small frame holding eyed slats with slots between) and others a set of cards (tablets) with holes at the corners. The Oseberg ship preserved a band loom set up with 52 threaded four-holed tablets. Such devices produced ribbons, belts, sashes, edgings, and tapes, both plain and elaborately patterned.

Netting called sprang, convenient for sleeves, stockings, hair nets, and other garments requiring elasticity, also needed small frames. (Knitting was probably invented in the late Middle Ages, but sprang dates from the Neolithic.) Sprang was often elaborately patterned.

Although linen cloth was typically plain weave, statistical analyses of burials and urban excavations show that woolen twill cloth (mechanically patterned with a simple diagonal, variable into zigzags and lozenges) was the most popular weave from 500 to 1000 C.E. in Europe, especially in Britain. Sprang and tablet-woven braids were also favored. Silk and metallic threads trimmed the cloth and clothing of the rich as well as fabrics for use by the Church. Velvet began in Florence about 1385, whereas lace first became popular—for Church textiles—early in the Middle Ages, spreading northward from Italy. Figured textiles existed, too: Church vestments with religious scenes and great wall hangings like the Bayeux Tapestry (actually an embroidery) or the Oseberg wool-on-linen tapestries depicting battles and other events.

Labor Organization

As in earlier times, household production of cloth, start to finish, was done principally by women, although such messy, smelly tasks as dyeing thread or fulling the finished cloth might be sent to specialists. (Some colors could be achieved easily with local herbs boiled in kitchen pots; but others, like woad blue and "royal" purple, involved complex processes.)

Archaeological finds show that coastal communities around the North Sea and the English Channel were almost the only places in which Roman-era textile industries survived; soon these began to drive the economy of the Carolingian Empire and Anglo-Saxon England. Cloth in recognizable local weaves (usually twills) from emporia in western Norway, Saxon England, Germany, and the Frankish areas were widely traded in Merovingian times; even silks and "Coptic" tapestries from the Middle East occasionally reached Western royal graves. Viking raids in the ninth century drove cloth workers (once dependent on sea trade) inland, but with the new loom and spinning wheel, textile trade throve again, each town attaching its seal to its brand of cloth. Cloth fairs developed into permanent covered markets, such as Blackwell Hall, built in London in 1397.

Some workers organized into guilds (such as Florence's Calimala wool-workers' guild); the destitute were organized by entrepreneurs. Thus, eleventh- to fourteenth-century documents from northern France and Flanders delineate a system by which the merchant imported wool from England and sent it in turn to people who each enhanced it with a single task in her (or his) own home and returned the wool to the owner. The initial tasks were sorting by quality, color, and type; beating to fluff and clean; washing and regreasing; combing or carding, as required; and spinning. Each week the *fileresses* "(female) spinners" came to town for weighed packages of prepared wool to spin, the returned thread being weighed to protect against loss or filching and sent on to the *dévideresses*, whose job was rewinding the thread into the bobbins or skeins needed for weaving particular items. Finally, the entrepreneur sent it to weavers, collected the cloth, and sold it. Legislation (including wearing leather aprons) was aimed primarily to prevent loss or adulteration of the wool.

Further Folklore

Most textile-related medieval folklore involves spinning, probably because—as for the ancient Greek *moirai* (fates) and the norns of Scandinavian mythology—spinning comprises an act of creation, when amorphous fluff "magically" grows into useful thread, even a thread of life (analogous to women producing a baby from nothing—attached by a cord?). Remembrances of Greece's Fates (spinning and clipping the thread of destiny) mixing with Rome's *Parcae* (female spirits who bestow gifts on newborn children) produced such beloved but technologically confused tales as "Sleeping Beauty" (AT 410): hand spindles themselves are not sharp, yet tradition associated them with death and birth.

"Magic girdles," common in European lore, may have been woven not only with talismanic motifs but also by counting number magic (an ancient Germanic belief) into the warp threads. Potent textile motifs included lozenges for female fertility, roses for protection, and a bell-skirted female with birds on her raised hands for protection in childbirth. Still used in Eastern Europe, these motifs can be traced back several millennia.

See also: Peasants

—E. J. W. Barber

Spirits and Ghosts. Usually unseen, often demonic presences attached to natural phenomena (spirits); or the spirits of the dead (ghosts), closely related to the animated corpses of the dead (revenants).

The fear of spirits and ghosts is extremely common. Medieval people often connected such unseen forces with natural phenomena, localities, objects, and activities, and they used cultic rituals and magical practices in attempts to influence them. The word *ghost* (from old Germanic *gast*) indicates an unspecified demonic being. The words *ghost* and *demon* are often used synonymously. The German scientist Theophrastus von Hohenheim, known as Paracelsus (1493–1541), set himself the task of describing "the creatures beyond the light of nature" (i.e., spirits) in his posthumously published *Liber de nymphis, sylphis, pygmaeis, et salamandris* (Book of Nymphs, Sylphs, Dwarfs, and Salamanders). For him, all these demons and ghosts are indisputably real; he characterizes the elemental spirits as "ghostmen," even though they were not descended from Adam. They are, so to speak, of human nature, but they have no soul:

> Therefore they are men and people, they die with the cattle, change [into] spirits, they eat and drink with men. Their dwelling is four-fold, that is after the four elements. One in the water, one in the air, one in the earth, one in fire. Those in water are nymphs, those in air are sylphs, those in the earth are dwarfs, those in fire are salamanders.

Paracelsus's writings on elemental spirits trace their roots to Greek nature philosophy and Neoplatonism; his characterizations grow from the prescientific speculation of a scholarly culture. While Paracelsus interprets these elemental spirits as a kind of human but without a soul, Martin Luther goes one step further and delivers a Christian interpretation, in which he explains lamely that all these are metamorphosed forms of the devil.

To be sure, the Christian interpretation met only partial success in folk belief, and many of the forms described here have kept their ancient substance to this day, in spite of all tendencies to demonize them. Medieval demonology, with its division of spirits according to four elements (water, fire, earth, and air), promises a logical taxonomy. But its logic descends from the speculations of the natural philosophers of the fifteenth and sixteenth centuries and, not least of all, from the Romantic nature poetry of the nineteenth century. Sylphs and naiads, undines and nymphs were never manifestations of folk belief; they were creations of prescientific natural philosophers who derived their inspiration from the demonology of late antiquity.

Folk tradition reports numerous supernatural experiences of numinous encounters with the Wild Hunt (also known as Woden's [Odin's] or Arthur's Chase; motif E501), people of the night, witches and druids, demonic beings of different kinds, spooks and poltergeists, (fairy) mounds and nightmares—apparitions that we would nowadays classify as psychological or parapsychological phenomena.

Among the most common personifications of spirits are the various forms taken by the vegetation deities that Wilhelm Mannhardt designates as "corn demons." These spirits reside in fields of grain and other plants important to the rural economy, such as flax, beans, poppies, and hops. They appear in human as well as animal form. They can be either male or female. Undoubtedly, they appear among all agrarian-oriented peoples. Over the course of time, the influence of the Christian Church demonized these vegetation deities; finally, they descended to the level of villains in tales told to frighten children.

Peasants made offering to such spirits so that they would protect and benefit the crops. When the wind moves through the fields, making the grain wave, the motion of the plants is said to be a sign of the presence of the corn spirit. Such phrases as "the Corn Mother is in the field" are used to describe the motion of the grain. Adults may say that the Rye Mother is sitting in the field holding her black breasts out to the children so that they will drink from them and die. Therefore, the Corn Spirit is sometimes called Langtüttin (Long Tit). The spirits are known by numerous personifying names and are said to take various human and animal forms: besides such humanized figures as a "rye-mother," "corn man," "corn angel," and "sickle-woman," plant spirits sometimes take the forms of wolf, bear, cat, or bogeyman, all of which are invoked to frighten children and keep them from trampling the ripe grain.

One of the most interesting forms is the *Bilwis*, which has undergone many transformations in medieval literature and subsequent folk belief. The little-known Germanic goddess Bil was first, apparently, a personification of the waning moon. Later she developed an elfin, dwarfish aspect and the ability to cripple people or cattle with the shot of an arrow—as in Wolfram von Eschenbach's poem *Willehalm* (c. 1218–1220), which mentions "Bilwis-shot": "Si wolten, daz kein pilwiss / si da schüzze durh diu knie" [They didn't want any Bilwis to shoot them in the knee].

During the course of the thirteenth century, the Bilwis is less and less frequently treated as the personification of a supernatural power but becomes increasingly identified as a malevolent human being, a witch. Still later, with the rise of witch persecutions at the end of the Middle Ages, the Bilwis was demonized; she becomes an incarnation of the devil for the witch and sorcerer. A final development has taken place since the sixteenth century, as, especially in northeast Germany, the Bilwis has been conceived of as a grain spirit bringing wealth; yet this latest manifestation of the Bilwis has its harmful side, the Bilwis-cutter, who is blamed for the unexplained patterns that are formed among the rows of standing grain. The cutter is a sorcerer or a witch that cuts down the corn with sickles that are fastened to its feet. He is classified as an essentially malevolent Corn Spirit. Thus, the Bilwis is exceedingly polymorphous, taking on many appearances and meanings in all German-speaking areas throughout the Middle Ages. The Bilwis is one of the strangest and most mysterious beings in all of folklore; its varying forms reflect the concerns of a farm culture, and it serves to explain the eerie appearance of turned-down rows of plants in cornfields.

To the class of anthropomorphic (human-shaped) spirits belong the revenants. The most common revenant of folk belief is a deceased person who must stay in one place because of some sin, crime, or other reason, in the shape in which it lived, as a living corpse or as the undead. Ghosts of the dead can appear in many shapes. They may appear to the living in their original human aspect, with the appearance and age they had at the moment of their death. But in folk belief they can also appear as fiery dogs, horses, pigs, or goats. Frequently the apparition is black or white, or half black, half white, to reveal its state of spiritual development—for example, the penance it is undergoing in purgatory. Sometimes, especially in Christian tradition, the ghost gives a sign. When a tortured soul from purgatory appears to a living person it often leaves behind a fiery handprint on wood or cloth that serves as a sign of its need for redemption.

Such medieval writings as the Icelandic sagas are rich in accounts of revenants. The haunting spirit takes on the shape that it possessed while living. As Claude Lecouteux describes these creatures of the sagas, "The dead are beings with flesh, sinews and skin; sometimes they speak; sometimes they cry for help or kill." It is noteworthy that pre-Christian (Germanic) concepts have held for such a long time in this realm, especially in light of the remarkable small number of Christian revenants. Devils and purgatory likewise play a very small role in the folk beliefs and portrayals, and, Lecouteux continues, "nowhere do we encounter the image of the decaying corpse." Revenants are not specters; they are "living corpses," human beings who died an unnatural death or who are burdened by some guilt and therefore must return without rest to the scenes of their crimes.

Recent research distinguishes between genuine and nongenuine revenants. Among the nongenuine revenants are the dead who are heard from immediately after death, who stir before burial, and those whose rest has been disturbed and who are resisting death. With these are classed the restless corpses that move or even speak during the wake and those that resist having their graves disturbed or robbed. And finally there are those who are summoned—that is, reawakened—with spells.

Among genuine revenants are the dead that the living sometimes dream about and thus are imagined in corporeal form. But the most important are those reported in Old Norse literature: the dead who appear as they died in life and retain their living shape. These are the actual demon revenants, the undead, that appear in various forms: sometimes headless, sometimes in the shapes of animals (such as dogs and horses). Sometimes they assume fiery shapes, when they return to avenge themselves, to make good on a debt, or to point out a failure or omission to the living.

The so-called White Lady or ancestress, associated with certain noble families in Germany (including the Hohenzollern family), plays a special role. She appears whenever death or misfortune is imminent for one of the members of the family. The fate of the family is intimately bound to her. She protects family members from treachery and misfortune and also appears to announce deaths in the family. The White Lady, therefore, assumes the functions of a house spirit, praising and punishing servants and offering invisible help. The woman who announces death appears in a story told by the Cistercian monk Caesarius of Heisterbach (c. 1180–1240) in his *Dialogus miraculorum* (Dialogue on Miracles), drawn from oral tradition:

> In the episcopacy of Cologne in a village called Stamheim lived two knights named Gunther and Hugo. One night while Gunther was beyond the sea, the maid took his children outside into the yard. … While she was standing next to them, behold, the form of a woman in snow-white raiment and with a pale countenance was looking at them over the hedge. While the maid was being seized by the horror of the sight, the specter went, without a word, to Hugo's estate, which was quite near, and looked over the hedge in the same manner, and then went back to the churchyard from which it had issued. After a few days Gunther's older son got sick and said, "On the seventh day I will die; after another seven days my younger sister Dirina will die." And so it came to pass. But after the death of the children the mother and the maid died. At the same time the knight Hugo and his son passed away. Our trustworthy subprior Gerlach attests to this.

These widespread stories about the White Lady vary according to the social status of the tellers. Peasant folk legends depict the White Lady as a guardian of treasure, a woman with a key. In such tales white tends to symbolize the color of the departing soul. In many legends the woman is partly black (or wears black gloves), or appears as a washerwoman: these indicate that she has not attained complete salvation. In the legends of the medieval nobility, however, the appearance of the White Lady proclaims impending death or danger of war.

See also: Fairies; Funeral Customs and Burial Rites; Wild Hunt

—Leander Petzoldt

Supernatural Weapons. In Germanic and Celtic cultures, spears, axes, swords, and bows (the chief weapons of these cultures in the early-medieval period), created and wielded by otherworldly beings or by mortals endowed with magic powers.

The spear, in particular, had associations with the divine world, and as early as the Scandinavian Bronze Age a gigantic figure brandishing a spear was carved on a rock at Bohuslän in Sweden, suggesting that it was the weapon of a god. In the Viking Age one of the many titles of Odin, ruler of Asgard and god of battle, was "Lord of the Spear." He carried the spear Gungnir, said to have caused the first war in the world when he hurled it against the Vanir, a rival family of gods. Odin's spear could determine which side would be victorious, and it was said that the first to throw a spear against the opposing force would ensure victory for his own side.

According to *Ynglinga Saga*, a man who died in his bed (a disreputable death for warriors) might still be dedicated to Odin and achieve the prospect of warrior status in the afterlife if he were marked with a spear. Odin himself was said to have been pierced by a spear as he hung upon Yggdrasil, the World Tree, and it is indicated in the literature that victims sacrificed to him were both strangled and stabbed.

Splendid spears, some marked with runic characters or decorative patterns, have survived from Germanic areas and appear to have been ceremonial weapons. The fact that the Anglo-Saxons were careful to place a spear beside a man in the grave, even though the length of the weapon often made this difficult, may be because it was a symbol of the cult of Woden, the equivalent of Odin in Anglo-Saxon England. In the royal grave at Sutton Hoo in East Anglia there were six large spears and three *angons*, or throwing spears, all of different types, and one spear was placed by the splendid sword, as if it were the chosen royal weapon.

The spear was also a divine weapon in Irish tradition. Lug (Lugh), who, like Odin, was identified with the Roman Mercury and held to be the ancestor of kings, had a great spear, perhaps accounting for his title "Long-Armed."

Lug became the champion of the gods against the Fomorians at the Battle of Mag Tuired, where he slew the terrible Balar of the Baleful Eye, his grandfather. Balar's destructive eye, opened only on the battlefield, killed all those on whom his glance fell. In the best-known version of the tale, Lug destroys the eye with a sling stone, but some postmedieval oral versions of the tale tell of the great spear forged for him by Goibhniu, the divine smith, with which he performed the deed and which afterward became one of the treasures of the gods.

Another divine bearer of a mighty spear, a spear that oozed dark blood, was Mac Cécht. T. F. O'Rahilly associated such supernatural weapons with lightning. Cú Chulainn had a special weapon, the *gae bulga*, given to him by the supernatural woman Scáthach, who taught him the skills of a warrior. It seems to have been a type of spear, and no defense against it was known, since once it entered the body of an opponent it opened out into barbed points, suggesting that it was based on memories of the barbed spear of the Continental Celts. One objection to taking the *gae bulga* as a lightning symbol is that it has connections with water and is said always to be sent downstream and cast between the toes. Another supernatural spear was that of Fíacail mac Conchinn, which he gave to the hero Finn to enable him to enter the otherworld and kill an enemy there; Finn kept this spear, and it protected him against otherworldly dangers.

Traditions of such supernatural spears appear to have influenced the descriptions of the bleeding lance in the accounts of the Grail in Arthurian romances. This was given a Christian setting and in apocryphal tradition was identified with the spear of Longinus, used to pierce the side of the crucified Christ. We find the lance in the narratives of Chrétien de Troyes and Wolfram von Eschenbach, as well as in the Welsh *Mabinogi* and in other, minor sources. Perceval and Gawain saw it in the castle of the Fisher King, and when Gawain asked the right question concerning it, the fertility of the Waste Land was partially restored. Traces of a bleeding lance outside the Grail setting can be found in Irish sagas, and some have argued that the motif goes back to Indo-European tradition.

The axe was another weapon associated with the supernatural world from very early times in northern Europe. Axes are depicted in the rock carvings of the Bronze Age in Sweden, some of huge size, as though intended for ceremonial processions, and some depicted beside sun symbols, as if connected with the sky god. Richly decorated axes have been found in graves in Scandinavia from very early times, and tiny axe-and-hammer amulets were worn in Anglo-Saxon England, while "Thor's hammers," some elaborately fashioned in silver, became very popular in the Viking Age. Such ornaments were associated with the sky god Thor, who bore the great axe-hammer Mjöllnir, forged by the skillful dwarfs. This was the most powerful weapon against the enemies of the gods, and it was reckoned their greatest treasure. In the Viking Age it was depicted as a hammer rather than as an axe, but in many legends of Thor's exploits it is featured as a deadly weapon. When thrown through the air, it never missed its mark, and it returned to the hand of the thrower; it could also be brought down to shatter an opponent's skull. Many were the giants and giantesses dispatched by Thor's hammer, and various unavailing attempts were made to steal it or to trick the god into leaving it at home.

This weapon was clearly identified with the

lightning, and bronze hammers were said to be used in the shrines of the god to imitate the noise of thunder. Long after anyone believed in Thor, prehistoric stone axes found in the earth were kept in houses as protection against storms and fire. The hammer was also used at marriage ceremonies, since Thor both granted fertility and solemnized legal contracts; it was also carved on memorial stones of the Viking Age.

A medieval example of the axe as a supernatural weapon is found in the Middle English poem *Sir Gawain and the Green Knight.* Here a mysterious green champion with a mighty axe rides into the hall of King Arthur and challenges any knight to exchange axe blows with him. He will accept the first himself, and in a year's time the knight must submit to a return stroke from his axe. Gawain cuts off the knight's head, but nevertheless he rides away. When Gawain encounters the knight again by the sinister Green Chapel, he hears the sound of a blade being sharpened, and the Green Knight rushes out with what is now described as a Danish axe, threatening his life. Whatever the significance of the impressive figure of the Green Knight, we have here a character from the supernatural world, armed with an axe that fits into the tradition of otherworld weapons.

Swords, too, were associated with the gods. Among the treasures of the Irish gods was the sword of Nuada. None could escape from it once it was drawn from the scabbard, and no wound dealt by it could ever be healed. Nuada was associated with the source of the Boyne, and his consort was the goddess of the river. Another famous sword in Irish tradition was Caladbolg, possessed by the mythical king of Ulster, Fergus mac Roig, who used it to cut off the tops of three hills and also to slay an underwater monster. Geoffrey of Monmouth called it Caliburnus, and from this was derived the name of King Arthur's sword, Excalibur, another weapon from the supernatural world. Excalibur was given to Arthur early in his career by the Lady of the Lake; it was flung back into the water at Arthur's death, and a hand came out of the lake to receive it.

It is noteworthy that though some of these supernatural weapons in Celtic tradition were associated with the lightning, others were connected with the underwater world and with the supernatural women who dwelt there. An early parallel can be found in the Anglo-Saxon heroic poem *Beowulf.* A number of fine swords are described in this poem, and one of them is a mighty supernatural weapon used by the hero to slay the mother of the monster Grendel. She dwelt beneath the waters of a sinister lake, and after she had come to the king's hall to avenge her son, who had been mortally wounded by Beowulf, the hero tracked her to her home. He plunged into the water to find her, taking with him the splendid sword Hrunting, but no normal weapon could wound the she-monster. Beowulf was getting the worst of the struggle when he caught sight of a gigantic sword on the wall, said to have been wrought by giants. This sword had runes on the hilt and curving patterns on the blade. With it Beowulf slew Grendel's mother and then cut off the head of the dead Grendel, whom he found lying in the underwater dwelling. This was the only weapon effective against these monsters, but their poisonous blood caused the blade of the wonderful sword to melt away, and Beowulf was only able to carry the hilt back to the Danish king. A similar tale of the overcoming of a giant with a magic sword beneath a river in Iceland is found in *Grettir's Saga,* and the tradition can be traced through a number of later legendary sagas.

Although Odin's own weapon was the spear, he gave out swords to chosen warriors, plunging the sword Gram into a tree trunk to be drawn out by Sigmund the Völsung. Various swords with special powers are found in Norse tradition, such as Tyrfing, in *Hervarar Saga,* fated to cause a man's death whenever it was drawn, and others destined to slay some particular supernatural being. Wonderful weapons were forged by otherworld smiths such as Weland (or Wayland) or by the skillful dwarfs, just as in the postmedieval poem the *Kalevala,* the Finns celebrate the mighty primeval craftsman, Ilmarinen, who began the forging of iron, and fashioned great swords, spears, and axes in his otherworld smithy.

The bow does not often appear as a supernatural weapon, although there are traditions of famous archers, such as Arrow-Odd—who possessed magic arrows obtained from the king of the Sámi (Lapps)—and in later times Robin Hood and William Tell. We know little about Ull, called "god of the bow" in Norse tradition; however the weapon was also associated with the northern goddess Skadi, who dwelt in the mountains and was a hunting goddess. The effects of a bow in the hands of a goddess are shown in the story of Thorgerd, the goddess worshipped with great devotion by Jarl Haakon, who ruled Norway in the tenth century, and possibly to be identified with Freyja. Thorgerd and her sister Irpa were said in *Flateyjarbok* to support the jarl in battle against the Jomsvikings, and after a terrific hailstorm had beaten his enemies back, a monstrous woman was seen supporting his army, using her bow with such speed and skill that it was as if an arrow flew from every finger, each causing a death.

The idea that certain illnesses or pain could be caused by spears or arrows shot by malicious supernatural beings is indicated in an Anglo-Saxon charm against a sudden pain said to be caused by mighty women hurling spears. Small prehistoric arrowheads found in the earth were said to be elf arrows, used in this way, and were blamed for sudden attacks of pain or mysterious illnesses among cattle.

Axes and spears are predominantly male weapons, but spears were carried by the Norse valkyries, while swords and bows both had associations with otherworld women. The significance of a supernatural weapon does not always remain the same, as some earlier scholars attempted to establish. However, such weapons persisted as potent symbols in both pre-Christian and Christian times, playing a major part in some of the most memorable literature of the Middle Ages.

See also: *Beowulf*; Scandinavian Mythology; *Sir Gawain and the Green Knight*; Sutton Hoo; Sword; Thor; Valkyries; Woman Warrior

—Hilda Ellis Davidson

Sutton Hoo. A small village on the coast of Suffolk, the site of the most remarkable burial ground of Anglo-Saxon England—indeed, one of the most important of early-medieval Europe.

The site contains 17 burial mounds, dated to the late sixth and early seventh centuries, though some are barely visible because of repeated plowing. All but one were plundered in later centuries; that one, however, was excavated in 1939 and yielded a pagan ship burial of unsurpassed wealth and archaeological significance. Recent research (1986–1992) revealed 55 more crude burials, often of mutilated corpses, believed to be victims of executions.

The great ship burial, under what is now called Mound 1, remained intact because it lay so deep—a trench descending 3.5 meters (11 feet) below the original ground's surface had been dug to receive the ship, within which a cabin-like chamber held the corpse and its possessions, and the whole was covered by a mound several meters high, baffling some Elizabethan treasure seekers who tried to open it. From the magnificence of the contents, it is virtually certain that the man buried there was a king, probably Raedwald, who died about 625 C.E. and was the last pagan king of East Anglia (the region which included Suffolk).

Although the corpse was destroyed by acid soil, much can be deduced from other contents of the grave. The coffin was large, containing clothes, cups, bowls, wooden flasks, knives, combs, and a coat of mail, all piled at the dead man's feet. Displayed on the coffin lid were treasures appropriate to his status: a sword, purse, sword belt, and shoulder clasps, all lavishly adorned with gold and garnets; a grim helmet of Scandinavian type with a face mask, bearing magical and protective images; two silver-mounted drinking horns; a huge silver dish from Byzantium, holding food; and a nest of ten silver bowls and two silver spoons with Christian inscriptions, also from abroad. Bulkier objects were arranged round the chamber: a cauldron and its hanging chains, spears and a shield, a lyre, an ornate hanging bowl, and two unique items—a spiked iron grid, perhaps the framework for a royal standard, and a massive faceted whetstone, carved with human faces and topped by a bronze stag mounted on an iron ring, which can only be a royal scepter. Taken as a whole, the assemblage of grave goods honors the dead man both as an individual and in his public roles as ruler, warrior, and giver of feasts; the foreign items may be diplomatic gifts and thus further evidence of his power.

Excavation resumed in the 1980s, revealing that Mound 2, which had suffered badly from robbers, had held the burial chamber of a well-equipped warrior lying with drinking horns at his feet; here, too, there had been a ship, but turned upside down over the chamber. In Mound 17 a young man lay in a wooden coffin, wearing his sword and a purse containing a few garnets; alongside his coffin were spears and a shield, a cauldron, a bag of lamb chops, a bowl, and a splendid harness with gilt bronze fittings and pendants; the horse itself had been buried separately, but under the same mound. In Mound 14 a woman had been buried in a wooden chamber, together with a silver bowl and various silver-mounted wooden vessels. Mounds 3–8 all covered cremations; in most cases burned animal bones were mingled with the human ones, showing that horses, cattle, pigs, red deer, and perhaps a dog had been laid on the pyres; the remains were sometimes gathered into a bowl, and further goods (e.g., gaming pieces) had been added. It is thought that these cremations began before 600 C.E., predating the burials, and that the first was probably Mound 5, which contained the burned bones of a young man who had died violently, his skull gashed by repeated sword strokes. There were also four graves, which may once have had mounds over them, containing small items of jewelry, buckles, or weapons; one was for a boy aged about seven.

Sutton Hoo was thus an exclusive cemetery for an aristocratic group, in use for some 60 years, which corresponds well to the known dates of the East Anglian royal dynasty that took power in the pagan period (late sixth century) and became Christian around 640. The funeral rites they favored appear, from our present knowledge, to be exceptionally lavish for Anglo-Saxon England, and the ship burials at Mounds 1 and 2 resemble those at two Swedish cemeteries of the same period. They symbolize the ethos of a pagan heroic culture, with its stress on personal glory and warlike achievements, and a belief in a material afterlife. It is currently thought that one reason for the rituals carried out here was to assert the paganism of the East Anglian kingdom and its affinities with Scandinavia in deliberate defiance of the politico-religious pressures from the Christian Frankish empire, whose influence in England was increasing.

Two groups of very different burials, without mounds or grave goods, have also been found at Sutton Hoo; one is at the eastern edge of the area occupied by the mounds, the other closely surrounds Mound 5. Most of the corpses here died violently and were then mutilated or contemptuously treated; some had been hanged, others beheaded and their heads misplaced; some were buried facedown, or trussed up, spread-eagled, or bent over backward. It is virtually certain that these were victims of public executions carried out on or near the mounds and that the rough way they were buried was a further mark of infamy—and possibly, in some cases, a way of preventing their ghosts from walking. Radiocarbon tests gave dates ranging from the sixth century to the eleventh; the first executions took place at the same period as the great funerals, but most date from Christian times.

Interpretation is difficult. Was Sutton Hoo first used for executions because the death penalty was a royal prerogative? And did this continue because to Christians a pagan burial ground was accursed, or merely because it was conspicuous yet away from habitations? Later, probably in the twelfth century, the gallows were shifted to a hill about a mile and a half upstream, still called Gallow Hill on a map of 1601; maps of the 1830s and 1840s name fields between the two locations as "Gibbett" and "Gallow Walk." So far, no "normal" cemetery has been found at Sutton Hoo, though large areas are as yet unexcavated; barring future discoveries, it seems that those laid here were either rulers and their kin or felons.

See also: *Beowulf;* English Tradition: Anglo-Saxon Period; Funeral Customs and Burial Rites

—Jacqueline Simpson

Swan Knight. A chivalric figure of chanson de geste and romance, associated with the House of Bouillon, as well as with the houses of Brabant and Clèves.

Tales of the Swan Knight served to explain the legendary genealogy of Godfrey of Bouillon (d. 1100), leader and hero of the First Crusade; the Swan Knight was purported to be Godfrey's grandfather.

The story's popularity in Western Europe is attested by its literary extension: Latin, French, German, Spanish, English, Italian, and Icelandic versions all survive. The legend exists in two major branches: Branch 1 deals with the childhood of the Swan Knight and runs parallel to the postmedieval märchen of "The Maiden Who Seeks Her Brothers" (AT 451). Versions of Branch 1 begin appearing in French chansons de geste around 1200. *Beatrix* is a famous example:

King Oriant and Queen Beatrix are childless. Beatrix, seeing a woman with twins, says enviously that multiple births are proof of adultery. She is immediately punished by conceiving seven children—six boys and a girl, all born with silver chains on their necks. Matabrune, Beatrix's cruel mother-in-law, arranges to have the children killed, and she tells Oriant that his wife has given birth to dogs and must be killed.

The servant entrusted with killing the children cannot make himself do it; instead, he abandons them in the woods, where they are raised by a hermit. Discovering that the children are still alive, Matabrune has a servant take their silver chains away; the servant retrieves only six of the seven because he cannot find one of the boys. As soon as the chains leave their necks, the six children turn into swans and fly to a pond near their father's castle.

After 15 years Matabrune finally convinces Oriant to have his wife executed: she will be burned alive unless a champion will fight for her. An angel appears to the hermit in the woods, declaring that the one son who remains in human shape must fight for his mother. The boy, ignorant of the skills of knighthood, goes to the city, receives baptism and the name Elias, defeats his opponent, frees his mother, and helps reclaim the chains that can transform his swan siblings back into people. One brother must remain a swan because his chain has been melted down and turned into a cup. Elias becomes the Swan Knight, and his swan-brother leads him to his next adventure but disappears to return only when his brother's interdiction has been broken (see Branch 2).

This tale, repeated in a fourteenth-century Middle English poem *Chevelere assigne,* so closely resembles later oral märchen that some believe it existed as an independent story before the legend of Godfrey of Bouillon took shape. Supporting this view is the fact that one variant of this plot, found in a late-twelfth-century Latin tale collection, contains no mention of Godfrey or his progenitors.

Branch 2 deals with the Swan Knight's adult chivalric adventures. Its plot is best known today through Richard Wagner's reworking of the story in his opera *Lohengrin.* A swan draws a knight down the Rhine in a boat pulled by a golden chain. He arrives to defend a damsel in distress (the widow of the Bouillon/Brabant/Clèves House); she asks him to wed her or her daughter. He agrees, but on the condition that she not ask his name. In the French version seven years pass before the wife breaks the interdiction; in the German version she does so on their wedding night. The following morning the boat pulled by the swan arrives, and the knight is led away forever.

The two branches probably stem from two independent stories. The appearance of swans in both may have suggested their association to the unknown authors of the written versions. The story seems to be associated with the lower Rhine region (Wallon, Lotharingia/Lorraine) and may have been inspired by the yearly migration of swans to the region.

The French versions, which include both branches, form part of the series of epic poems written about the First Crusade and known as the Crusade cycle. The German versions, on the other hand, contain only Branch 2. Wolfram von Eschenbach includes the tale at the end of his *Parzifal* (Book 16), explaining that Loherangrin is Parzifal's son; Wolfram thus links the Swan Knight to the Arthurian cycle.

Some scholars have connected the Swan Knight tales with Celtic traditions because swans appear frequently in medieval Irish narratives and decorative arts, in which they are often represented as being linked together by a yoke or by a chain made of a precious metal. An analog to the Swan Children story, discovered in an eighteenth-century Irish manuscript and named "The Fate of the Children of Lir," suggests a distant common Celtic origin. Some speculate that the connection between the two traditions was made as early as the ninth century, when Irish monks settled in the lower Rhine region.

See also: Accused Queen; Chanson de Geste; Crusades; Folktale; Nine Worthies

—Paul B. Nelson

Sword. A powerful symbol in the heroic literature of the early-medieval period and in later epics, sagas, and romances.

The sword was an aristocratic weapon associated with kings and heroes and used against human and supernatural foes; receiving his sword was a major event in the initiation of the medieval knight. Swords were frequently buried with their owners or hung above their tombs in churches, but they might also be passed on from father to son and treasured for several generations. They might be won from an enemy on the battlefield or in a duel, or presented to a valiant youth in recognition of outstanding achievements. Sometimes they received names of their own, such as Hrunting or Durendal; their histories were remembered and related when they were passed on to new owners, while the efficiency and beauty of famous swords was a favorite subject for poets and storytellers. A warrior's sword was the weapon on which his survival and his fame depended; he took it with him everywhere and took care to preserve it in good condition. Good swordsmanship was an essential skill for princes and leaders, as early battles largely depended on a series of duels between swordsmen or between two champions. Inevitably, swords play a major part in the folklore of the Middle Ages.

Early-Medieval Swords and Legendary Smiths
Some very fine weapons were produced by the sword smiths of northern Europe from about the fifth century onward. Many of these have been recovered from graves or rivers, amazingly well preserved, and we now know a good deal about their making. To compensate for the absence of good-quality iron and the limitations of small furnaces, the method once called "false damascening," but now known as pattern welding, was developed. Swords made by this process had a decorative panel, with herringbone or chevron patterns or covered with twisting wavy lines, down the center of the blade. They were weapons of great beauty and outstanding efficiency, although they might be produced from bog ores of mixed quality. In a letter written at the close of the fifth century, Cassiodorus, secretary to the Visigoth ruler Theodoric, acknowledges a gift of such swords from a Germanic chief and describes the blade as seemingly grained with tiny snakes and interwoven with many colors. Such weapons, he says, "might be deemed the work of Vulcan, who is said to have perfected his craft with such art that what was formed by his hands was believed to have been wrought by power not mortal, but divine."

The Western method differed from that used to produce the fine damascened swords of the East, with their patterned blades. Narrow strips of iron were twisted into bars and welded together, and then filed down rigorously; the cutting edges, of good-quality iron, would be welded onto the central panel. With skill, patience, and good luck, splendid blades could be made in this way in a simple forge, as was proved in 1955 when John Anstee succeeded in producing such a sword at the Museum of Rural Life, in Reading, England.

Much trial and error was involved in the process, and the blade was very likely to break before it was completed, so it is not surprising that there was much folklore concerning skilled smiths who worked for years on a famous sword; Tribuchet, in the romance of *Perceval*, forged only four in his lifetime. They were reputed to know special secrets, such as the virtues of certain liquids for quenching the hot iron, varying from the water of certain rivers to the urine of a red-haired boy or the juice of radishes mixed with earthworms. In the thirteenth-century Norse *Thidrek's Saga* the famous smith Weland (Wayland) is said to have remade a famous sword by reducing it to small filings, feeding them to poultry, recovering their droppings, and using the harder parts of the iron that survived. This may have been based on actual practice and was perhaps a means of retrieving iron filings from the smithy floor.

A smith who could produce outstanding weapons was a man whom any king would welcome into his service. Indeed, the great smith Weland himself was said to have been kidnapped and lamed by a king in order to keep him captive, a deed for which a terrible vengeance was exacted. Weland was more than human, and many famous swords were tied to the supernatural. Odin plunged the sword Gram into a great tree trunk in the hall of the Völsungs, and only young Sigmund was able to draw it out. Arthur became king by being the only one able to draw out a sword plunged into a stone; Galahad also drew from a stone floating in the river a sword destined for the world's best knight. Odin himself shattered the sword Gram when it was time for Sigmund to fall in battle, and Excalibur, obtained by Arthur from the Lady of the Lake, was returned to the water as Arthur lay dying.

Some renowned smiths belonged to the otherworld; Weland appears to have been of a supernatural race, and another celebrated smith,

Regin, who reforged the broken fragments of Sigmund's sword for Sigmund's son Sigurd, was a member of a family of shapeshifters. Regin's sinister purpose was to persuade Sigurd to slay his brother Fafnir, who had taken on dragon form and guarded a great gold hoard, and he meant to kill the young hero after the deed was done. But Sigurd was warned of the treachery, cut off Regin's head, and bore the great sword Gram thereafter.

Swords of High Quality

Recent work has shown that good pattern-welded swords and those made of good iron could be refurbished for effective use after years in the earth; the sword of Henry V, from Westminster Abbey, could still be used if burnished and re-sharpened. An Arab writer of the early eleventh century, Ibn Miskawayh, records that the Muslims took swords from the graves of Scandinavian fighting men in Russia, after the northerners had left, because of their sharpness and excellence, and there are many traditions of swords taken from graves. However, such trophies might not always bring good luck to the new holder. The Icelandic hero Grettir the Strong was given a famous family sword by his mother. Though the sword was said to bring fortune and victory, he afterward replaced it by a short sword that he took from a burial mound after a battle with its dead owner. He passed on the family sword to his brother, and from that time on his fortunes gradually declined, until he died as an outlaw. The famous sword Tyrfing in *Hervarar Saga* also came from a burial mound, obtained by the fearless girl Hervör from her dead father in spite of his warnings, and this sword had a curse laid upon it and caused much calamity.

Medieval swords of good quality cut like razors, as is known from examination of the terrible wounds left on the skeletons of men who fell in warfare, such as those killed in the Battle of Visby in Gotland (off the coast of Sweden) in 1361. Both legs might be cut off by a single stroke, steel coifs on the head hacked to pieces, and repeated wounds dealt in the frenzy of battle—any one of which could have caused death. It is not surprising, then, to find fantastic sword strokes attributed to heroes in medieval tales, and claims of stupendous cutting power made for the famous swords of legend. The sword Gram reforged for Sigurd was tested by using it first to slice the smith's anvil in two and then to cut through a strand of wool floating down the river; this resembles a test recorded in a recent technical report on a damascened sword from Eastern Europe, which was said to have cut through a gauze handkerchief thrown into the air.

The sword and the scabbard in which it was kept could be elaborately decorated, sometimes with gold and precious stones, and might bear symbols, inscriptions, and amulets to bring luck and protection to the weapon and its owner.

Runic characters were seldom inscribed on the blade, but they might be found on the hilt or scabbard, while little crosses are said to have been set on the sword of Charlemagne "for the destruction of the heathen."

The guard and the hilt formed a cross, and Christian knights might swear oaths on a sword hilt. Of special interest are the rings occasionally set on Anglo-Saxon and Continental hilts, sometimes loose and sometimes fixed or in the form of a ring-knob. We read of the followers of a king laying their hands on his sword when swearing oaths of loyalty, and it seems possible that they touched this ring as he held out the hilt to them, as a symbol of the pledge between them. It was the king's responsibility to provide his warriors with swords when needed; in return, they bound themselves to follow him until death.

Symbolic Swords

The sword was an effective symbol outside the realm of warrior leaders and champions on the battlefield. A naked sword was a symbol of justice and of the enforcement of royal power, and in England a sword is still introduced at the sovereign's coronation and the opening of Parliament, although the axe rather than the sword was formerly used to execute traitors.

In medieval Germany the sword might be used in marriage ceremonies, and there are accounts of a ring being handed to the bride on a sword hilt, possibly to mark the solemnization of a contract. There are records from Norway as late as the seventeenth century of the bridegroom plunging a sword into the roof beam to test the luck of the marriage, and here it may have been more than a phallic symbol, for it also stood for the continuation of the family. A sword might be taken from the grave of an ancestor to present to a newborn child, as was said to have been done for St. Olaf, who ruled Norway in the eleventh century; as was often the case, Olaf's mother preserved the weapon for her son until he grew up.

A different use of the sword as a symbol of separation and chastity is found in a number of medieval tales; in *Tristran*, the twelfth-century romance by Béroul, King Mark discovered his wife Iseut and Tristan sleeping with a naked sword between them and assumed that this proved the innocence of their relationship (motif T351). This idea is found again in the story of Amicus and Amelius, probably going back well before the twelfth century. When Amicus takes the place of his friend in a duel and leaves Amelius to impersonate him in his castle, Amelius sets a sword in the bed as a barrier between himself and his friend's wife, and so proves his loyalty to Amicus. This motif has found its way into Norse tradition: in two poems in the *Poetic Edda* and in the *Völsunga Saga*, Sigurd uses the same method to keep apart from Brynhild after wooing her for Gunnar. The separating sword was a popular motif among the Arabs and in Eastern Europe, and it apparently became familiar in Western Europe in medieval times.

Folklorists have shown much interest in the origin of the sword dance, which some have tried to trace to pre-Christian customs. It is unlikely that the sword dance as practiced in England goes back to Viking tradition, as has been claimed, since tools or staves appear to have been used before the introduction of swords. Dances with swords or spears, however, were known among the Germanic peoples, and dancing warriors were represented by the Anglo-Saxons and the Alemanni on buckles and helmets.

There is no doubt that the sword was a multifaceted and powerful symbol, linked as it was with family ties, the attainment of manhood, loyalty to one's lord, justice, sovereignty, and the last funeral rites, as well as with the excitement of battle and adventure. As the weapon of the aristocratic leader, it played a major part in heroic and courtly literature, but it also remained a potent symbol in legends and märchen.

See also: Supernatural Weapons; Sword Dance
—Hilda Ellis Davidson

Sword Dance. A popular and widespread style of performance in late-medieval urban festivals, characterized by groups of dancers linked by holding the swords hilt-and-point, and sometimes featuring pyrrhic or mock-combat dances.

The first records of sword dances date from the end of the fourteenth century, and they multiply through the fifteenth and sixteenth centuries. The oldest records come from the cities and towns of Flanders and elsewhere in the Low Countries, but the style was also well known across central Europe, in Sweden, and on the Iberian Peninsula. The performers were typically the young men and boys of a community, often journeymen and apprentices in craft guilds, members of religious guilds, or simply young citizens. In the Low Countries and central Europe Shrovetide festivities provided the most common occasion for the dance, though a given community's main holiday (such as the *omgang* in the towns of Flanders or Brabant) could also be used. In Spain and Portugal Corpus Christi became an important occasion. Everywhere, royal visits, weddings, Joyeuses Entrées, and so on were appropriate occasions as well.

Contemporary documentation comes chiefly from town records, which show payments for performances as well as permissions and prohibitions. Literary and descriptive evidence includes several poems by the Meistersingers of Nuremberg in 1560–1600 (Hans Sachs among them); the description of Swedish dances of about 1500 by Olaus Magnus, bishop of Uppsala, from his *Historia de gentibus septentrionalibus* (History of the Nordic Peoples); and comments and descriptions from Spanish plays (including the works of Lope de Vega).

Several contemporary pictures show the danc-ing in the mid- to late sixteenth century: a tapestry woven in Brussels in the 1540s; *The Fair of St. George's Day*, by Pieter Brueghel the Elder, showing a Flemish village fair (c. 1560); several pictures from the Nuremberg manuscript *Schembart* or *Schonbartbücher* (c. 1560–1600); and one from the Wickiana manuscripts of a performance in Zurich in 1578. These clearly show the groups of dancers (5 in the Brussels tapestry, 11 to 13 in Flanders and Zurich, up to several hundred in Nuremberg), linked by holding swords with a hilt in their right hands and the point of the next performer's in their left. They are performing such figures as stepping over the swords (Brussels, Zurich), passing under them (Flanders), and weaving the swords together to create platforms on which fencers could stand and fight (Nuremberg). The dancers in the pictures from Nuremberg and Zurich are accompanied by musicians (fife and drum) and Shrovetide fools. Besides swords, they wear more-or-less elaborate costumes—bells at their knees in Brueghel's picture; white shirts, blackface, and garlands in Zurich; and rich and elaborate clothing in Nuremberg.

Sword dancing achieved its peak of popularity in the Low Countries from the mid-fifteenth century to the 1560s, in central Europe from the late fifteenth to the early seventeenth centuries, and in parts of Spain and Portugal from the fifteenth to seventeenth centuries. It thereupon declined because of warfare (the Netherlands' wars with Spain beginning in the 1560s and the Thirty Years' War in central Europe, 1618–1648) and because of the "victory of Lent" in the war of Lent against Carnival, as religious and political authorities cracked down on the older, rowdier popular festivals such as Shrovetide. Other factors, such as changing fashions in types of performance styles, were no doubt important as well. Nonetheless, in some regions styles of linked-sword dances continued into the twentieth century (the Basque regions and elsewhere in Spain, upper Austria, and the town of Überlingen, Baden), or even appeared for the first time in the eighteenth and nineteenth centuries (Moravia, Slovakia, northwestern Italy, southeastern France, and northern England and the Shetland Islands).

The documentary records strongly support the view that sword dancing developed as a performance style in urban festivals of the late Middle Ages, an era in which carrying swords was a mark of honor and respect and in which styles of linked dancing by groups of boys and young men were often a part of local festivities. But contemporary and later scholars have come up with a variety of often fantastic explanations for the origins of the dances. As early as the mid-sixteenth century, commentators and scholars began to link the late-medieval dances to Tacitus's comment in his first-century *Germania* that the Germanic tribes would dance with swords and spears. This explanation became particularly popular among highly nationalistic German and Austrian writers of the nineteenth and twentieth centuries. More classically minded writers have said that the dances derived from ancient Greek or Roman dances (an explanation that turned up in Spain, France, and Italy) or medieval Viking dances (this origin has been used by writers looking at later dances, known since the eighteenth century in the north of England and the Shetland Islands). Some writers have also tried to explain the dances' origins as survivals of ancient rituals, tied to human or animal sacrifices, an approach that has drawn upon the "doctrine of survivals" developed by such scholars as Wilhelm Mannhardt in Ger-

many and E. B. Tylor and James G. Frazer in England. These sorts of bizarre origin stories reached their climax from the 1920s to the 1940s, under the influence both of extreme nationalism (and in Germany and Austria, Nazism) and of romantic views of primitive humanity in general. Since World War II, scholarship, though sparse and scattered, has been somewhat more rational, and writers have been more inclined to see the international nature of the style, or better, of the clusters of apparently related styles.

See also: Dance; Sword

—Stephen D. Corrsin

*T*aliesin (sixth century). Welsh poet, archetypal bard, and legendary seer.

The historical Taliesin is named in the *Historia Brittonum* (History of the Britons) as one of the north-British poets who flourished in the time of Ida of Northumbria in the second half of the sixth century. Some 12 poems in the thirteenth-century manuscript known as the Book of Taliesin are regarded as being the authentic work of the historical poet (or at least as belonging to his period). These poems, addressed to Urien of Rheged and his son Owain, Gwallawg of Elmet, and Cynan Garwyn of Powys, are classic examples of celebratory heroic poetry. Taliesin's praise to Urien and Owain became the model for later medieval court poetry, whose ethos modern critics have termed "the Taliesin tradition."

Taliesin's status in the poetic tradition was such that he developed a body of folklore relating to the role and concept of the Welsh bard, and the allusions to him by later poets do not distinguish the historical, legendary, and divinatory aspects of his persona. The Book of Taliesin is an attempt to bring together a corpus of poems, composed at different times and in various contexts, associated with him, so that together they represent all the facets of his character. Some poems are prophecies of the fortunes of the Welsh and foretell the return of the redeemer-hero. In the Black Book of Carmarthen (c. 1250), the poem "The Dialogue of Myrddin and Taliesin" (c. 1050–1100) brings together the two major prophets of Welsh tradition, and there are other indications that each has been influenced by the other's legend. Other poems in the Book of Taliesin present Taliesin as an omniscient seer boasting an encyclopaedic knowledge of medieval learning and science.

The all-knowing Taliesin has personally experienced many episodes in Welsh myth and legend, and the learned and legendary aspects of his knowledge are combined in other poems, most notably in "Preiddau Annwfn" (The Spoils of Annwfn), where the speaker, by inference Taliesin, describes an expedition led by Arthur to the otherworld (Annwfn) to recover a cauldron, to win a treasure, and to free a prisoner: "Three ship-loads we went, save seven none returned." In addition to this narrative of the otherworld, there is another version of this disastrous raid that shifts the location to this world, becoming here an account of the invasion of Ireland in *Branwen*, the Second Branch of the Mabinogi, where Taliesin is named as one of seven survivors. The poem ends with Taliesin's taunting his monkish audience with his superior knowledge of their own culture. Geoffrey of Monmouth's *Vita Merlini* (Life of Merlin) also combines the mythical and learned Taliesin when the two seers, Thelgesinus and Merlinus, have a learned conversation in the course of which the former describes the *Insula pomorum* (Isle of Apples) where he and others took Arthur after his last battle, Camlan. Other poems in the Book of Taliesin allude to a number of other legendary locations and adventures in which Taliesin claims to have taken part, some of which are versions of episodes in the Four Branches of the Mabinogi.

The origin of Taliesin's preeminence as bard and omniscient seer is described in his legend, "The Story of Taliesin." This composite narrative is preserved in sixteenth-century copies, but it appears to provide the context for poems in the Book of Taliesin and probably contains archaic elements of the myth of the origin of poetic inspiration that endows the traditional bard with his prophetic power and wisdom. The first part explains how Gwion Bach inadvertently swallowed the three drops that are the distillation of the brew of the Cauldron of Inspiration, which the hag Ceridwen had prepared for her son Afagddu and which gave Gwion his visionary powers. After a series of metamorphoses, the boy is reincarnated as Taliesin. The rest of the tale recounts his bardic exploits. Fostered by Elffin, he contends with and defeats the bards of Maelgwn Gwynedd and reveals his poetic and prophetic powers. In terms of his mythic role as the archetypal Welsh bard, and his status in the bardic tradition, Taliesin is "Chief of Poets," the title given to him as a member of Arthur's court in *Culhwch and Olwen*. The legends of Taliesin have been relocated in Wales, especially in north Cardiganshire. His grave, Bedd Taliesin, is a tumulus near the village of Tre-Taliesin.

See also: Annwfn; Camlan; Maelgwn Gwynedd; Myrddin; Owain; Sleeping King

—Brynley F. Roberts

Tannhäuser (fl. 1240–1266). Poet and knight, central figure of a legend pitting Christian piety against erotic love.

The famous early-fourteenth-century *Codex Manesse*, created in Zurich for the Manesse family, contains a collection of the most important Middle High German courtly love poetry composed between 1170 and 1330. Among them we find the work of the thirteenth-century poet Tannhäuser, who may have been related to a Franconian family of minor nobility from *"auf dem Sant"* in the vicinity of Nuremberg or who may have been a descendant of an Austrian family in the region of Salzburg. In the illumination accompanying Tannhäuser's texts the poet is depicted as a Teutonic Knight, wearing a white coat with a black cross on the front. The coat of arms above his head has nothing in common with the Franconian family, but it seems very likely that Tannhäuser was indeed a member of the Teutonic Knights.

From some statements in his songs, we may deduce that Tannhäuser took part in the Fifth Crusade (1228–1229) under Emperor Frederick II. He also lived at the court of Duke Frederick II in Vienna for some time, and later at the court of Meissen and some other east German locations. The Austrian poet Neidhart exerted some influence on his work, but Tannhäuser never treated peasants in his poems as Neidhart did. Some of Tannhäuser's stanzas, forming the so-called repentance song, which may have been the original source for the later Tannhäuser ballad, and a poetic treatise on courtly manners are found in another manuscript (the Jena song manuscript, c. 1330), but their authenticity is debatable.

Tannhäuser's poetry contains extensive lists of geographical names of countries, cities, rivers, and winds. He discusses his travels and provides us with some autobiographical references. His lament about his poverty, like his various other comments about his personal life, so closely follows the conventions common in poetry of his time that we cannot say much about him as an individual.

Tannhäuser's lyrical output was fairly slim, but it nevertheless provided the basis for a highly influential legend that sprang up in the late Middle Ages. Most of his songs treat the traditional theme of courtly love, emphasizing the experience of nature reawakening in spring and the rejoicing over new love. Sometimes he also expresses his dismay because of the arrival of winter and includes specific references to Church holidays. Tannhäuser was apparently quite familiar with Middle High German literature, as we can tell from his allusions to various courtly romances and their protagonists. At times he assumed a very satirical stance, for example, in ridiculing his lady for imposing impossible tasks upon him as a condition for granting him her love. Often Tannhäuser also included didactic elements and dealt with political issues.

Whereas the historical Tannhäuser can be identified through his songs in the *Codex Manesse*, the late-medieval legendary figure of Tannhäuser, first mentioned in a song entitled "Das Lied von dem Tannhäuser" printed in a Nuremberg broadsheet in 1515, has no historical basis, yet the figure has exerted a tremendous appeal throughout the centuries. The ballad tells of a knight who, driven by lust, enters the Mountain of Venus, pledges allegiance to Lady Venus, promises to stay with her forever, and enjoys all imaginable erotic pleasures. Suddenly, however, his heart is filled with remorse and fear of the punishment awaiting him in the afterlife. After praying to the Virgin Mary he obtains a leave of absence from Venus and goes to Rome to beg absolution of his sins from Pope Urban IV (1261–1264). The pope, doubting that God will ever forgive Tannhäuser's sins, states that a dry wooden staff planted in the earth would sprout leaves before Tannhäuser could gain God's grace. Filled with sorrow, Tannhäuser returns to his mountain, appealing to the Virgin Mary once

again for his salvation. Three days later the staff begins to sprout leaves, offering divine proof that Tannhäuser has been saved. The pope sends out messengers to bring back the repenting sinner, but nobody can find him. As a consequence the pope is condemned to eternal punishment in hell for his harsh treatment of the repentant knight.

The ballad treats the conflict between worldly love—represented by Lady Venus, who threatens to rob Tannhäuser of his eternal life—and God's power to forgive the sins of penitent Christians. Tannhäuser and Lady Venus have a long altercation before she allows him to leave the cave on the condition that he sing her praises all over the world. Only after Tannhäuser prays to the Virgin Mary and condemns Lady Venus as a she-devil can he gain permission to return to the world.

Evidence indicates that various legendary accounts existed before the ballad was published. In 1483 the Dominican monk Felix Fabri wrote of a Venus Mountain on Cyprus and also mentioned a popular song, known all over Germany, featuring a Swabian noble named Tannhäuser who had experienced the temptations of Venus. In his satirical *The Ship of Fools* (1494), Sebastian Brant included a reference to the Tannhäuser tale, condemning all those who become followers of Lady Venus and hence of the devil. In an account of his journey to the Holy Land (1499), Arnold von Harff mentions that he took a detour in Italy to visit a Mount Venus near Noxea, of which many rumors had been spread back home. References to the Tannhäuser tale appeared in many forms after 1515. The famous Nuremberg shoemaker and Meistersinger Hans Sachs created a Shrovetide play, "Das Hoffgesindt Veneris" (1517), and several other satirical plays with the Venus Mountain motif were written between 1545 and 1559. Many versions of the Tannhäuser ballads were copied in fifteenth- and sixteenth-century German songbooks. The legend remained popular in Germany into the seventeenth century but then lost its appeal until the early nineteenth century, when the German Romantics, enraptured by medieval themes, rediscovered Tannhäuser. Richard Wagner, inspired by Heinrich Heine's poem "Der Tannhäuser: Eine Legende," created his opera *Tannhäuser und der Sängerkrieg auf der Wartburg* in 1848; it was followed by a large number of literary adaptations, translations, and dramatizations well into the early twentieth century. Popular songs (*Volkslieder*) of the last two centuries indicate that this motif has never lost its pervasive appeal.

See also: Courtly Love

—Albrecht Classen

Thomas Rhymer (fl. thirteenth century).

Scottish poet at the heart of an interesting complex of literature and legend.

Thomas Rhymer was first of all a man whose historical existence is vouched for by contemporary documents, and he was the first poet on

Scottish soil using the "Inglis" language (that is, Scots as opposed to Cumbrian or Gaelic) whose name is known. He was called "Rhymer," perhaps from his vocation, and he was also called "of Erceldoune," from a small piece of land he owned at the place of that name in the Scottish Borders, which is present-day Earlston.

Thomas was reputed to be a prophet as well as a poet, and he may well have composed some of the lines of poetic prophecy ascribed to him, though most of the prophecies given out under his name are later compositions. Some of the prophecies are of a millenarian cast, announcing a time of chaos and disaster preceding the coming of a new king. In more than one place in Scotland Thomas entered the legend himself and is spoken of as the sleeping warrior in the hill who will one day waken to return as a savior. Thomas's legend is most strongly localized at the Eildon Hills near Melrose, in the Scottish Border country, where he is not only represented as the sleeping warrior but is also said to have met the Queen of Elfland.

This otherworld encounter forms the subject of a verse romance-prophecy in three fits (or sections) called *Thomas of Erceldoune*, an interesting but poorly composed piece written in northern English and datable through contemporary allusions to the fourteenth century. Six versions are known, the earliest in fifteenth-century manuscripts and the most recent in a seventeenth-century printed collection. Most of the prophecies, which appear in Fits 2 and 3, have an English slant, and this suggests that the work as a whole is English, but the romance element, which is mainly to be found in Fit 1, may be Scottish. Its localization in the Eildon Hills certainly suggests that it at least had a Scottish source, either a prose legend or a verse narrative whose nature we can glimpse through the later Scottish ballad, Child 37: "Thomas Rymer."

The romance tells how a lovely lady on horseback comes to Thomas while he is reclining under a tree one May morning. She is so beautiful that he thinks at first that she is Mary, Queen of Heaven, and he prepares to worship her. But when he discovers he is mistaken he immediately urges her to lie with him. When she does so she becomes for a time ugly and distorted, but she later regains her initial beauty. She leads Thomas "in at Eldone hill," and Thomas, walking beside her horse, up to his knees in water in darkness under the earth for days on end, becomes faint with hunger. She brings him into an orchard but forbids him to eat the fruit. She then tells him to lay his head on her lap and shows him five roads—to heaven, paradise, purgatory, hell, and Elfland. She reveals that she is the Queen of Elfland and leads him by the last of these roads into her castle, warning him not to speak while he is there. After a period of festivity, which Thomas thinks lasts for three days but which is actually more than three years, the queen returns

him to "Eldone tree" in order to save him from the possible fate of being chosen as sacrifice when the devil comes to demand his due from the Fairy People. The queen then recounts to Thomas a series of future events involving battles and politics. At their parting, she offers him the choice of one of two powers: "to harpe or carpe." He chooses speech (to "carpe") in preference to music, saying that "tonge es chefe of mynstralsye," and she promises that he will never thereafter tell a lie. This gift of truth, which makes him a seer-poet, is also present in the ballad and connects with another name by which the poet is known: True Thomas.

Thomas is presented as becoming a poet not only through an initiatory otherworld journey but also, as a more personalized complement to that concept, through a gift from the woman of the otherworld to whom he is bound. In a postmedieval version of the legend he is said to have returned to her when summoned by a hart and hind that led him away into a forest, never to be seen again.

Analogs to the motif of the otherworld woman on horseback selecting and favoring a mortal lover occur in the Arthurian lay *Sir Launfal* and in the First Branch of the Mabinogi. The visit to the fairy realm may be compared with that in the lay *Sir Orfeo* and its associated ballad, "King Orfeo" (Child 19).

See also: Fairies; Fairy Lover; Scottish Tradition; Sleeping King

—Emily Lyle

Thor. Major deity in Scandinavian mythology and Germanic religion.

Onomastic evidence (that is, evidence based on personal and place names) indicates that Thor's cult was more widespread than that of any other god. His name is compounded with many nouns to make place names indicating cult activity, such as "holy place" and "stone altar," and with others perhaps suggestive of such activity through their association with field, meadow, and grove as well as with numerous other features of the physical landscape, including headlands, valleys, plains, islands, lakes, mounds, ridges, mountains, and so forth. Theophoric (that is, based on a god's name) place names associated with Thor are found in all the areas of oldest settlements in Scandinavia: Jutland, Sjælland, and the Danish islands; Götaland and Svealand in Sweden; and the Oslo Fjord and southwest Norway. Iceland, too, has many place names containing Thor's name, and the English place name *Thurstable* (probably "Thor's pillar") locates the god there as well and associates him with a world axis, symbolic of cosmic unity. Similarly, Thor was an extremely popular first component in personal names, and nearly a fourth of the early settlers in Iceland, both men and women, bore such names. Other gods' names were hardly used at all.

In the written texts of the later Middle Ages,

Thor is equipped with a hammer, and Viking Age graves contained miniature hammer-like objects now usually called "Thor's hammers." Most are made of silver or iron, although bone, amber, and bronze examples are also known. Some are highly decorated; others are plain and coarsely made. Archaeologists assume that Thor's hammers were worn as protective amulets to ward off evil. Those made of iron are sometimes attached to iron rings and are found in both cremation and inhumation graves from the earlier Viking Age, with an especially high concentration in Sweden. The silver rings, on the other hand, date from the later Viking Age and continue into the early Christian period. These at least must be seen as reactions to the Christian cross, and their continued use after the conversion to Christianity is reflected in one Icelandic find that appears to be a hybrid hammer-cross and by molds that might be used to smith either hammer or cross.

The hammer was a powerful symbol, for it was inscribed on Bronze Age rock carvings, Migration Age runic stones, Northumbrian coinage, and even on a loom weight from the Viking Age settlement in Greenland. In addition, swastika-like symbols used in more recent times in Iceland to separate districts and to help catch thieves have been called Thor's hammers.

To judge from this material, then, Thor was a highly popular god who could protect both the living and the dead from the forces of evil. His cult spread with the Scandinavian expansion of the later Viking Age. Thor's appeal beyond the conversion to Christianity is consistent with the picture given in texts about the missionary period, which conceive of the mission precisely as a struggle between Thor and Christ. Icelandic verse from around the time of the conversion ascribes to Thor the shipwreck of a missionary, and a few other poetic fragments may have called on Thor to slay Christian missionaries just as he slew the enemies of the gods in the mythology. These fragments list giants who fell victim to Thor, unnatural beings with a surprisingly large proportion of females. Besides the poetic fragments, only a few runic inscriptions are contemporaneous to worship of Thor, and when, for example, they call on Thor to hallow the runes, one may glimpse once again a late pagan synthesis with Christianity.

As is generally the case with Scandinavian mythology, all the rest of the textual material was written down in the thirteenth century, more than two centuries after Iceland had converted to Christianity. Although these texts manifestly retain much from pagan times, they are the product of Christians, and both of the most important texts, Snorri Sturluson's Edda and the anonymous collection of verse called the Poetic Edda, show a strong tendency toward systematization.

Poems about Thor follow the synoptic Völuspa and poems about Odin and Frey in the Poetic Edda. They show Thor fishing up the Midgard serpent, obtaining a kettle and killing giants (Hymiskvida), putting an end to Loki's insults to the gods (Lokesonna), getting back his hammer from a giant and killing that giant and his family (Thrymskvida), and tricking and killing a dwarf (Alvissmal). To judge from its location in the manuscript, the compiler apparently also regarded Harbardsljod as a poem about Thor, but in content the poem highlights Odin's mental superiority to Thor.

Snorri's Edda retells other noteworthy myths of Thor, of which perhaps the most important is his slaying of Hrungnir. This slaying is mythologically significant because Hrungnir is the most powerful of all the giants, who, according to Snorri, recognize their danger if Hrungnir cannot overcome Thor, and because it occurs in the context of a duel with ritual trappings; each contestant has a companion, and Thor's companion defeats the giant's companion, an artificial creature with the heart of a mare. Many scholars have seen here the reflection of actual initiation ritual. Snorri also tells of Thor's journey to and beguiling by the giant Utgarda-Loki (unknowingly, Thor lifts the Midgard serpent, drinks much of the sea, and almost succeeds in defeating old age in a wrestling match) and of his journey to and slaying of the giant Geirröd and his daughters.

The Thor of the Eddas is a large, red-bearded fellow with great strength and an enormous appetite. He spends much of his time traveling to the East, where he slays giants, and he frequently operates in conjunction with a smaller companion. The mythology equips him with a wife, Sif, and two sons, Magni and Modi. Goats and the hammer are his accoutrements. His greatest enemy is the Midgard serpent, whom he fished up once and will fight later at Ragnarök, the end of the world.

Thor's fishing of the Midgard serpent (which itself may not be free of the influence of the story of Christ and Leviathan) is depicted in stone carvings from Viking Age Sweden and on the Gosforth cross in Cumberland. The use of a pagan scene on a Christian artifact shows once again that Thor flourished in a mixed context and the figure's power to persist. Later folklore also reflects that power: Thor's retrieval of his hammer was made the subject of a ballad, the only pagan myth to be so treated, and numerous references to Thor are to be found in practices and lore from Scandinavia and northern Germany down through recent times.

See also: Giants; Scandinavian Mythology

—John Lindow

Thousand and One Nights [Thousand Nights and a Night; Arabian Nights]. An Arabic frame tale dating from the eighth or ninth century C.E.

Still surviving in the modern oral tradition, Alf Layla wa-Layla, as it is known in Arabic, has its roots in the medieval oral traditions of Persia and Arabia. The Arabic version takes its name from the Persian *Hazar Afsaneh* (A Thousand Stories). The frame tale concerns Shahrazad, who must narrate a tale every night to entertain her tyrannical husband, Shahrayar, who has executed each of his previous brides the morning after consummating the marriage in order to prevent any future infidelity. Shahrazad's storytelling so enthralls her husband that he spares her life night after night, giving her the opportunity both to give birth to three sons and to demonstrate her moral virtue; thus, she saves her own life and those of the remaining unmarried women of the kingdom.

The length of the collection varies from manuscript to manuscript, the shortest being also the earliest extant version, from fourteenth-century Syria (recently edited by M. Mahdi). The loose structure of the frame allowed numerous stories to be added over time; indeed, many tales, including "Aladdin," were first included by European translators and then eventually made their way into later Arabic versions. Such contamination has led to much confusion and debate as to precisely which tales constitute the *Thousand and One Nights*. The fourteenth-century Syriac manuscript contains just 40 stories, filling 270 to 280 "nights," whereas the nineteenth-century manuscript known as Calcutta II contains hundreds of tales.

The stories in the collection represent the variety of medieval Arabic, Indian, and Persian storytelling—fables, anecdotes (both historical and fictional), and folktales—and take place throughout Asia and the Middle East, although most are centered around Baghdad and Cairo, the local cultural centers of the time. The themes are also varied, although love and marital infidelity play a large role in the interpolated tales, as they do in the frame story. The sheer numbers of tales and narrators also make storytelling and the power of the tale a primary theme of the *Thousand and One Nights*. Many of the interpolated stories parallel the situation of Shahrazad in that a narrator must narrate a wondrous tale in order to ransom his or her own life or that of another. Jinn and sorcerers add to the fantasy of many of the tales, a quality that led to the popularity of the *Thousand and One Nights* in Europe when it was first translated into French by Antoine Galland in the eighteenth century.

Though one might assume that the subject matter, which contains many un-Islamic elements such as extramarital sex and the drinking of alcohol, led the Arab literary elite to reject the *Thousand and One Nights*, a more accurate analysis is that the form of the work led to such disregard. The tale was not considered a literary genre in Arabic until the modern period, and in the history of Arabic letters the *Thousand and One Nights* was disdained as mere diversion for the masses until the recent awakening of interest in folk arts throughout the Middle East. The themes of the *Nights* have often led to controversy, but the value of the collection as entertainment inspires greater loyalty in its audience than does the periodic banning of text editions, as is evident in the facts that the stories have circulated orally and that written selections of the *Nights* have been read by adults and children since the medieval period.

Despite past Arab disdain toward the *Thousand and One Nights*, its impact on literary tale collections and its contribution to the international corpus of folktales are great. Its structure, which can have as many as five layers of narrators, is the archetype of the frame tale. Its survival for 1,000 years in the oral tradition attests not only to its popularity but also to its probable influence on other frame tales. Many of the interpolated tales have analogues in the European, Asian, and African traditions, but tracing lines of transmission and influence has been difficult because of a lack of early manuscripts.

See also: Arabic-Islamic Tradition; Frame Tale; Harun al-Rashid

—Bonnie D. Irwin

Totem. In tribal society, a symbol that associates the individual with his or her kin group (motif B2), from the Ojibwa *ototeman* ("he is my clan brother"); not to be confused with the personal animal guardian, a shamanic attribute.

Though diverse lore is drawn into orbit around it, the totem is above all a kinship sign. As a mystic guardian or a deity (A113, totemistic gods) it protects an entire clan, not just an individual. Like the modern surname, it identifies the lineage of the bearer. Usually it takes the form of an animal, although plants and other natural phenomena (e.g., earth, cloud, or rain) figure as totems, too.

Generally, taboo restricts interaction with the totem (e.g., C221.2, eating totem animal), especially where clan symbols correspond with food species. In such cases the clans may conduct seasonal rituals aimed at propagating their eponymous species; these ceremonies occur among agrarian as well as hunter-gatherer tribes. Thus, magico-religious cults arise based on the belief in a mystic, symbiotic bond connecting tribe and totem.

The bond is sometimes expressed as kinship between individual and totem, human and animal (B600–699): the lines between species fade, erased by myths of origin. Viewing the totem as a mythic progenitor (B1) leads naturally to ancestor worship. Rich mythology evolves (e.g., B601.1, marriage to bear), adapting itself to the changing contours of the clan system. Myths of shapeshifting, in which humans assume animal form and vice versa, are especially common.

Marcel Mauss would call totemism a "total" social phenomenon: one in which "all kinds of institutions find simultaneous expression; religious, legal, moral, and economic." Not all tribes have totems; however, those that do often build elaborate classificatory systems around them. Kinship units can be subdivided into complex categories; a clan that arranges its clans in two main divisions has moieties; three or more subdivisions, phratries; and these in turn can fall into sections and subsections.

Exogamy (marriage outside one's birth group) is the usual motive for such divisions; people are expected to marry outside the natal clan. Aside from signifying the bearer's group, each totem may be associated with its respective color, crop, cardinal direction, tribal office, and so on. People are named after totems: members of a Siouan buffalo clan have names like "Curved Horn" and "He-Who-Walks-Last-in-the-Herd." Rich artistic traditions revolve around the totem, the subject of myth and folktale as well as representational forms; again, animal transformation is a common theme.

While there is considerable anthropological literature on totemism, the topic has not yet been systematically applied to the folklore of medieval Europe. But various aspects of Celtic and Germanic lore suggest obscure totemic origins. In earlier phases, both cultures venerated horned deities (A131.6); for example, ceremonial headgear is depicted on the Celtic Gundestrup cauldron and one of the four Germanic Torslunda dies. The die shows a one-eyed man in a horned helmet dancing with a warrior who though human from waist to toe is otherwise a howling wolf (D113.1.1, werewolf).

The horned man—also carved in Bronze Age Scandinavian petroglyphs—may stem from a totemic ancestor figure, with typical zoomorphic traits (shamanic interpretations are equally feasible). The horns of the Torslunda dancer terminate in bird's heads; one apparently represents an eagle, the other a raven; could these have been the totems of prehistoric moieties? Various Anglo-Saxon artifacts depict these bird's-head horn terminals, stylized, without the Torslunda distinction of species.

Otherwise, in its very obsession with zoomorphic design, the animal interlace so common in Germanic and Celtic art may reflect a totemic worldview—though not necessarily that of the artist, who may have simply copied ancestral motifs. Different species may have had multiple referents we can scarcely imagine. Group-related symbols are most susceptible to totemic interpretation: regarding the stone scepter from Sutton Hoo, for instance, A. C. Evans writes that "the whetstone may have been vested with a totemic significance that cannot easily be translated into modern concepts." Here she is discussing the "ancestral portraits" on the stone shaft; however, the bronze stag mounted on top may represent the totem of a royal clan. Similarly, *Heorot* ("hart"), Hrothgar's antler-adorned royal hall in *Beowulf*, may have been named after the Scylding dynasty's totem; and the boar standard bestowed upon the hero may represent the totem of Hygelac, head kinsman of the Hrethling clan.

The origin of heraldry itself may lie forever lost in the totemic systems of preliterary Europe.

Tales of transformation into animals may reflect totem lore (again, shamanic overtones are also present). Shapeshifting themes recur in such Celtic sources as the poetry of Taliesin as well as in Germanic sources like the Icelandic *Eddas* and sagas. *Hrolf's Saga* tells of a were-bear family (B601.1, marriage to bear; D113.2, transformation: man to bear). The motif of animal kindred, enmeshed here with shapeshifting, parallels totemic myths of origin. Furthermore, this saga may illustrate a breach of taboo, when a pregnant mother is forced to eat bear meat, with the result that her offspring have animal traits (B635.1.1, eaten meat of bear lover causes unborn son to have bear characteristics; cf. C221.2). Widespread tales of swan or goose maidens and men also suggest totemic mythology (D150, transformation from man to bird). This motif appears in Old Norse (*Völundarkvida*), Middle High German (*Lohengrin*), and late Middle English (*Chevelere assigne*).

The search for European totemism involves sifting disparate traces; the most telling evidence probably lies in the reflexes of a prehistoric kinship system. Notable here are the animal names preserved in earlier Germanic literature: *wulf* (wolf) is the most common root for personal names recorded in Anglo-Saxon writings; Old Norse and Old English retain names based on words for bear, raven, seal, swan, boar, hart, and so on.

At some point in Germanic prehistory, people were probably named after totems, whether their own or those of the clans with which they intermarried. The special relationship connecting a son to his mother's brother may reflect totemic systems of exogamy. Old English retains a distinctive term, *eam*, for "mother's brother," whereas the term for "father's brother"— *fædera*, a backformation from *fæder* (father)—seems later and less distinctive. The heroes' strong ties to their mother's brothers affect plot and character in *Beowulf*, as well as in most of the Middle English Arthurian romances, where Gawain, for instance, has high status as the king's sister's son. Totemic elements in medieval folklore thus seem rooted in Celtic and Germanic traditions, but it could be that these are simply the traditions that managed to survive intact. Sámi drums depict animal figures; Pictish symbol stones may preserve proud clan symbols, incomprehensible nowadays; and we should recall the lupine foster mother of Romulus and Remus (depicted on the Anglo-Saxon Franks casket).

See also: Bear; Shamanism; Swan Knight; Wolf and Werewolf

—Stephen O. Glosecki

Tournament. A contest of skill between armed and (usually) mounted knights.

Tournaments were at once a form of sport, entertainment, and ritual during the more than four centuries in which they played a central role in the life of the European aristocracy. Tournaments evolved from fairly spontaneous and extremely violent martial exercises to highly elaborate and carefully staged performances that made up in pageantry what they eventually lacked in danger. As social forms, tournaments were crucial to the development of what has been called the "chivalric ethos" and to representations—both serious and parodic—of that ethos in literature and the visual arts. Their role in defining the knight and his class over and against the rest of medieval society cannot be overestimated.

While the exact time and place of the tournament's origin is unclear, its rise can be securely dated to the late eleventh century. It was at this time that a new military tactic—the charge by a group of armed knights on horseback with lances couched (tucked) securely under their arms rather than held like spears in their hands—appeared and was used to great success by the Franks during the First Crusade. We cannot be sure that the French invented the strategy, but we do know that it was in northern France that its *practice* first became part of the essential training of the mounted knight. In its early days the tournament was just barely distinguishable from actual warfare. Two groups of knights would agree upon a space for a mock combat that could range over several miles of open country and between towns. Though certain "safe havens" were agreed upon and the battle was not meant to be hostile, this early form of the tournament was extremely dangerous, not only for the knights who participated but also for the countryside (and its inhabitants) that they ravaged in the process. Indeed, tournaments were often used as excuses for physical manifestations of personal rivalries and as covers for political treason. It was largely because of their violent nature that the Church, from a very early date, condemned tournaments in no uncertain terms; in 1130 at the Council of Clermont the pope himself prohibited "those detestable markets or fairs at which knights are accustomed to meet to show off their strength and their boldness and at which deaths of men and dangers to the soul often occur." Jacques de Vitry, a well-known preacher of the early thirteenth century, went so far as to claim in one of his sermons that the tournament led participants into all seven of the deadly sins. But the sheer number of repeated ecclesiastical prohibitions of this sort, until their general repeal in 1316, makes it clear that tournaments were fast becoming a popular form of secular entertainment, and the Church, its protests falling on deaf ears, was unable to eradicate them. In addition, as is already evident in the pope's allusion to markets and fairs, tournaments were soon important sources of revenue both for the successful knights, who stood to prosper by the capture of their opponents' horses, and for the towns that hosted them.

At the same time, a more organized version of the tournament began to appear in courtly literature designed for the entertainment, and possibly the instruction, of the knightly class at the courts of northern France and Anglo-Norman England. One of the very first literary references to a tournament appears in the pseudohistorical chronicle of Geoffrey of Monmouth, *History of the Kings of Britain* (c. 1138). It lays the groundwork for future elaborations of the tournament in both literature and life by setting the event at the legendary court of King Arthur and representing it as both a celebration of knightly prowess and an exhibition of chivalric valor for female spectators. At a victory feast, Arthur's knights

> went out into the meadows outside the city and split up into groups ready to play various games. The knights planned an imitation battle and competed together on horseback, while their womenfolk watched from the top of the city walls and aroused them to passionate excitement by their flirtatious behavior....Whoever won his particular game was then rewarded by Arthur with an immense prize. (Trans. L. Thorpe [1966], pp. 229–230)

Here we have in miniature the form of the tournament that was shortly to become a central part of the chivalric romance as it developed in the last quarter of the twelfth century; in particular, in the romances of Chrétien de Troyes and his followers the tournament provides the arena within which various knights of Arthur's court receive their training, demonstrate their valor, and prove their love for their ladies. It was partly through the romance's image of the tournament that the knight, at least ideally, began to aspire to that mixture of physical prowess and courtly eroticism with which chivalry is often associated today. From the thirteenth century onward life imitated art, and art, life as real knights across Europe and fictional knights in the romances traveled great distances to test their skills, fulfill vows, and win lucrative prizes as well as fame.

The tournament evolved into three basic forms, each with its own rules. The *tilting course* (so called because of the *tilt*, or central barrier, often placed down the center of the playing field between the surrounding *lists*, or fences) was held on horseback with lances, and the participants' aim was to unhorse their opponents. It could be either a *mêlée* or a *joust*, the former a contest between groups and the latter a single combat between a pair of knights. Other forms included the *baston course*, also on horseback but fought with blunted swords or wooden clubs, and the *foot combat* with lances or swords. In addition, the later fourteenth and fifteenth centuries saw the rise in popularity of the *pas d'armes*, a special kind of tournament in which one or more knights would proclaim their intention to defend a specific place for a defined period from all comers. As the sport's forms proliferated, tournaments led to the creation of a new literary genre, the *tournament books* that recorded spectacular events in words and images and gave advice to the would-be champion. Tournament armor, which at first was no different from the armor worn in battle, evolved to accommodate both changes in the sport and its increasingly ceremonial function. A special shield for the joust, the *targe*, appeared in the fourteenth century, and it soon became customary for the knight to have one *garniture* (set) of armor "for war" and another "for peace." The need to identify individual armored knights for the benefit of spectators led to the adoption of devices, decorative forms painted on shields and placed on the top of helmets as crests; the proliferation of such devices created, in turn, the art of heraldry.

For the most part tournaments were held at courts, hosted and attended by kings, princes, great lords, and their ladies as celebrations of aristocratic births, marriages, and political alliances. However, particularly in the urban centers of the Low Countries and in Italy, tournaments were also civic events in which members of the rising middle classes participated. In Germany tournament societies arranging such events on a regular basis and restricting participation by aristocratic bloodline were an important part of tradition in the later Middle Ages. Some tournaments, most famously that of l'Espinette (the Thorn) at Lille in Flanders, were held annually as part of Carnival festivities and as lucrative tourist attractions. Irrespective of where and by whom they were held, tournaments in the later Middle Ages and until their decline in the early seventeenth century were usually elaborated by parades, pageants, and feasts held over periods ranging from several days to more than a week. They were themselves increasingly spectacular affairs involving role playing, complicated scenery, and costumes drawn from Arthurian and other popular legends. Mock tournaments fought with tubs, buckets, and clubs seem to have been a regular part of folk culture in town and countryside, and they appear in comic literature, such as the French tale of *Aucassin and Nicolette* and the English *Tournament of Tottenham*, to great humorous effect. Finally, the marginalia of many medieval manuscripts are filled with seriocomic representations of jousting knights, women, and animals and testify to the central place of the tournament in the medieval literary and visual imagination.

See also: Courtly Love; Games and Play; Knight

—Lisa H. Cooper

Travel Literature. Treated here as first-person travel accounts dating from circa 400 C.E. to the end of the fifteenth century.

Numerous such writings are extant, including accounts of merchants' travels, religious and diplomatic missions, and Crusades, with destinations ranging from the Holy Land to East Asia and points between. Within these four broad "types" of medieval travel, however, amount of description, focus of description, development of narrative, inclusion of folk materials (European or Asian), and purpose of writing vary greatly.

Nevertheless, a few general statements about these travel accounts can be made. Because medieval travelers were frequently readers of other travel accounts, those who wrote their own often incorporated into them portions of what others had written. In addition, medieval travel writers often established analogies between familiar objects and the unfamiliar, aiding their readers' (and their own) understanding of the unfamiliar. In fact, travelers to the Holy Land were likely to create an allegorical landscape as they described sacred sites, thus grounding beliefs in physical locations. Travelers to places outside the Holy Land often compared unfamiliar or apparently bizarre beliefs and customs with beliefs and customs of their own cultures. These comparisons can provide the twenty-first-century reader with a range of medieval responses to otherworlds, from the extremes of appreciation or condemnation to more moderate or ambivalent ones.

Tracing a chronology of medieval accounts illustrates another general point: the more recent accounts focus greater attention on the travelers and their curiosity, the journeys themselves, the exotic sights and peoples met along the way, the variety of folklore encountered by the travelers, and their interpretations of sights and stories, rather than attending exclusively to the destination (whether that be the Holy Land or East Asia). For example, in many pilgrimage accounts of the fourteenth and fifteenth centuries much of the works' attention is focused on the sights and on the travelers' curiosity; thus, these travels become less sacred trips and more excursions to exotic places that also happen to be sacred. The increasing interest in and attention to the real world led to works filled with detailed descriptions. A reliance on past travel accounts, combined with the travelers' curiosity and excitement, creates a blend of what modern readers might refer to as factual writing tempered by—or tampered with—fiction. The traveler, however, was probably writing what he or she perceived to be true. The author's attitude toward the truth value of the account, then, can allow the modern reader of medieval travel accounts to gain insight into medieval perceptions of the world.

There are too many extant travel accounts to discuss each one individually here, but a chronological presentation of some particularly noteworthy examples can provide a sound overview of the genre. Though most of the accounts included are those of Christian European travelers, two by non-Christian travelers are also presented, for their works provide alternative medieval perspectives.

Early Pilgrims' Accounts

The earliest extant medieval travel account to a destination outside Europe is *Peregrinatio ad Terram Sanctam*. The Spanish (or French or Italian) pilgrim Egeria (also known as Aetheria or Saint Sylvia) traveled to the Holy Land in the late fourth (or fifth or sixth) century. She addresses her account, in letter form, to her "venerable sisters." In her account she focuses on Christian beliefs, customs, and sacred places, showing little interest in the actual journey or in purely secular sites. Essentially, she created an iconographic map of the Holy Land, with few marvels noted and paying no attention to the beliefs or customs of non-Christian peoples. Egeria's account makes it clear that Christians in the Holy Land had already established definite itineraries for pilgrimage; monks guided her on prescribed routes to such traditionally established locales as the sites of the Burning Bush and the Golden Calf or the "Mountain of God" (Mt. Sinai).

In comparison, Antoninus Martyr, or Anthony of Piacenza, circa 565, writes primarily of the marvels and miracles he sees during his pilgrimage in Palestine. While describing sites in "Of the Holy Places" he interprets them in terms of Christian beliefs, turning descriptions of man-made objects, such as a Roman-built aqueduct, into descriptions and stories of miracles. His account, reflecting early-medieval beliefs, perceptions, and legends about the Holy Land, is a rather well developed tale of wonders.

In the late seventh century, Bishop Arculf of Gaul told the story of his pilgrimage to the Holy Land to Abbot Adamnan of Iona, which Adamnan wrote in *De locis sanctis* (Of Holy Places), also known as *The Travels of Bishop Arculf*. In his story Arculf focuses much attention on the customs of peoples, the supernatural, miraculous signs, places of martyrdom, and miracles and marvels, both on the journey and in the Holy Land. He retells legends to validate the miraculous nature of holy sites and relics that he has seen. Although the stated purpose of the narrative is to advise future pilgrims, Arculf's interest in the world around him is evident.

In the early eighth century, Willibald, from Wessex, traveled to Rome and then to Jerusalem. His rather short pilgrimage narrative, *The Travels of Willibald*, focuses attention on biblical sites, miracles, and religious legends. At times he connects his experiences with legends or beliefs in order to validate the truth of his story, as he does when describing his attempted visit to Theodoric's Hell in the Isle of Volcano. This is the earliest extant travel work that includes a description of Theodoric's Hell.

Because of intermittent hostilities between Saracens and Christians, pilgrimage routes sometimes changed. In the late ninth century a pilgrimage route through Egypt was frequently used. Bernard, a Breton monk, recounts his journey to Palestine by way of Egypt in *The Voyage of Bernard the Wise*. He includes descriptions of some wonders of Egypt, such as Joseph's granaries, along with methods of providing himself with safe passage. He describes holy sites in Jerusalem and notes which relics are contained in which churches. Bernard's account is the earliest extant travel work that tells the legend of "the miracle of the holy fire" (an angel lights the lamps in the Church of the Holy Sepulcher on Holy Saturday). Besides containing material about Christian beliefs and legends, Bernard's account also provides some insight into medieval European perceptions of Arabic beliefs and customs.

Travel Writing and the Crusades

In 1095 Pope Urban II proclaimed the First Crusade. Two travel accounts of that crusade are extant: *Gesta Francorum et aliorum hierosolimitanorum* (Deeds of the Franks and Other Pilgrims to Jerusalem) and Fulcher's chronicle of the First Crusade. *Gesta* was written by an unknown minor French crusader and thus provides insight into the life and perceptions of a medieval soldier. It includes views about Saracens and their beliefs as well; epithets appear to be based on the religion and country of origin of the people being described.

Fulcher's chronicle includes descriptions of signs and portents, which the author interprets using biblical and historical analogies. The beliefs and customs of peoples are discussed, along with histories and genealogies. Fulcher, a member of the clergy, describes the physical world through which the crusaders pass, stating that he wishes to delight and move his audience to greater faith.

Saewulf, an English merchant, traveled to Palestine in 1102–1103 and wrote an account of his journey, *The Travels of Saewulf*, a portion of which is extant. His interest is focused primarily on sites related to Christian beliefs and legends, such as those concerning martyrs and miracles. He interprets historical events, both recent and legendary, as either the fulfillment of prophecy or as the means of carrying out God's will. The beliefs or legends of non-Christians are important only insofar as they can be interpreted as part of medieval Christian history.

Benjamin of Tudela, a Spanish Jew, traveled to Palestine in the mid-1100s to determine the state of Jewish communities, taking a wider circuit in his journey than that usually taken by Christian pilgrims. His account, *The Itinerary of Benjamin of Tudela*, provides information about medieval Jewish life as well as about marvels he witnesses or hears of. He describes the marvelous events in detail and discusses their possible validity. His perspective as an "outsider" provides another view of medieval beliefs and customs.

Ibn Jubayr, a Spanish Moor, wrote an account in 1182–1185, *The Travels of Ibn Jubayr*, that focuses much attention on the beliefs of Muslims and of people of other faiths. His few negative statements about non-Arabs seem to be conventional, for the discussions about beliefs of nonbelievers are presented in a manner that conveys an appreciation of differences. This "outsider" perspective presents mainstream medieval beliefs in another light. In addition, his detailed descriptions of mosques and of Muslim relics and rituals provide the modern reader with an insider's view of the medieval Arab world.

Accounts of Central and East Asia

The History of the Mongols, John of Plano Carpini's account of his diplomatic mission to the Great Khan in Karakorum in 1245, portrays the Mongols as monstrous. An envoy of the pope, he details cultural information, including their religious beliefs, practices, and character, and ties these to their treatment of prisoners and the devastation left behind as they conquered parts of Russia, Poland, Western Europe, central Asia, Persia, and China. The Mongols are presented as alien and as a threat to the medieval European way of life.

William of Rubruck, another envoy to Karakorum, traveled in 1253. A native of Flanders, he was sent by Louis IX, king of France (St. Louis). Because Rubruck's goal was to persuade the Mongols of their common interests—with the hope of converting them to Christianity—his account, *The Journey of William of Rubruck*, written to the king, focuses in part on the beliefs and practices of the Mongols. Rubruck includes his perceptions and feelings as he searches for understanding based on European beliefs and customs. He describes superstitions and related behavior, presenting the inhabitants as real people living in a real world.

The communication between Christian political and religious powers and the khan eased the way for enterprising merchants such as Marco Polo. Polo's late-thirteenth-century travel account *Il milione*, dictated to and embellished by Italian romance writer Rustichello, contains descriptions of marvels and wondrous sights as well as personal experience narratives and tales of unusual peoples, strange customs, and legends. The world he describes is filled with exotic wonders—otherworldly and dream-like places, events, animals, and peoples.

Odoric of Pordenone emphasizes the marvelous and exotic in his xenophobic account of his journey, completed in 1320, through East Asia, *The Travels of Friar Odoric of Pordenone*. He provides detailed descriptions of places he visits, animals and plants he sees, customs, superstitions, and beliefs of the peoples. His *Travels* may provide modern readers with insight into medieval European biases and negative perceptions about the Other.

Two German pilgrims traveled to the Holy Land in the 1330s and left narratives of their journeys. Wilhelm von Boldensele's *Itinerarium* (1337) and Ludolf von Suchem's *Description of the*

Holy Land (1350) contain detailed descriptions of marvels, exotic animals and plants, beliefs and customs of Christians and "infidels," superstitions, and legends. Von Suchem also relates what folklorists call a personal experience narrative.

There are a number of extant accounts of travels from the fifteenth century. One of these travelers, Bertrandon de la Brocquiere, a Burgundian pilgrim (1430), focuses much attention on the beliefs and customs of the Turks. His curiosity about and fascination with this group of people is apparent in his *Travels*, which provides detailed descriptions of their lives.

The most famous pilgrimage of the fifteenth century (1483–1484) left several travel narratives. Two of the most detailed are those of Bernahard von Breydenbach (*Peregrination in Terra Sanctum*) and Felix Fabri (*The Wanderings of Felix Fabri*). Von Breydenbach includes maps, describes Christian shrines, relics, and rituals, and tells personal experience narratives in which he describes encounters with people of other cultures (Egyptian camel drivers, for example). Details of marvels and natural wonders are highlighted as well.

Fabri, who had made an earlier pilgrimage to Jerusalem, wrote a long and intricately structured narrative after the 1483–1484 pilgrimage. His curiosity during the trip is obvious, and his use of rhetorical strategies arouses a similar feeling in his readers. Fabri includes graphic and concrete detail regarding both the positive and negative aspects of the pilgrimage, details that draw the readers into the narrative. For example, most modern readers can appreciate Fabri's growing boredom as he visits innumerable churches that all begin to look alike to him. He presents his emotional responses to the travel experience in a way that elicits similar responses in readers. Thus, while he, too, provides information about legends, relics, and beliefs, Fabri's work displays a strong and well-developed narrative presence. In fact, the work as a whole can be seen as a personal experience narrative with shorter embedded narratives. Fabri also focuses on the voyage home, with a homecoming scene that includes a dramatic recognition of the changed traveler. Fabri's work, then, contains information about various genres of folklore, but the material has been interpreted by a perceptive and changing narrative persona.

These medieval travel accounts incorporate, to varying degrees, numerous types of folklore and thus present the modern reader with an opportunity to learn about the beliefs held by medieval Europeans. Because they often focus on the beliefs and practices of other people as well, we can gain some insight not only into how Europeans saw themselves but also how they perceived others. The variety of extant travel accounts and the information contained within them may also help counter oversimplified assumptions we might make today about the attitudes and beliefs of peoples who lived and traveled several centuries ago.

In addition to the Eastern travels dwelt upon here, there is a diverse and significant literature concerning travels by Muslims and Christians to various European outposts. These include Ibn Fadlan's accounts of Viking settlements among the Russians in present-day Ukraine and Gerald of Wales's twelfth-century *Journey through Wales*, *Description of Wales*, and *Topography of Ireland*.

See also: Baltic Tradition; Crusades; Foreign Races; Gerald of Wales; *Mandeville's Travels*; Pilgrimage; Slavic Tradition, East

—Elizabeth MacDaniel

Triads of the Island of Britain [Trioedd Ynys Prydein]. Collection of allusions to Welsh legendary heroes and episodes, arranged in groups of three.

Triads, a method of classifying names, events, rules, maxims, or other items of information in groups of three on the basis of a shared element, are a common device in medieval Welsh pedagogy in, for example, law, bardic grammars, and bardic instruction. The most comprehensive series is the Triads of the Island of Britain, a collection of names of traditional heroes from history, myth, and legend grouped under a common epithet or descriptor. The title "of the island of Britain" signifies that the frame of reference for the collection is the concept of the Welsh as the residue, and expectant heirs, of a single unified Island of Britain. This is not so much a geographical entity as a cultural and ethnic one that has its origins in an awareness of Brittonic unity and a recollection of Roman Britain. The Brittonic hegemony was finally shattered in the fifth- and sixth-century wars for the kingdoms of north Britain; the "Old North," its dynasties and heroes, came to represent the Welsh Heroic Age, the inspiration for the remnants of the Britons, the Welsh.

The Triads are based on the corpus of oral literature that circulated in early and medieval Wales and that represented the Welsh view of their legendary history. This body of literature is now largely lost, apart from the fragments preserved in the *Mabinogi* stories, the "Stanzas of the Graves" (in the Black Book of Carmarthen, c. 1250), and allusions by medieval poets. The Triads, however, are the largest and most important single source of reference for these fragmentary traditions. The collection appears to have been compiled for poets and storytellers to facilitate the recall of narratives and also as a store of personal names and epithets that could be used as resonant metaphors and comparisons in eulogies to contemporary patrons. The Early Version appears to have been compiled in the twelfth century and was elaborated and expanded in a more comprehensive collection, from a variety of sources, by the thirteenth century. This later version, found in the White Book of Rhydderch

(mid-fourteenth century) and the Red Book of Hergest (end of fourteenth century), has additional entries and explanatory comments on key epithets and obscure allusions. It developed its own status as a text and may have become an antiquarian collection rather than a mnemonic aid. There are indications that the allusions have become separated from their narrative context and that the main purpose of the collection was to supply traditional references for poets who may not have had a deep knowledge of the tales themselves. Both the Early and White/Red Book versions testify to the wealth of the medieval Welsh narrative tradition, and both reveal the increasing popularity of Arthur's name in that tradition as a magnet for other independent characters and episodes.

See also: Arthurian Lore; *Mabinogi*; Welsh Tradition

—Brynley F. Roberts

Trickster. A pervasive figure in worldwide folklore, appearing in medieval myth, animal tale, legend, drama, chronicle, fabliau, and romance.

Tricksters not only love to deceive; typically they also violate the moral codes of their communities. They tend to possess great sensual appetites: for food, sex, and other bodily pleasures. Their tales are generally a source of humor in storytelling communities, as listeners delight in the narration of the trickster's blatantly amoral, antisocial, and self-serving exploits. When the society thrown into confusion by the trickster's antics is itself morally corrupt, however, the trickster often assumes a positive moral stature, for he is fighting the good fight against an oppressor. Such is the case in certain postmedieval oral traditions, including African American animal tales and jokes, in which figures like Brer Rabbit or the wily slave John assume heroic stature as they deceive Brer Fox and Old Master, who are cast as the leaders of slaveholding societies.

Tricksters appear at every social and supernatural level in oral and written traditions: they may be deities, spirits, witches, animals, or simply human beings. Though the great majority of tricksters appearing in medieval tradition are male, female tricksters exert a significant presence in the fabliau.

Mythic Tricksters

In cultures as diverse as the Navajo and Ojibwa of North America and the Yoruba of West Africa, mythic tricksters are both creators and destroyers, bestowing substantial gifts upon humanity and alternatively threatening the world with chaos and destruction. These figures tend to place their own appetites and cunning ahead of any other values, and often both the "good" and the "evil" resulting from their acts are the incidental effects of their own love of deceit, which constitutes the highest good of the mythic trickster.

Folkloric approaches to the Trickster developed largely from the study of Native American and African traditional figures, such as the Ojibwa Winabijou and the Yoruba Eshu. Among surviving medieval mythic traditions, the Scandinavian god Loki most closely parallels these figures: he uses his cunning both to help the other gods and to harm them. Loki's mixed parentage—his mother is a god and his father a giant (or Jotunn)—neatly sums up his two-sided character, for in Scandinavian mythology, the gods and giants are mortal enemies.

The positive and negative extremes of Loki's actions are both expressed in the story of Loki and Svadilfari, as told by Icelander Snorri Sturluson (1179–1241) in his *Edda*. To protect their realm, Asgard, from invasion by giants, the gods commission a Jotunn builder to erect an impenetrable wall. Loki engineers the bargain. The builder demands excessive wages: If he finishes the wall in one winter's time, the gods must give him the sun and moon and Freyja, the goddess of fertility, a certain death sentence for the world. But if his work remains unfinished as summer begins, he will receive no compensation at all. By the terms of the bargain the giant can receive help from "no man," but he skirts the contract by relying upon a powerful giant horse, Svadilfari, that hauls stones for him so quickly that the builder seems certain to finish the wall by winter's end.

To thwart the giant, Loki displays another aspect of his ambivalent nature, a fluidity of form (commonly found in trickster traditions): he switches gender and species, transforming himself into a mare to lure Svadilfari away from work and then copulating with the giant horse. Without the help of Svadilfari the giant loses the contest, and Thor crushes him to death with his hammer, Mjöllnir. After mating with Svadilfari Loki gives birth to Sleipnir, Odin's eight-legged horse, an inadvertent benefit of his trickery.

As Snorri's narration of the history of the gods continues, Loki assumes a progressively sinister nature. Through his trickery he engineers the death of Baldr, "the white god," a figure of such goodness that many scholars see him as having been influenced by the figure of Christ (a distinct possibility, as Iceland had officially converted to Christianity more than two centuries before Snorri wrote). Once Baldr has died, the gods seek to rescue him from the Norse underworld, Hel. If every being on earth will weep for Baldr, he will be allowed to return to Asgard. Loki, once more using his shapeshifting abilities, transforms himself into a giantess who refuses to weep and thus seals Baldr's doom. When the gods learn of Loki's treachery, they hunt him down, finally capturing him after he has assumed the shape of a salmon. They tie him to a rock under a serpent that drools venom over his face. When splashed by the venom, Loki convulses—his convulsions, states Snorri, are the earthquakes that periodically wrack the earth. Loki will remain chained to the rock until the final battle of Ragnarök, when he will fight on the side of the giants against the gods and the world will be destroyed.

Although surviving Celtic mythological records feature no trickster god as fully developed as Loki, there are figures such as the Dagdae—called "the Good God" in the tenth-century *Wooing of Étaín* because he is a force of fertility. The Dagdae also possesses a Zeus-like propensity to use his divine powers to seduce women and deceive their husbands. In the *Wooing of Étaín* the Dagdae casts spells over Elcmar, sending him away on a one-day journey, in order to sleep with Elcmar's wife and impregnate her. The Dagdae distorts Elcmar's sense of time: Elcmar returns, believing he has been gone for only one day, but actually nine months have passed; his wife has given birth to the Dagdae's son, and the Dagdae has spirited the child away.

Human Tricksters

In medieval humorous literature, humans play tricks that, while occasionally purely selfish, are often directed against representations of authority or higher social classes. Among such figures are men of the people, figures closely related to the outlaw—for example, Robin Hood—or the fool, who often functions as a caustic social critic. Such lower-class heroes as Eulenspiegel, Unibos, and Marcolf are fundamentally uneasy with authority. Their attacks on "civilized values" are often mounted via their bodies. Eulenspiegel often uses his feces to level the score with his rich and powerful opponents, while Marcolf uses his sexuality.

Of special interest is the figure of Marcolf, who matches wits with King Solomon in a comic dialogue known in Europe as early as the tenth century. The earliest full-blown text, *Dialogus Salomonis et Marcolfi* (c. 1190), falls into two parts. The first is a parody of the learned disputations practiced by Church-trained scholars. Solomon poses proverbial questions, and Marcolf responds with obscenities, blasphemy, and nonsense. The second part comprises a series of anecdotes in which Marcolf solves various riddles posed by Solomon in an unexpected and sometimes scatological manner. The iconography of Marcolf is also of great interest: his hunchbacked figure owes much to the traditional portrait of Aesop. Elsewhere, in thirteenth-century Spanish cathedral facade sculpture, he is portrayed as a dwarf with a giant phallus. The climactic anecdote, in which he hides in an oven and exposes himself anally to an outraged Solomon, is depicted in a manuscript margin, the early-fourteenth-century Franco-Flemish *Hours of Marguerite de Beaujeu*.

In the late Middle Ages Marcolf assumed the identity of a wily peasant, striking back at the entrenched power and conventional wisdom represented in the figure of Solomon. Between 1482 and 1509 numerous translations appear, in English (1493), Dutch (1501), Italian (1502), and

French (1509), but particularly in German (in which more than 20 separate editions were published between 1482 and 1670). The *Dialogus* was also adapted for dramatic presentations in the Nuremberg *Fastnachtspiele* (Carnival plays) written by Hans Folz (c. 1482–1494) and Hans Sachs (1550).

As a type, the Trickster is particularly well represented in medieval Germany, not only by Marcolf but also by Eulenspiegel and by Der Stricker's thirteenth-century *Pfaffe Amis* (Parson Amis, said to be English!), the subject of one of the earliest surviving versions of one of medieval Europe's favorite trickster tales. An English bishop, jealous of Amis's prosperity, demands payment from the priest, but Amis will give him only a meal. The bishop threatens to seize Amis's church unless he can answer five impossible questions, to which Amis responds with even trickier answers. For example, to the question, "How many days from Adam to our time?" Amis answers, "Seven, for as soon as seven are gone they begin again." Amis keeps his church. In later versions of the plot, known to folklorists as "The Shepherd Substituting for the Priest Answers the King's Questions" (or "The King and the Abbot," AT 922), a powerful ruler threatens an abbot or other Church official with death if he cannot answer enigmatic questions. A peasant or shepherd takes the abbot's place and uses his wits to save the life of the clergyman.

Fabliaux Tricksters
Trickery in fabliaux, perpetrated by both males and females, most often concerns illicit sex, and a common situation is for a woman and her lover to conspire to cuckold her husband. In certain cases the female appears merely as an accessory to male-engineered sexual exploits, as in Jean Bodel's *De Gombert et des ii clers* (French, c. 1192), or Chaucer's adaptation of the same plot in "The Reeve's Tale" (c. 1390, AT 1363), in which the wife of the miller Simkim, through no plotting of her own, simply enjoys a night in bed with a wily clerk at her husband's expense.

On other occasions, the woman in the fabliau comes into her own as a coconspirator and even overshadows her partner, as in Chaucer's "Miller's Tale" (AT 1361). Here the crafty clerk Nicholas is one of those tricksters so in love with his tricks that he trips himself up: he passes up an opportunity to sleep with Alison when her husband is out of town in order to devise an elaborate plan to sleep with her while her husband is present. At first, Alison may seem the mere tool of Nicholas's scheme, but when another suitor, Absolon, arrives on the scene as Nicholas and Alison are enjoying each other in bed, Alison takes over. Absolon is waiting for a kiss at Alison's window. Rather than her face, she offers her buttocks, which Absolon kisses "ful savourly" before realizing that he has been had. Rendered stupid by his own love of guile, Nicholas tries to duplicate Al-

ison's perfect trick without reckoning that Absolon will not fall for it a second time. Absolon, with a thrust meant for Alison, strikes Nicholas in the rear with a red-hot coulter. At the end of "The Miller's Tale," all three men—the husband and the two suitors—have been injured by their own foolishness and others' trickery; Alison emerges as the master trickster. Only she escapes unpunished.

Some female fabliau tricksters author and execute their own plots. A notable example is Guérin's *De Béranger au lonc cul* (Beranger of the Long Ass; French, c. 1200), which concerns the daughter of a poor aristocrat given in marriage to a rich userer's son. The lazy rich man tries to trick his wife into thinking that he is a fearless warrior: he rides into the woods, shatters his own lance, batters his shield with his sword, and returns to his wife claiming that he has defeated rival knights in fierce combat. As he repeats his ruse on successive days, his wife follows him into the woods, discovers the trick, dons armor, and rides out to challenge her husband, demanding that he fight her to the death or kiss her ass. Unaware of his wife's identity, the cowering husband elects the anal kiss. His disguised wife announces that she is "Beranger of the Long Ass, who brings shame to all cowards." Still undiscovered, she rides home and invites a knight into bed with her. When her husband returns and discovers the lovers, he threatens his wife, but she replies that she will seek help from Beranger of the Long Ass, which silences her husband.

These examples demonstrate a few of the roles of the female fabliau trickster. Sometimes a personification of male fears of uncontrolled sexuality, she can also be, like Alison, a devotee of pleasure, as witty as and more common-sensical than her male counterpart—or, like "Beranger," a resourceful agent for leveling male pretensions and questioning the powers that men exerted over women in medieval societies.

See also: Animal Tale; Celtic Mythology; Fabliau; Fool; Myth; Scandinavian Mythology; *Unibos*

—Carl Lindahl and Malcolm Jones

Tristan and Iseut [Isolde]. The central figures in one of history's most famous love stories; also two sides of a famous and fatal love triangle.

The story of Tristan and Iseut is a tale that undeniably fascinated and beguiled medieval audiences. In addition, it evidently troubled those same audiences, not so much because it featured an adulterous relationship, for those were commonplace in lyric and romance literature, and perhaps not even because Tristan's mistress is a queen and married to Tristan's uncle, King Mark. Rather, the story may have been troubling because—depending on the particular account—it either emphasizes pain, suffering, and destruction (with none of the ennobling effect that more commonly accompanies such love in medieval texts) or depicts the lovers as blithely indifferent to the effect of their relationship on Mark or on society.

The tale has nearly endless complications and convolutions, owing to the number and variety of texts that recount it. The basic story contains a number of motifs that quickly became popular and led to their depiction in literary texts and numerous other artistic media. After recounting Tristan's birth and youth, the legend tells of Tristan's defeat of an Irish knight (and uncle of Iseut) known as the Morholt. During this battle a piece of Tristan's sword is embedded in his opponent's skull. When he later returns to Ireland to find a bride for his uncle, the king, he defeats a dragon but is poisoned by the flames from its mouth; he is cared for by Iseut, who sees the notch in his sword and recognizes him as the killer of her uncle. On the voyage back to Cornwall they mistakenly drink a love potion intended to bind her to Mark. She marries the king but loves Tristan, and the lovers are periodically separated, threatened with punishment, and reunited. Exiled at one time, Tristan marries another woman, named Iseut of the White Hands. Eventually poisoned or fatally wounded, he sends for the queen, asking that when the ship returns a white sail be flown if Iseut is aboard, a black sail if she has not come. Iseut of the White Hands learns of the plan and informs him, deceitfully, that the sail is black. Despairing, he dies, as does Iseut when she comes ashore and learns that her lover no longer lives.

The Tristan story draws upon elements of Celtic British tradition. The characters' names themselves go back as far as the sixth or seventh century, the Pictish name Drust having been identified with Tristan. The Welsh Triads of the Island of Britain, mostly in manuscripts of the thirteenth to fifteenth centuries but doubtless dating from much earlier, preserve the name of Drystan, identified as one of the "Three Powerful Swineherds," charged with caring for Mark's pigs. The earliest surviving versions of the tale, in French, owe something to an intermingling of French, Norman, Welsh, and Breton artistic and cultural influences that converged during the twelfth century.

Tristan and Iseut stories appeared in romance form in the late twelfth century and immediately captured the imagination of authors and their audiences. Within a period of two or three decades, several versions of the Tristan legend were elaborated. Two of the earliest are French, by Béroul and Thomas d'Angleterre (that is, "of England"), both of them dating perhaps from the 1170s. These two, which have been preserved in fragmentary form, are radically different in tone and inspiration, leading scholars to identify them as belonging to separate traditions, known as the "common" (or "primitive") and the "courtly." Béroul's belongs to the former, which is assumed to be closer in tone and inspiration to the original and less influenced by court culture and the

conventions and rhetoric of romances. Thomas's, on the other hand, is a fully courtly romance, intensely concerned with literary psychology and devoting long passages to the analysis of the lovers' pain and alienation.

Two German compositions date from roughly the same time as the French. Eilhart von Oberge's Tristrant is the earlier of them and is the earliest Tristan romance preserved in its completed form. His text is related to Béroul's, and the two doubtless drew from the same (presumably) French source. Thomas's courtly version served as a primary source for Gottfried von Strassburg's Tristan, a very long and complex, though still incomplete, romance dating perhaps from the very first years of the thirteenth century. Gottfried combined classical material with his borrowings from Thomas, and he composed a romance that is both an important elaboration of the Tristan story and an encyclopedic investigation of the humanistic tradition; his hero represents that tradition and is depicted more as poet and singer than as knight.

King Arthur and his knights appear in Béroul's Tristran, but not (for example) in Gottfried's romance. This tentative mingling of Tristan's world with Arthur's was obviously appealing to authors and audiences, and in the French Prose Tristan (an enormous romance composed in two versions, the first from around 1230) the integration of Tristan into the Arthurian context is completed. Tristan is there presented as a knight of the Round Table and a companion of Lancelot, who was of course part of a love triangle that mirrors that of Tristan, Iseut, and Mark. In the prose Tristan, however, Mark becomes a genuine villain who eventually kills Tristan and is to a considerable extent responsible for the ruin of Camelot and the Round Table.

The Tristan story is treated in numerous other literary forms, from Old Norse to Italian to the Middle English Sir Tristrem. But the most persuasive evidence of the medieval fascination with the story may be found in the number of literary allusions to it and the number and variety of its treatments in other media.

The greatest French author of medieval romance, Chrétien de Troyes, used the Tristan legend as the very basis and structure of an entire romance, Cligés (c. 1175). The relationship of Tristan and Iseut is reflected in that of the hero, Cligés, and the woman he loves, Fénice, who is married to his uncle. The text, which also turns on a magic potion, appears to be a kind of "anti-Tristan," as the heroine seeks to avoid duplicating the situation of Iseut, whose heart belonged to one man while two possessed her body.

The Tristan story also served as a source of inspiration for medieval lyric poets. The surviving corpus of love songs composed by the troubadours of southern France and by their northern counterparts, known as trouvères, preserves scores of references to Arthurian characters and serves as conclusive evidence of the popularity of such figures. Judging from the number of allusions, Tristan and Iseut, not Lancelot and Guinevere, were the most common images of ideal lovers. Indeed, Tristan, named almost 30 times in troubadour lyrics, was clearly taken to be the embodiment of passionate, fated, and tragic love, and he served no doubt as a fitting symbol for the love-stricken poet himself. As the troubadour Bernart de Ventadorn put it, "Plus trac pena d'amor / De Tristan l'amador, / Qu'en sofri manhta dolor / Per Izeult la blonde" [Love torments me more / than it did Tristan the lover, / who suffered greatly / for Iseut the blonde].

Similarly, the visual arts provide ample evidence of the medieval world's fascination with the lovers. Tristan scenes are numerous, not only in manuscript miniatures, where we would expect them, but in sculpture, jewelry, textiles, and other media. Whether the subject was Tristan or some other character or theme, it was important that it be easily recognizable, and thus certain scenes predominate; notable among them are Tristan as a harper, the lovers' sea voyage, and their tryst beneath the tree in which Mark is hiding. The last may well be the most frequently depicted Tristan scene of all, both because it is a distinctive feature of the legend and, perhaps, because its shape and symmetry make it particularly appropriate for presentation within a confined space.

In depictions of the tryst scene Mark's face is typically seen reflected in water between the lovers, and one of them is gesturing toward the reflection in an effort to warn the other. Thus, it is on a remarkable Parisian ivory casket (jewelry box) now in the Metropolitan Museum in New York; similar caskets with Tristan carvings are preserved in London, Florence, and elsewhere. The lovers' tryst (either this meeting beneath the tree or another) is carved on combs, mirror backs, misericords (carvings on the underside of choir seats, visible only when the seats are raised) in the choirs of Lincoln and Chester Cathedrals, and a corbel of the town hall of Bruges, Belgium. The Tristan legend was also a popular theme for embroideries and quilts, especially in Germany and Italy.

One of the most extensive nonliterary interpretations of the Tristan story from the Middle Ages is preserved in a series of tiles that were originally part of a pavement at Chertsey Abbey in England. The tiles, from about 1270, preserve 35 scenes from the legend, from Tristan's birth to his death. Among the most remarkable of Tristan artifacts is the magnificent Burghley Nef, now in the Victoria and Albert Museum in London. This nef is a ship model of nautilus shell and silver gilt, dating from circa 1527 and depicting the lovers sitting at a chessboard on deck, but holding hands instead of playing.

All these objects and a great many others offer irrefutable evidence of the medieval fascination with the love story of Tristan and Iseut, and Tristan's popularity remained undiminished through the Middle Ages, though the story's popularity was perhaps less long-standing in Britain than on the Continent. Only a single Middle English romance (*Sir Tristrem*, c. 1300) has Tristan as its central hero, and Sir Thomas Malory devoted a book or section ("Sir Tristram of Lyonesse") of his *Le Morte Darthur* (1470) to Tristan. Malory, however, appears to be more interested in Tristan as a knight errant, the focus of adventures, than as a lover; and moreover, Tristan himself is shown to be a libertine, more concerned with the satisfaction of his appetites than with selfless devotion to his fated love.

The origins of the Tristan story have not been identified with certainty, despite repeated attempts to do so. The majority of source studies have focused on Celtic tradition, and familiar elements of the Tristan story occur in such early tales as the ninth-century *Diarmaid and Grainne* and the tenth-century Irish *The Wooing of Emer*. A number of Irish tales offer striking similarities to the pattern of the Tristan story, although the generality of those similarities (accounts of sea voyages, bride winning, or elopement) may be insufficient to establish origins. Some scholars have also argued that in some form the story we associate with Tristan and Iseut was known in Cornwall as early as the tenth or eleventh century. Arguments have been advanced as well for Persian, Germanic, or other origins. Well over a century ago scholars identified analogies between, for example, the Persian *Wîs and Râmîn* (eleventh century) and the familiar Tristan story. Similarities include the notion of a love triangle, the role of a nurse/confidant as go-between, a stratagem to prevent the husband from sleeping with his wife (in the Persian) or from learning that she is not a virgin (in later tradition), and the lover's eventual marriage to another woman. Ultimately these parallels, like those adduced between Celtic legends and the Tristan narratives, suffice to demonstrate only that the stories belong to the same or similar tale types.

Scholars have often hypothesized that there was an archetypal tale, known as the *Ur-Tristan*, probably composed in France during the mid-twelfth century. This *Ur-Tristan*, whose existence is now doubted by some scholars, would have served as the ultimate source of the medieval Tristan texts in French, German, and other languages.

See also: Courtly Love; Harp

—Norris J. Lacy

*U*lster Cycle. A term used by scholars since the late nineteenth century to describe that part of the body of medieval Irish pseudohistorical narrative that concerns itself with the first-century warrior society of the tribe called the Ulaid (Ulstermen).

The bulk of the surviving Ulster cycle stories (generally referred to as "Irish sagas") are found in two major manuscripts, *Lebor na hUidre* (The Book of the Dun Cow, often referred to as LU) and the *Book of Leinster* (properly the *Lebor Nua Congbhalla*, referred to as LL). The stories range in size from a few paragraphs to epic length. The language of these tales is, for the most part, Middle Irish, dating the composition of the tales as we have them to the period 800–1200 C.E., though some material is in Old Irish, indicating a manuscript origin earlier than 800 C.E. *The Book of the Dun Cow* was compiled prior to 1106 and the *Book of Leinster* in the 1160s. A number of the surviving tales are accompanied by the claim that they were copied from the lost ninth-century manuscript *Cín Droma Snechta* (The Quinium of Drumsnat—so named because it was compiled at the monastery of Drumsnat [snowy ridge]). The relationships among the 15 or more existing manuscripts containing Ulster cycle material are far from clear-cut, indicating considerable scribal editorial activity and a good deal of fluidity in the tradition.

The Ulster cycle tales themselves center on the activities of the warriors of the court of King Conchobor (sometimes referred to as the "Red Branch") at Emain Macha (now Navan Fort, county Armagh) around the year 1 C.E., a dating for which there is no modern archaeological support. The pseudohistorical dating is established from entries in annals concerning Ulster cycle figures such as the premier hero Cú Chulainn (The Hound of Culann), from genealogies involving these same characters, and from internal references in the tales themselves. Conchobor's death, for instance, is triggered by his anger at hearing of the Crucifixion. The milieu of these sagas is fundamentally Iron Age, complete with chariot warfare and druids, though the later Christian redactors of the tales are unclear both on the terminology and on the function of many of these archaic features. The centerpiece and longest example of the surviving Ulster sagas is the *Táin Bó Cúailnge* (Cattle Raid of Cooley), which tells of an expedition against the Ulaid by all the other "men of Ireland" led by Queen Medb and King Ailill of Connacht to capture the Brown Bull of Cooley. Because of a mysterious nine-day debility (the *cés noinden*) that afflicts the Ulster warriors whenever the province is attacked, the entire defense falls to the young hero

Cú Chulainn who, as a boy and as only a half-Ulsterman by descent, is exempt from the debility. The bull is eventually captured by the attackers, but they suffer ultimate defeat when the Ulster warriors recover from the *cés noinden*. The Brown Bull of Cooley, however, then engages in combat with Medb's prize bull, Finnbennach (Whitehorn), and both bulls perish.

The tales are in prose, but the longer ones usually contain embedded verse of two kinds: end-rhymed stanzaic bardic meters that reflect composition in the ninth century or later and alliterating cadenced meters, some of which show extremely archaic lexical or syntactic features. Verse of this latter kind, though, could certainly have been convincingly produced by archaizers well into the period of our surviving manuscripts. The verse tends to be vatic (prophetic) and to appear at points of heightened dramatic interest, much as in modern musical drama. The information contained in the verse sections seldom if ever adds to that provided in the prose, and some of the verse seems to have circulated separately, at least at times, from the prose.

It is to be emphasized that the very term *Ulster cycle* reflects a kind of nationalist bias proper to modern scholarship. The term occurs nowhere in the native tradition, and the tales themselves, as we find them in manuscript, are mixed freely with other kinds of lore (e.g., genealogies, saints' lives, place name legends) and with tales involving other times, tribes, and social and political matters. The modern concentration on the Ulster saga material arises partially from the simple fact of its relative fullness and partially from its Iron Age setting, which promises information about pre-Christian Celtic culture. The promise is only partially fulfilled, however, for while many of the customs reported of Continental Celts by Greek and Roman ethnographers are present in the Irish sagas, and many of their characters can plausibly be related to pre-Christian mythic figures, the tales as we have them were actually produced by medieval Christian intellectuals, who were often as puzzled by the material as we are. For example, although druids are often mentioned in these sagas, their actual functions, aside from general prognostication, are rarely properly assigned to them. At the same time, however, the hero Cú Chulainn's birth story indicates that he is an avatar of the chief Celtic deity, Lug, after whom such important European cities as Lyon and Leiden are named. It thus seems clear that the tradition embodied in the Ulster cycle stories contains material of great antiquity, but material that has been repeatedly adapted to changing times and mores.

The larger sagas, such as the *Cattle Raid of Cooley*, begin *in medias res*, relying on an audience familiar enough with the entire tradition to know the explanatory fore-tales. The existence of the native term *remscela* (fore-tales) as early as the tenth century indicates both the existence of a popular tradition of saga cycles and a scholarly appreciation of the structural problem posed to written narratives by the existence of such a tradition. Indeed, the *Book of Leinster* version of the *Cattle Raid of Cooley* provides an entirely innovative beginning to the story, in which a quarrel between Queen Medb and King Ailill is offered as its origin.

The problem of the origin of the Ulster cycle material has been much debated since the first modern editions began to appear at the beginning of the twentieth century. There is no question that the manuscript texts as we have them are the product of an established culture of writing, both in the vernacular and in Latin. The surviving manuscripts often show identical or nearly identical wording, to the point that editors have felt free to supply material missing from *The Book of the Dun Cow* by reference to the *Yellow Book of Lecan*, which has an exactly parallel version of the *Cattle Raid of Cooley*, a state of affairs that demonstrates that the texts as we have them were circulating in written form in the ninth to twelfth centuries, if not earlier. We also know from surviving copies of correspondence among scribes and churchmen, as well as from marginalia, that some of this very material was borrowed in written form for the purpose of copying. That being said, there is little reason to question the general antiquity of the narrative in its origins. There is too much verifiably early ethnographic material and too many linguistic archaisms to imagine that the Middle Irish saga material is a recent concoction as we find it. The tales, for instance, know a great deal about chariot vocabulary and chariot use, although it is almost certain that no chariot culture ever existed among the Celts in Ireland itself, indicating that such lore must be embedded in the literary tradition and must have come to Ireland in oral form before the introduction of Christianity and writing in the fifth century C.E.

The narratives themselves bear strong structural resemblances to other early epic traditions—including the *Iliad* and the central narrative of the Sanskrit epic *Mahabharata*—which cannot be explained, even indirectly, as borrowings, implying that they all have in common ancient structural features carried over from oral versions to written. Additionally, no rational stemma can be drawn of the surviving manuscripts of the *Cattle Raid of Cooley*, implying that the introduction of variants into the narrative was going on even as manuscripts were being written. We cannot thus be sure by what process the Ulster cycle tales came to be written down, but we can have some confidence that in the written versions we are seeing texts that strongly resemble their oral forebears.

See also: Celtic Mythology; Fenian Cycle; Irish Tradition

—Daniel F. Melia

Unibos [One Ox].

Title of a facetious trickster tale, first appearing at the end of the tenth century and sharing its plot with many later written narratives and oral folktales.

The plot of the medieval Latin poem *Unibos* has often been reworked in European facetious literature, but it is also immensely popular in oral tradition as "The Rich and the Poor Peasant" (AT 1535), collected in many variants over large parts of the world. Basically, it is the story of a poor man deceiving a rich one, for revenge or for fun, by playing upon his gullibility. The combination of episodes and their order of appearance are treated with great freedom, but the following episodes are the most stable elements of the tradition: (1) The trickster sells a pseudomagical cowhide or bird skin to an adulteress or her husband or exchanges it for a chest in which the woman's paramour is hidden and gets money for setting the latter free. (2) After the trickster reports the price his cowhide has brought him, his enemies kill all their cows to sell their hides or burn their houses to get high prices for ashes. (3) The trickster, by means of a pseudomagical object, resuscitates an apparently dead woman; his enemies buy the object, kill their wives, and try to resurrect them, with disastrous results. (4) In revenge, his enemies put the trickster in a sack to drown him. As they leave the sack unattended, a shepherd comes by. Claiming he is there as punishment for refusing high office or an advantageous marriage, the trickster convinces the gullible shepherd to change places with him. The trickster goes away with the sheep, and the shepherd is drowned in his place. (5) The "dead" trickster reappears with sheep, which he claims to have found underwater. His enemies, seeking underwater riches for themselves, jump into the water and drown.

Some of these episodes are also part of a very closely related tale type, "Cleverness and Gullibility" (AT 1539), which centers on the sale of worthless animals and objects under the pretense that they are magical (such as a rabbit as letter carrier, a pot that cooks without fire, a horse that excretes gold, or an object that resuscitates the dead).

The final episode of "The Rich and the Poor Peasant"—the exchange in the sack and its fatal consequences—also exists as an independent tale, "The Parson in the Sack to Heaven" (AT 1737), in which the trickster trapped in the sack tells the gullible shepherd that he is the Angel Gabriel on his way to heaven. This scene is also often used as the denouement for another trickster tale, as popular and widespread as *Unibos*: "The Master Thief" (AT 1525), in which a cunning thief is challenged by his squire to accomplish increasingly difficult thefts, and in yet another tale, "Two Presents for the King" (AT 1689A), in which a poor but generous farmer finds an extraordinarily large beet, presents it to the king, and receives a large reward. The farmer's rich but avaricious companion, eager for a reward, gives a stallion to the king, who rewards him with the beet. In his anger, the rich man tries to drown the poor farmer, who saves himself by the trick of the exchange in the sack.

The earliest attestation of the tale of "The Rich and the Poor Peasant" is a poem in Latin, *Unibos* (One Ox), written by a cleric from France, Lorraine, or the Netherlands in the eleventh (and perhaps as early as the tenth) century. It tells of a poor peasant who never owns more than one ox. Every time he buys a second one, it dies, so that in jest, the villagers nickname him Unibos. On his way to town to sell his ox hide he finds some silver. In order to weigh it he sends his young son to borrow scales from the parish judge. Accused of stealing, he claims that he got the money in town in exchange for his ox hide. The judge confers with the farm bailiff and the priest, and they all decide to kill their cattle and sell their skins. Demanding high prices for their skins at market, the three men are unable to sell them. Seeking revenge, they find Unibos, but he tricks them again, this time by smearing pig's blood on his wife, having her play dead, and then "reviving" her—more beautiful than ever before—by playing a "magic" flute. The men buy the flute at an enormous price and then attempt to beautify their wives by killing and reviving them. When their wives remain dead, the men search for Unibos again. This time he sells them a mare that excretes silver when petted; his enemies pick through the horse's dung but never find riches. They condemn him to death. The poem ends with the episode of the sack and the drownings: Unibos trades places with a swineherd, and the judge, priest, and bailiff all jump into the sea and drown.

The next literary treatments of the tale of Unibos are Italian *novelle*, appearing in the fourteenth through sixteenth centuries. However, as an independent tale, the episode of the exchange in the sack appears in animal fables, mostly with the fox as trickster.

The tale type "Two Presents for the King" has appeared in edifying stories written by both Christian priests and Jewish rabbis, as well as in the Latin poem *Raparius*, attested in four German manuscripts from the fourteenth and fifteenth centuries. The episode of the pseudomagical object supposed to resuscitate the dead and its fatal imitation is used in a Carnival play by Jakob Ayrer.

Trickster by vocation or trickster in self-defense? The various versions, literary as well as oral, of the *Unibos* tale oscillate between these two poles, stressing social protest, when the tricks are motivated, or the laughable gullibility of the victims, when the tricks are not motivated by the rich man's maltreatment of the poor man.

See also: Folktale; *Novella*; Peasants; Trickster

—Michèle Simonsen

Unicorn. Legendary beast resembling a horse or wild ass with a single horn in the middle of its forehead.

Descriptions of the unicorn date back to the ancient Greeks. About 398 B.C.E., Ctesias wrote the earliest European description of the unicorn. His information came from travelers' tales and officials' reports, which he heard while serving as a physician at the court of the king of Persia. According to Ctesias, the unicorn is a type of Indian wild ass, as large as a horse, with a white body, a dark red head, and blue eyes. He says the horn is about a foot and a half long, with a white base, a black middle, and a bright red tip. This horn, he claims, has special properties. If it is hollowed out and made into a drinking vessel, anyone who drinks from it is protected from poison, convulsions, and epilepsy (the "holy disease"). Ctesias also describes the unicorn as large and powerful, a ferocious fighter, with solid hooves, and so swift that no other animal can overtake it. Where this description came from is difficult to say. Since Ctesias never visited India, he would have had to rely on stories and objects that others brought back from the mysterious East. Possibly he saw a rhinoceros horn, decorated as he describes, sold as a drinking vessel. Ctesias speaks highly of Indian dyes, and a picture of a rhinoceros on a piece of fabric might have been as colorful as an imaginative artisan chose to make it.

Our present image of the unicorn owes more to the *Physiologus* (Naturalist) than to Ctesias. First compiled in third-century Alexandria, the *Physiologus* was a collection of descriptions of animals, accompanied by moralizing explanations of their traits. There the unicorn is described as small, about the size of a young goat, but so fierce that it regularly kills elephants. Like Ctesias's unicorn, it is too swift for any hunter to catch.

In medieval Europe the tradition of the *Physiologus* was elaborated by authors over the centuries and developed into the bestiaries, books that further moralized and Christianized the descriptions of animals, The only way to catch a unicorn, says the Bestiary, is to bring a virgin to its dwelling place and leave her there alone. The unicorn will run to her, lay its head in her lap, and go to sleep. (See illustration.) The hunters then capture it and lead it to the palace of the king. (Why they do this and whether the virgin is informed of the ruse is unknown.) Because of the fierceness of the animal and its improbable tameness with the virgin, unicorns came to represent both power and purity. The Bestiary draws an explicit connection between the unicorn and Christ, who could not be captured until he humbled himself, entering the human condition through a virgin.

In spite of such chaste interpretations, the erotic symbolism stands out in many of the illustrations and descriptions of the unicorn capture. An early medieval Syrian version is quite explicit: The unicorn approaches the virgin, "throwing himself upon her. Then the girl offers him her breasts, and the animal begins to suck the breasts of the maiden and conduct himself familiarly with her."

The small, bearded, goat-like unicorn of the Bestiary also appears in the late-fifteenth-century Unicorn Tapestries, a series of intricate, highly symbolic portrayals of progressive stages of the unicorn hunt. An even smaller depiction of the unicorn appears in the Lady and the Unicorn, another series of tapestries also produced toward the end of the fifteenth century. There the unicorn is about the size of a large dog.

The reason for the hunt may lie in the magical powers that ancient and medieval medical writings attribute to the horn. Ctesias's claim that drinking from it would protect one from poison appears in many places with embellishments. Many writers recommend it as a detector of poison, claiming that it will sweat in the presence of any venomous substance. Physicians prescribed the horn of the unicorn, ground into powder, to cure and prevent a variety of illnesses, including plague and leprosy. Most physicians seem to have prescribed only part of the horn in powdered form, probably because a "genuine" unicorn horn would have been prohibitively expensive for most of their patients. Since such a horn would sell for twice its weight in gold, the challenge for those who did not wish to be cheated was to distinguish between a real one and a fake. Ancient writers suggest several tests, the most common of which was to submerge the horn in water: the horn of a real unicorn would bubble, and the water would seem to be boiling, even though cold.

See also: Bestiary

—Leigh Smith

Valentine's Day, Saint [February 14].

Date of a late-medieval festive custom, best documented in France and England, in which lovers chose their mates for the coming year.

There is no clear tradition connecting the two premedieval Italian saints named Valentine to the courtship ritual enacted on their day. In hagiographic writings dating back to the sixth century, Valentine of Rome enraged Emperor Claudius II by curing a blind girl and converting many Romans, acts that inspired his beheading circa 270. The second Valentine, of Terni, first appears in eighth-century *vitae* as the worker of a similar miracle, for which he was beheaded in Rome circa 270. Neither saint was associated with lovers or the sending of Valentines until well after the Middle Ages, when clerics attempted to find sacred meanings for the playful customs of February 14.

The earliest evidence of mating rituals on Valentine's Day is found in fourteenth-century works by the English court poets Geoffrey Chaucer (*Parlement of Foules* and *Complaint of Mars*, dating from the 1370s) and John Gower, several Old French poems by Oton de Grandson (including *Songe Saint Valentine*, c. 1370), and a song composed circa 1400 by the Valencian knight Pardo. All of these works refer to a tradition holding that birds mate on Valentine's Day. Indeed, in Chaucer's *Parlement*, birds play the roles of human lovers: three noble male eagles protest their love for a lady bird, who refuses all three while other, nonnoble birds lock wings, entwine their necks, and sing a song in praise of spring.

Apparently, by the late fourteenth century noblemen and -women were playing courtly love games on February 14. The most detailed evidence is in the form of two charters announcing the foundation of the Cour Amoureuse (Court of Love), which would hold its first annual feast on St. Valentine's Day 1400 or 1401. More than 600 people, including the king of France and the duke of Burgundy, are mentioned as participants in this amorous society. They are divided into 17 ranks, ranging from Grand Conservateurs to Gardeners, and led by a Prince of Love. At their yearly meeting they are supposed to compete in presenting love poems, with ladies awarding prizes to the finest compositions. Some scholars caution that the Cour's charter may be an elaborate fabrication because none of the highest-ranking nobles named there was present at the time and place the charter was issued, but the celebration described in the document closely resembles contemporary song competitions known to have taken place.

In the fifteenth century Charles d'Orléans, Christine de Pizan, and John Lydgate continued to create poems celebrating Valentine's Day rituals of love. Christine invokes the "law" that lovers rise early to choose their mates and the "custom" that the pair exchange green chaplets to seal their love. Because such descriptions of the festivities are all poetic, we cannot be certain which rituals were actually practiced and which were simply literary fictions.

Because eleventh-century English calendar traditions associate early February with the beginning of birds' songs and nest building, it is possible that a folk tradition of mating games on Valentine's Day existed before the fourteenth-century noble entertainments just described. Yet our earliest evidence that Valentine's Day was celebrated beyond the noble courts dates from the late fifteenth century. In letters written to John Paston in Norwich in 1477, Margery Brews addresses John "my ryght welbelovyd Voluntyn," and her mother Elizabeth asks John to visit and propose marriage to Margery on "Sent Volentynes Day," for that is the time that "every brydde chesyth hym a make" (every bird chooses a mate for himself).

There is some indication that late-medieval Valentine's Days may have been celebrations of neighborly as well as romantic love. A charter of the city of Norwich dated 1415 states that since Valentine's Day is the time when creatures "chesen her make," citizens should come together, settle their quarrels, "make pees [peace], unite, and accord, poore and ryche to ben oon [one] in herte, love, and charite."

See also: Chaucer, Geoffrey; Courtly Love

—Carl Lindahl

Valkyries.

Supernatural figures who play a considerable part in the medieval literature of Scandinavia, Denmark, and Iceland.

In their most familiar form valkyries are the battle maidens of the god Odin, who sends them down to earth before a battle to decree which leaders are to be victorious and which must die, according to his choice. They ride through the air, armed like warriors with shields and spears, and it is their responsibility after the battle to conduct the illustrious dead to Valhalla, the hall of Odin. Here a life of perpetual fighting and feasting awaits kings and other leaders who die heroically on the battlefield. Odin's purpose was to collect outstanding warriors around him in preparation for the last great battle at Ragnarök.

It is possible that in early times these followers of the god of battle were destructive spirits who feasted on the dead. The word *wælcyrge* (chooser of the slain) was known to the Anglo-Saxons and was used as a term for the Furies of classical tradition. A spell against sudden pain has survived from Anglo-Saxon England that describes the pain as caused by the spears of a troop of mighty women riding over the hill, and this might be a memory of such spirits of vengeance and slaughter. In another spell a swarm of bees is described as "victory women." However, by the eighth century valkyries are pictured on memorial stones on the island of Gotland as dignified women welcoming dead heroes to Valhalla and offering them a horn of mead. This became a popular symbol of a heroic death, depicted on many carvings of the Viking Age and even found in the form of a silver amulet in a Swedish grave on the island of Öland.

Another picture of valkyries deciding the fates of warriors is preserved in a poem known as "The Song of the Spear," quoted in *Njal's Saga*. It is said to have been chanted by 12 valkyries in Caithness in Scotland on the morning before the Battle of Clontarf was fought in 1014, between the Vikings and the Irish, to decide the future of Dublin. They sat weaving at a grisly loom formed of arrows and spears, severed heads and entrails, and their weaving was to decide the fate of the kings who were to fight in Ireland that day; when it was completed they rode off through the air to reach the battlefield and choose the slain.

Poets as well as artists delighted in the image of these maids of battle; the Scandinavian poets known as *skalds* made many allusions to them, bestowing them with lists of suitable names, such as *Hildr* or *Gunnr*, words meaning "battle." Some poems relate that they conversed with ravens—birds that haunted the battlefield—and in funeral poems for kings of Norway in the Viking Age, Odin was represented as calling on his valkyries to welcome the dead ruler arriving in Valhalla after his last battle. The very popular King Haakon the Good, who died in 961, was a Christian, but he, too, is welcomed by valkyries into Odin's hall in the poem commemorating his death in battle.

A slightly different picture of valkyries is that of guardian spirits who encourage and support young warriors, especially princes, throughout life. They appear in this guise in some of the poems of the Icelandic *Poetic Edda*, particularly in a group of three fragmentary poems dealing with one or more heroes called Helgi, thought originally to have been Danish. In one of these a valkyrie gives a name to the young hero and tells him how to win a sword.

The hero takes a valkyrie as his wife; she supports him in battle and welcomes him into the burial mound when he is slain. In the last of the poems, *Helgakvida Hundingsbana II*, his valkyrie wife is called Sigrun. When he falls in battle he rides home to the ancestral burial mound, where Sigrun awaits him. They spend the night together within the mound; however, in the morning he departs on his journey to Valhalla. Here we seem to have traces of an earlier concept than that of kings joining Odin in his hall; instead, they return to their ancestral burial places, to bring blessing on their people, and a guardian spirit is there to receive the dead warrior.

Saxo Grammaticus, the learned Danish histo-rian, writing at the beginning of the thirteenth century, collected many myths and legends for the first section of his Latin account of Danish kings, and he, too, is familiar with the concept of a female guardian spirit helping a young prince. He has an account of one named Svanhvita, who appears with her sisters to a young prince Regner. Svanhvita inspires the prince, who had been deprived of his kingdom. She gives him a sword and becomes his bride, fighting off hostile supernatural enemies on his behalf.

A valkyrie of this kind is represented in the *Edda* poem *Sigrdrifumal* as giving counsel to the young hero Sigurd the Völsung and teaching him the spells that he would need as a warrior prince. In other *Edda* poems dealing with the Sigurd cycle, and in the late legendary *Völsunga Saga*, the heroine Brynhild takes over the role of a valkyrie. She is said to have offended Odin by granting victory to a leader against the god's decree and to have been imprisoned in an enchanted sleep on a hilltop surrounded by a wall of fire. Sigurd rode through the flames and awakened her, but after drinking a magic potion he forgot her and married Kudrun. It was Brynhild's anger at Sigurd's faithlessness that caused his early death. The story is told differently in the medieval German *Nibelungenlied*, wherein there is no role for valkyries as guardian spirits or as battle maids of the god. The composer Richard Wagner (1813–1883), however, deliberately brought the valkyries of Scandinavian tradition into the role of Brünhilde in his opera cycle, *The Ring of the Nibelungs*.

See also: Burgundian Cycle; Eddic Poetry; German Tradition; *Nibelungenlied*; Otherworldly Journey; Scandinavian Mythology; Woman Warrior

—Hilda Ellis Davidson

Vampire. A revenant, reanimated corpse, or phantom of the recently deceased, which maintains its former, living appearance when it comes out of the grave at night to drink the blood of humans.

Vampires share traits with, yet are distinct from, cannibals or corpse-eating demons such as zombies, as well as certain blood-drinking witches, such as the Russian Baba Yaga, the Austrian Perhta, and Lilith, the succubus and destroyer of infants in Jewish legendry. Although the word *vampire* postdates the Middle Ages, vampirism recalls the bloodthirsty gods of death from Greek antiquity, like the Lamia, a blood-sucking child-stealer. The vampire's ability to change its outward appearance can lead to its being confused with animal-men, such as werewolves. In cases of acute vampirism, such as reported in the years 1731–1732 in Serbia, people claimed that they could identify a vampire in almost any animal—in blood-sucking parasites such as fleas or bugs as well as in dogs, pigs, or toads.

Distinguishing vampires from other demons

has always been problematic. The *Nachzehrer*, a particular kind of revenant in German legends, appears frequently, but not always, as a vampire. This being can be identified audibly by the loud smacking it makes in the grave as it eats its own shroud and sometimes its own body. A *Nachzehrer* becomes a vampire upon sucking the blood of its relatives.

Typical characteristics of a vampire's outward appearance are the lack of decomposition or rigor mortis, a pallid face, and sharp protruding canine teeth. Vampires usually have to suck blood from humans or mammals for sustenance. Their victims are turned into vampires themselves when they are killed or forced to drink vampire's blood. One can return from death as a vampire either through a desire for revenge or in punishment for former sins. At daybreak the vampire must return to its grave or coffin.

In postmedieval European tradition, elaborate rituals and many precautionary measures have been handed down to protect the living from vampires and to prevent the transformation of a dead body into one. These are usually combined with Christian funeral rituals. A corpse has to be buried facedown, or it has to be decapitated, or the tendons and muscles of its legs have to be cut, or else nails have to be driven through its heart, hands, and feet. Most procedures are characterized by ruthless brutality, demonstrating the sheer horror inspired by the living dead. Few are the ways to put a vampire to its final rest: one must drive a stake through its heart, or decapitate it and put its head between its legs, or burn its corpse—procedures marked by considerable bloodshed and usually accompanied by drastic protestations from the creature. Other methods for warding off a vampire's night visits are wearing a crucifix or sleeping with a wreath of garlic. Further fantastic and pseudoscientific properties have been added in the nineteenth- and twentieth-century literature, with Bram Stoker's *Dracula* (1897) and other horror novels.

Early legendry and folktales rarely differentiated vampire stories from similar accounts regarding blood as the source of life. The eleventh book of Homer's *Odyssey* (eighth century B.C.E.) presents such an instance of blood transferring new life to dead persons. In *Bride of Amphipolis*, Phlegon tells about a revenant in a story of a loving union between the dead bride and her unsuspecting groom (first century). Thus, the phenomenon had long been known before the word *vampire* was established in European languages.

The first revenant in surviving medieval literature to possess the characteristics of a vampire is described in William of Newburgh's *Historia rerum Anglicarum* (1198). William tells of an Englishman killed in an accident and buried without the last rites. He appears at night in his village and brings illness, pestilence, and death to the people. When his grave is opened his corpse is found fresh and full of blood "like a leech." His heart is extracted and his body is burned, thus saving the village. Other medieval records of revenants are found in England (end of the twelfth century), in Germany (1336/1337), and in Bohemia, where a revenant was reported as having howled terribly while being staked (1336).

One of the first instances of the word *vampire* occurs in Charles Forman's *Some Queries and Observations on the Revolutions in 1688, and Its Consequences*, written in 1688 and published in 1741. In the seventeenth century, the term appears in English, German, French, and Hungarian. The various theories of its etymology reflect the multicultural spread of the phenomenon. The term *vampire* derives from Serbian tales about vampirism, a concept borrowed from Slavic, Hungarian, and Greek sources (Serbian *upirina*, "ghost, monster"). The same word was used metaphorically to designate an exploitative, malevolent, and greedy person.

The historical figure Count Vlad[islaus] Dracula (1431–1476) was nicknamed the Impaler. The word *dracula* (Latin for "little dragon") refers to a member of the military Order of the Dragon, but it also means "evil" in Serbian. Dracula fought in bloody encounters in Transylvania until his capture in 1462, when he was accused of secret contracts with the Muslims and condemned for his well-known cruelty, particularly for impaling his enemies on stakes. At this point was born the image of Dracula as a diabolical and bloodthirsty monster.

This monstrous depiction of Dracula became very popular through fifteenth- and sixteenth-century exemplum literature. In these pamphlets particular regional traditions and imported elements blended with special religious or political interests, such as those first reported in Dom Calmet's *Dissertation sur les apparition des esprits et sur les vampires et revenants* (Treatise on the Apparition of Spirits and on Vampires and the Undead, 1749). In modern times the vampire has stepped out of the context of independent folk legendry and has turned into the fictionalized figure of popular culture.

See also: Blood; Lilith; Witchcraft

—Ruth Petzoldt

Virgin Mary. The mother of Jesus.

The Virgin Mary is obviously an indispensable character in the opening chapters of the two New Testament Gospels that include episodes concerning the birth of Christ, Matthew and Luke, but she hardly appears elsewhere in the New Testament. The earliest Gospel, Mark, names her as the mother of Jesus once (Mark 6:3). Paul refers to Jesus' birth but does not mention Mary by name. John's Gospel has Jesus' mother in two episodes—the wedding at Cana and at the foot of the Cross—but she is left unnamed. Even Matthew and Luke virtually ignore her after the opening chapters. References in the Gospels to the family of Jesus are generally hostile (e.g., Mark 3:32ff. and parallels).

However, the Acts of the Apostles has Mary alongside the disciples at work in Jerusalem after Jesus' death within the nascent Church. Whatever the historic circumstances of Mary's relationship to Joseph and indeed to Jesus during his ministry and after his death, her role changes dramatically in second-century literature and beyond. The restraint of the New Testament authors and their eclipsing of Mary outside the nativity stories are not mirrored in the later, apocryphal tradition.

One of the main vehicles for enhancing Mary is the second-century Protevangelium of James. In this influential noncanonical Gospel, Mary's parents are introduced and her birth is described. Then follows her presentation in the Jerusalem Temple, where she is received as a ward of the priests and "nurtured by an angel" for nine years before being entrusted at the age of 12 to the elderly widower Joseph. The story then leads on to her pregnancy and the birth of Jesus. The midwives present at his birth declare that Mary remains a virgin even after parturition. The popularity of this Gospel and its subsequent use by other, later accounts reinforced the belief in Mary as a perpetual virgin, and this guaranteed devotion to her as mediatrix and as a miracle worker in her own right. Other apocryphal texts such as the Arabic Infancy Gospel detail many miracles effected by Mary.

One document in particular, the Gospel of the birth of Mary, written perhaps in the fifth century, was responsible for disseminating many of the early legends in the West, especially after its contents had been taken over later, in the thirteenth century, by Jacobus de Voragine in *The Golden Legend*. That medieval collection of stories about the saints perpetuated many of the earlier apocryphal stories and maintained their popularity over many more centuries. Medieval art, including the cycles of the life of Mary in such places as the Arena (Scrovegni) Chapel in Padua and in Chartres Cathedral, owes much of its artistic inspiration to the apocryphal stories, as known in many cases through their having been retold in *The Golden Legend*. Some religious art of the medieval period is understandable only with the aid of the apocryphal traditions, and this is especially true of depictions of Mary, particularly her childhood and death.

Just as Mariology throughout many parts of Christendom may be attributable to these stories of her birth and life, so, too, can Marian doctrines about her death be traced to written, apocryphal sources. Accounts of her bodily ascent to heaven at death, known as her Assumption, or *transitus*, occur in several apocryphal texts from the fourth century onward. They occur separately in several languages: Greek, Coptic, Syriac, and Latin. These legends led to increased devotion to Mary, to her canonization as a saint, and to the many holy days set aside to mark incidents in her career, particularly August 15, which was eventually declared the date for the commemoration of the Assumption.

The preeminence of Mary also spawned a vast corpus of theological writing. In addition, it has encouraged a high degree of popular piety leading to claims of individuals' visionary experiences of her, to private devotion, to intercessional prayer, and to pilgrimages. All of these seem a far cry from the biblical narratives, but it is the Gospels' accounts of her as the mother of the one the Christians claim is divine and the sole savior of all mankind that prompted theological questions about God's choice of Mary, and her worthiness for this role, as well as interest and speculation about her whole life. *The Questions of Bartholomew*, dated possibly as early as the second century, raises this problem in the form of questions by the Apostles to Mary: "Tell us how you conceived the incomprehensible, or how you bore him who cannot be carried?" In that book it is said that Mary is unable to reply without thereby destroying the world through the fire that would issue from her mouth. Thus, the author raises a continuing problem while leaving the answer a mystery. And this is how most Christian thinking has left the matter. That mystery has helped to preserve the uniqueness of Mary in ecclesiastical debate and in popular piety. This has encouraged folklore associated with virginity in general and with Mary in particular as the virgin of virgins par excellence.

See also: Anne, Saint; Jesus Christ; Joseph, Saint

—J. K. Elliott

Votive Offerings. Gifts presented by believers to a saint or to a holy place, in order to obtain material and spiritual favors, to fulfill a vow, or to thank God for miraculous help.

Votive offerings might consist of any number of possible gifts, ranging from real estate to wax, candles, or bread. In any case, a specific sort of standardized object set apart as a sacral offering is properly called an *ex-voto*, such as ancient *donaria* (wax or wooden reproductions of parts of the body), metallic hearts, or painted tablets.

In the early Middle Ages, laypersons in Gaul and in the area of present-day Germany offered anatomical reproductions in wax (perhaps figures of the part of the body that had been healed), bread, and candles at healing waters, trees, and crossroads in the countryside. Despite the fact that authors often condemned these offerings, similar practices are attested in liturgical contexts and at such pilgrimage centers as the tombs of saints in the Frankish kingdom, where gifts of wax, wooden donaria, animals, cheese, and other agricultural products were common. Sixth-century Palestinian shrines housed many different kinds of votive offerings, including wax, clothes, food, silver and gold objects, jewels, and animals. In other cases, some people chose to give monasteries and cult centers real property and money; some may possibly have offered to help construct or repair sacred buildings. Graffiti (most frequently signs of the cross) and inscriptions on the walls of a sacred place often revealed a petitioner's request. A special category of gifts was represented by sacred images. Such images, which might serve to express either a request or thanks for a miracle, could be carved in wood, painted, or rendered in other artistic media. Among the earliest preserved monumental ex-votos, one may cite some mosaics in St. Demetrios, Thessalonike (sixth century), which show donors being escorted by their holy patron.

Gold votive crowns, to be hung over the tombs of the martyrs, constituted a common votive object for Byzantine emperors and their Lombard, Frankish, and Visigothic imitators in the West. Merovingian and Carolingian sovereigns used to offer sumptuous reliquaries to famous saints; from the eleventh century onward such donations were commonly made by simple priests and even by laypeople in northern France. Cult centers usually housed many objects (crutches, for example) offered by people miraculously cured by saints' intercession; thanks for graces received was sometimes signified by images representing perilous scenes (e.g., as shipwreck graffiti in the burial crypt of Hosios Lukas, Greece, tenth to eleventh centuries).

No less than pilgrimage centers, simple churches could be the object of pious gifts; donations of liturgical furnishings were well diffused. Frequently an inscription bearing the petitioner's name and a request for aid was intended to express his or her desire for a more personal and somehow privileged relationship to the saint.

During the course of the Middle Ages such relationships were to become more and more "asymmetrical," the axis tilting toward a greater share of power for the saint. Whereas early on votive offerings could be interpreted as a way of manifesting and cementing a sort of alliance or client-like affiliation with a saintly patron, donations later became clearer expressions of the donors' need to submit to the saints in order to ensure salvation; in some posticonoclastic Byzantine votive images, for example, donors are represented in the act of bowing down at the feet of the saints and imploring their protection. Fear of the afterlife was surely one of the major driving forces behind donation, and in the later Middle Ages, in the thirteenth and fourteenth centuries, this is indicated by the development of testamentary practices. Originally restricted to gifts of land, precious objects, and money to ecclesiastical institutions, such acts attest a widespread phenomenon of donations for the soul's sake. Donors embellished churches with precious cloths, liturgical furnishings, wooden statues, frescoes, decorated windows, altars, altarpieces, and chapels. In Trecento (fourteenth-century Tuscany), mendicant orders were among the main beneficiaries of such practices. A great number of votive images—bearing inscriptions, coats of arms, or donors' portraits—were intended as a way to seek protection for oneself or on a loved one's behalf by introducing an individual, somehow "private" nuance into standard religious things and symbols.

Wax long continued to constitute one of the main kinds of sacral gifts: along with common people's oblation of candles and anatomical reproductions (as witnessed, for example, by Boccaccio in the *Decameron* 1, 1), wax portraits of donors were widespread. Life-like wax portraits are known at least in the second half of the thirteenth century; in the fourteenth and fifteenth centuries a Florentine sacred place, Santissima Annunziata, housed quite a number of them. In other instances such objects could reproduce the donor only metaphorically, as in the case of wax measures corresponding in their weight to the healed person's age. Contributions to the lighting of a church, both of candles and oil for lamps, were also quite common throughout the Middle Ages.

Late-medieval votive images are of great interest because of their particular status as objects both constituting the material gift and representing the donors' dedication to a saintly interlocutor through donation. The little painted panels that emerged during this period probably owed much to the highly ornate Byzantine icons set aside for private devotion. These little panels manifested the donors' desire for salvation either by publicly displaying their petitions or by depicting them making vows or praying. Though it originated in monastic and mendicant circles, this practice also enjoyed wide popularity among laypeople. Pious behavior and ecclesiastical attire were often displayed pictorially: portraits of donors in the habit of mendicant *conversi* (people affiliated with a religious order who offered periods of their lives to God) recur frequently in fourteenth-century votive images (e.g., in ancient frescoes preserved in the church of San Giovenale, Orvieto, Italy). Painted ex-voto tablets, which are widely diffused in present-day Catholic practice, are first known from late-fifteenth-century examples in the shrine of Madonna del Monte, Cesena, Italy, and have their iconographic roots in dedication images of earlier centuries; tablets displaying a prodigious event (e.g., a shipwreck) appear in the sixteenth century, although their iconographic patterns owe much to representations of miracles in late-medieval painted cycles of saints' lives. Silver hearts are known from the fifteenth century as offerings to St. Anthony in his basilica in Padua, Italy; they, too, were intended as symbols for the donor's full self-dedication and submission in the votive relationship to the saint.

Along with pilgrimage centers, mendicant and parish churches, and cathedrals, other beneficiaries of votive offerings were confraternities, charitable institutions, and hospitals. Beds destined for the poor and the sick or for pilgrims and other wayfarers were a quite common sort of gift, since the prayers of such people were commonly thought to be extremely efficacious for the soul. As with liturgical objects and embellishments, the beds could be marked by an image displaying donors in the act of dedicating themselves to holy patrons, as is shown by a rare votive bed preserved in the church of St. Maria del Letto (St. Mary of the Bed) in Pistoia (1326–1327).

Earlier scholars tended to consider Christian votive practices to be a legacy of ancient paganism, largely the result of widespread belief in folk magic. Ex-votos, mainly identified in anatomical donaria, were interpreted as direct substitutes for diseased organs and constituted a specified subject for such historians of medicine as O. Weinreich. Interpretations from a juridical point of view exercised great influence on such European folklorists as G. van der Leeuw, who conceived votive offerings to saints as being ruled by a contractual relation of people to holy counterparts, best expressed by the Latin formula "*do ut des*" [I give so that you give]. Some scholars have considered a distinction between offerings for thanksgiving and offerings expressing desires and requests to be important in folklore studies, but most scholars prefer to consider the two kinds of votive gifts as functional variants of one phenomenon.

A systematic interpretation of votive phenomena is provided by the folklorist L. Kriss-Rettenbeck. While refusing to relate sacral offerings to "popular religion" or magic, Kriss-Rettenbeck analyzes their plurivocal functions and forms in Christian culture as being relatively independent from social or educational backgrounds and proposes that there are three main semantic patterns in every votive practice: (1) The *repraesentatio*, or the particular sign to manifest the donors' relation to sacred counterparts, can consist in acts of submission, promise, request for a privileged position, and so on; nonetheless, the offering may be the gift of an actual object, an image of the invoked saint, a partial or full painted or written reproduction of the donor, or a representation of the event causing the donation. (2) The *promulgatio* is the public, social, and representative side of donation. (3) The *dedicatio*, devoting oneself to saints, is metonymically symbolized by the offering of meaningful objects.

However, according to G. B. Bronzini, it is necessary to avoid a taxonomic or statistical approach to religious folklore studies. Indeed, we may say that studying different religious practices within their specific social contexts appears more likely to reveal the meanings these practices have for the people who valued and performed them. In this view votive practices are not simply characterized by a progressive chronological development, nor can they be reduced to schematic rules. They respond to a wide range of functions: in pilgrimage centers, graffiti inscriptions and symbols are intended to express the pilgrim's effective presence in the sacred site, while the act of recording one's name on the walls possesses a commemorative meaning; material gifts, which express the donors' desires for protection and favors, are ruled in every historical context by contemporary conceptions of gift exchange. Whereas in ancient agricultural contexts exchange could be conceived in a somewhat direct and coercive way, medieval votive practices were characterized by the human subjects' need for submission and self-devotion, an act expressing a ritualized request that might also be unsatisfied.

See also: Saints, Cults of the

—Michele Bacci

Wandering Jew. Figure of medieval Christian legendry (motif Q502.1), a man who roams the earth eternally as punishment for an act committed against Christ on the day of the Crucifixion.

There is no biblical source for this legend, but the figure of the Wandering Jew has been strongly influenced by two characters who appear in the Gospel of John: John Cartaphilus (Dearly Beloved), who waits for Christ (John 21:20–22), and the soldier who strikes Christ (John 18:22), traditionally identified as Malchus (John 18:10).

The legend began to develop in premedieval times and apparently spread in two waves: Eastern versions, which survived primarily in oral tradition, were told in Anatolia, the Balkans, and Slavic countries. Western versions spread through Egypt and North Africa to Italy. Although a written account emerges as early as the sixth century in the Middle East, the earliest surviving European legends do not appear before the thirteenth century (1223 in Italy; 1228 in England).

Typical of the early Wandering Jew tales is this one told in 1238 by Matthew Paris, a monk of the Abbey of St. Albans, England. Paris writes that in 1228 an Armenian archbishop visited the abbey. The archbishop was asked if he knew anything about a man named Joseph, who was widely reported to have seen Christ on the day of the Crucifixion. A knight in the archbishop's retinue replies that, indeed, the archbishop had seen Joseph many times and had learned the story of his life. On the day of the Crucifixion, Joseph—then named Cartaphilus—was working as a servant of Pontius Pilate. As Jesus was being dragged toward his execution, Cartaphilus struck him contemptuously, saying, "Go quicker, Jesus." Jesus looked sternly back at him and said, "I am going, and you will wait till I return."

Thus cursed by Christ, Cartaphilus must wander the world until the Second Coming. He has himself baptized as a Christian and changes his name to Joseph. He travels in Armenia and throughout the East, visiting with Church leaders. He does not speak unless holy men ask him to do so; then he talks about his personal knowledge of Christ and early Christianity. Every time he reaches 100 years of age, he reverts to the age of 30, his age when he witnessed the Crucifixion.

In 1242, a few years after Matthew Paris's account, Philip Mouskes (who was to become bishop of Tourney, France) also wrote of the Wandering Jew, also citing the Armenian archbishop as the source of his tale. According to Philip, Joseph was now wandering through Western Europe, visiting the shrines of St. Thomas Becket in England and St. James the Elder in Spain, as well as the relics of the Three Kings in Cologne. Shortly after 1500 a Bohemian tale reports the existence of the Wandering Jew, and an Arabic account states that the ageless man has been preaching Christianity to a Muslim soldier.

In some medieval accounts the Wandering Jew ages continually, but in others—as in Matthew Paris's version—he reverts to the age of 30 every 100 years, usually experiencing a dramatic seizure as he grows suddenly younger. In the Icelandic *Magus Saga,* the Wandering Jew sheds his old skin like a snake as he regains his youth.

Agelessness is not the only supernatural attribute of the Wandering Jew: in a fifteenth-century Italian tale, as in later central European legends, he has the power to locate hidden treasure as well as to heal miraculously.

To judge by surviving manuscripts, the Wandering Jew piqued the imaginations of medieval people for many reasons. Most obviously, the tale provided support for Christian beliefs by alleging the existence of an actual, living witness to the Crucifixion. Furthermore, the eternal life of the Jew was interpreted as evidence that the Christian God could be merciful to all people. Also, emerging during the era of the Crusades, a time of heightened curiosity regarding the wonders of the East, this tale—like the stories of the Islamic Assassins and the Indian ruler Prester John—served as an expression of European awe toward a region in which the miraculous seemed to be an ordinary occurrence.

In postmedieval times, particularly during the seventeenth century (when he was a major subject in chapbooks) and the nineteenth century (when Romantic poets and novelists made him a widespread literary symbol), the Wandering Jew has become very well known among Western European Christians, but the tale has always been an outsiders' legend; it was never a significant part of Jewish tradition.

See also: Assassins Nizari Ismaᶜilis; Jews, Stereotypes of; Prester John

—Carl Lindahl

Wells and Springs. Frequently sites of veneration in the Middle Ages and often associated with local saints or the Virgin Mary.

One of the main features of holy wells lay in the healing power of their waters, attributed to the power of the saint. Votive objects dedicated to the saint were often hung about the well, and water from a holy well was used as a cure for skin ailments, eye diseases, infertility, and other illnesses. Apart from the therapeutic value of their waters, sacred springs and wells were also sites of prayer and devotion.

The veneration of such bodies of water in Western culture can be found in antiquity; Greco-Roman mythology contains several instances of fountains and springs inhabited by nymphs (known as naiads) or other minor deities (for example, the naiads who lure Hylas, the companion of Hercules, to his death in their spring). Both Greeks and Romans attributed a prophetic power to certain wells, such as the spring at Delphi. Celtic mythology endowed several bodies of water with an attendant spirit; the cult of Coventina, strongly associated with water, flourished in northern Britain, and that of Sequana, personification of the source of the Seine, in France. Mineral springs and natural hot springs were often revered for their medicinal properties; the British Roman town of Bath or Aquae Sulis, also dedicated to a Celtic goddess, is but one example of several throughout Europe. Votive offerings from antiquity have often been found in what were once sacred springs or wells (such as that of Coventina); in areas of Roman settlement, tablets with requests to the local attendant deity or curses have been found, probably a precursor to the modern "wishing well" idea. While there is a popular tendency to attribute the origin of hydrolatry, or well worship, to the ancient Celts, its prevalence in most European cultures suggests otherwise. The motif of the holy well or spring also has a widespread distribution; it exists in Eastern traditions (most notably Hindu), in ancient Egyptian cults, and in biblical tradition—for example, the well of Hagar (Gen. 16:7–14); the well of Moses (Exod. 17:6–7); and the healing well of Bethesda (John 5:2–4). An example from Norse mythology is the spring of Mimir at the base of Yggdrasil, the World Tree, whose waters conferred wisdom.

Although some pre-Christian sites in Europe became rededicated to Christian saints, lack of historical or archaeological evidence in most cases precludes any conclusion regarding continuity of worship; only the impulse to venerate wells and springs can be attested in local folklore. Wells that were never considered sacred or therapeutic may have been dedicated to a saint in the Christian era to promote either the saint's cult or the authority of the Church, and some sites, such as Bath, were never Christianized. Some wells became hallowed simply by virtue of being the property of a church and used for baptism, especially in towns; in the countryside pagan survivals are more likely but have less documentation. Saints were often credited with the miraculous creation of wells and springs, either by praying, by striking a staff into the ground (in imitation of Moses), or by shedding their own blood on the ground. The early-medieval Church more often than not condemned any custom that smacked of the veneration of wells and springs as heathen practice, but the later medieval Church embraced the reverence of its wells, and numerous wells and churches were dedicated to the Virgin Mary. Several healing wells associated with saints became pilgrimage sites, and certain wells became the focal point for gatherings and rituals (such as circumambulation, prayer, or well dressing) at significant times of the year, most often in the summer. Drinking or washing in the water of a holy well, along with prayers to the saint, could effect a cure, but desecration of the water was thought to cause injury, disease, and even death. The custom in England of well dressing, decorating wells with flowers and green branches at a certain time of the year, seems to have survived, although intermittently, from the Middle Ages, and in some areas it has undergone a revival. The earliest recorded instance is at Tissington in 1350. Folklore studies of holy wells generally depend on postmedieval documentation and modern field research.

See also: Pilgrimage; Scandinavian Mythology

—Dorothy Ann Bray

Welsh Tradition.

The folkloric culture of the Welsh.

Early History

Celts, or more specifically, speakers of two forms of Celtic, entered Britain and Ireland from Continental Europe over an extended period and in successive waves in the fifth, third, and first centuries B.C.E. Ireland was settled by speakers of Goidelic, from which is derived the Gaelic of Ireland and thence that of Scotland and the Isle of Man; mainland Britain was settled by speakers of British (or Brythonic), which developed into Cornish, Breton, Welsh, and Cumbrian (among other forms of northern British now lost). Though Goidelic and British were significantly different, and early forms of Irish and Welsh even more so (none of the modern Celtic languages is mutually understood), and though separate national identities had developed by the early Middle Ages, nevertheless, contact among all these peoples was maintained, and their religious and social institutions and culture had much in common. The Britons, in spite of their tribal divisions, were conscious of their strong linguistic and cultural affinities, and in historical times, from the first Roman subjugation in the first century C.E., they can be recognized as inhabiting Britain south of the Antonine Wall. Following the collapse of Roman rule toward the end of the fifth century C.E. and the subsequent Anglo-Saxon invasions and settlements, the area now known as England was thoroughly colonized, and an almost complete language replacement resulted. British kingdoms remained in north Britain south of the Clyde and the Forth, in Wales, and in Cornwall, and though separated from one another geographically (by land though not by sea), the links between them remained and their shared traditions continued (e.g., Cornish dynastic traditions were preserved in south Wales and in Brittany, and the Welsh [*Cymry*] and Cumbrians shared a common ethnic title, "compatriots"). The sixth and seventh centuries, when the northern kingdoms struggled against the Anglo-Saxons and among themselves, became the heroic age of Welsh history, and the northern traditions and their heroes were to be its classical, defining historical horizon. Cornwall had been absorbed into Wessex by the tenth century. Most of the northern British kingdoms were subjugated in the seventh century, but Strathclyde remained until the late eleventh century, when it became part of the kingdom of Scotland. Its continuance probably allowed it to act as a conduit for the preservation of northern traditions and their transmission to Wales.

Welsh Geography and Economy

Wales is a land of mountains and high plateaus cut by deep valleys with low-lying arable land around the edges. Tempered in winter by the sea and in summer by high altitude, Wales has a moderate climate marked by heavy rainfall, particularly in winter. In the medieval period it was still heavily forested, with woodland extending high up the slopes. There were also extensive marshes and bogs. From the literature we know of oak, ash, elm, hazel, alder, holly, thorn, apple, willow, yew, broom, gorse, meadowsweet, heather, and reeds. Wild animals included stags, wolves, boars, and such small mammals as pine martens and stoats. Among the birds were cuckoos, eagles, crows, jays, and thrushes. Domesticated animals included cattle, swine (the most-eaten animal, according to archaeology), sheep, goats, horses for riding, asses, oxen for plowing, cats, dogs, and poultry. Bees were also kept.

Settlements were generally dispersed, though there was some nucleation around royal courts and religious houses. Construction was mainly of timber and wattle, although stone huts were common in the northern mountains. There is evidence of some transhumance (i.e., the practice of driving cattle and sheep up to summer pastures), as is suggested by the nomenclature of dwellings: hendref (old home, i.e., permanent settlement) and hafod (summer home), as well as other names denoting this type of temporary dwelling. In general, people lived off the land, with hunting, fishing, and nut gathering and with a mixed farm economy based on wheat, barley, some vegetables and herbs, dairy, and flax for linen. Ale, cider, wine, and mead were the common beverages. The economy was one of interdependence and gift exchange. Currency was used to some degree, and the commutation of renders and taxes from kind to currency was accomplished mainly in the thirteenth century; nevertheless, currency did not become significant until after the Edwardian Conquest (1282). Clothes included jerkins, cowls, cloaks, and shoes or boots and might be made of skins, silk, or linen, depending on the period and individual wealth. The law texts provide a partial inventory of medieval material culture with references to household paraphernalia, such as cauldrons, vats, sacks, jars, meat forks, sieves, weaving frames, various types of axes, knives, ropes, nets, armor, bridles and leashes, jewelry (rings, bracelets, brooches), bedding (pillows, sheets, and brychans—woven, usually woolen coverlets, sometimes used as cloaks by day), harps, and game boards with pieces made of whale bone, hart's antler, steer's horn, or wood. The Welsh had three primary musical instruments, the harp, the crwth (a stringed instrument), and pipes, and were noted for their part singing. According to contemporary accounts, the Welsh were especially attentive to personal hygiene: bathing, washing and dressing their hair, and brushing their teeth.

Medieval Welsh society was highly stratified socially rather than economically, with status based on birth, family, and occupation. The kindred, which was patrilineally defined, formed the basic unit of support, protection, and legal responsibility, such as for payment of galanas (blood price) or sarhad (compensation for insult or injury) in a legal system that emphasized compensation of the victim over punishment of the offender. Economically, although there were rich and poor (with slavery persisting as late as the eleventh century), there appears to have been little destitution (records indicate that even the poorest might be expected to have owned one or two cows) until the late eleventh century, when poverty became intense.

Welsh History

Wales emerges in the early Middle Ages as a number of small autonomous kingdoms. Politically separate, they were nevertheless bound together by a common language that attained a standard literary form very early, an essentially common system of law and legal training, and a common view of their origins as Cymry. British overlordship of the island of Britain is the most integral feature of Welsh legendary history, and this concept was a potent force in Welsh resistance to incursions by the English kingdoms of Wessex and Northumbria. The Norman Conquest of Wales was a piecemeal penetration along strategic routes from newly established lordships on the border in the North (Chester), mid-Wales (Shrewsbury), and the South (Hereford). The units of conquest were the cantrefi, native political entities that were autonomous and royal by Welsh law and that became quasi-autonomous Marcher lordships. The initial Norman thrust was swift and powerful, penetrating deep into the heartland of the country. By the end of the eleventh century, in spite of a respite in the southern kingdom of Deheubarth under Rhys ap Tewdwr in the years 1075–1093, Wales appeared to have fallen to the invaders. The return from exile of Gruffudd ap Cynan in 1094 to assert his claim to the northern kingdom of Gwynedd marked a change in the fortunes of the Welsh as lost lands were regained and new conquests consolidated. The uprising in the South initially had more limited success, but in the confusion following the death of Henry I of England the Welsh reasserted themselves, and the years 1135–1197 were to be a period of national awakening in state and Church under Owain Gwynedd (Gruffudd's grandson) and Rhys ap Gruffudd (ap Tewdwr's grandson). When the latter died in 1197, a balance had been struck between the major Welsh princedoms—Gwynedd, Powys (in mid-Wales), and Deheubarth—and the Norman Marcher lordships to the east.

The conquest was political, for even within the Norman lordships there existed the division of Englishry (around the castle and its borough) and Welshry, where Welsh law and custom remained. There was considerable interaction between native and foreign features in society, in the economy, in political developments, and in literature, not only in the Marcher lordships but also in the native princedoms of *pura Wallia*. Thirteenth-century Gwynedd under Llywelyn I and his grandson Llywelyn II sought to create a united Wales, each province paying homage through the prince of Wales (Gwynedd) to the English crown. This ideal, briefly achieved during 1255–1267, was finally shattered in the Welsh wars of Edward I of England in 1277 and 1282, when Llywelyn II was killed. The Treaty of Rhuddlan (1284) created the king's domain of the principality of Wales governed under the English administrative and economic system. Nevertheless, some aspects of governance were devolved to the local level, and there developed a class of native administrators and crown servants who grasped the opportunity to create estates as their economic base and to use service under the crown as their source of influence and leadership. These local leaders, the *uchelwyr* (gentry), some of whose forebears had held office under the native Welsh princes before 1282, became the dominant class in fourteenth- to sixteenth-century Welsh society and the new patrons of Welsh literature, replacing the pre-1282 royal courts. From one of the oldest and most influential families among them, the Tudors of Anglesey, came Owen Tudor, who married the widow of King Henry V of England. Under his grandson, Henry VII, the first of the Tudor kings, the principality of Wales and the Marcher lordships were brought together, and Wales became assimilated to England in the Act of Union (1536). The structure of traditional Welsh society disintegrated, and the gentry became increasingly anglicized.

Pre-Christian Religion

Celtic religion was oral, and it is only partially recoverable, therefore, from its material remains (dedications, inscriptions, effigies, votive offerings), from descriptions by classical authors, from medieval vernacular literature, and through what light historical linguistics can shed on the nomenclature of deities. The archaeological evidence is mainly Gaulish and Romano-British; most of the vernacular literary evidence is Irish. Together these sources can be used to present an overview of Celtic religion and its structures.

Though predominantly tribal and local, there were nevertheless some gods worshipped across the Celtic realms and others who were more functional than local. Some gods had marked zoomorphic elements, and goddesses of rivers and *matres* (denoting fecundity) were widespread. The Celts had a strong sense of place, and particular regard was paid to the tribal goddess of the domain, its "sovereignty," whose union with the king was a sign and cause of prosperity and well-being. Transcending local manifestations were other mythologically and culturally homogeneous aspects apparently shared by all the Celtic peoples, such as the cosmological cult of the center and the five divisions of land, and a tripartite learned class represented in Gaul and early Ireland by druids, bards, and seers, who were responsible for safeguarding and transmitting traditional lore. This latter function was fulfilled in Wales by *cyfarwyddiaid*, "knowledgeable ones," who are described as being the conservers of knowledge of local custom and rights. Though the usual meaning of the word in Middle Welsh is "storytellers," this refers to the medium and is probably an indication of their wider role as transmitters of traditional lore of all kinds: genealogies, origin legends, cosmology, boundaries, history, religion, and so on. Court poets, whose main function was the praise of rulers, were knowledgeable in these categories, and there was some overlap in the roles of storytellers, poets, lawyers, and mediciners as the learned classes of medieval Wales. Unlike in Irish literature, the content of *cyfarwyddyd*, "traditional lore," is poorly preserved in Welsh literature. The medieval prose tales in their extant forms belong to the late eleventh to the thirteenth centuries and are sophisticated compositions; their authors were more concerned with using traditions for literary ends than with safeguarding and transmitting them unchanged. The other chief source of information about *cyfarwyddyd* is the Triads of the Island of Britain, a schematic collection of references to heroes and their legends. The evidence for pre-Christian religion in Wales is, therefore, late, sparse, and allusive and consists of references, named characters, and episodes; it is to be read in the light of the Gaulish, Romano-British, and Irish evidence but with careful regard to the danger of putting undue weight on the detail of cultural affinities between these Celtic peoples.

The characters of the Four Branches of the Mabinogi share their nomenclature, though not their legends, with some of those in the Irish mythological cycle. The children of Dôn are reflected in the Irish family of the goddess Danu, though the only correspondence of names is the smith (Welsh *Gofannon*, Irish *Goibhniu*); another son is the Welsh Amaethon, "cultivator." The children of Llŷr also feature in the *Mabinogi*—Brân, Branwen, Manawydan (with whom is to be compared the Irish Manannán mac Lír). The First Branch of the Four Branches tells of Pwyll, called "Head of Annwfn" (the otherworld), though he is actually king of Dyfed in southwest Wales; his otherworld wife Rhiannon (*Rigantona, "great queen"); and their son Pryderi, who is in fact reared by Teyrnon (*Tigernonos, "great king"); That there has been some confusion or manipulation of material here seems to be confirmed by the account of the snatching of Pryderi from his mother's side, which is echoed in a reference in another tale, Culhwch and Olwen, to Mabon (Maponos, "great youth"), who was lost when three nights old from his mother Modron (Matrona, "great mother"). These deities are attested from north Britain and Gaul. The Lleu of the Fourth Branch corresponds to Irish Lug (Lugh) and the Gaulish Lugus. Other mythological themes that appear in the Welsh sources are the sovereignty myth of the sacral marriage of king and goddess and the interrelationship of the otherworld and the land of mortals.

Christianity had been introduced into Britain by the mid-third century and seems to have been widely established by the fifth century. Western and northern Britain saw a vigorous flowering of monastic and hermetical Christianity in the sixth century, the "age of the saints" whose names are commemorated in their churches throughout Wales (usually prefixed by llan, "ecclesiastical settlement"). There was inevitably some fusing of the two religions (e.g., the otherworld became hell, and its ruler Gwynn ap Nudd came to be seen as the king of devils). The monastic leaders became the heroes of popular religion as healers and protectors and also as symbols of the victory of a new local hero over pagan rulers. Saints' legends are probably the best-reported category of medieval Welsh popular beliefs.

Narratives, Customs, and Beliefs

Medieval Welsh folk narratives are poorly preserved, and some allusions become clear only in the context of folktales noted more recently. The historical tradition of the lost overlordship of Britain by the Welsh (as the Britons) and its prophesied restoration under a national savior remained a political force throughout the Middle Ages. Historical legendry was popular, as is clear from The Dream of Maxen Wledig and the tales about Lludd and Llefelys, Vortigern and the Saxon conquest, and many dynastic legends and anecdotes. Topographical and onomastic legends were popular, and there appears to have been a rich and varied folk narrative tradition of sunken cities, giants, wells, caves, and fairies.

Information on the folk customs of medieval Wales is scant, with most of it concerning customs related to religion and rites of passage, such as pilgrimages, attention to relics, attendance at healing wells, and celebrations of the local saint's day (gwylmabsant). We know of infant baptisms, wedding feasts, and burial in graves, sometimes with wooden coffins and sometimes with stone markers, but we know few of the details. Although, aided by assumptions about pagan fertility rituals, we might extrapolate backward from seventeenth-century and later accounts of such Christmas and New Year's customs as the Mari Lwyd (a horse's head carried into individual households by revelers in search of food and drink), wassailing, hunting the wren, and having good luck and prosperity brought into the house on New Year's morning by boys sprinkling fresh spring water with an evergreen twig (box, holly, myrtle) or by boys carrying a calennig (an apple decorated with corn and evergreen sprigs), we lack direct and precise evidence of these customs in medieval Wales. The few extant references, found most often in poetry, tend to be fleeting allusions.

See also: Annwfn; Arthurian Lore; Culhwch and Olwen; David, Saint; Gerald of Wales; Gwynn ap Nudd; Maelgwn Gwynedd; Map, Walter; Maxen Wledig; Myrddin; Nennius; Owain Glyndwr; Sleeping King; Taliesin; Triads of the Island of Britain

—Elissa R. Henken and Brynley F. Roberts

Wild Hunt [German Wilde Jagd, French mesnie Hellequin]. Legend complex (motif E501) concerning a ghostly hunter, often accompanied by dogs or spirits and often hunting a woman, who is frequently one of the supernatural beings.

In many Scandinavian and German versions the hunter captures or kills the woman and carries her off like a game animal. The hunter may be unidentified, or he may be a historical figure like Dietrich von Bern or the Danish king Valdemar Atterdag, Satan, or some reflex of the Norse god Odin. The woman being hunted is most often a local forest being; in some Scandinavian versions she is said to have huge breasts that she slings over her shoulder as she runs from her pursuer. The fullest versions of this form of the legend tell of someone who witnesses first the woman running by, then the hunter, and then finally the hunter with the captured or killed woman. In other forms of the legend more common in Germany, the hunter may be a lost soul, or he may lead lost souls on a wild ride through the sky, rather like the Norwegian oskorei, a band of spirits who rush about and often overrun farms, especially at holiday periods like Christmas. Sometimes a rushing noise high in the trees is called Odin's hunt, even in locales where the legend plot is not present, and indeed there is much variation among the medieval and more-recent recordings that are usually discussed in connection with this complex. Postmedieval legends following this pattern are known from southern Sweden, Denmark, and Germany, and there are a few from Norway also. The medieval recordings are mostly from Germany. In Reider Thorvald Christiansen's catalog The Migratory Legends, "The Fairy Hunter" (ML 5060) is based on postmedieval Norwegian variants.

The identification of the hunter as Odin and

the rushing of spirits around him has led scholars, especially O. Höfler writing in 1934, to consider a connection with an ecstatic Odin cult and to draw on recent popular customs from German-speaking areas. More-recent scholarship, however, would argue for a basis in an Indo-European warrior cult in which young warriors imbued with life force fight with the characteristics of animals, especially those of wolves, and are initiated into a warrior band that unites them not just with other warriors but also with the spirits of the dead warriors who had been members of the group. Even if such a cult existed, however, we are left with no clear interpretation of many of the motifs in the legend complex of the Wild Hunt.

From the twelfth century forward the Wild Hunt appears as a major theme of legend in England and Wales. In the *Peterborough Chronicle* the anonymous author notes under the year 1127 the supernatural occurrences accompanying the arrival of the new abbot of Peterborough, who was despised by the monks:

> Let no one be surprised at the truth of what we are about to relate, for it was general knowledge throughout the whole country that immediately after [the new abbot's] arrival … many men both saw and heard a great number of huntsmen hunting. The huntsmen were black, huge, and hideous, and rode on black horses and on black he-goats, and their hounds were jet black, with eyes like saucers, and horrible. (*The Anglo-Saxon Chronicle*, trans. G.N. Garmonsway [1953], p. 258)

Writing in 1191 and narrating the tale of the Welshman Meilyr, Gerald of Wales depicts a similar spectral band. Meilyr, after sleeping with an otherworldly woman, was able to see and communicate with "unclean spirits.… They would appear in the form of huntsmen, but it was human souls they were pursuing, not wild beasts" (*The Journey through Wales*, trans. L. Thorpe [1978], p.117). These references, written by clergymen, depict the Wild Hunt as diabolic. In later English romance traditions, however, such ghostly hunters are associated with a fairy otherworld distinct from heaven or hell. In the fourteenth-century English romance *Sir Orfeo*, the "King of Fairy" is seen riding through the woods with 1,000 armed knights blowing horns and accompanied by barking dogs, but the huntsmen never captured any animals. In the Scottish *Thomas of Erceldoune*, composed at the end of the fifteenth century, the queen of fairyland appears blowing a horn, armed with arrows, and accompanied by dogs; after Thomas sleeps with her she guides him past heaven, hell, and purgatory to her fairy realm, where he lives with her for three years.

See also: Fairies; Fairy Lover; Gwynn ap Nudd; Scandinavian Mythology; Thomas Rhymer

—John Lindow

Wild Man [*Wodehouse, Wodewose*]. One of the most important cultural figures of the late Middle Ages, typically representing the animal side of human nature, though occasionally his bestial nature is capable of being interpreted *in bono*, when he becomes a sort of "noble savage" who purposely stays aloof from the corruption of the world.

Of all the "monstrous races," the Wild Man is the most autonomous and least monstrous; indeed, with his wife, the Wild Woman, he is often to be found living an idyllic sylvan existence, *en famille*, even if he does have a regrettable tendency to abduct human women whenever the opportunity presents itself. One early-sixteenth-century tapestry depicts a band of Wild Men fighting against another band of "exotic" people who are probably intended to represent Native Americans—an interesting stage in the process of assimilation of this newly discovered "wild" people into European culture.

His origins are not to be fixed definitively, and, indeed, it is likely enough that such a figure should emerge independently in a number of European regions, especially in areas of dense forest; he is better seen as a cousin of the classical satyr than as a direct descendant. The Celtic reflexes of the Wild Man type are especially important, as they include the Irish *geilt* (madman) Suibhne and the Welsh Merlin.

Two of the earliest references to the figure are in fact to the Wild Woman, in the form of a *wildero wibo hus* (wild woman house) named in an eleventh-century German charter and even earlier in that rich source of Germanic folklore, the *Penitential of Burchard of Worms* (c. 1000), in which penance is prescribed for anyone who believes in *silvaticae* (forest women), who take human lovers and materialize and disappear at will. In later German tradition the epic hero Wolfdietrich is forced by just such a Wild Woman to live for six months in the forest with her as a Wild Man, and sixteenth-century illustrations of the Nuremberg *Schembartlauf* (carnival processions) show small, helpless human males being carried along by Wild Women.

The "classic" Wild Man of the later Middle Ages is covered in shaggy hair (except for face, hands, and feet), frequently wears a wreath of leaves around his head, and wields a club, usually a branch. Some of the earliest representations are found on capitals in Romanesque churches; the one at Semur-en-Auxois of circa 1250 appears as Esau—a hairy man, of course—paired with his brother, Jacob. But there are also early representations in wood, and the Wild Man is especially popular as a supporter for coats of arms: by the mid-twelfth century, it has been calculated, he appeared in the arms of no fewer than 263 noble families—a function that he was to continue to fill throughout the later Middle Ages.

In iconography, humans who take to the wild or become wild are readily approximated to the

Wild Man: such are the Old Testament king Nebuchadnezzar (usually depicted as covered in shaggy hair, despite the "eagle's feathers" that cover him in the Book of Daniel) and a number of saints who become "hairy anchorites" (one such appears as a marginal illustration in the early-fourteenth-century Smithfield Decretals). The most popular saint to play this role is undoubtedly St. John Chrysostom, seen creeping about in the background of the well-known engraving by Albrecht Dürer. (Curiously, St. John of Beverley appears in the same posture in a woodcut illustrating his Flemish "Life," printed in Brussels, c. 1512.) St. Mary of Egypt is the best-known example of a female "hairy anchorite."

The Wild Man was a convenient figure onto which medieval doubts about aggressive male (and sometimes female) sexuality could be projected. In the late-fourteenth-century *Wars of Alexander* (a translation of the Medieval Latin *Historia Alexandri Magni de Preliis*), Alexander is confronted by the sudden appearance of a Wild Man described merely as hairy, of great size, and having a voice like that of a boar. The English translator, however, prompted by no textual hint in his original, informs us that "large was his odd lome the lengthe of a yerde" [his "extra limb" was huge, a yard in length]. Clearly an aspect of the Wild Man's inhuman monstrosity is the extravagant sexuality implied by his outsize penis. Setting a trap reminiscent of the traditional mode of capturing the Bestiary unicorn—another long-horned beast—Alexander orders a naked maiden to be set before the Wild Man, who is then swiftly bound by the king's men while he is still drooling over his prospective prey. Like the unicorn (though not so fatally), the Wild Man, seen on one tapestry now in Frankfurt storming the Castle of Love in the urgency of his desire, can indeed be tamed by the love of a good woman. On another tapestry, he precedes the lady like a dog on a leash attached to his ankle and says, "I shall always remain wild until I am tamed by a Lady," to which she responds, "I think I can well tame you, as in fairness I should."

The scene of the Wild Man's abduction of a (noble) maiden seems to have been particularly popular in fourteenth-century art and has been shown to be an episode in a lost romance in which an elderly knight, Enyas, rescues the lady from the clutches of a *wodehouse*; the scene of the knight spearing the *wodehouse* appears on ivory caskets, an enameled amulet case, the silver mount of a horn, the foot of a monumental brass commemorating two princely bishops of the Bulow family in Schwerin, and in marginalia in the Taymouth *Hours* (to a caption to which we owe our knowledge of the knight's name), the Smithfield Decretals, and the Bodleian *Romance of Alexander*, not to mention three separate precious vessels depicting the scene, enumerated in the inventories of Louis, duke of Anjou.

By the fifteenth century the Wild Man appears in every conceivable type of decorative art: as a popular terminal knob on English silver spoons ("vj gylt spones with wodehowse at the endes" reads an inventory of 1509), as feet or finials for goblets, and on a wide variety of jewelry, from the richest brooches to the humblest lead badges.

The Wild Man's favorite steed is the stag, on which he may be seen abducting the maiden (as in the Taymouth *Hours*), jousting, or merely out hunting, as on a fifteenth-century German biscuit mold. In a most suggestive incident in Geoffrey of Monmouth's mid-twelfth-century Latin *Vita Merlini* (Life of Merlin), the Welsh magician becomes a Wild Man, rides a stag up to the house of his former mistress on her wedding night, and in a fit of jealous rage tears off his mount's antlers and hurls them at the couple—an intriguing early British reference to the horns of cuckoldry.

Other artistic media in which the Wild Man was especially popular are tapestry and woodwork. English inventories often record the content of *wodehouse* tapestries that are no longer extant: "*wodewoses joustantz a chival and lestorie dun descomfiture dun wodewose et dun Leon*" [jousting *wodehouse*s on horseback and the story of the discomfiture of a *wodehouse* and a lion] (1397); "*j wodewose and j chylde in his armys*" [one *wodehouse* and a child in his arms] (1459); "a wilde man Ryding on a horse" (1513). Germanic tapestries, in particular, often depict the cozy woodland family life of the Wild Man, the Wild Man domesticated, as it were. In English misericord art he is often to be seen fighting with a lion or dragon—which might suggest a positive reading of his role here.

He is a very popular figure in late-medieval romance, and by the late fifteenth century the Wild Man had reached print in the tale of *Valentine and Orson* (French edition, 1489; English, c. 1510), based on the fourteenth-century Germanic *Valentin und Namelos*, a classic twinning of cultured and wild brothers. Orson, having been abandoned, was raised by a bear (French *ours*). A dramatized version of the brothers' story in a village setting was famously portrayed by Pieter Brueghel the Elder, and the brothers were also among the characters who welcomed Edward VI on his way to his coronation in London in 1547 in a pageant staged at the great conduit in Cheap.

The popularity of the Wild Man in folklore led to his appearance in various forms of popular drama: in Padua in 1208 there is already mention of a "*ludus de quodam homine silvatico*" [play about a certain man of the forest], and another is recorded from Arau in 1339. The famous illustration of charivari in the *Roman de Fauvel* manuscript of 1314–1316 includes at least two participants dressed as Wild Men. But Wild Folk were also a part of courtly entertainment: twelve *wodehouse*s appeared in a Christmas masque before Edward III in 1348, and in a tragic 1393 incident a group of such Wild maskers at the French court were burned to death; the incident thus came to be known as the Bal des Ardents. Wild Folk were in evidence at tournaments (le Pas de la Dame Sauvaige of 1470), royal entries (Brussels, 1496; Bruges, 1515), feasts (la Fete du paon at Tours in 1457), processions (e.g., Nuremberg's *Schembartlauf*), and even in snow sculpture (Brussels, 1511).

See also: Bal des Ardents; Charivari; Cuckold; Green Man; Iconography; Myrddin; Wild Woman
—Malcolm Jones

Wild Woman. A female figure often represented as covered with hair or fur and situated ambiguously between the human and nonhuman worlds.

The figure of the medieval Wild Man was manifest in both generic and specific models: the first is exemplified by biblical figures (e.g., Adam, Cain, Ham, Nebuchadnezzar, Nimrod) whose rebellion against God or the local cultural norms expressed their essential "wildness"; the second is the familiar quasi-human wilderness denizen recognizable for his beast-like hirsutism, aphasia, hunting lifestyle, mastery of flora and fauna, and sexual excess. A similar duality characterizes paradigms of medieval feminine wildness. In addition to the companion of the hirsute Wild Man was a more generic Wild Woman, a figure who pushed the parameters of medieval female otherness to the limit.

Although the hirsute Wild Woman was depicted less frequently than her male counterpart in medieval material culture, enough examples in manuscript marginalia, engravings, tapestries, wood carvings, and stone sculptures remain to attest that a consistent physical appearance was attributed to her. The hirsute Wild Woman usually presented a seductively pretty face surrounded by a coiffure of luxuriant, long, unkempt hair. In contrast to the thick, almost costume-like coat of fur covering the Wild Man's body, a somewhat sparser coat seems to sprout visibly from the skin of her body, with her feet, elbows, knees, and especially her breasts left erotically exposed. Artists thus rendered the Wild Woman's body in more sexualized and anatomically accurate, if more animalistic (that is, less human), detail than that of the Wild Man.

The hirsute Wild Woman's reputation for alluring sexuality was represented iconographically in subtle visual allegory (e.g., scenes of her capturing and subduing a unicorn, a mythical beast who emblematized almost unseducible chastity). Artists also domesticated her uninhibited sexuality by promoting her as an emblem of carnality legitimized through procreative fertility, either depicted on the face of or supporting heraldic crests. The family life of the Wild People was portrayed in engravings and tapestries showing Wild couples and their children or images of the Wild Woman suckling a baby. Artists transferred the iconography of the Wild Woman to images of female saints associated with the wilderness, such as the desert ascetic Mary of Egypt, and to Mary

Magdalen, the sometime patron saint of prostitutes, whose nude body was depicted covered with long hair that, like the hirsute Wild Woman's, covered her body from head to toe.

The generic Wild Woman's mixed provenance includes Maia the Roman goddess of fertility and Lamia (the Latin word literally means "witch" or "vampire"), a child-devouring, libidinous hag from Hebrew and Greek antiquity. The lamia had a beautiful woman's face, an animal's hairy body, large shapely breasts, and no voice except a dragon's hissing. In revenge for Hera's murder of Lamia's children from an affair with Zeus, Lamia herself turned to kidnapping and child killing; she gradually multiplied, and these lamias, known to haunt pools of water and wells, became associated with the practices of witches: vanishing; shapeshifting from ugliness to beauty; and seducing and sucking the blood of young men, in the manner of a succubus, and devouring them. In the late Middle Ages the word *lamia* denoted a witch, as is evident from the title of Ulrich Molitor's 1489 treatise on witchcraft, *De lamiis*. In the lamia figure we can discern the source of the medieval Wild Woman's attractive face, bared breasts, hairiness, and the speechlessness she shared with the aphasic Wild Man.

Whether representing the specific hirsute companion of the Wild Man or the generic female Other, visual representations of the Wild Woman often were more extreme than those of the Wild Man. In some cases within the same book, the respective depictions of the Wild Woman and Wild Man seem to assign them to different species, she looking "wilder" and he more recognizably human, or at least like a human in a costume. This paradigm is exemplified in the *Nuremberg Chronicle*, an early printed book compiled by Hartmann Schedel, printed in 1493 by Anton Koberger, and illustrated with more than 1,800 woodcuts. More than 3,500 copies of the original Latin and subsequent German translation of this book were printed, making it a late-medieval–early-modern "best-seller" whose wide circulation would promote its interpretations of gendered wildness equally widely. In a hand-tinted copy of the *Nuremberg Chronicle* now owned by the National Gallery of Art, the book's only depiction of a pair of Wild Men is placed prominently on its frontispiece, whose central subject is a majestically enthroned God the Creator. The Wild Men stand upright, wear hat-like headgear and girdles, and sport coats of artificial-looking, green-tinted fur, all of which makes them resemble civilized humans masquerading in green ape-suits. Whereas these "noble savages" are placed in the context of God, the book's lone Wild Woman is included on the margins of a *mappamundi* (map of the world), where she represents the Wild People among exemplars of other physically grotesque "monstrous races" such as hermaphrodites, sciapods, centaurs, crane men, and six-armed men. Relegated to a place of abjection among her "fellow" monsters (all male), she is posed against a bleak backdrop of sparse vegetation, while the Wild Men are situated in the splendor of God's court. She is represented in the "wildest" possible way: entirely covered, except for one exposed breast, with sparse, naturalistic-looking, brown fur and long, obviously uncombed hair that, had she been permitted to stand upright, would reach to the tops of her thighs. Her legs are splayed in an ungainly pose, and she is forced (by the squares depicting other monsters framing her) to sit hunched over and contained. The artist limits her humanizing elements to a pretty face topped by abundant hair.

Similarly, a pair of *bas-de-page* scenes in a circa-1500 antiphonary (book of verses to be sung by one choir in response to another) in the Pierpont Morgan Library (M 905, vol. 1) portray a Wild Man and a Wild Woman, respectively. (See illustrations.) Folio 205 depicts a thick-furred Wild Man aiming a bow and arrow (rather than the more traditional club) at a sleeping stag. This dapper *wodewose* carries a quiver of arrows attached to his waist by a red girdle and wears an ivy garland on his head. The manufactured weapons and costume accessories suggest Chaucer's Yeoman or Robin Hood rather than a fierce *homme sauvage*. Folio 122, on the other hand, reveals a long-haired Wild Woman, breasts protruding prominently through her light brown fur, as she brandishes a club in one hand while holding a dragon by the tail in the other. This winged, web-footed monster (who is gendered female by the nippled udders that mirror the bare breasts of her captor) in turn clutches a flailing human baby in her mouth (details that reflect the Wild Woman's origins in the lamia). It is unclear whether the Wild Woman and the she-dragon, two examples of female monstrosity, are in collusion in the abduction of the baby or whether the Wild Woman is fighting the dragon for the baby, either to rescue it or to abduct it herself. In any case, within the pages of the same book the female exemplar of wildness is rendered far "wilder" than the male.

Shaped by the prevailing patriarchal misogyny of the period, the profiles of both the generic and the hirsute Wild Woman comprise an array of the negative roles and conventions commonly attached to the female sex in the Middle Ages. Her prototypes were ancient, and her period analogs were numerous and included the lamia, the witch, the Sheela-na-Gig, the siren/temptress, the fairy mistress, and the Loathly Lady. Examples of Wild Women in medieval literary texts are rarer than in visual images. However, one unquestionable example would be the sexually aggressive *serranas*, a group of mountain women encountered by the archpriest in Juan Ruiz's late-fourteenth-century *Libro de buen amor*. A woman capable of being seductively attractive at one moment and grotesquely ugly and malevolent the next (or vice versa), the generic Wild

Woman took on many more forms than her male equivalent, the hairy *wodewose* or *homme sauvage*. As imagined by a culture that gendered voracious sexual appetite, excessive physicality, and lack of reason as female, the Wild Woman literally incorporated and personified traditional medieval anxieties and stereotypes about the power of women.

See also: Iconography; Wild Man

—Lorraine K. Stock

William of Orange [Guillaume d'Orange].

Hero celebrated in chansons de geste.

Guillaume d'Orange appears in one of the oldest medieval French epic legends, *Chançun de Willame*, and is one of the most popular epic heroes of the Middle Ages. The epic cycle named after Garin de Monglane features Guillaume and his family. There are six poems that specifically focus on Guillaume. He is known as much for his distinctive nose as for his heroic exploits and his strong wife. Scholars are divided, however, on whether his epithet, *al corb nez*, implied a hooked nose or a short one.

The *Chançun de Willame* (c. 1185) begins with a Saracen attack upon 700 French knights. Guillaume counterattacks with 30,000 men but is defeated in a battle that he alone survives. Eventually he defeats his opponents, but only after being rescued by his young nephew Gui. The poem treats many of the themes that made Guillaume a celebrated hero and the chansons de geste so popular in the twelfth and thirteenth centuries. It focuses on warfare against Islamic forces, a topic of great interest in the era of the Crusades. Yet the importance of lineage and the noble family is also stressed, for Guillaume fights to avenge his nephew at least as much as to further the cause of Christianity. His wife, Guiborc, plays a crucial part in the family drama by urging Guillaume to fight, running the household in his absence, rounding up knights to join him, and caring for the men upon their return from battle. The heroines of the chanson de geste vary greatly in type and character. Guiborc, for example, is not only a leader and the wife of a hero, but she is also fiercely independent, in stark contrast to "la belle Aude" in the *Chanson de Roland*, whose fragility causes her to expire upon the news of Roland's death. In most cases, chanson de geste heroines are very different from those in chivalrous romances.

Several scholars have tentatively identified Guillaume with William, count of Toulouse. William of Toulouse was a military leader and administrator under Charlemagne and founded the Benedictine Abbey of Gellone (now St. Guilhem-le-Désert) in 804, retiring to it in 806. This is paralleled and expanded in the legend of Guillaume. William of Toulouse was canonized in 1066, and his feast day is May 28. Joseph Bédier suggests that inconsistencies came about as various writers seized upon the exploits of other men named William and incorporated their legends into the evolving cycle. Guillaume's battles against the Saracens, for example, have been identified as possibly those undertaken in the tenth century by the brother and son of Arles-based Count Boso, both named William.

Guillaume's legend was at its height in the twelfth and thirteenth centuries, and his exploits were widely known outside the French-speaking world. For example, he is mentioned in Dante's *Divine Comedy* and is the protagonist in Wolfram von Eschenbach's *Willehalm*. In the *Historia ecclesiastica* by Ordericus Vitalis he is treated as a warrior saint, and there is an Italian cyclic compilation of his legends *(I Nerbonesi)*.

See also: Chanson de Geste

—Gillian S. Polack

Wine. The fermented juice of the grape.

Fermented beverages called wines are also made from some fruits and plants, but the names of these wines generally contain the name of the substance from which they are made, for example, "dandelion wine" or "currant wine." Wine was originally a product of the Mediterranean region, but the remains of Greek amphoras found in France that date to the sixth century B.C.E. show that there was an early market for Mediterranean wine in the northern countries. With the growth of the Roman Empire, trade in wine increased and viticulture spread into Gaul. The fall of the Roman Empire disrupted trade but seems not to have had a serious effect on local production.

From the fifth to the tenth centuries, princes, bishops, and monks continued to cultivate vines on their properties, even as far north in England as Ely. A factor in the preservation of viticulture during this time of transition was the requirement for wine in the celebration of the Christian Mass. Just as much a factor, however, was the association of wine consumption with high social rank in the northern, non-wine-producing areas. Along the Mediterranean wine was drunk at all levels of society, whereas in the North, beer was the common beverage and wine was consumed by the elite. Another effect of the fall of Rome was the shift from the use of airtight amphoras, which allowed long-term storage of vintage wines, to the use of wooden barrels, in which wine remained potable for only about one year. Throughout the Middle Ages, therefore, wine was produced for immediate consumption.

With the growth of towns from 1100 on, the rise of wealthy craftsmen and merchants created a new market for wine. Their riches allowed them access to the status symbols of the upper classes, including wine. At the same time, the reestablishment of trade routes and relative peace led to long-distance merchandising of wine. Production in the parts of the North inhospitable to viticulture waned, and wine making began to be centered in the areas most favorable to the growth of wine-making grapes. Thus, many northern areas came to rely on imported wine.

Wine from the Mediterranean was favored for import. These heavier, sweeter wines (especially malmsey and romney) were both valuable and popular, for the high sugar content made them travel better and last longer than the lighter, drier wines of more northerly wine-producing regions such as Gascony and Germany. England in particular depended on wine from Gascony (which includes the Bordeaux region), which was linked to England after the marriage of Eleanor of Aquitaine to Henry II in 1152 and stayed an English possession until 1453. During this period the monastic orders were important in the development of wine making. Many of the great foundations, such as Cluny and Cîteaux, had extensive vineyards, which had been bequeathed to them over the years. The stability of vineyard ownership and the high educational level of the monks enabled growth in knowledge about the growing of grapes and the production of wines.

The trade in wine was lucrative, and much documentation has survived about volume and source of import, taxation, and pricing. In the southern production areas the supply of wine was steady, but in the North the rhythm of supply was controlled by time of vintage and seasonal weather patterns. The first shipments of new wine would be made in October or November, after harvest and production. The feast of St. Martin (November 11) marked the normal date upon which new wine was ready, and in wine-making areas processions and festivals could take place on this date. In March and April, after the worst of the winter, a second shipment would go out. Then, in July and August the sweet wines from the Mediterranean would arrive in the North.

The documents and literature of the medieval period reveal much about the quality of different wines and of the social significance of wine and wine drinking. A particularly valuable document is Henri d'Andeli's *Bataille des vins*, dating from the first half of the thirteenth century. In this poem an English priest judges an array of wines for the king of France. The sweet wines from Cyprus are judged the best, and wines from the Champagne region are also ranked highly, while wines from the northwest of France are condemned for being too acidic. This ranking of wines is reflected in the tradesman's call at the end of the prologue of *Piers Plowman*, which mentions the wines of Oseye (Portuguese), Gascony, Rochelle, and the Rhine. Chaucer's *Canterbury Tales* reveals many attitudes about wine in fourteenth-century England. His portrait of the Shipman shows both the continuing importance of the wine trade between Bordeaux and Gascony, for the Shipman sails this route, and reveals one of the dangers of the trade, for the Shipman has the habit of drawing wine from the barrels while the merchants sleep. "The Shipman's Tale" shows the prosperity of the merchant husband and the merchant's esteem for his monastic guest when the merchant serves malmsey and vernaccia, both costly wines.

In "The Merchant's Tale," Januarie prepares himself for his wedding night by drinking vernaccia and two types of spiced wine, hypocras and clarree. Clarree was usually served at the beginning of a meal and hypocras at the end. Both, however, were also considered medicinal, and Januarie's use of both and his use of vernaccia (some white wines were also considered to have health properties) form part of a depiction of overpreparation for the consummation of his marriage. The medicinal properties of wine were part of medical tradition. For example, it was used for dressing wounds, to relieve fever, and as a general antiseptic and restorative. Because of its alcohol content, it could also dissolve and render palatable other medicinal substances.

Chaucer's Pardoner may inveigh against drunkenness—ironically, since he is drinking while delivering his "sermon"—but he also comments on the adulteration of wine. He warns of the wine of Lepe in Spain, known to be very strong, and describes how it is mixed with other wines. The customer might expect to be purchasing a wine from Bordeaux, but in reality it has been cut with wine from Lepe, a cheaper wine, so the mixture yields a higher profit for the seller. Numerous laws deal with this and other types of adulteration, and a merchant caught tampering with wine would be forced to drink a draught of the bad wine. The rest would be poured over his head. Yet simple mixing seems a small offense when compared with descriptions of how wine that had gone to vinegar could be cooked and doctored with noxious substances and then passed off as a high-quality product.

Wine-drinking rituals were part of student life at the universities, serving as rites of initiation, community, and passage. The students' daily rations in their colleges included wine, and some colleges would drink a *potus caritatis* (cup of mutual love) at the end of the evening meal. Fines would often be paid in wine, and taverns were places where all levels of the university would meet to celebrate passing exams and other events—often at the cost of the individual promoted. Songs in the *Carmina Burana* bear ample testimony to the place of wine in the lore of student life, depicting how wine and love go together for better or for worse, and lauding, perhaps ironically, wine's use in keeping the wits sharp for learning. Wine also played a social function in feasting, in which watered wine was served to most guests, while pure wine was served to the head table, where guests could water it or not according to taste. Records show that a copious wine supply was one hallmark of a good feast.

See also: Festivals and Celebrations; Foodways; Harvest Festivals and Rituals; Inns and Taverns

—Mary Agnes Edsall

Witchcraft [French *Vauderie*, German *Hexerei*]. Discussed here in a sense that emerged in the fifteenth century: a set of alleged actions centering on conspiratorial association with other witches and usually involving a pact with the devil and attendance at nocturnal assemblies (first called "synagogues" and, later, "Sabbats").

Associated with the assemblies were homage to and veneration of the devil, sexual intercourse with the devil, flight through the air to and from the meetings, eating of human flesh (especially that of unbaptized babies), and repudiation or blasphemous parody of Christianity. The devil reportedly gave witches the means for bewitching people (e.g., powders and ointments) at the Sabbats and exhorted them to use them.

"Witchcraft" is difficult to define, partly because the Middle English *wicchecraft*, like the French *sorcellerie*, was used for various forms of maleficent magic; the use of curses, potions, wax images, and the like might still be spoken of as "bewitchment" or "witchcraft." But when the charge of practicing such magic was combined with other accusations in the late Middle Ages, the term took on the more complex range of meanings treated here.

Belief in these notions was in large measure an extension of the traditional Christian belief that magic was inspired, taught, and made possible by demons. Augustine's *De civitate Dei* (The City of God) and Isidore of Seville's *Etymologiae* (Etymologies) were among the classic texts responsible for establishing the idea that magic worked because, wittingly or not, it invoked demons. Geiler von Kaisersberg reiterated this notion in 1508, arguing that the witch who sprays water over her head with a broom and pronounces some incantation in the process can cause hail only because her action and her words constitute "signs" to the devil, who sees and hears these signs and carries out her desire. This interpretation was commonplace in medieval theological literature. In the central and late Middle Ages an alternative notion of "natural magic" became widespread: magic that was accomplished not through demonic agency but by exploiting "occult virtues" (or hidden powers) within nature. But the concept of natural magic remained controversial, and many writers insisted that such claims were false and that magic was in fact demonic even if it purported to be otherwise.

When people were accused not simply of sorcery but of conspiratorial witchcraft, even the nature of their alleged magical acts assumed greater gravity. The individual sorcerer or sorceress was likely to attack individual neighbors through indirect means (image magic or the hiding of magical substances). The conspiratorial witch was thought of as an enemy of society in general and was thought more likely to inflict destructive storms or epidemics or to attack not just enemies but also infants (to eat their flesh and use their fat for ointments). When such conspiratorial witches attacked persons, they were more likely to do so with direct, physical means; they smeared unguents on them or entered through windows and strangled babies. The devil not only gave them the means with which to accomplish their antisocial deeds but called them to account and punished them if they were insufficiently miscreant.

The social distribution of such notions is a controversial issue. Margaret Murray's now dated work on witchcraft argued that the Sabbat involved pre-Christian fertility rituals and that its demonization was the product of Christian bias. The element in her theory most subject to criticism is the assumption that witches were organized into underground covens, self-consciously opposed to the Christian Church. Jeffrey Russell also sees witchcraft as an alternative to mainstream religion, but for him the Sabbat was not a pre-Christian fertility rite but the ritual of anti-Christian, devil-worshipping heretics. Carlo Ginzburg and others have argued that the alleged witches did not in fact attend the Sabbat but, rather, entered into shamanistic ecstasy and imagined that they were transported to such assemblies. For Ginzburg the mythology of the Sabbat is built mainly upon archaic beliefs about people whose souls leave their bodies on shamanistic nocturnal journeys, in some cases to fight against witches or other enemies of their villages.

When the trial records disclose the dynamics of prosecution, however, it seems clear that in most cases the original accusation was of practicing some type of maleficent magic; the mythology of the Sabbat is superimposed on this original charge, often via leading questions asked under torture. When the trial records (and a fortiori, the fifteenth-century theological literature about witchcraft, such as the *Malleus maleficarum*) talk about pacts, Sabbats, sexual intercourse with demons, and related notions, it is safest to assume that the voice we are hearing is that of the judges and theologians. Their ideas about witchcraft may have been rooted partly in surviving notions about shamanistic journeys and other sources, but they were chiefly grounded in a long tradition of polemical calumny that had earlier been directed against heretics. This is not to say, however, that there was a sharp division along class lines in thinking about witchcraft: there were always possibilities for the diffusion of ideas. Thus, in 1448 a man in the diocese of Lausanne told his judges that, if tortured, he would confess anything, including eating his own children. Evidently this man had heard what other people were confessing, and he knew that torture would induce him to echo their confessions. In 1477 a woman in the same diocese heard rumors of witches who flew on brooms to meetings where they ate children, had intercourse in bestial fashion, and could not make the sign of the cross, but she could give no further details on these occurrences.

Trials for witchcraft became common in the fifteenth century, but prosecution for maleficent magic (which some historians refer to as "sorcery," analogous to the German *Zauberei*) had in fact occurred earlier, and these sorcery trials served as important background for the witch trials. There is some evidence that legal action for sorcery became increasingly common in the late fourteenth century, perhaps in large part because Inquisitorial methods of prosecution (including torture) were being widely adopted by secular courts. Particularly important were the trials for sorcery that involved major political figures. In the early part of the fourteenth century, as the last of the Capetian kings of France died in rapid succession, various people were thought to be using sorcery against them and others at court. Several times Pope John XXII (reigned 1316–1334) expressed concern about his own vulnerability to sorcery, and he had various enemies tried for this offense. Similar trials occurred in England in 1376, when Edward III's mistress was tried for using love magic against him; in 1419, when Henry V's stepmother Joan of Navarre was accused of trying to kill him with magic; in 1441, when the duchess of Gloucester was punished for involvement in intrigues against Henry VI; and in 1470, when the duchess of Bedford was accused of using image magic. Trials of this sort served to publicize and stimulate anxiety about maleficent magic.

The earliest evidence for trials involving the fully developed concept of witchcraft comes from around the 1430s. During that time there were extensive trials in southeastern France and southeastern Switzerland, trials in which is is possible to see the concept of witchcraft emerging. Of particular importance in this development was a series of writings produced in and around the 1430s detailing the new concept of witchcraft. An anonymous work called the *Errores gazariorum* stated that people joined the witches' "sect" to gain revenge or to sate their gluttony or their lust and described attendance at assemblies where they kissed the devil in the form of a black cat, ate their own offspring, and obtained unguents and powders to kill people and destroy crops. The Dominican Johannes Nider's *Formicarius* (Ant-Heap, 1437) reported trials from a generation earlier in the Simme Valley in Switzerland but may have revised some details in accordance with the latest theories about witchcraft. The municipal chronicler Johann Fründ gave a detailed and lurid account of witchcraft in the Valais (his account bears little resemblance to the judicial record of prosecution from that region). And the secular judge Claude Tholosan wrote a similar account based largely on his experience in trying witches. The witch trials became yet more virulent, and witchcraft literature was penned, in later decades of the fifteenth century. The 1450s witnessed heightened concern about witchcraft, most obviously in Arras, where 34 people were arrested and 12 burned for *vauderie*.

The most vigorous prosecution (followed by something of a lull) came in the 1480s, the decade in which Heinrich Krämer (or Institoris) was active against witches in southern Germany and in the Tyrol. At Innsbruck in 1495 Krämer tried 48 women and two men, chiefly for a wide variety of sorcery. Krämer was the chief author of the *Malleus maleficarum* (Hammer of Witches, c. 1486), the most important medieval writing on witchcraft. Although the work does not discuss the Sabbat, it does deal with the pact with the devil (which can either be explicit or implicit), sexual intercourse with demons (which, as Thomas Aquinas acknowledged, can result in the procreation of children), and other phenomena generally associated with the Sabbat, and the book repeatedly emphasized the demonic element in sorcery and the conspiratorial nature of witchcraft.

In only two types of trials did males figure prominently among the accused. Trials for "necromancy" tended to involve clerics in particular, and in trials focused specifically on the Sabbat and related activities rather than on sorcery, women were not singled out for prosecution. This is especially the case in the trials for *vauderie* in the 1430s and at Arras in the 1450s. Indeed, as late as 1481, when a man in the Val de Travers in Switzerland told of all of the men he had seen at the Sabbat, his puzzled judge asked specifically if there were no women.

In most cases, however, and especially when sorcery was a prominent charge, women were the chief subjects of accusation. One might explain this fact as a realistic reflection of women's greater role in the actual practice of magic, but it is not clear that most forms of magic were specifically associated with women. Some forms, to be sure, were connected with women; Matteuccia Francisci, burned at Todi in 1428, and Maria Medica, imprisoned at Brescia in 1480, provided love magic and other services for their mainly female clientele, and both were tried as witches in the fully developed sense of the term.

The primary cause for the gender imbalance seems to have been that women were more deeply feared even if they were practicing the same kinds of magic that men also used: a female healer and diviner was more vulnerable to suspicion than her male counterpart. Furthermore, a woman who had no immediate family or whose family was not well integrated into the community was more vulnerable to suspicion and attack: A woman tried for witchcraft at Kriens around 1500 was from a family that had migrated into that part of Switzerland in recent years and had become quite prosperous but had not intermarried or become otherwise integrated into the local community. In her case, as in many others, suspicion of witchcraft developed gradually over many years and finally led to prosecution. Witchcraft in the fully evolved sense does not figure prominently in the professed fictional literature of the late Middle Ages, but there are interesting representations of witches in art. By the mid-fifteenth century treatises on witchcraft were already sometimes illustrated with depictions of the Sabbat (especially Jean Tinctoris's *Sermo de secta Valdensium* [Sermon on the Waldensian Sect] of 1460), and in more than one region of Europe. Wall paintings in churches depicted witches flying on brooms.

The witch trials and witchcraft literature of the fifteenth century are often seen as a prologue to the great "witch-craze" or "witch-hunts" of the sixteenth and seventeenth centuries. The late Middle Ages is important, however, not simply as prologue but as the formative period in which ideas about witchcraft were first fully developed and given theological articulation, and in which the means for both ecclesiastical and secular prosecution of witches were first established.

See also: Folklore; Magic; Magic Manuals; Satan
—Richard Kieckhefer

Wolf [Canis lupus] and Werewolf.

Quintessential carnivore, a common figure of a dangerous predator throughout medieval legendry.

Throughout the Middle Ages wolves thrived from the Arctic southward, with subspecies found even in India and Arabia, whose wolves Aristotle said were smaller than the Greek. The wolf embodies wilderness, inimical to medieval minds. Its howl bodes death, as in the Eddic *Gudrunarkvida II* (Second Lay of Kudrun), which is resonant with lupine lore, including the symbolic beasts of battle—wolf, raven, eagle—familiar in Anglo-Saxon poetry. Although opposed to civilization, and so in mythologies the archetype of chaos, the wolf has inspired profound ambivalence among humans, who have simultaneously abhorred and admired this complex creature, the subject of scientific inquiry only since the 1940s. That it was the first beast domesticated—as *Canis familiaris,* a civilizing force—is one among many canine ironies. Never has there been a single, simple human response to the wolf.

Ambivalence marks Norse myth, for instance; it is haunted by wolf beneficent and wolf malevolent. Two serve as Odin's noble guardians, another as his nemesis. In the great Scandinavian myth of the end of the world, three more (Skoll, Hati, and Managarm [Moondog]) pursue the sun and moon each day across the sky until their quarry is crushed at Ragnarök. These and other wicked wolves are spawned by Loki's lover Angrboda (Harbinger of Grief), the giantess of Ironwood. Doomsday machine or gentle nursing mother—as in myths of Leto and Romulus and Remus (see motifs A511.2.2.1, L111.2.4), or in legends of the Irish bishop St. Ailbe—the wolf has evoked aesthetic responses as diverse as its spectral howl.

Various influences, however, from Germanic myth to the biblical exegesis of St. Augustine, reinforced revulsion in the medieval mind.

Whereas Rome venerated the wolf-mother, Dante's she-wolf deteriorated to a flat symbol of excess: lust, gluttony, greed, and wrath. The Inquisition linked the wolf with lechery (especially inaccurate vis-à-vis actual pack behavior, yet persistent in slang and such sayings as *elle a vu le loup* [she's seen the wolf], that is, lost her virginity). Edmund Spenser's wolf, on the other hand, equals envy. Thus, the animal sagged under the chains of humankind's own sins.

If we could write it, the history of medieval lupine lore would chronicle a millennium of decline. Exegetical applications—first in *Physiologus*, later in bestiaries, tracts, and homilies—doomed the image of the wolf to infernal typologies. Instrument or avatar of Satan, the wolf had become wholly wicked by about 1486, when the text *Malleus maleficarum* appeared (Hammer of Witches, literally "evildoers," who were said to shift shape and couple with demons). Inquisitional propaganda, this text condemned the shapeshifting werewolf as an enemy of God and Mother Church, as a sinful puppet and devil's plaything. Folklore fused into doctrine. The most ambiguous figure of all wolf lore, the lycanthrope (motif D113.1.1, werewolf), became monochromatically Satanic, ready for Shakespeare and his even more macabre contemporary, John Webster, whose Doctor could be describing lycanthropy before a heresy tribunal. But in works from the early Middle Ages the primeval ambivalence grows more apparent. Some of Aesop's fables—ostensibly Greek but in fact a corpus with Asian links, expanding throughout the medieval period—depict the wolf as an emblem of liberty ("The Dog and the Wolf," motif J953.5; cf. B267.1), forbearance ("The Wolf and the Crane," W154.3), or victimization ("The Wolf and the Shepherds," cf. U21.4). Others convey the "bloody, starved, and ravenous" associations more familiar in folktales of today. Beyond Aesop, the Reynard cycle, collected in the thirteenth-century French *Roman de Renart* and rendered in other vernaculars, also depicts a more ambiguous wolf figure. In these beast epics, Renard the wily fox (usually taken to be the oppressed but resourceful peasantry) repeatedly dupes Isengrim the unwitting wolf (apparently the greedy, bullheaded overlords). Presumably well established by oral tradition, the Renard story first appears with the *wolf* as title character in the Latin poem *Ysengrimus* (Ghentish, mid-twelfth century). By personifying the wolf these beast fables all subtly suggest the shapeshifting motif never wholly absent from medieval representations of *Canis lupus*.

Sometimes the motif surfaces in romance and saga. The late-twelfth-century *Lai du Bisclavret*, attributed to Marie de France, recounts the misadventures of a baron trapped in lupine form by his unfaithful wife. In the *Völsunga Saga* wolf pelts transform Sigmund and Sinfjötli (a kenning for "wolf") into the beast itself (an analogous

theme figures in Irish legends about the werewolves of Ossory). Later in the saga, conspirators embolden Guttorm Sigurd's-Bane by feeding him wolf meat, magic also mentioned in the *Edda* (D1358.1.2). Later still, Kudrun warns her brothers of impending treachery via a single wolf's hair looped round a gold ring (H75.5).

According to the principle of *totem ex parte* (the whole can be inferred from a part), which is elemental in sympathetic magic, wolf parts conjure up the entire creature, or at least its essence, its "spirit." The skin transforms its wearer, man to wolf. Wolf flesh instills wolfish ferocity. A single slap from a witch's wolf-skin glove turns a prince into a were-creature (*Hrolf's Saga*). Scratching runes on a wolf claw brings the warrior luck (*Sigrdrifumal* 17), as does hearing the howl before battle (*Reginsmal* 23). More graphically, a figure on a sixth-century Torslunda die represents either a werewolf or a warrior dancing in a wolf skin, complete, teeth to tail. In either case, as in the preceding examples, sympathetic magic is involved: lupine aspects equal lupine identity. "A wolf will be found where a wolf's ears are" (*Fafnismal* 35). Ultimately, medieval wolf lore reflects lost rites of prehistoric cults and clans.

As omens of violence and revenge, wolves loom large in the Norse dreamtime: in *Njal's Saga*, Gunnar's wolf dream foreshadows ambush (ch. 62); later, in an eerie vision, Njal sees the "fetches" (ghostly counterparts) of Gunnar's enemies lurking in the woods, massed in a pack for the kill (ch. 69; E423.2.7, E731.9). Suggesting second sight and shapeshifting, this Icelandic motif, the "fetch" or *fylgja* (possibly from *fulga*, "skin"), thus has shamanistic implications. A doppelgänger, or "shadow self," the *fylgja* resembles the Ojibwa *nigouimes*, a personal animal guardian. Norse myth exalts the feature in Odin's wolf companions, Geri (Hungry) and Freki (Ravenous); the "man-between-monsters" plaque from Sutton Hoo, now in the British Museum, probably represents Woden consulting his wolves.

Totemic implications arise when the wolf symbol becomes group-related. Such is the case with úlfhethinn (wolf-jackets) in Harold's ships at Hafrsfjord (*Grettir's Saga*, ch. 2); they are the most likely referents of the Torslunda wolf dancer. Seen now through the lens of literature, this Norse lore reflects proto-Germanic cults that used lupine rites, fetishes, and nomenclatures. Lingering fear of their sorcery is implicit in an Old High German charm against male or female wolf attack. Such cults generated poetic terms for warrior that are preserved in Old English and Old Norse, for example, *freca/freki*, "ravenous (wolf)," and *wælwulf*, "slaughter-wolf." As the wolf image became more pejorative during the Middle Ages, these terms grew increasingly unfashionable and obscure.

Yet as late as 1014 Wulfstan could still echo their thunder in his *Sermo lupi* (Sermon of the

Wolf). Righteously wrathful, the bishop preached as a Christian wolf soldier; nor had the animal referent of his name, "Wolf-stone," lost its mythic resonance (cf. the fourth-century Visigothic bishop, Wulfila, "Little Wolf"). As such works as *Beowulf* show, no onomastic element was more common in Germanic masculine names than *wulf* in one of its forms. Totemism is implicit here, too, where men named for predators evoke a forgotten culture that once merged its identity with that of the pack. For the Norse audience, Brynhild's bloodthirsty demand was far less figurative than it sounds today: to avert vengeance she ordered the death of Sigurd's three-year-old son, called "wolf cub" in *Edda* and saga. The audience knew an older name for the Völsung dynasty that died with the toddler: Ylfingar, "Children of the Wolf" (cf. the Wylfingas of *Beowulf* and *Sigrdrifumal* 35).

And thus the ironies reverberate. Noble children were called "wolf," but so were outlaws and crop diseases. Zeus (via Lycaon) and "wolf-born" Apollo (B535.0.9, B535.0.11), like the shaman-god Odin, had celestial lupine attributes, reflected in the constellation Lupus. But by the Renaissance the associations were mainly infernal. Since the Mesolithic, when wolves and people hunted symbiotically, human regard for canines—howling from the forest while growling by the hearth—has mingled love and loathing. Medical terminology also echoes the ancient ambiguities. Names for diseases retain traces of terror: bulimia nervosa was once called "the canine hunger"; lycanthropy still denotes a clinical psychosis (perhaps formerly associated with rabies); congenital nevus was the "werewolf syndrome"; and lupus designates an array of complaints, some severe. But, homeopathically, cure and consolation in the medieval pharmacopoeia took wolfish form, too, in dried and powdered wolf parts or in extracts from herbal genera, including *Lupinus* and *Lupulus*. On the other hand, *Aconitum lycoctonum*, wolfsbane, was notoriously toxic. Thus, at one and the same time this powerful beast lent its name to hero and villain, saint and sinner, disease and cure, medicine and poison.

As with the lore at large, these ambiguities belie human ambivalence toward one of our species' oldest adversaries and staunchest allies. Even while naming princes after totems, Germanic society proscribed the outlaw as *warg* (wolf; *Grettir's Saga*, ch. 72). To the West Saxons he was *wulfheort* (wolf-hearted, vicious), legally outcast as *wulfesheafod* (wolf's head), and worth a bounty when turned in for execution on the *wulfheafodtreo* (gallows). Beowulf's demonic foe Grendel (a shapeshifter?) grows more frightful through wolfish imagery in the epithet *heoruwearh*, "sword-warg" (i.e., "condemned sociopath"; cf. Old Norse *mordr-vargr*, "killer wolf," the legal term for a condemned murderer). Wolf imagery also darkens the horror of Grendel's mother, the troll wife called *brimwylf*, *grundwyr-*

gen, "she-wolf of the sea (floor)." Yet along with five other characters in his epic, the hero who quelled these monsters also bore a name with the wolf referent.

To this day in northern Norway an angry father might scold his reckless son as a "wolf in the temple." Morning twilight in Sweden can still be called "the hour of the wolf" (even though in 1996 there were perhaps 30 wolves in all of Scandinavia). The Romans, too, called dawn *inter lupum et canem*, "between the wolf and dog." And vague links with moonlight persist: our ancestors saddled their lunar lore and fear of the dark upon these shaggy shoulders. At last, the true identity of medieval folklore's strange familiar beast—that liminal predator so alert when its groggy prey first lurches toward lake water— glimmers in half-light, a shadow at sunup. Mammals are most vulnerable from dusk till dawn. Scarcely discernible, the wolf is most active then. Hence its haunting power, in forest as in folklore. And so, recalling *vargöld*, the "wolf age" when, in Scandinavian myth, Fenrir will break free to devour Odin and the waning sun, we should rest content with a symbol of wildness, beyond ken, ultimately untamable.

See also: Scandinavian Mythology; Scandinavian Tradition; Totem

—Stephen O. Glosecki

Woman Warrior. A familiar figure in both Scandinavian and Celtic medieval myth, legend, and chronicle.

On the Celtic side, there is historical evidence from the British Isles for queens leading their armies into battle. Boudicca of the Iceni is the best known of these: she headed a savage revolt against the Romans in the first century c.e. Another example is that of Cartimandua of northern Britain, who took over the leadership of the Brigantes from her husband. In 697 c.e. the "law of the innocents" was adopted at the Synod of Birr through the efforts of Adamnan, abbot of Iona, forbidding women to become warriors or military commanders, something that was evidently an established custom in Ireland. There was a tradition that Macha of the Red Hair became the first ruler of Ireland in 377 c.e., taking the kingdom by force.

In the Irish sagas there are some redoubtable women leaders, such as Queen Medb of Connacht in the *Cattle Raid of Cooley*, who took an active part in battles, and the mighty hero Cú Chulainn learned the most effective and dangerous of his skills in warfare from a woman warrior, Scáthach, the instructor of the greatest champions. She had an even fiercer sister called Aife, whom Cú Chulainn only overcame by a trick when they met in single combat but who afterward became his lover. Another woman warrior who raised an army and pursued Cú Chulainn when he eloped with her sister, Emer, was Scenmed, whom he defeated and killed. There are other references to women taking a leading part in warfare in the sagas and chronicles.

It was still possible for an Irish woman to command her ships and to fight at sea in the sixteenth century, as can be seen from the career of Grace O'Malley. Of royal descent, she not only took an active part in fishing and trading but also led her galleys against merchant ships as a successful pirate chief. She visited Queen Elizabeth I as a sovereign in her own right and was received with much ceremony at the English court. There is a wealth of folklore about the exploits of Grace O'Malley, who is said to have had fantastic powers, and she became an almost supernatural figure in local legend. Another famous woman warrior was the fifteenth-century Joan of Arc, who carried a sword and was said to have led the French army into battle dressed as a man, and again many legends gathered around her.

Women warriors also abound in Scandinavian tradition. The early-thirteenth-century Saxo Grammaticus mentions a number of them in his *Gesta Danorum* (History of the Danes). He may have been partly inspired by his knowledge of Virgil: the death of the shield-maid Vebiorg in Book 8 bears a close resemblance to that of the Amazon Camilla in the *Aeneid*. However, there is no doubt that the figure of the shield-maid or supernatural woman warrior was a familiar one in Scandinavian medieval tradition, and Saxo in Book 7 claims that girls of strong character and powerful physique often chose to live the life of warriors. Certainly women skilled in warfare play an important part in the legendary Icelandic sagas known as *fornaldarsögur*, in which princesses sometimes take up the role of shield-maid, and belligerent supernatural women either attack heroes or give them special weapons and support them in battle. The favorite term is *shield-maid*, but they may be called *valkyries*, *giantesses*, or even *troll-women*, and there is clearly confusion here between traditions of the shield-maid and the valkyrie as a guardian spirit who may appear on the battlefield bearing weapons like a warrior.

The familiarity of the woman warrior in popular tradition in the twelfth century is shown by legends of the appearance of Eleanor of Aquitaine and her ladies, mounted on white horses and dressed as Amazons, on their way to the Second Crusade.

The medieval romances continued to introduce women disguised as warriors in armor taking part in jousting and single combat. One of the main characters in *Orlando furioso*, a long epic poem composed early in the sixteenth century by Ludovico Ariosto, is Bradamante, known as "the Maid." A woman warrior, she appears in Book 1 as a mysterious knight clad in white armor who overthrows the Tartar king. She is aided in her brilliant career as a warrior by the use of a magic lance belonging to the hero Astolfo. After many complex adventures, she marries Ruggiero, whom she loves, and a brilliant line of descendants is prophesied to her by Merlin. Spenser's noble Warrior Maid, Britomart, in *The Faerie Queene*, also destined to marry a hero and to have distinguished descendants, is clearly influenced by Ariosto's heroine. She is involved in the restoration of the British dynasty in Tudor England and also plays a major role in the allegory of the poem.

There were female leaders of the Wild Hunt, the company of dark and menacing riders who were said to pursue their victims through the air or along forest paths and who appear to be made up of those who had died untimely deaths or led wicked lives. Sometimes, in medieval times, their leader is Satan, hunting down such sinners as priests' concubines. However, female figures such as Perhta and Herodias in Germany or Kudrun, wife of Sigurd, in Scandinavia, have been represented as belligerent leaders of this dangerous host of destructive riders.

The concept of the warrior woman has had a considerable impact on folklore and legend and also on the serious literature of the Middle Ages. While the influence of women warriors in classical literature and of the tradition of the Amazons had some effect on medieval literature, the concept can also be seen to have roots in traditions of supernatural guardians giving assistance in battle in northern Europe, as well as in memories of some outstanding women who took a direct part in warfare in their lifetimes.

See also: Irish Tradition; Valkyries; Wild Hunt

—Hilda Ellis Davidson

World Turned Upside Down [Latin *mundus inversus*, French *monde renversé*, German *verkehrte Welt*]. A complex of motifs representing reversals of the status quo.

Depending on one's perspective, these motifs may be seen as positive or negative, as revolutionary portents of a new order to come or chronic, unnatural symptoms of a world in terminal decline.

Isaiah proclaimed fierily that "the Lord maketh the earth ... waste, and turneth it upside down," and Jesus himself preached that "the last shall be first, and the first last." Such reversals of the "natural order" were therefore not inevitably seen as negative.

There are many conceivable types of reversal: between human and animal (the man carries the horse, the cow milks the woman, the ox slaughters the butcher), between predator and prey (the hare hunts the hound, the mice hang the cat, the geese hang the fox, the hares roast the huntsman), between men and women (most notoriously, the woman "wears the trousers" and the man spins with her distaff, the quintessentially female implement), and between social groups (the pupils flog the master).

Such world-turned-upside-down motifs are related to proverbial follies and to impossibilia (or *adynata*, impossibilities) and indeed, to the realm of nonsense represented by the French *fatras*.

The world is frequently turned upside down by divine intervention through the medium of the saints; the miracle is an inversion of what we have learned to expect from the natural world: Jesus walks on the water, various Celtic saints sail across the sea on a millstone. It is noteworthy that some of the miracles that turn the workaday human world upside down would be proverbial follies if attempted by ordinary mortals: In medieval iconography, fools tried to pen in a cuckoo by erecting a fence around the bush on which it alighted. It flew away—but St. Werburg of Chester was able to contain a flock of wild geese within just such an open enclosure, to the evident incredulity of the servant she ordered to so pen them, according to her late-medieval *Life* by Henry Bradshaw (d. 1513):

> Knowynge that well it passed course of kynde
> Wylde gees for to pynne [pen] by any mannes polycy
> Syth nature hath ordeyned suche brydes to fly
> Supposynge his lady had ben unresonable [irrational, mad]
> Commaundynge to do a thynge unpossyble.

But *unpossyble thynges* become possible in the topsy-turvy world of the saint.

In the visual arts it is not until the 1560s that broadsheet anthologies of world-turned-upside-down motifs (which thereafter enjoy an enormous popular success) are found (the earliest in Italy), but almost every individual subject can be traced in antecedent medieval art: an ox plowing with two men, for instance, can be seen in a fourteenth-century manuscript in the Bibliothèque Nationale; in the cathedral in Breisach is an early-fifteenth-century carving of an ass with a purse round its neck driving a man carrying a sack on his back. A thirteenth-century German poem describes several world-turned-upside-down motifs, including the sack of flour that carries the ass to the mill, the geese that roast the cook, the hares that chase the hunter, the sheep that devour the wolf, and the frog that swallows the stork. The fox is popular in such reversals and is barbecued by a cockerel in a Flemish book of hours or—frequently in England—hanged from a gallows by a collection of geese and other prey.

The cat hanged by rats or mice was a popular subject; in manuscript illumination it is found as early as the Rutland Psalter (c. 1260), and it is carved on misericords at Great Malvern in Essex (c. 1480) and Talavera de la Reina in Spain. A carved stone capital from the twelfth century in the cloisters of Tarragona Cathedral depicts a cat bound to a litter carried by a number of rats or mice to a place of execution, but the cat subsequently escapes and pounces on the "mourners." A *Katomuomachia* (Cat and Mouse War) was composed by the Byzantine writer Theodoros Prodromos (d. c. 1166 C.E.), and there is a contemporary wall painting of rats defending a castle besieged by cats, perhaps part of such a war, in a church in Obersteier-mark, Austria. Cats hanging from gallows also feature as part of the depiction of another such war in an early-fifteenth-century mural in the Jagdzimmer of the Ansitz Moos-Schulthaus in Eppan, Austria. An interesting historical employment of the figure occurred in 1493, when Emperor Maximilian took the town of Arras and caused to be inscribed over one of the gates the couplet "Quand les François prendront Arras / Les souris mangeront les chats" [When the French take Arras / Mice will eat cats]—which Louis XIII, when he retook the town in the seventeenth century, is said to have wittily adapted by merely causing the *p* of *prendront* to be erased (so that the rhyme read "When the French give up Arras / Mice will eat cats").

A Toledo misericord (1489–1495) carved by the Fleming Rodrigo Aleman depicts the pig turned butcher with a knife at his belt, while a similar notion is expressed in a ceiling painting of 1437 in the Swedish church of Tensta depicting an ox slaughtering a man.

The world turned upside down in terms of gender roles is a common fear, expressed in such popular images as the woman pulling on a pair of breeches while her husband spins with her distaff. Chaucer picks up this image in *The Canterbury Tales* when the Host quotes his wife as shouting, "I wol have thy knyf, / And thou shalt have my distaf and go spynne!" Even more badly humiliated husbands are threatened by their wives while washing clothes or are beaten on the bare bottom with a switch or foxtail. The foolish Aucassin is held to be a wise man in the topsy-turvy land of Torelore, where he finds the king lying in childbed and his queen leading the country's army into the field.

The thought that women might gain the upper hand in the domestic ménage was bad enough, but the idea of *mulier super virum* (woman on top) during intercourse was denounced by all right-thinking theologians—according to the sixteenth-century writer Thomas Sanchez, whose *De sancto matrimonii sacramento*, was not published until 1607: "This position is absolutely contrary to the natural order.... If the man is beneath, by the very fact of this position, he submits, and the woman plays the active part, and it is obvious how much Nature herself abhors this reversal."

According to another theologian it was precisely because "women [had] gone mad and abused their husbands in this way" that God had sent the Flood to destroy humanity. Similarly bent on the destruction of humanity, but also an embodiment of women's notorious lustfulness, was the witch. By the time that Ulrich Tengler's *Neu Layenspiegel* (New Mirror for Laymen) was published in Augsburg in 1511, the mounting witch-craze hysteria was such that the woodcut depicting the evil deeds of witches included a scene of a devil copulating with a witch—"naturally" with the far from hag-like young witch on top; just as witchcraft represents an inversion or perversion of the natural order, so the sexual proclivities of the witch herself are portrayed as similarly inverted and indeed—in the world of orthodox late-medieval misogyny—perverted. In his *Life and Death of Cardinal Wolsey*, alluding to events circa 1530, prior to the Dissolution of the Monasteries, George Cavendish reported a prophecy notable for its sexual inversion, that "whan [the] Cowe ridyth the bull / than prest beware thy skull," which was popularly interpreted to have come true upon Henry VIII's marriage to "Anne *Bull* eyn."

The *monde renversé* is the natural habitation of all such unnatural elemental reversals, where, for example, fish fly in the air—a frequent *adynaton* used (in Archer Taylor's phrase) as one of the many colorful locutions for "never"; cf. from William Caxton's *Jason* (c. 1477): "Certes that shal not be unto the tyme that the fishes flee in the ayer. And that the byrdes swymme in the water." It is a land where pigs really do fly—long before its first appearance in English vernacular literature, in the 1616 edition of John Withal's dictionary, this still-popular absurdity occurs in the mid-thirteenth-century *De mundi vanitate* (On the Vanity of the World) by the English poet Walter of Wimborne: in a lengthy list of the impossibilities that will come to pass when the poor man finds friends, the penultimate absurdity is that *"uolabit sus pennata"* [the winged pig will fly].

In French literature the motif is found in chapter 41 of Rabelais's *Quart livre* (1551), in which *"un grand, gras, gros, gris pourceau, ayant aesles longues et amples"* [a great, fat, huge, gray pig, with great long wings] suddenly appears flying toward Pantagruel and his companions and bombs them with mustard pies! The Rabelaisian flying pig appears to be male, as, evidently, is the winged boar in a woodcut probably issued in the 1530s by the Dutch artist Cornelis Anthonisz—significantly, this print clearly associates the flying pig with the *monde renversé* by representing the marvelous animal standing on a symbolic world-orb, the world turned, if not entirely upside down, then at least on its side!

In 1480, however, in his long satirical poem, *Les droitz nouveaulx* (The New Laws), Guillaume Coquillard alluded to a Parisian tavern called La Truye Vollant (The Flying Sow), but the animal depicted in a little contemporary lead badge, barely an inch wide, recovered from the Thames foreshore in London seems to be a flying boar.

The Anthonisz pig, balanced tipsily on a toppling world-orb, signals by means of that symbol the wider theme, and the inverted globe is also used elsewhere to great effect, most notably in Pieter Brueghel the Elder's *Netherlandish Proverbs* (1559), where it functions as the sign of the village inn, the badge of the chaotic world in which we are presented with so many proverbial follies.

See also: Iconography; Misericords

—Malcolm Jones

INDEX OF TALE TYPES

The following index catalogs the plots of folktales referred to in this book.

This numerical list is based on Antti Aarne and Stith Thompson's *The Types of the Folktale,* 3rd ed., Folklore Fellows Communications 184 (1961)—a systematic classification of internationally distributed fictional narratives. Following the conventions of folklorists, the prefix "AT" (for "Aarne-Thompson") is used to designate tale types. For example, AT 300 refers to "The Dragon-Slayer," one of the most widespread medieval and modern European tales.

The great majority of tale types in the Aarne-Thompson index are based on oral narratives told widely in Europe and Asia in the nineteenth and twentieth centuries. Although there is considerable continuity between medieval and modern folktales, *The Types of the Folktale* is not an ideal guide to medieval traditions, for there are many current oral tales that cannot be documented as having existed in the Middle Ages, as well as many medieval tales, now known to us only in written form, that have not thrived in recent oral tradition. Furthermore, the fact that a medieval narrative shares a plot with a twentieth-century oral folktale is no guarantee that the medieval tale was in fact a folktale—that it was part of a community-based oral tradition. Nevertheless, such indexes are useful in helping researchers both to identify and compare different versions of a widespread medieval plot and to discover significant differences and continuities between medieval and recent storytelling traditions.

For a more detailed discussion of tale types and their relevance to medieval folklore studies, see the entry titled Folktale above.

The contributors to this volume vary significantly in their approaches to tale types. Some used the Aarne-Thompson catalog profusely, others not at all. The following list represents a middle road, directing the reader to the major tale types discussed above, but it does not present an exhaustive list, nor does it refer the reader to every minor allusion to a given tale type. In a few instances, the index below directs the reader to a discussion that refers to a given tale type but does not cite that tale type by number. For example, the entry on George, Saint, mentions the saint's famous fight with a dragon. This narrative is the most famous medieval example of the plot known to folklorists as AT 300, "The Dragon-Slayer." This index cites the page (173) on which this famous narrative is mentioned, although the text on that page does not contain the tale type number AT 300.

According to Aarne and Thompson's system, a number followed by a letter indicates a significant subtype. For example, AT 425C, "Beauty and the Beast," represents a subtype of AT 706, "The Search for the Lost Husband." A number followed by an asterisk [*] indicates a tale with limited distribution.

INDEX OF MOTIFS

The following index lists the folk motifs cited in this book.

This catalog is based on Stith Thompson's six-volume *Motif-Index of Folk-Literature: A Classification of Narrative Elements in Folktales, Ballads, Myths, Fables, Mediaeval Romances, Exempla, Fabliaux, Jest-Books, and Local Legends*, 2nd ed. (1955–1958)—a systematic attempt to assemble the motifs of world folk tradition.

According to Thompson, a motif is "the smallest element in a tale having the power to persist in tradition" (S. Thompson, *The Folktale* [1946], page 410). For a lengthy discussion, see the entry Motif in this encyclopedia.

The contributors to this volume varied significantly in their approaches to motifs. Some used the Thompson catalog profusely, others not at all. The following list represents a middle road, directing the reader to the major motifs discussed in the book, but it does not present an exhaustive list, nor does it refer the reader to every minor allusion to a given motif. In a few instances, the index below directs the reader to a discussion that refers to a given motif but does not cite that motif by number. For example, the entry Baltic Tradition refers to a divine smith named Kalvelis, who serves as an example of the motif A142, "smith of the gods." This index cites the page (31) on which Kalvelis appears, although the text on that page does not contain the motif number A142.

According to Thompson's system, each motif begins with a letter, and each letter represents a certain traditional subject category. For example, "A" refers to "Mythological Motifs."

Thompson entertained no illusions about the completeness of his catalog. He knew that additional motif numbers would be proposed, and he encouraged other indexers to add them. This encyclopedia follows scholarly convention by using asterisks [*] to mark those motif numbers that have been added since Thompson's index was published. In the following list, additional motifs—for examples, *F811.14.2 and *V331.5.2—generally come from Gerald Bordman's *Motif-Index of the Middle English Metrical Romances*, Folklore Fellows Communications 190 (1963). There is one exception: motif C999.1.1.4* is found in Tom Peate Cross, *Motif-Index of Early Irish Literature*, Indiana University Publications, Folklore Series 7 (1952).

A. Mythological Motifs

A113	Totemistic gods, 407
A131.6	Horned god, 408
A132.5	Bear-god, 32
A142	Smith of the gods, 31, 111–12
A162.1.0.1	Recurrent battle (everlasting fight), 90
A511	Supernatural birth of culture hero, 339
A511.2.2.1	Culture hero suckled by wolf, 440
A524.2	Extraordinary weapons of culture hero, 378, 395–97
A580	Culture hero's expected return, 22, 388–89
A671.2.2.3	Rivers of fire in hell, 281

B. Animals

B1	Animal elders; mythical ancestors of the present animals, 407
B2	Animal totems, 407
B11	Dragon, 100, 280
B11.2.13	Blood of dragon, 379
B11.11	Fight with dragon, 190
B124.1	Salmon as the oldest and wisest of animals, 90
B267.1	Alliance of dog and wolf, 441
B297.1	Animal plays musical instrument, 169
B301	Faithful animal, 280
B331.2	Llewellyn and his dog, 159–60, 188–89, 209, 284
B365.2.1	Ant grateful to hero for preventing destruction of nest, 90
B481.1	Helpful ant, 90
B524.1.4	Wolf defends master's child against serpent, 281
B535.0.9	She-wolf as nurse for child, 441
B535.0.11	She-wolf cares for baby exposed in the forest, 441
B600–699	Marriage of person to animal, 407
B601.1	Marriage to bear, 32, 407, 408
B635.1.1	Eaten meat of bear-lover causes unborn son to have bear characteristics, 32, 408
B771.2	Animal tamed by holiness of saint, 278
B841.1	Animals debate as to which is the elder, 90

C. Tabu

C31.9	Tabu: revealing secrets of supernatural wife, 281
C94.1.1	The cursed dancers (Dancers of Kölbigk), 61–62, 91, 93, 141, 177
C221.2	Eating totem animal, 407, 408

GENERAL INDEX